SAVIOR
Book 1

SAVIOR

BOOK 1

BY JENNIFER SAVIANO

This is a work of fiction. Names, characters, places, and incidents
either are the products of the author's imagination or are used
fictitiously. Any resemblance to actual persons, living or dead,
businesses, companies, events or locales, is entirely coincidental.
For permission requests, write to the author at
authorjennifersaviano@gmail.com,
or on Instagram @the_saviors_mc

ISBN : 979-8-9886863-0-9

NOTE:
This is a work of fiction, liberties may have been taken in regards to
rules and regulations involving Law Enforcement, Motorcycle Clubs, &
Underground Fighting Rings, to fit the narrative of the story.
It takes place in a fictionalized region of the Eastern Carolinas.

The Saviors MC Series deals heavily with characters navigating life and
relationships through and after trauma. Trauma can cause your brain to remain
in a state of hypervigilance. It can cause you to suppress memory and impulse
controls, and trap you in a constant state of intense emotional reactivity.
As I write my characters true to who they are, they will be far from perfect,
and might not make the same decisions you would. We all deal with things
in our own ways. This is their story.

Trigger Warnings
Contains Explicit Content:
Graphic Sex, Violence (Gun/Knife/Fighting/Murder,
Domestic Violence, Attempted SA) Profanity,
Blasphemy, Stalking, Substance Abuse Alcohol/
Drugs, Manipulation/Blackmail/Exploitation,
Vigilantism, Prostitution

Acknowledgements:

Thank you to my husband, Frankie, for loving me like crazy
all these years & always having my back.
Your love and support is unwavering.
I love you.

Thank you to my parents and sister, for your love
& support, as well. Though, I hope you never read this book.
If you do, please skip the pages I tell you to. Trust me...

And to the Biker who tried to save me from a monster
when I was barely a teenager...
I wish I knew who you were. Thank you.

TERMS ASSOCIATED WITH MOTORCYCLE CLUBS

Biker - a person who rides a Motorcycle.

Cage – a vehicle, car/truck/van etc. of any kind that is not a Motorcycle.

Citizen – a person that isn't a member or affiliated with a Motorcycle Club (MC).

Church - a Motorcycle Club Meeting / a conference room where meetings are held.

Colors - the Patches / Logos worn to represent who you are / are with.

Cut – a leather or denim vest that has the Motorcycle Clubs colors / patches sewn onto it. Worn almost always, even over leather jackets / other clothing.

Getting Patched / Patched in - being accepted into a Motorcycle Club officially, moving up from being a Prospect.

Hang Around – a person interested in Prospecting to eventually become a full member of a Motorcycle Club.

House Mouse – a female, usually related to a Motorcycle Club member, who gets paid to keep up with daily or weekly house chores (cleaning, laundry, shopping etc.) for members of the MC.

Ink – tattoos

Ink Slinger – a tattoo artist.

Nomad - a member of a Motorcycle Club that is not a member of a specific charter, they are not bound by geographic province. A nomad can also be a lone Biker, or may have been sent to a new region with permission to form a new chapter of the Motorcycle Club with which they are affiliated.

Old Lady / Ole Lady – a woman who has been with a specific Biker for a while and has earned the Motorcycle Clubs trust. She is either a wife or long-time girlfriend, and is respected by the Club and completely off limits to anyone but her Biker / Old Man / Ole Man.

Patch Wearer / Patch Holder – a full member of a Motorcycle Club that wears a clubs' patches/colors on his cut.

Rockers – another term for the patches / logos on the back of a cut.

Sweetbutt / Lady Lay / Lay Girl / Patch Whore / Party Favor – a female who hangs around Bikers, equivalent to a Groupie. Usually makes herself available and open to sleeping around with Bikers in the hopes of becoming an Old Lady.

"DOUBT THOU THE STARS ARE FIRE;
DOUBT THAT THE SUN DOTH MOVE;
DOUBT TRUTH TO BE A LIAR;
BUT NEVER DOUBT I LOVE..."

HAMLET – WILLIAM SHAKESPEARE

Dedicated to
the leather clad Lancelots
the Ladies that love them

Chapter
one

DEAN

3 YEARS BEFORE COLLISION

THE MC PATCH ON MY LEATHER CUT SAYS I'M A SAVIOR. ONE MIGHT think that word implies we're men of God. Some of us are. Some of us are simply trying to atone for sins of our own. Buying our way into Heaven. If there even is a Heaven. I'm haunted by the things I've seen. Things that often make me doubt the existence of a God, or Heaven, all together. Heaven might only be what we manage to find within fleeting moments of happiness. If we're lucky.

I had it once. Happiness, that is. Or so I thought, at the time. Gave that whole settling down thing a shot, when I came back to town and joined my late Uncle's MC. I thought I could try to put the darkness behind me. Carve some kind of semblance of a normal life out for myself. It wasn't in the cards for me, I suppose. My little piece of Heaven quickly turned into Hell, when she ripped everything away from me... *Everything*...

Happiness often lacks the stamina misery has. It doesn't seem to last very long. It'll slip right through your fingers. But *Hell*... Hell will grab a hold of *you*... Hell exists. It exists all around us. In all different forms. Hell isn't particular about what form it takes, either. You can find it anywhere. Within a beautiful home with manicured lawns in a picture-perfect neighborhood. You can find it hiding behind the eyes of the beautiful, dutiful wife living inside it. And you can find it, just the same, in dark, dank rooms with filthy, crimson stained mattresses on cement floors... Handcuffs hanging from rusty metal bedframes, below tiny barred windows... There are many Hells on Earth. And the Devils are among us. They live within the cold hearts of men. Men, who far too often, go unpunished for their crimes against the innocent.

Life has taught me that the law doesn't guarantee justice. And that's why I'm here. To pick up some of the slack.

Tonight, I sit atop my motorcycle in the shadows of a large oak tree over-hanging the street. The thick branches and foliage block out the glow of the streetlights in this affluent little neighborhood. It's a chilly night for early spring. But I'm wearing my leather jacket, my second skin, over my cut. So, I'm fine. Even if I wasn't fine, I'm not going anywhere until this job is done. This mission. This little ember of what's left of the dwindling fire inside, keeping me alive.

I lift the binoculars to my eyes once more. Viper's in the black van parked across the street from the woman's house. I'm backup this time, in case the as-shole decides to come home early and throw a wrench into the proceedings. It happens. Can't always count on things to go smoothly. More times than not, there's an issue. People aren't always predictable. Especially women. Especially women under duress. Like this one, tonight.

We've tried to rescue her several times before. But each time, she's backed out at the last moment. Sadly, that's common. Some never reach their breaking point. For others, it's even worse than that. I've seen it far too often.

Axel is a few blocks away, watching for the prick's Mercedes Benz. He'll shoot me a heads up via text, if he spots him. I'll stop him if he does show. Pull out in front of him. If he wants to get violent, all the better. I love that shit. I live for it now. My fists are itching to connect with someone's face. Even better if that face belongs to a woman beating sack of shit. The sound their noses make when they break is rather soothing, also. I enjoy it. Maybe a lot more than I should...

For *her* sake, I hope the bastard doesn't show. It will be less stressful on her to escape without his interference.

Viper flashes me the brake lights, twice. That means he sees her. She's actually coming out this time. I shift my focus back to her driveway, hoping to see her with a bag or two, hurrying to the van. Once inside, Viper will transport her to a safe house. We don't own any, yet. We work with orga-nizations that run shelters for domestic abuse victims and their children. Not only do we assist, on occasion, with helping victims get out, we also provide free security to the safe houses as well. That's why we're called The Saviors MC. We save people. Women and children. We also run fundrais-ers to raise money for the shelters and organizations that work with us to help make this shit happen.

However, this part and the security, we don't advertise to the public. It's kept secret for the victims' safety and privacy. One of our set-in-stone MC rules. I don't break *that* one.

I barely hear Viper start the van, but it means he sees her coming towards him. That's good. I silently hope she chooses freedom this time. Some of the women make it to the end of the driveway, hesitate, then run back to the house. She's done this before. And there ain't anything we can do about it.

Come on... Come on... Come on, baby... You deserve better than this life. Go with Viper. You can do this!

I see her, she's speed walking with a backpack and a bag, hurrying down the driveway. So far, so good. Though, I notice she's got an arm in a sling this time. Fucking piece of shit fiancé... I hope she kept the ring so she can hock it. She only hesitates this time to look both ways before she darts across the street to Viper. The side door of the van opens as she approaches and jumps inside. We have her. She's safe now. The door slams and Viper hits the gas. I watch the van speed off. No time to hesitate once we have them. It's for the best. I watch him take the first left and disappear down a neighborhood side street.

Fuckin' Aces!

Tucking the binoculars back in the saddle bag on my bike, my cell phone chimes. It's Axel with a heads up. Dirtbag just passed him, in route to me now. Five minutes, max. Axel is following him. I was supposed to take off when the van did. But I wait, glancing around at the neighboring houses. Doesn't appear that anyone has noticed me here, yet. I keep waiting.

My cell rings this time. It's Viper. I only answer it in case he's encountered a problem with the woman. I already know why he's calling. He doesn't see me in his mirrors. He's calling to remind me about another MC mission rule. A rule I break every chance I get. Old habits die hard. And like I said, I'm here to pick up the slack where the law falls short of *true justice*.

"What are you doing?" Viper's tone betrays the fact he already has a solid idea. I simply clear my throat. We both know what's about to go down. "Dean... Come on, man. It ain't worth the risk." He pushes. I know he doesn't want to say anything specific, in case the woman overhears him.

"The law let him walk... *I won't*." He broke her arm. For that, I'll break both of his legs.

"Fuck!" Viper hangs up on me. I slip the cell phone back in my jacket pocket and wait some more.

Shitbag's Benz blows by me and turns into the driveway a few houses up, where we snatched the woman and spirited her away to safety only minutes ago. A moment later, Axel's bike pulls up alongside me. He shuts it down and looks at me, but I stare straight ahead towards the house up the street.

"Dean, man. We gotta go." He pushes. "Protocol, remember? You told me it's always important to stick to the plan."

I glance over at him. Axel is a good kid. Just started prospecting for us. He's looking at me through his black helmet with worry in his young, blue eyes. Can't help but smile back at him. He gives a shit about me. Looks up to me. I actually saved him myself a few years ago. Him and his mother. Same fucked up situation. I was stationed at their safehouse for a while, too. Got to know him. He took a liking to me. To the bikes. To the cause. Joined up with us as soon as he was old enough to get his own bike. Now, he does these missions with us, as a look out, for the time being. He's got a few years before we can patch him in as a full member of the MC. I vouched for him when I still had pull within our MC, before my uncle, the founder, passed away. Before I was demoted from Sergeant at Arms to just a patched member. I'm glad I was able to do that for him, though. I'm proud of Axel. If I ever had a son, I'd want him to be just like Axel.

"Bro, come on." He urges me. "We got her. He can't get her now. She's safe."

"Alright." I sigh. I'm not going to let Axel down. He's one of the few threads still holding me together.

We fire up our Harleys and take off.

Tonight, the scumbag narrowly escapes the beating of his life.

Back at The Twisted Throttle, I down a double shot of Jack at the bar, savoring the burn as it slides down my throat. The warmth it creates in the empty pit of my stomach. One look at Cherry, my vibrantly red headed bar-maid, and she pours me another. I tank that one too. She looks concerned. I know she is. Cherry is a good girl. She's Axel's babe.

But I don't want to hear it tonight. I avert my eyes to the mirror behind the back bar counter, behind the shelves of liquor. Staring into my own dark, dead, fucking eyes. I don't even recognize myself anymore.

I slide the shot glass to Cherry again, across the smooth polished mahogany wood bar counter. Instead of pouring me another shot, she grabs a glass with ice and opens a can of coke, pouring it over the crackling ice, then slides it back to me.

"*Come on*, Cherry." I mutter.

"*No*, Dean. That's enough." she tells me, firmly, but I can hear the undertone in her voice. Sadness. Fuckin' pity... *I hate it.*

Reaching over the bar, I grab the bottle of Jack Daniels myself. She can keep the shot glass. And the coke on the rocks. The bottle is mine now. Literally. I own the bar. The attached clubhouse. The motorcycle repair shop across the lot. The deeds are all in my name. Have been for a few years.

"Dean, give it back." Cherry insists, though there's a sympathetic look in her pretty green eyes. I lift the bottle to her in mock salute and take a swig, like an asshole. She looks like she wants to cry.

Fuck this. Can't take it.

Pushing away from the bar, I get up, taking the bottle with me. I'll drink outside on the wooden bench, by myself. I'm shit company anyway, these days. Shoving the steel door open and stepping outside, I let it clang shut behind me. Forgot how chilly it was out here tonight. Unusual this time of year. No matter, though. Hopefully I won't feel anything soon. Not the cold. Not the heartache. Nothing.

14

I settle down on the bench just outside the steel door of the roadhouse, against the brick wall, and let my gaze surf the sea of motorcycles, trucks and a few cars in my lot. My patrons. Why they love this hole in the wall, I don't know. But it pays the bills. Sometimes I'm grateful for it. Tonight, I don't care about anything.

The steel door opens and clangs shut again. Viking, my bouncer, MC Brother, and friend for years, steps outside. His huge body looming over me. He's called *Viking* because he looks like one. Like somebody yanked him out of some historical docu-series about them and gave him a Harley Davidson Fatboy and a black leather Saviors' cut. You'd never guess he comes from a well to do family. Or that his real name is *Gunther Westergard*. He'll break your face though, if you call him anything other than *Viking*.

He clears his throat, but I don't bother looking up. I know I'll see the same thing in his eyes. Cherry probably sent him out here, anyway. I take a drink instead.

"Heard the mission went well tonight. Extraction went smoothly, according to Viper. Says the woman is safe and sound." Viking says.

I nod. "There's that."

Viking lowers his hulking form down next to me. "Can I get a swig?"

"No."

"The fuck not? Greedy dick." He elbows me in jest with his massive tattooed arm.

"You won't give it back. Then I'll have to fight you for it."

"We both know how that will end." He laughs. "I'll knock your ass out."

Now there's an idea... "Promise?"

He sighs. "Bro... I get it."

"You don't." No one does. Or can.

"Lucinda is a -"

"Don't fucking say her name!" I snap. Don't mean to. It's an instant reflex to the pain. I take a breath and let it out slow, attempting to shove the pain back down. It's not working. I take another swig of Jack.

"The MC needs you. You gotta stop this shit, Dean." He's growing impatient with me. And not just about tonight.

"Cherry needs you inside, incase somebody gets rowdy." I attempt to deflect.

"Cherry is on break. Crying her eyes out. She asked me to come out here." Viking's tone is noticeably sharper. None of us want our women crying. She's one of ours. Saviors' Property. It's not as misogynistic as it sounds. Just means she's under our protection. Nobody can mess with her. We all look out for our own.

But *I* made her cry... And I feel like shit for it. I do. I swear. I just don't want to feel anything tonight...

"You have all of us, Dean. We all love you, Bro." Viking continues to push me.

Fuck! No more...

I lift the bottle and chug the alcohol into my system now.

Viking jumps up and knocks the fucking bottle out of my fist with a hard swat of his giant hand. It shatters on the pavement beside me. I stare at the shards of glass and dark liquid spreading across the shadowed pavement.

"The fuck, Dean!" He shouts at me. "You trying to kill yourself? *Death* by fucking *Jack*? You asshole!"

"*That* was alcohol abuse..." I mutter, gesturing to the broken bottle on the pavement. I sit back against the bench again and wait for the alcohol to kick in. Didn't eat today. Shouldn't take too long.

"Maybe I *should* kick your fucking ass!" He shouts again.

I lift my arm and gesture with my hand for him to bring it on. "Promises, promises. Nobody keeps them."

Especially not Lucinda...

Viking grabs me by the lapels of my leather jacket and hauls me to my feet, glaring in my face. He looks like he wants to punch me, so I grin back at him to egg him on. He just shakes me, frustration etched across his expression. Guess I'm going to have to work for it.

"You're going to kill yourself if you keep this shit up!" He shouts at me some more. "Is that what you want? You want to die over that fucking twat, *Lucinda*? You fucking asshole!"

I struggle to get out of his grip. The Jack's finally kicking in. *Figures.* Now that I might actually *want* to hit him. "Ain't about *just* fuckin' *Lucinda!*" I say, or try to say. Maybe it came out coherently. I don't know. Does it even really matter anyway?

"Yeah, I know there's a bigger picture here, Dean... But you gotta move on. Life fucking goes on, Bro." Viking urges. "You have other people counting on you! You're going to lose this fucking MC! Do you want that?"

"Lost everything else." I mutter.

"No, you didn't, Dean. You beat her in court. You keep everything."

I shake my head. "Lost what mattered most."

"Maddie wasn't yours... Take solace in -"

I clock him in the face for saying it. True or not. That shit hurts too much. Ain't enough Jack in this entire fucking bar to numb that pain out.

Viking slugs me in the gut and I want to puke. Knocks the fucking wind right out of me with one of his goddamned, ham sized fists. *Fucker...* Couldn't do me the damn favor and hit me in the fucking head! He holds me up while I'm keeled over, trying to fuckin' breathe. But I'm not done yet. He promised to knock me out. I'm through with broken promises. Throwing an elbow at him, I catch him sharply in the ribs.

"Stupid dick!" He winces, releasing me as he takes a step back.

I stagger to stand straight and square off with him. All I need is one good shot. I don't even care if they leave me in the dark fucking parking lot. "Come on, asshole!" I raise my fists, as if I actually want to fight him. "You couldn't kick my ass *wasted*." I taunt him, but he just folds his massive arms across his barrel of a chest and looks at me stoically. "*Come on!*"

The sound of heels clicking hurriedly on the pavement towards us from the patio out back, down the lot, echoes behind Viking.

Shit. It's fuckin' Cherry. She must have heard us shouting. I might still have time.

"Fight me, asshole!" I yell at him again.

"You really going to do this in front of her?" Viking's disappointed expression irks the shit out of me. Cherry walks around him and I drop my fists in defeat.

"Fucking dick." I say to him, as she looks between the two of us, back and forth. Her watery eyes land on me. I look away from her and stare at Viking. Resenting him for letting me down. This fucking alcohol isn't working fast enough.

"Fine! I'm out of here." Pulling the keys to my motorcycle out of my pocket, I turn and walk towards the shop where I parked her. I'm confident that this will work. I'm almost at my last resort. If this doesn't work, I'm just going to ram my skull into the fucking brick wall of the Twisted Throttle Roadhouse.

"No!" Cherry shrieks, throwing her petite little body against me, grabbing at me to stop my progression towards my motorcycle.

"You fucking prick!" Viking scowls. "You want to wrap yourself around a tree?"

"Dean, you can't ride like this!" Cherry cries.

No. I can't. Viking better stop me. I don't look at him though. I don't want him calling my bluff. I try to get past her, gently. I don't want to hurt Cherry. Either Cherrys. Great. There are two of her now. Maybe the end is near after all. "Cherry, let me have them." I say.

"No!" she shouts at me. "I'm getting Axel!"

Fuck... Don't get the kid...

I glare at the Vikings. "All you had to do, was either let me fucking drink myself into oblivion or knock me the fuck out!"

"You need to let Cherry go, Dean." Viking sounds pissed again. But I'm not going to use Cherry to get my way, so I let her go.

"I'm sorry, Cherry." I mean it, though I'm sure I still sound like an asshole, regardless. The other motorcycles in the lot are spinning now. Fuck yes, it's almost over. For a time, anyway. I grin at Viking as my head reels. "Looks like I don't need your fucking assistance after all." I sway on my feet. Going down soon. Would have preferred to have been left the Hell alone to pass out on the bench. *Whatever...* Maybe I can make it to the bench. Cherry helps me, tucking herself under one of my arms as we head back in the direction of the roadhouse.

"I wasn't going to ride..." I whisper to her. Or I think I whisper, as we stagger back towards the Twisted Throttle. "I'm an asshole... But I wouldn't actually do that. I just wanted him to hit me..."

She's crying. I'm such a prick.

"I'm sorry." I say again.

Viking grabs the collar of the back of my leather jacket, hauling me back up to my feet. I guess I fell. Didn't even notice. *Aces...* He tosses me at the bench. I land half sitting up and mostly on my side, before I straighten myself out somewhat as he sits down next to me.

"I got it, Cherry." He sighs. "Don't tell Axel. He doesn't need to come out here and see this." I'm still conscious enough to be relieved by that. I don't want Axel seeing me like this, either.

I hear the loud burst of noise from inside the bar, laughing and loud talking and rock music, when Cherry opens the door to go back inside. Then the loud clang shut and it's quiet again, for the moment. I let my head fall back against the bench.

"You're a fucking prick." Viking mutters. I grumble in agreement. "This shit needs to stop."

"Let me pass the fuck out in peace." I groan.

"What's it going to take to bring you back, Dean?" Viking asks. I don't know the answer to that. "There's a woman out there that needs you."

I scoff. Nobody needs me. Lucinda even said I was useless...

But the nagging thought of his last words haunt what remains of my consciousness, as Jack pulls me into the dark oblivion I seek...

S OMETHING SLAMMING INTO THE BOTTOM OF MY BOOT, SEVERAL TIMES, wakes me up. Sending shock waves all the way up my body, to my throbbing brain. I don't even want to open my eyes. I know it's going to hurt.

"Wake up, shit head." Viking says, kicking my boot again.

Now that I'm conscious, and my eyes have rolled forward behind my lids, I throw an arm over my eyes to block the light coming through the broken blinds. It's daytime. Don't know what time. Don't know what day. Don't really care, either.

"Bro!" he shouts this time, his voice a *sonic boom* that I feel in the actual core of my brain, radiating outward to penetrate even the bone of my skull. For good measure, he kicks my boot again. *Hard.*

"*Fuck!* What?" I groan, sitting up on my elbows, refusing to open my eyes. Feels like I'm in a bed, though. He probably dragged me to my room in the back of the club house, on the other side of the building attached to the Twisted Throttle Roadhouse.

All members of the Saviors MC have a small room here, regardless if we live elsewhere. I do. Just haven't actually been home in a while. I've been staying in my clubhouse room. A convenient place to crash after getting wasted. The rooms are meant to prevent MC Brothers from getting DWI's after partying, and a convenient place to bang around with patch whores and sweetbutts. Or as we lovingly call them, *Lady Lays.* We're Saviors... *Not Saints.*

"Get up. Wash up. And let's get going." Viking says.

"Going?" My eyelids feel like they're made out of lead. "Where are we going?"

"First things first. Get the fuck up and get in the shower. You look like shit."

I push myself up and put my feet on the floor. I'm still fully dressed. I can feel all my clothing on my person. Don't want to open my eyes yet. My head's fucking throbbing. I lean forward, elbows on my knees, palms against my eye sockets, willing the throbbing to subside.

"What time is it?" I ask.

"It's *fuck this shit O'clock*, Dean." He grumbles. When I don't respond, he finally gives me an actual answer, "Two fucking thirty in the afternoon. You've been out cold since last night. *Get up*."

"I'm fucking *up*." I groan.

"Yeah, you are *fucking up*. Fucking up everything!" He barks at me.

I'm not in the mood for this shit right now. I crack an eye open slowly and glance up at him. "Can we not right now? My fucking head feels like it's going to split in two."

"You're lucky I didn't split your damn head in two last night."

I barely remember last night, at first. But it's slowly starting to come back. Letting out a long, remorseful sigh, I admit, "I wasn't actually going to ride Serene like that. I told Cherry the same."

"Just get up, asshole. Get cleaned up."

"Is Cherry okay?"

"She's fine. Worried about you, as usual." He frowns at me. "Like the rest of us."

I nod. Alright. I'll fucking get up and go apologize to her for being an asshole. Again.

Standing up, I unzip my leather jacket, pulling it off and dropping it on the bed behind me. Peeling off my t-shirt, I catch a glimpse of the tattoo on my right, inner forearm. *Lucinda...* in thin, fancy script. I grimace at it and move on to my belt, undoing the buckle and pulling it through the belt loops, dropping it on the bed as well. Feeling his eyes on me, I glance over at Viking. "You gonna watch me strip?"

"Just making sure you get in the fucking shower."

"The fuck are you riding me for?" I kick off my boots and move around the side of the bed, past him, towards the bathroom.

"Shit's been going down lately, that you've been too fucking wasted to notice."

I turn around and look at him. "The fuck does that mean?"

"Preacher wants to vote you out now, too." Viking replies. "Says you're a loose cannon. A wild card. Violence prone and it's just a matter of time before you make trouble for the MC."

"Because I beat the shit out of a couple of scumbags every month? Ain't like they didn't have it coming."

"Ever since Lucin..." Viking clears his throat before he continues, "That whole thing went down... You aren't yourself. You spend half your days drinking and fighting."

"I'm functioning. I'm dealing with it." I grumble. But even I know, that's not even a half truth. I'm raging... Self-destructing...

"No, you're not. You're drinking and you're fighting." Viking counters.

I stare at him for a moment. "How am I supposed to be my old self, when that guy's dead?"

Viking takes a long breath and exhales slowly. "We know you're hurting, bro. What she did to you... It doesn't get more fucked up than that. But you gotta pull it together, man. You gotta *live*."

I suddenly want to throw up. From his words. From the memories of what she did to me. From my massive hangover. But I pull my shit together. "When are they voting?"

"Dunno yet. Soon. A majority vote. We'll all be called to the table."

"Do I get to be there?"

Viking nods. "You were demoted, but you're still a fully patched member. And you still have too many bros that like you. I don't think they'd stand for any backhanded bullshit like a vote behind your back. Even if Preacher pushes for it."

"Asshole." I mutter. "I don't know why my uncle ever hung around with that jerkoff. Co-Founding member or not."

"Get it in gear, bro." Viking gestures towards the bathroom behind me. "Cherry's making lunch and then you and I have an appointment."

"The fuck for?"

"Getting that shit off your arm." He nods to Lucinda's tattooed name. "Today is a new day, Dean. Time to start living like it again."

If only it were that easy. "A cover up isn't going to erase what's in here." I tap the side of my temple. "Or heal the heart she rammed a dagger through." Then pulled out and stuck in my back a few times, for good measure.

"No. But it's a start." Viking shrugs. "And I already paid for it. You know Diesel doesn't do refunds. *You're going*."

"I'll give you your money back."

"No. I'm doing it for you. That bitch's brand needs to go. Now get the fuck in the shower. Put on new clothes and get your fucking ass out here and eat with us." Viking insists. "*We're* your family. Like it or not. And we're not putting up with this shit from you anymore."

Damn it. "Alright."

"And trim your fucking beard. You're beginning to look like a *dirty, English Knight*. Gonna start calling you *Sir Lancelot*." Viking jabs at me as he heads for the door. "Scrub your balls good too. I'm getting you fuckin' laid tonight. Burying yourself in pussy is better than drowning yourself in alcohol." He slams the door behind him, making me wince.

I finish undoing my pants and toss them on the floor as I head to the bathroom in search of some fucking Advil, Tylenol, whatever the fuck. Catching a glimpse of myself in the mirrored cabinet above the sink, I can't help but crack a grin. I kinda do look like a dirty Knight. The salt and pepper (mostly pepper) beard on my chin coming to an odd point in a way I never keep my facial scruff. *Sir Lancelot*, I chuckle to myself. I've had a few names thrown at me in jest over the years, running with different MC's, but an official road name never stuck.

Grabbing the buzzer out of the bathroom drawer, I place it on the counter, then snatch the bottle of Advil as well, popping two into my mouth and swallowing eagerly. Plugging the buzzer in and clipping on the shortest guard, I go to work on my facial hair. Chicks seem to dig short scruff on me. Once I'm through with my beard, I remove the clip and buzz the sides and back of my head. Leaving the dark hair on top longer, so I can slick it back. Staring into the mirror now, though a little thinner than I used to be, I look a bit more like my old self.

"I don't hear any goddamned water running!" Viking shouts from outside in the hall.

"Jesus fuck! I'm on it!" I shout back at him. The throbbing in my skull making me instantly regret it. Yanking back the shower curtain, I twist on the water and grab a bar of soap and a razor blade from the mirrored cabinet. Stepping into the *hot as I can take it* shower, I slide the bar of soap over Lucinda's name and drag the razor blade across it. I'd be lying if I said I wasn't tempted to push down and skin the fucking thing off my arm, myself.

Freshly showered and clothed, I grab my leather jacket and head down the hall.

Cherry's carrying a tray out of the kitchen with food on it. Looks like a huge pile of sandwiches. I'm actually starving. I'm happy to eat whatever she threw together for us.

"Hey, Cherry." I say, kinda low, embarrassed of my behavior last night. "You want some help?" I ask, shrugging into my jacket to free up my hands to assist her.

She smiles, passing the tray to me. "Yeah, can you bring these out back? The guys are out on the patio. I'm gonna grab some more drinks."

We walk out together so I can hold the door for her as well. Axel and Viking are already seated outside. I don't even have the tray set on the table before Viking snatches four sandwiches. Half of this tray will end up down his gullet, easy. Cherry doesn't even bat an eye, though. She's used to it by now. Having to cook food enough to feed eight people, when it's only the four of us on a regular basis. The other ranking members of the MC have wives and girlfriends, and don't live at the clubhouse the way we do.

Glancing at Cherry as she hands out bottled lemon iced teas, she hands me one also. *"Green tea* for you, mister." She gives me a faint smile. "Good for *detox.*"

I accept it and sigh with remorse. "I'm sorry." I tell her. "I know I upset you last night. I just... I don't know how to..." She hugs me around the waist. Her bright red little bob against my chest. I shut up. Didn't know what I was going to say anyway. I rub her back and kiss the top of her head. She lets me go after a moment and holds out my motorcycle keys.

"You know I'll always forgive you, Dean. You're still my guardian Angel." Cherry smiles up at me.

"Even Angels have Demons, doll." I sigh, taking my keys from her.

We sit down and eat together, like the fucked up little family we are.

21

Viking and I ride our bikes up to the front of Ink Slingers Inc. A Tattoo parlor owned by Diesel, one of our MC Brothers, on the other side of town. He uses one of the guys here, so I know he's good. Viking's got quite the collection of ink on his body, including full sleeves on both arms of Nordic Runes and other Pagan themes.

We walk in together and Buck, our artist, is waiting. He's a light haired, thin, sinewy guy, covered in tats himself. He's also got more piercings and jewelry than I care to count.

Removing my leather jacket, I toss it to Viking. Buck tells me to have a seat so we can discuss my cover up. I take a seat in the black vinyl chair and lay my arm out for him to inspect.

"What are you thinking of getting?" he asks, prodding my skin. "Was this a bargain basement job?"

"Everything about it."

He chuckles. "Bitch broke your heart, huh?"

I just force a smile.

"Well, what are you wanting over it?"

"Something Dirty Knight related." I grin at Viking.

Viking laughs. "Your call, bro. Even a black dildo over it would be better than what it is." We all chuckle at that. But no fucking way am I getting anything *dick related* tatted on me. Not even over the bitch's name.

"Actually, wood grain would hide this nicely. How about one of those club weapons Knights used in medieval times?" Buck says. "Or one of those rods with the spikes at the top? Wouldn't even have to go too much bigger than what it is currently."

I nod. "Sure. Serene has spikes. That works."

"Cool. Let me draw it up and we'll get it done." Buck says, moving over to his work station with his computer and printer.

"My appointment here yet? Piercing some titties today." A voice says from the back of the parlor. Buck's co-worker, Jarred, approaches us to say hello. We bump fists with him and exchange greetings, before his punk rocker looking ass goes back to his station.

Viking grins at me. "We might get to see titties, Dean!" he says, with mock exaggerated excitement. I shake my head at him. "*Pregame* titties!" He continues with his adolescent badgering, until the two chicks walk in. They're pretty fucking hot. A blonde and a brunette. Young. Tan. Wearing Daisy Dukes and tanks. Beachy looking college girl types.

"Hell yeah." Viking says, unabashedly. *And loud*. Making no attempt to hide the fact that he's checking them out from head to toe. Neither of them seems to mind in the slightest though, as they walk right over to him.

"Oh my god, look at all your tats. That's *so* hot." One of them says, touching his arm. I grin as he flexes his muscles for them. Chicks always dig Viking. Even when he's a crude asshole.

The other girl looks at me. She smiles. I smile back. "Are you guys bikers?"

"Fuck yeah." I grin as she checks me out. It's been a while since I've bothered paying attention to female attention. Kinda feels good knowing

22

she's eyeing me up, even though I wouldn't actually make a real play for a girl her age. But, *lookin' ain't touchin'.*

"Are you guys like, in a motorcycle gang or something?" she asks. I can't help grinning wider and glancing at Viking. He's grinning too, and I know it's coming...

"You bitches seen SOA?" He asks. We're used to outsider girls asking us about *Sons of Anarchy.* I shake my head when he refers to them as bitches. For some fucking reason though, they seem to like it. Maybe he actually knows what he's doing. I've been out of practice the last half a decade. Loyally married to a disloyal bitch, myself.

"Oh my god, are you guys like that?" The blonde chick asks.

"Fucking, *just* like it." He lies. Bald-faced lies. I have to bite my tongue not to laugh. The MC we're with now, is nothing of the sort.

The brunette eyeing me, eyes me a little more. "That's hot... What are you getting done?"

Viking chimes in before I can reply. "This fucking guy right here, blood of the founder of our MC. Gonna be fucking president some day soon." A pipe dream at this point. My ass is about to be voted out. But I smile and let him say what he's going to say. "He's newly single. Getting his ex-bitch's name covered up."

"Cool." The brunette says to me. "Which ones your bike?"

"The expensive one." I tease her, though I'm not lying. My girl, *Serene,* is a custom lady.

She smiles, peeking back at the motorcycles through the front window, then at me again. "I can't tell." She giggles coyly, as if she doesn't want to offend me. It's cute.

"The one on the right, doll." I wink at her. She smiles bigger. *Doll* works better than *Bitch* any day of the week, and twice as well on Sunday. "You ever been on the back of bike before?"

She shakes her head, kinda slowly. Bites her bottom lip a little, in that way that makes a man pay extra attention. I glance over at Viking. He's still grinning.

His blonde touches his arm again. "I haven't either." She volunteers that bit of information.

Jarred pokes his head out from behind his curtain. "Are you getting piercings today or what?" he impatiently asks them.

"We'll be back in a bit." The brunette says to me with another smile. Viking and I watch them walk away behind the curtain together.

I look back at him once they're gone. "SOA. Seriously?"

He shrugs. "You're never gonna see them again. Who cares?"

I shake my head as Buck comes over with the transfer paper of my new tat. He wipes my forearm down and lays the design on. Peeling the paper off slowly, the outline is down. He sets his ink colors up on a tray next to me and the tattoo machine buzzes to life.

"Alrighty, say bye-bye, bitch." Buck says.

I lean my head back on the headrest. If only memories were as easy to cover over as shitty tattoos.

It's not long before the girls return from getting their piercings done. Didn't even hear them make a peep back there. I wonder if they even went through with it.

"What did ya's get?" Viking asks, clapping his hands together and rubbing them in anticipation of seeing some boobs.

The brunette lifts her tank up slightly, and pulls down the front of her shorts. She twists to show me first, her dangly little belly button jewelry... Hot.

"That hurt?" I ask her.

"Not really." She smiles. "I did my nipples last year."

I grin at her. "Did *that* hurt?"

She shakes her head again, biting that lip. She teases me like she's going to lift her shirt higher to show me, but she doesn't. I flash her another grin anyway and lean back again, as Buck wipes at my arm and goes back to it.

"What about you?" Viking asks the blonde. This chick does lift her shirt to flash us her perky tits. "Nice." Viking nods his head appraisingly.

"So, like, do you guys have biker names?" The blonde asks.

"Yeah. My buddy right there, they call him Lancelot. That's why he's getting that weapon tattooed over that bitch's name." Viking says. Again, I have to bite my tongue to prevent myself from laughing at the shit that comes out of Viking's mouth at any given moment.

"Oh, like the Knight?" the brunette asks.

"Fucking, *exactly* like the Knight." Viking says. "Bitches even call him *Sir* sometimes. *Sir Lancelot.*"

I'm dying of laughter inside. But I keep a straight face, clearing my throat before I speak. "Yeah. And we call him *Thor*." I say, cocking my chin at Viking. Even Buck is trying not to laugh now.

"Oh, like the God Thor?" the brunette asks.

"Hell yes. Look at me. I'm built like a God." Viking says. All the confidence in the world. I wait for it. No way the braggart ain't mentioning it... "Packing a fucking *hammer* too." He grabs a handful of his crotch.

Fucking called it.

The brunette loses interest in me and shifts her focus to Viking. I can't help but laugh. Wasn't going to go for her anyway.

Thirty minutes later, Buck's wrapping up my tat. Lucinda is gone. No trace of her. Does feel better not having her on me. The weapon looks realistic with the woodgrain and shading, and the spikes look pretty bad ass. I tip him, after he plastic wraps my tat and gives me the run down on aftercare. Not my first rodeo. I slide my leather jacket back on and notice the brunette is really eyeing me now. There's something about women, and men in leather jackets.

"So, um..." The brunette steps closer to me. "We walked here from campus. Can you guys give us a ride back on your bikes?" she asks, batting her eyes at me. I glance over at Viking. He shrugs with complete indifference.

"Sure, doll." I smile at her. The last chick on the back of my bike was my ex-wife. Fitting that streak should end today, too.

We drop the girls back at the campus and they linger a few minutes to flirt, while their frat looking boyfriends shoot glares at us. Viking revs his bike at them, and the loud roar of his straight pipes visibly shakes their confidence. We both laugh.

The brunette leans closer to my ear and asks for my cell phone. But the way she does it, the way she stands with her back directly towards the frat boy, and the way he's looking at her longingly, tells me she doesn't want him to know she's giving me her number. And it tells me he's got feelings for her.

I'm not going there. Not doing it to him. Not after the shit I've been through the last year over a woman.

"Watch your feet, baby." I say to her, slowly backing up Serene.

She looks baffled. Must not get rejected much, because her expression slides right into annoyance. She throws her arms up at me, like *what the fuck?*

I simply smile. Not going for this type, ever again.

Fuck Lucinda types everywhere.

T HE JOCSAN COUNTY JOKERS MC CLUBHOUSE, IS ALWAYS BANGING ON A Saturday night. I should have known Viking would drag me to one of their weekend parties, to fulfill his unsolicited promise to get me laid. The Jokers are well known for their generosity regarding *party favors*... Namely, their patch whores. Which they have more of, than any other MC in a three-hundred-mile radius, easy. A big part of the draw these women have to this particular MC, has a lot to do with the Jokers' distribution business. As well as the couple of Gentlemen's Clubs they own across their county.

Where it's typically uncommon practice for an MC's club girls to inter-mingle with members of a different MC, The Jokers are one of the exceptions. The sweetbutts and patch whores, though primarily there to cater to the Jokers at their beckoned whims, are basically a draw to attract potential prospects, and ease alliances between the JoCo Jokers and other MCs.

All MCs are by invitation only, regarding members of other MCs inside their club houses. The Saviors and the Jokers have been friendly with each other throughout the history of both of our clubs. I'm not surprised we're let right in without question, after the three prospects standing guard out-side the front door, pat us down and let us by.

I've always favored their choice of location for a clubhouse over others I've been to. Even our own. Not only do I find their choice in real-estate *sin-fully amusing*, but it was smart of the Jokers to purchase a former *Nunnery* years ago, tucked away in the woods, and transform it into the perfect club-house. The old Convent has lots of open space, and plenty of rooms upstairs turned into studio apartments for the Brothers and Prospects to crash in. It's funny to me, to imagine what the Nuns might think of what actually goes on here, now, in this *Den of Sin*. The downstairs consists of a large open space, with scattered couches and chairs arranged in a bunch of separate seating areas, generally centered around a raised platform with a stripper pole. There are several pool tables and pinball machines, as well as a long bar full of alcohol, and a huge industrial kitchen off to one side of the mas-sive open space.

In the center of the main wall, there's a large mural of their MC's logo. A skull wearing a three-pointed jester's hat. Down the hall, more rooms for their members and guests to crash in, probably even rooms for the live-in patch whores, as well as a huge conference room where they hold Church.

There's also a large marble water fountain in the main foyer. Which is currently spilling over with soap suds and bubbles, as several wet bikini babes wrestle inside it. Brothers gathered around laughing, goading them on and spraying them with beers. As we pass by, we tilt our chins up in greeting to those that notice us.

Slice, the President of the JoCo Jokers MC, a well-built, middle-aged man, with a buzz cut and a thin scar down the left side of his face, spots us and waves us over to his seating area. We shake hands, accept a couple of beers from the scantily clad sweetbutts making the rounds, and take a seat with him and three of his jacked-up Sergeant's at Arms. With a snap of his fingers, both Viking and I are surrounded by a few chicks each.

After about twenty minutes of having my balls broken over my bitch of an ex-wife, how nobody's seen me in months, how I'm about to lose my cut and how a good *pot fuck* will set me straight again, they finally quit ragging on me and move on to other neutral topics. It isn't long though, before Viking steers the conversation back to *pot fuck*... As in, *get high and get fucked*.

"You wanna blaze, let's blaze." Slice nods at a girl sitting on the arm of the couch near Viking, across from me. "Mary Jane, go grab us a few samples." He orders her. She gets up and walks away, down the hall somewhere out of view, and returns a few minutes later with a tray of joints and a small blown glass pipe, packed with weed, and unfortunately, shaped like a dick.

"What's your pleasure, gentleman?" She asks, bending to place the silver mirrored tray on the table before everyone. "We have AK-47 joints, here." She points to the pairs of rolled joints, naming each, "Purple Haze, Sour Diesel, Blue Dream and Gelato."

"My broken-hearted bro needs a mood booster." Viking says. I glare at him and take another swig of my almost empty beer.

Slice snaps his fingers and I've got a new one before I can blink. It's cold, too. And she even cracks the top off for me. "Thanks, doll." I say to the little blonde beer wench. She gives me a smile before she scurries off to cater to someone else.

"*Blue Dream* always makes me feel better." The brunette on my left smiles sweetly as she touches my arm. "They call me *Trippy*, by the way." She giggles. With all this weed, I can hardly imagine why. I clear my throat and smile at her.

"Dean." I say, switching my beer to my other hand to offer her my right one. She seems surprised by the gesture, but shakes my hand anyway. I guess a greeting around here towards a female is a slap on the ass or something. That's not how I roll, though. I hold the fairer sex in a higher regard than that.

"You don't have a road name?" Trippy asks.

I shake my head. "No. And I'm really not as miserable as he says I am, either."

"Bullshit. *He's worse*." Viking scoffs, they all laugh at me some more.

26

"Blue Dream it is, then." Mary Jane says, tucking her long, blue-black hair behind her ear and lifting the joint to spark it up. Viking sticks his greedy hand out first and she passes it to him, before offering the other contents of the tray to a few of the others sitting around us. One of the girls grabs the dick pipe and hits that too, bitching about how its packed too tightly. Another girl passes her a bobby pin to fix it. The tray ends up back on the table between us. As Mary Jane takes a seat on the arm of the couch across from me again, I notice Viking leans back and looks behind her.

"What do you have handcuffs for?" He flirtatiously asks.

"Why do you think?" She takes a drag from the joint.

Viking glances at me. "Why don't you show these bitches your party trick, Dean?"

"She might not want me to break her little bedroom accessory." I say, before taking a swig of my beer.

Mary Jane gives me a sly little grin. "These aren't some weak little set of cuffs from a sex shop." She taunts me. "You might be able to pick them, *if* you had something to pick them with. But you can't break out of them. They're real."

I can't help chuckling at *they're real*. "Oh yeah, doll? What do I get if I do break out of them?"

Slice laughs at me. "You don't have to bargain with her, bro. She'll spread for anybody with a cock and a cut." He says, then flicks his tongue salaciously at her between his two fingers. Mary Jane smirks back at him, opening her legs wide, dropping a hand between them and flipping her middle finger up at him in front of her panty-less snatch.

She snags the joint back from Viking, taking a hit herself as she turns to look me over. "What do you want?" she asks.

I shrug. "I'm going to break your toy, baby. You tell me what that's worth to you."

Mary Jane stands up to pull the cuffs out of her denim skirt's back pocket. She saunters over to me, dangling the cuffs in my face before she sits down next to me. Taking another drag of the joint, she blows the smoke at me. "They're not toys. They didn't come with fur." She says, "And neither does my pussy."

"I noticed." I grin back at her.

"Can you really do it?" Trippy asks. She sounds excited as she scoots closer to my left side. I just smile and hand her my beer. Turning back to Mary Jane, I hold my wrists out for her to cuff me.

"The tighter, the better, doll."

She places the joint between her lips and puts the cuffs around my wrists, squeezing them tightly. Holding the joint in her two fingers now, she licks her lips and smiles at me. "I've got you now, *Dean*."

"You're supposed to read him his rights." Viking jokes.

"You've got the right to remain silent, though once I'm toking on that cock, I doubt you'll be able to." She taunts me some more. The brothers and other sweetbutts around us join her in laughing at her little joke.

27

"I know where she keeps the spare keys." Trippy volunteers, her arm draping across my shoulders now. "I'll free you if she gets all power hungry on you."

I give Trippy a little smile before I glance back at Mary Jane. "You gonna bogart that joint all night?"

She gives me a playful scowl before she places the joint to my lips. I pull a long hit from it, then turn to Trippy. With a grin and a cock of my chin at her, she smiles back at me, her hand reaching up to hold my chin as she presses her lips to my mouth. Her tongue slides across my lips and I part them, shot-gunning the smoke into her waiting mouth.

"Thanks for looking out, doll." I wink at her. She half chokes, half giggles.

"Won't the fact that they're so tight make it harder to break out of?" Mary Jane asks.

I shake my head. "No, you want them tight, for this move. Otherwise, you'll really fuck up your wrists. You can still get out, but the less they rock back and forth, the less damage they'll do to you, for this move."

"Well, these are cop issued handcuffs. Good luck." Her confidence in these cuffs amuses me.

"Here we go." I say, stretching out my arms in front of me to force my leather jacket up my forearms slightly, getting it out of my way.

"Gonna be calling him Houdini instead of Lancelot after this." Viking jokes, reaching his hand out for the joint again. Mary Jane passes it back to him, then it's all eyes on me.

I grind the cuffs together between my wrists, twisting the chain around, trying to get it to kink and lock up on itself. It takes a minute or two, to finally get the chain to lock up correctly. When I do, I jerk my elbows out with a little torque, and snap the cuff at the swivel where the chain attaches to the metal ring, separating my wrists.

"Oh my god." Mary Jane says with surprise. "Those cuffs are by *Smith and Wesson*! Cops use them!" She reiterates. "I can't believe they just broke like that."

"The swivel is a weak point, even on cop issued cuffs. That's why it's best to always cuff behind someone's back. This move is basically impossible to pull off with your arms behind your back, because you can't lock up the chain and throw your elbows out at the right angle to break the swivel, or in some cases, the chain itself." I explain.

"So, what if your arms are cuffed behind your back? How do you get out of that?" Trippy asks, looking at me like I'm some kind of science professor. It's cute. I can barely keep from grinning at her excited curiosity.

"You either get your hands back in front of you, by tucking your legs through your arms. Or, you have to pick them. Which can be done on a double lock too, like these. You just have to knock the pin out. That can be done with your hands behind your back too, with practice."

"Show us!" Trippy says, excitedly, her little hands gently gripping my arm.

I slam the cuffs down hard on the table, dislodging the pins. Picking up the bobby pin one of the girls was using to stir the end of the glass dick pipe, I pick both cuffs and drop them on the table, one then the next.

"See. Fuckin' Houdini over here." Viking says.

"That's impressive!" Trippy says, eyes wide as she grabs one of the broken cuffs, examining it. "How were you able to even do that?"

"Knock the double lock pin out. Then place the shim between the ratchet arm and the pawl," I say, holding up the cuff to point to the components as I explain, "Just enough to force the shim down into the pawl. That will allow the cuff to be opened. You can do it with any small, stiff object similar to a paperclip or a hair pin." I say, chucking the busted cuff back on the table and sitting back. "I've seen it done with a tooth from a comb, too."

"Where did you learn to break the chain?" Mary Jane asks, taking a drag from the joint and leaning into me to press her lips to mine. I let her shotgun me.

"I was a bad, bad boy." I smile, smoke drifting out of my mouth as I speak.

"I like bad boys." She says, her eyes slightly hooded now as she looks me over.

"Me too." Trippy volunteers, handing me back my beer.

Mary Jane takes another long hit, before she leans across me towards Trippy, reaching out to pull Trippy's face to her. She shotguns the smoke into Trippy's mouth this time, making a sexy little show of their literal *smoking* hot tongue action. I lean back against the couch and take another swig of beer as I watch them French kiss and fondle each other in my lap.

After a few moments, Mary Jane turns her head slightly to look at me, as Trippy continues to lick her neck, reaching her hand up Mary Janes tank top to grab at her tits as she does. "You ever have two girls pleasing your cock at once?" She asks.

"What do you think?" I smile.

She bites her lip as she looks at me, contemplatively. "How about one girl blows you while the other rims you?"

"Fuck, bro..." Viking groans on the couch across from me. He's intently watching the girls fondling each other in front of me.

I can't help grinning back at Mary Jane, though. "Is that what you're offering?"

"Is that what you're into?" She smiles back.

"No."

She pouts at me for a moment, but then a smile pulls at her mouth as something seems to spring to her mind. "Do you know why we call her *Trippy*?" She asks, stroking her gal pals face, before she slowly pushes Trippy towards me. Trippy leans into me, ducking her head down and starts to place soft kisses on my neck. Her hands slipping up the bottom of my shirt to stroke her fingers along my abdomen. "Trippy is short for *Triple Threat*..." Mary Jane says, holding up three fingers. "You've got *three ports of entry* with her." She smirks with a naughty gleam in her eyes. I did not anticipate *that* being the origin of her little pet name...

"I want Trippy!" Viking immediately announces, hand raised high in the air. Slice snaps his fingers, and within an instant, Trippy is off my lap and into Viking's, faster than I can blink.

"You bastard." I mutter at him. Trippy seems sweet. I sense a bit if a bitch streak in Mary Jane. But whatever, it isn't like I'm ever going to pursue any of them at any point. The last thing I want is another Old Lady. Plus, they're property of the JoCo Jokers MC. The Jokers don't mind sharing their sweetbutts on occasion for a quick bang, but that's it. The girls belong to their MC.

"Looks like it's just us then." Mary Jane says, her fingers curling into the lapel of my leather jacket.

"I'm down." A pretty, petite red headed girl says, sliding her hand up my arm as she seats herself right in my lap. "The boys call me Lucky." She smiles, looking at me with her bright green eyes.

"Told you I'd get you *lucky* tonight, bro!" Viking laughs, before he gets up, grabbing Trippy and tossing her over his shoulder. She squeals and laughs, letting out a little shriek as he slaps her on the ass.

"You said I'd get *laid*." I correct him.

Viking shrugs. "Same shit." He glances at the other girls around us. "I've got more cock than Sig Sauer. Trip's gonna need a hand. Any of you bitches interested?"

I watch as one of the girls walks over to him. "Fuck yeah." He says to her, looking her up and down quickly, before he grabs her and flings her over his other shoulder. "Where can we get our fuck on around here?"

"Guest rooms, last two doors at the end." Slice cocks his chin in the direction of the hall on the far side of the room. "Wrap your shit up. There are condoms in all the night tables. Or in your case, plastic bags under the sink." That one earns him a round of laughter as well.

Viking grins, taking pride in the fact everyone knows he's got a huge dick. He turns and lumbers off in that direction, the two girls laughing, their long hair swaying with each of his strides down the hall. A door slams behind them and it isn't long before we all hear a pair of shocked female voices... *"Oh my god!"*

As for myself, I finish my beer, then spend a good portion of the evening on my knees, balls deep in Lucky, while she goes down on Mary Jane. Viking is right. Pussy is better than booze.

A FEW WEEKS LATER

VIKING AND VIPER HAD COME TO MY REPAIR SHOP, TO SOLEMNLY INFORM me that there would be a mandatory member vote tonight at the table. I knew then, that the axe was about to drop, severing my membership with The Saviors MC.

Now, I sit at the long, polished wood table in the meeting room of our clubhouse, surrounded by my MC Brothers. Staring at the carved skull and wings logo of our MC in the center, I listen stoically, as Preacher chunters on about my various infractions and misconduct against the rules of the MC.

"You're also committing a string of felonies." Preacher shoots at me. "That right there is plenty reason enough to trigger the morality clause to strip you of your cut and membership in this MC."

When he finally stops talking, I turn to glare back at our President. "First, I haven't been *convicted* of anything." I say. "Second, I haven't even been arrested. Not only have I not been arrested, I haven't even been fucking *questioned*." I try to keep my cool, taking a breath before I continue. "Finally, there's no proof I ever did anything to anybody. And it isn't like we're talking about innocent men. I don't see a problem. Sometimes it's the only justice these people get."

"You wouldn't see a problem, would you?" Preacher replies. "Your morals are in serious question, Dean. And if we're being honest, they always were, as far as I'm concerned. Your uncle was a forgiving man."

I force a thin, joyless smile. I've never been a saint, true. Never claimed to be either. But I never used my acquired skills on anyone that didn't have it coming to them. So what, if I made a living off it for a while? That was before my uncle brought me into this MC. At least I came at my targets head on. I didn't wait until they were brought to their knees by... other means. The way Preacher is doing to me.

"You're the last person I'd listen to a lecture on morality from, Preacher. Should rip your own fucking patch off and call yourself Snake." There are a few grumbles from the other members around the table in response to my words, but I keep my focus on Preacher.

"You haven't been convicted or arrested. But you could easily be questioned at any time." Preacher says smoothly.

I briefly glance around the table, at my soon to be former MC Brothers, trying to assess where their own feelings on this impending vote on my membership may lie. My gaze settles back on Preacher again. "You saying you gonna snitch on me? You don't have any proof either."

Preacher leans forward and folds his hands on the table beside the gavel. "I said nothing of the sort."

I scoff at him. "Of course not." I can read between the lines, though.

Preacher sighs, his expression mock sympathetic. "Dean, I'm only concerned with your behavior in recent months tarnishing the good name of this MC. Your past, prior to your uncle bringing you in, has nothing to do with the present issues. Your current unlawful actions and disorderly conduct makes us all look bad, and it puts this club at risk."

"That's a load of bullshit. Ain't looking like anything to anyone because nobody outside of this MC knows about my... extracurricular activities. Hell, *you* don't even actually *know*. You just read about the occasional story in the local news and *assume*. I've got alibis for every one of those events. Fucking try me." I growl at him. "You want me out because I'm a threat to your fucking throne. Let's call a spade a spade, Preacher. You hold the gavel only because I didn't want it."

My words don't seem to affect Preacher in the slightest. His smile only broadens. "I can't kick you out of this MC, Dean. It has to come to a vote."

The confidence in his tone tells me that he already knows which way this vote is going to go. Viking was right. Moves were being made to take my cut behind the scenes while I was too deep in the bottle. Wallowing in my misery over my ex-wife's treachery. Too fucked up to notice what was happening. To notice, or to care. Once again, clarity comes too late.

As I stand back from the table and await my obviously predetermined fate, I glance phlegmatically around the table at my MC Brothers. How I managed to convince myself that being voted out of the MC my late uncle founded, wouldn't bother me, I don't know. Because it feels like being slugged right in the liver.

The vote against my membership comes down, five to seven, in favor of stripping me of my patch. I'm surprised it wasn't closer. However, I keep a straight face as my eyes shift to each of the men who cast their votes. Most of them can't even look at me. Or won't, for whatever their reasons were for siding with or against me. My gaze finally lands on the oldest biker in this MC. The Club President. The snake. Preacher.

I should have challenged him for the gavel when I had the chance, a few years ago. When my uncle passed away. Before things happened in my private life that derailed me. I should have stepped up... I made it an easy power grab for Preacher.

"You're out of control, Dean." Preacher says. "That's why you're out of this club."

I glare at him. "*Out of control* would be slamming your fucking head through that wall behind you."

"Are you threatening me?" He raises his voice as he stands from his seat. His two Sergeant at Arms stand on either side of him, prepared to fight his battle for him, like good little soldiers. I suddenly feel better about having been demoted from Sergeant at Arms to a lower ranking member. He's not worth protecting.

"I'm telling you I'm in total fucking control." I growl back at him.

"Your actions prove otherwise, Dean. Turn in your cut."

When I don't remove it fast enough, one of my so-called Brothers, Ruger, the Sergeant at Arms that took my position, makes a move to reach for me. As if he's going to pull it off of me himself. A major sign of disrespect. He re-thinks his decision when Viking stands up from his seat beside me and steps towards him.

I grab Viking's arm, halting him. Though I feel somewhat betrayed, I don't want Viking to pound anyone into the foundation. The members of this MC are decent people. With one exception. But I'm the one who fucked up. Viking was right. He tried to warn me this would happen. I was too fucked up to listen at the time. Too absorbed in my own personal Hell.

Shrugging out of my cut, I toss it down on the table.

Viking snatches it up before any of the other members can take a knife to the patches.

"This cut is staying whole." He announces. "Dean is blood. The founder's nephew. It ain't right to vote him out on these bullshit grounds. And it ain't right to strip the patches off this cut. He's done more for the causes we support than anyone at this fucking table. He's done shit some of you only wish you had the fucking balls to do."

"Dean can remove them himself." Preacher interjects.

"You make him remove them, or anyone else, then you can remove me, too. Snowy, Dozer and Chopper will go with me. We already discussed it. And you can forget about patching in Axel. He'll join up with us. If you want this MC to remain whole, then you allow this fucking cut to remain whole." Viking says, he glances at Viper. "You fucking disappoint me, Brother."

I suppose Viking is as surprised as I am that Viper voted against me.

Viper says nothing, only continues to stare back at him.

"He's out, Viking. He can't keep his cut." Preacher says.

"Then I'll keep it." Viking glances around the table. "Unless any of you want to try to take it from me?" No one makes a sound, let alone a move. They all know it would take quite a few of them to bring down Viking. I don't give a shit about the cut anymore. But if they move on Viking, I've got his back, too.

"Fine. Take his cut." Preacher concedes. He looks back at me. "It's just a scrap of leather now, as far as I'm concerned. But if you've got club ink, you know what needs to be done about it."

Fortunately, I don't. Never got around to it. I've done the nomad, freelance thing for the majority of my MC experience, until my uncle talked me into settling in with the Saviors MC. Because of my former freelance life style, I was never too keen on branding myself with any club ink. Though I'm sure he wishes I had, just to put me through the humiliation of having my tattoos blacked out. I've done freelance work with harder MC's, who cut or burn them off ex-members. Seeing that once or twice was enough to put me off rocker tattoos.

"For the record, this is bullshit. And you're wrong about me not having control. I fucking own this building. The lot it sits on. That means I own this clubhouse. The Roadhouse, the bike shop. Legally, it's all mine. *Under my fucking control.*"

"That's fine. We're taking the MC in another direction." Preacher says.

"The fuck does that mean?"

"Well that no longer concerns you, Dean." Preacher's smile tells me there is more to voting me out than simply his perceived threat to his throne. "Remove yourself. We have other Club Business to discuss."

When Viking moves to follow me out of the meeting room, I stop him. "No. I'm out. You're still a Savior."

"I'm your Brother first."

I nod, forcing myself to give him a slight grin as if everything is alright. "A scrap of leather on our backs doesn't make us Brothers, bro. We're Brothers regardless." I extend my hand to him, and when he accepts it, I pull him in for a quick embrace. Unnoticed by the rest, I take the opportunity to whisper in his ear, that Preacher is up to something, and we need a man on the inside. Viking gives me a single nod before he resumes his seat at the table.

"I suggest you find yourself a new Church." I say to Preacher. "I'm taking things here in another direction as well."

He looks at me with the nerve to appear astonished. "You're throwing the MC out? This has been The Saviors clubhouse for over two decades!"

"The Saviors are welcome. You're not." I say with a shrug, then knock my knuckles on the table. "Feel free to take this table with you. I think I'm going to knock that wall down behind you, after all. Turn this whole area into a private gym or something. Would love to get some equipment in here. Maybe even a boxing ring."

He glares at me. "Part of me is glad your uncle isn't around to see what you've become. He'd be so disappointed in you."

I nod. "Without a doubt, he would be. For a lot of reasons. Top of the list would be allowing you to take over. I'm not a complete asshole though, Saviors can still drink for free at the bar on weekends. They can still use the rooms. That is, until you line up another clubhouse. However, the cash flow from the bike shop, ends tonight. I'll no longer be contributing to your coffers."

"What about the mission?" Viper chimes in.

And that's when it clicks. My uncle left everything to me, not the club, for a reason. To make sure the mission continued, lived on after his passing. He expected me to take his place and keep moving forward. He knew by leaving the property, the clubhouse, the businesses, to the MC, that everything could potentially fall into the wrong persons hands. That it could be transformed into something else entirely. With me out of the way, Preacher would have had everything he needed to take this MC in any direction he wanted. My uncle trusted me, me alone, not to let this mission fail. Clarity always comes too late...

"As long as the mission continues, I will continue to support it." I say to Viper, before addressing the other members sitting at the table. "As long as The Saviors MC remains on course, I will not turn my back on you guys. Only one thing needs to change. Preacher isn't welcome here. I don't trust him." I turn to face my glaring, former President. "And neither did my uncle."

As I exit the meeting room, parting ways with the Saviors MC, I feel my phone vibrate to a ringtone I haven't heard in almost a year... Thinking my mind is just rattled, I pull the phone out of my pocket to see if I'm mistaken.

I'm not. Her name is right there on my screen.

Fuck... What the fuck?

Storming down the hall back towards the bar, I stare at her name, warring with myself over whether or not to answer. I don't want to give her the satisfaction of picking up. Not after she's blown me off for a year. I shift my focus to the time on my phone. Eight pm, Sunday. As I move my thumb to hover over the little green phone icon, I hesitate, missing the call. Within seconds, she's calling me back again.

Something must be wrong... What if it's about Maddie?

I don't hesitate this time. I hit the green icon and brace myself as I say her name out loud, "Lucinda?"

"Dean..." her voice is low, barely a whisper. It sounds tight, strangled even. Like she's been crying.

"Is Maddie alright?" I immediately ask. She doesn't answer me, all I hear is whimpering. "Lucinda, what the fuck is going on?" I demand, my anxiety rising as the second's pass.

"I need your help." She cries.

Before I even realize what I'm doing, I'm walking hurriedly towards the front door of the bar to get to my motorcycle parked out front.

"Where are you? What happened? Where's Maddie?" I ask, fishing my keys out of my pocket as I shove the steel door open. I storm out towards my bike, parked near my repair shop across the lot. "God damn it, Lucinda! Fucking talk!"

She finally rattles off a cross street. I tell her I'm on my way, shoving the phone back in my pocket and mounting my bike. I fire her up, twist the throttle and take off to rush to my ex-wife's rescue.

When I find Lucinda, she's standing on the side of a back-country road, alone, in the dark. Leaving my headlights on, I kick the stand of my bike down and dismount to approach her. "The fuck are you doing out here? Where the fuck is your car? Where the fuck is Daniel?" I have a million questions, but I fire those off first as I walk up to her. Even in the mostly dark, only illuminated by the light on my bike, there are slight, visible traces of mascara running down her tear-streaked cheeks. She's holding her black riding helmet in her hand, wearing a cropped leather jacket, tight blue jeans and boots. "Did he fuckin' leave you out here?"

She swipes her blonde hair out of her face and nods, staring up at me. "He kicked me off his bike a mile back. I tried calling him. He didn't pick up. I tried calling Jason, but the signal back here is hit and miss. I don't even think Jason heard me. He might be on duty tonight. Then as I was walking, I called you. My parents are with Maddie. I didn't want to call them."

"Did he fuckin' hit you?" I demand. She shakes her head, no. Good. I have no intention of ever laying eyes on Daniel again. But I would make the exception to kick his ass if he had hit her. That shit will never, ever fly with me. The last time I saw him face to face, was when he was voted out of the MC like I'd just been. Only he was thrown out for fucking a Brother's wife. *Mine*.

"We were arguing, and I-", she begins to say, but I lift my hand to shut her up.

"I don't want to know. Just get on my bike." I cut her off. "I'll take you home. We don't need to talk about anything."

"Dean, please, don't be this way." She whimpers.

I'm so not doing this in the middle of bum-fuck-back-woods on a dark country road. I turn from her and walk back to my bike. "Come on. Get on the bike." I tell her again. "All I want to know from you is if I'm taking you to your house or to your parents' house?" Behind me, I can hear her boots slowly click on the pavement as she approaches. Headlights slice through the dark night from up the road. As the car approaches, I glance back to make sure Lucinda is near the side of the road. I fucking hate her. But I don't want her to get hit. Not by her boyfriend, or by a car that might not see us in the dark. I step slightly further out, so the driver's headlights catch me, and they approach with more caution.

When I recognize the vehicle as a white Dodge Charger, I sigh with minor relief. The driver bright lights me, making me squint and lift my arm to block my eyes. Then he flashes the red and blue lights on top of his patrol car, pulling over behind my motorcycle.

"Looks like Jason heard you, too." I say over my shoulder to Lucinda. I wait by my bike for Jason to step out of his police cruiser.

"Didn't expect to find you two out here...*together*." Jason says, shutting the door of the cruiser as he approaches us. "Everything okay here?" he asks, stopping a few feet from me. He places his hands on his tactical belt and glances between Lucinda and me.

"Yeah, you showed up in the nick of time to give her a ride home, so I don't have to."

Jason studies me for a moment before he looks at Lucinda. "You okay? All I heard was a cross street and you sounded upset."

"I'm fine. Daniel kicked me off the back of his bike. I couldn't get a signal. I didn't think you heard me at all. So, I tried calling Dean, too." She explains.

"And now that you're here, I'm off the hook." I say to him, turning and grabbing the handlebars of my bike to sling my leg over the seat. "She called you first, anyway." I loathe myself for actually feeling slightly bitter about it.

The radio on Jason's broad shoulder goes off, a female voice speaking in code, talking about a suspect fleeing a scene. Jason tilts his head to his shoulder, grabbing the radio and answering back that he's on it. *Fuck...*

"Sorry, brother." Jason says, before he turns and hurries back to his police car. I watch him over my shoulder as he jumps in the Dodge Charger and takes off, leaving me alone with Lucinda. I try not to resent him for leaving. He's on duty. He can't help it. He probably would have taken her if he could have, just to spare me from having to deal with her myself.

Taking a deep breath of muggy night air, I exhale slowly and attempt to brace myself for the next twenty minutes I'll have to be in her presence. "Alright. Let's go. Get on." I say to her. Lucinda puts her helmet back on and climbs on behind me, wrapping her arms around me to hold on. I tense at the feel of her body wrapped around mine. It's been more than a year... Hell, way more than a year, since I've had her on the back of my bike. Before she was too pregnant to ride with me. Before she had Maddie and left me not long after... The feel of her arms around me is a reminder of how much I miss what never fucking was... Melancholy slips back into hate.

"Where am I taking you?" I force myself to speak. "Your place or your parents' place?"

"*Your* place." She says softly.

36

"Fuck no." I pull my riding goggles back over my eyes, then fire up Serene. Kicking up her stand I ask once more, "Daniel's or your parents'?"

I feel her squeeze me a little tighter. "Dean, please? I want to talk."

"I've got nothing left to say to you, Lucinda." I sigh.

"But you came." She says. "I called you for help, and you came."

Of course, I did. It's what I fucking do. But I wasn't lying when I told her I've got nothing left to say. I don't. I've tapped out of this fight. I tapped out a long time ago.

"I'm sorry, Dean."

For what? There's quite a lot for her to be sorry for. But I choose not to acknowledge her words. It doesn't matter anyway. What's done is done. There's no going back. No undoing the past. I clear my throat, and after a moment, I ask her once more, "Daniel's or your parents' place?"

"My parents' place." She finally answers. I twist the throttle, taking off.

When I get her to her parents' house, I pull Serene to the end of the driveway. I'm not going up and risking them coming outside. I keep her engine running, so Lucinda doesn't get any ideas about trying to talk to me. She climbs off and rushes to the front of my bike, straddling the front tire and holding onto the handlebars, staring me in the face.

"Let go."

"Five minutes." She says, her blue eyes pleading.

My eyes narrow at her. "No. Get the fuck off my bike, Lucinda."

"Do you hate me?"

"Honestly, you make it real hard not to."

She stares at me. "But you came."

I let out a long sigh. "That's what the fuck I do, isn't it?" I snap. "When shit doesn't go your way. When you get your ass in trouble. You call me to fix it. You always did."

"You always come through for me."

I shake my head. "Except where it mattered most, right?" She puts her hand on mine, but I immediately sit back and pull away from her.

"Maddie is inside. Would you like to see her?" she asks, after a few moments of our stare down. Now I'm outright scowling at her. It's been a year and a half since I've seen her. Since they kept her from me. I probably wouldn't even recognize the baby I knew for six months before she was taken from me. I don't even have words to respond to her offer. All I have is a simmering rage inside me. "Dean?" she says my name, her eyes giving me that pleading look again.

"I gotta go. Get off my bike. Take your hands off of her, now."

"We need to talk." She pushes. "I miss you. I'm sorry." She's going to push me into losing my shit. I lean forward, gripping the handles of my bike, twisting the throttle to make her engine roar loudly as I glare in Lucinda's face. I want to tell her to go fuck herself, but as I angrily rev Serene, I let her tell Lucinda for me.

Lucinda lets go of my bike, but she doesn't move. She pulls off her helmet and chucks it onto her parents' front lawn, before she turns back to me. Her eyes are watery, but that defiant, determined look, is still there. "I miss you, Dean."

"I don't care how much it hurts." I snarl at her. "You broke me first."

When she finally steps aside, I take off so fast I damn near wobble the bike. Serene's back tire peels out with a scream upon the asphalt, leaving Lucinda in a little blue smoke cloud of burnt rubber.

T HE SUN IS SETTING ACROSS THE RIVER, CASTING A DEEP ORANGE GLOW over everything. I'm sitting on Serene, in the parking lot of the small riverfront park. The sound of kids playing on the nearby playground echoes across the lot. I glance in their direction. Two young mothers are seated on a bench, watching their boys play on the monkey bars. One of them has a stroller with a baby as well. They're the only people around.

I glance at my watch. The playground closes in less than thirty-five minutes. Though I'm here waiting for a specific purpose, I resolve myself to remain here until the women and their kids leave. Regardless of whether or not my business concludes before that time. This part of town changes after nightfall, when the dregs emerge looking for entertainment. Usually in the form of trouble, and often times, at the expense of innocents.

Twenty minutes later, Officer Jason Caldwell parks his squad car a few spaces away. He gets out and makes his way over to me, a file in his hand at his side. I notice the women spot the police car, and the cop coming up to me. They gather their kids and make their way to their mini vans. I can't help grinning.

They didn't notice me the whole time I've been watching over them. The cop approaching me automatically paints me as the leather clad bad guy biker in their minds, though. They'll never know the cop and I are childhood friends. That the cop comes to me to see to it that justice is served to those who manage to skirt the system. They'll never know how safe they were in my presence. But it's okay. I'm the scary biker. What matters is, they're leaving now. I no longer have to concern myself with their safety.

"I heard about the vote." My cop friend says, running his hand over his crewcut. "I'm sorry."

"Shit happens. I've gotten a lot of work done these last few weeks. Frees me up to do other things." That's a half-truth though. I can't do the missions alone. For that, I am sorry, and do harbor some regret. Though, not for myself. For the Madelines...

"Preacher's backing the MC out of everything. Not even working with safehouses anymore." Jason informs me as if I didn't know.

"Fucking prick. He didn't have the balls to tell me to my face either. I suspected as much though. When he couldn't even look me in the eye."

Jason shakes his head. "Shame. The Saviors are an MC the community approves of." We stand in silence for a moment before he brings up, "What was that with you and Lucinda a few weeks ago?"

"There's no *me and Lucinda*." I want to make that perfectly clear. "And you heard her. Daniel dumped her ass on the side of the road. I dropped her off at her parents and took off like a bat outta Hell."

"He's an Asshole." Jason sighs.

"They deserve each other." I mutter.

After a few moments of awkward silence, Jason lifts the folder he's holding. "I'm gonna say some shit to you Dean, that I never fucking said to you. Got me?" His tone is serious. He seems tense.

"All these years, the shit we've done together. You still feel the need to say that to me?"

He shakes his head. "Just had a rough couple of days." He hands me the folder. "I was the responding officer a few weeks ago to a domestic call. Husband beating on his wife. Took him in. She got an order of protection against him. They let him walk, though. Last night he put her in the hospital. Broke her face. An arm. A few ribs." He folds his arms and turns toward the river. "Paper doesn't do shit. When they violate, they barely get a slap on the wrist. It's a joke. All we can do is arrest. Sit back and hope a judge tosses them away for a while. But it's never long enough. They never get what they actually deserve. And the victims are left not only beaten and broken in more ways than one, they get to live looking over their shoulders for these bastards to come at them again. Knowing that the next beating is going to be worse than ever for getting them locked up, regardless of how temporary it is."

He's right. The justice system is a joke in many cases. Set up to protect the criminals. Sucks for the victims of violent crimes. I flip open the folder and take a glance. "There are six guys in here." I thought I was only going after the one he just mentioned.

Jason nods. "Was thinking you and I could come to a new arrangement." He turns back to me. "Broaden your scope... There are more than just women beaters in this file... I'll get you the intel you need. You deliver your special brand of street justice. Preferably on nights I'm working, just in case. That way there's a chance I'm the first responder, if anything should go wrong. You get a chance to slip away."

"Haven't been caught yet." I shrug.

"First time for everything."

True. I notice him look down at his boots. He seems agitated. More so now than when he got here. "What's the matter, Bro?"

"That last guy." He tilts his chin to the folder I'm holding.

I flip the pages to the last one to study him for a moment. "What about him?"

"Within an inch of his life. Got me?" his tone is grave. I look back up at my friend. His mouth is a hard line. Jaw tense. Eyes glaring down at the photo in the file.

"That bad, huh. She alive?" I ask.

"Barely. She's in a coma. Cracked skull. Broken hands... *defense wounds*, you know." His voice trails off on the last part.

My blood boils. "I'll do him first."

"Just watch your ass. He's into that MMA shit like you." Jason sighs.

"Why don't you do him with me? Might make you feel a little better."

He shakes his head. "Can't risk it. Got a wife and a baby. My jobs a risk as it is. As much as I'd love to unleash on these bastards, deliver the justice they deserve, my hands are tied. I'm bound to uphold the law. What I'm doing right now, handing you this information. It's a risk I'm willing to take. But that's as far as I'll go. If I can cover a scene long enough for you to get out, if shit should go wrong. I'll do what I can. But you're pretty much on your own there, bud. Best I can do."

"Not going to involve you. Don't worry. You won't know till it's done." I say, glancing down at the MMA guy. Looks like a big dude. I can imagine the damage he did to her. It's always extra impressive when trained fighters pummel a chick.

We're both silent for a few moments. Jason is staring at the setting sun. He looks troubled though, discontent. Frustrated. I don't blame him. Jason always wanted to play the hero growing up. He was born to be a cop. To serve and protect. A real good guy. To see him standing in his blues, so disgusted with a system he dedicated his life to, it evokes a somber feeling.

"You're a good cop, Jay." I remind him. "A good man."

"Am I?" I barely hear him.

"Never doubt it. It's not your fault we operate within a flawed system. You're still delivering justice." I pull the papers out of the file and roll them up, tucking them into my jacket and hand him back the file. "You're still the hero, Jay. I'm just the hammer. But you help me, too. I get to use my skills for good now. You give that to me. A worthy purpose. I get to be good, too."

He scoffs, but he nods. "You're good, Dean. You're just a psycho."

I grin. "Yeah well, some things can't be heled."

IT'S A QUARTER PAST ELEVEN ON A THURSDAY NIGHT, WHEN I PARK SERENE halfway down the long, wooded driveway of the wife beater's home. Far enough in so that she isn't seen from the road, and far enough away from the house, that she isn't noticed. I'll have to jog back to her once the job is done. As I walk within the shadows of the tree line towards the house, I pull the skull print mask up over my nose to obscure my face.

The house is fairly large. All slate and stone. Manicured lawn and gardens. A large water fountain in the driveway, which turns from pea gravel to cobble stone once I'm closer to the house. This place definitely has an alarm system. Fortunately, I do not see any cameras outside. There's a red corvette parked in front of the house. Must be the prick's car. He's home. Breaking in the old-fashioned way isn't going to work here, but there are two large, nine-foot potted Arborvitae bushes, on either side of the front door. They will work nicely.

The car is parked under a large Poplar tree, and I walk over to the tree line to find a decent sized branch. Once I do, I approach the car and place it carefully on the hood, nearest the house so that it will be easily noticed.

Then I grab a quarter sized stone from the garden and walk up the front steps. Turning, I hurl the rock at the red corvette, nailing it on the front quarter panel. Its alarm blares and lights flash, as I tuck myself behind one of the decorative bushes by the front door.

Within moments, the douchebag emerges from the front door with his keys, wearing shorts and a t-shirt. He's fucking ripped too. I already know I might be feeling this job tomorrow if he gets a shot in.

He beeps the alarm off and descends the stone steps slowly, cursing the tree for dropping a branch on his precious car. I slip out from behind the bush and through the front door, into his house, unnoticed.

It's a nice fucking house. Marble floors, cathedral ceilings. The furnishings and décor look straight out of a snooty magazine shoot for a lifestyle of the rich and shameless article. There's even an open top mahogany grand piano sitting in the living room. So pristine, it doesn't even look like it gets played. Actually, the entire room doesn't look like it gets touched by anyone but a maid. I scan the space for camera's inside, but I don't spot any. If he beats his wife, I'd imagine he wouldn't want cameras inside, either.

I hear him muttering on his way back into the house, and get into position beside the front door. As he crosses the threshold, I slug him in the face, knocking him sideways, then kick him in his side, sending him sprawling onto the marble floor of the grand piano room. I shut the front door and I make my way into the room with him.

"Oh, you're fucking dead!" He says, pushing himself to his feet. "You picked the wrong house to rob motherfucker!"

"Ain't here to rob you. Here to deliver a message." I tell him. He looks at me, confused, though still pissed off. "You lay a hand on your wife again, you're the one who ain't gonna be waking up. Got me? And I'm not talking about a coma. I'm talking dead."

"Who the fuck are you?" he demands.

"Just a messenger with a special delivery." I smile, unseen beneath my mask. I pull the brass knuckles out of my pocket and slip my gloved fingers through them. Then gesture for him to bring it on.

"Fucking prick!" he roars as he charges me. I sidestep and grab him again, twisting him back around, using his own momentum to hurl him back into the room. This time I rush him while he's off balance, nailing him in the face with a downward slug, then crouching slightly to upper cut him, sending him stumbling backwards. He recoups quickly though, grabbing at me as we grapple with each other.

He's fucking strong. I quickly realize I shouldn't have let him get close enough to get a hold of me. He slugs me in the ribs, two solid punches to my right side, then he grabs me by the collar of my leather jacket in both fists and hurls me sideways through the air. I crash down hard, feeling splintering wood beneath me as I'm momentarily stunned by the deafening, thunderously loud vibration of landing solidly on top of piano wires. Despite the ringing in my eardrums, I scramble to get out from *inside* the grand piano, before he can grab me again. I shove the lid off my body, making a less than musical racket as I climb out quickly.

Once on my feet, I snatch the splintered lid prop from the now busted up instrument and throw it at his face, using his instinct to block the sharp wooden object to my advantage. I tackle him full force and we land hard on the marble floor. Slamming my hand against his forehead, I crack the back of his head against the floor, semi knocking him out. His body squirms beneath me, fighting to remain conscious.

If I had intended this to be a fair fight, I'd have gotten off him. But he didn't show his woman any mercy. And so, he will not get any mercy from me.

"Can you hear me? You fucking sack of shit. This is for your wife. You hurt her again, I'll kill you." I say in his ear, then back hand him across the face. He groans. "You hear me? You're fucking dead if you do it again."

With that, I slam my fist into his face, again and again. I feel the crunch of his nose breaking against my knuckles on impact, and the blood begins to flow. I grab him by his hair and slam his head against the floor. Not hard enough to crack his skull, but he's out, like a busted light.

Taking a moment to catch my breath, I get off him and stand up. Pain shoots through my side and keels me over, forcing me to brace my hands on my knees. Fuck, landing inside that piano hurt. The fucker can throw a solid punch too, I can feel that already in my ribs. Son of a bitch. I really need to start hitting the gym harder than I've been lately. Get the ball rolling on putting a gym in the clubhouse. This *out of fighting shape* shit is unacceptable on my part.

I glance back down at him. Fucked his face up good. But it's not good enough. He beat her within an inch of her life. So, I straighten and kick the shit out of him, landing my steel toe motorcycle boot into his stomach and ribs until my own body is nearly screaming at me to stop. His ribs have to be broken at this point. I'm pretty sure at least one of mine are. Crouching down slowly, I check his pulse. He's still alive.

I make my way back out the front door and down the stone steps, walking at a steady pace towards Serene. I don't call emergency services to come get this trash bag, so there's no need to jog. Making it to Serene, I sling my leg over her, sinking down onto her seat carefully. I'll text Jason when I get back to the clubhouse. Bending to retrieve my cell phone from the side bag right now isn't that appealing. I fire up Serene and kick her stand up, riding out of the driveway and back into the streets. This piece of shit is on his own. I left him alive. He should stay that way. If he doesn't wake up, the maid or somebody will eventually find him. I don't care.

Serene carries me over the streets towards home. With every dip and bump in the road, I'm glad I improved her suspension system when I upgraded her to make her the beautiful, smooth riding Dame she is. Within thirty minutes she's got me riding through the open gates of my lot. In front of the repair shop, I shut her down and dismount her slowly, walking over to press the code into the keypad to unlock the garage door. Bending carefully to lift it just high enough to walk her inside, I tuck her in for the night before shooting Jason a text that the job is done.

As I walk the short distance across the lot towards the Roadhouse, I glance at my watch. It's a little after one, so the place is still in full swing. The crescendo of loud music, billiard balls cracking and conversation bursts through the door as I enter The Twisted Throttle.

Viking is sitting on a bar stool near the front door, keeping an eye on the room. Cherry is behind the bar serving up drinks. As I shut the steel door behind me with a clang, Viking turns to look at me.

"Any problems tonight?" I ask.

"Nope." Viking says, then sighs as if he's bored. I have to chuckle.

"Don't look too eager to fuck up my bar." I tease him. He grins.

Walking over to the bar, I check in with Cherry, and greet a few of our regulars as well. Cherry gives me a smile as she reaches under the bar into the fridge and grabs me one of those damn Green Tea bottles she keeps there just for me. With a little wink, she tosses it to me.

I shake my head and grin back at her as I twist the top off. I actually am thirsty as fuck and would probably drink just about anything. Plus, it makes Cherry happy to think she's helping me better myself in some small way. I chug the whole damn thing down and toss the empty bottle back to her.

"It's not that bad, right?" she smiles. I give her a wry look, which earns me one of her eye rolls as she grabs a rag to run over the polished bar top. "What happened to your hand?"

Glancing down, I notice a few scrapes on my knuckles. Probably the jerk's teeth when I fucked his face up. But I go with a sarcastic, "*Serene bit me.*"

Cherry's green eyes narrow slightly, but she's still smiling. "Like your darling Serene would ever bite you."

I walk into my room at the club house, flicking the dim light on and chuck my keys onto the dresser top. Shrugging my leather jacket off carefully, I drop it onto the chair as I walk across the room to the bathroom to take a leak. Flipping the seat up with my boot, I relieve myself. Cherry's green tea concoctions have me pissing like a damn racehorse. I suppose that's part of the "cleanse" she keeps reiterating every time she hands me a bottle of the shit. Shaking my dick off, I kick the handle to flush and tuck myself back in my pants. Zipping up my fly, I step back into the bedroom.

"Thought you'd be interested to know, Daniel's prospecting with another MC."

Her voice scares the shit out of me, damn near giving me a fucking stroke. I wasn't expecting to find anyone in my room. Least of all, *fucking Lucinda*, in my goddamned bed.

"Jesus fucking Christ... The fuck are you doing in here?" Willing my heart rate to come back down to normal, I lean back against the dresser and try to avoid looking directly at her.

She grins at me. "That was some impressive pissing." She teases.

"What do you want?" I'm not in the mood for her games.

She pouts at me. "You didn't hear me?"

I heard her. And I couldn't care less what the man she cheated on me with is doing with his life. "I don't give a fuck. Don't really care what you do either."

She gets up off the bed and saunters towards me. She's wearing a tight leather skirt, low on her hips. I can see her pink thong peeking out the top. It matches the pink bra I can see through her black lace top under her crop style open leather jacket. She looks like a fuckin' sweetbutt.

"He fucking lets you leave the house dressed like that?" She keeps coming towards me and I put my hands out to object. "Stop! Close enough, Lucinda. What do you want?"

She snatches my wrist, holding out my arm to inspect the cover up tat. "I can't believe you actually did it." She scoffs. "You told me you'd cherish it forever."

I pull my arm back, mocking her with a scoff of my own. "You made similar statements about things. Now look where we are."

She turns and pulls down the top of her skirt, exposing the upper portion of her ass cheek to me. The Tattoo she got of my first initial, a cursive letter D with a little fancy heart beside it. "I've still got your mark on me." She smiles at me over her shoulder.

"Well, now it can be *D* for *Daniel*. Lucky you." *Or D for dick in general.* I keep that thought to myself.

"It will always be you, Dean." She sighs, turning back around to face me with a pout. "Do you miss me at all?"

I stare at her coldly for a moment. "I miss what I thought we had. But it was a lie. So, there's nothing to miss."

She grins. "Why are you living at the club house when you've got the ranch house and the farm? If you were just going to let it sit empty you should have let me have it in the divorce."

"I think you took enough, Lucinda." I sneer. Besides, it's none of her business that I'm having the whole damn place renovated and redecorated to erase all traces of her presence from it. "Get gone. I'm tired."

"I brought you some pictures of Maddie." She says, and my guts twist at the mention of her name. "Would you like to see?"

Yes. "No." My heart thumps painfully in my chest. God, I miss her. I swallow hard.

She folds her arms. "Really? You hate me that much? You don't even care about Maddie anymore?"

I glare at her, my pulse quickening. "Of course, I fucking care about Maddie!" I snap. Even I can hear the venom in my voice on that one.

Lucinda grabs her purse and sits down on the black comforter on my bed, pulling out an envelope. She fans herself with it and pats the bed beside her. "I come bearing gifts, Dean." she winks at me. "Come see. She's gotten so big so fast. I've got pictures of her new room in here too. I put a photo of you in there, so she knows who her uncle Dean is."

It's like a fucking knife in my gut and my heart at the exact same time. For a moment I can't breathe, stunned by her callous words. I force myself to pull my shit together and suck in a breath. *"So she knows who her uncle Dean is?"* I repeat her words back to her. She blinks at me, as if she is oblivious to the pain I'm in over Maddie. "She'd know me if you didn't *keep her from me."*

"Daniel doesn't think it's a good idea...you know that." Lucinda's tone is irritatingly placating. "He is her father."

I scowl at her. "How well I know."

She cocks her head to the side and looks at me as if I'm the one being unreasonable. "Come on, come look at the pictures. I made you some copies to keep. Do you really not want to see her pictures?"

Against my better judgement, I join Lucinda at the foot of the bed. She hands me the envelope, leaning against me to look at the photos, as I pull them out and slowly flip through them. Maddie has grown so much in the year since I saw her last. A beautiful, little blonde girl, with brown eyes and lots of smiles. At least she looks like a happy baby. I can find some solace in that. I have to try to, anyway. Or succumb and let the pain eat me alive.

Lucinda narrates each photo, the wheres and whens and whys of each, but I barely hear her. In my mind, I hear Maddie crying at two AM for her bottle or a diaper change. Which I always jumped up immediately to attend to without hesitation or complaint. I hear her little coos and gibberish as she squeezed my finger in her tiny fists when I held her every chance I got. I can hear her little sneezes that always melted my heart and how she giggled when she'd reach up and grab the rough stubble on my chin. When I close my eyes, I can smell that amazing newborn scent of her head, that I locked into my memory forever...

Lucinda's squeezing hand on my knee brings me back to the present. When I open my eyes there are drops of water on the top photo. I wipe it off on my chest.

"Dean," she whispers, reaching up to touch my face. I feel her brush away more water from under my eyes.

Pulling back from her, I impatiently wipe my face against the back of my arm. Swallowing hard, I try to compose myself, looking through the rest of the photos more hurriedly this time. Once I've seen them all, I place them back in the envelope and hand it back to her.

She pushes it back to me. "Keep them."

I swallow the lump in my throat before I attempt to speak. "Thanks. She's beautiful."

"I'm so sorry. I thought the photos would make you happy. I didn't think they'd upset you so much."

"I just miss her." I reach over to the dresser and place the photos on top of it.

Lucinda rubs my arm and places her chin against my shoulder. "What if you didn't have to miss her so much?"

I glance at her. "What are you talking about?"

"What if we worked something out... like a special visitation thing every now and then?"

"Daniel doesn't want me having anything to do with her. He's her father. You like to remind me of that." I say, bitterly.

Lucinda leans her head against me, draping her arm across my chest, her hand holding onto my shoulder. "There are times, Dean... many times... I have wished... and still do wish... that Maddie was *ours*." She whispers.

"But she's not. And we both know all the reasons why." Reasons I don't like to think about, let alone speak of.

Lucinda blows out a long breath. "If you don't want her in your life, just say so. I'm not going to force her on you." she snaps at me.

If I don't want Maddie in my life!

"Fuck you, Lucinda." I mutter. "Callous bitch."

In an instant Lucinda is in my lap, straddling me, her hands holding my face to hers as she roughly crushes her mouth to mine. I grab her arms and twist my face from her. "The fuck are you doing?" I demand, anger rising inside me.

"Do you want to fuck me, Dean?" She whispers in my ear. "Fuck me for fucking Daniel behind your back?" She licks my ear, bites my neck. Her hand reaching down to grab at my dick. Her other hand grabbing my face and pulling me to meet her eyes. "Tell me a revenge fuck doesn't appeal to you. I'm ready and willing to give it to you."

It is appealing. I do owe him one. Would be poetic justice to fuck his woman after he fucked mine. Sick that it's the same fucking woman. She was my wife when he did it to me, though.

She shoves her tongue in my mouth and groans, fumbling with my belt and the zipper of my pants. "Fuck me, Dean." She pants like a bitch in heat. "We were hot together, don't you remember?" Yeah, I remember. We had some hot times. Lucinda was a wild one in the sheets. I doubt much has changed. Except the fact that I kind of fucking hate her now.

She's got my cock out and she's jerking me, getting me semi hard. "You'll have to do better than that, Lucinda." I mock her.

She shoves off me and drops to her knees on the floor before me, taking me into her mouth and sucking me off with a vengeance.

Fuck!

Nothing like an angry blow job to get things going. I wrap my fist in her hair and twist it until she whines, but she keeps sucking me off. Determined little bitch. I debate busting a nut in her mouth without giving her a heads up. After a few moments though, she claws my arm away and stands. Ripping off her clothes and tackling me like a Hell cat, she grabs my cock and guides it into her, about to ride me like a bull.

"Oh, fuck no!" I growl at her, ignoring the pain in my rib as I grab her and pull her off me. I pin her face down on the bed, my hand pressing against her shoulder blades. My other arm lifts her hips up off the bed so I can fuck her from behind. "I don't want to see your fucking face!" I snap at her, shoving my pants further down to grab my dick and line it up with her treacherous snatch.

46

She's begging me to fuck her so I don't bother being gentle, I ram all the way into her, balls deep, and she cries out as I pound her mercilessly.

"You better fucking come, Lucinda, I'm not waiting for you." I warn her. "I don't give a shit if you get off or not." I can feel her fingers rubbing her clit, her sharp nails occasionally jabbing my cock, her hips moving to fuck back on me. I slap her ass hard and she lets out a sharp little cry.

But she's *yessing* me, and *Oh God'ing* the whole time. I'm not hurting her. As much as I fucking hate her, I don't want to actually hurt her physically. Fuck her feelings though... *Heartless. Callous. Bitch.*

I can feel her pulsating and rippling around my cock. She begins to pant and then clenches around me, crying out, her body shuddering. I was hoping I'd beat her to the finish line, but at least she can't say I'm a lousy lay. I pump her furiously for a few more moments, until I come inside her with a grunt, biting my tongue to prevent myself from saying anything she could take as complimentary. I pull my cock out of her and slap her ass hard, once more. Should have used a wrap. Too fuckin' late.

"Take that back to Daniel, bitch." I step back from her to shove my junk back in my pants. I don't bother zipping up. I'm getting in the fucking shower after this dirty fuck.

Lucinda rolls over onto her back, still catching her breath. "Oh my God that was amazing! For whatever it's worth Dean... you still fuck like a rock star."

I grab her clothes off the floor and throw them at her. "Shut the fuck up, Lucinda. Get dressed and get gone."

She laughs, but grabs her clothes and starts to get dressed. "When is a good time for you? We can try to work something out."

I look at her incredulously. "Fuck no. This was a one-time thing."

She grins at me, watching me closely now as she pulls on her clothes. "I mean about Maddie. You *earned* it." she winks.

I'm pretty sure my jaw just hit the fucking ground. "I fucked you to get a visit with Maddie? That's what the fuck this was?" Emotions I didn't even know I had start to wash over me. "You're a *sick* bitch, Lucinda."

"You want to see her, or no?" she demands, pulling up her skirt. No qualms about it what so ever.

"Of course, I want to see her... But what about Daniel?"

"He doesn't have to know about any of it." She says, nonchalantly, pulling on her jacket and slipping into her heels. I don't even know what to say as I watch her move about the room, dumbfounded. "I'll text you." She says, reaching for her purse and heading for the door. She stops before she opens it. "*Oh!* I almost forgot." She turns back to me, reaching into her purse and removes a small, pearly white envelope with a familiar faded picture of a purple jar of hearts. "I wanted to hand deliver this to you."

"The fuck is it?" I ask, reluctantly taking it from her.

"Daniel and I are getting married. That's your invitation."

"You really are a cold-hearted bitch, Lucinda." I sigh.

She steps closer to me, running her hand down my arm, her fingers lingering over the tattoo where her name used to be. "You might have removed

47

my name from your arm. But you'll never remove the scars I've left on your heart." She sneers at me, before she turns and slams the door behind her.

I CLOSED THE REPAIR SHOP EARLY TO BE DOWNTOWN. NOW, I WATCH MADDIE and Lucinda from a distance at the park across the street from the ice cream parlor. She's almost twenty months old. I've missed thirteen of those months. She's walking on her own now, running awkwardly to and from Lucinda as they play together in the grass with a bright pink rubber ball. I can hear her shouting words excitedly, though from this distance, they're hard to make out.

A big part of me wants to sweep her up in my arms and hold her tightly. Spin her through the air like some cheesy fucking movie where everything always works out Aces in the end. Where life is always as sunny as this summer day in the park. That through some act of God, the kid remembers me and loves me.

But my life ain't sunny. Never has been. And so, my rational mind reminds me that Maddie most likely doesn't remember me at all. That I'm a stranger to her. That I might even scare her. That there's a good chance she'll reject me and fearfully cling to Lucinda when we meet. I have to brace myself for that probable outcome. She won't have any idea that her first six months of life were spent in my arms. Until she was ripped out of them... out of my life... thirteen long, miserable months ago.

When Lucinda finally looks around the fairgrounds, she spots me sitting on the picnic table in the shade, across the lawn under an oak tree. When we set this meeting up, a few weeks after our little *arrangement*, I had asked her to bring Maddie to me. I thought it would be less intimidating for the kid if they were the ones to approach, as if it were on their terms.

Lucinda lifts her arm and waves, then bends to say something to Maddie as she points in my direction. The little girl finally looks my way as she picks up her pink ball and clings to Lucinda's finger. They begin their walk towards me.

My heart starts to beat faster in my chest, the closer they get. Maddie doesn't look scared yet. She's focused on me, breaking her concentration on the stranger at the picnic table only once, when she drops her pink ball and has to stop to pick it back up. I'm practically strangling the stuffed animal I brought for her. A monkey. Lucinda told me Maddie had a thing for monkeys. So, I made damn sure to bring her one. I am not above a bribe for Maddie's affection. She doesn't remember me. I need to pull out all the stops I can, to make a worthwhile first impression on her.

More than halfway to me, Lucinda bends to lift Maddie into her arms and carries her the rest of the way. Saying something in the child's ear that I cannot make out either. My eyes are locked on Maddie though, searching incessantly for any sign of fear. So far, I see only curiosity in her little brown eyes.

She is only a few feet from me now. I smile at her gently, but I don't move from the table. I don't want to appear to be any form of threat to her or her mother.

"Do you know who this is?" Lucinda says to her daughter, kissing her cheek. Maddie shyly tucks her head against Lucinda's face, but she doesn't look away from me. "This is your uncle Dean. Remember?" Lucinda gives her a little gentle bounce in her arms, as if that will jog her memory. "You have uncle Dean's picture in your room. We say *night-night* to him, right?"

What sounds like "*Yeah*," squeaks out, barely audible from Maddie. I lift the monkey a little higher, so she notices it, and I make it wave at her. Her eyes light up and she beams a smile at it. When she looks back up to meet my eyes, the smile doesn't fade. My heart skips a beat.

"Hi Maddie." I smile back at her.

"Hi." She says to me, clearly, and still smiling. Lucinda sits down on the table beside me, propping Maddie up in her lap to face me. I shift slowly to face her more directly.

"I brought this little guy for you, Maddie." I say gently, extending the toy to her. She reaches for it, dropping her pink ball without much of a care now. It rolls a few feet away. I make a mental note to get it for her, but I don't want to move just yet.

"*Oooh wow!*" Lucinda plays it up for her daughter. "How cool is that!"

"*Coo.*" Maddie agrees, in that little voice that melts my fucking heart. Nothing is cooler than '*Coo*'.

"What do we say?" Lucinda prompts her.

"Tank you."

"Thank you..?" Lucinda prompts once more.

"Tank you... *Unka Dee.*"

I'm sure I'm grinning like an asshole, but I can't help myself. "You're welcome, princess."

Lucinda jostles her playfully. "Uh oh, somebody thinks you're a princess!" Maddie giggles, still focused on me as she holds her new toy. "Uncle Dean has another surprise for you. He's gonna get you some ice cream!"

Yup. Attempting to buy the kids favor. And thankfully, the kid appears to be a huge fan of ice cream, because her little hand darts out at me and I can't resist reaching back to her. She grabs onto my index finger, the way she did as a baby. Her fist is still small, though she's grown since then. I fight the urge to kiss her hand. But I let her keep my finger for as long as she wants it.

"Eye keeem!" she squeals, smiling back at me. She tugs my finger as if to say, *let's get a move on.* I can't help but laugh. Demanding. Just like her mother. But that's as far as I allow that thought to go.

Across the street at the Ice Cream parlor, Lucinda and Maddie are sitting at a round table. I bring over a small serving of Vanilla soft serve for Maddie, and a milk shake for Lucinda, as per Lucinda's instructions. We prop the monkey up on the table so he can see the ice cream too, whilst remaining out of the reach of inevitable sticky fingers.

I don't order anything for myself. My insides are still doing flips and all I want to do is stare at Maddie. She digs in eagerly to her ice cream as I sit down beside her.

"What do you think? Did they make it good?" I ask her.

She nods, going to town on it. I can't help chuckling.

Maddie looks over at Lucinda to see what she's got. Lucinda shows her and tells her it's a Milk Shake. Then Maddie turns to me, her little eyebrows moving together as she gives me a puzzled look, realizing I don't have anything. She jams her little spoon into her ice cream and sticks a heaping scoop in my face.

"I share Dee." She insists, holding her spoon out to me.

I'm touched, truly, but I don't know the protocol on this one, so I look to Lucinda. She shrugs and tilts her head as if to say it's okay.

I look back at Maddie, who's staring at me as if she's wondering what the hell my problem is. As if she's thinking 'this is fucking ice cream, dip shit. Nobody says no to ice cream'.

I grin at her and let her shove it in my mouth. Most of it ends up on my face, but It's *Coo*. So fucking *Coo*.

She's squealing with laughter as it melts down my chin. Lucinda hands her a napkin to give to me, but instead of handing it to me, she insists on wiping my face herself. I let her do that, too. I'm fucking putty in this kid's hands. It's all down the front of my leather jacket too, but I don't give a shit. Lucinda sneakily hands me a few more napkins behind Maddie's back, and I use them to wipe my jacket off while Maddie crams her napkin around my face.

"Aw keen Dee." She smiles at me. I doubt it, but...

"Yes, all clean, baby." I smile back at her. "Thank you so much."

She takes another scoop of her ice cream and then insists it's my turn again. "You go Dee." I shift myself towards her a little better and she gets it in my mouth a lot cleaner this time. "It good?" she asks.

"So good."

She grins and wiggles in her seat, as if she made it herself and I'm complimenting her culinary skills. Fucking adorable. I could watch her eat ice cream and laugh forever. We go back and forth a few more times. Her aim gets better each time. Even if it didn't, I don't mind at all. She's taking to me, and it's all I could have hoped for.

"Can Mommy try some?" Lucinda asks.

"No, Dee." Maddie cold shoulders her and twists back towards me with her spoon ready.

I can't help grinning in Lucinda's stunned face, as Maddie shovels another scoop of ice cream into my mouth.

At least Lucinda looks amused. "You know you're a hot sticky mess, right?"

"I don't care." I smile down at Maddie.

"Uh oh, I think uncle Dean loves you, Maddie." Lucinda says to her daughter.

Maddie smiles up at me. "Wuv unka Dee too."

My heart skips a beat. Cloud fucking nine.

"I love you lots, baby." I say on a sigh as I watch her finish her ice cream.

"Okay munchkin, you have to come with Mommy to the ladies' room so I can clean you off before we get in Mommy's car." Lucinda says. She looks at me. "You might want to use the facilities yourself, uncle Dean."

Lucinda picks up Maddie and the Monkey and I escort them to the ladies' room, before ducking into the men's room, myself.

Yeah... total sticky mess. But so worth it. I rinse my face off and grab a few wet paper towels to wipe off my jacket. No harm no foul.

I wait for them outside and then walk them to Lucinda's SUV across the street at the fairgrounds. I'm sad our meeting is coming to an end, but ecstatic it went so well.

She'll remember me next time. I won't have to be afraid...

Assuming there is a next time. Shit.

"Okay, it's time to say bye-bye." Lucinda tells Maddie as we walk up to the back door of the SUV where Maddie's car seat awaits her.

She turns from Lucinda and reaches her hands up to me. I immediately bend and lift her into my arms, and she wraps hers around my neck. I hug her back and kiss her soft little cheek.

"I love you, Maddie. Forever and ever." I say to her. She leans back to look at me, touching the scruff on my chin the way she did when she was a baby.

"Wuv Dee... bye-bye." It pains me to do so, but I hand her off to Lucinda and open the car door for them so she can strap her in her seat. Lucinda gives her the monkey and shuts the door. I walk her around to the driver's side.

"Thanks for letting me see her... Means a lot."

Lucinda turns to face me before she opens the car door. "It was fun. Maddie enjoyed herself."

I look past her through the window at Maddie. She appears to be having a private conversation with the monkey. I smile.

Lucinda reaches up to stroke my face, but I step back from her and shake my head. "Not a good idea... We're out in public, Lucinda. Anyone could see and tell Daniel."

She grins at me. "So, you're on board with this arrangement?"

"I'm going to need you to be a bit more specific... And explain how you expect a barely over two-year-old, to keep a secret from her father."

Lucinda laughs. "It's a small town. We ran into you. No big deal." She says, placing her hand on my chest. She runs her hand up to the top of my shoulder and squeezes it. "Besides, it's not going to happen too often anyway."

My heart sinks at her words, but I knew it was going to be this way. It has to be. Something is better than nothing though. A little time with Maddie is better than no Maddie in my life at all. Sucking in a breath, I nod. "I'll take what I can get."

She grins at me, letting her hand drift down my chest, down my abdomen, until her finger hooks into the top of my belt at my jeans. She tugs me and bites her lip, then whispers "Same here..." as her finger brushes the denim over my cock.

An unfamiliar feeling washes over me as I realize Lucinda is actually going to put me through this ordeal. This twisted *"fucking"* arrangement. I shift my gaze back to Maddie. I don't need to convince myself that she's worth the anguish.

She is.

I love her.

ONE YEAR LATER

"HARDER! FASTER!" VIKING SHOUTS AT ME FROM BEHIND THE TAN leather punching bag in our clubhouse gym. He's bracing the bag for me as I throw several combination punches and a hook round house kick with every ounce of might I've got left in me. We've been working this bag for the last solid thirty minutes.

"Great, now two sets of jabs, cross jab, switch kick!" He barks. "Higher! Go for the fucking neck, Dean!" I attack the bag with his instructed combination of strikes.

"Alright, you're almost done. Home stretch. Jab, cross punch, switch kick, sprawl. Ten times." He says, slapping the side of the bag enthusiastically. I must have given him some kind of look that conveyed my exhaustion, because he adds an encouraging, *"You got this, Bro."*

"You're fuckin' killing me." I pant, but I push myself. Viking is a seasoned pro in Muay Thai Kick Boxing. He knows what he's doing. So, I throw his combination of strikes, kicks, then drop to the floor in a sprawl, jump back to my feet, throw his combination of strikes again and drop to the floor in a sprawl. Rinse, repeat. Ten. Fucking. Times. On the tenth sprawl, it's definitely a struggle to get back up to my feet.

Viking slaps my sweaty back as I drop my arms and try to catch my breath. "You're a fucking killer, Bro!"

"Yo, those sprawls look like they suck to do." Axel says, curling dumb bells a few feet away. Axel is right. They do suck. "When's your next fight?"

"Friday night." I say, grabbing my water bottle and chugging half of it.

"Can I come this time?" Axel asks, placing the dumb bells back on the rack beside him.

"Only if Viking goes too. It can be a rough crowd." I say, catching the towel Viking tosses to me. I wipe the sweat off my face and throat.

"They still got ring girls?" Viking asks.

I chuckle. "Only on Friday and Saturday nights."

"They worth looking at?"

I shrug. "Not bad."

"I can work with *not bad*. We can go." He says to Axel.

"Better ask Cherry, first." I tease him.

"Ask Cherry what?"

We all look towards the gym door at the same time, where Cherry has apparently been watching us. She's wearing a white tank top and a girlie pair of pink gym shorts with socks and sneakers.

I glance at Axel as he stands up straighter, shoulders back. A determined look on his face. "I'm going to Dean's fight Friday night." Axel says. It's clearly a statement. In no way asking for her permission. Viking and I just stand back and watch, amused by his display of Alpha Male posturing. We both look at Cherry next, curious how she will respond. Cherry is a smart cookie. I expect her to be fine with it. Even to let him get away with his posturing in front of his guy friends. At least, for now. Behind closed doors, however, can be another story. As all men learn, sooner or later. But a good woman won't deliberately embarrass her man in front of others. Especially not an Ol' Lady in front of her man's MC Brothers. Cherry knows the deal with MC life.

"Dean's been working really hard." Axel adds after a moment, as if that will edge her towards an affirmative answer.

Her gaze shifts to me. "I can see that. Looks like the Green Tea is working on you, Dean. Looking good." She teases.

"Yeah, it's definitely *just* the Green Tea, doll." I tease her back, curling my arm to flex a bicep at her. It took a year, but I actually don't mind the shit anymore.

She rolls her eyes at me then shifts her gaze back to Axel. "Okay." She says, nonchalantly, then makes her way over to the treadmill to get in a workout of her own.

"Cool." Axel nods with satisfaction. Viking and I grin to ourselves.

T HE RESTAURANT IS MODERATELY UPSCALE. ENOUGH TO WARRANT THE OF looks of disdain from patrons, as I follow the hostess to my waiting party. I had to bribe her with a pair of twenties and a promise that I would not be staying long. The softly lit dining area with classical music playing in the background, paired with cloth covered tables set with wine glasses and fine china, are a clear indication that I am far from being dressed for the atmosphere of this place. Compared to the sports jackets and little black cocktail dresses of those glaring at me, my biker boots, faded black jeans and leather jacket, do not fit the bill.

Fuck them, though. I don't even want to be here right now.

"Your party, sir." The hostess says smoothly, as she stops and gestures to the empty chair across from Lucinda.

"Thanks, doll." I give her a quick wink and a grin, before I slide into the cream-colored fabric chair. I can't help but wonder if she thinks I'm going to dirty the fabric. The hostess gives me a curt nod, then glances at Lucinda for a brief moment before she walks away.

I shift my focus back to Lucinda, who's almost shooting daggers at me with her eyes. She's wearing dangly earrings, a slinky, champagne colored sparkly dress and a wrist full of gold bangle bracelets. They slide down her arm as she lifts her wine glass.

"Thirty minutes late, thought you'd at least show up dressed properly. You know this place." She says, coolly.

"Not my choice of places to meet. You insisted." I shrug, grabbing her glass of ice water and taking a sip. "Bet everybody in here is wondering why the hell you're here with me."

"It isn't obvious?" she smiles slyly over her wine glass at me.

I take a quick gander across the room, noticing the looks I'm still getting from the other diners. Glaring men. However, more than a few of the women they're with are looking at me as if they are hoping I'm on the dessert menu.

"I guess I'm the proverbial pool boy." I mutter, making sure Lucinda notices me winking at the woman in the red cocktail dress across from us. The lady in red blushes. Her date, or husband, or whatever her male companion is to her, glowers at me. I grin at him and shift my focus back to Lucinda.

"You guessed right." She says with a grin of her own. "Now about that."

"Yeah, *about that*. I want to renegotiate the terms of our little fucking arrangement."

"Our *fucking* arrangement, indeed." She purrs at me, and I suddenly feel her foot under the table brushing against the denim over my leg.

"Let me pay you."

Her expression darkens, though she's still wearing that smirk of hers. "Pay me?"

"Yes. Let me pay you for visitation with Maddie. Instead of this sick arrangement."

Her deep blue eyes narrow at me. "I've heard you've more than gotten back on your feet, financially, anyway."

"That surprises you?" I sneer back at her. I suppose I'm still bitter over one of her reasons for leaving me. Money, being one of the top two of those reasons. "I keep my fucking word. I always told you I'd get it all back and then some. Would have happened faster if I wasn't... *derailed*."

"I derailed you?" she says, humor in her voice.

"That's putting it mildly."

"I suppose you've made profitable use of your free time then, after being kicked out of the Saviors." She swirls the red wine in her glass before she takes a sip.

"You suppose correctly. Now let's talk numbers. What's it going to take to drop this current arrangement?"

She lifts a shoulder in a slight shrug. "I'm content with the current arrangement."

"We can't keep doing this, Lucinda." I say, trying to keep the clawing feeling of desperation out of my voice.

"Do you feel bad for Daniel?" she asks.

"No." I don't.

"Are you seeing someone *special*?" she says the words with a tinge of mockery.

"I'm seeing a lot of someones. No one special." I say, hoping that will push her towards agreeing to my offer. Knowing I'm fucking other women. *A lot* of other women.

She laughs. "Well, I never demanded exclusivity from you. I'm still fucking Daniel, anyway."

"Shoot me number." I push.

"*Sixty-nine.*" She nearly whispers, then slides her tongue over her red lips. Her reply begins to sink any hope I had coming in here to negotiate. I'm going to have to offer her a significant number to even pique her interest in changing the terms.

"Five hundred per visitation." I can make that in one or two underground fights.

She looks surprised, but she doesn't answer me. Instead, she lifts her arm to grab the waiter's attention. He eyeballs me as he comes to stand beside our table.

"We're ready to order." Lucinda says to him.

"The gentleman requires a jacket." He replies.

"I'm wearing a jacket." I grin, though I'm not amused by anything going on here tonight.

"A material other than *blackened animal hide*, sir." He responds, with the balls to look down on me in his fuckin' penguin suit.

"Guess I'm shit out of luck then." I shrug, glancing back at Lucinda. "Order whatever you want. I'll cover the bill. But I gotta go. Promised the hostess I'd make this quick."

She's glaring at me. "Our arrangement stands."

The waiter chimes in again, "If you don't have a sports jacket, sir, I'm afraid you will have to leave."

"How much will five fucking minutes cost me?" I glare up at him. I notice him look at the hostess, then back to me. I'm not surprised word is already out that I paid her off and this guy's here to shake me down as well. "Forty? Fine. Five minutes." I dig into my wallet and pull out another pair of twenties. "Now fuck off." I crush the bills into his palm and turn back to Lucinda as he walks away.

"That was kind of hot." She smirks at me.

"I can't do this with you anymore, Lucinda. Please." I sigh. "Let me pay you off. Let me pay you to see Maddie."

"Every *other* visitation." She says. "But that's it. I want what I want. And you're going to give it to me."

Fuck. "Lucinda... name your price. Please." I press once more.

"I just did, Dean. I want *you*, when I want you." She smiles.

"One thousand per visitation. Cash. Quarterly. I can do that. Hell, I can do that more than quarterly if you're open to letting me see her more often than that."

"Is that all your dignity is worth to you?" she chuckles.

"Jesus fuck, Lucinda. What's it going to take?"

"I'll think about it." She says, taking another sip of her wine. "In the meantime, our arrangement remains. If you want to see her, you know what I want from you."

I ball my fist and slam it down on the table, making the silverware clang. From the corner of my eye, I catch the woman in red across from us jump, startled by the sudden bang that cut into the soft classical music drifting through this ritzy place.

Her husband, or date, or whatever he is to her, waves the waiter over to their table, pointing at me, demanding I be removed from the restaurant.

"Nice going, brute." Lucinda huffs at me.

The waiter turns, his hands extended, palms up, as if to say he has no choice but to insist that I leave, now. I just nod at him in defeat and turn back to Lucinda.

"Think about it. An easy grand." I urge her.

"An *easy lay*, too." She smirks.

"Go fuck yourself, Lucinda." I mutter, standing up from the table to show the waiter I really am going to leave.

Lucinda chuckles. "That's what you're for, darling." She taunts me. "See you in a few weeks. Don't forget to foot the bill on your way out. I think I feel like lobster tonight." She smirks at me. I don't respond, instead, I turn to the woman in red and approach their table.

She looks up at me, timidly, as her male companion stiffens in his seat. I watch him for a moment, to see if he's got the balls to say anything to me himself. But he doesn't. My focus shifts back to his cute date.

"My apologies, ma'am, if my presence here tonight put a damper on your evening." I say to her, as charmingly as I can muster. Her teeth sink into her bottom lip as she stares up at me. I can't help but grin down at her. Must not have dampened her evening too much. Or perhaps I did. Between her thighs.

"It's... It's alright." She says, flustered.

"Can I offer you dessert?"

"That's not necessary." Her date interjects, with an attitude.

I don't look at him, I keep my eyes locked with hers. "For you and your husband."

"He's not my husband." She says, her left hand touching her face. Clearly, she wants me to notice the absence of a ring. I grin at her once more. But damn, now I almost feel bad for the guy she's with.

I shift my gaze back to him. "The lady might fancy a gentleman," I cock my chin at his attire. "But a *woman* craves a *savage*." I add, tugging on the cuff of my leather jacket. I give her a wink before I head to the front desk to foot the bill for Lucinda's dinner alone. The hostess is fighting a smile.

"You must really have a thing for the blonde." The hostess nearly whispers to me, brushing a strand of her straight brown hair behind her diamond studded ear.

"What makes you think that?" I ask, handing her my credit card.

"Oh, I don't know. The fact that you paid off two employees' upwards of eighty bucks for ten minutes just to talk to her. Now you're paying for her meal." She chuckles.

56

"If I liked her, I'd have come in the appropriate attire. Actually, I hate the bitch." I smile. She looks at me, surprised, but she smiles back. "That reminds me, one hundred bucks is my limit. Anything over that, is on her."

"Noted." She giggles. I let her notice me checking her out. She's pretty. Slender. Cute face. Why not?

"What time do you blow this joint?"

She stares at me. "Eleven-thirty."

"I own a bar. I'll be there tonight. I'll buy you a few drinks if you want to meet up with me. Unless you have a guy."

"Nothing serious." She replies, handing me back my credit card.

"I'm not looking for anything serious." I say, making that damn clear right off the bat. I slip the card back in my wallet and pull out a business card to hand back to her. "That's the address. Just ask for Dean, if you decide to show up."

She looks at the card. "A Biker bar?" she asks. I nod. "Won't I be a little over dressed?" she gestures to her ankle length black dress with a thigh high slit over one leg.

I grin at her. "Maybe you won't be wearing it long enough to worry about that."

She smiles back at me, slowly sliding my card into the low-cut neckline of her dress. "Maybe I'll see you tonight, Dean... I'm Kimberly, by the way."

She'll be the fourth Kimberly, Kim or Kimmie I've fucked this summer...

I smile. "Lovely name, *Kimberly*."

S TEELING MY RESOLVE, I OPEN THE DOOR TO MY DIMLY LIT ROOM AT THE clubhouse. As expected, Lucinda is on the bed waiting. I step inside and close the door behind me, chucking my keys onto the dresser.

"Did anyone see you come in here?" I ask.

She rolls her eyes at me and lets out a long sigh, as if she finds my question exasperatingly annoying. "You ask me that every time... *No*. No one knows I'm here. Your dirty little secret is safe."

I glare at her. "Great. You're finally seeing this sick arrangement for what it is. A dirty, fucking secret."

She gets up off the bed and walks towards me. "You don't complain when you're getting your rocks off inside me." She leans forward and sniffs at me. "Are you fucking drunk?"

"Not drunk enough." I mutter.

"Are you even going to be able to do this?" she looks me up and down, with the audacity to appear disgusted with me.

I rip my jacket off and chuck it on the chair on the side of the room. "You make me feel about this fucking big, Lucinda." I stick my hand in her face, gesturing with my nearly pinched fingers.

She laughs at me. "You sell yourself *short*, Dean. Add at least seven inches to that."

I scoff at her. "Right. That's all I am to you."

She crosses her arms and stares at me. "I didn't think you wanted to be more. Do you?"

"Not in a long, long time."

She scowls at me. "Then we're both getting what we want."

"I can't imagine that Daniel isn't built similar, Lucinda. You fucking cheated on me with him. Left me for him. Now I'm willing to pay you every few months... instead of this." I try once more to renegotiate.

She steps closer to me, grinning that fucking grin of hers. Once upon a time it turned me on. Now, it only triggers anger deep within. Lucinda is an attractive woman. A natural Blonde, with a slender athletic body. A typical biker's dream babe. But she no longer holds any attraction for me. Whatever I used to feel for her has been twisted into something that turns my stomach now.

"You're right. You're similar." She glances at my crotch before she looks back to my eyes. "But he lacks your *ardent zeal*."

I look past her, running my hand through my hair. We've met like this at least twenty times now, since the start. Each time it bothers me more than the last.

"It's Maddie's birthday next week." Lucinda says.

I close my eyes and clench my jaw. I haven't seen Maddie in three months. "Does she still ask about me?" It's a worry I can't shake, basically only getting to see her quarterly throughout the last year and a half. It's a question I always ask.

Lucinda touches my arm, sliding her hand up to my shoulder as she steps closer to me. "She does. She's campaigning for you to be invited to her birthday party." Sweet kid. Though I can't imagine that working out for either of us. "Daniel of course said you couldn't make it. But I could bring her to you sometime after next week. If you want to give her a gift then, I'm sure she will be happy to see you. She always is."

"So, I'm banned from Maddie's life events, but he's fine with you bringing her to see me a few times a year? Are you paying him off with your fucking ardent zeal?" I sneer at her.

She laughs at me. "Sex gets you what you want. Gets me what I want. Are you jealous I'm fucking both of you?" She tries to taunt me.

"No. I wish he had the fucking *ardent zeal* you crave. Then maybe you'd be willing to just take my fucking money instead of my goddamned dignity." I glare at her.

She pouts at me, mocking me as she starts to take off her clothes. I watch her. I don't even try to hide the contempt in my eyes. "How do you want me?" she whispers huskily, sliding her tongue across her bottom lip.

"I don't."

She drops her last article of clothing and reaches out to grab my junk, squeezing me, hard. I grimace, can't help it. But I take it in stride. Part of me is happy she's surprised my dick isn't hard for her. She looks a little pissed off. I grin in her face, until she fucking twists her fist. "*Fucking bitch!*" I hiss through the pain. Now she's grinning at me.

58

She releases her death grip on me to start undoing my belt and fly. "You better get your shit together." She says, fumbling with my zipper. "Don't fucking drink so much next time. I don't have all fucking night either."

I laugh at her. "I had a shot, baby. To take the edge off. Not nearly enough to put me out of commission. *This is all you.*" I sneer.

She glares up at me, abandoning her task. "Have it your way." She shoves me in the chest. "Maybe you need to go another six months or so without seeing her."

I swallow hard, closing my eyes and forcing myself with every ounce of my will power to keep my shit together.

"You do realize that just because Maddie is older now, that she knows who you are and wants to see you, doesn't mean you have any right or claim to her!" Lucinda hisses at me. "I decide if you see her or if you don't for the next thirteen years of her life!"

I can't do this sick shit for the next thirteen years. These last years have taken a toll on my wretched soul. Opening my eyes, I glare back at her. But I have no words. All I have is Rage. Pain. Disgust, for the both of us.

"What's it going to be?" she demands.

"Were you always so hateful?" I manage to choke out. Is love so blind that I never saw this side of her? "I loved you once, Lucinda. You almost destroyed me then. I'm not going to let you do it again."

She looks at me with disdain, then hurriedly gathers her clothes and starts to get dressed. "I'll be sure to tell Maddie you said happy birthday, since you won't be doing that yourself any time soon." She hisses at me. "And don't send her anything either."

"That's spiteful even for you."

She shrugs with indifference, pulling her skirt up. "And don't even think about *accidently* running into us anywhere. I'll get another restraining order if I have to." She threatens me. "I'll tell the MC you're threatening me. You'll never get back in with the Saviors either."

I shake my head. "*You* left *me*, Lucinda. How can you hate me for the choices you made for yourself?"

"How can you think I hate you?"

"You think this shit has anything to do with love?" I demand. "Love for Maddie, yes. *For Maddie,* I've done what I had to do, to gain a small place in her life. I love *her*. Always have. Always will. But you and I, Lucinda... We're fucking broken."

"I don't hate you, Dean." She says, her voice soft now. "How can you even suggest that?"

"Look at the last years. This dirty, fucking secret." I sigh. "Was never about us, to me. It was what I had to do for Maddie."

"I only took what I could get. I never stopped loving you, Dean."

"There's nothing left to get. I can't do it anymore, Lucinda." I brace myself for what I have to say next. The odds are not in my favor, but I'm finished, regardless. "So, if you truly do love me, you won't force me to do this with you anymore. You'll let me see Maddie... you'll let Maddie see me... because you love me? Maybe. That's debatable. But mostly... Because you love *her*."

She stares at me for a moment, and I can see the rage building in her eyes. Her body tenses. She grabs the photo of Maddie I have on the dresser and storms up to me, jamming the frame into my chest, forcing me to take it from her. "This is all you get to see."

"Lucinda..." I already know it's useless, but for Maddie, I lower myself once again, and utter a desperate plea. "*Don't do this.*"

"Go fuck yourself, Dean." She spits the words at me. "You act like I put a fucking gun to your head. You fucking came every time."

"That's fucking *biology.*" I snap back at her, placing the picture frame back on the dresser. "I did what I had to do. It ain't working for me anymore. I'm willing to pay you for visitation. Shoot a number at me, for fucks sake. Consider it, please."

"Consider yourself out of her life. You can see her when she's eighteen, if she still cares enough to know you by then." Lucinda grabs her purse and starts for the door.

I block her from it. "*Wait.*"

She stops to stare at me. "*What?*"

"Tell me why it has to be this way?"

"Tell me why it's such a problem now!"

"It's never *not* been a problem, Lucinda." I sigh. "Why this? You hold all the fucking cards. We both know it. I'm willing to pay you off."

She glares at me. "Because you're *mine*. Because you'll always be *mine*."

"You think fucking me makes me yours?" I look at her incredulously. "Do you know how many women I've fucked since you left me? I've lost count!"

"Doesn't matter. We have a connection." She insists. "Sweetbutts don't count for anything. I know the life. I know *you*, Dean. You may have fucked other women, but whose face were you seeing while you did it? *Mine?*"

For a long time, yeah. She's right. Then nothing. Then it was just sex. A way to relieve stress. A way to detach from the pain for a fleeting time. Like Alcohol. Like fighting. Fucking is just fucking. Just like this. Our little arrangement... *Just* fucking...

"Give me what I want, or get out of my way." She insists.

If I do this one last time, I can at least have a chance to tell Maddie I love her. Make up some fucking reason why I have to go away for a while, why she's going to see me even less. I'm a fucking shit *uncle* to her anyway, though not by choice. I'd see her far more than every few months if it were up to me. I'd be a real presence in her life, if I had the power to be. But she has no idea about any of this. No idea why her Dee only bothers with her a few times a year.

I grab Lucinda by her arms and shove her backwards on to the bed. "This doesn't mean you fucking own me." I snarl at her.

She grins up at me, victory in her glacial eyes, as she begins to strip off her jacket. "*Whatever.*" She taunts.

"Don't bother getting naked. Just get on your fucking knees so I can get this over with."

She drops down in front of me without protest or hesitation, hurriedly working to get me into her fucking duplicitous mouth. I don't look at her. I stare straight ahead at the blank gray wall, the broken black blinds. When she takes me, I shut my eyes and let it happen. Auto pilot. Just fucking. After nearly ten years, she knows how to work me. To get the response out of me she wants. It's just fucking biology. Shit happens when shit happens.

After a couple of minutes, she stands up to slide her panties off. I shove her backwards onto the mattress. "Turn around."

"Not this time." She says, defiantly.

"I ain't fucking you missionary. Out of the goddamned question."

"Fine." She huffs. "On your back then. I'll do all the work."

"*Whatever.*" I throw back at her, shoving her out of my way as I crash down on the bed, hands behind my head. "Hurry up. Got shit to do." I stare up at the ceiling. I'm not giving her the satisfaction of looking at her. She's nothing now. Just a fuck. A faceless, meaningless fuck.

She yanks my pants and boxers down my thighs. I let her take me again, riding me like a mechanical bull. Mechanical is exactly what this is. Her hands raking down my chest, her moans and pants and gasps blend in with the sound of the creaking mattress springs beneath us. I continue to stare at the ceiling.

"You're mine." She gasps. "You belong to me." I don't bother responding. There's no point. "I belong to you too. I'm yours, Dean." She squeezes me inside her, fucking me a little harder, a little faster.

"Whatever you gotta tell yourself to get off, Lucinda." I mutter.

She laughs as she bounces up and down on me. "Get off, or *get off*?" her words, breathy from exertion. She can take it however she wants. I continue to stare at the ceiling.

"Are you gonna come, baby?" she asks after a while.

Eventually. "Just shut up." I sigh.

She laughs again, but her laughter is interrupted by her orgasm. She shudders on me, her pace hiccups, momentarily losing control of her body as it squeezes and pulses around me.

Against my will, my body reacts. It's fucking biology. Shit happens when shit happens. I squeeze my eyes shut, tilt my head back and let the shit fucking happen. She keeps going though, drawing it out for all its worth. Torturing me for as long as she can until I finally go soft inside her.

She gets off me slowly, sliding me out of her before she walks to the bathroom to clean up. That was intentional. She wanted to leave a fucking mess all over me. No matter. I have every intention of showering this fucking encounter away the moment she's out of here. For now, I just wipe myself off on her skirt, pull my clothes back up, tuck my cock back in my pants and zip up, keeping my emotions in check as best I can.

"I'll text you a time to meet up with Maddie." She says, when she gets out of the bathroom and throws her clothes back on.

"Yeah." I mumble. "You fucking do that."

"Dean."

"What?"

"Look at me before I go. I'm not leaving until you do." She insists.

That's all I want right now. For her to leave. So, I sit up and look at her.

"That's round twenty-five." She grins at me. "You can pretend all you want that you don't like it. Deep down you know you still have feelings for me and that we belong to each other."

I look away from her, at anything else in the room. I only feel contempt for her. On my dresser I spot a framed photo I didn't have before. It's a photo of me and Lucinda. She must have put it there with the few pictures of Maddie I have. It's a photo of she and I, shortly after she told me she was pregnant. We both look happy in it. When I thought the kid was mine. Is this supposed to make me think of happier times? Is this bitch *insane?* What a fucking joke.

"The fuck is that?" I ask.

"I thought you'd like to have it. It's one of Maddie's favorites of you and I. She thinks it's cool that she's technically in the photo with us."

I fucking lose my shit, slamming my fist through it, shattering the glass, busting the frame. Lucinda jumps, startled. A shard of glass about an inch-long sticks out of my hand between my index finger and middle finger. I hold it up to look at it as the blood trickles down the back of my hand. I don't really feel anything, physically. I'm too pissed off. I don't feel things when I'm pissed off.

I stand up and turn to give Lucinda a look as I pick the bloody piece of glass out of my flesh and flick it at her.

"That's how you make me feel, Lucinda." I glare at her. "Shit between us is twisted enough as it is. Don't get this fucking twisted. And I fucking hope you're not twisting Maddie's mind about us. There is no *us*. We ended a long time ago. You're with Daniel. Her father. Don't fuck with her head, too."

"I don't know what you're talking about." She snaps.

"There's no fucking reason for you to be giving her photos like this of us. The subtle manipulation might not be obvious to anyone else, but I fucking *see you*, Lucinda. You're fucking sick!"

"It's just a picture."

I glare at her. "A picture speaks a thousand words, doesn't it? Especially that one."

She doesn't bother trying to deny it. She just folds her arms and looks back at me.

"You want to fuck with me, fine." I'm fighting to keep my voice steady. "But you better stop fucking with Maddie's head. You and I, we're done, *forever*. Make it work with Daniel. Her father. You're not going to fuck me back into your life. You're not going to manipulate Maddie into accepting me as anything other than her so called *Uncle*. That's all I am. So fucking stop the games. This shit ends now."

"So, am I to take that as you *don't* want to see Maddie for her birthday?" she asks, but it's a threat to keep me in line, not a question.

I don't know what to say any more. This arrangement isn't what I thought it was. It was fucked up when I thought it was just about Lucinda using me for sex, controlling me in a twisted way. But this whole thing is spiraling out of control now. She's got a much bigger end game in mind and it ain't happening.

"What am I really to you?" I ask. "You're still with Daniel. Living with him and Maddie as a family."

"I want the best life for Maddie and myself."

I stare at her. "The fuck are you saying?"

She shrugs. "For a while, that was with Daniel. But you're doing so well now..." She smiles at me. "As soon as you're in with the Saviors again, we can..."

"Get the fuck out." I'm barely holding on. The blood dripping down my arm reminding me how good it feels to make somebody bleed. I need to slam my fists into something, or someone. As much as I hate Lucinda right now, it won't be her. I don't hit women.

She starts to talk. "You didn't answer my que-"

"Get the fuck out!" I shout at her as my bloody fist slams the door beside her fucking head. I see a flicker of fear in her eyes. Normally, that would have bothered me a lot more than it did right now. I don't enjoy scaring women. Grabbing the door knob, I open it for her, like a fucking gentleman. She leaves quickly and I slam it behind her, giving her a few moments to get out of here before I go on a fucking rampage.

That fucking photo catches my eye again in its busted frame. I grab the edge of the dresser and toss the whole fucking thing on its side with a crash. Snatching my jacket and my keys, I storm down the hall towards the bar as I pull the jacket on. When I reach the bar, I glance around the room, looking for any motherfucker that might want a fight. Any asshole that might be hassling a girl that doesn't look happy about it. Cherry is behind the bar, nobody bothering her. The sweetbutts and other waitresses are fucking fine. I should be happy about it. Normally I would be. But I need to fight somebody.

"Bro, what happened?" Axel asks, suddenly by my side. "You're bleeding and you look like you want to kill somebody."

"I'm fine." I lie.

"You don't look like it, Dean." He presses.

I walk away from him. I have to. I'm not looking for conversation. I'm looking for a fight. Someone to purge on. Axel ain't it.

Worse comes to worst, I can always go to a bad part of town and wait for a fucking moron to try to jump me. I storm out the front door past Viking, who says something to me, but I don't bother stopping.

I sling a leg over my bike. My beautiful Serene. The only loyal lady I've ever had, and fire her up. She comes to life beneath me and I already feel slightly better. She fucking gets me. I rev her up and make her roar before we take off together, barreling out of the gated lot and into the city streets to look for trouble. I'm Hell bent on finding some tonight.

EIGHT MONTHS LATER

IT'S BEEN THE BETTER PART OF SIX MONTHS SINCE MY LAST UNDERGROUND fight. The years on the circuit prior to my divorce, I had been a bet-to-win fighter. Top physical condition. Fast. Brutal. Other fighters hesitated to step into the ring with me. I only fought the top dogs. Taking names and making bank.

After my divorce... my self-destructive behavior trickled down into every aspect of my life. Including this. I stopped fighting to win. I fought to feel pain. To inflict pain on others, yes. But also, just to feel something other than the twisting knife inside me. I fought when I managed to numb myself to the point where I was genuinely curious if I was even capable of feeling anything, anymore. I also took beatings to punish myself, for all of my wrong doings and short comings.

Through this self-destructive behavior, I tarnished my reputation. I lost my rank within my former MC, then lost my membership all together. In the underground fighting circuit, I was no longer known as a top fighter. I stopped caring enough to hone my skills in the gym. To work out at all. I was stuck in a repeat cycle of drinking, fucking and fighting, without any real will or desire to go on living this way. If I didn't wake up after a binge, fuck it. If someone killed me in the ring, so be it. And if one of the dirtbags on Jason's hit list managed to take me out, then maybe I had it coming, after all the shit I've done in my life.

I didn't care. Not for the last three years. But something changed that last night with Lucinda. When I saw that she had gone far beyond simply attempting to control me via our arrangement over Maddie. The subtle manipulation of her daughter broke whatever chains she had around me.

I am not Maddie's father. I never was. I never will be. And I could never be with Lucinda, or anyone like her, again. I wouldn't survive it. Maddie deserves to live a happy life with her father. If cutting myself out of her life, gives her that chance; If it strips away Lucinda's motivation and ability to manipulate her, then that's just another sacrifice I'm willing to make. Her life will go on without me. And my life can go on, too. Even if it means loving her from afar. For now. It's out of my control, anyway. All I can control, is my own life. I just have to find the will to live it. To go on fighting for myself.

I just have to catch my second wind...

The gritty, underground fighting rings were once my way to center myself. A way to let everything fall away. For the brief period of time inside a ring, slugging it out with another man, that's all there is in the world to concern yourself with. To focus on.

Now, standing in my corner of the makeshift ring, surrounded by shouting men placing cash bets, in the grimy basement of a former brewery in downtown Wilmington, I await my first challenger.

It's been six months since I broke free of my chains. Six months of reconditioning my mind and body for a real fight. Viking and I have been working out together almost daily. And he's a hard driver. His eighty percent in a sparring match is most guys one hundred and twenty percent. I'm not here to take a beating tonight. I'm here to give one and win.

Physically, I must look like I'm back on my game. There are men here, fighters, that had beaten me in the ring before. A year ago. Two years ago. When I was at my lowest. But these same men are looking at me now, like I'm someone they wouldn't fuck with. I wish they would.

"I'll fight him." A familiar voice from the crowd calls from somewhere behind me. I'm grinning before I even turn around to face him.

Kenny O'Keefe. I've fought him twice before, when I was in my prime. Once here in North Carolina, once when I spent some time out in Arizona. Both fights had been close calls. But I beat him. He's a known underground fighter, and his challenge to face me in the ring has the crowd buzzing. I'm sure he's the one they're all betting on to win this match. Many of the men here tonight have witnessed my downfall. Tonight, they'll get to see me rise up from the ashes of my scorched reputation. And with a worthy opponent at that.

O'Keefe strips off his shirt, tossing it to the red headed woman he's with, and makes his way over to the ring, ducking under the ropes. We're still evenly matched, physically, with the way I've been training hard the last half a year.

"Heard rumors you called it quits and retired." O'Keefe says, as we wait for the betting to be closed on our match. "That you let yourself go and threw in the towel. Glad to see that isn't true. I was pissed, thinking I missed my shot at beating you."

"Third times a *lucky charm*?" I joke, watching him warm up in his corner. We've both got Irish blood pumping through our veins, but I'm a bigger mutt in that department than he is. I'm also half Scottish. His body is covered in tattoos that display his Celtic pride and fighting spirit.

"Laugh it up, Keegan. I'm going to sham-*rock* your block off." He sneers back at me. I just grin.

"Bro," Viking calls to me from the crowd, beside Axel. I shift my gaze to my two brothers watching near the edge of the ring. "You got this. You got the speed. You got the skills. You never lost your instincts. You just gotta put your heart into it." Viking says. "We put all the money on you to win, don't break our wallets."

I nod, reaching over the ropes to fist bump both him and Axel. "Thanks, coach." I jest.

The organizers announce that all bets are closed for this fight now, and for the first time in a long time, I feel a little sliver of excitement. I want this fight. Not just for the pain. Not just to blow off steam. I want to *win*.

O'Keefe wants the win as well. He charges me before the word "Fight" is even fully shouted by one of the organizers. Attacking me with a flying knee kick that would have landed directly in my face. Instinct and reflexes are still on my side. I pivot out of the line of fire and square off with him as he lands and spins around to face me.

The crowd of bettors and spectators roar as we circle each other in the ring, throwing quick jabs, each waiting for the opportunity to throw a cross punch, or an opening to land a solid kick. He tests me again with another charge. This time, I bend my knee and lift my leg, nailing him in the chest with a push kick that shoves him backwards, creating enough space between us for me to attack him immediately after, with a round house hook kick to his rib cage.

The pain he's feeling weakens his guard enough for me to slip in an upper cut to his jaw, then a right hook to the side of his head, rocking him sideways. It would have been a knock out, but he managed to soften the blow just enough, by getting his arm up to semi block my punch in the nick of time. He nails me with a shin kick to my thigh, then a left hook to my body and his own push kick, knocking me away from him as we square off and circle each other once more.

The crowd is as loud as ever, and as I hear the tone of excitement begin to turn to anger, it confirms my earlier suspicion. There are quite a few bettors that are worried about losing a lot of dough. They bet against me, and now they're not so confident in those bets.

O'Keefe isn't so eager to charge me a third time, as we continue to circle and jab at each other, testing and waiting for that opening to take the other out. He presses forward, jabbing fast, trying to get in closer to nail me with an elbow, or a knee to my solar plexus. I keep my guard up, blocking his assault, when he suddenly drops low, grabbing me around the back of my thighs and lifting me up.

I attempt to wrap my arm around his neck in a guillotine head lock, before he slams me backwards to the ground, hard. Nearly having the wind knocked out of me from the impact, he escapes the head lock and rains down punches from above me while I block him from below.

The crowd is in an uproar again, thinking their man is going to beat me. But I'm not done. Sometimes you have to take a hit or two to make a move of your own. Which is what I have to do to get myself out of this situation. I buck my hips upward, knocking O'Keefe forward and slightly off balance, forcing him to plant a hand on the mat beside me to break his fall. And that's exactly what I wanted him to do.

Curling my body up towards him, I grab the wrist of his hand planted on the mat, simultaneously wrapping my legs around his body, locking him in. I throw my other arm around his shoulder and wrap it under, latching onto my own wrist around him. As I pivot my position beneath him, I twist his arm backwards as if I'm going to bend his arm to the back of his head, in a most unnatural and painful position.

With an agonizing shout, he slams his other hand down on the matt repeatedly, signaling his submission. I beat him by way of a painful Judo style Kimura arm lock. Had he not tapped out, it would have resulted in a spiral fracture of his humerus bone, or at the very least, a dislocated shoulder and damaged rotator cuff.

"Motherfucker!" O'Keefe gripes, shoving himself off me as he gets to his feet. He's glaring at me, but he still extends his hand to me, pulling me to my feet as well. "I'm going to beat you some day, Dean Keegan. Someday real soon."

"You're a year late. You probably could have."

He looks at me with disdain, as if he resents me for saying it. "Fuck that. Beating you when you're down and out for whatever reason, isn't beating you." He grunts. In a way, I'm glad someone thinks so. "I want to beat you and have it count. Got a special place for you right here." He grins, pointing to a spot on his inner arm among a dozen or so tattooed clovers. "Each of these represents a worthwhile fighter I defeated. You're going right here, Keegan. You're gonna be one of my lucky clovers."

I can't help grinning back. "Maybe the fourth times a lucky charm, then." I shake his hand before we exit the ring and part ways again.

"That arm bar was brutal, Bro!" Axel says excitedly as I approach him and Viking. My thigh where O'Keefe nailed me with that shin kick is a little tender. I expect to find a decent bruise there in a few hours.

"We should collect your winnings and get the fuck out of here, Dean." Viking says, shoving my shirt at me. "A lot of guys are pissed you won."

"Fuck them. They're gonna have to get used to it again." I say, slipping back into my shirt. Axel hands me my boots and socks and I slip those back on as well.

"Head for the exit, I'll grab your cash and we'll hit the road."

"Shit, are people really that surprised?" I ask, glancing at the crowd. I am getting more than a few dirty looks. I can't help grinning to myself, though. It feels good to win. "Alright, grab the cash. Axel and I will meet you by the bikes, just in case." I say, taking my leather jacket from Axel and sliding it back on.

"Roger that." Viking makes his way through the crowd towards the bookies table.

Axel and I head in the other direction towards the exit of the old brewery. Once we're outside in the run-down lot, we hang by the bikes, waiting for Viking.

"I think I want to get into this." Axel says, sitting on his bike sideways. "I want to be able to do what you do."

"Learning to fight is one thing, kid. But this shit," I gesture toward the old brewery, "This shit is illegal."

"So? You're not hurting anybody that isn't asking for it."

Yeah, he's right about that. But... "Cherry is going to kill me if she hears you talking like this."

"Let me worry about Cherry." He says, all the confidence in the world.

I can't help but chuckle. "You should."

Axel looks at me, a serious expression on his face. "A man should know how to fight. I want to be able to protect Cherry. She ain't gonna be mad at that."

I can't disagree with his reasoning. "We'll teach you to fight, kid. But this underground shit is a no go, for now, anyway. You're not even old enough to patch into the MC yet. This shit, here, tonight, can be really dangerous." I try to make him understand. "Not every man you fight has integrity. Not every man who seeks this underground shit out, fights fair. Bad shit happens in places like this."

"I should learn what you know, Dean. You and Viking." Axel insists. "I will be a Savior someday, soon. I'm almost twenty-one. It will be something I can fall back on incase I need it on a mission, too." I watch the determination on his face transform into disappointment... "One day." He sighs.

My heart sinks a little as his words hit me. The MC's mission. It's former mission, anyway. I swallow hard, unsure of what to even say to him now. The kids basically dedicated his life to joining up with the Saviors MC, just to be able to take part in the missions we used to carry out.

I nod and force myself to smile at him, patting him on the shoulder. "Okay, kid. You're right. We'll teach you how to fight."

PRESENT DAY

S TANDING BESIDE THE BED, I GRIN DOWN AT THE SEXY BRUNETTE I JUST spent the last hour and a half fucking. As I zip up my pants and redo my belt, her hands are still bound together and tied to the headboard with a red scarf. Her idea, by the way. It was also her idea to meet up in this hotel room.

"*Fuck*, that was *amazing*." She croons, slowly wriggling on top of the comforter, like some kind of sated serpent. "God, I wish we lived closer. I don't think I could ever get enough of you." She smiles up at me.

Crystal. Nice woman. Classy. We met a year and some months ago, around Christmas. She calls me when she's in town and we usually meet up for a quick bang when she's available. Some kind of medical supply sales woman or a pharmaceuticals rep, that gets paid to travel to different hospitals across the state. Something like that. I don't remember exactly, and I don't care enough to ask again.

I make it a point not to comment on her last statement. I'm glad she only calls me when she wants to hook up. It tells me she's not serious about me, either. I'm not interested in anything more. She's hot. She can fuck. She's smart. And seems nice. But I just don't feel anything more for her.

"Are you going to untie me or leave me here at the mercy of housekeeping?" she giggles.

I give her a sinister smile. "Now there's an idea." I tease. Of course, I'd never do that. Grabbing my shirt off the chair in the room, I slip it on, before I sit down on the bed beside her and untie her wrists, freeing her. I bend to grab my boots and pull them back on as she twists onto her side to face me.

"Do you really need to go?" She pouts. "I usually have you longer than this. It's only eight o' clock. Can't you stay longer?"

Shit. I'm supposed to be at a friend's birthday bash across town around nine tonight. My junior mechanic's, Derek.

"Got someplace I need to be, doll. Sorry." I say, jumping back up to my feet to glance around for my leather jacket. I spot it flung over the flat screen TV on the dresser and move across the room to grab it and slip it on as well.

"Another woman?" Crystal gets up off the bed, draping the red scarf across her shoulders and saunters towards me.

"Yeah. I've got them lined up waiting for me. Like I'm sure you do with men." I joke, but for all I know, she actually does have a few fuck buddies she meets like this at the different towns she travels to throughout the year.

She chuckles, but then gives me a flirtatious look. "If you come back later tonight, I'll make it worth your while." She purrs, flinging the scarf around my neck and wrapping it around me.

"*Oh yeah?*" I say, watching her tuck the scarf into the lapels of my leather jacket. "You realize it's spring time, right? No reason to bundle me up with a scarf."

"It's *your* scarf, silly. You forgot it last time we were together. I brought it to give it back to you."

Oh, right. It is mine. "Thanks." I say. "I really gotta book now, doll. Tonight, was great." I reach for the black motorcycle helmet sitting on the dresser that I got Derek for his birthday.

"Are you gonna come back for round two? Might lead to round three and four? Maybe even *five* if you're... *up* for it." She winks at me.

"We'll see. Will have to grab some more rubbers though, if that's what you've got in mind."

"I have a box of condoms in my purse. No need to stop anywhere on your way back to me." She smiles.

"Aces." I say, trying not to sound as impartial to the idea as I really feel. Her major stock in condoms answers the fuck buddy question, too. I make my way towards the door to leave.

"You're not going to come back, are you?" she pouts again, following me to the door, naked.

"I can't promise you." I say, I'm not going to lie.

"I'll let you fuck me in the ass." She grins.

Well, damn... Not every chick puts that offer on the table!

I smirk at her. "I'll text you later. What's your cut off time?"

She shakes her head. "I'll wait for you. I check out tomorrow morning." It just feels wrong, to think of her waiting up for me. Like we're something to each other that we aren't. I can't do it...

"Don't wait up for me, doll. It was great seeing you again." I say, trying to sound sincere. "But I can't promise I'll be able to get back here tonight. Between meeting up with some people, and the roadhouse tonight, I just don't know if I'm gonna have the time to get back here."

"Promise me you'll try." She pushes.

I really don't like making promises. My word is important to me. And I'm tired of broken promises in my life. I refuse to contribute to the words decay.

"We'll see what happens, doll." I say, and it's the best I can do. She just needs to accept that. I bend to kiss her briefly, and basically meaninglessly, on the lips, before I shove the helmet on my head and walk out the door, closing it behind me.

It's a breezy night, a slight chill in the air for mid spring. Still not scarf weather, but I don't have the time right now to care. Sliding the face shield down on the helmet, I walk quickly to my bike parked in the lot below. I don't think Derek will mind me testing out his gift tonight. After all, it's too big to fit in either of my side bags.

As I mount my favorite lady, Serene, and fire her up, I feel my cellphone vibrate in my jacket pocket. I pull it out and look at the screen before I leave. A text from Crystal. I open it, just in case she's watching me from her hotel window. I don't want her to see me blow her off.

"I'll be waiting up for you." Her text says, with an attached photo of her naked ass to remind me of her offer, should I return to her bed tonight.

I tuck the cell phone back in my jacket without responding. I don't know what to say. I didn't promise. I'm not going to promise. I'm not even sure I want to return to her tonight. I'll take another look at her photo later and see what my cock thinks about it then.

Kicking Serene's stand up, I take off out of the hotel parking lot and head across town to Kelly's Tavern for Derek's birthday gathering.

As I pull Serene into a parking space in front of K.T.'s on the other side of town, I'm hit with an odd feeling. An overwhelming, nagging feeling. That I'm supposed to be here, right now, this exact place at this exact time. And for some strange reason, it's got nothing to do with it being Derek's party.

I kick her stand down and dismount, glancing around at the seemingly happy crowd gathered outside of the bar. Pulling off the helmet, tucking it under my arm, I make my way inside the Tavern. The feeling just gets stronger.

Scanning the room, there are many faces I recognize. From town. From my own bar. From the farm. The repair shop. So far, nothing is different, other than the atmosphere. I casually walk through the crowd of strangers and acquaintances, greeting people I do recognize, as I continue to play hot and cold with this peculiar sensation. It seems to grow stronger still.

When I turn back towards the bar, the feeling becomes more magnetic, as if something is pulling me in a more concrete direction.

The fuck is happening?

I study the people around me, who don't seem to notice a damn thing. They're talking, laughing, drinking. Carrying on as if this is a normal night out, in a normal bar. Surrounded by normal people they encounter normally. Everything is totally fucking *normal*, exactly as it should be. As I would expect it to be.

The song playing on the jukebox switches to a mellow, bluesy, rock jam. Ed Sheeran's, *Make It Rain*. The lyrics resonate with me, very much so. The music, and the vibe pulling me into this bar, is almost trance inducing.

70

I stand where I am, trying to fight the trance like state my mind seems to want to be lulled into. I slowly scan the room once more. I don't like this unfamiliar feeling. My curiosity about it is shifting towards high alert. My body instinctively tenses. I've never felt anything quite like this before. My eyes roam down the length of the bar counter as my heart rate quickens. Yet no one at the bar is paying any attention to me, or anything else going on around them. They're wrapped up in conversations with other people or throwing back drinks.

I don't understand it.

Until I do.

Until an energetic charge hits me like a fucking bolt to my heart.

I lock eyes with *her.*

Her dark, penetrating stare, holding me in place from across the room. As If I've just gazed upon a gorgeous, dark-haired Medusa, and she's turned me to stone.

She gives me a shy, timid little smile, before she looks away from me, and suddenly I can breathe again. I didn't realize I wasn't breathing, as I take a gulp of oxygen and continue to stare at her.

The guy sitting next to her shoves a bottle of beer in her hand, and I'm suddenly, unexplainably, completely and irrationally, *jealous* as fuck!

Though, she doesn't look interested. Not in him. Not in the beer either.

Now in full possession of my faculties, I quickly make my way through the crowd to watch her, from a distance, without her noticing. I lean up against the wall, behind a group of people shooting pool.

Another guy, a big dude in a Knights MC cut, is talking to her now. The guy who gave her the beer scurries off, abandoning his seat to the big biker.

She laughs at something he says. Her smile is fucking beautiful. So are her ample fucking breasts that rise and fall as she takes a breath after laughing at whatever he said to her.

I was jealous of beer guy, but now I'm murderously envious of the Knight. She's letting him buy her a drink. Lucky bastard.

I notice she's looking around the bar as the Knight goes on about something. Her brows furrow slightly. Is she looking for me? Is she disappointed in my abrupt disappearance? Could *I* be that fucking lucky myself?

The Knight sure does seem to be doing most of the talking. She looks bored as she sips her drink... Fool. I'd be fascinated to know what her favorite color is. What her damn dog's name was in kindergarten. Where the fuck she bought that dress she's rocking the absolute fuck out of... *Fuck me...* Curves for days on this woman...

She can't see me, stalking her like a fucking creep from a dark corner of the bar. Since I'm already being a creep, I allow myself the liberty of roaming my eyes all over her, from head to toe. Best to do it now, unbeknownst to her, so I'm hopefully in better control of my urge to do so when I get the opportunity to go up to her.

Perfection. From her long dark hair, to the arch of her brows, the fullness of her breasts and curvature of her hips. Those thick legs, crossed. Her booted foot twitching like a cat's tail at random... The Knight *is* boring her... *Aces!*

71

She finishes her drink. I watch her lick her lips, and my desire to press my mouth to hers and taste her is almost overwhelming.

Before I even realize what the fuck I'm doing, I'm walking towards her. I catch myself in the nick of time, before she sees me, turning sharply into the dark corridor that leads to the restrooms. Only a few feet from them. I can hear her, though her back is to me now.

The biker is looking at her like a parched, desert stranded man, and she's a tall drink of water he wants to reach out and consume. Though I don't fault him for it, he's looking a little too eager.

I don't fucking like it.

She says she doesn't drink. He offers to escort her to the alley for some air. She slides off the bar stool, shaky on those sexy fucking stems. The Knight offers her his arm, and she takes it, allowing him to lead her towards the corridor.

I back against the wall, tucking my head down. They pass with their backs to me as I remain unnoticed in the shadows.

No way I'm letting her go to the alley with him alone. Not with him looking at her the way he is. Not with her clearly unable to handle her liquor.

I glance at the new black helmet in my hand. I can use looking for Derek as my excuse to go out there with them. Then strike up a conversation. Throw her a few flirty grins. He ain't gonna like it, but I couldn't care less. All's fair in love and war, Bro. You just met her. I'm not breaking any codes. She's not his Ol' Lady.

They don't make it to the back-alley door. He shoves the door to the men's room open and pulls her inside...

The fuck? Hell no... No. No. No! She's not that type of girl... She doesn't even drink for fucks sake...

Anxiety and rage hit me like a ton of bricks, and I storm towards the men's room. Shoving the fucking door open, I can already hear her in a stall begging him to stop, to get off of her.

Motherfucker!

I put Derek's gift on the sink counter, then turn around quickly to slam my boot into the door of the stall, forcing it open. Grabbing the piece of shit by the collar of his leather cut, I haul him away from her, out of the stall, and slam him up against the solid wood door of the men's room. He doesn't get to speak. There's no fucking excuse. I immediately go to work on him. Rocking him sideways with a hook to his fucking jaw with my right, then rocking him back with a punch to the other side with my left. I ram my knee up into his gut, knocking the wind out of him, and upper cutting him in the fucking nose when he crumples forward. Grabbing him by the back of the head, I slam his face down into my knee and let him fall unconscious to the dirty bathroom floor.

The woman is still in the stall. I can hear her whimper, then the all too familiar sound of throwing up. I step over the trash on the floor and push the stall door open. She's struggling to stand in front of the john, keeling over, expelling her guts.

Poor thing. I wrap an arm around her to prevent her from hitting the filthy floor and sweep her gorgeous hair back to hold it with my free hand. One of her hands clutches mine, as if she's afraid of my grip on her, but she can't stop herself from throwing up.

"Shh...shh...shh... You're okay." I say, as gently to her as I can manage. "I've got you. I won't let you fall." I try to reassure her. "You're safe with me."

After a few moments, her body trembling, she's finally through.

"Let's get you out of here and over to the sink, okay?"

I back out of the stall, my arm still around her waist, just in case the sight of this asshole bleeding on the floor makes her faint. I get her over to the counter, where she turns on the sink, cupping her hands in the running water. She brings them to her face, rinsing out her mouth and splashes her face.

The prick on the ground lets out a slight groan, but she doesn't hear it over the water. I glance down at him, lining the back of my heel up with the back of his head. I give him another good backward kick to the skull. Discretely knocking him the fuck back out again.

She finally lifts her head out of the sink, glancing around for the paper towels. The dispenser is near me, I grab a few sheets and step closer to her.

"Here, doll." I say, offering them to her.

She turns around to somewhat face me, leaning back against the counter. Keeping her head down, her hair remains falling around her face. Probably embarrassed by this entire ordeal. She timidly accepts the towels from me and presses them to her face, hiding herself in them. She mumbles something into the towels, but I didn't understand her.

"What's that, baby?" I ask.

"I had a purse." She says again.

I glance back inside the stall. It's on the floor beside the toilet.

"I got it." I say, entering the stall and reaching down to grab it. I bring it back to her, but I let go before she grips it and it falls to the floor again.

Before I can bend to grab it for her again, she beats me to it. Though, she doesn't get up right away. She lingers for a moment, seemingly staring at my boots, before she begins to stand back up, slowly. As if she's taking a real close look at every inch of me.

As her eyes finally meet mine again, for the first time since we locked eyes from across the room, she takes in a little surprised gasp.

"It's you." She says, barely above a whisper.

Guess I made my own impression on her... Aces!

I can't stop myself from grinning. "Hi." I say, in the most charming tone I can muster, "I'm Dean Keegan."

She extends her hand to me, and I eagerly take it.

"Thanks for saving me, Dean Keegan." She smiles shyly. "I'm Vanna."

Vanna

Fuck, me.

And just like that, my second wind hits me like a freight train.

Chapter two

Vanna
3 Years Before Collision

ALL I EVER WANTED WAS FOR HIM TO LOVE ME... I never imagined he would turn into a monster. He was supposed to be a good guy. A hero. A member of the Thin Blue Line to serve and protect.

Standing beside him now, wearing the deep blue gown that he chose for me to wear tonight, I keep my eyes cast down to the floor. God have mercy on my soul if he should ever think I was looking at one of his Brothers in Blue. Especially on a night like this. His precinct's Christmas Eve party. All of his higher ups are present tonight as well. I must be on my best behavior. I know this. He didn't even have to warn me.

"Giovanna, darling," he says so smoothly.

My eyes meet his now. "Yes, my love?" I respond. It's expected.

"Would you be a sweetheart and order me another scotch? *Neat.*" he hands me his empty glass and gestures to the bar across the room.

"Of course." I smile sweetly.

He snakes his arm around my waist, pulling me against him. I place my hand on his chest and he kisses me chastely on the cheek, before he whispers in my ear, that I'm never to wear this shade of *trollop red* lipstick again.

He approved my entire ensemble for this evening, a week ago. But I don't argue with him. I smile as if he just whispered something sweet in my ear, before I walk to the bar to retrieve him his drink. Knowing full well, he's watching my every move.

The bartender is a woman, thank God. Or he would have gone himself. I place his glass on the bar and wait for her to finish serving another few officers before she gets to me. One of the cops at the bar turns to me to tell me I look great tonight. I immediately lift my left hand to my clavicle and smile back, thanking him for his compliment and wishing him a Merry Christmas. I turn my head and smile back at my fiancé, making sure he sees his diamond ring on my finger, sparkling in the dim lights above the bar.

Yes, dear, I made sure he saw it too...

When dinner is served, I know not to finish my plate. To say that it was wonderful, but that I couldn't possibly eat another bite. I've never been a skinny girl, though. He reminds me often. I'm to play the part of the figure conscious *bride to be*, especially in public.

The heels he chose for me are killing my feet after three hours of this. So far, aside from the lipstick I'm wearing, that apparently makes me look like a whore, I think I may make it through this evening unscathed. I don't think I've made any mistakes, thus far.

His Captain approaches us, wanting a word with him. He excuses himself from me and suggests that I go to the ladies' room to freshen up. I do as I'm told, and I take my time in here. He won't want to have to watch me when he's speaking with his Captain. Sending me to the ladies' room puts his mind at ease, that I will not be around other men unsupervised.

As I stand before the mirror above the sink, I remove my lipstick, and retouch my makeup around my mouth, blending it out carefully, before applying a slightly tinted lip gloss. Then I brush my long, dark hair out, killing time while I wait for him to come get me. He will use me as his excuse to leave. Say that I'm not feeling well, and that he must take me home.

There's a light knock on the ladies' room door. It's time for us to leave. I open the bathroom door and look up with a smile, happy to see my adoring, attentive, fiancé.

However, it isn't my fiancé. It's his partner.

My heart sinks as I realize I've made a terrible mistake.

"Is everything alright, Giovanna?" he asks, his seemingly kind hazel eyes searching mine. "The last few times I've seen you, you just haven't been yourself."

"I'm fine." I keep smiling, I don't know what else to do. I glance past him, looking for my fiancé. My left hand clutching the base of my own throat.

"Vanna... you can tell me, if there's something..." he begins to say, when my fiancé rounds the corner and catches us together.

I catch the flash of rage behind his eyes.

"Actually, I don't feel well." I manage to choke out.

"What's going on here?" My fiancé asks, smiling at his partner.

"Bumped into Giovanna on my way to the bathroom. Just wishing her a Merry Christmas. You both should come to dinner some night with me and the misses. It's been a while." His partner says. "Now that you're getting married, it would be good to induct Giovanna into the *wives club*."

My fiancé pats his partner's arm. "We'll have to do that, Kyle. Have June call Giovanna and set something up." He says, shifting his gaze back to me. "Let's go, darling. The cab is outside waiting."

I'm not even three steps inside the front door of our home, before he shoves me hard between my shoulder blades, knocking me off balance in these pointy heels. I land on my hands and knees on the hardwood floor.

"Stupid bitch." He mutters, slamming the door shut and stepping around me. "Get the fuck up and get out of that dress. We need to have a little talk."

A little talk...

I slip the heels off my feet before I stand back up. When I start to make my way towards the master bedroom, he grabs my arm, hard, stopping me.

"You don't have anything to say to me?" he growls.

"I'm sorry." I quickly reply. "I thought it was you at the bathroom door when-"

He back hands me across the face and I'm on the hardwood floor again. My mouth and the side of my face, throbbing. I bring my cold hand up to cup my cheek, trying to stop the painful pulsing there.

"You want to fuck him, don't you?" he says, standing over me.

"No... I thought it was you."

"Stupid bitch." He mutters again, shoving me with his foot to knock me back over as I attempt to stand up again. "On second thought, stay the fuck down there, where you belong. I don't care if you ruin that slutty gown."

"You picked it out." I say, using the back of my hand to dab at the little bit of blood in the corner of my mouth now.

"Then you've gained weight. Because it shows off everything!" he shouts at me.

I don't bother arguing. It seems as though everything he once liked about me, he hates now. My hour glass figure. My sassy attitude. The confidence I once had. If I argue, I'm just going to make this *little talk* worse for myself. I reach for the beaded clutch I had with me tonight, but he kicks it away from me.

"You think you're gonna call the cops? You stupid bitch. They're not going to help you." He reminds me. *Again.*

"No, I just wanted a tissue." I can hear the defeat in my own voice. I called the cops on him once. When this first started. His buddies showed up. Talked me into not pressing charges. Told me how a restraining order was just a piece of paper. That he really loved me anyway. Through their smiles I saw the threats. I don't bother calling anyone now. I'm on an island alone with him. The cops are on his side. Our parents think he's wonderful. A real prince charming. A hero cop that fell for the former spitfire he's loved since high school.

What happened to us?

"You're a fucking whore, that's what happened!" he shouts at me. I didn't realize I said those words out loud.

"You're the one that cheated on me." I whisper. For some reason, it still hurts. Once upon a time, I loved him. I loved him all through high school and my first years of college. It didn't matter that he was a few years older than me. Our families have been close friends for years. I believed we were meant to be, *once upon a time...*

He grabs my arm and hauls me back to my feet, shoving me up against the wall. I wrap my arms across my body, hoping he doesn't crack any ribs this time. It's so painful, and they take so long to heal.

"What the fuck are you doing?" he demands.

"Please... I'm sorry... I am. I love you." I whimper, pleading as my vision begins to blur with tears as I stare into his cold as ice, blue eyes. I used to think they were beautiful...

"Put your hands against the wall and fucking take it." He growls in my face.

I instinctively clutch my abdomen tighter, and he slaps me for it, snapping my head to the side. Tears fall, but he doesn't care. He grabs my hair and yanks my head back, slugging me in the stomach, so hard it knocks the wind out of me. My body wants to crumble as I gasp for air, but he doesn't allow it. He slams me back up against the wall, so hard a framed photo bounces off its hook and smashes on the floor beside us.

"Now look what you did!" he snaps, shoving me towards the living room couch. My shin hits the side table, rocking the lamp on top of it.

I desperately reach to grab for it before it hits the ground and breaks, but I'm not fast enough. It slips through my fingers and topples over, smashing on the floor. The rolled-up bills I had hidden inside of it, lay on the floor now, exposed among the broken glass.

I'm frozen in place as I stare at the money I've managed to hide over the last two years. It's not a whole lot. He watches every penny I make. I never had a solid plan of escape, either. I just knew I'd need cash to make it happen, if I ever did figure something out.

As my eyes shift up to meet his, I can see, beyond a shadow of a doubt, that he truly meant what he said to me two years ago. The night I actually did try to leave him.

He said that he would kill me. That no other man would ever have me, if he couldn't. He would kill me, and he knew how to get away with it.

His fists clench at his sides. The muscles in his jaw rippling, he makes a move towards me.

I've hated my life these last few years. But I don't want to die. I dash for the front door.

Wrenching it open before he manages to grab me, I run out onto the porch, barefoot, in an evening gown, screaming into the snowy night for someone to help me. Before I even make it to the steps, his foot slams into my back, sending me soaring off the porch steps, landing face down in the snow on the front walk.

I continue to scream as he jumps on me, yanking me over so that I'm on my back in the cold snow. He punches me, again and again, shouting at me to shut up. But I don't shut up. I continue to scream as I try to shield myself. He hits me over and over. I keep screaming, until I feel his hands around my throat, choking off my cries for help.

"I'll fucking kill you, Giovanna!" he shouts in my face, the pressure increasing around my throat. *"I'll fucking kill you!"*

I can't breathe... I can't breathe at all!

I claw at his hands and try to kick beneath him to escape, but I can't get away.

He's too strong... And I can't breathe...

Two Years Later

A S I WALK INTO THE LITTLE VOODOO SHOP, THE THICK MUSKY SCENT OF incense and oils permeates the air. Candles and jars of assorted herbs and other ingredients for spell work line the shelves of the shop. It isn't a large space, but it's full to the brink of spiritual supplies.

R&B music is playing quietly in the background. I make my way further into the shop when a woman appears from behind a tapestry in the back. She is strikingly beautiful. Tall, slender, dark skin with long box-braided hair partially piled atop her head and tied with a scarf. Her seashell earrings clinking as she turns to face me.

"May I help you?" she asks.

"Yes. Are you Marie Delai?"

"I am."

"I was referred by a client of yours. Laura Percy? You helped her with something a few years ago. I was wondering if you could do similar for me."

She studies me for a moment before walking in my direction. Then reaches past me and locks the shop door.

"Follow me." She says softly. I follow her behind the tapestry, which conceals the back room where private readings and other magical services must take place.

"What is it you believe I can help you with?" she asks, gesturing for me to take a seat at the small, round table draped in a dark cloth. I do.

"I've created a big problem for myself. I've managed to escape, thus far. But I know time is running out for me. I will have to face it again."

"Sounds insidious." She says, studying me.

I nod. "I don't think I will survive next time. I think I'm in bigger trouble than I ever anticipated. I need protection."

She stares at me for a long moment, then holds out her hand across the table. "Let me see your palm." I place my hand, palm up, in hers as she gazes into it.

"You're a witch. Whatever you do is automatically more potent." She says simply.

"I made a terrible mistake in desperation, that has to run its course, I know. But I am in very real danger... I've learned the error of my ways."

"In this man, you awakened a sleeping demon. Everything he's done, or will do, was already a part of him." She says, as if she can sense the guilt inside of me.

"What do I do now?" I ask. "A talisman, a crystal. That isn't going to be enough. How do I stop him from coming after me when he is eventually released?"

She pulls out a deck of tarot cards from a velvet pouch on her table and slowly shuffles them. Her dark eyes seem to look through me. She spreads the cards across the table between us. Taking my hand once more, she guides my palm over the cards, back and forth three times. Almost midway through the third pass, she stops abruptly.

"There. Lift the card." She says. "It will reveal to you the solution to your problem."

I slowly lift the card and turn it over.

"The Knight of Wands." She smiles, looking oddly pleased with herself. "You're correct. A talisman or a crystal won't suffice. But a *Knight* surely will. If you summon a worthy one."

"*Summon?*" A feeling of uneasiness washes over me.

"Yes. Summon a guardian. A savior. A man who will rise to the challenge, eager and willing to provide you with the protection you desire."

"But, aren't I in this mess, this karmic shit storm, because I did a spell to influence another man's free will?" I ask. A love spell, to be precise.

She laughs at me. "Do you have a specific man in mind to put to the task?"

"No."

"Then fear not. Your spell will summon a man *meant for you.* You will not be targeting the free will of a specific person. The man you will call to your side will happily rise to the challenge."

I still feel uneasy about it. "Is there another way?"

She gathers her cards and shuffles them, once again she spreads them across the table and instructs me to carefully select another card. I select one and place it on the table, face up. My breath hitches slightly as my eyes take in the answer.

The Knight of Wands.

"No. There isn't." she replies.

There has to be something going on here. How does that card come up twice in regards to this situation? Maybe third time's a charm.

"May I?" I ask, nodding to the cards. She bows her head slightly with consent. I scoop the cards up, shuffling them thoroughly myself for a few moments. Placing the deck on the table, I cut it in half, then select the first card on top and flip it over.

The Knight of Wands. *Again.*

"Perhaps this man is seeking *you* as well." She says, almost absentmindedly.

I shrug that comment off though, as I have zero interest in working a spell to forge a relationship with a stranger. Especially after things went so horribly wrong after working magic on my ex. The thought of even entertaining the idea of having another man in my life any time soon, doesn't appeal to me at all.

"Alright. So, the solution to my problem is to enlist an unsuspecting man to fight my battle for me?" I say, more so to myself.

"This dangerous man, the one you bewitched. You are certain he will come for you?" she asks.

"I put him in prison. A *cop*. In *prison*. I'd say he can't wait to retaliate against me."

"Do you wish to face his vengeance alone?"

"No." I sigh. I'm scared to death of that...

"Then you have your answer."

We sit silently for a few moments. I know she's right. "How do you suggest I go about this? I don't want to make any mistakes this time around."

She smiles at me knowingly, and rises to fetch a pen and paper. She scrawls a list of ingredients and instructions, then picks up the Knight card and hands it to me with the paper folded over it.

"Keep this card. Look at it often. It will assist you in your workings." She instructs me.

I take them from her and tuck them into my purse, still unsure if I'm actually going to go through with this plan of action. "What do I owe you?"

"An update." She smiles. "When everything comes to pass."

I SIT ALONE ON THE FLOOR OF MY BEDROOM. THE VOODOO PRACTITIONER'S ingredients and instructions laid out before me as I finish sewing the two poppets that she instructed me to make. One to represent myself. One to represent the Knight.

As I sew, I try to imagine what kind of man would be protective and willing to do whatever it takes to stop *Him*? What kind of a man could be seen as a modern-day *Knight in shining armor?*

Most would automatically say a police officer... But *He* has ruined that for me. It isn't fair, I know there are good cops. But I will probably fear cops for the rest of my life because of *Him*. I have to come up with another answer.

I stare down at the Knight of Wands tarot card. The Image is quite simple. A Knight clad in black armor, atop a Black Horse, wielding a morning star weapon, waving a red banner. What could these symbols represent now, in present day?

Leaning back against my bed, I glance around the room as I contemplate this question. I need someone tough enough to handle *His* level of crazy. Someone brave enough, and willing to possibly go beyond the law to do what may be necessary. What kind of modern-day male would have their own set of moral codes, yet still be willing to cross legal lines if need be?

My black cat walks into the room, brushing against me. I stroke his fur as he purrs and chirps his little greeting. "Who will our Knight be, huh, Nico?" I ask him. Like he can actually answer. He doesn't, of course. Instead, he does what cats do and jumps up on my dresser, knocking over a box. I stand and walk over to pick it up, gathering the few items that fell out back inside, when I spot an old gift from a friend.

A Tasmanian Devil doll, wearing a leather motorcycle jacket. It occurs to me right then.

A Biker.

Bikers are tough guys, aren't they? They certainly have that type of image, at least in my mind. Not that I've ever actually met a real biker before. And couldn't a motorcycle be considered a modern-day black steed?

Pulling the mini leather jacket off the Taz doll, I sit back down on the floor with my spell work ingredients. I slip it onto the Knight poppet. A badass biker. That could really work. And I'm not a biker girl type, so I wouldn't even have to worry about the *love thing...*

I'm not casting a love spell!

I'm summoning a savior!

Grabbing the red scarf that fell out of the box as well, I cut a strip off and tie it around the Knight's neck. "This will represent the red banner in the Knight of Wands tarot card. Let this be a sign so that I recognize him. My Knight will be clad in black leather, with a red banner, on a black motorcycle."

What about the morning star weapon? Would that be a club of some sort, nowadays? I suppose so. Perhaps a baseball bat? There needs to be another sign that involves the morning star, so I know it's him. Leather and black motorcycles are far too common, I need that additional sign to know for sure. My savior needs to stand out to me, or I know I will doubt.

I place my petition paper between the two poppets and tie them together with the remaining fabric of my red scarf. Red doesn't always have to represent love. Red is also a color for protection, I remind myself. My savior does not have to love me, he just needs to be devoted to keeping me safe from *Him.*

I place the poppets together inside the wooden box. Marie Delai told me to tuck the box away some place safe where it will remain undisturbed. For now, I shove it under my bed. The voodoo priestess also instructed that I look at the Knight of Wands Tarot Card often, so I wedge it into the corner frame of my mirror where I will see it every day.

As I climb into bed, I stare at The Knight card once more before I close my eyes, silently pleading to the universe to send me a savior...

Present Day

THE OLD TWO-STORY FARM STYLE HOUSE IS TALLER THAN IT IS WIDE. AND it needs a lot of work. Both outside as well as in. However, it does have a cool wrap around porch. The peeling beige paint on the wood siding is in need of a good scraping so that it can be repainted down the road. So does all the faded away white trim work. The brick chimney appears as though it could crumble at any minute. And the windows look original, the old-style wood pane kind with the storm windows and screens you slide up and down. They are probably drafty, too.

The lawn is large, but patchy and overgrown in some spots. It is more weeds than actual grass as well. The flower beds and bushes have been completely neglected for a while. Overgrown with weeds and tall grass. The bushes are way too big and sun burned.

"Home sweet home." I sigh.

"It's... cute." Laura says, but I can tell she's just trying to be nice. "A bit of a drive from the shop though, isn't it?"

It is a forty-five-minute drive into the country from where I work, but... "It's what I can afford. Utilities aren't in my name. The owner didn't make me sign a lease. So, I can't be traced here."

"Then it's perfect. For now." Laura says.

I nod. "I'll make it work. This is a small town. Everyone probably knows everyone. If I can make friends here, in time, maybe they will watch my back."

"Definitely make friends with your neighbors. Their land surrounds your house." Ethan says. On either side of my little two-acre lot, there is a large farm to the left, up the hill. And a pecan orchard to the right. Both on acres of land. Behind my little farmhouse is a patio and then a patch of woods that divides the two farm properties. I have no idea how deep the woods go.

"Yes, I plan to." I say to Ethan. "As soon as I'm settled, I'll bake them both some muffins or something and introduce myself."

"You should charm them." Ethan suggests. "Bake some honey jar magick into them so they take an instant liking to you."

"Good idea." Laura agrees. "But you might want to keep the whole *witch thing* under wraps for a while. Most people this far out from the city limits are bible thumpers."

Right. "I'll try to keep what I do private."

"Well, let's get you moved in. We're losing day light." Ethan says.

It only takes an hour for the three of us to move my twenty or so boxes inside and disperse them to the rooms in which they belong. Mainly the bedroom, bathroom, living room and kitchen. I don't own much, anymore. Just clothing and some personal items. My books and crystals and witchy things I acquired while working off the books for Laura in her metaphysical shop.

The interior of the old farmhouse is just as dated as the outside. It is fully furnished, however, and looks as though you've just stepped into the 1950's. The front door opens to a small foyer. To the left, a staircase which leads to the master bedroom and bathroom. The kitchen, coat closet and downstairs bathroom are to the left as well. To the right, a living room or a study. No dining room. The kitchen is large enough though. There is a table that sits four in front of a picture window, and it has a small island by the sink and oven. I can see one of my neighbor's houses, from the window behind the sink in my kitchen. The one that lives on the farm on top of the hill, about a quarter mile up the road. It looks like a nice house, a ranch, from what I can tell at this distance. I hope the owner is nice, too.

"Well, that's everything." Laura says.

"Thanks for helping me move in." I say, to both of them.

Ethan pulls a small, empty jar out of his pocket and hands it to me. "Fill it with ingredients for protection and bury it in your yard for luck. You're going to need it."

"Thanks. You shouldn't have." I joke.

Laura hands me four quartz crystal points from her purse. "And bury these at the four corners of your house for protection as well."

"I will, thank you."

Hugging them both good-night, I watch them leave from my screened storm door and wave them off. Once they're out of sight, I close the big solid oak door and lock it. Now that the door will be shut, no more consistent in and out of moving boxes, it's safe to let my cat out of his carrier to explore his new home as well.

"Come on Nico, let's make something for dinner." I say to him, as he stretches and proceeds to rub his solid black body against my leg. I bend over to pick him up and carry him into the kitchen with me, placing him on the island. His pretty green eyes scan the room. "What do you think, bud?" I ask. He leans to headbutt me. "This is home." For now...

P ULLING INTO THE BACK GRAVEL PARKING LOT OF THE OLD PURPLE VICTORIAN house, I'm surprised to see that the parking lot is empty. I didn't expect to be the first one to work this morning. I'm glad, in a way, that I am the first to arrive. The new house I'm renting is a bit further away from my job than my last rental, and I don't want my boss thinking it will hinder my work performance at all.

I park my little gray Honda Civic under the shade of one of the big old trees over hanging the parking lot, and make my way up the steps of the back porch. Fishing the shop keys out of my bag, I unlock the old door and let myself in.

There are quite a few little lamps with fancy shades around the shop. Jewelry and specimen display cases, salt and selenite lamps, that all need switching on, before I unlock the front door for business. As I plug in the last display case of essential oil blends, I finally make my way to the front door. Flipping the blue and white CLOSED sign back around to OPEN, I notice there's a brown box outside on our front porch. I unlock the big old door to retrieve it and bring it to Laura's desk.

An order we placed last week, to replenish our shelves of Spell and Ritual Candles from Country Coven Creations. I grab the scissors from Laura's cauldron shaped mug of writing utensils, to cut the tape and open the box.

The candles are packed with black tissue paper and a handwritten letter on top, thanking us for our business. As I pull out the first candle, a bright Magenta one with swirls of black within its wax, I can't help but smile. It's almost the exact shade of Laura's crazy colored hair. I leave that one on her desk to see if she comments, then go about restocking our shelves with the rest.

"Hellooo! I'm heeeere!" Laura calls from our back room, in her familiar upbeat, but hoarse smoker's voice. I just finished lighting a few incense sticks and tucking them into the potted plants around the shop, when she bursts into the main display room. She's dressed in her typical hippie slash bohemian attire, complete with her fringed hobo bag slung over one shoulder, a Starbucks cup in her other hand.

"We got the candle order in this morning." I tell her. "I left one on your desk that you might like. The blessing candle in the foyer is low. Might want to swap it out."

There's a little table against the back wall of the foyer when you enter the front door. We keep a lit candle on it during shop hours. Laura calls it our blessing candle, and her intention is that it keeps negative energy out of our shop. Customers have to walk past it in order to enter between the two white columns on either side of our main show room, once they walk through the front door.

"Oh my gosh! It matches my hair!" she laughs, immediately peeling off its plastic packaging and sniffing it. "I guess witches brew smells like Amber and Patchouli." She says, grabbing one of her many lighters scattered on her messy desk. She carries it over to the glass plate on the foyer table to swap out the candles.

"Is Ethan working today?" I ask.

"Yes, he'll be in any minute." She says, taking a seat behind her desk to turn on her laptop. I sit in the single chair across from her, glancing out the big picture window behind her at the traffic backing up on Wrightsville Avenue.

I wonder what the traffic will be like going home in that direction after closing up shop later this afternoon.

"How was it getting here this morning? Did it take long?" she asks.

"No. I've been here about twenty minutes already. I gave myself an hour to get here. Didn't take that long." I say, debating whether or not to mention the idea of picking up extra work on the weekends closer to my rental house. I need something to make up the gas money, but I don't want to put any doubts in her mind about my ability to keep working here.

Ethan arrives within a few minutes, carrying a stack of papers.

"I printed out this month's event calendars." He says, placing them on Laura's messy desk. She has to slam her hand down on the stack to prevent it from falling to the floor and scattering everywhere. Ethan and I laugh at her. "Maybe you should try organizing this disaster zone." Ethan says. "Then again, why bother. You will have it trashed by the end of the day anyway."

"It's an organized mess!" Laura insists, moving the calendars to the top of the essential oils case.

Ethan rolls his eyes at her. "*Aquarius.*" He sighs.

Laura scowls back at him, then turns to me. "So, what are your big weekend plans in your new place?" she asks, taking a sip of her Starbucks.

"Besides the thrill of unpacking and food shopping?" I laugh. "Latisha invited me to her brother's Birthday Bash at some pub in town. She said she'll introduce me to some of the locals and let me know which ones to stay away from."

Ethan leans against one of the columns, ankles crossed. He reminds me of Pan for some reason. His thin build, rust colored short hair, and short, pointed goatee scruff of a beard. "Which pub?" he asks.

"Kelly's Tavern, or something. I think that's what she said." I notice Laura and Ethan exchange glances. "What?"

"It's kind of a rough place, at times." Laura says. "It has a reputation."

I have a hard time believing Latisha and her brother would want to hang out anywhere that would actually be dangerous.

Laura grabs her purse and pulls out her deck of tarot cards. "Let's see what the cards have to say about these weekend plans."

I can't help laughing. Laura *always* consults her cards about everything. I humor her and watch her as she shuffles them, then pulls three cards, laying them down on her desk.

When she turns them over, my heart literally skips a beat. I stare back up at her.

"What's wrong? The Knights are all great cards to pull, Vanna."

I swallow hard. "You're never going to believe this." I manage to say.

She smiles wide at me, lifting one more card from her tarot deck. "Try me." She says, placing the fourth card next to the first three.

The fourth Knight card... *Are you freaking kidding me?*

"I told you I went to the Voodoo priestess. But I never told you I actually did the spell." I say. Laura and Ethan both stare at me, as I relay the entire experience to them, including how I worked the Knight Summoning spell.

"Oh, you're going to that bar this weekend! You have to." Laura insists. "This kind of a sign isn't one to ignore."

"When you say this is rough place, is it a Biker bar?" I ask.

"It's not exactly a Biker bar, but it's always been one of the places they hang out." Laura says.

"I did that spell over a year ago. Or just about a year ago. Nothing ever came of it." I say. "In a year I've never crossed paths with a single Biker."

"Sounds like you might get the chance this weekend though. And more than one chance, if it's a hang around place." Ethan says.

"Could it really take this long to work though? I don't know if I did it right. And what if he actually is there, and I don't recognize him?" I ask, suddenly feeling overwhelmed.

"Don't look with these eyes, look with this eye!" Ethan flicks my forehead where the third eye is located between the eyebrows. "I doubt a Knight in shining armor atop a white horse, wielding a sword, is going to sweep you up into his arms and ride off with you into the sunset to live happily ever after." He says, his voice dripping with his typical sarcasm.

"*Bitchy Sagittarius.*" Laura playfully gripes at him. We all laugh.

"No, he'll be riding a black horse, wielding a morning star." I say, recalling the artwork on my original Knight of Wands tarot card. "And I don't expect him to whisk me away. I didn't work a love spell."

They both have a confused look on their faces.

"You don't want him to fall in love with you?" Ethan asks.

"Not after the last time a love spell went horribly wrong." I sigh. "I didn't know what I was doing when I did this spell though. I was summoning a savior. Someone to protect me, if *you know who,* decides to..." My voice cracks. I swallow hard again. They both nod, knowing better than to push me to talk about *Him.*

"Were you specific at all?" Ethan asks.

I shrug. "I mean, kind of. I used the depiction of the Knight and some other things that might help me recognize him. But I don't know if it even worked. It's been a whole year."

Laura taps the cards on her desk. "Someone is coming. Nobody ever pulls all four Knights in a row."

"The card you used, in your summoning, the Knight had a morning star? The club with the spikes?" Ethan asks.

I nod. "Yes, a morning star. A black horse. And a red banner."

"That card symbolizes the Knight of Wands then." He says.

"That's what the Priestess said."

"Well, the Knight of Wands represents one ready for action, prepared for what's ahead. Someone with determination of wanting to be successful in his endeavor. Fire is a dominant factor in the Knight of Wands symbolism too. So is the red banner." Ethan explains. He taps on the Knight cards on Laura's desk as he explains the others. "The Knight of Pentacles is a harbinger of money. The Knight of Swords represents a person with quick wits, intense responses and assertion. A fighter. Protective."

"Maybe my cards are giving you an idea of what to look for?" Laura says, thoughtfully. "Sounds like quite a catch so far." She teases me.

"The Knight of Cups is the card of falling in love at first sight, too." Ethan adds.

I stand up from the chair, smoothing out my skirt, while simultaneously wiping the clamminess from my palms. "I didn't work a love spell." I insist. "And I wasn't that specific about the Knight. He could be anyone."

Laura shoves the four Knight cards towards me. "Vanna, there's no way you can miss this guy. These cards don't just happen to present themselves like this."

Taking a deep breath, I exhale nervously. "I'm scared."

Laura laughs at me. "Of meeting a smart, possibly wealthy man who may fall head over heels in love with you and want to protect you?"

"Okay, for the last time, I did *not* work a love spell!" I insist, wishing they would stop with all the love talk. "I didn't target anyone specifically. I have no idea who he is. If he's even out there. If the spell even worked. It's been a year."

"That's perfect, Vanna. So, you don't even have to worry about all that *free will* guilt trip mumbo jumbo." Ethan says. "Girl, go get him!"

I stare at the cards on Laura's table, before I'm saved by the bell on the front door. It jingles as our first customer of the day enters our shop.

N OTICING THE IMPRESSIVE ROW OF MOTORCYCLES LINED UP IN FRONT OF the tavern, I turn to look at my friend. Completely unfazed, as usual. Latisha is a party girl. An adventure junkie. Nothing ever intimidates her. I wish I could be more like her. Seemingly carefree, up for anything at any time. Completely open to meeting new people and even more eager and enthusiastic about new experiences. I used to be like her.

"I never took you for a biker bar type of chick." I comment, as we start our walk towards the establishment.

She flips her dark dreads over her shoulder and slides her purse strap up her arm, glancing over at me, a knowing look on her face. "Derek hangs out with a lot of bikers. Relax, Vanna. The actual biker bar is on the other side of town. This is just a bar. That some bikers happen to come to, too."

"There's a difference?" I ask.

She laughs. "Depending on the MC's, *oh yeah*." Before we reach the curb, she touches my arm lightly, stopping me to face her. "Don't be mad at me, okay?" she suddenly says, a mischievous expression on her face.

Oh, no...

My anxiety level immediately increases. I knew there was something more about tonight. This wasn't just a party for her older brother. She has something else up her sleeve.

"What did you do?"

She looks at me pitifully, then laughs as she rubs my arm, her way of trying to comfort me. "There's actually somebody I want you to meet to-night." Latisha takes a quick step back, throwing up her arms as she pretends to block a punch. As if I'd actually hit her. Of course, I don't. Even if I want to.

"*Now?*" I almost shriek.

"Well not *now*, now. He's not even here yet, I don't think." She glances around at the bikes for a moment, as if she's looking for a specific one owned by a particular person. "No, he's not. Some of his people are though." She nods her head toward one bike in particular.

My heart nearly skips a beat when I read what the lettering says on the bikes tank. Saviors MC. *Saviors...* Is this a sign? After so long? I had just about given up on the spell I worked.

"What's the matter?" she asks, snapping me out of my daze.

"Nothing. Just a strange name for a motorcycle gang." I say, trying to cover.

She laughs at me. "Not a *gang*. A *club*. Do not say *gang*, Vanna. They're just motorcycle clubs. If you say *gang*, you're going to offend someone." She explains. I must look more nervous now because she sighs and continues. "A lot of MC's donate the money they raise to charity. The Saviors specifically, do a lot of charity rides and fund-raising events. They're just people. Some are a little rough around the edges, but still. Just people."

That doesn't sound so bad. "You're right."

"Come on, let's get you a drink. You're really uptight tonight, Vanna. Being weirder than usual." She teases. Hooking her arm around mine, she pulls me towards the door to the Tavern.

I had specifically requested a *savior*. I can't help but wonder if the Knight Summoning is finally working. Or was this simply a funny coincidence? I have a feeling I'll know soon enough.

The bar is crowded as Hell. Loud. There's rock music playing from a juke-box in the back, pool tables and darts. The bar is really long with lots of stools lined up. There are tables and chairs littered about and a small open floor area for dancing, near the jukebox. I glance around looking for a less crowded area, and spot one, down near the very end of the bar in a darkened corner.

"Can we go sit over there?" I ask.

"How are you going to meet new people hiding in a corner, Vanna?" she rolls her eyes at me.

"Just let me adjust!" I say, jokingly, but not. "I'm not used to all this. This isn't my kind of atmosphere." I can already feel people starting to notice me. The odd girl. The outsider. The Witch in the country. I should have worn jeans and a flannel shirt, or something more 'country'. Not a long, black lacey wrap dress. Someone is going to hit me with a bible. That last panicked irrational thought has me inwardly laughing at myself, though. Of course, that won't happen. Right?

She rolls her eyes at me. "Fine. *Go adjust*. I'm ordering us a shot though. A double for you!" She lets go of my arm and immediately disappears into the crowd. Abandoning me. Damnit. I didn't even have a chance to protest. Now I'm standing here awkwardly by myself, contemplating leaving. But I can't do that to her and her brother, Derek. I don't see him anywhere either.

I make my way carefully, but quickly, towards the end of the less popu-lated area of the bar and hop up on a bar stool. Fixing my skirt, so that it falls neatly around me to my ankles, I wait for my friend to come back, smiling shyly at anyone who happens to glance my way in the sea of people here.

Suddenly the bar tender is across from me, throwing down a napkin and placing a big shot glass on top of it before me. He's youngish, cute. Wearing a tight t-shirt and jeans that compliment his athletic physique. Blonde. Not my type, but definitely cute. His vibe is very friendly though.

"Latisha said to drink up!" He gives me a quick smile before hurrying off to tend the busy bar.

"I can't believe she's not even going to drink with me." I mutter to myself, wondering where my little social butterfly wandered off to. I lift the shot glass to sniff its contents. I'm not a drinker. I have no idea what this actually is.

An older guy in a ball cap and blue jeans clanks his beer bottle to my glass. "I'll drink with you." He winks at me.

I laugh, attempting to be polite. "Thanks, I don't know where my friend disappeared to."

"Who's your friend?" he asks.

"Latisha." I say, avoiding eye contact with him. He seems friendly enough, but his vibe is off-putting.

"Drink up, I'll buy you another."

"No thanks. I'm really not much of a drinker."

His demeanor changes upon my refusal. It's subtle, but I notice.

Latisha comes up to me, finally, exchanging a look between me and this guy and gives me the slightest shake of her head in disapproval. I nod in agreement. He's a *Hell no*. She knows him, or at least knows about him.

"Girl, you shoot that you don't sip it!" she teases me. "Come on, you need to loosen up!"

I sigh, but I take the shot to appease her. Awful, as expected. "What the hell was that?"

"Jack Daniels. You're such a lightweight." She says, grabbing my arm again and yanking me off the bar stool. "Come on, I'll introduce you around."

A whirl wind of faces and handshakes for the next twenty minutes takes it out of me. Everyone is of course friendly and welcoming. The double shot is doing its job. I'm feeling loose and a bit dizzy, but nothing I can't handle. I just need some fresh air. I excuse myself to step outside for a few minutes.

Once outside in the cooler air, I feel a little bit better. Like I can actually take a breath. I lean up against the brick wall behind a group of people chatting casually, and pull my cellphone out of my purse. I'm about to text Laura about the weird Saviors connection, when I hear another loud motorcycle roll up. I glance up to see if it's another Savior's bike.

The motorcycle is a huge Harley Davidson. No chrome. Completely blacked out. It's actually an intimidating looking machine. The man riding it, is wearing a full helmet and black leather jacket, of course, and a red scarf around his neck. As he dismounts the bike, a cool breeze catches the scarf... and it billows out, like a red banner.

A red banner.

My heart sinks and then suddenly beats faster.

The red banner. The black armored Knight. The black horse.

The Knight Tarot card.

He's still wearing a full helmet. I can't see his face. But he's glancing around as if he's looking for someone.

Is this him?

As he's about to pull off the helmet, I scurry back inside the bar.

Latisha is MIA again, so I retreat to my comfort zone in the back corner and wait for her to find me. It's farther back from the entrance and it will give me a chance to get a look at this biker without him noticing me.

"You're like a magnet." The guy in the blue hat from earlier says to me, a little too close to my ear. I recoil instinctively, then laugh at my own awkwardness.

"Yeah, in a lot of ways." I joke, more so to myself. A magnet to this corner and a magnet for pushy men. Maybe even a magnet for something else... I focus on watching the door in the front of the bar. Waiting for the mysterious man to enter.

This guy in the hat is saying something to me about buying me another drink, but I don't hear a word. The biker finally enters the bar. And now that I can see his face, I'm instantly fixated on him.

He is handsome. *Really* handsome. The definition of *ruggedly handsome*. Dark, almost black hair, buzzed short on the sides, longer on top but slicked back. A short scruff of facial hair, like he hasn't shaved in a day or two, but it looks damn good on him. And he's tall. Taller than a lot of the guys in here tonight.

He's wearing a black leather jacket with silver zippers, belted at his waist. It accentuates the broadness of his shoulders and the narrowness of his waist. He has a nice physique. Not *overly* muscular, from what I can tell. His build is more athletic muscle. He looks *dangerous*. A threateningly masculine type of dangerous.

The red scarf is now tucked in neatly beneath his jacket. He's got a large hunting knife of some kind strapped to his side, hanging down in a black sheath over his dark gray denim pants. And he's wearing big black biker boots, double buckles on the side of each.

People want to greet him as he moves through the room. Especially women. He's being polite, but I can tell he's searching for someone. When he walks, he walks with a kind of authority. An air of power about him. A noticeable confidence.

The jukebox starts playing a slower song. Ed Sheeran's *Make It Rain*. Slower and bluesy. It seems to almost mellow out the crowd. Funny how music can affect an environment so fast.

When he smiles at people, I can see the brackety dimples through his short facial scruff. I notice his strong, angular jawline as well, his high cheek bones, as he scans the crowd.

Unable to take my focus off of him, we lock eyes from across the room. A sea of people between us. His eyes are dark, and full of *darkness*... When he doesn't look away from me, I smile at him. My awkward habit of avoidance, however, gets the better of me. Averting my eyes, I turn slightly away, in time for this pushy guy in the hat to shove a bottle of bud lite into my hand.

"*Oh*," I say, surprised. "Thanks, but I don't drink beer..."

A large hand, attached to a heavily tattooed arm, plucks it from my grasp and places the bottle back down on the bar in front of hat guy.

"Heard her turn you down before." A gruff male voice says. I look up to see a big guy with a shaved head and blue eyes, which are scowling at the guy in the hat. "Beat it." He out right orders him.

To my astonishment, pushy guy grabs the beer and walks away, leaving his bar stool for this man to take. Which he does. He sits down next to me and gives me a friendly smile.

"Hi, I'm Shane." He says, his voice suddenly a lot less gruff.

I quickly glance back in the direction I last saw the attractive guy with the red scarf and leather jacket, but he's nowhere to be seen now. And for some reason, disappointment washes over me.

I shift my attention back to Shane. "Hi, I'm Vanna." I smile back, glancing over him. He's well built. Definitely works out. My eyes zero in on a symbol on his leather vest, though. Two Swords crossed, with the letters A.K. between the blades.

"My MC." Shane says, noticing me staring at the swords. "Asphalt Knights, MC."

First, the Saviors MC. Now, the Asphalt *Knights* MC. Are you kidding me?

"Cool." I smile at him, hoping I don't sound like a dork. I don't know how to talk to bikers!

"Since I rescued you from that weasel, would you let me buy you a drink? I'd really enjoy the pleasure of your company." Shane asks.

"Oh, you rescued me?" I can't help giggling, which makes him smile wider at me.

"I know a damsel in distress when I see one." He grins. "I *am* a Knight, after all."

For the Knight reason alone, I let him buy me a drink, *with ice*. I'm already buzzed from the double shot Latisha made me drink when we got here.

We have a casual, mostly one sided, conversation. Mostly about his bike and his workout routine. Shane is a decently attractive man, but I find myself feigning interest, and continue to occasionally scan the bar for that tall, dark and dangerously handsome biker I saw pull up on that solid black motorcycle. He wasn't wearing any patches. So, he probably wasn't another Knight, or a Savior.

As I finish my drink, I realize it wasn't the best idea. My dizziness has gotten worse, and my skin feels cold and clammy.

"Are you okay?" Shane asks.

"I never drink." I say, a little embarrassed.

"You want to get some fresh air?" He asks. "There's a door to the alley back there past the bathrooms. I can go with you. That way we don't have to shove through this crowd to get out the front." It has gotten rather packed in the half hour we've been chatting. As I slide off the bar stool and grab my purse, I realize just how badly buzzed I am. Even my legs feel a little shaky.

"Sure, fresh air sounds great." I say. Shane gets up and extends his muscular arm for me to hold onto. "Thanks." I actually do appreciate the chivalrous gesture, and he escorts me towards the back of the bar where the sign for restrooms hangs above the corridor.

As we make our way towards the back-alley door at the end of the dark hall near the bathrooms, Shane's arm drops around my waist as he pushes the door open to the men's room and swings me inside. I'm stunned, my voice catching in my throat as he manhandles me into a stall. Panic begins to set in as I attempt to get past him, but he's a brick wall, taking up the entire space inside the stall, forcing me to stumble backwards and land sitting on the toilet behind me as he shuts the stall door.

"Shane...please..." My voice is trembling as much as my body now, and I feel like I could hurl. He reaches down to stroke my hair and touch my face, but I twist away to avoid his caress. "Stop!" I snap, trying to stand up. He shoves me back down. "I'm here with someone." I try to warn him off, as I attempt to stand again. This time, he grabs me and slams me up against the wall of the stall, his big hands roaming greedily over my body as I try to shove at him, telling him again, to stop. He's so strong though, so much bigger than I am.

Suddenly, there's a loud bang, a door busting open. The creep is yanked away from me and I struggle to stand on my own. The combination of my stupid drunkenness and fear wreaking havoc on my shaking body.

The stall door slowly swings closed and I try to focus on what's happening outside of the stall. I can hear shuffling, then the familiar sound of fists meeting flesh, again and again, until a body flops down on the floor just outside the stall. The creep is on the ground. His face a bloody mess, unconscious, visible to me under the door.

I'm nauseous now. I can feel my stomach lurch up my throat as I spin around and face the toilet to heave, emptying its contents until it hurts and I'm gasping for air.

Someone is behind me, holding my long hair back. Another strong arm, though not quite as big as the creeps, holds me against them and prevents me from crumbling to the dirty floor.

"*Shh, Shh, Shh,* you're okay." A male voice says, "I've got you. I won't let you fall. You're safe with me." His tone sounds sincere, and for some inexplicable reason, I feel completely safe in his arms.

Chapter
three

Vanna Collision

I'M SO EMBARRASSED.
Having let myself get drunk with a stranger, then puking my brains out in front of *another* stranger. After being attacked by the first stranger! I should have stayed home.

I rinse out my mouth and splash my face with cold water. The guy who just rescued me from being attacked, then held my hair for me while I puked alcohol, hands me some paper towels now. I reluctantly turn around to accept them, unable to bring myself to even look him in the eyes. Pressing my face into the paper towels, I wish I could just disappear. I rinsed my mouth out thoroughly, but I'm pretty sure I've got spearmint tic-tacs in my bag. Shit, where is my bag?

"I had a purse." I say, my voice muffled in the paper towels.

"What's that, baby?" the guy asks.

"I had a purse." I say again, louder.

"I got it." He says, after a moment. I remove the wad of damp paper towels from my face and reach for the purse he's holding out to me. It slips through my clumsy fingers and falls to the floor between us. I immediately squat down to retrieve it, fishing for the tic-tacs, when I notice his boots... Black biker boots. Buckles on the sides. I stare at his body as I slowly stand back up. Dark gray pants. Black sheathed knife. Black leather jacket, belted. Silver zippers. Red scarf... And a devastatingly handsome face, with deep, beautiful, soulful dark eyes.

I take in a sharp breath.

"It's *you*." I manage to whisper. The black clad biker on the black motorcycle, that I locked eyes with earlier tonight. He saved me.

"Hi," he says, low. His voice immediately has an effect on me. It's deep. Growly. I can't help sinking my teeth into my bottom lip as his eyes roam over me. He wets his lips briskly with the tip of his tongue and grins. "I'm Dean Keegan."

Automatically, I extend my hand to him, which he grips in his large, hot, rough hand.

"Thanks for saving me, Dean Keegan." I smile slightly, looking up at him. He has to be two or three inches over six feet tall. "I'm Vanna."

"*Vanna...*" Dean says my name like it means something to him. "It's a pleasure to meet you." That vocal fry of his is giving me butterflies. And he hasn't let my hand go. I decide he can keep it. "We have a decision to make, Vanna." Dean speaks again, breaking me out of my daze.

"We do?"

"We call the cops on this prick, or we get the hell out of here?"

No... No cops. Cops will want my information. I can't have that...

"Let's get the hell out of here." I say, quickly. "But I came with a girlfriend tonight, she's still in the bar somewhere. I can't just disappear on her."

"I got you, doll." He grins at me, still holding my hand. "We'll sneak out the alley and come back in the front, find your friend."

As I nod in agreement, he grabs the helmet off the sink counter and gently tugs my hand, leading me out of the men's room, down the dark hall and out the back alleyway door.

"What if somebody finds him? Someone is bound to go in the bathroom soon." I ask. Dean continues to hold my hand while we walk towards the street that will bring us back to the front of the Tavern.

"Don't worry about it. He's got more to be afraid of than we do." Dean says. He walks purposefully ahead, as if he's on a mission.

"What if he wakes up on his own and comes after us?"

Dean chuckles. It's a low, dark sound that sends a shiver through my body. And not in a bad way, either. What the hell is wrong with me?

"Then I'll lay him the fuck out *again*. There's nothing for you to be afraid of, Vanna. Not while you're with me." He says, this time looking down at me with a smile. For some reason, I believe him.

We make it to the street and around the corner of the brick tavern, heading back to the front door. As if we had nothing to do with what went down in the back bathroom.

"Who's your friend?" he asks, releasing my hand for the first time to hold the Tavern door open for me.

"Latisha Wallace." I say, stepping back inside.

"Derek's little sister?" Dean asks, his hand on my lower back, guiding me gently through the crowd.

"You know them?" I ask, surprised. Though maybe I shouldn't be. It's a small community. I'm the newcomer. They all probably know each other.

"Derek is my junior mechanic." Dean says. "I was just going to wait to give him this helmet at work, but he told me Latisha wanted to see me."

I spot Latisha near the pool tables and wave to catch her attention. She sees me and immediately grabs her beer and heads for us. We meet her halfway, near the edge of the little dance floor in front of the jukebox.

"Girl! Where did you disappear to?" She demands, then looks up at Dean. "I see you found each other, though."

"Found each other?" I ask.

"Dean's the guy I wanted to introduce you to." She says to me, before she steps closer so Dean can hear her better. "I wanted to tell you about my friend, Vanna. She's looking for some off the books work. Very part time. I thought maybe you could use her at the roadhouse?"

This is a work thing? Damn. For once I wouldn't have minded being set up. He's gorgeous. Probably out of my league, though.

"Alright." Dean says, lifting the helmet and plopping it down over Latisha's head. He slides the face shield up for her. "Go give your brother his new helmet. I'm gonna talk to Vanna."

I can't help giggling at the whole scene. He must really know them well. Latisha gives him a thumbs up, before she waves to me and heads back over to the group of people she was hanging out with. This time, I don't mind her leaving me alone.

"I had no idea I was being set up on a job interview." I say to Dean, trying to sound humorous about it.

"Disappointing." He sighs. I must have reacted to his comment in some small way, because he immediately adds, "Not like that." As if he read the insecurities in my mind. "I'd like to offer to buy you a drink, Vanna. But I have a feeling you might turn me down for multiple reasons, at this point."

"What's in a Shirley Temple?" I ask.

His expression brightens with a smile that actually makes my heart flutter. "Ginger ale, grenadine, lime juice and maraschino cherries." He replies.

"Wow, you really fired those ingredients off." I giggle. "Do you tend your own bar?"

"I used to. It was my uncle's before it was mine. I tended bar for him often when I was a teenager." He notices me give him a look about the age, and grins at me. "Yeah, we live by our own rules, doll." He smiles, gesturing for me to head towards the bar. Once we make it through the crowd, Dean leans between two people, grabbing the bar tender's attention. He orders two Shirley Temples and drops some cash on the bar. "Keep it. We'll be down the far end." He says, pointing to where I had been sitting earlier.

"Shall we?" Dean steps back to me, offering me his arm as the Knight did before. I have no reservations about sliding my hand under it and holding onto his leather clad bicep. I allow him to escort me to the other end of the bar.

We sit down together, facing each other. Dean's back is to the guy with the blue hat who was hitting on me earlier as well. I notice the guy turn slightly to give Dean a dirty look. I try to hide the smirk on my face at hat guys jealousy.

Dean notices. "What?" he asks, with a curious smile.

"Nothing," I say, trying to think of something else to bring up. "You ordered two Shirley Temples. You don't seem like a Shirley Temple kind of guy." I tease.

The bar tender swings by with our drinks, placing them down on two napkins before he hurries off to tend to another customer.

Dean hands me one of the glasses. "I'm not. But here's to solidarity." He teases me back, clinking his glass to mine before he adds, "And maybe I was curious how it tastes." He watches me over the brim of his glass for a moment, before he takes a gulp.

"You're very brave." I take a sip and placing it back down on the napkin.

"For kicking that guys ass?" he asks, placing his glass beside mine.

"Well, that too." I say. "But mostly for looking the way you do and drinking a pink girlie virgin drink with me, where all these other biker men can see you doing it."

He grins at me again. And God, he's so handsome. "I can kick all their asses too." He says, with more than a hint of cockiness in his voice. "Pink drink or no." I bite my lip to prevent myself from giggling again, like an infatuated idiot. "Is Vanna short for something?" he asks. "Can't say that's a name I've often heard."

"Giovanna, actually. But everyone calls me Vanna." I shrug.

"Beautiful." He winks at me this time, and I feel a slight flush in my cheeks. He takes another swig of his Shirley Temple, watching me as I follow suit. "You're not from around here. I'd have heard about you."

"Heard about me?" I ask, wondering what that meant.

"Most definitely." He smiles, the tip of his tongue peeking between his teeth quickly to touch his upper lip. Is he trying to entice me with it? It's working.

"I just moved here, actually. I haven't had much time to venture out into the community between the move and work."

"What do you do, *Vanna*?" he says my name again, in a way nobody ever does.

"I work in the next county over. A metaphysical shop. Not sure I should be talking about that out here though." I glance around quickly to see if anyone over heard. No one seems to have. "I've been warned people sometimes have particular ideas about that sort of thing down here."

"Down here?" He asks. I'm not so sure I want to get into being from New York just yet, so I deflect with a question of my own.

"So, you have a bar too? And a repair shop?" I ask.

"A roadhouse. It's a biker joint. And I own a motorcycle repair shop." He replies. "I live on a small farm too, open to the public also."

I smile. "I *love* that. The little house I'm renting is between two farms. Well, one is a Pecan orchard, actually. The other one is a farm. It's a quarter mile up the road from me, but my yard is against their corn field."

Dean is grinning ear to ear now, as if I've said something he finds exceptionally amusing. I can't help smiling back at him suspiciously. I reach to take another sip of my drink. His smile is infectious.

"What?" I ask.

"I hope you buy locally." He says, in such a way that I can't help feeling like there is so much more behind that comment. But I don't get the chance to ask him.

A woman drapes herself over him, sloppily. Hanging over his shoulder, her arms around his neck. She's wearing ripped jeans and a low-cut top. I can see her red lacy bra at the edges. Her hair is blonde with black streaks in it. She's wearing a very wrong shade of bright pink lipstick and too much eye makeup.

I shift my focus back to Dean as he places his drink down, and I notice he's staring at me more intently now. Watching my reaction to this encounter, as if he's concerned.

"Dean!" she squeals. "When are you going to take me for a ride on that big, beautiful bike of yours?" she asks, laying the flirtation on thick. His smile is thin and doesn't seem genuine, though.

He clears his throat. "Connie, this is Vanna." He says, watching me.

She glances at me, but says nothing, immediately going back to flirting with him.

"Okay, then." I say, under my breath. I turn away from them and take another gulp of my drink. If that's the type of girl he's into, I'm seriously wasting my time. She and I haven't got a damn thing in common, except the fact that we both find Dean Keegan attractive.

"I'm a busy man, Connie." He says flatly to her, shifting in his seat as if he's uncomfortable with her proximity, or behavior.

"I'll make the time, baby." She pushes. "You just say where and when."

She's really annoying me. I take another sip and place the drink down beside his, before I slide off the bar stool and smooth out my skirt. My long hair falls over my shoulder as I bend to do so, and I brush it back impatiently.

"Dean, would you please excuse me for a few minutes?" It's really not a question. It's just a courtesy statement.

"Of course. I'll be right here." His tone is different. He's definitely concerned about something.

Connie looks at me again. This time she actually speaks and acknowledges my presence. "The ladies' room is back there." She gestures towards the corridor behind me, dismissively, as if I don't know where the bathrooms are. I'm very familiar with that bit of information, thank you very much. "Who does your extensions, by the way?" she asks.

"I'm not wearing any." I say, glancing at Dean. He's smiling at me again. A genuine smile. I smirk back at him, before I turn and start walking towards Latisha and her group of friends. I glance back in his direction before I get to her, and I'm pleased to discover he is still watching me... Maybe Connie isn't his type after all.

"He is *so* into you." Latisha says. We watch her brother and his friends shoot pool for a few moments.

"What are you talking about? I thought this was a job interview?"

She shrugs. "I mean, *technically* that was the point of the introduction. But he *likes you*, likes you." She says, reaching into her purse to pull out a small mirror and a liquid lipstick. She opens the little clam shell mirror and applies another coat of that deep navy blue that looks really cool with her dark complexion.

"How do you know?" I ask, afraid to get my hopes up with Connie over there, hanging on him. I haven't actually been remotely attracted to a guy in a long time.

"It's written all over him. These biker bitches are practically foaming at the mouths, they're so jealous." She laughs.

"Oh, so he's the *unattainable* bad boy biker of this town." I sigh, my excitement dropping a few notches. Of course, he is. He's *gorgeous*. He looks dangerous. And he saves women in bathrooms. He's probably every biker girl's fantasy. He could get any woman he wants. Why would he bother with me?

"Not exactly. He's actually not real big on dating."

"One-night stands?" I sigh again. The thought is tempting, but I'm not the type.

"He's a really genuine guy, Vanna. I wouldn't introduce you to a prick." She seems offended. "Not after you know who." She knows better than to mention *His* name.

I glance back in Dean's direction, in time to see him pull Connie's arm off him. I watch her walk away before I look at him again. He's still watching me.

"Well, if he's so great, why aren't you after him?" I ask.

Latisha laughs. "I'm not the one into the *Daddy thing*."

I gasp and actually do smack her on the arm this time. "You bitch!" We both laugh. "He's not that much older than I am. What is he, eight or ten years older?"

"No more than that, if that." She shrugs. "I'd be open to getting to know Dean though, if that was my thing."

"Please. He isn't old enough to be my Daddy." I scoff. "But what makes you actually think he likes me and isn't just being nice as a favor to you? Maybe he doesn't want to offend you. You clearly know each other. And why didn't you tell me before hand? I would have worn something different."

She purses her lips for a moment and raises a brow at me. "Because I know you. You wouldn't have come. If I told you I was introducing you to a guy you would have made up some lame-ass excuse not to come out with me tonight." We both laugh again, because she is one hundred percent correct in that assumption. "He's sitting over there, patiently awaiting your return. Normally he'd be shooting pool or talking to somebody. It's a party." She says. "But no, he's waiting for you. Guarding your drink."

I didn't even think of that. I left my drink out in the open. Between the Knight and the guy in the blue hat, I should kick myself for being so stupid and reckless.

"So, he's a good guy." I say, mostly to myself.

"Definitely. And you should go back over to him before he thinks we're cooking up a scheme to help you bail on him."

"Okay, I'm going." I sigh. "I'll just talk to you later, I guess."

"Go get him, tiger!" she teases me, slapping me hard on the ass as I turn to walk back to Dean. I try to keep a straight face as I approach him, knowing he saw all that from a distance.

I watch him, watch me, as I walk back to him. He stands up as I approach and only sits back down when I do. I note the chivalrous gesture.

"Thanks for guarding my drink." I smile at him.

"You trust me?" he teases.

I lift my drink and salute him before taking another gulp. "If my friend says you're good people, then I trust you."

"I'm sorry about before." Dean says. "Connie. I hope I didn't offend you."

"Don't worry about it. I hear you have quite the harem." I joke.

He clears his throat and his expression looks slightly concerned once again. "That's false information." His tone is low. Did I offend him?

"I'm sorry. Maybe groupies would be a better description?" I tease. He's staring at me, though.

"I don't know if you're aware of your influence in a room, Vanna. But you've got quite the number of male admirers yourself." He grabs his glass and downs the rest of his drink, before placing it back on the bar.

I glance around the room briefly. There are a few guys looking my way. "I'm just new." I shrug.

He laughs, incredulously. "Right." He says, but decides not to comment further.

Over his shoulder, I spot Latisha's brother, Derek. He's a handsome guy with a gym sculpted body as well. He's almost as tall as Dean, too. I wave to him and he comes over, hugging me hello. I notice Dean is watching us intently. If we hadn't just met, I'd even venture to say his gaze is borderline territorial.

"Happy Birthday!" I say to Derek.

"Thank you!" he smiles brightly, then turns to Dean. They bump fists as Dean wishes him a Happy Birthday as well. "Bro, I can't thank you enough for that GT Air Helmet. I had my sister lock it in her car. I don't want to leave a six-hundred-dollar helmet sitting on my bike unsupervised."

Damn... that was a generous gift.

I take another sip of my drink, acting like I didn't notice. They talk for a few minutes about the specs and performance ratings on this apparent top-quality helmet, before Derek moves on to greet a few more of his friends. I finish my drink and place the glass beside Dean's on the bar.

"Would you like another?" Dean offers.

"No, thank you." I say. He nods, but he's staring at me. "What's wrong?" I ask.

"Our mutual friend sprung this whole job thing on me, Vanna." Dean sounds almost regretful.

Of course, she did. I just nod and glance around the room, waiting for him to let me down gently on the job prospect.

"It's a little rowdier than this place at times." He continues. "It's an *actual* biker bar."

"You don't seem too enthused." I force myself to chuckle. I think I read the vibes wrong. I must have. He's not that into me. Latisha was wrong. He's just a nice guy.

"I want to help you out, Vanna. I'm just..." I watch as he brings his hand up to the back of his neck, rubbing it for a moment before he drops his arm back to his side. "I don't know if it will be a fit, for you." He attempts to explain. "I'm not really sure it's *your* scene."

I nod, contemplating his words. I wouldn't fit in.

"Plus," he begins to say, then hesitates. He runs his hand through this hair, then strokes the stubble of his jawline.

"I don't fit the aesthetic." I say, finishing for him. "Not that *skinny* biker babe type, like Connie... I get it. It's fine. You have a specific type of customer. They want something to look at. Bikers like biker chicks." Maybe Connie is his type after all.

Dean looks at me like I've sprouted a second head. "*Really?*" he says, seemingly astonished. He's staring at me now. His expression is a mixture of puzzlement and concern.

"Well, this has gotten awkward." I say, folding my arms across my abdomen.

"Vanna, I-", he begins to say something, but I don't let him finish.

"It's okay, Dean. Don't feel obligated to give me a job. You know your business. Customers like what they like. I understand, really."

"No, Vanna, I really don't think you do." His tone is insisting. "It would be a conflict of interest. That's all."

"How?" I ask. "I don't know anyone in this town, besides Latisha."

"I'd be your boss."

We stare at each other for another long moment. "Am I missing something?"

"I can think of a few things." He sighs, an almost rueful look in his eyes. "Self-esteem, for starters."

"That was presumptuous." I almost snap at him. He isn't wrong, though.

"Not really." He shrugs slightly, almost wincing as he says the words.

I try not to frown at him. "I thought you were a nice guy."

"I can be." He says. I'm so confused right now. How did we get here? I just stare back at him, hoping he will explain. He laughs, getting off his stool to step closer to me. He places his hand behind me on the low back of the bar stool on which I'm sitting, and leans slightly in to me. "Vanna, I like you. If I hire you, I'd be your boss."

"My other boss likes me." I shrug, wondering what the big deal is.

"I bet he does." His expression darkens, his hand drops back to his side.

"*She.*" I correct him. "And shouldn't bosses like their employees? I mean, for the most part. You just gave Derek a six-hundred-dollar gift. You must like him, too."

Dean is smiling at me again, but he shakes his head as if he's in disbelief. "You break my heart, baby." He says with a sigh. I can't help wondering if I'm still drunk. Dean reaches into his back pocket and pulls out his wallet, extracting a business card and hands it to me. "That's the address to my roadhouse. It's attached to the Saviors MC club house. Across the lot from my bike shop."

Oh my God...

"You're a *Savior*?" I ask, wondering how I let myself get so distracted from the Knight Summoning signs. I must be tipsier than I think. Or just dazzled by his rugged good looks.

"Technically, no. I'm not a member of the MC anymore. But I own the buildings." He explains. "Stop by tomorrow, after you get off work. We'll talk about possibly giving you a shot, okay?"

"Okay." I take his card and stick it in the front zippered pouch of my purse. As I do so I notice him pull his cellphone from inside his jacket and glance at the screen. He must have gotten a text. Probably a chick. He's probably got a contact list full of booty call babes.

"You will come tomorrow, right?" he asks, his eyes suddenly searching mine. I wonder why he's seeking reassurances from *me*, now? A moment ago, it didn't seem like he wanted to hire me at all. Now all of a sudden, he wants to confirm my interest.

"After I get off work tomorrow, yes. I'll come to the address on the card."

He nods. "There's somewhere I need to be, now, unfortunately." His tone sounds almost regretful. "Had I known I'd be meeting you tonight, Vanna..." he hesitates, looking me over again. "Well, I'd have cleared my night to spend it with you."

"It was nice meeting you, Dean." I smile, extending my hand to him again.

He takes it, gently this time. "The pleasure has been all mine, Vanna. I look forward to seeing you again tomorrow." He smiles. "Good night."

"Good night." I smile back.

When he releases my hand, he steps past me, and walks towards the hall-way in the back of the bar that leads to the bathrooms and the alley. I find that strange, considering his bike is parked near the front door of this tavern. Why would he leave out the back?

Curiosity drives me to linger near the entry way of the corridor, and peek down the hall. As I do so, I watch him approach the men's room, pushing the door open. He doesn't step inside though. He continues to make his way to the back door and exits into the alley.

Dean must have been checking on the Knight, and now I can't help but wonder if that jerk is still in there on the floor. He can't be though. Would people have just left him in there stepping over him? Not called the cops?

I scurry down the hall and push the bathroom door open to look for myself. I'm not surprised to find the Knight is gone. He must have come to and left out the back as well.

Hurriedly, I make my way through the crowd back towards the front door of the tavern, in time to see Dean straddle his motorcycle. He's got his cellphone to his ear, talking to someone. I inch my way closer, hiding among a group of people crowding around the sidewalk in front of the entrance.

"You know where to find me if you think he isn't lying." I hear Dean say. "But I give you my word, Shane *is* lying. He's also lucky he's still breathing."

Shane. That was the Knight's name. The jerk Dean beat up and saved me from. Is he in trouble now with the MC over it? Is that why he had to leave so suddenly? Shane deserved what he got.

"Twenty minutes then. I'll be there." I hear Dean growl into the phone, before he shoves it back into his jacket and fires up the motorcycle.

I hurry over to him, grabbing his arm before he can pull away. "Wait!"

"Vanna?" He looks surprised and concerned to see me again.

"Are you in trouble because of me?" I ask. "Because of that jerk in the bathroom?" He stares at me but doesn't answer. "I'm sorry, I overheard the last part of your conversation and I can't just let you ride off if something bad is going to happen because you gave that creep what he deserved." I blurt out.

He smiles slightly at me. "Nothing for you to worry about, doll."

"That's not really an answer." I realize I'm squeezing his arm nervously, when he glances down at my hand. I let him go, wrapping my arms around myself instead.

He shuts the bike off, kicking the stand down, before he gets off of it and takes a step closer to me. Placing both of his now black leather gloved hands on my arms, he bends to look me in the eyes.

"Vanna, nothing that happened tonight and nothing that will happen tonight, is your fault." I'm sure that was supposed to sound reassuring, but it isn't.

"Oh God, you are in trouble, aren't you?" I stare up at him. "Call them back, I'll tell them it was all his fault. That you were only helping me."

Dean chuckles. "I'm not the one in trouble, doll. But that's all I can say about it. Got me?" he says. I nod, mostly because that's what I think is expected of me. "Besides, I can take care of myself, even if there was a problem." He tries to sound reassuring again.

I nod once more. Maybe he's right. Shane was a lot bigger than Dean is. And Dean dropped him hard. And fast. But if Shane's MC is mad at Dean, who knows how many of them might be involved now.

"Okay, *promise* me, then." I say. "*Promise* me that you're going to be alright."

He gives me a crooked, bemused smile. "You want a *promise* from me?"

"Yes. I know we just met and maybe I'm crazy, but promise me that you're not in danger." I insist. "I'm not going to be able to sleep tonight if you don't promise me, Dean."

Something flickers behind his dark eyes as he removes one of his hands from my arm. He places his forefinger and thumb beneath my chin, tilting my face up slightly higher. "You're really sweet, Vanna." He says, his voice softer now. "Do you promise to come to the roadhouse tomorrow?"

"Yes." I say. "I already told you I would."

"Then I promise I'll be there, too."

I really must be crazy. Out of my damn mind. Because all I want to do right now, is kiss him. Kiss a man I just met not even an hour ago. And he's looking at me as if he wants to kiss me, too. Though, as he releases me and takes a step back towards his bike, his expression reads as if he's forcing himself to do so.

"Good night, Vanna." He says again, climbing back onto his motorcycle. "I *will* see you tomorrow." Firing up his bike, he winks at me, kining the stand back up. He walks the bike backwards, positioning himself to take off down the street. With one last look in my direction, he revs the motorcycle and takes off into the night.

Now that Dean is no longer here at this tavern, I suddenly want to leave as well. I want to go home and look over what I had written down in the Knight Summoning spell. Could it possibly be Dean? Am I reading too much into the signs? What the hell was that wave of emotion that washed over me when I thought he was in danger? And how badly I wanted to kiss him. I haven't wanted to kiss anyone in years. He stirs things that have been dormant inside of me for a long time.

I push those thoughts back down as I reach into my purse to pull out my cellphone. It's almost ten thirty. Laura is probably sleeping already. I'll just talk to her about everything that happened tonight, when I see her at work. Instead, I shoot Latisha a text to tell her I'm leaving, before I grab my keys and head for my car parked across the street.

Chapter four

Vanna

I'M IN THE SIDE ROOM OF OUR LITTLE WITCH SHOP, REORGANIZING the book shelves to make room for the new inventory order that arrived today, when I notice Laura and Ethan standing in the doorway, staring at me. Arms folded, each leaning against opposite sides of the frame.

"What?" I ask, holding an arm full of books as I stop what I'm doing.

"Are you really not going to talk about what happened this weekend?" Ethan demands.

"Did you meet the Knight last night or not?" Laura chimes in.

"I'm... not exactly sure." I stammer.

Ethan rolls his eyes, dropping his arms to his side as he walks up to me. He takes the books from me and piles them on the edge of the shelf I'm organizing, then grabs my hand and pulls me across the room. There's a round table we have set up with a few chairs, in front of a picture window, for patrons to read from books Laura keeps in the shop as reference material that aren't for sale.

"Sit." He points to a chair, pulling one out for himself and one for Laura as well. We sit down together, the two of them still staring at me. "Spill it." Ethan insists. "Did you meet him or no?"

"I met two. One was a Knight. One was a Savior." I say. Laura looks ecstatic, with a huge grin, practically bouncing out of her seat. "Wait, don't get too excited." I warn her. "The Knight was a dirt bag. And the savior isn't a Savior."

"What the Hell?" She asks, both of them looking at me with furrowed brows, confusion etched across their faces.

"I don't know if I met him or not. If the spell even worked." I sigh, frustratedly.

"Should I go get my cards?" Laura asks.

I give her a wry look. "No, no more cards."

"Okay, start with the actual Knight. What happened?" Ethan asks.

"I thought he was nice, at first. He chased away some really pushy creepy guy who kept trying to buy me drinks. He had a patch on his leather vest, saying he was part of the Asphalt Knights MC."

"Well, if that isn't a sign, I don't know what is." Laura smiles.

I hold my finger up to her face. "Yeah, that's what I thought. Until he dragged me into the men's room and shoved me into a stall with him."

Both of their eyes widen at the same time. "Oh my God!" Laura exclaims, shock in the rasp of her voice.

"Well, that's not very *Knightly*." Ethan frowns. "You obviously look like you're okay, but what happened?"

"That's when I met the savior who isn't a Savior."

Laura looks contemplative for a moment. "The Savior... that sounds familiar. That's another MC out that way, isn't it? They hold a motorcycle rally in the fall. I think they raise money for charities of some kind. The Saviors."

"Yeah, I think so. The part about being an MC called The Saviors, anyway. I don't know much about them. Any of them." I say. "Anyway, the guy... he said he used to be a Savior. He isn't anymore. I don't know the details."

"But he saved you, from the douchebag Knight?" Ethan presumes.

I nod. "Yeah, he beat the shit out of the Knight, then held my hair for me while I puked my guts out in front of him." Laura's hand flies to her mouth. Ethan bursts out laughing at me. I let them compose themselves before I continue with the events of last night. "Yeah, so, the Savior saved me. Or, the former Savior did."

"I'd still take that as a sign." Laura shrugs.

"You would." Ethan teases her, then looks back at me. "But were there any indications it was this guy, according to the summoning spell you did?"

I take a deep breath and let it out in a huff. "Kind of. But, hear me out and maybe you'll see why I'm not convinced." I fold my arms and lean back in the chair. "He was riding a black motorcycle. All black. Not a glint of chrome at all. He was of course, wearing a black leather jacket too."

"Black horse. Black armored Knight." Laura says, her voice hopeful.

I nod. "Right. But... isn't that like, *ninety percent* of bikers out there? That's not really a *sign*, sign. You know?"

"What about the morning star? Anything that could represent that?" Ethan asks.

I shake my head. "No. Nothing that stood out to me. He had a knife hanging from his belt in a black sheath. But bikers carry knives, don't they? I've noticed, anyway." I shrug, looking down at the purple velvet table cloth. "But a knife would make more sense as a sword connection. Not a morning star."

"The Red Banner?" Laura presses, still hopeful for another sign.

I glance back up at them. "That part was a little odd."

"What was strange about the red banner?" Ethan asks.

"It wasn't a banner. It was a scarf. A red scarf. When he pulled up on the bike, the wind caught it and it billowed out, like a red banner." I explain. "It wasn't scarf weather. I thought it was odd he was wearing it, once I thought about it."

Laura looks excited again. "Because it was a sign!"

"Maybe... Or maybe when you're doing seventy miles an hour on a motorcycle, on a breezy night, that explains having a scarf? I don't know."

"Red banner. Black horse. Black armored Knight." Laura pushes. "Look at it all together. Plus, he saved you from that asshole."

"How much importance did you place upon the morning star?" Ethan asks.

"My intention was that it be a key symbol for me to determine, so pretty major. When I did the spell, I figured black motorcycles and black leather would be common place among bikers. I knew I'd need something else to distinguish." I explain. "And there was no morning star representation that I could see. At all."

"I think it's him." Laura says, stubbornly. "I think you need to give it more time for the morning star to reveal itself." I don't have a problem with giving Dean time. I try to keep my smile to myself, but they notice. "What?" Laura asks.

Ethan looks at me, suspiciously. "How hot was the Savior?"

"*Former* Savior." I correct him, hesitating to answer. But they're both looking at me with excitement in their eyes again. "He is *gorgeous*." I can't help grinning.

Laura laughs excitedly, bouncing in her seat again. "Tell me! Tell me!"

Even Ethan is smiling. "What's his sign?"

"I don't know what his sign is. I didn't ask." I say, then look at Laura. "He's tall, dark hair, dark eyes and ruggedly handsome. He was fully clothed, of course, but even wearing his leather jacket, I could tell he's got a nice body. The way he beat up that huge Knight jerk, a man almost twice his size in bulk... Dean has to be in real good physical shape underneath that leather."

"*Dean!*" she nearly shrieks. "His name is *Dean*?"

I smirk and nod. "Uh huh. Dean Keegan. I think that's Scottish. Or Irish."

"When are you going to see him again?" Laura asks.

"Umm... about that." I hesitate, unsure how she's going to take the idea of me needing to take a weekend job. But I've got to find something to cover the extra expense of moving further away from her shop, and a higher rent than I was paying for a small apartment within city limits. "I'm supposed to meet him after work, tonight."

"Oh my God! Is he taking you to dinner?" she asks.

I shake my head. "No... he didn't ask me out. He didn't ask me for my number either. And he didn't give me his."

She looks perplexed. "What the hell?"

"I'm meeting him at a bar he owns. A roadhouse, actually." I hesitate as they're both staring at me, waiting for me to clarify the situation. "I asked him for a part time, weekend job. To cover the extra expenses of my new place... I'm going there tonight to try to convince him to give me a chance, even though I've never worked in a bar before. It's really close to my new place. It'll be weekends, so I'll still have during the day off, and it won't interfere with me working here."

"It'll give you a good chance to find the morning star and fire connection with him." Ethan says. "If it actually is him. And if not, you'll be in a hot bed of bikers, regularly." He laughs at his own puns. "Maybe you'll find him there?"

"True." I look back at Laura. "You don't mind, right?"

"Of course not." She says. "You have to do what you have to do."

"Great." I sigh with relief, feeling silly for worrying about it to begin with. I have an admittedly terrible habit of worrying about things and over thinking.

"What time are you meeting Dean?" She asks.

"He just said to come after work. He promised me he'd be there." Now I'm worrying about the call I overheard him on last night, wondering about the Knights and what could have happened. I stand up and walk back over to the bookshelf to busy my mind with work, organizing the new inventory into the old stock.

Dean promised. For whatever reason, I trust him. He knows what he's doing better than I do. I have no idea how MC life works, but he didn't seem too concerned for himself. Not even a little bit. Not even drinking Shirley Temples with me knowing the Knight was still out cold on the men's room floor.

How the hell was I not bothered by that? What is wrong with me? Dean says don't worry about it, and just like that, I'm not? What the Hell is that about?

"You can go after your last Reiki appointment, if you want." Laura says, pulling me out of my thoughts. "Just let me know what happens, as soon as you know."

DEAN

A LOT OF THE GUYS IN THE MC ARE FITNESS FANATICS. I DON'T CONSIDER myself to be one. A fanatic, that is. Though I do stay in shape for obvious reasons. My body is a weapon. I like to fight. Hell, I love to fight. Gets me high. Makes me feel alive. But I don't spend *all* my free time pumping iron and slamming my fists into sand bags. Especially not the way Viking does. He's even got a set of dumbbells he keeps behind the bar for less eventful nights.

I suppose the women who hang around the club assume we all prefer that slender body type of gal, because of the overall commonality of our gym sculpted physiques. Truth is, we appreciate the female form in all its glory and varieties. At least I do. Whether they work for it or are just metabolically blessed, I don't know. Don't really care either. Most of the chicks that hang around here are definitely on the petite side of the body type spectrum.

That's what first caught my eye about *her*. The fact that she *isn't*.

In the best fucking way, she isn't.

She's got hour glass curves. Pick your fucking jaw up off the floor, feminine curves.

Big, home-grown boobs. More than a handful. All natural in the way that they bounce and jiggle when she moves. No implants in those bad girls.

A luscious ass I want to drop to my knees and worship. Sink my fucking teeth into while I'm down there. Die happy thick, American thighs, I wouldn't mind suffocating between. She's smoking hot. Voluptuous. Soft looking and sensual. She looks like she's built for sex, all fucking kinds of sex. Love making to hard fucking. And I want to have it *all* with her.

Even her damn near ass length, wavy dark hair, makes me want to run my fingers through it. Wrap my fist in it. Breathe the scent of it deep into my lungs. Her full pouty lips, instantly make me think of her lipstick leaving a ring around the base of my cock. When she smiles, it accentuates her cheeks. Her voice turns me the fuck on as well. Sultry, all woman. When she says my name, I feel it in my dick.

Her eyes, though. Her eyes are mysterious. Alluring and dark. Almond shaped, beneath her perfectly arched brows. Long lashes that flutter when she's excited. Her eyes look innocent one moment, soul penetrating the next. Eyes I could see myself getting lost in, and I wouldn't mind it one bit.

And her name. *Giovanna.*

But don't call me that, she had said. *Call me Vanna...*

Sure, baby. I'll call you anything you want. What I really want to call you, is *mine...*

Viking walks into the Twisted Throttle where I've been sitting for the last thirty minutes on a bar stool. My back and elbows against the polished mahogany wood top of the counter. I'm just staring at the jukebox across the room. Gotta get some Ed Sheeran in that thing. *Make It Rain.* That song was playing when I first saw her. I want to hear it again. I only played it ten times last night when I got home and whacked off about her.

Shit... I never texted Crystal back last night. Between Vanna and having to have a rather frank conversation with the President of the Asphalt Knights MC, I completely forgot about Crystal.

"Why are you sitting out here?" Viking asks. "Shipment isn't for another hour. Snowy and the prospects were gonna handle it."

"Yeah, I'm supposed to meet somebody here. Not exactly sure when. Didn't give me an exact time but I don't want to miss them."

He looks at me curiously. "What about?"

"A job."

"What kind of job? A hit?"

"No. They're looking to work here, part time."

"Another Bouncer?"

I shake my head. "No. We've got that covered."

"A chick then." Viking says, knowingly. I only sigh. "You skirt chasing motherfucker." He shoves my arm. "She must be hot, because we're pretty well covered as far as females go in here, too."

I don't answer. And in not answering, he gets his fucking answer.

"Fuck. She must be real fucking hot." He sits down on a stool, two over from me. "Guess I'm waiting with you. I gotta see the female that's got you so sprung. Waiting here like a puppy she left tied to a post. Ain't seen you this way about a chick in a fucking decade."

I toss him a "Fuck you."

He laughs. "Well, we've established she's hot. Does she have bar experience? Is she a biker bitch?"

I let out an exasperated sigh. "We might need another bouncer." *Me.* More like a personal security detail, though.

From the corner of my eye, I can tell he's looking at me again. "The fuck did you hire, Bro? Who is she?"

"Truthfully, I don't want to hire her. I'm not sure she can handle a rough place like this."

"You mean *you* can't handle a bunch of dudes eye fucking her and trying to pick her up." Viking laughs.

"There's that, too." Gonna be like throwing fresh meat to hungry wolves. *Shit.* I'm definitely back on Bouncer duty if she's gonna be working here weekends. No fucking way is any other guy getting a shot before I do. *No. Fucking. Way.*

"Damn, Bro." Viking shakes his head. "So, she's an outsider. Maybe that's a good thing for you."

"Wish I could give her a job at the farm stand or even at the bike shop. But she works a day shift elsewhere. Can only do nights." I don't want to let her down. That would be worse than having to beat away the hounds sniffing around her every night. Still, I really don't know if this is such a good idea. I'd fucking pay her to date me, but I know she'd take that the way wrong way. Probably slap the shit out of me if I ran that idea by her.

"What is she? A kindergarten teacher or something?" Viking jokes. "*Sexy.*"

"No. She ain't a kindergarten teacher, asshole." I mutter.

"A Librarian, then? Fuck, that's hot."

"No." *Dickhead.*

Viking grins. "No fucking way I'm missing this. I need to see this chick for myself."

"*This chick*, is off limits." The words fall from my mouth. I can already feel it. The territorial urge kicking in. "I don't want to hire her because I want to *fucking date* her, okay? *Off fucking limits.*"

"Then why is she coming if you don't want to hire her?" Viking persists.

I let out another exasperated sigh. Because I'm a fucking sucker for a dame in distress. Because she's so fucking hot my will power to resist her plea equates to zilch. Because it gives me an excuse to be around her... I lean forward and run my hand through my hair, resting my elbows on my knees.

I twist my head to look at him. "Viking, do me a solid. Don't break my fucking balls in front of her, okay?"

He grins at me. Wide. Way too wide for any hope of coming out of this unscathed. "I cannot wait to meet her." He taunts.

"You need to back the hell off, bro. I'm not playing."

"What's her name?"

"*Giovanna.*" I literally sigh her fucking name.

"Fuck you... Are you fucking with me?" He says, leaning back against the bar, genuinely looking at me as if I am indeed, fucking with him. "*Giovanna!*" He exclaims, with unbridled amusement. "The fuck kind of name is *that* doing in a shit little town like this?"

"She doesn't like it. Want's to be called *Vanna.*" I say, ignoring his question.

"Bro. What does she look like? You're gonna have to brace me for this one." He taunts me some more. "*Giovanna.* Fuck. I'm already hard. When did you meet her?"

"Last night."

"You jerked off to that fucking name, didn't you?" He grins at me.

Not just her name. "Shouldn't you be bench pressing something? Or clearing out the fucking refrigerator?" I ask, not bothering an attempt at hiding my agitation.

"Viper's in the gym right now with Dozer and Chopper. And Cherry said if I opened the fridge, she'd kick my ass." He shrugs.

"Cherry is literally like a buck ten. If that." Though, I wouldn't cross her either. Out of respect. If she doesn't want us in the fridge that means she made something good for us for dinner and doesn't want it disappearing. Viking's a fuckin' magician when it comes to food.

I wonder if Vanna can cook? Giovanna. That's Italian. I bet she can. *Fuck.*

"So, what does she look like?" Viking asks again. *Trouble.* That's what she looks like. I keep my mouth shut. "Fine. Don't answer. Gonna see for myself anyway." He folds his massive arms across his broad chest and leans back against the bar.

Snowy walks in, looking less than thrilled.

"What?" I ask.

"Fucking Preacher." He mutters.

"What now?"

"The truck's here. Ready to be unloaded. They went by Preacher's place first. You're gonna have to go over the order and see what they shorted us this time. The driver says since it's all under Saviors MC he didn't see an issue since he dealt with the President directly."

Fucking Preacher. Always out to subtly screw me any chance he gets. Skimming off the top of deliveries while he's at it. I'm ending that shit now.

I look over at Viking. "Let's go get this shit straightened out."

"Who's gonna wait for your girlfriend?" He asks. I stand up and glare at him. He rolls his eyes, getting up too. "Fine. Let's go."

Vanna

"HELLO?" I CALL INTO THE SEEMINGLY VACANT TWISTED THROTTLE Roadhouse. I showed up after my day job as promised. The front door wasn't locked but there's nobody inside. No cars or bikes in the front lot. The inside is empty. There are tables and chairs, a few pool tables. A large jukebox and two stripper poles in the back. Along the red brick walls, there are black leather couches that match the black bar stools. The actual bar counter is a long, polished dark cherry wood, or mahogany. The back shelves packed with liquor match the bar, with a large back mirror. The brick walls are covered in motorcycle memorabilia and random parts to old bikes, framed photos and other posters of leather clad biker babes. Some practically naked. There's also a large American Flag tacked up on the back wall behind the jukebox and stripper poles.

"Hello? Is anybody here?" I call out again, towards a corridor past the bar on the other side of the room.

"We're closed till seven tonight!" A man's voice calls back from somewhere in the back.

"I'm not looking for a drink, I'm looking for Dean." I call back, walking timidly towards the other end of the bar in the direction of the man's voice. The sound of heavy boots coming down the hall thump closer and closer. I stop and wait.

A big, burly man dressed in jeans and a leather vest, rounds the corner into the bar room where I'm waiting. He's carrying a case of liquor, which he plops down on the bar and looks at me. I can see his grin behind his thick white beard as he looks me over. He kind of reminds me of a biker version of Santa Claus.

"*You* want to work *here*?" his tone is full of amusement. Before I can reply, he cocks his head over his shoulder and shouts for Dean to get up here.

I adjust the strap of my purse on my shoulder and wait.

Another pair of heavy boots stomp down the corridor. This time, it's Dean who rounds the corner. His eyes fixed on what looks to be a few pages of stapled inventory sheets.

"What Snowy?" Dean grumbles.

He's wearing the same leather jacket I met him in last night. And he's just as handsome as I remember. Shadowed, angular jaw line, high cheek bones. Tall, dangerous looking. All alpha male, tough guy vibes, but with an aura of depth about him that pulls at me.

I clear my throat, and he glances up at me with those deep, dark eyes. He arches a brow at me appraisingly and grins, creating those brackety dimples through his facial hair that I find so attractive for some reason.

"You showed up... *Aces*." His voice, deep and growly. God, I love that vocal fry of his. I could listen to him talk about motorcycle parts all night and not get bored. That growl in his voice is downright sexy.

"Of course, I did. I told you I would."

"Looks like we both kept our promises." He flips the pages back to the front of the stapled inventory sheets and shoves them to Snowy's chest. "Have a prospect finish unloading. Then double check the rest of the inventory." He says, authoritatively.

I bite my bottom lip and glance away from his fixed gaze, as he takes a few steps towards me. I peek up at him through my lashes and he grins at me again. "*Vanna*," he breathes my name in that damn way he does... "How can I be of service to you?"

I force myself to focus on the reason I'm here. "There aren't many places willing to hire off the books these days. I was hoping you could hire me a few hours on weekends, for whatever, really. I've got my other job at the witch shop, as you know. But it's not quite full-time hours. I'm hoping to make a little extra income."

"This can be a rough place, sometimes." He exhales, but it's not quite a sigh. "I'm a little concerned you may-"

"*Please*." I cut him off. "I could really use the money." I push. Something in his eyes softens at my plea. "Just give me a shot, Dean." I press him a little more.

"You own any jeans?" he asks, after a moment.

"Yes."

"Boots or sneakers?"

"Both." I answer, feeling a little more hopeful.

He nods. "What kind of schedule are you looking for?"

"Weekends. I work Monday through Friday until five thirty. I can be here by seven, whatever days you want me." The conflict he feels over this arrangement is still evident in his expression. "One chance," I urge, folding my fingers together and bringing my hands up under my chin. "If you don't like me, no hard feelings. I still appreciate the shot."

"Damn it." He almost whispers under his breath, reaching into his jacket pocket. He pulls out his cellphone and brings up someone's number.

We both wait.

"Axel, is Cherry there?" Dean asks. "Put her on a minute." A few moments pass as we wait some more. Dean's looking at me differently now. No longer appraisingly, more like slight concern. "Cherry, yeah it's Dean. Listen. I got a gir- *Lady* here. I'm gonna need you to show her the ropes, Friday night... Uh huh. No, she ain't a sweetbutt. Not even close."

What the hell is a sweet butt? I can't help but wonder.

"All right. Thanks, doll." He hangs up the phone, then his eyes are back on me as he tucks it back into his pocket. "Well, Vanna. Let's see how this plays out. You'll meet Cherry. Friday and Saturday nights. Ten until closing at two am. You'll probably be out by two thirty."

I can't contain my excitement as I throw my arms around him, hugging him briefly. He doesn't make any moves to discourage it, but I release him quickly and step back from him anyway. "Thank you! I really do appreciate it so much."

"Happy to help." He smiles at me, though he seems suddenly more tense than he had been a moment ago.

Snowy storms back with another huge biker trailing behind him, looking none too pleased as he comes to stand before Dean. "They shorted the order." He grunts.

This part is none of my business. I decide to get out of his hair and go home to tell Laura I got the job. "I'll let you get back to it, then." I say, smiling at him again. "Thank you, Dean. I really appreciate you, so much."

He grins at me, raising his arm to grip the back of his neck, almost as if he's anxious. "See you Friday night, Vanna."

"Promise." I smirk back at him. Glancing at the biker he calls Snowy, and the other freaking huge biker, I smile briefly at them both, then turn to walk towards the door to leave. Looking back over my shoulder, I smile at Dean once more, before I close the door behind me.

DEAN

"I CALL..." I BEGIN TO SAY, WAITING FOR THE STEEL DOOR OF THE BAR TO shut all the way behind Vanna. "Dibs!" I announce. "I'm staking my claim on her. She's mine." I sound crazy, even to myself, but I don't care. I can still feel her body pressed against mine when she hugged me. Took every ounce of whatever gentlemanly inclinations I have within me, not to wrap my arms around her and *really* get a feel of her.

Viking is still staring at the front door. "*That.*" He points in the direction she left. "*That* right there... Is the type of chick a guy wouldn't mind burying his cock in, for the rest of his life. I think I could die happy never fucking anything else ever again." Viking says, staring at the closed door.

There's a lot of shit Viking says that pisses me off from time to time. Over the years I've known him, he's been a world champion ball buster. However, this shit is really grinding my gears.

"*Claimed her.* Bro." I remind him.

"That ain't a *chick*, Dean." He's still staring at the fucking door. "That's a fucking *Goddess*! Did you see the tits on her? The fucking hips on her? I wouldn't even be upset if I knocked that up. Hell, *I'd do it on purpose.*"

I can feel the muscles in my jaw rippling. Did he really just fucking go there? "Fuck off, Viking. I mean it." I growl. "She's *mine*."

"Maybe she's into threesomes." Snowy shrugs.

I glare at him. He backs up. "She look like a lay girl or a sweetbutt to you?"

"I'm just gonna go double check that inventory." He says, clearing his throat and walking away.

"Yeah, you do that." I mutter after him, before I turn back to Viking. "Are we going to have a problem, Bro?"

He finally shifts his focus from the door, to me. "I anticipate many problems, Bro. You're definitely gonna need another bouncer."

"Yeah. *Me.* I'll watch her." I growl.

"Me too."

I don't like the way he said that at all, either. "I was referring to a problem between us. Can't have you making crude comments about my woman. Shit ends here and now." I warn him.

His eyes narrow and the corner of his mouth turns up. "You fucking serious?"

"Yep. Something about her. A lot of somethings. Gotta have her. I staked my claim. She's mine." I repeat my lunacy once again.

"What if you give me one shot? Just one. I won't even put it in. I'll just oil up those thick thighs and squeeze em around my-"

My fist connects with Viking's mouth, shutting him the fuck up for five seconds. I didn't hit him that hard. Enough to knock his head to the side. Enough to convey I'm not fucking around.

He looks back at me. "Dick." He mutters, touching his jaw.

"You earned it... And if you try to fuck her, I'll castrate you."

"What happened to *Bro's before Ho's*?" he mocks me.

"She look like a ho to you?" I ask. "Be careful how you answer that." He notices my fist still clenched at my side.

Viking cracks a smile. "No. She looks like a sweet girl. And you deserve something good after all the shit you've been through. I'm not gonna fuck with your woman, Dean. She's club property now. Specifically, yours. I'll keep an eye out on your behalf."

He slaps me on the back, hard. Knocking whatever air I had left in my lungs, out of me with a rasp. I can't help grinning. I know it's revenge for the sucker punch in the mouth. His way of reminding me he's a fucking powerhouse.

"You're so fucked, Dean." Viking laughs.

He isn't telling me anything I don't already know.

Chapter
five
DEAN

THE TWISTED THROTTLE IS ALWAYS PACKED on a Friday night. Tonight, is no exception. Bikers and truckers and other blue-collar locals are here to blow off steam at the end of a work week. The crack of pool balls, classic rock and conversation, fills the room, as I slide onto a stool near Cherry. She's been slinging drinks for the last hour.

"No hard liquor for you, Dean." She says. "I can tell you're anxious about something, though, so I'll let you have a beer."

"You'll *let* me?"

She swipes a wisp of her bright red hair from her eye and throws the look I'm giving her, right back at me. *Sassy*. Gotta admit, the fact a girl like Cherry isn't afraid to cop an attitude with a guy like me, gives me a warm feeling. She's come a long way since I first met her, and I'm glad I didn't shoot her trust to shit these last few years. Having to not only witness, but also put up with, my self-destructive behavior.

"Miller. A bottle. Though I'm shocked you're not insisting on *green tea*." I tease. She's eased up on me in regards to consuming healthy foods and drinks, since I've been working out and staying in shape for my underground fighting and other extra-curricular activities I've gotten back into the last year or so.

Grabbing a bottle from the large fridge beneath the bar, she cracks it open and hands it to me, then clanks her club soda to it with a smile. "Cheers." She teases me back. "So why are you so wound up tonight? Is it the new girl coming in?"

"Just hoping it all works out for her." Though it's so much more than that. Still, I'm not lying to Cherry. I do hope this all works out for Vanna. All of it. Everything I have in mind for Vanna. I've been obsessing over her all week. Both looking forward to seeing her, and dreading how her presence here is going to play out.

Vixie, one of my other barmaids, and kind of a lay girl, approaches Cherry with a drink order for a table. She smiles at me, the diamond stud piercing above her lip catches the lights above the bar. I lift my chin at her in greeting, but before she can try flirting with me again, I twist around on the stool to overlook the rest of the bar, sipping on the beer.

Viking is by the front door, watching the room as well. We rarely have problems with unruly patrons, but the potential of a brawl breaking out in a biker bar is always ever present. Especially on Fridays and Saturdays. As much as I love to throw punches, kicking the shit out of my patrons isn't ideal for business. Fortunately, Viking's presence as a bouncer is generally enough of a deterrent for guys to take their issues outside. I don't really care what they do in the parking lot. This ain't a cop calling type of crowd, but on occasion, shit happens.

It's only eight o' clock. I told Vanna ten pm. Yet every time I hear the door swing open, my eyes shoot in that direction. Hoping it's her, yet at the same time, relieved it isn't. As I take another swig of my beer, I sincerely hope I'm not fucking up. Not fucking up by allowing her to work in a potentially rough environment. Not fucking up my plans for her and I. I should have just asked her out the night we met at the tavern. The fuck is wrong with me? I didn't even ask for her number. No wonder she didn't think I was interested. I need to rectify this, asap.

The front door swings open again and an older man enters. He doesn't look like a biker to me. He looks like he just stepped off a tractor after a long day of tilling fields. Viking bends to hear him better. Something about the old timer's expression though, he's here looking for someone. Viking points to me and the old guy cranes his neck to see around him, looking in my direction. I take another swig of beer and watch him as he slowly approaches me. He looks nervous, fidgeting with a small yellow strip of paper in his withered hands.

"Mister Keegan?" he asks, but I know he knows who he's talking to. I can see it in his face.

"That's me."

"I was hoping I could have a conversation with you." He says. "I knew your uncle from grade school." He adds, as if he needed to in order to convince me to hear him out. His shaky hands are still toying with the paper.

"What can I do for you?" I ask, trying to sound a little friendlier to put him at ease. Something's got this old guy worked up. The look in his eyes is full of distress as he stares at me for a moment, before shifting his gaze to the floor. He takes a deep breath before he lifts his head again.

"I knew your family, so it pains me to have to come to you with this."

I take another sip of my beer as I look back at him. "My family's been dead years now. What are you hoping I can do for you?"

"My granddaughter, she's been in the hospital. She's supposed to be getting out in the next day or so, going back to her home." He fidgets with the paper some more.

"Alright." I say, wishing he would just cut to the chase and ask me whatever he's going to ask me. "She need a fundraiser or something for medical bills? Preacher is the president of the MC now. He can help you with that."

The old man shakes his head. "Don't need to talk to Preacher... Her fiancé is the one who put her in the hospital."

Oh. I get it now. And yeah. Preacher is a waste of time.

"She doesn't want to go back to him. She's got cousins that will take her in, a few states away, but he ain't gonna let her go." The old guy says, pain in his eyes now. "This ain't the first time he's done this to her either."

I inhale through my nostrils and let it out slowly. "That his information?" I nod to the paper he's been fidgeting with since he got here. He hands it to me. It's the guys name and an address. "What's her name?"

"Janie." He says. "Janie Lynn Dawson."

"They got kids?"

"Thankfully, no."

"Are you asking me to get her out of there?"

He shakes his head. "No. We can get her out. If he... isn't there to stop it." The old man says, looking at me intently as if he hopes I was able to read between the lines. I hear him, loud and clear.

"She gets out of the hospital tomorrow and is going back to him. You're sure she wants out?" I ask. Sadly, that's not always the case. Often times, it isn't. I try not to think of *Madeline*...

"She don't want to go back to him. But he's gonna come get her."

"Cutting it a little close, no?" Of all the nights he could have sprung this on me.

"Out of respect to your uncle, I came to you last. I know how he felt about your past. Cops even admit a restraining order is just a piece of paper. I tried asking others. They didn't want to get involved. I'd do it myself, but..." His words drift off as he looks at his own shaking hands.

Fuck. That gets me right in the ticker.

He'd take the son of a bitch out himself if he were physically able to. I let out another long sigh as I lean forward to pat his shoulder. "Is he here, tonight?" I ask, holding up the paper. The old man nods. "I'll take care of it." I say, tucking the address into my jacket pocket.

He looks up at me. "I can pay..."

"I don't want your money. Are there any security cameras I need to know about? Dogs? Weapons? Roommates? Anything?"

"It's a trailer on a wooded lot. No security. No dogs. He's alone, but might have a weapon."

I nod. "Just so we're clear, I'm not going to take him out. I'm going to put him out of commission for a while. I'm gonna buy you and your family a little time free of him. So, move quickly."

He reaches into his pocket and pulls out two photos. "This is him. And Janie." He says, handing me one of the photos.

I study it. Janie is a cute, trim, blonde woman with a pixie style haircut. Young. Maybe only a few years older than Cherry and Axel. The prick is a dark-haired juice head looking bastard. Could be somewhat of a gym rat, but I'm not worried. I've taken on all kinds of gym rats before. This guy doesn't deserve a fair fight, anyway. So, I'm not the least bit concerned about dealing with him. I hand him back the photo and notice he's hesitant to show me the other one, but he does. He hands it to me slowly, face down. I have a feeling this photo is for *motivational purposes*. I brace myself for what I'm about to see.

As I turn the photo over and glance down at it, that's exactly what it is.

It's a photo of Janie. Almost unrecognizable. Purple bruises all over her face. A busted lip. Eyes swollen shut. If not for her distinguishable blonde hair style, you'd never know it was the same girl from the other photo.

I swallow hard. The rage inside me at a low boil now. Nothing gets me like this shit does. Women or kids harmed by the men in their lives that are supposed to care for and protect them. It enrages me. I shift my eyes back to Janie's grandfather. "You didn't have to do this to me, old man." I say, handing him back the photo.

He nods slowly, understanding exactly what he's done. "Son, I had to do it to *him... For her.*"

On my way out the door, I grab Viking and pull him aside.

"I'm hoping to be back here not long after Vanna shows up. But I might not be." I say, cursing the old man for not bringing this shit to me *last night*. "I need you to keep an eye on her, for me."

"Where are you rushing off to? What did that old man want?" Viking asks. "Gotta be important, you've been waiting for Vanna all damn week. Not to mention, staring at the damn door all night."

I let out an exasperated sigh. "Believe me, I don't want to go. But this has to happen tonight."

"What does?"

"A special delivery. Some prick missed the life memo about not bashing women's faces in." I growl. "It's time sensitive."

Viking shakes his head. "Alright, I got Vanna for you. I won't let her out of my sight." He grins.

I glare at him. "I'm serious, Viking. I fucking like her."

"I know, Bro. I'm not going to fuck you over. I'll barely say anything to her. Promise."

I don't have time to waste threatening him, I have to get a move on if I'm going to be back before she's here very long without me. Giving him a quick nod, I grab the keys out of my pocket and jog across the lot to Serene.

WHEN I GOT HOME FROM WORK EARLIER THIS EVENING, I DUG OUT A pair of blue jeans from one of my boxes, as well as a pair of black sneakers. I have boots, but I don't want anything slowing me down tonight, like sore feet. I imagine working in a bar, you're on your feet a lot. I decide to go with efficiency over fashion. Dean pretty much implied I could wear either, anyway.

As I pull on the jeans, I'm relieved they still fit me like a glove. I haven't worn them in a while, having typically been wearing long skirts and dresses to work at Laura's witch shop.

Yanking open my bedroom closet door, once again, I search for a suitable top to wear. I'm not exactly sure what *Twisted Throttle Roadhouse* attire looks like, but I assume since jeans and sneakers are okay, a simple top should do as well. I grab a black, open shoulder top with a scoop neckline, just to look slightly more presentable. It shows a little cleavage, but nothing too dramatic. I don't want to come across as trying too hard for tips, but I don't want to look like a Nun, either.

In front of my bathroom mirror, I give my long dark hair a brush through, then bobby-pin a portion of the top back so it won't fall in my face, or anyone's drinks, while I'm working.

I go light on the makeup as well, a barely there look. Some mascara, a tinted lip gloss. I toss both into my purse just in case I have to reapply later.

Glancing at the clock on my night table, I see that it's time to go.

"Wish me luck, Nico!" I say jokingly to my sleeping cat on the foot of my bed. Grabbing my keys off my dresser, I bound down the stairs.

Five to ten on a Friday night and the parking lot of the Twisted Throttle is already full of bikes and a few trucks. I walk hurriedly across the gravel lot to the front door.

As I pull the door open, I'm hit with the smell of booze and loud rock and roll music. The crowd is loud and lively as well, but the vibe is over all positive. Unsure of where Dean is, I step inside and start my way to the bar to ask for him.

A big, blonde biker stands up and steps into my path. I lift my chin to look up at him, *all the way up* at him, and can't help the little smile that crosses my face. He looks like a modern-day Viking. Huge muscles, blonde hair, shaved on the sides, but the top is long and braided, pulled back in a mohawk style ponytail. Tattoos cover both of his massive arms and I can't help noticing the Nordic theme of them. A large Odin on his shoulder, with runic symbols interwoven among wolves and ravens in the art work from shoulders to wrists.

Awesome, maybe I'm not the only pagan in this town after all.

"Hi." I smile at him, having to raise my voice to speak louder than I normally do on account of the noise around us. "I'm looking for Dean."

The biker just stares at me for a few moments.

"I'm supposed to help out tonight." I add, beginning to feel a little awkward. "Nice Runes. You look like a Viking." I smile at him again. Nothing.

Does this man not speak? What the Hell?

He finally points to the bar and lets me pass.

"Thanks." I say, not wanting to be rude to anyone, especially not before I even start working. I make my way towards the bar.

There are a couple of girls walking to and from the bar with trays, stopping at tables. They're all dressed similarly in some variation of leather and denim. Biker babes.

A woman with a bright red bobbed haircut comes up to me, smiling. She's wearing ripped up jeans and a black wife beater with The Saviors MC logo on it.

"Are you Vanna?" she asks.

"Yes, you must be Cherry." I say. "Cool hair."

She smiles and tells me to follow her, leading me past the bar and down a corridor into a small room with mini lockers. "You can lock up your stuff in here." She says. "I recommend bringing a spare top or two, just to have here in case you ever need to change. Do you want me to see if I can find you an MC shirt?"

"Is it required?"

"Not exactly." She says, but she's looking at me kind of funny. "Don't be shocked if Dean eventually asks you to wear an MC property shirt."

"MC property?"

"Have you ever worked in a Biker bar before?"

"No." I admit. I can tell she's trying to stifle a grin. "Am I wearing the wrong top?" I ask, looking down at myself.

"No, it's fine. It looks really good on you, actually." Cherry says. "Consider an MC shirt, though. That way it's not a big deal if someone spills a drink on you... or something."

Or something? Why do I get the feeling there's more to it than that?

"I left my purse in my car. My cellphone is in my back pocket, unless I can't have it on me?" I ask.

"That's fine. Dean doesn't care about that, as long as you pay attention to the patrons first." Cherry says. "Come on, I'll show you around."

Once she shows me where everything is behind the bar, the price charts, how to use the taps, etc., I notice the Viking guy is still staring at me.

"Who is that big guy I ran into when I came in? The Viking looking one." I ask.

Cherry laughs. "*Viking*. He's our bouncer and a member of The Saviors." That makes sense on both accounts. "He's nice, don't be afraid of him. The patch whores and sweetbutts love him, he's really just a big teddy bear."

"What's a patch whore? And a sweet butt?" I can't help asking, after hearing Dean say those words on the phone earlier this week. Cherry nods towards the side of the room lined with black leather couches, where men are sitting with beers and scantily clad women in their laps.

"You see those girls over there, grinding their asses on those bikers? Those are patch whores." She says. "Some guys call them sweetbutts, lay girls, *Lady Lays*."

"So, women who have a thing for bikers?"

"Not exactly," Cherry shakes her head, "Patch whores are cum dumpsters." She says, and I am sure my expression gives away my surprise. She obviously doesn't like these girls, but she laughs at my reaction. "They'll fuck anything with a patch and a bike. Including married MC guys. Their end goal is to become somebody's Old Lady. But most of them just get passed around. None of the guys take them seriously." I don't even know what to say to that, it makes me feel a little uneasy, but I keep my mouth shut. "Don't let any of these guys in here call you a patch whore, or a sweetbutt. Most of the guys who hang around here are pretty decent. But some of them are going to try you. If you carry yourself with respect, they won't treat you like a dick motel."

I can't help but wonder if I've made a mistake begging Dean for a job here. Maybe he was right to try to talk me out of it...

"Flirting will get you bigger tips, naturally. So will boots and a low-cut top." Cherry adds, with a nonchalant shrug of her thin shoulders. "And one last thing before you hit the floor. The guys with Saviors patches don't pay for drinks on Friday and Saturday nights. It's included in their dues. Everyone else pays." Cherry hands me a tray and smiles. "Good luck."

DEAN

I T DOESN'T TAKE ME MORE THAN A FORTY-MINUTE RIDE TO GET TO JANIE'S home. I shut Serene down at the end of the driveway and walk her up to the house, turning her around so I can hop on her later and take off quickly. The wooded lot is nicely secluded from his neighbors, so they won't see my bike. Plus, it saves me a jog down the driveway if I were to leave her in the street. Less potential witnesses this way too.

I slip on my gloves and a set of brass knuckles as I walk up to his front door. I could break in, if I want to, but this sack of shit isn't worth the extra effort. Or the time. I just want to toss him a beating and get back to Vanna. Knocking on his front door, I pull down the red bandana over my nose and mouth so he can hear me clearly.

"Yeah, who's there?" Tough guy calls from inside.

"The guy who's been fucking Janie." It bugs me slightly to say those words about her, but it'll get me in the door faster and I don't have time to waste. I hear the dead bolt unlock. Yep, that did it. Pulling the red bandana back over my nose and mouth, I open the screen door.

As soon as the idiot swings the door open, I slam my fist between his eyes, knocking him backwards, straight to the floor behind him. I let myself in, closing the door behind me.

"Fuckwit." Stepping over him as he groans on the floor, trying to come to, I grab the bat he's got by the front door and stand over him. I watch him try to focus his dazed eyes and move his limbs on the linoleum floor. "Pussy. I didn't even hit you that hard yet." I mutter, giving him a decent kick in the ribs and he jerks and flops over like a fish out of water, curling on his side and grunting in pain. "That wake you up?"

"What the fuck, man!" he groans. "What do you want? Money? All I got is fifty bucks in my wallet. Take it."

"I'm not here to rob you, prick." If I had a dollar for every time I've had to say that to a guy... I chuckle to myself.

He turns his head to look up at me. "The fuck you want then, asshole?"

"I want you..." I point at him with the bat, inches from his face, "To stay the fuck away from Janie."

The mention of her name throws him back into a rage. "You fucking Janie? That filthy whore!" He shouts at me, attempting to get up, but I plant a boot in the center of his chest, kicking him hard and sending him onto his back again. Bringing the bat up over my head, I slam it down on one of his shins. The bone cracks. I feel the vibration up the wooden baseball bat, and he wails in pain.

Damn, that felt good. Reminds me of the old days...

"Nope." I say, standing over him as he clings to his leg, crying like a little bitch. I mean, yeah, it probably hurts. *A lot*. I can see the bone sticking out of his skin. "I guess you're one of those guys that can dish it out but can't take it, huh?" I taunt him. "I saw your handy work on Janie."

"I'll fucking kill you!" he shouts again.

"Oh, I doubt that." I take a swing at his other leg. He lets out another wail, cursing me. After a few moments, he's trying to drag himself backwards, away from me. "I don't know what you're bitching about, bro." I say, taking slow steps toward him as he drags himself. "I'm trying to give you clean breaks. Faster heal time. But if you want to get nasty with me, I can get nasty with you. I'm the one holding the fuckin' bat, asshole."

He lifts his hand out to me, "Stop, please... please, stop." He begs, almost panting.

Casually resting the bat against my shoulder, I look at him sideways. "I bet Janie said similar to you, didn't she? But you didn't stop, did you?" I can see it in his eyes now. He knows how fucked he is. "I'm not going to stop either, Ralph. I haven't even gotten to your face yet."

He looks like he's going to cry. The tough guy has officially left the building. "I won't touch her again, I swear!"

"Bet you told her that, too. You sorry sack of shit."

He whimpers and reaches for a kitchen chair to try to pull himself up, unwittingly giving me a perfect angle. Holding the Louisville Slugger with both hands now, I swing down on his fucking arm. More wailing, more crying.

"Now that one *had* to be a clean break." I mock him, letting him scream it out for a few more moments, before I slam my boot down on his stomach, taking the wind out of him.

"Shut the fuck up, you're starting to annoy me with all that noise." I toss the bat somewhere behind me. Sounds like it lands on a piece of furniture and rolls onto the floor with a light thud on the carpet. Then I hold up my hand with the brass knuckles, so he can get a good look at the next course on tonight's menu.

"I'm sorry... I'm sorry..." he wheezes, trying to get air into his lungs.

I kneel over him, grabbing him by the collar of his shirt and yanking him up for a better angle. "I do *not* accept your apology." I let him know. His good hand grabs at me, but he can't do shit. I cock my fist back and smile at him, unseen behind the red bandana. "Face time, asshole." I clobber him in the eye socket, haul back and hit him in the other one. Cock back twice more and hit him in the mouth and the side of his jaw. I remember Janie's picture accurately. Busted mouth Swollen eyes. Bruised jaw. I shove him backwards and let his head smack on the linoleum floor. He groans and twists his head to spit out a bloody tooth... or several. Standing up, I survey my work. He should probably be in the hospital at least a few days. "What did we learn tonight, prick?" I ask him. "Are we gonna hit women anymore?"

"N-no..." he groans, blood sputtering out of his mouth as he coughs.

"Are you going to stay the fuck away from Janie?" I ask. He hesitates, so I remove the huge knife I carry with me and hold it up for him to see. "I asked you a question, Ralph. If you go near Janie, I'm going to have to come back and use this on you. And it won't be quick. And you won't be getting up afterwards." He groans some more. "Are you going to stay the fuck away from Janie?"

"Yes." He finally says.

"Great. Where's your cellphone, I gotta make a call." I say, glancing around the room. I spot a cell on the coffee table behind me. "Don't move." I can't help joking, as I turn to grab it and power on the screen. It's locked. "What's your passcode?" He just groans again. "I don't have all fucking night, Ralph!" Vanna's gotta be with Cherry by now. "Passcode!"

"Four... three... two... one."

I shake my head as I type it in and unlock the screen. "You really are a fuckwit." I say, jamming the phone in my pocket.

"Are you going to k-kill me?" he mumbles.

"No, not tonight. Though If you say anything to anyone about me, someone *will* kill you, Ralph." I say, matter-of-factly. "And if you go near Janie again, someone *will* kill you, Ralph."

I glance around the room, making sure I didn't drop anything. I didn't get much blood on me either, just the brass knuckles and my disposable gloves. "Are we clear?" I ask him. He groans. "I'll take that as a yes... I'm gonna do you a solid and call an ambulance for you. Let them know you somehow managed to fall down a flight of stairs in a one-story trailer." I joke, making my way back to his front door. "Or you can make up something, so long as it ain't the truth. You know, the way poor Janie has had to do to cover for your abuse in the past when people have asked her about her injuries." I turn around to kick him once more solidly in the ribs. "Piece of shit."

I leave him bleeding and broken on his kitchen floor and walk to Serene. Mounting her, I fire her up and off down the driveway, out onto the street. When I'm a few miles away I pull over and use his cell phone to call 911, then smash it before chucking the shattered cell into a dumpster, along with the bloody gloves. I'll get a prospect to detail Serene tomorrow, just in case.

I ride directly back to the Twisted Throttle, where I've been all night. Cherry, Axel and Viking can confirm that alibi for me, should anyone come asking, but they won't. They never do.

I'VE BEEN SO BUSY WITH DRINK ORDERS AND SERVING FOR THE PAST HOUR, I don't notice Dean until I collide with him. Smacking my face right into his hard, leather clad chest, nearly dropping my tray. Thank God I didn't have anything on it.

"I'm sorry, I didn't see you." I apologize, taking a step back from him. But damn, he smells good. Rich and woody. "You smell like a Western." I find myself absentmindedly smiling at him. Like Leather, Sandalwood and smokey cedarwood. Musky and damn near intoxicating.

He grins at me. "How's it going so far?"

"Busy. But okay. You're my first *collision*." I joke. He smiles, but there is something off about him. He's not the same as he was when I first met him last weekend. "Are you okay?" I ask. The way he's looking at me, there's something in his eyes, but I can't decipher it. "Sorry, none of my business. Can I get you anything?"

Before he can even respond, he's bombarded by three women fawning over him. I decide to just get back to work and leave him to his groupies. Of course, a man like Dean has groupies.

I walk quickly past them to get back to my rounds and distract myself with work. Spotting a table with quite a few empty bottles, I walk over to get them out of the way.

"Can I get anyone anything else?" I ask, collecting the bottles and placing them on the tray. I glance around at the five men sitting at the table, checking for patches. They aren't Saviors.

"Another round, sugar." One of them says, dropping two twenties on my tray.

"Sure thing." I smile politely.

I carry the tray full of empties to the far side of the bar to discard them in the glass bin and ask the girl behind the bar with the diamond stud in her lip, for five more Millers. She takes the cash and brings back change as well. I glance around the bar quickly and spot Dean watching me. He's leaning against the wall by Viking. His groupies must have dispersed. The girls that interrupted us before are nowhere near him now. I flash him a quick smile and grab my tray of new bottles to bring back to the table of five.

"You're fast." One of them says, as I place the tray down and begin to crack tops off with my bottle opener and pass them out.

"I'm trying. Never worked in a place like this before." I pick up the cash from the tray and hand the guy who paid, his change.

Instead of taking the money, he grabs my wrist and pulls me forward, off balance, forcing me to twist and land ass first in his lap. I immediately try to get up but he holds me in place.

"Easy sugar, I'm not going to bite you." He says in my ear, his bushy beard touching my face. His nasty beer breath hot on my skin, making it crawl. "I might lick you though, see if you're as sweet as you look."

"Let me go!" I demand, struggling against him as his buddies laugh. He grips my thigh harder and I slap him across the face.

Blonde lightning strikes as Viking is suddenly at my side, grabbing the jerk by the back of his leather vest and hauling him up out of his seat. I'm able to jump away and take a step back. Viking's strength is impressive, as he hurls the guy to the dirty floor. I take another step back as the other four guys stand up abruptly from the table as well, muttering what the fucks and professing they were just fooling around.

I bump into someone behind me and turn to see Dean. His glowering expression is unnerving and I hope he's not going to yell at me.

"She was looking at me like she wanted it!" The jerk on the floor says, instantly flipping my switch from nervous to pissed off.

"You wish, asshole! You grabbed me and probably left a bruise on my leg!" I shout at him.

"You broke a rule. I saw it." Viking finally speaks.

"No, I didn't!" The jerk protests.

"You touched Saviors' property." Viking cocks his head towards me. I stand here feeling as confused as the jerk on the ground appears to be.

I glance back at Dean, who is standing rather close to me. He's glaring at the jerk on the ground as he steps around to my side.

"Oh shit, Dean, I didn't realize! She isn't wearing your patch or nothing!" He scrambles back to his feet. "I've never seen her here before, man. Come on."

Dean shifts his steely gaze to me. "I heard you mention a bruise. Did he hurt you?" There's something dangerous in Dean's tone. Something that makes me think this idiot might actually be in serious trouble. Maybe even danger.

"I'm not hurt." I answer quickly. "He just wouldn't let me go. I didn't ask for it. And I didn't like it. But I'm not hurt." Dean's dark eyes slowly look me over before he shifts his attention back to the jerk.

"Dean it was an honest mistake, c'mon." The biker says. I wonder why he seems more afraid of Dean than Viking. Viking is a mountain of a man compared to most of the men here. Hell, most men period.

"You know I can't let this stand." Dean's voice is low and serious. "There are rules for a reason. And there are consequences for breaking those rules."

The biker looks more nervous by the minute, eyes shifting between Dean and Viking. "Dean, she ain't got nothing on her saying she's yours. Come on man, I'd never pull that shit on you knowingly." He insists. "It'll never happen again."

I touch Dean's arm lightly to get his attention. He turns his head and looks at my hand on his arm, then into my eyes. There's something there, burning behind them, but I'm not sure what. "I'm okay." I say softly. "I'm not hurt or scared."

He stares at me, seeming to consider my words. After a few moments he says, "Apologize. And mean it."

The jerk sighs with relief, then begins to say, "I'm sorry, Dean, it won't hap-"

Dean's head snaps back to the biker. "Not to me! *To her. Vanna.*"

The biker looks surprised, but immediately complies. "Vanna, I apologize for putting my hands on you. It will never happen again."

I just nod, silently hoping that's the end of it.

"Tip her and get the fuck out." Dean mutters.

The guy shoves the fifteen dollars in change I gave him back at me.

"Oh, you better be joking!" Dean says, aggression returned to his voice.

The biker fumbles for his wallet and pulls out a fifty, handing it to me. Dean glances at my hand, then back at the dumbfounded biker.

"Tip her more. Tip her *good*." He growls.

The biker hands me five more twenties.

I nervously whisper, "Okay." Unsure if I have any influence here at all, but I want this to be over. Feeling like I'm part of a shake down isn't sitting well with me.

Dean steps in close to the biker's face and threatens him, "If you ever lay a hand on her again..."

"I won't. I swear." He says, before Dean can finish his sentence.

"Get out." Dean says in a low, but sinister tone.

I've never seen a so-called tough guy, haul ass out of a place so fast...

Dean turns to the guy's abandoned companions. "Are we going to have any more problems?" He asks.

Viking cracks his knuckles, then his neck, as he sizes up the other four.

"No, but we'll go too." One of them says.

"Suit yourselves." Dean smiles. He turns to me. "Vanna, a moment of your time in private, please."

I glance around for the first time and realize a majority of the room has been watching. "Okay." I say quietly. I stuff the cash into my pocket and follow Dean past the bar, through the corridor and down the hall towards the back exit. Dean holds the door open for me and I walk through into a gated parking lot. I notice there's a motorcycle shop across the way. '*Mean Dean's Repair Shop*', the old withered sign above it reads. *Mean* indeed.

I turn around to face him. "Are you firing me?"

The corner of his mouth curves up slightly. "No, Vanna." He says, and I sigh. "Sit down." He gestures to the two sets of outdoor tables and chairs.

I sit in the chair nearest me and look up at him. "Am I in trouble?"

He chuckles. "You *are* trouble."

I don't know how to respond to that, as I watch him slowly circle around to the other side of the table.

"I'm sorry that happened to you." He says, pulling out a chair across from me. "A lot of these guys are used to... agreeable women. But I don't allow that shit. If a woman is willing, fine. If not... They don't get off that easy." He lowers himself into the seat.

I don't say anything. I just look back at him as he looks at me.

"Cherry says you're doing well." He seems to be making an effort to lighten his tone now.

"It's not that difficult to run drinks back and forth and clean up." I shrug.

"Are the girls being nice?" He asks.

"I've only really had conversation with Cherry." He smiles knowingly and chuckles again. "What?"

"It takes some of them a little time to accept new girls. You're not the type one usually encounters in a place like this."

I hesitate for a moment, before I decide to ask, "What's all this property talk?"

"Saviors' women are under the MC's protection. Nobody but their men can touch them." He replies.

"Are they actually property?" I'm not very comfortable with this terminology.

He's watching me intently, as if my question gave him answers. "Of course not." He finally says. "Not in the sense you're probably thinking. But they're off limits to anyone else."

"That biker apologized to you for not realizing I was *yours*." I say.

"He did."

"When did I become yours?"

"My employee." He says smoothly, but there's something more behind his slight smile.

"It didn't seem like that's what was being implied." Dean remains silent, but I can feel a tension in the air growing between us. His eyes are searching mine again. "Dean?" I press him for a response.

"Do you still want to work here, Vanna?" He asks.

"I need the money, so yes."

"Then just be glad nobody will get out of line with you again."

I stare back at him. "I'm not a sweet butt."

He bites his lip to keep from laughing at me, and it takes him a solid moment to respond. "I am well aware, Vanna."

"What does *call* mean? I heard you say it earlier this week, as I was leaving."

I can tell his eyes are searching mine for some kind of clue that I know what he had meant. Another grin creeps across his face as his hand rubs the stubble of his jaw.

"You're very observant." He finally says. "And I'll venture to say you already know."

"I have a theory."

"I'd love to hear it."

"Did you think leaving off the *Dibs* part would be less offensive? Or did you just think I didn't hear you at all?"

"Have I offended you?" He asks, sincerity in his voice.

I stare at him for a moment. "I haven't decided yet."

Another smile etches across his face. "I like you." He reaches into his wallet and fishes out a hundred-dollar bill, folding it a few times and leans across the table, handing it to me. "For tonight. You can leave when you want."

I take it and slide it into my pocket with the rest of my money, watching him sit back again. "There's two hours until closing. Is this a permanent pay raise? Or is tonight special?" I ask. He only continues to grin at me. "Cherry said it's fifty plus we keep all our tips." I say, folding my arms and looking at him curiously. "So why am I getting double?"

"You earned it."

"I earned it, or I *will* earn it?"

His expression doesn't change, but something flickers behind his eyes again, like he took offense to my question. "I don't have to pay for women, doll... And I wouldn't insult you like that."

"Yeah, I noticed your groupies were glad to see you. So much for that being false information."

"I've never touched a single one of them." He says in earnest. He wants me to believe him. Why does he care? "I like you, Vanna." He says, as if he read my mind.

"Why don't you ask me out then?" I challenge him outright. "You never even asked me for my number." He smiles at me, but says nothing. So, I stand up and walk back to the door to get back to work.

"Vanna." He calls after me.

"Yes, Dean?" I glance back at him.

He gets to his feet, adjusting the cuffs of his leather jacket. "Can I take you out?"

"I'm working." I smile back at him, before I step inside and let the door close behind me. I only get a few steps down the hall before I hear him shout the word "*Fuck!*" frustratedly outside. I smile to myself.

The next two hours to closing pass without any further incidents. The guys are all respectful. The women continue to avoid me. Whatever though, I'm here to make money, not girlfriends. Dean however, has made himself so scarce, I'm beginning to wonder if I hurt the bad boy's feelings out back. Baiting him and then leaving him hanging. Guys like him probably aren't used to that. They way these girls around here throw themselves at them.

"You don't have to take the glass bin out, Vanna. The prospects will do it." Cherry says, as I'm about to attempt to pull it out. "We just sweep up and wipe tables down. They'll mop the floors when we're done."

"Is Dean still around?" I ask, walking back around the bar.

"Saw him cut out a while ago." She says.

I nod. Disappointed. I guess I did hurt his feelings. Damn. Dean was hot.

"He's not a bad guy, you know." Cherry says.

"I never thought he was."

"They're tough guys, yeah. A little rough around the edges. But the Saviors are all really decent men. Especially Dean."

I finish wiping down the last table and come back to the bar to ask her, "Did Dean say something to you?"

"He said he thinks he struck out with you, and that he's not too happy with himself."

I'm surprised to hear that. "He really said that?"

Cherry laughs. "Yeah. Poor guy." She pouts. "Dean comes across as a cocky asshole sometimes. But he's got a big heart. A lot of girls have been trying to nail him down for a while. You're the first woman he's shown any real interest in since..." she hesitates, as if she's said too much. "Since a while."

"Well, I was just teasing him a little. I'm not used to this biker culture."

"Yeah, I told him that too. But anyway, will I see you again?" she asks.

"Unless he fires me." I shrug. Cherry assures me, he won't.

We say goodnight and I head out the door to walk to my car in the front lot.

Parked next to my little gray Honda Civic, straddling the huge black Harley Davidson Motorcycle I had seen him on the night we met, Dean is waiting for me. My heart skips a beat and I realize, I'm really glad I have another chance to speak to him. Under the street lights, a top his bad ass motorcycle, clad in that sexy belted and zippered leather jacket, buckled biker boots, he is a dangerously attractive man.

"Hi." I say, a little timidly as I come to stand near him.

"Hi."

"Are you waiting for me?"

"I am."

"Cherry said you left."

"I did."

We stare at each other for a moment, before he reaches inside his leather jacket and produces a red rose. He holds it gently between his leather gloved fingers, twisting it around, almost nervously, as he glances back at me.

"That's for me?" I smile.

"It is." Dean smiles back.

I can feel my face flush with heat as he extends his arm to hand the rose to me, and I'm glad for the darkness that hides my blushing face from him.

"That's really sweet of you. Thank you." I say, accepting it. "It's beautiful."

"Pales in comparison if you ask me, doll." He smiles.

I can't help but giggle at him and he seems to light up a bit at my laugh. "*Smooth.*" I tease him. "Where did you find a rose at two am?"

"*Magic.*" He replies, and I giggle again. "I'm not sure what kind of impression I made on you earlier... but I'm not a bad dude." He insists.

"So, I've heard."

"I'd like to take you out on a date, Vanna. Tomorrow night. I'll give you the night off." He says with a hopeful smile. "Some place nice. Not like here."

"I don't know if dating my boss is a good idea." I tease.

He grins at me. "Alright. You're fired. Now say yes." He teases me back. I can't help but laugh at him again. "One chance, if you don't like me, no hard feelings. I still appreciate the shot." He winks at me, using my exact words against me that I used on him, to get him to hire me.

I bite my lip and bring the pretty flower to my nose. I sniff it and admire it for a moment, making him wait again before I meet his eyes once more. "Alright, Dean. I'll go out with you." I smile.

"*Aces!*" he grins, his eyes look genuinely happy. "Shoot me a text around three tomorrow." He says, firing up his bike.

"How am I going to do that? I don't have your cell number."

"Yeah, you do, doll. You've had it all night." He smirks at me. "Get home safe, Vanna. Really looking forward to our date." He says, before he rides off, leaving me confused.

Was this some kind of joke? When did he give me his number?

I get in my car and drive home, confused about the number thing the whole way back, until I'm in my room, counting my earnings. The one-hundred-dollar bill he folded up and handed to me. The words "*Give me a chance*" and a phone number are written in black ink across it. I smile to myself as I enter his information into my cell phone, then tuck the one-hundred-dollar bill into my night table. Why couldn't he have written it on a napkin?

Smiling to myself as I bring up my messaging app in my cell phone, I text Dean before I go to sleep, **'You're so smooth.'**

DEAN
Chapter SIX

HAVEN'T SET FOOT IN THIS RITZY RESTAURANT since that night, almost a year ago, when I met with Lucinda. Tonight, as the hostess shows me to the table I reserved for Vanna and myself, I'm not getting the dirty looks I did last time. No, quite the opposite, actually.

Tonight, I left my leather jacket with Serene parked out front. Tonight, I pulled out all the stops to impress Vanna. To make her see me in a different light. She's seen me as the rugged, knock around biker. I want her to see me as a gentleman, capable of having class and manners as well.

I left the biker boots at home. Instead, I'm wearing deep burgundy Italian leather dress shoes, so dark they're almost black. Instead of my leather jacket, I'm wearing sharp black slacks with a black sports jacket, over a dark burgundy button-down collar shirt. No tie though, I don't want to bull-shit the woman. I did trim up my facial scruff, though, a little more than a five o'clock shadow. Same as my fresh haircut. Buzzed low on the sides.

The longer hair on top, I slicked back a little tighter than I usually wear it. Topped the look off with a spritz of that cologne she said makes me smell like a Western. I took that as a compliment. She seemed to like it. After all, what's cooler than a Western?

Glancing at my watch, I see that I'm still ten minutes early, as I sit down at our table in the back. I wanted something tucked away, as much privacy as I could get in a packed-out restaurant. My one-night stand with Kimberly, the hostess, paid off. I must have made a decent impression, since she pulled some strings to get me a reservation tonight. The table is more than decent, too. I'm seated at a cloth covered table for two, in front of a large wood paned picture window, overlooking the scenic landscaped garden and pond in the back. Though the sun has just about set, the garden is softly lit with tiny golden hued string lights on the cherry blossom trees, that glitter against the reflecting pond.

It actually is a nice place. I had forgotten how nice and didn't bother noticing last time I was here with Lucinda. Though, I hadn't been here long that night, anyway.

The bus boy swings by with a glass of ice water while I wait, listening to Vivaldi playing softly in the background. I glance around the dining room as my anticipation builds, attempting to distract myself by admiring the ornate crown molding and fancy millwork throughout the place. The filigree patterns in the cream and gold textured wall paper panels, match the style of the trim molding throughout. The crystal sconces that dangle from the walls above the tables catch the light from the candle lit dinners beneath them. I absentmindedly pass my hand back and forth through the flame of the white tapered candle in the center of our own table, while I wait, playing with the fire.

As the violins of Vivaldi's *Winter*, pick up the pace in a beautiful melodic crescendo, so does my heart rate, the moment I spot her from across the room... *And Jesus Fuck...* I ain't the only one either.

Vanna is a goddamned knock out, breaking necks as she moves through the room in that body con, nude illusion, ruched black mesh dress. Not only does this killer dress make her look like she's naked, wrapped in sheer black, but it's got a thigh high slit up her leg and a low-cut neckline. Her dark hair done in long, old Hollywood style waves. She looks like she just stepped off the cover of *Italian Vogue*.

I can feel her presence before she even reaches me. Fucking Divinity in motion. Completely lost in her image, I forget to move my hand from the flame of the candle and burn myself, snapping me out of my trance. I jump to my feet, immediately moving around the table to pull out her chair for her, ignoring the burn in my finger. I'm ogling her covetously and unabashedly. Summoning a small, chivalric gesture is the very least I can offer her, as I've lost control of my ability not to stare.

"Your guest, sir." I barely hear Kimberly, the hostess, say. In my peripheral vision, I manage to notice she places two menus down on the white cloth table. "Enjoy your evening."

"Hi." Vanna smiles at me, her lips a deep, seductive shade of red. Her dark eyes smokey and equally as alluring. She doesn't sit though. She steps closer to me, lifting an arm to drape gently around my neck in a light hug. I hug her back this time, mustering the self-control to not crush her body against mine. To feel those voluptuous breasts pressed against my chest. Lacking the self-control, however, to not smell her as we embrace.

Fuck me... Whatever she's got on hits me square in the olfactory bulb as I breathe her in deeply. I fight the urge to let my hand slide down her back to the generous curve of her perfect ass. If one could bottle lust, that's what she's got on. Pure, unadulterated lust.

"I hope you weren't waiting four seasons for me." She says, as she pulls back from me to take her seat.

Four seasons? Right... Vivaldi.

I smile back at her as I take my seat again. "Only since the end of *Spring*."

"*Winter* is my favorite. Glad I made it in time to hear it." She says, placing her little black sparkly clutch on the far side of the table nearest the window.

She glances outside to admire the view, and the candle light catches the highlight on her cheekbones and the shimmer on her smokey eyes. She's fucking gorgeous.

"I'm glad I Googled this place when I got your text. Though, I hope this dress is okay. I don't own anything really fancy." She says, shifting her gaze back to me.

"You look like a model in Italian Vogue." I just say it. I'm not lying.

Vanna giggles, but gives me a skeptical look. "Right, the controversial issue in demonstration against anorexic models?"

The fuck? Does she not realize how damn beautiful she is?

"The hottest fucking issue they ever put out." I counter her. "You look absolutely stunning, Vanna. I think I dislocated my jaw when you walked in here."

She bites that full bottom lip of hers. White teeth on deep red, and my cock twitches at the sight of it. "Well, you look like you just stepped out of a GQ magazine yourself."

I give her a modest shrug and a grin. "I try."

A waiter arrives, placing a tall glass of ice water down for Vanna, as well as a basket of fresh baked bread and a little dish of olive oil and herbs. He takes our wine orders before he leaves us alone again to look over the dinner menu. I watch as Vanna's eyes skirt across the items listed inside. Debating with herself, I'm sure, over whether to pull the typical girl move and order a Caesar salad, instead of the steak or lobster.

"Order anything you want." I encourage her. "You really can't go wrong here."

Her eyes flick up to look at me through her dark lashes over the menu. A little smile crosses her lips as she folds it closed and places it on the edge of the table. "I think you should order for us both." She says, a sultry hint in her voice.

"Alright. I'm up for that challenge. Any allergies I should know about?" I joke.

"No. But that was a very thoughtful consideration." She teases me back.

The waiter returns with our drinks. Her Pinot Noir, my Red Cabernet. He asks if we're ready to order. I glance back at Vanna with a grin, "Last chance." I warn her. But she only smiles back at me and gestures with her hand for me to proceed. "We'll both have the steak and scampi scallops with shallots and French string beans." I say, handing him back both menus.

"Very good, sir." He replies. "Will that be all for now?"

"No. An order of *Lumache* as well, for the lady." I grin, shifting my gaze to watch Vanna's reaction. Her mouth drops open to form a little O, as a tiny gasp escapes her. I can't help grinning wider.

"No, cancel the *snails*, please." She says, smiling up at the waiter. "My date thinks he's funny." Her gaze shifts back to me as our waiter walks away. She snatches a crust of bread and pinches off a crumb. "I can't believe you did that." She says, playfully chucking the crumb at me, which hits me in the chest and falls onto the table cloth. She lifts her wine glass to take a sip. "You're not so nice after all, are you?" I can tell she's teasing me though, she's still smiling, feigning upset. The snails amused her.

I pick up the bread crumb. "You didn't mention any exceptions. I gave you the chance. Fair game, Vanna." I smile, gently tossing the bread crumb back at her.

It hits her wine glass though, ricocheting right off of it, falling down into her cleavage, into her dress. Deep down in there. Right where I want to shove my face.

I'm half mortified at having just done that to her, though, half stifling a laugh as I watch her shift in her seat slightly, away from the rest of the room of diners. She places her wine glass down on the table and attempts to discretely fish the bread out of her breasts with her fingers. I can tell it isn't working. It's in there. Way down in there between those gorgeous tits.

"I'm very sorry." I try to whisper, still fighting the urge to laugh.

"You're not nice at all!" she whispers back to me, teasing still. "It's really down in there." She sighs, sitting back in her chair normally again to face me. She takes another sip of wine and places it back down on the table. "Well then, Dean. Please excuse me, while I visit the Ladies' room."

I stand up from my seat as Vanna does hers, grabbing her clutch and making her way towards the bathrooms near the front of the restaurant. God damn, she's a vision from the back as well. The curves on this woman. Viking wasn't wrong at all when he called her a Goddess. As I lower myself back down to my seat to await her return, I can't help noticing more than half the guys in this place are admiring her fine ass as well. I don't blame them. I can't blame them. But I don't like it.

Jamming my burned middle finger into my ice water while I wait, I can't help hard eyeing a couple of these jagoffs. Eat your hearts out, fellas. She's mine.

LAUGHING TO MYSELF AS I PICTURE DEAN'S MORTIFIED EXPRESSION WHEN he threw the bread down my dress, I fish it out of the bottom of my bra easily enough without an audience. Chucking it into the waste basket, I place my little black clutch on the fancy gold and black colored granite bathroom counter, and glance in the ornate gold framed mirror.

Dean thinks I'm pretty enough to be in Italian Vogue. I almost believe he meant that. But then, it could just be the cleavage, combined with my signature scent, *Seduction*. A musky, feminine blend I created myself with essential oils, including Hawaiian Sandalwood and Styrax. He didn't comment on it, though I know for a fact I've turned heads with it before.

Not wanting to keep him waiting too long, I adjust my dress, check my lipstick, and add just a little dab more of my concoction behind my ears.

When I return, Dean gets up to help me to my seat again.

"I really didn't mean to." He says quietly in my ear. He lingers for a moment, before returning to his own seat. *Seduction*. He does like it.

"It's okay. I was just playing with you. No harm done."

"You really look very beautiful, Vanna. Turning a lot of heads in here tonight." He says. That last part. There's a tinge of something in his words. Jealousy? I'm not quite sure.

"I haven't noticed. I'm here with you. And you look very nice yourself." I remind him.

The waiter returns with our meal, and as we dine, we ask each other the typical first date questions. He learns that I've recently located to NC for a fresh start and live alone with my cat Nico, whom I love. That I also love the beach at night, star gazing and astrology.

I learn that he's originally from Virginia, but that his family bought a farm house in NC when he was about five years old, his father, also named Dean, opened up the Motorcycle shop and was a member of an MC as well. His parents passed away years ago and left him everything. He's divorced, has no children, and is a Scorpio.

We are working on our last sips of wine when the waiter returns with our check. Dean picks it up immediately and places his card inside the leather folder, handing it back to the waiter without looking.

"I hope you enjoyed the meal?" Dean says, inquisitively.

"Yes, very much. Thank you." I smile.

"There's a really great coffee and dessert café that's open till eleven. It's just a few blocks from here. Would you like to go for a walk and stop by there?" He asks.

"That sounds really nice... Let's do it."

We walk along the side walk, chatting casually, peeking in little boutique shop windows. It's a pretty area. Fancy, triple globe style street lights with flower baskets hanging from them, and cobble stone streets. When we reach the café, Dean opens the door and I step inside to the amazing aroma of freshly made desserts and artisan coffee.

"Oh my gosh it smells so good in here." I say, glancing back at him and catching him looking at my ass.

He grins, knowing he got caught, but then I notice him scan the room. "Where do you want to sit? They come to you."

"How about near the window so we can look outside. It's a pretty town."

We find a half-moon booth near the window and slide in. I sweep my hair to the side and bring it in front of my shoulder.

"No extensions, really?" he teases me.

I feign insult. "Absolutely not! Everything about me is home grown, honey." I tease him back. "Don't believe me?" I slide a little closer to him so we're only inches apart. "Touch it. Feel it for yourself. Get your mitts in there." I taunt him.

He does. He isn't intimidated at all. He slides his hand right up the back of my skull. "Okay. No tracks. I apologize." He smiles, but he doesn't remove his hand. He keeps stroking my hair.

I smirk at him and whisper, "Doesn't even hurt when it gets pulled."

Why the hell did I say that? Why does this man have such an effect on me?

A grin begins to creep across his mouth. I feel his fingers begin to twist lightly into my hair as he gives me a slight and gentle tug. There's something stirring behind his dark eyes as I stare into them. He doesn't look away from mine and moves his hand over my hair, taking a hand full and bringing it to his face. He inhales the scent of my hair deeply, boldly, and unashamed, never breaking eye contact with me.

It turns me on. I lick my upper lip slowly and then bite into my bottom one again. That seems to stir something inside him as well.

I straighten back up in my seat and as I do so, my hair slowly slips through his fingers until it falls back against my body. I smile coyly and look away from him as a young waitress walks toward us. Crossing my legs under the table, I slyly pull the slit of my skirt over to flash him a generous eye full of thigh, discretely under the table.

"*Fuck...*" he mutters under his breath, his voice thick with desire as he writhes slightly in his seat.

It gives me butterflies, and I squeeze my thighs together. Just knowing his eyes are on me, the bare skin of my thigh, affects me in a way I haven't experienced in a long time. I can't help wondering what he's thinking. Though I could imagine, if I dared.

"Hello! Welcome to the *Dream Bean*." Our young waitress cheerfully greets us. "May I take your orders?"

I smile at her. "Thank you. I'll have a small chai tea Frappuccino, please."

Dean is silent. I turn to look at him and find that he's still staring at my leg. "Dean, would you like something to drink? Some dessert maybe?" I ask.

"*Cherry pie*." He blurts out, with a wicked grin.

I can't help letting out a stifled giggle at his completely inappropriate, yet still kind of appropriate, response. I really hope his inuendo went over our young waitress's head.

I turn back to look at him. "No really, is that your order?" I ask, giving him a look that I hope conveys, *knock it off, she's a kid.*

He looks at the waitress for the first time and smiles politely. "I'll have a coffee, black with honey. And absolutely, some cherry pie."

"Thank you." I say to her again, and she scampers off behind the counter. I look back at Dean. "You are so bad!"

"You started it." He smirks.

After our dessert, we walk slowly back towards the restaurant, neither of us seemingly too eager for the night to end.

"Thanks for a really lovely date." I smile at him, as we approach my car parked across the street from the restaurant. I hit the key fob to unlock it and place them back in my clutch.

"You're off tomorrow. Come out with me again." I know he intended it to be a question, but his demanding delivery of it makes me giggle.

"You really want to see me again?" I tease. "So soon?" He nods, his expression serious. I lean back against my car, looking up at him as I pretend to consider his request. Of course, I want to go out with him again. I really like him. "What would we do?"

Dean steps closer to me, removing the clutch from my hands and places it on the roof of my car. He takes my hands in his and gently holds them between us.

"Whatever you want to do, we'll do." His thumbs lightly stroke my skin. So lightly, it almost tickles, making me think of other ways I want him to touch me. I push those thoughts aside though. I barely know him.

"What is there to do on a Sunday?" I ask, trying not to look flustered, as I shift my eyes from his penetrating stare. I notice a blonde woman standing near his bike, across the street behind him. She's got her hands on her hips and she seems to be glaring at his back. "Who's that by your bike?"

Without releasing my hands, Dean glances over his shoulder for a moment, before turning back to me. "Nobody." He says, as if he couldn't care less. "Let me take you out again tomorrow, doll. You ever been on a motorcycle before?"

I look back at him, shaking my head. "No. Are you going to take me for a ride on it?"

He smiles at me. "*Her*."

"Her?"

"My Harley. *Her* name is *Serene*." He grins. I can't help wondering if this is a biker thing. I giggle, it's kind of cute. "We can pick you up tomorrow, before noon."

"We?"

He nods. "*We* can take you to lunch. Cruise around. Have dinner again someplace, maybe by the river." He pushes.

"Oh, you want my *whole* day?" I tease.

"I'll take what I can get, but I'm shootin' for the moon, doll." He grins back, squeezing my hands slightly tighter.

At least he seems to be an honest man. "Okay. I'll text you my address."

He presses his lips together for a moment and nods. "Yeah, text that to me, baby."

I find his response a little odd, but then I remember, I actually do have something I was meaning to do tomorrow. "Can we make it a little bit after noon? I have a couple of things I have to do in the morning." I've already been in my new place a week, and haven't gotten a chance to bring charmed muffins to either of my neighbors yet. I can do that tomorrow before Dean and I meet up again.

"Sure, doll. Whatever you want."

"Then it's another date." I smile.

"*Aces.*" He grins, lifting my hand to his lips to kiss me. My heart flutters a bit. I didn't know guys still did that, let alone *bikers*. I bite my lip to keep from giggling like an idiot again. He has a way of making me feel things I haven't in what seems like ages.

Releasing my other hand, he reaches for my car door and opens it for me. "Thank you, Vanna, for spending your evening with me. I really enjoyed your company and look forward to tomorrow." God, he's so polite. I guess bikers are more than just tough guys. At least Dean is.

"Thanks for being such a gentleman. It's appreciated more than you know."

His eyes narrow ever so slightly, as if he's reading into my words. Maybe I said too much. Dean grabs my clutch off the roof for me as I get into my car. "I'll never be anything less with you, Vanna." He says with sincerity as he hands me the clutch. I believe him.

"Good night, Dean."

"Good night, Vanna." He says, stepping back. I close my door and start the car.

As I drive off, I watch him in the mirror. He doesn't walk to his bike when I leave. At least not while I can still see him before I turn off the street to head home. He stands and watches me go until I'm out of sight.

DEAN

"WHO WAS THAT?" LUCINDA ASKS, AS I REMOVE MY LEATHER JACKET from the left saddle bag on Serene. I act like Lucinda isn't there, giving my leather jacket a quick shake before I slip it back on. She's not going to ruin my night. Not with visions of Vanna in that dress still fresh in my mind. Never gonna forget the way she looked tonight. Burned it into my mind forever. Burned my fucking hand, too. Totally worth it though.

"Dean!" Lucinda raises her voice, cutting into my thoughts. I almost forgot she was still there. Slinging a leg over Serene, I take a deep breath through my nose and exhale slowly as I lower myself onto her seat.

"What?" I reluctantly ask.

"Who were you with just now?"

"Not *just now*. All evening. Seeing her again tomorrow, too."

Lucinda looks at me as if she's in a state of shock. "You have a *girlfriend?*" she asks, the displeasure notable in her tone.

I smile to myself. I will. If I keep playing my cards right, I will make Vanna mine. She already is, she just doesn't know it yet.

I don't bother responding to Lucinda. Instead, I fire up Serene and kick up her stand, revving her up as Lucinda attempts to ask me again.

It's really none of her damn business what I do, or who I'm with. Serene agrees, her exhaust pipes blocking out Lucinda's sidewalk hissy fit.

Before Lucinda can pull any bullshit, like grabbing me or jumping on the back of my bike, I take off into the night. Visions of deep red lips, thick thighs and smoldering dark eyes, are dancing through my mind to the classical Baroque Concerto of Vivaldi's *Winter*.

For the first time, in a long time, it feels damn good to be alive.

Chapter Seven

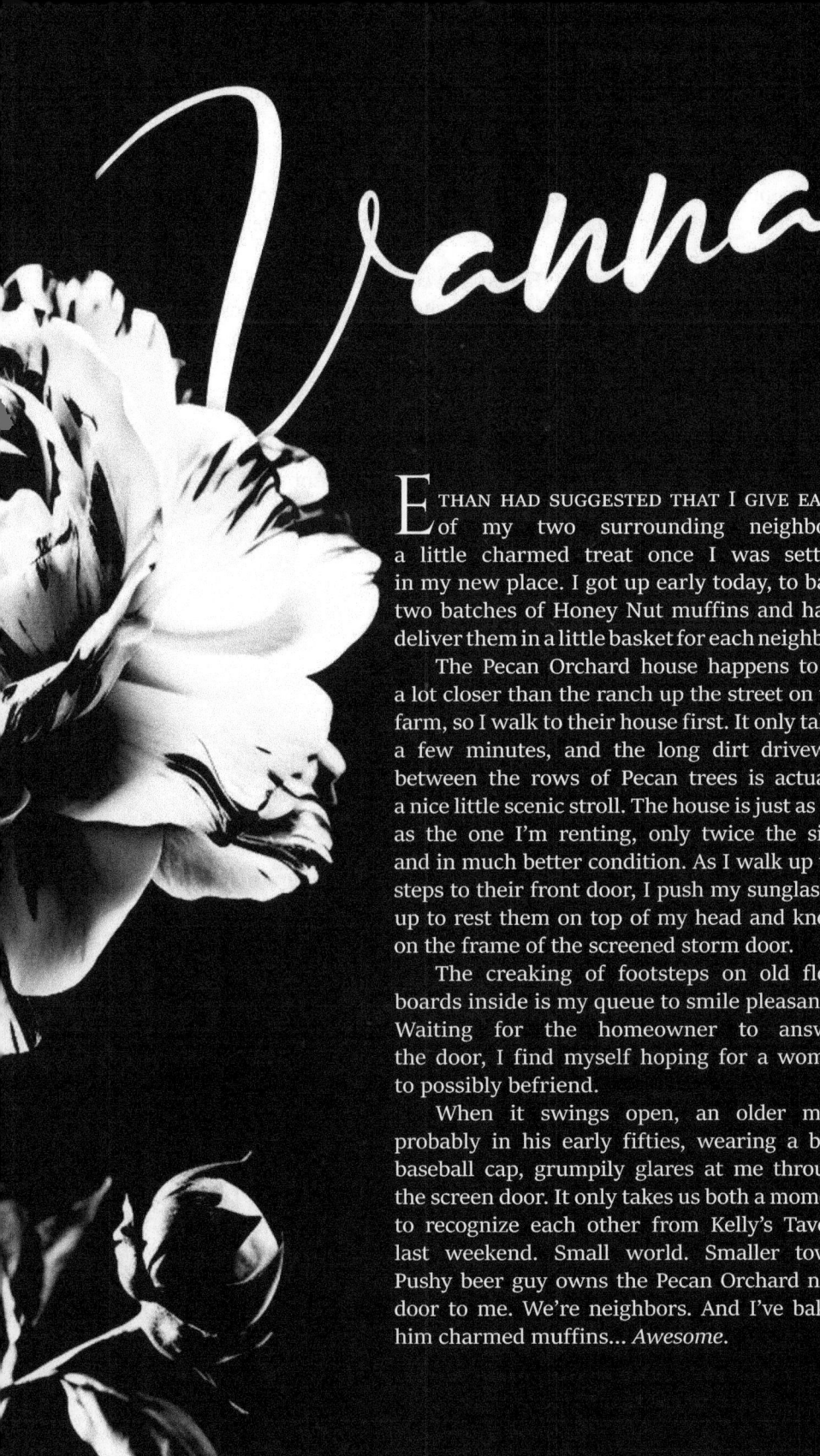

Vanna

Ethan had suggested that I give each of my two surrounding neighbors a little charmed treat once I was settled in my new place. I got up early today, to bake two batches of Honey Nut muffins and hand deliver them in a little basket for each neighbor.

The Pecan Orchard house happens to be a lot closer than the ranch up the street on the farm, so I walk to their house first. It only takes a few minutes, and the long dirt driveway between the rows of Pecan trees is actually a nice little scenic stroll. The house is just as old as the one I'm renting, only twice the size, and in much better condition. As I walk up the steps to their front door, I push my sunglasses up to rest them on top of my head and knock on the frame of the screened storm door.

The creaking of footsteps on old floor boards inside is my queue to smile pleasantly. Waiting for the homeowner to answer the door, I find myself hoping for a woman to possibly befriend.

When it swings open, an older man, probably in his early fifties, wearing a blue baseball cap, grumpily glares at me through the screen door. It only takes us both a moment to recognize each other from Kelly's Tavern last weekend. Small world. Smaller town. Pushy beer guy owns the Pecan Orchard next door to me. We're neighbors. And I've baked him charmed muffins... *Awesome.*

He suddenly goes from grumpy old man, to grinning hound dog again. I can feel my plastered smile fading and catch myself. "Hi." I say, with forced pleasantry. "I'm your new neighbor. I just wanted to introduce myself and bring you some muffins."

He pushes the screen door open and steps out onto the porch with me. I take a step backwards, keeping the basket of muffins in front of me. Effectively, between us.

"That's real sweet of you." He says, eyes roaming over me.

"Well, I'm Vanna." I attempt to retain the pleasant tone in my voice. I don't want to make enemies in this town. Especially not one within a five-minute walk from my front door.

"That's a real pretty name, Vanna. Suits a real pretty woman."

I continue to fake my smile. "Thanks. And you are?"

He extends his hand to me, which I very reluctantly accept. "I'm Garrett Johnson." He grins. "Real pleasure to see you again, Vanna. You should let me buy you a drink sometime."

I don't respond to that, changing the subject instead. "How long have you been here? This orchard is lovely."

"Was my father's, passed down to me. Worked it as a boy. Where do you work, missy?"

"The next city over." I attempt to keep it vague, but I already know that's not even remotely close to an answer.

"What do you do, specifically?" he asks again.

I don't want to be rude. I don't want to raise suspicion. I just want to live next door in quiet peace. "I work at a little holistic gift shop." Not technically a lie, but I imagine it sounds less threatening than a *Witch Shop*.

"One of them New Age places?"

I force myself to chuckle again. "You could say that." I smile, extending the basket of muffins to him. He takes them, making sure his hand touches mine as he does so. I fight the urge to grimace and keep this damn smile on my face. "Anyway, enjoy the muffins. I have to go, but it was nice meeting you, officially." I turn and head back down his porch steps.

"Pleasure's all mine, sweetheart." He calls after me, as I walk briskly down his unpaved driveway towards the road. "Wait!" he suddenly shouts. I halt in my tracks and look back at him. "There's a path a yard or two up, through the Orchard. Leads to the property line, so you don't have to walk all the way down to the road."

"Oh, thanks." I say, giving him an awkward wave.

"I'll definitely enjoy your muffins, honey." He calls after me once more.

"Have a great day!" I say back, ignoring the innuendo. I take the path through the orchard back to my house. At least it's shaded and more scenic than walking back home along the street. I can't believe I made *that guy* charmed muffins! I hope they're duds. I don't need him liking me. Although, with my awful track record regarding spell work, they will probably work too well.

After a pit stop at my house to grab my purse and my next neighbor's basket of muffins, I walk the quarter mile trek up the road to the ranch house on the hill overlooking acres of farm land. I plan to buy some fruit and veggies from their farm stand on my way back home. Hopefully this time, there will be a woman I can make friends with.

Deciding it might be better to see if the owners are actually working the farmstand, before I walk all the way up to the house, I turn right at the gravel paved drive way that leads to the farmstand and a little parking lot. The barn style farmstand is adorable. Red with white trim, and there are decorative barrels with thick bunches of flowers growing out the tops on either side of the entrance. Hanging flower pots with cascading plants along the overhang in front of it. Across the way are several long greenhouses, which are parallel to a *pick your own* strawberries field.

As I step inside the little barn, it's full of wooden box shelves containing produce along the walls, and in the center of the space. The register and scale are at the front counter, with jars of local honey and homemade jams. The two girls behind the counter smile and greet me pleasantly.

"Hello," I smile back, "Do you two live here?"

"No ma'am. We just work here." The taller girl with the straight chestnut hair says. "Can we help you find something?"

"I actually just moved in next door, and was hoping to meet my neighbors. Do you know if they're home?"

"He was just here a minute ago. I'll see if he's still nearby."

Smiling in thanks, I decide to browse around for a few minutes, before I hear him behind me.

"I thought the plan was that you were going to text me your address and Serene and I were going to pick you up at your place?" I'd recognize that sexy, growly, baritone voice anywhere. Slowly turning around, I come face to face with a grinning, handsome as ever, Dean Keegan. He's leaning against the frame of the barn doors, wearing jeans, and a button-down flannel shirt. "A little after noon time, wasn't it?"

"You knew we were neighbors this whole time, didn't you?" I ask, remembering his comment about hoping I *buy locally* when I told him I lived near a farm. And last night when he told me to text him my address, I thought he was being weird.

He shrugs. "I knew you'd figure it out, eventually."

The two girls are looking at me differently, now that they realize I actually know Dean. The taller one with the chestnut straight hair looks less than thrilled. I wonder if she has a crush on her boss, too.

Dean notices us looking at each other. "Vanna, this is Jessica and Veronica. My cashiers and helpers around this place."

"Nice to meet you." I smile, but don't say anything to me now. I shake my head at Dean and chuckle. "Anyway, this really is a small world."

"Even smaller town." He winks.

"I was just thinking that earlier, when I stopped over at Garrett's house."

The grin on Dean's face slowly fades before he asks, "Why were you over at his place?"

"I brought him some muffins to introduce myself. You know, doing the *new neighbor* thing. I made you some, too." I say, lifting the basket slightly to show him.

Oh crap... These are not just muffins... They're *spell casted* muffins. I charmed them. I can't let Dean eat these! Not after what happened when I... No. I'm not risking it.

"But you can't have them now." I say quickly.

His brows furrow. "Why not?" he asks, pushing himself off the door frame and walking towards me.

I swing the basket away from him, holding it somewhat behind my back. "Because... you... you knew we were neighbors this whole time and you never said a thing about it!"

"Well, I didn't know there would be muffins involved, Vanna." He grins at me.

"That's too bad." I say, trying not to smile back. His playful grin is so damn infectious though. I have to press my lips together to fight it.

"Those are *my* muffins, Vanna. You said so yourself." He presses, taking another step closer to me.

"No, you lost your muffin privileges." I barely get the sentence out without laughing. Even the two girls who work for him are trying not to laugh at us.

"Fine. Let's barter. You can fill a basket up with whatever you want here, in exchange for the muffins." He says, pointing at the basket I'm clutching.

"I brought cash. I don't need to barter." I hold the muffins further away from him.

"Then your money's no good here." He grins, with another shrug.

"Dirty pool! That is not fair. I came here to buy some produce for the week."

"No, you came here to give me muffins. Shopping for produce was secondary." He waggles his finger at me and takes another step closer.

"It wasn't secondary, it was equally in addition to!" I insist.

He stares at me for a moment. "Are you really going to stand there and deny me my muffins?"

I can't help laughing now. Those words. Him standing there with his fists on his hips. This utterly ridiculous situation I've managed to back myself into. "I am, yeah." I laugh even harder. He snatches the basket from me, faster than lightening. "*Hey!*" I protest, trying to snatch it back, but he's too fast, and too tall, holding the basket high above my head. "I am not above tickling you, Dean Keegan! You give those back!"

"Tickle me. Revenge is sweet." He insists. "Maybe even as sweet as these muffins."

I fold my arms. "Fine. Keep them. Just don't eat them."

He looks at me suspiciously, lowering his arm to examine the muffins. "Why? What's wrong with them?" he asks, lifting up the little checkered piece of fabric I covered them with. "They look like perfectly good muffins to me. You bake them with ex-lax or something? Not a good way to make nice with your neighbors, Vanna." He teases.

"No. But you still shouldn't eat them." I sigh.

"Tell me why." He persists.

I glance at the two girls who have been silently watching our exchange. I don't want to come clean with an audience. If I say I charmed them, word could spread like wild fire in this little town that I'm a witch. I look back at Dean, before I start to walk out of the little farm stand, intending to lead him towards the pair of picnic tables outside. He follows me, basket of muffins under his arm, before the chestnut-haired girl reaches out to touch his shoulder as he passes, stopping him.

"Dean?" she says, looking up at him through her lashes. Oh yeah, she definitely has a crush on him. "My car's been making a funny sound all week. Could you check it for me before I leave this afternoon?"

"Sure, doll." He casually replies. I note the *doll* part, though. Must be the way he talks to women. The way she lights up at his answer, it's like she won the lottery. As he turns from her to follow me out, I notice she shoots me a little glare, as if to curse me for leading him away from her.

Once we're out of earshot, I turn to face him. "I charmed them."

"What the hell does that mean?" he asks.

"I'm a Witch. When I was baking the muffins, I charmed them so that my neighbors would like me. Just in a friendly way. Nothing major. But, you can't eat them, because I don't want to influence you into liking me."

"What if I already like you?" he asks, pressing his lips together. I can tell he wants to laugh at me and is not taking this seriously at all. He doesn't laugh, though. He doesn't want to offend me.

I run my fingers through the top of my hair, shaking it out. He's going to eat these damn muffins. I know it. "I don't know. It's just a little nudge towards liking me."

"I'm way past a nudge." He grins, and I can't help smiling, even though I can feel my skin flush at his words.

"Can you just, not eat them? I'll make you a normal batch, instead." I offer, attempting to reach for the basket, but he twists slightly away from me.

"Are they baked with *eye of newt or toe of frog* or some shit?" he jokes.

I roll my eyes at him. "No, you jerk. They're normal Honey Nut muffin ingredients."

"So, what charms them, as you say?"

"The metaphysical properties of each ingredient, paired with my intentions."

Dean's just staring at me now, like I'm a freak.

"Okay, like for example, I used honey. One of the ways honey is used in magick is to sweeten people up towards a person." I explain, "I just wanted to get along with my neighbors. I want to fit in here, you know? If people find out I'm a witch, they might not like me." I sigh, trying not to sound flustered. "I figured, at least if my neighbors liked me, maybe I'd have a safe place to live, even if people in town don't like me. That if somebody ever came to my house to harm me, and my neighbors saw something, they'd be more apt not to turn a blind eye... See. Nothing nefarious."

Dean puts the basket of muffins down on the picnic table beside us. "Vanna, I'll never let anyone harm you." He says, placing his hands on my shoulders. I can hear the sincerity in his words. "You are extremely likeable." He adds. "You don't need muffins to charm people when you're already charming, yourself."

"So, you don't have an issue with me being a witch?"

"No. I don't want to offend you, but I don't buy into all that spell casting, *magic muffin* stuff."

I can't help giggling at the way he says *magic muffin*. "Okay. I don't mind that you're a skeptic, either." I happen to glance back towards the farm stand to see Veronica still watching us. I hope she didn't hear anything. Looking back at Dean, I continue, "You should visit the shop I work at some time though, I bet I could change your mind about a few things. Introduce you to the Hermetic Principals."

"Whatever the hell that means." He smiles at me. "But I'll take you up on that offer."

"So, do you want a new batch of muffins?"

"Nope. These will do just fine." He says, picking up the basket of muffins again. "Go grab some produce. A deal is a deal. I'll give you a ride home so you can change into some jeans. Then Serene and I will come get you at noon. I'm going to bring these up to the house and get my truck."

"Don't say I didn't try to stop you." I sigh.

"They're just muffins... I already like you. I'm *immune* to your witchcraft." He winks at me.

That has yet to be determined. I sigh to myself, thinking about the Knight Summoning spell. "Well then, don't tell anyone I'm a witch."

Dean touches my chin, lifting my face to make sure I'm looking at him when he speaks. "You, and your secrets, Vanna, are always safe with me." He promises.

As Dean carries the two bags of produce to my front door, my cellphone receives an urgent text. Shoving my hand into my purse, I grab it and shut the blaring caution zone themed ringer off and immediately open the text. I already know what it's about. It can only be one thing. My heart palpitates, and I try to keep a straight face, so as not to draw suspicion from Dean.

The text is from Joey, my former roommate. **'CALL ME ASAP'.**

Damn it. I don't want to get into this in front of Dean. I don't want to have to explain anything just yet. I'm supposed to have more time to figure things out.

"Everything okay?" Dean's question brings me back to the present.

I plaster a fake smile across my face. "Yes. Let me take those, inside." I say, hurriedly making my way up the porch steps to open my front door. I didn't lock it, knowing I'd be back within the hour and having only been next door. Dean hands me the two bags, but I notice his expression looks slightly concerned. I must not be acting well enough.

My cellphone blares that horrible caution alarm ringtone again. *Damn, damn, damn!*

"I'll be right back." I say, leaving him on the front porch and hurrying into my kitchen to place the bags on the center island. I grab my cell phone out of my purse as Joey is now impatiently calling me. This has to be bad. I have no choice but to answer. I try to remain calm, to keep my voice low, knowing Dean is only a few steps away, by the screen door of my front porch. "Hello?" I whisper into the phone.

"It happened." Joey says.

I already knew it did, but the confirmation still makes it worse. "*Shit.* Did it come direct?"

"Two of them did, Vanna. I'm out." Joey's voice, as nervous as it is serious.

"You're out? What do you mean you're out?"

"One of the letters came to *me*, Vanna. From *him!*" Joey nearly shrieks in my ear. "He's threatening *my* life now!"

My blood runs cold in my veins as I lean back against the door frame of my kitchen. "How is he doing this?" I ask out loud, to no one in particular.

"I don't know, but I didn't sign up for this."

"I'm sorry I dragged you into this."

"I'm sorry too. But I can't risk him coming after me."

"I don't want you to. This is my mess. I'll figure it out. I need to see the letters, though. Can I come get them now? I don't want to wait for the mail. I need to see them now."

"Yeah. I'll be here for a couple of hours. When are you coming?"

"I'll be there in an hour. Give me yours too. I don't want you to respond to anything he sends you. He's just trying to scare you into giving up information."

"I'm not going to tell him anything, Vanna. He's still in prison, right?"

I nod, even though Joey can't see me through the phone. "Yeah. For a few more years, hopefully."

"Are you going to move again?"

I glance at the screen door, noticing Dean's shadow. "No. Not yet... but if he..." I catch myself, hoping Dean hasn't heard anything.

"If he finds your current address, you will." Joey sighs.

"Yeah. Something like that... I'll see you in an hour." I hang up the phone and shove it back inside my purse.

One step ahead, now... Only one.

Closing my eyes for a moment, I try to compose myself before I go back outside to let Dean know I have to postpone our second date. I remind myself that I've done things differently this time. Nothing is in my name here. There's no lease, the utilities are in the home owners name, included in my rent. Which I pay in cash, since I don't even have a bank account or credit cards. I don't get mail here. My cell phone is a burner phone. And my car is still registered to an old address. Most importantly, He is still locked up. He still cannot get to me. Even if he does somehow manage to figure out where I am, he wouldn't send anyone else to do his dirty work. He wouldn't deny himself the pleasure of doing it himself. I've got two years before I have to worry. Before I have to *really* be afraid. Four years, if he doesn't get early parole.

I have a little time, I remind myself. A little more time, to make and save as much money as I can. To figure out a plan. To find the Knight who will protect me from *Him*.

Glancing back at the shadowed form lingering on my front porch, I wonder if Dean really could be the Knight I summoned. And if he is, just how exactly do I truly feel about it?

Forcing another fake smile across my face, I grab my purse and walk back to the front door, prending like everything is just fine.

"You alright?" Dean asks, as I step back onto the front porch with him, closing the oak door behind me and locking it.

"Yes, fine." I lie. "I'm afraid I'm going to have to postpone our date with Serene." I let the screen door slam shut behind me. I can see he's concerned. It's written plainly on his handsome face. "I'm sorry, I just have to go all the way to Wilmington for some important paperwork. I don't want to wait for the mail. It just takes so long and things get lost and I would just feel so much better if-" I ramble on, before Dean cuts me off.

"I'll take you." He says, gesturing to his Chevy. "My trucks right there. I wanted to spend the day with you anyway."

I try to quickly assess the pros and cons of his offer, but I can hardly think straight. "But, what about Serene?"

"She's not going anywhere." He smirks at me, the intentional double meaning behind his words making me smile back at him.

"But, all the way to Myrtle Grove? That's actually closer to Carolina Beach than Wilmington."

"I'll take you all the way to Myrtle Beach, *South Carolina*, if you want. I don't care how far you need to go, Vanna."

It's probably better to act like this isn't a big deal and go with it. If I resist him, it might make him more suspicious than he already might be. "Alright. Let's go." I smile. "I wanted to spend the day with you anyway, too."

"Aces." He grins back at me.

I DIDN'T HEAR EVERYTHING. IN FACT, I BARELY HEARD ANYTHING. IT'S HER demeanor, her body language, that is a dead giveaway something isn't right in Vanna's private life. I want so badly to ask her about it, but I don't want to push. If I can get her to trust me, she'll eventually tell me on her own, right? I try to convince myself of this on our little excursion to Myrtle Grove.

Now, as I sit in the parking lot of a large apartment complex, watching Vanna knock on the door of a second story apartment, I can't help but stare at the door, wondering. What kind of paper work does one rush out of town to pick up on a Sunday that cannot wait until Tuesday? Which is about as long as it would take for whomever is inside that apartment to send her. She tried to play it cool at her house, in the truck with me the whole way here. But I know a fake smile when I see one. I could feel her tension even as we bullshitted on the drive down here. I can read people. I've honed that skill my whole life. She's hiding something. And she might need help. I want to help her, but I don't want to push her away. I have to play this cool. Act like everything is fine, the way *she's* pretending it is. Just long enough for her to trust me. I need to have a little patience...

My patience already starts to wear though, when a fuckin' dude answers the door. I watch with irrational jealousy as they talk. He hands her an envelope, which she hurriedly stuffs into her bag. My fist squeezes the steering wheel as she hugs this guy. Briefly, but still. Another man touching her, even that seemingly innocent, admittedly quick hug, twists my guts up.

"*Ex-boyfriend?*" I ask, trying to keep the tone of my voice level, as Vanna hops back into the passenger seat of my truck.

"No," she chuckles. "Ex roommate. I used to rent that apartment with his girlfriend, before I managed to move next door to you."

She's doing that thing again, where she's trying to sound upbeat and chipper. Trying to sound like there isn't an envelope in her purse right now containing something she was desperate to get her hands on an hour ago. Willing to blow me off for.

"I haven't had a boyfriend in years." She volunteers, her expression suddenly serious. She can tell I'm off my game. She affects me too strongly. I can usually hide my discontent from others, but she's seeing through me.

"You want one?" I ask, trying to sound playful to throw her off.

She smiles back at me. It looks genuine this time. "You offering?"

I grin at her, but I don't answer. "Where to now?"

"I'll buy you lunch for driving me out here."

I can't help cocking a brow at her. "We'll go to lunch, but you're not buying. Doesn't work that way with me."

She looks at me, surprised, but not displeased. "You paid last night."

"Yeah. What's your point?"

"You don't think I owe you a meal after paying last night? Or at least gas money for this?"

I stare at her. "Did I ask you out to that restaurant, Vanna?" She nods. "And did I ask if I could drive you here?"

She smirks, giggling this time as she tells me, "Actually, it was more like you *insisted.*"

"When you're with me, Vanna, I pay. That's just how it is. You don't owe me shit."

Her smile fades. "Are you mad at me?"

The question catches me by surprise. Why would she even ask me that? Am I behaving as less than a gentleman? "Of course, not." I automatically say, continuing to study her as I reach for the shifter, throwing the truck in reverse. I pay particularly close attention to her body language, as I drape my arm across the seat in preparation to check my blind spot. She doesn't flinch, but she tenses, ever so slightly. I glance over my shoulder as I back the truck out of the parking space and throw it back into drive. "Why would I be mad at you?" I can't help asking, cutting the wheel and heading for the exit of the complex.

I don't get a verbal response. I get a shrug.

"I think you've dated some shitty guys, Vanna." I sigh.

She's staring at her hands in her lap now, fidgeting with her fingers.

Fuck.

I'm not wrong about the shitty guys. For her sake, I hope going Dutch on dates was the worst of it. I'm not going to push her. She's not commenting. She obviously doesn't want to get into her dating history. I get it. God knows I would rather talk about anything other than Lucinda. Or the train of women after her...

"Fear not, my lady." I try my best to sound playful again, for her. "That streak is over. You're with me now."

We end up having lunch at a nice little Mexican place, seated on a covered balcony outside, overlooking the town of Carolina Beach. Enjoying a view of the pier on the opposite side of the road and the ocean beyond.

I had expected Vanna to excuse herself immediately to the ladies' room, in order to get away from me to read whatever this important paperwork is that couldn't wait. But she doesn't. To my surprise, she remains with me the whole time. Smiling and chatting, as though the urgency of retrieving this piece of mail never occurred. Like the plan was always to drive my truck all the way out to this specific restaurant, for tacos and tequila margaritas. As if this mysterious mail didn't exist.

And I realize, that's how she wants me to feel. She wants me to forget about it.

The waitress swings back around to clear our plates and pick up the check. I lean back against the chair in which I'm seated and wait until we're alone again.

"So, what did we drive all the w-" I begin to ask, before she cuts me off.

"Your farmstand set up is adorable. I love it. I really hope my money will be good there next week." She fires off at me, turning from admiring the view of the ocean to face me once more. She's smiling, leaning forward to take another sip from the margarita straw. Before she does, she adds, "I really do try to shop locally. And you have a great selection. Do you grow everything you sell in those greenhouses?"

She uses the tip of her tongue to hook around the straw, positioning it center of her lips, before she sucks in a little sip with a smile that accentuates her cheek bones. The whole fucking ordeal was only a few brief seconds. And would have been a mundane, regular action by any other person. For some insane reason, she's got me hot under the collar about it.

The fuck was the first question?

"*I, uh*... Yeah, we grow everything in the greenhouses. Except the corn, the different berries and the pumpkins." I say, reining in my focus again. "I actually lease the entire place out to a farmer, he runs everything. I get to keep the farm stand stocked, and we go halves on the farmer's market. And no, it isn't... Your money, I mean. I'll let the girls know."

Her brows furrow. "What do you mean? I have to keep paying in muffins?"

I grin back at her. "I'm not going to turn down homemade dessert. But no, I mean it's on the house. Get whatever you want for the week. The only exceptions are the jarred goods. Jessica's grandmother supplies the home-made jams and local honey."

"Which one was Jessica?"

"The blonde. The brunette is Veronica. Nice girls." She looks at me through slightly narrowed eyes, a playful suspicion. "I know what you're thinking. But they're way too young for me. Plus, they're related to two of my MC brothers, which makes them *completely* off limits. Jessica is Chopper's granddaughter. Veronica is Snowy's niece. They work at my farm stand and do a little house mouse-ing for me."

"*House mouse-ing?*" She looks perplexed.

"Like a house maid. Cleaning, light shopping. Laundry." I shrug. "A lot of the younger women connected to the MC do it for some extra pocket money."

"I see."

"Anyway, I'll let them know the deal, for the next time you stop by."

"You don't have to do that." She shakes her head in refusal of my offer. "I know I told you I needed the part time work, but I can afford to pay you for your produce."

"I wasn't implying anything. Just being a nice guy, doll."

She lets out another sigh, watching me for a moment before she speaks. "I know, I'm sorry. I wasn't implying anything about you either." She says, a slight wave of her hand as if she can swipe her words away. "Thank you, it's very generous of you."

"I'll let the girls know."

"Are they the ones who decorate the outside? With the flower pots and such?"

"I keep it the way my mother had it. The flowers change as the seasons do. But I haven't changed a thing, otherwise."

"It's adorable. She must have been a sweet woman. She raised a good guy."

I fight back my kneejerk reaction to scoff at her last statement. Instead, I force a smile. "She was a sweet woman." That much of what Vanna assumes is true.

"What was your mother's name?"

"Madeline." I try not to think of her as I speak her name.

"*Madeline*. It's pretty."

"She was."

Vanna looks at me, in a way that tells me she's getting a read on something. "Were you close with your mother?"

Mercifully, our waitress returns with my credit card and the receipt, buying me time to contemplate a simple answer to what shouldn't be a complex question. "I loved my mother, very much." I sigh, grabbing the pen to scribble my signature on the receipt and add a tip. Placing the pen back down inside the booklet, I lean back against the chair and meet her curious eyes once more. "And my mother loved us." Despite the men in her life failing her at every turn. Myself included, in that sorry lot.

"You and your father?"

"She must have." To have stuck it out for so long with the vicious bastard that was my father. "But I was referring to my brother and I."

"Oh, I didn't know you had brother."

"I don't."

Her puzzled face is adorable, before her expression slowly turns to one of regret. "Oh my gosh... was he in the accident too?" She looks concerned for me, and the way she begins to reach for my hand across the table, then hesitates, thinking better of it as she pulls back from me, makes me smile. Her concern for me is touching. Her hesitance to *touch me*, however, makes me wonder what that's about. I can't help the slight feeling of loss that washes over me, at her reluctance to do so. I more than welcome her touch.

"No. He wasn't. My parents were killed in a freak motorcycle accident. My brother is alive and well, last I heard. Though, I try not to hear much."

She nods. "I'm sorry for your loss... You don't get along with your brother, then." She continues. It isn't a question, though her tone tells me she feels as if she needs to tread carefully with me on this topic. And honestly, it wouldn't bother me much if she did feel that way. Family history isn't one of my favorite topics.

"He's dead to me." I shrug.

We stare at each other for a few moments, before Vanna breaks our silence. "I'm sorry. Do you have other family?" she asks, as if she's concerned for me again.

"Lost my uncle, a few years ago. He never really got over the death of his sister. My mother... I've got my MC Brothers, though. Viking, Axel, Viper and the others. Viking and Axel are closer to me than my own blood is. And Cherry. She's like a sister to me. I'm not alone in the world, if that's your concern."

She nods. "I'm glad."

"Are you?"

"Why wouldn't I be? I'm sorry you've had so much loss in your life."

I shake my head. "No, I mean, are *you* alone, Vanna?" I clarify. "I know you live alone. You moved to our little town, an hour from where you work. What's up with that?"

She laughs, but it's without amusement. "I got sick of the traffic around here. Of sharing walls with people." She sighs. "I've always wanted to live in the country. The little farm house I'm renting needs work, but it's perfect for me, right now."

Fair enough. Can't say I blame her. But... "Where's your family?"

"Back in New York. We don't talk either." Before I can ask anything else, she continues with, "The ocean always makes me feel better. Since it's right there, do you want to go sit under the pier for a bit? Unless you want to head back?"

"Would *you* like to go sit beside the ocean, Vanna?"

"I miss it. Though, I do prefer it at night. It's cleansing, don't you think? The fresh air. Grounding in the sand. Releasing the negative vibes and letting all the quartz and the sea salt just transmute it to positive energy."

I can't help the grin tugging at the corners of my mouth as I listen to her speak.

"What?" she tries to fight her own grin. "Do I sound like a weirdo again?"

"I don't think you're a weirdo, Vanna. You're just different."

Her brown eyes narrow at me, but she's still smiling. "Different is a polite word for weirdo."

"I don't make a habit of insulting the fairer sex."

She looks at me, contemplatively. "You don't, do you?" she says, though I get the impression it's a rhetorical question.

"I'm not perfect. But I follow my own unwavering moral code."

"Like paying for dates." She teases me. "And rescuing women in bathrooms."

I shrug. "I do what I can." My attempt at modesty.

"Like giving the new comer in town a job, against your better judgement, because she needed it." Vanna smiles at me.

"You did well, though." It's not her fault I'm already territorial about her.

"Like ordering me a real meal, instead of a salad, last night. And not commenting that I ate both of my tacos today." Her smile hasn't faltered, but there's a rueful look in her pretty, dark eyes.

"Only a fucking prick would do something like that, Vanna." I say, trying not to frown at the thought of some fucking idiot having the audacity to make a comment like that to any woman. Especially a woman as gorgeous as Vanna. Now I know for sure there's a history of shitty guys in Vanna's past. Though, she did make it a point to tell me that she hasn't had a boyfriend in a long time. A woman as gorgeous as Vanna, single for a long time? Must have been a major asshole to put her off men. I can't imagine I'm the only guy in her life that's slipping into madness for her. Just the thought of other guys even attempting to court her elevates my blood pressure. I selfishly rejoice in silence as I remind myself, she hasn't had a man in a while. I understand where she's coming from, though. Lucinda messed me up for a few years myself. I'm not going to press her on this. At least, not yet.

"I think you're a good guy, Dean." Vanna says, pulling me out of my thoughts.

That makes one of us. "I try to be."

"Am I wrong about you?" she asks, searching my eyes.

"I'll be good to you, Vanna." I say it, because it's the truth. I would be good to her. I'm going to be good to her.

"I've been wrong before." She sighs.

I nod. "Then we've got something in common."

THE LETTERS ARE BURNING A HOLE IN MY PURSE AS I SIT BESIDE DEAN IN his truck. We're almost back to my house, after having spent the day together. I haven't mentioned them at all to him. I haven't looked at my bag once. I didn't excuse myself to the ladies' room to run off and read then, either. Though I wanted to, badly. I know he's curious about why I had to go all the way to Wilmington for an envelope that I haven't even bothered to open yet. I'm just not ready to talk about it. Any of it.

It's been a really long time since I've even considered dating anyone. Every time I look at Dean, every time he smiles at me, or finds some way to touch me, it feels like it's been even longer than it actually has. What started out as a mission to simply find the Knight, is slowly turning into something more. Something I didn't intend.

I like Dean. More than I should, having only known him a week. And this only being our second, somewhat, date. He really seems like more than a decent guy. Could he actually be my Knight? Some of the signs fit, technically, but not all. The morning star was supposed to be a key element to signify the Knight. But I haven't seen anything on him or around him that could represent that specific detail.

"So, when do I get to see you again?" Dean asks.

When I turn from the truck window to look at him, I find him smiling at me. His eyes are kind, and hopeful. The more time I spend with him, the less rough around the edges he seems. It's almost difficult to picture that other smile he's capable of. That smile that's fiercer, more intimidating, than some other men's glares.

"You want to see me again?" I tease, biting my lower lip lightly. It seems to have somewhat of an effect on him. Stirs something behind his eyes. Seeing him respond, even in the slightest ways to my subtle attempts at seduction, affects me too.

He doesn't answer me right away. He gives me a little smirk as he pulls the truck up my driveway, stopping behind my car beside the walk way to my front porch. Throwing it in park, he twists the keys to shut the truck off and leans back against the seat to look at me.

"I want very much to see you again. Throughout the week, not just when you're working for me. Not just on Sundays."

I can't help giggling. "That often? You'll be sick of me in a month."

He shakes his head, slow and serious. "I won't."

Squinting my eyes at him in mock suspicion, I jokingly ask, "Did you eat any of my muffins?"

"No. Not yet." His smile turns into a wicked grin. "However, I have every intention of eating your muffin, Vanna."

A little gasp escapes me at his bold inuendo. *"Muffins!"* I correct him, though I can't help returning his grin. "And here I thought you were a gentleman." I tease, reaching across the seat to playfully smack his arm. The motion causes me to accidentally knock my purse on the floor at my feet. I reach down to grab it, placing it back on my lap.

"I'm always a gentleman." He insists, that low, growly voice giving me butterflies again. "I promise."

"I'll hold you to it."

"Hold me to anything you want."

Playfully rolling my eyes at him, I grab the handle of the door and slide out of the passenger seat. My boots hit my driveway and I hear Dean exiting the truck as well, coming around to meet me.

"I'll walk you to your door." He insists.

"It's only ten or fifteen steps." I chuckle.

"You haven't answered my question, though." Dean says, walking beside me on the cracked cement walkway that leads to my porch steps.

When we make it to my front door, I stop to face him. "You never answered mine either."

He looks at me, one eye brow arched. "I didn't?" I shake my head. "Ask me again."

My lack of confidence strikes again. I veer the conversation slightly away. "Anyway, I don't get home from work until after six most nights. Unless it's a slow day, sometimes Laura, my boss, will let me leave early."

"I can work with that." Dean says, looking at me contemplatively for some reason.

"You can stop by the shop anytime you want, too." I lift my shoulder in a slight shrug.

"I intend to take you up on that, as well."

Pursing my lips and suddenly feeling awkward, I turn to open my storm door and unlock the solid oak one. As I twist the key, the dead bolt slides open with a soft clunk. "Well, thank you for spending the day with me."

Dean reaches to remove my hand from my keys, leaving them in the lock as he lifts my hand to his lips. "The pleasure was all mine, Vanna." I can't pull my eyes from his as I watch him kiss my hand. The sensation sends a shiver through me that I try to hide, but the mischievous look in his eyes tells me that it didn't go unnoticed. "And to answer your question, Vanna. I *am* offering." He winks at me.

My breath hitches for a brief moment, and I'm sure he noticed that, too. He slowly lowers my hand, but doesn't release it yet. He holds it between us, stroking the back of my fingers with his thumb, as we stare at each other.

"Any thoughts on the matter?" he asks, obviously feeling the need to prompt me due to my silence.

161

Feeling like a bashful idiot, I giggle and look away from him. "I suppose I'll have to think about it." I try to tease him, not wanting to appear too eager. Though, it is something I should think about. I haven't dated anyone in a long time, for a reason. Am I really ready for another relationship? How would the Knight fit into everything? *Is he the Knight?* If so, this isn't supposed to be happening this way... I wasn't supposed to develop any feelings, and neither was the Knight. Is the fact that we might be developing feelings for one another, a clear sign that he *isn't* the Knight? Though, who's to say Dean's feelings actually go beyond the physical aspects of a dating relationship? The way women fawn over him, I can't imagine him not being a very virile man...

I watch as a slight grin tugs at the corner of his mouth. "Fair enough. I'm not going anywhere. Hold me to that, too."

"I might." I smile back, releasing his hand. "Good night, Dean." I say, twisting the door knob as I'm about to walk inside.

"Wait."

I freeze, looking back at him. His playful expression has transformed into something more stoic. Unreadable. "What's wrong?"

Dean reaches into his back pocket and produces two envelopes, folded in half, holding them out to me. "These must have fallen out of your purse in my truck."

Though I'm fully aware of him watching me intently, I cannot help snatching the letters from his hand and clutching them to my chest as my heart pounds.

"*Oh,* thank you." I say, willing my voice to sound calm, though my re-action clearly spoke volumes on its own. And to the contrary, damnit. It's probably too late to down play anything. I look up into his eyes in an attempt to read him.

"No problem." He says, his tone even. His expression still unrevealing of anything. "After our little excursion to retrieve them, I didn't think you'd be too pleased to find them missing."

I force myself to laugh a little bit. "Right." I agree, but I'm not willing to talk about them. I glance at the letters in my hand for a moment, wonder-ing if he looked at who they were from. I wait to see if he brings up the fact that they're from a prison in upstate New York.

"Well, good night then, Vanna." Dean says, after a few more moments of silence between us. I look up into his eyes. It's only an instinctual feeling, but I don't think he pried. Behind his eyes, I do see curiosity, but not paired with a level of concern that might reveal to me he did see the origin of the let-ters. Perhaps, he is now wishing he had taken a peek when he had the chance without my knowing. But he didn't. I can just tell, he didn't. And I'm grateful for that seemingly small act of kindness. That sign of respect he must have for me and my privacy.

"Thank you."

He nods once, as if he knows I don't *just* mean thank you for giving them back. I also mean thank you for taking me to get them in the first place, and not asking me questions about it. Thank you for dinner. Thank you for saving me, and giving me a part time job when you didn't have to. Thank you for being a decent man.

As I take a step closer to him, raising myself up a little higher on my tippy toes, I lean towards him as he bends slightly, allowing me to kiss him on the cheek.

"Good night, Dean." I say again, before I step back from him.

"Will *you* promise me something?" he suddenly asks. I look back at him with piqued curiosity. "We both work during the week, and so... I mean... It doesn't have to be permanent, or even long term." He says, almost stammering. "A *for now*, type of thing. Hell, you don't even have to promise me... *Fuck...* I was wrong to even spring this on you." His expression no longer stoic, he looks more regretful than anything else, and runs his hand through the dark hair on top of his head. "Never mind. Have a good night, Vanna." He turns, walking hurriedly down my porch steps.

"What is it?" I call after him.

He stops, turning back around to face me at the bottom of my steps. "It's wrong of me to ask."

"Ask anyway. I can always say no, can't I?"

"Always, Vanna." He says, in such an impassioned way.

"So, ask me." I push.

He takes a breath, studying me for a moment before he decides to go for it. "I was going to ask you to promise me Sundays." He sighs. "But you don't owe me anythi-"

"I promise you Sundays."

A slight smile pulls at his mouth, relief evident in his kind eyes. "I really don't want you to feel obligated, Vanna."

"Maybe I want to spend Sundays with you." I give him a little shrug. "I kinda like you, Dean." I can't help smirking at him.

He grins back at me. "My offer wasn't really an *offer*."

Placing a hand on my hip, I pretend to glare at him. "Oh, now you think you have the upper hand, do you?" I tease.

"Never." He shakes his head. "It wasn't an offer, so much as it was a *hope*. You asked me if I was offering when I asked you if you wanted one. A man."

"And you didn't answer me. You left me hanging." I pretend to pout.

"No, few things hurt quite the same as the sting of rejection." He shrugs. "You're different, Vanna. I like that about you. But I think I might be different to you, too. I know I am."

"What are you trying to say, Dean?" It's not like him to beat around the bush, at least that's the impression I've gotten from him so far.

"Guess I was just afraid if I said, yeah, I am offering to be your guy, it would have come across all wrong, because I didn't mean for it to sound as if I would ever believe I'd be doing you any favors by it."

"I wouldn't have taken it that way."

"I'm glad... But I still wouldn't be doing you any favors. It's more like the other way around."

I cross my arms and lean against the door frame, asking, "How do you figure that?"

"I think you're a sweet girl, Vanna. A classy woman." He sighs. "I'm a dreg by comparison. You could do a lot better than a guy like me."

"Dean..." I try to interject, but he doesn't let me finish.

"You could, Vanna. You really could... But... *I don't want you to.*" His grin returns. "I'm going to be a selfish prick about it. I'm warning you now."

I can't help giggling at him again. "Are you?"

He nods. "Last night, the way every man in that restaurant was looking at you..." he brings his fist to his mouth, biting his knuckle, jokingly.

I laugh again. "Stop it. Nobody noticed me."

"Oh, they did. They always do." He insists. "But nobody does, more than me."

"That's all that really matters, then." I tease.

"So, you will consider me, then?" he asks, his tone hopeful.

"*And* promise you Sundays?" I smirk.

He shakes his head. "No, I won't hold you to that. I shouldn't have asked that of you."

"Will you promise me Sundays, then?"

"Yes." He says, instantly. "At your discretion, yes, I promise you Sundays."

"Deal, then." I smile at him.

"Aces." He smiles back at me.

I watch the tail lights of Dean's truck drive up the road to his ranch on top of the hill, before I close and lock my front door. The letters in my hand, the only thing that could put a damper on our sweet little exchange.

I think I could really like him. I *do*, really like him. But I also need to be careful. These letters are a stern reminder of that cold hard fact.

As I move to the hall closet to remove the box where I keep the collection of His letters from prison, I force myself to read what it is He has to say, this time. Not much has changed in the three years since He went away for nearly killing me that night on Christmas Eve. Nearly beating me, and strangling me to death in the cold snow.

I shudder at the memory. Thank God a neighbor heard my screams for help...

Opening the letter to Joey first, I skim over it. Veiled threats of bodily harm if my former roommate didn't get in contact with him to tell him where I was. This is why I never told Joey, or anyone else, besides Laura and Ethan, where I was moving. Joey has no idea where I am, either. Not that I think Joey would contact him and tell him. It's just another level of precaution I took. I'm so tired of moving. Running from a man who can't even physically chase me... *yet.*

Tossing Joey's letter into the box, I move on to the one addressed to me. *Giovanna, my love... I'm sorry...*

Remorse... Remorse is better than hate... but he's flipflopped back and forth before. In his letters, as well as in our relationship. I've heard

164

all the promises before. To never hit me again. Only to hit me again. To be less controlling, only to tighten the chains...

I place his letter in the box as well. There's no need to read the whole thing. I don't believe him, for one. Secondly, I've read similar a dozen times over. The next one he sends will detail explicit, violent fantasies of his revenge. I don't want to think of those letters now. I place the lid back on the box and shove it onto the shelf in the closet beside another box of odds and ends left behind by the landlord.

I'm still one step ahead of Him. And I've done things differently, this time. I have two years to live my life without having to look over my shoulder. Four if I'm lucky.

Closing the closet door on the letters and my shameful past for now, I allow myself to wonder what these next two years could possibly look like... And if these two years might include Dean Keegan. For the first time, in a long time, I let myself hope for something more...

One Month Later

THIS SUNDAY MORNING IS MY FIRST VISIT TO THE FARMERS MARKET. DEAN said it would be set up near the water front down town, around the large Gazebo in the grass lot. He would be stopping by again sometime after eleven to make sure everything was going smoothly. His set up looks to be one of the more permanent ones. Not a tear down at the end of the day type deal, but actual heavy wooden box tables and a sturdy fixed shelter to keep his staff and produce in the shade from the hot sun. Jessica and Veronica are manning the stand for him. I know neither one of them are fans of mine, so I wait a little while before I go over, browsing the other tables and booths that are here.

There are other fruit and vegetable vendors, but there are also craft tables, jewelry tables and tables selling homemade pies and other desserts, as well as local honey and jams. I approach the table selling the honey and jam, recognizing the label as the same maker Dean sells at his farm. The old woman smiling at me from behind the table, under her umbrella, must be Jessica's grandmother. I smile back at her.

"I've purchased your honey before, from the Keegan Farm."

"Oh, yes!" she says, happily. "My granddaughter works for Mr. Keegan. He's such a nice man."

Mr. Keegan. I giggle inside. *Why is that funny to me?*

"This honey is great. I've never tasted better before."

"Clover honey, dear. The bee's harvest pollen from a huge clover field." She explains. "A distinct taste. Straight from the hives. In late summer through the fall, they harvest Golden Rod."

"It's wonderful. I'd love to try some of your jam, too. Do you have a favorite?"

"The blueberry jam is a popular one. Blackberry too. We actually source the bulk of our berries from Mr. Keegan's orchards."

Then I'll have to try both. I place one of each on the table in front of her. "I'll take these two. Thank you." I say, pulling out my money from my purse. I hand her a ten and she hands me a small bag with the jars inside.

"Have a blessed day, dear." She smiles.

"Blessed be."

Damn it... It just slipped out of my mouth.

I smile back at her, then walk away before anything can come of it. It's annoying that such a peaceful saying could be construed negatively simply because it's a *"Witchy phrase"*, but you never know how people in the Bible Belt will react. And I don't want any trouble. This isn't Laura's shop, which is located in a more city like area, near colleges and more religious and spiritual diversity. This is out in the country with the Bible Thumpers, where they probably still think Witches are the Devil's Whores and we dance naked and steal husbands and drink the blood of children.

I shake it off and peruse the next couple of tables and booths, killing time. It isn't long before I hear it whispered, though, I try to ignore it. I never should have told anyone what my day job was. It's a small town. Word travels fast in a small town. And I'm the new comer.

"Witch bitch." Someone sneers at me.

I keep my chin up and stay on course. Making my way casually towards *Mr. Keegan's* set up.

"Devil worshipper." This time I can tell it's a man's voice. "Whore!"

Okay. That does it. Whore is pushing it, who does this jackass think he is to judge me? He's probably banging Peggy Sue at the Piggly Wiggly behind his wife Mildred's back.

I turn around to see who is taunting me. It's a guy, older than me. Probably early fifties, wearing overalls and standing with a bunch of his farmer looking buddies. There's a younger guy with them too, maybe about my age. Probably his son, who's looking at me with a little less disdain than the older guys, but I still don't like it. It makes me feel uneasy. Even in a crowd of people on a bright sunny day.

"You heard what I said, bitch." The ring leader scowls at me.

I'm not taking on five men. I turn back around and try to distract myself with the lovely array of homemade pies and fudges at the next table. The woman behind the setup is kind of glaring at me too. She must have heard them, took one look at me and decided I was exactly what they called me. I pull my cell phone out of my purse and glance at the time. It's eleven now. Dean should be here soon. Shoving my cell back in my bag, I decide to just head straight over to his stand across the lawn and wait for him.

Stepping away from the table with the pies, I walk across the grass, glancing at the group of men in time to see them shove the younger guy in my direction. Taunting him, as if daring him to come up to me and say or

166

do something. I walk a little faster, creating as much distance between us as possible.

"Good morning." I say with forced pleasantry to Veronica and Jessica, though I'm somewhat relieved to have made it here before any of those guys could come up to me. I glance over my shoulder to see them lingering near the big oak tree in the middle of the lawn a few yards away, watching me.

"Dean isn't here." Veronica mumbles, not bothering to return the greeting since Dean isn't around to witness her rudeness. "He was here this morning setting up, he might not be back." She adds. I know it's a technical lie. He told me he would be. She just wants me to leave before he gets back.

I roll my eyes behind my sunglasses. Veronica must still think I'm just the neighbor with the hots for him. I doubt Dean talks to her about anything other than her car problems and farmstand business. She probably has no idea we've been on dates, or that I've been working for him, too. She's obviously not significant enough in his life for him to have mentioned any of it to her.

I decide to just let it go for now and watch as Veronica walks away to help a customer with a purchase. She's all smiles and *thank you for your business* with everyone else. More clear evidence she's definitely got an attitude with me. When she walks by me again, I ask to buy a bottle of water. She tells me it's three bucks, I pay and she places the water on the counter, walking away to put the money in the cash box. No pleasantries at all.

The hate all around me at this market is really starting to get to me. I should just go home and text Dean to get up with me after he's done with everything he has to do for the day. But unless I want to walk all the way around the market, to the street and around the first block of buildings to get to my car, I have to cross the five guys who were saying vulgar things to me, and are clearly up to something.

Screw it. It's not like they can actually hurt me in front of all these people. Shoving the bottle of water in my purse, I adjust the strap on my arm and grab the wide brim of my garden hat. Tugging it slightly down so it blocks the side of my face from them, I walk back across the open lawn towards the parking lot. If one of them comes up to me, I'll hit them in the face with the bag holding the two jars of jam.

"You're gonna burn, bitch!"

Just keep walking... Just keep walking...

The jam lady waves to me. Seems like she's the only nice one here. I wave back to her, but I keep up my hurried pace, until a hand grabs my elbow, halting me. My heart racing, I whirl around expecting to see one of the mean rednecks gripping my arm.

"Where you running off to, baby?" Dean asks, his handsome face smiling at me. I let out a sigh of relief, gripping the leather on his arm as I try to steady my nerves. He's wearing his jacket. That means he came on his bike. "Vanna? What's wrong?"

I shake my head, quietly telling him, "Nothing. I didn't hear your bike. I thought maybe you got tied up and couldn't make it. I was going to text you later."

167

"I had to park the bike a block away. And I'd have text you if I wasn't going to meet you."

"Right. Sorry." I briefly glance past him at the five guys who are watching us. "Um... Veronica... She said you might not be coming." He looks at me, perplexed. Probably wondering why she would say that to me, when she knew he'd be back. He probably told her so himself. "Doesn't matter. I was going to text you to see if you just want to meet up later. I was leaving."

"Did something happen?"

"Not really."

"*Not really*, isn't no." his brows pull together as he studies me. "So, what happened?"

"Those guys behind you, by the oak." I glance past him again. Dean immediately twists around to look at them.

"Yeah, I see them. What about them?" He demands. The tone in his voice already tells me he's about to go over to them.

"They were calling me things. Saying I'm gonna burn."

He turns back to me. His eyes dark angry slits. "What kind of things?"

"Witch. Bitch. Whore. I'm pretty sure they were trying to get the younger one to come up to me for something."

"*Right.*" Dean growls. He grabs my wrist and pulls me with him as he makes a beeline for the five men standing under the shade of the oak. I have to hold my hat on my head to keep it from falling off, nearly jogging to keep up with his long, determined strides.

The five men suddenly don't look so tough in Dean's presence, now that we're only a few feet apart from them.

"You limp dicks got something you wanna say?" Dean asks them, point blank. He sounds pissed. None of them say anything. "Of course not." He says, eyeing each of them. "Take a good look at her. Take a real good look, fellas. Pretty, ain't she?" He steps back from me, looking at me himself. "Yes indeed. A fine fuckin' woman. Sexy as Hell." He strokes the stubble on his jawline, looking me over, appraisingly.

I look at him like he's crazy, standing here stunned. He glances back at the guys, as if they're all suddenly friends. The men are looking at him like he's lost his damn mind too.

"Baby, give us a little spin. Show off that pretty dress you got on, doll." He says, cocking his chin at me, and gesturing with his finger for me to spin around. "Go on, baby." He insists.

As awkward as I feel right now, I do what he asks, and turn around for him.

"The body on this one, am I right?" Dean says, "Fuckin' gorgeous. You can say so." He taunts them. "You'd have to be blind, or fucking gay to disagree with me. Are you fuckers blind or gay?"

None of them say a word. They look a little more nervous too.

Dean takes a few steps back towards me. "Well, I hope you thin dicked weasels enjoyed yourselves." He says, his tone sliding from mock friendliness, back to sinister and threatening. He pulls the huge knife from the sheath that hangs from his belt and holds it up, twisting it so that it glints in the sunlight. "Because if you ever fucking look in her direction again, I'll cut your fucking eyes out." He growls. Inwardly, I jolt at his sudden, serious threat. "If you ever say another fucking word to her, I will cut your fucking tongues out. And if you should ever *fucking touch her*, I'll cut your fucking junk off and feed it to you... You pricks picking up what I'm putting down?"

The five men are just staring at him. A few moments of silence pass.

"Maybe you need a demonstration?" Dean asks, waggling the tip of the knife at them. "Which one of you called her a whore?"

They suddenly look even more afraid, especially the ring leader. None of them say a word.

"Baby, which one of them called you a whore?" he asks me.

I look at the ring leader, who suddenly looks like he's about to shit himself. Dean sees it and guesses for himself, walking closer to the guy.

"*This guy*, doll?"

"Yes." I say, barely. My voice almost cracking on that one simple word.

Dean drops his arm with the blade in a circular motion and brings it up between the guy's legs, holding the blade against the denim of his overalls.

My hand flies to my mouth, stifling a gasp, as everyone's eyes widen, including mine.

"You called *my* woman, a *whore*?" Dean asks him, his tone low, deep and scary as Hell.

"*I – I- Uh...*" the guy stutters. "I'm sorry. I apologize."

"Do you know who I am?" Dean asks. The man nods. "Who am I?"

"Know you're a biker."

Dean shakes his head. "That's not good enough. You got a wallet on you?" The guy nods. "Grab that for me, *carefully*. I got a real sharp knife to your dick right now."

The guy reaches into his back pocket slowly, then hands Dean his wallet. Dean flips it open casually and glances at the guy's license.

"John McKinney. 3405 Packard Lane." Dean says, flipping the wallet shut and handing it back to him. "Got a few friends that live around there. Nice area. Anyway, my name is Dean Keegan. In case you decide you want to call the police and make a complaint about me."

The guy shakes his head. "No, I ain't gonna do that."

"Why's that, John McKinney, of 3405 Packard Lane?" Dean asks, obviously demonstrating there's no question as to whether or not he retained the guy's information.

"I was in the wrong, and I apologize to your woman and to you, for my poor behavior. It won't happen again."

Dean glances at the other four guys. "How about you fuckers? We clear on this whole situation?" They all nod and express nervous words of agreement. "So, what happens next time you happen to notice this pretty lady?" Dean asks.

"We're gonna leave her alone." John McKinney says. "Right, fellas?" They all agree again, and Dean takes a step back from John, flipping his knife up and back down into the sheath at his hip with a flourish. As if he's done it a million times... I wonder if he has.

"I really think that's best for everyone." Dean comes to stand by my side, wrapping his arm around my waist. "Have a nice day, fellas." His words are anything but friendly. He escorts me away from the group of men that he basically just verbally castrated... and the one he almost actually did. "You okay, baby?" he asks me, now that we're a few yards away from them. Part of me is still in shock over what he did.

"Are you a criminal?" I just blurt it out.

Dean laughs at me. A genuine, hardy laugh, as he touches my face gently, taking a breath before he speaks. "Oh, baby... That was *adorable*." He says with a grin. Dropping his hand from my face, he takes the bag of jams from me to carry it, like a gentleman. His other hand raising to wave to Jessica's grandmother. "Good morning, Mrs. Townsend!" He calls to her, a beaming smile on his handsome face. "Real nice lady." He says, as we continue to walk across the outdoor market together.

I can't help noticing that Dean didn't actually answer my question...

Chapter
eight
DEAN

SLAMMING MY FISTS INTO THE LEATHER punching bag, I attempt to focus on my workout. Doing my best to tune out Viking's incessant pestering about my relationship status with Vanna. It's a losing battle, though. I know this. The man is relentless.

"If you're going to stand there busting my balls, you might as well brace the fucking bag for me and make yourself useful." I snap at him.

"Somebody hasn't gotten laid yet." He mutters, grabbing hold of the bag from behind. "Now let's see you throw some real hits, since you ain't hittin' it with *Vanna*." He taunts.

I let out a half-suppressed laugh, throwing a combination of punches and a swift side kick. "You don't know shit about me and Vanna." I grunt through a few more strikes.

"I know you guard that pussy like a fucking wolf watches over its mate."

"She's not just pussy." I try to keep the growl out of my voice, focusing on expelling my aggravation on the bag.

"Not *just* pussy... So, it's *Sunday Funday* after all." He grins at me, slapping the side of the bag enthusiastically. "No wonder we haven't seen a trace of you these last seven Sundays. A fuck-a-thon on a Sunday, beats dragging your ass to the gym another day."

I can feel myself wincing at his words. It feels wrong to let him think I am fucking her, when I'm not. I haven't even gotten close. I haven't even really kissed her yet. A chaste kiss on the cheek or the hand, a hug now and again. Taking things slow. There's something in her past she hasn't told me about. My instincts are telling me not to press my luck, though every time I'm near her, it's a challenge not to. I want to grab her and kiss her, but she seems content with where we're at. I don't want to fuck it up. It's been a long time since a woman has mattered to such a degree with me.

"Must be some grade A puss-" Viking starts in again, but I cut him off.

"Enough." I warn him. "I'm being a gentleman. You should fucking try it sometime."

His shit eating grin makes me want to swing around the bag and nail him square in the face. *"Bro..."* the laughter in his voice is palpable.

"Shut up." I warn him again, striking the bag a few more times.

"Bro... You're not telling me that you haven't sampled that-"

I take a quick step back from the bag, lifting my foot to kick it solidly dead center, rocking it backwards into his chest with a thud. The giant ass-hole only laughs at me.

"Shut the fuck up." I mutter at him, ripping off my open fingered gloves and chucking them on the bench against the wall. "I came here to get a work out in, not have my balls busted."

"Gotta get something in somewhere if Vanna ain't putting out." He snickers.

I glare at him, moving over to the dumbbells and grabbing a pair without looking. I get to pumping iron, staring ahead at the half black, half gray painted cinderblock wall of our makeshift gym.

"She ain't like the chicks we're used to." I mutter.

"I've noticed. Believe me." He says, his tone still dripping with crudeness. "I still can't believe you've known her almost two months and haven't tapped that."

I shake my head. "Some things are worth the wait. We're getting to know each other. This can't be that much of a foreign concept to you."

"The concept, no. I get it, in theory. But fuck that. I'm not looking to settle down any time soon. Not when there are so many hotties that practically throw themselves at us." He grins at me, in a way I know that I need to brace myself for whatever the Hell is about to spill out of his goddamned mouth next. "Unless Vanna's got a twin sister you can set me up with."

I don't bother responding. It's no use. It's fuel to the fire of his burning need to aggravate the shit out of me.

"I'm just fucking with you, Bro." Viking sighs, after a few moments of blissful silence between us. "It's good to see you somewhat happy for a change. Instead of the mopey dick you've been the last few years. Vanna seems nice. A sweet girl."

"She is." I agree, continuing to curl the weights as if I haven't been tempted to throw them at him.

"*Bet she tastes sweet, too.*"

I slam the weights back on the rack. "Ring. *Now.* You and me."

He looks surprised. "The fuck, Bro? You can't take a joke now?"

"I've asked you *repeatedly* not to talk about Vanna like that. Obviously, I need to beat it into you." I growl at him, getting in his face, though to do so, even I have to look up. "I'm not fucking around. I'm serious about her."

"Alright, *Lancelot.* Calm down." He says, hands up in mock surrender.

We both know it would be a knock-down, drag out fight if Viking and I actually did go at it. It wouldn't be unlike the first time, almost fifteen years ago, before we became brothers. It would be another blood bath. We're both skilled fighters. Though I've stayed in practice in the underground fighting circuits. He gave it up a few years ago.

"Mock me with that *Lancelot* shit all you want. I will defend her honor." I scowl at him.

"I'm not mocking you, Dean. I was just fucking with you. I didn't realize you were already in *this* place with her." He sighs. "I thought you just wanted to bang her for a while. But you're right, she's not like the usual chicks that hang around."

"The fuck did I just walk in on?" Axel's voice interrupts us as he walks into the gym.

I take a step back from Viking, turning away from him to face Axel. "Nothing."

"Was just telling Dean that Vanna seems like a nice woman." Viking says.

"Oh yeah, I like her." Axel smiles as he approaches us, flipping the towel he had draped over his shoulder onto the rack of dumbbells. He sets his water bottle down on the ground. "Cherry thinks she's nice, too. She's glad she's stuck it out working the bar with her. They get along well." He glances at me. "Why do you look pissed, then?"

I shake my head. "I'm not. Warm up with Viking on the bag. I'll spar with you after."

"Uh... I've seen what you do to Viper when you look pissed off, Dean. I'm not so sure I want to spar with you, Bro. No offense or anything, you know I love you." Axel says.

I can't help chuckling at him. "Would I ever hurt you, kid?"

"Not intentionally." He grins.

I reach out and dishevel his dirty blonde, slicked back hair. "Not *ever*, is more like it." I say, letting him push my arm away after a moment.

"I gotta talk to you about something." He says, looking between me and Viking. I notice Viking shake his head slightly at Axel, then Axel nods.

"What?" I ask. "Is something wrong?"

"Everything is fucking wrong." Axel heaves a sigh. "But I've prospected all these years, I'm not giving up the hope that you'll come back. I'm getting patched in, on my Twenty-first Birthday. The club voted me in, officially... I'm finally gonna be a Savior."

173

I was only a few years older than Axel is now, when I first met him at 8 years old. Nobody has wanted to be a Savior longer, or worked harder to become inducted into the Saviors MC than Axel has. He started prospecting as soon as he was old enough to ride a motorcycle. It's a bitter sweet moment.

"Congratulations, kid." I say, squeezing his shoulder. "You've more than earned your patch."

He nods. "Too bad it ain't the same club, though. Ain't the same without you in it, Dean... You're the reason I ever even wanted this."

"I don't need a cut to be your brother, Axel. We've been brothers for thirteen years. Club or no. Nothing is going to change that. Same goes for this asshole." I cock my head towards Viking. "Even when I want to kill him."

"So, you'll come, then? To my patch party?" Axel asks.

"I wouldn't miss it for anything, kid." I promise, patting him on the arm. "Go warm up, so I can toss your scrawny ass around the ring."

He grins at me. "While you still can. I'm gonna be like you some day, Dean. Watch me."

Axel is already a better man than I ever was, but I grin back at him. "I'm watching, kid." And I do just that, taking a seat on the workout bench to watch them warm up.

Axel has come so far from when I first met him. His mother was a woman in one of the safe houses we worked with, years ago. He had lived there with her for eight months. I spent a lot of time with Axel when I was on guard duty at their safe house. He loved the motorcycles. Always wanting to sit on them, twist the throttles and make them roar. It brings a smile to my face, remembering him as that little dirty blonde boy, fascinated by our Harleys and our MC cuts.

He took a particular liking to me, though. Probably because I would play catch with him outside on the lawn, the days I was there. And his mother trusted me enough to take him around the block a few times on the motorcycle at least once a week. He has always been a very positive natured individual, even despite the Hellish environment he was raised in with an abusive father. Something else we have in common. One would think he would have been a fearful child of adult males. Especially us rough, tough bikers. Not Axel, though. He looked at us like we were heroes. I guess, in a small way we were, to him. Though, I'm not sure if Axel realizes how much I admire him. Even as the little kid he'd been.

There was a day, when I was on guard duty, a rainy shitty day, where I spent the majority of my shift under the carport on my bike to keep somewhat dry. Axel had poked his head out and asked me if I wanted to come inside. We could play video games, he had suggested. Or his mom could make us soup.

I had to explain to him that we weren't allowed inside the house. That there were other women who lived with him there, that would not be comfortable with a man in the house. Especially us. He had looked at me, and I remember that puzzled expression on his face, because he didn't say a word. He marched back inside and returned five minutes later, wearing a garbage bag like a poncho, his head poked through the top, and his mother's too big for his feet purple rain boots. He dragged a folding chair out with him and set it up next to my bike. He sat with me until his mother had to physically drag his stubborn ass back in the house after an hour or so.

We didn't really say a whole lot though, that whole time he sat with me. I had asked him what he was thinking about. He wore such a contemplative expression for a little kid, sitting in his makeshift rain gear, staring ahead at the end of the driveway. A Ziplock of Cheez-Its in his lap. All he had said, was that we were *the good guys*...

I made sure I was there the day Axel and his mom were moving out to a place of their own. Something had happened to Axel's deadbeat father and he was no longer a threat to them. They were free to go live their lives without fear of him. I remember being happy for them. His mother was excited about the little single-family home with a small yard and a garden, just a county away, that she had found for them. Axel had been anxious since he found out they would be leaving. For two weeks, he had been extra full of questions about the bikes. Extra curious about how far we would ride the bikes. As if he were afraid that he'd never see us again, and this was his roundabout kid way, of trying to figure out if we'd visit him at his new house.

The day of their move, was the first time I had seen a tear in the kid's eyes. I had gone with them to their court dates before, where Axel faced his dirtbag father. There had been no tears. I had been there when he'd skid his knees in the driveway, trying to show off a skateboarding move. There had been no tears. But this day, there had been tears.

I walked over to assure him he would be okay. That he and his mom were safe now, and if they ever felt like they were not safe, they could call me and I would be there. He looked up and point blank told me he wasn't afraid of anybody. That he was tough and he was strong, like me. Like the bikers that guarded the safehouse. That he was gonna be a *good guy* with a motorcycle, too. I had asked him, well then what's with the waterworks, kid? And he had taken a breath, wiped his nose with the back of his sleeve, and looked me in the eyes when he told me that he wished I was his big brother, so he'd never have to say goodbye.

The little shit choked me up. Damn near broke my fuckin' heart. I had to pull him into a hug so he wouldn't see it. Told him I was his brother, that this was *see ya later*, not goodbye. And that if he wanted to be an MC Brother when he was big enough, he had a spot waiting for him.

Now, I look at Axel, a young man throwing combination strikes and kicks at the bag, working up a sweat. About to become a fully patched member of the MC he's looked up to all these years. The way he wears his Prospect cut proudly, all day every day. He practically lives in it. And I'm proud and disappointed at the same time. Proud of the man Axel grew up to be. How could I not be? He's as loyal as they come. To me. To Cherry. More loyal than my own blood brother, by leaps and bounds. And Axel is tough, brave and smart. Never lost his positive outlook on life, either. Always the eternal optimist of our fucked up little family. He was one of the lights in the darkness that consumed my life in the not-so-distant past. Axel means more to me than I could ever express.

The disappointment I feel is for the MC, though, I'm partially to blame for not fighting hard enough to keep things going the way they should have stayed. For getting kicked out and losing my influence. The MC who's cut Axel proudly rocks, is dead. A lost cause. An abandoned mission. One that was close to both of our hearts for exactly the same reasons.

Now, the Saviors MC exists in name only. A shame. Just another typical social club. Axel's heroes hung up their capes.

"Alright, Bro, I'm warmed up!" Axel says, making his way to the ring. Viking tosses him a set of head gear. "Remember, I said Vanna was nice." He says, slipping the gear on.

I grin and shake my head. "Eighty, Forty, kid."

"Yeah, but your forty percent is a regular guys eighty percent." Axel says, hopping around in his corner of the ring as I grab my MMA gloves and slip them back on. "Plus, Viking already pissed you off, I can tell."

Viking and I glance at each other, before we look back at Axel. "He apologized. We're good." I say.

"Oh, I did?" Viking pipes up.

"Didn't you?" I growl.

"Whatever." Viking grunts.

"Thought so." I say, jumping into the ring with Axel. It's the closest thing to an apology one can ever expect from Viking. I'll take it, this time.

"Oh shit." Axel says under his breath, squaring up with me, though I can tell he's nervous as he watches me raise my fists to a fighting position. "Vanna's so pretty, Dean. So pretty, in the most respectful way a guy can call a girl pretty." He rambles.

I can't help chuckling and shaking my head at him. "Axel, relax. Throw a few shots at me, I'm just gonna block for now."

He nods, moving forward and throwing a few jabs at me, half-heartedly.

"Eighty, kid. That's more like twenty. Come on. Show me what you've got." I push him.

"I've got mad respect for Vanna, that's what I've got, Dean." He says.

I can't help shaking my head again, dropping my fists and looking between the two of them. "Am I really that bad, guys?" I have to ask.

Axel presses his lips together, wide eyed, and looks at Viking.

"Yeah. You are." Viking says. "You get a little *psycho territorial* when it comes to a chick you like. Granted, it's been a long time since you've been this way about a chick, but a psycho you tend to be, Bro. When you're *in love*."

"*In love*?" I look at him incredulously. "I've known her barely more than seven weeks. I've only been out with her a dozen or so times."

Viking scoffs at me. "I'm sayin!" he shakes his head. "Fuckin' *psycho*."

"Look, guys, I like her. I like her a lot. But *in love* is a stretch." I say. Axel still has his lips pressed together, his fists up, looking between me and Viking silently. And Viking is looking at me like I'm the one that's late to the party.

176

I take a deep breath and let it out slowly as I contemplate what they're saying. It would be easy to fall in love with Vanna. I love everything about her. But *In love... already*? Is that even possible?

"You look confused." Viking says. "Like you're trying to figure out the *Riemann Hypothesis* or some shit."

I shake my head and turn back to Axel, lifting my fists up again to continue his sparring lesson. "Hit me, Axel. Come on." I encourage him.

"Yeah, hit him, like Cupids Arrow!" Viking taunts us from beside the ring. "Or at least try to knock some sense into his brain."

"Bro, shut up!" Axel practically begs Viking, though he's afraid to take his eyes off me.

"Maybe if you hit him hard enough, he'll see better." Viking continues. "See what we see."

"Just ignore him, Axel." I say, circling to his left, forcing Axel to move around the ring at least.

"Yeah Axel, ignore me like Dean's ignoring his feelings right now." Viking pushes.

"Throw a few combos at me. I'm just gonna block. Get comfortable in the ring, kid." I try to coach Axel once again. Axel nods, moving towards me again to throw a few jabs and cross punches. "Good form, kid. Just throw them harder. Come on. Sixty percent isn't going to hurt me." I push him. "Bring it up to Eighty."

"That's right, Axel. No *love* taps. Leave that to Dean." Viking comments from the one-man peanut gallery.

I can see Axel fighting hard not to laugh at that one, and I can't help cracking a grin at Viking's stupid joke either.

As I allow myself to be Axel's moving punching bag, I can't help my mind drifting back to Vanna. It really would be so easy to fall for her. Not allowing myself to fall for her, however, that would be the challenge. That would be like fighting thirteen grueling rounds in a ring with a skilled opponent. A goddamned knockdown, drag out battle.

Vanna, however, doesn't seem quite so inclined when it comes to me. Not saying she doesn't like me. She must. She spends her free time with me, even after working her weekends in The Twisted Throttle. But, Hell, she hasn't even *kissed* me yet. I'm in that dangerous territory of having stronger feelings for her than she does for me.

Fuck! I need to rein in my emotions. My Brothers are right. This is crazy. This thirteen-round battle has already begun, and I'm already losing it. I can't lose again. Not after last time.

My heart feels heavy, though, as my rational mind steps back into the ring with it. Feelings vs Rationality.

Round one...

Fight...

Vanna

L AURA CALLS ME DOWN FROM UPSTAIRS, TO INFORM ME OF A WALK IN REIKI appointment. As I descend the staircase and round the corner between the two columns to enter our main display room, I find myself face to face with a familiar townie. Garrett Johnson. My neighbor.

"Oh!" I can't help my surprised reaction. "Garrett, I didn't expect to see you all the way out here." I should be friendly and professional towards him. He is one of the few people that have, for the most part, been over all welcoming to me. And he is, after all, my direct neighbor. "How can I help you today?"

"I was hoping for a massage." He says. There are at least three massage parlors that even I know of, between our hometown and this shop. Several in this area alone. He has another agenda, but I smile sweetly.

"Have you ever experienced a Reiki massage?" I ask, already knowing the answer will be No. I try to give him the benefit of the doubt though. At least he's here. In a witch shop. As a patron. He isn't holding up a protest sign or a bible quote.

"No ma'am." He says, adjusting that blue ball cap over his short, white hair.

"It's not the same as a regular massage. It's strictly energetic." I explain. He looks intrigued, but there's something else about his vibe and his expression. I'll flush it out of him momentarily. He's here for me. I smile again. "There's hardly any touching with a Reiki massage." I add, waiting for his expression to give away his true intentions.

He looks slightly disappointed.

Yep. He came here hoping for an intimate, physical connection. Latisha was right, warning me to keep away from him in the bar. What a perv. Now I want to mess with him for thinking he could come here, seeking me out for a cheap thrill.

"Still interested?" I ask, biting my lip and tilting my head slightly. He nods. "Okay, then. My room is upstairs. Follow me." I can practically feel his eyes glued to my ass as he follows me upstairs to my room. I have him lay down on my Reiki table, face up, as I come to stand behind him at his head.

"Would you mind if I place my hands on your shoulders? I'd like to get a feel of your energy."

"Touch me wherever you want." He says, making no attempt to mask his desires.

I place my hands on his shoulders and he closes his eyes, imagining who knows what at the feel of my touch on his body. His energy is so full of sexual tension. So thick I could cut it with a knife.

"You do have some tension in your lower body. I can feel it." I say, after a few moments. Removing my hands from him, I walk over to my little table of crystals and select a selenite rod. "I'm going to place this on your lower stomach." I say, holding it up so that he can see it. "This will help amplify the healing energies I'm about to send through you. Any objections?"

"None. Do what you want with me." He says, his hungry eyes watching my every move. I step back to him and gently lay the selenite just below his belt, watching his reaction. His expression looks as though his imagination is working overtime at the feel of the pressure of the stone down there.

"I'm going to touch your shoulders again, and this time, I'll be channeling the Reiki energy to your lower back. Just relax. Keep your eyes closed and allow yourself to heal." I say in a soothing voice. He follows my instructions for the duration of the thirty-minute session.

Once his time is up, I remove my hands from his shoulders again, moving down his body to remove the selenite from his lower stomach as well, and place it back with my other crystals.

"You're all done." I say. "Feel free to sit up when you're ready."

He does, twisting his back slowly, as if to test the pain level. "Well, I'll be damned." He says in surprise, looking at me curiously. "Maybe there is something to this *Hocus Pocus* after all."

"It's Reiki." I correct him.

He reaches to remove his wallet. "How much do I owe you?"

"Oh, you can pay Laura down stairs. She pays me at the end of the week. It's fifty dollars for thirty minutes."

"A tip then. I insist." He pulls out a twenty-dollar bill and hands it to me. For some reason, I feel awkward accepting the money from him, but I do. It isn't like I'm not going to need it at some point. The sand is running out of my hour glass, after all. I may need every penny I can scrounge up in two to four years. Plus, he did come here with the intention of a cheap thrill at my expense.

I take the money and smile. "Thank you."

"Can I take you to dinner some time?" he asks suddenly. "Tomorrow night?"

"I'm sorry, I actually have dinner plans tomorrow night."

"Tonight, then?" he presses.

I see where this is going. Better to just fess up. "Actually, Garrett, I am kind of seeing someone. So, I can't have dinner with you, any night."

He looks at me for a moment. "Do you do this Reiki outside of work? House calls?"

Technically, I could, but I see where this is going also. "No, I prefer to meet clients here." I say, before he can get any further ideas. I turn to grab my smudge bundle off the little dresser so that I can clear the energy from my room and table once he does leave.

He nods. "Well, since we live so close, it would save me a trip out here if you could do Reiki on me at my house now and then. You wouldn't have to take a cut in your price either, cut the middle man out." He says, tapping his foot on the floor gently to indicate my boss down stairs. "Would save me some gas money too. Might increase your tip." He grins.

Hell no. "That's against shop policy." I lie. "I could lose my job here for that." I don't think Laura would mind if I did take clients out in the country where I live now, but no way I'm going there with Garrett Johnson. "Anyway, Laura can help you check out downstairs. I have to prep the room for my next client." Not that I'm expecting a specific client, but I want to get him out of here.

"You probably have them lined up for you." He sighs, standing up.

I simply smile and light my sage. Maybe the smell will expel him from my presence.

"This was great, Vanna. I'll be sure to recommend you." He winks at me, before he leaves, closing the door behind him.

Suddenly feeling gross in the aftermath of this session, I decide to smudge myself as well.

R UNNING A RAG ACROSS THE BAR IN THE TWISTED THROTTLE, I NOTICE Dean's watching me, as usual, from across the room. I give him a little smile and he winks back at me. He's sitting in Viking's usual spot, on a bar stool near the front entrance, leaning against the wall where he can pretty much see the whole room.

Vixie walks up to the bar, placing her tray down in front of me. "I'm taking my break now." She informs me. "Cherry should be back soon, but until she is, it's on you to cover tables."

"Okay." I say, ignoring the hint of hostility in her voice. I get along well with Cherry, and most of the sweetbutts are civil with me. For some reason, Vixie just doesn't seem to like me at all. Watching her storm off, I move her tray to the side of the bar and get back to work waiting tables and filling shots for the next twenty minutes, until Cherry returns.

"I don't think Vixie likes me." I say to her, as she flips the side counter up to come behind the bar with me.

"Vixie doesn't like anyone." Cherry says, as if I shouldn't worry about it. "She likes *you*."

"Because I'm with Axel. And Axel is too young for her taste." Cherry says, grabbing a towel to finish drying a batch of shot glasses. She gives me a look, then tilts her head in Dean's direction, without being too obvious about it.

"Oh... Vixie has a thing for Dean."

"And Dean's got a thing for you." Cherry says. "Vixie's been after Dean for a couple of years. She's bitter because he's not interested. Never was."

"So is she one of the... um... you know... the *patch chasers*." I ask.

Cherry laughs at my reluctance to refer to them as patch *whores*. "Technically, though, she's probably not quite that easy. She won't roll over

180

for just anybody." Cherry shrugs. "But Dean, Viking, Viper... maybe even Chopper. All they'd have to do is snap their fingers and she'll be on her back like the rest of them. At least she has a few standards, though."

A loud whistle in the back of the bar grabs my attention. A group of guys wanting another round of whiskey and beer where they're playing pool.

"I'll get it." I say, grabbing a tray and loading it up with the same shots and bottles they ordered previously, before I make my way over to them. One of them slaps the money on the tray as I hand the drinks out to them and collect their empties.

"Ain't seen you here before." One of the guys wearing ripped jeans and a half way unbuttoned long sleeved shirt under his leather cut, says to me. I reach for the last empty bottle on the table near them.

"This is only my sixth or seventh weekend working. I'm part time." I smile politely.

"You with the Saviors?" he asks.

I glance towards the front of the bar, where Dean is watching me intently now. I try to suppress my chuckle at his territorial nature. "You could say that." I reply, shifting my focus back to the customer. "Can I get you anything else?"

"Some luck. I'm losing every rack so far." He sighs, chalking up his cue stick. "Been paying for every round all night."

"Maybe you should ask a pretty girl to blow on your cue stick for luck?" I joke. "You know, like in dice games. Craps, for example."

He looks amused. "That's not a bad idea, sweetie." He grins at me. "Would you mind?"

"I meant, you know, one of the other girls..." I begin to say, gesturing randomly behind me, but he thrusts the cue stick right in my face. "Sure, why not?" I silently wish him luck and blow the blue tip of the cue stick, as if it's a birthday candle. "There, I hope you win."

"I'll let you know." He smiles back at me.

As I make my way back to the bar, grabbing more empty bottles from a few tables and noting who wants refills, Dean is waiting for me by Cherry. His back and elbows resting against the bar counter.

"What was that?" he asks, cocking his chin towards the group of guys playing pool.

"Oh, he wanted me to blow on his cue stick for luck. Says he's been losing all night." I say, sliding the tray over to Cherry for her to toss all the empties. "I need two pitchers of draft each for the two tables in the middle over there." I tell her.

"When are you planning on taking your break?" Dean asks.

"Whenever my boss wants me to." I laugh.

Dean glances at his watch, then looks back at Cherry. "I'm stealing Vanna for a bit."

Cherry rolls her eyes at him as she finishes filling the four pitchers, then places them on the tray. "At least let her run these back over to those two tables before you two pull a disappearing act." She says. "Maybe by then, Vixie and Viking will be back from their breaks."

Dean chuckles. "They're at it again?"

"I'm pretty sure. Might want to avoid the back patio until they're back up here." Cherry says.

"Roger that." Dean nods.

I grab the tray with the pitchers of beer from Cherry. "I'm going to pretend not to know what you two are talking about."

"You know?" Dean asks, seeming somewhat curiously amused.

"Patch chaser business." I try to suppress a giggle. Cherry laughs at me again.

"Patch *chaser*?" Dean repeats my words as if he's mulling them over.

"Vanna prefers not to call them patch *whores*." Cherry replies.

"How *PC* of you." Dean chuckles.

"Well, she already hates me. I don't want to call her a *whore* and make it worse." I shrug, then walk off to deliver the pitchers of beer. On my way back to the bar I notice Dean is talking more seriously with Cherry, but they stop talking as I approach, all smiles again. I look at him suspiciously.

"What? Did I miss something?" I ask.

Dean shakes his head. Cherry just sighs and says that Vixie must be losing it because normally it doesn't take her this long to get back on the floor.

Dean chuckles. "If she's with Viking, though." He lets that sentence hang between them.

Cherry laughs. "Good point."

"You know, inside jokes aren't fun for the ones on the outside." I say, crossing my arms at them.

"Oh, you'll know soon enough." Cherry giggles.

Dean shoots her a look that only makes her laugh harder. "Fucking better not." He mutters. "And just for that, I'm kidnapping Vanna for the rest of her shift."

She scowls back at him, but there's still a slight smile on her face. "You were planning to do that anyway." She accuses him.

"Now you'll never know." He shrugs.

"I just love, how you two act like I'm not here. And you," I playfully jab Dean in the chest with my finger. "Kidnapping me for the rest of my shift? I don't get a say in this?"

He grins at me. "That's why it's called *kidnapping*."

Now it's my turn to roll my eyes at him. "What about my hours though? It's only eleven."

"I'll still pay you for your shift." He says.

I glance at Cherry who is busying herself with refilling shot glasses for customers at the bar. "How is that fair to Cherry?" I ask, trying to keep my voice down, even though it's a loud bar and she probably can't hear us now anyway.

Dean is still smiling at me. "Cherry lives here with Axel rent free, doll. Plus, I pay her and she keeps all her tips, too."

"She lives here?" I ask. "How can she live at a bar?"

"There are about twelve bedrooms with bathrooms in the back of this building, babe. Plus, a full kitchen." He says. "This place used to be the Saviors headquarters. We've got a decent gym back there too."

"Wow." The building does look fairly large from the street, but I guess I never really thought about what else was potentially here.

Dean's eyes follow someone behind me. "About fucking time." Glancing over my shoulder, I realize he's talking to Viking, who just grunts back incoherently and returns to his watchful post as bouncer near the front of the bar. "So, can I kidnap you now?" Dean tugs at the strings of my apron.

I shrug, letting him remove it for me. "You're the boss."

"Aces." He tosses the apron behind the bar. "There's somebody who's been wanting to meet you."

"Well, she's a Harley Davidson Road Glide Special." Dean says. "A few years old now. Though, she came out of the factory sweet as Hell, I did do a few things to her." He steps closer to the blacked-out motorcycle, which still looks intimidating, even under the bright lights in the garage of his Motorcycle shop. "Custom wheels and rims. I modified her engine a bit, made some air and fuel improvements, added a stage five kit, a cam..." He goes on to explain, gesturing and pointing to parts and areas on the bike as he does. "I upgraded her to a blacked-out thunder header exhaust system to make her sound a little deeper and raspier. Sexy as fuck. Plus, it liberates some extra horse power and helps combust fuel more efficiently. I added drag bars with risers, added some detailing with dark gun metal accent spikes, just to give her that *bad ass bitch* aesthetic. And of course, custom black powder matte paint and parts to murder her out."

"*Murder her out*? That sounds scary. She already looks intimidating."

He grins at me. "Just means no chrome, baby." He says, then goes back to talking about the work he did on her. "I made some changes to the suspension, swapped some parts out to bring the ride height up and make her an even smoother ride. Stretched her out slightly to accommodate my height. Then I swapped out the single seat for a better two up one and some passenger foot pegs for the ladies... Although, I'll be honest with you. Serene is very particular about who rides with me. She's a picky lady." He looks back at me with another smile.

"Oh. Those bikes aren't?" I ask, turning towards the other several bikes in his collection.

"My side chicks? Nah. Not really. They're for banging around." He does that thing with the tip of his tongue again as he smirks at me. "Don't get me wrong, I take care of all my ladies. The Sport Glide, the Night Rod low rider. The Rebel. All great bikes. But *Serene*..." He pauses and looks back at his pride and joy. "Me and Serene... We have a *relationship*."

The way he looks at *Serene*... if she were a woman, I'd be very jealous. It's kind of cute though. His attachment to his favorite bike. I wonder if all bikers have a deep love for their motorcycles the way Dean does. Or maybe, he's just crazy.

"So, do you build custom bikes for people?"

He shakes his head. "Rarely from the frame up. I mostly do custom modifications and repairs, tune ups, paint jobs, inspections. That sort of thing."

"You did Serene on your own?"

"Yep." He says, looking over his baby again. "Took a little while. Had to work on her during spare time, after hours in the shop, and before the Twisted Throttle at night. So maybe a few hours a week. She's mine so I don't make money doing shit for myself." He turns back to me. "So, what do you think of my *actual harem*?" he teases.

"I think they're all beautiful." I say, looking around at the different style bikes. "Though, Serene looks like she could kick someone's ass. She's big and intimidating."

"She *is* a bad bitch." He pushes me towards her, as if I'm actually afraid of her.

"She might not like me." I tease him back, pretending to struggle against him.

"We're both sweet on you, doll. And you'll know how much she likes you when I finally get you on the back of her one of these days."

I glance up at him. "What do you mean?"

He grins and bites his bottom lip. "You'll just have to wait and see."

I turn to face him more directly, hands on my hips. "No, why are you smiling like that?" I look at him suspiciously, though I'm smiling too. He just has that effect on me. "What do you mean?"

"Harleys, they have a *reputation...* And with the improvements I made on her engine and exhaust system... she... *purrs* real nice." He grins at me wider.

Now I cross my arms and look up at him. "I've never been on a motorcycle before. I have no idea what you're trying to allude to, Dean."

That little tip of his tongue peeks out to touch his lip again as he smirks down at me, stalling for a moment before he says, "Let's just say, you're in for *a pleasant surprise*."

I roll my eyes at him. "Fine. I guess I'll wait to find out."

"It'll be more fun for the three of us that way." He insists, though humorously. "Not only would telling you take the fun out of it, *saying it* might be considered *ungentlemanly*."

"Since when do you behave like a gentleman?" I shove him playfully.

He stares at me for a few moments, looking me over slowly. Something darkens behind his eyes. He cocks his chin towards the murdered-out Harley. "Get on her." He growls, his tone a lower octave than before. "I want to see her between your legs."

His words catch me by surprise, giving me instant butterflies. The way he's looking at me, the words he chose to say just now and the *way* he said them... I bite my bottom lip and step closer to Serene.

DEAN

V ANNA FLIRTATIOUSLY SHOVES ME. "SINCE WHEN DO YOU BEHAVE LIKE A gentleman?" That playful look in her eyes. That almost unspoken *dare* in her voice.

It's getting harder and harder to behave myself around you, Vanna.

Especially when I'm thinking about her clinging to my back, her body pressed tightly against mine, as I whip us around these country roads... I've wanted to get her on the back of a bike for weeks now, especially Serene.

Fuck.

I could take her, now. God knows I want to. Serene is down for it, too. Vanna is wearing appropriate attire for riding tonight as well. She's got on a denim jacket, though leather would be better. I'll have to rectify this in the near future. She's wearing jeans tonight... fucking tight, curve hugging jeans that make it even harder to behave myself. Sexy boots that complement her shapely stems as well.

Since when do I behave like a gentleman? I *try* to at all times... But...

Fuck it. Not tonight. I'm in the mood for a little *girl on girl* action.

"Get on her." I cock my chin towards Serene, keeping solid eye contact with Vanna. "I want to see her between your legs."

Vanna seems a little surprised by my request, though the slight flush of her complexion, the dilation of her pupils, leads me to believe she isn't displeased. Not with the way she sinks her perfect teeth into that lower lip of hers as she looks up at me.

She moves towards the bike.

Fuck yes.

My pulse quickens as I watch her grip Serene's handle bars. She swings a leg over the leather seat and straddles her, settling down on her. She looks real fucking good on my bike.

Serene... you lucky bitch. I wish she'd mount me like that.

I watch Vanna as she looks away from me, down at Serene, admiring my girl up close. Her custom paint. Her instruments and gauges, carefully touching her...

Fucking sensual!

When her hair falls forward, over her shoulder, blocking her face from my view, she whips it back and straightens herself up on the seat. My fucking cock jerks in response. She doesn't notice, thankfully.

"This is really cool." She sounds happy and looks back up at me, smiling.

Fuck. That makes me happy.

"Ain't nothing like it, baby. The power. The freedom. You can't beat it."

She's got her teeth in her bottom lip again as she grins excitedly. "Will you take me now?" She asks, her expression hopeful, playful even, her fingers absentmindedly caressing Serene's tank...

So. Fucking. Hot.

As if I could say no to her, especially when she's looking at me the way she is. "Well, it is a nice night." I say, walking up to them. I don't want to sound as I eager as I actually am to make this a threesome. "I suppose I could take you for a little *joy ride*." I wonder if she'll catch my drift when Serene's giving her the *good vibrations*.

I reach into one of the side bags to pull out the spare helmet and place it on Vanna's head. She's still smiling as I strap it on to her. Once I check it to make sure it's secure, I hand her a pair of riding glasses. She slips them on eagerly.

"Gonna have to scoot you back a tad if I'm gonna join you ladies."

Vanna pushes herself back on the seat. "Good?" she asks, looking around the bike for a place to put her feet. She spots the passenger foot pedals and places her boots on them. "Good?" she asks again.

I can't help smiling back at her. She's so fucking cute. "*Good*, babe." Reaching back into the side bag I pull out my helmet and night goggles, strapping them on before I mount Serene, too. "You're going to have to hold onto me tight." I tell her. Vanna puts her arms around me. I adjust them around my waist. "Here, but tighter." She holds me tighter, scooting herself up against me. "Don't let go, ever. If you want me to pull over just pat my stomach and I'll find a spot, okay?"

"Okay."

I kick up the stand and start Serene. Even over the roar of her motor and rumbling of her exhaust pipes as I give her a few revs, I hear Vanna squeaking excitedly. I can't help grinning. She's going to be a biker chick. *My biker chick.* I know it. She's already this excited and we haven't even rolled out yet.

"Hold on tight!" I remind her one more time, before Serene barrels us out of the garage, through my lot and into the city streets beyond.

I take Vanna through town first. It's a slower ride, but I just want to be sure she's comfortable on the bike, before I take her on the highway and over the bridge to a little spot I know down by the river. I think she'll like that. It's a nice night, and hopefully Serene will work her magic and wing woman me into a hot kiss under the bridge or along the board walk with Vanna. I think I might lose my mind if I don't get to kiss her soon.

Before we leave the town and hit the highway for a quick thirty-minute ride over the bridge to the waterfront park, we stop at a red light. I turn my head to ask Vanna if she's okay. She confirms she is, that she's having a blast. I remind her to keep holding on tight because we'll be going a lot faster on the highway in a few short minutes. She holds me a little tighter and for the duration of the red light, I give Serene a constant rev, smiling evilly to myself. Poor, innocent Vanna has no idea what Serene and I are up to.

The light turns green and we take off again. The last red light before the highway, I hit her with another solid rev session, twisting the handle bar just enough to catch a peek at Vanna in the mirror. She still doesn't suspect anything, as far as I can tell. She's glancing around at the historical buildings of down town. She doesn't look flustered yet either, but we haven't been riding long. Still, I make a mental note to hit the fucking rumble strip before we exit the highway to get to the waterfront board walk. That ought to seriously kick start her first experience.

We hit the highway, finally. Serene glides over the asphalt as I accelerate her speed. A nice thirty-minute ride with no stops. If Vanna is feeling anything, she's taking it like a champ and not letting on. Makes me wonder if she's the type to really make a guy work for it in the bedroom. I'm definitely up for the challenge.

Twenty minutes down the highway, I take the exit for the bridge over the inter coastal waterway. In a few minutes I'll hit the rumble strip on the way to the next exit that will bring us to the river walk. When I do, I ride that bitch for a solid minute straight, grinning as Vanna's grip gets a little tighter. Though I can't tell yet if it's from pleasure or because it startled her. I'll know soon enough when we reach the park.

We hit two more red lights before we get to the river front park, both lights I rev Serene consistently. Vanna squirms a little against me, and I grin. It's working. Good job, Serene. By the time I pull us into the parking lot near the board walk, Vanna has her fingers digging into my abdomen. I debate whether or not to finish her off or keep her wanting... I might get further with the latter...

Fuck it. I'll do her a solid. I am a gentleman, after all.

Before I shut Serene down, I rev her rpms high for another few moments until I feel Vanna's thighs clench tightly against me, her fingers digging into my body, her body shuddering against mine, a little stifled whimper...

Fuck. Now I'm hard.

I stop revving her and shut Serene down. In the now mostly quiet, I can hear Vanna's quick breaths as she comes down from her orgasm, courtesy of Serene and I. I grin secretly to myself and pat Serene's tank. *Good girl.*

"You okay, baby?" I ask, kicking the stand down.

"Yes. Fine. Great." She says, quickly, loosening her hold on me, unclenching her thighs from my sides.

"Stay put. I'll help you *get off.*" Serene gets it.

I dismount, keeping my back towards her as I adjust my fucking wood without her seeing. I take off my helmet and goggles, hanging them on the handle bar as I turn back to Vanna. Reaching out, I remove her riding glasses, slipping them into the side bag, then unstrap her helmet for her and pull it off her head.

She's staring at me as he runs her fingers through her long dark hair, which looks sexy and windblown now. Her cheeks a cute rosy shade. Lips dark. Apparently, I missed some good lip biting action with her behind me. Damn. I tuck her helmet in the side bag as well, then offer her my hand to help her down.

"Did you enjoy the ride?" I ask as she dismounts Serene.

She nods, looking at me as if she's trying to determine whether or not I'm aware that Serene got her off and got her off good. She's got that hot as Hell *just got fucked* look.

"Are all bikes like this?" She asks, her gaze shifting back to Serene.

A forty-thousand-dollar *vibrator? Afraid not, doll.*

"Not exactly." I say instead. "Serene has a little more power than stock bikes with the modifications I did on her."

"You did a good job." She says softly, almost as if she didn't mean to say it out loud.

That makes me grin. "Do you want to take a little walk along the river? At the end of the dock there are benches. We could hang out for a little bit before I take you back."

"Sure... Is Serene safe here by herself?"

"Should be." I offer Vanna my arm and she takes it without hesitation. I lead her towards the river and we walk out onto the dock. In the dark, the water looks like black oil. The small waves gently slapping against the dock posts. The further we walk out, away from the lights in the parking lot, the darker it gets. Vanna tucks herself closer to me as we venture out.

"Nervous, doll?"

"It's a little eerie for some reason, isn't it?" she asks, glancing around.

I stop walking, tugging her hand to stop. She looks up at me with a questioning expression. "If you don't like it here, all you gotta do is say so. I ain't gonna force you to do anything you don't want to do, baby."

She looks back at Serene, waiting for us alone in the parking lot, then back up at me. "Are you going to keep me safe?" It's a serious question. I can hear it in her voice. Now is not the time to even make a dark joke. She wants an honest answer. I give it to her.

"Fuckin' A, baby. You know it."

"Okay." Her demeanor suddenly seems much more at ease after my reply. She trusts me. "Then let's go all way."

"Wish that wasn't in reference to the dock." I tease her. She smacks my arm then tugs me to keep walking.

We sit down side by side at the end of the dock. In the dark. The only light now coming from the moon above that sparkles across the dark water of the intercoastal. We're completely alone out here. Vanna doesn't seem afraid any more, looking up at the stars. But a nagging feeling inside forces me to ask, "What are you afraid of?"

She doesn't look at me. "What do you mean?"

"You seemed nervous before." We'll start here. A safe place. And I'll keep digging until I know the truth.

"It's just really dark... and there's nobody out here but us."

"Well, you're not afraid of me. Thought you were gonna jump in my pocket before." I tease her. "So, what is it?"

She sighs. "Anybody could show up here and give us a problem."

"Nobody's gonna do anything. And even if they tried, you still wouldn't have to worry."

She looks at me now. "Why? You got a gun or something?"

"Well, I do agree with our founding fathers. Stay strapped or get clapped." I jest.

She giggles. "Oh really, which one of them said that?"

"Pretty sure it was Washington." My reply makes her laugh again.

"Are you really carrying a gun?"

I shift to face at her a little better. It's difficult to really get a read of her features in the pale moon light. "Why? Would it bother you if I did?" She shakes her head no. "Alright. I do have a gun. But I'd only use it as a last resort."

"So, it's on you, right now?"

I wonder what her interest is about the gun. "Yeah, baby. It's on me. Locked and loaded. Got a knife too. In case you were curious."

"Yeah, I know about the knife you wear on your belt. Anyone can spot that a mile away."

"Actually, I was talking about this one." I say, pulling out my Balisong knife. With a quick flick of my wrist and a spin the knife flips open with a flourish, reflecting the moonlight on its blade.

"Holy cow. That was cool." She says. I can't help grinning as I show off, dazzling her with a few more butterfly knife tricks to open and close it. "You're a badass." She says with another little laugh.

I can't help chuckling this time. "That's exactly what it's for. Intimidation. Whip out a knife with some fancy wrist work like you dice people up for a living and suddenly you're not worth fucking with. It's just a little butterfly knife though. Basically, a fidget spinner."

"A fidget spinner for bad asses."

"I'll teach you. It's easy. Just, not in the dark." I slip it back into my pocket. "Still a knife. Still gonna stab and still gonna cut."

"Where's the gun?" she asks.

"What's with the gun, baby?"

She shrugs. "Just curious."

"It's on me. Don't worry."

"I'm not worried. I feel safe with you." Her words warm my heart, but I'm still curious...

"Are you gonna tell me what you're afraid of, Vanna? Why you want a gun?"

She peers up at me. "I didn't say that." I just stare back at her and wait. She shrugs. "Maybe I don't want to get clapped either."

Hiding behind humor. I can relate to that. There's something, though, my instincts can feel it. But she doesn't want to talk about it. I'll try again, once more, then let it go for now, if she resists. "Who's gonna clap you?"

She swallows. "A robber, maybe?"

It's a valid response. But not the whole truth. I haven't earned it yet. I can't let myself get upset or offended. I should back off and keep it light for now.

"So, did Serene make you come?" Even in the dark I can tell her eyes get wide and I can see her jaw drop. I press my lips together firmly to prevent myself from laughing. Though I can't see it in the darkness, I'm sure she's blushing.

"So, that's what you were alluding to." She finally says. "A *pleasant surprise.*"

"Told you she likes you." I tease.

Vanna glances at me from the corner of her eye. "You're a bit of a rogue, aren't you?"

"I've been accused of worse."

"I'll get you back for this." She warns me, though her words are still playful.

Intriguing. "I sure hope so." I grin, trying not to let my imagination run wild with the possibilities of what Vanna might do to me. Get me back for getting her off. Damn. "Though, I hope whatever you do to me is more along the lines of *reciprocation* than revenge."

She laughs, smacking my arm before she gets to her feet and walks to the railing of the dock, looking over the dark waters. I stare at her profile as she lifts her face to the night sky. The moon light on her face, her dark hair flowingly softly in the slight breeze. She's so damn beautiful.

"We're a little backwards, aren't we?" she says.

"What do you mean?"

"You give me a job before you ask for a date. You give me an orgasm before you've even kissed me." She sighs, glancing over her shoulder at me. "Maybe Serene likes me better than you do." She teases.

I like you more than I should, Vanna.

I push myself off the bench and walk towards her. She turns around swiftly at my approach, her back against the rail of the boardwalk, facing me now. She tilts her head to look up at me. I stand before her, so close I can feel her breath on my face as I hover my lips above hers.

"Do you want me to kiss you, Vanna?" I ask, wondering if she can hear the desire I have for her in my tone. The way my voice wraps around her name.

"I don't want anything that isn't real." She nearly whispers.

I slide my hand into her thick, soft hair, gently holding the back of her head as my other hand slides up underneath her denim jacket, pulling her body closer to mine.

"It's fucking real, baby."

Her hands reach up between us and grip the lapels of my leather jacket. She bites her bottom lip again, eyes flicking up from my mouth to meet my gaze. And I can't even remember the last time my heart beat faster in anticipation of a kiss...

Blue and red lights suddenly flash across her face, as her eyes shift from mine to glance past me. "Serene." She says, her grip on me loosening as the moment slips away from us. "There's a *cop*, by Serene." Her voice is somewhat nervous now.

I reluctantly release her, removing my hand from her hair to turn and glare at the cop responsible for interrupting what would have been our first kiss. A kiss I've been craving for fuckin' weeks.

Reaching for her hand, she places hers in mine, as I let out frustrated sigh. "Come on, doll." I say, "There's someone else I want you to meet tonight."

A COP! DEAN WANTS TO INTRODUCE ME TO A COP!
I try my hardest to remain calm as Dean leads me back down the dark boardwalk, towards the semi lit parking lot where an officer stands waiting beside Serene. My heart is fluttering in borderline panic, as I attempt to keep my expression neutral.

"Noticed Serene sitting here all by herself." The cop says, his arms folded across his chest as he sits back against his squad car. He's built, bigger than Dean, though they seem to be about the same height. The cop is clean cut though. A smooth-shaven face with light brown hair buzzed to a tight crew cut. He gives off a military type vibe. "Thought I'd pull in and make sure you were alright."

"Doing just fine, bro." Dean says, still holding my hand as we approach the police officer. "Hope it's been a slow night for you."

The cop's eyes shift to me, giving me a once over look. "Nothing serious." He says. "Who's your lady friend?"

Dean lifts my hand in his, turning his face to look down at me with a smile, as if he's proud to be seen with me. As if he wants the cop to see us holding hands. I'd find it endearing if I wasn't so nervous.

"This is Vanna." Dean says, releasing my hand only to slip his arm around my waist.

"It's nice to meet you, Vanna." The cop says, extending his hand to me. I shake it and smile. His hand is a lot gentler than I anticipated it would be. "I'm Jason." He says. "Caldwell. Jason Caldwell." I notice he's attempting to hide a bashful smile at his slight stammering of his name. "Dean and I go way back. Childhood buddies."

"It's nice to meet you, too." I say, politely. The officer releases my hand. I'm about to stuff it into my pocket, but Dean gently takes it again, holding it in his between us.

"I don't think I've seen you around town before." The cop says.

"I... I... um... I just moved here." I say, noticing Dean looking down at me from the corner of my eye.

"Sick of city limits. Wanted to come kick it with us country folk." Dean says, his thumb gently caressing the back of my knuckles. "We're actually neighbors. Imagine that."

"Oh, nice." The cop smiles at Dean. "That how you two met?"

"No, actually..." Dean begins to say, when my nerves get the better of me and I squeeze his hand anxiously, afraid he's going to say something about the Knight that attacked me in the stall. It's bad enough the cop knows where I live now. He glances down at me again, clearing his throat. "Vanna was looking for some part time work, so I offered her weekends in the bar." Dean continues, shifting his focus back to the officer. "She's on her break." He jokes.

The officer laughs. "I'd say. Long break. This sure isn't the parking lot of your bar." He chuckles. "Good thing your boss is a generous guy, Vanna."

I force myself to laugh with them, hoping it sounds genuine. Jason Caldwell seems nice enough. And if Dean has been friends with him since childhood, I can't see him being a bad guy.

"So, I guess I'm interrupting an impromptu date, huh?" the officer says, his hands resting on his utility belt now, as he looks from me to Dean with a slight smile. I glance up at Dean in time to catch his grin.

"You could definitely say that."

"Well alright then," the cop pushes himself off the hood of his squad car to stand at his full height. He's slightly taller than Dean, but only by an inch. "I'll be on my way. You two kids have yourselves a nice time." I'd tell you to be careful out here, but, you're already with the one the bad guys should worry about." He says to me with a smile, before he pats Dean's shoulder.

"Be safe yourself, brother." Dean nods to him. "Tell Casey and the kids I say hi."

"Will do." The officer says, getting back in his squad car. We watch him pull out of the parking lot, back into the city streets to continue his patrol.

I try to take a deep breath and let it out subtly.

"Why don't you like cops?" Dean asks, point blank.

I try to play stupid to buy myself time to think of an excuse for my obviously blundered attempt at hiding my reaction. "What do you mean?"

"You were afraid of him, Vanna. Your palm's sweaty." He says, tucking his thumb in between our clasped hands to stroke the inside of my palm. "You squeezed my hand when you thought I was actually going to say something about that night in the bar." Dean turns to stand directly in front of me so that I have to face him. "Even that night we met. You didn't want me to call the cops on that dirtbag that tried to ra-"

Don't say it!

"I'm not!" I insist, cutting him off before he can get the *R word* out. "I thought you were going to get a ticket tonight. And that night in the bar, the bathroom... You beat the shit out of that guy. I didn't want you to get in trouble for it." Dean stares at me, obviously trying to determine if I'm being truthful with him. I force myself to smile and look at him as if he's the one being weird. "I'm not afraid of Jason. I didn't know he was your friend.

I thought we were going to get in trouble for being here so late." It's not technically a lie. I did think that initially.

Dean is still silent, his penetrating stare unwavering.

"What did he mean when he said you were the one bad guys should worry about?" I ask, desperate to steer this conversation in a different direction. Even if I have to do it slowly.

"Like I've told you before. You're safe with me, Vanna." Dean replies, rather stoically, however.

"I know."

"Do you?" he asks. "Do you *really* know, Vanna?" I nod slowly. "Then why don't you tell me what's going on?"

"I think you're making a big deal out of nothing." I say. "I got nervous because I thought we were about to get in trouble. That's all. It's after midnight, in a dark parking lot. A cop showed up. I got nervous. Is that really so hard to believe?"

"No. It isn't." he concedes, after a moment. I can tell he isn't completely convinced. Arguing the point with him will only make him more suspicious. I need to move this along to lighter topics, as if everything is just fine. Because it is just fine. The cop left. The cop is a friend of Dean's. He didn't ask me much about myself at all. Everything is fine.

"What now? There's only about an hour before the roadhouse closes."

"Whatever you want." Dean almost sighs. He still seems a little stoic. I find myself hoping he isn't thinking back on the letters after this.

"My car is still in the lot. We have to go back there anyway. I should help Cherry and Vixie clean up for the night." I say. "Since you're still paying me, might as well get something out of it."

Dean releases my hand to retrieve the extra helmet and goggles from the saddle bag on his bike. "As you wish." He says, though he seems disappointed.

DEAN

S HE'S HIDING SOMETHING. I'M SURE OF IT NOW. BETWEEN THE RUSH TO Wilmington to retrieve those mysterious letters weeks ago, and her obvious aversion to police. There's something going on with Vanna.

I brought her back to finish her shift, as per her request, without any shenanigans with Serene. Now, I watch her, though trying not to be obvious about it, for the remainder of the last thirty minutes the bar is open. Pretending to listen to Viking's tales of his latest conquests, though I barely hear two words he says to me.

He shoves me, nearly knocking me off the bar stool I'm sitting on beside him. "Bro, the fuck is the matter with you?" he demands, glaring at me.

"Nothing. Tired. That's all." I say, not wanting to mention anything about her to him.

"Bullshit. You left with her happy. You came back gloomy."

I let out a disheartened sigh. "Tried to kiss her. Didn't happen." That was disappointing. I would have kissed her. I wanted to kiss her. We both wanted it.

"Oh shit... Did she reject you, bro?" Viking seems genuinely sorry for me.

"No... we were interrupted by Jason in his squad car."

Viking pats my back now. "Alright, so she didn't reject you. The cop cock blocked you. Try again." He attempts to sound encouraging.

I just nod, glancing back in Vanna's direction. She's smiling at customers as she collects the empty glassware and bottles from their tables, being sweet, wishing them all a good night and telling them to get home safely as she goes about her routine. The *blow on my cue stick* guy from earlier spots her, and looks a little too happy to see her again, as she nears the back pool table he's at with his buddies. I can't help gravitating closer to listen to their exchange.

"Where'd you disappear to?" the guy asks, grabbing a few empties and putting them on the tray for her.

Vanna giggles, tucking her hair behind an ear as she smiles back at him. I know she's just being polite, but for some irrational reason, I don't like it.

"How did you end up fairing?" she asks, grabbing a few glasses from another table before she turns back to him.

"Very well." He grins, showing her a wad of cash. "You'll have to swing by and blow on my stick again, regularly."

Fuck you, asshole.

Vanna laughs, but doesn't reply to his obvious inuendo.

"Well, here." The guy says, peeling off a twenty from his cash and holding it out to her. "Figured I owed you for the good luck."

She seems hesitant to take it. "Oh, you don't have to do that. I'm glad your luck turned around, though."

"It did, thanks to you." He insists, smiling as he folds the bill and steps towards her. In a bold move that sends a jolt of anger through my body, he reaches out and tucks the money into the front pocket of her jeans. The muscles in my jaw clench as tightly as my fists.

Vanna seems surprised, frozen in place by his unforeseen action, staring down where his fingers had just shoved inside her pocket.

"Um...thanks." She says, her voice quieter than only moments ago. "I... um... I should get back to work, now." She stammers, carefully lifting her over loaded tray of bottles, shot glasses and beer mugs. It's an accident waiting to happen. It's also my opportunity to back this motherfucker off.

I step around the small crowd, walking up to Vanna and taking the tray from her. "I got this, doll." I smile at her, before shifting my glare to her new admirer. He glances between the two of us for a moment, before his eyes fix on mine. "Bar's closing. Might want to head out." I say to him. The guy doesn't move. Just looks back at Vanna. Subtle isn't going to work with him. "Baby, go see if Cherry needs anything." I say to her, though I'm still dead eyeing this fuck.

"Okay." She says timidly, then walks off towards the front of the bar. I break eye contact with him, only to check to make sure she doesn't stop. Though, she is peeking over her shoulder to see what's happening here.

Placing the tray back down on the table, I shift my focus back to him.

"I do something wrong?" the guy asks.

"You're definitely skirting the line." I warn him. "That move with the cash... I better not ever see something like that again with her."

"Was just tipping her."

"I know what it was, *cue stick*." I growl at him.

He looks at me a little harder, as if it finally clicks. "She yours?"

"She's mine." I concur. "You pull a stunt like that again, or a stunt like you did earlier, we're gonna have a problem, you and me."

"That blow for good luck was *her* idea." He says. "But alright. I don't want any trouble."

I give him a single nod, before heading back to the bar where Vanna and Cherry are talking.

"Is everything okay?" Vanna looks concerned, her brows slightly pinched together.

"He asked you to blow on his stick?" The question comes out more heated than I intended it to.

She hesitates, glancing at Cherry before she looks back at me nervously. "I was just kidding when I told him to ask a girl to blow on it for luck. Like in craps, you know?" she says, her fingers fidgeting with her apron pocket. "I never meant myself. But when he held it out to me, I didn't want to be rude, so I just did it. It was just a joke." She insists. "I didn't mean anything by it."

"He thought otherwise."

Vanna steps away from the bar, glancing at the guy before she looks back at me. "Should I go apologize to him?" she asks, her eyes almost wide with worry.

"Fuck no." *Shit*. That wasn't supposed to sound as harsh as it did either.

She stares at me with that worried look. "What should I do? Are you mad at me?" That's not the first time she's asked me that.

"No." I sigh. "You didn't do anything wrong."

"But you seem upset."

"He slip you his number with that cash, when he had his fingers in your pocket?" I ask, making an effort to keep my tone level.

"I don't know, I don't think so." She says, reaching into her pocket and pulling out the money. She unfolds the twenty to reveal a slip of paper with his phone number and name. *Jake*. She looks back up at me as if she expects me to lose my shit. "I'm sorry, I had no idea." She insists, immediately handing the paper to me.

I glance in *Jakes* direction, as he and his buddies are leaving the bar. He looks at me as I hold up the slip of paper between my two fingers for him to see as he makes his exit. I just want him to know that I figuratively, and literally, had his fucking number the whole time.

Reminding myself that Vanna is a pretty woman and guys are going to try this shit on a regular basis, I take a breath and rein in my jealousy. Turning back to Vanna, I hold out the slip of paper for her to take back.

"I don't want it." She insists, stepping back from it as if it's some kind of grotesque insect she wants no part of. "I promise you... I didn't even know I had it."

I believe her, but... "Would you have told me?"

Her eyes look almost regretful, but she answers me with the truth again. "I would have just thrown it out."

I nod. "Fair enough."

"Would you prefer that I tell you?"

"I suppose it doesn't matter."

"I can see that it does." She's looking in my eyes as if she can see something in them. A window into my broken soul perhaps. The damage Lucinda left in her wake. My broken ability to fully trust.

"You told me tonight on the dock, that you don't want anything that isn't real." I say to her. "I feel exactly the same way. I'll never settle for anything less, again." She nods in understanding. "Honesty is important to me, Vanna... I'll just leave it at that."

"I swear, I didn't know he slipped me his number." She insists.

"I believe you." I say to her, hoping it puts her mind at ease.

Though, I know she's hiding things from me. I also realize that trust goes both ways and so I'm willing to be patient with her. To give her a little more time to see that I am worthy of her trust as well.

Vanna takes a step closer to me as I toss cue stick's number on the bar. "I'd have just thrown the number away, and not said anything about it, because I'm not interested in anybody else." She says quietly, as if she's still afraid I might lose my temper.

"I'm afraid to ask how many you've thrown out in the weekends you've worked for me."

"All seven." She says. *Seven!* "Though, Vixie took one."

"So, this makes eight... We might need to talk about you wearing a PO top when you're here." I sigh.

"What's that?"

"Property Of." I say. "Like Cherry's got on."

Vanna doesn't say anything at first, but she eventually responds by reminding me that I told her she could wear her own clothes.

"I'm not going to force you." I say.

"I'd rather hand you the numbers as they're given to me than wear that." She says, nearly glaring at the back of Cherry's cut before she looks back at me. I note the flash of defiance in her eyes. Alright. There's something behind that reaction as well. Seems as though Vanna may turn out to be quite the little book of secrets.

"Doll, it doesn't mean what you think it d-"

"I should finish cleaning up." She cuts me off, turning from me to walk straight back to the over loaded tray I took from her before.

I beat her to it before she can pick it up. "I got this."

"You said that before."

"Why are you mad at me?"

"I'm not." She insists.

"You dont seem happy." I press.

"My feet hurt. I should go back to sneakers, if I'm still *allowed*."

"Vanna, I didn't mean -"

"Great." She says, cutting me off again. She spins back around, grabbing more items off empty tables, and brings them back to the bar for cleaning or disposal. I decide to give her a little space, since I've clearly managed to offend her somehow. I wait for Vanna to grab a rag and move away from the bar before I bring the loaded tray up to Cherry to clear.

Viking is ushering out the last of the patrons for the night when we step outside together.

"What happened by the pool table? Looked like you were laying down the law with somebody." Viking asks.

"I was. He made a subtle move on Vanna." I say on a sigh laced with frustration. "Can you believe she's had eight motherfuckers pass her their numbers since she's been working weekends?"

"Uh. *Yeah*." He says, like I'm the idiot.

I shake my head. "Right under my fuckin' nose. And she just told me now that she's been tossing them."

"Isn't that good?" He asks. "She could have saved them... Then called them... Then fucked them." I glare at him. "I'm just saying. It's good she tossed them. Obviously, she likes you too."

"Yeah. It just fuckin' burns me. And she won't wear a PO top."

"Maybe because you're too busy being *mister nice guy* and you forgot how to lay your fucking claim on a chick. Make that yours, bro. She's gonna start thinking you don't want it like that." Viking says. "You're going to *friend zone* yourself, bro."

"Well now she's mad at me." I mutter.

"This is why I *tap and go*, bro. Bitches are complicated." Viking shakes his head.

As I glance across the lot at Vanna's car parked under a floodlight, I have the distinct feeling, that when it comes to Vanna, things might turn out to be very complicated indeed.

Chapter nine

Vanna

Our Sunday date was at a Fifties themed diner, complete with Doowop and old rock music playing from an antique jukebox, black and white checkerboard décor and candy apple red vinyl booths. The neon pink and blue track lighting and all things fifties, displayed in every nook and cranny against the walls. The front of the diner even has a life size Betty Boop figurine. Our burgers and fries were served in baskets and checkerboard paper, alongside our ice cream floats, by waitresses on roller skates.

I was relieved when Dean called me to ask me out, after our awkwardness at work the night before. He promised me Sundays and I'm glad he chose a fun, relaxed place for us to go to together, packed as it is. We needed something a little care free to shake off the slight turbulence that occurred the other night.

We stumble out of the crowded diner, onto the sidewalk with our to-go ice cream floats. It's already dark out, mostly due to the encroaching rain clouds. Taking his truck tonight, instead of the motorcycle, was a good call. The air feels heavier now, as if it's about to pour.

"That was really cute." I smile up at him, as we start walking back in the direction of his truck parked a few blocks away.

"Bet you'd look real cute in a poodle skirt." He winks at me, grinning as he bites the straw sticking out of his float.

"Complete with a bullet bra?" I tease him.

"You'd kill somebody in one of those." He says, "But at least they'd die happy."

We both laugh, until Dean notices a guy pull his motorcycle over a few yards up ahead, beside the sidewalk. The rider is wearing all black, including a full coverage black helmet with a tinted face shield. Completely obscuring his features from view. He doesn't remove it as he kicks the bike stand down and kills the engine, sitting back on his bike. He seems to look in our direction as well.

Dean scowls at the guy as he reaches for my hand, clasping it in his. We continue to walk in the biker's direction, however. And just as we pass him, Dean chucks the remainder of his ice cream float into the open trashcan the biker parked next to.

There was something about that action though. The way he threw it. It was almost as if he meant some form of disrespect by it. Like he was throwing trash *at* the mysterious rider, without actually throwing trash at him.

When I glance over my shoulder to peek back at the biker, he's still looking in our direction. I notice the patch on the back of his leather vest is a skull with horns.

"Somebody you know?" I ask.

"Nope." His reply is clipped and cool.

"You tossed your drink at him." I say.

He looks at me, arching a brow with a slight grin. "I tossed it in the trash."

"There was weirdness." I push, though I smile back at him. "Is he part of a rival MC or something?"

Dean lets out a sigh and shakes his head, then chuckles at me. "He's nobody, Vanna. And we're about to be soaked. The sky is going to open up and rain buckets on us any second."

I look up at the dark clouds in time for a raindrop to nail me right in the eye, making me flinch and laugh. Dean laughs at me too, as I glance up at him with one eye shut. He stops to swipe his thumb gently across my eye, wiping the water away for me.

With the loud rolling of thunder, the clouds open up and big, cold raindrops begin to fall all around us.

Dean lifts the side of his leather jacket, holding it out and wrapping his arm up and over my head to shield me from the rain. As I tuck myself against his body beneath his arm, we scurry together towards the direction of his truck.

"This rain is crazy! I don't think I've ever seen raindrops so thick. They're practically the size of my index finger!" I say in amazement.

"Welcome to eastern NC, babe." Dean chuckles.

Puddles are forming everywhere, almost instantly, even on the sidewalks. People are ducking into shops and restaurants for shelter. My feet are already soaked to the point my sandals are beginning to slip off my feet as we hurry along.

"Wait!" I tell him, stopping to pull them off my feet and carry them so I don't end up twisting an ankle as we run.

"You can't run to the truck barefoot, Vanna!" Dean protests, as I hurry over to throw my drink in another trash can and run back to him. He's glancing around, as if deciding which establishment on this strip of downtown businesses we're going to duck into as well. "Fuck, come on! We'll just wait it out in the tavern. I can't have you cutting your feet, Vanna." He insists, wrapping his jacket around me again and ushering me towards the entrance.

Once we're inside, he releases me and steps back to look me over.

"Well at least your dress didn't get too wet." He says, running his fingers through his soaked hair, slicking it back. It looks solid black now that it's wet.

"You practically stuffed me in your jacket pocket." I giggle, shaking out my sandals.

"Your hair looks sexy wet, though." He grins.

"You don't look bad yourself." I say, gripping his wet, leather clad arm for balance, as I slip my sandals back onto my feet.

We spend the next forty-five minutes throwing darts, while the rain hammers down outside. A rougher looking crowd of people file into the bar. Louder. Rowdier. They look like bikers with their women. Dean's playful mood seems to shift upon their arrival and I immediately wonder about that strange, silent standoff he had with that biker earlier in front of the diner.

"Is he here?"

Dean looks at me, confused. "Is who here?"

"That biker guy. The one with the black helmet, earlier."

He stares at me for a brief moment, before he replies, "I doubt it."

"What was that about, anyway? Seemed like some serious tension between the two of you." I notice Dean, notice someone across the room, and he looks less than thrilled. Following his line of sight, I notice this *some-one*, has noticed him, as well. A pretty blonde someone, among the bikers, who starts to make her way in our direction.

"*Shit.*" I hear him mutter under his breath. "This town is too god-damned small."

I tear my attention away from the attractive blonde woman walking towards us, to look up at Dean, as he goes back to throwing his last two darts at the dart board. He then slides his arm behind my back, gently guiding me in the opposite direction towards the juke box in the back of the tavern.

"Vanna, why don't you pick out a song to play?" Dean pulls some change from his pocket and hands it to me.

"Okay. What kind of music do you like? Just Rock? Or?" I ask, since the jukebox at his roadhouse strictly plays Rock N' Roll.

"Any kind." He glances over his shoulder. "I have to deal with something. I'll be right back. Stay here where I can see you."

"Is everything okay?" He seems even more agitated.

"Just unavoidable, inevitable bullshit." He sighs. "Pick a song you like, doll. I'm curious." He winks at me, though it's an obvious attempt at trying to be reassuring. His tense energy tells me otherwise.

I glance past him and see that the blonde is coming in fast, and she does not look happy. I look back up at him curiously. He must have been reading me because he turns immediately, lifting a hand to her and growls one word, stopping her dead in her tracks.

"Don't!"

She's angry now, glancing back to her biker companions and throwing up her arms. One of the men shrugs back and waves her off dismissively, before he goes back to his buddies and beer at the bar. I wonder if she's an ex-girlfriend of Dean's. She's a blonde, like his ex-wife was. She's also taller than me and slender. Wearing tight black jeans and a red low-cut top that matches her red lipstick and finger nails. Tough looking, but pretty, as all of these biker babes seem to be.

"Vanna," Dean says, bringing my attention back to him. "Wait here. I'll be right back. Pick a song you like. I want to hear it."

I nod and turn towards the jukebox, looking over my shoulder to watch Dean whirl around towards the angry blonde woman.

"Over there." He growls at her, pointing to the bar in the front of the room. "This is fucking bullshit and you damn well know it." He's definitely a little scary when he's angry.

The blonde storms off towards the bar, and Dean glances back at me once more before following her over. I pretend to look for music. There are seven songs ahead of whatever I end up choosing, and I wonder if we'll even be here long enough to listen. Every time I glance over towards Dean and the blonde, they're animatedly arguing, but I can't hear what is being said over the music and the crowd. There's definitely some kind of history between them though. She could very well be an ex. At least she's got a little more meat on her bones than that trashy girl that was hanging on him the night we met. This one is still on the skinny end of the spectrum though. I go back to looking for something to play on the jukebox while I listen to the current song playing, *Every Breath You Take*, by the Police.

A Brunette in blue jeans and a leather vest walks up to me, leaning against the jukebox. "Hi, Vanna." She says to me.

"Hi." I say, immediately suspicious, looking her over. The patch on her vest says her name is Daisy – Property of Knuckles, JoCo Jokers MC.

"I'm-"

"Daisy?" I cut her off, nodding at her vest.

She laughs. "Yeah, it's nice to meet you."

I tentatively shake her hand. "How did you know my name?"

"Small town. Word travels fast." She shrugs. "I want to apologize for Tamra, over there." She gestures towards the bar where Dean and apparently, *Tamra*, are talking. Less animated now, but he still doesn't look happy. "She's way out of line, breaking up your date with Dean like this."

"Oh, is that what this is? Isn't she somebody else's *property*, too?"

Daisy looks at me as if she's taken aback. "You're kinda spunky, huh?" I don't say anything to that. "Yeah, she is. She's with Dawg. She's Lucinda's sister."

"I don't know anything about Lucinda."

"*Oh...*" Daisy seems genuinely surprised. "Sorry, I thought Dean would have said something about her." Her *yikes* expression doesn't go unnoticed and I wonder if that's her intention.

Before I can say anything, I hear Dean shout "*Dawg!*" across the bar, grabbing Tamra's man's attention. The big burly biker starts to head in their direction, shaking his head. He doesn't seem too happy with Tamra either.

Dean looks back in my direction, taking notice of Daisy. He looks stressed by this and runs his fingers through his dark hair. "One minute, baby." He mouths to me.

I nod, watching as Dawg reaches them. Dean points at Tamra while saying something angrily to the biker, who puts his hands up in a gesture that seems to convey something along the lines of *I don't want to get involved in this*. Dean says one more thing before turning from them and heading back over to me.

Tamra shouts his name.

"Tell Lucinda to fuck off!" Dean shouts back at her. He looks frustrated, though as he strides toward me, a determined look begins to etch across his handsome face.

"Damn it, Dean!" Tamra shouts at him again.

As Dean reaches me, he grabs me around my waist, pulling me against him as he spins us to the side so we're in profile to Tamra.

"Report *this*." He growls at her, before he leans down abruptly and takes my mouth with his, kissing me in front of everyone in the bar.

I'm completely stunned, but as his arms wrap around me tighter and his tongue slides across my lips, seeking entry, it's like a bolt of electricity rips through me and every nerve in my body is humming with energy. I automatically part my lips and return his kiss, grabbing onto his leather jacket and pulling him even closer as we deepen the kiss. His hand slides up by body, into my hair at the back of my head, holding me to his mouth as his tongue dominates mine. My knees actually weaken and my entire body flushes with heat. He holds me tighter against him as if he can tell I'm trembling inside.

An involuntary whimper escapes me and I can feel his deep, primal growl in response, before he breaks the kiss. His stare is a lustful blaze.

Did he feel that too?

We're both nearly panting. I can feel my heart beating against my rib cage. He still has me pressed against his body.

A hoot and a whistle from someone in the bar, snaps me back to reality. I glance around briefly to discover we've drawn quite an audience. I bite my lip and look back up at him. He's still staring at me, but now he looks conflicted. He releases me and I step back slightly, leaning against the jukebox, still whirling from our intense kiss.

I watch as Dean's eyes shift around the room for a second, before he grabs my hand and pulls me, leading me towards the front exit of the bar.

It's dark out now and still raining, though not as hard as earlier. Dean stops and releases my hand before we step outside. Removing his leather jacket, he drapes it over my shoulders, placing his arm across the small of my back, he guides me away from the tavern, towards an awning a few shops down. Once sheltered from the rain beneath the awning, Dean stops and turns to me.

"Vanna," he breathes my name. "I'm so sorry I did that to you." He runs his hand through his wet hair. "I shouldn't have done that. I was way out of line... I...I just... I'm an asshole, baby."

I'm shocked. Words escape me as I stare back at him, dumb founded. He's *apologizing*? For a kiss? An amazing, earth moving, sensual, *electrifying* kiss? The best kiss I've *ever* had in my life? What?

"Vanna, please." He says, "I fucked up, I know it."

I open my mouth to speak, but words fail me. All I can do is shake my head in bewilderment.

He runs his hand over his whiskered jaw, then clenches his fist before he shouts, "Fuck!", making me jump. "Shit," his expression looks pained now as he realizes he startled me. "I'm sorry, damn it." He sighs. "Let me go get the truck. You're gonna be soaked to the bone. God, I'm an asshole. I'll take you home, you don't have to be afraid of me, Vanna." He says, so much regret in his voice.

Before I can say a word, he turns and heads out into the rain. His fists are balled at his sides, his body rigid as he stalks away in the down pour.

"Dean, wait." I say, finally finding my voice. He doesn't hear me over the clapping of the rain and his own self-loathing muttering.

"Dean!" I say louder, slipping on his leather jacket and following him out into the rain. He turns and hurries back to me.

"Vanna?" his expression is wrought with concern. "Are you okay? Do you prefer a cab?"

I let out a sympathetic sigh. Poor guy. There's only one way to put his conscience at ease. "You didn't feel it?" I ask, looking up at him, blinking from the rain hitting my cheeks and splashing up into my lashes.

He hesitates. I don't. I wrap my arms around his neck, sliding my hands up the back of his skull, pulling his face down to mine. On my tippy toes, in the pouring rain, I kiss him again.

I can tell he's surprised at first, but it only takes him a second to wrap his arms around me and kiss me back, deeper and more feverishly than even the kiss before. The electric current is back and we're lost to the world again, there's only us, this kiss, our bodies pressed together.

Without breaking our kiss, he backs me up so we're under the awning again. As my back hits the front display window of whatever closed shop is behind me, I break the kiss momentarily to take a gasp of air and tell him, "I'm not mad at you, Dean. I'm not afraid of you."

He swipes a wet strand of hair from my face and cups his hand against my cheek. Rubbing his thumb gently across my bottom lip, he stares at me. That hot blaze in his dark eyes. "I feel it, baby." He whispers.

"I do want your kiss, Dean." I whisper back, and before I can utter another word, his mouth instantly takes mine again. Holding me tightly against him, his hand tangles in my wet hair as the other wraps around my back. I submit to him, his tongue sweeping through my mouth once more. My body responds to his deep, sensual kiss, his warm, hard body pressed against me, with a flutter in my lower abdomen.

It's been a long, long time since I've felt any kind of carnal desire. This man stirs something inside of me that I can't deny. And I don't want to. Even his seemingly chauvinistic, alpha male, macho tendencies that flare up on occasion, are a turn on to me, though I try to hide it. I'm not hiding it very well now, however, as our tongues and lips thoroughly explore each other. Sharing our breaths, our bodies melding together more and more as each moment passes. I feel his leg press between my thighs as he attempts to get as physically close to me as we possibly can on this soaking wet, public sidewalk.

"Save some for us, pal!" A man's sneering voice says from the bar not far away from us.

Dean immediately breaks our kiss and steps back from me with a growl, facing the crude man a few yards away.

I'm trembling. Partially from being soaked by the cold rain and losing the warmth of Dean's body pressed against mine. But it's mostly from his passionate kiss. I brace myself against the sill of the large window as I catch my breath.

"The fuck you say, asshole?" Dean snarls.

"Oh shit," the man says. "Didn't realize that was you, Dean. Carry on, brother!" he laughs, returning to the bar with his buddies.

Dean turns back to me, looking me over. I attempt to hide my shivering by pulling his jacket around me a little tighter and sweeping my wet hair to one side.

"I should take you home. You're soaking wet and cold. I don't want you getting sick. Let me go get the truck. Stay here." With one last longing look, as if he's forcing himself to part with me, he turns and jogs off into the rain.

DEAN

THIS SHOULD NOT HAVE HAPPENED THIS WAY. OUR FIRST KISS SHOULD have been more romantic. Not an impulsive, misogynistic display of rage driven rebellion. I used her... Initially. That's what it was. Me using her to convey to all concerned, that I *am* over Lucinda.

Our first kiss should have been the other night, on the boardwalk. Alone. Without an audience of drunken spectators. Without a group of Lucinda's spies to witness.

It should have been private. Respectful. Intimate. Vanna deserves that. She wanted *real* from me. What she got was a *real* dick move.

But God damn... Do I want to kiss her again!

I turn the heat on in the truck, low. Just to keep her shivers at bay. I can't help glancing at her in the passenger seat, as I drive her back to her home. She's avoiding eye contact with me, fidgeting with the zipper on my leather jacket. Her teeth gently biting her bottom lip again. However, in this moment, I realize she's unaware that she's even doing it. It's subconscious. She's thinking about something that either has her tense, or dare I wish it, *aroused...* I find myself hoping it is the latter.

"Are you alright, Vanna?" I ask, finally breaking the silence between us as I pull my Silverado up her driveway.

"Yes." She says, peeking over at me. "Are you?"

"I'm sorry about tonight." I put the truck in park and shut it down behind her car. Shifting in my seat, I study her in the lambent glow of my trucks interior lights before they fade. She turns slightly towards me as well, tucking a strand of damp hair behind her ear with a shy smile.

"I had a nice time." She says softly, as if she's trying to reassure me.

I nod, halfheartedly. "Yeah, you seemed to enjoy the diner." I sigh.

"And getting caught in the rain." She smiles, tugging my leather jacket around herself a little tighter. I can't resist smiling back at her. Though...

"I should probably get you inside. You need to change into some dry clothes. Maybe take a hot shower first."

"Who was that woman?" she asks.

I take a breath through my nose and exhale, trying to hide my discontent. "Lucinda's sister." I reply, figuring it's better to keep my answers short and as to the point as possible regarding this subject.

"You seemed very angry." Vanna has that searching expression in her eyes again.

"This town is just too fucking small. The past is always right there to slap you in the face." I mutter. She nods and I can tell by her demeanor, she agrees with my sentiments. "That why you left New York?"

"I needed a new start. But I'm glad you didn't leave this little town. It would really suck without you in it." She smiles at me again. "You know, you don't have to take me places." She adds, as if something has just occurred to her. Vanna's looking at me as if she's concerned about something. "If it's a problem."

"If what's a problem?" I ask. She hesitates, shifting in her seat and fidgeting with the zipper on my leather jacket again. "Vanna, why would me taking you out be a problem?" I press her.

She lets out a little sigh. "The small town. Running into people you know." She says. "Being seen with... somebody like me-"

"*Is something I'm proud of.*" I interrupt her, before she can say anything else. "I think you're a fucking knock out, Vanna. You can't not know that about yourself." But she nearly winces at my words. As if the compliment hurt her in some way. "Do you really not know?" I can't help asking now, it's impossible that's the reason.

She shakes her head, her nose scrunched up and her hand lifting slightly as if an attempt to physically push my words away from her. "Don't, I'm not asking." She says. "All I'm saying is we don't always have to go out. You're right, it's a small town and-"

"I kissed you in front of everyone in a crowded bar." Granted, it was the wrong move under the circumstances, but goddamn, I fucking did it. How can she think I wouldn't want to be seen with her?

"Which you regret doing." She glances at me, but only for a moment.

I can't help shaking my own head, incredulously, now. How can a woman like her harbor such deep insecurities? "Because you deserve better than that. That's *all*. I've been wanting to kiss you for weeks! I wanted to throw Jason in the river for interrupting us on the dock!" I say, realizing I'm losing my cool to a slight degree. Taking a brief moment, I try to rein myself back in. "Vanna, I wanted to kiss you the night I met you. And every night since."

She glances timidly towards me again, that absentminded nervous lip biting, as she lowers her hand to fiddle with a few wet tendrils of her long dark hair. A little smile pulls at the corners of her mouth. "Really?" her whispered question is barely audible.

I nod. "I kissed you in the rain, too."

She stifles a little giggle. "Actually, I think it was *I* who kissed *you* in the rain." She says, averting her eyes from me again.

Smiling back at her, I slowly slide across the seat of the truck to get closer to her. She watches me intently, twisting in her seat to face me head on, her back now against the passenger door of my truck, her eyes staring into mine as the interior lights finally begin to fade to dark.

The only illumination in the truck now, is what's being cast from her porch light, a few yards away. But I can still see her. Her slight smile, her dark almond eyes becoming slightly more hooded as the seconds tick between us. I can hear her breathing through the constant tapping of the rain on my truck. The rain is getting harder again. Louder. I reach my hand up slowly, to gently stroke her face before I cup my hand against her cheek.

"You're fucking beautiful, Vanna." I tell her softly, my thumb caressing her bottom lip. I move closer to her, so that my lips are only centimeters from hers. "Tell me to stop." I whisper, unable to take my eyes off her sexy mouth. This time, when her teeth sink into that full bottom lip, it's because she wants it. And she doesn't tell me to stop.

I press my lips to hers, gently at first, testing the waters. She responds, her eyes fluttering closed. Long, dark lashes fanned atop her cheeks, which look ivory by comparison, in the gloomy lighting. Her soft lips press against mine, molding to my mouth and then part slightly. An invitation I'm all too willing to accept.

Moving closer to her still, my body presses hers against the passenger door further. I slide my hand to the back of her head, protecting her skull from the cold, hard glass of the truck window, now against my knuckles through her hair. I accept her invitation. Tasting her sweet, sensual lips first, with the tip of my tongue, before I slide inside her hot, smooth mouth.

Her hands are against my chest now, but she isn't attempting to push me away. Her fists are gripping and twisting into the fabric of my damp shirt, as if she wants to pull me closer still. She tilts her head slightly, teasingly, as her tongue gently wrestles mine. I kiss her a little more amorously now, pulling a wanton moan from her, which immediately stokes my carnal fire.

Removing my free hand from the dashboard of the truck, I grip just above her knee, gently, waiting to see if she protests. She doesn't. She's kissing me back, matching my rising passion. I slide my hand up her thigh, roughly, gripping her sexy body over the cool, wet fabric of her maxi dress. Feeling her soft, sexy, feminine curves that arouse illicit fantasies of what it would be like to be between these thick thighs. How fucking badly I want to take her to bed. How hard and vigorously I want to thrust myself inside her. Thighs made to cushion a man's pounding hips. She's built to take all I've got to give her. *And Jesus fuck! Do I want to give it to her!*

"You perfect fucking woman..." I growl against her lips, my fingers now digging into her thigh as I kiss her deeply, possessively, once again. Taking her to bed would be a damn good way to make sure she gets out of these soaking wet clothes. I'd be the lucky bastard peeling them off of her curvaceous body...

Her hand is suddenly gripping mine. Her fingers attempting to curl under my hand, to pry it away, as I'm kneading the flesh of her thigh so shamelessly. But I can barely help myself.

"Dean," she pants my name against my lips, my mouth capturing her little plea.

My guess is she wants me to stop groping her, so I force myself to give up her sexy thigh, gripping her intruding hand instead and lifting it to pin back against the rain drop beaded glass of the window, beside her head. The back of her hand slides across the rapidly fogging glass with a slight vibrational squeak. I feel her lips curl into a little amused smile against mine, but she doesn't pull or twist away from me. She allows me to conquer her mouth once more, kissing me back ardently.

I have no idea how long we've been making out for, but I could keep kissing her. I'm lost to her. Completely captivated by our sensual osculation. Never in my life, have I kissed, or been kissed, the way Vanna and I are kissing tonight. Not even the Devil himself could pry me away from her. No, it would take something far worse for that to happen...

I hear the familiar, dreaded ringtone inside my leather jacket, which Vanna is still wearing. I can feel her attempting to pull away from me, but I have the back of her head in the palm of my hand, holding her mouth to mine.

"Ignore it..." I whisper against her lips, trying to coax her back into our make-out session. I can feel that she's not as into it as she was only moments ago.

Fucking Lucinda! Damn you!

I keep trying, for a few moments longer, but she twists her mouth from mine, releasing my shirt that was clenched in her fist, to reach into my jacket pocket and retrieve my phone.

"Lucinda?" she barely whispers, glancing up from the screen of my phone to look at me, questioningly. "Her ringtone is Eminem's, *Love The Way You Lie*?"

I sit back slightly, releasing her hand from against the window as she passes me the phone, then brings her freed hand to her sexy, kiss swollen lips. Her eyes no longer hooded and alluring. They look troubled now, clearly wondering why my ex-wife is calling me.

"Aren't you going to answer it?" she asks, her voice faint, nearly inaudible through the torrent of rain still clattering down on my truck.

"No."

"Do you know why she's calling?"

"No... And I don't care."

Her brows furrow slightly as she glances back down at my phone. I hit it to silent and let it keep ringing. When she looks back into my eyes, it pains me a little, to see distrust in them. I hold the phone back out to her. "Answer it. If you want to."

Her expression transforms to slight surprise. "Why?"

"I've got nothing to hide. I've got nothing to do with her, anymore... Haven't for a while. I've got nothing left to say to her. If you want to know, answer it."

Vanna glances back at the phone for a few moments, her fingers still gently touching her rosy lips, contemplating God only knows what. I lick mine briskly, finding it difficult to look away from her mouth. But I do, when her eyes flick up to meet mine again.

"Does she look like her sister? Tamra?" Vanna asks.

I shrug. "A little, I suppose."

Vanna's eyes widen slightly, before they tighten a bit, as she comes to a realization about something. I wait patiently to hear it. "That was her." She says. "By your bike. I saw her. Our first date. You brought me to that fancy restaurant. You told me she was nobody."

"She's nobody to me."

"She's your *ex-wife*."

"*Ex* being the key factor here." I remind her.

My phone starts to buzz again. Lucinda, of course. She must have spoken to Tamra about what happened between her sister and I. And how I basically ravaged Vanna in front of a bar full of people.

"You gonna get that?" I ask Vanna, holding the phone out to her again.

She slowly shakes her head. "No."

I hit the red ignore call icon and shove the phone in my back pocket.

"What about kids?" Vanna asks.

"Lucinda has a daughter."

"With you?"

"No. Her current husband." I reply. Why she's asking me about kids again, could only mean there is still a level of distrust in her mind. I told her I didn't have kids over dinner that first night. She thinks she's going to catch me in a lie.

"That girl Daisy, with the JoCo Jokers..." Vanna starts to say, but hesitates. "What is a JoCo?"

"Jocsan County. Two hours away." I say. "What about Daisy?"

"She said Tamra was trying to bust up our date. Why would she do that?"

"I didn't ask her."

Vanna stares at me for a moment, searching my eyes. "Before you kissed me, you told her to *report this*... That's why she's calling, isn't it? Lucinda would only want a report if she wanted you back."

"I don't care what Lucinda wants, baby."

"Does she want you back?" Vanna presses.

I turn to lean back against the seat of the truck, letting out a frustrated sigh as I run my fingers through my hair, slicking it back. I'm fairly certain Vanna's not going to want to kiss me again tonight. I make a mental note to change Lucinda's ringtone to silent at all times. It's been eight whole months since she's let me see Maddie. I'm pretty sure that's not going to change any time soon, anyway. And even if she did offer, it would come with a price. A price I'm sure I wouldn't be able to pay. Not now. Because it wouldn't have anything to do with a monetary amount. It would cost me any chance I've got with Vanna.

"Lucinda wants a safety net." I finally reply to Vanna's question. "I used to be that for her. For years. Even before we got together. Whenever she got her ass in trouble, I was there to fix the problem. She can say she misses what we had, but I ran out of every reason to care. What we had was a lie." I glance back at Vanna and find her staring back at me.

"She really hurt you." Vanna says.

"What doesn't kill you, makes you stronger. Right?" I try to laugh, but it sounds dark, even to myself.

Something flickers behind Vanna's eyes. "Right." She seems to force a smile.

"You don't have to worry about Lucinda, doll. That ship sailed and sank a long time ago."

Vanna nods, straightening herself back up on the seat as well, then leans forward to shrug herself out of my leather jacket. She passes it back to me. "Thanks for the jacket." She says. "And for dinner."

I reluctantly accept the jacket. This means she'll be leaving me shortly. "You're welcome... Sorry about tonight..." I begin to say, but then I stop myself. "You know what... *No*, I'm not fucking sorry." I glance back at her to find a somewhat surprised expression on her face. "I'm not sorry at all."

Vanna presses her lips together, as if she's trying to suppress a laugh at my sudden outburst.

"I wanted to kiss you. I took the fucking shot. I don't regret it."

She clears her throat, averting her eyes from me as she timidly smiles. "It was a pretty good kiss." She damn near whispers.

"Fuckin' *A* it was." I concur, unable to keep from smiling myself when she giggles at me. "So, you don't want to go out with me anymore?" I ask, ready to clear that shit up next.

"I never said that." She insists. "I just meant you don't have to take me out. We don't have to go places. If you don't want to."

"I want to be with you. If we go out. If we stay in. If we sit all night in this fucking truck. I don't really care what we do, Vanna. I just want to do it with you."

"Okay." She says, smiling at me, like she might actually believe me this time. "I'm a pretty good cook. Would you like to have dinner with me one night this week?"

She wants to cook for me! Fuck yes!

"I would love that, Vanna." I smile back at her, dialing down my excitement, but keeping the sincerity in my voice. "Just tell me what day and what time and I'm here."

"Any requests?"

I shake my head. "Anything you want to make is fine by me, really."

"Okay, I'll surprise you." She says, then turns to look out the window. "I think the rain is finally just a light mist. I should probably make a break for it."

"Let me walk you to your door." I insist, jumping out the driver's side before she can protest. She watches me through the windshield as I make my way to her door and open it for her.

"Such a gentleman." She teases me.

I hold the screen door for her as she unlocks the deadbolt on the solid oak one and pushes it open. A rather large black cat, with stunning green eyes, is there to greet her. She bends to lift the animal into her arms, turning to face me as she kisses it on the head.

"This is my boy, Nico." She smiles warmly at it and I can see the love in her eyes as they look at each other. I try not to allow myself to be envious of a cat, but I do find myself hoping to see that look in her eyes towards me some day.

"Handsome cat." I say, as its eyes stare into mine, almost giving me an appraising look.

Vanna giggles, nuzzling her nose against the cat's cheek, kissing it again. "Mommy's little boy is handsome, isn't he?" she says, in a high-pitched little baby voice.

I'm grateful she's too distracted to see me flinch at her words. It isn't from the pitch of her voice, however. I console myself with the knowledge that we are still in the early stages of our budding relationship. There's no need yet, unless she should bring up the subject herself, for me to rip open this barely healed wound inside of me.

"I hope he's friendly." I say. "Looks like a mini panther. Could probably kick my ass if he decides he doesn't want me around you." I try to joke.

Vanna turns her focus back to me. "He's a sweetheart. A big mush. Just don't make any sudden moves at me and he won't attack you." She smiles.

"*Damn.* My plans are foiled." I smirk at her, teasingly, before I glance back at the cat. He's still hard eyeing me. "May I?" I ask, lifting my hand to ask if I can pet it.

Vanna twists slightly to bring him a little closer to me and I gently stroke the soft fur on his head. He allows it. I'm glad. I'm not afraid of him, but it would really suck for her precious feline to take a disliking to me. I don't push it, though. After a moment, I drop my hand back to my side.

"Well, he didn't bite the shit out of me." I say. "Nice to finally meet you, Nico."

Vanna giggles. "He knows about you. He wouldn't bite you."

"You told your cat about me?" I know it's just a fucking cat. Feels good anyway though, to think of Vanna thinking of me enough to speak about me to another... Even a cat.

"Yes. I'm afraid I'm a crazy cat lady. You might want to cancel our dinner plans." She jokes.

"Never. I'd expect a Witch to have a black cat, anyway." I tease, which thankfully makes her giggle some more. She kisses Nico again and he head-butts her back. "I hope you have a few more of those left for me."

She glances back at me, a little smirk on her face as she nibbles that bottom lip. "Okay, Nico," she says to the cat, turning to place him back inside the house. "Mommy has to say good night to Dean."

Ugh... that word. Please let it just be a crazy cat lady thing...

She steps back towards me, closing the screen door behind her to keep the cat in, now sitting there watching us.

"I did have a really nice time with you tonight." She says, reaching her arms up to wrap them loosely around my neck. I wrap my arms around her waist.

"Me too." I say, trying not to stare at her mouth again. I doubt I'll ever get enough of her kisses. I bring my lips closer to hers, waiting for her to close the rest of the distance between us.

Nico meows, making Vanna chuckle again, but she doesn't look away from me.

"Sorry, buddy." I say to the cat, though I'm staring in Vanna's eyes as I pull her body closer against mine. "You're gonna have to get used to this." I grin, before she seals my words with another one of her exquisite kisses.

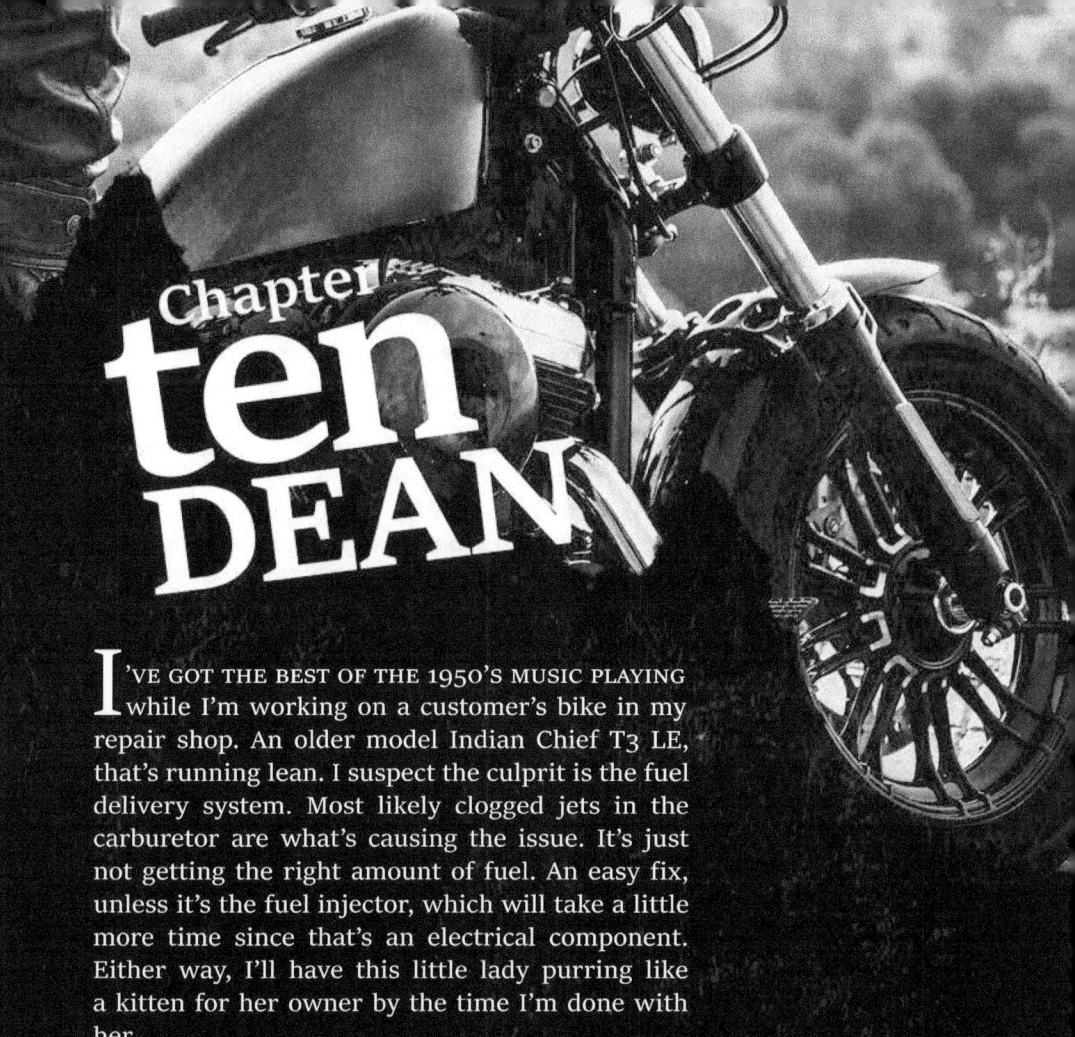

Chapter
ten
DEAN

I'VE GOT THE BEST OF THE 1950'S MUSIC PLAYING while I'm working on a customer's bike in my repair shop. An older model Indian Chief T3 LE, that's running lean. I suspect the culprit is the fuel delivery system. Most likely clogged jets in the carburetor are what's causing the issue. It's just not getting the right amount of fuel. An easy fix, unless it's the fuel injector, which will take a little more time since that's an electrical component. Either way, I'll have this little lady purring like a kitten for her owner by the time I'm done with her.

Glancing at my shop clock, I've got three hours before I plan on stopping by Vanna's day job. We've been dating almost two months now, and I haven't been able to find the free time during our nine to fives', to get over there. Today's an easy day though, so I intend to take advantage of it.

"The fuck you listening to?" Viking says, walking into the shop from the door nearest the back lot. I've got the clogged carburetor off, sitting on my work bench as I look over my shoulder at him. Viper's with him, too. I turn my back to him and continue clearing out the jets.

"Not even a hello?" Viper says behind me, dragging a rolling stool out from under a work bench and sitting down on it. I continue to ignore him. "You sure hold a grudge, Keegan." He mutters.

I suppose a part of me still harbors a little resentment towards him, for voting to strip me of my membership in the Saviors MC. Though, I do let him use the gym in the former clubhouse, our friendship has never been the same since that day I was voted out.

"What do you guys want?" I ask. "I'm on a personal deadline."

"Vanna, again?" Viking's tone is dripping with mockery. "She like this type of music?" I don't bother responding to his questions. However, I can't hide my grin. "Yep. Vanna." He sighs. "You making any headway there?"

"Finally kissed her. And I met her cat." I say.

"Is that a weird 50s *Rockabilly way* of saying you fucked that pussy?" he asks.

I just shake my head. "Seriously, what do you want? I've got shit to do today before I go to her place tonight. She's cooking for me." I can't help being a bit of a braggart as I glance at Viking. "And no, you can't third wheel."

Viper clears his throat before he speaks, pulling my attention back in his direction. "Preacher has an offer. He wants me to relay that offer to you."

"There's not a damn thing he can offer me, Viper. Save your breath." I don't bother looking at him as I lift the carburetor and inspect the jets.

"He wants to buy you out. Fair market value. The Bike shop, the roadhouse. The clubhouse. The lot. Everything." Viper says.

I scoff. "And just what does he think fair market value translates to?"

"He's open to negotiations, but his offer is seven hundred thousand." Viper says.

That is fair market value, but... "Tell Preacher it's a hard *fuck no*." I watch Viper this time to read his reaction.

"I'll let him know." Viper says, seemingly pleased with my response. I can't help wondering why he'd be happy I refused his presidents offer.

"Let him know I'm fed up with his bullshit, too. This MC was meant for more. We both know it. We were taking it in a direction that actually had a purpose." I say, placing the part down and turning to face Viper head on. "Hell, man. It's how you met your wife. Are you going to look me in the eyes right now and tell me I'm wrong? That what we *were* doing wasn't worth while?" Viper's body tenses up, but he doesn't speak. "Alright. Tell it to your wife then. If you can. That what we... That what the MC stood for, isn't worth it." I challenge him.

"Don't fucking talk about my wife." Viper mutters spitefully.

"You know what the fuck I mean, Viper. This MC was meant to be more than a damn social club. We were *The Saviors* for a reason. Whatever the fuck Preacher is up to, isn't what this MC was meant for."

Again, Viper is silent, though he glances at Viking.

"Tell me I'm wrong." I push him. "Tell me it's not worth it. Tell me that last extraction mission wasn't worth it, Viper. Especially to you. You wound up marrying the woman we saved that night."

I can tell his glare at me is half-hearted, though he gets to his feet, taking a step towards me. I place the carburetor back down on my work bench. If he hits me, I don't want to risk breaking my customer's part. But I'm not afraid of fighting Viper. He packs a punch, but he's never beaten me when we've sparred. He runs a hand over his short black hair, then drops his arm in a balled fist at his side.

"How is Rosita, by the way?" I ask him.

"Preacher's counter offer is five hundred thousand. And you keep this shop, a fraction of the lot as well, for customer parking. He'll pay for the permits to divide the property." Viper says.

I lean back against the work bench, resting my hands on the edge. "No."

A slight grin creeps across Viper's face. "Why not, Dean? What are you doing with all this? You hanging onto everything out of sentimental obligation to your uncle?" he asks. "Or do you have plans we don't know about?"

"You think I'd tell *you*, if I did? So, you can run back to Preacher."

"It's your fault, you know. That the mission failed." He sneers at me. "That the MC is divided. That these fucking assholes are still waiting around for you to step up." There is a level of disdain in his words.

"These *fucking assholes* are still your brothers." I remind him. "And maybe you forgot, but you were one of the ones that voted me out. How much of the current state of affairs is really my fault, Viper? You turned on me. Maybe you need a new president... Preacher is the reason the MC is divided and failing. Not me."

"Right." He glares at me. But there's no trace of sarcasm in his tone this time. No real resentment in his eyes, though his expression is hard. I glance towards Viking, who's simply staring at us, uncharacteristically quiet as a church mouse.

"The fuck are you guys really here for?" I ask. They're both silent. "Viking?" I look back to him, as he's the only one I trust for an honest answer.

"Just here to make sure Viper comes out of this alive." Viking shrugs.

"Why wouldn't he?" I ask, my eyes sliding back to Viper.

"Don't shoot the messenger." Viper shrugs. "I know you think I betrayed you."

"Didn't you?" It sure felt like it at the time.

"You were out regardless of which way my vote went, Dean." He says. "I'll let Preacher know there's no deal. See you around." He glances at Viking once more, before he walks out of my shop. I look back at Viking as the shop door slams shut behind Viper.

"Seriously, what the fuck was that?"

"Preacher doesn't trust me. This MC *is* divided, bro. I don't know." Viking says. "He hasn't bitched about not getting dues from us. He doesn't let the brothers that sided with you know about meetings or votes on anything. It's like our half is out, but we've still got our cuts."

"What about Axel? Are they not patching him in next month?" I ask. Preacher has to know that Axel solidly has my back. President of the MC or not.

"Far as I know, he's still patching him in. Maybe even a few others."

"None of this makes any damn sense. Why would he want to buy me out of everything Saviors if he's not even filling the coffers?"

Viking shakes his head. "I don't even think Viper knows."

"This is a whole lot of clubhouse for a dwindling MC." The building that houses the Twisted Throttle Roadhouse, the gym, the club rooms and full-sized kitchen, isn't a small space by any means. The only reason

Preacher would want it if is he's planning on growing the clubs' numbers. There has to be a reason he's walling out the brothers that didn't vote against me though, if he's trying to grow. Letting them keep their cuts when he wanted mine so badly, is strange, to say the least. Though, I'm pretty sure Preacher has always hated my guts.

"I don't know what he's up to. But if you plan on hosting the bike rally in the fall to raise funds for the safe houses, you might want to keep that cash far away from any accounts Preacher has access to." Viking says.

I nod. "I'll make the donation myself. On behalf of the Saviors."

"Preacher doesn't deserve the credit." Viking grunts.

"In honor of my uncle, it'll be done in the Saviors name. It's got nothing to do with making Preacher look good to the community." I reiterate. "My uncle started the mission. It's the least I can do." After losing his MC to Preacher. For the first time in a while, I'm starting to have some regrets. Especially with Axel about to be patched into whatever the fuck Preacher is cooking up.

"There is something else you could do, Dean." Viking says. "The brothers who backed you then, will back you now. If you still want it. I know a lot has changed. But they would."

"Even if I wanted it, and I'm not saying I do, but *if*... I have no footing to even bring it to the table. I'm out, bro."

"I'm not suggesting that. I'm saying start again. A new MC. You have Jason. Your uncle's connections still. The same mission can be possible under a new MC. Hell, you still own the club house. You've got enough brothers on your side to patch in and fill the necessary ranks to start a new MC."

Turning back to my work bench to finish up the jets, I admit to myself the thought used to cross my mind. Before everything fell apart. That I'd one day be the leader of the Saviors MC. It's been a while... Two years to be exact, since I've let myself entertain the possibility. But this county has been Saviors territory for decades. A new MC just doesn't feel right.

"You gonna tell me you don't have any regrets?" Viking asks.

"I have a lot of regrets, bro. About a lot of things." I mutter. "I just don't know if I've got it in me anymore, to lead. And I sure as hell don't have it in me to follow."

THE BELL ON THE FRONT DOOR JINGLES AS I'M RESTOCKING THE BOOK-shelves in Laura's shop.

"Welcome to the Ametrine Cauldron!" I call from the side room. "I'll be with you in just a minute, feel free to browse!" Shoving the last of the books onto the bottom shelf, I stand up and smooth out my skirt before walking out into the main room to greet our latest patron. As I round the corner, I'm met with a very pleasant but unexpected surprise.

"Dean." I smile. "I wasn't expecting to see you here."

He's standing in the center of the room, clad in that belted leather motorcycle jacket, dark jeans and biker boots. He grins back at me, those sexy, brackety smile lines showing through his short facial scruff.

"Thought I'd stop by and see if there was anything you wanted me to bring to your house tonight for our dinner date?" He asks.

"You could have just called, you know." I tease him. "And no, just bring yourself."

He grins back at me. "Well, I've also been meaning to come visit you at work for a while. Finally got the chance. Serene and I needed to take a ride anyway. Get outta town a while. Thought maybe you'd like to grab some lunch with me?"

"I just have to wait for my boss friend to get back, so she can keep an eye on things while I'm out. She should be back soon."

"*Boss friend?*"

I laugh. "Yes. Sorry. Laura. I call her my boss friend because, well, that's what she is. I'll introduce you when she gets here. You'll love her."

"If Laura is your *Boss Friend*, what am I to you?" his brow arches inquisitively to pair with his crooked smirk.

I look at him for a moment, biting my lip to prevent a smile as I contemplate his question. "I haven't decided yet." I tease him.

"Ouch." He pretends to grimace in pain.

"More than a Boss *Friend*, though."

"I'll *survive* with that, for now." He teases me back, then glances around the shop at all of our eclectic merchandise. It must seem odd to him. He doesn't strike me as the type to have ever set foot in a witch shop before. I can tell he's trying hard not to look judgmental, or disinterested, at the same time. At least he's making the effort.

"Shall I give you a tour?" I offer.

"Sure. I've been a bit curious about what you actually do here..."

"Well, you're standing in our main room. Downstairs is where we keep the tangible items. The used books at discounted rates are there," I gesture to the shelves on either side of the room, across from him, "Laura's desk slash register, is behind you with the mess of crap neither one of us can keep organized for more than a day. The new books and tarot card decks are in the room behind me. The foyer you walked through to get in here is where we keep the blessing candle lit during store hours." I walk past him, gesturing with my finger for him to follow me further back into the shop. He grins at me and follows. "This is our crystal room, as you can see. The back wall is all of our spell and ritual candles, incense and smudge supplies." I turn around in front of the candle shelves to face him. "Questions?"

A smile creeps across his face as one of his eyebrows raise. "Yeah, is that a *dick* candle?" He tilts his chin to the shelf behind me.

"Yes. It is." I grin back at him. "We carry a variety of colors and sizes."

"Why?" In this moment he reminds me of an immature little boy.

"For a variety of reasons. We supply Yoni candles too." I smile at him. "*Balance.*"

"What?"

I realize he must not have noticed those because I'm standing directly in front of them. I turn to pick one up off the shelf and show him. "Vaginas." I clarify.

He clears his throat, folding his arms across his chest, then strokes the stubble on his jawline. "What for?"

"They're used to represent the masculine and feminine. The different colors correlate with the intention of the spell." I say, placing the Yoni candle back on the shelf and retrieving a bright red penis candle. *Play time*, my inner demon sneers. I turn back to face him, holding up the penis candle as if I'm modeling it for him.

"Let's say I wanted to work a spell on a man I wanted. Maybe I only want him for a few hot nights. Or maybe more long term. I'd choose a color, let's use this bright red one for example." I smile at him. He's staring at me intently, though his grin hasn't wavered. I have his undivided attention. "This color represents lust, sex, passion. I would take this candle and carve his name into the shaft." I run my finger slowly down the side of the wax penis. "Then I would anoint it with a specific oil of the same intention, and rub it down, from the head to the base. Like this." I stroke the candle a few times, working my hand around the head and down its length, before I shift my focus back to him.

"You're fucking with me." He says, though he still looks uncertain.

I shrug innocently. "If you don't believe me, you can ask Laura when she gets back." I smile. "There are a few more steps to working candle magick, but I think perhaps you've heard enough." I place the candle back on the shelf and turn back to smile at him, making sure he notices that I glance at his crotch. "And in case you were curious, size doesn't matter." I wink at him.

"You'd need a bigger candle, baby." He winks back at me. "What's upstairs?"

"That's where we do readings and teach classes on essential oils. My reiki table is up there as well. Have you ever had a Reiki session before?"

"Nope."

"Well, if you're curious I'd be happy to give you a demonstration." I offer. "I know all this might be a little overwhelming, so if you're not into it that's totally okay."

"Lead the way." He says, as if I had dared him. I can't help but giggle. I walk towards him and motion with my finger again for him to follow me up the stairs.

I lead him into the first room, which is basically just tables and chairs with spiritual art hanging on the walls. "This is our little class room and where Laura brings clients for readings if they want a little extra privacy. My room is over here. It's smaller but all I have in here is a Reiki table and a little dresser." I walk into the room first and step to the side so there's room for both of us. "Hop on." I say, gesturing to the massage table. "*This is where the magick happens.*" I tease him. He looks at me skeptically, as if I'm still messing with him. "I'm not going to hurt you. I was teasing you with the candle, okay? But come on, Reiki never hurt anybody. It's all love and light.

Lay down." I insist. He eyes me for another moment, but complies with my request as he gets up on the table and lays flat on his back. "I'm going to give you a quick Reiki massage." I smile down at him.

"Shouldn't I at least take off my jacket?" he asks, more confused by the minute.

I can't help but giggle at him as I lean over and kiss the tip of his nose. "Dean, I never thought I'd say this, but you are so adorably out of your element right now, it's kinda cute." He just smirks at me and settles down. I touch his shoulder. "Just relax. I'm going show you real magick, that even you, *Mister Skeptic*, are not going to be able to deny."

"I'm all yours." He smiles.

"That's what they all say." I tease him.

He frowns slightly. "You have a large male clientele, don't you?"

"What's large?" I playfully taunt.

"Fuck. I don't want to think about it." He grumbles.

"You can keep your clothes on because I'm barely going to touch you just yet. I may not have to touch you at all."

"How is it a massage then?"

"You'll see." I pull out a quartz crystal pendulum from the tiny dresser behind me and let it dangle over him so can see it first. "This is a pendulum. I'm going to check your chakras with it. All you have to do is lay there and relax."

"I still feel like you're fucking with me, but alright."

"Just shut up and let me do my thing." I proceed to move the pendulum over his major chakras, from head to toe, paying attention to how the dangling crystal point moves.

"There's something creating a sight blockage in your heart chakra. But otherwise, you're not in too bad of shape. I'll clear some of that up for you." I say, coming to stand at his side again. I close my eyes for a moment and hold my hands in a prayer position, rubbing them together three times as I chant the words to activate the Reiki energy, before I hover them over his heart.

"Vanna, seriously, are you messing me with me?" his eyes are open now, watching me.

"Just let me know if you feel anything, and if you're comfortable with hearing any messages that might come through." I say, focusing on sending healing energy into his heart. He stays quiet for a few moments and lets me concentrate. It's a stubborn blockage. He's very guarded. I can feel it. I decide to scan his body for physical injury and perhaps any discomfort or pain I can remove for him, even if it is only temporary. Maybe he'll notice and won't be such a skeptic any more. I place my hands lightly on his shoulders, and as I do so, I feel a tingle in my right knee.

"Do you have any pain in your right knee, ever?" I ask him. "Your aura is slightly weak there."

He glances up at me, curiously. "I injured it years ago. Doesn't bother me much, but on occasion."

I nod. "I can feel it. I'd like to try to relieve it for you, though it may only be temporary."

219

"Psychosomatic?" Dean says with a cocky grin.

"That's what I thought my first time, too. But you're in for a surprise. I'm about to make you a believer." I say. "Close your eyes and relax. Let me know when you feel it."

"Feel what?"

"You'll know it when you do. *Now shush.*" I say, concentrating on sending healing energy to his old injury. It only takes about a solid minute before he sits straight up and gets off the bed. "What are you doing? I'm not done yet!"

He's smirking at me, but there is something in his expression that tells me he just had his mind blown a little. "How did you do that?" he asks, bending to inspect under the table near where his knee had been. He stands to look at me again. "You were up by my head the whole time. I was watching you."

"So, you felt something... Let me guess. A kind of tingling in your knee, behind the cap. Deep." He nods slowly. "Oh good!" I smile at him. "It was working."

"That's some freaky ass shit, Vanna." He says, amused, but I can tell he's slightly unnerved.

"Feel how hot my hands are." I show him the redness in my palms.

"What the shit?" he touches them gently to confirm that they are indeed, very warm. "There wasn't enough friction to cause that amount of heat."

"That's Reiki. It's energy healing."

"Maybe you actually *are* a witch." there's something off about the way he said it.

Before I can respond, I hear the door open down stairs and Laura's familiar, raspy, "*Hellooo!*"

"My boss friend is back." I say. "Come meet her. Then we can get out of here for a bit." I suddenly have the urge to get him out of this environment as fast as possible.

"Laura, this is Dean. Dean, Laura." I introduce them once we're down stairs.

Dean smiles brightly and extends his hand to her. "I've heard great things, Laura. I am very happy to meet you." Dean says, polite as can be.

"Such a gentleman." She teases. "Vanna speaks very highly of you. And you are as gorgeous a man as she's told us you are."

"*Laura!*" I scold her, embarrassed. I should have expected that though. I glance at him and he's grinning, loving it. "Anyway, Dean rode out here to take me to lunch. Do you mind if we cut out for thirty minutes or so?"

"Not in the slightest." She says. "You kids have fun."

Once we're in the parking lot, I touch Dean's arm and he stops walking to look at me. "Are you really that freaked out about what happened upstairs?" I ask him. "It was all positive. Healing. Nothing dark."

"I looked up the seven hermetic principals, after you said something about it a few weeks ago and I didn't know what the hell you were talking about." He says. "I read about balance and duality. Those capable of healing are also capable of harming. That kind of shit."

"Okay. That's true. Are you saying you think I'd harm you?" I ask.

"I'm saying after seeing penis candles to control men and feeling a weird sensation in my body I've never felt before, I should watch my ass if I ever piss you off." He grins at me. He meant it as a joke, and I would have laughed, but I know he is at least half serious, and that this could be a potential problem.

"Fortunately for you, I've learned my lesson in dabbling with spells. You don't have to worry about me manipulating your feelings."

"What do you mean?"

We are so not going there! "Look, I'd never do anything to mess with your free will, Dean." Not intentionally, anyway. "That's all you really need to know. The only magick I do now is Reiki, and little things for myself. Reiki is healing. It doesn't hurt anybody."

"Are you upset because I called you a witch?" he asks, looking at me curiously. "To be fair, you've called yourself a witch before."

"It's just the way you said it." I sigh. "I am what I am."

"Well, *I like what you are.* Relax, baby. Nothing wrong with an open mind, right? You just blew mine open a little more." he says, trying to reassure me. "You can blow me any way you want any time you want." He winks.

I smack his arm. "You're such an asshole."

He grins wider. "Yeah, but you like me anyway." He takes my hand, leading me over to Serene.

"How is this going to work? I'm wearing a dress."

"I don't particularly like doing this, but we aren't going far." Dean says, kneeling down at my feet. He reaches between my ankles, grabbing the back of my skirt and pulling it forward to tie it with the fabric in the front of my skirt, making a knot. He looks up at me with a sly smile. "I can hike your skirt up for you, if you'd like."

"I've got it, thanks."

Dean stands back up as he watches me pull up my skirt to just above my knees. "Nice." He teases me.

"Please, I look ridiculous." I roll my eyes at him.

"Give me your hand, I'll help you get on Serene." He says. "You're going to bunch the extra fabric between your legs, and make sure you hold it there, or Serene will rip your skirt off." He grins. Dean helps me gather the remaining fabric so that it doesn't get caught in his bikes tire before he mounts in front of me. "We're going to go slow, but hold on as best you can without letting go of your skirt. There's an Italian deli right around the block." He says. "Next time, I may just bring you something, since you seem to have something against pants."

I can't help laughing at his comment. *"I don't have anything against pants."*

"This witchy, long skirt thing isn't conducive to riding on the back of a motorcycle, baby."

"Right. You're probably used to chicks in leather miniskirts." I say. He fires up the bike without responding to my comment. "Yeah. I thought so." I mumble to myself.

W HILE I SET THE TABLE IN MY LITTLE EAT IN KITCHEN, I HOPE DEAN doesn't mind too much that my farmhouse rental probably isn't nearly as nice or as spacious, as his large ranch a quarter mile up the street. It really does need a lot of work.

I had gone shopping for all of the ingredients I'd need to cook tonight, earlier this morning, before heading to Laura's shop. Glancing at the old clock on the wall, I expect him to arrive any minute.

The roar of his bike barrels up my driveway, and I make my way to the screen door to greet him. Naturally, he's wearing his leather jacket, which has a bouquet of red roses sticking out the front top of it. I giggle as I imagine him riding his bike with flowers under his chin. He unzips his jacket and removes them as he makes his way towards the steps of my front porch, finally spotting me watching him. He grins and takes two steps at a time to my porch door.

"Hey, darlin'." He greets me. I flick the latch unlocked and push the creaky door open for him to enter. He stomps his feet on the door mat before stepping inside, bending to kiss me briskly on the mouth and hands me the flowers. I thank him as I take them from him, letting the spring on the screen door slam it shut. "Smells great in here."

He follows me into the kitchen as I glance around for something that will pass for a vase. I spot one with a wide mouth on top of the kitchen cabinets. Dean must have noticed me contemplating how my short ass was going to reach it, because he stretches his arm up and gets it down for me.

I suppress a chuckle as he hands it to me. "Thank you."

"How'd you get it way up there to begin with?" he teases.

"Actually, a lot of what you see in this house was here when I moved in." I explain, rinsing the vase out in the sink and filling it halfway with water. Grabbing a set of kitchen scissors, I cut the roses out of their cellophane. "I didn't move in with very many belongings. The house was fully furnished with pretty much all of the previous owner's stuff." I say, arranging the roses in the vase. "I pretty much just brought a mattress, my clothes and a few personal belongings."

He's leaning against the kitchen counter, watching me and listening. He's quiet, as if in thought, before he decides to say, "I knew the old woman who lived here. She was a sweet lady. There's actually a trail in the woods behind the house that leads to my blueberry orchard. She used to pick them. I never minded. Feel free to do the same, by the way. I think she passed away about a year ago."

"That's what her son told me. He owns the house now. I rent from him." I say, lifting the vase of red roses and bringing them over to the little kitchen island, placing them in the center. "I have the option to buy, if I want. I actually have to give him an answer by the end of my sixth month here, or he raises the rent and puts it on the market to sell. He's not really cut out to be a landlord. Plus, he lives out of state."

"Do you like the house?" Dean asks.

"It's cute and cozy, it's nice having a yard, too. But it really does need a lot of work." I say. "Come on, I'll show you around, real quick. Dinner's almost ready."

After his quick tour, we have the dinner I made for us. Baked Linguine pasta and clam sauce, with muscles and shrimp, home-made garlic bread on the side, paired with white wine to drink. Dean seems to have really enjoyed it, as he ate every bite and soaked up every drop of sauce with his garlic bread.

"Good?" I ask, still hoping, though I'm fairly sure he liked it.

"Amazing!" he wipes his face with his napkin and sits back in his chair. "You made all this from scratch?"

"Of course. Check the garbage." I blurt impulsively, immediately regretting the words as they left my mouth. He looks at me inquisitively. "I just mean, all the packaging is in there. I went to the market today and got everything fresh."

He keeps staring at me, as if he expects me to elaborate further on my strange response.

I let out a faint sigh, unable to think of a way around this stupid slip up on my part. "I had an ex that would check to make sure everything I cooked was from scratch."

Something flickers in Dean's eyes, and I notice a slight flinch in the hand he has resting on the table. He takes a sip of his wine, but he doesn't look away from me. "What an asshole." He nearly growls.

I get up to collect our plates to bring to the sink. "Yeah, you could say that." I comment under my breath.

As I reach for Dean's plate, he gently catches my hand and looks up at me. "Thank you, for a spectacular dinner, Vanna. I sincerely appreciate your efforts." His tone is genuine and his eyes are serious.

"I'm happy you enjoyed it." I smile back at him.

Taking our plates to the sink, I rinse them off and load them into the small dishwasher. Dean is beside me suddenly, with the remaining wine glasses and bread basket.

"I really want to ask you something, Vanna." He says, placing the basket on the counter. I try to keep my anxiety under control. "How long ago was the garbage checker?"

"The what?" I try to stall, uselessly.

"The unappreciative asshole ex."

"Oh." I know I can't keep *Him* a secret forever. Everyone has a past. But I will keep the ugly secrets hidden for as long as I possibly can. If only forever were possible. "A few years ago."

"He what you left New York over? Or is he from around here?" Dean presses. The tone of his voice tells me that if *he* actually was somewhere in this state, *he* might soon meet the very much darker side of Dean Keegan.

"God no." I say. I need to change the subject before Dean starts asking questions I really don't want to answer. I smile and act like everything is fine.

"He's definitely not from around here. You sweet southern boys appreciate a woman who can cook, right?" I joke.

"New York, then." Dean says, seemingly more to himself.

"Speaking of southern, I made sweet tea. Laura taught me how to do it the right way. Would you like some? We can go sit out on the porch." I attempt to steer this in another direction again. He nods, but I'm not sure if he's nodding because he wants sweet tea, or because he's figured out something about my past for himself. *Damn it. Stay chipper.* "Ice?" I offer with a smile.

"Sure, doll." But he seems discontented. Like he knows I'm faking an upbeat mood. "I'll meet you outside."

I reach for two tall glasses in my cupboard, as I hear the screen door creak and slam, genuinely glad for the moment alone to compose myself. He must have known I needed it. I have to be more careful. He is too observant of a man. He picks up on too much, even the unspoken. I both admire that about him, and stress about it. I can't keep him waiting too long though, so I grab some ice out of the freezer and the pitcher of fresh sweat tea from the fridge and pour us our drinks.

Dean's sitting in one of the old rocking chairs on the porch when I bring the glasses out. I hand him one and sit down in the chair next to him.

"I'm excited to go for another ride on your bike tonight." I say, breaking the silence between us and hoping it pulls him back to the present moment. Away from any dark concerns he may have about me and my past.

"*Serene.*" Dean corrects me, taking a sip of his tea before he looks at me. "Think it's safe to say you two girls are on a first name basis." He jokes, though his tone is still a little dry. "Anywhere in particular you want to go tonight?" He's trying. I appreciate that.

"I don't really know where anything is." I shrug. "I've basically only been around this little town, and Laura's shop. The beach. I don't get out a whole lot."

"Why is that?" he asks, still rather stoic.

"Work, mostly... Did I make the tea right?" I ask.

"It's great, doll." He says. "And even if it wasn't, I'd still appreciate it."

I don't say anything. I sip my tea and glance out across the front yard, shifting my gaze to his bike, trying to think about another topic or question I could ask him about to shift him away from this.

"How about a different section of beach? I know a spot where there aren't any lights and you can really see the stars." He says, suddenly sounding more up-beat. He's really trying, and it's for my sake. I really like this guy.

"Yes!" I say, excitedly. "I'd love that. Should I bring a blanket or anything?"

"Yeah, I've got room in one of the saddle bags."

"Okay," I say, standing up. "Do you want me to bring your glass inside? Or would you like to finish?" I ask.

"I'll finish and bring it in. Maybe use your bathroom if you don't mind."

"Of course not. It's the door to the left of the kitchen, across from the stairs." I say. "I'll go get ready."

Before we head out, I feed Nico and change into a pair of jeans. Removing my cellphone and house key from my purse, I stick the cellphone in my back pocket and tuck the key in my front one. Brushing my hair quickly, I pull it back in a pony tail for the ride, then put on my denim jacket and head back downstairs.

Dean is out on the porch. He says he's ready to go so I lock the big oak door and we walk over to his bike. He pulls a spare helmet out of the saddle bag and hands it to me while he pushes the folded blanket into its place. I put the helmet on my head and he helps me adjust the straps so it's on correctly, then gets on his bike. I use his shoulders for balance as I climb on behind him. He fires Serene up and she roars to life.

"Hold on to me tight." He always reminds me, reaching back to grab both my arms and wraps them around his waist. He backs the bike up to turn around in the driveway so we're facing the street.

"This is already fun!" I say excitedly.

He glances over his shoulder and grins at me. "You're adorable." He says, then turns back to face ahead, revs the bike and takes off quickly.

I can't help the little shriek of excitement that escapes me as we barrel down the street and head for the beach. Dean is right. There's really nothing like flying down the highway on a badass motorcycle. It does feel a little bit like freedom.

A little over an hour later, the sun already set, we pull into a small parking lot at the very far end of the beach near a small boat launch. There are only a handful of people here. And one car is already leaving. Dean offers me his hand to help me get off the bike before he dismounts as well. I take off my helmet and stretch.

"Was that more exciting than the driveway?" he teases me, placing his helmet on the handle bar and reaches for mine.

I hand it to him. "Yes." I laugh. "I definitely get it now. The whole bike thing. That was awesome." I grab the scrunchie from my hair and pull it down, freeing my hair from the pony tail as I shake my head, letting it fall naturally.

Dean catches himself staring, then turns back to the bike to open the saddle bag and retrieve the blanket, putting my helmet in its place. He pulls out a small flashlight and clips it to his belt.

"Where do you want to go?" I ask, scanning the area for a nice spot as I shove my scrunchie in a pocket. "There's a long jetty, but it looks like it ends if we walk about ten or fifteen minutes that way." I say, pointing. "Or we can climb the rocks. High tide isn't for a few more hours."

"There's a small gap in the jetty. Come on, I'll show you." He says, tucking the blanket under one arm and then offers his hand to me. I take it and we start walking towards the beach. Dean finds the break in the rocks and we climb through to the sand on the other side. It's like our own private little beach down here. A section of sand, surrounded by the boulders of the jetty, obstructing anyone from being able to see us, unless they enter through the break in the rocks as we did.

"This is great." I say. "Thank you so much for bringing me."

"My pleasure, baby." He smiles.

I grab an end of the blanket and help him spread it out on the sand near the boulders, before we both plop down on it to admire the ocean and take in the fresh air. The sound of the waves lightly crashing a few yards away is soothing to the soul, and the stars are already beginning to become visible in the darkening sky. There are sparse clouds of deep pink beginning to turn more purple as the minutes pass and the darkness deepens.

I glance at Dean, curious to see his expression, only to find him staring at me. "The view is over there." I giggle and point to the ocean.

"That, baby, is a matter of opinion." He says smoothly. I roll my eyes at him playfully and look back at the waves.

We're both quiet for a few minutes. I wonder if he actually enjoys the ocean. He must though. Who doesn't? Plus, he knew about this little private nook.

"I never realize how badly I need to come here, until I'm actually here." I sigh. "It's like, all the tension in my body, even tension I don't know I'm holding onto, just washes away. As if the ocean knows, and that's what it's here for. That's what it does for us. That's it's job."

Dean remains silent, and I know he's taking in my words. Reading between the lines. Watching me closely. I glance at him for a brief second, confirming for myself. I smile at him and look away again, pulling off my sneakers and socks. "I'm going to touch the water." I say, stuffing my socks into my sneakers and rolling up my pants, just below my knees. "Will you come with me?"

"I'll follow you anywhere." He replies.

I chuckle at him and crawl down to his feet, pulling off his boots and socks and stuffing them inside as I did mine. Placing them in the bottom corner of his side of the blanket and my sneakers on mine, I stand and reach down to help him up. He takes my hand as I haul him to his feet playfully. He doesn't let go of me though, so we walk to the shoreline holding hands.

The water is warmer than I thought it would be, as the first waves touch my feet. He lets my hand go so I can go a little further in while he bends to roll his pants up a bit as well. I venture out just a few more steps. It feels so good, letting the water wash away all my stress. I take a deep breath as I reach my arms up to the brightening stars and stretch them out to my sides before I let them fall and exhale. Closing my eyes, I focus on the feeling of the waves pushing and pulling the sand around my feet, creating that dizzying, sinking sensation.

Giggling as I lose my balance, Dean is there to catch me. "It happens to me too." He knowingly says, as he holds me from behind. His embrace feels safe and comfortable. We stand together, letting the ocean do its thing.

When we've sunken past our ankles, we pull our feet out and laugh at the slurping sounds the wet sand makes as it sucks at our feet. I turn my head towards him so he can hear me. "Do you want to help me find a hag stone?"

"What's that?"

"It's a stone with natural holes worn through it. They're good luck for witches."

We stroll along the beach for a while, not saying much but enjoying each other's company. No hag stones were spotted, but I did pocket some beach glass. We decide to head back to the blanket and look at the stars as it's now too dark to see much in the sand. When we get to the blanket, I take off my denim jacket and roll it up to use as a makeshift pillow. Dean settles down beside me, doing the same with his leather jacket.

"You're right about this spot. You can see a lot more stars." I sigh contently. He's quiet, so I glance over at him. "Are you okay? Do you want to leave?"

"No, I don't. We're not leaving at least until we see a shooting star."

"I'm totally fine with that. I could sleep here."

"I hope that's not something you do."

I laugh at his protective tone. "No. I know better. But it's so peaceful, I probably could." I glance over at him again. He is actually looking at the stars this time. "Do you come here a lot? This spot?"

"Not in a while."

"Is it a place you used to come to with somebody special?"

"No. Nobody special... But I'm hopeful it could turn into that." I can see a crack of a grin on his face.

"Me too. I have a hard time seeing you coming here alone, though."

"You asked if I came here with somebody special. They turned out to not be so special."

"I'm sorry."

"Don't be."

"She's an asshole." I say. "She has to be."

"So's your ex. A fucking huge one, I gather." He grumbles.

I force myself to laugh. I don't want this to take a turn for the dark. Asking him questions about his ex means it's fair game for him to ask me questions about mine. And I don't want to lie to him. "I only say it because you're a really nice guy."

"I'm not that nice..."

"You told me you were."

"I told you I wasn't a *bad* guy." He clarifies.

I swat his arm playfully. "Whatever. I think you are nice. But feel free to elaborate."

"I don't think I should."

Turning on my side, I prop my head up on my elbow to look at him. "Why not?"

He turns his head slightly to look back at me. "Because you're alone with me." His voice a low growl, as he speaks slowly. "Far away from anyone who could hear you scream. With no way of getting away from me. I have you trapped. Right where I want you."

My instincts tell me he wouldn't hurt me, but his words are sobering and unnerving as I consider the cold hard truth in them. I swallow hard, before I speak, "But... That would make you more than not a nice guy... that would make you a bad guy."

"I'd never hurt you." There is sincerity in his words, and what looks like pain in his eyes.

"I don't believe you would. But... why did you say all that?"

"You might have those worries if I tell you why I'm not such a nice guy." He says. "I don't want you to have those worries about me. But I also don't want to lie to you."

"Okay. I don't. I trust you." I say, a little warily now. "Why aren't you that nice of a guy?"

He turns to stare back up at the stars. "I can still say I'm not a bad guy, because I'd rather die than hurt you. But a nice guy wouldn't be thinking about how easy it would be to take you right here, willing or not. That you drive me so crazy, I'm actually capable of even having such filthy thoughts." He growls. "But that's what you do to me, Vanna. That's how strong of an effect you have on me. And to be honest, sometimes I hate myself for it. I've never had these types of thoughts and feelings before about a woman."

I don't know how to react to that. I lay back against my makeshift pillow and stare back up at the stars as well.

We're both silent for a few moments, his dark words hanging between us. I can feel the pull too, but I dare not admit to it, not now. Not out loud. I am strongly attracted to him. I felt that strange magnetic pull to him when we first locked eyes. That electric current when we kiss. If we were to kiss again, here, alone, I don't know if I would want to stop him. And if I did at some point, I know I wouldn't be able to stop him if he didn't want to stop, himself.

"If I say I want to go home-"

"I will take you home right now." He says, before I can even finish asking the question. "Do you want to leave?"

"No."

"You're not in danger with me, or from me." His words, spoken as if they are a promise.

I hesitate before I ask my next question, but it's something I want to know now. What kind of darkness was he capable of? What is it about him that radiates danger so potently? We sit in another few moments of silence before I ask. "Dean?"

"Yes?"

"What's the worst thing you've ever done?"

He scoffs. "That's a long list, doll. I don't know what the worst would be."

"What springs to mind?" Though part of me is afraid of what he might say, I want to know. "Something, recent?"

He takes a long breath, then exhales slowly before he elaborates. "I almost committed cold blooded murder." He says flatly. "Do you want to leave now?"

"No. You said, *almost*. And I'll listen, if you want to tell me why."

He clears his throat before he begins to speak. "It was four years ago. After my wife left me for him. I was drinking a lot at that time. I went to their home after dark. Stood outside their living room window. I had the gun

aimed at him, for what felt like forever, and was about to pull the trigger...
When Lucinda walked into the room. She handed him their baby daughter."
His voice lowers. "The baby was smiling. She looked happy. And I couldn't
bring myself to do it after that."

"You still loved her... Even though she hurt you."

"I thought so. Once upon a time. If the baby wasn't there, I'd probably
be four years into doing hard time right now."

"I'm glad you didn't do it."

He chuckles darkly. "I am, too."

"Maybe he'll get hit by a bus." I joke, trying to lighten the mood a little.

"Or you could drop a house on him." A Witch joke. Funny. But I can still
feel something dark in his mood.

"So, this was your old spot... with Lucinda." I say, resenting the stain
she's left here in this beautiful, perfect little private nook of beach tucked
behind the jetty.

"Are you upset I brought you?"

"No. It's a nice spot. You shouldn't let her ruin it for you."

"That's why I brought you here." He sighs. "I haven't been here in years."

"I'm glad you did. I think it's time we exorcise her lingering presence
out of here." I say, sitting up to look down at him.

He glances up at me curiously.

I bite my lip, hesitant for a moment, trying to gather my nerves. I really
like Dean. And he does turn me on. Some of the things he says should really
be a red flag, but for some reason, I just trust him. I *have* trusted him, since
day one. And if I'm being honest with myself, those same things he says that
should be red flags, also turn me on.

Twisting towards him, I throw my leg over his waist so that I'm straddling him before he can even react.

"Vanna!" He says with surprise, but I silence him by placing my hands
on his face and lowering my mouth to his with a kiss. He immediately wraps
his arms around me, twisting me back down to the blanket. Only when he is
on top of me, does he pull back, breaking our kiss. "Are you crazy, Vanna?
Did you not hear *anything* I said?"

"You said you'd never hurt me, and I believe you. Kiss me." I demand. "Or
take me home."

He hesitates, as if he's conflicted. I wrap my arms around his neck and pull
him back to me, kissing him again. He gives in to me quickly. Wrapping my legs
around his waist, I hold him to me as I open my mouth and allow his tongue
inside, deepening our kiss. My hands slip under the bottom of his shirt.
His skin is smooth and hot, and I rake my nails lightly across his lower back.

He grabs the hem of my shirt and shoves it up over my breasts, exposing
my bra. His hot, rough hand skims across my stomach up to my chest, gently
grabbing at my breasts as his tongue continues to tangle with mine.

I place my feet back down on the blanket, straightening one leg and pushing my pelvis into his, as I try to twist. No way I'm strong enough to roll
him over on my own, but he takes the queue. Wrapping his arms underneath

me, he rolls to his back, pulling me on top of him. I bend my knees so that I'm straddling him again and pull back, breaking our kiss to sit up on him and pull my shirt off. I drop it beside us as my hair cascades down over my shoulders and back.

"You're fucking beautiful, baby... but you're playing with fire." He pants, running both hands up my denim clad thighs, his strong fingers digging into my flesh through the fabric.

"Kiss me again." I breathlessly demand.

He sits up immediately, and our mouths come together hungrily once more. He wraps his arms around me tightly, one low around the small of by back, the other sliding up between my shoulder blades. I feel his fingers curl into my hair at the back of my scalp as he pulls my head back. His lips parting from mine, find my chest. I slide one hand up the back of his skull as well, pulling him to me as he buries his face in my cleavage, kissing and sucking the swells of my breasts. His short facial hair is rough like sand paper and scratches my sensitive skin, but I don't care. It turns me on more. He's going to think of *me* the next time he thinks of this place. Not Lucinda...

I rock my hips forward and roll my body, grinding against his lap. He lets go of my hair and stares me in the eyes, both of his hands now grabbing my ass as he pulls me forward, tighter against his front and more directly against his lap. I roll my body against him again as he groans and takes my mouth hungrily once more, pulling me harder still against his erection. I grind on him a little faster, pushing my tongue into his mouth now. My arms are around his neck again, one hand snaking up his skull and finding his hair. I grip it and pull his head back this time, kissing him even deeper, sucking his tongue.

He's groaning into my mouth as I mercilessly grind on him, fast and hard and rough. After a few minutes, his hands, that have been tightly gripping my ass, release me, grabbing my hair and pulling my head back to break our kiss again.

"Vanna, you're going to make me come." He pants.

I slow down for a brief moment, ducking my head down to press my lips to his throat, kissing him there. "Serene and I owe you one." I whisper teasingly against his Adams apple. I giggle and lick him some more when it bobs from his hard swallow. "*Tell me to stop.*" I whisper again, the way he did to me in his truck, the night he first kissed me.

"*Jesus fuck...*" he groans, and I can hear the desperate conflict in his voice.

"Do you want me to stop?" I whisper my question against his lips and kiss him again. He kisses me back hungrily, his arms still holding me tightly against him. I tuck my hand down between us, sliding my fingers down over his impressive erection. Smiling at the little spot of dampness I find there. I nibble his lip gently. "I can finish you off." I taunt him, slowly making circles with my hips again as I rub against his trapped erection. "You're already a mess."

He groans and clenches his eyes shut, but he's still holding me tightly against him. I pick up the pace on him once more, writhing and grinding on him. Pulling his head back again, I kiss him deeply for a moment before

230

I whisper against his mouth, "I'm wet for you too, Dean." Baiting his tongue with mine, he plunges his tongue fervently into my mouth, and I suck on him once again.

His body shudders as he lets out another groan, before I hear him desperately whimper, "Stop!"

Immediately I cease what I'm doing and shove myself off him, landing next to him on the blanket where I had tossed my shirt. I grab it and pull it back on as he lays back against the blanket, catching his breath. I lay back as well, and once again we're both staring up at the starry night sky. The only sounds around us are his labored breathing and the waves crashing against the shore.

It's a good five minutes before either one of us speaks.

"*What*... the *fuck*... was *that*?" He asks, bewildered. "Where did you learn to *kiss* like *that*?"

"I don't know... I've never kissed like that before." It's the truth. I don't know what came over me. He really turns me on.

"Fuck..."

"Did you like it?"

"I almost busted a nut in my fucking jeans, Vanna." He says, as if that should be answer enough. I bite my lip to keep from giggling. "That was some wicked witchcraft, doll. I don't know if you're half angel or half demon."

"The Hermetic Principals would say both." I tease.

"Right." He takes a deep breath and lets it out slowly.

I can't help laughing. I really don't know what came over me. I've never behaved in such a manor with any man before. Not only does he make me feel safe with him, but something about him makes me feel safe to be myself as well. I can't remember the last time I felt this way. Being with Dean actually feels like a little bit of freedom. I haven't felt any sort of freedom in years.

"We probably missed a few shooting stars." I say.

"They were all in my fucking brain." He sighs. "You fucking wreck me."

"You wanted me to stop before you... got there." I say. "I just wanted to give you something else to remember here."

He's quiet again.

"Are you mad at me?" I ask, wondering if maybe I pushed things too far.

"Mad *at* you? No... Mad *about* you... that's a safer bet."

"Thanks for bringing me to this spot." I look over and smile at him.

"Pretty sure the pleasure was all mine." Dean says, glancing back at me with a smirk of his own. "*Almost*, anyway."

Chapter eleven
DEAN

MY BACK IS FACING THE STEEL DOOR OF MY shop when it creaks open. I hear the all too familiar sound of spiked heels clicking on the cement floor. It's been years since she's set foot in my shop. But I know the sound of her footsteps in a pair of designer heels. The sound of a tight, leather skirt rubbing over her ass and thighs as her hips sway. I don't bother turning around to see if I'm correct. Instead, I continue working on a rebuild of a customer's suspension forks.

"I've been trying to call you for days." She says, a hint of aggravation in her voice. The sound of her clicking heels stops a few feet behind me.

"Been busy." I say, without turning around. "Besides, you have a *husband* for whatever task you could possibly ask of me."

"So, Maddie is a *task* now?" she gripes at me.

I turn my back on the suspension forks to glare into Lucinda's piercing blue eyes. "You mean the little girl you punish me with? The little girl you've kept me from the last... what it is now... eight months? *Nine*?" She crosses her arms, but the hard look in her eyes fades quickly. There's no way she can justify the way she uses her daughter as a pawn to manipulate me. "*That* Maddie?" I sneer at her.

"That's the one." She sarcastically replies.

I can't help shaking my head as I brush past her, grabbing an oil pan to drain the fork cylinders into. She wants me to ask about Maddie. And I want to, but I fight the urge. I don't want to play into her hands. Maddie is the only hold Lucinda knows she still has over me, and probably always will.

"She misses you." Lucinda pushes when I don't say anything. Instead, I slam the oil pan down on my work bench near the partially dismantled suspension forks and grab for a box of rubber gloves on the shelf above my work space. "I have her in the car outside."

I scoff, trying to rein in my building temper as I stare straight ahead at the shelf in front of me. My hands gripping the edge of the work table.

"She wants to see you... What should I tell her?"

"What *have* you told her? What excuse has she been given for my absence in her life this time around? Has her *dear uncle Dean* just been so swamped with work, he can't find any time at all to even *call* her on the fucking phone? Let alone visit!" I turn to glare back at Lucinda again.

"She's a little kid, Dean. She has no idea it's been months." Lucinda sighs, as if I'm being irrational. "She's a very active little girl, time flies for her."

"I'm sure she misses me." I say, keeping my tone as level as I can manage. "Like I've been missing her. For *nine* fucking months. Why now? Why is today our lucky fucking day, Lucinda? Might your sudden change of heart... and I use *that* word lightly... have anything to do with the fact I'm dating someone steadily now? Afraid that death grip of yours is slipping?" I sneer at her. "That safety net disintegrated a while ago."

I can see she's fighting the urge to scowl at me. "Of course not. You think I don't know you're out fucking women every chance you can get? You told me so yourself."

The grin widening across my face is impossible to stop. Her desperation to convince herself that there's no way I could be serious about someone else, is plain to see. "Only I'm not fucking *women*. I'm only seeing *one* woman. And that's what's got your panties twisted."

She rolls her eyes at me. "*Oh, please.* That frumpy, gypsy looking wallflower you've been galivanting around town with lately?"

"*Frumpy wallflower*?" I can't help laughing, heartily, at her utterly obvious attempt at convincing *herself*, that Vanna isn't a total fucking knock out. "Fuck... Lucinda... I needed that laugh today." I say, catching my breath and trying to compose myself as I lean back against the work bench. "If you're absurdly referring to *Vanna*, then yes. I am only seeing her. Quite contently, as a matter of fact."

"I see you've *lowered* your standards then." She smiles contemptuously.

"Get your sight checked."

Lucinda rolls her eyes at me again. "I'm going to have to meet her if you're going to be around Maddie, and this... *Vanna* person, is going to be around you." She says, with an air of authority in her voice, as if she's got any over me.

"You're just full of jokes today, aren't you?" I shake my head at her. "Go fuck yourself, Lucinda. I don't want Vanna anywhere near you."

She looks taken aback. "You're the one that must be joking!" she snaps. "A woman you've known barely more than a few months, over the little girl you've known and *supposedly* loved for five years!"

I glare at her. "Only a manipulative bitch like you would see it that way, Lucinda."

"What other way is there to see it?" she demands.

"Another one of your control tactics. Another manipulation using that little girl to weasel your way into my life again!" I nearly snarl at her, fighting the urge to get in her face. "I'm not going to let you keep doing that to her. Bringing me in and out of her life at your twisted whim whenever you want something from me. Leaving her wondering why I suddenly don't care enough to bother with her, every time I fall short of your fucking demands or expectations!" I only realize I'm shouting at her, when my junior mechanic, Derek, walks into the shop from the front lobby.

"Dean, everything okay in here?" he asks.

I take a few steps back from Lucinda. "Yeah, fine." I mutter, shooting him a look that lets him know he needs to get back to work.

"Aight, man. I'll just give you some privacy, then. Got a customer up front." He says, clearly warning me that we need to keep it down. I nod once to him, before I look back at Lucinda.

"You need to leave. I've got work to do."

"You're really not going to walk outside and see her?" she stares at me in disbelief.

"I'm not going to let you keep hurting her." I say, turning back to the suspension forks on my work bench. "Even if it means I have to hurt myself."

"You're unbelievable."

"According to you, time flies for Maddie. She'll be eighteen before she knows it." I glare at her with contempt, an overwhelming feeling of disgust for both of us washing over me.

"Stubborn asshole!" Lucinda hisses, before she turns on her heels and storms out the way she came in.

I try to focus on the work in front of me. Attempting to push the image of little Maddie waiting expectantly in the car to see her asshole *uncle Dean*. Her spiteful mother spinning some pathetic excuse as to why she can't see me. The disappointed, possibly even saddened expression on her little face... Will she wonder why? Think it's somehow her own fault I can't be bothered with her?

The sound of the steel door opening with a loud clang, and those fucking heels clicking on the cement, fill me with barely containable rage again. I whirl back around with every intention of lacing into Lucinda, customers in the lobby or not. But my heart sinks, and my rage momentarily dissipates, as Maddie runs towards me ahead of her mother. A bright, happy smile across her little, innocent face.

Dropping to one knee, I capture her in a tight embrace, crossing my forearms behind her small back, careful not to let my oil dirty hands touch her pretty little sun dress.

"Uncle Dean!" she exclaims, with such glee it nearly breaks my scarred-up heart. It's as if this child harbors no resentment towards me, no blame for being so inconsistent in her life. I rest my chin on her little shoulder as her arms squeeze around my neck. I can't help glaring up at her mother with new found disdain, as she grins triumphantly back at me.

Lucinda... I fucking hate you...

V ANNA SPOTS ME FROM ACROSS THE BAR AS SOON AS I WALK INTO THE Twisted Throttle, shutting the steel door behind me with a clang, barely audible over the loud rock music and boisterous conversations. Her smiling face, initially happy to see me, morphs instantly into worry, as she realizes I'm sporting a freshly bruised cheekbone, and a cut above my eye brow. I give her a little wave, as I walk over to Viking, eager to take a seat beside him on the extra bar stool. My leg hurts, from being nailed by a solid kick to my thigh in the ring, a mere hour ago.

"I see you had a therapy session tonight." Viking says, looking me over. "You lose this one?"

"I thought about throwing it." I confess. I wanted to punish myself... The first two rounds, I let myself take somewhat of a beating. After the stunt Lucinda pulled earlier today with Maddie... I don't deserve the love that girl has for me. "But I didn't want to throw away all the work I've put into climbing back to the top of the circuit." I shake my head. "I let him get a few good shots in, then I KO'd him in the third round."

"Your girlfriend know about your little hobby?" Viking asks.

"No." I watch Vanna hurrying with getting an order out so she can come over to me.

"What brought this on?" he asks.

"What else?"

Viking lets out his own sigh. "Fuck, Bro. What did she do to you now?"

"Ain't just what she's doing to me. I honestly don't know what to do anymore." I watch as Vanna places her serving tray down on the bar near Cherry then starts to head in my direction. "Do me a favor and don't say anything about any of this." I sigh remorsefully, already feeling all kinds of wrong about not being up front with Vanna in a moment.

"Oh my God! What happened to you?" Vanna asks, concern written all over her face as she rushes up to me. Her hand gently touching the unbruised side of my face. I reach up to touch her wrist, and she spots my bloody knuckles. "Did somebody jump you? What happened?" she asks, taking my hand in hers now and inspecting it.

"I'm okay, doll. Just got in a fight."

"We should clean these cuts out, Dean."

"Go let your Lady clean you up, bro." Viking says. "I got my eye on things."

Vanna's pleading look won't allow me to deny her. "Alright." I say, getting back to my feet. I let Vanna lead me over to the bar by Cherry, who's looking at me knowingly already. I shake my head slightly at her, hoping she won't make a comment about my condition, or my situation. She doesn't, she just puts some ice in a towel and hands it over the bar to Vanna.

"I'll be back as soon as I get this one straightened up." Vanna says to Cherry. *This one.* I chuckle to myself, following obediently as Vanna leads me into my office and sits me down at my desk. She fishes the first aid kit out from the large bottom drawer and removes the antiseptic and cotton swabs.

"So, are you going to tell me how all this happened?" she asks, placing the towel of ice gently against my cheek. "I need you to hold this here so I can clean that cut above your eye and your hand." I do as I'm told, watching her soak a swab with antiseptic and carefully dab the cut above my brow bone. "Are you going to answer me?" she asks, before she lightly blows on the cut, as if she's worried the antiseptic might be causing me further discomfort. I think it's sweet. Reminds me of the way my mother used to blow on my skid knees as a kid, after dumping hydrogen peroxide on the cuts. I can't help smiling at her now.

"I just got in a fight. Nothing serious." I say, hoping she won't force me to lie to her.

"Did you rescue another damsel in distress in a bathroom stall?" she teases me.

"No." I chuckle. "Some guy thought he could beat me in a fight. He was wrong. Guy stuff." I shrug, hoping that will satisfy her. Technically, I'm not lying to her.

"Oh, so this is a *I should see the other guy,* type thing." She smears a dab of Neosporin across the cut.

"That's right."

After she places a little butterfly bandage across the cut above my eye, she moves on to my hand, carefully cleaning the scrapes on my knuckles, blowing on them as she goes, as well. "I don't think band aids are going to work well here." She says, dabbing a little more Neosporin here and there on my hand. "You might just need to be careful with this."

"Whatever you say, doc." I tease her.

"I noticed you weren't walking right when you came in. Is there something wrong with your leg?" she asks, packing the first aid kit back up.

"Took a kick to the thigh. Probably bruised. Just a little tender. I'll drop my pants though if you want to have a closer look." I grin at her.

"You're so naughty."

"You're one to talk... after that beach exorcism the other night." I have not been able to get that demon kiss she laid on me out of my head.

Vanna giggles, bringing her hands together in front of her, as if in prayer position. I watch as she rubs them together, whispering her little chant in that witch language I don't understand.

"Oh shit, are you gonna *freaky deaky* me again?"

She nods, smiling, and places both of her hands on my thigh as she bends forward. I can feel the heat of her touch right through the denim instantly. But I don't know if it's her so called *energy healing*, a psychosomatic influence, or if I'm just hyper sensitive to her touch in general. What fucking ever though... She's got her hands on me. No complaints here.

"It's called *Reiki*, by the way." She corrects me. "Just give it a few minutes. I know this *witchy shit* isn't your cup of tea."

"Your hands are on my thigh. I'm content to sit here and take it." I grin. "Where would your hands be if he kicked me in the balls?"

She smirks at me, one of her perfect eyebrows arching slightly.

"Well damn." I smile.

"I wouldn't do that for just anybody though."

That didn't even occur to me. Her disproportionate number of male clientele, seeking her services at her day job. This healing touch of hers...

"Fuckin' better not." I try not to frown at the thought of the possibilities.

She giggles at me. "Shush. You've been such a good patient so far. Don't ruin it."

"Do I get a lollipop or something?"

"I'm afraid I'm all out of lollipops."

"That shit just ain't fair." I sigh.

"How about a kiss?" she offers.

"Aces." I grin, lowering the towel of ice from my cheek to collect on my prize. Vanna leans in closer to my face, her lips mere centimeters from mine, smirking teasingly at me. I only wonder why she hesitates for a moment, before my desire to have her lips against mine overrules my instinct to interpret her actions. I reach my hand up gently to wrap my fingers around the nape of her neck and pull her the short distance to my mouth.

Her kiss instantly washes away some of the turmoil that's been clawing at me all day. Taking the edge off the pain eating away at the hole in my soul. The deep wound Lucinda seems determined to continually rip back open, every chance she gets.

She kisses me for a few moments, chastely by comparison to the way she kissed me that night at the beach. Her sweet little tongue only teasingly touching mine, before she smiles against my lips and pulls back from me. A sigh escapes me at the loss.

"I should really get back on the floor." She says quietly, her proximity still allowing her soft breath to reach my lips, tantalizing me again. "My shift barely started when you walked in."

238

I know I should let her go. Back to work, and to retract my hand from her neck. But my will power is rather weak at the moment, and she isn't fighting me either.

"One more?" I whisper my request. She smiles and allows me to gently pull her the short distance back to me, pressing her soft lips to mine once again. Her tongue barely touches mine before there's a frantic knock on my office door.

Vanna immediately pulls back and straightens, turning towards the door. I want to slam my fist on the desk, momentarily angry for the interruption, but as my wits return, I realize that we are at the roadhouse, and there could be a potential problem on the floor. I immediately rise from my desk and step around to open the door.

"Viking is asking for you." Vixie quickly informs me. "Nomads at the door wanting to come in. A group of them."

I nod and she quickly turns back down the corridor to return to the bar.

"Nomads?" Vanna asks. "Is that bad?"

"Not necessarily. You can wait in here, if you'd like, but I have to go."

Vanna picks up the towel of ice I left on my desk. "Be careful." She says, a nervous tone in her voice.

I don't have time to answer whatever questions she may have. Viking needs me to make the call on whether or not they get in, or need to be encouraged to leave. I nod at her and head down the corridor to return to the bar. Viking is standing by the front door waiting as I approach.

"They got an MC name?" I ask him.

"Chrome Demons." Viking replies.

"Shit." I mutter. "How many?"

"Only five." Viking says. "We can take them."

"Let's try to do this tactfully." I don't want to make enemies with a nomad group of unknown numbers. I am somewhat familiar with the Chrome Demons MC. Familiar enough to hope they're just passing through our little town.

"Gentleman," I keep my tone steady, "What brings you here tonight?" I ask, looking the five men over as they stand around their bikes in the lot outside. Viking is behind me, arms folded and silent.

"Are you Dean Keegan?" The one nearest me asks, leaning on his bike. He's standing in profile to me, slouched slightly. A glowing cigarette between his fingers of the hand that's resting against the clutch of his Indian Chief motorcycle.

"I'm Dean Keegan. There a reason you're asking for me?" I inquire, my eyes continually scanning their group spread out in the darkness. Seemingly just enough to avoid the illumination of the flood lights, intentionally.

He chuckles, a low sound emanating through the dark lot. "Now, *you...*" he says, standing up from his bike, pointing at me with the two fingers holding his cigarette. Even in the darkness, I can see that he's looking me over, appraisingly. "*You,* I get." The Demon is about my height, though he's got a slimmer build on him. Lanky, even. A thin, clean shaven, sharp featured face, that's evident, even in the shadows.

"I'm gonna need *you*, to *get* to the point." I say.

The Demon laughs again. "Our intel was that Preacher was the man to see in this town. The *President* of the Saviors." His words are somewhat mocking.

"He is. And you are?"

"*Legion.*" He replies. "Vice President of the CDMC. Word on the street, is that *you're* the gatekeeper in this county."

"I'm the gatekeeper of this establishment, *Legion*. And I'm afraid we don't permit out of state Nomads. This is a place for locals... Locals that don't want any trouble."

"Not here to give you any trouble, Dean Keegan." Legion says. "Just wanted to meet the man."

"Well Preacher isn't here. And you'll never find him here." That's all *they* need to know. But... "What's your interest in the Saviors anyway?"

"Networking." Legion smiles at me, before he takes a long drag off that cigarette. "And I wasn't referring to Preacher. We've met." He says, the smoke billowing from his mouth as he speaks.

The thought crosses my mind, that Preacher may have enlisted this MC to encourage me to sell him the clubhouse. An attempt to intimidate me into taking his offer. Strong arm me via hired thugs. From what I remember of my time out West, the CDMC were a nasty crew. I laugh internally at the possibility of him sinking to that tactic. But why reach out to an MC based out of the desert? Seems extreme to go to those lengths, when hiring local thugs would be easier and achieve the same results. Another firm *fuck no* from me. I don't roll over. There has to be another reason why the CDMC is littering my parking lot tonight.

"So, what do the Chrome Demons want with me, Legion?" I ask. "You've come an awful long way to seek me out. Arizona, that's where you originate from, isn't it? Nevada maybe? Somewhere hotter than Hell."

"Oh, not quite that far, Keegan." Legion chuckles. "Our new club house is only a forty-five-minute ride from your establishment's front door. We've chosen your lovely state to lay down roots for a permanent charter."

Fuck... And weak ass fucking Preacher let it happen! At our back door, no less!

"So, you see, we're not exactly nomads." He continues with a grin, taking another step towards me as he flicks his ash. "In fact, one could even call us *locals*."

"This county is Saviors' territory. You're over stepping."

"We're over the county line, brother." He shrugs. "No worries."

"Forty-five minutes? *Barely*." I counter.

"Your President didn't have an issue. Preacher gave us his blessing." Legion sneers.

"Preacher isn't my president. I'm not a Savior anymore. This establishment is beyond Preacher's reach. I call the shots here. And until you and your crew, show me just what *kind* of crew you are these days, these doors remain closed to you."

Legion takes another drag from his cigarette, nodding at my words. "Preacher said as much. That you lost your cut. Consider joining *our* merry little band of bikers." He smiles, gesturing to his crew. "We could use a man of your... *talents*. And we wouldn't even make you prospect long."

"No thanks. I'm good." I reply.

Legion pinches off the cherry of his cigarette with his fingertips, then walks towards the ashtray trash bin a few feet away from me. I can hear Viking's body shift slightly towards him as he does so, following his movements. Legion grins at him as he chucks the butt into the trash bin, then shifts his gaze back to me. "Perhaps you'll have a change of heart. We're not here to cause you any trouble tonight, Keegan. Savior or not." Legion says, extending his hand to me.

In the dark, illuminated only by the flood lights in the parking lot, his pale, long fingers, actually do remind me of a fucking Demon.

"*You*, we actually respect." Legion says. Though I can tell he's smiling at me, I can't read his eyes in the darkness. Reluctantly, and for the sake of keeping peace alone, I accept the Demon's hand shake.

KEEPING MYSELF BUSY WITH WORK, FILLING ORDERS AND COLLECTING empties around the bar, I try not to focus on what might be going on outside with the Nomad situation. It seems like Dean has been out there with Viking a long time. Yet as I glance at the clock above the bar, it's only been about twenty minutes.

"Should someone check on them?" I ask Cherry, when she's through pouring a few shots at the bar. "Would we even be able to hear them if they're out there fighting?"

Cherry shakes her head. "Axel's watching on the camera's outside. And there are only five of them. Even if they do get into a fight, between Dean and Viking, those nomads aren't going to come out on top."

Only five of them. "Dean fights a lot, doesn't he?" I ask.

Cherry presses her lips together, her eyes slightly widening as she finds something to busy herself with behind the bar, instead of answering me.

"I'll take that as a yes." I sigh, wondering if I should add this to the list of red flags about Dean that I continue to notice, then chose to willfully ignore.

"He's fine." Vixie says, coming up behind me and placing her hand on my shoulder as she smiles. "Dean is a badass. And Viking... well, who in their right mind would pick a fight with that man?" she laughs. "If there were ten of them, I might be *slightly* concerned."

"Right." I say, wondering why Vixie is suddenly being nice to me. The whole two months or so that I've worked here, she's been rather cold towards me. Maybe she found a guy to take her focus off of Dean? Or maybe Dean was right about the girls here. Maybe some of them just take time to warm up to new comers. I decide to give her the benefit of the doubt, for now.

While I'm serving tables in the back, Viking finally enters the bar. Alone. I finish cracking bottles open for the group of men at the table I'm working, before I grab my tray and walk over to Viking.

"Is Dean still out there with them?" I ask.

Viking looks at me, settling back down on his bar stool. He takes his time responding to my question. "Dean told me to watch out for you till he gets back. He had to run an errand." He says, folding his massive arms across his chest and leaning back against the brick wall.

"With the Nomads?"

"No. But you're skirting the line on club business." He says, more firmly now. My perplexed expression makes him sigh with a detectible level of annoyance. "Women stay out of club business." Viking grumbles. "MC doesn't just stand for Motorcycle Club. It's also a Man's Club. You should commit that to memory. If you plan on sticking with Dean for a while."

Sticking with Dean for a while? "Did I do something to piss you off?" I ask, crossing my arms to match his tough guy posture. I notice a little grin begin to creep across his otherwise impassive expression.

"Not yet." He says. "Go waitress. I'm in charge when Dean isn't here."

"You're rude." I glare at him.

"*And you're on the clock.*" His smile seems to widen the more he aggravates me, but he's right. I am being paid to work here. Dean gave me this job when he didn't have to. The least I could do is be a good employee. Not attempt to pump his rude bouncer for information.

"Fine." I scowl at him, before I return to waiting my tables.

Halfway through my shift, Dean still hasn't returned. I let Cherry know I'm taking my break, and head down the corridor towards the back of the building. Pushing the back door open to the patio, I find Vixie talking on her cellphone in one of the chairs at the nearest table.

She smiles at me, kicking a chair with her foot towards me. "Sit down." She says, cocking her chin towards the chair. I take a seat, pulling out my cellphone as she tells whomever she's talking to that she'd give them a call back later. I bring up Dean's number and send him a text, asking if he's okay and if he plans on being back before the bar closes.

"So, you and Dean, huh?" Vixie says, shoving her phone in her pocket before she leans back in her chair and looks me over.

"We're dating, yeah."

"How did Dean meet a girl like you?" she asks.

"Like me?" There are too many ways she could have meant that.

"Clearly not an MC woman, that's all." Vixie says.

"We met at Derek's Birthday party."

"And you're a... *Witch*?" she asks, almost humorously.

I try to keep my expression neutral. I'm used to people not taking me seriously, thanks to preconceived notions about witchcraft and paganism. Mostly thanks to Hollywood's over the top depictions of witches in movies and television. "I work at a metaphysical shop." I shrug. "Why do you ask?"

"Word travels fast in a small town."

I highly doubt it was Dean who said anything about it. He promised not to say anything. The only other person in this little town who knows what I do, is my other neighbor, Garrett Johnson. He must have really meant it when he said he would recommend my services to others. I silently hope this doesn't cause me any more issues down the road. Things have been quiet on that front, since the incident at the farmers market... But if Dean keeps pulling knives on people, someone is going to call the cops on him.

"So, you are?" She asks. "That would explain a few things."

"What do you mean?"

"You're just not Dean's typical type, that's all." I don't know how to even respond to that remark, but I get the feeling, Vixie isn't trying to be my friend. When I don't respond, she continues to drive her point. "He's just a through and through MC guy. We just never expected him to bring in somebody like *you*."

"Who is *we*?" I ask. "And what do you mean by somebody like me?"

She scoffs. "Hell, *everybody*."

My thoughts go back to Viking's rudeness earlier, and I wonder if maybe Dean's friend doesn't like me either. In fact, besides Dean's customers, none of the members of the Saviors MC ever even speak to me, unless they have to. Except the younger one, Axel. He seems genuinely friendly, at least he was the handful of times we crossed paths for brief moments around the roadhouse.

"You're just not the type of woman he's always gone for in the past, that's all." Vixie adds. "Not to say you don't have any assets that appeal to these guys." She says, waving her hand at my chest. As if big boobs are all I've got that are worth anything to these MC guys.

"Maybe he's not as shallow as you might think he is."

"Oh, no. I don't think that at all." Vixie says. "You're very pretty, Vanna. Dean is clearly playing it safe with you, though. But who can really blame him, after Lucinda."

"And just what the hell is that supposed to mean?" I demand, positively sure now that Vixie hasn't changed her feelings about me at all. This fake friendliness at the bar was just a ploy to trick me into giving her the time of day so she could mess with my head.

Vixie shrugs. "Just that he never really got over Lucinda leaving him. She was the love of his life, the poor guy never recovered. Probably never will. Lucinda ruined him for other women. She's basically every biker's dream babe. He's playing it safe with you because he thinks you'll never cut him as deep."

"I wouldn't want to hurt him."

"You couldn't. Not like she did. That kind of pain takes *real* love."

Right. And Dean could never really love somebody like me. Her words bother me more than they should, having only known Dean barely more than a few months. But if he is the Knight, isn't that what I asked for? That the Knight *not* fall in love with me...

I swore to never do another love spell after the nightmare my life became. Now, I find myself regretting putting the intention of blocking love all together, in the Knight Summoning spell. Vixie might be right after all, if Dean is indeed, my Knight. He can't fall in love with me, can he? He can only care enough to want to keep me safe.

There is still a chance though, that he isn't the Knight at all. There is no sign of the Morning Star weapon around him. In which case, there's still hope, isn't there?

"Look, you seem like a nice person, Vanna." Vixie says, pulling me from my inner thoughts as I look back at her across the table between us. "You're just ... kind of the *opposite* of Lucinda. In a lot of ways. I'm sure Dean likes you, but he's killing time knowing you're never going to break his heart. He's never going to love anyone the way he loves Lucinda."

I force myself to smile, as if her words didn't hurt to hear. "Well, we are only dating. He's a good friend."

"Should probably keep it that way. Dean is a good friend to have." She says. "I hope we can be friends, too. I didn't mean to say anything to offend you." Her smile doesn't reach her hazel eyes.

Yeah, right. But I'll continue to be civil, for the sake of this job. "Sure." I say, trying to ignore the cold feeling in the pit of my stomach. I feel like I could lock myself in the bathroom and cry. Standing up from the chair, I rub my clammy palms on my jeans and check my cellphone once more. No reply from Dean yet.

"Are you going in already?" she asks.

"Yeah. Time goes by quicker when I work."

She nods, pulling her cellphone back out of her pocket. "See you in there, then." She grins, more to herself, than at me, texting someone on her phone again.

Yanking the back door open, I walk down the corridor towards the bar, making a pit stop in the bathroom to compose myself.

Vixie basically said that none of Dean's people understand what he's doing with *somebody like me*. That he's still hung up on Lucinda. Could that be true? She was calling him the other night. And that ringtone he has her saved under... *Love The Way You Lie*... a song about a toxic relationship that neither lover can walk away from. Another red flag waving in my face that I've refused to fully acknowledge.

Is he only spending time with me because I'm so vastly different from everything Lucinda? That I'm a safe bet because he will never fall for me the way he fell for her, and therefore, never risk getting his heart broken again?

244

Staring in the mirror behind the sink in the bathroom, I try to recall what Lucinda looks like. I had only seen her across the street, that night. Our first date. But she was tall, slender and had long blonde hair. She was wearing some kind of tight black dress and heels.

I really look nothing like her. Or the women that hang around Dean. He keeps company with slender, leather clad biker babes, naturally. Not wild haired, curvy bodied, witchy looking chicks.

And the way Vixie said that me being a witch would explain a few things. Like I bewitched him or something, because there's no way I could attract a guy as gorgeous as Dean on my own looks alone. My heart sinks a little as the point actually does resonate with me. If he is the Knight, that's the only reason a man like Dean is even giving me the time of day, let alone wanting to be around me. He might not even understand why he wants to, himself. It's the spells influence, driving him to want to be near me. He's confusing that desire with actual desire, and just going with it.

Glaring at myself in the mirror, I wish now I hadn't added that clause in the Knight Summoning spell about not wanting the Knight and I to fall in love. I wish I had left the whole concept out of it all together. I was just trying to be fair to this unsuspecting Knight. It was bad enough I was summoning a man to deal with another problem I created myself. I didn't want to influence his emotions on top of putting him in danger with my exes impending wrath.

Cranking the sink on, I rinse my face, wishing I could wash away all my mistakes and just start over. My only shred of peace in this entire situation with Dean, is that thus far, there is no third sign confirming he actually is the Knight. That was a key point. It still might not be Dean.

Angrily grabbing a few paper towels to dab my face dry, that little bit of peace is short lived. Even if the Knight Summoning Spell was a complete flop, and there is no Knight, Dean could still be playing it safe with me, as Vixie said. I am, after all, no *Lucinda*.

DEAN

"YOU WANNA TELL ME WHAT THE FUCK PREACHER'S DOING MAKING NICE with the fucking Chrome Demons MC?" I demand, when Viper opens his front door. "Giving his fucking blessing for them to set up shop right in our fucking back yard!"

Viper steps outside onto his front porch, closing the door behind him, glaring at me as if I've got some nerve pounding on his door at eleven at night. Fuck him.

"A fucking phone call would have sufficed, asshole." He growls at me. "And *Our* back yard, is a stretch, isn't it? You turned your back on the Saviors."

"Start talking. Or I'm going to start swinging." I threaten him.

"Rosita is inside. Your psychotic ass already scared her." Viper snaps at me.

"Then I suggest you don't ruin the rest of her night by forcing me to lay you the fuck out in her flower beds."

"The fuck you want to know? This is all club business. You're out, but I'm sure you remember the rules."

"I want to know about the Demons. The fuck is going on with that?"

Viper lets out a long sigh as he looks me over. "They made their presence known a few weeks ago. Met with Preacher privately. All I know is they set up shop in an old rundown diner off the service road on thirty-three. Just past the county line. Been turning that condemned lookin' shit hole into a clubhouse. *The Demons' Den.*" He tilts his head, as if something just occurred to him. "How do you even know they met with Preacher?"

"Because five of them showed up to the Twisted Throttle tonight. Claiming they sought the Saviors blessing before laying down roots."

Viper scoffs. "They didn't seek shit. Those roots were laid before they ever spoke with Preacher. The Jokers and the Knights had no idea either. Nobody was approached by the Demons until they already moved in. Why were they at your bar?"

"Wanting to meet me." I watch Viper intently. "Funny how just the other day you were asking me not to shoot the messenger."

"And that's all I was. The go between for you and Preacher." Viper sneers at me. "I don't know what the deal is with the Demons. They've been fairly quiet so far. So has Preacher. He told me to make you an offer, I did. I don't know why the Demons were at your place. But I've got a question for you. Why do you suddenly care about the Saviors after all this time? You haven't given a shit these last three years, up until recently."

"Letting a crew like the CDMC slither their way into this state, let alone this close to our community, is a huge fuck up. *Huge.* I've heard about them, out West, years ago. They're nothing but trouble this community doesn't need."

"That's the impression I got." He mutters.

"So, what the fuck is Preacher doing?"

Viper lets out a sigh. "I don't know."

"The fuck you mean you don't know? You're his VP."

"That patch doesn't mean shit. He's blocking out all of us, but the four or five that are still close to him." Viper says. "I don't know shit. He doesn't trust me anymore. Like he doesn't trust Viking, or the other guys who sided with you."

"You sided against me. Why wouldn't he trust you?"

"Maybe he can tell a few of us regret the way we voted."

Too little, too late. "He still patching in Axel?" I ask, feeling even more uneasy about the whole idea now.

Viper nods. "That's still a go, as far as I know. Preacher doesn't trust us, but hasn't tried to take anyone's cuts for some reason. He doesn't even like Axel much, because the kid is such a *fan* of *yours*. It's like he doesn't want to drop numbers, but he doesn't trust any of us either."

"That's what Viking said. It doesn't make any sense. He says Preacher isn't even making a stink over some of you not contributing to the coffers anymore either."

"He isn't."

"How does he think he's going to buy me out of the club house with a dwindling MC?"

Viper shakes his head. "I told you, he doesn't tell me shit."

"How do you know the Jokers and the Knights weren't consulted? That diner is in the Knights' County."

"I spoke with their VP's. They didn't know moves were being made by the CDMC until they were already made. My guess, the Knights are a smaller MC than the Demons. Between being outnumbered, and the Demons reputation for being an MC you don't want to fuck with... they decided not to fuck with them. The Jokers aren't much larger than the Knights, and they're not as close territory wise as the Saviors and The Knights."

"How many Demons are there that we know of?" I ask. Being formerly nomadic, there's really no way of knowing exactly how many there are settling in. Or how many might still come.

"I rode by about a week ago. Counted eleven bikes. But who really knows?"

"What time?" I ask, glancing at my watch. Eleven thirty on a Saturday night. If that rundown diner is their clubhouse, a majority of them will be there tonight.

"My way home from work. So around six pm." Viper says.

"Tell Rosita I apologize for frightening her. I gotta go." I say, turning from Viper to head back to Serene.

"Don't kick the hornets' nest." Viper mutters after me.

I pull Serene into a dirt lot on the opposite side of the highway, across from the old rundown diner. It sits just outside of the county line, and there are sixteen bikes parked out front. Hidden in the darkness, I remove my binoculars from Serene's side bag to take a better look. The place is indeed, a shit hole. The diner closed down well over a decade ago, and as far as I can remember, nothing has ever been done with it since that time. It's been left to decay, nature attempting to reclaim the structure with over grown grass, creeping vines and large gangly bushes. Even the parking lot and walk ways are cracked with weeds growing through them. In the middle of nowhere out here, it's really no surprise nothing ever became of it. It's actually a perfect place for the Demons to set up, even if it's temporary. Even if it's a shit hole. The windows are still boarded up, though, through the cracks of the boards, I can make out the glow of some kind of red lighting inside. If the aesthetic they're going for is *Creepy Demonic*, they're fuckin' nailing it.

I want to get a closer look, though, so I'm going to have to sneak over there and take a peek through the boards. Glancing around the property through the binoculars one more time, I make sure there aren't any prospects keeping watch.

"I'll be right back, baby." I whisper to Serene, tucking the binoculars back into her side bag. Pulling my cellphone out of my jacket pocket, I switch it to silent before heading across the highway.

I approach the building from the far left, the opposite side of the structure that's without a side door or a flood light, and make my way stealthily towards a boarded window. Conscious of casting a shadow, I chose one in total darkness and peek through the crack. From what I can tell, the inside of this rat's nest diner, is just as run down as the outside. Though, they've got a bar, and a pair of pool tables inside. The dining tables have been removed from the center floor, only the booths remain along the perimeter walls. Red track lighting along the ceiling and floors is the source of the red glow emanating through the cracks of the boards. The sixteen riders are lounging around inside, either at the bar, scattered in a few of the booths, or shooting pool.

Roaring straight pipes barreling down the highway interrupt my surveillance, and I duck back down into the shadows to wait them out. The loud Indian Motorcycles pull into the lot in front of the Demons' Den. I make my way carefully and quietly to the edge of the structure, glancing around the corner to get a look at the new arrivals. Three more bikers, bringing their numbers to nineteen, have brought a few women with them. And by the disheveled, strung-out look of these women, they're most likely prostitutes.

"*The party's here!*" One of the Demons shouts, throwing both arms around two of the women's shoulders on either side of him. They laugh as they make their way to the front door.

The third woman is so out of it, she's having a difficult time getting off the back of one of the bikes. The Demon she rode with impatiently grabs her off the bike, throwing her over his shoulder to carry her inside. His companion yanks her already short skirt up, and slaps her bare ass before they go, *hard*. She barely even reacts...

A queasy feeling over comes me as I lean back against the building. *Three* women... *Nineteen* men... And I didn't even see Legion or his other four riders inside.

Stepping back into the shadows near one of the boarded-up windows, I'm almost afraid to look inside again, now that *the party's here...*

D EAN HASN'T RETURNED SINCE HE STEPPED OUTSIDE TO DEAL WITH THE
nomads. Nor has he returned my text. The bar is closing for the
night, and Cherry and I are already starting to clean up the tables. Viking
seems unfazed by Dean's absence though, so I keep telling myself that he is
probably fine. He's off doing MC business. Whatever the hell that means.
Whatever the hell that *is*, at two thirty in the morning. It isn't like him to
ignore my texts though. For all I know, he could be with his precious Lucinda.

I try to push that thought out of my head. It's Vixie's fault I'm even worried
about it now, not Dean's. As far as I know, he hasn't wronged me in any way.
We're only dating. And if anyone has possibly wronged anyone in this... *rela-*
tionship?... It's me that has wronged him, with that damn Knight spell.

"Have a good night, ladies!" Vixie calls, as she heads to the front door
to leave for the night. "See you next weekend, Vanna." She smiles at me.
I give her a quick nod, not bothering to stop wiping down the table I'm at.

"What the hell was that?" Cherry asks, as I move on to the last section
in the back.

"Nothing." I sigh, vigorously wiping down a table top, before I chuck
the rag in her bucket.

"Did Vixie say something to you?"

"Nothing I didn't already know." I say, heading back behind the bar
to rinse my hands in the sink before I head home.

"Alright, well... I guess we'll see you next weekend?" Cherry asks, trailing behind me, her tone somewhat suspicious, but I really don't care at the
moment. I just want to get back to my rental house, cuddle up with Nico
and go to sleep. Forget that conversation with Vixie. Though, I know I won't.
It's going to eat at me.

"Have a great night." I smile as best I can at Cherry. I walk by her and out
the front door. I don't even bother acknowledging Viking as I leave, though
I hear his heavy footsteps behind me, crunching on the gravel in the lot as
I walk towards my car.

"What do you want?" I demand, whirling around on him.

Viking's expression is as impassive as ever. "I'm supposed to make sure
you're safe." He says, "That's what I'm doing."

"Oh, like *you* care." I scowl at him.

"Dean cares. *Ergo,* I care. Keep walking."

"Where is Dean?" I ask. "He never responded to my text." Viking just shrugs. "Let me guess, *Biker business* I'm not allowed to know about?" I cross my arms, glaring up at him.

Another grin starts to crack his previously blank expression. "It's *MC business*. *Biker business* just sounds corny." He says, then points towards my car. "Walk, woman."

Woman! "You're such a jerk. Do you know that?" I snap back at him.

"The sooner you're safe and sound in your car, the sooner I can find Dean."

"Find Dean?" My annoyance evaporates instantly. "Did something happen to him?"

"That's for me to find out, and for you to *get in your fucking car*." Viking says. "Don't make me carry you over there and put you in it."

I'm not as dainty as the chicks that hang around this MC, but Viking is huge. I don't doubt for a minute, his ability to carry out that threat.

"*Okay, okay.*" I say, taking a few steps back in the direction of my car. "Do you know where to look for him at least? Can you give me something? I'm really worried about him now."

He lets out an exasperated sigh, that actually sounds closer to a groan, as he takes a big step towards me. Before I can even attempt to stop him, though I'm sure it would be useless anyway, I'm being flung over Viking's shoulder. His massive arm pinning both of my legs to his chest as he starts walking across the parking lot with me.

"Put me down!" I protest, pushing against his muscular back as I attempt to look up. My thick, long hair swaying in front of my face with every one of Viking's long strides.

The familiar sound of a motorcycle racing into the lot, has me struggling with my hair flopping in my face as I try to see. The bike rides right up next to us, with a loud rev as Viking finally flings me forward and drops me back to my feet, rather unceremoniously, as I stagger for balance.

Finally flipping the hair out of my face, I'm relieved to see Dean sitting on top of Serene, though I take a quick second to smack Viking on his arm for being such a brute.

"The fuck's going on here?" Dean demands, shutting his bike down and kicking the stand. He dismounts and walks the couple of feet up to us, his glaring eyes fixed on Viking.

"I was about to go looking for you, but she wouldn't get in her goddamned car. I was making sure she was safe first. Like *you* wanted." Viking says. "But bitches be stubborn, bro." He adds, shooting me a look of his own. I roll my eyes at him.

"Where have you been? And why haven't you responded to our texts?" I ask Dean, now that Viking's said his peace.

"I'm sorry, I had my phone on silent." Dean says, pulling it out of his pocket and turning it on. He holds it out so I can see that my text, as well as Viking's, are still unopened. "Might not seem like it, but I actually did rush to get back here." Dean shoves the phone back in his pocket. "If anybody asks... And I mean, *anybody*..." Dean begins to say, when Viking cuts him off.

"You've been here all night." Viking finishes Dean's sentence, then gives him a tight-lipped look, cocking his thumb at me, as if Dean shouldn't have said even that much in front of me.

"Biker business?" I fold my arms, looking between the two of them. "I'm not going to tell anybody. I have no idea what's going on anyway."

"Keep it that way." Viking lets out another aggravated sigh. "And it's *MC business*." He corrects me. "*Man* Concerns. Go home, *woman*."

I glare at Viking for another moment before I turn back to Dean. "He's been talking to me like this all night."

"She doesn't listen." Viking says. "Like, *at all*, bro."

Dean is looking at the both of us like we're two squabbling kids.

"Bro, handle your woman!" Viking throws his arms up, as if he's astonished Dean hasn't sent me packing already.

"I'll meet you inside, Viking. Just give me a minute with Vanna." Dean says. We wait a few moments as Viking storms off back to the roadhouse, mumbling something about bitches.

"Are you okay?"

"I'm fine, doll." Dean says. "But Viking's right. You should head home."

"I was worried about you." I sigh, disappointed he's already trying to get rid of me.

"You don't have to worry about me, baby." Dean says, reaching out to stroke my cheek.

"What am I supposed to do? You show up beat up earlier, then you disappear all night after some nomad situation, next thing I know, Viking is trying to get rid of me so he can go find you." I ramble off. "And now you're trying to get rid of me, too."

Dean presses his lips together in a sympathetic frown. "Never, baby. If it wasn't so late, I'd ask if I could meet you at your place later. But it is late, and we have all day tomorrow. You promised me Sundays, right?" He pulls me in for a hug. "I'd like to reciprocate, for dinner at your place the other night." He says, pressing a kiss to the top of my head. "But I want to be greedy and monopolize your whole Sunday as well. I need it." He sighs.

I wrap my arms around his waist and look up at him. "You need it?" I smile.

He grins down at me. "Badly." His eyes tell me he means it. And so does his kiss.

DEAN

"**B**RO, YOU MUST HAVE A THING FOR DIFFICULT BITCHES." VIKING GRIPES at me, as I walk into the Twisted Throttle after seeing Vanna off. "Vanna's got some sass hidden behind that sweetheart act."

"It's not an act." I grab a chair off one of the tables, straddling it to face him on the bar stool he's sitting on. "I went to the Demons' Den tonight." I say, cutting right to the point.

"Alone? Are you fucking nuts?" Viking shakes his head, then lifts his hand as if to wave the question away. "Don't bother, I already know the answer to that."

"There's gotta be at least twenty-four of them. There were nineteen there tonight. Legion and the other four weren't there."

"You fucking went inside?"

"No. I just scoped them out. Tried to get a lock on their numbers. Viper thought there were about eleven of them. There's a lot more than that." I sigh. "Wound up putting in a blocked call to the local fire department too. Before I got the hell out of there."

Viking looks at me, perplexed. "Why? Just to fuck with them?"

I shake my head, letting my arm hang over the back of the chair. Running my other hand through my hair, I take a breath, trying not to think too much about the fucking *party* they were having. "No. They had three women in there with them." I swallow, clenching my fists. "I'm pretty sure they were prostitutes. They all looked pretty fucked up. But the third one... She was way out of it before they even went in on her..."

"Oh, fuck." Viking mutters.

"I wanted to break in... to stop it... but..." I can't even say the words, partially disgusted with myself for not doing it.

"Bro... there were *Nineteen* of them. What were you actually going to be able to do?" Viking sighs. "They might have killed you. Plus, the women were prostitutes. They were probably paid for whatever went down. As long as they were consenting adults."

I nod. "Yeah, they weren't that young. At least, they didn't look it. They definitely looked strung out though. Rough looking. But, the two of them at least, didn't seem like they were being forced to do anything they didn't want to. It was the third one that got to me. I put the call in as soon as I knew what was about to go down in there. That she wasn't going to be left alone. Thankfully, it wasn't long before the fire trucks showed up. I passed them going the opposite direction when I took off."

"So, their train got broken up pretty quick." Viking says. "You did stop it, bro."

I shake my head. "Not fast enough. I should have broken a window or something."

"And got caught? You did what you could. Not even you can take nineteen guys on. Hell, you and me together couldn't take nineteen of those guys. They got a rep for fighting dirty, too."

"Nothing good will come of them moving in." I sigh.

"No shit. What are we going to do about it?" Viking asks.

I wish I knew...

DEAN

Chapter
twelve

S INCE VANNA SEEMS TO HAVE DEVELOPED SOME
aversion to being out and about around our little
town, I take her to the Wilmington Arboretum, where
we can walk together and admire the different style
gardens and various artistic sculptures on display
across the acres of perfectly manicured grounds.
In the center of the whole place, there is a giant
koi fish pond, with a bridge to walk to the island in the
middle. A large rose garden, with paths throughout
to admire the different varieties of roses, towards
the front. And in the back, a Japanese Zen rock garden,
complete with ponds and small waterfalls, as well
as a Japanese Tea House with rice paper windows.

It seems like a place she would enjoy. Though
after my last twenty-four hours, I could do for a little
Zen myself. I find that lately, in her.

"This is really pretty." Vanna says, taking in all
the deep greens of the plants and shrubbery and colorful
flowers. I watch her as she walks towards the rose
garden. She pauses to admire the little yellow roses,
no bigger than a quarter in size, that are growing

all over the trellis of the entry way to the rose garden. "You go to places like this?" she asks, glancing at me over her shoulder, as I follow her down the pea gravel path.

"No. Not really. Just thought you might enjoy a change of scenery."

"You don't like it?"

I grin at her. "You're the prettiest thing no matter where you are. No need for me to seek beauty elsewhere when I'm lookin' at you, doll... We're here for you."

She rolls her eyes at me and goes back to admiring the flowers. I watch as she spots a species of rose that is yellow with pink tips. She touches one of them gently and bends to smell it. "I love these. Peace and Love roses, or Josephs Coats."

"They your favorite?" I ask, prepared to make a few mental notes for the future.

She smirks at me, knowingly. "I love roses. And Peonies, which are technically roses. But they are so pretty, I consider them apart from roses. Different colors mean different things though, when it comes to roses. So, it depends what you're trying to convey."

"What if a guy just wants to bring a smile to your face?" I ask, watching her walk towards another type of rose bush to admire it. They're white. That's all *I* know.

"Then it doesn't really matter." She sighs. "And it doesn't need to be roses."

"Why are you being difficult?" I ask, keeping a playful hint in my voice.

She giggles as she glances over her shoulder at me again. "Am I?"

"Just tell me what your favorite fucking flower is, Vanna." I smile at her, watching her bite her bottom lip coyly, before she laughs at my request again.

"You can't really strike out with red roses. Or Peonies." Still not exactly a straight answer, but as with most things regarding Vanna, I'll have to take what I can get.

I smile back at her and just shake my head. "I have no idea what the fuck a Peony is."

"It looks like a really big, fluffy rose." She replies.

"But it is a rose."

"A rose apart from roses. Stand-alone beauty."

"Like you." That was supposed to be a compliment. Supposed to make her feel good. For some reason, the little twinkle in her eye fades away, and the smile on her face is no longer genuine. She turns from me and walks towards the far side of the garden, to the path that will lead us to the Japanese gardens. *What the fuck was that about?*

Towards the end of the rose garden, she spots a low bush, and squats down to take a huge flower in her hands, bringing her face to it, then looks up at me.

"This is a Peony." She smiles. It's a fluffy rose like flower, almost the size of her face. It is actually impressive, as far as flowers go.

"I see what you mean... Standalone beauty." I watch her as she looks back at the flower, touching its petals, as if she's petting it.

Alright. Filing Peonies away under Vanna's favorite flowers.

She reaches her hand up to me, and I take it, assuming she wants me to help her stand back up, but she doesn't. She tugs my hand, wanting me to crouch down beside her. I do.

"Look at it." She says, as if she's in awe of the thing. "I mean, really admire it. For a moment."

"It's beautiful." I agree.

"Why is it beautiful?" she asks, her eyes searching mine.

"Is this a trick question?"

She lets out a soft sigh and turns back at the flower. "They represent romance, a happy marriage, honor and compassion." She says, thoughtfully. "They also symbolize bashfulness. There are two myths about the Peony flower. One is about a beautiful nymph named Paeonia, who attracts the lustful attention of Apollo." She pauses to look back at me for a moment, as if she's trying to unravel something about me, before she continues, "He pursues her, but when Paeonia and Apollo are caught by Aphrodite, she becomes bashful and turns a bright shade of red. Aphrodite then transforms the nymph into a red Peony flower. They come in lots of colors, though. This one's pale pink, obviously." She smiles, *bashfully* might I add, as she looks back at the flower.

I can't help slightly grinning. "That's really interesting."

"Is it?" she sounds as though she doubts the sincerity of my comment.

"What's the other myth? You said there were two." I ask, hoping to demonstrate that I really am listening to her. She studies my face for a moment again, before she speaks, still trying to decide if I'm being genuine.

I am genuine, Vanna. I wish you would trust me.

"Peonies were valued for their medicinal uses. In ancient and medieval times, their roots and seeds were believed to cure many diseases. Even heal snake bites." She says. "The other myth is that they're named after Paeon, the Greek physician of the Gods. According to legend, Paeon was a student of Aesculapius, the God of Medicine. When Paeon used a Peony root to heal Pluto, Aesculapius became very jealous of his medicinal abilities, and tried to kill him. So, to save Paeon, Pluto transformed him into a Peony, because he knew it was a flower that people would admire. That's how Peonies came to represent compassion."

"You sure know a lot about Peonies. Is it safe to assume it's your favorite?"

She lifts her shoulder in a slight shrug, touching its fluffy petals once more before she stands. I stand up with her. "I research things I like. The symbolism. The meanings behind things. I guess it's a quirky hobby."

"Not really." I say, walking beside her on the wider path that brings us around the giant Koi Pond. The pond is full of flowering lily pads, surrounded by different types of native water plants. There's also a giant metal sculpture of a dragon in the center of the pond.

"Do you know what your name means?" She asks, stopping to sit upon a large rock. The Koi fish spot her and swim towards her, expectantly.

"No. Do you?" I ask with a grin I can't fight back. The thought of her actually taking the time to look into the meaning of my name, gives me a buoyant feeling.

She peeks up at me as she bites her bottom lip lightly, before she speaks. "Dean is of Celtic origin. It's a locality name, like, *at the dean*. A valley."

"My name is *Valley*?"

She giggles. "It gets better."

I smile wider at her. "I'm listening."

"Well, *Keegan* is an Irish clan name, of Gaelic origin, which means 'son or descendant of fire'," She explains. "Some translations say *Descendant of the Fiery One*. Others, simply a flame, or *ardent*."

How fitting. Though, I'm not about to bring up why *Descendant of the Fiery One*, actually fits me fucking perfectly. Or another person's use of the word *ardent*... No reason to taint a nice day by mentioning either my violent father, or Lucinda.

"Since you research things you like, is it safe to assume you like me?" I ask, veering the conversation away from the possibility of her asking about it.

She gives me another eye roll. "Of course, I like you, Dean." She stands, brushing her hands together to wipe the little bit off dirt from the rock off her palms. "I'm just not..." She begins to speak again, but stops herself.

"You're just not what?" I ask, making a real effort to keep sounding casual. Inside I'm stressing out over the possibility of her next words being something along the tragic lines of *'I'm just not that into you.'*

"No, it's nothing." She says. "Let's go see the Tea House. That sounds cute." She starts to walk away from me, further down the walk way towards the Japanese themed gardens.

I catch up to her within a few strides. "You're just not what, Vanna?" I ask again as we walk along the path side by side. "Not into me the way I'm into you?" She doesn't answer me, but she stops walking when we cross into the Japanese garden section.

There's a Zen rock garden with a wooden rake and three small boulders in the sand. Across from the rock garden, stands the little Japanese Tea House, surrounded by little waterfalls, small ponds and connecting streams. A small bridge allows one to walk up to the tea house, accented with bonsai bushes and miniature red maples.

I'm feeling anything but Zen, as Vanna still doesn't respond to my question. I follow her across the bridge towards the tea house, and grab her hand before she steps off it to walk inside.

"Just tell me." I sigh.

"Standalone beauty." She says, pointedly.

"What?" She had said that about the Peonies, that they were roses, but so pretty, they stood apart from them. When I told her she was like them, she didn't seem to appreciate that. "Vanna, just tell me what you were going to say. You're just not, what?"

She stares at me for a moment, and I can tell by her slight fidgeting, the way she curls the bottom length of her long dark hair around her finger, she's uncomfortable.

"I'm just... Can we forget that part and leave it at, I like you?"

Leave it at *she likes me*. Alright. That is a positive. But you can like someone as a friend, too. And I want far more than friendship from her. I watch her, watch me, consider her request. I can tell she's taking my silence for acceptance, as she gives me a little grin before she attempts to turn from me and walk towards the tea house.

"Not so fast." I gently snatch her by the hand again.

She lets her head fall back dramatically, before she turns back around to face me, as if she's grown tiresome of this topic. Too bad. "What?" She sighs, as if she doesn't know.

"You're not allowed in the tea house until you answer my question." I say, trying to sound playful about it. Though, I'm serious. She's going to answer me. Not only will I deny her the little tea house, but we'll camp out here, in the damn rose garden until I get an honest reply.

"What was it again?" She asks with another tiresome sigh.

She knows damn well. "You're just not what?"

She looks up at me, as if she's nervous to say the words. "Don't get mad, okay?"

Well, fuck. That doesn't bode well for me.

I brace myself and force a smile. "I won't."

"Promise?"

"God damn it, Vanna." I say, through nearly gritted teeth.

More lip biting. Normally it makes my dick twitch, but not right now. "I'm just not sure."

It's like pulling teeth! "About?"

More fidgeting.

"Standalone beauty. The Peonies. The roses. Throw me a fucking bone, woman." Again, trying to sound playful, while my sanity is slipping. "You're not sure about what?"

"Do you have a favorite flower?" She asks.

"No. They're all pretty, Vanna." I sigh. "But I'm a guy. We're not as complicated as you females. Especially *you*, in particular."

"So, the Peony wasn't prettier than the other roses?"

"They're all beautiful in their own ways, Vanna. I can see how it would be your favorite, though. It does stand out. What does this have to do with you, liking me, but being unsure? Did I offend you when I said you were like the Peony? That you stand apart from other roses? It was a compliment."

"It wasn't a trick question." She says, her eyes shifting from mine to look at the little stream below the bridge we're still standing on.

I try to tamper my frustration and think back to what the question had been. It was centered on the flower. She had asked me why it was beautiful. Why the hell does she care? Why would it matter? This can't be about flowers.

"What aren't you sure about?" I try again.

"I'm not sure I'm... that I... I'm... I don't think..." she stammers.

"This ain't about flowers."

"Not exactly." She shrugs.

"I was paying you a compliment."

"I know."

259

"You're very frustrating."

She giggles. "That's not a compliment."

"You're a Peony among Roses, Vanna. You're a stand-alone beauty." I tug her hand gently, trying to get her to look back at me.

"But you're a guy. You said flowers are all the same to you. The Peony may as well be a Dandelion... A flower is a flower is a flower."

Fuck. I walked right into that. This is definitely not about flowers.

"The Peony wins, hands down. It's the prettiest." I say, attempting to back pedal.

"Why say that now?"

I shrug. "Maybe I didn't want to look like a sissy." Perhaps I can get my ass out of this sling with a touch of humor.

Her slight smirk is now paired with slightly narrowed eyes. "*Bikers can't like flowers?*"

I try to keep a straight face, failing miserably as I lie, "It's frowned upon. We're supposed to be bad asses. I'm not even supposed to *be* here. That's how much I like you, Vanna. I risked my man card by taking you here to look at pretty flowers."

This time, she laughs. The melodic sound of her laughter relieves some of the tension in my body. "You're a liar." She finally says.

"And you still haven't answered my question." I remind her.

"Can you ask me in the tea house?" She gives me a playful grin, tugging my hand this time.

"Only if you promise to actually give me a straight answer."

"I'll try."

"Vanna."

"*Okay.*" I let her lead me into the little Japanese Tea House. "There's nothing in here." She turns around and pouts at me.

I can't help laughing. "Looks like somebody had a few preconceived notions."

"You made it seem like there was something in here to see." She frowns.

I shrug. "A deal is still a deal."

"Fine." She looks me up and down as she stands on the other side of the empty room, in front of the rice paper windows. "I'm just not sure I'm actually your type."

"You are. Come over here and I'll prove it to you." I tease her.

"Your track record says otherwise. So do the girls in your bar."

"Do you see me chasing after anyone but you?"

"Maybe I'm convenient. Maybe what I look like isn't important because in the end, it boils down to just *one thing*, anyway."

Right. A flower is a flower is a flower. I lower my eyes from her, for one reason, and one reason only. To hide my aggravation. To prevent myself from glaring at her. Not only is she insulting me, she's insulting herself. And for some reason, the latter bothers me more.

"Vanna..." I try to keep my tone calm and steady. "I've never had a problem getting a woman for a night. Believe me when I tell you, you're not that *convenient*. In fact, you can be quite the pain in the ass." I glance back up at her to gauge how she took that last part.

She's actually glaring at me, arms folded. A little scowl on her face that is honestly more adorable than it is intimidating. I won't tell her that though. *We're being serious.* I fight back the grin that wants to creep across my face. It's only fair that I get to aggravate her back. God knows she drives me crazy enough on a regular basis.

"Oh, I'm aware of your groupies." She sneers at me. "It proves my point."

"You think so, huh? What point is that?" I'll play along for another few minutes.

"That I'm not actually your type."

"When have I ever said anything about you that wasn't complimentary?"

"You just called me a pain in the ass." She shrugs.

"About your fine physique, baby. We both know the answer to that is never." She stares at me for a moment, it's as if she's actually trying to find something to argue with me about. *Women.* I don't think I'll ever fully understand them. I wait for the next bullet to dodge.

"Maybe you're smart enough to realize it's easier to get a woman in bed if you don't insult her." She says.

"That's typically the case, though, some might surprise you." I say, just to annoy her further. It works. Her brows furrow a little tighter, her eyes squint just a tiny bit more. And I'm oh so tempted, to push *her* buttons, for a change. "Maybe you're one of those women, Vanna. Compliments obviously don't work on you. Should I insult you? Will that get me up your skirt? These rice paper windows might not be sound proof, but they do provide a little privacy. If you can be quiet, I can." I slide the divider in the room to close it off, as if I'm serious.

I watch as her resolve is shaken for a moment, but she quickly composes her surprise, uncrossing her arms and placing her hands on her sexy hips, where her waist dips in before they curve out. Accentuating her hour glass figure. "Try me."

Vanna is right about one thing, though. I'm smart enough to know that would be a stupid move. Just to ruffle her feathers a moment longer, I look her over, as if I'm attempting to find something about her that I don't find attractive. I cross my arms and stroke my chin, just to play it up for her. As if I'd actually try to hurt her feelings on purpose. As if I'd say something to deliberately make her feel insecure about herself.

She suddenly looks uncomfortable, though. As if she's bracing to hear something negative about herself. That bothers me. The look in her eyes tells me someone has before... I don't want to play this game anymore. "There's nothing about you I'd complain about."

"You're smarter than you look, then."

"Then I must be a fucking genius." I smile.

She ignores that comment. "Your ex-wife looks like a Barbie. Perfect."

Oh, baby... she was far, far from perfect.

"*Ex-wife.*" I reiterate that back to her. "And so, what?"

"So, you agree?"

I'm not falling for this. "She's definitely my ex." I smile.

She lets out a sigh with annoyance. "About the body type."

"Beauty is in the eye of the beholder."

"You married her."

"Unfortunately."

She stares at me for a few moments. I keep a smile planted on my face, waiting for whatever comes next. "I'm nothing like her." Vanna finally says.

"I agree with you."

"Ah ha!" She points at me.

That was cute. I grin wider. "What?"

"I'm nothing like her." As if saying this in a higher pitch explains everything.

"Thank God."

She frowns. "Do you not get it?"

Oh, I get it. I'm just not playing into this so easily. "I agree, you're nothing like Lucinda. It's a good thing."

"We don't look alike at all. We're polar opposites, as your groupies like to remind me."

"Pretty much, yeah. It's great."

"Or is it just about one thing?"

"If that's all I wanted, I'd fuck Vixie. Or any of the other ones that hang around waiting for it."

"Why don't you, then?" She crosses her arms again, studying me.

"Vanna. You're clearly the only one here who doesn't get it."

"I'm listening."

"Well listen good, because for some reason, you have a hard time letting it sink in." She's thick in more ways than one, but no way am I saying that bit out loud. I take a few steps closer to her, so we're both standing in the middle of the little tea house. "Vanna, before today, before you, I had no idea a Peony existed. Never heard of it. Never seen one. I have a favorite flower now that you opened my eyes to its existence. Okay? Do you get what I'm saying? I feel the same way about you. I didn't know you existed, until you walked into my life and knocked my fucking block off."

I take another step closer to her, so that our bodies are nearly touching, and tip her chin up with my finger to make her look me in the eyes.

"You're right. I do only want *one thing*." I sigh. "*You*. Vanna. The *one thing* I want, is *you*."

DEAN DROPPED ME OFF AT MY HOUSE AFTER OUR EXCURSION TO THE gardens in Wilmington, so I could change for dinner and feed Nico, while he went back to his place to prepare everything for us.

Now, as I pull up Dean's driveway, parking my car in front of the detached four car garage, it's the first time I'm actually at his home. I've seen his house from a distance, being his immediate neighbor a quarter mile down the street on the other side of his farm land. But this is the first time I've seen it up close. Grabbing the blueberry pie I made us for dessert, I make my way towards his front door.

Dean Keegan lives in a one level Country Ranch style home, with a stacked stone style exterior combined with plank siding. The trim around the windows matches the rustic style wood of the wrap around porch. There are a few Adirondack chairs and two rocking chairs on the front porch as well. The steps up to the front door are wider at the bottom step and become slightly narrower at the top. The porch columns are half stone on the bottom, half rustic barn wood style on top with wrought iron twisted spindles beneath the wood railing along the porch. Between each column there's an empty hook where I assume plants once hung.

So far, his house is really nice. It's classy, yet still has a masculine vibe about it.

As I lift my hand to knock on the door, it swings open before I get the chance, startling me. I clutch the blueberry pie to myself so I don't drop it and raise my eyes to meet Dean's. He's smiling, wearing a deep blue but-ton-down shirt and a pair of light-colored, loose fitting, frayed blue Jeans. He looks hot. Casual hot.

"I made pie..."

"Can't wait to eat your pie, Vanna." Dean grins at me, stepping aside as he gestures for me to enter his home. I would normally smack him for the comment, but this is his actual home and I know he's only teasing. Maybe. Either way, I let it slide.

I step inside his house and look around as he closes the door behind me. It's just as beautiful as the exterior.

The inside is a very open floor plan. I can see the entire modern French country style kitchen, dining area and living room as I stand inside the front door. The floors are all a rustic barn wood throughout. The kitchen, I love. It's white with some black accents, marble counter tops, a marble back splash behind the stainless-steel appliances, and there is a huge marble topped kitchen island lined with seven dark wood bar stools on the side opposite the living room. The ceiling beams are exposed barn wood that match the floor throughout as well.

I glance into the living room, where there is a stone fire place with a large flat screen TV over the mantel. The couches are a brown medium dark leather 4 piece set with studded details, like you would probably see in a ranch. The end tables are a rustic style as well, repurposed barn wood with slate stone tops. In front of the picture window there's a small round table with a built in chess board and two smaller leather chairs on either side.

To the right, front of the kitchen area, closer towards the front door, there's a large dining room table, rustic country style as well, with a dark stained top and white legs to match the kitchen. The chairs match the bar stools as well.

"Wow... Dean, your house is beautiful." I shift my eyes back to him and realize he's been watching me look around in awe at his home.

"Were you expecting something else?" he asks with a sly smile. "Something a little less sophisticated perhaps? A little more of a *dirtbag biker motif?*"

"No!" I shove the pie at him. "Take a compliment, jeez!"

He laughs as he grabs the pie against his abdomen so it doesn't drop. "Take a compliment, she says!" he mocks me playfully. "You're one to talk, Vanna, but I'll let you get away with it, this time. Come inside." He says, walking over to the kitchen island to place the pie down. "Let me show you the rest of the place since you're so impressed with my humble abode."

I cross my arms and take a few steps further into his house, playfully scowling at him. "Maybe I don't want to see now."

"Oh, come on. This place took me three years to renovate. And the best part is in the back."

"The bedroom? *Where the magic happens?*" I tease him.

He walks over to me and grabs my hand, pulling me towards the hallway beyond the kitchen. "Only if you're in there, baby." He teases me back.

"You're skipping a few rooms you know." I say as we pass several closed doors.

"Empty guest rooms. An office. A bathroom." He says, as if they're boring and of no consequence.

"I like offices and bathrooms."

"Then you'll love my master bathroom." He says, opening the door at the end of the hall and pulling me through behind him.

The master bedroom is a large room with a huge king-sized bed. A dark wood headboard with matching night tables on either side. The dressers match the night tables, and there's a leather chair off to the side of the room. I expected another huge TV in here as well, but there isn't one. And there isn't much in the way of décor either. Just the basics and a simple solid cobalt blue bed set. The windows on the opposite side of the bed are curtained over with blue fabric that matches the bedding.

"No TV? Weirdo."

"I don't come in here to watch TV, baby."

"Ew." I roll my eyes at him.

He laughs. "I sleep in here, Vanna. You're the first woman to set foot in this room since my divorce. And I burned that fucking bed. I haven't decided what to do in here. I kinda lost steam after the front of the house and the bathroom. But... *This*, you will like." He releases my hand and walks over to the bathroom door, pushing it open and gesturing for me to walk inside.

I make my way towards it. "I wasn't knocking your bedroom, just so we're clear on that." I say to him, as I step inside the bathroom. He flicks on the light once I'm inside.

The whole room is stone. Floor to ceiling, tiled stone in neutral earth tone shades. The bathroom counter is one large piece of stone in front of a wall sized mirror, where the double sinks have actually been carved into the stone.

The drawers and cabinets beneath are a light-colored stained wood that looks like teak. There is a large tub towards one side of the bathroom, big enough to fit two people inside, and it's sitting in front of a round stained-glass window, which appears to be depicting a scene of wisteria vines with their purple flowers cascading down in front of scenic rolling hills.

When I turn around, there is an enormous walk-in shower, with a huge clear glass wall running the length of it. The shower is all stone tiles too, with a polished solid stone bench inside it, below three raised small windows to let in natural light. There are three shower heads, one large rain drop head in the center of the ceiling, and two others on either side on the walls.

"Holy smokes." I barely hear myself.

"The lighting in here is adjustable too. The shower has settings also." Dean says from behind me.

I turn around to look at him. "This is fancy spa level nice."

He grins. "Feel free to get naked and enjoy it, any time."

I smack his arm playfully and pretend to be appalled. "Is that before or after you eat my pie?" I throw his overtly sexual flirtation back at him, trying to throw him off.

"Any way you fucking want it, baby." That salacious smile creeping across his face.

"When you invited me to dinner, I assumed you meant... you know, actual dinner."

"I did. I'm not pressuring you." he says, taking my hand and leading me back towards the kitchen. "Not only do I have a kick ass fancy spa level bathroom," he brags, using my words, "I can also cook!"

Beef tenderloin with a wine reduction sauce, oven roasted herb potatoes and string beans. Dean was right, he can cook. The meal was delicious and I tell him so. He pours us both another glass of Cabernet Sauvignon to finish off the bottle. I'm sure I'll be feeling buzzed by the time I finish this second glass.

We decide to take our wine to the front porch and sit back in the Adirondack chairs to enjoy the evening air.

"Were you really that surprised by my house?" he asks.

"Not surprised... I don't know what I was expecting, really. More motorcycles, maybe?" I joke.

He nods towards the detached four-car garage across the driveway. "The motorcycles are in there."

"I figured that. Did you do the renovations yourself?"

"Not all of it, an interior designer did most of it. I wanted a whole new vibe after the divorce. Didn't want to recognize the place when I came home."

"When you came home?"

"Yeah. I stayed away for a while, after the divorce." His voice is low as he looks out across the front yard. "Did some cross-country riding. And was staying at the club house when I got back. Had a room there for a while. Still got some shit there."

"Did you really burn the bed?"

"Fuck yeah." He takes a gulp of his wine. A big one.

I take a sip of mine as well and look away from him. Must have been a pretty bad divorce for him to want to erase the memories of his ex-wife from the entire house. I'm not going to ask about it. He doesn't seem like he likes talking about it. Who would? And secondly, it would give him the right to ask me questions about my past, that I might not be willing to talk about. I don't push the issue any further, curious as I may be.

"Great bathroom, though." I comment, trying to turn the conversation back to positive territory. I glance at him from the corner of my eye and see him smirking.

"Yeah, that offer still stands, by the way."

"Tempting." I tease him.

"Not as tempting as your pie." He teases me back.

I cover my eyes with my hand and giggle. He really has no shame at all. Peeking over at him through my fingers, he's grinning at me, swirling what's left of his wine in his glass before he gulps it down and places it on the little table between us. I take another sip of mine as well, deciding I'll play along with his little flirt game.

"I hope you like the way it tastes." I say, leaning back in the chair as I re-cross my legs to face a little more towards him. I casually pull the hem of my dress up a little higher to my knee.

"I'm sure I'll love it." He says, staring at my leg for a moment, as if he's hoping I hike it further up.

"I hope so. You own it. It's all yours." I smile at him, playing it up to that possessive, macho, virile male side of him.

"Your pie?" He looks directly in my eyes now, a slight grin on his face, but I can tell he's searching my eyes for something.

I bite my bottom lip and nod. "You can eat it any time you want." I say, taking my last sip of wine and placing my glass next to his.

"I know you're fucking with me, but God damn." He swallows hard. "We're talking about the pie on the counter, right? Just so I don't miss the opportunity of a fucking life time, would you clarify for me?"

I can't help chuckling again. "The blueberries I used are from your orchard. I took you up on your offer. I followed the trail in the woods behind my house and picked them this morning. So yeah, technically, the pie belongs to you."

"I knew it. But the confirmation still hurts."

"I'm sorry." I pout at him teasingly.

"You should be... You're missing out. Bet I could eat your pie for hours." He grins as he winks at me. He isn't giving up.

I shift toward him a little more and lean the side of my head against the back of the chair, smiling back at him. "I like you, Dean. You make me laugh. But if it takes hours to get it done, maybe you're not as good as you clearly think you are." I laugh, immediately regretting my words. It must be the wine. I cover my mouth with my hand and stare at him. "I'm sorry, I didn't mean that."

His grin widens as he arches an eyebrow. "You never had a man go down on you, have you?"

I turn away from him immediately and fix my dress. "I'm not answering that."

"You don't have to. I can tell." He says, all ego. Totally confident. "Look at me, baby." He taunts me.

"No." I try not to giggle.

"You either never had it, or never had it done right." He pushes. "Which is it?"

"No!" I refuse. "I'm sorry I said anything, it was the wine. I told you before, I don't have a high tolerance."

He chuckles. "You don't get to insult me then deny my rebuttal, doll."

I take a deep breath then let it out before I turn to face him. "I take it back, okay? I was rude."

"It wouldn't take me hours to make you come. I'm fairly certain I could get you off rather quickly."

I cover my face with both hands, hiding my flushed cheeks from him as I bite my lip, trying hard not to burst out laughing at the embarrassing situation I created for myself.

"I could eat your pie, Vanna, for hours. Because it would be my pleasure, and yours. I'd make you come over and over again while I did it." He continues.

"Oh my god, please stop!" I laugh through my hands.

I can hear the humor in his voice as he continues to torment me for my mistake. "I would go down on you so good, baby, you wouldn't be able to stand up. You'd be so weak from the multiple orgasms I'd bestow upon you." He relentlessly persists. "Your legs would be trembling from the pleasure."

"Okay, okay, okay! I get it!" I say, putting my hand out in his face as I take a breath from laughing. "I'm sorry I dissed your oral skills."

"Ain't the only skills I got either."

I shake my head. "You are having way too much fun with this!"

He grabs my hand playfully to hold it away from his face, continuing to make me pay for my insult. "I would drive you wild, Vanna. As mad as you drive me." He insists. "And I wouldn't stop until you were begging me to fuck you."

And suddenly, it isn't funny anymore. Suddenly, in my mind, I'm on a hard, cold floor... my arms are blocking my face as a leather belt whips down on me, biting into my body as He taunts me... *He will beat me until I beg him to fuck me...*

I rip my arm away from Dean, accidently knocking over the wine glasses. The shattering glass brings me all the way back to the present moment again, as I jump up from my seat.

"Vanna... where the fuck did you just go?" Dean asks, a fearful expression etched across his handsome face.

DEAN

"*OH MY GOD, I'M SO SORRY!*" SHE SAYS, LOOKING DOWN AT THE BROKEN wine glasses. She's about to bend down and pick up the sharp shards with her bare fingers. I stand up to block her from doing so.

"Don't worry about it. I'll get a broom. Don't touch the glass." I say, more sternly than I actually intend to, but I want her to obey me. She won't meet my eyes, and I'm not sure what triggered this reaction in her, whether it was the way I grabbed her hand, or something I said. I observe her demeanor for a few moments, making sure she's cognizant enough not to touch the broken glass.

Vanna is trying to hide the shaking in her hands, but I see it. The trembling in them, even though it is slight now, it pisses me off. Someone hurt this woman. And she's going to try to play this off as an accident. As if she didn't just go somewhere dark in her mind. I don't think she even realized she hit the glasses until the sound of them breaking snapped her out of it.

"Why don't you just have a seat, and I'll be right back?" I intentionally block her so her only real option is to just sit back down in the Adirondack.

She moves slowly to lower herself back down in the chair, avoiding my eyes still. "Don't touch the glass." I remind her. "I'll be back in just a minute." Only when she gives me a slight nod of comprehension, do I go inside to retrieve the broom and dustpan from the closet in the kitchen. I make quick work of the broken wine glasses and discard them in the trash bin.

Before she gets the chance to try to cut our evening short, I grab the tea pot and throw it on the stove and plate up two pieces of the blueberry pie she made. I don't bother making coffee. She rarely drinks it. She prefers tea and I'll have the same. If I can stall her with having dessert with me, there's a chance I can distract her long enough to make her comfortable again, and she'll change her mind about wanting to bail on our date. I don't want her to go. I'm not going to pressure her for details either. The last thing I want to do is to scare her away. I'll play the fool and pretend to believe it was just an accident. That I didn't notice the way her mind took her back to something unpleasant. For now, for the sake of her comfort around me, I will hold off.

As I stare at her through the front window on the porch, I try to think back on what my exact words had been at the moment she was triggered. I don't think it had anything to do with teasing her about oral sex. She was laughing. And she took that dig at me first. No, it had to have been something else. I've also taken her hands before, without any kind of reaction like this.

So, it couldn't have been that either. What the hell did I say? That I'd make her legs shake? She'd beg me to fuck her?

Real fucking classy, asshole.

I will the teapot to hurry the fuck up as she stands and smooths out her dress. I watch her walk slowly towards the front door to come inside. Her eyes are cast down as she moves, and I know exactly what she's going to pull.

Fuck!

I crank the flame up to high on the teapot and grab two mugs from the cabinet, placing them by the two slices of pie on the kitchen island. Turning back to the cabinets above the stove to get the tea sampler box, I hear the front door open and shut quietly behind her. I chuck the box casually onto the kitchen island, making it spin with a flick of my wrist. It slides across the marble toward the two mugs as I give her a playful smile.

"Ladies choice! I got all kinds." I say, cocking my chin towards the tea.

She gives me a timid, awkward smile.

Shit. Here it comes.

"I'm really sorry I broke your wine glasses."

That's better than starting off saying she's gonna leave. I've got a shot at salvaging this date. "Don't be. I'm actually switching to stemless." I keep smiling at her, trying to be reassuring. *Note to self; Order stemless wine glasses.*

"Oh... Okay." She says, still looking painfully uncomfortable.

The teapot finally starts to steam. Doesn't quite whistle, but fuck it, close enough. I grab it and switch off the flame before I pour some into the mugs.

"Sit down and have some dessert with me." I say. "You want sugar or milk with your tea? Got some of that clover honey you like too." I put the teapot back on the stove and wait for her reply. I can see her hesitation, how she wants to tell me she is going to leave. But seeing everything already set up makes her feel bad about walking out on me. Just like I intended it to. When she finally steps forward to come sit at the island, I let out a breath I didn't realize I was holding.

Thank fuck. It worked.

"Honey would be great, thanks." She says, climbing onto a stool and situating herself. I watch her as she reaches to open the lid of the tea sampler box and her eyes scan the options inside. "What kind do you want?" she asks.

"I'll have whatever you're having." I have no idea what's in the box. Cherry left it here. I go back to the cabinet to grab the jar of honey and a spoon from the drawer then make my way over to the stool beside her. "What are we having?" I ask, handing her the spoon and opening the jar of honey for her.

"I like Earl Grey." She says, sliding my mug closer so she can put the tea bag she opened into it. I notice she smirks slightly. Thank God something has lifted her mood.

"What's funny?" I ask.

She bites her bottom lip as her adorable grin widens. "Nothing." She lies.

I duck down and lean a little closer, trying to force her to look me in the eyes, but I'm smiling back at her.

I'm a playful, tea drinking, charming asshole, Vanna. I am not a threat to you.

I watch as she brings her mug closer to her, placing the Earl Grey inside it as well. She's still smiling.

Is it the mugs?

"Is it because I don't have teacups?"

She giggles. "Do you really not have teacups?" she finally looks me in the eyes. Damn, she's pretty. Even prettier when she smiles playfully at me like this.

I can't help grinning back at her. "Do I look like I'd have teacups?"

She lifts a shoulder as she glances around my home briefly. "Well, before I saw your house I'd have guessed not. But you're fancier than I thought." She teases me.

"Nobody has *ever* accused me of being *fancy*. Congratulations, that was a first." I tease her back.

She giggles again as she reaches for the honey jar and dips her spoon in, carefully putting a little dollop into her mug of Earl Grey. "You want some?"

"Please."

She does the same to mine and gives it a little stir before she pulls the spoon out and brings it to her lips. I watch as she sticks the spoon inside her mouth and sucks off the residual honey as I will my blood not to rush to my dick. Damn, I want to kiss her right now. Taste that honey right off her tongue. She slides the spoon out of her mouth slowly before she places it down on the counter top.

It occurs to me that I'm staring at her, hard. I force myself to stop and shift my eyes to something else. The damn mugs. She thought they were funny. I'll try to work with that.

"So, you think I'm fancy, huh?" I ask, picking my mug up and lifting it towards her, inviting her to cheers me. She smiles and gently clanks her mug to mine.

"Well, not anymore." She smirks.

"No?" I grin at her. "How about now?" I ask, lifting my pinky up off the mug.

Her laugh is soul soothing. Her genuine smile, so beautiful. "That helps a little." She giggles. "But I like mugs, so you're safe."

"I like your mug." I tease her back. "Especially when you smile."

She takes a careful sip of her tea, averting her eyes again as she places her mug back down on the kitchen island top. I take a sip as well, watching her pick up her fork and poke at the blueberry pie. That's not the first time she hasn't responded to a compliment. I wonder what that's about.

I resolve myself to refrain from making any more sexual pie innuendoes. I want her to forget about whatever happened on the porch earlier, and just be relaxed around me. I'm capable of being a gentleman. She deserves that. I place my mug back down as well and grab my own fork to dig into the blueberry pie.

"Do you like it?" she asks, after we've both had a few bites.

"Very much, thank you for making it. Where did you learn to bake?"

She shrugs. "YouTube, mostly. You can learn a lot on that site."

Not the answer I was expecting. She doesn't mention much about her background. Ever. That makes me wonder too. Vanna has a talent for speaking without saying much. However, I'm supposed to be keeping this light. I don't want her to feel interrogated.

"I'm not real big on social media." I throw out there.

She agrees. "Yeah, I'm not either, anymore. But I'll go on YouTube to figure out how to do things in a jam if I have to."

"What kinda jam?"

"How to change a tire, or fix a leaky sink. Those kinds of things."

"I can do those things for you." I offer. "You got a leak in your house?"

"The Landlord is supposed to take care of it, but thanks." She says. "I'm afraid my little farm house rental isn't as nice as your beautiful luxury Ranch." Her tone is humorous, but I can read between the lines.

"I don't care about any of that shit, Vanna. I lived in a dumpy room at the clubhouse for almost three years after my divorce. No way your place is worse than that."

She smiles at me. "Yeah, but then you got fancy." She teases, taking a bite of pie.

"But I don't even have Teacups." I tease her back. She giggles, covering her mouth as she chews, all polite like. "The only thing I fancy is you, baby." I push my luck. Fuck it. Her cuteness is my weakness.

"You're so smooth." She rolls her eyes, taking a sip of her tea.

"Well, I'm serious about my offer. If you ever need a hand with anything, just let me know. The house. The car. Whatever."

"So, you're a handy man too? On top of everything else?" she asks, but I still detect a level of playfulness. "How are you single?"

That question catches me completely off guard. I don't consider myself *single* anymore. Not with Vanna in my life. The way we try to spend as much time together as possible. It bothers me that she's even asking this. That she doesn't think of us as more than what she's clearly thinking. *Shit.*

"How are *you* single?" I toss the question back to her, because I don't know how to respond right now.

She shrugs. "Maybe I'm hard to love."

That was a loaded response, joking or not. And I call bullshit. No way is Vanna hard to love. How could she even say that about herself? I've only known her a few weeks over two months and I'm... *Fucked. Totally fucked...*

I clear my throat. "I find that hard to believe."

"You've got a lot of admirers. So how are you single?" she asks again, ignoring my statement.

She doesn't want another line. She doesn't want to hear some smooth talk about how I've been waiting for her. She wants honesty. She deserves that too. So, I'll suck it up and give it to her.

"I kinda dated some, after the divorce." That's a stretch, though, but I'm going with it. I didn't date. I fucked around. However, I'm not about to paint that picture for her. Hell no. She's too much of a good girl. I've never had to take things so slowly with a woman in my entire life. I continue, uncomfortably, but I want to be clear with her, for both our sakes. "I never found anyone I considered getting serious with. But, to be honest with you, Vanna." I hesitate, shifting in my seat. "I'm not sure how you feel, but... I don't feel like I'm all that single. I mean, anymore. Since, you know... *We've* been seeing each other. I don't want to spend my time with anybody else, doll. Just you."

She's staring in my eyes now, holding more contact than she has all night with me. "Are you saying we're not single? That we're an item and *exclusively* dating?"

My fucking heart sinks into the cold pit in my stomach as a feeling of panic washes over me at the thought of Vanna possibly dating other men.

Fuck! Has she been? She's got more free time than I do. She's hot as fuck and sweet and who wouldn't want to date her? Even if they somehow knew she wasn't exclusive with them and I missed the goddamned memo somehow? *What the fuck?* Is there some prick that lives closer to her job that I don't know about?

My mind is racing with images of some other fucking dude with his hands on her... Vanna smiling at some other guy... laughing at his stupid fucking jokes... Putting on a pretty dress and doing her hair for another man.

I run my fingers through my hair and lean closer to her. "Baby, are you fuckin' with me?" I ask, hoping with all sincerity that she is.

She shakes her head no... *No*, she's not fucking with me.

Jesus Fuck!

Has she done shit with somebody else? Been intimate with another man? That will fucking kill me! Just the thought of that makes my ears ring painfully as my blood pressure spikes.

"Are you seeing someone besides me?" I force myself to ask, as calmly as I can manage, even though I'm afraid of what I'm going to hear.

"No. I'm not seeing anyone else."

Thank Fuck! I nod. Okay, there's time to remedy this. I can try to calm down. I take a large gulp of tea, wishing there were a few shots of whiskey in it. The burn sliding down my throat isn't the same, and she's shot my nerves to shit.

"I just wanted to make sure we were on the same page. Dating is so confusing, you know?" she sighs.

Do I know? Now more than fucking ever, Vanna!

"I ain't interested in any other women, Vanna." I say, point blank, period. "I want exclusivity with you." *I fucking demand it.*

She shifts her focus from me, back so her tea. "You just have a lot of admirers." She says quietly into her mug.

"What does that matter? I told you I'm only interested in you."

"Being with me might bring you trouble." She says, after a moment's hesitation.

"I don't give a shit. Are you worried about the witch thing? If you're with me, baby, loud and proud, nobody is going to say shit to you in this town. And if they do, you just tell me about it and I'll handle it."

She lets out a soft sigh as she pushes the remainder of her pie away from her, then picks up her tea to finish the last few gulps. I can tell something is bothering her still. And I don't know if it's related to earlier or not.

"Vanna, talk to me. Something is clearly bothering you, and if it's making you question us, or me, you need to tell me what it is so I can fix it."

"Maybe it's not like brakes or a leaky pipe under a sink. Maybe you can't *fix* it."

"Tell me and I'll figure it out." I push.

"Lucinda." She sighs.

The wrecking ball. Why wouldn't this tie back to fucking Lucinda? All roads to Hell in my life lead through Lucinda! "What about her?"

"Vixie said you're still crazy about her."

"I'm not. Anything else?" I lean against the back of the bar stool and fold my hands in my lap. I hate talking about Lucinda, but if Vanna needs to, I'll fucking do it.

"I want to be exclusive, too."

"Done deal. Was already on that page the night I asked you out." I say, somewhat annoyed that this didn't go without saying, but fuck. I try to hide it.

"I'm serious." She says, looking at me almost sternly.

"You think I'm not? I meant it when I said you were mine. You are mine. I didn't mean just at the bar. I mean it period. I don't share. I thought we were on the same page all along. Just thinking you weren't concerns me, Vanna." For more reasons than she can ever know. That I'll never admit to her out loud.

"I'm not seeing anyone else." She insists.

"Were you, at any point, since I asked you out?" I have to know, or it will eat me alive.

She shakes her head. I stare at her, needing to hear the words. She gets it. "No. I haven't dated, or been with anyone." She says. "In years, if that helps."

"Years?" how is that possible. She's fucking gorgeous. I remember her telling me she hasn't dated in a while, but *years*?

She lifts her shoulder in that timid shrug she does when she's either embarrassed or uncomfortable. "Yes, years." She says again, though more quietly. "So, don't hurt me."

I don't want to get hurt either. And I certainly don't want to hurt Vanna. "I'd never intentionally hurt you, baby. I've never been the cheating type either. When I asked you out, and continued to ask you out, I meant it exclusively. You're *not* single. You're with me. Nobody else, got me?"

I force myself to take a breather and grab the empty mugs and plates to take to the sink, making every effort not to just drop them in. I'm sure that would scare her and I don't want to do that. I do want to fucking hit something though.

I grip the edge of the sink and just take a moment to fight the urges inside. I'd never lay a finger on Vanna. On any woman. But I can feel myself spiraling. I can feel the rage boiling up inside me. Why the fuck am I reacting so strongly to this? Her concerns and questions were valid. We never had the conversation about exclusivity. She's an outsider. In more ways than one. She doesn't know anything about MC culture. How men like me are about our women. I shouldn't be this upset. And she says she hasn't seen anyone else. How the fuck did this rattle me to my fucking core?

"Dean?" Her voice is quiet.

"Yeah, baby?"

"Are you upset with me?"

"No." I turn around to face her, but remain leaning against the sink. "I'm not upset with you. I'm just surprised, I guess. We've been dating and I suppose I should have been clearer."

"It's just that Vixie and some of the girls told me that MC guys are different... I assumed we were exclusive too, but Vixie said until you're an *Ol 'Lady,* bikers can do whatever they want... And even after, they can still get with sweetbutts if they want."

I'm going to fire Vixie.

"Baby, I'm just a man. I'm *your* man. I ride motorcycles. I run a bar. I'm not a member of the MC anymore, either. I'm sure Vixie knows guys that are that way with women, but I'm not like that."

"But what about Lucinda?"

"What about Lucinda?" *Let me guess... Vixie said?*

"Vixie said that you and Lucinda were together a long time. That you're still hung up on her. Why would she say that to me?"

"I don't know, baby. But I will have a little chat with her about all this." I bang my knuckles on the edge of the counter, just to kind of hit something. It doesn't do shit for me.

"And Lucinda?" she asks again.

"Lucinda is my ex-wife. She's remarried with a kid. I have zero interest in Lucinda." I feel like I've said this twenty times already to her.

"Am I really her polar opposite?"

"In all the right ways." I sigh, but something changes in Vanna's demeanor. She seems suddenly a little withdrawn. "I said in all the *right* ways... That's a positive, baby. What's the matter?"

She shakes her head, again with the fake smile. It bothers me. I can't stand fake. Especially when it comes to Vanna. Especially not now, after her shaking me up this bad over fucking nothing.

Is it nothing, though? I've seen her flirt at work. Didn't think a whole lot of it at the time. Seemed more like a game to me. Like a waitress trying to get a few extra tips. And those dweebs that go to her shop, If Vanna's into me, how could she be into them? I ain't like those dudes. Two different species, practically. No. I'm fucking paranoid now. There's nothing going on with guys at her job. She's asking about club life.

"Do me a favor, baby. Next time you want to get some behind the scenes info on me, or MC life, just ask Cherry, okay? Stay the fuck away from Vixie." The look in her eyes tells me I'm being a fucking asshole.

Why am I being a fucking asshole?

Nothing happened. Everything is the same.

She want's exclusive. She's been exclusive.

The fuck is my problem?

"I'm sorry, baby." I push off the counter and walk over to her. She won't look at me, so I try to gently lift her chin up. "I didn't mean to be rude to you. I care about you, a lot."

"I just don't want to get hurt." She says, eyes still cast to the floor. "I haven't dated in a really long time."

"I haven't either. Not seriously."

Her eyes finally look up to meet mine. "Why me, then?" she asks, and I can tell, by the way her eyes shift back and forth in mine, that she's really searching for truth. Or lies. I don't lie. Not gonna start now.

"A lot of reasons." Though, leaving it at that would be a total cop out and a bullshit response to a question she obviously needs answers to. "I'm more than simply attracted to you. Yes, I think you're gorgeous. Everything about your physical beauty turns me on. But I'm also drawn to you like nothing I've ever felt before. Beyond looks. Beyond an intellectual connection, which we do have. You're very smart, Vanna. I like that too. But, there's also something about you that's hard to explain." I pause, taking a moment to try to put into words this fucking pull she has on me. I drop my hand from her chin to run my fingers through my hair again, before I attempt to explain something I've never felt before.

"I can feel you, before I see you, sometimes. It feels that way, anyway. I feel better when I'm around you. The closer I am, the better. When we're apart, I think about you all the time. And when we touch, especially when we kiss... *fuck*... I don't even have words for that feeling. I've never felt it with anyone else, though. That much I can say."

She's still staring deeply into my eyes, but there is something behind hers. And I can't help the nagging feeling inside me that my answer did not bring her the reassurance she was searching for. It makes me feel uneasy and wonder why. "Do you not believe me?" I ask.

"I feel the pull too." She says softly. "That night I first saw you, I felt your presence before I spotted you. I think it was a sign we were supposed to meet."

"Like fate?" I ask, stroking her cheek with the back of my hand. For some reason, she averts her eyes from me now.

"Something like that." She replies, but I detect a sadness in her.

I let my hand drop. Have I been fooling myself this whole fucking time? I thought she was really digging me. All she's mentioned out of everything I said was about the pull. The weird connection. She didn't say anything about attraction. She didn't agree with me about our kisses either.

Fuck. I'm not playing the fool. I am the fucking fool. The one who fell harder. The fatal mistake that seems to be a pattern with me. And last time, I got burned. Bad. I'm not willing to go through that shit again. It cost me too much. I've made it back to solid ground, only to meet with Vanna. Another woman who has the potential to fuck me up, again. Wields the power to take me higher, or back into the choking darkness.

"You don't seem too thrilled with what fates messenger brought you." I sullenly say.

She looks up at me again, her brows furrowed. "It's not that at all. You're exactly what I was looking for."

That should make me feel better. Maybe I'm too much in my head about everything. But... "*Was* looking for?"

She gives me a half smile. "Yes, *was*. I'm not looking anymore because you finally showed up." She says the words as if she's accusing me of being late to something.

"I've been here. You walked into my life." Like a whirl wind.

For some reason that makes her smile. "You're right. I did." Whatever uncertainty was behind her eyes seems to have faded away. She's looking at me like I'm something to her again. "It really doesn't bother you that I'm a witch?"

"No. Does it bother you that I don't exactly buy into all that?"

She laughs now. "No. I actually like that about you. A lot."

I can't help the corner of my mouth crooking upwards into a slight grin, amused by her enthusiasm. "You're happy about that? That I don't believe in magic?"

She slides off the bar stool and steps up to me, throwing her arms around my neck. My arms automatically circle around her, pressing her body harder against mine. "I'm thrilled about it." She smiles up at me.

"I'll say one thing about you, Vanna. You certainly keep me on my fucking toes." I say, watching her sink her teeth into her bottom lip. "Thought the fact I just told you I might think you were a little cooky would piss you off."

She tosses her head back to laugh again, eyes closed, her body moves rhythmically against mine as she laughs. Her hair brushes against my hands at the small of her back. Her sexy throat exposed and expelling her laughter. I want to slide my tongue along it, feel the vibration, but my eyes drift lower to her tits pressed against me, heaving along with her glee at the fact that I just told her I thought she was a little out there.

What the fuck? Why are the crazy ones always so fucking hot?

I pry my eyes away from her dick hardening cleavage as she tilts her head forward again to meet my eyes. Hers are blazing.

Fuck. Now I'm really hard.

"Kiss m-" I take her mouth before she even finishes her request, and she's kissing me back with just as much fervor as I feel for her. Her hands are gripping my neck and shoulders, pulling me and kneading my muscles before her fingers are sliding up my neck, my skull, pressing her mouth to mine harder. She's never kissed me like this before. With this level of almost aggression.

And just like that she breaks the kiss to stare me in the eyes, as we both catch our breath for a moment. A very brief moment. Because her eyes are hooded and dark with desire. Her lips are reddened and pouty from just being kissed roughly. I watch those seductive eyes slide to the side towards my living room. The three-seater leather couch facing the fireplace. Her eyes meet mine again. She doesn't have to say anything.

Fuck yes!

I grab her again, taking her mouth once more as I simultaneously haul her towards my living room where we topple onto the couch together. I do my best not to crush her beneath me, but she doesn't seem to mind at all. In fact, she seems pretty fucking eager to have me on top of her. And I'm pretty fucking thrilled to be here myself.

She lifts her head to bring her lips to mine and I slip my hands to the back of her skull, my fingers buried in her dark, silky hair, elbows digging into the leather cushion. My body is completely pinning her down into the couch, she couldn't move if she wanted to. I can feel her shallow breaths, her diaphragm struggling beneath my weight. I kiss her mouth a moment longer, not wanting to stop, but she needs to breathe. I kiss down her jaw, her throat, lifting my body slightly off her as I move to kiss her clavicle, the swell of her breasts, which are heaving now that she is able to take deeper breaths. I bury my face in them, moving my arms to slide them under her back and grip the top of her shoulders from underneath her.

"Are you mine?" I hear her nearly whimper beneath me, as my tongue slides around the soft curvature of one of her ample breasts.

Fuck. I know I am. I lost myself somewhere. She fucking owns me. It should concern me more than it does at this present moment. But my throbbing hard cock is grinding into her hip. Her hot fucking body melded to mine, has my mind focused on only her. Her scent. Her taste. Her breaths and whimpers.

"I'm yours, baby." I growl against her soft flesh, twisting my face to kiss her other breast. I feel her fingers slide up my neck again, to the back of my skull and into my hair. After a moment she twists her fingers and tugs the longer hair on top of my head with a roughness that only gets me hotter.

"Kiss me again." She demands, breathlessly, coaxing me back to her waiting mouth. Her lips are parted for me before I'm even there. I crush my mouth to hers, thrusting my tongue inside as I capture her little groan. Hits me right in the dick again as I flex it against her, wondering if she can feel it through the denim. She barely manages to squirm under my weight, but she tries to rub against me. Fuck yeah. She feels it.

"Do you want me, baby?" I ask against her lips, grinding myself against her.

"Yes." She whispers.

Fuckin' Aces!

"Fuck, Vanna. I want you so bad. *Been* wanting you." I growl, before I shove my tongue in her mouth again, wrestling hers into submission. I slide my hands down her curvy body until I reach the sides of her thighs. Shoving my hands down against the leather cushion to get them under her, I grip her sexy ass. My body pressed down on hers has her dress trapping her legs down, preventing them from wrapping around me. That's alright. I've got other plans first. Words to live up to.

"I want to taste you first, baby." I whisper against her lips, before I trail more kisses back down her chin and throat. I shift my body to kiss her further and further down.

"How do I divest you of this dress without rippin' it off you, doll? You got a zipper somewhere or do I just wish you out of it?" I teasingly ask. There's way too much fabric hiding her from me. Separating us. And I want to see and feel every fuckin inch of her. I lean back slightly, still hovering over her, so I can watch her face as I unbutton my shirt.

She's biting on her lower lip again, watching me, but there's more than lust in her eyes suddenly. There's... apprehension.

Shit.

She did tell me it's been a while since she's dated. Years, she had said. And Vanna isn't the fuck around type. Not even close. We've been dating for months now and this is the furthest we've gotten. She's just gotta be nervous. Probably never been with a guy like me, either. I wonder if I scare her in some ways. The rough biker. Not the love making type. The *wham bam thank you ma'am* type of dick. Hell no. Not with Vanna.

"What do you need from me, baby?" I ask, halting with my shirt halfway undone. I want her to be completely comfortable with me. I'm in no rush. Not with Vanna. I want to savor every moment of being with her. I've never wanted to be with a woman as badly as I do Vanna.

She doesn't answer me, though. She kinda seems to have frozen.

"Baby? You nervous or something?"

"A little." She whispers.

"Not gonna hurt you, doll." I promise. "Not gonna lie either. I fuckin' want you. *Bad.* But if you don't want to do this, you just have to say so. I'm not going to force anything on you." I watch her throat swallow, hard. Something isn't right. "Are you afraid of me, doll?" Could that really be it? "I know you've seen me get a little threatening from time to time in the bar. But I don't hurt women, Vanna. I'd never hurt you."

"I'm not afraid of you." She says.

"Good. All I want to do is make you happy, baby. Make you feel good. I'm not going to rush anything." I try to reassure her some more.

"You'll keep me safe?" she asks. And I wonder why she always asks me that question.

"*Always.*" I swear to her. "They call me Lancelot for a lot of reasons, baby." Her eyes widen at the mention of my unofficial road name, as if she's astounded for some reason.

"They call you *what*?" she nearly gasps.

Vanna

L ANCELOT! THEY CALL HIM LANCELOT!

"Yeah, doll. Lancelot." Dean says, hovering over me, a disconcerted expression on his face. "Like the Knight." He adds. "Why do you look like you've just seen a ghost?"

I try to sit up and push myself away from him, scooting back along the leather cushions until my back is against the arm rest of the couch.

"Vanna?" he looks worried, but he doesn't make a move towards me.

"We can't do this."

Dean is staring at me intently, but he doesn't move. "Okay, baby. We don't have to do anything you don't want to do." He says again. "Can you tell me what's wrong, though, Vanna? What just happened?"

"You don't want to do this." I say. "Not *really*, you don't."

Dean must be the Knight. Morning Star or not. Maybe I messed up the spell in some way and it's just not coming through for some reason. But Ethan said the Knight of Wands is connected to fire as well. Dean's name literally translates to fire. I wrote that off as a mere coincidence, since it wasn't something I directly addressed in my spell. And I've foolishly been burying my head in the sand, hoping the spell was a bust. Just for my own selfish desire to pursue a relationship with him. But now with the Lancelot connection... He has to be the Knight! And if he is the Knight, that's the only reason he feels drawn to me. It isn't real. I can't take advantage of him like that. It's bad enough I've already doomed him to a collision course with my revenge driven ex! And you can't turn a hostage situation into a relationship. I should know this better than anyone...

Dean clears his throat. "Um... Vanna... I'm not sure what you mean, doll. But... not to sound crude... all systems are definitely a *go* on my end." He sits back slightly, his hand dropping to somewhat cover his erection, still trapped in his jeans. "So, *really*, I *do*. I want to... But not if you don't." he adds. "And it's okay, if you don't. Maybe I jumped the gun... I just... I like you so much. But I know there was something that happened on the porch earlier... Vanna, you can tell me anything."

No. I definitely do not want to get into that. This situation is humiliating enough. I don't need him knowing about my shameful past on top of everything else.

"That was an accident." I manage to say, twisting to get up off the couch. Dean jumps to his feet as well, taking a few steps back from me, but only to block my path to his front door as I start to walk in that direction.

"Vanna, baby." I try not to pay attention to the way he attempts to adjust his jeans. "You can trust me, I promise you. Just, talk to me. Tell me what's going on here. Did I do something you didn't like?"

"No, you're perfect." That's what makes this so difficult. "Dinner was great. I gotta go, though." I say, taking a few more steps towards him, hoping he'll stand aside. He doesn't.

"Vanna... come on... Dinner was great? I gotta go? What the fuck, baby? Talk to me."

That old familiar claustrophobic feeling starts to rise up inside me. I take a deep breath, closing my eyes for a moment as my hand involuntarily clutches at the base of my throat.

Do not have a damn panic attack in his living room! Stupid bitch! You are fine!

"I think I just need some air." I manage to say, taking another step towards him. He still doesn't make a move to let me by. My anxiety rises, another few notches. "Are you just going to keep me trapped here?" I snap at him, regretting my harsh words immediately, but I feel like my emotions are about to spiral out of control. I'd rather have a break down without his audience.

"*Trapped* here?" he looks genuinely hurt by my words. His brows lifting and knitting together.

"I'm sorry... Just, let me go. I'll call you later." I say, attempting what must be the most unconvincing smile ever plastered across someone's face in the history of pretending to be fine.

"Vanna..."

"Dean, *please*." My voice is on the verge of begging.

I watch the muscles in his jaw ripple, as his fists clench at his sides. He takes a few slow steps back, allowing me passage to his front door. I hurry past him, grabbing my car key off of his kitchen island and bolting out the front door. I practically jog the short distance to my car, hitting the unlock button on the key fob.

Once I'm inside, I lock the doors and crank the ignition. I know if I just go home, he's probably going to come over to check on me. Because he cares. And he's a decent person. Spell or not. Dean is a good man. And I'm clearly not okay.

I glance towards his front porch as I make a U-turn in his wide driveway. Dean is standing at the top of his steps. He looks furious. His stance is rigid, his eyes glaring. His fists still clenched at his sides. I'm actually afraid to look at him for more than a moment. Turning away from him, I take off down his driveway and into the street. When I get to my driveway, I don't stop to pull in. I continue down the road towards an undetermined destination.

The cellphone on my passenger seat buzzes. I glance down to see Dean calling me. Probably to ask me where I'm going. He must have expected me to go directly home. I don't know if I should answer though, he looked so angry standing there on his front porch, watching me bail on him. If I don't answer, will that just make everything worse? I don't want to lose him as a friend.

Grabbing the cell, I hit the answer icon.

"Vanna, what are you doing?" his tone is wrought with concern.

"I'm just going for a drive. I'll call you later, I promise. I'm sorry." I say quickly.

"Vanna, plea-" I hit the end call and place my phone back on the passenger seat.

Staring at the blurry road ahead, I wonder if the damage I'm causing between us is irreversible. Then again, what does it even matter? A relationship with the Knight would be doomed anyway.

Brushing the tears from my face impatiently, I force myself to acknowledge that I sabotaged us the night I worked the spell... Dean and I never stood a chance.

DEAN

Chapter
thirteen

S HE CALLED ME LATER THAT NIGHT. ONLY because she promised me she would. I don't believe for a moment, however, that she actually wanted to make the call.

Serene and I, we tried to find her that night. Rode all over town. Checked every river front park and boardwalk. Even made the hour ride to the ocean in record timing. I thought for sure I'd find her there. The way she talked about how the ocean always makes her feel better. Washes away her troubles. I guess whatever these troubles are, aren't the wash away kind.

Old habits die hard, too. I wanted to break into her house. Look for anything that might indicate what the fuck is going on with her. Maybe come across those letters she had to have night, at the man who hurt Vanna... causing her to run, *from me!* It's pushing me over the edge. Seeing her car, finally parked in her driveway later that night, was both a relief, and the *only* thing that stopped me.

I wanted to pull up her driveway. Knock on her door. Get her to talk to me. But I didn't. For her sake, I forced myself to go home. To wait for her call. Holding onto the hope that she would keep her promise about calling me, as I paced my front porch, watching her house. For what, I don't even know. But knowing she was there, was a sliver of peace.

She must have heard my bike. Assumed I had gone looking for her. It wasn't very long after, when she called me. The call itself, wasn't very long, either. An apology. Multiple, actually. But also, an open-ended request for space.

That was like a knife in the gut. It hurt more than I would have anticipated, had I seen any of this coming. It still hurts. The pain hasn't dissipated in the six days since I saw her last.

Now, as I sit against the wall at the Twisted Throttle beside Viking, staring at the clock above the bar, I wonder if she'll show up tonight. Her shift starts at ten. It's five to, now. If she doesn't show, I know we're over, before we ever even got to really start. As the hands on the clock move closer to ten pm, the tightness in my chest increases with every passing second.

I force myself to close my eyes. To lean my head back against the brick wall and attempt to calm my nerves. As fate would have it, whether to mock me, or to help me keep hope alive, a familiar song begins to play on the jukebox. That dark, bluesy rock ballad by Ed Sheeran. *Make it Rain.* The song that was playing when I first laid eyes on her. I focus on the hauntingly relatable lyrics, about pain and purification. And wait to see which hand fate will deal me tonight.

As the song comes to its close, I know it's a little past ten. And that steel door to my right, only a yard away, hasn't swung open. Vanna's late. She's never been late. I remain where I'm seated, eyes closed, head against the bricks. With a hard swallow, I attempt to fight the tidal wave of disappointment that washes over me. The little candle flame of hope I was holding onto in the darkness, wavering now.

"Bro... she's only a few minutes late." Viking says at my side. I must look as miserable as I feel, for him to have remained silent for this long. To have resisted his natural inclination to break my balls. "For all we know, she's having car problems. She does drive an old cage, you know."

He isn't wrong. It's a possibility. And she probably wouldn't have called me to help her, even though I'm her only real connection in this town, despite the current situation. She'd be on the side of the road by herself, *fucking YouTubing a DIY video* on how to change a tire or attempting to diagnose the reason for a car to stall out.

"You're right." I say, getting to my feet and heading for the door.

"What are you doing?" Viking calls after me.

"She could be on the side of the road having car trouble. Won't be hard to find her this time if she's actually trying to make it here tonight." I say, my flame of hope refusing to extinguish. I won't fucking let it.

"Bro..." the pity in Viking's voice at my evident desperation to hold onto her, any way I can, grates my nerves.

"Shut up. I'm going. I have to." God forbid she has to call a tow truck and spend a night's earnings to have her car brought three fucking miles to her home or a repair shop.

Do you see, Vanna? My willingness and desire to protect you from everything!

I jerk the steel door of the bar open, rushing through it. In too much of a hurry to notice the person on the other side of it as I step through. The door slams shut behind me, as I collide with a smaller figure outside, nearly knocking them backwards. I grab them by the arms to steady them on their feet.

"Shit, I'm sorry... I..." I begin to say, when I realize, who it is I'm holding. "Vanna..."

"Run me over why don't you." She laughs. "Where are you rushing off to without looking?"

Why does she sound so happy? I've been in fucking agony... and she's talking as though nothing happened. As though it hasn't been six long days since...

"You're late..." I say, trying to gather my thoughts. "I was afraid you might be on the side of the road or something. Flat tire... you know... *something*."

She giggles again. "You're right. Kind of. I'm sorry I'm late. When I went out to my car earlier, one of my tires was flat. I tried to change it myself, but it's just too dark. I couldn't see what I was doing."

I glance across the lot. Her car isn't here. "I'll fix it for you."

"You don't have to. I know how to put the donut on. I'll buy a new tire tomorrow." She says, like it's no big deal. It isn't. Not in that sense. Swapping out a flat tire for the spare is simple. It's that she doesn't want me to help her that bothers me.

"Did you pay for a ride to get here? I would have come if you called."

She clears her throat. "No, actually... our neighbor... Garrett Johnson, saw me outside, messing with the car, and offered to drop me off."

That bothers me. A lot. I try not to let it show too much. The urge to ball my fists brings me to the realization that I haven't let her go yet. "You should have called *me*, Vanna." I say, trying not to clench my jaw as I finally release her arms from my grasp.

Even in the darkness, I can see her perplexed expression. "I didn't *call* anyone." She reiterates, insisting. "He saw me with a flashlight in my driveway."

Right. So that makes two of us watching her fucking house at night. Something tells me his intentions aren't on par with mine, however. I force myself to rein it in. This shit will be dealt with accordingly.

"Anyway," Vanna sighs, "I am sorry I'm late. Please don't fire me." She seems slightly flirtatious for a moment. "If it's okay with you, I should get in there and earn the tire I have to buy tomorrow."

"I know a guy, don't worry about it."

"Well, Walmart's website says it's going to run me about a hundred. I can swing that." She says, "So, *you*, don't worry about it."

285

"I can beat that price for you, doll. Would be a better-quality tire, too."

"Okay. Who's your guy?" she asks.

"I'll put the donut on it in the morning, so you can get here tomorrow night. We'll go Sunday and have it replaced."

"Dean..." I don't like the way she says my name this time... Her patronizing tone makes my guts feel like they're twisting up.

"Vanna?" Can she even hear the sincerity in my voice when I speak her name anymore? What the fuck happened? What is she trying to do to me? "You promised me Sundays."

I watch as she wraps her arms across her abdomen, a sign of discomfort I've come to recognize in her. She averts her eyes from me, as well. "About that..." her words are barely above a whisper.

No. Fuck. No. I'm not letting it happen.

I turn from her, before she gets the chance to sever that promise she made me. I'm not giving that up so easily. I'm not giving *her* up. I grab the handle on the steel door, yanking it open for her. Without speaking, because I fucking *can't* right now, I gesture for her to proceed inside.

As if she can sense my own aversion to this subject, she grants me this temporary mercy and steps inside, without saying another word about our Sunday promise to each other.

Once she's inside, I close the door behind her, lingering outside in the dark, alone. I lean my back against the brick wall and stare off into the shadows. I need a moment to compose myself. To give her time to busy herself with work, and hopefully forget about trying to end our one promised day a week together. I know she was about to try. But why? What the fuck happened between us? How were we on the verge of *making love,* for the first time, on my living room couch, and the next moment she doesn't want me anymore? She asked me if I was hers... I admitted I was... And now, after barely responding to my texts all week, she's acting as though we were never more than friends.

No. Fuck this. She doesn't get to do this to me. To us!

If she's throwing me away, I need to know why... So I can change her mind.

M Y HEART IS POUNDING AGAINST MY RIB CAGE AS I WALK ACROSS THE BAR. Dean doesn't look like he's doing too well. I don't know what I expected of him, though. It hasn't been a walk in the park for me either. I've missed him. More than I thought I would. I force myself to focus on the job though. It's a Friday night, and the place is packed with bikers and truckers, wanting to have a good time and kick back. If I keep myself busy, I won't have to think so much. And I'll try to keep myself from looking in Dean's direction. It's only two nights a week. We're all adults. Keeping this job should be manageable. If not, then I'll just make the most of it while I'm here.

"Hi Cherry." I smile pleasantly at Dean's friend. She just finished pouring shots for a group of patrons and turns to face me. "Sorry I'm late. Car trouble."

"Did you talk to Dean?" she asks, a detectable level of concern in her voice.

"I saw him on my way in. He's outside, I think." I say, attempting to sound casual, as if all is well. "Can I get a tray? That table in the back looks like they might be ready for another round."

She hands me a tray over the bar. As I start to walk away, Cherry stops me. "Vanna, is everything okay?"

I force myself to smile back at her, but I don't know what to say.

Forty minutes into my shift, I've just brought a table a bunch of shots and chasers, when I suddenly feel an arm wrap gently, but possessively, around my waist. Lips close to my ear, a growly voice I'd recognize anywhere whispers to me. "I need to talk to you. Come with me, now."

I turn slightly in order to look up into his eyes. They look pained. I imagine they looked the same earlier, though I couldn't see them very well in the dark outside. I did hear the uncertainty in his voice when we spoke briefly, however. I don't know what to say to him, now.

"I'm working." I sigh.

"And I'm still your boss." Dean pushes.

"Well, you have me there." I try to make light of the situation. I know this is going to be an uncomfortable conversation.

"I'll have you however I can." He says softly. "Come with me." He moves his hand from my waist, to take my hand. I let him lead me towards the corridor past the bar, where I leave my tray as we pass. Once we're walking down the hall that leads to the back patio, he walks a little faster, pulling me in tow. I'm tempted to ask him to slow down, but if we're going to the patio, it's not that much further.

He uses the palm of his hand to slam the back door to the patio open. It hits the back wall with a loud bang, as Dean steps outside, pulling me with him.

Vixie is sitting at one of the patio tables, looking startled by the door.

"Get back inside." He stonily orders her.

She gets to her feet without hesitation and hurries back inside, shutting the door Dean left wide open as she does. Part of me is a little surprised at how she jumped at his command.

Dean turns around to face me, releasing my hand, only to cup both of his on either side of my face. He backs me up quickly, against the brick wall of the building beside the patio door. The instant my back hits the wall, his lips are pressed to mine, kissing me hungrily, as if he were starving for it.

I must have been too, because I have zero will power inside me to stop him. I want to kiss him back. To hold him close. To tell him I'm sorry for the pain I've caused him. For all the pain I *will* cause him. I let him kiss me. Though, I barely kiss him back.

"Vanna... *why?*" His whispered plea against my lips nearly breaks my heart. He stops kissing me, only to press his forehead to mine, eyes squeezed shut. His hands are still holding my face, the front of his body against mine. "What did I do, baby? Please..." he whispers again.

I hate myself... I literally, whole heartedly, hate myself.

"Nothing." I manage to choke out. "You didn't do anything to me."

"Then why are you doing this to us?" he asks. "Why did you run away from me? Why are you pushing me away?"

I don't know what to say to him. All I can do is reach up and hold onto his wrists as his hands continue to cradle my face. Closing my eyes against the burning tears that are threatening to well up and over flow. I can't let myself cry in front of him. I just can't.

"This isn't fair..." he whispers again. "I can count on these two hands how many times I've gotten to kiss you... *really* kiss you..." he strokes my cheeks with his fingers gently, his forehead still pressed to mine, before he holds my face again. "It wasn't enough, baby. It isn't enough."

"I'm sorry." I whimper.

"I don't need to hear apologies. I need to know what happened. You said you wanted exclusivity, you had that from the beginning... You kissed me like I meant something to you... asked me if I was yours ... and then you ran out on me, Vanna." His thumbs gently brush the dampness beneath my eyes.

Nothing but the truth makes any sense as to why I did what I did, but I can't tell him the truth. Hating myself is one thing... I have a lifetime of practice in that. Especially these last few years. The thought of *Dean* hating me though, I don't think I could stand that. I need to keep him in my life, however. If I'm going to come out of this nightmare alive.

"You do mean something to me, Dean. I care about you." I say. "I'm just... not like these other girls. I'm not like Vixie, or Lucinda... or even Cherry. I just... don't fit."

"You fit with me. *Be with me.* Nobody else matters." He insists.

Under normal circumstances, he'd be right. Had I not set us on this course of turmoil and destruction ... But the spell could be the only reason he ever even looked at me twice... I can't lose sight of that. If I do, I'll cave to him. And when he eventually fulfills his purpose, he'll most likely drop me. Snap out of it and wonder what the hell he was ever even doing with someone like me. I don't think my heart could take that.

If I have feelings for him already... I'm afraid to even try to imagine the pain I will feel in a year or two, when everything comes crashing down. And if he ever knew what I did to him...

No. It has to end here. As much as it hurts now, it'll hurt so much more in the long run. I've had to do worse to survive. I'm doing him a favor if I end the romantic pursuit.

"I think we'll be better off... if we just stay friends." I manage to choke out, my voice barely an octave above a whisper.

"You're lying to me." He growls. I try to shake my head, my face still in his hands. "Open your eyes and tell me you don't want me the way I want you." He challenges me. "Make me believe you. Look me in the eyes and fucking *lie* to me, Vanna."

I'm about to try, when there's suddenly a loud electronic buzzing noise coming from somewhere above us. I realize immediately, it's the emergency button under the bar. The one we're supposed to hit if a fight breaks out. My eyes open and focus on his, which are glaring into mine now. A painful rage in them. The buzzer goes off again, almost frantically. Like someone ringing a doorbell.

"*Fuck*!" Dean shouts, as he uses the brick wall behind me to shove himself away from me. "Stay here. This isn't over. Not this conversation, and not us!"

Before I can respond, he's gone. The patio door swinging on its hinges, the faint sound of his motorcycle boots pounding down the corridor towards the bar.

R OUNDING THE CORNER OF THE CORRIDOR, I BURST INTO THE BAR, scanning the room to assess where I'm needed first in the fight. I'm ready and eager. Tonight, is not the fucking night to get on my bad side.

I don't see anything awry. There is no fight... Everything is fine. Viking is sitting on his bar stool in his usual spot by the front door, now looking at me like I'm crazy. Cherry is behind the bar, cracking tops off bottles for a few patrons sitting near her, oblivious to my hasty arrival. Fucking Vixie is waiting tables across the room.

I storm up to the bar to Cherry. "Did you hit the buzzer?"

She looks at me with her brows pinching together, puzzled. "No, everything is fine up here."

I walk around and step behind the bar to check the buzzer. Maybe something got wedged up against it accidently. I crouch down to check under the bar near the button. All is clear. I inspect what I can see of the wiring for any indication of something coming lose that could have caused a false alarm. There's nothing. Everything is intact and as it should be.

"Were you the only one back here within the last three minutes?"

"Vixie grabbed a few bottles for the table in the back. I was down this end serving when she did." Cherry says.

Fucking Vixie.

I stand back up, turning my back to the bar so Vixie can't see my face. I know I must look pissed, because Cherry looks concerned.

"Do you know what happened between Vixie and Vanna last weekend?"

"No. I thought maybe Vixie said something to Vanna, but Vanna didn't tell me anything. I asked her." Cherry says. "I thought she was mostly just worried about your disappearing act with the nomads... But something was definitely a little off between them. Vixie has been cold to Vanna, up until last weekend. Suddenly she decided she was going to start talking to her. But about what, I have no idea."

"I was out back with Vanna. Sent Vixie inside so we'd have some privacy. Next thing I know, someone's hitting the buzzer like a speed addict on a game show. Thought I'd be running into a fucking riot."

Cherry scowls, her gaze shifting to Vixie out on the floor. "You know that bitch has wanted you since she started here. She probably got in Vanna's head. Hit the buzzer to prevent you guys from working things out."

"That's my guess, too."

"Fire her." Cherry says, coolly.

"You won't have any real help if I fire her. I don't know how much longer Vanna's going to be around..." I sigh, shaking my head. Vixie might be part of the reason, but there's more Vanna isn't telling me. I can feel it in my fucking bones.

"What are you talking about?" Cherry asks.

"She's saying she just wants to be friends. That we just don't fit."

"I'm sorry, Dean." Cherry says, a sympathetic look in her pretty green eyes. "I know you really like her."

"I think she's lying to me... Am I wrong?"

"You know her better than any of us do. Vanna really doesn't say a whole lot." Cherry says. She's got that right. Vanna is like a fucking vault of secrets. That I'm determined to crack.

"So, she doesn't talk to you, I'm gathering."

"Nothing of any real significance. I don't think she's got many friends, though... That might be something you should think about, Dean."

"I do think about it. I worry about her." She's so... *alone.*

"I mean... there might be another reason she doesn't have friends, Dean. She's nice and all, but... Don't you think there's something a little... *off* about her? What do you really know about her?"

"I know she's been hurt. I don't think I'm going out on a limb here saying it was bad... I know she's not used to relying on anyone but herself. She's resilient. Smart. She's sweet and considerate."

Cherry giggles.

"What?"

"You could be describing yourself."

I scoff. "What's with women thinking I'm sweet and fancy?"

Cherry laughs at me. "*Fancy*? Who accused you of that?"

I can't help the corner of my mouth curling into a half grin, at the memory of Vanna's laughter. Her beautiful smile, as she playfully teased me over mugs of tea, barely a week ago.

"Vanna... I don't want to lose her, Cherry. You're a woman. Tell me what to do."

"Give her what she thinks she wants." Cherry shrugs.

Not what I wanted to hear. A tinge of panic jolts through me. What if she thinks she's right then? What if that feeds directly into her insecurities about herself? That would be taking ten steps backwards in our relationship. What if she fucking believes me and some other prick asks her out, and she says yes? I'm not going to be able to stand there and watch that shit go down... Fuck no.

"Doll... I think I'm past the point of no return here..." I swallow, hard. My fingers digging into my own chest anxiously.

"Are you saying you fell for her?" She's giving me that sympathetic, pitiful expression again.

"I... I don't know... *Falling*... maybe." I stammer, like a fool. I'm not ready to throw around certain words just yet. *Self-preservation* is a hell of thing...

"Maybe she feels like things are moving too fast between you two? Vanna's not like these girls." Cherry suggests, tipping her chin to indicate the women behind me somewhere, most likely hanging on other bikers. "You MC guys are used to fast bikes and faster women."

Did I rush her? I thought we were moving at a slow pace. I followed her lead, didn't I? I never tried to rush a kiss. Was I too forward? I could have sworn she wanted to take things further that evening at my house. Could I have read the signs wrong?

I notice Cherry glance past me, then look back up into my eyes, her brows slightly raised. Vanna must have just walked into the bar through the corridor.

"Is everything okay?" I hear her ask as she approaches us.

"False alarm, apparently." Cherry answers her.

"I'm gonna go relieve Viking for a bit. Cover for him so he can take a break. You can let Vixie know she can finish her break too, if she wants. I made her cut it short, before." I say to Cherry.

"Is that *all* you want me to tell her?" Cherry asks.

"For now."

I turn around to walk out from behind the bar. Vanna is standing there, timorously, as if she expects me to yell at her or something. I don't say anything though. I walk past her and head to the other side of the bar to sit beside Viking. Resolving myself to be content for the moment, with watching her from a far.

C HERRY AND I ARE ALMOST FINISHED WIPING DOWN THE TABLES AFTER the Twisted Throttle closed for the night. I'm still debating whether I should call a cab for a ride home, or ask Dean. He hasn't said a word to me since he left me on the back patio. I'm not sure if asking him would be sending him mixed signals, or if calling a cab, when he passes my house to get to his, would come across as being overly dramatic about the whole situation. Or possibly worse, coming across as intentionally trying to hurt him.

Once the tables are cleaned down, I walk behind the bar to wash my hands in the sink and remove my apron. Emptying the remaining bottle caps from it into the collection bucket, I hear the sound of motorcycle boots approach the bar.

"You got a ride home?" Dean asks. He sounds as though he's trying to seem detached.

Folding my apron quickly, I tuck it in the far corner drawer below the back bar, before I turn around to face him. "I wasn't sure if I should call a cab, or ask you." I say, placing my hands on the lower front bar counter, trying not to appear as awkward as I feel. "Garrett offered to come get me, but..." No way I was going to take him up on that. Not at two thirty in the morning. I can't help feeling like he would expect something from me, if I had said yes. It was uncomfortable enough in his truck with him when he was dropping me off. Thank God it's less than a fifteen-minute drive, but he knew he was taking me to work. If he were to drive me home, without the time restraint of needing to be somewhere, I'm not sure what he would try.

"*Fuck that.*" Dean growls. His eyes slightly narrowing, as if he's imagining the same scenarios in his mind about Garrett, that I am. "I'm taking you. Let's go."

"Are you sure?" I ask, "I know you're my neighbor, but-"

"I'm more than your *neighbor*, Vanna." Dean cuts me off. "I'm not going to let you fool yourself into reducing me to just your *neighbor... Boss... Friend...*" His words are leaden with indignation.

"I... I'm not trying to do that." I nearly stutter under his crushing glare. "Do you really believe I just suddenly don't care about you at all?" That couldn't be further from the truth.

He shakes his head slowly, his eyes boring into mine. "No. But please, feel free and encouraged, to explain to me why you're determined to push me away so suddenly?"

Because I care, that's why. But I don't respond.

The steel door of the bar opens as Viking walks in. "The lot's clear." He says, glancing at both of us for a few moments, before he asks, "Did I walk in on something?"

"I'm taking Vanna home." Dean says to him, without taking his eyes off me. "Lock up behind us." His authoritative tone is slightly unnerving. My mind thinks back to that night when I first started working for him. How that biker that grabbed me seemed more terrified of Dean, than he was of a much bigger Viking.

In the parking lot outside, I follow Dean over to Serene, where she's parked under one of the flood lights by his shop across the way.

"I'm surprised you don't have her in the shop's garage. I'd think you'd be afraid of someone bumping into her accidently or something." I say, attempting to make neutral conversation to fill the uncomfortable silence between us.

"There are multiple cameras in this lot." He says, cocking his chin towards a camera on the building, angled directly at his precious motorcycle. "And people know to stay away from her." He adds. I watch as he removes the extra helmet from one of the saddle bags.

"Right. I remember the golden rule. Never touch a biker's motorcycle." I say, attempting a little smile at him.

Dean takes a step towards me, gently placing the helmet on my head, and fastening the strap under my chin. "Or his woman." He says, his eyes staring into mine again, his gravelly voice low and borderline sensual. I want to look away from him, his penetrating gaze. But as I feared would be the case, I'm warring with myself. I find him far too attractive for either of our own good.

He touches my face lightly, his thumb brushing across my bottom lip, gently tugging it free of my teeth. "The way you're looking at me, doll..." he growls, making me want to clench my thighs together. I can smell his scent on his fingers, that intoxicating smokey wood and leathery aroma that seems to always be lingering on him. "You're mine, Vanna. As much as I'm yours." He says the words as if they are set in stone. A cold hard fact. Non-negotiable.

I force myself to take a breath. But before I can speak, he gives me a command, in that same authoritative tone he spoke to Vixie and Viking, that had them complying immediately to his orders. *"Get on the bike."*

Taking his offered hand, I climb onto the back of Serene without hesitation. He looks at me on his motorcycle for a moment, as if admiring the view, before he mounts her in front of me. As Dean fires her up, revving her loudly and kicking up her stand, I wrap my arms around him, holding onto him tightly. As we take off out of the lot, flying through the city streets towards our homes in the country, I press my cheek against his leather clad back.

A part of me wishes this didn't feel so right. The other part of me craves the peace in knowing that something... *someone*... finally does.

E IGHT-THIRTY IN THE MORNING, AS HE PROMISED... OR MORE LIKE, *insisted*... Dean is at my house to change my tire. Now, as I sit on my front steps, after handing him my keys, watching him swap out the flat tire for the donut, my thoughts drift back to six hours ago. My failed attempt at the *just friend's* plan.

We only kissed good night. Though... it was a kiss that left us both breathless. There was no talking, either. Dean made that impossible. I'm sure that was part of his plan. To prevent me from speaking... even *thinking* straight. Dean Keegan knows how to kiss... and the man is fully aware of the effect he has on women. He's dangerous in more ways than one.

"I've got a question for you, Vanna." he says, breaking the silence between us, as well as pulling me out of my day dream about our steamy make-out session last night... That began on Serene, and ended up with me pressed against my storm door...

"Huh?"

"When's the last time you had your brakes changed?" he asks, looking over his shoulder at me as he tightens the lug nuts on the donut.

"Um... I don't know." I say, trying to remember. Must have been a year or two ago, though... Maybe?

"How about your oil, doll?"

"Umm..."

He chuckles. "That's what I was afraid of." He says, standing up and brushing his hands on his pants. "I'm not even going to ask about the tranny fluid or power steering."

"There's fluid in the steering?"

He smiles as he shakes his head, making his way around my car to the driver's side door. He opens it and pops the hood of my car to check my oil and other fluids I assume.

"Is there something wrong with my brakes?" I ask.

"Only that they're basically gone." He shrugs, then lifts the hood to poke around at a few things in there. "At any point, did you hear any squeaking or grinding of any kind when you were driving?"

"About two months ago... but it stopped. I thought it worked itself out."

Dean chuckles again, shaking his head some more as he pulls out the oil stick. "This is terrible, Vanna." He sighs.

"I need oil and brakes?"

"An oil change, power steering service, tranny service. Yes, you need brakes, desperately. New rotors, since you ground the shit out of them. And it looks like there's something wrong with the axle... You haven't heard anything when you make a right turn?"

I bite my lip. "Only a little when I make a sharp right." I admit.

"Did you hit something recently?"

I shrug. "Not that I remember."

He lets out another sigh as he pulls the hood back down. "What am I going to do with you, Vanna?"

"I'm guessing lecture me on being a bad car mom." I giggle.

"Didn't anyone ever tell you how important these things are to the life of your car?"

"I lost track of time. Sheesh." I say, watching him pull out his cellphone and text someone.

"What were your plans today?" he asks, glancing up from his phone to look at me.

What were *my plans?* "Not a lot." For the last months, I have been spending a lot of my free time after work and on weekends with Dean. "I was going to sleep in a little today. But you had other plans." I wave my hand at him and my car.

"Didn't get much sleep?" He asks, a slight, crooked grin on his handsome face.

I can't help the smile he pulls out of me. "Not really. Did you?"

"I haven't gotten much sleep at all this week." He says, his grin fading. He doesn't have to elaborate. I know it's because I ran out on him, and then spent a week avoiding him. I didn't think it would bother him as much as it apparently has. God... I have so much to feel guilty over. The consequences of my actions just keep piling up.

His cellphone chimes, pulling his attention back to whomever he was texting. "Have you had breakfast yet?"

"No. But I don't always anyway."

"Go put your sneakers on. You can follow me to my buddy's shop. I'll take you to breakfast while he straightens your car out." Dean says, shoving the phone back in his pocket.

"Wait... How much is this going to cost? This sounds like a lot and I don't know if I can afford it all at once."

"Okay, well I'll tell him to look everything over, and come up with an estimate while we have breakfast." Dean suggests. "That sound good?"

I suppose it wouldn't hurt to find out exactly what I need to keep this car going. Whatever it is, is still probably cheaper than having to buy a new one. "Okay."

"What do you think you can swing today, if you had to?" He asks.

"I have three hundred."

"Three hundred that you can use for this? You have grocery money? Rent?"

I nod. I have more in my emergency reserves, but sticking to my budget, without having to dip into my escape money savings, I can swing three hundred for my car. "I have three hundred I can spare."

"Counting what I owe you for last night?"

"No."

Dean nods, pulling out his wallet and removing some cash as he walks over to me. "Here's for last night and tonight's shift. Now you have five hundred. That will at least get you a tire, front brakes, an oil change, new rotors and maybe even the axle."

"Are you sure? That seems like a lot for five hundred."

"I'm sure, doll." Dean smiles.

"Okay, I'll take your word for it." I sigh, standing up to go get my shoes and purse. "I don't know cars."

"You don't have to convince me of that, baby." He teases me.

I follow Dean across town to his friend's repair shop. After handing over my keys to the mechanic, Dean takes me to a little family-owned breakfast nook on the outskirts of town. We take our time enjoying a country style breakfast while we wait for word on my car.

"I was right about the price in case you were wondering." Dean grins at me over his glass of orange juice. "I gave him the go ahead to make the repairs before we left."

"How long did he say it would take?"

"A few hours. Why? You want to run from me again?" I can detect the dark humor in his words, but still. I look back down at my plate, avoiding his gaze, uncomfortably. He sighs. "I'm sorry, Vanna. Part of my asshole charm is bad timed remarks... But we should talk about what happened. A serious conversation."

"Can we do that somewhere a little more private?" I ask, glancing at the other people having breakfast at tables around us.

"Sure, doll." Dean says. "Let me settle up here and you can tell me where we're going after this."

As I watch Dean walk up to the register, I can't help but wonder if he meant where we're going in our relationship, or where we're going to talk about said relationship.

We end up near the river bank of the intercoastal. Down a trail in the state park that leads to a secluded little beach like area. There are a few sun-faded picnic tables, under the shade of Pine, Poplar and Old gnarly Oak trees, dripping with Spanish moss. It's actually a beautiful place. With lots of driftwood washed up along the bank that would make for some pretty, natural art projects.

"You know where the best little tucked away places are." I say, watching him hop up onto the picnic table to sit with his boots on the bench. "Is this another Lucinda location?" I ask, though I'm mostly just teasing him. I assume, after a few years of marriage, he probably brought her everywhere.

"If it is, can we do what we did at the beach to get rid of her energy?" he asks with a sly little smirk. "You know, exorcise her out of here?"

I can't help giggling, thinking back on the way I practically attacked him on the beach behind the jetty. "I don't know what came over me that night."

"Whatever it was, it can come back any time it wants. I'm game." He teases me. "I've got a little rustic log cabin in the mountains too, that we could exorcise as well."

I loved going to the Pocono's as a kid on family vacations. I try not to smile at the thought of Dean's cabin in the mountains. Not when I don't know what's going to happen between us. Though, if things were to somehow work out for us, I'd love to visit it with him.

"That sounds nice." I say, then catch myself before he can make another comment, "A cabin in the mountains, I mean... I've always loved the mountains. I haven't been since I was a kid."

"I'll take you one day. It's rustic... I'm talking wood burning stove, antique steel steam radiators and a fireplace for heat." Dean says. "My great, great grandfather built it. Built the furniture inside too. There's not a lot to it, but the views are spectacular, no matter what time of year. I bet you'd love it." He smiles faintly, as if he's picturing us there, and isn't sure himself, if we'll ever get to go.

"I bet I would." I sigh, turning to walk closer to the river bank. I squat down to arrange a few small sticks of driftwood in the sand into the shape of a pentagram.

"Trying to freak out the locals with that witch stuff?" he jokes.

"There's nothing scary about a pentagram. Or a pentacle. The star, or pentagram, represents the elements. Earth, air, fire and water. The upright top point represents spirit." I say, picking up a few more sticks to make a circle around the star, turning it into a pentacle. "When the pentagram is inside

296

a circle, it's a pentacle. And the circle represents the universe. Everything is connected. These symbols are used as talismans, or in evocations. They're protection symbols." I explain, keeping things simple and to the point. I know Dean doesn't believe in any of it, anyway. Glancing up, I find him looking at me. "See, nothing scary about it."

"And when it's inverted?" he asks, thoughtfully. A genuine curiosity. Though I'm sure he's asking because he's probably seen an upside-down pentacle in horror movies or used by satanic groups.

"Right side up, represents masculine energy. Spirit ruling over matter. Grounded in duality." I explain. "When the symbol is inverted, it represents feminine energy. Matter ruling over spirit. Grounded in spirituality. As above. So below."

His eyes meet mine. "So, no devil shit, then?"

I'm not exactly sure if he's asking a question, or just stating what I see as the obvious. But I can't help a little laugh. "No, there's no devil in the craft. The physical material the universe is made of, is in essence, feminine. Matter equals mother. The conscious phenomenon is masculine. The body, and all living things are vessels with at least some form of consciousness." I shrug. "But people see things differently. To some, the inverted pentacle represents the horned God, Pan. And other occult groups, like Satanists, adopted the symbol of the inverted pentacle as well. That doesn't make the symbols evil, or something to be afraid of. Witches aren't inherently bad, either."

"Kinda like bikers." He jokes. "Some people think we're all criminals."

"Aren't you?" I tease him, standing up, I brush my hands off on my jeans.

"I suppose that would depend on what you consider a crime." He grins at me.

"Do I even want to know what you're alluding to?" I ask, only half joking this time.

Dean's grin only widens, but he doesn't comment further. After a moment, he pushes himself off the table and walks towards me, his hand outstretched, inviting me to take it. "Walk with me. This place won't be very private for very long. I know another."

Of course, he does.

We follow the hiking trail along the river, through gnarly scrub oaks and pines until we come to a large, fallen Oak tree. Its main trunk is massive, and its numerous limbs stretch across the ground, even jutting out across the river, hanging just above the surface of the water. There are shoots of new life growing from the trunk. The tree is still living, despite having fallen some time ago.

Not letting go of my hand, Dean leads me over a few of the limbs and branches, until we come to the center of the tree. Limber as a cat, and somehow unhindered while wearing heavy biker boots and a leather jacket, Dean climbs up to the top of the trunk with ease. As he crouches low, to offer me his hand again to help me up there with him, I can't help thinking that comparing him to a cat was an understatement. He's more like a mountain lion.

Hoisting me up on top of the tree with him, he directs me to sit down on the edge, facing out over the river. My legs dangle down between the large V where the limbs of the tree shoot off from the main trunk. Dean takes a seat behind me, his legs on either side of mine, as he wraps his arms loosely around me, holding me against him.

"This is one of my favorite places." He says softly beside my ear. "When I was a kid, this big old tree was still standing. My brother and I used to look for the civil war bullets that are embedded in the trunk. That's how old this thing is. A hurricane took it down ten years ago. But it refuses to give up. It's still alive." His words are full of admiration. I agree with him though, impressed by the Oaks tenacity towards life as well.

"The view isn't bad either." I say, staring out across the sparkling river.

"This is also a spot I never brought Lucinda." He adds.

I actually do like that. "Even better." I smile to myself as he hugs me a little tighter to him, his nose nuzzling my ear through my hair. I can hear him breathing in my scent.

"I really like you, Vanna." He whispers. "I've really come to care a lot about you."

I try not to let myself tense up. There's no way I'll be able to hide it from him, not with him holding me the way he is.

"Why?" I ask. Though, I'm fairly certain I already know the answer. "Our worlds are so different... I'm not your type of woman... the MC thing isn't a world I'm used to... and you don't believe in my world."

"There's only one world, Vanna." Dean says on a sigh. "One miserable, fucked up world. That got a whole lot less miserable when you stepped into it, for me. I've never met anyone like you before. I don't... come around to people, the way I've done with you. If you told me right now, that you put a spell on me, I might even believe you. And I wouldn't even be mad about it."

I try not to cringe at his words. God, if he only knew the truth. He'd feel so much differently about me.

"You, Vanna... you brought light back into my life. I don't want to go back into the cold darkness. Not after feeling your warmth." He says, pressing his lips to the side of my face as he holds me tighter still.

"We've only been seeing each other a few months. This doesn't seem fast to you?" I ask. He loosens his hold on me, slightly, but doesn't let me go.

"Is that what this is about? You think we're moving too fast?" He asks. "We've only kissed... if you aren't ready to go further, I respect that. I didn't mean for you to feel pressured that night. I thought I made myself clear, you could, and can, always tell me no, Vanna... If I didn't make that clear, I'm sorry. I never want to make you feel like you have to do anything, baby. Or make you feel... *trapped*."

I remember the look on his face when I said that to him. Like I had slapped him. "I'm sorry I said that to you. I didn't mean it."

The truth of the matter is that Dean actually makes me feel freer than I've felt in a long time. Admitting that out loud though, would invite questions I'm not prepared to answer yet.

"I just... I didn't want you to go. And then when you did... and later, when you told me you wanted space... I can't lie to you doll, that shit *hurt*."

"I'm sorry. The last thing I want to do is hurt you." *Or get you hurt!*

"Would you give me another chance? I know you said you want to try the friend thing, but... I want to be more than just your friend, Vanna. And I believe that's what you want, too. Can we try again? Slow?"

"Why are you so sure you want me?" I sigh.

Dean holds me a little tighter in his arms again. His lips near my ear as we both look out over the intercoastal waters, shimmering in the sun light as the water gently laps at the sand below us. "Sometimes, a person walks into your life... and suddenly, your life is different. Your world is changed. Sometimes, you can meet a person, and feel like they've always been a part of you. You can look in a person's eyes, and recognize aspects of your own soul in them. Your heart's just like mine, Vanna. We hold our pain inside. I can see that in your beautiful, dark eyes. We're the same in a lot of ways. Our jagged edges fit, doll. We fit together. You're wrong when you say we don't. And we've got more in common than I think either of us even know, yet." He reaches up to touch my chin with his fingers as he turns my face gently back to look at him. "I'll follow your lead. You dictate the pace. Just... don't push me away. I want to be with you, doll."

Damnit. Damnit. Damnit! I close my eyes so I don't have to look into his. It's so much harder when he looks in my eyes. The concern I see in them for me. The adoration. I crave it so much, yet at the same time, the guilt feels like it will rip me in half.

"Can we try again, baby?" he asks, his thumb gently brushing my lower lip again, tugging it from my teeth. I can feel his soft breath against my face... my lips. Knowing his mouth is so close to mine only zaps my will power further. "Vanna?" he breathes my name in that way that only he does.

I tilt my face up to him, ever so slightly, closing the distance between our lips a little more. I can almost feel his.

"You're mine, doll." He whispers, his hand sliding up my cheek, his fingers burying themselves in my hair, curling around the base of my skull, ready to pull me and hold me to his mouth. "*Tell me.*" That deep, sensual, growly baritone voice of his... My undoing.

"Yes." I whisper.

"Aces." He growls, pulling my mouth to his.

Chapter
fourteen
DEAN

ONE MONTH LATER

"IT WILL BE A GOOD WAY TO SEE IF VANNA CAN REALLY HANG, BRO." VIKING had said to me earlier in the gym today, during our workout. My original plan was to go to Axel's patching in party alone. Just not mention it to her, under the guise of "MC Business." Biker parties are known for getting a little wild. Especially when there are multiple MC's involved. Our two closest allies, The JoCo Jokers MC and the Asphalt Knights MC, would be in attendance tonight as well. Had it just been the Saviors MC, I wouldn't be too concerned. But alas, Axel invited Vanna. I couldn't leave her home.

As I ride Serene up Vanna's driveway, she's already outside waiting for me. "Do I look like a biker chick?" She asks, excitedly.

Vanna is standing at the bottom of her porch steps, wearing tight black jeans with slashes across her thighs, allowing peeks of her skin beneath. Black boots, a black top with some kind of lace up lowcut neckline that's going to distract me all night, and a cropped leather jacket that barely makes it to her rib cage. But damn, does it accentuate the curve of her body. The way her waist dips in and her hips swell back out. A perfect hour glass, with a few extra minutes in all the right places.

Fuck. I'm going to have to be on her all night. "You look hot, baby."

She turns around to grab something off one of the steps of her porch, and I can't help admiring her ass. Imagining my hands holding onto her hips and...

"Can you put this in the side bag?" she asks, turning around with a black box wrapped in an orange ribbon. "I got Axel a little gift."

"What is it?"

"A little Motorcycle figurine. The front tire is a clock. I thought it was cute." She says, walking over to me.

"Very sweet of you. I'm sure he will love it." I say, getting off my bike to retrieve her helmet from the saddle bag and tuck her gift in its place. "Where'd you get this little jacket?" I ask, placing the helmet on her head and strapping it on her.

"A second-hand shop. Same as these jeans." She laughs. "I couldn't find anything motorcycle related at the thrift store. Sorry."

"Well, nothing says *Biker Chick* like being on the arm of an actual biker." I tease her. "And I plan to keep you that way, all night." I'm not kidding about that part, even though she giggles.

The party is in full swing by the time we arrive, almost a full lot of motorcycles parked behind Ink Slingers Inc. Under normal circumstances, this Saviors hosted party would have taken place in the lot behind the Twisted Throttle. But since my falling out with the President, they chose another spot. The place is owned by one of my former MC brothers, Diesel. He owns the couple of acres of field behind it as well, where a large bonfire is already raging, blazing high in the center of the clearing. Behind the bonfire, a few yards back, there's a makeshift stage with a live band playing rock music. Posts with lights strung up on them, crisscross over the main area of the gathering. The heavy aroma of a whole pig roasting on a spit is wafting through the night air as well, mingling with the smell of the raging bonfire.

As I pull Serene off to the far side of the lot, I feel Vanna squeeze me suddenly. When I glance back at her, I notice she's looking at a motorcycle with the AKMC logo on it.

"There are *Knights* here..." She says, worriedly.

"He isn't a Knight anymore. You won't see him here with them." I assure her, kicking Serene's stand down and dismounting to help Vanna off. She looks up at me, apprehensively, as I unstrap her helmet and remove it from her head.

"Are his... *Brothers*... going to be mad at me?" she asks.

"Why would they be mad at you? You didn't do anything wrong that night in the bar. He was a predator. That shit doesn't fly in our MC's. I dealt with it that night, anyway. And besides, nobody knows you." A big part of me wishes I could slap a cut on her with my patch on it. Clearly marking her as mine and off limits to anyone looking her way. Though, even if I could, she'd probably still fight it. I haven't forgotten her aversion to wearing a Property Of MC shirt around the bar when she works. "Relax, baby. We're just here to party and have a good time." Though I'm not sure who I'm trying to convince more. Vanna, or myself.

Throwing an arm across her shoulders, we start walking towards the gathering. I'm slightly relieved to see a lot of women here wearing MC Property cuts. That means although things could get a little wild later, after we've all had a few drinks, at least there aren't as many Lay Girls and Patch Whores around, making themselves available to any guy who wants it, *anywhere*. I'll just have to keep Vanna away from the shadows of the outskirts of the party, where the *free love* goes down.

There are tables lined up with catered food and coolers of beer and sodas, as well as a small selection of hard liquor. The usual shit. Jack Daniels, Bacardi, Tequila and Vodka. I grab a soda for Vanna, handing it off to her, and a beer for myself, as we walk together across the grounds. I cock my chin to those who acknowledge my presence as we move through the crowd in search of a spot to land for a few minutes.

I find us a picnic table towards the border of the party, not quite in the shadows. It's still early yet, so it should be a safe spot for now. I hop up on the table and sit with my boots on the bench. Vanna moves to sit between my feet, but I tug her hand and scoot back a little further.

"I want you right here, doll." I say, spreading my knees and patting the table in front of me between my thighs. "Nice and close."

She climbs up onto the bench and plants her fine ass right where I want her, nestling up against my crotch with a playful little giggle. I clamp my legs against her hips and lean back slightly to twist the cap off my beer, taking a quick swig. Setting it down beside me, I wrap my arms around her.

"You want me to open that for you?" I ask, nodding at the soda in her hands.

"I don't really want it yet." She says, glancing around at the scene before us. Placing my chin on her shoulder, I attempt to follow her eyes. She seems to be looking towards the raging bonfire. The women dancing around it to the rock music playing. Their bodies, dark silhouettes against the bright leaping flames, twisting and swaying to the rhythm. The *pagan-esque* scene reminds me of her. As if Vanna is ever far from my thoughts at any given moment anyway. Even with her here in my arms.

"So, it's really just a party. Nothing crazy."

"The night is still young." I whisper in her ear, teasing. She squirms in my embrace and giggles. I've come to learn she's quite sensitive around her ears and neck. And though I promised infinite patience, I yearn for the opportunity to explore just how sensitive these little spots on her body are. What she'll respond to. What gets her really hot.

"I was expecting things to be a little wilder." She shrugs.

"An orgy?" I joke, sliding one of my hands up her thigh and hooking a finger into one of the cuts in her jeans.

Fuck. She's so soft.

It occurs to me in this moment, I've never touched her bare thigh before. I've only groped at her over her clothing. I fight the urge to jam my whole hand inside her fashionably ripped jeans. However, I resolve myself to simply stroking her soft skin, slowly. Savoring the feel of her on my finger tip.

"Not exactly an orgy. But Vixie said…"

I sigh. Of course, *Vixie said*. "What did she say?" I reluctantly ask.

Vanna twists around to whisper in my ear, as if she's embarrassed for anyone else to hear her. Not that they could. The music is loud, and we're three yards from the nearest people.

"Vixie said a lot of sex happens at biker parties… like, *public* sex." She whispers, then pulls back to look me in the eyes. Her fingers now pressed to her lips as if she just said something really naughty and would be reprimanded for it. Only, there's a playful little twinkle in her dark eyes.

"Vixie would know." I mutter, still harboring some resentment towards her for the stunt she pulled a month ago with the buzzer, and for trying to get in Vanna's head. I hope I was effective in backing her off, after our frank little chat a few days later.

Vanna looks at me, curiously. "You wouldn't?"

I grin at her. "I'm not falling for this."

"Falling for what?" she eyes me with playful suspicion. "You've never gotten a little *wild* at one of these biker parties?"

"Can I plead the fifth on that?"

She smacks my chest, pretending to look appalled. At least, I hope she's pretending.

"Not since I met you."

"You told me you never slept with a patch chaser."

"I said I never slept with any of the current Lady Lays at the Twisted Throttle." I remind her. "As this party goes on, you might want to avoid any areas in the shadows." Not that I'm going to let her wander off alone anyway.

She twists back around to look at the fire. "So, you've had sex at parties like this with patch chasers." I can't tell if it's a question, or if she's just thinking out loud.

"I was young once, babe… One of the perks to rolling with MC's… *the willing women.*" I slip my finger out of the slit in her jeans and lean back to take another swig of beer. She doesn't attempt to shove me off when I wrap my arms around her to hold her again. Maybe she accepts that I have a past and is willing to let it go. She doesn't ask me anything else about it.

Axel spots us and waves, then gestures with his hand to wait one minute. I notice him and Cherry pouring some liquor into a couple of solo cups, before they start heading over in our direction. I can't help chuckling.

"You mind doing a shot with him? He just turned twenty-one on top of getting his patch. I'm sure they're bringing one or two for you."

"I'm sure I'll be fine. I'm safe with you, right? And you're sure that Knight isn't here?"

"The safest place you can be is in my arms, doll. And I have no intention of letting you go." I kiss her head, breathing in her coconut scented hair. "The AKMC kicked Shane out. Like the Saviors, they hold their members to a higher standard." I say, hoping that is still the case with the Saviors. Patching in Axel, knowing the kid's loyalty lies with me over him, has me wondering just what the fuck Preacher is up to lately. Axel is as good as they come, so there is hope.

"Congratulations, kid." I say to Axel, as he and Cherry walk up to us. Unable to stop me with his hands full, I reach out to tousle his dirty blonde slicked back hair, thoroughly messing it up. "I'm proud of you, kid."

"It's *Brother* now, Bro!" he says, ducking out of reach of my arm with a big grin. "I wish you could have been there to see me get my patch. Finally cutting off that Prospect one. Man, it felt great."

I smile back at him. "So do I, Brother. I hope you hold onto that prospect patch though. Nobody's ever put in the work like you did to become a Savior. You'll be president some day with that dedication." God knows the MC would be better off with Axel running it someday instead of Preacher.

"Should be you, Dean." Axel sighs. "And don't say *it is what it is*. Because what it is, is bullshit." I try to keep the smile on my face for him. When I fell from grace, Axel took my ousting harder than even I did. He hands me one of the red solo cups, and runs his fingers through his hair, slicking it back loosely again. "Most of the guys still think it should be you running this MC. Fuck. I joined because of *you*, bro."

I glance at Cherry, who suddenly smiles, handing Vanna one of the extra solo cups she's holding. "Well, let's drink to Axel's twenty-first birthday, shall we?" She chimes in cheerfully, thankfully taking charge of the conversation and steering it in a happier direction. I'm grateful for Cherry's astute ability to pick up on my subtle ques when I need her to bail me out of a situation. "A shot for his birthday, and a shot for his patch." She says, raising her cup.

We wish him a happy birthday and shoot the whiskey together.

"Where's Viking at?" I ask, taking Vanna's empty cup from her and placing it inside of mine on the table beside my beer.

"Sampling one or two of the *party favors* the Jokers brought with them." Axel laughs, dodging Cherry's swat at him.

"Party favors?" Vanna asks.

"Lay girls." I say. "Sweetbutts. Patch whores. Take your pick."

"He's a legend at these parties." Axel says with a shrug.

"A legend for what?" Vanna asks. Of course, she would.

None of us get to answer her question, though. The roar of at least twenty-five or so motorcycles pulling into the lot has everyone's heads turning in that direction. I recognize Preacher at the head of the pack, as they file into the lot, parking among the bikes that were already here when I arrived with Vanna.

I jump to my feet, standing over her, when I realize just who the fuck is riding alongside him... *Legion*... Along with his twenty Demons and the few Saviors still backing Preacher.

"What the fuck is this?" I ask, scanning the crowd to gauge the reaction of the rest of the bikers here. They seem to be as surprised as I am to see the Chrome Demons roll up with Preacher, as if they're a crew now. "Do you know why they're here?" I ask Axel, "Why Preacher is with them?"

Axel shakes his head. "I have no idea."

"Where's Viper?" I ask, jumping down off the bench. Maybe he knows what this is about.

"He's here somewhere." Axel says.

I look back towards the lot, as Preacher and the Demons dismount their bikes and begin to walk towards the field where the party, previously in full swing, comes to a grinding halt. He's carrying a mega phone in his hands, which he raises and orders the band to stop playing.

The music stops, and the crowd quiets down. Preacher raises the mega phone once more. "In the interest of keeping the peace between our MC's, as President of the dominant club in this region, I have invited the CDMC to join us here tonight." Preacher announces. "I expect you all to be welcoming of our neighboring MC. Both here, and in the streets of our cities."

"Not the dominant club for long." Axel says, looking up at me. "They outnumber the Saviors already... by a lot."

"This isn't all of them. I counted twenty-four at their club house a month ago. And fuck knows how many more there are. Or if they're recruiting new members. This isn't the type of MC we want to be associating with either." I say, remembering their little *party* at the Demons' Den.

Watching Preacher turn to shake Legion's demonic hand, and the sly grin on both of their faces, tells me this is far more than just an introduction due to club proximities.

As the music picks back up, people go back to enjoying themselves, albeit, not as at ease as they had been prior to the CDMC's arrival.

"Should we just leave?" Vanna asks. I can tell she's a little nervous.

"No, don't go." Axel says, glancing back up at me. "I've Prospected way too long to let some new club run me out of my own MC's party."

"Axel's right. About being run out. To leave now would look weak." I mutter, glancing towards Serene in the lot. She's blocked in by a few bikes behind her. I could always jump the curb and ride across the field to the road, though. "They might outnumber the Saviors, and the other MC's individually, but not together. I doubt they're here to start anything. They're here to feel us out. For what purpose, I'm not sure yet."

"So, what do we do?" Vanna asks.

"We appear to have a good time." I say, turning to Axel. "And we stay sharp. Got me?" I make sure he sees me glance at his solo cup before I meet his eyes again.

"Right. No more alcohol. Stay alert. Just in case." He nods.

My guess is that the Demons aren't here to cause any trouble. Not tonight, anyway. Tonight, they will *play the part* of the new comers, looking for acceptance among the closest MC's to their shit hole headquarters. But it is a part they are playing. I can see it in Legion's eyes, the way his smile doesn't reach them when he speaks with Preacher. It isn't genuine. He's tolerating Preacher. There's no respect there. And he said as much to me the night he showed up with four of his men at the Twisted Throttle. Preacher gave his blessing to save face. Legion didn't need it, or want it. Preacher had no choice but to act as though he was fine with them moving in so close to our territory.

"They showed up late to make an entrance. Though, this isn't all of them, it's enough of them to demonstrate that they would be a force to be reckoned with." I say to Axel. "Notice where they parked their bikes also." I cock my chin towards the lot behind us. "Do you see what I see, Bro?"

Axel follows my gaze towards the lot, studying where the clusters of Chrome Demons motorcycles are parked. "They've got you blocked in. There are four bikes around Serene." Axel says, looking further across the lot. "There are five around the President of the AK's too. And their Sergeant at Arms. They've got five bikes around the Jokers President's bike, too... and his Sergeant at Arms." He says, looking back up at me. "No way that's a coincidence."

"It's not. It's strategic. It's a subtle message." I concur.

"You're not even in the MC anymore. Why did they target you?" Vanna asks. I know she's nervous and has been listening to us intently. I wish I hadn't brought her tonight, but it is what it is. And if these Demons are going to pose some kind of a threat in the future, I'd rather her be aware that they are not to be trusted. I can't shelter her from everything regarding the darker side of MC's. Not if she's going to be with me.

"Some kind of a power play. This is strictly psychological." I say. "Though, I don't know why they're involving me. I have no influence in how the Saviors run their club or territory anymore."

"Uh... actually, bro..." Axel chimes in, hooking his thumbs in his front pockets as he looks at me. "That's not entirely accurate."

I turn to face him a little more directly. "What isn't?"

"There's been talk, among the Saviors." Axel says. "That the majority of us want to vote you back in. And once you're back in, bring a vote to the table to have you replace Preacher as Club President."

Oh fuck. Here we go.

"How would the Demons know about any of this?" I ask, not wanting to indicate any interest, or lack thereof, in what he just told me.

"I'm not sure. But they must. Otherwise, why are you grouped in with the top dogs of the other MC's?" Axel asks. "They might see you as a potential shot caller."

"I'm not sure. But they're counting on us noticing. Whether it's something as petty as forcing the leaders of the MC's into having to ask them to move the bikes in order for them to leave as if they need permission, or some other form of subtle intimidation, I really don't know." I say, reaching back to grab my beer off the table and taking a swig. "I really don't care either. They're not going to do shit tonight."

"How are you so sure?" Vanna asks.

"There are seven Saviors here that I'm fairly certain will follow me into a fight, if it comes down to that." I glance at Axel. He nods in agreement. "There are thirteen Jokers and twelve Knights that would follow suit. That's not counting prospects, either. The Demons are outnumbered. If they wanted a fight, they wouldn't do it with the odds stacked against them. Three MC's against one, all at once, is a foolish move." And something about Legion tells me, he's not foolish.

"Then why the intimidation tactic?" she asks.

"Just a head game, doll. They lose if we don't give a shit. Or at least appear not to. The way they appear to want to play nice with the rest of us."

I glance in Legion's direction, in time to see him spot me. He grins at me. Then pats Preacher's arm, before he starts walking in my direction, flanked by two Demons.

Fuck. I'm not so sure I want him to see me with Vanna, for her sake. It's too late. And as they approach us, Vanna instinctively tucks herself against me anyway. One of her hands grips my leather jacket nervously.

"Relax, baby. They aren't going to do anything." I say quietly to her. Her grip loosens, but only slightly.

I glance at Axel, who throws his arm over Cherry's shoulders, tucking her in close to him as well.

Fixing my gaze back on the approaching Legion, I notice Preacher standing off in the distance behind him, looking our way. He doesn't seem happy. That could be because he fucking hates me, though. Or, he resents the fact that Legion is approaching me, for what I assume to be a greeting, as if I'm of some significance.

"Well, well, well. If it isn't the man of the evening." Legion growls, with a sharp grin across his thin, sinewy face. He's staring at me as he says the words, but then turns to Axel suddenly, extending his hand to shake. "Congratulations, Brother. I've heard a lot about you. Your dedication. Can't say I've ever had the pleasure of meeting such a determined prospect. The Saviors are lucky to have you, Axel." His gravelly voice sounds genuine enough, but as with the last encounter I had with Legion, I can't help feeling like there is something more behind his words.

"Thanks." Axel says, uncharacteristically cool.

Legion's eyes shift to Cherry. "And is this vibrant, charming little pixie, your Old Lady?" Legion asks, extending his hand to Cherry now. She reluctantly accepts it.

"Cherry." She says flatly. "And yes, I belong to Axel."

"How fitting." Legion grins, holding her hand a moment longer before he lets her go. He turns back to face me.

"Looks like the gangs all here." I say to him before he can speak to me, hoping he will slip up and reveal something about their true numbers.

He grins. "Not exactly. A few... *Brothers*... were asked to stay behind." The two Demons behind him chuckle, and with one sharp look from Legion, they shut the fuck up immediately.

What the fuck was that about?

"Too bad." I say, pretending not to notice. Though, I can tell Legion knows I did.

His cold eyes slide to Vanna, still pressed to my side. And as his gaze roams over her, something in them changes for a split second, and I wish once again, that I hadn't brought her tonight. He steps slightly closer to her, his hand extended towards her, but not in the way one would offer a hand shake. I steel myself as he watches my reaction.

"And this dark beauty is?" He asks, as Vanna slowly places her hand in his.

"Vanna." She quietly replies.

"*Vanna.*" Legion repeats her name in a way that grates my nerves. "How have I not heard about you?" he asks, bringing her hand to his lips and pressing it against them. I try not to clench my jaw, though my fist is white knuckled behind her back. "Sandalwood... Sage... and a hint of Lavender." He grins widely at her, a knowing look in his eyes. "Not your perfume, however... *You're not wearing any.*"

The way he says that last sentence, sends a surge of rage through me.

Vanna awkwardly giggles as she gently pulls her hand from his, wrapping it back around my arm. I try to focus on the feel of her body against mine, to calm my simmering temper. This motherfucker just kissed and *sniffed* my girlfriend, right in my face. I glance at his two Demons behind him and notice that they are watching me, both slightly grinning.

This was some kind of test.

"No, it isn't." she says in response to his statement.

"A dark lady indeed, then." Legion smiles, shifting his gaze to me. "Is she also your Old Lady, Dean Keegan? Is this lovely, *bewitching* creature, sadly off limits to the rest of us?"

"She's mine." I try to keep the edge off my voice. "*Off limits.*"

"Of course." Legion sighs. "*Our* loss." That sinister grin of his as he says those last two words, makes me think of what I had seen go down in their club house with the three women. As I watch the grin on his face widen, I can't help but wonder if he knows I was there that night. If he knows I was responsible for breaking up their little *party*. If he knows, that I know, about the sick shit they're into.

I grin back at him, throwing a little test of my own his way. A simple, loaded statement. "You got that right." I smile. "Vanna is my four-alarm fire."

Something shifts behind Legion's eyes, but he composes himself immediately and smiles back at me. "Well then... enjoy the *party*." Legion replies. As he turns to walk away, I notice he looks at the two of his henchmen briefly, before they walk off into the crowd.

"Okay, what the actual fuck was all that?" Axel asks, once they're out of ear shot. "That guy is creepy as fuck!"

"I think I want to wash my hand." Vanna says. I actually wouldn't mind if she did.

"I could use the ladies' room too." Cherry says.

"Go together. The back door of the tattoo shop is unlocked. Why don't you escort them, and wait for them, Axel? I'm going to see if I can find Viking and Viper."

I watch them walk across the field, towards the back lot of the tattoo shop. Once they get inside the building, I go in search of my missing Brothers.

I'm glad Vanna isn't with me when I finally find Viking in the shadows at the far end of the clearing. His back against a tree. Two women on their knees in front of him.

I clear my throat, grabbing the threesome's attention. Though, none of them seem to be hindered by my intrusion in the slightest. "Not sure how long you've been back here having your own private little party." I say. "But twenty-five or so Demons just rolled up on us."

"Nothing little about this party, bro." Viking grunts.

"Any thoughts on what I just told you about the Demons?"

"Thought I heard Preacher yappin' about something CDMC." Viking says.

"Finish up and meet me lot side of the fire. I'm gonna find Viper."

"Rosita isn't with you?" I ask Viper, when I find him sitting at a picnic table on the opposite side of the clearing. He's leaning back, elbows resting on the top of the table.

"She ain't real big on crowds." Viper says.

"Or did you leave her home because you knew this stunt with the Demons was going to go down here tonight?" I don't bother attempting to hide the suspicion in my voice.

Viper glares up at me. "My wife doesn't like crowds." He growls the words at me slowly.

"You know what I'm asking you. Don't make me ask you again."

He scoffs at me. "You really turned into a fucking prick you know that?"

"Can you blame me?"

"I do, actually. If you want to know the truth." He says, standing up to get in my face. "I blame you for a lot."

"Easy bro's, take it down a notch." Viking says, coming from somewhere in the darkness, finally, and stepping between us. My eyes are locked with Viper's steely blue glare as we continue to glower at each other.

"Viper was about to say something. Should let your brother speak his peace." I mutter.

"He's your brother too, Dean." Viking sighs.

"That's debatable." I say.

"You don't know shit, Keegan. You arrogant asshole." Viper snaps at me. He takes a step back and looks at Viking. "I'm sick of this shit. And it's been for fucking nothing."

Viking places his hand on Viper's shoulder. "We don't know that."

"The fuck is going on with you two?" I ask.

Viper's turns back to me with a resentful scowl. "For three fucking years we've waited for you to bounce back. But you only drifted further away from us."

"Waited for me? You fucking voted me out." I say.

"I voted you out! I voted you out!" He mocks me. "You were out regardless of my vote!" he nearly shouts at me, before Viking grabs him by the collar of his cut and shoves him backwards.

"Viper! Shut the fuck up!" Viking threatens him, his low, yet harsh tone a clear indication that they're up to something they don't want to draw attention to. "You want to fill him in, that's fine. I get it. But don't bring the whole fucking gathering here down on us!"

I glance around to see if we've attracted any attention from the crowd of bikers partying around the fire near us. They don't seem to have noticed. Shifting my focus back to Viking and Viper, I ask, "Fill me in on what?"

Viking releases Viper and walks a few feet over to a cooler, grabbing three beers and tosses one to each of us. "Let's have a drink together. Viper could use it."

He's glaring at me again, but as I look closer at him, there's something besides anger in his eyes. Sadness? Disappointment? Something remorseful...

"Tell me, Viper."

He shakes his head and lets out a long sigh. "I only voted against you because you were out anyway."

"So you've said."

"Yeah, well what I never said was *why*." Viper cracks the top of his beer off on the edge of the table and takes a swig. "Preacher was never going to trust anyone who voted with you. The only way for there to be a man on the inside, for your benefit, would be if I voted against you. If I made Preacher think that I lost all faith in you. I only voted against you, to do you that fucking favor. To be your man on the inside. Your fucking spy." He shakes his head. "A lot of good it did. Somewhere along the line these last few years, you stopped giving a shit."

"What's that supposed to mean?" I ask.

He shrugs. "Life goes on, right? You spent your time revamping the Twisted Throttle, building up the business at the repair shop. Occupying yourself with other things like your *underground hobby*." Viper says. "Hell, even found yourself a new woman, though that's fairly recent."

"You resent me for getting on with my life?"

"*I resent you*, for turning your back on us. The mission. I believed you cared." Viper snaps.

I nod. "Right. Because I haven't been doing my part at all, in that regard. I've just been playing with bikes, fucking women and tending bar?" I shake my head. "You have no idea what I do. And if you did, you'd probably take issue with it anyway. Like you always have."

"The fuck does that mean?" Viper asks.

"You want to point the finger and blame me for the mission being abandoned. The fuck did you do to keep it going? Huh? You let Preacher kick me out. You let him cut ties to the organizations we worked with. For what? To be a social club? To pal around with the fucking Demons now?" I take a breath and regain my composure, so as not to draw any attention to our conversation. Cracking off the cap of my beer, I take a swig too. "Unlike you, I never abandoned the mission. At least not the entire mission. I'm still putting scum in the hospital. I just do it through other channels now."

I can tell by the slight widening of Viper's eyes, that he's surprised. "How long?"

"Never fuckin' stopped." I reply, glancing at Viking. "You never said anything to him?" Viking is the only one who knows about my connection to officer Jason Caldwell.

"You told me to keep my fuckin' mouth shut about it." Viking shrugs. "So, I kept my fuckin' mouth shut about it."

Viper nods. "Well then, maybe there's hope after all. And for the record, asshole." He takes a step closer to me. "I only took issue with you putting scum in the hospital because I was afraid it would jeopardize our connections with the agencies. If it ever got out that it was a fuckin' Savior tossing those beatings, they'd never work with us again." He sighs. "I never would have ratted you out though."

"I never thought you would. I know Preacher put it together for himself." I say, looking at Viper and then at Viking. "That whole fucking thing at the table was an act, then? You two have been in on this together from the beginning?" They both nod.

"No way Preacher was ever going to trust me." Viking says. "It had to be Viper."

"I guess you can keep your fucking mouth shut after all." I say to Viking.

"Don't act so surprised, Bro. You might hurt my feelings." Viking grins, clanking his beer to mine.

I turn back to Viper. "Sorry for being a dick to you. Obviously, I didn't know."

Viper clanks his beer to mine as well. "I'll forgive you when you save this MC."

"YOU DO REALIZE THAT DEAN IS PROBABLY GOING TO INSIST YOU START wearing his PO cut at these parties, right?" Cherry says, leaning into the bathroom mirror to reapply her red lipstick. "Probably at the bar, too."

I'm not sure how to respond to that. The thought of being branded some guys property again just doesn't sit well with me. Even though Dean isn't just some guy. And he's nothing like my ex.

I notice Cherry watching me through the mirror. "Property Of doesn't mean what you think it means, Vanna." She sighs. "Axel doesn't treat me like I'm his personal servant. Like I actually *belong* to him, like his bike or his leather jacket or something."

He doesn't. I've seen the way Axel looks at Cherry. He worships her. He'd literally do anything she asked of him. If anything, Axel was property of Cherry, but she treats him lovingly, too.

On the flip side, I've seen a little of the way sweetbutts and patch chasers are treated by MC guys. Not specifically the Saviors, but other MC's. The women are passed around and ordered about. Expected to cater to their every whim. Dean was even telling me earlier tonight there was a chance I might see one woman with multiple men at this very party.

"I can't lie to you and tell you that Dean isn't staking his claim on you when he's trying to get you to wear his Property Of tops." Cherry says, turning around to face me as she leans against the edge of the sink. "He is. You agreed to date him. You took a job at his bar. You didn't say anything when he staked his claim on you in front of that Legion ghoul."

I can't help giggling at her description of Legion. "He was creepy, wasn't he?" Though, there was an aura about him. A type of sly confidence. A self-assuredness that was... notable. And that *Dark Lady* talk. He somehow knows I'm a witch. I shake my head and focus back on what Cherry had said. "Anyway, so I'm Dean's property because I'm his girlfriend? That gives him ownership of me?" It sounds so barbaric.

Cherry lets out another sigh, and I can't tell if she's frustrated with my resistance to the idea of all of this, or if it's because she wants to defend Dean out of loyalty to him.

"It's not exactly ownership. Think of it more as *Protection Over*, if *Property Of* bothers you so much. It means the same thing. If a Savior sees another guy giving you a hard time, it's his duty out of loyalty to Dean to come to your defense. You're protected. *Protected Over* by the Saviors MC. All of them. Mostly Dean, but also Viking, Axel, Viper. The rest of them. All of them. And other MC's know that means you are off limits as well."

"But Dean isn't even a Savior anymore."

"That's complicated. Technically, he isn't. But you heard what Axel said. It's a matter of Dean deciding what he wants. Preacher is delusional if he thinks Dean couldn't over throw him. Dean just has to want it."

"What do you mean? Dean might actually take over the MC?"

"It's club business. I'm really not supposed to say anything. Women aren't club members. It's boys only."

I remember Viking rudely mentioning something similar a few weeks ago, when these Chrome Demon fellows first showed up.

"We're connected to the club through our men, but we don't have any part in club business. If the women know anything about what the club is doing, it's because their men slip up and tell them." She smiles. "You know, *pillow talk*. Behind closed doors, our men might seek our counsel, but they're technically not supposed to let us know about anything."

"Clearly you have Axel wrapped around your finger then." I smile back at her.

She shrugs. "I'm sure all the guys talk to their Old Ladies. It's just not something they advertise."

"Does this protection extend beyond the roadhouse and parties?"

She nods. "Yes. This is how we live. Outsiders might not honor the patch, because they don't understand what it means. But if they approach you and a brother sees it, or if you tell someone. They're going to handle it."

"Does this just go for being hit on?"

She shakes her head. "No. For anything. If you have a problem, you tell Dean. He makes that problem go away for you. I mean, within reason. They aren't exactly outlaws. Though some of them..." she lets her sentence trail off as she turns back around to face the mirror, fixing her hair.

"Some of them are?"

"Some of them are a little less concerned with civilian laws than others. I'll just leave it at that."

"Dean?" Again, she lifts a shoulder as if it's an answer. "Are all MC's like the Saviors?"

"What do you mean?"

"With these rules about women? And property?"

"Not exactly the same. But most guys from other MC's will not hit on a woman wearing a Property Of patch. That much is pretty standard across the board. If her Property Of patch doesn't have a man's name on it, and it's just Property of the MC, then they might. But typical protocol is to approach a male member of the MC to ask about any woman they might be interested in talking to."

"I've seen guys in different cuts hit on some of the girls at the bar. Some of the sweet butts and patch chasers." I point out.

"They're free agents. Not really respected. It is what it is. If you don't respect yourself you can't expect these guys to respect you either."

"I don't understand that at all. Why would they want to be passed around like that?"

"Some are hoping to find a sponsor." Cherry shrugs. "Some are hoping to become somebodies Old Lady. Some are just here to party hard and like fucking around with rough men."

"You don't seem to care much for them."

"Some of them not only lack respect for themselves, they lack respect for the sisterhood of the MC by trying to go after another woman's Old Man. That shit will get you jumped."

"There's a sisterhood?"

Cherry nods. "In most MC's. The women usually stick together."

"The Saviors?"

"The Saviors are drifting apart. The men. The sisterhood. This is becoming a dwindling social club more than an MC with a mission." She sounds sad.

"What mission? I thought they just rode motorcycles, drank beer and fought over pool games." I joke.

"Some actually use their connections in the communities for good. Fund raisers for special causes. A presence in the community that keeps certain undesirable elements out of the area." Cherry sighs. "But then there are clubs

his feet. The other one attempts to reach around me to grab her. I have to un-clench my jaw to let out a growl of "Back off!" The Demon I nearly knocked off his feet steps back to me, eyes glaring.

"She ain't claimed." He has the balls to snap at me. "Not yet, anyway."

"The only claim you're gonna be making is to your insurance company when I bust that fucking jaw and both your arms!" I snatch Vanna around her waist and spin her away from him. The second guy glances at his buddy and nods. I notice he's wearing a Prospect patch on his cut. "You too, fucker. Try patching in to any club, when you can't ride a bike. Prick."

"Who does this guy think he is? Snatching away prime pussy and he ain't even wearing a cut of any kind himself?" The Prospect says, eyeing me up like he wants to throw down.

"This your man, sweetie?" The other asks her, then shifts his focus to sneer at me. "From what I hear about him, he doesn't mind sharing his woman with a *Brother*."

Of all the fucked-up shit I've done in my life, *this* is what fucking sticks? A dirty fucking *lie*! God damnit, Lucinda... Bitch doesn't even have to be fuck-ing me anymore to fuck me.

"You heard wrong." I say to the ballsy bastard. He's about to regret ever laying eyes on Vanna. "Square up, bitch." I warn him, as I make a move in his direction.

He's just beyond my reach, when Viper and Ruger get between us.

"He's prospecting to be a Savior!" Preacher shouts at me from the side line of the growing crowd.

A Savior? He was partying with the Demons not even five weeks ago!

"He ain't Savior material." I mutter. "You may have lowered your stan-dards, Preacher. But I'm not going to let the disrespect go unpunished."

"This is why you're out!" Preacher shouts, storming up to me and nearly shoving Ruger out of his way to get in my face. "You're out of control!"

"Lucky me, you ain't my president. I don't take orders from anyone, least of all you. Now get the fuck out of my face, unless you want your jaw cracked first." I snarl at him. Preacher's eyes are ablaze, but he doesn't make a move on me. He knows I'll lay him out with one swing.

"Is there a problem here?" A gravelly voice emerging from the circling crowd around us asks. It's a voice I've come to recognize instantly. Legion.

"I made it perfectly clear this woman is off limits. Yet I come to find two of your Demons trying to put their hands on her." I shift my eyes from Preacher's to look at Legion, who comes to stand alongside Preacher. "One of which was standing right behind you earlier, when I informed you of the fact."

"I see only one Demon involved in this dispute here." Legion says, glanc-ing at the two men standing a yard or two back now, before he turns back to look at me with a slight smile.

I know what I saw. That guy posing as a Saviors Prospect was a fucking Demon five or six weeks ago. There's something else going on here, but I've got a more pressing issue to deal with at the moment.

"Call him whatever the fuck you want. We're throwing down. Here. Now. Or I'll hunt the fuckers down and handle it without any of your interference." I say, looking at Legion, then at Preacher. "You know I will."

"Dean... maybe you ought to calm down..." Viper says quietly.

"What if some prospect called your wife prime pussy like she was just some patch whore to pass around? You gonna let that shit slide? Gonna let that shit roll off your back if she heard it? A piece of shit like this, talking to Rosita that way?"

Viper's expression slides to one of annoyance. "Fuck." He knows damn well he wouldn't tolerate that shit for one second. Viper cocks his head over his shoulder to look at the prospect. "You said that shit?" he shouts to him over the gathering crowd around us.

"I didn't know she was spoken for." The prospect says.

"Your fucking Demon pal does." I say, cocking my chin at the grinning Demon standing beside him. I look back at Legion. "And you fucking know it yourself."

"That's the Vice President of an MC you're talking to, Keegan!" Preacher snaps, but I ignore him. Preacher means nothing to me. I continue to glare at Legion. Something tells me he's the one calling the shots anyway. That hunch is confirmed for me, when Legion places a hand on Preacher's shoulder.

"Keegan has a right to protect his property. My man was made aware this woman is off limits." Legion says. "Keegan is right."

Though I'm highly suspicious of Legion's stance, I shift my focus to Preacher, just to take in the look on his face, as he's undermined by Legion in front of everyone. Preacher looks pissed, as I allow the slightest grin to crack my expression. He begrudgingly steps back to the side lines of the crowd around us. Ruger walks away from me as well, to stand with his subverted President.

Now, the only two standing between me, and the two assholes about to learn a lesson in proper MC etiquette, are Viper and Legion.

"It appears you have a debt to pay tonight, gentlemen." Legion turns towards the Demon and the prospect.

"Ain't afraid to fight the cuck." The Demon shouts back, a grin on his face at getting that verbal shot in at me for all to hear. The balls on this motherfucker. They're about to come off.

Viper puts his hand on my shoulder. He knows why that fucking word stokes my rage. "Dean, don't fucking kill the guy." He sighs, a sympathetic tone to his words.

I wait until Legion walks a few feet towards the two men I'm about to fight, before I look at Viper. "I want to know why he keeps making that dig at me." I mutter. "How are the Demons privy to my ex-wife's infidelity? Did Preacher say something?"

"I wouldn't put it past him to want to make you look weak." Viper says, "He knows something is brewing within the MC. I'm sure he suspects it has something to do with you. But I don't know for sure if he's the one who said anything to the Demons about Lucinda."

Viper releases me and I start removing my knife from my belt.

"No fucking weapons!" Viper turns and shouts so all can hear. "No fucking jump ins! And no permanent damage!"

"Agreed." Legion says, then gestures to the two men to remove their weapons as well.

I glance around at the crowd circled around us to watch the entertainment, before I turn to hand my sheathed knife to Axel, now standing beside Vanna.

"I'm fucking sorry, Bro. I should have been paying closer attention to her." He says, looking as remorseful as I've ever seen him look.

I pat his arm. "Not your fault. Just, stay with her now." I say, before I turn to Vanna. Her eyes are wide. She looks nervous, troubled even. "Don't be scared. Just settling a score. They had no right to pull what they did."

"You're going to fight them?" I almost have to strain to hear her over the music and the buzzing crowd. "*Both* of them? At once?"

"I am."

"Why? This is crazy, Dean." She looks almost panicked. "You don't have to do this."

"I'm defending your honor, babe." I smile at her with a wink. Mine, too, but I'm not going to admit that out loud. Especially not to her. The thought of Vanna thinking of me in that way... *A fucking cuck...* it makes my stomach churn. Removing my leather jacket, I hand it to her to hold onto, before I turn back to face my human punching bags.

"Why don't we make this more interesting?" the Demon shouts at me, "*Winner gets the girl...* At least for a night."

Viper grips my shoulder as I walk back towards them. "Dean, don't kill him." He says again. I don't respond, to either of them. I just dead eye this prick and await the signal that this fight is on.

"You afraid you're going to have to antiup?" The asshole continues to taunt me.

Viper whirls around on the guy. "You're about to dance with the fucking devil, prick. You might want to shut the fuck up and stop making it worse for yourself."

I can't help noticing that Legion looks rather eager to see this fight go down. He's grinning at me, ear to ear now, as he stands between the two soon to be bloody bastards and the raging bonfire. A freshly lit cigarette between those long, thin fingers of his. He takes a drag from it as he stares back at me, blowing the smoke out of his nostrils.

"Let's keep this fight clean!" Viper raises his voice again above the crowd, so both I, and my two opponents, can hear him clearly. "No dirty bullshit, no stomping the unconscious!"

I nod once in agreement. I don't have to fight dirty to beat these assholes. The two pricks who have about ten seconds of consciousness left, nod also.

Viper steps aside, getting out of my way, as I raise my fists and take a few steps forward, squaring off with them.

The Demon charges at me first. I side step him and slug him in the jaw, rocking him sideways, into the crowd. The Prospect who circled me on my right, wrongly assuming I was distracted by the Demon, makes a move to grab me. But all he catches is my elbow to his face. I hear his nose crack on impact and he's screaming like a bitch, hands on his face, leaving his body wide open for another attack. Which he gets, as I step forward with a little momentum and slam my boot into his gut, sending him flying to the dirt beside the fire on his back.

Spinning around to face the Demon, I can hear nose bleed on the ground struggling for air, groaning. Getting the wind knocked out of you sucks. He'll be down there for a few, while I deal with the mouthy shit talker.

I let him swing on me a few times, ducking and blocking his blows for a few moments. Then I slug him in the ribs and shove him backwards. I know the crowd is shouting, but I don't hear what anyone is saying. If they're rooting for me to win or to fall. I don't know. I don't care. I watch the Demon as he staggers back and winces, but recovers. This time he isn't as quick to rush at me.

I move towards him now, throwing a few jabs at him. Just fucking with him really. Just waiting for the kill shot. I can tell he's afraid of me, after seeing his buddy get his nose broken barely two seconds into this fight.

He throws a quick punch at me, his fist narrowly connecting with my cheek bone, but he did clip me. I use his momentum against him, grabbing him by his cut, swinging him down to the ground, tossing him like the trash he is. I could jump on him right now and pummel the shit out of him, but I don't. I glance up for a moment to look at Vanna, who is clutching my leather jacket tightly to her body, holding her own cheek as if she were the one who just got punched. I grin at her and touch my cheek, then glance at my fingers. A little blood. It's fine. I wink at her to let her know I'm perfectly okay.

The Demon gets up and squares up with me again. He's smiling now that he sees he drew first blood between us. As if it means shit. Idiot doesn't realize I'm allowing him to remain in this fight. That lucky clip is all he's going to get though. I'm going to put the hurt on him momentarily.

I drop my arms and extend them outward, leaving myself open for attack to sucker him in. The Demon lunges at me and I tighten my core to brace for his shoulder driving into my abdomen. He wraps his arms around me as I bring my elbows up high and slam them down into his back, hard, before he has the chance to get me off my feet. His arms drop from around me, his body in shock from the jolt of sharp pain in his back. Grabbing his collar, I drive my knee up into his gut, and when he tries to back away, I upper cut him, sending him back on his ass on the ground with his shit talking buddy. Again, I could jump on him and pound him to sleep, but I don't. I wait to see if he wants to get up for more. He's taking his sweet ass time though, so I shift my focus to the prospect beside the fire, pinching his still gushing nose.

"Take that fucking Saviors cut off." I growl at him. He freezes, looking up at me before he shoots a look towards Preacher, and then Legion. "I said take it off or I will."

I glance back at Legion, who is glaring darkly at the prospect on the ground. There's definitely something going on here. Why would Legion give a shit about a prospect's cut being taken from another MC? I know I saw this prospect with the Demons. I'm sure of it now.

Legion shifts his focus from the prosect, to the Demon I just put in the dirt. "Get the fuck up." He snarls at the guy.

The Demon starts to slowly stagger to his feet. I realize he's playing it up too late though, as he flings a fist full of dirt at me. I turn my head quickly to avoid any of it getting it in my eyes, and he uses my reflex to his advantage, tackling me to the ground.

I block as he slams punches down on me, mostly nailing my arms. He's tired though, I can feel it. He's still hurting from the elbow shot to his back. I hit him just right. He'll be feeling that strike for days.

Vanna doesn't know I'm still okay, though. I can hear her freaking out, even over the shouting of the crowd around us. I have to end this now. Her fear is too much for me to let this go on any longer.

My arms are blocking him, vertically in front of my face, when I curl upward into his body. As he swings with one arm, I grab his other one, holding onto it tightly, bringing my knee up behind him, I knock him forward, off balance. Twisting him down onto his back quickly, I'm on top of him now. I don't let go of his arm until I sock him in the face several times and then once in the fucking nuts for that dick move with the dirt. For good measure I get up and kick him in the stomach, leaving him curled on the ground, clutching his balls and gasping for air. He's out of commission now.

I glare back at Legion as I walk towards the Prospect, again. Legion flicks his cigarette at the downed Demon, as if he's disgusted with him for failing some unspoken mission. I only turn my attention away from him once I'm standing over the prospect again.

"The fucking cut. Hand it over. You're not worthy to wear the Saviors name."

"That's enough, Keegan!" Preacher shouts at me. "You have no authority to lay a finger on that fucking cut!"

"I've seen this motherfucker before." I say. "Aside from the bullshit he pulled tonight, he was running with another MC barely a month ago. Since when do we entertain patch jumpers? Have you done away with the hang around policy as well? Background checks to make sure you aren't recruiting scum?" I glare at Preacher. When this club was led by my uncle, it had standards. Men of integrity. Our mission required it. We didn't accept dregs. We didn't accept men who jumped from club to club. These last few years I've watched Preacher run the MC into the ground. Abandon the mission. For what?

"There is no *we*. You're nobody, Keegan. You shouldn't even be here." Preacher says.

I shift my focus to Legion as he snaps his fingers and points to the Demon I left in the dirt. Two of his men hurry over to pick him up off the ground.

"And you don't take issue with one of your former Demons patching over to the Saviors?" I ask Legion.

"I think you're mistaken." Legion says with a smile, knowing I can't say exactly where I saw him with them, without revealing myself as the reason their little gang bang got shut down a few weeks ago.

I grin back at him. "How does that little school yard rhyme go again? *Liar, liar... something's on fire?*" I taunt him with what I know, he knows.

His smile only broadens. "I'm quite sure *you've made a mistake.*" He insists. I know that's a veiled threat. I can read between the lines as well as he can. "Your fighting skills are impressive, though. If the Saviors don't want you, my offer still stands for you to join the CDMC. It isn't unheard of for a man to join up with another MC after being so ... unceremoniously cast out.... *We accept the fallen.*"

That demonic grin on his face. "No thanks." I say, shifting my attention back to the bleeding prospect. "Cut. Now."

"Oh, come now, it wouldn't be the first time we've taken in Saviors scraps." Legion says, stepping towards me and effectively pulling my attention back to him. He's way too concerned about this former Demon crossing over to the Saviors. Way too determined, to prevent me from getting in the way of that.

What former Savior could have possibly patched over to the CDMC without me hearing about it? Then it hits me... And the taunts that dragged me into this little shit show make sense now... The fallen Savior that was cast out, turned Demon, is Lucinda's husband...

Fuck. Me.

The sinister grin across Legion's mouth broadens, as I'm sure the expression on my face clearly indicates I've received the message loud and clear...

This certainly explains the Demon's cuck jokes...

I force myself to pull my shit together, turning back to the prospect. I grab his cut and rip it off him, tossing it into the bonfire. "You can take this piece of shit back too." I mutter to a still grinning Legion.

Preacher storms back up to me, as if he's got the balls to actually do something. "Take your bitch and get out of here."

"My *what*?" I'm about to grab him myself, when Legion steps between us, shoving Preacher out of my face, and out of my reach.

"The man was disrespected." Legion says to Preacher. "Things got heated. Let's let this little incident slide. For the sake of keeping the good times, rolling, eh? It's a party. Let's consider this little scuffle, live entertainment!" Legion raises his voice and waves his arm as if he's the fucking ring leader. I'm really beginning to believe he is, as the crowd cheers in agreement with him. "Let's set the example and lighten the mood, shall we, Preacher?"

Preacher doesn't speak. He just continues to glare at me, but he does take a step backwards.

"Very good." Legion pats his shoulder again, in that condescending way. Undermining him yet again. "And how about you, Dean? Are you satisfied now? You beat the shit out of two men. You took a man's cut and burned it. Are you willing to let this go now that you've settled the score? Can we all get back to the party? That pig is just about done. Let's all break bread together, instead of bones, eh?" He smiles at me, bringing his hands together in gesture of a mock plea.

I suddenly feel a hand touch my arm, gently squeezing my bicep. I don't have to look back to know that it's Vanna. That this is her silent plea for me to end this. That this was probably too big of a dose of MC culture for her.

For her sake, I nod once at Legion, before I turn to take her hand and walk away, leading her from the crowd, back towards the outskirts of the party.

Making a pit stop at one of the last tables, I flip open a cooler and dip my cupped hands into the ice-cold water inside it. Splashing my face off a few times, I rinse the blood off my cheek so she doesn't have to see it. It's already stopped bleeding. I'm a fast healer. Using the sheet draped over the table, I wipe my hands dry before I clasp her hand in mine again. Continuing back towards the dark edge of the clearing, I lead her back to the picnic table in the shadows where we started our night.

The crowd is centered around the fire still, and the food being served up. We're a good hundred and fifty or so feet from the party now, and between the live band and the darkness, we're basically alone here.

"This was probably a lot for you." I say, turning to face her, but I don't let go of her hand.

"This was my fault." She says. "I went to get Axel's gift, and when I came back, those two guys wouldn't let me pass. Axel had no idea I walked away from him. I'm sorry. And I should apologize again to Axel, too. He thinks it's his fault."

"It's not your fault. I shouldn't have walked away from you. None of this would have happened if I would have stayed with you." I say, realizing she's still carrying my jacket and knife for me. "You don't have to hold that." Taking them back from her, I slip my leather jacket back on and reattach the knife to my belt.

"You aren't mad at me for ruining Axel's party?" She seems almost astounded.

"You didn't ruin anything." I insist. If anyone ruined anything, it's Preacher and this stunt with the Chrome Demons. "It's not a biker party without a fight or two."

"I think I'm starting to piece together your reputation." Vanna says, after a moment.

A cold feeling starts to wash over me, and I'm grateful for the darkness enveloping us. She probably can't tell I'm rattled by her words. I clear my throat before I attempt to speak, hoping she didn't over hear any of that bullshit cuck talk.

"Oh yeah? What's my reputation?" I force myself to ask.

"Certified badass." She giggles. I want to allow the wave of relief to wash over me, but a life time of darkness won't allow me that reprieve. Instead, I wait for the other shoe to drop. "I should be afraid of you." She says, after a few moments of silence.

Fuck. I knew it. This was too much.

The cold feeling turns to a sinking, cold feeling. She's going to bolt on me again. "Don't be. Please, don't be." I sigh, gently placing my hands on her arms. The last thing I want is for her to pull away from me again. "You're the last person who needs to be afraid of me, Vanna."

"Sometimes I worry that I'm making a mistake. That I shouldn't want to spend so much time with you." She says, looking away from me. "That I should just run for the hills. But... when I think about running... All I can picture is running *to* you."

Okay, I can work with that. In the moonlight above us, I can tell she's abusing that bottom lip of hers, her mind dueling with her emotions. I keep my mouth shut, waiting for her to continue.

"Nobody's ever made me feel the way I do, when I'm with you." She looks back up at me. "Everything about you, should be wrong for me. But, somehow, it isn't."

Thank fuck. Though, my heart still races with the anticipation of rejection.

"I try to resist this...this *pull*." She says, her frustration evident in her words. Her hand gesturing back and forth between us. "To hide from my feelings, but the more I'm with you, the more I just want to surrender. I'm so tired of feeling like I'm fighting *everything*. Like I'm running from *everything*." She sounds resentful of herself, letting out another exasperated sigh. "I just want to be *free*. Like you. You're not afraid of anything."

"What are you afraid of?" I ask, placing my hand gently on her cheek.

"I should be stronger than this." She says, biting that bottom lip again. I softly swipe my thumb across it, trying to coax her into releasing it. Sometimes I pity that sexy bottom lip, wondering how her kiss is so soft and smooth, with how often she absentmindedly abuses it. Then there are times, like now, when I want to bite it myself.

Her hand reaches up to touch mine, before her fingers lightly wrap around my wrist. "I should be stronger than this..." she whispers again, her eyes flicking up to look into mine.

I'm not sure what to say. I just stare back into her eyes, admiring her beauty in the moonlight as she tilts her head slightly, pressing her face against the palm of my hand.

"I don't want to fight it anymore."

"What are you fighting, Vanna?" I ask.

She turns her face slightly, her hand sliding up from my wrist, to the back of my hand, guiding my thumb closer to her mouth again. She parts her lips, and I can feel her warm breath against the pad of my thumb, before the tip of her tongue slides against it.

Fuck me...

I reflexively push my thumb a little further into her mouth, her teeth gently biting down on me just past my nail, as if to warn me that this is far enough. Her lips encircle it and I feel the gentle suction as the tip of her hot, wet tongue swirls around the tip of my finger.

Sucking in a breath of air with a hiss, I fight the urge to grab her and throw her up on the picnic table beside us in the dark. I know I can't do that. Not with her. Not yet.

"Fuck, baby..." I growl, unable to really form a coherent sentence, when my mind is swirling with images of everything I want to do with that sexy fucking mouth of hers.

Her teeth loosen their bite on me, as she closes her eyes and slowly moves her face forward, taking my finger deeper into that hot, slick mouth of hers. I watch the hollows of her cheeks sink in, accentuating the high cheekbones of her gorgeous face. The smooth, tight ring of her lips, sliding over the skin of my finger as she sucks my fucking thumb... There's no stopping the rush of blood to my jealous cock.

"*Fuck*... You're killin' me, baby." I manage to breathe.

PULLING BACK, I RELEASE HIS THUMB FROM MY MOUTH AND LOOK UP AT him. I don't want to hear how *I'm* killing him. I don't have the strength to stay away from him. I want him too much. I need him now, not just as my probable Knight. I think I'm actually falling in love with Dean Keegan. Which makes talk like that even harder to hear.

He slides his hand to the back of my neck, curling his fingers around me and pulling me closer to him. "What, baby?" he asks, leaning closer to me, hovering his lips above mine.

"What if I was?" My guilty conscious unable to give me a moments peace. I run my hands up the front of his leather jacket, gripping the lapels in my fingers.

"What if you were what?" his other hand slides around to my lower back, pulling my body against his.

"Killing you."

"Then I die happy, as long as you're with me. Tell me what you're fighting, Vanna." He sighs, his breath against my lips. "Just don't tell me you're fighting me."

I can't. I lost that fight. I wasn't strong enough to do the right thing and walk away from him. I barely lasted one, miserable week away from him, when I tried to end us a month ago.

"I just want to be free." I whisper. Free from my past. Free from my guilt. Free to be with him without worrying if it's what he actually wants. "How do you do it?"

"Do what, baby?" his lips brush against mine, tempting me to kiss him.

"Live your life so free?" I whisper.

"I take what I want."

"No, you don't." I can't help but smile. "You're too nice for that."

"*Nice?* I just broke a guy's fucking nose, not ten minutes ago." He says softly, but I can hear the humor in his voice.

"That was... impressive." He can certainly handle himself. Dean, against two guys at once. And he took them down so efficiently. Like a trained fighter, just toying with them. Like he beats the crap out of jerks as a regular hobby. Should it be turning me on, though? His violence? What is wrong with me? I should forget the Knight's red banner. Dean Keegan is a walking red flag! Biting my bottom lip, I try to think of something else to distract myself. It's impossible, but I try. "How's your face, by the way?"

"Fuck my face, Vanna." He growls. I can't help giggling at his choice of words. That isn't helping. He grins salaciously at me. "*Freudian slip...* But I'm down if you are."

"You're so bad." I tease him.

His hold on me tightens. "Now you get it." He jokes back. "If you don't kiss me soon, though, Vanna, you *are* going to kill me."

"I don't want that." I sigh, wishing he'd stop saying that.

"What?"

"To kill you."

"Aces." He closes the short distance between our lips. I don't fight it. There's no use. I want him. Evidently as much as he seems to want me. Curving his body into mine, his hips press forward and I can literally feel his desire jutting against me.

Parting my lips, I invite him inside. My arms reach up to wrap around his neck, resting on his strong, leather clad shoulders. His kiss is hungry and full of fervor, his tongue demanding and dominating as he sweeps it through my mouth. In a whirlwind of movement, quite literally being swept off my feet, I find myself seated between Dean's legs again, on top of the picnic table, where this whole night started.

His fingers slip under the opening of my little jacket near my shoulders, pulling it down my arms. He discards it somewhere beside us on the table in the dark. One arm wrapping around my lower abdomen, his other hand sweeping my hair back from my neck, he presses his lips to the top of my exposed shoulder. His rough whiskers brushing against my sensitive skin as he trails soft kisses up to my ear.

"I want you to feel free, baby." He whispers against my ear. "I want to shoulder your burdens. Battle your demons..." His tongue flicks my ear lobe, making me tilt my head to give him even more access to do what he will with me. As he tongue kisses my neck, I place my arms on top of his thighs, my hands on his knees on either side of me. "You just have to let me." He wraps his other arm around me, holding me tighter against, nibbling my ear gently.

I shouldn't, but I try to forget my guilt as I close my eyes and focus on the way his warm breath feels against my skin.

"I can make you happy, Vanna." He whispers, one hand still pressed against my lower abdomen, keeping me where he wants me. The other, gently sliding up higher, over my breast. I can feel myself harden, even at his barely-there touch. His thumb gently brushes back and forth across its peak over the fabric of my top. Even through my bra, I'm sure he can feel the hard, little tip responding to his touch.

Reaching my hand up, I place it over his, encouraging him to fondle me without feeling the need to be overly gentle. Sliding his other hand up my body, he cups my other breast over my top. Squeezing them both gently, as if he's testing me. He pushes them up slightly, pressing them together, feeling the weight of them.

"*Fuck...*" The word hisses from his lips. Kissing my neck as he continues to fondle me, his tongue slides up from the base of my neck, to my ear, making me shudder against his body. An involuntary gasp escapes me.

"Bingo..." he growls, and I can feel his smile against my skin. He found one of my erogenous zones. One that's been neglected for years.

"What are you going to do about it?" I whisper, hoping I can tempt him into giving me more. He bites me, giving my neck a quick, teasing suck. The unexpected sensation startles me for a brief moment, pulling another gasp.

"You like that, doll?" he trails kisses back up to my ear again as he continues to massage my breasts.

"It's been a while."

"This? Really?"

"Yes... I've told you." I frustratedly sigh. "Do you not believe me that I haven't been with anyone in-"

"Years... You'll have to forgive me for finding comfort in that." He slides one of his hands down from my breast, to my abdomen, slowly pulling up the hem of my top, feeling my stomach.

I squirm against him, grabbing his wrist as he touches me there, suddenly self-conscious. "Don't." He stops moving his hand over my body, but he doesn't remove it from my flesh.

"Why not? You don't like to be touched here?" When I can't find the words, he gently stroke my skin again, until I press my hand against his to more firmly. "You're crazy, Vanna, if you think I don't find every fuckin' inch of you sexy as sin." He kisses my neck and behind my ear again.

"Maybe *you're* crazy." I mutter.

"Crazy about you." His other hand moves from my breast to my stomach as well.

"I'm serious. Maybe Lucinda messed you up more than you realize." *Or my spell did.* I half-heartedly attempt to pull his hands away.

"I resent that. And we'll revisit this. I promise you that." He actually does sound slightly annoyed with me. Taking a breath, he exhales slowly before he speaks again. "Right now, I want you to put your hands back on my knees. And keep them there." His voice is softer now, though there is an edge of that authoritative tonality within his words.

"Why?"

"Just do it."

"But why?"

"Because you think too much. You want to be free, Vanna? I'm gonna free you, if only for a few minutes." I hesitate. "Try to trust me, baby." Dean whispers. I reluctantly place my hands back on his knees, resting my arms along the top of his thighs. "Was that so hard?"

I can't help a nervous giggle. "Like whatever you have planned ends here."

"You want a safe word?"

My body tenses. I wait for him to assure me he's only kidding. "Are you serious?"

"If you want one."

"What's the safe word?"

"*More.*" He growls against my neck. I can feel his salacious grin against my skin. I giggle and twist slightly to look him in the eyes. He lifts his hand to my chin, holding my face as he brings his mouth to mine, kissing me deeply. "Trust me, Vanna." He whispers against my lips. We spend a few more moments making out, before he speaks again, "Lose yourself with me for a little while. Listen to the music, and just let go... This is a great song. I hope you'll remember it. It already makes me think of you. I listened to it on repeat for a week... the first time you bolted from me." Pain still lingers in his voice.

"What is it?" I turn to face the bonfire where the band is playing. The party continues to rage on without us. It's a cover of some rock ballad.

"*Still Loving You*, by Scorpions." Dean places his hands on mine. "Keep these here." He reminds me, gently running his fingers down my arms until he reaches my elbows, giving me a soft, tickling sensation as he does. He then sweeps my hair to the side, this time exposing the opposite side of my neck, and gently tilts my head back against his shoulder.

Wrapping his strong arms around me, he brings his mouth to the top of my exposed shoulder, kissing me once more. I close my eyes, listening to the music, focusing on his lips and hands moving over my body. His thumbs tease my nipples, bringing them to hard little pebbles beneath his touch once again.

"Sometimes I feel like I can't figure you out, Vanna." He whispers between licks and kisses along my neck. "You're a yes, then a no. You tell me nothing... then everything... but only in your kiss." His hands slide slowly down my abdomen again, making their way to the hem of my top. "You push me away, then have me crawling back to you, on my fucking knees." he growls against the side of my throat. "Do you like me there, baby? On my fucking knees for you?" He sweeps his tongue up my neck, pulling another gasp from me as I shiver and grip his thighs. "Worship is better done in that position, isn't it?" He lifts the hem of my shirt. This time, he doesn't touch my stomach. He grips the top of my jeans. "You are a fucking Goddess, Vanna ... And you *could* kill me... but only by leaving me."

"You don't even know what you're saying..." His teeth skim my neck, pulling another wanton moan from me, as he undoes the button on my jeans, slowly unzipping the fly. My fingers dig into his thighs, both in nervousness and anticipation.

"The safe word is *Stop*, by the way, as it should be." He whispers, roughly jerking my pants open wider, making me jump at his unexpected forcefulness.

"Oh God..." I whimper, glad to be in the darkness. I'm sure I'm flushed with a mixture of desire and bashfulness. His hand slides lower down my body, into my open pants.

"You're so fucking beautiful, Vanna... and God, you're so soft." He kisses my jaw. *"But are you wet for me?"*

Another hot flush washes over me as I tremble against him. His hand moves lower still, fingers reaching my panties now, rubbing me gently over the cotton fabric. I bite down on my lip to prevent myself from making another desperate sound.

"*Fuck*, baby..." He groans, his hand sliding slightly back up my panties, toying with the elastic band. "You have no idea how many times I've wondered what you've got going on down here." He growls against my throat, tucking his hand inside my panties now, inching further down. His tongue works its magic on my neck, as his fingers find their way to my wet slit. Strong, rough hands, stroke me slowly. His touch is warm and gentle.

"*Perfect.*" He whispers against my ear, sinking his fingers between my slick folds as he carefully strokes me, seeming to intentionally fall short of directly touching my clit. His fingers massage me in a soft, circular motion, matching the swirling of his tongue kisses on my neck. "Do you like that, baby? Do you want more?"

"Yes." My body jerks against him reflexively when he touches my clit, but he doesn't stop. He continues to gently stroke my most sensitive spot. A tingling pressure builds in my core. I flush with another wave of heat, fingers digging into him harder. I'm only barely aware I'm doing it.

He gives me longer strokes when my hips begin to thrust. My body craving more as the tips of his two fingers tease entry.

"Fuck, baby... you're so wet." He growls, nibbling my lobe and tweaking my pebbled nipple over my clothes with his other hand. "I want to be inside you so bad... Do you want me inside you?" His fingers curl into me a little deeper, his middle finger going further than before. His thumb flicks and rubs against my clit a little rougher now, making me groan, jerking and rocking my body forward against his hand. "Tell me, Kitten." His hand releases my breast for a moment, only to shove it under my shirt and pull the cup of my bra down, exposing my breast fully to his touch. He teases me with the gentle scraping of his finger nail against my hard nipple, as his hand inside my panties continues to work my clit and tempt me with the promise of penetration at any moment.

"Oh... God...yes..." I think I gasp, I'm not even sure at this point. I can hardly think straight.

He slides his middle finger inside me, slowly thrusting it in and out, and as my body shudders against him, he curls a second one into me, penetrating me deeper, rubbing my clit rougher still. My back arches, pressing my bottom into his crotch, shoving my breasts into his hand as my arms reach up and back to grip his leather clad shoulders. The top of my head presses against his chest, as he fucks me roughly with his fingers, driving me closer to the edge.

Thrusting against him faster, my legs fall open wider. It's not entirely involuntary, however. My body wants him. Badly. My desire spiraling out of control. He's lucky he's wearing his leather jacket. My nails are digging into his shoulders and upper back as I grab and claw at him, panting and whimpering, more desperate for release with every passing second.

"I want to fuck you so badly, Vanna... but I *won't*." he growls against my jaw, relentlessly working me over. "Sometimes I'm afraid that if I fuck you... you'll be gone... the only evidence that you were ever with me... that you were ever mine... the scent of you that lingers on my skin... and the scratch marks you'd leave down my fucking back." Abruptly he releases my breast and grips my jaw, forcefully pulling my head to the side. His teeth bite into the base of my neck, lips suctioning against my skin as he leaves his mark on my body. Curling his fingers deeper and tighter inside me, he roughly strokes my g-spot, thumb grinding my clit mercilessly, shoving me over the edge.

My entire body tightens like a spring, before the pressure that has been rapidly building up inside me, explodes. Spasming around his fingers, my body shudders and jerks as he rips the orgasm out of me. I cry out into the night, barely aware of anything but the uncontrollable convulsions in my body, my fingers desperately clawing at the leather of his jacket.

Before I lose my mind completely, I drop one hand between my legs, gripping his hand over my panties and clenching my thighs tightly together. I beg him breathlessly to stop. Slowly withdrawing from me, I shudder once more as he slides his slick fingers over my sensitive clit, removing his hand from my panties. I slump exhaustedly against him, attempting to catch my breath. My body continues to hum from the intense orgasm he just gave me.

Resting against his torso, I feel him moving slightly, doing something with his hands and his jacket pocket, before he wraps his arms back around in front of me. He's got a red handkerchief in his hands, wiping off his fingers with it before he dangles it in front of me.

"You're welcome to use it, but I want it back." He growls, pressing a kiss to my head.

"*Kinky.*" I chuckle, weakly. Once I've cleaned myself up, I hand him back his naughty souvenir. He folds it up, tucking it into the front zippered pocket of his leather jacket.

"How do you feel?" he whispers against my ear, holding me in his arms again.

"Oh my god..." Is all I can muster after what he just did to me, but I do feel somewhat relaxed, and more than content in his arms. "No wonder you're a mechanic." I giggle. "You're very good with your hands."

Dean chuckles, his finger gently touching the slightly sore spot where he marked me, right where the top of my shoulder meets the base of my neck. I imagine it's probably a pretty noticeable hickey.

"I'm not going to be able to hide that, am I?" I tease, my voice sounds sated, even to my own ears.

"That's the idea." He growls, though I can still detect his smile.

"What about you?" He doesn't answer, only continues to gently stroke the mark he left on me. "Dean?" I slide one of my hands back to press against his hardness, attempting to curl my fingers around him over his jeans. He drops his hand to grab my wrist, pulling my hand away from him.

"This wasn't about me." He pins my hand down against his thigh. "I meant what I said before."

"But you must be uncomfortable?"

He scoffs. "You think this is the first hard-on I've had around you? Fuck, Vanna. When I'm near you... when you kiss me... it's practically my default state of being."

I sigh, knowing that was supposed to be a joke. "I heard what you said. But I don't understand you. You say you want to be with me, but you won't?"

"Frustrating, isn't it." His words are a statement, not a question. I know I frustrate him, but his words were spoken with passion before. A desire I could hear in his voice, and feel pressing into my lower back. Hell, I almost wrapped my hand around it until he pulled me off him.

"I don't understand you. Are you mad at me?"

His arms tighten around me as he buries his face in my hair, breathing me in. On a long sigh he asks, "Why do you always ask me that?"

"I don't know... Bad habit, I guess."

"Or perhaps ... it's *conditioning*." He barely whispers, but there was something in his voice as he said the words. I try not to let my body tense up, not with the way he's wrapped around me. He'll feel it.

I force myself to laugh a little. "What in the world does that mean?"

"You don't have to do this with *me*, Vanna."

"I'm not doing anything." I insist, as casually as I can manage.

He presses his forehead against the back of my head, his fingers moving my hair to the side once more. "Do you know that this is the only kind of mark I'd ever leave on your body?" his finger gently touches the love bite at the base of my neck.

"I don't know what you're talking about." I lie. "It's just a hickey. You're lucky you're wearing that leather jacket, or I probably would have scratched you up. You'd be worse off than I am." I try to fake a playful giggle, hoping it disguises my rising anxiety.

"Physical wounds heal much faster than other kinds do, Vanna." He says the words as if he knows from personal experience. I know where he's trying to take this. Dean knows... Or at least has a damn good idea about my shameful little secret. But it's *my* secret. And I don't want to be forced to talk about it. I have to steer this in another direction.

"Right." I say, remembering the way he reacted to something that Demon taunted him with earlier. I don't actually want to hurt him. I just want to back him off. But I say the words anyway, because he's the one backing me into a corner, now. "Like the wounds Lucinda left inside of you... when she... *cucked* you."

This time, I feel *him* jolt. A solid minute passes before he responds. And when he does, his voice sounds strained. "Yes... But I didn't *know* she was sleeping with him...let alone *condoned* it."

"I'm not asking you about it." I don't want to say anything that might hurt him, I just want to make my point. "That's your private business."

"I need you to know that I would *never, ever* accept that. It would destroy me if you ever slept with another man, Vanna." His arms curls tighter around me. "I do have some deep wounds inside, too. That's why trust and honesty is a major factor with me. I need them both from you if we're going to go the distance together."

"Is that some sort of ultimatum?" My anxiety morphs into annoyance. "Did you finger fuck me thinking you were going manipulate whatever information you want out of me? Like you did me some fucking favor? Like I owe you!" I snap, struggling against him, shoving his arms from around me. I hop off the table and spin around to glare at him, trying not to focus on the hurt that is evident in his expression. "Nice try, but if I needed help in *that* department, there specialty shops for the things you just did to me!"

There's a stunned kind of pain in his eyes as he swallows hard, then slowly stands up from the table. Hesitantly, he extends his hand to me, as if he wants me to take it. "Vanna... of course not..."

"My secrets are mine to keep!" I snap at him, redoing my jeans. "They have nothing to do with you!" Yet even as the words regretfully leave my mouth, I know it's a damn lie. He is directly connected to my secrets, and it's my damn fault that he is. That I'm wrongfully lashing out at him when it's my fault he ever even laid eyes on me. It's my fault he thinks he wants me, yet for some reason he holds back. Perhaps his subconscious knows he'd never actually want to be with me of his own free will. He'd never choose me. I'm not his type. Getting me off wasn't about him. He said it himself. He was doing me a favor. Helping me feel free, if only for a moment. My selfless, steadfast Knight... *I feel so filthy now.* Loathsome and disgusting...

Storming back over to the table, I grab my jacket and pull Axel's little giftbox out of its pocket, staring at the little black box with the orange ribbon. Harley Davidson colors. I hope Axel likes it. I hope he and Cherry will know that I tried. I wanted to be friends with them, but it's not going to work. Not if it isn't going to work with Dean. They're his friends. His circle of trust and honesty. And I'm on the outside, where I belong. Dropping the leather jacket on the ground at my feet, I brush a tear from my cheek angrily, and adjust the little orange bow on top of the box.

"Baby..." I can hear the caution in Dean's strained voice.

"Make sure Axel gets this." I turn to shove the box in his outstretched hand. "Tell him I'm sorry. For everything." I don't bother picking up the leather jacket when I turn to walk away. I don't even care that my cellphone is still in its pocket. It's a piece of shit burner phone. There are only three people's numbers in it that matter, and I have those numbers committed to memory anyway.

"Where are you going?" Dean asks, keeping pace alongside me. He's got my jacket in his hand. Of course, he does. "Let me take you home. If you won't talk to me, at least let me take you home."

"*Home.*" I scoff. I haven't had a home in years. "My shit hole rental, you mean. I'll find my own way, thanks."

Dean grabs my arm, halting me from my ill-thought-out escape. I didn't think I'd be needing one tonight. I managed to fool myself into thinking things were going okay with us these last several weeks. Shoving my stupid head back in the sand.

"Vanna, don't do this. Don't run away from me again." He pleads. "You told me you were tired of running. That when you think about running, it's to *me*, baby. *I'm right here.*" He slides his hand down my arm to grip my hand in his. "*Run to me.* You can trust me, Vanna. I'll never hurt you."

"But I might hurt *you.*" *Or get you hurt...*

He shakes his head, completely unaware of my trespasses against him. "Only if you give up on us."

We stand in silence for a few moments, as I try to calm myself down. As much as I hate myself for dragging him into my messed-up life, I know he's the only way my nightmare eventually ends. "You were right. What you said earlier. This was all too much."

"Let me take you home." his thumb gently strokes the back of my hand, the way he usually does when he wants to comfort me. Though this time, I'm not sure if he's trying to soothe me, or himself. "Just promise me we still have tomorrow."

Closing my eyes, I nod slowly. We still have tomorrow. In fact, we still have two years. Four if we're lucky. Maybe we'll both even come out of it alive.

Chapter
fifteen
DEAN

NOBODY RIDES A MOTORCYCLE TO FEEL SAFE. IN A WORLD WHERE everything is delineated to reduce risks and eliminate the dangers in our lives, Bikers ace out that societal inclination. Serene makes me feel alive. Forces me to be in the present moment with her, or die. She helps me clear my mind. Control my emotions. Recenter myself, when pounding the shit out of someone isn't a viable option. She's uncomplicated. Dependable. Loyal. When something is wrong with her, she tells me so, and I fix it. I fix *her*. No pretenses. No games. It's what I do.

Officer Jason Caldwell is waiting for us in the parking lot of the river walk pier. Our usual meeting place. The folder he has for me tonight, isn't a hit list, however. It doesn't contain the names and information of abusers of women and children. It contains information I really don't have any right to lay my eyes upon, but I don't think I can help myself. Not at this point. Because even though she refuses to speak the words out loud, Vanna is telling me there's a problem in her life. I can see through the pretenses. I can read between the lines. And I want to fix it for her. However, that doesn't change the fact I'm still conflicted about my methods. I realize what I'm doing is unethical. A transgression. Just plain fucking wrong.

As I pull Serene into the parking lot and up to Jason's squad car, my guts continue to twist up inside me. They haven't stopped since I asked him for this nefarious favor, three days ago. After the night of Axel's patch party. The night I may have pushed things a little too far with Vanna.

Kicking Serene's stand down and removing my helmet, I hang it on her handle bars, before I hang my head in wait. And in shame.

Jason steps out of his squad car, shutting the door behind him. Attempting to steel my resolve, I glance up, out over the intercoastal river. The sun has already set behind the tree line, making them look like a black, jagged ridge across the surprisingly still waters. The sky, deepening shades of purple and hues of dark blue.

As Jason comes to stand beside me, I force myself to meet his eyes, avoiding the manilla envelope in his hand. "It's sealed, right?" I requested that he seal it. As if that final, barely-there barrier, might prevent me from invading her privacy. That small detail, a thin line that I hope I possess the self-restraint, not to cross.

He nods. "Yeah. It is. But you're going to wa-"

I raise my hand, silencing him. "Don't." Taking a deep breath, I let it out slowly. "I just want to know one thing, for now. Is she in danger?"

"Not presently."

I nod. "Not presently... But that could change."

Jason glances down at his tactical boots for a moment, before he speaks. "You, more than anyone, knows how these bastards are."

The muscles in my jaw ripple. I knew it. I don't need the file containing the information he dug up on Vanna's past to tell me anything. I knew it all along. She's told me all about it, though rarely with her words.

"Where the fuck is he?" Bloody fantasies already dance through my mind. I'll never let him get near her again.

"Prison."

"*Prison*... for what he did to *her*?" My guts twist a little more, as my body fights my minds inclination to imagine what she must have endured. What he could have done to her to have landed in prison, when these sick fucks usually get to walk after a short stint in county.

Jason holds the manilla envelope out to me. I reluctantly take it, beating down the urge to tear it open and page through her dark secrets.

"She can't know I've done this." I've hated myself since I caved and asked Jason for this fucked up favor.

"She won't. Not unless you tell her. This stays between us."

I dismount Serene to tuck the envelope into her side bag, then step back, staring at it. My hand finds the back of my neck as I grip myself. I have all the answers to the burning questions that have been swirling in my mind since Vanna entered my life. They're right there. In my possession. A letter opener's slice away... or in my case, a switch blade's.

"I should not have asked you for this."

"You already knew." Jason says, as if that makes any of this better. "You just don't know the details."

I stop wringing my own neck, dropping my hand back to my side, and look up at him. "Do I need to?"

"You might." He sighs.

I swallow hard. "Is it that bad?"

Jason looks out at those dark, jagged trees, this time. His hand brushing back and forth over his short crew cut, before it comes to rest on his tactical belt. "It's always bad. Some are worse than others. But it's always harder when you love them."

When you … *Love* them. I try to push that thought aside. "But you said not presently."

"I'm not just talking about him. He's looking at another two to four years. I'm talking about you."

"*Me?* She's not in any danger from *me*."

"The details might explain a few things."

I stare at him for a moment. "You're not helping me prevent myself from tearing into that fucking file, Jason."

"I suppose not. Since I'm the one that gave it to you." He chuckles, though without humor.

"I hate myself for even asking you to do it." I mutter.

"I know. But your heart's in the right place, as usual."

"Does that excuse my actions?"

Jason shrugs his broad shoulders. "*All's fair in love and war.*"

There's that L-word again. I stare at the leather strap on Serene's side bag, containing Vanna's secrets. "What is it you think I *need* to know?"

"The Devil's in the details, brother." Jason sighs. "She's the way she is for a reason. Taking it slow with her, is probably your only shot."

I instinctively knew this as well. Perhaps the whole file is just confirmation of everything I already know. Maybe I don't need to see the details, after all.

"Would you read it?"

"*I'm a cop.*" He chuckles.

"I mean if you were me."

"Have you tried just asking her?"

"In a lot of ways."

"Maybe try a more direct approach. Or just read the damn file, Dean."

I wince at the pang of desire I feel to do just that. To rip through that envelope. Rip through her fragile trust, that I've only barely begun to gain. "I'm an asshole."

"She's been with worse."

I try not to glare at him. "Not funny."

"It isn't. But facts are facts."

"Right." I mutter, grabbing my helmet off Serene's handle bars and slipping it on.

Jason looks at me for a moment, his head cocked to the side. "You resent me for doing something you asked me to do for you?"

"Of course not. *I resent myself* for asking you to do it in the first place."

"Dean." He says, as I throw a leg over Serene and kick up her stand. The punching bag in the gym back at the clubhouse is calling my name. I need to blow off a little steam before the bar opens tonight. Vanna's working, and I haven't gotten to spend any time with her since Axel's party. I'll take whatever I can get of her.

"What?" I halfheartedly reply.

"*Love and war*, brother." Jason says.

"Right." I nod once, before firing up Serene. "Love and war…"

WHEN I PUT AXEL'S GIFT IN MY GLOVE BOX SO THAT I WOULDN'T FORGET to bring it to the Twisted Throttle tonight, I found something in there that I didn't expect to find. A receipt from Dean's auto repair friend. In the amount of twelve hundred dollars. Paid for with a master card. It was folded up around the five hundred dollars cash I had given to Dean to pay the guy with.

Now, as I sit on my porch steps, holding the cash and receipt in my hand, I glance back at my car. He never said a word about it. And now that I'm actually looking at the car, I'm not sure how I over looked the fact that it's got four brand new tires on it, not just the one that went flat.

I feel worse now. Since Axel's party, I haven't spoken to, or texted Dean much the last few days. Feeling too awkward and guilty, unsure of what to even say to him. What *do* you say to a guy that you wrongly flipped out on, after he finger bangs you at a biker bash? God, it still sounds so raunchy, even though it wasn't. Not really. It wasn't just about that... or he would have let me reciprocate. I never thought I would have ever taken part in something like that, though... not before Dean.

Staring at the money in my hands, I let out a remorseful sigh. I really don't deserve him. His level of generosity. His determination to keep working through my bullshit. I'm not worth it. He's too good for me.

My cellphone buzzes in my pocket. A silly meme from Ethan. I should probably text Dean. On second thought, perhaps a text isn't enough. The right thing would be to thank him in person. Insist that he at least take the five hundred cash back. Though he probably won't. I find myself smiling at the thought of his stubborn generosity. Maybe I should sneak the cash back to him. He hasn't said a word to me about it. It's been a month since my car was worked on. For all he knows, I'm still unaware of what he did. At the very least, we should talk.

As I stand up to head inside and grab my purse and keys, my cell phone rings. It's my mother this time. She hasn't called me in months, and our conversations are never pleasant. Hitting *ignore call,* I swing open the screen door and walk inside.

DEAN

MY FISTS SLAM INTO THE PUNCHING BAG WITH CONSECUTIVE BLOWS, thumping against the leather. Viking is standing behind it, holding it steady, while Viper and Chopper stand off to the side, occasionally heckling me to hit the bag harder. I barely hear them. My mind is still racing with everything that transpired at Axel's patch party the other night. The Chrome Demons MC. Lucinda's husband joining them, and apparently running his damn mouth. Preacher and whatever scheme he's cooking up with Legion. My own MC brothers pushing me to take over the Saviors. Even still, I find my thoughts circling back to Vanna, as they always do.

I should be hard as a fucking rock right now. Thinking about how amazing she felt beneath my hands. So fucking tight and slick and responsive to my touch. My stress level is actually working for me right now. Warding off a raging boner. Though, if I keep thinking about touching her... fucking her...

No. I can't fuck her. No way...

As I pound the bag harder, pushing those memories to the back of my mind, I replace them with the acknowledgement that I went behind her back with Jason. A dick softening act of betrayal. What the fuck was I thinking? I can't look in that file. I just can't. She'd never forgive me. She may never forgive me for even obtaining it. Maybe I've got a chance at redemption, if I never look inside. If I never confess this momentary lapse in judgement.

"You're swinging like a bitch, Dean! Focus for fucks sake!" Viking shouts, pulling me out of my thoughts as he slaps the side of the punching bag. "Don't you hear these pricks calling you a pussy?"

No. No, I didn't. I've been preoccupied in my own mind.

"If I'm such a pussy why don't one of you get in the ring and spar with me?" I challenge them, throwing all my effort into this cross punch, then striking the bag with a solid side kick.

"Why, so you can tickle me too?" Viper sneers. "You ain't even rocking that bag with those hits."

"Viking is almost three hundred pounds of solid muscle. Why don't you hold the bag for me? See if it rocks, since you're too chicken shit to get in the ring with me lately." I toss back at him, then hit the bag with another combination of far more efficient strikes than I have been this session.

"Yeah, pussy." Axel taunts him from the other side of the room where he's curling dumbbells. I can't help a little grin. Axel, my loyal hype man.

"I ain't afraid to get in the ring with you." Viper snaps back.

"Now would be the time. I've been at this bag for thirty minutes straight. Expelling energy." I say, slamming the bag a few more times before I turn to look at him. "You're coming into it fresh. I've been busting my ass." I wipe the sweat off my forehead with the sweatband on my forearm. "You got the advantage."

"*Do it! Do it! Do it!*" Axel says the words slowly, taunting Viper some more. Viper shoots him a look then shifts his focus back to me, contemplating my challenge.

"Come on, Bro. I promise. No cheap shots. I ain't gonna hit you in the balls." I know he and his wife are trying to have a kid. I overheard a few of the MC wives talking about it at the party a few nights ago. "Rosita would have my ass for that. And I don't fight girls. I'll make an exception for you, though, *sweetheart*." I wink at him.

"All right, asshole. Let's do this."

"Yes!" Axel shouts, slamming the dumbbells back on the rack.

"Fuck yeah. I'll get the gear." Viking releases the bag and walks to the supply locker.

Chopper tosses me my water bottle with a knowing grin. I catch it and take a swig, finding it funny how eager they all are to see Viper get his ass whooped.

THE SPARRING MEN ARE TOO CONCENTRATED ON EACH OTHER TO NOTICE when I enter the gym. Circling and jabbing at each other, both are topless and barefoot, only wearing shorts and head gear. I realize immediately, one of the men fighting, is Dean.

His bare skin is slick with perspiration. I can't help staring at the muscles in his back and arms, rippling with every powerful punch he throws at his opponent. I've never seen Dean without a shirt on. All sweaty and...*hot.*

I lean quietly against the wall beside the door and admire him. He's fast on his feet. Even faster than the other night I saw him fight beside the bonfire. He moves with ease, without the leather jacket and heavy biker boots. I don't know how long this sparring match has been going on, but I can tell Viper is winded.

Dean has more tattoos than I thought, though I'm not surprised. These Biker's all seem to be pretty inked up. There's a black scorpion on Dean's chest, to the left side. I caught a peek of that one a few weeks ago. A gun on his left forearm, partially covered by one of the sweat bands he's wearing on his forearms. There's another tattoo on his right forearm, but the sweatband is obscuring it too much, I can't tell what it is. There's a large Celtic cross on his right shoulder that extends down almost to his elbow. On his other arm, an old school style red heart with a ribbon around it that says *MOM*. Below that, a skull with a knife plunged through the top of it, engulfed in flames. As he moves around the ring, I notice there's one more on his right shoulder blade. A circle of thirteen stars, three bullets lined upright in the center.

Viper has a collection of ink as well, including a coiled snake around a big gun on his back between his shoulder blades. I'm admiring the detail of that tattoo, when Viper suddenly whips around in a spin kick at Dean, who takes the blow, gripping Viper's leg and charges forward. Dean knocks him off balance, shoving him to the floor of the ring. Viper lands hard with a grunt as Dean flips him the bird. The men around the ring are laughing and taunting. I recognize Axel and Viking, but not the third guy. Another tall, muscular, tattooed, bearded blonde guy.

Viper shoves himself back up to his feet and the two of them circle each other once more.

"Come on Dean! Knock his ass out! Fight like you're fighting to get out of the friend zone with Vanna!" Viking cackles.

The friend zone? What is that about?

Viper notices me first, cocking his chin over Dean's shoulder. "Speaking of *friend zone*." He says with a sneer. "Your woman is watching."

Dean side steps him in order to shift their positions and take a safer glance in my direction. I give him a little wave. He gives me a quick chin lift. Obviously knowing better than to be distracted in the ring, he shifts his focus immediately back to Viper.

"Guess that means I gotta stop taking it easy on you, Bro. Got a female to impress now."

"Fuck you Keegan, bring it!" Viper snaps.

"At least Rosita isn't here to see this." Dean taunts him some more.

Viper moves quickly, lunging forward with a powerful kick to Dean's core, rocking him backwards against the ropes and attacks him. Dean drops low, grabbing Viper by the back of the legs and lifting as he drives forward, flipping him backwards as they both crash to the floor of the ring, grappling and wrestling on the mat.

The guys around the ring are shouting and pounding on the mat excitedly. Viper manages to get on top of Dean, but Dean's got one of Viper's arms in a death grip, and he's bringing his legs up Viper's body slowly. Viper fights for his life, punching Dean in his thigh muscle, but it's as if Dean doesn't even feel it.

I step closer to the ring to watch what seems like it must be the end of the fight at any minute. Viking and Axel are going nuts, cheering Dean on, cursing out Viper, seemingly all in good fun. Dean lurches back with Viper's arm, twisting it sideways, distracting Viper just enough with that bit of pain, to get his legs up around Viper's neck and under his shoulder, pulling on that arm against his chest. Viper looks like he's hurting, but he's still struggling.

"Don't make me break it! Submit!" Dean yells, almost drowned out by the other men's excited shouting.

341

Viper lets out a loud groan. "Fuck! Fine!" He taps Dean's leg with his free hand and Dean releases him, unwrapping his legs from Viper's body. Rolling away from him, Dean gets to his feet. Viper sits up on the mat, clutching his arm to his chest with a grimace.

Dean pulls off his head gear and hands it to Viking, before he walks back towards Viper, offering his hand to him. Viper reluctantly takes it and allows Dean to help him up.

"A fucking armbar." Viper glares at him.

"I didn't want to knock you the fuck out in front of everyone. Had to end it somehow. Good try though." Dean slaps Viper's sore arm, making him wince even more.

"Fucking asshole." Viper mutters, turning to get out of the ring.

Dean fist bumps Viking and Axel before he climbs out as well, walking towards me with a satisfied grin.

I can't help sinking my teeth into my lower lip as he approaches me. Hot. Sweaty. His broad shoulders contrast his narrower hips, where his shorts are hanging low from fighting on the mat. My eyes gaze down his hard, sculpted, athletic body. I notice he has a collection of thin scars across his chest and abdomen, but my eyes are distracted by the dark, thin line of hair that trails below his belly button, leading down into his shorts. My gaze lingers there as I imagine licking that little bit of man fur.

"Hey, baby." He says in that growly, sexy tone of his. "Wasn't expecting to see you so early. Got a few hours before your shift."

"Figured I'd see what my *friend* was up to." I tease him.

"Working out." He flexes his chest, making that scorpion move. I fight the urge to lick my lips.

"I see that." I smile. "Looking good."

"You like what you see?" He runs his fingers through his almost wet hair, looking me up and down as he steps closer to me. "Was gonna shower, you wanna join me?" he asks, laying it on thick. I can smell his body. Sweat and man and leather and... *Yeah, I kinda do.*

"No." I smile up at him.

His eyes squint slightly, but his grin remains. "*Liar.*" I let my eyes roam over his glistening body again. He really is a sexy bastard. I peek around his shoulder to see if the others are still around. They seem to have cleared out. "We're alone." Dean says, confirming my assessment.

"I brought Axel's gift." I say, adjusting the purse strap on my shoulder. "But I was hoping you and I could talk."

Dean takes another step closer, forcing me to back up, or I'll be wearing his sweat. "You ain't looking at me like you want to *talk*." I try not to have a physical reaction to his words... or the way he's looking at me right now. Can he tell he's got me flustered? Are we both thinking about his hands all over me the other night on that picnic table in the dark?

"We should... talk, I mean." I say, taking another step backwards as he moves towards me again.

"What do you want to talk about, Vanna? You've barely responded to my texts since... well, you know... Am I due back on my knees?" He asks, though his tone sounds slightly sarcastic.

"Huh?" Is all I can manage.

He reaches out to brush the back of his fingers against my cheek, softly. "Your little game of push and pull. You let me... *touch* you..." he pauses, biting his own lower lip for a moment, his jaw shifting slightly forward. I can tell by the look in his eyes, he is thinking about having touched me on that picnic table. *More* than simply touched me. His fingers lightly trail down my skin, moving to that spot where my neck meets my shoulder. His eyes linger there on the now faded mark he gave me. "And then you pushed me away, again." He's staring at me as if he'd like to give me another one. I have to close my eyes for a moment, as his fingers curl around the nape of my neck, his thumb stroking that mark. "So, are you here to bring me to my knees again, baby?" He asks. "I'm already there."

"I'm not trying to push you away." I sigh, forcing myself to open my eyes. I take another step back from him and watch as he drops his hand back to his side. "And I'm not trying to bring you to your knees."

He grins libidinously. "You'd enjoy it. I guarantee it."

I narrow my eyes. "You're just hopped up on testosterone and adrenaline from fighting Viper... Do you always get this horny after working out? Is this an endorphin thing?"

"You lookin' at me the way you're lookin' at me gets me horny." He steps forward once more.

The back of my legs hit a solid object and I teeter backwards, landing on my ass on a bench, eye level with his crotch, and that thin line of hair peeking out the top of his waist band. I swallow and gaze up his athletic body until I meet his eyes again. They seem to darken now, as he takes in the proximity of my mouth to his manhood. There's no way he would ask me for head in the gym where anyone could walk in. Dean isn't like that. Not with *me*, anyway...

"You said you didn't want me like that..." I manage to whisper.

"The fuck I did." He growls, using his legs to knock my knees apart as he steps between them. I let my purse slide off my arm, setting it down on the bench beside me as I stare up at him. That craving inside of me, wanting to test his words.

Hesitantly, I reach up to touch his thigh, sliding my fingers under the bottom of his shorts, feeling his hot skin as I squeeze him. He flexes the muscle, wanting to impress me. I can tell by his crooked grin. I dig my fingers into his muscle. His thigh is like a rock covered in skin and hair. So different from my own. Now seeing him half naked, he must work out far more often than I thought. Sliding my other hand up his other thigh, I stroke him some more. His jaw begins to clench, though he's still staring at me, still grinning.

I twist my hand around inside the bottom of his shorts, grabbing the fabric, giving it a slight tug as I lean my face closer to his body, inches from the top of his waist band. As he stares at me intently now. I part my lips and let him feel my breath against his lower stomach. He tenses beneath

343

my touch, but I don't look away from his eyes as I slowly stick my tongue out, licking him up his happy trail, from the top of his shorts half way up to his belly button.

He lets out a hiss of air, his fists clenching at his sides. Dean's reaction stirs that lustful craving inside of me. Spell or no spell... I'm not sure I can resist the desire I have for him. Not even with the nagging guilt in the back of my mind. Seeing him fight... his half naked, sculpted body... remembering the way he touched me with those skillful hands...

I run my tongue across his hot, salty skin to his hip bone, where I nibble him gently and kiss him, pressing my tongue against his skin and swirling it. A low growl escapes his throat. I work my way across to his other hip bone, this time biting him a little harder and sucking at his skin. He groans, rolling his hips towards me as he buries his fingers in my hair.

His erection is jabbing against my throat through his shorts. I trail kisses and nibbles back down towards the waist band of his shorts, along his impressively cut Adonis belt. Digging my nails into his thighs and slowly raking them down his muscles, I bring them up to tuck my fingers into the elastic waistband. Dipping my tongue down between the fabric and his body, I'm about to pull his shorts down to free his erection, when he grabs both of my wrists and hauls me to my feet.

"Jesus fuck, Vanna." He says the words on a breath, before he releases my wrists and grabs me around my waist. Crushing his mouth to mine, he plunges his tongue inside. I wrap my arms around his neck and kiss him back, our tongues wrestling. His hands slide down to my ass as he grabs two handfuls, squeezing me, hard and rough, before he slides them down slightly lower, bending and then lifting me quickly and spinning me around until my back hits the nearby wall beside the boxing ring. His body pins me against it, his arms force my legs around his waist, his powerful thighs beneath mine, bracing me up against the wall. My maxi dress, now hiked up my legs, is cradling his trapped erection between us, but I can feel the head of his cock bumping up against me through the fabric draping down between my legs.

He pulls back from our kiss, his voice thick with desire. "I can taste my sweat on your tongue."

"Well, I was licking you." I pant.

"I like it." He takes my mouth again, roughly. Thrusting his hips forward, his hard cock rams against me, turning me on even further.

I slide my hand up the back of his neck, my fingers skimming up his fresh buzz cut, finding the longer hair on top of his head, I run my fingers through and pull, making him groan. But he doesn't let up. He rams his cock against me harder, making me whimper with desire into his mouth. We have too many layers of clothing between us and he's thrusting against me like he actually *does* want to fuck me.

His hands slide under my ass and he hoists me slightly higher. This time, when he thrusts his hips against me, the head of his cock is hits me dead center. Dry fucking me, his tongue invades my mouth with matching vigor.

I wonder how far he will take this. At the beach, when I was grinding on him, he wanted me to stop before I made him come. Right now, he doesn't seem too worried about it. The way he's going at me, I think he wants to come. His fingers are digging into my ass as he pulls me to him with every thrust, his grunts and groans sound almost as if he's frustrated as well. I break away from our kiss to breathe and he buries his face in my neck, his body continues to go at me at a determined pace. I have the opportunity to say something to him right now, but I don't know what to say. Maybe he needs this? To fuck me without *actually* fucking me. I guess I pushed him too far this time and technically, he is keeping his word, even if I don't want him to. Even if I don't understand why he even said it to begin with. All I can do is hold on...

"You drive me fucking crazy, Vanna." His words muffled against my throat. "Do you see what you fucking do to me?"

"Just take me." He groans and bites me gently at the base of my neck. "I want you, Dean." I whisper again, licking his ear as I reach between us, yanking at my dress to get it up higher and out of the way, but it's no use. The way he's pressed against me, it's just not working. "Damn it!" I say with frustration. "Let me get my skirt up at least, we can slide my panties to the side if you want me to keep my clothes on."

"No." he growls against my neck, before he lifts his face to take my mouth roughly once again.

"Why?" I demand against his lips. "Are you *friend zoning* yourself?"

"Ain't fuckin' you." He slides his tongue across my lips, then shoves it back in my mouth, grinding against me a little harder, a little faster.

I moan into his mouth. The pressure and friction of him rubbing on me is so tempting, but it's not enough to get me off. "*Dean...*"

"*No*, Vanna." He growls. "Ain't fuckin' you."

"You're practically fucking me!"

"*Practically,* doesn't count. *This* doesn't count." He pants.

"*This* isn't fair!" I *practically* whine like a brat.

"Nope." He concurs, taking my mouth again with another aggressive kiss.

I hold onto him tighter and try to roll my hips forward in unison with his thrusts, grinding his cock between my legs as best I can with all this damn fabric between us. I'm starting to wonder if he's trying to punish me with a lesson in frustration. Maybe he does think I tried to *friend zone* him again. Maybe that's why Viking said something about it before. Maybe this is some kind of twisted revenge on his part for *making him crazy!*

I twist my mouth away from his and slide my hands to his chest, pushing against him so my back is straight against the wall and I can look him directly in the face. His eyes are dark with lust, almost scowling at me, but he's wearing a wicked grin. He is trying to frustrate me! The bastard. Maybe punishing me for avoiding him again. There's no way I'm going to get off like this, and he knows it.

I reach down and grab his cock over his shorts, curling my hand around it as best I can over the fabric. His grin turns into a grimace, as he squeezes his eyes shut and continues to thrust. I rub my thumb over the wet spot at the head of his cock, swiping it back and forth, smearing his precum onto my finger through the slick fabric. Shoving his cock back down against me, he opens his eyes in time to see me stick my thumb in my mouth and suck him off of it. I moan around my finger, naughtily playing it up for him. "*You taste good.*" I whisper, expecting him to either drop me, or give in to me. I don't expect him to crush his mouth to mine again, shoving his tongue inside, pinning mine down aggressively with his and groaning loudly. He thrusts hard against me twice more, then his entire body tenses. His cock jerks against me and he shudders before the tension leaves him.

Dean kisses me gently then, releasing my legs and letting my feet back down on the ground, though he still has me pressed up against the wall. After a few moments of gentle kissing, he presses his forehead to mine as we both breathe against each other.

"Did you seriously just do that?"

"I did."

"That was definitely against *friend zone* policy." I sigh.

"Guess I busted out again." He grins. "Speaking of which, you might wanna get some club soda on that dress, baby. Got some behind the bar."

"Oh, so I'm dismissed now? You got off, that's all that matters?" I tease him back.

"Gonna hit the shower. You're welcome to join me. I'm happy to reciprocate."

I playfully try to shove him back from me, but his hips keep me pinned against the wall.

"I actually did come here to talk. I wasn't expecting all this." I can't help admiring his physique again as I touch the scorpion tattoo on his chest.

"Are you leaving, then?"

"If you aren't going to talk to me, yes. I have laundry to do now, *thank you very much*. And my boss doesn't allow me to work in a dress."

"Your boss has good reason." He smiles, his hands running up the sides of my thighs, making the fabric against them rise with his firm touch. "Don't like the easy access."

"Wasn't all that easy just now." I joke. "Or is there another reason why you seem to prefer me with my clothes on?"

His eyes squint slightly as my words register. He almost looks offended. "You drive me nearly insane, Vanna. Fully clothed. Can you imagine what you'd do to me if you weren't?"

I shrug. "You're the one who keeps saying you don't want to fuck me."

He shakes his head. "And you're the one with an obvious hearing problem."

"I heard you just fine. Though, you're sending quite a few mixed messages."

"*I* send *you* mixed messages?" he asks, incredulously.

"I'm not the one turning you down." I sigh. "Not a few moments ago... and not the other night, when you... did what you did."

"*What did I do?*" he whispers, grinning that salacious grin again. His hand slides over the curve of my hip, dipping down against the fabric of my skirt to trace my inner thigh with his finger. I grab it before he can touch me *there* again.

"I'm not going to say it out loud."

"Don't play prude with me, doll. Not after letting me... *do what I did*, the other night." Leaning closer to my ear, he whispers teasingly, "My bashful little *Peony*... Can I see you later? Take you to dinner before your shift tonight?"

"Wasn't that supposed to happen *before this*?" I joke.

"*This* didn't count. Still didn't fuck you." He insists.

"You're going to have to explain what just happened here."

He shrugs. "Nothing happened."

"There's evidence to the contrary all over both of us."

"Touché." He grins. "So, am I picking you up in a little while? Grabbing something to eat before your shift starts?" he asks, dodging my question again. "I can give you a lift home afterwards, too."

"Sure."

"Aces. I'd walk you to your car, but..." he arches a brow and looks down between us. I press my lips together, curling them in as I try not to laugh. He steps back from me, dropping both hands to cover the front of his gym shorts. "Sorry about the dress." He smirks.

I glance down at my skirt. Fortunately, the dark patterned fabric makes it difficult to spot, unless you're really looking. "Don't worry about it." I shake my head in minor disbelief at the whole situation. "But we do need to talk." I say, walking over to the bench to grab my purse. I sling it over my shoulder as I make my way back towards the exit of the gym. "So, no shenanigans."

"My word as a gentleman." He winks at me as a pass him.

I can't help laughing at that. "Right. This screamed *romance* and *chivalry*." I roll my eyes at him.

As I walk down the corridor and enter the empty roadhouse bar, my cell-phone rings in my purse. I recognize the ringtone. It's my mother again. And it isn't like her to call me twice in one day. Let alone twice in several months.

Pulling the phone out of my bag, I make my way hurriedly across the bar to the front door. Once I'm outside in the parking lot, I hit the answer icon.

"Giovanna?"

"Yeah, I'm here. Just let me get in my car. Hold on." I say, not wanting to chance anyone overhearing anything. Even though I know Dean has se-curity cameras outside, it's still dark out and I prefer to be aware of my surroundings. I make it to my car, sliding into the driver's seat and shut the door. "Okay. What is it?"

"Johnathan Nero passed away."

I can literally feel the blood drain from my own face. Johnathan Nero's death will only add fuel to the fire of my current problem.

"There will be a memorial service Monday." She adds.

347

"Okay..." I manage to get the words past my lips. "Are they letting... *Him*... out?"

"To attend his father's funeral? Of course, they are." She sounds annoyed with me for even asking. "With a prison escort, no less. And probably in cuffs." Her tone sounds as though she's appalled by the idea of the man, who nearly killed me, having to grieve the loss of his father under such conditions.

I don't even know how to respond. Nothing's changed. Nothing at all...

"Poor Katherine, can you imagine?" My mother continues. "Her husband in a casket. And her son in shackles... It's such a shame."

I choose not to respond to that. Obviously, my parents still believe *His* side of the story. The fact that he was convicted and locked up, just makes me look worse in their eyes. I shake my head and squeeze my eyes shut, gripping the steering wheel until my knuckles turn white.

"Can your father and I expect you to come up and pay your respects?"

"With *Him* there?" I almost shriek. "No! Absolutely not!"

"The Nero family has been a friend of ours for years." She pushes. "After everything you did! After everything you put them through, you owe-"

I hang up on her. I can't do this. I want to scream at the top of my lungs. I owe them? *I owe them!*

Their son tried to kill me, was abusive for years, and they always blamed me... all of them. I somehow pushed him to it and it was only a crime of passion. I did something and he loved me so much, he lost it once... Only it wasn't once... What he did to me that night... Even if it had been once... There's no excuse.

The rage inside me at the injustice of it all, boils over into tears, and I slam my fist against the steering wheel, letting out a scream of frustration. I don't stop hitting the wheel until my hand aches from the abuse.

Slamming my head back against the driver's seat, I wipe the tears from my eyes and try to compose myself. I have to drive back to the house. Change. Feed Nico. *Pretend* to be a *normal woman* for Dean. For fucking society... As normal as I can muster, anyway.

I remind myself that Johnathan Nero's perfect son will have guards with him at the funeral. He won't want to screw up his possibility at early parole. I've cut ties with everyone I know in New York. Nobody knows where to find me. Not even my parents. Even though he's going to be out of prison, it's only for a few hours. And we're hundreds of miles apart.

I'm fine. I'm safe. He can't get to me...

He can't get to me... And even if he tried... Even if he somehow managed to escape and hunt me down... I'm pretty sure I found my Knight in black leather armor.

DEAN

WHEN SERENE AND I ARRIVE AT VANNA'S HOUSE TO PICK HER UP FOR dinner, I'm pleasantly surprised when I'm greeted with the mouthwatering aroma of Vanna's cooking. I guess she had other plans. Or that strange aversion of hers to going out in public with me has kicked in again. The tantalizing smell of Vanna's cooking isn't the only thing drifting from her open front door. She's got some fifties or sixties music playing pretty loudly inside as well. Loud enough that she doesn't hear me knock on the frame of her storm door. The light on the front porch flickers through the wings of a large moth. Next the mosquitoes will descend.

"Doll?" I call through the screen, not wanting to enter her home and possibly frighten her. She still doesn't hear me.

I walk into her home with the intention of proceeding with caution, making my way towards the kitchen where the blaring music is coming from. As I cross the foyer, I can't help noticing a box of letters on the little foyer table beside the stair case. It piques my curiosity, though my conscience reminds me that I'm already on thin ice as it is, as far as her privacy is concerned... My gut, however, tells me that the letters we rushed to Wilmington for, are in that fuckin' box. And I'm willing to bet one of my side chicks, they're from that piece of shit in prison, Jason told me about. If I'm correct in my suspicion, why would she keep them?

I hesitate. She doesn't even know I'm here... And they're *right there*... A mere five steps from where I'm standing. She wouldn't even hear me...

I pull my gaze from the box, glancing towards the kitchen. She's singing sweetly along to the music, completely unaware of my silent inner battle. My moral dilemma. The second one concerning her in a matter of hours. Talk about a damn test of ones will, for fucks sake.

Vanna's black cat, Nico, descends the stairs. He stops to sit on the bottom step, staring at me. As if he knows *exactly* what I'm thinking, and disapproves. His vibrant green eyes even seem to slightly narrow at me in a harshly judgmental way.

I didn't do it! I find myself shouting in my mind at the feline, as if we can suddenly communicate telepathically.

The cat flicks its tail and scowls at me a little harder. *Well damn...*

"*Snitches get stitches.*" I whisper at it, with equal hostility.

Glancing one last time at the box, I take a deep breath. She'll tell me when she's ready. I need to muster up some more patience. Flipping the cat the bird, I walk towards the entryway of her kitchen.

I'm glad I do. She still doesn't know I'm here. And I've walked in on a little pre-dinner show to the tune of The Righteous Brothers *Unchained Melody*, performed by the one and only, Vanna.

Leaning against the door jamb, I watch her. She's in front of her old stove. Probably from the damn fifties or sixties itself. Wearing a fuckin' apron, tied behind her back, accentuating that fine ass she's slowly swaying back and forth to the music. My eyes are glued to those tight denim clad globes as she moves, stirring whatever she's got cooking in that pot as she sings along to the music. She reaches for a wooden spoon in the large tin can on her counter. Instead of cooking with it, she brings it to her mouth, using it as a microphone, and belts out the last few verses of the song.

I can't stop the grin on my face as she sings. The music is loud, but even over the music, I can tell, she's got a fuckin' set of pipes on her. The best part though, is the slight smile on her beautiful face as she sings, eyes closed. I can't help but wonder who it is she's thinking about. I can hope. I only need your love, too, baby. I've hungered for your touch, a long, lonely time, as well. And I will wait for you, doll. No matter how slowly time seems to go by. I'm still yours... And you're still mine.

As the song ends, she turns to lower the volume on her little old portable boom box on top of the kitchen island, still oblivious to my presence.

I clear my throat, making her turn abruptly in my direction. She looks momentarily mortified, embarrassed that I've been watching her.

"Now all we need is some wet clay and a potter's wheel." I grin at her, attempting to make light of the situation for her sake. "I surely wouldn't mind getting dirty and making a sensual mess with you."

She giggles coquettishly. "I think we already played that game in the gym today."

"Oh, come on, my mess was definitely bigger than yours." I say, walking into the kitchen to pick up the CD case and glance over the contents of what she's listening to.

"I believe you." She says, shaking her head. "How long were you watching me?"

"Nico let me in a few minutes ago. I caught most of that last performance." Her cheeks turn a shade of pink as she shyly covers her face. "I loved every minute of it."

"Yeah, I bet you had a good laugh at my expense."

"No. But you did make me smile." I say, placing the case back down. "And not because I found it funny, either."

"Well then, you owe me a performance." She unties her apron, placing it on the kitchen island. "Music is like the ocean. It makes me feel better." She says with a sort of sigh. There's something slightly off about her. I wonder if she'll tell me what, on her own. She turns back to her oven and grabs a mitt. I watch her as she slips it onto her hand and pulls out a tray of chicken parmesan.

"Hell yeah, baby. Did you make that from scratch too?"

She looks at me as if the question was an insult. "I can make chicken parm from scratch, blindfolded."

"That sounds dangerous. But I believe you." I chuckle, glancing towards the foyer beyond the kitchen doorway. "I'm sure you can remember a recipe, *to the letter*." I don't think she'll catch the reference. If she does, maybe she'll throw me a fucking bone and tell me what's going on with her.

"I can." She smiles, pulling off the mitt and tossing it back onto the counter. "These need to cool off for a few minutes. In the meantime, we should talk."

"What about?"

"I know what you did." She says, crossing her arms at me.

Fuck me... No way... I wait for her to speak again. There's no way she could know about the damn file. I've got it locked in the bottom drawer of my desk at the repair shop. It's barely been in my possession a few hours. Only Jason and I are aware of its existence. Aware of my betrayal.

When I don't speak, she walks around the small island and out of the kitchen towards the foyer. I follow her. When she realizes the box of letters is on the table, she looks over her shoulder at me. I wonder if she's wondering if I looked inside. I can tell, by her expression, she knows damn well I had ample opportunity. After a moment, she seems to rule in my favor and simply opens the closet under the stairs. Grabbing the box of letters, she stuffs it onto a shelf, before closing it again, then grabs her purse.

With an air of skepticism, she asks, "Do you not remember?"

"Enlighten me, doll." I say, mentally repeating to myself that there's no way she knows about the file. Unless she's got a damn crystal ball in here and witchcraft actually exists. I scoff inwardly at myself at the silly thought. Snitching black cats and crystal balls... Yeah right. I did something else. Or, she thinks I did, anyway.

She reaches into her purse, pulling out a folded paper before she places the purse back down on the foyer table. I recognize the heading on the paper, it's the receipt I left in her glove box with the five hundred cash. Inwardly, I sigh with relief.

Vanna looks at me for a moment, as if she's waiting for me to speak. I'm not sure what to say. I'm not sure how she feels about it.

"Four new tires. Balanced. An oil change. Tranny flush. Power steering service. New brakes and rotors. A front axle." She says, unfolding the receipt and removing the cash that was inside. "Twelve hundred dollars, Dean... And you didn't even take the five hundred?"

"No. I left it in your glove box." I try to sound humorous with the obvious statement.

She smiles slightly. "You should at least take the five hundred." She holds out the cash to me. "I'll work off the rest."

"I don't want it." I refuse to lift a hand to accept the cash from her.

"Dean, twelve hundred isn't like lending someone twenty bucks."

"I'm not *lending* it. Save it for your next couple of tune ups."

She stares at me, lowering her hand holding the cash. "You don't have to do this."

"I realize that... But I wanted to."

"Why?"

I shrug. "I just wanted to do something nice for you… I feel like you haven't had a whole lot of that, baby."

She smiles at me, but there's something almost rueful in her eyes. "You'd be right." She practically whispers. Her words tug at my heart. Turning to put the cash back in her purse, she lingers there for a moment, head down, facing somewhat away from me. Is she going to cry? Shit… I reach down to take her hand in mine, but she flinches, rather sharply, pulling her hand away from me and holds it to her chest.

That's a new reaction… "Baby?"

"I'm sorry, I just hurt my hand earlier." She says, twisting her wrist to show me the bruising on the side of her hand.

"Jesus fuck, Vanna. What happened to you?" I ask, placing my hand on her arm instead.

"I um… I tripped. On my walkway." She says, nodding towards her front door. "Caught myself though, with this hand on the steps." She won't look me in the eyes as she gives me her explanation. "Damn cracks."

"That landlord ought to fix it for you." I say, immediately annoyed by the fact she got hurt due to his neglect of repairs needed around this place.

Now she really scoffs. "Yeah right. I was serious when I told you he's really not cut out to be a landlord."

"I'll talk to him."

"No." Her widened eyes finally dart up to look at me. "Don't do that. I don't want to make any waves."

"He's got legal obligations to…" I begin to say, when she reaches out to grip my leather jacket over my bicep.

"Dean, *don't*… Mr. Blackthorn isn't that bad. He just lives out of state. It's not a big deal. Just, don't."

I glance at her fingers clutching my arm, before I meet her pretty brown pleading eyes. I nod once, curtly agreeing to her request. She said she had a six-month lease before either having to purchase this place, or he'd be raising the rent until it sells. She's got a few months before she has to decide. Perhaps in a few months-time, I'll be able to make her a better offer to move into a place with a *spa-level nice* bathroom and a large kitchen she really seemed to admire, and would put good use to. Not to mention, a leather three-seater couch and a king size bed that still need christening…

"Let's have dinner." She says, releasing my arm. "My shift starts in less than two hours." She starts walking towards the kitchen.

"Not if that hand is hurting you." I follow her.

"I can manage, it isn't difficult to carry a tray or crack open bottles." She insists, opening a cabinet and grabbing two plates. She places them on the counter beside the stove, grabbing a spatula from the array of kitchen utensils inside that large tin can. As she plates the chicken parm and pasta, I go to the fridge and open it up.

Looks like we're either drinking water or sweet tea, which is fine by me. "What are you drinking?"

"A bottled water is fine."

I grab two, content to have whatever she's having, but I notice she's watching me, her eyes slightly narrow, the corner of her mouth turned up in a suspicious smile. "What?"

"I knew you didn't like the sweet tea I made that first night I cooked for you." She accuses me.

I open the fridge again, putting one of the water bottles back and grabbing the pitcher of sweet tea. Moving to the cabinet she keeps the glasses in, I snag one and pour myself some. After taking a few large gulps, I refill my glass before placing the pitcher back in the fridge.

"Happy now?" I try to sound like I'm teasing her.

"Not if you don't like it. Don't choke it down for my sake." She says, carrying the two plates over to her little kitchen table.

"I only grabbed the fucking water because I figured I'd just have what you were having. I actually wanted the damn sweet tea. So there." I say, perhaps a little more snarkily than I intended. "I don't lie to you. Why would I lie to you about sweet tea?" I place the water beside her plate and pull out a chair to sit. She doesn't answer me. Grabbing my fork and knife, I cut a decent sized piece of chicken parm, stuffing it eagerly into my mouth. *Fuck that's good.* I almost close my eyes, just to focus on how fucking good it is before I swallow. "It's your cooking that's God awful, not the tea." I joke, shoving another piece in my mouth. I almost choke trying not to laugh, when her eyes widen at me and her mouth falls slightly open in surprise. Her lips quickly curl back into a smile. She knows I'm joking. Thank God.

"Asshole." She whispers, then shakes her head, twisting her fork in her pasta.

"Your cooking is fucking amazing, doll." I say it, just to make sure she really does know. I don't want to take any chances. "*You're* fucking amazing."

She rolls her eyes, though I can tell she's being somewhat playful about it. "You just know you're on thin ice."

"I fuckin' live there. Can I trade the twelve hundred bucks for another inch or two?" I joke. "Despite popular opinion, I'm not all too eager to fall through this thin ice."

She giggles, covering her mouth as she chews her food before speaking. "Fair enough."

DEAN DROPS ME OFF IN FRONT OF THE DOOR TO THE TWISTED THROTTLE before he parks Serene under the flood light and security camera on his repair shop. As I pull the door open and step inside, I'm *welcomed* by a dubiously faced Viking, as he folds his massive arms and looks down at me.

"Late again." He grumbles. "Must be nice to date the boss. Get away with all kinds of shit that way."

I roll my eyes at him. "Five minutes. Must be how you get away with your extra-long breaks, though." I snap back at him. "Being the boss's best friend seems to have its perks, too."

He grins at me, but doesn't respond. I look away from him to glance around the packed roadhouse. Cherry is serving drinks to a nearly full bar. Vixie and a couple of the patch chasers are running trays. I spot Axel surveying the room from the opposite side.

"I guess he's the new bouncer." I say, waving at Axel. He smiles and waves back. "You two are like night and day."

Viking chuckles. "He can fight. Dean and I have been training him."

"I meant personality wise. Axel seems too nice to do the same job you do." I really don't care if any disdain is detectable in my tone. Viking deserves it for always being a jerk.

He taps his wrist. "You're on the clock. Go work, woman."

I roll my eyes at him again. "Caveman." I sigh, storming over to Cherry to see if she wants me behind the bar with her, or running trays tonight.

About an hour into my shift, the crowd in the bar goes nuts as soon as Def Leppard's *Pour Some Sugar on Me,* blares over the jukebox. Hooting and hollering, cheering loudly as they bang on tables and whistle, getting all rowdy.

"What the Hell?" I ask Vixie, since she happens to be nearest me at the moment.

She nods towards the back of the bar where the stripper pole platforms are. "Unspoken House rule. There are a couple of songs, that any time they play, a girl has to get up there and dance. This is one of the songs. Could be any of us, if we want to. Even a customer. Looks like Cherry is gonna take the lead tonight."

I turn back to face the two stripper pole platforms on either side of the jukebox. Cherry is up on the right pole, working it to the music as the crowd cheers her on.

"I'm surprised this doesn't happen more often. The crowd seems to love it."

"Dean rotates the songs out often or it gets abused." Vixie laughs. "But we're allowed to jump on a pole whenever the mood strikes. *Cherry Pie, Pour Some Surgar On Me* and *Shook Me All Night Long,* are the songs that customers seem to really go crazy for."

They really do seem to, too. One of the other patch chasers jumps up on the other pole. I glance around looking for Axel. I'm really curious to see his reaction to his woman dancing for all the men in here tonight, after experiencing just how territorial Dean normally is.

I spot him sitting on one of the leather couches near the back. He's watching her with a big smile on his face and doesn't seem to mind at all. He looks like he's beaming with pride, actually. Even sticking his fingers in his mouth to whistle at her.

I can't help but laugh. "Damn. We should all strive to land a man that looks at us the way Axel looks at Cherry."

"You must not notice the way Dean looks at you." One of the sweet butts, Kelly, a skinny girl with long bleach blonde hair, says to me as she grabs four beers. "A lot of women would kill for that." She almost sounds bitter as she brushes past me.

I glance over towards the door, where Dean is standing with Viking. He is watching me. I give him a little wiggle to the music and point to the poles in the back. He shakes his head sternly and mouths "No." with a slight frown. I can't help laughing at his jealousy. I guess I'm the one girl in this bar not allowed to attempt the pole show, though I would never have the guts to do it anyway. Still, I pout at him playfully, then turn back to watch the rest of Cherry's performance.

She moves like she's definitely done this before. Maybe even professionally. Makes me wonder how Cherry and Dean actually met, and became as close as they are.

Axel is nearer to the platform now, arms up clapping for her. They're actually adorable. She ends her little show by jumping down into his arms. Everybody claps and cheers for her, guys in the bar throwing cash. Axel helps her collect it as they both laugh together. You can't watch them together and not smile.

The next song playing is Bon Jovi's *You Give Love A Bad Name*, which earns another patch chaser up on the pole Cherry was on. Seems she got some kind of a ball rolling tonight, but the crowd is loving it. I walk behind the bar to grab a quick sip of water before I go back to working tables.

"Vanna!" I hear Viking shout over the music. I turn to look at him in time to see him shove Dean playfully. "This song is for you! For *friend zoning* my bro!" he yells at me.

I can't help laughing, but I flip him off anyway.

Dean shoves Viking back, then turns to look at me, studying my reaction to the song. He actually looks concerned that I might be offended by Viking's joke. I decide to play along and get Dean back for joking about my cooking earlier. Acting like I've never paid attention to the lyrics before, I look at him and drop my jaw as if I'm offended and turn away from him abruptly.

One of my tables waves for me, holding up empties. They want another round. I duck under the bar to grab six more beers, placing them on a tray to carry them over. As I make my way, I shoot Dean another look. Viking is laughing hysterically. Dean looks heartbroken. I have to turn my head and make a real effort to keep from laughing. As I crack the tops off the bottles and pass the beers around, I spot Dean storming over to the jukebox.

I notice Cherry looking at Vixie, as if this is an odd occurrence, then at Viking, who is now leaning against the brick wall for support, shaking with laughter, tears in his eyes.

Dean's nervously tapping on the jukebox, his back to me, scanning through music as if he's in a mad rush to find something.

I collect the empties from the table, balancing them on my tray to take them back to the glass bin behind the end of the bar.

355

Dean is still at the jukebox, searching for a song, when a new one starts playing. Joan Jett and the Blackhearts – *I Hate Myself for Loving You*. Another great song.

"Vanna!" I hear Viking shout at me once more. Dean whirls around to face him, making a cut throat gesture with his hand across his neck, as if he's begging his buddy to stop. Viking has no mercy though. "Vanna!" Viking shouts my name again. I turn to look at him with a knowing smile. "This one's for you too!" I can't help cracking up. Dean won't even look at me now, he's back at the jukebox, scanning through its huge selection of music.

Cherry walks up to the bar and asks for eight bottles of Miller. I grab them for her and put them on her tray. "Just so you know, Dean *never* touches the jukebox during bar hours." She says. "You and Viking must have really broken his balls to get him to do this."

"I didn't do anything. This is all Viking." I laugh.

"He thinks you got your feelings hurt by these songs. And just so you know, he feels fully responsible for whatever went down between you two. Maybe you should cut him a little slack." I know Cherry is just protective of Dean and feels bad seeing us mess with him, when he's taking it seriously.

"You're right. I'll let him know I was just playing along with Viking." I say to her with a sigh. "He started it though."

She smiles and grabs her tray. "Viking usually does." Cherry heads off to her table and I notice Dean walking hurriedly towards me. I guess he found a song. His expression is a mixture of pissed off and concern.

"Hey." I say, about to tell him I was just messing with him.

"Vanna, these songs just happened to come on." He still looks slightly distraught.

I laugh. "I know. They're great songs."

"I overrode the play list. The next song is actually for you. It's the best I can do in a crunch. I'm sorry if you were offended. Listen to the next one."

Before I can respond, he storms off towards the front door. Viking tries to stop him, and actually looks like he's trying to apologize. Dean blows past him and walks outside. Viking looks at me like he fucked up and was sorry about Dean. He sits back down on his stool shaking his head. I can see him debating with himself whether or not he should go outside and talk to him.

The next song kicks on. An electric guitar rips the intro. It's a song by Scorpions, *No One Like You*. I sit down behind the bar to listen to it, focusing on the lyrics. It's a rock love ballad. A man longing to be loved by the woman he loves. Missing her and thinking about the things he wants to do with her, how it's hard for him to stay away from her. It's sweet, actually, and it makes sense he would pick this song. Now I feel bad for messing with him. This song says a lot about him.

I glance at Cherry. She's looking at me like I better go after him. He asked me to listen to it though. So, I will listen to the whole song before I go outside. Viking is sitting back against the wall. Arms crossed. Watching over the crowd. I know he regrets busting Dean's balls a little extra, but I can't read his expression any more. He's back in bouncer mode.

356

As the song comes to a close, I walk over to Viking. "Are we in trouble?"

He shakes his head. "He'll get over it. But I'm supposed to apologize to you, so there you go."

"That was literally the worst apology in the history of apologies." I laugh. "Fortunately, I know you were just joking around so I don't think you need to anyway."

"Tell that to Dean." He says. "Tell him to get his sulking ass back inside here too, I want to take my break."

I wave to Cherry, grabbing her attention to let her know I'm stepping outside for a moment, like she wanted me to do, anyway. Shutting the door behind me with a clang, I spot Dean on the bench right outside the entrance, sitting in the shadows.

"That was a great song." I say, feeling a little guilty now for teasing him. "For the record, I know Viking was only joking. I wasn't offended. I was just playing with you."

I can tell he nods, but he doesn't look at me.

"Are you mad at me?"

The frustration in his sigh is evident, and I remember the last time I asked him that question. It was at Axel's party, in the after math of our little picnic table session. The question led to another downward spiral between us. Me pushing him away.

"I'm sorry, forget I asked... Viking wants to take his break," I quickly add, "so I guess you need to get in there and cover him. I'm going to grab Axel's gift from your bike."

"I'll get it." Dean says, standing up. I know he's just being his usual protective self.

"Thank you. My feet are actually killing me. I think I'll take my break and give Axel his gift now." I say, looking across the lot towards his motorcycle parked under the flood light. She looks even more intimidating in the dark, the light cast down on her from above, creating even darker shadows on parts of her already black form.

"Why do you wear those if they hurt your feet?"

I lift my shoulder in a half shrug. "Bigger tips for some stupid reason."

"Right." He mutters. "I'll be right back."

After he retrieves Axel's gift, he opens the bar door for me and we step inside. Viking is already gone. And I don't see Axel either.

"Fucking impatient asshole." Dean says, shaking his head as he takes a seat on Viking's usual bar stool.

"I'll tell him you said so." I try to joke. Dean's expression remains stoic. When I turn to walk away from him, he grabs my wrist, careful not to grab the hand I lied about injuring on my steps earlier. I look back to find his eyes a bit remorseful.

"I'm sorry I can't take a fucking joke when it comes to you, Vanna. I don't mean to be a dick. I'm just..." he runs his fingers through his hair with his other hand. "I'm just a little fucking sensitive where you're concerned. And sometimes it feels like shit just wants to work against us... and..."

I lean into him, placing a finger against his lips. "Shh... it's fine, Dean. I really liked the song you actually picked. I'm going to add it to my favorites."

He cracks a slight smile. "I've got a play list a mile long of songs that make me think of you."

That actually makes me curious. "You'll have to show me."

"Maybe." He shrugs.

"I'll be back in fifteen." I say, as he releases my wrist.

He glances down at my boots. "Take your time."

I give him a little smile before I head across the bar and down the corridor towards the door to the back patio. I figure Axel is probably back there taking his break as well.

As I push the bar on the back door and shove it open, stepping outside onto the patio, I'm greeted by the distinct sound of moaning. Automatically turning my head in the direction of the noise, I see Viking leaning against the wall, head back, with Vixie on her knees in front of him... *both* hands *and* her mouth, working his huge cock as she sucks and moans on it.

"*Oh, my god!*" I say with surprise, immediately turning away from the scene and lifting my hand to shield my eyes. Now I know why they say he's a legend at those biker parties. Holy cow! I'm only barely aware of the patio door shutting behind me. I should probably grab the handle and run back inside, but I'm stunned. Momentarily frozen in place. I didn't expect to walk in on this.

I don't look, but I hear Vixie shuffling back to her feet, Viking muttering some kind of disgruntled curse words, and the heavy sound of his footsteps approaching me. I turn back to look at him, only to realize he's still tucking himself back in his jeans. I force myself to look up at his face instead, only to find him grinning.

"*Nice package.*" He winks, grabbing the handle of the patio door and walks back inside. It takes me a moment to register his words, realizing I'm still holding Axel's gift in my hand.

Vixie brushes off her knees and sits down in one of the patio chairs. "First time seeing it?" She chuckles.

I shake my head in an attempt to break out of my stupor. "I'm sorry, I didn't know you two were back here doing... *that*. I had no idea you and Viking were a thing."

She laughs. "We're not. Viking enjoys the variety of life too much. Though, he's too sexy to say no to. Not every man is packing a python like that." I'm speechless. I have no idea how to even respond to that. The shock has my brain momentarily scrambled. He's *huge*... In *every* way. Viking is *huge*. "How's Dean's, by the way?" she smirks at me. I look at her, confused by the question. "Please tell me he isn't packing a little garter snake." She giggles.

I shake my head, stammering, "I... I wouldn't know..."

She actually looks surprised by my response. "*Really?*" She sounds almost happy about it. "You two haven't fucked? Are you a virgin or something?"

I'm not having this conversation with her. "I have to find Axel." I say, grabbing the door handle and yanking it open to walk back inside. I wonder if Viking told Dean what happened out here. And what the hell Dean's reaction is going to be. He isn't packing a garter snake, that's for sure. I've semi grabbed him over his clothes before. But he isn't a python either, thank the Gods! I'm surprised the patch chasers Viking's been with aren't in wheel chairs...or dead. I shake my head, trying to get the image of Vixie going down on him out of my brain.

As I walk back down the corridor, I bump into Axel, finally.

"I've been meaning to give this to you for days now." I say to him, handing him the black and orange box.

His handsome face lights up with a bright smile. "Wow, Vanna. You didn't have to get me anything." He says, accepting the box from me and running his fingers through his dirty blonde hair, the way Dean does. I notice the leather jacket he's always wearing beneath his Saviors cut is similar to the one Dean wears as well. I think it's adorable, and I can't help smiling at him. "This is so cool of you." I watch him as he opens the gift to reveal the little chrome motorcycle clock figurine. "This is awesome. I'm going to put it right on my night table in my room here." He smiles at me, then pulls me in for a hug. He smells like leather and Aqua Di Gio.

"I'm so glad you like it. I wasn't sure what to get you. And I'm also very sorry I wandered off at that party and caused all kinds of trouble. I should have told you I was going to Dean's bike. I meant to give this to you then, before things... got a little crazy."

He releases me to look me in the face. "I'm not mad at you. Though, if you'd wear Dean's patch that probably wouldn't have happened." He grins at me, stroking his short blonde neatly groomed facial scruff.

"So I've heard. But I'm not sure how that works, since he isn't even a Savior anymore."

"We'll see." He smirks. "I have to get back on the floor. I'll give this to Cherry to bring back to our room. She's going on break when I get back." He adds, before walking away. "See you around, Vanna."

The rest of the night passes uneventfully. Viking doesn't appear to have said anything to Dean about what I walked in on earlier, thankfully. Though, the jerk grins at me every so often when he catches me glancing in their direction. I do find it humorous, however, the way Dean shoots him a sideways glare every time he catches him doing it.

By the time the Twisted Throttle closes, the balls of my feet feel like they are going to split in two. I decide right here and now, the slightly higher tips are not worth this amount of pain. I practically limp to my last table and wipe it clean, sitting down in one of the chairs once I'm done, content to remain right here while I wait for Dean to give me a ride home.

Putting my foot up on one of the chairs, I pull out my tip money to see how I actually made out tonight. It isn't long before Dean comes over to me, lifting my foot to sit down in the chair nearest me, then rests my foot in his lap.

"How'd you do tonight?" He asks.

"My feet are killing me. I don't know how these biker babes do it."

"For starters, the heels they wear are thicker. That's not a bad thing." He smiles. I feel like there might be something behind his words, but I'm too tired to try to decipher his meaning right now. "Biker boots are more comfortable than this type of witchy looking torture device you've got going on here." He says, pulling at the laces of my boot in his lap.

I laugh at his accurate description of my choice in footwear. They're tight, pointed, laced up past my ankles and have a spiked heel. "Stop messing with my laces." I playfully swat at his hands.

He grins, ignoring me as he continues to loosen them, then pulls my boot off and places it on the table. He cocks his chin at the spike heel. "That shit looks painful. Sexy, but definitely not comfortable."

"I'm going to have to clean the table again. And, I could see that just fine when it was still on my foot."

"Yeah, but I can't rub your feet with your boots on." He winks at me, then immediately begins to massage my aching foot before I can protest.

I let out a slight groan as any will to stop him evaporates. It does feel great. "Oh my God, yes." Leaning back exhaustedly against the chair, I plop my hands in my lap, holding my tip money, and tilt my head back. It feels too good to tell him to knock it off. He's grinning as he rubs my foot, obviously pleased with himself. "You're going to do the other one too, right?" I jokingly ask, though I hope he does.

"Of course. I'll just take it out of your pay." He teases.

I giggle. "You better not." I reach down to untie my other boot and slip it off, twisting in my seat to bring my other leg around and place my right foot in his lap as well. "You're such a good *friend*." I tease him back.

"That hurts."

I chuckle and lean back again, fanning myself with my tips. "Maybe *you* should be paying *me* extra, for allowing you to touch my feet?" I joke. "You ever think about that? That's a real fetish thing, you know. Foot worship."

He laughs. "Don't push your luck, Vanna. I don't do this shit for just anybody."

"I must be really special, then." I giggle.

"You are." His expression tells me he isn't joking. I close my eyes to relax and decide not to comment, enjoying the foot massage more than I ever thought I would.

After a few minutes of silence between us, he asks, "Feeling any better?"

"Mmmhmm." He begins to massage my other aching foot. "You're really good at this."

"I'm good at a lot of things." He growls. I can't help smirking, but I don't open my eyes to look at him. I know he's wearing that naughty grin of his. I can hear it in his voice. "You've never had a man massage your feet before?"

"I didn't say that." I bite my bottom lip and peek at him through one eye. He's wearing a slight scowl at my words now. I can't help but giggle. "Jealousy is not allowed in the friend zone." I tease.

"*But foot massages are?*" He teases me back, though there's still a trace of darkness in his eyes.

"Well, it's a *friendly* foot massage." I giggle again, wiggling my toes at him.

Faster than I could have ever reacted to, let alone seen coming, he yanks off my sock and lifts my foot, gently biting the inner side of my arch. My eyes snap open wider and I sit up straight to look at him, shocked, but not at all appalled by his action for some reason.

"*Friendly* enough?" he asks, wearing that salacious grin that always does things to me. He presses his thumb into a nerve in my foot, making me gasp out loud, as he triggers another pleasure zone I didn't even know I had. He clearly did though, and was waiting to attack it. "Bet I can guess where that nerve shot to." He whispers, grinning wolfishly as he drags his middle and ring finger up and down the center of my foot, stroking me in a way similar to how he stroked me that night on the picnic table... Only his fingers had been a lot closer to that area that nerve just shot to between my legs...

I can't help but grin back at him, amused by his boldness and clever strategy. He's going to tear down the friend zone. He's not the type to play by any rules but his.

We stare at each other a few more moments as he continues to massage, never skipping a beat. I find myself wondering what other sensual tricks he knows. What secret skills intended for pleasure did he have at his disposal?

"Oh fuck, get a goddamned room already." Viking grumbles as he walks past us. I cover my face and laugh, slightly embarrassed, but Dean doesn't even flinch. He doesn't even look at Viking. His eyes are fixed on me as I peek through my fingers at him. He's staring at me, almost hungrily, as he continues to work my foot in his strong hands.

"Seriously, Bro. Take that shit to your room." Viking says again. "You want to be seen like this?"

I glance up at Viking. "It's just a foot massage. What's the problem? The bars closed anyway."

He just shakes his head. "What you two do behind closed doors is one thing, but this is downright inappropriate behavior." Viking looks back at Dean. "The fuck is the matter with you? What if the other guys see?"

Dean grins and lifts my foot to his face again, looking Viking right in the eyes as he gently bites me once more, making me stifle a little squeal at the sensation.

"You make me sick." Viking grumbles at him, though there is a slight grin on his face now. When he starts to walk away, I notice Vixie is staring at us also. A look of shock on her face. Viking grabs her by the arm and they head towards the corridor together. I guess they're going to finish what I interrupted on the patio, earlier.

I look back at Dean. "What the hell was all that about?"

He shrugs. "Nothing."

"That didn't really sound like nothing."

"Some MC guys are still a little... *old school*."

"What's that supposed to mean?" I ask. He hesitates to answer my question, though he doesn't stop rubbing my feet. "Tell me." I push, bending

361

my knee slightly to rub his thigh with my other foot as I attempt to flirt the information out of him. He grins, knowing exactly what I'm up to.

"In a lot of MC's, women are here to service *us*. Not the other way around. At least, not in public. It's expected for our women to cater to our needs in public. It's quite rare to see things go the other way around. Behind closed doors, however..."

I can't help rolling my eyes. Viking really is such a caveman. "Like a foot massage is worse than what I walked in on earlier." I say, then immediately regret my words as Dean's expression changes to one of piqued curiosity. I press my lips together and look down at my tip money.

"What did you walk in on?" he asks, when I don't elaborate.

"Nothing." I manage to say, trying not to burst out laughing.

"Vanna... what did you walk in on?" he asks again. When I don't answer, he presses his thumb sharply into that nerve in my foot again, making me gasp and clench my thighs together with a groan.

"That's not fair."

"Tell me." He insists.

I stare at him for a moment, before I can no longer hold back a giggle. "Let's just say... I know why the girls call him *Thor* sometimes."

Dean's look of suspicion slides into shock, then horror. "How the fuck..." his tone sounds rather angry.

I can't help laughing as I nod. "Yeah... I saw his dick. It's enormous." The laughter doesn't stop, even though I can tell Dean is clearly jealous, and maybe even a little insecure now. When he stops rubbing my feet, I bend forward to touch his hand. "I'm sorry, I didn't mean to cut you off, go on."

"You go on!" he insists. He's barely smiling at my hysterics, but I know if I don't tell him exactly how I came to see Viking's member, Viking may end up in serious physical danger from Dean.

"Earlier tonight, when I went looking for Axel, Vixie was blowing him on the patio. I walked in on them." I explain, fighting back another bout of laughter as I raise both of my fists, one on top of the other in front of my face. "She was using *both* of her hands... *and* her mouth... and it *still* wasn't *all* of it." I bust out laughing at Dean's expression. His lips pinned tightly together, his nostrils flared, eyes glaring.

He gives me a moment to catch my breath before he asks, "Does he know you saw?"

I nod. "He was still shoving himself back in his pants when he walked past me." I chuckle. "It actually felt rather intentional."

"Fucking *asshole*." Dean mutters. "I'm never going to hear the end of this. He's going to break my balls about this, *indefinitely*."

"I'm sorry." I say, attempting to compose myself again, but Dean's face makes me burst out into another fit of laughter.

"Vanna, I am shocked and appalled." He teases, finally cracking a slight grin again. I know he isn't, not really. But he definitely seems a little jealous, and perhaps a bit insecure about what he's got in comparison.

"For whatever it's worth, I really hope you're not packing something like that." I tease him back, though I'm being honest. "I don't know how these biker girls that have been with him walk around, period. Let alone parade around in heels."

Dean frowns, grabbing my sock and sliding it back on my foot before he stands up and places my feet back on the chair. "You *know* I'm not." He grumbles. "Viking might be bigger than me, over all. But his balls aren't bigger than mine. I've got half a mind to go throat punch that motherfucker."

I can't tell if he's actually serious. "Don't, it was an accident. I'll just make sure not to take my break the same time he does any more." I say, putting my boots back on.

"Son of a bitch." He mutters, glancing around the room as he runs his hand through his hair.

"I meant what I said." I sigh, seeing that he's still a bit distressed by the situation. "I have an *idea* about... *yours*. And I am very glad it is what it is." I don't know what he's so upset about, really. I've had my hands nearly around Dean. Though, it had been over clothing. He has *nothing* to be ashamed of.

"Are you ready to go?" he asks, barely looking at me.

I fold up my tip money and jam it in my pocket as I stand up. "I'm sorry."

"You didn't do anything." He reaches in his back pocket and pulls out his wallet, handing me two, one hundred-dollar bills.

"One hundred per shift was our agreement... What's this for?" I ask, holding up the extra bill.

"That's for letting me touch your feet." He winks.

I gasp at his boldness, but cannot hold back another giggle. He can be so deliciously dark and unexpected. And I'm also relieved that he seems to be moving past this not so *little* incident.

"You know I'm keeping this, right?" I smile.

"I wouldn't have it any other way." He smiles back. "I'm not at all thrilled about you seeing what you saw tonight, Vanna." Dean lets out a sigh, before that grin of his returns and he takes a step closer to me. "But I gotta tell you, doll... I am pleased beyond measure, to know you think about my dick."

Chapter
sixteen

Vanna

S ATURDAY MORNINGS, ARE MY MORNINGS to sleep in late, ever since I started working for Dean at his roadhouse on week-ends. That has become my norm. Sleep in, drink a cup of tea on my front porch, then off to the grocery store to get my shopping done for the week ahead. Or at least, try to. I usually end up having to stop somewhere on my way home from Laura's shop, at some point during the week, regardless.

I haven't taken Dean up on his free produce offer at his farm stand in a while. For one thing, he goes out of his way for me enough as it is. Secondly, Jessica and Veronica are definitely infatuated with him, and the daggers they shoot at me with their eyes, just isn't worth the couple of bucks I'd save having to deal with that negativity.

Dean's motorcycle shop has Saturday hours. Since he didn't mention anything last night after dropping me off, about us getting together today before my shift at the roadhouse later tonight, I assume he's working. Maybe I'll stop by the shop and surprise him with a little homemade lunch. I have a few breaded chicken cutlets left over from last night, that would be good on a sandwich. I make a mental note to grab some fresh Italian bread.

The thought of cooking for him brings a smile to my face, as I peruse the isles of our local grocery store. He really does seem to enjoy my cooking. And maybe he did actually like the sweet tea, chugging a damn glass of it just to prove it to me. I giggle at the memory of that. And the jukebox last night. The song he wanted me to listen to, Scorpions, *No One Like You*...

Damn... I really am falling for this crazy biker.

A familiar voice in the next isle pulls me out of my thoughts about Dean. Rounding the corner, I spot Vixie chatting with a tall, slender blonde woman. My breath hitches upon realization that I'm looking at Lucinda. Before I can back away with my cart to hide and wait them out, Vixie spots me. A wide grin crosses her face. Suddenly, a few things start to make a little more sense about her and the things she's said to me the last few months.

"*Oh my god*, Vanna. Wow. Speak of the devil." She says, her voice high pitched and fake as hell. She turns towards me with her basket on her arm. Lucinda is standing beside her with a cart full to the brim.

I force a little smile, deciding to ignore that choice phrase. Obviously, she wanted me to know that they were talking about me. I don't say anything though, unsure of how Lucinda is going to receive me.

"Lucinda, this is Vanna." Vixie says, barely looking at me, though she's watching Lucinda with a slight grin.

I turn back to Lucinda, who is wearing skin tight, white low-rise jeans on her long slender legs, heels that look designer and probably are, since she's got a white leather Prada bag on her arm as well. Her slender wrists are stacked with multiple thin gold bracelets. Her black blouse is low cut and also mid drift, showing off both her perfect breasts *and* her flat, tanned stomach at the same time. She's even wearing a dainty gold body chain. Just to draw attention to how perfect her body really is. You know, in case you were somehow unaware of that fact at first glance. *Here's some jewelry to draw your eyes to my tight, flat stomach.*

Her expression is unreadable at first. Resting bitch face, definitely. There is no denying she is pretty. Her makeup is flawless. So is her blonde mid-length hair. She actually looks like she was just at a salon before she stepped into this grocery store.

I don't even want to think about what I look like right now. I'm not wearing a stitch of makeup. I threw on a pair of well-worn in jeans with holes in the knees, sandals and a cream-colored peasant style blouse. *Peasant* style... how fitting by comparison to her. My hair is mostly down, except for the top portion, which I clipped back in one of those cheap plastic claw things. She probably wouldn't be caught dead with one of these things in her hair.

I force myself to smile at her, but I'm not sure what to say.

I watch as she steps around Vixie and to the side of my cart, as if she wants to get a better look at me. I can only imagine she's wondering what the hell Dean is doing with someone like me, after being married to someone like her... We truly are polar opposites.

To my surprise, she sticks her hand out to me, and I notice her long pointed fingernails, are dark matte black. The same matte black as Serene. That has to be a coincidence.

Not wanting to be rude for the sake of being rude, I accept her hand shake. She says nothing either, as she looks me over. It's an entire awkward minute before she says, "So, you and Dean... *Interesting.*"

"Is it?" I'm not going to allow her to speak down to me, though I hope we can keep things civil.

The corner of her red lips curve upward into a slight smile. "What are your lunch plans, Vanna?" she asks, catching me completely off guard with that question. I glance at Vixie. Even she looks surprised.

"Errands. Mostly." I say, guarded.

"Nothing you can't put off and join us for lunch?" she asks, "We can meet up down town in an hour or so?" her smile widens, revealing her perfect white teeth. At least we have that in common.

"Thank you, but no. I have an appointment today." I can count surprising Dean with lunch as an appointment, can't I? I mean, it's technically a *plan,* at the very least. Even if I'm the only one aware of it. Besides, I'm not sure how Dean would feel about me meeting with his ex-wife behind his back.

"Oh, come on, reschedule and have a girl's day with us. I've been asking Dean to let me set something up for us to get to know each other." She pushes.

"He hasn't mentioned that." And why on earth would we do that to begin with? It isn't like they have a kid together or anything, where she'd want to get to know me on account of spending time with a child they shared.

She smirks and semi rolls her eyes. "That's *our* Dean." She chuckles.

Our Dean...

"Maybe another time." I decline, deciding I've done enough shopping to last me a couple of days. "I should get going."

"Lovely to finally meet you, Vanna." Lucinda smiles.

"You too." I'm about to start pushing my cart towards the front registers a few steps away, when she grabs the side of it, preventing me.

"Oh, Vanna..." she says, her voice a few octaves higher than before. I notice she glances somewhere past me, before her eyes meet mine again. "I just want you to know, that I will be praying for you. Dabbling in Witchcraft is the Devil's work."

I'm only stunned for a moment, before I realize what she just did. Glancing over my shoulder, I see the cashier and several shoppers in line, staring at me. Lucinda really is an evil bitch.

It takes everything in me to keep my chin up. She just dropped a bomb on me. It would probably be best for me to just abandon my groceries and walk out. Do my shopping on the way home from my day job, in the next county over, where nobody knows me, like I end up stopping anyway. I can't show my face in here again. Not after this. It isn't worth the trouble and I can't afford the extra attention in a town I'm trying to disappear in.

Taking a deep breath, I turn back to look her in the eyes, plastering a fake smile on my face. "Thank you, and I'll do the same for you, Lucinda... *Adulterer's* burn in Hell right beside Witches."

Her eyes widen in surprise, before those perfectly plucked blonde brows pitch downward into a glare. Her red lips press together in an angry grimace.

"You, bitch!" Vixie snaps at me.

"So do *whores*." I snap at Lucinda's sidekick, before I glare back at Lucinda. Shoving my cart so that it slams into hers with a clatter, I turn and head for the automatic doors.

Standing by my driver's side door, I dig for my keys, which have of course managed to get lost in my bottomless pit of a purse. I look up in time to see Garrett Johnson approaching me. I am *so* not in the mood for his not-so-subtle inuendos.

"Are you heading home?" He asks.

"Yes." I automatically answer, finally snatching my keys and wrenching them out of my purse.

"My pickup truck just died on me. Would you mind giving me a lift, since you're going that way anyway?"

It would be a total bitch move to say no to him. He literally lives next door. And he did give me a ride to work that one time I had car issues. I can't say no. "Sure. Get in." I sigh, beeping my car unlocked.

As I pull out of the parking space, I see Lucinda standing outside of the grocery store, on her cell phone, looking pissed. I wonder if she's calling Dean, since according to her, they talk far more often than he cared to mention.

"No groceries?" Garrett asks, surveying my back seat.

"Forgot my wallet." I lie. From the corner of my eye, I notice him pull out a pack of cigarettes and remove one. "No smoking, sorry." I really don't care if I still sound annoyed. I am. And him not asking for permission if he can even smoke in my car, has me aggravated too.

He tucks the cigarette behind his ear and leans his elbow on my center console, intentionally trying to get closer to me. I'm glad we only live a few miles away. "So, when are you going to let me take you to dinner?" he asks. Though my eyes are focused on the road ahead, I can feel him looking at me.

"I'm seeing someone." I remind him. *Again.*

"Exclusively?" he presses.

"Yes."

"Who?"

"Our neighbor, actually. You probably know him." I say, glancing at him in time to see him frown slightly.

"That biker?" he asks, resentfully. "That guy really gets around."

His comment irks me, but I tell myself that Garrett could just be saying that to get under my skin. I notice him looking at me again. As I fix my eyes back on the road, I can still feel his scraping over my body. Like dirty hands on my skin. I push the gas pedal a little more. Only a few more minutes until I can make the turn onto our road.

"So, you work nights at that biker clubhouse?"

He knows I do. "Weekends."

"What's that like?"

"It's a bar." I shrug.

"I hear those bikers get a little wild." I can hear the grin in Garrett's voice. I don't respond. "That what you into? Do I need to get me a motorcycle and a leather jacket to take you out?"

Oh great, I see where this is going. "I don't know what you mean." I say, finally making the turn onto the long, mostly wooded road we live down.

"You one of them pass arounds?" his hand drapes off the side of the console, inches from my thigh.

"No!" I snap at him, really hitting the gas now. I can hear him chuckling over the sound of my engine accelerating.

When I get to his house, I hit the brakes, hard. Jolting both of us forward slightly in our seats and then back, at the abrupt stop. I hit the unlock button on my car door so he can get out, but he doesn't. He reaches his hand down to grip my leg, just above my knee.

"Thanks for the ride, darlin'." He growls at me.

"You need to take your hand off me, *now*." I warn him.

He turns away from me and shoves my door open to get out. As soon as he closes it, I hit the gas and speed towards my driveway.

As disgusted and annoyed as I am by what he just had the nerve to pull with me, I know it's something I'm going to have to keep to myself. Dean would probably kick his ass if I said a word to him about it. And I don't want him getting in trouble. I remember what he did to those guys at the farmers market, and they only said things to me. Not to mention, how murderously angry Dean looked that first night I worked for him and that jerk pulled the same move. And that was before we even started dating. Then there was the fight with the two guys at the bonfire... *No.* I can't tell Dean about this.

That's two losses in one day. Not that Garrett Johnson is really a loss. However, now I definitely have to avoid him, as well as the closest grocery store to my rental, thanks to that bitch Lucinda. *That*, I will have a talk with *our Dean* about.

DEAN

"FUCK OFF." I WARN HIM, THE SECOND HE STEPS INSIDE MY SHOP. "You're the last person I want to deal with right now."

Viking shuts the door behind him and takes a seat on one of the metal stools at the work bench across from me. "Come on, Bro. It was a fucking accident. Ain't like I propositioned her."

"Oh, you'd be fucking dead if you did." I growl, turning my back on him to finish repairing a stabilizer for a Harley Davidson Fat Boy.

"You sure you're just not pissed that I've gotten further with her than you have?"

I scoff. "How do you figure that one?"

"Well, she's actually *seen* my dick, Bro." He chuckles.

Fuck, I want to punch him so bad!

"Playing footsy with her, like that Beta bullshit you were doing last night, isn't going to get your dick wet, Dean."

"Do me a favor, and don't worry about my dick." I grumble.

"Are *you* worried about it?" He taunts me. "I mean, like, in the stage fright sense. Now that Vanna's seen my huge cock and yours is still in the *friend zone.*"

"Not that it's any of your fucking business, but I've never gotten any complaints in the dick department. So, no. I'm not worried about it. And I'm *not* in the fucking *friend zone.*"

"Bro... you're over four months into this chick... if that ain't the friend zone, you're teetering on the fucking edge of it." Viking scoffs. "Seriously, what is the problem? You seem into each other. You've been with her long before she saw my dick. Maybe I can help you. Wing man you in there or something."

"You should leave before I ram this stabilizer down your throat."

"Dean." He pushes.

"I'm a gentleman. I may be a violence prone asshole, like you. But I am a gentleman."

"You know what they say about nice guys, Lancelot? They always finish last."

"They should. Maybe if you'd *finish last* now and then, you wouldn't be a perpetual bachelor." I toss back at him.

Viking laughs. "It's a choice, Bro. And fuck you. My bitches leave satisfied. I'm single because I want to be. I'm not looking for a ball and chain. Bitches complicate shit. There ain't a sissy bar on my motorcycle for a reason. Getting rid of yours after Lucinda was the right move."

"If that's how you feel, why are you so concerned about my progress with Vanna?" I ask, though I probably shouldn't have.

He lets out a long sigh. "Because, Dean. You're the type that needs a woman behind him."

I scoff. "Yeah, that worked out really well for me these last fifteen years."

"Lucinda wasn't always a soul sucking demoness, though, was she?"

I don't know. At this point, I don't really care. Nothing I can do to change the past. I don't respond.

"She was the hottest piece of ass in ten counties though. And you had to have her." Viking chuckles, a nostalgic tone in his voice.

"I'm really not interested in a trip down memory lane. Not about her."

He's quiet for a minute. And I've got a fifty/fifty shot of that either being a good thing for me, or a bad thing. I keep my mouth shut and hope for a good thing.

"That's it, isn't it?" he says.

Fuck me. Of course, it's the latter. I continue pretending to ignore him as I work on this part.

"You're gun shy, aren't you? You think Vanna might wreck you like Lucinda did. But you still can't resist chasing after her. You're a fuckin sucker for those big hot pouting lips... and big brown eyes... and that big rack... and that big..."

"Viking. One more word, and I swear to fuck I will hurt you."

"I was gonna say big heart." He chuckles.

"The fuck you were."

"Is that it?" He asks. I refuse to answer. "Damn. You got it bad, don't you? I was just breaking your balls with the *in love with her* shit... But you are, aren't you? You're not fucking her because you're in love with her... Fuck, bro... No wonder you're a miserable prick."

I reach over to my sound system and raise the volume a little more on the classic rock station currently pumping out a love ballad by Scorpions, *You and I*. I try to focus on the lyrics and tune out whatever Viking is droning on about. I'm quick to realize, this is another Vanna song. And though she drives me crazy, both in good ways and bad, I find myself smiling over the lyrics of the song. Klaus Meine must have loved a Vanna, too.

A FedEx box slamming down on the work bench beside me, snaps me out of my day dream of making sweet love to Vanna to this song.

"You got a delivery. I signed for it." Viking says. "And that stupid grin on your face paired with this sappy ass song, tells me you didn't hear a fucking thing I said either, did you?"

I grab the knife out of my pocket and slice the long box open, revealing something I ordered for Serene. A grin pulls at my mouth as I hear Viking let out a disgruntled sigh beside me.

"Oh, for fucks sake..." Viking mutters. "A goddamned sissy bar! You run this shit by Serene?"

"You should see Vanna and Serene together..." I dreamily sigh. Just picturing my girls together gives me instant wood.

Viking shakes his head. "I fucking love you, Bro. But you're crazy as fuck."

I smile. "I know."

"Since you just spent the last five minutes ignoring my words of wisdom, I'm sure you missed the bit about the meeting tonight."

I look at him, curiously, because I did miss that part. "What meeting?"

"Nine O'clock. In the empty room across from the gym. Everybody. The prospects are going to watch over the bar in our absence, till we get shit straightened out."

"Fuck." I have a feeling I know exactly what this meeting is about. "I'm gonna step out on a limb here and assume Preacher doesn't know about it."

"Fuck no." Viking says. "You nervous?"

"Fuck no." Nervous isn't the word I'd choose. More like...*reluctant*. For a few reasons.

"You had to know this day was coming, Bro."

371

I nod. Part of me hoped it wouldn't, though. "I suppose we have the Chrome Demons MC to thank for kicking this into gear."

Viking slaps me on the back. "Was bound to happen anyway, bro. Was just a matter of time." He says, walking towards the door to leave.

"Fuck me..." I mutter.

"Someone should. You sure ain't getting any in the *friend zone*." He laughs, slamming the door behind him. *Asshole*.

I THOUGHT FOR SURE, VIKING WAS GOING TO SEE ME DUCK INTO DEAN'S office, when he walked by to sign for that FedEx package in the front lobby. Thankfully, I managed to avoid his detection by hiding against the wall as he passed through the little hallway. I usually don't park my car in the street by the front lobby, either. But I've never walked in the back door to Dean's shop without him. I figured coming in the front would be best. I didn't expect to over hear them talking about me. And part of me wishes I didn't. Ignorance really can be bliss.

The loud clang of a metal door shutting, and the silence that follows, tells me that Viking left. I should leave, too. I'm not sure what to even say to Dean after what I overheard.

Placing the brown bag containing the chicken cutlet hero I made Dean for lunch on his desk, I grab a post it and write *From Vanna* on it, before sticking it to the bag.

Peeking out into the hall, towards his work shop, I see that he's still working on whatever part he's got on his bench. I scurry quietly back to the front lobby. Just as I do, a man grabs the front door from outside, making the bell above the door jingle loudly. He sees me standing on the other side and holds the door for me. I smile at him in passing as I hurry back to my car.

Cranking the ignition, I slap on my seat belt and check my blind spot before pulling out. Garrett Johnson wasn't lying when he said Dean really got around. According to Viking, Dean went on one hell of a bender after Lucinda. Booze. Screwing countless, random women... And the way he spoke about Lucinda... the hottest chick in ten counties. Dean had to have her. And apparently, they talk far more often than he let on. As far as Lucinda claims, anyway. At this point, I don't think I'd be surprised. She was calling him the night we were making out in his truck in the rain. The night of our first kiss. Maybe I should have called his bluff and answered the damn phone when he offered.

Stopping at a red light, I grab my cell phone to text Latisha.

"What are you doing tonight?"

"It's Saturday. Getting my drink on. You down? Been a while."

"I'm down. Text me time and addy."

"Cool Beans. 9 at Bill's Bar on main street. C-ya there!"

I back out of her text and bring up Dean's number.

"Not coming in tonight. Sorry. Lunch on your desk." I type to him. As the light turns green, I hit send.

DEAN

S HE DRIVES ME FUCKING CRAZY. UP A GODDAMNED WALL! SHE ISN'T responding to my calls. Or my texts. She isn't home. I checked. Multiple times. She isn't coming in tonight. She leaves me lunch on my desk this afternoon, then blows me off. What the fuck kind of mixed message is that? We didn't argue at all the night before. Hell, I even gave her a damned good foot massage last night. Took her home, where we kissed good night for at least twenty fucking minutes, before I had to pry myself away from her and go home to jerk myself off. What the fuck, Vanna? Where are you?

My fingers rapidly and incessantly tap on the table Axel set up in here. There are a bunch of folding metal chairs surrounding it as well. More than I expected. He's sitting a few chairs away from me, as we both wait for the rest of our MC Brothers to pile in. It's five to nine now. This sit down I've been expecting, since the Chrome Demons rolled into town, is about to commence. And I can't tear my thoughts away from Vanna.

I know what my Brothers want from me. Hell, *expect* from me. Taking over the Saviors MC will complicate my life. Not only have I grown accustomed to my total freedom, I've grown very attached to Vanna. And that is an issue. That is an issue now, and will be an issue moving forward. For all kinds of reasons. All kinds of reasons I can't even attempt to sort out right now as the scenarios flash through my mind.

If I were the President of the Saviors MC, my focus should be one hundred percent on this meeting. But it isn't. I'm completely distracted. Wondering where she is and why she's blowing me off again. If I ever get to claim her, really, truly claim her, I'm putting a tracker on her fucking phone. And her goddamned car. Maybe I'll even look into having some kind of tracking device worked into a piece of jewelry I could give her. God damn it, I sound crazy even to myself. *Fuckin' Vanna!*

If I ever do claim her, as President of this MC, thereby making her my Ol' Lady, my Brothers will have to vote on it. They will have to trust her too. Without their votes, she'll remain an outsider. That's a fucking complication to consider as well. I don't see her being the type not to ask questions about MC life. It only works one of two ways when it comes to Ol' Ladies. A Brother either tells them everything, or tells them absolutely nothing. Keeps them completely separate from the MC. Basically, living a double life. I don't want that. I don't believe she'd want that either. Vanna would be a need to know everything type.

And if I'm bugging out about her whereabouts right now, if I have trust issues, *now*... How the fuck can I expect my MC not to have even more about her? Their trust in me would dwindle if I pushed for it and didn't even appear to trust her myself.

I'm jumping the gun here. She doesn't know everything she needs to know about me. Before she can even decide if that's something she wants. She might not want me once she learns the secrets I'm keeping, myself. It's presumptuous for me to assume she'd allow me to claim her that way. Making her an Ol' Lady is basically the MC equivalent of putting a ring on her finger. I'm not sure if I'm ready for that. And I know for a fact, she isn't.

It isn't that I don't trust her... I don't actually believe she's fucking around on me behind my back. I just wish she'd fucking trust me enough to stop pushing me away whenever something seems to spook her. This disappearing act bullshit needs to end. It's the not knowing why she's doing this that's driving me mad. If we had argued, I'd think she was doing it to punish me. But we didn't. I'm at a loss...

"Dean, you nervous about the meeting?" Axel asks, nodding to my tapping fingers.

I ball them into a fist against the table top, forcing myself to stop. "No. Vanna's MIA."

"Maybe she's with friends? Forgot her cell phone or something." He suggests. Axel. Our eternal optimist.

My phone chimes and I grab it out of my leather jacket, hoping it's a response from Vanna. Of course, it isn't. It's the alarm I set letting me know it's nine o'clock. Time for our meeting. Shoving the phone back in my pocket, the patched members of the Saviors MC start to enter the room, including Viking, who's holding a large, shallow black box for some reason. I watch as the eight men pull out chairs and take their seats at the table.

Viking tosses the black box into the center of the table with a loud thwack, before he takes his seat at my right.

"You bring donuts or something?" I joke. "What's with the box?"

"We'll get to that. Let's talk first." He says.

"Maybe you should be sitting at the head of the table?" I suggest.

"You're right where you belong. Let's get this show on the road, shall we?" Viking says, addressing the guys around the table.

As I scan the familiar faces lining both sides of the table, my eyes rest on one Brother in particular. Ruger. Preacher's Sergeant at Arms. His rugged face glances back at me, not exactly scowling, but there's something in his dark eyes.

I lift my chin at him. "Gotta say, I'm surprised to see you here."

"But I'm here." He nods.

"Is this everyone?" I ask. "Nine of us are going to take over?"

"Torque, Gears, Rider, Kace, Slugger and Dutch are outside. They don't have voting power yet, but they're with us. So, sixteen of us are going to take over." Viper says, sitting to my left. "All Preacher's got left is Kruger and Maverick. We'll have to look into the five Prospects again once we're under new leadership. If they don't make the cut, they don't get a cut."

"Fuck. You guys have been busy." Viper and Viking must have been working overtime behind the scenes to convince all but two of Preacher's crew.

"We want our MC back. Preacher is looking more and more like he's in bed with the CDMC." Ruger says. "I didn't sign up to be a fuckin' Demon."

I narrow my eyes at his words. "Are you saying he's looking to patch over the Demons to the Saviors?"

"It's looking like it." Viper says.

"Well, that's one way to let them take over our territory... I knew that prick in the Saviors prospect cut was at the Demons' Den that night." I shoot a look towards Viking. "So, Preacher and Legion were going to Trojan Horse our community. That can't happen."

"Fuck no, it can't." Viking shakes his head.

"Legion was fronting Preacher the money to buy you out of this place." Viper says. "I found out after the fact."

"If I were you, I'd expect another offer." Diesel chimes in, leaning forward and placing his massive, dark-skinned tatted arms on the table before him. He's almost as big as Viking. "They purchased that shit hole diner on thirty-three as a temporary spot. Got it real cheap, too. Twenty grand. A drop in the bucket. Legion's got money, and he's got his eyes on this place. On this county. He wants in. He want's control."

I pinch the bridge of my nose, closing my eyes for a moment and leaning back in my seat. I knew it was going to come to the CDMC wanting to push into our territory, eventually. I didn't think it would be happening upon their apparent immediate arrival.

Some civilians might view MC's over all, as undesirables. Criminal organizations. Gangs. To be fair, some MC's are, and are deserving of that rep. Like the Chrome Demons MC. When I crossed paths with them during my time out West, they were dealing mostly in drugs and prostitution. Keeping their girls hooked on meth and heroin, and therefore, more compliant. That's never been us. Not by a long shot.

Our presence has always played a role in keeping the worst criminal elements out of our county. Especially out of our town, where our club house is located. It also helps public opinion of us, that we're pretty open about our charitable acts and donations. The fundraisers we run a few times a year for different causes. Not to pat ourselves on the backs or anything, but to show the public that we give a shit and want to better the community as a whole. That we're a part of them. Invested. And just like them, we want our neighborhoods safe. Free of gangland bullshit. No hard drugs. No shootings. No prostitution rings. We keep that shit out of this county.

That's not to say our territory lines haven't ever been challenged before, in the years The Saviors MC has taken up residence here. Especially in this city, specifically. A small police force is a tempting draw to criminals, but they have to go through us. And once upon a time, that wasn't so easy to do.

With Preacher handing Legion the keys to the fucking door though...

I shake my head. I've got too much invested in this town to allow Preacher to let everything go to Hell.

Curling my fist and placing my hand back on the table, I glance around at my Brothers. "So, what's the play, gentlemen?"

THROWING THE SHOT OF WHISKEY BACK, IT BURNS MY MOUTH AND THROAT, and I know I'm wearing an ick face as I place the shot glass on the bar, because Latisha is laughing at me.

"Girl, you work in a *Biker Bar* and you still can't take a shot?" she jabs at me.

"I *work* there, I don't drink there." I say. "Well, maybe *worked* there, is more accurate." I add, on second thought.

She looks at me with her head tilted slightly. "Dean fired you?" she sounds as though it would surprise her if he had.

"Not yet. But I blew off my shift today." I say, lifting the second shot and taking a breath to brace myself for it. "I let him know, like, seven or eight hours in advance, though." I shrug. "So, we'll see what happens, I guess." I take the second shot and practically gag once it's down. "Besides," I slide the shot glass back to the cute dirty blonde bar tender in the tight muscle shirt, and shake my head when he looks like he wants to pour me another. He grins at me and moves on to another patron. "I kind of called one of his long-time employee's a whore to her face today." I say, turning back to my friend. "She probably wants to kick my ass. It's a good idea to let her cool off."

She laughs. "What spurred this whole situation?"

"They all hate me." I force myself to smile.

"They're probably just jealous, Vanna." Latisha says. "I mean, you stroll into town and land Dean Keegan with one look."

I scoff. "*Land him?* Hardly." Should I tell her he's still supposedly talking to his super-hot ex-wife? Or what he said about not wanting to sleep with me, yet has apparently fucked half the women in ten counties? No, that's the Whiskey talking. That's definitely TMI. It's definitely also the spell screwing with his mind and emotions.

"What do you mean, hardly?" She asks, looking at me suspiciously. "Aren't you guys, like, *together*?"

I stare at her for a moment, before blurting out, "I don't know what the fuck we are."

Her eyes widen at my extremely rare use of the word *Fuck* out loud, then we both laugh. "Girl, trust me. They're jealous." She sighs.

"His best friend, too? That jerk Viking is always such an asshole to me." She's looking at me with a sympathetic expression on her face. "It's fine." I say, waving my hand in front of myself as if I can brush the situation away. "I'm just there to make money while I can... We're here to have fun, not talk about work, right?" I make another effort to smile and reassure her everything is fine.

She nods in agreement. "Let's hit the dance floor before you can't stand anymore, lightweight." Latisha laughs, grabbing my hand and dragging me off the bar stool.

"**O**NE LAST THING BEFORE THIS FIRST MEETING THAT NEVER HAPPENED IS adjourned." Viking announces, standing up from his seat at the table. "We voted prior to this meeting. And I know you're going to have a bunch of bullshit to say about it. Act like you don't want it. So, let's just skip all that fucking crap and cut right to the point." He says, looking at me before he shoves the box at me. My hand reflexively grabs it before it slides off the edge of the table. "The vote was unanimous. When it happens, you're it. Congratulations, and shut the fuck up."

Letting out a long breath at the conclusion of Viking's closing statements, I flip the top of the black box open and find myself staring down at my old Saviors MC cut. The one Viking refused to let Preacher take from me, three damn years ago.

I honestly don't know how I feel right now.

"For motivation." Viper says.

"Was kinda hoping there were actually donuts in here..." I sigh, attempting humor to stall. Viking reaches into the inner pocket of his leather cut and pulls out a black and white patch, tossing it down on top of my old.

"You get to stitch that on the next time we meet like this." Viking says.

The patch says President on it. "Guys..." I sigh, staring at the patch for a moment. "I'm really honored you think I can do this, but-"

"I said *congratulations* and *shut the fuck up*." Viking interrupts me to reiterate.

"Why me?" I ask. "Why not Viper? Why not you?"

"Viper's gonna be your VP. I'm your Sergeant at Arms. Ruger, your Road Captain. Chopper and Diesel will be Secretary and Treasurer. If you want to appoint additional SA's or enforcers, you'll get the chance later. This isn't going to happen overnight, unless we go the hostile takeover route. Which I know you're opposed to at the moment."

"That doesn't answer my question."

"For one thing, Legion appears to have a certain level of respect for you." Viper says.

"That respect gonna hold him off when his crew eventually out numbers us five to one?" I ask. "Or most likely worse."

"Quality versus quantity." Axel says, pulling my focus to him. "The CDMC look like a bunch of strung-out junkies. Their numbers don't mean shit if they're just a bunch of pussies who will run from a fight if things get tense." I can't help grinning slightly at Axel's remarks. He reminds me of myself, at his age.

"Legion doesn't strike me as a strung-out junkie." I say. "He seems calculating. Orchestrating." I think he may have even orchestrated that fight I got into at the party. Playing the entire event like a chess game. He wanted to see me fight. To discover what triggered me. What buttons to push to get a reaction. Without being too obvious about it. It's pretty much a guaranteed fight to make a move on a man's woman. Ol' Lady or not. Off limits means off limits. I could tell Legion took a liking to Vanna, but he wouldn't dare make a move on her himself if he still thinks he's got a chance at bringing me to his side. He had his goons do it for him. To take the beating for him as well. And manipulated the entire scene to make himself look like the fair one. The man who understood where I was coming from and agreed I was justified. Wanting to win me over, in some small degree. Even undermining Preacher multiple times to make that point. I saw it all playing out that night, but I couldn't not fight. Making a move on Vanna put me in checkmate. The cuckold bullshit was just to spur me on and to let me know, he already has a fallen Savior in his ranks. I'm not sure if Legion realizes, or believes, that I couldn't give less of a fuck about Daniel. I stopped thinking of him as a Brother the moment I realized he'd been fucking my wife behind my back. And when I read Lucinda's letter, Maddie's paternity test, he was stone cold dead to me.

"Legion's one man." Axel says, pulling me out of my thoughts.

I shift my gaze back to him. "So am I, kid."

"But you're the better man." He smiles.

I nod in acknowledgement of his high regard for me. It truly means a lot coming from Axel. "Every man at this table is a better man, kid."

Viking lets out a loud sigh that borders on sounding like an exasperated groan. "It's you, *Washington*. Accept it. You were always meant to eventually become the President of the Saviors MC. So, step up. It's your duty, Bro. And we all know you fuckin' eat duty for breakfast."

I stare back down at the leather cut and rockers. "*Fuck.*"

"Don't worry. We don't expect you to start wearing it yet. Don't want to give Legion or Preacher any kind of heads up. As far as Legion is concerned, you're still a free agent." Viper says.

I nod, slowly closing the top of the box. "When's the vote on removing Preacher as president?"

"Now that we have the majority, we can call an emergency vote any time we want. His new prospects and newly patched members don't hold any sway, yet. It's the Eight of us against Preacher, Kruger and Maverick." Viper says. "Once he's out, we'll see where Kruger and Maverick land. I suspect Preacher will go Demon. Those two might follow him. And even if they don't, I'm not so sure I'd trust them."

I nod in agreement. I'm not so sure I'd trust them either.

"Once Preacher is voted out, there will be an immediate vote to fill the President's seat. That vote will go my way." Viper continues, glancing around the table to nods of agreement from our MC Brothers. "At which point, I replace Kruger and Maverick, with Chopper and Diesel, as Secretary and Treasurer. That will give us possession and control of any and all accounts and legal documents. Once that business is secured, we vote you back in as a fully patched member. I wave the mandatory seven-year rule for you to be able to throw your hat into the running for President. Technically, you've got those years as a Savior under your belt, anyway. We vote again, and you take control of the gavel. I'll act as your VP, unless you want someone else."

"Majority rules. I don't want to be the King." I sigh. "But you've always cared about the mission, Viper. And I know you will do everything in your power to make it our mission again. So, I'm good with you being my VP. There is something for us to consider, going forward with this move. Preacher, Kruger and Maverick, can't leave the room until everything is secured. How ever that has to be ... *arranged*." I glance at Viking with a grin. "I'm thinking duct tape. It hurts more to take off than cuffs." I say, only half joking, but a few of the guys chuckle. Part of me would love to force Preacher to watch me take his seat at the head of the table.

"You sure you don't want to go the hostile take-over route?" Viking grins. "Could be... *therapeutic*. And definitely more fun."

"And well deserved on his part." I sigh, thinking about the relationships he's probably destroyed with the organizations we used to work with. I look over at Viper. He seems to know exactly what I'm thinking, as he shakes his head with disgust. "The fundraiser in the Fall, we should go all out. Rake in double what we have in the past, at least. Approach the organizations with a substantial donation, when we reach back out to them. I want to get our mission back on track." I say. Viper nods in agreement, so do the other Brothers. "But we've got a lot of work to do on all fronts. Before we can even think about reaching out to our connections regarding the mission, we need to neutralize the CDMC. Dues are going to increase, to speed that along. We're going to have to amp up security here. Fortification. Replenish our arsenals. This could get ugly when Legion's plan A, goes to shit." I glance around the table, looking for any sign of reluctance that might forewarn me of a potential turncoat. For now, every man seems to agree with me. I look back at Viper. "Do we have any idea what's still in the coffers?"

"Afraid not." Viper says. "Could be cleaned out for all we know." That actually wouldn't surprise me. I just nod. "So, you're in?" Viper asks. I can tell he's attempting to hide the hopeful tone in his voice.

"He doesn't have a choice." Viking chuckles.

379

"We always have a choice." I sigh. Glancing around the table, my eyes come to rest on Axel, sitting proudly among his MC Brothers. His young blue eyes, looking back at me with hope as well, not even expectation. Even though I know he's wanted this for me since before he was even old enough to prospect.

"I don't want Ruger as Road Captain." I announce. "He's better suited as the Sergeant at Arms Enforcer, under you." I say, glancing away from Axel to look at Viking. "Along with Trigger." It's true. They are better suited in these positions, but it also puts Viking between us. I'm not one hundred percent certain of them yet, and as my Sergeant at Arms, it's Viking's job to watch my back at all times. To protect this MC. Putting them in this rank, slides them closer to Viking, and it's still a respected rank.

"Alright." Viking agrees.

I look at the two men I just named. Ruger and Trigger both seem pleased with their newly appointed ranks, and nod in agreement.

"I concur with appointing Chopper and Diesel to Secretary and Treasurer." I say. They both run successful businesses outside of the MC, and they both voted in my favor, three years ago. Diesel is also a whiz with numbers, and is a tough motherfucker who doesn't take shit from anyone. He can be trusted with the club's bank account.

"Making a lot of calls for a guy who doesn't want to be the King." Viking jokes.

"I don't want to be the King. But if... *If*, I'm going to do this, I want to be *efficient*."

"Fair enough." Viking nods.

Turning back to Axel, I can see him smiling, looking at his MC Brothers, as if he's trying to contain his excitement at witnessing me taking charge. Even if it's unofficially. And in secret.

"Kid." I say, bringing Axel's attention back to me.

He smiles. "It's *Brother*, now." He corrects me, slapping the leather cut on his chest with pride.

I can't help cracking a grin. "Oh, come on, this might be the last time I get to call you *kid*." I tease him.

"I know you sometimes still see me as that eight-year-old, Dean. But, I promise, I'm going to hold a rank someday in this MC. And you'll be proud."

"I've been proud of you for thirteen years, *kid*. And I don't foresee that ever changing. I love you, *Brother*. And I might get some flak for this." I say, glancing around the table at my MC Brothers. Some of them seem to know what's coming, attempting to hide their grins while they watch Axel for his reaction. I look back at Axel, who's staring at me now, a bemused look on his face.

"I love you, too, Dean." He says. "What's going on?"

"You nervous, *kid*?" I tease him.

"*Brother*." He grins back at me.

"How does *Road Captain*, sound? *Brother*."

His eyes widen as he stares back at me with surprise for a moment, before he glances around the table, as if he expects one of the men to have a problem with it. We all know how many years Axel put in as a hang around, before he even prospected for five years on top of that. Holding an official rank with voting powers in this MC requires a member to be fully patched at least a year or two before they can be voted into any official rank. Axel has put in his time, in my eyes. And our Brothers seem to be of that same mind.

Axel's eyes find their way back to me after a moment. "I'm Road Captain?" He says, as if he can't believe his ears.

"If you want it. Otherwise, I'll toss it to Snowy. You don't have to take the position if you don't-"

"I want it." Axel says, with a single nod and a serious face. "I want to be Road Captain. I can handle this rank, Dean."

"I know you will." I say, before I glance at Viking. "And so, I guess that means, I'm in, too."

Viking grins at me as he slaps me hard on the back. "Adjourn the meeting then, Prez. We got shit to do."

Indeed, we do. "Meeting adjourned, gentlemen." I slam my gavel-less fist on the table, to a mixture of applause and fist pounding from my Brothers.

It's a quarter after ten pm, before I'm alone in our impromptu conference room. Pulling my cellphone back out, I've still not received any word from Vanna. I attempt to call her once again, only for it to go directly to voicemail without a single ring. Her phone is off. Whether it's intentional or the battery died, I don't bother leaving another voicemail.

Walking down the corridor into the bar that's packed and in full swing, I give Cherry a quick chin lift, as I make my way across the room, to the front door where Viking is seated, watching over the floor.

"Sup, Bro?" He asks.

I grip the back of my neck, attempting to stave off my aggravation at the situation. "Vanna's been MIA all day. Can't get in touch with her. I'm about to go look for her. Swing by her house again to see if maybe she's home now."

"She just blew off her shift tonight? No word at all?"

"She sent me a text around one thirty this afternoon, that she left me lunch on my desk and wasn't coming in tonight. What the fuck is that about?" I say, though I already know I'm asking the wrong person. If Viking were in my situation, he wouldn't give a shit. Even at this very moment, he's probably just wondering what she left me for lunch.

"One thirty? Weren't we both in your shop around then?"

"Give or take. I'm pretty sure I was by myself working on that stabilizer. Though, I did have a customer come in right before I got that text. Why?"

"No reason." He says, looking back out across the room.

Before I can ask him why he's being weird, my cell phone rings. Yanking it out of my pocket, I see that it's an incoming call from Latisha, Derek's little sister. Before I even answer the phone, I'm sure Vanna is with her. Should have thought of that possibility. I hit the green icon and place the cell to my ear. "Latisha, is Vanna with you?"

"Oh, yeah. You might want to come and get your girl." She says.

My girl. Even when she has me aggravated, the thought of her as *my girl*, elates me.

"Where are you two?" I ask.

"Bill's Bar. And I did *not* call you."

"Got it. Be there soon." I say, before I hang up the phone and shove it back in my pocket. So, she is mad at me about something. What the fuck did I do now?

"Found her?" Viking asks.

"Yup. You wanna give me a ride to Bill's Bar? Got a feeling I'm gonna have to drive her cage home."

"Alright. You wanna ride bitch on my bike, or should we take my truck?" he asks, as if it's a serious question, though I know he already knows the answer to that. No way I'm holding onto him, dick to ass, on his bike.

I shake my head at him. "The truck, asshole."

When we arrive at Bill's Bar, a thirty-minute drive just outside our county line, Viking pulls the truck over across the street, and I jump out. I hear his door shut as well and glance back at him slipping his cut back on, right side out.

"You can head back." I say.

"Hell no. I might have to back you up." He insists, already taking his secret rank as my Sergeant at Arms, seriously. "I let Axel know I'd be a little while. He's got a few guys with him still. No worries."

I don't bother arguing with him.

Walking into the establishment, Viking in tow, I immediately spot Latisha sitting at the bar and approach her. Before I can ask where Vanna is, she just points her finger. I turn my head in that direction, and when I spot her, my whole body goes completely rigid. Vanna's dancing. Alone. Her arms up over her head. Her curvy hips slowly swinging, her head swaying, working that long dark sexy as fuck hair, as she moves way too sensually to Nirvana's *Smells Like Teen Spirit*. She closes her eyes and does this thing with her body that I thought only snakes could do... I feel it all the way in my dick.

Fuck me. I swallow hard.

She's wearing those tight slashed black jeans she wore to the bonfire party. Those *follow me home and fuck me* boots, that I need to do something about. And an off the shoulder black blouse. She looks hot as fuck.

"She been dancing with anybody?" I growl, trying to remind myself that dancing isn't cheating. I just can't stand the thought of any motherfucker getting that close to her. Touching her... I scan the room and notice quite a few guys drinking their beers and watching her move. Especially the pricks at the pool tables not too far from her.

"Nope. Just me." Latisha says. "She turned down everyone else."

I nod once. *Good.*

"Can I get you guys anything?" the bar tender asks.

"A Miller, and whatever these two, want." I say, gesturing to Viking and Latisha. "Thanks." Viking says he'll have the same and Latisha orders a Bud Lite. I hand the guy some cash. "Keep it."

Turning back to face Vanna, I lean against the bar beside Latisha. "So, what did I do?" I ask, as Viking hands me my beer and takes a seat on the bar stool next to me with his.

"All I got, was that she thinks everyone hates her." Latisha shrugs. "She seemed a little down when we met up. And not to throw your buddy over there under the bus," she says, nodding towards Viking, "but *he* was specifically mentioned."

I glance at Viking, who's pretending he didn't hear. "*Oh, really.*"

"Next round of beers, says that dude by the pool table makes a move on your chick." Viking says, using his beer to point in the guy's direction.

"Nice try." I say, knowing he wants to side track me from interrogating him. "What did you say to Vanna? Was this last night when you had your dick out?" I demand. Latisha damn near spit her beer out beside me.

He glances at me. "No."

I glare at him for a moment, before I take a swig of my beer and shift my focus back to Vanna. Viking wasn't pulling my chain. There is a guy taking way too much of an interest in Vanna. The prick's eyes are roaming all over her, as he hands his buddy his pool stick and starts dancing his way closer to her. I take another swig of the Miller before slamming the bottle roughly on the bar. "Watch my beer." I can hear the snarl in my own voice.

"Glad you said *watch*, not *hold.*" Viking jokes.

I move towards her through the thin crowd, reaching her before he does, stepping directly into his path, only a foot from her back as she dances, oblivious at the moment. He damn near bumps into me. Too bad he didn't.

"The fuck, dude. Get out of my way." He says, like he's going to step around me. I move with him to show him that isn't going to happen. "I saw her first, asshole!" he gripes at me. "I've been here all night, you just walked in minutes ago. Take your shot at someone else."

I'm about to tell him exactly who I'm going to take a shot at, when I feel a hand on my arm. "Dean?" Vanna says, obviously surprised to see me here. I don't look at her yet. I'm still staring down one of her admirers.

I watch his eyes slide to Vanna, her hand on my arm, then back up to meet my glare.

"You were fuckin' saying?" I growl at him, now that he knows I'm not just some random dude in the bar eye fucking her like the rest of them.

"Sorry, didn't know she was with you."

"Now you do. Fuck off." I wait for him to turn and walk away before I look at Vanna.

"What are you doing here?" she asks, as if she's annoyed with me.

"You lose your cellphone or something?"

"It's in my purse. In my car." She says.

"You couldn't text me and let me know you weren't going to be reachable all day and night, after blowing off your shift? You pissed at me for something I don't know about? This isn't like you. I've been worried about you all fucking day. You want to talk about mixed messages? You bring me lunch then blow me off for hours? What the hell is that, Vanna?"

She frowns at me. "Well excuse me, *stud!*"

Stud? What the fuck was that?

"You'll have to forgive me for not *loving the way you lie!*" She shoves my arm and almost stumbles backwards as she attempts to turn away from me. I grab her around her waist, partly to stop her from walking away from me, partly to prevent her from falling. She's definitely had a few drinks.

"What are you talking about, Vanna? It's like you're speaking in riddles."

"Get off me." She pushes against my chest.

"Let me walk you to the fucking bar so you don't break an ankle. We clearly need to talk about something."

As I escort her towards the bar, she catches sight of Viking talking to Latisha and stops in her tracks. "You brought *him* with you?"

"Are you pissed off about something Viking said? Tell me, I'll fix it."

She scoffs at me. "You can't *fix it*. You can't *undo* anything. I can't either."

"Vanna, I'm fucking lost, doll. I have no idea what you're so mad about. I thought we parted ways last night on good terms."

She's quiet for a moment, listening to the music, I think. She starts to laugh, turning to pat my chest. "This song, this is for you." She says, before she leans slightly to look around me. "Right, Viking!" she shouts at him, "This is Dean's anthem, isn't it?"

Shit... Maybe she was offended by Viking's fuckery last night with the jukebox. Listening to the song playing, I'm a little taken aback by her saying this is my song. It's Pat Benatar's *Heartbreaker*. What the fuck?

She suddenly throws her arms on my shoulders and starts to dance against me to the music. Whipping her hair back and forth and getting a little wild. I'd be turned the fuck on right now if she wasn't acting so out of character. If she wasn't so pissed off. If she wasn't insinuating that I was some kind of fucking player.

I hold onto her body loosely, keeping her near me, in case she stumbles on these fucking heels again as she dances. When the slower verse plays, she grips the lapels of my leather jacket, yanking me closer to her, and lips the words to me, essentially calling me a Heartbreaker to my face. She presses herself up against me and does that fucking snake move down my body, her hand grabbing my fuckin' belt as she works her way back up. She's got some pole worthy moves... *Fuck*... Again, I'd be rock fucking hard, *if* she wasn't calling me a player as she did it. Spinning around in my arms, she leans back against me, pressing her ass into my crotch, her arms reaching up to wrap around the back of my neck as she writhes against me to the music. I can't help but think about our similar position on the picnic table in the dark... how she felt in my hands... how they felt in her...

I might be getting a little hard now, damnit.

Her fingers slide up my neck and the base of my skull. When the guitar solo hits, she drops her arms and places her hands over mine, which I've got firmly planted on her hips. She pushes her ass harder against my junk, grinding against me as the fast-paced rock song races to its finish. I glance over at Viking and Latisha, who are staring at us, wide eyed. Shocked amusement written on both of their expressions. Viking lifts his beer to me in salute. The song comes to its end, with Vanna straightening back up, whipping her hair back and whacking me in the face with it. She then shoves me away and walks over to the bar by Latisha.

For a moment, all I can think about is how Vanna is probably... No... *Most definitely*... A fucking Hell Cat in the sack.

Reminding myself that something is very wrong here, I will my dick to forget about what just happened for now, and approach her again.

"What the fuck, Vanna? I told you, I didn't have anything to do with that last night. Viking was just being a dick to both of us." I say, leaning close to her ear so she'll hear me.

She ignores me, waving to the bar tender to order another drink. I'm standing behind her, signaling to the bar tender that she's cut off. He nods, and carries on with his other patrons. She turns around to glare at me, knowing I had something to do with her being passed over with only an awkward, apologetic smile from the bar tender.

"*Heartbreaker*? Really?" I sigh, placing my hand on her arm.

She shrugs her shoulder almost violently, attempting to get my hand off her, then pushes me away as she slides back off the bar stool, storming over to Viking, who appears to be hitting on Latisha. Great. Like I need him pulling moves on Derek's little sister.

"*You!*" she says, pointing in his face. I'm right behind her, grabbing her arm to pull her back from him. He'd never lay a finger on her, but I have no idea what's got her so heated, or if she'd lay one on him in this state.

"What's up, Vanna?" Viking smiles his asshole grin at her.

"Thank you." She says, unexpectedly.

Viking and I look at each other. We're both confused.

"He's been less than honest with me." She jerks a thumb in *my* direction. *What the fuck?*

"But *you*, in all your mega asshole, bad boy biker glory... With your macho man's club... no girls allowed... MC... He-Man-Woman-Hater's... Caveman bullshit..." She's rambling on and on at him. Viking is clearly loving every second of her drunken barrage of scrambled words, which I know are meant to be insults in her inebriated mind. But he's taking every one of them as compliments. She stops for a moment to take a breath, before she continues. "You actually spoke the truth, and now I know. So, thank you," she slaps his cut with the back of her hand, "for being the fucking asshole that you are."

He doesn't say anything. Continuously smiling at her and grabs my beer. "You gonna finish this, Bro?" he asks, as if this cryptic torrent didn't just pour out of Vanna, directly at him. He seems completely unfazed.

"No." I say, looking back and forth at them suspiciously. Vanna is still glaring at him, as if she's waiting for him to say something about whatever this situation is.

"I'll drink it then." He says, taking a swig. "Ain't like we've never drank from the same bottle before." He grins at Vanna slightly and winks.

Her mouth drops open at his words, before she spins around, clenching her jaw shut now as she death glares at me. She looks like she wants to slap me in the face.

"Doll, please tell me what the fuck is going on here? What's going on between you and Viking?"

She scrunches her nose. "*Ew*. Nothing."

"I second that." Viking raises my former beer and takes another swig.

"He's a dick. A huge one. But at least he seems to be honest." She scowls at me.

"Okay, so clearly you think I've lied to you about something. Fill me in so I can fix this."

She shoves her middle finger in my face. "Fix, *this!*"

Alright. Enough of this shit. "Where are your keys? We're leaving."

"I'm here with Latisha. You two are party crashers." She says, hopping back on a bar stool next to Latisha.

"We need to talk, Vanna." I step closer to her again.

"You have plenty of women to talk to, Dean. Why don't you call up your favorite?" she says, leaning back on the bar as she crosses her legs and stares at me. It's as if she's waiting for me to make some kind of connection.

"My favorite? I'm *looking* at her." I sigh, attempting to touch her, but she halfheartedly kicks her boot at me, scoffing. Then shoots a look at Viking on the other side of Latisha. What the fuck is up with her and Viking? I'm about to drag his ass outside and ask him with my fists.

"But I'm not even the hottest piece of ass in ten counties." She says, her eyes sliding back in my direction to glare at me.

Oh shit... What the fuck did she hear in my shop?

"Fuck..." Viking mutters.

I turned the music up when he was droning on about something in my shop. So even I'm not one hundred percent sure of what he said in those five minutes. She must have been listening when she came to bring me lunch, and obviously heard something that pissed her off.

"The fuck did you say?" I growl at him.

He puts his hands up, palms out in a placating gesture. "Bro, nothing bad, I swear!"

"Don't be mad at that asshole." Vanna says, surprisingly coming to Viking's defense again. "You're the one who lies to me."

"Vanna, baby, what did I lie about?"

She doesn't say anything. I look to Latisha, pleadingly, hoping she's got some other intel she could help me out with.

Latisha clears her throat and touches Vanna's arm gently. "Vanna, does this have anything to do with the girl you ran into today? You, know... from the bar? The one you called a whore?" Latisha gives me a quick look.

I pick up on that clue immediately. "Fuckin' Vixie again?"

Vanna rolls her eyes at me. "Don't worry, I know she's at least one of these patch chaser's you haven't put your dick in." she mutters at me with a dirty look, before she suddenly starts laughing, hysterically. "I guess she and I have a few things in common after all!" she manages to say through her laughing fit.

Viking is laughing hysterically along with her now, and suddenly they're both feeding off of each other's laughter.

Latisha and I look at each other, completely out of the fucking loop.

I step over to Viking and punch him in the arm. Hard enough to let him know I'm not playing. "If you know something you better start fucking talking." I warn him.

"Bro, this relationship shit is between you and Vanna. I'm not getting in the middle of this crazy shit." He says, catching his breath and taking another swig of beer.

Vanna stops laughing to point up into the fucking air at nothing. "Listen!" She says, "It's another Dean song!"

Paula Abdul's *Straight Up*, is playing over the sound system now. Another song I'm taking as a Player dig again.

I glare at Viking. "You realize you started this bullshit with your fucking jukebox antics last night, right?"

He presses his lips together for a moment, in an attempt not to laugh again. "This is why I hit it and quit it, Bro. Bitches be crazy."

"I wish they'd play Dean's *favorite song*." Vanna taunts, glaring at me again.

"And what song might that be, Vanna?" I ask, trying to tamper down my aggravation.

"You don't know?" She asks. I don't say anything. I'm trying not to glare back at her. "Maybe you're sick of it, after hearing it so much."

"Vanna... enough with the cryptic bullshit, and just tell me what the fuck you *think* I did."

"I'll give you a hint... It's about a couple who are toxic for each other, but they can't give each other up. They can't walk away from each other."

"Give me your keys, we're going." I say, holding my hand out to her. I'm over the games.

"No. You're not the boss of me." She says, shifting her body sideways, as if she wants to keep that right pocket of her jeans away from me. That's the first place I'll check when I get the chance to grab them.

"You can't drive yourself home in this condition, regardless of how you feel about me right now, Vanna. Or what you think I did. I've been loyal to you the entire four months and counting that we've been seeing each other."

"I love the way you lie."

"I'm not fucking lying to you, Vanna."

"Your ringtone, asshole!" She snaps at me.

At least that much clicks, now. *Love The Way You Lie* is Lucinda's ringtone, but what does Lucinda have to do with this fucked up situation? I stare at her, waiting for her to elaborate. She doesn't say anything, until she turns to Latisha and hugs her friend. "I'm gonna go. Thanks for hanging out with me." Latisha hugs her back, telling her to feel better and to call her soon.

I look at Viking. "Make sure she gets home safe." I say, pointing to Latisha. "This is Derek's little sister. Don't fucking forget that." I warn him. Derek is a good junior mechanic, and without him working for me, I'd have less free time, which I don't have an abundance of to begin with. Viking nods.

Vanna slides off the bar stool and tries to storm past me again, but I grab her arm and walk out of the bar with her. Once we're outside, I ask her where she parked her car. She indicates that she had to park a few blocks down the street to the right.My aggravation kicks up a few notches at her reply. This isn't the safest neighborhood, and the thought of her walking to her car, alone, in the dark, late at night and possibly drunk, pisses me off.

"So, what was your master plan, doll?" I ask her, as we walk down the sidewalk in the direction of her car. "Get wasted, drive your car and wrap it around a tree on the way home?"

"I wasn't going to leave until I was okay to drive. I only tried to order another drink because you and your sidekick showed up. Besides, I could have called a cab."

"This isn't a great neighborhood at night, Vanna." I sigh. "You could have gotten mugged, or worse."

She scoffs. "I walked back to put my purse in my car and nothing happened to me."

"You're fucking lucky. And let's hope your car window isn't smashed out and your purse is still in there."

"I shoved it under my seat. Nobody can see it if they look in my car." She says, clearly still annoyed with me.

As we approach an alley between two buildings, I can hear a hushed conversation between men in the dark, and wrap my arm around her, keeping her close to me. Tonight, is not the night to fuck with me or my woman. I will lay a dreg the fuck out if they're stupid enough to look for trouble in our direction. She's got me that heated. We make it to her car without any issues.

"Keys." I say to her again. She turns with her back to the passenger side door and leans against it, arms crossed as she stares down at the sidewalk. Suddenly she doesn't seem as angry as she was in the bar, and I take the opportunity. "Talk to me." I try again.

"I ran into Vixie today." her voice quiet, almost defeated sounding. "At the grocery store."

"Was she mean to you again?"

"She called me a bitch. I called her a whore."

"What brought this on?"

Vanna shrugs slightly. "I told Lucinda she's an Adulterer who is going to burn in Hell right alongside us Witches."

Wait... Fucking rewind. "*Lucinda*?" I sound shocked, even to myself.

Vanna nods. "Yeah. She was with Vixie. Apparently, they're quite close."

"Jesus fuck, Vanna. Why didn't you tell me?" Of course, this whole thing would be Lucinda related. And fuckin' Vixie's bullshit makes sense now. I run my hand through my hair, then grip the back of my neck. I can only imagine what the fuck Lucinda could have said to Vanna. I know it's nothing good.

"I brought you lunch today. I was going to tell you what happened. But then I walked in on your conversation with Viking." She says, finally lifting her eyes to look at me. They look so glassy and sad now... "She's really pretty. I can see why you had to have her. How she's the hottest woman in ten counties... or whatever Viking said."

I reach out to touch her face. "Baby, she's got nothing on you, I swear. You're so-" I try to tell her she's so beautiful, in so many more ways than Lucinda ever was or could ever hope to be. But Vanna pulls away from my touch, twisting to lean against the car on her side, and brings both of her hands up to cover her face. A slight sob escapes her.

Fuck. She's crying... "Baby, please. What is it?" I ask, stepping closer to her to rub her back. Why is it, whenever I try to compliment her, it goes so fucking south? Most women I've known fish for compliments. Vanna is the complete opposite. It's as if compliments *hurt* her, and I don't understand. "Vanna?" I wrap my arms around her gently, holding her to my chest. I'm relieved that she lets me, resting my chin on the top of her head, I stroke her hair. "What did Lucinda say to you, baby?"

"She said she'd pray for me because I was doing the Devil's work." She says on a quivering breath. "She said it loud, so the cashiers and other shoppers heard her."

Fucking spiteful bitch. Pressing a kiss to Vanna's head, I say on a sigh, "I'm sorry, doll."

She sniffles and moves in my arms to lean back and look up at me. Her glassy eyes, tear streaked cheeks and wet lashes tug at my heart. "Has she spoken to you about wanting to meet me?" Vanna asks, her eyes searching mine for truth. I can't lie to her.

"Yes. But I told her I didn't want her anywhere near you."

Something flashes in Vanna's eyes. Some kind of realization that seems to harden her slightly, once more. She reaches up to brush the tears from her cheeks, then reaches into her pocket and hands me the keys. "I want to go home." She nearly whispers.

I beep the car unlocked and hold the door open for her as she climbs in. Once she's safe inside, I shut the door and get in on the driver's side to take her home. My mind races with all the possibilities of what else Lucinda could have said to Vanna, as I drive her home in her car. I'm honestly afraid to even ask. There's so much shit she could say to tarnish me in Vanna's eyes. But I know I need to know what was said, so I can fix this situation with her.

"You awake, baby?" I finally ask after a while, glancing over at her. She's curled towards the passenger side door, her head leaning against the side of the seat away from me. She gives me an affirmative little mumble. "What else did Lucinda say?" I ask. All that I'm a Player bullshit in the bar has me wondering if Lucinda flat out lied and told Vanna we're still fucking. I haven't touched that bitch in almost a year. And even then, I didn't want to.

"She wanted me to go to lunch with her." Vanna says, sleepily and quietly, to the point where I have to make a real effort to hear her. That would be bad for me on an epic scale. "I turned her down, though." Vanna yawns. "I wouldn't go behind your back like that." I suddenly feel a fresh wave of guilt about the file on her locked in my bottom desk drawer at the shop.

"Thank you... What's with the Heartbreaker shit?"

"I heard Viking say something about the hundreds of girls you've slept with trying to get over her."

"Fuck." I let the word out on a sigh. "Vanna..." I don't even know what to say about it.

"It's okay... I *don't* want to hear about it. And I *don't* want to know if I work with any of them. I don't want to know anything about any of it." Her voice is tight and has a slight tremble in it.

The thought of her being disgusted with me churns my insides. How could she not be? "Doll... I was in a real bad way..." I try to begin.

"Dean, please." She whispers. "If I have to hear it again, how many women you've been with... especially from you... And how *in love* with her you were... or *are-*"

"I'm not in love with her... Vanna... sometimes I fucking hate her."

"There's a thin line between love and hate."

389

"There's no line. There's hate. I fucking hate her." I insist. "I say some-times, because I don't want you to think I'm cold enough to truly hate. But I am. I'm capable of that kind of cold. And I hate her."

"Because you loved her so much." I can hear the tightness in her voice again.

"Years ago, I thought so." I sigh. "I've long since moved on."

She doesn't respond to my statement. I drive in another stint of silence towards her home. Both of us alone with our thoughts, together.

I pull into her driveway all too soon, not ready to part ways with her for the night. There's still so much unresolved between us. I put her car in park at the top of her driveway and kill the engine, pulling her keys free of the ignition.

Sitting back against the driver's seat, I look over at her. She hasn't moved from that curled up position, and I realize she's fallen asleep. She looks so peaceful, almost cherubic. Beautiful and innocent. Her lips slightly parted, her long, dark lashes against her pale cheeks. I hope her mind is at ease. That if she's dreaming right now, it's pleasant. I hate to wake her up, but I know she's better off inside her house, in her bed, than in her little car.

I reach over to gently rub her back, stirring her. "Vanna, you're home." She blinks her eyes awake, then stretches with a yawn and unbuckles her seatbelt. "Which seat is your purse under?" I ask, leaning back and glanc-ing in the back of her car.

"Mine." She answers groggily.

I reach under the back of her seat, feeling for the purse and grabbing it when I do. As I'm about to lift it over to hand it to her, I spot something on her back seat.

A cigarette... Vanna doesn't smoke. Neither do I. And neither does Latisha.

Handing her the purse, I wait for her to start getting out of the car before I reach in the backseat and grab it, tucking it into my jacket pocket before I get out of the car as well.

"Did you walk to your car alone when you decided to put your purse under the seat?" I ask, walking her to her door.

"Yes." She says, fumbling with her keys.

"You had a lot of eyes on you tonight in that bar." I mutter.

"Don't worry. Your fan club is bigger." She says, sarcastically, pulling open her screen door and sliding the key into the dead bolt.

"Were you with another guy tonight, Vanna?"

She turns to look at me, a mixture of what looks like surprise and anger. "Why would you even ask me that?" she snaps. "Because guys were looking at me? You've got some nerve. I'm not the one who can fill an arena with all of their one-night stands!"

"I've been loyal to you... When I told you that earlier, you called me a liar."

"Because you're still talking to your ex-wife all the time! You still have a relationship with her! She told me in the grocery store! Called you *Our Dean...*" The words spill out of her again like a torrent. "I guess it's a *biker MC thing* to juggle multiple women, but I'm not into that, sorry. I'm not a patch whore. And don't bother trying to tell me otherwise, you already ad-mitted you talk about me with your precious Lucinda!"

"Whoa... hold up there a minute, doll." I say, pushing the screen door away from her. I grab her and pull her back to me before she gets inside and slams the door in my face. She's already got it unlocked when I do.

"Don't *doll* me!" she says, trying to turn from me to get the screen door open again. "You've got some nerve trying to accuse me of what you've been doing!"

"And just what have I been doing, exactly? You think I'm fucking Lucinda behind your back? I'd rather stick my dick in a meat grinder than go near that snatch again."

"Well, you're sticking it somewhere! You think I don't hear that loud fucking bike late at night when you go out? Serene is the perfect wingman, isn't she?"

"You're fucking serious, aren't you?" I ask, half pissed off, half in disbelief of what I'm hearing right now.

"Guilty conscience?" she sneers with an inquisitive tone. "Over four months we've been seeing each other. And I'm supposed to believe someone *like you*, with your *track record*, your *life style*, hasn't fucked *anyone* in that time? Because you aren't fucking me! And for some reason, *you don't want to!* You're obviously getting it elsewhere. You don't go from the numbers and frequency Viking was talking about, to *nothing*. Where else are you randomly going late at night?"

"You want it that bad, baby, all you have to do is say so." I try to keep the anger out of my voice. But even as the words leave my mouth, I don't mean them. I love her too much for our first time to happen in anger. For it to be when she's fucking drunk. I stand by what I said. I ain't fucking her.

She tries to shove me away. "We already played that game. A few times. And you flat out told me you aren't going to sleep with me."

I let out a long, exasperated sigh. I'm too pissed off to give her my heartfelt confession about that. About everything. I'm going to fuck it up if I do, and I don't want to fuck it up. Tonight, has been all kinds of fucked up already. And even though she's got me royally pissed off right now, Vanna deserves all the best I can ever give her.

Taking my hands off of her, I step back from her, shaking my head. "Go to bed, Vanna. You're drunk."

She glares at me one last time tonight, before she steps inside her house and slams the door in my face.

I wait until I hear the deadbolt slide into place, before I start walking home.

Chapter
seventeen

ONDAYS AT LAURA'S SHOP ARE USUALLY the slowest day of the week. Which sucks. Because I could use the distraction after the horrible weekend I just had. Not to mention, today is Johnathan Nero's memorial and funeral service, which has had me on edge all day. I know his son can't get to me, but the thought of *Him* being out of prison, even in shackles, even with guards, is unnerving to me. I have no idea what span of time he will actually be allowed out to attend his father's funeral, or when he will be returned to his cell. I imagine by night fall, he will be back in prison. Maybe I'll be able to calm down a little by tonight.

The other situation plaguing my mind is how I left things with Dean. On a hostile note, late Saturday night. And neither one of us reached out to the other yesterday. Sunday. *Our* day.

I thought about texting Dean that I was sorry, several times throughout the day. I didn't tell him where I was Saturday night, because I didn't want to get into anything with him, especially not after having a few drinks. I'm not even sure if I remember everything I said that night, but I know it wasn't good. It couldn't have been. I wasn't expecting him to show up to the bar. Especially not with his jerk best friend, *Viking*. He should change his name to Caveman. It's better suited. Vikings actually had some level of respect for their women. He might look like one, but he plays the part of the other so much better.

For a majority of the day, I busy myself with reorganizing merchandise and dusting. Sweeping the floors and the front porch and steps. Anything to keep myself as preoccupied as possible. Willing the hours to pass. Laura's busy with quite a few tarot reading appointments today, and has spent a majority of the day upstairs.

I'm in the back breakroom, slash, storage room, making another pot of coffee for Laura, when my cellphone chimes. Fishing it out of my purse from the cubby I usually jam it in for the day, I see that it's a text from my mother.

Last time we spoke, I hung up on her. Since I don't have to actually speak to her, I go ahead and open the text.

It's a photo of flowers in a vase. A funeral arrangement. The text accompanied by the photo reads, *"Since you're not here, we took the liberty of having a sympathy arrangement sent in your name."*

You've got to be kidding me... I use my fingers on my cellphone screen to enlarge the photo, trying to see the card attached to the flowers. Sure enough, written in my own mother's hand, the card reads, *"My deepest condolences to you and your family. All my love, Giovanna."*

All my love... to that monster... I could scream at her!

I'm in the process of texting her back *How dare you*, when my cellphone rings in my hands. It's my mother. I answer it in anger.

"How could you do that? You have no right to speak for me! Especially not when it comes to-" I begin to unleash on her, when I hear what sounds like a man clearing his throat on the other end of the line. I pause. "Dad?"

"No... It's *me*, sweetheart. Your lovely mother let me use her phone."

My skin crawl and I feel cold all over, frozen in place. Completely stunned. I haven't heard *His* voice in over three years, but I'd recognize it anywhere. And though he's speaking sweetly, because I'm sure my mother is right there with him, I can still detect the underlying hate in his words.

"It's so good to hear your voice, Giovanna... my love. I've missed you so much."

"Oh my god..." is all I can manage to whisper. I hear him almost growl an "mmmm" through the phone, as he relishes the fear in my voice. It's even more unnerving.

"I have a surprise for you... Where are you, my darling? I'm getting warmer. Can you feel me?"

That jolts me, snapping me out of my frozen state. I jerk the phone from my ear and hang up on him. A moment later, before I can even take a breath, the phone is ringing again. My mother's number. Only I know it's *Him*.

I hit ignore call, but I'm aware, this isn't going to stop. My cell phone chimes with a text, and I glance down to look. Of course, it's from my mother's phone. Though, she isn't the one who wrote it.

"You cost me three years with my father. Now he's gone. But don't worry, my darling. I will forgive you."

Will forgive me... After what? I don't even want to imagine... I need to cut this channel now. I can't have him calling me from prison now that he's seen my number. Having people call me and harass me, as well. My family has proven time and again, they believe his version of events over mine.

With trembling hands, I dial my network provider, and request to have my phone number changed, due to harassing calls. They process the number change right away, instructing me to restart my phone once our call ends. I jot my new number down on an old piece of mail I spot on the table beside me, before I hang up with the representative.

Shutting my cellphone down to restart it and activate the new number, I attempt to regain my composure.

I remind myself again, he's more than six hundred miles away from me right now. He's with guards. He's going back to prison for at least another two years. He cannot get to me now. He cannot get to me tomorrow. For the time being, I'm safe...

But he did get to me. And he knows it.

I hear the bells on the front door of the shop jingle.

I'm still shaking when I force myself to smile and walk out of the break room.

M ARLBORO REDS. THAT'S WHAT THE FUCKER SMOKES WHO WAS IN Vanna's car. The back seat, no less...

I'm sitting at the bar in my empty roadhouse. Elbows on the polished counter top. Twisting and rolling this fucking cigarette in my fingers in front of my face, as I stare at it and think about Saturday night. I was hoping Vanna would have called or texted me Sunday, but she didn't. I didn't either, only because I figured she needed some time to cool off. And I didn't think attempting to have another conversation with her while she was suffering a hangover, would work in my favor.

She said nobody from the bar she was at walked her to her car. That she wasn't with another guy. There's a slight chance this fucking cigarette could belong to Laura. They could have taken Vanna's car together to lunch or something. Maybe I shouldn't have jumped the gun on asking Vanna about another guy. Especially since it reinforced her insane suspicion that I'm fucking around on her, my guilty conscience that made me ask her about other men.

I'm tempted to crush the fucking cigarette between my fingers, just because I'm pissed off. I want to wreck something, but I know I won't derive a sliver of satisfaction from it. I need something more to burn off this rage. And I know where to get it. Monday nights are newbie nights, in the underground fighting circuit in Wilmington. The chance of possibly fighting a new guy with some skills, is tempting. Besides, my gut tells me this isn't Laura's brand. This is a guy's cigarette. I can fucking feel it.

The steel front door opens to my right, a flash of sun light bursting through into the semi dark and vacant room. I only bothered to turn on the lights on the back bar. The space behind me is black.

"What are you doing sitting alone in the dark?" Viking asks, shutting the door with a clang, before he walks up to me. He slaps down two bags of food from a local burger joint on the bar and sits on a stool beside me.

"Thinking." I mutter.

"About taking up smoking?" He asks. I shake my head. "Your body is a temple, Bro. Don't do it." He jests, pulling out a few burgers and a couple of boxes of fries out of the bags. "You hungry?" he slides a burger towards me.

"No, thanks."

"You on the outs with Vanna still?" he asks. I can hear him unwrapping a burger and shoving half of it in his mouth.

I don't bother responding to that question. It's obvious at this point. I'm only happy when she and I are happy. I'm well aware of the miserable prick I am when we're on the outs.

"What the fuck was with you two Saturday night?" I ask him. I haven't seen much of Viking since that night. "You've made yourself oddly scarce the last two days."

"Went to visit my folks estate up in Cary. Been a while." Viking says. "And nothing is going on with me and Vanna, Bro. Pretty sure she hates me."

"She thinks *you* hate *her*." I say, twisting around in my seat so that I can look him in the face. "Why would she think that?"

Viking shrugs. "Maybe because you treat her like a fragile little princess and I don't." He says, then shoves a fist full of fries in his mouth.

I wait for him to finish chewing before I ask, "You got some animosity towards her for some reason?"

"Animosity is a very strong word, Bro."

"Then why don't you tell me what the fuck you'd call it." I say, trying to conceal my own animosity.

Viking stares back at me for a moment, and I can tell he's trying to read me. Gauge my level of anger. "Did she say something to you about me?" he finally asks.

"No." I say, laying my arm down on the bar counter and gently rolling the cigarette back and forth with the tips of my fingers. "Not to me. Latisha said Vanna told her she thinks you hate her."

He nods. "You gonna rip my head off if I tell you the truth?"

"I'll try not to."

Viking chuckles. "I don't hate Vanna, Bro. I just hate seeing you this miserable."

"Vanna doesn't make me miserable. Not being with Vanna, makes me miserable." I correct him.

He nods again, as if he's considering my words. "You took a nose dive for this woman, Dean. Faster than even Lucinda back in the day. I'm just concerned for my best friend. That was a dark time, and you only just started to bounce back before you met Vanna. She isn't like any of the chicks that hang around us. It's not that I don't like her... I just don't know enough about her, yet. I don't really have an opinion either way."

"Fair enough." I sigh, feeling a little sorry for Vanna. No wonder she feels uncomfortable around my crew. Not only is she an outsider to this life style, but the closest people around me haven't taken to her.

"And just so you know, that whole jukebox thing, I was more so fucking with *you* than I was with her." He adds.

"Funny." I mutter, stoically. "She's right. You are a fucking asshole."

Speaking with his mouth full, he says something that sounds like a muffled, "I never denied that." He hasn't. Viking wear's that title like a badge of honor. A loud and proud asshole. "Not to pile it on or anything," Viking begins to say, when I give him a wry look.

"Oh, really? Because the last fifteen years or so I've known you, that really seems to be one of your fucking specialties."

He grins back at me. "Well, I'm one of those things in life that will make you stronger if I don't kill you first." He chuckles. That's actually a fair assessment. "If I'm your Sergeant at Arms, you're going to have to start taking my concerns seriously."

"And I suppose you have concerns over Vanna." I saw this shit coming.

"She's a spitfire under that sweet exterior. I got a kick out of that temper the other night." Viking grins. "She gives as good as she gets, you know. But no, I don't think Vanna is a danger to the club, in and of herself. I think she's a major distraction to you. And with what we've got coming up for the Saviors MC, gotta admit, Bro... You can't be distracted."

I nod. "Guess it's a good thing I'm a multitasker. I eat duty for breakfast, remember?"

"That's the fucking truth." He chuckles, before he pauses to look at me once more. "But I'm serious, Dean. If you can't work it out with her, you gotta let it go. Gotta let her go."

I feel those words stab me like a dagger in the gut. I know he's right. The thought of not being able to work it out with Vanna... Not make it to a place with her, where we're both happy and content, *together*... Hurts to even think about. For me, it's not an option. There's only her.

"And I don't want to watch you go to war with yourself over it." Viking sighs. "If you can't do what you have to do, regarding her, I'll have to do it for you. For your sake. And the sake of the club."

For what feels like a long time, we sit in silence as his words hang between us. I love my MC family. I love Viking more than my own blood brother, but this would tear something between us that I know would never

397

mend. Tucking the cigarette back into my jacket pocket, I get up from the bar and start walking towards the front door.

Viking attempts to stop me, placing his hand on my shoulder. "Bro, that day isn't today." He sighs, as if I should find that reassuring. Somehow be comforted by the fact that he has no immediate plans today to run Vanna off... Out of my life.

"That day isn't for *you* to decide." I growl. "*Ever.*"

"I'd talk to you, first, Dean. I'd never try to hurt you, Bro." there's sympathy in his sigh.

Just thinking about this scenario, hurts. I really don't have anything to say to him, now. Except maybe that it would be in his best interest to get his fucking hand off me. He seems to sense that on his own, though.

"I'm just saying, I'll do it for you, if you can't."

"Then this is a conversation that will never fucking come up again. You're over stepping, *Brother.*"

The bright sun has me scowling as I cross the lot to my shop. Though, even if it was night out, I'd probably still be scowling. If I thought I was in a shit mood before Viking showed up, I'm about to be Hell on two wheels now.

Pulling my motorcycle keys out of my pocket, I approach my girl, Serene. Grabbing my helmet and shades from her side bag, I slap them on before I straddle her and bring her to life beneath me. The rumbling of her mufflers and roar of her engine, send a soothing sensation through my body as I twist her throttle and kick up her stand. We cruise out of the lot, into the city streets, and she takes me where I need to be.

Across the street from the old Victorian house that serves as Vanna's witch shop, there's a huge brick church with a parking lot shaded by Willow trees. As I park Serene and shut her down, I hear the hand on the large clock tower of the church move to strike the hour with a heavy clunk. The bell slowly chimes twice a few seconds after. I can feel the vibration in my chest cavity as it rings out loudly across the entire area. Sticking a finger in my ear, I jiggle the ringing of my ear drum away, glad I didn't decide to show up at twelve o' clock. Next time I stalk my woman, I'll be sure not to sit directly under the fucking clock tower.

Two o'clock seems to be the ticket though, because Vanna's *boss friend* is exiting the parking lot in her little black Jetta, and it doesn't appear as if her coworker is working today. There aren't any other cars in the parking lot, either. I guess it's a slow day for her.

Pulling out my cell phone, I decide to text her a heads up that I'll be there in a few minutes. She's not expecting me. And I'm not so sure I'm going to be a very welcome surprise.

The text bounces back as undeliverable. That's odd. I hit resend and get the same result. *What the fuck?* There's no way she changed her fuckin' number on me... is there? I immediately hit call, and put the phone to my ear.

"*We're sorry, but the number you've dialed has been changed or is no longer in service...*"

Hanging up, I shove the phone in my pocket and dismount Serene. Fuck that bullshit. Removing my helmet and shades, I tuck them back in her side bag and head towards the street, looking both ways as I jog across. I make my way up the sidewalk towards the rainbow painted steps of the witch shop, staring through the big picture window in the front. She must be in the back, or upstairs in her Reiki room.

Pausing for a moment, hand on the door knob, I ready myself for part two of the riot act, written and performed by the one and only, Giovanna...

The little bells hanging on the door jingle, announcing my arrival as I step inside and close the door behind me. I hear her boots on the wooden floor as she heads in my direction, turning the corner, her eyes are cast down at the several books she's got in her arms. Before she even realizes that it's me standing between the two white columns in the entry way of the foyer. Several emotions flitter across her expression.

First, a friendly, but blank smile, that I'm sure is a force of habit when greeting customers all day, and an almost robotic greeting of "Welcome to The Ametrine Cauldron." As she enters the main display room, her eyes lift to meet mine. I see her expression change to one of recognition, then surprise... then what looks like, relief?

That look in her eyes... almost a rueful kind of relief. It only lasts but a few fleeting seconds, before that fake smile fades. The books drop to the floor with a loud thud that makes these old floor boards beneath the large area rug nearly jump.

I clear my throat. "You know, for a second there, I thought you looked relieved to see me."

"Why are you here?" Her expression now as stoic as I'm pretending to be.

"Why else, Vanna? I'm certainly not in the market for dick candles." I can tell she's trying to suppress a slight smile. And though I know she's still pissed at me, I'm elated at that small sign that I can still reach her. "Why did you change your number on me?"

She shakes her head. "I didn't. I mean, I did change it... But not because of you." Another wave of relief rolls through me. But I don't respond. I wait for her to elaborate. "I just keep getting these relentless robo calls... Telemarketers... You know? Anyway, it was driving me crazy. I just changed it not even that long ago. I was going to text you today... So, you'd have my new number."

As she moves to pick the books up off the floor, I move faster, stepping forward quickly and crouching to collect them at her feet. Standing up with the books neatly stacked in my hands, I ask her where she'd like them. She gestures to the disorganized desk to my right, in front of the big bay window.

"Anywhere on Laura's messy desk."

I chose a somewhat level spot on top of some printed calendars, and place the stack down on top of them. "What time will Laura be back?"

"She won't be. She wasn't feeling well." Vanna says, crossing her arms as if she's uncomfortable. "I'm running the shop by myself for the rest of the day."

Aces. "Maybe we can talk a little bit about what happened this past weekend?" I lean back on Laura's desk, crossing my own arms.

"Not here." She shakes her head. "I'm supposed to be working."

"We're the only two here." I point out.

"I have a customer coming any minute to pick up an order." Vanna insists. "I'd rather not get into this mess here."

I nod in reluctant understanding and glance down at my boots. From the corner of my eye, I spot a small trash bin to my left, beside the desk. I wonder if there might be a discarded cigarette pack, or two, in there. Vanna has mentioned that her boss is a bit of a chain smoker. Perhaps I'll be able to confirm or deny my suspicion.

"Well then, can I at least ask you how you are?" I say, shifting my focus back to Vanna. She's still standing in the middle of the room, looking as though she feels rather awkward.

"Alright, I suppose. All things considered." She sighs. "You?"

"Miserable. Can't you tell?"

"I know I behaved terribly. I don't usually get like that." She insists, and I can hear an honest level of remorse in her words. But then her brows furrow slightly. "You weren't supposed to be there, though. I was just hanging out with a friend."

"Well, I'm glad I spoiled your fun. What I walked in on was unacceptable." I say, sternly. If I'm going to make her my Ol' Lady someday, she can't be running off on me like this. Blowing me off and dancing for other men to fuckin' drool over... Fuck no.

Her eyes widen for a moment, before they narrow at me. "*Unacceptable?* Who do you think you are?" she demands, then continues without letting me answer that question. "You don't own me. I'm not your patch whore. I don't wear your leather brand on my back. I swear, that night you reminded me of Viking. Bulldozing in there and yanking me off the dance floor. Then have the absolute nerve to ask me if *I* was with another man! How dare you?"

The cigarette in my pocket feels like it lit itself, that's how badly I want to bring it up right now. I lower my gaze from her, glancing back down at that trash bin to my left. I want to press her on this, but I need to make damn certain that Laura isn't a Marlboro smoker before I step back into this ring with her. I notice a lighter on the edge of the desk...

Uncrossing my arms, I place my hands on Laura's desk, at my sides, letting my left hand *accidentally* knock that fucker off the edge.

Bullseye.

We both heard it land in the trash bin. So, I move to retrieve it. That's the right thing to do, isn't it? And it could have slid to the bottom of the bin, couldn't it have? I might have to fish around for it... My jaw tenses though, as I shove a few crumpled wads of paper aside to reveal not only the lighter, but a crushed pack of *Virginia Slims*... I straighten back up, tossing the lighter back onto Laura's disaster zone of a desk.

"Everything about this weekend was unacceptable, Vanna. I never say anything I don't mean. Especially to you. I wish you'd remember that... I wish you'd believe me." I back up from the desk to lean against one of the white columns near the foyer and look at her. "I want us to work, baby. More than you seem to know."

"Then maybe you should run that by *Lucinda*." She scowls at me. I watch as her eyes suddenly dart towards the front bay window, then back to me, her expression changing from one of annoyance, to concern. "They're here." She says, dropping her arms, her hands nervously smoothing out her skirt. "Please, don't make a scene." As if I'd ever do anything to cost her her job. Sometimes it feels like she doesn't trust me at all.

I don't say anything. I don't take my eyes off of her, though. I hear the door open, the bells jingle, then the door shut. Footsteps walking up behind me, then around to my side, as a man steps into the main room with us. My eyes shift from Vanna, to him. He looks real happy to see her. And I just fuckin' bet he is.

"Hi Paul," she says to him, with her *work smile*. Acting pleasant as pie.

Paul walks right up to her, arms open, giving me a quick look as he wraps his arms around *my woman*... For a *not quite quick enough* hug.

I actually suppress what would have been an audible reaction... One more second of this *friendly embrace*, and I'm going to rip him the fuck off her, and toss his narrow ass down that rainbow stoop.

Vanna takes a step back from him, ending their little hug session, but she continues to smile back at him. "Your package is in the back. I'll go get it for you." She says, and turns to walk back towards the far end of the shop.

I watch her go. Leaning forward and making it obvious to *Paul* here, that I am blatantly admiring the sway of her ass in that lacey, curve accentuating, Stevie Nicks looking dress she's got on. When Vanna's out of sight, I shift my focus back to Paul, looking him up and down for a few moments. I want to make it weird for him. Make it awkward and uncomfortable. Slowly taking in his beige fuckin' cargo shorts. His tan-colored sandals and odd textured button down short sleeved shirt. The fuck is that even made of? Hemp? Fuckin' hippie. He's probably a damn vegan too. Skinny fucker.

"You smoke?" I ask, after a moment. Though, I seriously doubt it. The question probably even offends him. Bet he drives a fuckin' Prius. I laugh inwardly at him.

"No." he says, looking at me as if I'm out of place here. Hell, I guess I am, in some ways. What he doesn't realize though, is that my place is wherever Vanna's at.

I adjust the cuff of my leather jacket with a slight grin as he looks me over. No fucking way Vanna's into this type of dude. Not if she's into me. He still needs to hurry up and get the fuck out of here.

"You need help back there, baby?" I call back to her, not so subtly marking my territory all over her. *Paul* looks away from me, and I watch him shift in his sandals uncomfortably.

Vanna returns a moment later with a medium sized box in her arms and hands it over to him. "There you go," she smiles at him again. "I put in a few extra incense boxes for you."

"Thanks, Vanna. See you..." Paul begins to say, shooting me a quick glance. "Next time."

I push myself off the column and take a few steps towards the front door. Grabbing the doorknob and pulling it open, I make sure the bells on the door jingle loudly to get his attention.

"Allow me, bro. That box looks heavy for you." I dig at him.

"It isn't." he says, turning from Vanna to head towards the door to leave.

"Must be dick candles, then." I grin. We glare at each other briefly as he exits. I slam the door behind him and twist the dead bolt.

"Dean... You can't lock the door." Vanna sighs, arms crossed again.

I flip the blue Open sign over to Closed, and step back into the main room with her. "So, where were we?"

She frowns. "You were about to give Lucinda a call."

"Vanna, I haven't given Lucinda a call since long before we met."

"She said you've talked to her, about her and I meeting. You admitted that, too. You can't backpedal now."

"Baby, Lucinda is a master manipulator. She phrased what she said in a way that would make you believe there was more going on between she and I. She knew you would ask me, and that I wouldn't lie to you. She knew, by me admitting that she mentioned meeting you, that it would appear that we talk more often than we do." I try to explain. "There is nothing... *Nothing!* Going on between Lucinda and I. I promise you."

Vanna doesn't say anything. She's just staring at me. I hope taking in my words and finding truth in them for herself. Jamming my thumbs in my pockets, I wait for her to say something. Hoping her silence bodes well for me.

Our silent standoff is interrupted by the distinct sound of a roaring set of dual header straight pipes. So loud, they rattle the glass in the wood pane windows of this old Victorian house. I only know one rider, with a custom set of aftermarket exhaust pipes, *this* obnoxiously loud, on his Harley Davidson Fat Boy... I groan and squeeze my eyes shut, letting my head fall back as I run my hand through my hair, and wish to whatever the fuck higher power is out there, that this isn't happening right now. But it is. And I'm not wrong. I did the fucking custom upgrades on his damn motor and exhaust system myself... It's Viking. On his Iron Horse.

Fuck me...

Within moments, his heavy boots are stomping up the front steps.

Opening my eyes, looking back at Vanna, she's even more livid with me now. I just shake my head. I can't even get the words out that I have nothing to do with Viking showing up here at her day job. Taking a few steps backwards, I unlock the front door and reluctantly let him in, glaring at him as he crosses the threshold. He looks back at me, before he shifts his gaze to Vanna.

"I guess my timing sucks." He jokes.

"Well, you suck in general, so yeah. I guess your timing would, too." Vanna mutters.

He nods, grinning slightly. "Okay, I deserved that." He says, patting my shoulder, almost gingerly, as he walks further into the room towards Vanna. He glances around at the witchy oddities around the shop for a moment, but brings his focus back to her.

"Tried calling you, 'bout an hour ago." He says to her. "You change your number on us, Vanna?"

She sighs with annoyance. "It had nothing to do with you two assholes."

He nods. "That's a relief. Honestly." He says, then turns to look at me. "I figured you'd be here, after we spoke earlier."

"Yeah. I meant what I said to you." I warn him.

"I know. But I came here to talk to Vanna, whether you were here or not." Viking says.

"So, I'm supposed to believe you two jerks didn't coordinate this?" Vanna asks.

I don't bother saying anything. I just hook my thumbs back in my pockets and brace for whatever's coming next.

"Dean didn't know anything about me coming here, Vanna." Viking says. "I tried calling you, because I wanted to talk to you about a few things. Then, when I thought you changed your number to cut Dean out of your life, I realized a phone call wasn't sufficient, anyway."

Vanna doesn't say anything, she just continues to stare up at him, with an almost impassive expression. *Almost...* But there's something in her eyes. Something that looks like she's more afraid, than she is angry, now. I can't help but wonder why. Her fear makes me draw nearer to her. My over protective instincts kicking in. Placing myself between her and whatever she's afraid of. Even if it's only Viking's words. I know she thinks he hates her. Maybe she thinks he's here to tell her off. Though, I know he isn't. If he was going to pull a stunt like that, I'd break his jaw in front of her.

His eyes shift to me as I come to stand by her side, and I know he can read my silent warning. He's familiar with my level of crazy.

"I know I crossed some lines. And I realize I may have made you feel like more of an outsider than I actually intended to." He sighs. I shift my focus to study her expression. Now that I know he's actually here to attempt to help the situation, for a change. "I said some shit just to piss you off, darlin'. It's kind of my thing."

"I noticed." She says.

"Anyway, I don't hate you. I thought you should know that directly from me. I'm not deliberately being a dick to you."

"So, what you said the other night in the bar was just to get under my skin? It isn't true?" she asks. Vanna glances at me for a moment, before she looks back to him for an answer. Viking doesn't say anything. His expression has gone a little imperturbable. "Well, is it true or not?" she pushes.

"Which part?" he asks.

"Well, all of it, I guess." Vanna says with a shrug. "Since we're all here, might as well lay it all out, right?"

I try not to swallow too hard.

"Gonna have to be more specific." Viking says. At least he doesn't launch right into recklessly airing out my dirty laundry. He's smart enough to wait to see what she's actually fishing for.

"Do you two still *drink from the same bottle*?" she sneers at him, then shoots me a dirty look as well.

Fuck.

"No. And that was never an intentional thing, Vanna. We don't outright share women. We just happened to bang a few of the same club girls and hang arounds. Not at the same time, just, over time. And it was only a handful of chicks. Hell, some of these girls have been with *all* of us." Viking says, as if it's no big deal. He even gestures with his fucking finger, making a circular motion between us, as if to visually connect us all to this dirty little fact.

Vanna grimaces and shakes her head in disgust. "Do they get a *special patch* for that too?" she shoots me another damning look.

Viking cracks a grin. "No, but... that shit would be funny. I bet some of them would actually think it was pretty cool. Kinda like collecting baseball cards." He says, looking at me. "Or like O'Keefe's collection of four-leaf clover tattoos on his arm for all the fighters he's beaten." He says, smacking my arm as if he expects me to laugh with him about this.

The fuck I do. I'm not a complete moron. I'm silently debating with myself whether or not I should tell him to leave right now.

"Or, like the patches you earn in the girl scouts or boy scouts?" Vanna chimes in, I can tell the enthusiasm in her tone is not authentic at all. It's dripping with venomous sarcasm.

"Yeah, exactly." Viking grins. Fucking idiot. I just shake my head. I don't even know what to say right now.

"Wow." Vanna says. She looks back and forth at the both of us for a moment. "I guess you really are what you hang with." She sneers at me, before she storms over to the front door, flipping the sign back over to Open. "You two need to leave." She insists. "Now."

"Uhh... I wasn't saying that you were like those chicks, Vanna." Viking says. "Dean would never share you with anybody."

"No. No I'm not." She smiles at us both, but it's a pissed off smile. "And there's nothing to share. Is there?" she glares at me, pointedly.

"Jesus fuck, Vanna..." I really don't want to get into this *no sex thing* in front of Viking, who is now looking at me like I'm crazy.

"Just give her the *D*, Bro." he says, lightly nudging me with his arm.

I shove him back, pushing him in the direction of the door. "Just go, you've done enough." He humors me and lets me shove him towards the door, but only to a point. He anchors in right in front of where Vanna is standing by the door.

"I don't hate you." He says to her again. I can hear in his voice that he's being sincere.

Vanna is looking up at him, less anger in her eyes for a moment. "Okay."

"You two should just fuck and get it over with though. I'm telling you. It'll be better for everyone if you two just go at it. *Hard.*" Viking says, slamming a fist into his hand a few times to drive his point home. I shove him again, and the jerk side steps, flinging a massive arm around my neck, grabbing me in a choke hold.

"Don't force me to have to get out of this." I warn him, grabbing at his huge arm.

"Oh my god, don't break anything!" Vanna says, nervously.

"Like merchandise? *Or his neck?*" Viking jokes, as I struggle.

"Either!" Vanna almost shrieks.

Viking chuckles. "Aww, see? She cares about you, Bro." He says, bringing his other hand around to painfully grind his knuckles into the top of my skull. I check him in the gut hard enough to make him grunt, and he stops.

"You two need to leave." Vanna says again.

"I'll go, but *you two* need to work shit out." Viking says. "My Bro here is crazy about you, Vanna. He's an insufferable prick when you two aren't meshing."

Vanna doesn't say anything, and I can't see her face the way he's holding me in this fucking head lock. I've got an excellent view of her boots and the wooden floor planks, though.

"I'm not joking. I'm talking lost puppy, sad." Viking persists.

Still nothing from her.

"Tell her." Viking says, yanking me more upright, so that I can look her in the face at least. "Tell her what a miserable shit you are."

I can tell she's trying to stifle a laugh, by the way she bites her lip then brings her hand up to cover her mouth as she looks at me.

"I am." I mutter. "And I really can get out of this, I just don't want to risk breaking anything in your shop, either."

"He's just embarrassed." Viking fake whispers to her. "He can't get out of this."

"Right now, there's a lot he can't get out of." Vanna says, crossing her arms again. "Like the *friendzone*, for instance." She glares at me.

"Oh fuck, Bro." Viking laughs. "Vanna is a savage!"

I watch as her eyes shift back to Viking. "Was that other stuff true?"

His grip loosens on me, and I take the opportunity to shove his elbow up hard and slip out of his hold.

"I told you, baby... That's my past." I sigh, running my fingers through my hair to slick it back again after being disheveled by Viking's stunt.

"How recent?" she asks, looking at Viking first. Viking keeps his mouth shut. She looks back at me.

"Before I met you." I say.

405

"That's a bit vague." Her eyes narrow slightly. She looks back to Viking. "Was it really hundreds?"

"I mean... not *literally* hundreds." He shrugs. "Maybe like... a hundred... give or take."

I can tell she's still disturbed by that answer as her eyes shift back to mine.

"I'm gonna go, now." Viking says, pointing towards the door.

"Yeah, you fucking do that." I mutter. He pats me on the back and walks out, closing the door behind him.

Vanna and I don't say a word to each other for a few moments. Listening to his loud straight pipes roar outside as he pulls out of the lot and tears down the street.

"Does it really matter, Vanna?" I ask. "So, I have a past I'm not proud of. Are you really going to hold that against me?" God knows I've done a lot worse than sleep around with a bunch of random women. Mostly in a drunken stupor, at that. I don't even remember most of them.

She lets out a sigh. "No... But I'm supposed to believe that you stopped whoring around the moment you met me?"

"Vanna, I haven't been with anyone since I met you."

"When was the last time?"

I really don't know how this is going to go over, but I don't do dishonesty. "An hour before we met. I was with someone. It was nothing. She asked me to come back to her hotel room, after Derek's party. I didn't."

She looks a little stunned. "*An hour...*"

"It's the truth. I met you... Something between us just... *happened...* I can't explain it." I really can't. Since I laid eyes on Vanna, she's the only one I want. "And I even completely forgot to text her that night that I wasn't going back. I forgot she existed until damn near midday the next day. At that point, I didn't even bother texting her. I knew she already left town." That probably makes me sound like a jerk.

"That's so *sweet* of you." Her sarcasm almost stings.

I try not to glare at her. "Since we're on the topic, when was your last fuck?" I demand. If she tells me the backseat of her car Saturday night, I'm gonna fuckin' die. She looks slightly rattled by my tone, though. And now I regret even asking. Fuck. However, she looks me in the eyes and answers me.

"Over three years ago."

Well, damn... I didn't expect it to be *that* long... Am I a complete misogynist asshole for being more than *A Ok* with that stretch of time? Fuck... "Oh..."

"Yeah. *Oh...* You can go now." She pulls the door open.

I don't want to go now, damnit. We haven't resolved jack shit. "Vanna... Come on, doll. Talk to me. I can't fix this if you don't talk to me." Silence. Nothing but a glare from her. "Do you really believe I still have feelings for Lucinda? That I actually talk to her behind your back in any meaningful capacity?"

Her eyes narrow at me again. "Actually, yeah. I do, Dean. And you admitted it the other night. Why did I have to hear from her that you two were talking about she and I meeting? Why would that even come up in conversation between you two? Do you run your girlfriends by Lucinda first or something? Get your ex-wife's approval? Do you have to get her permission to sleep with them too? Is that why you wont?" she snaps at me.

"What? Fuck no." I say. "Vanna, this is crazy..."

"Yeah, it is. This whole situation is crazy. And I need to get back to work. So, go." I hesitate. She's got this all fucking wrong... "Go!" she shouts at me.

"Fine." I force myself to keep my cool. "You want your fucking space again? Have it! But this isn't over." I promise her. I'm barely out the door before she slams it shut behind me.

RINSING OFF THE LAST PLATE IN THE SINK, I PLACE IT IN THE DRAINING rack. The familiar roar of Dean's motorcycle in the distance as he fires it up for another evening ride, travels through my kitchen window.

He must be feeling just as restless as I have been, since our semi fight a few days ago at Laura's shop. I have yet to text him my new number. I just know, the moment I do, he's probably going to blow up my phone. Or, he won't... He could be just as angry with me now. Maybe he doesn't want to hear from me. I hate to admit to myself, I'm actually a little afraid to text him my number... and him not respond at all.

I wish silently to myself, that he will be safe and protected, though. These country roads at night are pitch black and dangerous. The only illumination from his headlights and the waxing moon, expected to be partially clouded tonight at that. The sun is just about set now. It won't be long before it's dark.

Through my kitchen window, I can make out the small glow of his headlights up the hill. Taking a breath and letting it out slowly, I will the stress my body seems Hell bent on holding, to go away. I was the one who lashed out at him for things beyond his control. It's not his fault my confidence is in the gutter. That I worry about how I measure up to the hundreds of women he's been with. How I compare to Lucinda, especially... Actually, I don't compare to her. She looks like a Sports Illustrated model... I keep letting my feelings for him cloud my judgment. It's not fair to him at all. Though, I'm less than thrilled about him keeping whatever is up with Lucinda, a secret. Then again, who am I to even talk? I never tell him anything about my past.

He said he wouldn't be with me, though. That sleeping with me would somehow destroy him. I don't understand him. Yet at the same time, I do. I understand what's going on with him, completely. He's as conflicted about us as I am. Though he doesn't realize, it's because of the influence of a spell.

Grabbing the dish towel, I wipe my hands dry before tossing it frustratedly back onto the counter. I need to burn some sage and lavender to relax. Maybe apply some essential oil blends to my wrists. I've always found aroma therapy to be a soothing practice.

Turning my back on the kitchen window, I make my way across the old farm house to my witch room. The curio cabinet is where I have been keeping a small collection of essential oils, blends and potions. Selecting one of my favorites, that contains sandalwood and lavender, I dab the oil on my wrists and rub them together, before placing the bottle back in the cabinet. The friction activates the amazing musky scent. I take a deep inhale of it and release my breath, attempting to focus on relinquishing the stress from my body. It works to a degree, but it's going to take more than aroma therapy to get over Dean. I've managed to stay away from him for three days. And I'm already struggling.

Grabbing a smudge bowl, I throw in some lose sage leaves and lavender, lighting them on fire. I let them burn for a few moments before blowing out the flame, allowing the smoke to billow forth. Waving the smoke towards myself to cleanse my aura of negativity, I walk out to the foyer to place the bowl on the little table. Might as well let the smoke permeate the house a little as well. Opening up the solid oak front door, I let the slight breeze outside help the little bit of smoke flow through the house.

Lighting a few candles, I shut off all the lights and decide to try to relax and meditate in the darkness of my witch room. As I lie down on the couch, I try to clear my thoughts of Dean.

A rapping on my screened storm door wakes me up. I must have fallen asleep for a few hours. Glancing at the clock on the table, I see that it's 9:57 pm. A bit late for a visit. I know it can't be Dean. I would have heard his motorcycle pull up. No, Dean is out cruising with Serene, blowing off steam. Possibly getting blown as well, after the way I acted with him. The thought of him distracting himself with another woman instantly undoes all the work I had been doing in an attempt to de-stress tonight.

Standing up tiredly, I make my way to the front door. As I recognize his outline, I wish I would have shut the oak door so I could have ignored him. Latisha was right about him. He really doesn't take no for an answer. I should have put ex-lax in that specific batch of charmed muffins.

"I came over to see if you were alright. Noticed the candles from your window and got to wondering if your electric was out." Garrett Johnson explains.

Reluctantly, I walk to the door and flick on the porch light, showing him that my electric is working just fine. "Can't a girl just light some candles and relax in this town?" It isn't really a question I want him to answer, though. I secretly hope the light attracts mosquitos and other bugs to drive him back to his house.

"Sure, she can." He smirks at me through the screen door. "You want some company?" The flirtatious tone in his voice actually gives me a tinge of nausea.

"If I did, they'd be in here with me."

He leans on the frame of the screen door and grins. "I'm here, ain't I?"

I make no attempt to hide my eye roll. "Did I extend an actual invitation to you, Garrett? I don't believe I did."

He nods to the candles inside my house, behind me on the little foyer table. "Maybe you just *summoned* me?" His grin widens, as he looks me up and down slowly, making me feel like I want to jump in the shower.

"Sometimes a candle is just a candle." I reach forward and place the latch on the screen door through the loop to lock it. It's not going to stop anyone from getting in if they want to, but I'm hoping it will drive the message home that I don't want him here.

His pale eyes follow my motion, and I notice a flicker of annoyance wash over his expression. He makes no movement to indicate any intention of leaving.

Anxiety begins to rise up inside me as I consider the fact, that way out here in the country, my closest neighbors, which are acres of farm land apart, are Garrett and Dean. Dean, is who knows where right now, down some country road, if he's not with a woman. And Garrett, is right here, looking at me, like a juicy plate of barbeque he can't wait to eat. I really should have locked the oak door. He had the nerve to grab my leg in the car. I can't help feeling a little nervous about what else he might try...

To my extreme relief, I hear a motorcycle in the distance, heading down our road. I know it's Dean. The black Harley turns into my driveway and rides up to the house. Dean must have seen the porch light on and a figure at my door, and stopped to make sure I'm ok. And for the right reasons, too. Unlike Garrett. My clearly visible relief seems to further annoy Garrett, as he continues to stare at me in silence. I look away from him again and shift my attention back to Dean as he dismounts the bike and makes his way to the steps of my front porch. Garrett doesn't turn around to acknowledge Dean's presence, until Dean is walking up the steps.

"The fuck is this?" Dean's words are leaden with disapproval. His stony expression displeased, to state the least.

Garrett moves back from his hovering position against my screen door. "I was only checking to see if our lady friend needed any help." He says, as if Dean has a nerve to inquire about his presence here.

Dean looks at him with annoyed surprise, his brows raised, leaning back slightly. "*Our,* lady friend?" He hard eyes Garrett, until Garrett averts his gaze. Dean shifts his focus to me. "Snake charming again, doll?" his words dripping with sarcasm.

I shake my head. "No."

"She's got this snake crawling." Garrett nearly growls, sneering at Dean.

Dean turns back to him with an expression that would make my blood turn cold if he ever looked at me that way. I know he won't throw the first punch in a situation like this, but his body language is clearly asking Garrett if he dares to take the first shot.

As the two of them stare each other down, I decide enough is enough. Garrett is delusional if he thinks he's going to survive a fight with Dean. He's also delusional if he thinks he's got a shot with me. I flick the latch off the screen door and push it open with a loud creak. As I walk out onto the front porch with them, letting the spring slam the door shut behind me, I walk up to Dean and run my hand up the arm of his leather jacket. I can feel the muscle flexed tensely beneath it.

"Dean, why don't you come inside?" I urge him, gently. "Let's talk."

He doesn't move, nor does he speak. He's still glaring at Garrett like he wants to fight him. I know he's been angry since last Saturday. I don't want him getting into a fight with Garrett. I try to distract him to calm him down a bit. Keeping my hand in contact with his tense arm, I move to stand a bit more in front of him, bringing my hand to the base of his neck and running it down the front of his leather jacket. I step closer so that the front of my body is touching his. "Please, Dean?"

Nothing. He's still glaring Garrett down.

Okay. Time to break out the big guns and make it clear to both men just who is actually welcome and who is not. I take Dean's wrist and pull his arm around me, placing his large, leather gloved hand on my ass.

"Come on, Dean." I whisper. "Don't you want to come inside?"

A grin finally cracks his stern face, even though he is still looking at Garrett. His hand squeezes my ass as he presses me closer against him.

Behind me, I hear the distinct ping of a zippo lighter, then a clang as it snaps shut.

"Let me bum one of those smokes off you." Dean growls.

I look up at him, confused. Dean doesn't smoke. I glance back at Garrett, who seems surprised by Dean's request as well. Still, he takes a step forward, holding out the pack of cigarettes towards Dean.

"Actually, never mind, I got one." Dean mutters, pulling a cigarette out of his jacket pocket.

"Since when do you smoke?" I ask him.

His eyes finally lower to meet mine as I stand looking up at him. "I don't. I found it on the backseat of your car. Saturday night. When I drove you home from the bar."

It suddenly clicks why he was asking me if anyone walked me to my car, and if I was with a guy that night. "You've got to be kidding me!"

Dean shifts his gaze back to Garrett. "You wanna tell me what the fuck you were doing in Vanna's car?"

"She gave me a ride home." Garrett says. "*She owed me one.*" I can almost hear the smile in his voice as he said that last part. I look over my shoulder at him and frown.

"You should leave, Garrett. I did you a favor because you gave me a ride to work, once. That's it."

410

"Well, I'm a pretty good customer too, aren't I?" Garrett says. He's definitely trying to start trouble between us. I consider telling Dean he grabbed my leg before getting out of the car... But Dean would kill him.

"The fuck's that supposed to mean?" Dean asks.

I turn back to Dean and place my hands on his chest. "Okay, don't get pissed. But he's been to the shop a few times... for Reiki. *That's it.*"

Dean doesn't look at me, but I can feel his grip on my ass getting noticeably tighter, as a slight growl rumbles my name in his throat. He's never growled my name like that before... It stirs something primal inside of me. I try to push those feelings back down.

"Go home, Garrett." I say, running my hand up the front of Dean's leather jacket until my fingers trail up to his face. I stroke his rough jawline, as if I can try to calm him down.

"You heard the lady." Dean's tone is low and ominous.

Garrett silently descends the porch steps and skulks away, disappearing into the darkness as he heads back to his house through the Pecan orchard.

I sigh, glad to be rid of him. I can feel the tension leaving my body once again. I expected Dean to relax a little as well, but his body remains hard, his hand still a firm grip on my ass. I lean back to get a better look at his expression, my lower half still pinned against his body. He looks down at me, but says nothing. I guess he's still upset with me. "I'm glad you showed up when you did." I say, hoping to break our silence, though it is a true statement.

Dean lets out a long sigh, closing his eyes and bowing his head lower towards me. "Me too."

"You don't actually believe I'd do anything with Garrett, do you?"

"No. I don't think you'd let that prick touch you." He sighs, tossing the cigarette over the railing of my front porch. "Why didn't you say anything about him coming to your shop? Or driving him home?"

"It doesn't matter. There's nothing going on." I reach up to stroke his hair and he catches my wrist, sliding his large hand over mine and bringing it to his lips. He kisses my palm then holds my hand against his face for a moment. I watch him as he closes his eyes. As if he's relishing my touch against his face. I can't help admitting to myself that I've missed him. Like I always do. He seems to have missed me too.

"You smell good." He almost whispers.

"It must be the oil blend I made tonight."

"Some kind of magic potion to bewitch a man?" he asks, a hint of sadness in his words.

Ugh... Of all the things he could have said...

"No." I say, grabbing his wrist and pulling his hand off my ass. I was right to avoid him. This isn't going to work. I let my other hand drop away from his face. "Is that why you're so hesitant to be with me? You think I put a love spell on you?" I take a few steps back towards my screen door. "Maybe you should go too, Dean."

I turn around to go back inside, but Dean's hand pushes the screen door shut as he stands behind me. I feel him press his face into the back of my head and stroke my long hair with his other hand. He breathes in my scent.

"I've never met anyone like you." He says quietly, removing his hand from the door and wrapping me in his strong arms. He gently pulls me back against him. I can feel the heat of his hard body on my back. "You're maddening, Vanna."

The combination of anger and sadness, mixed with the usual strong desire I can't help feeling for him, which is always amplified in his presence, frustrates me to no end. Tears prickle behind my eyes. "I don't want anything from you that isn't real." I say, unable to keep the anger out of my voice. I did not, nor would I ever, put a love spell on him or anyone else, ever again. But I've managed to screw up a real chance at being with a decent man, for once. Dean says nothing, just continues to hold me. His silence further angers me. "I am who I am." I say, as I begin to struggle to get away from him. He releases me and I turn to face him. His expression looks as pained as I feel. "And if that's not good enough for you..." My voice wavers and I can't finish the sentence. Anger and sadness overcome me, and the stinging tears fill my eyes. I squeeze them shut to clear my vision and they roll down my cheeks. I brush them away angrily. When I open my eyes, I can't bring myself to look him in the face.

"You think I don't believe you're good enough for me?" Dean sounds genuinely shocked, the tone of his voice softer now. More caring than before. "Vanna... that couldn't be further from the truth."

"Then what is it?" I demand, looking up at him. He looks like he does want so say something, but he hesitates. "What is it?" I demand, more harshly this time. "You touch me like you want me, then you tell me you don't."

His brows furrow then pitch upward as he shakes his head. "*I never said that,* doll." He insists. "And I gotta say, I worry about the way my words translate in your head, baby. I know it's not your fault, though. We can work through all of it." He runs a hand through his hair. I can tell he's frustrated as well, when he does that. "I like you. A lot. And it happened quickly. Way quicker than I've ever come around to anyone before. It's way out of character for me."

"I don't understand." I'm so turned around and upside down about this entire situation between us. It's an uphill battle, fighting my own feelings for him. And the more I fall for him, the more I try to talk myself out of feeling guilty over the Knight Summoning Spell. But the guilt only grows, as my feelings do.

He stares at me for a few moments then turns away, walking to the porch steps to lean against the post as he looks out into the darkness.

"I see how men react to you, Vanna." He says. "I know you can't help it. It's just a part of who you are. That little need to flirt in you, like most women have. That desire to be reminded that you're wanted. You've got this aura about you... this, undeniable... maybe unattainable, energy that just draws men to you... draws *me* to you... like a moth to a flame. And we all know what happens to the fucking moth." His sigh is wrought with frustration.

"So, you're calling me a flirt?" I ask. "I flirt with guys to hurt you?"

Dean turns around to face me, but there is something dark behind his eyes and I can suddenly feel that electric current between us pulsing stronger, pulling at me.

"Oh no, baby. I get why you do what you do... I understand you. That need in you to cock tease these pricks. I see you, doll." He steps closer to me, breeching the line of personal space as he reaches out to skim my cheek with the back of his knuckles. I can smell his skin. A mix of leather, that cologne and machine shop.

I avert my eyes from his and focus on the cuff of his leather jacket, the silver zipper there halfway unzipped. Moving closer to me still, I find myself backed against the frame of the screen door.

"I also know that you like to help people." He continues. "So, let me help you, help yourself, to help others." He pauses to grip my chin with his thumb and forefinger, gently lifting my face so that our eyes meet. "If you *ever* let another man lay a finger on you, I will kill him." He growls. "You got me, baby? I don't care whether or not you actually belong to me. Understand?" I attempt to nod. He leans in closer, his face mere inches from mine. "Let me *hear* it." He whispers, his breath on me...

"Yes."

The grin on his face is borderline lascivious as he rubs his thumb across my lower lip.

"So, your problem is that you're jealous?"

His grin remains, but something darkens behind his penetrating stare. *"Of every man who's ever touched you."*

It's a short list. Definitely shorter than his. But that statement. His possessiveness. It should be a red flag. Instead, it turns me on to know that I affect him as much as he intoxicates me. I close my eyes, relishing the rush his jealousy gives me. As if he can sense what he does to me, he steps even closer, our bodies now touching. My chest pressed against his leather jacket, my back firm against the house.

"I'd hurt somebody over you, Vanna." He murmurs. "The thought of other men out there that have kissed you... fucked you... that you've come for." He growls in my ear. "You drive me crazy."

Once again, he seems to want me, at least as much as I want him. So why doesn't he act? The moth to a flame? Does he think I'll burn him? "There's no one else." I say, my eyes fixed on his hot mouth. "I don't want anyone else."

I watch as his mouth grins. The tip of his tongue peeking out to tap the corner of his upper lip then slides across his teeth before disappearing inside again. I bite my lip, my mind swirling around our last kiss. It's been days since we've kissed. Before things seemed to get so complicated so fast. Mostly in my own damn mind. My own guilt. But there is something he isn't telling me about Lucinda.

"What do you want?" I ask.

"*You.*" He says simply, as he gently places both of his hands on my hips.

I look up into his dark eyes, trying to read him. He searches mine as well. "Why did you say it?"

"It's abundantly clear to me that you could have any guy you want."

"That's bullshit."

"It isn't. You can't not know your effect on men. I've seen you toy with them."

"You think I'm toying with you?"

"The thought crossed my mind. I won't lie to you... But even if you are, I'd still feel the same. You could have any guy you want, Vanna." He sighs. "But if that guy isn't me, I'm gonna beat the fuck out of him."

That really shouldn't turn me on. What is wrong with me? "I still call bullshit."

"Then you're oblivious." He seems annoyed.

"If I could have any guy I want, I'd have him... Instead, here we are second guessing each other. Wondering who is playing who."

"I'm not playing you, Vanna." Dean says earnestly. "I'm not a fucking robot. I know I come across the way I come across. But I do have emotions, too."

I nod. "You're right. And you're entitled to them. I think it's best we give each other time. We're both fucked up from our pasts."

He takes a breath, then removes his hands from me and steps back. "If that's what you want. I'll stay in the fucking friend zone." He sounds bitter. "But I meant everything I said. Everything, Vanna." He growls. "You can friend zone me, but I'm still not going to let another guy near you."

"If I gave you the shot right now would you take it?" I ask.

"Define *shot.*"

"If I invited you into my bed tonight. Right now. Would you take me up on it?"

He stares at me, that dark shift evident behind his eyes again. "I'd want to... Badly."

"But you'd say no?"

He swallows, hard. His eyes flickering back and forth in mine as he attempts to read me. "I'd have to."

"Why?" I demand. He only stares at me, as if he can't figure out the word's he wants to say to me. "Why!" I yell at him, though I already know the answer.

"You're not ready. I haven't earned it. You want me in the friend zone. I'm there until you let me out." He says, his tone resigned.

"You prove my point... Good night, Dean. See you at the bar."

"What point?" he demands, reaching to stop me again.

"That you're full of shit."

"How am I full of shit, Vanna?"

"You said I could have any guy I want. Clearly that isn't true. Even with a golden ticket offered on a silver platter!" I yell at him.

"You were speaking hypothetically!" He shouts back at me.

"I'm not now!" I shove him. He steps back just to humor me. I know I'm not that strong. "Is it because I don't look anything like her?"

"No." he shakes his head. "And it kills me that you even think like that."

"Why don't you actually want me? What guy who claims to be attracted to a woman turns her down at a free pass?"

Dean stares at me for a moment. He looks conflicted. Like he wants to say something, but asks me a question instead. "Is that what you're doing? Offering me a night with you?"

"I'm calling you out."

He looks at me sideways, but takes that step forward again. "I need you to say the words, Vanna. I need you to be real clear, about what you're saying to me right now." He says, pointing as if to indicate the importance of this request.

"I'm saying if you want me, *come and get me*. I'm all yours tonight." I stare him down. Why do his eyes look so pained?

"I don't want *one night* with you... I'll stay in the friend zone if those are my two choices."

If he was really attracted to me, he wouldn't pass up the opportunity to screw around. What guy would? This Summoning Spell has him all kinds of messed up. And even knowing that, I still can't help lashing out at him. Even knowing that it's myself, not him, that I'm so angry with.

"Remember it was *you* that made the call." I snap at him. "*You* turned *me* down. Good night!"

I turn to walk into the house but he grabs me and spins me around to face him again. His arms wrap around me, pulling me up against him as he crushes his mouth to mine, kissing me roughly. I try to shove him off but he pins me up against the frame of the door so I can't back away from him, and continues to kiss me. All I can do is try to push him away but he's so much stronger than me it's useless, he has me pinned and trapped. I open my mouth for a breath of air and he takes full advantage, thrusting his tongue inside to kiss me deeper. I surrender to his kiss, thinking he will eventually back off if he thinks he's getting me to respond to his aggressive advances. It doesn't work. Only when I whimper does he pull back to look at me. I shove at him angrily.

"What the fuck!" I shout at him.

"I'm not turning you down." He sighs. "I'm doing what I think you actually need right now. And I need you to know me, *first*... So, it's fine, Vanna. I'm in the fucking *friend zone*. Happily and fucking willingly." But his fists are clenching at his sides as he steps back from me.

"Are you sure about that?" I nod towards those fists. "I wasn't the one who put you there."

"You are beyond frustrating, Vanna. But I'll show you what you need to see from me. I have no problem with earning it." He stares at me for a moment, dragging his fingers back through his hair, before continuing, "You are worth it. Whether you believe that or not. I'll be the man that proves that to you." He starts to leave but hesitates at the edge of the steps before turning to meet my eyes once more. "I am serious about what I said. About other men... I will hurt someone over you. So, consider that, before you play your little games with me again. I can only take so much torment from you, Vanna. *You're mine.* Even if you're not. Nobody else touches you. Or they get hurt, Vanna." His tone is serious. "And so do I."

"You still see her, don't you? It isn't just the phone calls. I hear you ride past my house late at night sometimes. You aren't going to the roadhouse. Are you still seeing Lucinda?" I demand. "Are you seeing anyone?"

This time, he glares at me. Hard. "Get on the fucking bike." He finally says. His voice is deep and a little unnerving. He never talks about Serene like that, *the fucking bike...*

I hesitate, and Dean storms up to me, grabbing my hand and pulling me with him towards Serene. Angrily, he yanks out a helmet and a pair of riding goggles from the saddle bag of his bike, handing them to me as he grabs his own helmet and eyewear, putting them on. Throwing a leg over the bike, he fire's it up.

"I said get on!" he shouts at me, making me jump.

"I can't! I have candles burning in the house."

He scowls at me for a moment. "Go blow them out. Then get your ass back out here." He growls. "Two minutes. Don't make me come get you, Vanna. I will."

I believe him.

Handing him back the riding gear, I hurry inside my house to extinguish the candles and lock my front door. Jamming the keys and my cellphone in my pockets, I walk back over to Dean where he's sitting on Serene, waiting. Putting the helmet and goggles on, I climb onto the back of his bike, almost afraid to touch him as I use his shoulders for balance. He reaches back to grab my hands and pulls me forward, wrapping my arms around his middle to hold onto him.

"Dean, where are you taking me?" I ask.

"I told you I'd show you what you need to see from me, Vanna. This is me, keeping my word to you. Now hold onto me." He growls, cranking up the sound system on Serene. Nine Inch Nails, *Closer*. Before I can even blink, we're down my driveway and flying up the street into the night.

Chapter eighteen
Vanna

DEAN LEADS ME UP TO A SET OF METAL doors at the back of a large brick building facing the waterfront. "Where are we? This is some kind of old warehouse. It doesn't even look like it's still used." I say, glancing up at the filthy, broken windows. The bricks are even eroded in some spots. The building itself looks like it's from the early 1900's. Actually, it's probably older. And it's big enough that it takes up a whole block.

"You asked what I'm doing when I sometimes leave late at night... It ain't fucking around on you... It ain't because I'm with *Lucinda*." He glowers back at me a moment longer before he grabs my arm and pulls me towards the big metal door. Yanking the door open with a loud creak, he pulls me through.

I'm startled to see two large men dressed in black inside, standing in the dark. They're muscular and they look mean and I back up against Dean's body, instinctively.

"Keegan. You partaking tonight?" One of them casually asks, as if Dean is a regular here. Wherever or whatever *here* is.

"Fuck yeah... New blood tonight?"

"Yup. Go on down." The guy says, as they step back to let us through.

Dean keeps a firm grip on my arm and leads me across the dirty cement floor of this old abandoned warehouse, to another metal door towards the back. This time, when he yanks the door open, I can hear what sounds like a crowd of people, shouting and cheering at the bottom of a narrow set of stairs.

"What is this?" I nervously ask, as he slides his hand down my arm to grasp my hand in his, leading me down the wooden staircase. It smells musty, and dirt and grime are caked all over the walls and the old boards of the steps. They look like they're from the 1900's too.

"Stay near me. Don't talk to anybody. I'm not fucking around, Vanna. Anybody says anything to you, you say you belong to me. And be fucking firm about it." His words sound ominous and angry still.

As we make it to the bottom of the basement steps and round the corner into the dimly lit concrete space, there are at least sixty men circled around a makeshift ring, watching two guys pound the shit out of each other inside a roped off area of the room. No protective gear. No floor mat. Just two guys, going at it, bare knuckled and bloody, as the room of men shout and cheer them on.

I squeeze Dean's hand and try to plant my feet to stop him, but he pulls me along. This place is scary and seedy. It smells like mildew and blood and stale beer. The dim lighting makes the whole scene look even more ominous. I yank his arm harder and he finally stops to look back at me.

"I don't like it here." I tell him, having to raise my voice so he can hear me.

"This won't take long." He leans slightly closer to me. "One fight, and we can go."

I stare at him. "You're going to fight?" I manage to squeak out. He nods. My eyes shift towards the ring, which is just a rope tied around four support columns in the center of the old basement. I notice the dark blood in droplets and smears on the cement inside that marked off area. My eyes shoot back to Dean. "You don't have to do this."

"I do this all the fucking time, Vanna. Nothing to worry about."

"There is blood all over the floor..."

"Ain't takin' my boots off, baby."

"But... what if..."

He shakes his head at me with a cocky grin. "Ain't hitting the cement *at all*, doll."

"I really don't like this..." I look up at him pleadingly. "It's gross here. It's scary and it smells bad and we're both going to catch a disease here."

Dean presses his lips together, rolling them inward to suppress a laugh, before he says, "It's not always held here. Underground fights move around."

"Is this illegal? This looks like a cock fight for humans."

Dean gives me another sly grin, but he doesn't answer me. Instead, he hauls me closer to his body and drapes his arm across my shoulders as he walks us into the crowd. We're walking up towards two guys that are just as jacked up as the guys standing guard upstairs. These guys are both open carrying shoulder holstered guns. They're standing in front of a smaller, dark haired, seedy looking man in a crappy metallic looking suit, behind a folding table and a bunch of metal boxes.

"I want in." Dean says to the guy. "Give me the motherfucker nobody wants to fight in this dump tonight."

"That would be a new guy tonight, Keegan." The man behind the table says, nodding towards one of his guys, who walks over to a chalk board closer to the roped off ring. He writes *Keegan* in a blank space next to the name Rocky. The crowd starts to stir as they notice a name go up next to Rocky's. Money starts to exchange hands and I look back at the man as he begins to speak again.

"Hope that's lady luck you brought with you tonight, Keegan." He looks me up and down before glancing back at Dean. "You might need some luck tonight."

"Yeah. Yeah. How soon till I get in there?" Dean asks, unrattled by his words.

"You're up after the next one." Cheap suit says, taking a huge pile of money handed to him by one of the big guys with the guns, then puts it into one of the metal cases.

Dean reaches into his jacket pocket and pulls out his wallet, removing some cash and hands it over to the guy.

"Bet yourself to win?" The cheap suit asks. Dean nods. The guy marks something down, then hands Dean a yellow ticket, which he shoves back in his pocket.

"Might take home a nice chunk of change if you manage to pull this fight off."

"Aces." Dean grins down at me, then steers us towards the makeshift ring, bringing me a little closer to see the fight.

It ends just as we get nearer, and one of the knocked-out fighters is dragged by his feet out of the ring, through the blood, smearing it across the concrete. The men around the ring are shouting and passing money around again.

I turn into Dean's chest and close my eyes for a moment. "I can't believe you do this."

"It's just a little blood." He says. "And most of the people who show up to fight aren't really trained in much. Amateurs at best. Just a bunch of guys looking to make some quick cash and blow off some steam. This isn't anything like some other places I've been to. Don't worry." Dean smiles at me. "This is tame and small time."

"Don't worry? Are you kidding me?" I stare up at him. "And there are worse places than this? This is a shit hole."

Dean chuckles. "I mean more dangerous fights. More skilled fighters. Less rules. Higher stakes. This is nothing compared to that shit." Dean makes it sound like this is no big deal. Like he's going to compete in a game of tic tac toe or something. "Here, there's no eye gauging allowed. No biting allowed. No weapons, *yada, yada*." He says as if he finds the rules boring. "Here, you can tap out and the fight's over. Some places can be a lot rougher. Some places, the fight isn't over until somebody can't get up." That sounds horrible. I look up at him as he's scanning the room, probably looking for whomever Rocky might be.

"You've fought in underground matches like that?" I ask.

"Oh yeah." Dean says nonchalantly, like it's nothing.

Someone shouts "Fight!" from the ring, drawing my attention back in that direction. The room goes wild again as the two new fighters circle each other before they start throwing punches. They both look like meth addicts, skinny and strung out.

"I hope you get tested for diseases often if this is your secret hobby, Dean."

Dean laughs. "I'm clean, baby."

"I'm serious. I want to shower just being here in this grungy place." I wrap my arms around myself. Dean removes his arm from around me and slips out of his leather jacket, draping it across my shoulders. Then he removes his large knife and hands it to me.

"This isn't going to be a long fight. I'm gonna be up any minute. I want you to stay close, where I can see you. Do not talk to anyone, unless it's to tell them you're mine." He reminds me.

"We can just go." I urge him. "You don't have to do this to impress me. I saw you spar that day, remember? And at the bonfire."

"Fuck yeah." He smirks, and I know which parts he's remembering. The part where he had me up against the gym wall. And the part where he had me on the picnic table.

"I know you can fight. Let's just go." I push.

He shakes his head. "Sparring is not the same as fighting, baby. I need to fight."

"Why? This is crazy, Dean. You could get seriously hurt."

"I need to." He says again, as if that's a legitimate answer.

The fight is called and the crowd gets loud again. I don't care about the meth heads. I'm frantically looking around the room now for anyone stepping up to the ring that might be Rocky. Nobody is stepping up so far. Maybe he backed out of fighting Dean? He does seem to be a known fighter among this group. Or maybe Rocky got tired of waiting for a challenger and left...

"You're up, Keegan!" Calls one of the organizers, or the ref, I don't know what he is, but a man shouts from the ring at Dean.

Dean takes my hand and leads me right up to the ropes with him. "Remember what I told you. Stay where I can see you. Do not talk to anyone. I won't be long." Dean says, shoving his sleeves up his forearms a quarter of the way as he looks down at me.

I stare up at him nervously. "Are you sure you want to fight somebody named *Rocky*?"

Dean chuckles. "Gonna be fine, Vanna. Watch." He winks at me. "You wanna knock me a little kiss for good luck?" He asks, a noticeable hint of flirtation in his voice.

Not wanting to take any chances, I clutch his knife to my abdomen and place my other hand on his shoulder to stand up on my tippy toes. He lowers his mouth to mine for a brief kiss.

"I don't need luck, baby. But I'll steal a kiss from you any chance I get." He whispers in my ear, before he pulls back from me to duck under the ropes and enter the makeshift ring. "Stay right where I can see you." He raises his voice to tell me once more. I nod and tug his jacket tighter around me, my eyes glued to him.

The crowd is getting rowdy again, seemingly extra excited about this particular fight. I watch Dean as he strolls to his corner, taking his position, he stretches his arms, then throws a couple of warm up punches, as his dark eyes scan the crowd with a scowl. I watch them settle on someone. The corner of his mouth curls up. I turn to see who Dean has zeroed in on.

My heart rate feels like it stutters and I can't even swallow at first glance... The guy making his way to the ring could be Viking's little brother. He's got to outweigh Dean by at least eighty pounds, and he's taller than him as well. My eyes shoot back to Dean. He doesn't look worried at all. He's grinning as *Rocky* ducks under the flimsy rope to step into the makeshift ring with him.

"Fight!" someone shouts loudly from the other side of the ropes.

As they approach each other, I notice that Dean isn't quite as light on his feet as he was when he was sparring with Viper in the gym. Then again, in the gym, he was bare foot and wore less clothing. I don't blame him for keeping his boots on with all that blood smeared on the concrete.

Rocky rushes Dean and throws a heavy fist at his face. But Dean jerks his body out of range and side steps him, grabbing the guy and slugging him in the ribs with two powerful shots before he shoves him back to avoid being grabbed or struck himself.

I remind myself to breathe as I watch Dean dodging and ducking punches, weaving around Rocky's attacks, sneaking in powerful jabs here and there.

As I watch them circle each other, sizing each other up again, I know that all it would take is one good hit to the head and it could be bad news for Dean. One shot to the mouth and that perfect, sexy grin of Dean's could be wrecked. They're not wearing mouth guards, gloves or any kind of protective gear at all. This is bare knuckled brutality in a dingy basement.

Just as I feared, the guy's powerful punch manages to break through Dean's block and clip him in the face. Luckily it seems to have just grazed his cheek bone and Dean doesn't appear to be fazed at all by it, repaying the guy with several blows of his own to his face and body. His opponent is definitely tiring. Obviously sensing this himself, Dean goes in for the kill, throwing fast combinations at the guy who can't seem to figure out where to block first or next, taking random swings as if he's just hoping to connect with Dean's body somewhere. But Dean is still on him like a savage, and the crowd is going wild, shouting so loudly I'm tempted to cover my ears.

With what seems like the last bit of the big guy's energy, he shoves Dean backwards and away from him, before he makes a lunge at Dean. I don't know what I was expecting to see, but it wasn't Dean charging forward at him as well. Only Dean jumps up, with his fist cocked back, and as he comes down on the guy, slamming his fist down into his temple so hard, it brings him to his knees at Dean's feet.

Dazed, Rocky makes no move to get up from his knees as Dean paces before him, a few feet away, watching his opponent. As soon as Rocky makes a move to stand up and resume the fight, Dean comes back at him with one more hard slug to the face, snapping Rocky's head to the side, knocking him down to the filthy floor. This time, Dean's opponent doesn't try to get up, and the crowd goes crazy again.

Dean's eyes lift from the guy's unconscious body to meet mine. He grins as he drops his fists and makes his way back over to me, ducking under the rope. "Was that so bad?" He asks, gently stroking a finger along my jaw. He's looking at me the way he was looking at me in the gym that day. Like he wants to attack me next, though not to fight. He must really get a rise out of this. A rush that gets him going.

I slip his leather jacket off my shoulders and hand it back to him. He's studying me intently as he slides it back on, searching my expression for something. I can only imagine he's trying to figure out if seeing him fight and win turns me on as much as it seems to have fired him up. I hand him back his knife, and he straps it back to his belt. He's about to say something when one of the armed guards in black, shoves a wad of cash to Dean's chest.

"Well done. Your payout and winnings are all here." The guy says to Dean, as Dean takes the money and stuffs it inside the inner pocket of his leather jacket. "There's a guy here, wants a word with you." He adds, cocking his chin towards the back of the room.

I watch as Dean twists his head in that direction. "About what?"

"He's looking for fighters. Runs a gig down near Myrtle Beach. Higher stakes. Invitation only. Thinks you could make some decent scratch." The guy says. Dean just told me higher stakes mean more dangerous fighters with better skills than these amateurs.

I grab Dean's arm, pulling his attention back to me. "Can we please go?"

"Yeah, we're going." Dean says. "Stay here for one minute. I'm just going to get his information."

"Why? You said this was nothing compared to that kind of underground fighting."

"This isn't. What that guy is offering is not easy to come by. I'll be right back."

I watch as Dean approaches the guy, who's wearing a nice suit and looks very out of place in this grungy warehouse basement. Dean stands beside him and turns to watch me as they hold a brief conversation. I cannot hear what is being said over the noise of rowdy men, entertained by whomever is fighting in this next round.

The guy in the suit pulls out a business card and hands it to Dean. Dean tucks it into his back pocket and heads back towards me, stopping at the old wooden stairs and gestures for me to come to him. I hurry over and he guides me to walk up ahead of him. When we get to the top, he reaches around me to shove the metal door open before we walk out across the main level of the old warehouse. The two guys in black are still standing guard.

"That was fast." One of them says.

Dean takes my hand as we approach the doors to leave where they are standing. "That was easy." Dean says, flatly.

"You usually stay for a few more rounds. You're not even bleeding." The guy says, shifting his gaze to me. "I guess you got a few other rounds in mind tonight." His eyes linger on me. "This shit get you hot, honey?"

Dean's hand grips mine tighter as we make it to the door. He shoves that door open as well, guiding me through it first, before he slams it closed behind us. Now outside on the sidewalk, he lets go to place his hand against the small of my back, as we walk towards the lot around the block.

"Can we talk?" I ask him, twisting to stop in front of him so he can't keep herding me in the direction of Serene. "Can we walk down to the boardwalk? Grab a bench or something?" I glance past his shoulder towards the riverfront behind him. There are a few empty benches, not many people walking around on the boardwalk tonight, despite the nice temperature and slight breeze.

He lowers his gaze to meet mine. "Thought you couldn't wait to get out of here?"

"Out of that scene in Fight Club, yeah." I say. "But we need to talk."

"Alright." He reluctantly agrees, and we change course to head towards the river.

DEAN

STANDING WITH MY BACK FACING THE WATER, I LEAN AGAINST THE guardrail, arms and ankles crossed. Vanna sits down on the wooden bench before me on the boardwalk, overlooking the Cape Fear. Soft music from an outdoor dining area of a restaurant on the river, drifts through the night. I notice her glance in its direction, and take a quick gander myself. You can just make out the white cloth covered tables and diners under the dim lighting. A few couples dancing, with the Cape Fear Bridge as a backdrop in the distance.

"Looks like a nice place." She says quietly.

"I'll take you one night, if you'd like?"

"Before or after your illegal fight?" her tone is full of sarcasm.

I was trying to lighten the mood. Hoping the romantic setting a few yards down the boardwalk would have a little influence on her mood. Guess that's not happening. "It's a nice place, would probably skip the fight. Keep it classy for you, you know?"

She turns her face back to look up at me. I can tell she thinks she may have insulted me. "I never said you didn't have any class... No need to project your insecurities onto me."

I have to smirk at that one. Is she kidding me? She's one to talk about insecurities. I clear my throat. "I just kicked a giant's ass in less than four minutes flat. No insecurities here."

She leans back against the bench and folds her arms, still studying me. "You mentioned class, not me."

I study her right back. "You mentioned wanting to talk. Let's talk. Why don't you start. I get the impression there's a lot you have to say, and I wish you would."

Her slight flinch doesn't go unnoticed. "Maybe you're right." She lifts one shoulder in a slight shrug. "Maybe you're right about more than you know." She shifts her eyes from mine to gaze across the dark river, looking in the direction of the NC Battleship and the other bridge beyond Historical Downtown Wilmington, the Isabel Holmes.

"Vanna." I urge her. "Is there something you want to tell me?"

"Lots of things." I barely hear the words escape her lips, and even under the partial darkness, illuminated only by a dim light post, yards away, I can see sadness in her eyes.

424

It stirs something inside me. Seeing her sad twists me up inside and my agitation melts away. Uncrossing my arms, I rest my hands on the railing behind me. "I'm listening." I say, gentler now, as I stare at her and wait.

She gives me the slightest nod, but doesn't say anything. Her gaze remains off in the distance. The sadness lingers in her eyes. I watch as her fingers fidget together in her lap, but the rest of her is still. The silence goes on between us. Only the soft music from the restaurant drifts in our direction, the rhythmic sound of the waves slapping against the small boats moored below us on the Cape Fear.

"Vanna?" I gently press her to speak, but she gives me nothing. Her demeanor says more about her than Vanna ever does about herself. It's frustrating. And disheartening. And it's moments like this that drag my thoughts back to that file locked in my desk...

I take a deep breath of the night air through my nose and let it out slowly, fighting hard to keep my frustration with her stubborn silence at bay. I'm about to press her again, when she finally turns to look at me.

"Why do you fight?" She asks.

I close my eyes for a moment and let my head hang down, not wanting her to detect any kind of disappointment in my expression at her deflective switch in subject matter. My fingers curl around the guardrail and I clench my jaw for a few moments, willing my frustration with her to subside.

Is there something you want to tell me?

Lots of things...

Yet she gives me nothing!

"Lots of reasons." I say. Maybe the taste of her own medicine will clear her throat and get her talking, when I turn the tables back on her. For now, I will try to lead by example, because I know she isn't through asking.

"You don't seem to need the money. Even though it looked like a lot for a five-minute fight."

"Four-minute fight. I don't need the money. And for four minutes, yeah, it was a lot." I say.

"If it's not about the money, then why?"

I lift my face to look at her again. "About a hundred dollars a minute still isn't anything to turn your nose up at."

She looks surprised. "Wow. You make that per fight?"

"Not always. Depends who I fight. Where I fight. What the odds are. If I can place a bet on myself to win. Not every ring allows it. The bigger the chance of getting my ass kicked, the more I make if I win, both ways."

"Do you ever lose?"

"Not often. But I have."

She stares at me a moment, before she asks me again, "Why do you fight?"

Lead by example. "To blow off steam. Relieve tension. Keep myself sharp." I fire off simple reasons.

"You could spar in the gym and accomplish that." She says. "It's a lot safer."

"It's not the same."

"There's more to it, isn't there?" She pushes, and my frustration with her begins to build again.

"Oh, you want *deeper*?" I ask, fighting to keep the edge out of my voice. I wish she would give me deeper. "How about to feel alive? To fucking *feel something*?"

Something changes in her eyes as she stares back in mine. It's surprise, mixed with concern. "You don't feel?"

"For a long time, I didn't. Lately, I feel too fucking much." I mutter, trying not to glare at her. I'm failing, because she looks away from me. Her hands no longer fidgeting in her lap, now she's holding herself, wrapping her arms across her abdomen in that way that tells me she's uncomfortable or nervous, maybe even afraid.

Fuck. I did that.

"Sometimes I fight to escape." I say. "When I'm fighting. When I'm in a ring. Or even in the street, or a bar. When I'm fighting, that's all there is. For that brief period of time, there's nothing else. I can focus on my opponent, and everything else falls away, even for a short time. I can forget everything. There's only the target in front of me. I get to feel alive, and free of all the other bullshit going on in my life. Sparring in a gym doesn't give me the edge I need to feel that."

I hope that's enough for her. I hope she doesn't need to hear how I enjoy the pain. How I enjoy inflicting it, and that breaking bones and spilling blood gives me a rush that I chase like a fucking junkie. And I hope she doesn't need to hear why that is.

"You need the intensity of the real thing." She says, her eyes finally coming back to me.

"I can't go full on when I spar. A real fight is real freedom. Real release. They want to hurt me, and I want to hurt them. When I spar, I have to hold back. I don't want to hurt my friends. But a stranger, who's asking for it, same as I. That's different. No holds barred. I don't have to worry about whether or not they deserve it, because they're asking for it. It's a safe outlet."

"Safe? But you said... And it's also illegal..." She stammers.

I shrug. "There's a lot of illegal shit that shouldn't be illegal, Vanna."

"You've been doing this a long time." It's a statement, she's not asking, but I confirm for her anyway.

"Over twenty years."

"You must not lose much then, anymore."

Sometimes I lose on purpose. To punish myself. For the fucked-up shit I've done. For the shit I didn't do... For the humiliation I allowed to be brought upon myself in the past. But I'm not going to admit that to her. I like the way she looks at me too much, to risk that ever changing.

"There will always be someone bigger and badder, than you. I don't lose often. But I have and do, on occasion."

"And how do you feel when you lose?"

That depends why I lost. If it's on purpose, the pain my body feels, is a distraction from emotional and mental anguish. If I legitimately get my ass handed to me, it's a learning experience.

"Doesn't feel as good as winning." I shrug. "Lets me know what my limitations and weaknesses are, so I can work on improving myself." It's true enough.

Her arms slip away from her abdomen, and she resumes her fidgeting fingers in her lap again. "That day in the gym, when I watched you spar... and before, when you won the fight. You had this look in your eyes." She begins to say, but I can tell she's slightly uncomfortable.

I allow myself a slight grin as I wait for her to find the words, to form the question she wants to ask me.

"You seem like you... I mean... it looks like you..." she stammers once again. "You seem to get..."

"A rush?" I throw her a bone.

"I guess." She swallows.

I cock a brow slightly at her and grin a little wider. "Not gonna deny it, nothing like a fight to get the adrenaline pumping. I do get a high from it. But there's one other thing that gets things pumping better." I smirk at her. I notice her thighs clench tighter together. It was a slight movement, but fuck, that was telling.

"So, it turns you on?" she asks.

I'm not the only one, baby. "The way you look at me, turns me on."

She bites her bottom lip, attempting to hide her shy little smile as she casts her eyes down from me. "But I've only seen you fight twice now. You don't get that way normally?"

"I get a high from the adrenaline rush from fighting, Vanna. But I get a fucking *rise* from you." I reply. "Thinking by the way you were looking at me, it might have had a similar effect on you." She doesn't say anything, nor does she look back up at me. "Nothing wrong with any of it, Vanna. It's natural." A little giggle escapes her, bringing a genuine smile to my face. "You have any further questions for me?"

She shakes her head, causing a few strands of hair to fall into her face. She brushes it back with her fingers and looks back up at me. "I'm sorry I frustrate you."

"You only frustrate me because I care about you." I sigh. "And I'd rather be frustrated by you than anyone else." She gives me a slight smile. "What am I going to do with you, Vanna?"

I notice her slight smile doesn't reach her eyes anymore. "You'll keep me safe." She says, but the way in which she says it, her underlying tone reveals her sadness again. "Of that, I don't have much doubt."

"I'll always keep you safe, Vanna."

"Why do you think so?" she seems to stare at me.

"That's part of caring about somebody, baby. Haven't you ever had anybody care about you before?"

"When I was a kid, sure."

427

Well damn. "You're younger than me, doll. But you haven't been a kid for a while."

"Guess I'm out of practice then."

"Of being cared about?" I ask. She doesn't answer me. *Fuck.* I knew she was alone. I wish I knew just how alone. "Thought you had family up north?"

"I do. We don't talk much."

"Why is that?"

"They don't agree with my life choices." She sighs, and I can see her tensing up. I need to tread carefully to keep the tiny bits of information flowing out of her.

"Mind if I sit?" I ask.

She shakes her head and scoots over, as if she needed to make room for me. I sit down beside her and drape my arm across the back of the bench behind her.

"They don't like the witchy shit?" I ask, wondering if this is a religious thing.

She lets out a fake laugh. "They don't even know about it. I was raised Catholic. Which, when you think about Catholicism, a lot of their practices are very Pagan. I won't bore you with a history lesson on all that, though." She seems to almost chuckle. "But no, they weren't aware. I took an interest a few years ago. But I didn't actually put a whole lot into practice until I met Laura. She taught me a lot... And I've learned that magick is nothing to fool with."

"Why witchcraft?" I ask, wanting to keep her talking. So far, this seems to be a safe topic for her to open up about with me. Perhaps, through witchcraft, I'll learn some of her secrets.

She lifts her shoulder slightly as she answers me. "Self-empowerment."

Interesting. I got into fighting as a teenager for the same reason. I must be looking at her, in some inquisitive way, because she seems to feel the need to elaborate a little further. And I'm all ears.

"You might pray when you find yourself in a seemingly impossible situation. Well, much of witchcraft is actually pretty similar to praying for something to change your circumstances, or situation... or whatever the case may be. It's like, creating a ritualized setting of intentions, and focusing on that intention, to bring about the change you want to see, or to bring something into your life that you feel you need... for whatever reason." She glances up at me, and I think she finds my expression reassuring. That I'm engaged in what she's talking about. At least, I hope so. I'm not sure if she realizes she's giving me a rather deep glance into the inner workings of herself. "Witchcraft has been around a long, long time. At least since humans have encountered any sort of hardships in their lives. One could argue that it dates back to human civilization itself." With that, she stops talking. I don't want her to stop talking. I try to think of something I can ask her about it, when she looks up at me again, her brows are slightly scrunched together. "Is this boring?" she asks.

"No. Not at all." I answer quickly. I'm not lying. Nothing about Vanna is boring to me. She's told me a lot about herself, just now, without even realizing she has. For instance, there was a time in her life where she felt powerless about her situation. Something made her feel trapped. Took her personal power from her... her self-worth... Drove her to a state where *ritualized prayer* was her only hope to escape something... And once again, my mind drifts back to that file locked away in my desk... A file about her, and the man that hurt her in more ways than one. A man that put her in an impossible situation...

The thought of anyone harming Vanna fuels that rage inside of me. Spurs every protective instinct I have within myself. I try not to let my mind imagine what those circumstances were for her... God knows I've seen enough to have an accurate idea of what she may have suffered through.

Fortunately, she speaks again, pulling me away from my darkening thoughts. "Anyway... No. My parents don't know about it."

"So, what's their problem with you?" I ask, hoping to be able to keep her talking. "You seem like you're doing alright. You're responsible. Working two jobs. Got your own place. Not into illegal activities like some people you know." I tease her, knocking my knee gently against hers.

"They had plans for me, I didn't want to throw my life away."

The vagueness of that reply is a clear indication to me that Vanna does not want to talk about this. I'll steer us back around and hope for the best.

"Well, I do care about you, Vanna. And I will keep you safe. You're not alone." I promise her. "Tell me something else I don't know about you."

She looks at me, "Huh?"

"Before, you said there were a lot of things you wanted to tell me." I remind her. "Tell me one thing. Just one."

"I – I don't know..." She stammers.

"If you don't tell me something, then I'll just have to ask you questions." I say, trying to keep my tone playful so she doesn't feel threatened. She's staring at me though, hesitant. "Hurry up, Vanna." I tease her.

"I don't know what to say!" she giggles.

"Times up!" I lean closer to her. "*Truth or Dare*, Vanna?"

Her eyes widen slightly. "Oh, I don't know about playing this game with you. You're naughty."

I can't help grinning at her accusation. *I'm* naughty, yet she's the one who's got the sweet, innocent thing down pat, when I know she can be a fucking seductress with the bat of an eye and a twitch of her smirk. That's part of her charm though. Part of what drives men crazy about her. How she can seem so innocent, yet sexy as fuck at the same time.

I hold up my right hand. "I promise not to push things too far."

Her eyes narrow at me with suspicion, though the corners of her mouth are still curved upwards. "Your idea of too far is what concerns me."

"I'll allow you two vetoes. How's that?" I offer, curling down three fingers of my raised hand. She hesitates, but I can see her playful side warring with her cautious mind. "Truth or Dare, baby?" I grin back at her.

"Truth." She replies, though I can see the slight worry behind her eyes. I will keep things light this first round.

"Chicken shit." I tease her, making her smile. "Okay, Truth. Are you a fugitive from justice?" I ask. When she hesitates at my joke of a question, I can't help arching a brow as I stare back at her, waiting for what should be a simple quick answer. Fuck... maybe I do need to take a peek in that file...

"No, I'm not a fugitive." She finally says.

"Way to make a guy wonder." I tease her.

"Truth or Dare, then?" she asks, cutting right to the chase.

"Truth." I smile.

"*Chicken shit.*" She throws back at me. "Tell me about your tattoo. What does your scorpion represent?"

"It represents a few things. Letting go of pain is one, another, intimidation. The scorpion also symbolizes strength and the ability to control and protect oneself. They also represent loyalty and powerful sexuality." I grin at her.

"Then it suits you well."

"I got it when I was out West for a time. When I was a nomad." But that's all I say about that time in my life. "Truth or Dare, baby?"

She squints at me before answering with "Truth."

I'll be nice, just this once more, then it's on. Though, this is a question I would like answered. "Does it turn you on to see me fight?"

"Yes."

"*Aces.*" Though, her body language already confirmed that for me. It feels good to know for sure.

"Truth or Dare?"

I lean closer to her face and whisper, "*Dare.*"

She smirks and glances around, trying to figure out something to have me do. I watch her as she twists around to look in the other direction, and then she points at something down the boardwalk. "I dare you to steal me a rose."

I lean around her to see where exactly she's pointing. There are a few potted rose bushes sitting in front of a closed shop down a few yards along the boardwalk.

"As you wish." I whisper in her ear, making her giggle. I stand up and remove my butterfly knife, flipping it open with a flourish that I know she finds sexy, and make my way towards the roses.

Selecting the prettiest one, I cut the stem, trimming off the thorns with my knife as I make my way back to her. Sitting back down on the bench beside her, I decide to cut the stem shorter, and tuck the rose in her hair above her ear.

"Thank you. It's pretty." She smiles at me.

"Pales in comparison to my little Peony." I smile back, reaching over to brush a strand of her hair behind the rose. "It's your turn, doll. Truth or Dare?"

"Truth."

"What life choice did your parents not agree with that put the strain on your relationship with them?"

She takes a breath, as if she's considering her answer, but then she hits me with "Veto."

I look at her, surprised by her response. "I should warn you, baby. A veto automatically bumps you to Dare."

"You didn't say that before we started."

I shrug. "My game. My rules. What's it gonna be? The devil you know? Or...?"

"The devil I know..." She whispers, seemingly to herself. She glances back at me. "Fine. It was over an ex. The Devil I know."

"They didn't like him?"

"You got your question answered. You get one. No more rule changes." She snaps at me, though remains playful. "Truth or Dare?"

"Truth."

"Did you sucker me into this game to fish for information?"

I grin at her. "That and then some." I reply. She's still looking at me suspiciously, but at least she's still smiling. "Your turn."

"Truth."

"Why didn't they like your ex?"

"They love him." She replies. *They* love him. She didn't? Interesting... "Truth or Dare?" she asks.

"Truth."

She's looking at me now, wickedly. Her eyes slightly hooded, her teeth lightly sinking into her lower lip as she twists in her seat to face me a little more directly. "If you really do imagine fucking me, how do you picture it happening?"

Fuck. This is a ploy to distract me, I know it. Turn this game to her advantage so I stop digging and default to testosterone driven sex hungry male. "Many different ways." I answer. "Every. Fucking. Way."

"That's not really an answer. I want details. Pick a favorite fantasy." She pushes, nudging my boot with her foot.

Images of the thousands of fantasies I've had about Vanna flash through my mind like an X-rated movie reel. A really, really long one. Fuckin A. My favorite? I'm staring at her as she waits for me to respond. I don't want to fuck this up. "I ... uh... My favorite fantasy of you..." I fucking stutter as my mind tries to latch on to something.

"Come on, Dean." She coaxes me, her foot now rubbing the side of my leg above my boot. "Don't worry about offending me. I won't hold anything against you."

Fuck! Pull it together, asshole! Forget the raunch, stick with romantic!

"The one where I'm going down on you in my bed, and you're loving every second of it... Calling my name out... that's hot as fuck." I manage to say, that fucking scenario front and center of my mind now, as I will my blood not to rush to my cock.

"That's it? You don't even fuck me in your fantasies?" She giggles.

431

I try not to chuckle at her sarcastic comment. "Truth be told, when I'm jerking off, thinking about that, I usually blow my load before I can even get to that part of the fantasy." I clear my throat. "Truth or Dare?"

"Truth."

I attempt to focus on a question I want to know about her past, but her sexy fucking thighs are squeezing my head between them in my mind and I can't think straight. "Uh... What are you afraid of?" I ask.

"Spiders." She says, simply and quickly.

"Fair enough." I sigh, disappointed with myself. I should have asked a more in-depth question about that, but her tactic is succeeding. Why are you always asking me if I'll keep you safe, for starters.

"Your turn." She smiles, stroking the back of my hand that I have draped across the back of the bench.

"Truth. Wait. Dare. I want a Dare." I need to get up and clear my damn head. No more pussy control mind tricks. I glance back at her and I can see her evil mind working behind those dark, mysterious eyes.

"I dare you... *to let me lick your scorpion*." She says, sliding her fingers inside the cuff of my leather jacket as she teasingly strokes my skin.

Fuckin'... What? I clear my throat again. "You want to...*lick* the tattoo on my chest?"

She nods, the little tip of her tongue sliding across her upper lip.

"Alright." As if I'd fucking veto this shit. I move to unzip my leather jacket but she grabs my arm to stop me.

"No, the dare was to let *me* do it."

I watch her as she slides closer to me, staring me in the eyes, inches from my face as she slowly pulls the zipper down on my jacket. In a move I sure as fuck was not expecting of her, she grabs my shoulders and throws her leg across my lap, straddling me on the bench, pushing my jacket wide open. As her hands touch my chest, running down to my abs and back up again, I come to the conclusion that there will be no turning the tables on Vanna. The table is broken. In my mind, we're fucking on the damn thing and it plain snapped in half. Her fingers unbutton the top of my shirt before she gives it a little tug, then pouts.

"What's the matter, baby?" I ask.

"Your buttons don't go down low enough. I can only get to the tip of the stinger."

"So, *lick the tip*." I grin.

She grins back at me, before she leans in closer and moves her lips to my ear, whispering breathily, "I want more than *just the tip*, Dean."

Fuuuuuuck! I'm pretty sure I just groaned. "Rip the fucking shirt, baby." I growl. I can already feel my cock pushing against the zipper of my fly.

She gives the shirt a pull, but then she giggles, tucking her face against my throat. "I feel bad ripping your shirt, Dean." She whispers against my throat, her breath and her lips touching my skin in a tantalizing way that drives me even crazier.

I reach up and rip the fucking thing myself, halfway down to my naval.

She leans back in my lap to look down at my chest, her hands reaching inside the tear to push the fabric apart, exposing my tattoo and then some.

I stare at her as she licks her lips, her eyes roaming over my body, her fingers doing the same. As her eyes flick up to meet mine, my heart damn near skips a beat. The way she's looking at me with those dark, hooded eyes, damn near evaporates my resolve. Makes me wish were in my bed, so I could show her in person, fantasy number one.

She leans in closer, so her lips are almost touching mine, but all I can feel is her breath as she whispers, "You're so beautiful. I'm gonna lick your scorpion now."

God, how I wish scorpion *was code word for something else!* But I'll take what I can get.

As Vanna moves to bring her hot little mouth to my chest, I tilt my head back and close my eyes, waiting for the sensation to hit me.

She teases me for a moment with her breath again, before I feel the warm, wet tip of her tongue on my skin, making my dick flex and the zipper of my pants that much more uncomfortable. She trails her tongue slowly across my pectoral muscle, following the curvature of the scorpions back and up the curl of its tail to the tip of its stinger, where it ends just under my collar bone. She stops there to tongue kiss just below my clavicle, before she kisses me that way back down my chest.

Vanna brings her lips back against my ear and whispers. "I pick Dare."

"I dare you to release me from the friend zone." I don't mean to sound as desperate as I do.

She bites my earlobe gently, then whispers, *"Veto."*

Fuck! "Truth then?" I open my eyes and try to focus on something to get my goddamned wits back. My eyes shift back and forth but there isn't much to see in this position. A light post. A flag post. Some fucking grass. I don't want to move either, I don't want her to stop touching me. I don't want her to get off of me.

"Your rules." She whispers in my ear again, her finger nails sliding down my chest lightly. God how I want to feel them digging into me... while she's writhing beneath me...

Fucking dick brained fool. I know exactly what she's doing to me.

"You ever think about fucking *me*, Vanna?" I ask. Perhaps I'll be able to find contentment in her answer. I can't go there with her... not yet. My little she-devil isn't going to take my soul tonight... But I just might let her drag me to the very edge of torment.

I feel her body rise up off me slightly and I lift my head to look back in her eyes for her answer. Her arms wrap around my neck as one of her hands slides up the back of my skull and pulls my face closer to hers. She stares me in the eyes as she gives me her answer.

"I'm thinking about it right now, Dean." She whispers.

Fuck... My hands reach up to hold her face as I press my mouth to hers, our tongues wrestling for control of the kiss. With a slight whimper, which ignites my flame further, she submits to me, allowing me full entry inside her mouth. Hot and smoother than oil. This woman drives me mad. In every fucking way.

Chapter
nineteen
DEAN

"I'LL BREAK." VIKING SAYS, GRABBING THE CUE BALL AND WALKING towards the end of the pool table as I finish racking up for the set.

"What are we playing?" I ask.

"Straight." He says, chalking up the end of his stick. "I gotta be somewhere before I have to come in tonight, so let's just go two or three racks." He says, placing the chalk back down on the cue rack. He slides the cue ball into position as I remove the triangle and hang it back up.

"Hot date?" I ask, watching Viking take aim.

"All my dates are hot." He says, breaking with a loud crack as the balls scatter across the green felt. He sinks one in the side pocket, then moves around to take another shot. "Four in the corner off the six." He makes that shot too.

"Was thinking about Bike Week down in Myrtle Beach." I say, watching him run the table. "You want to pick one of your hot chicks and go next weekend?"

Viking takes aim on his now fifth shot. "Nine, straight down, left corner pocket. Why Myrtle Beach? We got the fund raiser here in a month. Plenty of bikes, booty and boobs will be here for you to drool over." He takes his shot and misses, finally.

I step up and eye the table as I roll his counter to four. "Haven't taken a long run on the bikes in a while." I say, bending down and lining up my first shot. "Seven, side pocket." I make the shot. "Axel and Cherry are down if we decide to go."

"That's almost a four-hour ride."

"Two in the corner off the eight ball." I say, taking my next shot. I sink it. "So what? When is the last time we actually took a decent ride? Ain't even that long. We used to ride a lot harder than that. Four hours one way is nothing."

As I eye up my next shot, I wonder what Viking's issue is about Myrtle Beach. Normally, he'd have jumped on it damn near immediately. The bikes. The babes. The beach. The bars. All right up his alley.

"Nine off the one, side pocket." I say, lining up my shot and sinking it. "That three so far?"

"Yup. Three." Viking says. "Weekends are our busiest nights of the week. You want all of us to go?"

"Okay, what gives?" I ask, no longer looking for my next shot, I'm studying Viking as he stands, arms folded with his cue stick wedged in the crook of one of his elbows. "You got a ball and chain I don't know about that doesn't want you leaving town or something?"

He scoffs. "Fuck. No."

"Why don't you want to go to Myrtle Beach?"

"Didn't say that." Viking grumbles. "Take your fucking shot, asshole. Don't got all afternoon."

I scowl at him for a moment, then eye the table again. "Eight ball, straight down, side pocket." I sink that too. "Seriously, Bro. Something going on I should know about?"

"Could ask you the same question, *Bro*." Viking says.

"Alright. Fine. Found out about a new underground circuit."

He lets out a long sigh. "Dean, come on."

"Just want to check it out. Not saying I'm going to fight. I just want to see what's out there." I say, eyeing the table for my fifth shot. There aren't any options, so I pull a dick move because he deserves it. "Gonna attempt the twelve into the ten into three into the corner pocket."

"Never gonna happen." He mutters.

"Nope." I grin, tapping the cue ball lightly and watching it roll into the cluster of balls I called, leaving him with no shot either.

"Fucking dick." He sighs. I roll my counter to four as well. Viking steps up to the table as I step back and watch him struggle to find a shot worth taking. "We both know you're gonna fight. I know about the circuit in Myrtle Beach. I don't think you should do it, Dean."

"How do you know about it? And why the hell didn't you mention it?"

"Because you need to back off that shit. Just because you're tapping a chick a decade younger than you, doesn't automatically make you age backwards." He says, angling his cue stick high. "Thirteen, side pocket."

"In your dreams." I mutter. "And fuck you, by the way. I'm in better shape than a lot of guys half my age, you prick. I'm also not quite a decade older than her."

"Stop fucking crying so I can focus on this shot, God damn it." Viking throws over his shoulder at me.

"You're only a few months younger than me, dick."

He misses the shot, but he didn't have a prayer anyway. "Still younger." He turns around to look at me, that fucking annoying grin of his. "I can't wait to throw you that *over the hill party* in three years. I can picture all the black balloons and the coffin shaped cake now."

He's such an asshole. "That's still three years away. And besides, forty is the new thirty." I glare back at him. "And I don't give a shit. I'll get you back soon after. Your theme will be dicks. Dick balloons. And a big dick shaped cake."

He's still grinning as he shrugs. "As long as there's cake."

Human garbage disposal. "Yeah, you would eat a dick." I mutter, walking past him to take my turn.

"Since we're on that topic, has Vanna let you out of your cock cage yet?"

Shit. Here we go! "Fifteen off the six and twelve. Fifteen in the left corner pocket, twelve in the right corner." I say, leaning down to angle this shot.

"Now who's dreaming." Viking says. "So, has she let you bone her yet or what?"

"Shut up and let me take this shot." It's not impossible, if I slice it just right. I slam the stick into the cue ball and it all works out Aces.

"Nice shot." Viking nods. "So, was she worth the wait or what?"

"Fourteen, straight down, corner pocket."

"*Bro...*" I can hear the taunt in his voice.

I take the shot and sink it. "That's three. Ten in the side."

"Bro..." he sounds like he's about to burst out laughing.

I sink the ten. "One. Corner pocket."

"You're still wearing the fucking cock cage, aren't you?"

I sink the one in the corner. "Four. The three straight up, corner pocket." I sink that too.

"No wonder you want to fight. Jerking it ain't cutting it anymore." Viking laughs. "Bro, I warned you about the friend zone. You *Nice Guy'd* your way right the fuck into it. You're the Mayor of the friend zone. But there are plenty of chicks that are more than willing to help you out."

"Not gonna do that. She's worth the wait." I say, angling my next shot. Only three left.

"I don't understand either of you." He sighs.

"You don't have to... Two, side pocket." I sink it. "That's five."

"Is she a virgin or something?"

"You really think I'm going to answer that?" I sigh, walking around the table to shoot from the other side.

"Vanna is hot as fuck..." he begins to say, hesitating to contemplate his words, before he continues, catching my glare. "Dude, maybe she's just playing you."

"Are you really still on that? She hasn't asked me for shit. It's been four and a half months. All she asked me for was a job here, two nights a week. What the fuck could she be playing me for?"

"Maybe she's just gallivanting around with you trying to make me jealous." He jests.

I laugh at that one. "Six, side pocket."

"She's seen my dick, bro." he reminds me for the hundredth time since it happened. I miss the fucking shot and glare up at his goddamned grinning face. Straightening, I walk to the end of the table to add five to my count, then sit back and watch him sink the last two balls before he racks them up for round two.

"If Cherry and Axel are going to Myrtle Beach with us, who are you gonna have running this place while we're there?"

"Snowy knows how to tend bar, so does Stacy. Dozer can fill in for you. I'll check in Saturday morning, if they say shit got too wild, we'll just close Saturday night. One night. No biggie."

"You want to fight that fucking badly? I could save us an eight-hour trip and just kick your ass here... Like last time." He grins at me.

"That was almost fifteen years ago. And you may have technically won, but I took your giant ass down with me."

Viking grins wider as he racks up the balls. "That was an epic fight." He nods, and I can tell by the expression on his face, he's thinking back on that night. "Man, we were local legends for a time after that."

I chuckle. "Legends in our own minds, maybe. But yeah, that was a goddamned fight."

"More than our own minds, bro." Viking says, lining up the cue to break. "We were top fighters on the local circuit for a long fucking time."

Yeah, we were. For a time.

As I watch Viking break, then proceed to run the table, I can't help thinking back on that night almost twenty long years ago. The night Viking and I first crossed paths. It was more like a collision though, as opposed to a crossing of paths. A collision in a makeshift ring in the cellar of an old beer distillery, surrounded by forty or fifty other men, shouting and cheering, chugging beers and placing cash bets.

Viking had been the guy to beat back then, an undefeated fighter in his region up near Raleigh. After watching him pummel the shit out of two other guys in the beginning of the night, nobody else was willing to step up to him. So, I did. I didn't have any defeats in the circuit in my own region, and was itching for a challenge. Most of my own fights never went beyond a third round. Viking was known for taking his opponents down within the first round or two. When I stepped into the ring with him, he didn't take me seriously. By our fourth round, he was taking me seriously. And by our twelfth round, I had his complete respect.

Twelve bloody, grueling rounds. No gear, no gloves, no mouth guards, no nothing. It was damn near unheard of for two underground fighters going twelve rounds, especially not from different weight classes.

For almost an hour, we fought. I had managed not to let him get his huge arms around me. Managed to avoid his powerful punches and kicks to my head, which undoubtedly would have resulted in a knock out and instant defeat on my part. But man, my body took a pounding.

The few punches he managed to graze my face with, left me with cuts and bruises, one eye damn near swollen shut, sweat and blood stinging my other from a cut above my brow. The body shots he nailed me with had my guts feeling like they had been rearranged. For all I knew, I was dying. Bleeding from internal injuries. The two things I had working for me for most of the fight, had been my speed and stamina.

I had managed to wear him down. Exhausted him, though I had been exhausted too by that twelfth round. I was running on fumes, staggering to keep myself upright between dodging and blocking against his punches. Bracing myself for his powerful kicks that I was becoming too slow to avoid, having to absorb them. In the final moments, he charged me, and I held onto him like my life had depended on it. It basically did, in my mind, in that moment.

When he finally got those huge fucking arms around me that I had managed to avoid up until that moment, I expected him to slam me down to the mat and pin me under his weight. There would have been no chance of me escaping him. I was dead tired, no strength left to have been able to fight him off me. I expected him to force me to submit by way of an Arm bar, or a choke hold until I passed out.

But he didn't. Viking had known I was spent. I had nothing left in me. He threw me to the mat, where I landed on my back. I remember feeling the wind rush from my lungs, and staring up into the glaring lights above the ring. I made no attempt to get up. I couldn't. They were going to have to drag me out, like I had seen happen with fallen fighters before.

I remember him standing over me, his big damn head and broad as fuck shoulders blocking out the light above me.

"Stay down there." He had muttered, before he raised both hands up in triumph to a crowd screaming louder than anything I had ever heard before.

I remember his words pissing me the fuck off. I had already come to terms with myself that I was not getting up. I didn't need him to fucking tell me that.

With the last bit of energy left in me, I jerked my knee back, and slammed my foot into the back of his leg, sweeping him off his feet and sending him crashing down to the mat flat on his back beside me.

I let my head flop to the side to look at him, grinning tiredly. Had I had any strength left, I would have given him the finger when he turned to me.

I wasn't expecting him to grin back at me when he finally did turn his head to face me.

"The fuck is your name again?" he had asked.

"Dean Keegan." I remember my voice croaking out.

"I'm Viking." He had said.

"I know who you are."

"You're a *crazy* motherfucker, Dean Keegan."

I remember attempting to shrug.

"Thanks for stepping into the ring with me."

"Thanks for fighting me."

"Best fucking fight ever." Viking had smiled.

"Fuck yeah it was." I smiled back.

At that point, Viking sat up and got to his feet, leaning down over me, his hand outstretched. "Can you get up, Bro?" he had asked.

"I can try." I said, lifting my arm to take his hand.

Viking hauled me back to my feet and made sure I could stand on my own. The crowd was still going crazy, apparently, they'd never seen a fight like this before either.

"Can you walk, bro?" he had asked.

"Think so." I said.

"Let's get our money and go grab some beers." Viking suggested.

We hung out the rest of the night at a 24-hour diner, talking about everything from fighting, to motorcycles to chicks. Laughing at how the waitresses were looking at us like someone ought to call me an ambulance. I looked like shit. At least I didn't piss blood that night. It had been a concern. But damn, it had also been one Hell of a fight...

"I'm going to Myrtle Beach." I say, looking back at him. "I want to go before things pop off with the Chrome Demons."

He shakes his head at me. "You don't have to go to Myrtle Beach to chase the dragon, Dean. The dragon is right here, willing to kick your ass again and save you the trip." Viking says.

I ignore his statement. "I'm going to Myrtle Beach." I reiterate.

He lets out a long, defeated sigh. "Fine. Fuck it. We're going to Myrtle Beach."

"ARE YOU SURE YOU'RE OKAY?" I ASK LAURA, HOLDING THE PHONE AGAINST my ear with my shoulder as I open up a box of new candles we ordered for the shop. She went home sick a few days ago, and I've been running the shop alone, since. Ethan has been away on vacation with his boyfriend all week as well.

"I have an appointment tomorrow. I think I've just caught the flu." She sounds terrible. Exhausted.

"Okay, well if you need anything let me know."

"Thanks, sweetie." She says, before we say our goodbyes and hang up. I place the phone back on the receiver on the edge of her desk and start unpacking the new inventory.

What I now recognize as the sound of a motorcycle, pulls into our parking lot in the back of the house. I smile to myself. Before Dean, the sound of a motorcycle was just white noise to me. Now, when I hear them, I take notice. Not many of our customers are the biker types, but I'm not expecting

Dean to show up today. And it isn't Viking, either. His bike is way louder than the one that just pulled in.

As I go over the inventory list, I curiously wait to see who walks through the front door. The little bells on the front door jingle, and I greet them with our customary, "Welcome to the Ametrine Cauldron."

The man that steps into the main room between the two white columns, is probably the last person I expected to see in the shop today. Or ever, anywhere, really. I met him in darkness, weeks ago. At Axel's patch party. I never got a really good look at him because of that. He was near the fight Dean got into by the bonfire, but I had been too preoccupied with what was going on to pay attention to him. Somehow though, I recognize him immediately.

Maybe it's his somewhat thin, toned build. His clean shaven, angular jawline. Dark, slicked back hair. He's wearing biker boots and blue jeans. A black leather cut that says Vice President of the Chrome Demons MC. And his name patch...

"Legion." I say, unable to hide the surprise in my voice.

A broad smile stretches across his features, that reaches his pale blue eyes. So pale, they almost look like a stormy grey. I never noticed how unique they were in the darkness. They're almost hypnotizing... in an intimidating kind of way.

"Vanna." He growls my name. "What a pleasant surprise this is." He steps towards me in two long strides, extending his hand to me.

I absentmindedly place my hand in his and watch him raise it to his mouth, bending his tall frame, as he places a light kiss on the back of my hand. After a moment, he releases me and straightens.

"I'm pleased that you would even remember me." he says.

"It's a memorable name." I smile. "Goes well with the name of your MC, too."

"Indeed."

"Well, since you're here, what can I do for you?" I ask, watching his unique eyes roam over me. I'm expecting him to have some sort of a message for me to relay back to Dean or something of the sorts.

"Figure candles." He replies. "I was also hoping to find a few specific ingredients."

"Really?" I say, unable to hold back my surprise. I never expected to encounter a biker who was also a male witch. "You practice?"

He runs his long fingers over his smooth jaw line as he continues to grin at me. "I dabble." He smirks, with a slight, flourishing wave of his hand that seems oddly inhuman.

"Well, we actually just got this new shipment of figure candles in this morning. I've just started to unpack them. Are you looking for a specific figure?"

"What's in your box?" He grins.

"Male and female figures. Yoni and... the male counterpart, candles." I look down and feel my cheeks slightly flush with warmth, unable to look him in the eyes as I avoid saying the term *Penis Candles* to him. I'm not usually shy about discussing these magic tools with people. But there's something about Legion's intense stare, that just makes me feel a little timid and embarrassed about saying those words to him. When I peek up at him, he's still wearing that grin on his face.

"How many of each are in the box?" He asks.

"Umm..." I glance around for the inventory sheet, then grab it to look over. "Six of each, except the... umm... you know... there are nine of those." I say, looking back at him. "They're a big seller." I shrug, biting my lower lip.

"I want your box." He licks his lips briskly and smiles again.

"Oh." I say, surprised. "I still have to calculate the prices... it'll take just a minute if you want to have a look around?" I say, gesturing towards the rest of the shop behind him.

"I'll do that, Vanna." He turns to explore the shop.

Sinking down into the chair behind the desk, I grab the calculator and a pen to tally up his purchase on a receipt pad. "It comes to one hundred-seventy-five before taxes... Is there anything else I can help you find?"

"Devil's Shoe String? Vervain?" He asks, glancing back towards me.

"Yes, we do have them." I walk around the desk in his direction. "We keep our herbs and smudge bundles on these shelves and in these drawers over here." I say, stepping over to our display area on the opposite side of the room. Pulling open the second drawer, I grab him a packet of Devil's Shoe String and one of Vervain. When I step back with the intention of giving them to him, I bump my back up against his front, and accidently drop the packets.

"Oh my gosh, I'm sorry, I didn't even hear you walk over here." I say, and before I can bend to grab the packets, Legion already snatches them up off the floor.

He smiles at me as he stands back up to his full height, which has to be at least six feet. "I'd love to get my hands in your drawers." he says, with a borderline flirtatious tone as he steps around to stand beside me.

I decide to ignore that possible inuendo, as I'm really not sure if he is flirting, or just wants to see the selection. Opening up the top drawer for him to see the first array of herbs and resins, I can't help noticing his long, pale fingered hands as he places one on the edge of the drawer beside mine. Very close to mine.

"Ah... Palo Santo... to blind an enemy." He says, lifting a piece of the holy wood out of the drawer.

"I hadn't heard it could be used for that." I say, glancing up at him.

His eyes slide to the side to glance back down at me. "You wouldn't need it. Your magic doesn't require tools to work."

"I just do Reiki, now... My spells always find a way to backfire on me." Why did I tell him that?

Legion chuckles, a low, deep sound. I close the top drawer and proceed to show him the contents of the other four. He selects a few more items from each drawer before we walk back to Laura's desk. I finish writing up his receipt, and he pays in cash.

"Do you have a card?" he asks, when I hesitate, he adds, "For Reiki. I'm curious. I may want to schedule something with you."

"Oh, right." Why am I such an air head around him? "I actually don't, I'm sorry. But I can give you the shops card, and you can always call here to make an appointment. My boss Laura usually picks up the phone. But I'm here weekdays."

He only smiles, so I grab a card and hand it to him because I don't know what else to do. He takes it from me and slips it into his vest pocket.

"Well, thank you for your business, Legion." I smile pleasantly at him.

"It was my pleasure." He grins back.

I chew my bottom lip lightly as I look down at the box. "You came on a motorcycle..."

"Yes. I did. Would you mind holding onto this for me? I'll send a prospect to come get it by the end of the day."

"Oh, sure." I say, grabbing the box and turning to place it on the floor behind Laura's desk. "I'm here until five."

"I'll be sure they don't keep you waiting." Legion smiles.

I walk him to the front door and watch him leave, before I sit back down behind Laura's desk and debate whether or not I should text Dean, or just mention it later tonight at dinner. Legion seemed like he was being polite. Curious about the specific herbs he purchased, I glance down at the carbon copy of his receipt, where I notice a business card sitting on top of it.

I pick the card up to examine it. It's just an address on one side, with a hand written phone number. The other side has a logo of a skull with de-mon horns on it, Chrome Demons MC written around it. I guess it's the ad-dress to their clubhouse. If I take the bypass instead of the main highway, I'd actually pass by it on my way home. If I was ever curious about it, that is. Why would Legion leave this? He knows I *belong* to Dean. I roll my eyes and smile to myself as I get up from Laura's desk and walk to the break room. Grabbing my purse, I tuck the card into the front zippered pocket. I wonder how Dean is going to react to this one.

DEAN

WHEN VANNA PULLS UP MY DRIVEWAY, I'M SITTING ON MY FRONT PORCH in one of the Adirondack's waiting for her. I know she stopped home to check in on her cat before she got here. I saw her arrive home a little while ago.

"How was work, dear?" I playfully ask, as she exits her car and strolls towards me. I get up to greet her properly, wrapping my arm around her waist and pulling her against me when she gets to the top of the steps.

She looks up at me, almost as if she's studying me, and the corners of her mouth are slightly curved up in a little smile.

"It was... *interesting.*" She says, reaching up to touch my face. Stroking the stubble of my jaw for a moment, she continues to look at me in this odd, appraising way.

"What?" I ask.

"You're definitely better looking." She says, then drops her hand to pat my chest and backs out of my embrace.

"Glad you think so... But who are you comparing me to?"

"Did you cook tonight? Or are we going out?" she asks, side stepping my question in true Vanna fashion.

"I cooked. Mind answering my question?"

"Which one?" she teases me, stepping towards my front door. I automatically grab it and hold it open for her to step inside, following her in when she does.

"Both, but the second takes precedence right now." I say, closing the door behind me as I come to stand before her. "Who are you comparing me to?"

"Legion. He came into my job today."

Fuck my life... I was not expecting that. My protective instincts kick into over drive, though I try not to let her notice the extent to which I am bothered by this. "The fuck was he doing at your job?"

"Shopping." She shrugs, then turns to walk over to the kitchen island where she slides her purse off her arm and places it down on the marble top.

"Did he fuckin' hit on you?" I ask, wondering if that's the reason for her comparison.

Her eyes squint slightly, as if she's contemplating my question. It's really not a difficult one, which fuckin' irks me that she has to think about it before answering me.

"I don't know... For a moment, I thought, *maybe.* But he was perfectly friendly. Polite. He bought a lot of stuff. He came on a motorcycle and bought a box of candles and herbs and such. He had to leave it behind and have a prospect pick it up before I left today."

I don't know if Vanna even knows when guys are hitting on her. She really doesn't seem to grasp how attractive she is. Not fully, anyway.

"He fuckin' touch you?"

She giggles at me. "No more than when he first introduced himself to me at Axel's party."

"So, he kissed your hand and fuckin' sniffed you again?"

She laughs a little more. "He didn't *sniff* me. But he did kiss my hand. *Briefly.* Don't worry." She says, walking around the side of the kitchen island and opening my fridge to grab a bottle of water. She unscrews the cap and takes a sip as she watches me. "Oh, and he said he wanted to see what I had in my drawers."

"The fuck!" I nearly shout, and she almost chokes on her water as she giggles at me some more. "He said that? *Verbatim?*"

The tip of her tongue presses to the side of her upper lip as she seems to think back. "I was showing him some herbs... and I think he actually said he wanted to get his hands in my drawers." I don't know what I look like right now, but it prompts her to hold her hand up and wave it in my face. "Okay, calm down, killer." She says, placing the bottle down on the marble counter top. "He was probably just talking about the display drawers. We were literally standing right at them going through herbs."

Or the sneaky, demonic fuck saw us that night on the picnic table... When I had my hand in her literal fucking *drawers!* No way I'm bringing that up though. She would flip the fuck out on me... I swallow hard and bite my tongue. "Right." I manage to choke out. *Fucking motherfucker...*

"Oh, he left this behind, too." She says, walking back to her purse and pulling out a card. I walk over to her and take it. A Chrome Demons' business card, with the address to the Demons' Den clubhouse, and probably his fucking phone number. He either knew she was going to give this to me, or he really fucking has the hots for my woman. Especially if he was in the shadows creeping on us when I was getting her off... The prick was probably whacking off to her too...

He knows I know where their club house is, though... So why would he want her to give this to me? He had to have been hoping she'd keep this to herself. We had argued that night, if he was watching that, maybe he's hoping she and I split and she's available.

I stuff the card in my shirt pocket. "How'd he seem?" I ask. "Was he surprised to see you, or do you get the impression he knew you worked there and just acted like he was shopping?"

"All I know is that he spent a little over two hundred bucks, and was looking for specific things." Vanna says. "I couldn't really tell if he was surprised or not. I was surprised, though. *A biker male witch.* Who knew?" She adds. I hate that this seems to impress her on some level. She hesitates for a moment before she continues, "Did you know he has gray blue eyes? They're really intense."

"Guess I do now." I hate that he's left any kind of lingering impression on her.

Vanna giggles again. "Your eyes are nicer. I actually don't like blue eyes very much."

"Lucky me." I mutter.

"Are you jealous?" she smirks.

"Are you testing me?"

She shakes her head slowly. "I'm just telling you what happened at work today."

"He shows up there again, or anyone in that fucking crew, Vanna, you better call me. I mean *immediately.* And you are never to go near that clubhouse."

"Okay."

"What did the prospect do? Did you recognize him?"

"Nothing. And no. He just picked up the box and left. He was there for less than a minute." She shrugs. "Just a young guy in a leather vest like all your friends wear, with brown hair and a mole or something on his cheek. I've never seen him before. Why would I?"

"Just asking... The prospect say anything to you?"

445

"He said Legion wanted my box and he was here to get it for him."
She shrugs.

He wanted her box...

Am I losing my fuckin' mind? Legion is definitely testing me through Vanna. He's testing me, or he fucking wants her for himself. Two solid innuendos about her fuckin' pussy... As far as he knows, I'm a civilian. I'm not a member of the Saviors anymore. He shouldn't be aware of my pending presidential status, anyway. If he is, then we've got problems. And we're dealing with more than just the *mole* on that prospect's face. We've got a traitor among us. If Legion is still under the impression that I don't belong to a club, that hands-off policy wouldn't apply as strongly to my claim on Vanna, in *his* mind. Even though that's fucking bullshit. Patch or no patch, Vanna belongs to me. I don't need a cut on my back to put him six feet under for touching my woman.

"Are we going to have dinner?" she asks, pulling me out of my thoughts.

"Yeah, doll." I say. "Coming right up."

After we finish our meal, Vanna gets up to collect our plates to bring them to the sink, but I stop her, gently grabbing her hand and asking her to sit back down.

"What's going on?"

"I want to talk to you about something." I say, watching her lower herself back into her seat. I loosen my grip on her hand slightly, to see if she wants to pull her hand back from me, but she leaves it in my grasp. I smile inwardly.

"Is it about Legion?" She asks.

"No. Forget about Legion." I beat down the pang of irrational jealousy I feel inside. "Just, stay away from him."

"I said I would. What else did you want to talk about?"

"I'm taking Viking, Axel and Cherry to Bike Week in Myrtle Beach with me next weekend. I want you to come with us... with me."

"*Oh.*" She says, seemingly surprised by my request.

"We'd leave Friday, probably be back here Sunday night. Do you think Laura would let you take off Friday?"

"Um... I mean... yeah, probably." She lifts her shoulder in a slight shrug. "I've been running the shop alone all week, she'd probably let me take an extra day off."

Aces... so far. "So, would you go with me? I've already booked three rooms. It's short notice, I realize. I was actually lucky to get the rooms with everyone booking hotels for the event in advance. Double beds in each. So, you'd have your own bed, but you'd be rooming with me." Somehow, what I had in my head sounded a lot smoother than what just came out of my mouth. Damn it. "It's actually a nice hotel. Over-looking the ocean. Private balcony." I grin, leaning into her slightly. "A *Spa level nice bathroom.*"

She bites her bottom lip as she smiles and looks down at our joined hands laying against the top of the dining room table between us. "Bike Week?" she glances back up at me inquisitively. "What does that entail?"

"A fuck ton of motorcycles. All kinds of vendors, but mostly geared towards bikers. Wet t-shirt contests." I smirk at her.

446

She rolls her eyes playfully. "Oh boy, I can't wait to see *that*."

I rub her hand with my thumb lightly. "It's basically what we do here in the fall, just on a much larger scale."

"Would we take Serene?" She asks, though one of her brows slightly arches as she asks. "It's kind of a long ride... and... well, you know how she gets." Vanna giggles.

I can't help grinning, catching her drift. "Right." I chuckle. Vanna and Serene *get along* a little too well when they're together for extended rides. "We can take one of my side chicks. You'll have to pack light though. Limited room on a bike. Essential items and two outfits, something to sleep in."

She nods in understanding, but then realization hits her. "Wait... *Myrtle Beach...*" she says, looking at me. "Are you going to that underground thing? That guy in the suit...you called him, didn't you?"

I take a breath and let it out slowly. I don't want to lie to her. Or get her there under false pretenses. "Yes. That too. Gonna be a busy weekend." I try to sound humorous about it. She pulls her hand gently, and I release her, leaning back in my seat to study her as she contemplates what I've told her.

"Higher stakes. More dangerous." She says, hands in her lap now, fidgeting.

"To an extent. But cleaner. *No diseases.*" I joke. She doesn't look amused. "Better organized. Higher pay out when I win."

"*If* you win." She sighs.

"Ouch." I say, though I grin at her to let her know I wasn't actually offended by that.

"There's a chance you might not. What if you get really hurt?"

I shrug. "I've lost fights before. Not a big deal. There are rules. No weapons. It's a cleaner version of what you saw. If you really don't want to go with me, you can wait for me in the hotel. But Axel, Cherry and Viking will be there, too. You'd be with them when I step into the ring."

"This is so sudden." She says, moving her hands to her arms as she crosses them casually, except for the fact that she's gently rubbing her own arms as if to soothe herself. She's concerned. "Why do you want to do this?"

"To do it." I shrug. "It's a circuit I haven't broken into yet. I just want to see what's out there. Test myself. I've beaten so many guys here. I'm looking for a challenge. The only real way to know how good you are is to push yourself." She doesn't say anything, she's simply studying me right back. "I might not even fight, Vanna. We might end up just watching a few fights... Placing some bets."

"What are the chances of that being the case?"

"Fifty percent." She looks at me skeptically. "Alright... more like seventy thirty."

"In favor of fighting?" She sighs, sitting back to look at me for a few moments. "You really like to fight, huh?"

"Guess it's in my blood." Though, I don't have to guess. I know. She doesn't realize how right she was about the origin of my name... Keegan, Descendant of the Fiery One. My father was a violent motherfucker. Full of rage. All the time. I tried to become a better man than he had been. Channel my rage into something more productive. Or at least, channel it into something that wasn't

447

my wife and children... Not that I have children, but I've never hit a woman in my life. Not even Lucinda. As much as I've wanted to kill her at times.

I shake my head, not wanting to take this trip down memory lane again, and bring my focus back to Vanna. "So, will you come to Myrtle Beach with me? I promise to be a gentleman."

The corners of her lips curve upwards slightly. "I'll think about it." She says, getting back up to grab our plates and take them to the kitchen sink. I get up to help her and follow her over. Standing beside her as she rinses them off, I bump her gently with my body to get her attention. She looks up at me as I reach over and shut the faucet off.

"It would really mean a lot if you came."

She shifts to face me more directly and leans back against the counter beside the oven, looking at me contemplatively. "It's not really seventy-thirty, is it? It's more like eighty-twenty." I don't say anything. "You really want me there?"

"Yes."

"Why?"

"I want you in my life, Vanna. This is part of my life... I promised you I'd show you what you need to see from me. I meant that in all aspects." I have yet to bring up the fact that I'm about to be patched in as the president of the Saviors MC, but as that's top-secret MC business at the moment, I hold back on that bit of information for the time being.

She nods. "I saw this part."

"What you saw was nothing. I barely broke a sweat."

"This is about more than just a fight. What is it really about?"

Funny how she tries to pull it out of me, but is a vault when I attempt to pull it out of her. I let out a sigh before I confess. "Mid to late thirties... It's considered old for a fighter. I know I'm in the twilight of my life in this aspect. I've got a few years left to do this. And with certain things coming down the line, I'm not sure when I'll get the chance again. Or *if*, I will."

Her eyes soften slightly. "You're not old, Dean. Please." She says, her gaze drifting down my body for a few seconds. "You're in amazing shape, for anyone." She adds. "I wouldn't even say for a man your age. Just... you're in amazing shape. Period."

I can't help the crooked grin on my face as I watch her check me out. It feels fucking great to know she appreciates what she sees. "Thanks, doll." I growl, reaching out to grab her hips and pull her to me. She lifts up her arms to place them on my shoulders as she leans her head back slightly to look at me.

"You're welcome." She smiles.

I pull her body more firmly against mine, and press my hips into her a little harder. "You're welcome *to it*." I grin, pulling another giggle out of her.

"You're such a rogue... A rogue, and a *tease*."

"*I'm a tease?*" I can't keep the bewilderment out of my voice. "You vetoed my dare to let me out of the friend zone." I jab back at her, playfully.

She bites her bottom lip as she grins back at me, shrugging her shoulders. "Pay back's a bitch. So am I, I guess."

"I don't mind a challenge. But if you call my woman a bitch again, we're gonna have words." I tease, and she rolls her eyes at me. "So, will you come with me to Myrtle Beach?"

She purses her lips, but the corners of her mouth are still curved upwards as she pretends to contemplate my question. "What about Nico? I can't board him."

"Give him extra food. Extra water. You'll be in your own bed by Sunday night. It's only Friday and Saturday night. Besides, he's a cat. He'll probably sleep until you get back."

She gives me a slight frown. "Over night is one thing. But..."

"Viper likes cats." I interject, before she can even entertain turning me down. "I can have Viper look in on him Saturday." I press. She arches one of her perfect little brows at me, skeptically. I release one of her hips to reach for my cell in my back pocket and bring up his number. He picks up on the second ring.

"VP... I have a favor to ask." I say to him.

"You're not the president yet." He grumbles.

"I'll remember this when I am."

He sighs. "What is it?"

"I'm taking Vanna to Myrtle Beach next weekend. Need someone I can trust to check in on her cat on Saturday. Make sure it's got food and water and shit." I say, trying not to laugh as I ask this favor of him.

There's a moment of silence, before he comes back at me with, "Are you fucking kidding me? There are prospects for this kind of bullshit." He isn't wrong.

"But I trust *you*. Besides, you love cats. Make a new friend." I joke, winking at Vanna as she intently listens to every word I'm saying.

He sighs. "I do love pussy."

"Wait a minute. Did you just make a god damned joke? I'm impressed."

"Fuck you, Dean." He grunts.

"Can I count on you?"

He lets out another annoyance ridden sigh. "Fuck it. Fine."

"Thanks bro." I say, before he hangs up on me. I grin and shove the phone back in my pocket, before I grab her hip and pull her back to me again. "Now that that's settled." I smile. "Will you come with me?"

She reaches up with one of her hands to run her fingers through my hair. I fucking love it when she touches me like this. It's such a soothing sensation, a calming effect that always manages to release the tension in my body that I'm not even aware I'm holding.

"*Alright...* I'll go with you to Myrtle Beach."

"Aces." I grin at her, leaning forward for a kiss.

Chapter
twenty

Vanna

WALKING DOWN MY PORCH STEPS, DEAN EXCITEDLY DISMOUNTS HIS motorcycle, jogging up to me to grab the little duffle bag I'm carrying for our trip to Myrtle Beach. I watch as he straps it to the backrest of the bike on top of his own duffle bag.

"You ready to go, baby?" he asks, with a beaming smile. I can tell it's genuine, even though I can't see his eyes behind his dark shades. His brackety dimples showing through his shorter facial scruff. He buzzed the sides of his hair, too.

"Well don't you look handsome." I smile back at him as I come to stand beside his bike. Not that he isn't handsome all the damn time.

Dean grins at me as he strokes the stubble of his jaw line. "You like it shorter?" he asks, one of his arching brows raising above the rim of his sunglasses.

I shrug. "You always look good. You do ruggedly handsome very well. Now, aren't you going to introduce us?" I joke, nodding at his motorcycle. I already know it's a *she*. One of his *side chicks*. This side chick happens to be candy apple red, with a lot of chrome, and black leather seats with matching studded side bags.

"This little lady is Betty. She's a Harley Davidson Heritage Softail Classic."

"She's lovely." I pull my sunglasses down for a moment to look at her. "Did you give my spare key to Viper?"

"Yes. He'll let me know when he comes and goes tomorrow." Dean says, grabbing the extra helmet from one of the side bags and strapping it onto me. "Don't worry," he continues, grabbing the handle bars of the bike and throwing a leg over to mount it. "Nico will be fine. Let's have a good time, doll."

"Let's." I sigh, grabbing onto his shoulders for balance as I climb onto the bike behind him. I'm comfortably wedged between his back and the duffle bags.

"You okay?" he asks. "You got enough room?"

"Yes. I'm fine." I say, situating myself and wrapping my arms around his middle.

Dean fires the bike up, twisting the throttle and kicking up the stand. "You know the drill, doll. Just pat my stomach if you need me to find a place to stop. It's a little under four hours to the hotel from here. I used to ride a lot harder than that, but you haven't. No shame in needing a pit stop."

"I'm not tapping out before Cherry does. We got this." I giggle, giving him a slight squeeze.

He glances over his shoulder at me with a little grin. "Aces, baby."

By the time we make it to the parking garage of the hotel, almost three and a half hours later, my legs are a little sore. Dean helps me off the back of his bike, and I play it off like everything is fine. He's got that knowing look on his face as he tucks his shades in the pocket of his leather jacket.

"I didn't tap out." I say, trying to stretch my legs a little.

"You did really good, baby." He winks at me as he removes his helmet and tucks it into the side bag. I hand him mine to put away also.

Viking and Axel, with Cherry on the back of his bike, pull into the space beside us and dismount their bikes as well. Dean grabs our stuff off the back of the bike and tucks the straps into the saddle bags on the opposite side.

Flinging his arm across my shoulders, we walk towards the elevator that will bring us down to the front doors of the hotel's main lobby. Once Dean has everyone checked in, we take the elevators up to the twentieth floor, where our three rooms are, side by side. Axel and Cherry take the furthest one, Viking in the middle, and Dean and I, the first.

"Let's rally in the lobby at six o' clock, sharp. You've got a couple hours to relax, explore, whatever. But I've got a van coming to take us over to fight night, tonight." Dean says to his three friends.

They all agree, and I wait until we're in our hotel room before I ask, "That's tonight? Already?" I can't believe he rode this far and is going to fight tonight. "Don't you want to rest and be fresh before you get in the ring?"

"We've got a few hours. I plan to kick back for a bit." Dean says, dropping his duffle bag on the bed nearest the door. He places my bag on the bed near the balcony doors. I watch as he pushes the curtains all the way over to expose the view of the ocean. The room is nice. Two queen sized beds, with pale blue bedding. The room is mostly hues of seafoam greens and light blues, accented with drift wood color night stands and dressers. There's a large flat screen tv on top of the dresser, and a round table with two chairs in the corner of the room near the balcony doors.

"Do you want to see the view first? Or the spa level nice bathroom?" Dean teases me.

I walk over to the balcony door where he's waiting, as he slides it open for me. I step outside onto our private little balcony and place my hands on the railing. looking out over the ocean before us. There are privacy walls on either side, as well as another set of chairs.

Dean steps up behind me, placing his hands on my hips and his chin on top of my head. The sky is clear and the ocean is a deep shade of blue. There are colorful umbrellas and beach towels scattered all over the sand below, and I can hear the faint sound of waves crashing along the shore. The breeze is nice up here as well.

"This is lovely." I sigh, feeling him shift slightly to place a light kiss on top of my head. He lingers for a moment, and I can feel him inhale the scent of my hair. I twist around to face him. "Are you sure you want to fight tonight? Doesn't this inspire you to relax a little?"

He just grins at me. "I'll have Saturday to recuperate, if I need it. Part of Sunday too. If I need more time, you can ride back with Viking, Sunday. He'll have you home in time to rest up for work the next day."

His words make me feel uneasy. And it must be written on my face, because he lifts his hand from my hip to stroke my cheek gently.

"That's worst-case scenario, Vanna. I have every intention of riding home as planned, with you on the back of *my* bike." After a moment, he takes my hand and leads me back into the hotel room. "Check out the bathroom. Let me know how it compares to mine." He teases me.

The bathroom is spacious, and is floor to ceiling glass tiles in all shades of blues and greens, with accent pieces of what looks like Mother of Pearl and Abalone shell. The shower isn't as large as Dean's, but it's spacious as well, with a huge raindrop style shower head in the center, as well as a detachable showerhead on the wall. There's also a hot tub, big enough for two.

"It's really nice. I think I prefer your style though." I say, stepping back into the room with him. He's sitting on the edge of his bed now, his leather jacket draped on the bed beside him. "What do we do now?" I ask, glancing at the clock on the night table behind him. "We've got four hours before we have to be in the lobby."

"Power up." Dean says. "You hungry? I've gotta get some protein in me and hydrate a little. Gonna take a couple hours nap, to reserve my energy. You're welcome to tag along with whatever the others are up to, just... nothing alone." I can tell he wants me to stay with him.

"I think I'd rather stay here. I'm a little tired from the ride, too." The vibration from the bike, though nowhere near as powerful as Serene, kind of lulled me into a sleepy state.

Dean orders room service, and after we eat lunch together, he kicks off his boots and sprawls out on his bed. I notice him watching me as I organize our plates and discarded napkins and such on the room service cart, so that everything is somewhat neat before I push it out into the hall for the staff to collect.

"You wanna cuddle with me?" He asks, a little smirk on his face.

I can't help smiling back at him. "Do you want me to close the curtains? That might help you fall asleep better with a little less light in here."

"Whatever you want."

I walk over to the balcony door and open it, sliding the screen door over, before I pull the curtains across, darkening the room.

"There, now we have the best of both for a nap. Darkness, and the sound of crashing waves." I say, toeing the back of my sneakers to pull them off without undoing the laces. I step out of them and walk to the side of his bed. I can still clearly see the outline of his form, as Dean lifts his arm, gesturing for me to join him when I linger for a moment at his side. He lets out a slightly discouraged sounding sigh at my hesitation.

"I gave you my word I'd be a gentleman."

Crawling onto the bed, I lay down by his side. His strong arm curls around me, pulling me closer against his body. I place my head against the side of his chest and listen to his steady heartbeat, unable to deny the feeling of safety and security that washes over me.

Before I even realize it, the alarm on Dean's cellphone is chiming that it's twenty to six.

"This...is...fucking...awesome!" Axel exclaims, his eyes wide as he takes in the massive space. I watch him as he removes his cut, flips it inside out and puts it back on, before we step inside. Viking does the same with his cut. Dean explains to me that there are no colors permitted inside the event.

As we enter the large warehouse, it's obvious to me, that whomever the people are that are running this illegal fighting club, are probably organized crime. There is big money behind this. It's nothing like the grimy shit hole Dean brought me to the last time I saw him fight. That fight was in a basement, with ropes for a ring, on a filthy cement floor. Big enough to hold forty men with a little breathing room.

This place though... This place charges a three-hundred-dollar a head cover charge just to enter, and has four professional grade octagon cages.

There has to be over two hundred people packed around the cages, watching men fight and placing bets. The crowd is loud and it smells like freon, sweat, blood and booze. The air is cold and crisp, probably to keep the smell at a tolerable level, and the betting crowds comfortable enough to keep lingering and placing bets. Anything to milk as much money out of them as possible. I wrap my arms around myself and regret not bringing a jacket. Dean notices and slips his leather jacket off, draping it over my shoulders before he puts his arm around me.

"Don't worry babe, you'll warm up in a little bit." He grips my shoulder gently, before he shifts his focus back to the goings on all around us.

Viking calls us over to a table where he had just been talking to a few men, who look like they are part of whatever, or whomever, is running this whole event. Men in sports jackets, that make no attempt to hide the guns they're carrying beneath those jackets.

"These guys do shit differently here. And they have a rule you might not like." Viking says to Dean. "If you want to be able to fight in this circuit, today, or in the future, you have to cycle through five fighters. It's how they find their money makers. The better fighters that draw the crowds in for bigger money events."

"Cycle through?" I ask, though I'm pretty much ignored, so I continue to listen closely to their conversation, hoping for clarification.

"Okay. Any mention of skill level?" Dean asks.

"It's a mixed bag. But each one you make it through, your cut goes up. Plus, a bonus depending on bets placed. No way to determine that until it's over." Viking says.

"How's the cut?" Dean asks.

"More than decent." Viking shrugs. "The other option pays a lot more, but it's crazy."

"I'm listening." Dean says.

Viking shakes his head. "Fuck no. Five is enough. You don't know what's getting in the ring with you. You don't know how long each guy is going to last with you. There aren't timed rounds."

"Humor me." Dean insists.

I notice Viking looks at me, then back at Dean. Dean notices too. He calls Cherry and Axel over to wait with me before he steps a few feet away to talk with Viking, out of my range of hearing. I have a really bad feeling about this. It can't be good if they don't even want me to hear about it. And Viking obviously thinks whatever the second option is, is a bad idea.

"Do you guys know what they're talking about?" I ask Axel.

He shakes his head. "No. I've never been to a place like this. I've been to a lot of Dean's fights, but they're never on a scale like this." I look to Cherry, who I'm sure doesn't know either.

"I've never been to one of his fights, period. It's usually a boy's night thing, or Dean goes off on his own without telling anybody. We get to put two and two together the next morning when he's got a bruised face or bloody knuckles." Cherry rolls her eyes. I can tell she's not exactly onboard with Dean's extracurricular hobby. I'm not either. "At least this place seems to be a bit more sanitary than the places this one has told me about." She pats Axel on the chest.

"This place looks almost professional by comparison." Axel says. "They even made him get a blood test to make sure he was clean if he wanted to fight."

I glance back at Dean and Viking, who are still talking in the corner. Viking seems to be doing less of the talking now. His huge, tattooed arms folded across his massive chest, semi glaring at Dean, as he occasionally shakes his head in disagreement with something Dean says.

"I don't have a good feeling about this." I say.

"I've seen Dean beat more than five guys in a row, Vanna." Axel says.

"Aren't the men who fight here, more skilled than what he's used to?" I ask. "Isn't that why we've all been suckered into coming all the way down here? Viking doesn't seem too thrilled right now."

"Probably because Dean told him he was just going to watch and maybe fight a round or two for fun." Cherry says.

"I don't think either of them anticipated any kind of initiation type entry shit." Axel says. "I've never seen that at the small-time fights. But none of this shit is regulated at all. They can make up whatever rules they want. There are circuits where you can even fight with weapons. Knives. Pipes. Chains. Whatever." Axel blows out a breath, as if he's thinking of something unpleasant. "Where the loser just gets dumped off in an alley somewhere."

That's insane. "Please tell me he's not into that." I stare back at Dean. He smacks the side of Viking's arm and cocks his head to the side, as if he's trying to convince Viking to come back over to us with him.

"Not as long as I've known him. He's been in a few knife fights, but that might not have been for sport." Axel shrugs. "I think those were legitimate fights."

Legitimate fights. Does the man have a death wish or something? I try to wipe the look of horror off my face as Dean and Viking approach us again.

"We're gonna watch for a bit." Dean sighs, as if he's obligated by some agreement he came to with Viking.

"Awesome." Axel says, seemingly down for anything.

"Back this way." Viking mumbles, still slightly glaring at Dean, before he turns toward the cages where most of the crowds are circled around.

"Axel, keep Cherry close." Dean casually warns him. Axel nods and slings his arm around Cherry's shoulders as we make our way towards the far-left cage.

Dean curls his arm around me as well. I notice there aren't that many women here, as we follow our group, led by Viking, through the crowd. There are few wearing bikinis near some of the cages as I look around. I guess those are what they call, *ring girls*. They hold up the signs indicating each fighting round.

"Don't be nervous, Vanna." Dean says, leaning into my ear. "You're safe with me."

"I won't need to be nervous if we're only watching." I glance up at him when he doesn't say anything, and notice his lips are pressed together in a hard line as he stares straight ahead. "We are only watching, right? You're not fighting?"

He lets out a huff of air, but pauses before he answers me as the crowd gets louder for a moment, towards the center cage. I look in that direction in time to see why everyone was getting excited. One of the fighters is being choked out from behind, his face crammed against the chain link fence of the cage. I stop walking and stare for a brief moment, but Dean pulls me along. "I know how to get out of that position, baby. Don't let anything you see here scare you. I know what I'm doing." He sounds confident, at least.

I turn my face back to him. "Watching. You said we're only watching."

"I said we're watching for a bit." I knew it was useless to hope for a minute that Dean wouldn't fight. "Baby, I didn't ride four hours to watch a fight and look at bikes." He sighs. "I came here for a challenge."

"I wish you would have said something about a brutal initiation clause. I might not have agreed to come."

"Who's gonna kiss me for luck?" he grins at me, trying to be smooth.

We finally make it to the far-left ring, right to the front of the crowd, thanks to Viking's ability to plow through people. We're only feet from the cage. Nobody seems to have any issues, that is, once they take a look at Viking. He looks like he could fight any man here and win without breaking a sweat, and clearly, nobody want's any problems with him.

"Why this cage?" I ask. "Why not the ring in the middle? Or the one on the other side of the warehouse?"

Dean hesitates before he answers me, but finally does after a moment. "This is where the new fighters start."

"Do you have to switch cages to fight five guys?"

"No." he says, but doesn't elaborate. He watches the fighters in the cage. I can tell he's trying to get a feel for skill level, based on what he asked Viking earlier. Viking had said it would be a mixed bag. Some would be a challenge, some wouldn't, but Dean wouldn't know what he was fighting, until he was actually fighting.

Shifting my focus to the two guys circling each other in the cage, throwing jabs and kicks at each other, I notice there isn't a ref in the cage.

"Who calls the fight?" I ask, looking back at Dean. He doesn't look at me, nor does he answer. I look over at Viking. "Where is the ref?" I ask him, instead.

"No bell. No timed rounds. No ref." Viking says. "It's over when somebody taps out, or gets knocked out."

The men around us shout loudly in a burst of excitement, and probably disappointment, too, depending on who they bet to win. One of the fighters has the other on the ground, ripping his arm back, forcing a tap out.

"That's not even the worst part." Viking raises his voice so I can hear him.

"Come on, bro." Dean gripes, his tone full of annoyance.

"What?" I ask. Viking just cocks his head back towards the cage. I turn to look. The fighter who tapped out exits the cage, as another fighter enters. He immediately charges the guy who just won the previous fight, tackling him to the ground where they grapple on the mat. The previous winner manages to get on top of the new fighter and pounds the shit out of his face until the guy isn't moving. He then gets off him and backs up, his fists raised once again as his focus shifts back to the entrance of the cage. Two guys drag the unconscious guy out, as another fighter enters the cage. He squares off with the guy who just won two fights... *back to back.*

"This guy has to fight five guys in a row? No breaks?" I ask.

"In this case, yes." Dean says. "He fights until he loses, or until he beats his fifth opponent. It takes as long as it takes. Some rounds are quick. Some might be a bit more... grueling."

"And this is what you want to do?" I ask him, incredulously.

"It's an option."

"What's the other option?" I ask. "The one you clearly didn't want me to hear about."

"The one I want."

Of course it is. "Which entails what?"

His eyes finally drop to meet mine. "I go until I can't anymore. Whether that be five fighters or twelve. Hell, could be twenty. Won't know until I'm in there fighting."

I suddenly feel like throwing up. "That's crazy. Why would you want to put yourself through that?"

"To see how far I can go. To push my limits. To win and to learn."

"You fight until you lose. That's not winning... I'm going to have to watch you lose?"

He turns to face me directly. "Think you can handle that?"

"What if I can't? Are you still going to chance it?"

He stares in my eyes for a moment, before he asks, "Are you going to see me as less of a man if I lose a fight in front of you?"

I watch him study me, as I contemplate his question. Would I? I try to imagine what seeing him lose would feel like. The crowd around us starts to go crazy again, and I glance towards the cage fight happening a few feet away from us.

I try to imagine Dean being the guy on the ground, having his arm twisted backwards and his head smashed against the mat, screaming in pain before he taps out of the fight. I realize the guy who just lost, was the guy who had won the last four rounds. This guy didn't make it through five... And Dean wants to push even beyond that.

"Like that fighter in there, I'm eventually going to get tired, Vanna." Dean says, bringing my attention back to him. "Losing is inevitable this time."

"Not if you go with the first option." I say, hoping that if Dean fighting is going to happen, regardless, maybe I can at least talk him into stopping at five. "Axel says you've done it before."

"Exactly." He sighs. "I've done it before."

458

"I don't understand why you need to do this."

"It's just something in me. A part of me... It's in my blood. Literally. You said it yourself. In the rose garden, remember?"

"What are you talking about?" I don't ever remember telling him that fighting was in his blood.

"Descendant of the Fiery One." He says. "It's in my blood, as well as my name. Violence is a part of who I am. This is a safe outlet for that violence. A way to keep it under control, for me to function in day-to-day life."

"What do you mean? How is this in your blood?"

He closes his eyes and shakes his head. "Just tell me. Are you going to be able to see me lose, and still see me the way you do now?" he asks again, opening his eyes to search mine once more. I can tell that the thought of me looking at him differently, bothers him. A lot.

"What if I tell you that I don't know?"

He takes a breath and lets it out on a long exhale. "There's always going to be someone bigger and badder. Someone tougher, and more skilled that will beat you." Dean has said this to me before.

"This isn't that." I say, pointing at the cage. "This is not a fair fight. You fighting, exhausted, against a fresh fighter with an unknown skill level, is not a fair fight."

"Remember that, when you see me go down, Vanna."

"Dean, this is insane. Did we come all this way just so you could lose a fight?"

"No. I didn't know they played by these rules. But it opens a door for me to do this. Gives me access to a new circuit with fighters I've never come across before. Higher stakes. Bigger challenges. After this initiation, I'll be able to fight actual opponents, where bets are placed based on individuals. Not on how many guys he manages to take down before someone takes him down."

I shake my head. "Don't do this."

"I've been doing this since I was seventeen, Vanna."

"Then just do the five. You don't know who you're going to fight. At least after five, if you make it, you can say you did it and we can leave with you in one piece." I plead.

"I've done five. I've never had the opportunity to go beyond that and really push my limits." He says. "I want to do this."

For the life of me, I cannot imagine why he would want to put himself through this. Imagining him fighting for his life, because let's face it, anything could happen in there, fills me with dread.

"I'm not going to watch this." I say, turning away from him and storming off in the direction of the exit in the front of the warehouse. The crowd is tight, and it's difficult to get through the sea of people quickly without pushing and bumping shoulders.

"Vanna, wait." Dean grabs my arm, but I twist and try to pull away from him, elbowing a guy in the crowd accidently.

"*Watch it, bitch!*" The guy snaps at me, attempting to get in my face, but Dean grabs him by the collar of his shirt and hauls him face to face with him instead.

"The fuck you *think* you're gonna do?" Dean snarls at the guy. There isn't a snowballs chance in Hell, this guy would last three seconds against Dean in a fight. They're the same height, but Dean has a body built for battle. This guy looks like he hasn't gotten off his couch in weeks, and his beer belly is the biggest part of him.

Fortunately, the guy isn't drunk enough to miss the murderous glint in Dean's eyes, waiting for him to give him a reason to pound him out right there on the spot. He lifts his hands in a gesture of surrender, but says nothing in the way of an apology.

It's good enough for me, though. I grab Dean by the arm, trying to haul him away from the guy, but he may as well be carved in stone. "Dean!" I raise my voice to get his attention. "Let him go."

The rage in Dean's eyes is still simmering. "If I hadn't been here, this piece of shit would have hit you." He growls. "I can fuckin' smell it on him." He says the words as if he's filled with disgust. With disdain. With hate.

"He didn't hit me. I hit him, on accident."

Dean twists the guy's collar in his fists, like he's begging the guy to change his mind and strike out at him. "You like to get in women's faces? You get off on laying your hands on 'em? When your dinner is late, or she spills your fuckin' beer?"

That was oddly specific...

The guy just swallows, glancing at his buddy as if that drunk bastard should jump in and help him. But his buddy is just staring at Dean, taking a swig of his beer now and again.

A huge hand lands on Dean's shoulder, and I turn to see Viking. He leans to speak in Dean's ear, "Save it for the cage, killer."

Dean scowls in the drunk's face for another second, before shoving him away and snatching me by the hand. Dean takes a step towards him again, though, and growls once more in the drunk's face, "Pray *fates messenger* never finds himself at your door!"

Before I can even think about what he meant by that, Dean turns his gaze to me for a moment, then pulls me back towards the cage through the crowd.

"What the hell was that back there?" I ask him. "That was more than just you standing up for me." We're standing a few feet from the cage again, not far from Cherry, Axel and Viking, who is now talking to one of the security personnel manning the cage.

"He was about to get physical with you." Dean growls. Staring at the cage fighters. I can tell he's itching to get in there, by the ripple of his jaw muscles, and the tightness with which he holds my hand. "You need to stay near me or Viking at all times. Do not run off like that again, Vanna. This is not the crowd you want to get lost in."

"I wasn't getting lost. I was going to go back to the hotel." I correct him. "And you could have started a damn brawl."

"I'd fight anyone for you." He growls, his dark gaze lowering to meet my eyes. "No matter the odds. No matter the risk."

I believe him. And that uneasy feeling begins to radiate through me again. I know exactly what it is. His vow only reminds me of the summoning spell that most likely brought him into my life. Morning Star or not. I force my mind to push the thought back down. There's too much going on right now for me to dwell on all that. Dean would be fighting tonight, whether he ever met me or not. Whatever this is for him, it's not about me. Not tonight. Not for the last twenty years of his life. Whatever this is, it was inside of him long before he ever met me. Long before I ever cast the spell that brought us together.

Dean isn't just fighting men in a ring. Dean is fighting inner demons.

Viking walks up to Dean, distracting me from my dark epiphany. "You're in there next, if you want it."

"I want it." Dean says, releasing my hand to reach into his jacket pocket that I'm wearing. He hand's Viking a thick wad of cash. "Pay them. Bet the rest on me. I'm not coming out of that cage until I at least tie their record tonight." He growls. "And while I'm in there, stay near Vanna, will you?"

"Yeah. Just stay focused." Viking's tone is low, almost grave, as if he himself wishes Dean would reconsider. "Pace yourself, and tap the fuck out when it's time to tap the fuck out, Bro. Use your head." He adds, before he pats Dean on the shoulder and walks off to place the bet.

Dean shifts his focus back to me. He looks like he wants to say something, but he doesn't. I have a feeling I know what he's worried about. And I don't want him going into the ring distracted by anything. Especially not over something that has anything to do with me.

"I won't." I say to him.

"You won't what?"

"I won't run away. And I won't see you differently..." I have to swallow the lump in my throat, before I can continue. "When you lose. I promise."

He finally cracks the slightest smile. "Then why don't you knock me a-"

I grab his shoulders and rise up on my tippy toes to plant a kiss on his lips before he can finish his request. *Kiss for good luck.* I finish his sentence for him, whispered against his lips.

I can feel his grin against my lips as he whispers back, "Aces, baby." He wraps his arms around me tightly, deepening our kiss for a moment, before we hear his name called.

"Keegan! You're up!" A loud voice shouts from near the entrance of the cage.

He steps back from me and glances at Viking as he returns with a yellow slip of paper.

"The bets in. Good luck, bro." Viking says.

Dean gives him a nod, before he smiles at me once more. Touching my chin with his thumb and forefinger for a moment, he then turns to jog over to the cage. I watch him hurriedly discard his boots and clothing, hand-

461

ing them off to Axel, until he's wearing only his gym shorts, and one of his thin, long sleeved white t-shirts.

"Is he crazy, Viking?" I ask the huge biker standing beside me, as we both watch Dean enter the cage to a roar of cheers. Dean takes his place on the far side of the cage, away from the entrance. He throws a few punches through the air, twisting his body, jogging in place. Warming up for what we all expect to be a long, hard battle.

"About a few things." Viking says. "You're one of them."

"That's Dean fucking Keegan! Holy shit!" A guy somewhere behind us exclaims. I can't help glancing over my shoulder in his direction, surprised by his reaction.

"Did you hear that?" I ask. Viking simply nods. "That was a little more enthusiasm than I would have expected to hear... And by name?"

"Dean's been in this game a long time. He's somewhat known. There was a time he fell off for a while, but... as you can see. He's back at it." Viking says, though he sounds less than thrilled.

"So, he's good." I'm not even sure myself if it's a question, or just a hope spoken out loud. I look back at Dean in the cage. He's finished warming up. Now he stands, eyes fixed on the entrance to the cage, waiting for his first opponent.

"Good enough to have gone pro if he wanted to." Viking says.

"Why didn't he?"

"Shit happens. But he never got into this to go pro, anyway. He's got his reasons."

This is probably a shot in the dark, Viking is loyal to Dean, just like Cherry and Axel. But I ask on the off chance he gives me some inside information. "What are some of those reasons?"

"Give the guy a chance with you, and I'm sure he'll tell you anything you want to know about him." Viking says. After a moment he turns his head to look down at me. "I'm just going to put this out there, and we don't have to talk about this again. In fact, I'd appreciate it if you kept it between us." His intimidating hard gaze makes me swallow nervously. Viking continues, "Vanna, when you and Dean are good, he's great. But the flip side, when you two aren't meshing, for whatever the reason may be..." he hesitates for a moment, shaking his head, before he looks back towards the cage. "You get where I'm going."

I take a breath and let it out slowly. I'm not getting into our complicated relationship issues with Viking, so I decide to change the subject. "Not that I want to see him fight again, but what is taking so long?"

"They have to give the crowd time to get their bets in. A death match doesn't happen very often." Viking explains.

"I really hate that they call it that."

Viking chuckles. "They're also probably having a hard time getting somebody to jump in the ring with him first. A *sacrificial lamb*." He adds, his tone full of humor, but his expression changes to something more serious when he continues, "Will be faster after he goes a few rounds. The sharks will smell the blood in the water, and want to take their shot at being the one to bring down *Dean Keegan*."

His words make my stomach churn.

It's only a few more moments before the crowd around Dean's cage goes crazy, as a fighter finally steps up to challenge him. A big guy, probably the same height as Dean, from what I can tell before he gets into the cage. He's fairly muscular too, definitely looks like he's got experience as well. Maybe even a few years younger than him.

"Oh God..." My heart rate is already beginning to increase. My palms feel clammy, despite the cold air pumping through this place. "Here we go."

"This will be quick." Viking says. "Dean isn't going to fuck around. He's going to try to conserve his energy as much as he can. I give the guy ten seconds. Dean's gonna kill shot him."

Someone shouts "Fight!", and the battle begins.

Dean and the guy circle each other, fists up, sizing each other up, until his opponent charges him. Faster than I'm even able to register at first, Dean lands a solid spin kick to the side of the guy's head. The way his opponents body hits the ground, dead weight, he had to have been unconscious before he even hit the mat.

"See." Viking says. "Just because a guy is jacked up, doesn't mean he's anywhere near Dean's skill level. Keep that in mind. Especially when this comes to an end. He may go down against someone who isn't anywhere near his level, just because he's exhausted. But I bet he comes looking for the guy who takes him down, next time." Viking chuckles.

Next time... "How often does Dean feel the need to do this?" I ask, honestly afraid to know the answer to this question.

"This type of death match, running a train on a guy, shit? Rarely." Viking says, as we watch the first fighter being dragged out of the cage. "Regular matches, lately? Once or twice a month, unless he's got issues to work out." I can't help noticing the side look Viking shoots me, as he says that last part.

As soon as they drag the unconscious guy out, another man enters to square off with Dean. A heavier set guy, in a sweaty stained undershirt, who's about three inches taller than Dean is. I watch as Dean easily avoids the guy's punches, agile and quick with his reflexes. After a moment, Dean socks the guy in the face with a solid blow, then slams his foot dead center of the guy's chest, rocking him back against the chain link fence of the cage, where he quickly proceeds to pounce on him, knocking him out cold with one more solid punch to the head.

The crowd cheers as another unconscious body is dragged from the octagon.

Over the next fifteen minutes, five more men are dragged out of the cage. Three knock outs, two submissions. One by way of an arm bar, one a choke hold. And Dean remains unscathed, thus far.

"He seems to be doing well." I say, still riddled with nerves.

"He is." Viking agrees. "But the moment is coming, Vanna. It's inevitable."

I close my eyes and take a deep breath, holding it for a moment before I blow it out. "I know." I say, opening my eyes to look back at Dean.

After that last bout of wrestling on the mat to get the guy into a choke hold submission, he seems to have finally broken a sweat. As he waits for his next opponent, Dean pulls his shirt off and tosses it over the fence to Axel, before he glances over at me and gives me a playful wink and a smile. I smile back at him, though I'm sure he can tell it was mostly forced and nervous. He grins wider at me and flexes his chest, making the scorpion twitch. I can't help grinning back at him, genuinely this time. He's the one facing impending pain and injury, yet he's trying his best to make me feel better. It's short lived, though, as Axel shouts his name, bringing Dean's attention back to the entrance of the cage.

A new fighter makes his way inside. Number eight is a bald black guy with an athletic build. The way he hops around the ring, circling Dean in such a fast-paced way, has my nerves on edge. He seems aggressive, experienced. Eager to defeat Dean.

"Bet he's trying to force Dean to over step, so he can attempt a round house kick to Dean's head." Viking says.

"Does Dean know that?" I nervously ask, watching the muscles flexing in this guy's legs as he moves. I imagine it would really hurt to be kicked by him.

"Watch how Dean moves," Viking cocks his chin, "He's baiting the guy into the kick. Using what he knows the guy wants to do, against him. Dean's smart. Calculating. I've seen him pull this before." Viking chuckles.

As the black guy twists, and brings his leg up and around in an attempt to knock Dean's head off his shoulders, Dean drops low to the mat, swiping the guy's leg out from under him, crashing him down to the ground. Dean is on him in a second, slamming his fist into the guys face several bloody times, until he doesn't move.

"Told you." Viking shrugs. Dean backs off the guy, but he's not exactly unconscious. He's still moving on the mat. "Unfortunately, for this dude, unless he taps out, Dean's gonna have to hit him again in another second or two. He hates having to do that."

I watch as Dean paces near the black guy, waiting to see what he's going to do. When the guy doesn't tap out, and starts to get up, Dean ends him with one more slug to the face. Another knockout. The crowd goes crazy again and Dean retreats to his preferred area of the cage to await his next opponent.

"He's normally not that quick to hit a guy in a situation like this." Viking comments. "In a normal fight, Dean would have let the guy get to his feet."

I know how this ends... But I'm glad he's not taking any chances like that. The next fighter has the look of a professional athlete as well, and I feel my blood run cold as I hear Viking mutter "*Ah, shit...*", under his breath.

"What?" I can't help nervously asking, though I'm pretty sure I can figure this out for myself. This is where things are going to start taking a real turn.

"That's Kenny O'Keefe." Viking says. He glances at me. "This isn't going to be pretty, Vanna." His words make me feel momentarily light headed with worry. We knew this was coming, I remind myself. Dean knows he's eventually going down. That time could be now. I have to brace myself for the brutality I know I'm about to witness.

Kenny O'Keefe is equal height and size to Dean, covered in what appears to be Irish Pride themed tattoos and wearing gym shorts as well. There is something about the look on their faces as they circle each other, sizing each other up. There's some kind of history here.

"What's the story?" I ask.

"They... have a rivalry thing." Viking says. "Dean's beat him three different times over the last several years. I'm sure they're shit talking each other, we just can't hear it."

"But he's beat him."

"It's been close. And the last three times, it was fair. He's got Dean at a disadvantage this time. And I'm sure that's being thrown back and forth between them as we speak." Viking says. He looks down at me, as I look up at him. "How are you with blood?"

"I guess we'll find out." I manage to say, my mouth suddenly feeling dry.

Viking was right. It wasn't pretty. Kenny definitely weakened Dean over their seven-minute fight. The crowd in an almost continuous uproar as they battled it out with punches, kicks, body slams and grappling on the now freshly bloodied mat. In the end, Kenny taps out, another casualty of Dean's brutal spinning arm bar submission. He reminds me of a python, the way he wraps his strong body around his opponents, and rolls with their arms trapped in his death grip before they shout in pain and tap out.

Blood is definitely in the water now, however, as Dean breathes slightly harder. His body glistening with sweat. A cut above his right eye, trickling blood down the side of his face. That same right eye, turning a light shade of purple with every passing moment. O'Keefe definitely landed a few solid shots before Dean took him down. It was stressful to watch, but I'd be lying, if I said I wasn't impressed by Dean's skill and stamina.

"Now's when the low lives will attempt to jump in at the chance to fight and beat a champion." Viking says, a detectable level of disgust in his voice. "O'Keefe should have been the first man up. He has so far been Dean's most worthy opponent tonight. But I've got more respect for the first few guys who entered the cage with him." Viking hooks his thumbs into the front pockets of his jeans and looks down at the floor for a moment. "From here on out, it's going to be scum. Dirty fighters. No holds barred type shit." He looks over at me. "Not sure you're gonna want a closer look at what's about to go down in that cage, but I promised him I'd stay with you."

As his words sink in, my heart sinks as well. "What do you mean?" I ask, hearing the slight tremble in my own voice.

"This is going to be hard for you to watch, especially up close, but I need to be closer to that cage in case things go badly." Viking says.

"Then let's get closer." I say, looking up at Viking. "Don't let him get hurt."

"I won't let him get *killed*." Viking says. "Hurt is out of our hands."

Right. Of course, it is, I acknowledge to myself, as I watch Dean wipe at the blood on the side of his face with the back of his wrist and forearm. He's staring intently at the entrance of the cage, waiting for the next fighter.

After what looks like a quick conversation, and a bribe from Viking, the guy working Dean's cage in this sick arena, allows Viking and I to stand closer to the octagon.

"You can stand with Cherry and Axel if this gets to be too much." He says to me.

"What's another five feet?"

"Blood splatter might miss you." He shrugs.

I close my eyes and try not to let the words he just spoke to me paint gruesome images in my mind. "Great." I whisper, mostly to myself. I follow Viking closer to the chain link fence, as Dean's gaze shifts momentarily towards us.

"No," he protests immediately, "Vanna, stay back by Axel. You don't need to be this close."

Before I can react, the roar of the crowd raises and another fighter enters the ring with him. Thankfully, his focus goes immediately to his attacker, as I freeze where I'm standing, unable to look away. The guy wastes no time in charging Dean, slamming him full force into his abdomen with his broad shoulders, rocking Dean backwards against the chain link fence of the octagon. Dean wraps an arm around the guy's neck, holding onto him tightly as he brings his other fist up, again and again, slugging the guy in the ribs and stomach, each blow forcing air out of the guy with guttural sounds. The pain brings the guy to his knees, where Dean then brings his knee to the guy's face, sending another fighter unconscious to the mat. The crowd goes crazy, so loud I can barely even hear my own thoughts.

As this guy is dragged out, Dean bends tiredly over, his hands bracing against his knees as the takes whatever moments he has between fights to rest. Catching the breath that had just been knocked out of him against the fence. The blood from above the side of his eye is still trickling down his right shoulder and arm. Down over his large Celtic cross tattoo and a smaller tattoo on the inside of his forearm. Some kind of a club or something, it's hard to really tell what it is at this angle, and it doesn't really matter now. I keep glancing nervously towards the entrance, expecting someone at any moment to step into the cage and fight him.

Dean lifts his gaze towards the entrance of the cage, before he glances back at me. He tiredly lifts his arm to wave me back again, without speaking. I do as he asks, backing up to Axel and Cherry. I don't want to be the reason he gets distracted in a fight.

Cherry touches my shoulder and asks close to my ear, if I'm okay. I just nod. It seems like the number of spectators have grown also, eager to see how long the apparently known underground fighter, will last in the death cage.

"I wish he would tap out, before he gets seriously hurt."

"Me too." Cherry says. "But Dean doesn't know how to quit." She squeezes my shoulder gently.

"I've lost count. How many men has he fought so far?" I ask.

"Ten." Axel says. "According to the bookie, twelve is the record. If he makes it past twelve and wins against his thirteenth opponent, he's leaving here with an even nicer chunk of change."

"I don't think he does this for the money." I say, mostly to myself. Dean lives a fairly comfortable life, from what I have been able to tell, with three successful businesses, his motorcycles, nice house and land. This fight club madness is not about money for him. This violent insanity is about something else entirely.

As the crowd begins to shout again, another fighter enters the cage with Dean. I watch as Dean straightens himself again, and moves into a fighting position. Fists up, legs apart, ready to kick or jump out of the way of a strike. The guy lunges forward with a kick aiming for Dean's throat. Dean grabs the guy's leg, shoving it up higher, knocking the guy off balance backwards as he drives forward into him. They crash down to the mat, the guy managing two wrap his legs around Dean's upper body, one leg wrapped around the top of Dean's left shoulder, the other leg under his right arm.

"Think he's going to try to arm bar Dean." Axel anxiously says.

I hear him, but I don't look away from the struggle going on inside the cage. The fighter does have Dean's arm, and he's taking shots to the face from Dean's other fist, as Dean battles to free himself from the guy's grip. The fighter isn't letting go.

In a move I never would have believed even possible, especially not after how tired Dean looked after O'Keefe gave him a run for his money, I watch in amazement, as Dean manages to struggle to his feet. The fighter, still clinging to Dean's body. His legs wrapped around Dean's neck and shoulder, his arms still controlling Dean's trapped arm. Dean dead lifts a full-grown man, then drops to his knees, slamming the fighter's body down, head first, into the mat.

The crowd, including Axel, jumping up and down beside me, goes absolutely nuts. I watch as Dean remains on his knees, the guy's limbs falling away from Dean's body. Obviously unconscious.

"Fuck yes! That's eleven Bro!" Axel shouts with excitement.

Dean pushes the guy's legs away from him, but he remains on his knees, eyes closed for a moment, breathing deeply. That had to have taken a great deal of energy. Energy of which he has to be running out of rapidly, because he hasn't gotten up. He has to be exhausted... Unless he hurt himself with that pile drive maneuver... I hurry over to the cage beside Viking.

"Get up, or tap out. You know what's going to happen if you don't." Viking warns him.

Dean looks absolutely spent, only opening his eyes when he hears someone coming to pull yet another guy from the cage.

"Dean, are you okay?" I ask, trying to keep the anxiety out of my voice.

He gives me a tired smile. "Yeah. I got this." He says between breaths.

"That was eleven, Dean. Eleven fighters. That's double what's required to pass the initiation, plus one." I say, hoping that will convince him to throw in the proverbial towel.

"I still got some juice." He pants. "The record is twelve."

"Then you need to get the fuck up. They aren't going to wait for you before they toss another guy in here." Viking says, his voice stern and demanding.

Dean nods, slowly getting to his feet again, but he isn't on them long. The next opponent comes in swinging fast and hard, clipping Dean in the mouth, as he manages to get a fist through Dean's weakened block, then slams his knee into Dean's stomach, before shoving him down to the mat.

I feel a shriek escape my throat, but it goes unheard, drowned out by the shouting crowd. The fighter, a younger guy with a muscular build as well, wrestles him down on the mat, attempting to land punches to Dean's head and face, until he loses one of his arms to Dean's death grip. I watch as Dean struggles to position himself beneath the guy, working his body to attempt another submission maneuver from the ground.

The guy notices me frozen in place, staring at them through the fence.

"This your bitch, Keegan?" the guy taunts him as they continue to struggle with each other. "Maybe after I submit you on your back, I'll do the same with her. Would rather have her legs around me than yours."

Dean doesn't respond with words, though I know he heard him. He responds by head butting the jerk in the mouth, busting his lips against his teeth, stunning him long enough to clock him in the jaw and roll over on him. Positioning himself quickly behind the guy, Dean wraps his arm around his throat, bringing his hand to his own shoulder and squeezes. Blood is dripping profusely from the guy's mouth, coating Dean's choke hold arm. I can tell that Dean is whispering something in the guy's ear with a fierce sneer, but I have no idea what is being said, as the crowd is louder than ever, clearly excited by the gory twelfth fighter finish.

After a moment, damn near purple in the face, the jerk reaches up to smack Dean's arm, tapping out. Dean lets him go, shoving him away from him as he staggers to his feet. It takes a moment for the guy to get up, but he does, and skulks out of the cage.

Dean's eyes shift back to me, and he gives me a weak smile, using his hand to try to swipe some of the guy's blood off his arm.

And that's when I finally get a good look at that tattoo on his inner right forearm.

It isn't a club at all... No... It's far, far more significant than that...

It's a *Knight's Morning Star Weapon*... And I suddenly feel like I could faint.

My eyes shift up from the tattoo on his arm, to his face, which is looking at me like he's suddenly concerned for *my* wellbeing.

"Viking! Grab her!" Dean shouts, as he rushes towards where I'm standing on the outside of the ring. Viking has his arm around my waist as I stare at Dean, dazed. "Vanna, the blood isn't mine, baby. I swear, I'm okay." Dean says, crouching down near me, convinced my state of shock is due to the blood all over his arm.

The blood. It's a good excuse to cover my reaction to the blatant sign that Dean is the Knight. The literal Savior I summoned. There is no doubt at all in my mind now. Everything adds up. How could I have possibly missed this sign for this long?

Dean smacks his hand against the chain link. "Vanna? Can you hear me? It's not my blood!" he shouts over the roaring crowd. I only hear him because I'm so near.

I force myself to snap out of it. "Yes, I'm sorry. I... I got scared." I stammer.

"Viking, take her back over to Axel." Dean says, still looking at me with concern.

"*Incoming!*" Viking shouts, the only one of us to notice the next fighter entering the ring with Dean.

Viking was right when he said there would be dirty fighters. This one didn't even wait for Dean to realize he was even in the cage with him before he attacked.

The guy rams full force into Dean, slamming him down on the mat. Anyone with one eye and half a brain can see that Dean is spent, though he continues to try to fight the guy off him, no longer landing any blows himself. All of what's left of his energy is going into blocking the blows from the guy on top of him. And the blows are raining down on him.

Dean makes a last-ditch effort to get out from under the guy by bucking his hips up, in an attempt to knock the guy forward, and wrap his arms around his neck to get him in a headlock from below. But after thirteen fighters in a row, his strength level just isn't there, and he can't compete with this fresh fighter's combination of strength and speed. Had this been a fair fight, Dean could have beaten him, too, but not in this condition. Not in this fight. The guy slams Dean back down on the mat with his forearm across his throat, his other fist landing shots into his side as Dean struggles against his throat being crushed.

"Tap out!" I scream, shoving away from Viking and slamming my hands against the cage frantically. "Tap out! Tap out!"

I can see him grimacing, but I can't tell if it's from being in physical pain, or the realization that he's lost this fight.

The guy leans harder into Dean's throat, forcing Dean to stop fighting and smack the guy's arm to tap out of the fight.

But the guy doesn't stop... He doesn't get off of Dean...

And I suddenly have the urge to throw up, as my fingers curl around the chain link, watching Dean give up on the tap out, and go back to attempting to get the guys arm off his throat... He's fighting for his life now... He can't breathe...

"Get off him or you're fucking dead!" Viking's voice booms loudly, as he grabs onto the chain link fence, about to climb over into the cage. The psychopath trying to kill Dean glances up into Viking's face and immediately removes his arm from Dean's throat, allowing him to finally gasp for air, which he thankfully does. "*You!* I want *you!*" Viking snarls at the guy, who is pacing the cage, glancing at Dean who's still on the mat, like he wants to jump back on him and finish him off. "Fucking pussy, fight a man who hasn't gone twelve rounds before you step in the cage with him! Try that shit with me you fucking punk!"

"Get him out of there!" I turn to Viking and grip his massive arm, "Please!"

"Dean's okay." Viking says, not taking his eyes off the guy.

When I glance back at Dean, Axel is in the cage with him, hauling Dean up by his hand. Two security guys, almost as big as Viking, are escorting the psychopath out of the cage. Viking is moving quickly in that direction, as if he's going to toss the security personnel aside to pound the asshole into the cement. Part of me hopes he does, but I just want to get Dean the hell out of this place.

Axel helps him limp out of the cage and down the few steps. As he makes his way towards me, I'm tempted to throw my arms around him and just hold him tightly, grateful that he's alive and that psycho didn't kill him, but I don't. And it's not even because I don't want to hurt him. Though, I'm sure his body is in pain and the last thing he wants is a hug. It's because I don't even know what to think or how to feel about anything right now. This entire Death Match concept is sickening. Watching Dean fight man after man, until physical exhaustion and inevitable defeat, has been a horrible experience I never want to witness again. How he could have even wanted to take part in this, knowing the inevitable outcome, is beyond my understanding.

As they make their way over to me, Dean is walking without Axel's support now, but he's clearly in pain. I don't say a word. And though one of his eyes is already turning shades of purple and black, and he can barely squint out of it because of the blood dripping in it, I can tell he's trying to read me. He reaches for me with his right arm, and I stare at the tattoo there on his forearm, now that I can see it up close. It's without a doubt, A Knight's Morning Star weapon. My mind searches for the memories of the times I've seen him shirtless. He always wore sweat bands in the gym. And he's never taken off his clothes around me, outside of the gym. It doesn't look like fresh ink, either. He's had this tattoo at least as long as I've known him. It was part of him the night we met, on his black steed, his red banner blowing in the wind...

"Vanna?" Dean's scratchy voice croaks my name, breaking me out of my trance. I lift my eyes to meet his. His good eye looks concerned. His lips pressed together, a little blood in the corner of his mouth.

"I want to get out of here."

Dean nods. "We're going to the hotel." He says. "We'll order some room service and kick back. Just waiting for Viking. Not sure where he got off to."

"He went after the guy who just tried to *kill* you." I say, having to make a real effort to sound calm about this entire situation.

"He wasn't trying to kill me." Dean insists, attempting an air of nonchalance.

"I know what I saw. The look on that guy's face..." I've seen that expression before. I know it all too well... "And Viking would not have reacted the way he did if you weren't in danger in there!" I snap at him. Feeling my heart begin to race once more, I close my eyes and take a few breaths.

"The human brain can go four whole minutes without much worry of brain damage. I'm sure he would have backed off me if I blacked out." Dean says, as if I should be consoled by that little fun fact.

"Or crushed your throat and killed you." I open my eyes and look up at him. "He knew you were tapping out, and he didn't stop!"

Dean reaches his hand out to touch my arm gently. "I'm all right, Vanna. I'm in one piece." He tries to reassure me.

"What now? When can we get out of here?" I ask, fully aware of how impatient and flustered I sound. My nerves are shot though.

"I collect my cash, find Viking, and we can go."

"Then let's do that." I glance past him to see that Viking is storming back towards us. He looks agitated, and he's holding a thick white envelope in his hand.

"Got your money for you. They said come back any time." Viking says, slapping the envelope to Dean's sweaty, blood streaked, bare chest.

"You count it?" Dean asks him.

"Yeah. But you're light a hundred bucks." Viking says.

"For what?" Dean looks at him curiously.

"A bribe. But trust me, you ain't gonna miss it, Bro. I took a hundred so they'd let me throat punch that cock sucker." Viking replies.

Dean hands Viking back the envelope. "Fair enough. Mind holding onto it for me, till we get to the hotel? I'm not going to be much of a challenge right now if some shitfuck decides they want to jump me for it."

Viking grabs the envelope back and shoves it inside his leather vest, before he turns to grab Axel and Cherry's attention, informing them we're leaving.

As Viking cuts us a path through the crowd, Cherry orders a van to take us back to the hotel, while Axel and I walk on either side of Dean to make sure he's alright. Before we exit the warehouse, Dean struggles back into his clothing, using his white t-shirt to wipe as much blood off his face as he can before our ride shows up. It's not much of an improvement, though. He definitely looks like he's been through Hell and back again.

"You gonna be able to ride back after the bike show?" Axel asks him.

Dean leans against the back of the folding chair after he gets his second boot back on. He glances at me before he turns to answer Axel. "I don't anticipate having to stay a third night. I'll take it easy tonight, tomorrow. A second night of down time and I should be good to go. Didn't fuck my hands up, so riding the bike won't be an issue." Dean says, looking at me. There is something of a sadness in his eyes. "Like I said, I don't anticipate needing a third night. I'm quite capable of powering through a bit of discomfort for a few hours. My only concern is your safety." He says to me.

My safety. Certainly not his own. Not after what I saw him put himself through tonight. But of course, my safety would be his only concern. I made damn sure of that, didn't I?

"Whatever you say."

Chapter
twenty-one

Vanna

When we get back to the Ocean front Hotel, Cherry and Axel decide they want to check out the local night life, so we say our goodnights to them and head for the elevators.

"I fucking hate these death traps." Viking complains, jamming his thumb against the buttons to close the elevator doors and bring us up to the 20th floor. I find it slightly amusing that someone like Viking would be uneasy about elevators. His general zero fucks attitude had me thinking that nothing really fazed him at all.

"I'm sure this won't be the night the cables break and we plummet twenty stories to our deaths in a steel coffin." Dean taunts him, leaning against the back wall of the elevator, eyes closed, a slight grin on his face. "*Wait...* did you *hear that*?" His grin widens a little more.

"Shut up, asshole." Viking mutters.

As the elevator lurches to haul us up to our floor, Dean winces slightly. He must be feeling more pain with each passing moment.

"I can run out and get you some pain relievers." I offer. "There's a CVS on the corner of the block."

"Got some in the room waiting on me, baby." Dean says, tiredly. "And I wouldn't want you running out on your own anyhow. But thanks."

The elevator chimes and the doors open on our floor. We say goodnight to Viking and head inside. Dean twists the bolt lock and semi limps over to the bed, where he sits down on the edge of it slowly.

I turn on the lamp on his night table before I walk towards my side of the room. "Do you mind if I open up the balcony door? We'll probably get a nice breeze off the ocean." I ask.

"You do whatever you want to, baby." Dean sighs.

I pull the curtains back and slide the balcony door open. We can hear the soft, steady crashing of the waves on the beach. It's a clear night with lots of stars, and a nice comfortable breeze. I grab the screen slider and pull it into place, before I turn around and notice Dean moving extra slow to pull off his biker boots. Not exactly struggling, but still clearly in pain.

"Wait, I'll help you." I say, hurrying over to him. Kneeling down in front of him, I gently pull off his boots and socks. When I look up at him, he's wearing a weak, crooked grin. "Why don't you take off that bloody shirt and let me rinse it out in the sink. I'll hang it outside to dry if it's salvageable."

"It's not." He says, slowly shrugging out of his open button-down shirt. I get up to help him out of that as well. "Soap and water in the bathroom sink aren't gonna get blood stains out of it. It's alright."

"I guess you'd know." I say, standing back to watch him pull off his bloody t-shirt. Even in the dim light of the table side lamp, I can see the bruises forming on his chest and abdomen. Remnants of every punch and kick and knee shot he took in those thirteen rounds. "Oh my God, Dean. Look at you." I barely whisper, my hand automatically moving to my throat. He doesn't take his eyes from me though. "Those will be even worse tomorrow."

"I'm alright." He quietly insists. "Been in worse shape and I'm still here."

"Well, it looks painful. Maybe we should clean out these cuts." I say, noticing a strand of his disheveled hair flopped forward, nearing the cut above his eye. I reach out and gently brush my fingers through the top of his fight tousled hair, smoothing it back for him the way he likes it styled. Dean is staring up at me as I do so, a mixture of emotions in his eyes that I can't quite place. "What is it?" I ask, letting my hand drop back to my side.

"I am in a bit of pain, Vanna." He says with a sigh. "Your touch brings me such peace, yet at the same time... delivers one hell of a punch itself."

"I'm sorry." I don't know how else to respond.

"Don't be." He reaches for my hand and takes it, holding it gently. For a few moments, he only stares up at me, as if he wants to tell me something, but is unsure of how to say it.

"Maybe I should get you those pain pills?" I suggest, breaking our silence. I slip my hand from his, and his expression reads as if it is some kind of a loss to him. "Where did you put them?" I ask, trying to keep my voice steady and nonchalant.

"Bathroom counter." He sounds almost defeated.

"Should I get the shower running for you since I'm going in there?" I offer. "So you can wash off this blood. Some of it isn't even yours." I add, looking him over again. My eyes come to rest on the Morning Star tattoo on his inner forearm. "I never noticed that before. What is that tattoo?" I ask, pretending not to know.

"A Knights weapon. A Morning Star."

"Does it represent something special to you?"

"I was really hung over when I got it. I don't even remember *why* I chose it."

That's Interesting... "How long ago?"

"About a year and a half now. Why?"

I don't know how to even answer that yet, so I go with a simple, flippant, "Just curious. I thought maybe it had something to do with why Viking sometimes calls you Lancelot."

"Right. Makes sense." He says. "Actually, it kind of does. That morning, he told me I looked like a dirty English Knight. I suppose the Knight thing stuck in my head and I just went with it. The tattoo was his idea. Getting it done I mean. It's a cover up." I watch as he drags his finger across his inked skin. "Lucinda's name used to be here."

At least he got rid of it, but, "Why didn't you want to?"

"I didn't realize I did." He lets out a long breath as he stares at me. "I was in a really dark place, Vanna. For a really long time. Lucinda... she... *hurt* me. In ways I didn't know how to deal with. Other than drinking and fighting. I was a ghost of myself then. I did a lot of dangerous shit because I really didn't care what the end result was. Thought I didn't have anything to live for, that I never would again."

"You must have really loved her, once upon a time." I say, trying not to let my voice reveal how much the thought of him loving Lucinda actually bothers me. What right do I even have to feel like this? Of course, he loved her. They were married for years. Probably were together a while before that, too. But it does bother me. What is wrong with me?

"Not as much as I thought." He says, locking eyes with me, as if he's willing me to read into that statement. Not as much as he thought because of what? Of me? Or the spell I enslaved his emotions with, to instill his need to be near me...

Dean finally pulls his gaze away from me and starts to stand up from the bed. I notice how stiffly he moves, and I take a few steps closer to him, unsure of what I can actually do to help him, but I ask anyway.

"I'm just sore. I'll be alright." He insists, his hands moving to his belt to undo it and his jeans. I step back from him and avert my eyes to a framed beach scene on the wall of our hotel room, as he shoves them down his legs. "I've got my gym shorts on under my jeans, Vanna." He says, noticing my avoidance. "Did you forget?"

"Oh, right." I say, awkwardly. I actually did manage to forget, somehow.

"I know I'm still in the *fucking friend zone.*" He says, a detectable level of aggravation in his words. His jaw clenching for a moment. His eyes tightening. "That's why there are two beds in here. I'm not going to get naked in front of you. I gave you my word that I'm not going to try anything with you. I'm in no condition to anyhow, even if I was a total scum-fuck dirtbag."

Where did that come from? I clearly have offended him though. "Let me get you those pain pills." I finally say, "And after your shower, I'll help you with the first aid kit and we'll find something to close up that cut over your eye with." I start to walk past him, but he grabs my wrist to stop me.

"This is the shit that hurts, Vanna. More than getting beat up by thirteen guys. Even more than..." He hesitates, then just shakes his head. "More than a lot of things."

All I can do is stare back at him. I don't know what to say about anything. There's so much I *should* say, but I can't. I'm not ready. If he hated me, it would kill me. I'm realizing that more and more. I can't lose him, for a lot of reasons. Some reasons I'm not even ready to examine, let alone acknowledge.

"The Friend Zone, Vanna." He says, as if he thinks I don't know what he's referring to. His eyes look pained as he stares into mine. His brows moving together. "It's killing me... You're killing me."

My heart breaks as his words sink in. *I'm killing him.* He has no idea what I've *actually* done to him. The dark course laid out before us. That I, once again, set in motion. I don't deserve him. I'm as toxic as Lucinda, just in a different way. A deadlier way.

"Dean... I..." I don't have words. All I have is immense, overwhelming, guilt.

He lets go of my wrist. His expression sliding from pained, to something more stoic. "I'm sorry. I'm making this an uncomfortable situation for you. Not my intention, at all. Despite the fight tonight, I was hoping this could be a nice time for us." He sighs, and I can tell he's making a great effort to reel himself in. "I'll go wash up and then maybe we can just relax."

I nod. "I'll get the first aid kit out of your duffle." I say, just to say *something.*

"You don't need to cater to me. I've patched myself up, alone, plenty of times. Why don't you check out the room service menu and order us some food? Surprise me." He smiles, though it's a slight smile. And I can't tell if it's because his cut lip hurts, or because it isn't a genuine smile this time. I don't blame him though, either way.

As the bathroom door closes behind him, I sit down at the table for two in our room by the balcony doors. The little blue menu with silver foil font is in the center. I pick it up and glance at the overpriced meals. He's got to be hungry after all the energy he expelled in the octagon, so I decide to order him a double steak burger fully loaded with a side of fries. I order myself a grilled chicken club wrap with fries as well. They inform me it'll be forty-five minutes.

Wanting to do something for him, anything at all, I grab his duffle and place it on the foot of his bed, pulling out some fresh clothes for him to sleep in and getting out the first aid kit. I lay them out neatly on the light blue comforter for him to find. Then I grab his belted jeans off the floor and fold them, along with his discarded shirts, and place them on the chair in the corner of the room... As if keeping the room somewhat tidy means anything. As if laying out his clothes for him makes up for anything. This small, insignificant gesture. If I were a decent person, I'd tell him the truth about our situation.

I don't know how he puts up with me. Any other guy would have washed his hands of me and my bullshit a long time ago. Yet here he remains. Undeterred. And I can't help wondering, for probably the thousandth time... If there was never a spell, would he still be this determined to win me over? Would he have ever even been attracted to me to begin with?

As I glance around our fancy double bed hotel room, an overwhelming feeling that I really never should have agreed to come here, washes over me.

He's right about the mixed messages. I was too carefree with him at the start. I let his charm and his good looks and his charisma cloud my judgement. I knew Dean was the Knight the first time I saw him. I let my attraction to him feed my denial. I didn't need to see this tattoo to know the truth. It just confirmed it beyond any shadow of a doubt. And now I've complicated everything. Feelings were never supposed to be a part of this. He thinks he feels for me. I do feel something for him, but this can't be. Not with what's coming. The thought of Dean facing off with my psychotic ex, has my heart beating faster.

I was not supposed to fall in love with the Knight. Nor him with me.

God what a mess I've made of everything. I'm the worst witch in the history of witches. My spells work too well, in all the *wrong* ways. My Knight, my summoned Savior, thinks he has feelings for me. And I can't even let myself trust it, because of the spell. It would be wrong for me to act on what I feel for him, if what he's feeling for me isn't real. I never should have come here. Even staying in this room with him, as "friends", is wrong. It's another mixed message.

I grab my duffle bag and sneak out of our room, closing the door behind me as quietly as possible. Then I hurry next door to Viking's hotel room to knock on his door.

Viking opens the door, shirtless and barefoot. Wearing only his blue jeans. He's got a family sized bag of Cool Ranch Dorito's in his hand. Probably ten of them in his mouth, crunching away obnoxiously. Leaning against the door jamb as he looks at me, his expression is somewhere between disinterested and disappointed.

"I thought my pizza was here." He grunts.

"Switch rooms with me." I blurt out.

Viking stares at me, his expression sliding from disappointment into vague curiosity, but he doesn't say anything.

"I'll bring your pizza when it gets here, and you can have my chicken wrap and fries when it gets to the room." I say, hoping more food will entice him. "And you get to room with your best buddy, Dean." I force a smile.

He shoves more chips in his mouth as he continues to study me while I wait for his answer.

"Will you please switch rooms with me?" I ask again.

"Fuck no." He finally says, over another mouthful of chips. "I just ordered porn." A piece of chip flies out of his mouth on "Porn", smacking me in the cheek. I brush it away impatiently. Under normal circumstances, I would have been grossed out, and probably said as much, but I want him to agree to switch with me, so I don't even mention it.

"Viking, please. There are two beds in there..."

"Nope." He says, stubbornly.

The sound of the door to Dean's room opening makes me jump back from Viking, as Dean steps halfway out into the hallway, looking at us, perplexed. He's wearing a white towel around his waist, his hair wet. His eyes shift from me, to Viking, to the duffle bag in my hand, then back to me. "The fuck is going on here?" He asks. When I don't respond, his gaze shifts back to Viking.

Viking shrugs. "I don't know. Think she's trying to see my dick again, Bro."

I bring my hand to my face to hide the flush of heat radiating through me, especially in my cheeks. The flush is almost painful. I peek through my fingers at a scowling Dean, hard eyeing Viking. He shifts his focus back to me, the scowl turning to something else. A mixture of concern and possibly frustration. I really can't blame him, either way.

"Vanna, come back inside so we can talk." He says, calmly. I can tell he's making an effort to keep his cool.

I hesitate for a moment, glancing at Viking, before I look back at Dean. "I was *not* trying to see his dick... I just thought that maybe you two would have more fun..." I stop talking as the sound of a woman gasping and crying out screams of an orgasm, emanates from Viking's hotel room.

Viking grins before he shoves another handful of chips in his face. "*Scissor Sluts Seven.*" He says, around another grinning mouthful.

I turn and start walking slowly back towards Dean, still holding the door open for me with his arm.

"I am *not* paying for your porn." Dean points at him.

"You just banked over twenty fucking grand, you tight wad." Viking grunts. *Twenty grand!*

"Keep making dick jokes." Dean snaps back at him. "And I know you won money tonight on me, too. Why are you even watching porn? Shouldn't you be out chasing the real thing?"

I glance at Viking to shoot him a glare before I enter Dean's room.

He's grinning back at Dean. "Nah, bro. I had a really *rough* night. I'm *beat*." He says, full of sarcasm, obviously mocking Dean's physical condition.

Dean scowls at him once more. "Fuck you." He snaps back at him, before he steps into the room behind me and slams the door shut. I hear the bolt lock as I walk to my bed, placing the duffle bag on it. "What the fuck, Vanna?" He understandably demands.

I hurry up and busy myself with the first aid kit, removing the antiseptic, wipes and different style bandages.

"You should probably come into the bathroom so I can see you better." I say, gathering the items into my hands. "Or at least sit down over there by the lamp." I gesture to the side of his bed. He moves slowly to the bed, his eyes watching me intently, a slight scowl in them, before he turns his bare, beautifully sculpted back on me to sit.

I take a deep breath, trying to compose myself before I make my way over to him, and place the first aid materials on his night table. Turning to face him, I try not to look him in the eyes as I assess his injuries. A decent cut above his eye brow. A cut on his cheek bone. A scratch across the side of his upper lip. The rest is a collection of bruises. As my eyes scan his body, I try to ignore the fact that he's only wearing a white towel wrapped around his waist.

The cut above his eye seems the worst, so I start there. Wiping it gently with antiseptic and a pad, I blow on it gently, hoping it helps with the sting. He barely reacts. I can tell he's staring at me. Grabbing the Neosporin, I smear a bit of it over the cut, and place several butterfly bandages across it.

Moving to his cut cheek, I grab a fresh wipe and apply some more antiseptic to it. Dabbing at his cheek bone, I pull the pad away to blow gently on it. I make the mistake of lifting my eyes to his, for what I intended only to be for a second. Just to make sure he wasn't squinting in pain or anything. But our eyes lock, his gaze is intense. Heated. And I'm not sure if it's because he's furious with me, or if he's aroused for some unfathomable reason.

"You drive me fucking crazy, Vanna." He growls. His strong hand suddenly at the nape of my neck, yanking me forward as he crushes his injured lips to mine.

I gasp with surprise, and in true Dean style, he takes full advantage, opening his mouth to push his tongue against mine. I drop the wipe, placing my hands on his damp shoulders, as I gently try to push back from him, but he isn't having it. His free arm wraps around my waist, as he leans back on the bed, pulling me with him so that I'm on top of him. Only for a moment, however, as he rolls us over to position himself on top of me, pinning me to the mattress beneath him, somehow managing to keep our mouths from parting during that whole maneuver.

My hands are still between us as I gently attempt to push against his shoulders, letting out a little moan to get his attention, but the sound only seems to spur him on. A low, primal growl emanates from his throat, as I feel him shove one of his knees between my thighs and bend it, pushing my leg open as he settles himself down between them. That thin towel

479

wrapped around his waist, isn't doing a damn thing to conceal his desire. I can feel it jabbing me as his body presses against mine. My body wars with my nagging conscience. *I want him, too...*

A loud knocking at the door startles me, and I flinch beneath him. "Room service!" A male voice announces from the hallway.

With another growl, though this time from annoyance, Dean shoves himself off of me, standing before me as he stares down at me on his bed. He licks his bottom lip, readjusting the towel around his waist, his eyes never leaving mine.

"You mind handling that, doll?" his voice is low and deep, doing things to my insides as I slowly sit up on the bed. "I gotta handle something myself, if I'm gonna keep that promise I made, tonight." Dean mutters, his hand moving in front of his towel to pull his erection to the side.

I watch him storm into the bathroom, shutting the door behind him. Getting up from the bed, I straighten myself out before I open the door and let the hotel worker in with our cart of dinner trays. I hand him the cash Dean left on the night table, and tell him I can set everything up myself. He takes the money and leaves quickly. I busy myself with setting up dinner on the table in the corner by the balcony doors.

Dean seems to be needing a few extra minutes in the bathroom. I decide to step out onto the balcony outside and look up at the stars, leaving the balcony door open this time, so he'll know I didn't try to escape again. The full moon is rising over the ocean and the stars are bright on this breezy, clear night.

"Come have something to eat, doll." I hear him call to me a few minutes later. When I turn back around and step into the room, Dean's wearing the pair of shorts I left out for him and a faded Sturgis t-shirt. "Some music with dinner?"

"Sure." I say, sliding the screen door shut behind me as I watch him bring up some app on his phone and set it up against one of the tray covers. As I take a seat at the table, I notice the playlist is titled *Vanna's Songs*. The song playing on low now is an oldie by The Platters, *Only You.* I know he intends for me to see the play list. To pay attention to the songs, but I act like I don't notice, and avoid looking at his phone, like it's the eyes of Medusa waiting to turn me to stone at first glance.

We're quiet for the first few minutes, as we eat our meal together. I listen to the next few songs without commenting, but the message is pretty clear. They're all love songs... Pining for love, songs. Songs about a broken heart. A desire for a woman. The pain of unrequited love, songs. They're all great songs, but it's loud and clear he's trying to tell me something. And that something just stirs the guilt up inside me again.

When Bon Jovi's, *You Give Love a Bad Name* comes on, I can't help looking up at him with a slight smile, which only grows when I see him grinning back at me, nervously now.

"You son of a bitch." I whisper, teasing him. I sit back in my chair to fold my arms, pretending to be offended again, like I had done so in the bar that night when Viking and I were messing with him.

Dean grabs the phone and immediately skips it to another song. Guns N Roses cover of *Since I Don't Have You*, begins to play instead.

"You've got a decent playlist." I say, grabbing my glass of ice water and taking a sip as I watch him finish the last couple of fries on his plate. "Do you have a favorite?"

"Depends on what I'm feeling." He says, and by the way his eyes are scanning my face, I can tell he's reading me.

I'm afraid to even ask, so I look back down at the ice water I place back on the table. I don't have to look at him to know he's reaching to the phone and scrolling with his finger to bring up something specific... and I know it's to show me what he's feeling, right now. I wait anxiously. Half of me is curious, genuinely wanting to know. The other half is afraid, wanting to jump off the balcony.

He settles on *Still Loving You*, by Scorpions. I recognize the song, it was playing that night, at the bonfire party for Axel. When we were on the picnic table together, alone in the darkness. I can't help biting my lip at the naughty memory of what we did that night.

"Nice." I tease him, as I glance up into his face, expecting to find a humorous expression.

He isn't smiling, though. "That's not why."

"Oh..." Is all I can manage, feeling a little embarrassed.

"I must have listened to this song a hundred times by now." He sighs, his eyes shifting to his phone, as if he's ashamed to admit this for some reason. "Hell, maybe more... I can relate to the lyrics. The wailing... *weeping*, electric guitar... It conveys the agony in my soul whenever you run from me." He says, lifting his gaze to mine again. "But I've come to realize, when you do that... when you run... it has more to do with whatever demons you're battling from your past, than it does with me."

Well, this took a turn for the worst. "I'm sorry I asked." I try to sound humorous, as I get up to clear the table and start putting things back on the tray for room service to collect.

From the corner of my eye, I see Dean reach for the phone again, switching it to another specific song. Ed Sheeran's, *Make It Rain*.

"Do you remember this one?" he asks.

I nod. "It was playing in the bar, when I first saw you." I say, keeping my head down, collecting napkins and silverware and transferring them to the cart on our mostly empty plates.

"It was." He says, his voice low and contemplative.

When I have everything on the cart, he gets up and grabs it, pushing it to the door and shoving it out into the hall, before locking the hotel room door and coming back to stand before me. As I stare up at him, I can't read his expression, there's so much in his eyes. Frustration. Sadness. Determination. I can see the muscle in his jaw tick.

"Are you okay?" my words are quiet, even to my own ears.

"I wish I knew the right words, Vanna. To really reach you." He sighs with discernible frustration. "I try…" he gestures to the phone on the table, "But you either don't understand… or, you won't let yourself."

"I… I *don't* understand." I stammer.

His brows come together slightly, pitching upward, a sorrowful expression in his eyes. "Yes, you do. You have to. You just won't let yourself *believe* it." He shakes his head slowly at me. "Why, Vanna?"

I quickly step around him to dig my long t-shirt and shorts out that I planned on sleeping in tonight. "How was the shower? I think I might give it a whirl." Maybe if I lock myself in the bathroom long enough, he'll go to sleep. He has to be exhausted after tonight.

"I think you're the most beautiful creature on this miserable fucking planet, Vanna."

I don't respond, rummaging through my bag as if he weren't there.

"I thought it was Lucinda, for a long time." He heaves another heavy sigh.

The mention of her name gets right under my skin, as I straighten and turn around to face him again. "Well, I'm fully aware by comparison to her, she's a Ferrari and I'm a-"

"Goddess." Dean cuts me off. He even said the word with a straight face.

I scoff at his response, though. My own inner demons won't allow me the serenity his reply should bring me. "Yeah, right." My words dripping with sarcasm. "Are you talking *Aphrodite* or *Venus of Willendorf*? Because there's a *very noticeable* difference!"

"I'm not familiar with your Witch Slang, Vanna. The hot one." He coolly replies. I can't help laughing at his use of the term *Witch Slang*. He continues without asking me for clarification. "Why does it hurt you, when I compliment you?"

"What, are you a shrink now, too?" I ask, unable to keep the bitterness out of my words.

"I'm just observant… And I've noticed a lot more than you think, doll. I care enough to notice. I want to know you, Vanna. All of you."

I can't fight the tidal wave of resentment that washes over me. The broken mirror held to my face that I despise looking into. I lash out at him because my inner demons aren't content with only devouring my own soul.

"If that was true, you wouldn't consistently reject me. You act like you want what you're alluding to," I snap at him, gesturing to his phone, which is still playing that damn playlist. Now, Guns N Roses, *This I Love*. "But when I've been willing to go there with you, you shut me down."

"*Reject you?*" Dean nearly shouts at me, as if he is beyond dismayed. He takes a deep breath, regaining his composure. "Why is sex with me easier for you to fathom than actually letting me in? Letting me know you? No matter what I do or say, I'm not sure you'll ever let yourself believe me. You won't take me at my word until I fuck you? Why is that? Would you believe me even after? Or would you let your thoughts poison that too? Convince yourself that you were just sex to me? I wonder, Vanna. I really do. And long before

482

tonight, by the way. That would hurt us both. And that's why I haven't fucked you, doll. Because I really, truly, actually do, fucking *care* about you."

We're both silent for a few moments. Seething quietly. My thoughts swirling around what he just said to me.

"Who hurt you?" Dean asks, the hardness around his eyes fading. Shit... I cross my arms and turn away from him so he can't try to read my expressions. "Vanna. Who was he?"

"Nobody." I say, panicking on the inside. I need to end this. I'm not ready to tell him everything. My anxiety kicks up a few notches. I'm not angry any more. I've switched over to panic mode. This whole situation needs to stop.

"Vanna... I've noticed a lot these last months. Your habits. Your reactions to little things. Don't make me drag it out of you." He says, softer now.

"I'm going for a walk." I turn towards the door, but he moves faster than me, blocking the door to the hallway.

"Don't run, Vanna, please let me in."

"Move. I want to leave." I demand, silently praying my voice doesn't betray the trembling I feel inside.

"Who is he? And what did he do to you?" Dean presses. I keep my mouth shut and close my eyes. Willing this situation to stop. "Give me his name, Vanna." Dean sounds more concerned every time he asks.

"No."

"I'll find it on my own, Vanna. You know I will." It's a promise. I can hear the sincerity in his voice. And I can't have him doing that.

"Dean, *please*..." I look up at him, and I know from his expression, that he can see the fear written all over mine. A flash of pain reveals itself behind his eyes, but it's replaced with a low boiling rage as he stares at me. He's figured it out. My dark secret is out. All I can do now is try to convince him to leave it alone. I try to speak, but my voice is barely a strained whisper. "You'll make trouble for me, *please*, Dean. Leave it alone."

He nods, slowly, but even I can feel the tension inside of him building rapidly. The darkness behind his eyes returns. His nostrils flair as he sucks in a deep inhale, barely able to control the rage. I can almost see the slight tremble within him before he explodes...

"Motherfucker!" He slams his fist into the door frame, so hard his knuckles leave a bloody stamp on the white trim. "I fucking knew it!" He whirls back around to face me, agony in his eyes. "What did he do to you, baby? Tell me." He begs. "Tell me his name."

"I can't." I shake my head, backing away from him until the back of my legs touch the side of his bed.

"The off the books jobs. The utilities included in the cash only rent. The car registered to an old address. The shitty burner phone... You're hiding, aren't you?"

My legs are shaking and I feel like I could throw up. He storms up to me, grabbing both of my arms and forces me to look at him.

"His name, Vanna. Give it to me."

"*Why?*" I cry, but I already know the answer. I did this. To him. To us.

"So I can cut out his fucking heart and drop the bloody thing at your feet." He growls.

My heart breaks a little more. Dean is just trying to do what I summoned him to do. And now it will be my fault if he gets hurt, or worse. Tears sting my eyes and I can't bring myself to even look at him. "You can't. Don't look for him." I plead.

"Do you love him?" Dean demands. *Him!* The absurdity of it renders me speechless. Dean shakes me again. "Are you in love with this bastard?" He demands again, more harshly.

"No!" I shout back at him.

He seems minorly relieved, though it's only temporary. "Then tell me his name."

"I can't do that. You can't go looking for him." I beg.

"The fuck I can't. Watch me, baby." He lets me go to grab the cell phone off the table, and his jeans that I folded on the chair.

"What are you doing?"

"Going to get answers."

I grab him, trying to haul him away from his boots and position myself in front of the door. I don't know what he means by that, or where he's going to go to get these answers in Myrtle Beach, but I know Dean is a determined man, so anything is possible and it scares me. "Please, *please*, Dean! Don't do this! If he finds me, he'll kill me!" I sob, all my walls are crashing down around me. "Just stay with me, okay?" I grab at the fabric of his shirt, curling it in my fists, trying to pull him to me. "Stay with me and I'll be better, I'll be good. I'll be worth it."

He drops the clothes and the phone on the edge of his bed and wraps his arms around me tightly, holding me against his chest. I feel him kiss the top of my head and stroke my hair.

"Nobody's gonna hurt you, baby." His whisper is rough, strangled with emotion. "I'm not going to let anything happen to you."

We're both silent for a few minutes as he holds me in his strong arms. His warm, hard body calming the trembling in mine. I do feel safe in his arms. I know he cares for me. I allow myself a few more moments of the peace and calm his warm embrace provides me, before I step back from him, wiping my tear-streaked face. I can see he's reluctant to release me, as he keeps both of his hands on my arms. I have to clear my throat before I speak again.

"I know you care about me." I say. "I'm sorry I lashed out at you."

"Just tell me the truth." Dean says, his expression still a mixture of rage and deep concern.

I nod. "He's in prison. He got seven years. Possibility of parole in five. That was three years ago. I have at least two years left. Four if I'm lucky."

"The letter I took you to get. At your old address. The one that was so important we had to ride to Carolina Beach to get." He says. I just nod. He already knows. "So, he doesn't know where you are now?"

484

"Not yet. But he will, eventually... He'll find me faster if you do anything to draw his attention. So please, if you truly care about me, don't do anything. Don't tell anyone about this." I plead with him again. Dean doesn't say anything. He just continues to stare at me. I can't read him. "Dean, please. I'm begging you. Not a word to anyone. If the wrong person finds out... I'll have to leave."

"Leave?" he suddenly looks alarmed. "You can't just *leave*." He insists.

"Then don't make me." I sniffle.

Dean seems agitated now as he releases me and paces in front of me for a few seconds, running his hand through his dark hair, then comes back to stand before me again.

"You can't just *leave*, Vanna. What about the life you're building here?" He asks, his voice riddled with anxiety. "What about the witch shop? Laura? You love it there."

I shrug. "I'll start over. I've had to before. It's easier than dying. And everyone back in town hates me anyway."

"That ain't even close to true." He says, a longing look in his eyes, that tells me he mostly means himself.

I smile at him, but respond as if I didn't read between the lines of his statement. "That's not enough to make me stay. I'm sorry. So, if you actually do care about me, you need to keep this between us. If you can do that, I'll stay as long as I can."

Dean is staring at me intently. *"If I actually care about you?"* He seems hurt by my words. "You know you put me in the friend zone as much as I fucked myself over with that. I don't want to be there, Vanna. This push and pull, has been our dance together. You can't put it all on me."

"You're right. I can't. I put the brakes on once, but I wasn't rejecting you."

"Maybe part of me thinks you deserve better." Dean sighs. "Better than at a biker party. Better than in the front seat of a truck. Maybe I just wanted it to be perfect for you. For us. And maybe..." He hesitates. And it's not like Dean to ever be at a loss for words about anything. "Maybe you deserve better than me, altogether."

"What?"

"Just shut up and let me get this out." He lifts his hand to stop me from talking, taking a moment as if he needs to brace himself. "I mean it when I say you're a Goddess." He drops his arm back to his side. "All the times I told you that you're beautiful, gorgeous. I meant every word, every time. Maybe you didn't believe me, or just took them as compliments from a friend. But I never wanted to be *only* your friend, baby. Is it really that hard for you to see?"

Not exactly. "I know what I felt when we've kissed. I imagine you might have felt something similar-"

"When you kiss me, Vanna, you set my soul on fire. I'm hyper aware of everything about you. You damn near push me to the brink of sanity. There's an aura about you, baby. A pull I can't wrap my head around. No woman, ever, not Lucinda, or anyone else, has ever come close to what you do to me. We all have darkness in our pasts, doll. I'm no exception. And Lucinda, she broke my heart. There's no point in hiding it from you, now. But Vanna, the way I feel about you..." Dean hesitates, as if he's trying to muster up the courage to continue. He takes a quick breath, reaching a hand up to rub the back of his neck for a moment, before he drops his arm and tries again. "You have the power to crush my soul. Destroy me completely. If I go all the way with you... I'm fucking done for, baby... *It was self-preservation*. Never rejection." His eyes look almost pleading, as if he's trying to will me to believe him. "I would kill and I would die for you... Being with you, allowing myself to fall all the way with you, I'd never come back from it. You'd own me. My heart, my life, my soul... Completely and forever." He pauses to take another breath before continuing. "And if you ever left me, I don't know how I'd be able to go on. If you leave now... I still don't think I'd be okay."

For once, my demons are silent. He's stunned me. And I feel cruel not having a response to his heartfelt confession. I turn away from him to gather my thoughts. I want to go to him, but the Knight Summoning Spell haunts my conscience. I have to tell him the truth, yet I can't risk losing him either.

"Vanna," Dean's voice is almost pleading. "Did I say something wrong?"

"No."

"Are we at least in the same ballpark together?" he asks, and I can hear the insecurities veiled in his humor. Dean has never left himself so vulnerable before. I nod, I can give him that much. "Alright. Well, I've basically just told you I'm in fucking love with you... So, perhaps you might find it merciful to give me a little more feedback on the matter?" He pleads.

He isn't wrong. I turn back to face him. My handsome, bruised up Knight, usually so confident and strong, looks scared shitless right now.

"I know you don't believe in magick." I say. "But I *wished* for you, Dean. For years. Long before I ever knew you existed." It's a half assed confession on my part, but it is a piece of the truth I owe him.

He smiles, and even I can feel his relief. "I'm sorry I'm late." He jokes. "I wish I met you first. For both of us."

Tears sting my eyes again, and I wipe them away. "Me too." I whisper. I wish I met him before everything. Before the nightmare. Before the spell. If we had somehow met before all of this, could we have been something special? Something real?

"I am here, now, Vanna. You aren't alone in the darkness any more. There's nothing I wouldn't do to protect you." He swears to me, and I believe him.

"I know. I've known that a while now." I say. "It was a comfort, at first. Now... it just scares me."

He looks confused. "Scares you?"

"I don't want anything bad to happen to you, especially not because of me." I clarify. That is the truth. Though only a layer of it.

"You really believe this prick from your past is going to come after you." It's a statement more to himself, but I nod.

"He promised." I whisper.

"Is that what his letter said?"

"Letters. Yes."

"Is he still harassing you?"

"I'm sure he's trying to. Joey moved out, after he got a threatening letter. Whomever is renting the apartment now is either throwing them out, or they're going back to the prison as undeliverable. I haven't gotten anything at my house or Laura's shop yet. So far, so good... One step ahead."

Dean stares at me for a moment before he asks his next question. "And if you get a letter? What then?"

I don't have an answer. I'm afraid to even tell him that I don't know, after he poured his heart out to me.

Dean steps closer and takes me in his arms again. And this time, I'm not completely sure if it's only to comfort me.

"I don't want you to get hurt." I whisper, gripping his shirt in my fingers.

He kisses my forehead and holds me tighter. "*We* have two years." He reminds me. "Four, if *we're* lucky."

DEAN

Chapter
twenty-two

MADE IT THROUGH THIRTEEN FIGHTERS. I'M BANGED UP. BRUISED UP. A little cut up. No broken bones, though. My heart, however... that's a different story. She fuckin' broke that tonight...

I'll be better... I'll be good... I'll be worth it...

Fuck, baby... What have you been through?

I'm standing in front of the balcony door. I left it open for her. So she can listen to the waves in her sleep. The ocean makes her feel better. She's told me this before. I tried to lay with her, but I'm restless. My body aches. My mind has been racing since she dropped that bomb on me about leaving town. It did not go unnoticed that she didn't answer me about what she'd do if his next letter reaches her. It did not go unnoticed either, that when I told her I'm in love with her... She didn't say it back. In a way, I'm glad. I don't want her to say it just because I did. I want her to mean it. But now, I don't know what to do with myself. I don't know where I stand with her. And so, here I stand. In the dark. Watching her.

The moon is high up over the black ocean waters. Casting my shadow across her sleeping figure in the bed before me. She's a little restless, too. Tossing and turning in her sleep. An incoherent whimper escapes her now and again. And I can only imagine what she's dreaming of. She turns over on her side, facing me now. I lean against the frame of the door, and raise the little bottle of whiskey to my lips that I snagged from the mini bar in the room. Pain killers need a fuckin' boost. I finish the bottle in two shots, dropping my arm and letting the empty bottle dangle between my fingers.

"He can't breathe..." she whimpers in her sleep. This time I understood her. And now I feel even shittier. Maybe this was too much for her. *"He can't breathe... he can't breathe!"*

Fuck. I chuck the bottle into the chair in the corner and walk over to the side of Vanna's bed, gently rubbing her back as I lower myself to sit beside her.

"Get off of him..." another whisper.

"Vanna... I'm okay." I gently say to her, hoping I reach her. I don't want to have to wake her up, but I don't want to be the reason for her nightmares, either.

"Jack..."

The fuck is Jack?

"You're hurting me..."

Oh... Shit. Don't tell me the fucker's name is Jack...

"Jack... I can't breathe... please..."

No. Fuck no. I can't allow this.

"Baby, wake up... you're having a nightmare, Vanna." I say, rubbing her back a little more vigorously. I don't want to wake her up too abruptly. I don't want to scare her. But I want to pull her out of this. I can't save her from her past. But I can stop her nightmare. And I can kill this motherfucker if he ever does come looking for her. Hell, I might not even wait...

She turns to face me, and in the moon light, I can see her blinking up at me. "Dean? Are you okay?" she asks me in her sleepy voice.

"I'm fine, doll. You were having a bad dream." I say softly.

"Did I wake you up?" she asks. "I'm sorry."

I shake my head. "I haven't slept yet."

"Are you in pain?"

I shrug, not wanting to make a big deal of it. After all, I did this to myself.

Vanna moves over in the bed. "Come back." She says, lifting the covers. I get up and slowly slide into the bed next to her. "Come here." She yawns, sliding her arm behind my shoulders, her soft fingers moving across my skin, as she gently pulls me towards her.

I'm a little surprised, and unsure of exactly what she wants from me, so I let her guide me into the position she wants. I wind up with my head on her chest, the length of my body against hers, my arm around her middle. Her arm draped over mine. When her fingers begin to gently stroke through my hair, in that soothing way she just seems to know how to touch me, I want to tell her I love her, again. But I don't. I close my eyes and listen to her heart beat. Allowing her tenderness to lull me to sleep. As I curl my arm around her slightly tighter, I drift off knowing that I'll never let her go.

The rustling sound of the curtain billowing in the breeze, stirs me. I awaken blinking from the sunlight shining through the balcony door, realizing I'm spooning her body, my face all up in her wild dark hair. She's still sleeping, wrapped up in my limbs. I don't want to wake her yet, as I carefully attempt to unwrap myself from her body. I'm so fucking stiff from having my ass handed to me last night. And as I roll away from her, I'm glad my equally stiff cock didn't wake her either. I'm not sure prodding her in her ass with my dick is the proper *thank you* for the sweetness she showed me last night. I don't think a woman has ever been that tender to me before... Besides my mother, when I was a kid. And Vanna did it so... naturally.

Fuck. I'm a goner. She may not have said she loves me back. But last night, the way she held me, her fingers stroking my pain away, soothing me to sleep. That felt like love.

Pushing myself slowly off the bed, I walk stiffly, but quietly, towards the bathroom to down some Aleve and take another hot shower to loosen up. I want my girl to have fun today. She deserves it.

Vanna's sitting up in bed when I step out of the bathroom, fastening my belt. Her hair all bed wild and fuckin' sexy looking. "Morning, babe." I smile at her.

"Morning." She smiles back. "Are you done in there?"

"Yeah. You want to have breakfast in the room or do you want to go out?" I ask her.

"Whatever you want." She says, climbing out of bed and tugging down her t-shirt as she makes her way over to her duffle bag. "I want to take a shower first, though."

"I'll text the others and see what their plans are." I say, walking over to what's supposed to be my bed. I lay down on it carefully and grab my cell off the night table.

"How's the body?" She asks me, gathering up a bunch of things to bring into the bathroom with her.

"Looking good from here." I wink at her.

She rolls her eyes at me. "*Your* body. Are you worse off than you were last night?"

"I'll live."

Shaking her head, she walks into the bathroom and shuts the door behind her.

When she emerges a half hour later, she's wearing a white, modern looking Grecian style dress and sandals.

"Fuck. And you say you're not a Goddess." I tease her, watching her walk across the room back to her duffle bag. The light fabric of the dress is flowy around her legs as she moves, but cinched at her waistline, showing off the sexy curvature of her figure. I can't help noticing, Vanna looks real good in white.

"Is this okay to wear?" She asks, as I realize I'm staring at her. "I mean, I can change into jeans if you want to ride your bike over... I just thought you were going to take it easy today and we'd take a cab to the rally thing."

"You look too pretty. I'm not going to ask you to change" I say. She gives me that uncomfortable smile she does whenever I pay her a compliment. And it jabs me in the heart, now that I know the reason why.

"LICK...SHOOT...SUCK." VIKING SAYS, THEN GULPS DOWN HIS SECOND glass of orange juice. That's Viking's vote on which bar to hit up at the Bike Rally in Murphies Inlet.

"Or, the Sissy Bar." Axel shrugs, munching on a piece of bacon and glancing across the table at Dean.

"Or both. Fuck it." Cherry says, swirling her straw in her brunch mimosa. "I hope you're wearing comfortable foot wear, Vanna. Because these guys are going to be ogling bikes and boobs all day and night."

"Fuck yeah." Viking scoffs, attacking his stack of pancakes and sausage. The way this man puts away food, is astonishing. He should be one of the world wonders. I force myself to look away from the human garbage disposal at work across the table from me, and glance up at Dean beside me.

"How are you feeling?" I ask him. Dean never eats nearly as much as Viking, but I've never seen him not finish a normal sized meal.

"Alright, doll. Just not that hungry." He tries to assure me. Something seems off about him, but maybe he really is just a little sore.

"I really don't mind keeping you company in the hotel room, Dean. I'm sure there's something we can order on the TV to watch, besides porn." I say to him, shooting a look at Viking.

"Why would you?" Viking asks, his mouth full of pancakes and syrup. I try not to grimace and look back at Dean. He doesn't say anything, he just takes my hand and kisses it.

"You better not punk out and bail, bro." Viking says. "It's bad enough your pussy ass isn't even riding your fuckin' motorcycle to the rally. Poser." He says, with an antagonizing grin.

Before Dean can answer, I frown back at Viking. "He happens to be in pain, you jerk. He isn't a *poser*." I snap at him. Dean slides his arm around my shoulders and leans into my ear.

"It's okay, baby. He's just fucking around." Dean whispers.

"Nah, bro, let her speak." Viking says. "It's okay if you can't fight your own battles today. We get it. Thirteen fighters is a lot. And I'd be bummed too if my girlfriend cost me the record breaking round last night."

"What?" I ask.

"You really are an asshole, Viking." Cherry sounds uncharacteristically annoyed with him as she gets up from the table. "I'm going to the ladies' room. Do you want to come with me, Vanna?"

I glance back at Dean, who actually appears to be pretty pissed off at the moment. "Did I cost you th-"

"No." he growls, cutting me off before I can get the question out. He doesn't look away from Viking. "I was fucking spent. I would have lost it regardless." Dean says, pointing at Viking across the table. "And you fucking know it."

"No, I don't. I know you weren't even looking when that guy attacked you, because you were too concerned with Vanna freaking out over a little bit of blood that wasn't even yours." Viking shrugs. "You were *distracted*." He adds. "*Again*."

Dean stands up from the table, then extends his hand for me to take it. "Vanna, go with Cherry." He says, assisting me out of the booth. I glace at Axel as I slide out, who's sitting there wide eyed and quiet, looking between Dean and Viking.

Cherry wraps her arm in mine and walks with me to the ladies' room.

"What the hell just happened?" I ask her, once we're inside the bathroom. I watch her chuck her purse up on the sink counter, and pull out her cell phone.

"Axel will text me when it's safe for us to come out." She says, apparently texting Axel to do just that.

"Did I do something wrong?" I ask. "Break some MC rule about talking back to a biker or something?"

"No. Viking is just in dick mode today. Probably just woke up on the wrong side of the bed." Cherry sighs. "Maybe he lost money on Dean's fight last night and is just looking for someone to blame it on. Don't worry about it. Sometimes we just have to ignore Viking when he gets on these kicks. Dean will straighten him out."

I glance in the mirror for a moment, realizing just how much I don't fit with my group of *"friends."* Cherry looks like the perfect biker chick, in her typical ripped jeans, and tattered t-shirt beneath her leather vest declaring her as Axel's property.

"Maybe I should just hang back at the hotel. This rally is more of a *you guys'* thing."

"You're with Dean. That means you're with us, too." Cherry says.

I sigh, looking down at my dress. "When he said ocean front hotel, I thought this excursion was going to be a little beachier. I did ask him if I should wear something else. I packed jeans. He said I looked pretty, though."

"You do. There's nothing wrong with what you're wearing. He shouldn't be on his bike until he feels a little better anyway."

"Maybe you can help me pick out a few things. Dean said there would be all kinds of vendors." I suggest.

Cherry giggles. "So, I'll be Frenchie, you be Sandy. And Dean is Danny Zuko." We both laugh at her Grease joke, until her cellphone chimes. "Oh, it's Axel. The coast is clear."

I'm eager to get back to Dean, but at the same time, I'm not thrilled about being around Viking again. When we walk back into the diner, the guys are getting up from the table.

"Is everything okay?" I quietly ask Dean.

He gives me a reassuring smile. "Fine, doll."

"Are you sure you don't want to just go back to the hotel?" I ask.

"And punk out?" He says, shooting a look at Viking. "Nope."

Viking lets out a sigh. "I was being a dick." He says, looking at me and then at Cherry.

"That's his version of an apology." Cherry says to me, before she looks back at Viking. "Shut up, Kenickie." She says to him, and we both laugh. The guys look confused by her Grease reference, which just makes Cherry and I laugh harder. It feels nice to have an inside joke with her.

Viking and Axel ride their bikes to the rally, Cherry went with Axel, of course, and we have plans to meet up there. Dean is pretty quiet in the cab ride over.

"What happened with Viking?" I ask. "I kinda thought he and I were on better terms after you both ambushed me at Laura's shop that day."

"You are." Dean says, turning his head to look at me. He reaches for my hand and holds it in his, against the top of his leg. "He just likes to break balls, and sometimes he pushes shit too far and needs a reminder."

"Is he really pissed that I cost you that round?"

Dean is quiet for a moment, as if he needs to think about his answer. "No, not exactly."

"I don't understand."

"I'm not at liberty to discuss this with you, yet." I can see regret in his eyes. He lifts my hand to his chest, stroking the back of my hand with his thumb. "I hate having to say that to you, Vanna. Especially after last night." He sighs. "Just, trust me that everything is fine."

"Biker business?"

He smiles at me. "Something like that, doll."

"Okay, but does he hate me again?"

Dean shakes his head and presses my hand to his lips. "No. He never hated you, Vanna. He's just a prick sometimes. You'll get used to it."

When we arrive at the bike rally, I'm amazed at the number of motorcycles everywhere. In every style and color. Filling every parking lot and then some, as far as the eye can see. There are booths with all kinds of vendors, mostly catering to bike enthusiasts, naturally. Live music is playing somewhere behind the main bar we are at, country rock, right now. Which I expect to hear, and will probably hear more rock n roll as the day and night progress. As we head into the crowd to explore, I try not to act so surprised when I see scantily clad women walking around like it's totally normal. And I guess, for this crowd, it is. I admire their confidence to be able to walk around in fishnets and daisy dukes. Some of them only wearing pasties and thongs as a complete outfit.

Holding onto Dean's arm, I turn my face into him to giggle. "I think I'm a little over dressed." I joke.

"Fuck no, you're not." Dean smiles at me. "I am in no shape to be fighting anybody off you. Not that I wouldn't anyway."

Behind the main bar, there are a series of elevated board walks, built around the perimeter of the lot in the back, where there are more motorcycles, the live band on a stage, some kind of a large box that says *Burn Out Booth* on it. There are multiple mini bars scattered about, which have half naked women walking around and dancing on them, and even more vendors.

"Is this what your bike rally is like?" I ask.

"On a smaller scale, yeah." Dean shrugs. "But we don't do the banana contest."

"The what?"

Dean cocks his chin in the direction towards the side of the venue. There are a bunch of guys lined up sitting in chairs on one of the lower makeshift stages. They're all holding bananas between their knees with women kneeling in front of them.

"The one to peel the banana and get as much in their mouth first, wins." Dean chuckles. "No hands allowed."

494

I don't comment, instead I look around at the elevated board walk and spot a few large cages spread out in each section. "Let me guess... this little gathering gets crazy at night too... and there will be naked chicks in those cages."

"Pretty much." Dean confirms. "There will be chicks in leather with whips giving free beatings too." He adds, cracking a grin at my surprised expression.

We bump into Viking, Axel and Cherry after a little while. The guys are looking at custom parts for their bikes, while Cherry and I check out a few booths with biker chick clothing nearby. I find a few tops that are kind of cute, and drape them over my arm. Cherry snags a black leather purse with silver spikes all over it, and a man's leather bracelet cuff that actually says *Axel* on it.

"Must be a popular Biker nick name."

Cherry giggles. "Actually, his parents named him Axel." She says. "Axel Rose Jacobson. He didn't get a road name."

"With a name as cool as that, why would he want one?" I laugh.

"Exactly. He takes after Dean in that way, too."

"I thought Dean's road name was Lancelot?"

Cherry shakes her head. "No, that's just Viking breaking balls again. Dean never took a road name. But I guess with names like Dean and Axel, you're automatically cool." She giggles again, pulling a little black dress off the rack and looking at it. It looks like something a shark attacked, but Cherry has the petite figure that could probably wear anything and make it look fashionable. "I think I want to try a few of these dresses on. I'll be right back." She walks into the makeshift changing rooms under the tent we're shopping in.

I glance over at the guys, in time to see Dean slap the side of Viking's arm and cock his head towards me, before he walks off with Axel in another direction. Viking comes walking over to me.

"Dean wants me to keep an eye on you. He's going with Axel to check out a bike for sale out front."

I just nod, and go back to flipping through clothing while I wait for Cherry to come back. I'm really not interested in making small talk with Viking today. He seems to pick up on that and doesn't crowd me, walking back over to another Vender selling custom bike accessories.

"Giovanna?" A man's voice says from somewhere behind me. It's vaguely familiar, and I turn around to see who called my name. "It is you..." He says again as our eyes lock. My breath hitches in my throat as I realize who the man with the military style brown hair and hazel eyes is, standing a few feet away. He walks up to me and wraps his arms around me. I'm too stunned to react.

Out of seemingly nowhere, Viking is at my side, yanking him off me. "Hand's off motherfucker!" Viking threatens him. The jolt of it snaps me back to the present. I cannot let Viking hit him. I grab his huge arm before he can do anything else.

"Stop! Viking, he's a cop!" I warn him.

"You know this guy?" Viking demands, hard eyeing my ex's former partner.

"Yes… His name is Kyle Monroe. Officer Kyle Monroe of the NYPD."

The two of them glare at each other for a moment, before Viking breaks the silence, "You're a long way from New York."

"My parents live in Murphie's Inlet. My younger brother is in one of the bands playing tonight. I'm vacationing with my wife. Visiting family." Kyle says, hard eyeing Viking back, before he looks at me again. "How are you, Giovanna? June and I have wondered about you, often." He says. "Do you live around here now?"

"No." I say quickly, glancing at Viking. I wish he weren't right here to witness any of this, but I can't trust that this chance encounter won't get back to my ex somehow. "Atlanta, actually. Just here because my boyfriend is a bike enthusiast." I lie. Viking's expression is momentarily surprised, but he quickly regains his composure, and fortunately for me, keeps his mouth shut.

"This guy?" Kyle gestures towards Viking. He seems surprised that I would even be associating with someone looking like Viking, let alone dating. My ex was clean cut. Sharp dressing, when not in uniform. Kyle seems to take an interest in the patches sewn on Viking's cut, before he looks back at me.

I force myself to laugh. "No, this is my boyfriend's *friend*, Viking."

"Well, you look great… He must be keeping you happy." Kyle says. "I hope he is. You deserve that." I try to ignore the look of remorse in Kyle's eyes.

"He's around here somewhere." I say, reaching for any excuse to end this surprise encounter. "I should probably get moving and find him." I add, taking a step back.

"Giovanna… I want you to know something." Kyle says, stepping towards me, but stops when Viking makes a move towards him. They hard eye each other again for a moment, before Kyle turns his attention back to me, his eyes softening again. "I didn't know the extent of it, Giovanna. I swear to you. I never would have let him continue what he was doing."

His words make my heart palpitate for a moment, as I force my mind not to allow his words to conjure up specific memories of the past. I don't want this conversation to happen in front of Viking, either. In the middle of a biker rally. I don't want my secrets exposed like this. Though, as much as I want to run right now, I'm tempted to ask him what he did know. At this point, it doesn't matter. It wouldn't change anything.

"I wanted to ask you at the Christmas party, that night." He continues. "I wish you would have told me what was going on."

I don't say anything. I just stare back at him. And he seems to understand that I don't want to talk about this. He nods, taking a step back again.

"Anyway, it's good to see you again after all this time. You look great. Really. I'm happy for you." Kyle says. "Take care." He gives me a low type of parting wave, glancing at Viking once more, before he walks away into the crowd.

I turn back around to the clothing rack I was sifting through. I don't even want to *look* at Viking, but his massive presence is still right at my side.

"*Atlanta, Georgia*? That's a bit of a stretch." His tone is wrought with suspicion.

I just shake my head and flip through a few hangers of tops, blindly. I can't focus on anything right now. I have no idea how to smooth this over with him. How to pretend this encounter was nothing of any significance.

"You know, I just thought you were a little strange." Viking continues. "Maybe because you don't know jack about MC life... But it turns out, there's *a lot* we don't know about you, *Giovanna...*"

"Viking, please. It's nothing." I say the words, already knowing they're useless.

He scoffs. "I should have guessed there was a lot more to your story." He pushes. "Dean's always been a sucker for a damsel in distress." He mutters, walking around me as if he's going to walk away, but he stops to bend and growl something near my ear as he passes. "You better not hurt him, Vanna." His warning sends a shiver through my body, as he walks away from me as well.

"You getting those?" Dean asks, coming up behind me a little while later, his hand touching my lower back as he kisses the side of my head. He sounds too upbeat for Viking to have said anything to him about Kyle Monroe.

"Maybe." I sigh. I'm tempted to put them all back. What's the point of trying to fit in with his life style if his best friend is always going to hate me? I might as well just remain an outsider. Glancing up at Dean as he removes his hand from my back to pull out his wallet, I catch a glimpse of Viking watching us, a few yards away behind Dean.

Dean pulls out a hundred-dollar bill and tries to hand it to me. "Here, get whatever you want." He smiles. I look at the money in his hand and shake my head, placing the clothes down on the table beside me.

"No, thanks." I say, "I changed my mind." Part of me really wants Viking to see me refuse Dean's money. I know he's concerned about his friend. That maybe I'm using him for something. I hate that he's right. But it isn't for his money. Dean is looking at me, perplexed. He follows my line of sight and realizes I had been looking at Viking.

"Did he say something again?" Dean asks, his tone a clear indication that he'd get in Viking's face about it if I say yes.

"No... I just decided I really don't need more t-shirts." I push his hand with the cash back to him. "You bled for that money, keep it."

"Doll..." he begins to protest.

"Buy me a drink, instead." I force a smile at him and turn to walk towards one of the mini bars, manned by a half-naked chick in leather chaps and pasties.

A majority of the day passes, before Viking comes back up to us. Dean and I are sitting at a table on the upper decks, eating bar food with Cherry and Axel, over-looking the event, and whatever the *Burn Out Booth* is in the middle of the place. The sun is almost set now, and the string lights dangling everywhere come on. So does the track lighting attached to all the mini bars around the event, lighting up the women dancing on the counter tops. As things get darker, the crowd gets rowdier, but everyone still seems to be in good spirits, drinking and having fun.

Except Viking, who seems Hell bent on making me miserable.

There's a bit of a commotion below us at the Burn Out Booth, as someone pulls a motorcycle inside of it. They proceed to rev the absolute Hell out of it while peeling out, creating a thick cloud of burnt rubber smoke that permeates the crowd. The back tire squeals until it pops. The crowd cheers.

I look at Dean and can't help laughing. He just shakes his head and smiles. "The longest burnout before blowing a tire, *wins*." He shrugs.

"I guess all bikers are a little crazy." I tease him.

"I'd never abuse Serene, or any of my side chicks like that." Dean grins. No. Dean wouldn't.

"Did Vanna tell you about her friend she bumped into today?" Viking decides to chime in. Dean doesn't say anything, just glances back at me with curiosity. "Some cop from New York." He adds. When neither I, nor Dean, says anything, Viking continues. "No? Well apparently, the two of you are visiting from *Atlanta*."

I glance quickly at Cherry and Axel, who seem confused, but don't comment, before I look back at Dean. I can see in his eyes, that he pieced the situation together within seconds, before shifting his gaze to Viking. He looks at him with a slight scowl, as if it's an unspoken warning. But Viking refuses to take the subtle hint, as he looks back at me.

"Tell us about that Christmas party, *Giovanna*. Officer Monroe seemed pretty concerned about it." He says, in an almost mocking way that triggers my anger.

There's another bike in the Burn Out Booth, and as it's engine and tires scream, I feel like I could scream as well. Standing up from the table I snatch what's left of my spiked lemonade, splashing it right in Viking's smug face, tossing the solo cup at him as well. "Asshole!"

Viking and Dean jump up at the same time, Viking smacks the cup away with a clatter as he steps towards me with an enraged look in his eyes. Reflexively, I jump back from him. Dean and Axel are in front of him in a second, blocking him from getting to me.

"You lose your fucking mind?" Dean raises his voice to Viking, grabbing him by his leather cut. "You *think* you're going to approach her like that? You fucking *must* be crazy."

"I ain't gonna touch her." Viking growls, shifting his angry gaze from glaring at me, to looking at Dean, as he runs a hand down his face to wipe off the drink.

"You need to take a fucking walk." Dean says.

"You need to start asking her some fucking questions." Viking snaps back at him. "Quit jerking your dick to some princess trapped in a tower fantasy and open your fucking eyes, bro."

"Don't make me hurt you." Dean warns him, his voice borderline menacing.

"So much for *Bro's before Ho's*." Viking mutters, shooting me a resentful glare.

"You're making the choice for me, *bro*." Dean shoves Viking back, taking a step away from him.

"Why do you always have to be such a fucking dick!" Axel shouts at Viking. I can tell both Dean and Viking come down a few notches at Axel's outburst. "Everything's about to be as it should have been all this time, and *you* have to fuck it up!" He shouts at Viking again. I'm not sure what Axel means by that comment, but Dean puts his hand on Axel's shoulder as Cherry hurries over to him as well.

"Axel, come on." Dean tries to calm him down.

"No, Dean. You get shit from every direction. You don't need it from him, too." Axel says, shooting daggers from his eyes at Viking again. I can see that Viking is hurt by Axel's words.

I can't be the reason this odd ball family comes apart. They're the only family Dean has. And I know, as big of a jerk as Viking is, he's just trying to look out for his best friend. His family. He doesn't know anything about me. For all he knows, I could be another Lucinda. She might have ruined Dean's life for a while. But I'm the one who's actually *risking it*. So, in actuality, who's the bigger bitch in this equation...

"Viking's right." I say, interrupting them. "There's a lot you all don't know about me... I thought I could keep my past in the past, but I'm starting to realize, that's impossible."

"Vanna, stop." Dean says, but I can't bring myself to look at him, so I focus on Viking, who seems surprised that I'm even saying anything at all.

"Viking loves you guys." I say with a shrug, gesturing to them as if they're one unit. They basically are. "He's just looking out for you. You should cut him some slack... Even I can tell he means well."

Dean steps away from them to walk closer to me. "It's fine, doll. You don't have to say anything else, Vanna. *Really*." His tone is insisting, as if he's asking me not to say another word. Though, I can't imagine why not.

As the screeching tires and smoke from the Burn Out Booth fill the air again, I have to cough and clear my throat before I can respond to him. "I think I've had enough of this."

DEAN

I COULD KILL HIM. I REALLY COULD. THIS IS THE THIRD FUCKING TIME I'VE had to tell Viking to back the fuck off my increasingly fragile relationship with Vanna. The adrenaline beginning to course through my veins as my anger spikes, dulls the aches in my body from the previous night, and I'm ready to throw down with him if he makes another comment about her. And God help him, if he thinks he's going to take another step towards her.

"Viking's right." Vanna says, her voice pulling my attention to her. "There's a lot you all don't know about me... I thought I could keep my past in the past, but I'm starting to realize, that's impossible." The look of defeat in her eyes, jabs at my heart.

"Vanna, stop." I tell her. She doesn't owe him, or anyone else a damn thing. She told me the truth last night. That's what fucking matters. I don't want her to feel that she needs to rip this wound open in front of him to gain our acceptance.

"Viking loves you guys. He's just looking out for you. You should cut him some slack. Even I can see that he means well." She actually looks sorry for the bastard. I take a few steps towards her.

"It's fine, doll. You don't have to say anything else, Vanna. *Really.*" I try to reassure her. It took her until last night to tell me the truth for a reason. It hurts her. It embarrasses her. And I understand her reluctance completely. I understand the desire to keep certain aspects of one's past hidden, whether it be because of shame, or fear, or just simply because it's too painful to talk about. I know her pain. I carry it in my own heart. And I don't want her to feel like she has to bare her soul to gain *anyone's* fucking approval.

"I think I've had enough of this." She manages to choke through the smoke blowing past us from the burning rubber of a bike tire below.

There are far too many ways one can interpret that sentence, and all the ways that spring to mind, leave me feeling unnerved. As Vanna turns to walk away from us... from *me*, Cherry grabs my arm before I can go after her.

"Let me, Dean." She insists, before she turns and runs after Vanna, the two of them now vanishing from my sight within the clouds of smoke.

The sound of Viking's voice pulls me back to rage. "Bro... I -"

"*You...*" I snarl at him, cutting off whatever he was going to say as I turn back to him. I don't give a fuck what he has to say for himself. "You better fucking pray to whatever Pagan Gods you may believe in, that she doesn't leave me over this!" My fists clench almost painfully. I want to wrap my hands around his fucking throat.

"Dean... listen to me, bro... come on." He says. "I was a little out of line in the diner, about the fight. I admit that, it's not her fault she was freaked out. And yeah, you were spent, probably would have lost the fight anyway. My point was just that she was a distraction again. It was petty, I know... But *this* shit...*Fucking Atlanta*, bro? ... And then not even telling you it happened, like *I* wouldn't tell you? What the fuck is she lying for?" He gestures in the direction Vanna ran.

I grab him again, my fists twisting in his leather cut as I glare in his face. I can feel Axel pulling on my arms, attempting to get me away from our brother, repeating my name again and again.

"She isn't lying *to me*! And that's all that fucking matters!" I shout at him. "I should fucking lay you out where you fucking stand!"

Axel's hands are on mine now, trying to pry them from Viking. And as I lower my eyes to look at the Saviors cut in my fists, I can't help but scoff.

"It might sway your *unjustly low* opinion of her, to know that she's *one of them.*" I manage to choke out of my tight throat. "Last night, was the first night I watched her sleep. I got to see her toss and turn through nightmares of her past... I would have told you what you needed to know, you fucking prick! But she only confessed to me last night." I let go of his cut, taking a step back as I stare at it. What it used to represent. For once, he's fucking quiet. "I told her I love her. She was already thinking about running... And now... *now*, that she's *had enough of this*..." I slap his cut with the back of my hand.

"Dean, she was probably just upset. Vanna loves you, too." Axel says, trying to comfort me. She never said it back. She said she *wished* for me... What does that really even mean? "She's not going to run away."

None of them seem to realize, though... That's what Vanna does...

I glare back up at Viking again. "You want to know something about Vanna?" I growl at him. "She's selfless. Caring. And she'll *leave me* if she thinks she's causing me pain or hardship. She'll fucking *leave me*, if she thinks she's coming between me and any of you."

"Bro... I didn't know." Viking sighs.

I just nod, unclenching my jaw to instill a little more information to him. "Well, here's something else I'll clue you in on, *bro*. If this fuckin' club is going to cost me Vanna... it's not a price I'm willing to pay." *There... I've said it.*

"That's fucked up." He mutters, the sorrow in his eyes turning back to anger.

"I've gotten by three years without it. I don't need the club. I need her." I confess. And it barely even bothers me to admit it.

"Dean... come on, man." Axel says, heartbreak evident in his expression.

I turn my head to look Axel in the eyes. I need him to understand more than anyone. "Cherry or the club?" I ask him. "Doesn't matter how or why. But you can't have both. You want to be with Cherry? Or say goodbye to her and chose the MC?"

Axel lets out a long sigh, but answers after a moment. "Cherry." He says, grasping my feelings on the matter and understanding my position. I'm glad he does. I would have been disappointed if he had chosen the club over Cherry. And not because he would have gone against my stance. Cherry is a good woman. They deserve each other. And I know, his greatest happiness in life, will be through Cherry, not the MC.

As I shift my focus back to Viking, all I can do is shake my head. "I wish you the exquisite pain of falling in love with a woman, brother." I say to him. "From the bottom of my twisted heart. Only then, will you ever actually understand..."

Chapter
twenty-three
DEAN

S HE HASN'T SAID IT BACK TO ME. I BROUGHT her home, and she didn't even kiss me goodnight. We're going on a week and a half since our last night in the hotel together. And I don't know how long I can go on, before this breaks me down inside. Every time I'm near her, which isn't much lately, she's avoiding me. I feel like I'm going crazy.

Not being with her, is not an option. I won't let myself give up on her. On us. I don't think I could, even if I tried. I'll wait for her, even though it's killing me a little more inside, every day. If not for the glimpses of truth in her eyes, letting me know there's still something between us, I'd be completely lost. Her distance though... her distance is troublesome, and different from the times she ran from me before. She's acting as though we're friends, as if that's all we ever were. *Just friends*. After confessing my love for her, I'd be lying if I said that didn't fucking sting. The thought of her finding some other guy, while I'm stuck here, in the cursed *friend zone,* burning in the Hell she shackled me in... I don't think I could handle that. I don't think I'm a big enough man to be able to love her from afar.

I swallow a gulp of Whiskey, letting it burn all the way down, concentrating on the warmth it creates in the pit of my stomach.

As much as I want her, I'm almost relieved I haven't had her. Not how I want to. Need to. Not until she's truly mine. Her kisses alone have too strong of an effect on me. If I give in, it's over. I've known this. I'll be worse off than I am now. I'll love her for the rest of my life. Though I've warned her on multiple occasions, she's mine, even if she isn't. The truth of it, is that I'm hers. And if she doesn't end up with me...

I chug another shot or two of whiskey. Doesn't burn enough to dull the pain of that thought. I don't think there's pain enough I could inflict physically upon myself, to over shadow the pain of the emotions that thought stirs inside of me.

No. I am not man enough to see her smiling in another man's arms, and not lose my shit. I am not capable of seeing that, and being able to smile at her and wish *them* happiness. At least, not man enough to mean it. I'm aware enough to know I would self-destruct. I've been on the verge of that before... I'm barely holding my shit together now, and so far, there's not another guy trying to take my place. I'd fucking know it if there was.

Speaking of knowing... I grab my binoculars out of the cupboard, the bottle of Whiskey I'm working on, and head for my front porch.

Far too often, I do this. If she knew how often, it would probably creep her the fuck out.

But I don't do it to be a creep. I do it because I *need* to. Just to watch over her. And I've been doing this long before she told me anything about *Jack*... Though, I'll admit, he's increased the frequency... *Quite a lot.* I don't try to get a cheap thrill. But I don't think I'd be able to look away if I did happen to see something. Maybe I am a creep... *Fuck...* It's still not going to stop me from what I need to do...

Leaning against the pillar at the top of my porch steps, bottle in one hand, binoculars in my other, I lift them to my eyes and zero in on Vanna's house.

Her car is in the driveway, by itself. I sigh with relief. I wasn't expecting to see anyone else at her house. Knowing for sure there isn't, is always a comfort. I shift my head slightly. The lights down stairs are all off. I hope she remembered to lock up. Vanna is a cautious person though. I know this, especially after the little she's told me about her situation. I'm sure the doors are locked... But I'd be lying if I said I wasn't tempted to check.

With a slight lift of my chin, I notice the light in her bedroom is still on. I wonder what she's doing. Did she fall asleep with the light on? Is she on her phone talking to someone? Some prick who slipped her another number when I wasn't watching?

Closing my eyes for a moment, I drop the binoculars from my face and lift the bottle to my lips again. Another shot of liquid pain reliever. I swallow, then glance at my watch. It's two am. Weekdays, it's usually lights out in Vanna's house long before two am. What has her up in her room so late? Is she awake, thinking of me, the way I'm thinking of her?

I let out a long sigh. Probably not. She's the one calling the shots. I'm right where she wants me to be. An arm's length away. Close enough to grab me whenever she wants me. Fuck me up in the head, and in the heart. Far enough away to torment the shit out of me with her distance. Pull me in and make me soar. Only to push me away again, shoving me back down. Like being body slammed on concrete. That shit hurts... Though I prefer the concrete to the turmoil.

I lift the binoculars to my eyes again and take another peek at her upstairs windows. The bathroom light off the bedroom is on now. She's definitely awake.

Moving to the Adirondack chair on my porch, I sit down and place the binoculars on top of the table beside me. Grabbing my cellphone out of my pocket, I bring up her number and type out a text...

You're up late. *Send.*

A minute later she hits me back with, **So R U.**

I text her back, **Miss you. What are you doing?**

Going back to sleep. What are you doing?

I take a breath, running my hand through my hair, before I hit her back with, **I'm Still Loving You, Baby - Scorpions**

It takes her three minutes to hit me back with a smiley face.

I hit the bottle again...

LAURA CLOSES THE DOOR TO HER READING ROOM UPSTAIRS, AND WE SIT down together at the round table near the bay windows. I anxiously play with the fringe of the purple velour table cloth between my fingers, waiting for her to bring up the inevitable.

"Spill it." She says. "You've been back from your trip to Myrtle Beach nearly two weeks, and have barely said a word about it. What happened?"

"He told me he loves me. At least, I think he did." I leave out the parts about the illegal underground fighting, and the fact that his best friend doesn't like, or trust me. Not that I even blame him at this point.

Her head tilts to the side as she asks, "What did he say?"

"That if I left, it would destroy him. And that he's basically in love with me." I sigh.

"*Basically?*" Laura laughs, rolling her eyes. "*Men.*"

"I believe his exact words were, *I've basically just told you I'm in love with you.*" I shake my head, throwing my hands up in frustration. "What am I supposed to do with that?" *Basically* in love, is not the same as *I'm in love.* Which only tells me that he isn't definitively sure, himself. And I know the reason for the confusion in his heart and mind. I did it, after all.

"He's in love with you, Vanna. Believe him." Laura says, interrupting me from my mental lashing of myself. "I know you second guess everything, but I've seen for myself the way he looks at you. Especially the way he's been lately. He adores you."

"I really want to believe him." Looking down at her pack of tarot cards on the table, the desperate side of myself wants to consult them for advice. The other side resents them. Swearing off *Magic* and *Witchcraft* altogether. "I believe he thinks he loves me. But I don't know if that's because he can't distinguish between actual feelings of love, or because he feels overwhelmingly drawn to protect me, because of the spell." I want to slam my head down on the table. "Maybe he's confusing devotion to duty, for love."

Laura looks at me, as if she's really considering my dilemma, before she asks, "Are *you* in love with him?"

"I could be. I don't know." I've been back and forth on this, more times than I care to count, but I always land on *yes.*

"You need to be honest with yourself."

"*Yes.* I love him." I confess, with a long, frustrated huff. "Which has me even more messed up. This wasn't supposed to happen. He could end up getting *killed* because of me."

"You're getting ahead of yourself. A lot can change in two to four years." Life is unpredictable. Tomorrow isn't promised. Any of us can die tomorrow. Don't you want to be happy while you can be?"

I know it's a valid point. It's one of the points I tell myself just to get through the day sometimes. When the guilt is crushing. *Tomorrow isn't promised! Live for today!*

"Yes, of course, I *want* to be happy. I just can't get out of my own head about everything."

"Did you tell him everything?" She asks.

"He doesn't know specific details. And he doesn't know about the spell."

"So, he won't be blindsided by your ex, if the worst happens. He's got a few years notice. And he seems like a capable man, Vanna."

I think about the times I've seen him fight. His quickness. His stamina. His skill. "He's definitely capable." *And he's got a gun.*

Laura leans forward to touch my knee. "I think you're torturing yourself needlessly, sweetheart... But if you want to know, why don't you just tell him about the spell? Just show him everything."

I know I should. More than should. I have to. For both of us. "I'm afraid." I manage to whisper. "What if he hates me for it? What if he really doesn't love me and this breaks the spell and I lose him?"

"It's a slight risk. But you're going to tear yourself apart until he knows. You're never going to be truly happy, because of yourself. Not Dean." Laura folds her hands in her lap, her expression serious, but her eyes are still kind. As they always are. "Vanna, you need to tell him. You need to do this for *you*."

I slump forward, putting my face in my hands and let out a groan. I know she's right. I feel her touch my shoulder, trying to be reassuring.

"For what it's worth, I don't think he's going to care at all. It's not going to make one bit of difference to him. He doesn't take any of this *magick stuff*, seriously." She chuckles. "And even if he did, just a little bit, he's mad about you. His type of love, you can do no wrong in his eyes. I can just tell. He'd forgive just about anything from you."

"I hope so." I mumble. "Because I'm a hot mess."

"Vanna, have you considered that maybe, he wished for someone like you, too?"

"No." I say, picking my head up and sitting back in my chair again. "You should see his ex-wife. I'm definitely not what he's used to. Think sports illustrated. And bitchy." I frown.

"That might be one of the things he loves about you. Sometimes it takes men a few tries to get it right." She jokes. "And men don't all have a singular type, you know. They're quite capable of appreciating all types of women. Those are your insecurities getting in the way of your happiness. You can't put that on Dean, either."

"*I know.*" I grumble.

"Good." Laura smiles. "So, you know what you have to do."

I nod, slowly and reluctantly. "I have to tell Dean about the spell." And hope like Hell, this falls under the umbrella of forgiving me for just about anything... My only course of action now, my only option. The only right thing to do, is to come clean to Dean... And see where we end up on the other side of truth.

DEAN

"FOR FUCKS SAKE, DEAN! DID YOU HEAR A GODDAMNED THING I SAID?" Viper snaps, slamming his fist down on the folding table we're gathered around. The impact makes the lose brackets at the joints rattle beneath it.

"Yeah... two fucking weeks from tomorrow. I fucking heard you." I mutter, leaning back in the metal folding chair I'm sitting in.

It's actually been two fucking weeks, as of today, that Vanna's wanted to spend any time with me outside of work. Two weeks since Myrtle Beach. And I've even gone to her job. *Twice.* And though she isn't behaving coldly towards me, she's not her receptive self, either. It's always two steps forward, three steps back with her. I try not to glare at Viking, seated at my right. I know he regrets his part in driving Vanna further away from me, but the rage inside me is still at a steady simmer.

"Two o 'clock. Sharp. We need to do this while the bank and the county clerk's office are open. I want to do this in one swoop. We'll leave the back door open, you wait fifteen minutes, and come in. Preacher will never see it coming." Viper says. He wraps up the meeting, and I head for the bar.

I don't really care what any of them think. I don't really care if Viper decides he wants to keep the gavel for himself, either. Vanna's working tonight. She hasn't been blowing off her shifts at the Twisted Throttle, thankfully. And she seems to have gotten a little closer to Cherry, which is my one saving grace in this whole situation. If Vanna and Cherry are friends, that's at least something else to keep her here. I'm also hoping that the fact that I canned Vixie, pleases Vanna as well.

I glance at my watch as I walk down the corridor. Twenty after Ten. Vanna's definitely here. Rounding the corner into the bar, I spot her immediately, behind the bar with Cherry, laughing over something together as Cherry is pouring shots. I grab an open bar stool near them and give Vanna my best, panty dropping smile.

"Hey, doll." I growl at her.

"Hey." She smiles back at me, friendly, but seemingly unaffected. "You want a drink?" Is she immune to my charms now? *Fuck!*

No, that's the last thing I want right now. What I want to do is kidnap her and take her somewhere, anywhere, where we can be alone together. I haven't been alone with her since I dropped her off after our excursion to Myrtle Beach.

I watch her as she lifts a glass from behind the bar and takes a sip, looking at me expectantly. "*Well?* Do you?" she asks.

Fuck. Did I not answer her? "Uh... no."

She bites her bottom lip before she takes another sip of whatever that peachy colored drink is, that she's not so subtly sneaking behind the bar. I'm not even going to give her shit about it. I'm not a fan of my girls drinking on the job, but I'm in the negative here. This is a battle I'm not picking. Not tonight.

"My boss says nobody's allowed to hang at the bar unless they buy a drink... But I guess I'll let it slide." She smiles coyly, giving me a little wink. "Don't tell."

Is she flirting with me? She hasn't been cold to me. She does smile at me. She hasn't avoided speaking to me. But lately she's been skirting my touch. Avoiding my kiss. And now, *now* she's flirting with me? I stare at her, unable to think of some clever remark to say back to her. But I can still see the spark of a flame in her eyes. There's still something there for me.

She takes another sip of that drink, and I watch her tongue slide over her lips, capturing the sweetness of it, moistening them. Her pouty lips glisten under the lights of the bar, and I want to kiss her so badly, it hurts.

My sanity slips. I reach across the bar and snatch her wrist, gently pulling the glass from her fingers with my other hand.

"Hey! That's mine." Vanna protests. She watches me, watch her, as I raise her drink to my lips and pour the last sip into my mouth. Allowing the cool fruity liquid to wash over my tongue. The thin slivers of two or three mostly melted ice cubes crunch between my teeth, as I savor the sweet flavor of what she must taste like right now... *Sex on the beach.* Oh, the mind fuck of it all... "What the hell?" she demands.

I let the drink slide down my throat. "Just wanted to know what your mouth tastes like." I answer, stoically. Though I know, especially now that I've said it out loud, and seeing the expressions on both Vanna and Cherry's faces, it sounds as insane as I feel right now.

"Bro..." Viking says, behind me. Clearly another witness to my mental break as he enters the bar.

I hand Vanna back her glass. "I'm not even sorry." I'm not. I've lost it. The world knows I'm mad about her. And for some damn reason, she can't figure it out. And that's why I'm damned to the friend zone. Burning in Hell for her.

After a few moments of her staring in shock at me, Vanna giggles. Of course, she does. I'm beginning to wonder if she gets off on my pain... No, she doesn't. She wouldn't. She's simply fucking oblivious to it. And I don't know which is worse.

Sometimes, in order to fix something, you gotta go to the manual. You gotta take a peek at the directions. And as I sit at my office desk, in my shop across the lot from the Twisted Throttle, that's what I'm contemplating having to do... I'm just having a real hard time opening it. I've gone the last two weeks, taking it out of my bottom drawer, just to stare at it for a while, before locking it back up, unopened.

When I got back to the hotel room with Vanna, that night of the rally, she barely said anything to me. Unwilling to talk about the shit Viking brought up when he tried to put her on the spot with me. I know the secrets she's keeping are in this file. I'm hoping, if I open this and read it, there will be answers. At least, lines to read between to show me the way to reach her. But I hesitate. Staring at her scribbled name on the envelope. The short note I left scrawled across it, *for her*, in case the worst ever happened...

Dear Vanna, if you ever find this, please know I never read it. - Dean.

Fiddling with my balisong knife, I wait for the feeling to wash over me, that this *is* the right thing to do...

"Hey, what are you doing?" Vanna asks, suddenly leaning in the door way of my office, scaring the absolute shit out of me. I drop the knife and grab a pile of receipts and a motorcycle magazine, placing them on top of the file.

"Just looking over some invoices from this week." I say, willing my heart rate to slow down. She can probably see my fucking pulse in my neck from where she's standing. A mere five goddamned feet away.

"I can't believe you didn't hear me come in... Must be some pretty important receipts." She teases.

I clear my throat, getting up from behind my desk to walk around and lean against the front of it. I really, really don't want Vanna in here right now. Not until I have that file locked the fuck up again. "What brings you over here?"

She gives me a little shrug. "I'm on my break." After a few moments, she asks, "Did you and Viking make up yet?"

"We're fine. He knows he fucked up."

"So, what's the matter?"

"Don't act like you don't know, Vanna, please. That'll only make me crazier." I groan.

She giggles at me, of course. "I've kind of missed your crazy... Always trying to bust out of the friendzone every chance you get."

I search her eyes for a sense of sincerity. "You *let* me. Doesn't that mean *something*?"

"You know it does." She sighs.

"You haven't kissed me in two weeks... What's changed?"

"Are you asking for a kiss?" she smirks at me, twisting her position in the doorway so that her back is against the door jamb instead of her shoulder.

No... Yes... No... Fuck... Yes! "Not if you don't want to kiss me."

She stares at me for a moment. "Did you mean what you said in the hotel room?"

510

"I mean everything I say to you. *Everything.*"

She gives me a slight smile, then an almost uncomfortable sounding chuckle. "My break is almost over." Always so quick to run at the slightest hint of progress between us. Ready to dash every time I might touch on something real with her. That bothers me, to no fucking end. "My boss might get pissed if I'm late." She teases me.

"Fuck your boss."

She giggles at me again. "Oh, he'd turn me down." She taunts me.

"No. He won't." I reply, catching her off guard. "You've worn him down."

She stares at me intently now, the jokes over. Her smart mouth doesn't have a sassy retort waiting for me. I push myself away from the desk and walk towards her.

"What are you doing?" She barely whispers, turning to face me as she backs out of my doorway into the hall. I take her face in my hands and pin her to the wall in the hallway, my mouth barely an inch from her lips. I can feel her breath in quick, soft pants against my face.

"I'm showing you what you need to see from me." Even if it's to the detriment of myself...

"I never pictured it in your office... *or, motorcycle shop...* I thought you said you wanted it to be perfect?" She whispers, a slight tremble in her voice. I slide one of my hands to the back of her head. My fingers tangling in her long, silky hair. My other hand drops to her waist, pulling her closer to me.

"You're perfect. You're all I need for it to be perfect... Tell me what *you* need."

"*A little time...*" the pleading tone in her words. The tension in her frame.

Push. Pull. Push. Pull... I swear, I have to strangle down a frustrated sob inside of me, as I lean to press my forehead to hers. "Away from me?" I manage to choke out from my tight throat.

"No." She says, surprising me, her hands reaching up between us to stroke my jaw. I close my eyes and focus on the feel of her touch. The way her fingertips stroke my face, the sound of her nails gently scraping over my stubble. The tingling sensation it sends through my body. "I don't want to be away from you. I never did. I just have my own shit to work out." She whispers.

"Tell me what you need... I'll do anything."

"I need help believing."

"*In me?*" I ask, afraid to even look in her eyes, wondering how that could be when I've been nothing but doting, loyal and steadfast. To think that she doubts my feelings for her, really twists my insides up. And the fact that she doesn't answer me, just drives that shit deeper. Does she really not believe me? Was I not clear the first time?

"*I love you, Vanna.*" I utter the words as if they're a plea. "I'm *in love* with you."

When I feel her tilt her face up slightly, I don't hesitate to seal her lips with mine. And as I kiss her like a man starving for her, because that's exactly what I am. I can taste her sweetness, mixed with salty tears, and open my eyes to look at her. Hers are squeezed shut.

"Vanna?" I whisper against her lips, wanting to ask her why she's crying. She doesn't say anything, though. "Why can't I reach you? What can I do to make you believe me?"

"I don't think there's anything you can do... and it's my fault. I'm a mess. I'm a huge burden... you don't even understand." She says on a ragged breath.

"Make me understand. I promise you, I will listen. I will do anything." I say, brushing the tears from her cheeks with my thumbs.

She barely shakes her head. "You won't understand."

"Vanna, please. Try me, just tell me. And if by some chance I don't understand, I promise to just accept whatever it is."

Her eyes open to finally look at me. A mixture of bewilderment and doubt in them. "You don't know what you're saying. And you shouldn't make promises you can't keep." Her bottom lip quivers as her glassy eyes search my expression for truth.

"I don't make promises I won't keep. Whatever it is you still think you need to hide from me, you don't. I love you. All of you."

"What if I'm a terrible person?" She whispers, her voice strained, as if she's truly horrified by that impossible possibility.

"Then that makes two of us." I tell her. But there's no way Vanna is a terrible person. Vanna may have lived through some terrible shit, but she's far from terrible, herself. Whatever transgressions she believes she's committed, I've done worse. Ten times over. Vanna is an Angel. And I'm the Demon that fell in love with an Angel, fighting to free her wings, so she can fly us both out of Hell. "We were meant to come together, Vanna."

"How do you know that?" She asks, her teary eyes staring deeply into mine. I can see a glimmer of hope behind all the doubt in them.

"I wished for you, too. Though, I didn't realize it until I saw you. I knew you were mine from that first moment. I felt it in my soul." I confess to her, but she's looking at me as if she's still waiting to hear something I haven't said, as if what I'm saying isn't cutting it, isn't convincing enough. "Baby, tell me how to reach you. I can't lose you. Tell me the magic words." She almost flinches at that, and I can feel her withdrawing from me. I can see it in her face. The wall going back up. Brick by brick. And I have to beat back the panic rising up inside of me.

"There's something I have to do." She finally says, after what feels like an eternity.

"If you say you have to leave, I swear to God... Vanna..." I manage to force the words out, despite my tightening throat. My hands automatically dropping to her arms, my fingers curling around them. As if I can hold onto her and keep her from running. "Don't tell me you're leaving..."

"I'm not. Not tonight, anyway."

"Not tonight..." It isn't a relief. "Not tonight, but you are?"

She looks away from me, and I feel her arms attempt a slight, almost defeated shrug. "I don't know what I'm going to do. I guess it depends on what happens between us."

"I'm all in. I'm just waiting for you, doll."

She nods, but she doesn't look at me for a moment. When she does, it's to tell me she has a shift to get back to, and would I walk her back to the roadhouse. Of course, I do. I'm at a loss for words anyway. Nothing I say is reaching her. Before we make it to the steel door of the Twisted Throttle, I tug her hand to stop her from going inside, and she turns to face me as we stand beneath one of the flood lights in the lot.

"Did something change between us, after the rally? You haven't been the same since." I'm afraid to ask her what I really want to know.

"We're still the same as before." She sighs.

"Then kiss me, the same as before... That will tell me everything I need to know." I don't give her the chance to think. I cup her face in both hands possessively, brining my mouth to hers. I know the kiss is almost hard, insisting and full of tension, to start. My tongue pushes her lips apart. She surrenders to my desperation and kisses me back. I lower one of my hands to her waist and pull her against me, my fist balling up in the fabric against the small of her back. My other hand slides from her cheek to the back of her head, into her hair, holding her to my mouth. She wraps her arms around me, sliding her hands under my leather jacket. I feel her press her hands against my back, pulling me closer to her as well. I kiss her deeper, feeling our tension fade away more and more with every passing moment, as we begin to lose ourselves in each other. Moments pass before she turns her face from me to break our kiss. I lean my forehead against hers again, my eyes still closed. I'm not sure if this kiss brought me contentment, or if I'm worse off than I was before.

She reaches up again and gently strokes my whiskered jaw line. "Okay?" She whispers. I don't have an answer for her this time. All I can do is hold onto to her. Like if I let her go, she'll vanish on me. If I let her go, I won't get her back again. "Dean?" She says softly.

"I'm sorry." I say, opening my eyes to look at her again. "I never thought I'd ever become a stage five clinger... but here we are." I try to joke. She humors me with a little smile. "I mean it, Vanna. I never thought I'd ever say the words to another woman, again. But I do. *I love you.*"

This time, her hands slide out from under my leather jacket, and she pulls her arms back to herself to clutch her abdomen. I've come to learn, in my incessant, obsessive observation of her, that she holds herself this way in times and situations, where she's afraid or uncomfortable. Her expression reads as if she's smiling through torment. She doesn't say a word back to me.

Fuck... I press my lips together and nod. Attempting to swallow my pride, in this awkward, painful as fuck, moment. The agony must be evident on my face, though, because as I drop my hands from her, she reaches out to grab onto them, squeezing them in hers. An anguished, pleading look in her dark, beautiful and forever mysterious eyes.

"It's okay, Vanna." I try not to let my voice crack, especially as I watch another tear roll down her cheek. It's truly amazing how many ways a human heart can break all at once. I slip one of my hands from hers to brush her tear away. I lift her other hand to press against my lips, before I tell her, "None of us can choose where we will love."

The torture in her eyes is too much for me to bear now. I can't look in those eyes any more tonight. I head for the steel door of the Twisted Throttle, pulling her behind me by the hand. Before I can reach for the handle, Vanna pulls my arm, telling me to stop. To wait.

"I need you back in there, Vanna. In there. Or go home." I say, unable to face her.

"Why?"

"Because I need to go. And I can't leave you in this fucking lot, alone. So, make your choice. Finish your shift, or go home for the night."

She walks around me to stand before me, but I keep my eyes fixed on the steel door behind her now. "Will you come back tonight? Before closing?"

"I don't know."

"Where are you going?"

"I don't know."

She's quiet for a moment, until I make a move to reach for the steel door again. "Dean," she says, her voice sounds strained. I force myself to meet her eyes, once more. For her. "*I don't want you to go away.*" She whispers.

I want so slam my head into the brick wall beside us. I want to scream until I tear my throat apart. I want to demand to know how she can possibly kiss me the way she does, without loving me back... Instead, I stand here. Burning for her, stoically, through the pain.

Vanna reaches down to take my hand in hers again. "There's something I need to do... I'm just afraid to do it." I don't know what to say to her any more. So, I just continue to stare at her. "I can see that I'm hurting you. It's the last thing I want to do, Dean. Please believe me."

"I'll believe anything you tell me." I sigh. "Just fucking tell me *something*. Even if it's what I don't want to hear."

"Tomorrow."

"Just put me out of my misery now, Vanna." I try not to growl. I don't want to sound resentful towards her. I don't resent her. I resent my unworthiness *of* her. "Just tell me you don't love me back." She's got that pitying, sorrowful look in her eyes again, that just twists the fucking knife in my chest a little more. "*Don't look at me like that.*" The words come out more harshly than I intended them to, and her bottom lip quivers as if I hurt her feelings. It makes me angrier with myself. "Just say the words, I can take it. Tell me you don't love me back, God damn it."

"*I can't.*"

"*Why not?*"

"Because I'd be lying to you if I say that... And I never want to lie to you again."

514

The lump in my throat is painful, and I can barely swallow it down. I swear to God, she has this uncanny ability to speak without saying much, or to say more in one seemingly simple sentence, than I can wrap my head around at once. This time what she says, hits me like a ton of fucking bricks.

"Are you saying you love me?" I ask, willing my pounding heart not to get ahead of itself.

"I'll tell you everything, tomorrow."

"Why not tonight? Why not right now?" I ask, my fingers curling around her hand a little tighter, now that I have a glimmer of hope again.

"I'm not ready."

"What are you afraid of? I'm not going anywhere."

She pulls her hand from mine, taking a few steps back towards the steel door. "Stop making promises you might not be willing to keep." She says, before she turns from me and walks back inside. As the heavy door clangs shut behind her, I'm left standing alone in the dark lot outside.

Tomorrow. She'll tell me *everything*, tomorrow. And I'll prove to her, I'm a man of my word.

Chapter
twenty-four
DEAN

"COME IN!" SHE CALLS TO ME WHEN I ANNOUNCE MY ARRIVAL through her screen door. Walking into Vanna's kitchen, I find her on her back, on the floor, partially inside the cabinets under her kitchen sink. Her denim jeans are soaked. From what I can see of her shirt, it didn't fair much better. I press my lips together tightly, stifling a laugh as I look at the array of tools she's got laid out on the wet floor all around her. They're practically antiques, but can still get the job done, *if* she knows what she's doing.

"May I be of any assistance?" I offer, watching her hand reach out from the cabinet, dropping another old rusted wrench down on the floor beside her. She scoots herself out from under the sink and sits up to look at me. Yep. She's drenched. Wet shirt clinging to her body. Hair drenched as well. But she looks good wet.

"A pipe cracked." She says, blinking up at me in adorable bewilderment. "How does a pipe just crack when it's warm out? And did you know this house has well water? The main shut off is near the pump... *outside!* I was looking everywhere in here for a shut off and it's outside. My landlord is going to kill me if I water damaged anything." She says, flicking her wrists in an attempt to shake her hands dry. "I'm lucky he lives in Maryland and can't pop in on a whim."

"Nothing a mop can't fix, doll. Doesn't look like anything's damaged." I reach down and offer her my hand to help her up off the floor. She takes it and I hoist her back to her feet.

"Do you mind if I run upstairs and change?"

"Not at all, doll." I watch her walk out of the kitchen and scamper up the stairs, before I squat down in front of the sink to take a quick peek at her handywork. It appears she's got everything in order, so I start gathering up her tools and putting them back in the metal tool tote she's got on the floor as well. "You keep these antiques under the sink or you got another spot for 'em?" I call up to her.

"They belong to the landlord... I found them in the closet under the stairs... Don't worry about it though, I'll be down in a minute." She calls back down to me.

I carry the tool tote over to the already slightly open closet door. Pulling it open the rest of the way, a couple of boxes fall down from the top shelf and topple to the floor at my feet, as her cat Nico leaps down from the shelf as well.

"Wasn't me, the cat did it!" I call up to her again, no way she didn't hear that commotion. And I'm not about to take the fall for his furry little ass, either.

"What happened?"

"Nico knocked a bunch of shit off the shelf in the closet... I'll put it back, no worries." I say, placing the tool tote on the shelf before I bend down to pick up a couple of shoe boxes.

"Wait! Don't! Leave them!" Vanna says frantically from upstairs. I can hear her rush across the floor towards the stair case.

"**N**O! *DON'T!*" I NEARLY SHRIEK AS I RUN DOWN THE STEPS AND ROUND the banister of the stair case to the closet door where Dean is standing. It's too late... he's already seen what's inside the box. Staring at the contents inside as he rises. After a long moment, he shifts his body slightly towards me, though he's still looking in the box. His lips pursed, his brows low, his expression perplexed, to say the least.

Taking a breath, he lets it out in a huff and points at the contents of the box. "Is this... *Witch shit*?" he asks, confusion deeply etched across his face.

"Yes, please, just put it down." I beg, my hand outstretched towards him, though I'm frozen where I stand a few feet away from him. He turns and slowly places the box down on the little foyer table behind him, still peering inside it.

"Is that... *doll thing*... wearing a *motorcycle jacket*?" he asks, looking more bemused with every passing moment as the contents of the box begin to piece together in his mind.

I don't even know what to say. I had intended to ease him into this whole situation. Explain everything *before* letting him see it...

He reaches slowly into the box and pulls out the Knight of Wands Tarot card, looking it over. Studying the image. After a moment, he glances up at me with an expression that looks too much like suspicion. Tucking the card back in the box, he uses one of its corners to fish around inside. "A motorcycle jacket... and a red scarf... That's specific."

"It's not what it looks like." I finally manage to find my voice, though it's difficult to hide the desperation in my tone.

He drops the tarot card back in the box and looks at me. "That's great, Vanna. Because it looks like you're doing witchy shit on me." His tone is level. Almost cool. His expression is becoming harder to read as he goes stoic on me.

"Not... not exactly." I stammer.

"What exactly?" he presses.

"I did it over a year ago. I didn't know you even existed then. I didn't even live around here yet."

He points back at the box, his eyebrows raised now. "This is some freaky ass shit, Vanna... Is there a dick candle with my name on it somewhere too?"

I try not to frown. "*No*, there isn't. And it's not like I stole a pair of your old boots and nailed them under the floor boards of my house." *That* would be an attempt through witchcraft to directly control him.

His head jerks back slightly as he stares at me, his brows moving together, looking even more confused now. "What the fuck does that even mean?"

"I didn't do a spell on *you*, not *directly*. Not specifically. *Not* on *you*."

With a sweeping gesture of his arm down the front of his leather jacket, Dean grabs the poppets bound together and holds them up out of the box. "The motorcycle jacket even looks like mine... It even has a red scarf around its neck."

"I know... I was freaked out at first, too."

"At first?"

"Yes, when I first saw you. When I did the spell, I imagined what a modern-day Knight would be."

He reaches into the box to grab the tarot card again. "This?"

"Yes. Please, just listen to me. Just let me explain." I plead. "Just listen with an open mind, okay?"

"I'm listening."

I take a deep breath before I continue, saying the words slowly as I attempt to explain. "The Knight, a modern day one. It could be interpreted as a biker. The black horse, a motorcycle. Your leather, the armor. I used the jacket to represent a biker. I picked a biker because you all have a tough guy reputation. I thought if I called for a bad ass biker, he could protect me. Or at least, act as a deterrent. The red scarf..." I gesture, nervously, to the card, "if you look at the Knight of Wands tarot card, he's got a red banner. I used the red scarf in the spell to act as a sign. So that I'd know him when I saw him."

"Him? The Knight, you mean?"

"Yes... Because I didn't know who the Knight would be. I needed signs to help me find him. Or at least, tell him apart from others."

Dean glances at the tarot card. "So, you're saying you summoned me? That I'm the Knight?"

"Yes... But without directly targeting *you* specifically, because I didn't know you existed over a year ago. That's important for you to understand, Dean. *I did not know you existed* when I did this spell. I couldn't have put a spell directly on you without knowing you. But I did *know* it was you, when I first saw you."

"Because I had a red scarf... and a black motorcycle... and a leather jacket... Vanna, that's a lot of guys."

"Mock me if you want." I sigh. I'd rather him not take me seriously at all and shrug this whole thing off as me being crazy or weird, but I haven't gotten to the worst part yet.

"I'm not mocking you... I just... I don't know what to say." Dean shakes his head.

"Tell me you didn't feel anything when you first saw me. That there wasn't some kind of electricity between us. *A magnetic pull.* Tell me that honestly."

"I can't. I did feel it. I felt it even before I saw you... and then when I did see you... it intensified."

"That was a sign as well. So was your tattoo. The morning star." I cross my arms and lift one hand to rest at the base of my throat. A nervous tick I developed years ago. My thumb automatically moves to my ring finger, to play with an engagement ring I no longer wear. Haven't worn, since I hocked it at a pawn shop three years ago. "I've been trying to deny the fact that you were the Knight... all this time." I sigh, knowing I have to come clean about everything. He'll most likely get over the whole poppet thing. He doesn't believe in magick or spells. But I have a feeling, what I still have to tell him, isn't going to go over well. "I didn't realize you had that tattoo on your arm, until that night in Myrtle Beach, at your fight."

His eyes narrow as he recalls the incident I'm referring to. "It wasn't the blood that scared you before the thirteenth round... it was my tattoo."

I nod. "I couldn't deny it after that. All the signs I worked into the spell point to you being the Knight."

Dean's brows furrow in confusion again. "Why try to deny it at all?"

I shake my head, knowing the answer to this question is the part that might hurt him. And I'm not ready to go there, just yet. "I did the spell because I was afraid. And alone."

His eyes soften a little. His hand moving to grip the back of his neck for a moment, before he drops his arm and nods. "Because of your scum-fuck ex. The one you're hiding from... He scares you enough to do something like this." Dean gestures to himself. "To *summon some guy* to protect you."

"I know it's wrong..." I start to say.

Dean shakes his head. "No, I understand where you were coming from, Vanna. I mean, *in theory*... I don't actually believe in-"

"I just wanted to find a *savior*." I know that word might sway him. "I tried to put a call out into the universe to send me a *savior*, so I wouldn't have to face him alone."

His eyes widen for a moment, before they tighten again as he asks, "A Savior? Did you actually use that word? A year ago, when you did this?"

I nod. "Yes... another sign... I was stupid to have denied everything this long."

Dean puts the poppets back down in the box, and places the card down on top of them. He takes a step back from the table, running his hand through his hair. After a moment he looks back at me. "Quite a few coincidences at work here, Vanna." I only nod. I don't know what to say to that. "So, I'm your Knight. I get to slay the dragon for you... You know I would do it anyway, without all this witchy shit."

"Maybe." I barely get the word out.

He looks slightly taken aback, offended by my response. "*Maybe?* You think I'd let you face this fucker alone?"

I swallow hard, wrapping my arms around myself again, trying to gather the courage I need to say what I have to say to him. "I never meant to manipulate you in any way."

"Do you not realize, I *want* to help you, baby? I've known you were afraid of something from the start of us. You think I can't read you? I fuckin' see everything, Vanna."

I close my eyes for a moment, taking a breath and attempting to steady my nerves. "There's something else about the spell that you should know." I begin, opening my eyes to look at him again. He's staring back at me, waiting. "Love was never part of it."

"What do you mean?" He asks, confusion in his eyes again.

"I never expected, nor did I put any intention into the spell, for the Knight to love me. It wasn't about that. I didn't want to manipulate those feelings, and I've tried to deny to myself that you were the Knight. Love was never supposed to be part of the spell."

"I don't understand what you're saying."

"The Knight wasn't supposed to love me."

"But what if the Knight *does* fucking love you, Vanna?" Dean asks, worry in his eyes now as what I'm trying to say sinks in.

My throat is suddenly very tight. I watch what I can only describe as panic slowly begin to etch across Dean's face. Tears begin to prick behind my eyes.

"Wait... Vanna..." Dean takes a few steps towards me, one fist clenched, the other hand pointing at me as he speaks. "If it was never part of your spell, the fact that I *do* love you, should tell you this is real between us."

I press my lips together, closing my eyes on the tears that threaten to over flow as I shake my head. "It's not that simple," I manage to choke out. "The signs... there were so many... even your name ties into the Knight's banner... fire... that pull we feel towards each other... the spell is so strong... Even though I didn't intend for love to be a part of it... It could be that you're just so strongly influenced to care about my safety that... that... you only *think* you-"

"*Jesus fucking Christ...*" Dean mutters, shaking his head slowly in disbelief, pain in his eyes now. He raises both arms to press the heels of his palms against his temples. "You don't believe me."

"I really *want* to..." I whisper through my tears. Even I can hear the trembling in my voice.

He runs his hand over his mouth and jaw. I can see the horror and despair in his eyes as he realizes what I'm trying to make him understand.

"This is a *curse*, Vanna!" He swings his arm behind him, pointing towards the box. "I know you have your insecurities, but I could have fought through those! I would have reached you!" The torment in his eyes and in his voice nearly breaks my heart as he wrings his fists in front of him now, desperate to fight some unseen force... But he can't. "We could have gotten past everything! We could have been happy! If you didn't do *this!* I'd have had a chance with you!" He shouts at me, the agony in his words, in his expression... is almost too much to take.

"I'm sorry." I cry.

He stares at me for a moment longer, and I watch the kaleidoscope of emotions flash behind his eyes. Rage. Despair. Desperation... Then defeat... Before he storms past me towards the front door.

"Wait! *Please!*" I beg him, frantically grabbing at his arm. "Dean, *please!*"

He whirls around on me, the fury in his eyes sickens my stomach and makes me wince, reflexively shrinking back from his contemptuous, deadly gaze. Being on the receiving end of that look is almost crippling.

"I never meant to hurt you." I manage to whimper.

"That fucking *Pandora's Box* says otherwise." He mutters, before he turns from me and shoves the screen door open violently, storming out onto the porch.

I follow him out and wrap my arms around his waist before he makes it to the first step, holding him tightly, my cheek pressed against the leather on his back. "Dean, please... please don't go!" I beg.

I feel his strong hands on mine, as they slide to my wrists, his fingers gently wrapping around, prying my hands apart as he pulls my arms away from his body. "I need to step away, Vanna. You need to let me go." His voice is a strangled whisper.

"I can't let you go... *I need you.*" I cry. *"Please."*

A long, shuddering sigh escapes him. "I could never *leave* you, Vanna." He says, the tone of his voice is still so pained. "But you made damn sure of that, didn't you?"

I can't even form words any more as I sob against his back.

Dean releases my hands and turns to face me once more. This time, the anger in his eyes is mixed with anguish once again. "When I told you that I loved you, you told me that you *wished* for me. Was that your way of clearing your conscience about this?"

"Dean, please..." I reach out and touch his face, gently stroking the stubble of his jawline. I can feel the muscles rippling beneath my fingers.

"You said you *wished* for me... But you've never said you *love* me. Can you not love me, Vanna?" His voice nearly cracks as he pulls my hand away from his face, his eyes desperately searching mine for an answer.

"Stay with me..." I manage to plead through my sobbing. *"Don't go..."*

Dean closes his eyes for a moment, shaking his head slowly. "Right now, I need to take a ride and clear my head, Vanna." He says, before looking back at me. "Give me that much."

He lets my hand go and turns, walking down the porch steps, his determined strides take him back to Serene, waiting for him in my driveway. I watch as he mounts the bike, revs the engine angrily and takes off without a backward glance at me. I stand on my porch and watch him go, until I can't see him anymore.

He promised me he wouldn't walk away from me. He promised me he would accept anything I told him. He promised me... but he left anyway.

FOR SIX MONTHS I'VE FOUGHT TO REACH TO HER. FIGHTING THROUGH DARK forests of thorns and demons... Only to be met with the insurmountable stone wall of her prison tower. Much of which she constructed herself, in her own attempt to protect herself from a monster.

I'm going to kill *him*... *Jack* did this to us! Forced her hand to set something in motion that came back to bite us both, in ways I don't even think Vanna saw coming, herself.

I don't give a shit about the spell. I forgave her for it the moment I saw the fucking thing. It's nothing more than a prayer. Her little *witchy way* of getting down on her knees and begging God for help in a seemingly impossible situation. Her desperate attempt at taking control over circumstances beyond her control. I get it. What's more, is that I would have been grateful that she interpreted her supposed signs indicating me as her Knight. Her fucking Savior. I *want* that honor. I *want* to protect her. I *want* to love her and have her love me back...

But her Knight spell twisted into a curse... poisoning and crippling our love long before it could have ever had a chance to soar... Warping her thoughts against me... As if her own demons needed any help with that to begin with. She doesn't believe I truly love her. She *can't* believe it. She only wants something real... And if I'm under some supernatural influence, my feelings for her can't be real. My emotions... my need to be near her... just an influence of her curse.

How do I even conquer this? How do I defeat this force that only exists in her mind?

Thinking back on the times I teased her about not believing in any of this magic bullshit, she always seemed relieved. I expected the opposite. That she'd take offense. But she was happy about it. *Liked* that about me... That I was a skeptic. I understand why, now. She was trying to convince herself that I might be immune to this very situation. That night, in my kitchen, after the broken wine glasses... She seemed to be relieved when I teasingly called her crazy for believing in this shit. She kissed me... *wanted* me... until I referred to myself as the Knight, *Lancelot*... I remember the look on her face as I said it... the surprised horror I couldn't understand in that moment. That was the moment I truly lost her. The moment she ran from me. And it's been an uphill battle since... An endless chase...

She wished for me... Then said she would leave me... Because she didn't want me to get hurt. By leaving, her ex would hunt her down elsewhere... away from me. She'd leave to protect *me* from him... She *does* love me... In a way, I'm elated by this realization. She just doesn't believe that I love her.

I need help believing... She cried those words to me last night. How do I do this for her? How can I make her believe me?

Staring at the bottle of Whiskey on the bar counter before me, I try to wrack my brain for an answer. Vanna does love me, so there's hope... *I hope...*

"What's eating you?" Viking is suddenly beside me. I didn't even hear him come in. I don't even know how long I've been sitting here, alone. In the dark again.

"I'm cursed." I mutter, slowly spinning the shot glass between my fingers on the bar.

"Vanna again?" He sighs, that exasperated tone in his voice as he takes a seat on a bar stool beside me.

"Vanna, again... My never... and forever..." I shake my head wearily.

"You're not making any sense, bro. What happened?" he asks, shifting his bulk to face me head on, a massive tattooed arm leaning on the bar.

"I lost her." The words sour in my mouth as I speak them. I shoot the shot and slam the glass back down on the counter. Doesn't do a fucking thing for me.

"Bro..."

"Just shut up." I growl.

"Dean..."

"Shut up!" I snap, glaring him in the face now. He looks surprised. He shouldn't be. "You never had my back about her..." I begin to go in on him, thinking back to his words about making her go away if we couldn't work things out. If she was too much of a distraction from the club to me. Hell, we were sitting in this exact spot when he went in on me about that shit the first time.

"Dean, I know you're upset, bro... but I always have your back in everything. Even if you don't see it that way."

I don't want to hear it. I'm not ready to give up on her. There has to be a way to reach her... to get over this fucking wall... To climb the jagged stones of her prison tower with my bare hands. Cracked and bloodied. I've arrived at the tower unequipped for this challenge. The weapons I battled through the thorns and demons with, are of no consequence to this wall I've been bashing my goddamned head against. All I've got is my determination, my iron will to claw my way to her. To ascend this obstacle and vanquish this blockade around her heart.

I have to. I have to convince her that I truly love her, or she'll run... And the real Demon responsible for all of this anguish... All of her pain and fear and insecurities... Will come for her. To hurt her worse than ever before, as they usually do. And she'll be alone again... defenseless. Without her Knight. Without a Savior. Fuck that. That ain't how I roll. Jack's going to die. And I'm going to win her, once and for all.

"I ain't tappin' out." I growl, shoving the shot glass and bottle of whiskey away from me with a sharp clink as the two glass objects collide. "I'm still in this fucking fight. I can save her."

"From what?" Viking sighs, looking at me like I've lost it.

"I can fucking save her."

He's staring back at me, swalling before he begins to speak, as if he knows he needs to proceed with caution. "Bro, some women don't want to be saved. You've seen it before, with your own eyes. On the missions. The women who run back to their houses. Back to the Hells they've been living in. You've watched them change their minds and run away from us, knowing we'd save them... If Vanna keeps running from you..."

"She isn't. She's trying to run *to me*, but she's trapped. I just have to figure out how to reach her. If I can do that, everything will be fuckin' Aces for us! I know it." I say, pushing away from the bar, I get up and head for the steel door. I never should have left her.

"Bro, I'm worried about you. This is the Lucinda obsession all over again." Viking sighs.

"Vanna is *nothing* like Lucinda!" I snarl back at him, wrenching open the front door of the bar. Storming outside, the first thing I notice is the Silver Lexus SUV parked across the lot in front of my repair shop.

Speak of the fucking devil and she will appear...

As I cross the lot towards my repair shop, I realize Lucinda isn't in her SUV. She's inside the shop... Most likely in my office... where I left Vanna's file on my fucking desk buried under a pile of receipts! *Fuck!* Like I needed this to happen on top of everything else! How could I have been so goddamned careless?

I high tail it into the shop, down the short hallway between the lobby and the garage, into my office, where Lucinda is sitting in my leather office chair. The fucking file splayed open before her. The manilla envelope with my scrawled letter to Vanna swearing I never read it, torn open and cast to the side.

Fuck! Fuck! Fuck!

Lucinda's eyes lift to meet my own, a sinister little smile pulls at the corners of her lips as she leans back, folding her hands as she rests them on top of the file. "*Fascinating...* Your little wallflower has quite the colorful past." She taunts me. "She's not as boring as I thought."

"You've got some fuckin' balls." I growl. "Close it. And get out."

She rolls her eyes at me. "Oh, come on. I saw your little note. That's what got me so curious in the first place. You haven't read it. Aren't you a little curious?" she smiles deviously. "Go on, ask me anything!"

I take a step forward with the intention of grabbing the file from her. She snatches it, getting up from the chair and backs against the wall.

"You know I can take it from you." I warn her. "Don't make me. Hand it over. *Now*."

"She got him locked up. Good for her." Lucinda grins, ignoring my warning. "Did she tell you what he did to her?" her eyes squint as she attempts to get a read on me. "Is that why you're so into her? That fucking damsel in distress *kink* of yours? I swear, it's the one thing about you that always pissed me off. Your fucking *Hero complex*! Your need to rescue these wilting flowers! Get over her! *Madeline is dead*, Dean. You can't save your mother through these women!"

Enough of this shit. I storm around the side of the desk, shoving the rolling leather office chair out of my way. Lucinda makes a move in an attempt to get away from me, but I grab her, shoving her back against the desk, pinning her between it and myself.

"Give it to me." I snarl at her.

"I'll give you anything you want." She growls back at me, licking her lips libidinously. She places the file down on the desk beside her then grabs a hold of my leather jacket, attempting to pull me onto her. When I don't budge, she glares at me, bringing her legs up around my waist, wrapping them around me. Her tight skirt rides all the way up her thighs as she does so. I grab her knees and shove them open, prying her legs apart from clenching around me.

"You know what I want." I mutter. For her to stay the fuck out of my life. To stay the fuck away from Vanna. To grasp the fact that she and I are over. *Forever.*

"*Dean?*" I hear my name spoken timidly from the doorway of my office.

Lifting my eyes, my heart sinks and my blood runs cold as I lay them on Vanna. Standing there. Looking at me with shock, which is slowly shifting towards hurt, as she takes in the sight of me and Lucinda...

I'm fucking standing between her splayed wide-open legs, my hands still on her knees, holding them open... Lucinda, leaning back on my desk, looking all too fucking eager and playing it up like Vanna just caught us in the act of something she's admittedly feared I was doing all along behind her back...

Jesus fucking Christ... Could this situation be any worse?

"Doll... *it ain't what it looks like...*"

Vanna

"YOU KNOW WHAT I WANT." HE SAYS TO HER, STANDING BETWEEN HER legs as he pushes them open wider. Lucinda is leaning back on his desk, clearly willing to give it to him. And why wouldn't she? *Our* Dean... But he's always been *hers*.

I must have said something, made a sound, because he looks up at me. What is most likely an impassioned glare in his eyes, turns into shocked surprise as he realizes I'm standing in his office, staring at them. *Interrupting* them. I pushed him away and he ran straight to his true love... *The quintessential biker bitch*. The woman whose name lies hidden beneath the Morning Star tattoo on his arm... *Lucinda*.

"Doll... It ain't what it looks like..." He has the nerve to say.

The obvious lie takes me from despair to anger in a flash. *"Are you fucking kidding me?"* I can't help the words flying out of my mouth.

He shoves away from her. "Vanna, please listen to me..."

"I can't believe I came here to try to talk to you... to work things out between us." I shake my head in disbelief, shifting my focus to Lucinda, who's sitting up on the desk now, grinning over her shoulder at me like she's won. I watch as her hand reaches for something on the desk, but Dean lunges for it, yanking it away from her. Some kind of file. She twists on the desk, reaching for something else quickly and shoves a manilla envelope off the desk towards me before he can stop her. It flitters to the floor at my feet. I can't help but notice my name written on it, scrawled in black ink. As I bend to pick it up and read what's written, Dean says something in protest, but I'm not listening.

Dear Vanna, if you ever find this, please know,
I never read it. – Dean.

"What is this?" I manage to ask, looking back at him. He's clinging to that folder against his chest.

"The only reason he's infatuated with you." Lucinda mutters. "You might not be a blue eyed blonde. But you're still one of his *Madelines*."

Madeline? That's his mother's name. "I don't understand." I say, reaching forward to drop the envelope on the chair in front of his desk.

Lucinda rolls her eyes at me as if I'm some kind of dimwitted nuisance. "You'll never be what he needs long term, honey." She says to me in the most patronizingly obnoxious way. "He needs a strong woman. Not a *victim*."

A what? "What did you just stay to me?"

She sneers at me "You're nothing more than a twisted man's passing amuse-"

"Enough!" Dean shouts, startling me. He grabs Lucinda by the arm, yanking her off his desk before she can finish her sentence. He pulls her around the side of the desk and shoves her towards the doorway. I reflexively move aside as she stumbles on her heels and catches herself against the door frame. Dean rips open one of the drawers in his desk and shuts the file away, before he straightens and steps around to stand face to face with her. *"Get the fuck out of here."*

Lucinda's eyes slide to look at me again. "Why? She's the one that interrupted us." She mutters, disdainfully. "Run along, *Vanna*. He likes to get a little rough some times. We've never been shy about an audience, but it might be a little *triggering* for you to stay and watch the show. I happen to like it... *when he chokes me.*"

My eyes shoot to Dean. He looks like he wants to kill her, his body literally shaking. If looks could kill, she'd be a smoking pile of ash on the ground. Lucinda doesn't seem afraid of him at all though. Not even when he grabs her roughly by the arm and shoves her into the hall, dragging her back towards the shop, where I assume, he's going to throw her out.

Before they make it to the door, she grabs his face and kisses him. He twists his mouth from hers, calling her a crazy bitch and kicks the door of the shop open with his boot, shoving her through it to the lot outside.

I follow them out with the intention of jumping in my car and leaving, but I hesitate when she trips because of his manhandling, landing on her bare knees in the lot beside her Lexus. He hauls her back to her feet, regret now mixing with the anger in his eyes. Her knees are scraped, slightly bleeding. Dean takes his hands off of her and steps back.

"Why do you always have to drag the worst out in me?" He laments.

"I know you better than anyone. Better than she ever will." Lucinda says, cocking her chin at me.

"Leave." Dean says. "I'm sorry I made you trip, but you need to leave, Lucinda. If you weren't such a treacherous bitch, none of this would have happened."

"He'll always be mine." She threatens me.

"Vanna, don't listen to her." Dean tries to reach for me, but I step back from him. "She's always been a conniving, lying..."

"You seem to have that in common." I manage to say. "Don't touch me. I've seen enough. I've heard enough. When you walked out on me, I should have let you stay gone."

He looks taken aback. "I didn't... Vanna... I just needed a minute to clear my head... I'd never-"

Cheat on me? Sneak behind my back to run to Lucinda? That's what I walked in on.

"Fuck you, Dean." I turn and run across the lot towards my car, Dean calling after me. It's parked near the front of the roadhouse, where Viking just stepped out of the steel door, walking towards his bike. He stops and looks at me as I approach.

"Vanna? What's going on?"

In a million years, I never thought I'd do anything like this. But Dean deserves it.

"I figure you're big enough to take him on if he's got a problem with this." I say, storming up to Viking. He looks confused, and then his eyes widen in shocked surprise as I jump up and wrap my arms around his neck, kissing him full on the mouth as my legs dangle in the air down the front of his body.

"*What the fuck!*" Dean shouts from across the lot.

I let go of Viking, sliding down his chest to land on my feet in front of him. His hands are up as if surrendering, and he still looks stunned, but not unamused.

"I still don't like you." I scowl at him.

"Sucks for me." He grins.

I can hear Dean's boots stomping across the lot, coming in fast behind me. I run past Viking and into the bar. I don't know if he's mad enough, or stupid enough, to assault Viking for what I just did. But I'm hoping whatever happens between them, stalls him long enough to let me get away. If Dean gets his ass kicked, he deserves that, too.

I run down the corridor and out the back door to the break area in the back, then carefully around the corner of the building, peeking to see if Dean is still outside. He isn't, he must be in the bar already, looking for me. I sprint across the parking lot back to my car, jumping in quickly and cranking the ignition. Flooring it, I cut the wheel and skid out of the parking lot in time to see Dean dash back out the front door, throwing his arms up at me. I flip him off and keep going. In my rearview mirror, I see him run across the lot towards his bike.

He's going to come after me. Serene is fast. My best chance to avoid him is just to go home and lock the damn doors. Stepping on the gas a little harder, I hope there aren't any cops around.

I pull into my driveway so fast, the front end of my car bottoms out with a loud bang and a scrape, but I know Dean is only seconds behind me. Flooring it up my driveway to my house, I then slam on the breaks, throw it into park, grab the keys out of the ignition and dart to my house. I can hear Serene coming, and my clumsy hands fumble with my keys as I scramble up the porch steps. Getting the keys into the lock, I twist it open, just as Dean's bike roars down the street and up my driveway.

He shouts my name just as I manage to get the big oak door open. Rushing inside, I quickly slam and lock the door behind me. Backing away as the sound of his heavy boots stomp up my porch steps. The screen door creaks on its hinges as he flings it open and bangs his fist on the door with loud angry thuds.

"*Vanna! Open this door, now!*" His thunderous voice is angrier than I've ever heard before.

"No! Get out of here!" I shout back at him. "Go back to fucking Lucinda! And take that however you want, asshole!"

"Vanna, nothing was happening!"

"I know what I saw!" I scream at him. "Leave me alone!"

"Vanna, it wasn't what it looked like." His tone doesn't sound as angry as it did a moment ago. "Open the door, doll. Let's talk all this out."

I kick my side of the door angrily. "No! Why should I? You wouldn't listen to me!" I shout at him through the door. "I can't believe I ever thought I could trust you! You son of a bitch!"

Glass breaks somewhere inside my house behind me and I turn around. "Nico?" I call to my cat, my first thought that he must have knocked something over.

The sound of my back door swinging open and heavy boots storming inside, crunching on glass, stuns me momentarily...

"You've got to be shitting me!" I spin back around to the front door, lunging at the dead bolt to unlock it, but I'm not able to get it open in time.

Dean grabs me by both arms and spins me around to face him, his eyes blazing with a mixture of anger and worry.

"Are you fucking crazy, Vanna?" He nearly shouts at me.

"Me? You just did a *breaking and entering!"* I struggle to get out of his grip, but it's no use. "Let me go! You're hurting my arms!" I lie, but I know it will work. He lets go of my arms, but grabs me around my body so I can't run off.

"Just listen to me, damnit!" He pleads. "Nothing was happening with Lucinda, I swear!"

I continue to try to fight him off me, but he's too strong. "Get off me! I'll bite you!" I threaten him. He pulls me across the foyer to the stair case, then lets me go on the steps. I'm trapped between a wall and the banister. He's in front of me blocking my path to the door.

"You're quite the talented escape artist, Vanna. I'll give you that." Dean says, wiping his brow with the back of his hand. "But you're not going anywhere, now. Not until we talk this out."

I glare at him as I lower myself to sit down on the steps. "Fine. Let's talk. What color were her panties? Or was she not wearing any?"

Dean sighs exasperatedly. "I don't know, Vanna, I wasn't trying to fuck Lucinda. I was shoving her off of me. I wouldn't fuck her with someone else's dick."

"You're a liar. You said she knew what you wanted and you shoved her legs open!" Jumping back to my feet, I slam my palms into his chest to shove him away. He barely lets out a grunt at the impact, and doesn't budge. He's like a leather mountain. An unmovable, six-foot three blockade. "Leave!"

"I'm not leaving." He says stubbornly.

I hit him harder with the same result. Barely a reaction. *"Leave!"*

"Punch me. Kick me. *Bite me.* I don't give a fuck, Vanna. I ain't leaving until I fix this." He insists, his expression calm as if he's stating facts. "This is happening, now. Like it or not. You can listen to me first, or I can listen to you. Lady's choice." He says, hands open, palms up, a pleading gesture despite his stony expression.

I glare into his eyes, watching his anger fade away with every passing second. "Fine. What the fuck did I walk in on with you and Lucinda? What did you throw in your desk that she clearly wanted me to know about?"

Something flickers behind his eyes. Something I haven't seen in them before. *Fear?* It only lasts a moment, then it's gone. He nods slowly, one hand reaching up to run through his hair before he slides it down the back of his skull, stopping to grip his neck for a moment, before he drops his arm. "Okay... I owe it to you to be honest... Just know this, first. What you read on the envelope, still stands true." He says, clearly nervous about whatever he has to confess. "Do you remember what I wrote?"

I try to remember exactly how it was worded. There was a lot I walked in on. Dean seems to realize this.

"Dear Vanna," Dean says, his eyes searching mine for some reason. "If you ever find this, please know, I never read it."

"Right... Read what?"

He shifts in his boots, jamming his thumbs in his front pockets. "You might want to sit back down for this."

I don't. I just continue to stare at him and wait, crossing my arms.

He nods once, accepting my choice not to sit. "You need to know that I did this before our little talk in the hotel room in Myrtle Beach... You need to know, that I did this, *because I fucking love you,* Vanna. Whether you believe that or not, I *do.*"

I swallow hard as I think back on what transpired in his office. The strange, vague things Lucinda was saying to me, obviously meant something. I have a really bad feeling about this. Dean reaches out in an attempt to hold my hand, but I pull back from him. He looks pained by it, and drops his hand back to his side.

"I was determined to understand you. I knew you were hiding things from me. I only wanted to get closer to you... and thought if I knew what you were keeping from me, that I could help you. That it would *help* me, *help* you."

A sinking feeling begins to form in my stomach, as I realize what he's about to confess. "Oh God." I whisper, my fingers gravitating to the base of my throat.

"When I noticed your aversion to police... your inclination to live life under the radar, I considered that there might be some kind of situation you were hiding from." Dean pauses, taking a moment to swallow, hard. "I asked my cop buddy, Jason, for a favor." He takes a step closer to me.

"Oh, god, oh, god..." My legs feel weaker by the second. He was right, I should have sat down for this. "You have no idea what you've done..." I whisper.

"I did it because I love you. But I couldn't bring myself to read it... I didn't want to betray your trust."

"Too late." I shake my head at him. "She read it, didn't she? She knows all about me. All about *him.* His name. Where he is. How to contact him..."

"Nothing is going to happen to you, Vanna." I can hear the vow in his tone. "I'm going to protect you."

"You couldn't even protect me from your *wife*." I glare at him. My words actually cause him to flinch.

"*Ex*-wife." He mutters. "And I'm sorry."

"If she reaches out to him, I'm dead." I say, trying not to think of all the ways this scenario might play out.

"He'll have to go through me first, Vanna. And he ain't going to make it through me." Dean utters the words as if they're a promise.

"There you go again... making promises you can't keep."

"I've never broken a promise to you, doll." Dean adamantly objects.

"Last night you promised you would accept me, even if you couldn't understand."

"I'm here, aren't I?"

"You ran out on me."

"I needed a moment, Vanna. You dropped a fucking bomb on me."

I nod. Yeah. I guess I did. "I guess you still think you love me, too."

Clearly at a loss for words, Dean scoffs, shaking his head as he lowers it, his hands moving to his hips, his eyes cast down at his boots.

"What are we going to do now?" I ask, after a few moments.

"You tell me, baby." He sighs. "How do I convince you my love is true?"

"In two years, it won't matter." I say, lowering myself back down to sit on the steps.

He looks down at me, concern returning to his eyes. "What's that supposed to mean?"

I just shrug. "I'll be dead or gone."

"Are we back to that bullshit again?" He raises his voice with renewed anger. "You saying you're gonna leave now?"

When I don't respond, he begins to pace the room, his hand running through his hair again. I can see his mind working overtime. He's not going to give up so easily. "The fuck do I have to do, Vanna? Just fucking tell me!" he demands. I don't know what to say, so I don't say anything. "If you fucking run again... if you leave town... you're just going to have two fucking psychos tailing you wherever you go. You're not going to get rid of me. So, save us both the trouble, and just stay here with me. Let Jack come to me. I'll end him, doll. And you'll be free."

Jack! "You said you didn't read the file! How do you know his name is Jack?" I demand.

Dean stops pacing to look at me, a sadness in his expression. "I didn't read it... You had a *nightmare* in Myrtle Beach, doll. You were saying his name... I just put it together."

I swallow. "*Oh.*"

He comes to kneel before me, taking my hands and holding them to his chest. "Tell me what I can do to convince you this is real." He says, pressing my hands to his heart. "I'll wait the two years, if I have to wait for you, Vanna... but if there's anything I can do to show you now, tell me, and I'll do it."

My mind recalls the conversation I had with Laura about my doubts. About Dean confusing being devoted to what he perceives as his duty, with being in actual love.

"Can you tell me what the difference is, between love and devotion to duty?"

He stares at me for a moment, his expression suddenly a bit more hopeful. "Devotion is loyalty. Unwavering loyalty to a person, or a cause. Like keeping you safe from that scum-fuck of an ex. Which is what I vow to do, Vanna. Whether you can ever love me, or not. I will not abandon you. It is my duty to do at least that." He squeezes my fingers but keeps my hands pressed against his chest. "But *love*, Vanna... is an intense, all-consuming affection... an unshakable attachment to another person. When you know deep down in your soul, life would almost be unlivable without them." He lets out a long, contemplative sigh. "There is a difference, Vanna. Love over powers everything. I am devoted to my duty to protect you, yes. But I'm so far beyond devotion to duty. I love you, truly. You have ruined me in the best possible way."

I can't speak. I can only close my eyes and absorb his words. Are they enough?

"If you still can't love me, Vanna, I will go on loving you." He whispers, his voice sounds strangled. "You need to get rid of that spell. You have to give me a chance to prove myself to you. To prove it to yourself, as well."

Could that actually work? Now that he knows...

"Let's do it now." I say, opening my eyes. I pull my hands back from him to wipe my face before I stand up and walk past him to the kitchen. Opening a drawer, I grab a lighter and walk back into the foyer, snatching up the spell box and heading for the back door. "Come on." I say, and he follows me outside. I grab the small tin of lighter fluid from the side of my outdoor grill and drop the box on my makeshift fire pit at the edge of the old patio.

Kneeling down to open the lid of the box, I remove the Knight of Wands tarot card, squirting the lighter fluid all over the poppets inside. I stand up and look at Dean as he comes to stand next to me. Holding up the Knight of Wands tarot card, I light the edge of it on fire. As we both watch it burn, I drop it into the box with the poppets, and everything goes up in flames.

Turning to Dean, I take his hands and look him in the eyes. "I release you from any and all obligations to me. I call back my power, my influence, any and all hold I may have ever had on you. You're free, Dean. As I will it, so mote it be." Releasing his hands, I turn to watch the spell burn, until there is nothing left but ashes.

"What happens now?" Dean asks.

"I don't know. I've never done any of this before... Do you feel any differently?"

He takes my hand and holds it in his. "I might love you more... Does that reassure you?"

I glance up at him to find him slightly smiling. "Not if you're full of shit."

His smile only broadens. "I don't lie."

I lift my shoulder in a half shrug. "Then I don't know, yet." I sigh. "Maybe we both need time to just... process everything."

"You mean you want me to leave you alone, again." I can hear the disappointment in his voice.

I turn to face him more directly. "I need you to walk away from me and see if you want to come back on your own."

"If that's what it takes, I'll do whatever you need me to do." Dean somberly agrees. "But I need you to know, that I don't want to leave in the first place." He reaches up his hand to stroke my cheek with the back of his fingers. I smile faintly at him. "How long do I have to stay away?"

"I don't know."

"Can I decide?"

I look at him suspiciously. "Yes, but you can't walk out the door and walk right back in."

He cracks a slight grin at me. "Alright. I'm not ready to leave yet." He says, pulling me to him as he presses his lips to my forehead.

"I've wanted to tell you everything, for a long time." I say, wrapping my arms around his waist. "I just didn't know how. I'm sorry."

"Vanna, there was never anything for me to forgive. And even if there was, I'd have forgiven you."

I squeeze him a little tighter. "You're such a good friend." I tease.

He laughs. "That shit ends here and now."

I can't help laughing either. "You need to fix my back door, too. My landlord is going to be pissed about that."

"I'll get right on it." He says, resting his chin on my head as he holds me tighter.

"And possibly the front end of my car." I add.

"What happened to your car, now?"

"I bottomed out pretty hard when you chased me home."

"I'll take a look."

"And you better burn that file on me." I squeeze him hard for a moment. "And get a handle on Lucinda."

Dean strokes my hair and kisses my forehead again. "Quite the list of demands, Kitten." He teases me.

"Get used to it." I smile to myself.

"I intend to." He chuckles. "Do you really want me to burn it? I can't see what's inside the file?"

"What are you hoping to find out?"

"I just want to know you, Vanna." He sighs. "And I want to know my enemy. It's my duty to protect you. Hell, you *summoned* me for the task." He says, jokingly.

"Too soon." I say, though I'm only half joking.

"The Devil is in the details, Vanna. And I prefer to fight a Devil I know." His voice is almost a low growl as he says the words.

"There's a better way for you to get to know Jack, than whatever's in that file on me." I say, hoping this will convince him to get rid of it. I don't know if what I did is in that file or not. I release him and start walking back towards the house. He follows me inside, and back to the closet in the foyer. Opening the door, I reach up and grab the other box, then turn and hold it out to him. "His letters... You can read them before you go."

I sit at my kitchen table, watching Dean read Jack's letters. His stone cold, unwavering expression, as his eyes dart back and forth across every line of each page of every letter. He doesn't skim. He doesn't rush at all. He's taking in every word with steady determination. Like a cyborg absorbing information about a target. The only time he moves is to turn a page or grab another letter from the box. Otherwise, he could be carved in stone.

There are three years of letters in this box. Some are declarations of Jack's undying love for me, remorse at what he did to me. Some are fantasies about what he's going to do to me when he gets out to exact his revenge. All are examples of his insanity, and how thin the line between love and hate actually is.

Exhausted from the events of today, I decide to leave Dean alone with his research. I pour a glass of sweet tea and leave it on the table for him. He doesn't even notice. I don't know if he even notices me walking away and going upstairs to my room.

I lay down on the bed and curl up on my side, waiting for him to finish. Hopefully those letters paint him a good enough picture of what it was like being with Jack for several years. I don't want to have to describe the details. Dean can use his imagination. He's a very intelligent and insightful man. I'm sure he won't be far off from reality.

Nico jumps up on the bed and curls up against me, and I pet him until I fall asleep waiting.

The feeling of my mattress sinking down behind me as Dean lies down against my back, wakes me up. I feel his arm wrap around me, his body conforming to mine. When I open my eyes to glance at the window, I can see that it's dark outside.

"What time is it?" I ask, my voice groggy from sleep.

Dean brushes my hair from my ear with a finger. "It's almost ten thirty." He says softly, placing a kiss behind my ear.

"Did you read all of them?"

"I did."

I twist around in the bed to look at him, face to face against the same pillow. It's dark, but I can still make out his expression. "Were the letters enough?"

"For now." He strokes my arm gently. "He's a sick fuck. I can see that clearly. You're very brave, Vanna."

"Yeah, really brave." I scoff. "I'm in hiding. Getting *you* to do my dirty work."

"You are brave. It's a shame you don't ever see yourself for what you really are. It breaks my heart every time... You're beautiful, too." He traces my bottom lip with the pad of his index finger, so softly it almost tickles. "Sexy as Hell. And strong." He adds.

I close my eyes, but I feel him press his forehead to mine, taking my hand and bringing it up to hold between us. "I know he said things to you... more than what's in those letters... but they aren't true. You are leaps and bounds above a piece of shit like him. Men like him are too weak to appreciate someone as special as you, Vanna. They feel a false sense of power over others when they abuse. He knew you were better than him in every way. That's why he tried to tear you down. That's why he tried to make you believe you are less than what you are." He brings my hand up to his lips to kiss me. "And if I have to tell you every day, how special you are, until you believe it too, then that's what I'll do."

I slide my body closer to him, tucking my head up under his chin. He twists onto his back, wrapping his arm around me to hold me against him as I rest my head on his chest. I breathe in his scent, that leathery, campfire and sandalwood aroma, that reminds me of a Western... Playing with the zipper on his leather jacket, I whisper *"I love you."*

His breath hitches for a moment, his body tenses, as if my words took him by surprise. "I love you, too." He whispers back, before placing another kiss on top of my head.

"I don't want anything bad to happen to you."

"It's out of your hands, doll." Dean says. "You never needed any spell with me. There's no way I wouldn't have fallen in love with you. And I protect what's mine." His fingers curl around my shoulder, squeezing me to him. "Jack *Zero* doesn't scare me. He's already dead. He just doesn't know it yet." Dean growls. "You don't have to be scared any more, Vanna. No more fear. No more shame."

"I don't know how you can see me as brave. Isn't everything I've done up to this point the exact opposite?" I ask.

"You know what I see?" I can hear the sincerity in his voice. "I see someone that's not only brave for fighting to survive. But somebody so brave, that they gave life another chance. They started completely over. Alone, at that. They gave a lucky bastard like me a shot, after all the bullshit a man fucking put them through. That's not cowardly, Vanna. And for you to throw in with a guy *like me*... Shit. I appreciate the Hell out of that." He sighs.

"Why wouldn't I?" I ask, remembering him saying something about thinking I deserved better than him, the night he first told me he loved me. Then there were those strange outbursts from Lucinda today, that he didn't seem to want to comment on at the time.

Dean exhales slowly. Not quite a sigh. I can sense his hesitation. "I wasn't always a Savior, Vanna. I mean, before I got thrown out of the MC. I used to do some fucked up shit myself. I never hurt women though. You need to know that much. I've never harmed a woman or a child in my life. But... I did hurt people for a living. I did some real outlaw type shit. I was a bad dude myself, in a lot of ways... You would have thought I was a real dirtbag."

Well, that explains why I have always felt that Dean is dangerous. That tough guy, I will fuck you up, vibe about him. He feels like he's dangerous, because he is dangerous. Not just because of his fighting. A former bad guy who seems to have turned his life around.

I pull the zipper of his leather jacket down and slide my hand inside, across his warm, hard stomach, hugging him gently. "Well, you're not talking about the man I know now. And you're far from a dirtbag, Dean. Whatever you think you were, you turned into a successful entrepreneur. That's something to be proud of. You have nothing to be ashamed of either."

He clears his throat, as if he's not in complete agreement with what I've said. "There's still a lot you don't know about me, Vanna. I'm not the *Knight in shining armor* you think I am. There's no shine. I'm tarnished as fuck." He sounds sullen. "But I am tough enough and mean enough, to handle Jack Nero."

I run my hand up his hard body to rest it against his chest, feeling his strong, steady heartbeat. I'm more than certain, Dean has lived a rough life. His need to fight in these bare-knuckled, underground, grimy dungeons is an outward manifestation of the demons he's fighting inside himself.

"*A Knight in shining armor is a man who has never had his metal truly tested.*" I recite a line from a poem I once read by Benedict Menda. "The Knight with the tarnished armor is the one who actually knows how to fight. Who's lived through protecting his loved ones. I don't care what you did in your past, Dean. I might not understand why you seem to find inner peace through violence, but you've only ever shown me kindness... I love the man you are now."

Dean places his hand over mine, his fingers curling around my hand. "That other guy inside me is never far away, baby... But he's in love with you, too."

DEAN

SHE LOVES ME... HEARING HER SAY THOSE WORDS TO ME IS EXHILARATING! More so than even flying down a desert highway at one hundred miles per hour on a badass bike, or riding the very edge of a winding mountainside road, skirting the deadly cliffs of the coastal Northwest.

I'm barely out of her driveway and the urge to turn right back around and kick her *front* door in this time, is too damn tempting... But she asked me for this... To walk away and to see if my feelings for her change. If I want to return to her. I could laugh. My elated half could, anyway. My feelings for her have only managed to get stronger.

I'm too wired to go home, finding myself back at my shop. Vanna asked me to burn the file on her. And though I'm admittedly curious to see what it says, especially since Lucinda has at least seen part of it, I will do as she requested, and burn it.

Having read Jack's letters, I've gotten to know him a bit through his own words. He's not much different from the abusers I've spent more than a decade delivering justice to. Justice they never see coming. Punishment I hope they never forget. Shame and degradation, they get to carry within themselves, forever. And deservedly so. They inflicted the same upon the women and children who trusted them to love and protect them. I have no mercy, nor do I feel pity, for such men.

I can't help but smile inwardly at the irony of this situation between Vanna and I. She has no idea I do these things. I imagine she would take it as another sign that I was called to her through her spell. A dark Knight who slays abusers of women and children, summoned to her side. She would call it magic. I just say, it's fate.

To Vanna, Jack is a larger-than-life monster. A powerful, threatening man that was able to isolate her and break her down. Bend her to his malignant will. Instill a fear in her that kept her trapped. Kept her under his boot. Keeps her living in fear even now. Chasing her away from any sort of happiness or peace she attempts to find, through these letters. Through this count down to his inevitable release, upon which he vows to return to her...

Well come on then, Jack. Fate's messenger awaits your arrival. And he will never be far from her side. You've got your work cut out for you, Jack. You'll never hurt her again. But you, Jack... You're going to know pain. I'm happy to make that introduction for you. You see Jack, you hurt someone I love. I'm not going to be able to separate myself from that... Not even after I repair some of the damage you've done to her.

Grabbing a lighter off the shelf above my work bench, I take the file outside into the lot and light it up without ever looking inside. As I hold the burning pages in my hand, twisting it around so the flames consume the entire thing, I don't drop it until the fire nearly reaches my fingertips.

"The fuck are you doing?" Viking asks, his shadowed, lumbering form walks across the lot towards me. "I saw you out here being a pyro on the security cameras. What is that?"

We both stand and watch the last corner burn, until all that remains are ashes, flittering across the dark lot in the slight breeze of the night.

"Nothing." I say.

"Why are you smiling?" He asks. "Not that I'm complaining, I was just expecting you to be pissed off when you eventually showed back up here." He folds his arms across his chest, looking at me inquisitively.

I take a deep breath of the cool night air and let it out on a tranquil sigh. "I've got nothing to be pissed about at the moment."

He cocks a brow at me. "Your mood swings are giving me whiplash."

"You're lucky that's all I'm giving you."

"Bro, *she* kissed *me*." Viking says, putting his hands up in mock surrender.

I try not to glare at him. "That's why I didn't knock your block off. I'm more annoyed that you fucking *tripped me* when I ran back out after her. I could have caught her if not for that. What are you, twelve?"

Viking chuckles. "I felt like helping her out." He shrugs.

I look at him suspiciously. "Because she kissed you?"

"That didn't hurt." He grins.

I shake my head, unable to help grinning either. Perhaps there is hope for Vanna and Viking to come around on each other. Even if it's at my expense.

"Why are you back here, setting shit on fire at damn near midnight?" Viking asks.

I shrug. "Can't sleep. Have a project in mind. Figured I'd come down here and get started on it."

"Probably for the best." Viking nods.

I look at him, cocking a brow at him, this time.

"Daniel was here looking for you, earlier." He clarifies. "Was fuckin' pissed off about Lucinda. Probably won't be back tonight, but he was livid, Dean. He's looking for a fight."

"Well, I'll be sure to give him one when he shows up."

Fucking Lucinda. I didn't mean for her to scrape her damn knees. I was wrong for that shit, though. I should let her husband get a shot or two in for her. The shit she said to Vanna about me... Trying to expose me like that... Deliberately attempting to fuck with Vanna's mind, turn her on me... It's infuriating, but I didn't mean for her to get hurt. Especially not by my hand.

"So, I assume all's well with Vanna *for the moment*?" Viking asks, distracting me from my downward spiral, his question laced with sarcasm.

"More than for the moment." I smile. "She told me she loves me. Doesn't care about my past. She fuckin' loves me." Just thinking about it again makes my heart beat harder and I bring my hand up to rub my chest, remembering the feel of her hand against me.

"So, you finally hit it then?" Viking grins at me, waiting for a response.

Fuck. Here it comes.

"Bro..." He looks at me, his head cocked to the side, his expression annoyingly full of mock disappointment.

"Viking... Fuck off." I sigh. Of course, he doesn't. Not even a little bit. His wide eyes and shit eating grin are a clear indication that I should brace for what's coming out of his mouth next.

"She loves you and I've still gotten further with her, than you have." He gibes at me. "Not only has she seen my *huge* cock, Dean. She fuckin' *kissed* me, too, Bro."

Shaking my head, I turn to walk back into my shop. I spend the rest of my night cutting, warping and welding steel, into a hand-crafted gift for Vanna. A gift that I hope will symbolically represent and convey, my complete acceptance of her, and our seemingly separate worlds, *finally* and *officially*, joining as one.

Chapter twenty-five

Vanna

"**W**AY TO MAKE A GIRL WONDER." I SAY, walking across my foyer and up to my screen door, where Dean is leaning against the frame, hovering on my porch. He's wearing a sexy playful grin across his face as he watches me approach. I'm still wearing the dress I wore to work in Laura's shop today. I haven't been home long at all before I heard the familiar roar of Serene barreling up my driveway. It's like he timed my arrival home.

"I don't know how this spell shit works Vanna, I just figured twenty-four hours ought to do it." He says.

I grin back at him, squinting my eyes suspiciously as I fold my arms and come to stand before him. "Oh really?"

"That and you were at work most of the day." He shrugs. "We've waited six months... what's one more nine to five?" he jokes.

"Well, it was your call when to come back. If you wanted to come back."

He arches a brow, looking at me incredulously as he removes his arm off the frame of the door to straighten himself. "I'm back, baby. Never left, though. Never gonna."

I smile as I unlatch the flimsy lock on the screen door and push it open for him to come inside. He steps through the door, grabbing me around my waist and pulls me against him, walking me backwards as he places a kiss against my lips.

"I fuckin' missed you." He growls, pinning me gently against the little foyer table. He tilts his head slightly to press his forehead to mine. "Wasn't easy leavin' you last night... after everything we talked about." His hands slide from my lower back to rest on my hips.

"How do you feel about everything?" I ask.

He gives me a salacious smile and presses his hips forward into me harder. "Like we got a lot of time to make up for... and to look forward to." He says, making butterflies flutter in my lower abdomen and my skin flush.

"What did you have in mind?" I manage to ask.

"The Harvest Festival starts tonight. You wanna go?" He asks, his grin never leaving his mouth, though his suggestion takes me by surprise.

I lean back a bit to look at him skeptically. "You want to go to that?" He doesn't really strike me as a *Harvest Festival* type of guy.

The corners of his mouth curve down for a second as he shrugs, before his smile returns. "They've got live music, carnival type shit going on. We can take Serene over if you throw on some jeans."

"Okay. If that's what you want to do." I say, reaching up between us to lightly pat his leather clad chest. "I'll go change."

He drops his arms from around me, but as I start to walk towards the stairs, he grabs my hand and tugs me back to him playfully, our lips colliding once again for another few moments.

"Cards on the table, baby." Dean says when we part again. "I kinda really just want to parade you around as my woman in front of the whole damn town." He says, wearing that sexy grin of his. "Chauvinistic, maybe. But what do you say? Would you do that for me, doll?"

I can't help but giggle at him, reaching up to stroke the short scruff of his jawline, coaxing him back down to my lips so I can kiss him once more. "Ace's baby." I tease him.

The festival is crowded. He was right about the whole damn town being here tonight. But for early October, there is a warm, slight breeze that carries with it the aroma of fried carnival food and cotton candy. The music and the laughter and screams from the crowds, as well as the brightly lit rides and decorative string lights strung up all over, must be enticing in a little town in the middle of nowhere USA. Especially when there isn't a whole lot to do normally, on a regular night.

"Shall we?" Dean asks, slinging his arm across my shoulders possessively.

I can't help smiling back up at him as I reach up to thread my fingers with his. "Let's do this."

As we walk among the crowd, I notice quite a few people nod or wave to Dean in greeting. I suppose I shouldn't be all that surprised though. He does run three businesses in this small town, and he has lived here most of his life. I guess it makes sense for him to know a few people around. And he is quite a charming fellow when he wants to be.

Glancing up at Dean, I catch him grinning widely as his arm tightens around me. Following his line of sight to see who in the crowd he's spotted, I realize it's Viking, across the way with another new girl, at the milk bottle toss game.

Dean extends his free arm towards Viking, flipping him off, as he turns his face to me and bends to kiss me on the mouth. I know full well Viking has most likely broken Dean's balls about the little stunt I pulled yesterday when I kissed him. Deciding it's only right to do Dean a solid now because of my actions yesterday, I make a little more of a show of it.

Twisting under Dean's arm to face him directly, I slide my hands up his chest, over his shoulders and up his neck until my hands are cradling his face as I kiss him back. His arm drops from my shoulders to the small of my back as he pulls me closer against him, kissing me deeper as I drop my jaw to give him full access for a few moments. After a minute of making out like horny teenagers, I can't help but giggle against his mouth.

Dean only pulls back from my lips slightly, just enough to look me in the eyes. "Is the bastard still looking at us?" he asks.

I glance from the corner of my eye at Viking. "Yes. And it looks like he's challenging you to the milk bottle toss."

"Fuck." Dean mutters, though he's still smiling. "That son of a bitch can't let me have anything. He wants to beat me in front of you, the merciless asshole."

"You can beat him. I have faith in you." I tease him.

"The pressure is on." Dean says, reaching up to take one of my hands in his. "Let's do this."

"You know this shit is rigged, right?" Dean says to Viking, as they square off together at the milk bottle toss game, ready to throw.

"My arm's strong enough, it doesn't matter if it's rigged or not." Viking cockily replies.

Dean sighs, shaking his head, but at least he's still smiling. "Curve ball don't fail me now."

They both throw at the exact same moment, and I'm actually a little relieved when they both knock over their bottles. I know Viking's was due to brute strength. Dean's could have been also, though he strikes me as being more strategic.

"You got lucky." Viking taunts him. "Best out of three. That arm will give out before mine does."

543

Dean chuckles. "You're an asshole. First you kiss my woman, then you trip me. Now, you're trying to take me down in a not so friendly competition. What gives?" Dean says, though his tone is still humorous.

"She saw my dick too, Dean." Viking grins back at him. "Don't forget that part."

"As if you'd ever let me." Dean mumbles under his breath.

I anxiously turn to the blonde girl Viking is here with. "It was an accident." I whisper to her. She seems nice, and I don't want her to get the wrong idea. She smiles back at me, fingers tucked into her little daisy dukes.

The two *biker bro's* battle it out twice more, tying both times.

"Again. Three more." Viking taunts him. "I will beat you."

Dean looks at the girl Viking is with. "He must really like you. He's not typically this big of a dick." Dean winks at her.

"Sure I am. Ask Vanna." Viking taunts.

I can't help giggling, as I try to cover my mouth before Dean hears me. He really wasn't joking about Viking's merciless ball breaking.

"Loser pays. Let's go." Viking pushes him. They go head-to-head three more times. Dean loses on the third toss. Viking grins and hands the girl he's with a little teddy bear as Dean pays the vendor.

I wrap my arms around Dean's waist and hug him from behind. "I'm still thoroughly impressed." I reassure him, though teasingly. It's just a game anyway. "You gave the giant a real run."

Viking shoves Dean's shoulder. "*Giant.* You heard it, bro. Right from her *lips.*"

"You know what they say..." Dean says, twisting around to put his arm across my shoulders again. "The bigger they are, the harder they fall."

Do they ever stop antagonizing each other? It may be time to humble these boys. "I challenge you both to the target gallery." I say, placing a hand on my hip. I look over at Viking's female companion for the night. I'm sure I'll never see her again either, but I don't want her to feel left out, all the same. "You too, if you're up for it."

"What are the stakes?" Viking asks. "If you lose, what do we get?"

I shrug. "I don't know. What do each of you want?"

Viking looks at Dean with a sinister smile. "Careful, bro." Dean growls the warning at him. This time, there's a whole lot less humor in his voice.

Viking doesn't miss it. "If I lose, I'll buy everybody food and drinks. If I win, then Dean does."

"Well, if I win, I want everyone to go on a ride of my choosing, too." I say.

"Deal." Viking agrees.

I look up at Dean. "What do you want if you beat me?" I ask. He grins back at me. I have a pretty good idea what he might be thinking. I smack his chest lightly. "*Something we can do, here.*" I bite my lip to keep from giggling at his naughty nature.

"You gotta do that thing I like. On the Ferris wheel with me, later." He smiles.

I look at him, confused. "What thing?"

He leans down to whisper in my ear. "The way you fucking kissed me at the beach that night. *That thing*." His voice is a sexy growl that sends a flush through my body again.

I clear my throat. "Okay. Deal."

On our way to the target gallery, I keep an eye out for the worst ride here. The Gravitron is here. Probably the worst one, but these bikers ride fast motorcycles and live dangerously. The Gravitron might not bother them at all. The Carousel ride might be funny just to see them on it. Bumper cars, maybe? No, that wouldn't work. Viking probably wouldn't even fit in one of those cars, and they slam each other constantly with brotherly insults all the time anyway, no need to have them slamming the shit out of each other on the bumper cars.

I finally spot the perfect ride and smile to myself. They're going to be so thrilled.

When we get to the target gallery, we each chose our target colors. Whomever takes out the most of their color wins. Simple. But they move faster and faster each round, and they're all mixed up. There's room for four shooters, so we each get a rifle style gun. On the vendors mark, we take aim and begin to shoot. We have twenty seconds to hit as many targets as possible in that time.

The first round, Viking's gal pal is out. The vendor resets the targets as we reload our rifles. The game is sped up another notch and it's blast off once again. Viking is out the second round. I beat him by several targets. Dean has me tied. As we reload and the vendor sets the game up one more time, Dean grins at me.

"I knew you were a badass." He says, almost pridefully.

I give him a playful scowl. "You better not be all chivalrous and throw this because I'm a girl."

"Fear not, my lady. I left my chivalry with Serene. I want that prize, doll. I'll be shootin' to win." He teases me. "You're going down, Vanna."

I smirk back at him, making sure he sees me glance down at his crotch. "Only if you're lucky."

"Damn... Had I known *that* was an optional prize." He grins back at me.

"I thought I saw one of those private photo booths somewhere around here." I tease him back.

"You trying to throw me off my game, doll?" he asks, then tsks me.

"Is it working?" I giggle.

Before Dean can respond, the vendor shouts "Ready!", calling our attention back to the game. We both raise our rifles and take aim, the bell rings, the targets zoom by, and we open fire. The targets ping rapidly and flip backwards as we unload on the game. Twenty seconds flies by. All but three of my targets are down. Dean has one left standing, and its partially flipped back at that. Damn. He beat me.

"Would you like a rematch?" he offers.

"No. It was a fair match." I say, handing him my rifle. He passes them back to the vendor. I look at Viking. "You're lucky Dean beat me. Or you'd both be on the little pink Tea Cup ride next." He laughs, knowing damn well how ridiculous they would both look on that ride. Two big, tough looking, leather clad bikers, swirling around in pink tea cups. That would have been hilarious to have seen.

"Well, I still owe you guys food so let's grab some shit and listen to some live music for a bit." Viking says, handing the target gallery vendor some cash.

Dean pokes me with something furry and I turn around to look at him.

"I know I beat you, but I would have tried to win you something anyway." He says, handing me a cute little stuffed animal fox.

"Aww!" I accept his prize and smile at him. He throws his arm around me once more, as we follow Viking and his date through the crowd, over to the food vendors, so he can make good on his loss.

Sitting down at a table together where the band is playing a cover of Sweet Home Alabama, we dig into our paper plates of carnival food, consisting of burgers, fries, hot dogs and funnel cakes with a round of iced sodas.

We're having a nice time together, talking and joking around. Viking is telling his date and I about the time he and Dean got drunk at a bar one night in Alabama, got into a fight with a few members of another MC, kicked their bikes over and climbed a water tower to wait out the cops. Dean says his only regret is kicking over the innocent bikes. That it wasn't cool of them to have dominoed the row of motorcycles outside. Viking didn't care and would have done worse if the cops weren't coming. They both assure us girls, that those wild days are behind them, though. I have a feeling there are many more stories of the Adventures of Dean and Viking. And they're probably worse.

I volunteer to collect our plates and cups and take them to the trash. Dean grabs the rest of my funnel cake and eats it before I take it away. On my way back from disposing of our plates, I spot Lucinda and a few of her girlfriends buying ice cream cones at a concession stand across the lot. She doesn't seem to see me, but stares at Dean when she spots him. I wonder if she knows we're still together. I hope she doesn't come near us tonight. Or ever again, for that matter. But it's a small town, and this just drives that point home. I realize Dean is watching me, watch her. So, I hurry back over to him and pretend I'm not bothered by her presence here.

"Forget about her, baby." He says, leaning with his elbows back against the picnic table as he smiles up at me. "It's you and me, doll."

I stand between his knees and run my fingers through the top of his hair, before I lean down to kiss him briskly on the lips. He winks at me, grabbing my hand as he stands then leads me in the direction of the Ferris wheel. Dean doesn't even glance at Lucinda as we walk past her. She looks pissed about it, too.

Once we're on the Ferris wheel and up in the air, Dean grins at me licentiously and jams his fist down his pants. I assume getting himself into a better position in anticipation of an erection. "Alright, baby." His tone is deep, growly and sexy as hell. "Lay it on me." He says, his arm snaking around behind me and pulling me against him. He drapes his other arm across the back of the seat.

I press my lips to his, kissing him gently at first, teasing him. Running my hand up the back of his skull, my fingers slide up into the longer hair slicked back on top of his head. I grip him gently, just enough to pull his head back as I press myself against him, positioning my mouth higher than his. Kissing him deeper, getting a little rougher with him, I tempt his tongue into my mouth. Sliding my other hand down his chest and stomach slowly, I reach down lower to skim my hand over his hardening cock and down one of his parted thighs. Digging my nails into his leg muscle, I drag them slowly towards his cock, then dip my hand down to cup his balls over his pants, squeezing them gently. He groans, thrusting his tongue deeper into my mouth. I tug his hair harder, and go in for the kill, sucking his tongue in that way that drives him crazy, dragging my hand up to stroke the length of his hardness and then back down again to massage his balls. He nearly whimpers, as his other hand slides up my leg, then moves to slip his fingers under the hem of my shirt, touching the skin of my stomach. Sliding his hand up further to my chest, he gently squeezes one of my breasts over the cup of my bra. I tuck my fingers into the top of his pants behind his belt, gently rubbing the hot, velvety head of his cock. He pulls his hand out of my shirt and grabs my hand, almost in a panic, but he doesn't have the will power to pull back from the kiss. Unable to keep from smiling, I pull back on my own.

He lets his head fall back against the seat and breathes deeply, lips parted, eyes still closed for another few moments.

"Holy fuck, Vanna." He groans. After a minute or so he straightens up and opens his eyes to look at me. "You fuckin' blow my mind."

I giggle and look around to see what we can actually see from way up here on the Ferris wheel. It's dark out though, so there isn't much of a view. Just the lights of the carnival below and the black woods around the large clearing where this little festival is taking place.

"So, what's next?" I ask.

"Anything you want." He says.

I smile at him. "How about your place?"

"*Aces.*" He grins.

Once we're off the Ferris wheel, Dean takes me by the hand and we walk back towards the dirt parking lot where Serene is waiting. When I hear the band begin to play a cover of Elvis Presley's *Can't Help Falling In Love With You*, I stop walking and tug Dean's hand. He stops to look at me. "We can't leave yet. I love this song." I say.

Dean smiles at me, pulling me off to the side so we're not blocking anyone. "Dance with me, then." He says, curling an arm round me and lifting my hand to place against his chest. We slow dance together in the shadow of the last concession stand. I rest my cheek against his chest as we sway together to this timeless classic, and when the song ends, I ask him to take me to his place.

547

Once we're inside Dean's house, I remove my jacket and place it folded on top of the huge marble kitchen island, sitting the little fox he gave me on top of it. When I turn around to see where he is, Dean is leaning back against the door, looking at me. His smile is telling, his eyes are hungry, dark, a primal glint in them. I know he's imagining having me right now. The knowledge stirs my own lust for him.

"Did you have fun tonight?" I ask, pretending not to notice the way he's looking at me.

"Absolutely." His hand locks the door behind him. "Did you enjoy yourself?"

"Yes, very much." I smile.

"Alexa, play *Make It Rain*, Ed Sheeran. Loop mode on." He says, an octave louder, in that authoritative tone of his. After a moment, the sultry, bluesy music starts to play throughout his house. He removes his leather jacket, walking towards me to drape it over a bar stool at his kitchen island, then he turns to me, reaching out to touch my face. His thumb gently rubs across my lower lip. "I must have listened to this song a thousand times, thinking of you." His voice is low, deep. "About all the ways I would have you."

I try not to audibly swallow.

He bends to kiss me, his mouth taking mine in that starving way of his. But he pulls back almost abruptly. "Do you want me, Vanna?" He asks, a yearning expression in his eyes. "Because I don't know if I can stop if you change your mind." He pulls me against him and kisses me again. That desperate, hungry kiss. I surrender to it. After a few moments, he asks longingly against my lips, "*Is this a yes?*"

"Yes."

Dean grabs my hand and nearly drags me down the hall to his bedroom. Once we're standing at the foot of his bed, he wastes no time in pulling off my shirt, tossing it aside without a care, then yanks his off as well, dropping it where he stands. He pulls me against him again and kisses me once more, before he pushes me backwards, onto the bed behind me. I land sitting back on my elbows, surprised, and wondering if he's going to be rough with me after I've tormented him all these months. I'm half turned on, half nervous.

Dean kneels before me, undoing my jeans, then hooks his fingers inside the waist band on either side of my hips and pulls them down roughly, to my knees. He stops to yank off my boots and socks, tossing them over his shoulders, then pulls my jeans off the rest of the way. Discarding them in the same manner.

His strong, hot, rough hands grip my ankles, then continue to slide up both of my legs as he makes his way up to the elastic band of my underwear. His fingers slip inside to yank them down as well. I sit up and reach out to touch his powerful bare shoulders.

"*Wait...*" I whisper, shakily. I can't help thinking back on what Lucinda said about Dean's proclivity for roughness in the bedroom... I don't want him to feel guilty if I were to react to something... I know he'd never do anything to hurt me... A triggered memory wouldn't be his fault. And I'm afraid of reacting in a way that would make him feel rejected if I have to tell him to stop. Though as nervous as I am right now, I'm glad to know that I can still respond to the right touch, from the right man. And that man is Dean.

He pauses at my hesitation. His dark eyes meeting mine, and I can see the burning lust in them as he searches my expression. "I'm not going to hurt you, Vanna." He says, as if he can read my thoughts. "I'm going to make love to you. All fucking night. To this fucking song. Until it's burned into your mind the way it is mine. Until we sear each other's souls."

I can't help the nervous giggle that escapes me. He has such a hedonistic way with words sometimes. Oftentimes.

Dean gives me that trademark devilish grin of his, as he pulls my panties down, discarding them wherever as well. He reaches up and behind me to unhook my bra, sliding it down my arms before he throws that away too. I cross my arms in front of myself, now that I'm totally naked before him for the very first time, grateful that he didn't turn any lights on. Hopeful, that he won't.

"Don't be like that, Kitten." He says, his voice is low, deep. "I think you're perfect. And I'm going to prove it to you."

He stands up, kicking off his boots as he simultaneously undoes his belt and unzips his fly. He shoves his pants and boxers down his legs in one fell swoop, stepping out of them. Bending to peel his socks off as well, he then straightens to stand before me. I stare nervously at his bare feet on the hardwood floor.

"You can look at me, baby. I'm yours." He says, encouragingly.

I smile shyly back up at him. Even with the pale glow of the full harvest moon coming in from the windows beside the bed, our only source of light, I can make out his gorgeously masculine form. His taught, sculpted body. So dangerously sexy and built for action. His rigid cock standing at full attention. I have no idea what he was concerned about that night I saw Viking's cock. Sure, he's not *as* big as Viking, *thank God*. But what he's packing is nothing to sneer at... This might actually hurt at first. It's been a long while since I've been with anyone. I haven't even been interested, until I met Dean...

"Lay back against the pillows. I want to look at you." That authoritative tone, now laced with a deepening desire.

Pushing myself back up the bed, until my head is up near the pillows, I watch him as his eyes roam all over me, his fist now wrapped tightly around his cock.

"You're so fucking beautiful, baby." His voice is an even lower, deep growl. "The curves of your body are perfect. So feminine. *My* fucking woman. I could come just staring at you."

I bring my hand to my face and bite my finger to keep from giggling nervously, watching him slowly stroke his considerable length, as he continues to look me over... It's as if he's lost in the music and whatever fantasies are swirling around in his mind. Every time I move an arm, or a leg, his head tilts to take in a new angle as he strokes himself.

"You're crazy, Dean." I half whisper, half chuckle.

He nods only once. "I'm fucking crazy about you."

"Come here." I smile, reaching out to him.

He kneels forward, onto the bed at my feet. I bend my legs so he can come closer, and I stroke his hard thigh with my foot when he does. He leans forward, his hands gripping the top of my knees before he slides them slowly down my thighs. Then between them, before he shoves my legs apart to position himself between them. I let out a surprised gasp at the abrupt move. He goes from gentle to rough and back again so quickly, my heart begins to beat a little faster. Lowering his lips to my hips, he trails kisses from one side to the other, his short scruff tickling me. I drop one of my hands down over my lower stomach, feeling a little insecure about him being so close to my soft body, but he grabs my hand and pulls it away, as if he knows.

"You have the softest skin I've ever felt." He breathes on me, continuing to place kisses on my body. "When I go down on you, are you going to let me kiss you after?"

That question catches me off guard, and I stammer, unsure how to answer that. No one has ever done that to me before. Not the first part, or the second.

Dean smiles at me, knowingly. "Okay, baby." He says, kissing up my body. His hands find their way to my breasts as he fondles them gently. Pressing his palms against my nipples as they harden beneath his touch. He lowers himself again to kiss and lick them, raking his teeth over them one at a time, sucking and flicking them with his tongue. The sensation causes me to arch my back involuntarily, as sharp jolts of pleasure pang through my body.

He kisses up my chest, across my clavicle and up my throat before he takes my mouth again, kissing me deeply. He lowers his body onto mine, pressing against me. I can feel his hardness trapped between us, against my pelvic and hip bone. His hand roams up my body from my thigh, up my side and to my face. He strokes my cheek, sliding his fingers back through my hair to the back of my head as he kisses me deeper.

"I fucking love kissing you, Vanna." He says against my mouth, as his hand runs back down my body. He lifts his lower half slightly to get his hand between my legs. I gasp at his touch as his fingers gently stroke my sex. "But I need to own you down here, too." He kisses me once more, before he makes his way back down, kissing and gently nipping me until he settles between my thighs.

I can feel his breath on me down there, as he tells me to bend my knees. I do as I'm told and he wraps his hands around my thighs to anchor me where he wants me. I let out a quivering breath in anxious anticipation...

"Relax, baby. I'm going to take real good care of you." He says softly. "And I'm not going to stop until your legs are shaking." With that, his mouth is on me, his tongue sliding between my lips as he kisses me where I've never been kissed before. I grab onto the comforter we're laying on and grip it in both hands, gasping as his talented mouth sends new shock waves of sensation though my body.

"*Oh my god...*" I moan. The tip of his tongue is rubbing and swirling around and against my clit, and it's beginning to drive me wild. My back arches and my body writhes against him beyond my control. He tortures me for an entire duration of *Make it Rain*, bringing me so close to the edge, and backing off, several times. Until my body is trembling and I'm on the verge of begging him for release. The song starts over again, but he doesn't stop. There is no indication he is going to stop... I'm going to lose my mind!

"Oh God... Dean... please!" I cry out.

"I can do this for hours, baby, you're intoxicating..." He growls against my body. Even his breath on me is delicious torture against my sensitive parts.

His tongue is back at my clit again, swirling around before he presses harder against it, stroking it with rougher consistency, a rhythm that he doesn't stop. I can feel the pressure building inside me again, rapidly. My body once again on auto pilot, my hips thrusting up, but he grabs them with his strong hands, forcing them down on the mattress. He holds me there until he drives me insane, all I can do is barely swivel them against his mouth, but I can't stop, I can't control it.

My hands shoot down to grab at his fingers that are clamped at my waist, but it's useless, he's got an iron grip on me. As my orgasm hits me, my upper body arches up off the bed, my head thrown back as I cry out. He doesn't let up at all and I thrash and shudder, my nails digging into his wrists, before my arms fly out at my sides gripping the bedding, as my body convulses beyond control. I realize I'm still shrieking... did I black out? He's still mercilessly working my clit as another wave builds rapidly inside me again and my entire body feels like I've been hit with a heat wave. Another orgasm tears through me as I attempt to clamp my legs together, but he slides his hands down quickly from my hips to my thighs, keeping them pried apart as he relentlessly works me over. I lift back off the bed again, crying out, twisting and writhing beyond my control. My body is shaking harder than it ever has before. Only when I collapse back down against the mattress, completely spent, does he finally, mercifully, stop.

For a few moments, as I literally pant to catch my breath, I'm only partially aware of him standing up to gaze down at me.

"You're a fucking Hell Cat." He growls. My eyes finally focus enough to see him staring down at me, wiping his glistening mouth with his hand. "I almost came just watching you come." I notice his wrists are both slightly bleeding.

"Oh my God, did I *cut* you?" My voice is low and shaky.

"You clawed the shit out of me." He grins. "So fucking worth it."

I can't help a weak laugh at his reaction to being wounded in the throes of passion. I lift my arms up shakily to see if there is any blood under my nails in the moonlight. Doesn't look like it.

"I'll be right back. Don't move." He says.

Letting my arms drop back down against the mattress, I close my eyes. That was mind blowing. No wonder Lucinda can't get over him. My blood is still humming from everything he just did to me, and I'm finding it hard to even hate her right now. She must hate herself plenty, for losing him.

The sound of water running, a cabinet opening and closing, emanates softly from the bathroom. Some kind of paper rustling. He must be bandaging his wrists. I can't believe I did that to him. I must have really lost it there for a minute. Or thirty. I don't even know how much time has passed. How many times this song has played. He literally threw me into another dimension.

His footsteps return to the side of the bed, and I turn to look at him, noticing his wrists are wrapped up. He tears open a condom with his teeth and rolls it down his erection. "This is for *your* peace of mind." He comments, watching me, watch him. "I'm clean and totally willing to prove it, if you would ever consider letting me at you *au naturel*."

I giggle tiredly. "Are you sure your wrists are okay? I barely remember even doing that to you."

"Aces, baby." He grins. "Are you ready for me?"

I stretch out my shaky limbs and let my arms fall back against the pillows again as I smile up at him. "I'm all yours."

"*Fuck*, I love hearing you say that." He growls, climbing back onto the bed and caging me beneath him. His breath smells like mint. I reach up and stroke his whiskered jaw line, coaxing him down to me.

"You're so considerate."

He shrugs. "I figured while I was in there. I love kissing you too much to let your prudeness interfere with my plans." He teases me.

"Is that not normal?" I ask.

He gives me a crooked, almost sympathetic smile. "*Our* normal is whatever you want it to be." He says, lowering his body onto mine. I part my legs so he can settle between them more comfortably, and giggle at how they still tremble. He brushes my hair away from my face as he looks down at me. "What?"

"My legs are so weak right now."

He grins. "Well, I have every intention of making it rather difficult for you to walk tomorrow." He teases, lowering his face to mine and kissing me gently.

"About that," I say, reaching down between us to wrap my fingers around him.

He tenses at my touch and lets out a slow hiss of air as I squeeze him gently. "What about it?" He asks, pushing his hips forward so my hand strokes his hard length.

"Be gentle with this. At first, at least."

"I'll be anything you want me to be."

He begins to kiss my neck, turning me on in the way he knows how. He pulls my hand away from his cock and pins it down beside my head against the pillows. His tongue sliding up my neck makes me moan and tip my head back to give him better access. His free hand runs roughly up my body to my breast, gently squeezing, his thumb toying with my nipple, making it harder. He kisses me on the mouth and I open mine to him, our tongues gently stroking each other as our passion begins to build again. His kiss trails down my jaw towards the other side of my neck as his hand runs back down my body. Sliding two fingers between the junction of my thighs, he strokes

552

my still sensitive pussy and another little moan escapes me. He captures it with his mouth.

I wrap my legs around his waist, tilting my hips towards him as he withdraws his fingers from me to grab his cock, pressing it to my entrance. He then pushes into me slowly, inch by inch as he kisses and licks my neck, keeping my arousal climbing. When he lets go of my wrist, I run both of my hands up his smooth, hot shoulders, to the muscles working in his rippling back. The thought of him claiming me, the way that turns me on, outweighs the initial discomfort of his considerable manhood slowly impaling me. I raise my hips to coax him deeper, and I bite my lip as he gives me what I'm asking for. The sharp feeling of him filling me makes me whimper, and I'm only slightly aware of his groan as he takes me for the first time.

I lift my head to capture his mouth with mine, kissing him for a moment before I gently nip his lower lip, giving it a little suck. He thrusts into me a little harder for that, making me release him as I gasp at another stab of sharpness. I don't know if it was meant as a punishment or a reward. Or if it's because it spurned him on. But every thrust, he goes a bit deeper now, until he's sheathed inside me to the hilt.

As Dean pumps inside me slow and steady, he's no longer kissing my neck, but watching my eyes, my face. My reaction to him being inside me. "You're fucking *mine* now, Vanna." He growls above me, his rough hand digging into the flesh of my leg that I have wrapped around him as he slides it lower, pushing against the mattress to grip my ass. "You belong to me." He fucks me harder to drive home his point, harder and faster forcing me to gasp and moan beneath him. The little bit of pain transforms to intense pleasure as I swirl my hips in time with his thrusts, squeezing and fucking him back. He grabs my arms and pins my hands back down to the mattress, driving into me harder still. "*Tell me*, say the words for me, baby." He urges.

"Yes, I'm yours..." I gasp, as he pounds me faster, "All yours!"

He suddenly releases me, curling his arms under me and rolls over to his back, pulling me with him so that now I'm on top of him. I sit up, my hands against his chest to push myself upright, adjusting to our new position of me riding his cock now.

"I belong to you too, Vanna. You fucking own me." He says, looking up at me as if I'm the sexiest thing he's ever seen in his life. I start to ride him slowly at first, getting used to the feel of him inside me in this position. He reaches up to touch my body as I rock on him and slowly move up and down, his hands holding my breasts. "You're fucking gorgeous. If I wasn't wearing a rubber, you'd have already made me come." He runs his hands back down my sides to my hips, then slides them back to grip my ass, pulling me forward as he thrusts his hips upward.

I start to ride him a little faster, swerving my hips to give us both another sensation, watching him as he leans his head back and bites his lip this time. I can see in his eyes, that he wants me to fuck him the way I was grinding on him at the beach that night. I must have really made a lasting impression. Smiling down at him I tell him to give me his hands, he does so immediately, and I grip them palm to palm, our fingers interlocking. I roll my body and writhe like a snake on his cock, using his hands for support so I can fuck on him rigorously and mercilessly.

Within moments he's grunting and groaning and the sound of his pleasure drives me higher. I tug his hands back, pulling him to come to me. He sits up instantly, releasing my hands to wrap his arms around my back so that we're face to face. I wrap my arms around his neck and kiss him, parting my lips to meet his tongue with mine as I continue to fuck him. He grabs my hair and pulls my head back to kiss my neck roughly. I feel him bite me and suck, marking me like he did once before. His leather jacket protected him from my claw marks last time he did this. Tonight, there's no armor.

The pressure is building inside me quickly again as he forces my mouth to his, kissing me deeply and passionately before he pulls my head back by my hair roughly once more. Dean marks the opposite side of my neck. The sensation, the balls of that move push me further to the edge. It isn't long before I begin to gasp and whimper, he grabs me again and slams me down on my back against the mattress, driving his cock deep and hard, pumping me with everything he's got. My back arches beyond my control, my head thrown back over the side of the bed as I cry out. My climax shatters my existence for the third time this night. Convulsing and pulsating around him, nails digging into the back of his shoulders, I feel him tense and thrust into me twice more as he groans, losing himself inside of me as well.

"*Fuck!* Vanna! *Fuck!*" Dean grunts loudly, burying his face in the crook of my neck, gently biting my shoulder as he shudders from his strong release. He wraps his arms around me as his body finally rests.

We lie together for a few moments, our bodies still entwined, catching our breath in the after math of our first official coupling. After a moment or so, he withdraws himself and rolls off me, pulling me toward him like a rag doll. I laugh tiredly as I lay my cheek against his damp chest now, his arm tucking me against him, his fingers lightly stroking my back.

"Are you alright?" He asks, his voice sounds like he's drowsy too. I'm not surprised. He really made an effort tonight.

"Mmhmm." I mumble tiredly, letting my eyes close. "Are you?"

"*Fuckin' Aces, baby.*" He sighs, bringing my hand up to his lips to press a kiss against my fingers, before he places it on his chest.

I feel him move slightly and assume he just got rid of the condom. Probably threw it on the floor, too. I laugh to myself. He's too tired to give a shit right now. I don't blame him.

"Alexa... turn off." He says, and Ed Sheeran's *Make it Rain,* is silenced.

"I will never hear that song and not think of tonight." I sigh.

"*Exactly.*" Though tired himself, I can hear the smile in his voice.

I cuddle closer against him, his arm curling tighter around me as I yawn, already falling asleep to the sound of his strong and steady, heartbeat.

DEAN

MY HAND REACHES OUT IN THE NIGHT, SEEKING VANNA. SHE MUST HAVE rolled away from me in her sleep. The cool, smooth comforter where Vanna *should be*, jolts me awake. I'm alone... *She left me?* Sitting up abruptly, I glance around the room. She's not in here. She's not in the dark bathroom either. The digital clock on my night table reads two am. Been sleeping solidly for hours. I haven't slept like this in ages. As my heart pounds in rising panic at the thought of Vanna just up and leaving me in the middle of the night, I jump out of the bed.

Clothes are still scattered about on the floor. Among them, a bra. Her leather boots...

Thank fuck!

I'm not too fucking proud to worry about my performance with her. Though she did seem satisfied before we both fell into an apparent coma. Hell, she was more than satisfied. I've got the claw marks on my body to confirm that.

Nearly six fucking months. I've never worked harder to win over a woman in my life. But damn, she is worth it. My dick's hard again just thinking about what we did last night. Waiting though, waiting was the right thing to do. I had to be sure she's in love with me, too. I knew all along, once I had her, I'd never be able to let her go.

I find Vanna in the kitchen, in the dark. The light emanating from the fridge is silhouetting her form before it. She's wearing my t-shirt. *Only* my t-shirt. Tight across those ample, gorgeous tits. Her hot, round ass, peeking out the bottom. That long, flowing dark hair damn near reaching the bottom of the shirt as well. Wild and *just fucked* looking. I stand on the other side of the kitchen island, silently watching her as she removes a bottle of water and quietly twists off the cap to take a sip. I think it's adorable, the way she replaces the cap and carefully closes the fridge. As if I could hear these faint sounds from my bedroom and she doesn't want to wake me.

"I thought you ran out on me." I say, my voice cutting through the silence in the room, startling her.

She jumps and lets out the slightest little shriek, dropping that bottle of water on the kitchen floor as she spins to face me. I don't laugh, but I can't not grin. She lets out an exasperated little huff at me, and even in the dark kitchen, the only light now coming from the floodlight outside in my driveway, I can see her little scowl.

"*Dean!* You scared me." She whispers sternly.

555

"Why are you whispering? It's just us here." I tease her. She giggles, ducking down behind the kitchen island to retrieve her water. Damn island obstructing my view. "And who said you could wear my shirt? Take it off, this instant." I joke.

She smiles, biting into that bottom lip. "I couldn't find mine. I didn't want to turn on a light and wake you. I know it's been a while, but I thought guys were into the whole *conquered fortress* thing. Seeing the woman you just slept with, wearing your shirt. Is that not a thing anymore?" She asks, her fingers playing with the hem of it.

"Oh, it's a thing." I assure her, silently hoping she lifts the front of it just a little more...

She giggles again. "Are you thirsty?" She tosses the bottle of water at me before I even respond, but I catch it and take a nice, long swig of it. Fuck. Guess I am. I cap it and slide it back to her across the marble.

"For a moment, I thought you left."

"I didn't." She says, awkwardly stepping closer to the kitchen island as if trying to hide her naked lower body from me now. That just won't do. I know she's got self-esteem issues that run deep. If not for her past with Jack, I'd wonder how this could even be possible. She's exquisite. And it's my honor, duty and pleasure, to help her rid herself of these insecurities.

"Scared me." I admit.

She stares at me for a moment, her fingers absentmindedly touching the water bottle sitting on top of the island before her. "I'm sorry. I wouldn't just up and leave like that."

"Not from my bed. And not from my life." I want to hear her promise.

"No." She sighs, turning to face me head on as I walk around the side of the island to her. I touch her face, holding her cheek. I watch as her eyes drop to the bandage at my wrist. She shifts on her feet and looks up at me guiltily. "I can't believe I did that to you."

"*Worth it.* Thought about rubbing ink in them and making them permanent." I tease her. Her eyes widen in surprise at first, then her perfect brows pull together in confusion. "I'm just kidding, doll." Mostly, anyway. "Was it good for you?"

She bites her lip again and looks at me in that way that stokes my fire and makes my balls fuckin' ache again. No words, just a slow, sultry little nod. *Thank fuck.*

"I'm glad I was your first, at least in that aspect." I confess.

"The other, too." She nearly whispers.

Say what? My expression must be giving away my surprised confusion, because she elaborates.

"You were very caring with me... *Giving...* I've never had more than... well, he never..." She stammers.

Jesus fuck... Jack is the scum of the earth! I can feel my jaw pop as she tries to find the words she's attempting to say.

"He just wasn't too concerned with..." She stops talking when her eyes tip back up to my face. I must look as pissed as I am. "Sorry." She quickly says.

"You don't have shit to be sorry for." I growl, my words coming out far more harshly than I intended them to. She shrinks slightly from my palpable hostility, though it's only meant for Jack. Her arms move to circle her abdomen, *in that fucking way*... "I'm sorry, Vanna."

She shakes her head. "You don't have anything to be sorry for, either." She says. "I shouldn't have said anything about him."

"No... you need to express yourself." I encourage her. "God knows... Fuck, *I know*, that you've kept shit bottled up for far too damn long." She only nods without speaking. I drop my hand from her face to place both of my hands on her arms that she has clutched around herself. "Come on baby, you're safe with me. Always. No need for this." I say, softly now.

She glances down at my hands on her arms, staring at them for a few moments. She loosens her grip on herself, allowing me to pull her towards me and wrap her arms around my waist instead. I stroke her long hair and hold her close as she rests her face against my chest.

"He... he used to... punch me there." She whispers.

My heart fuckin' lurches in my chest and my whole body tenses as her words hit me. My blood pumps hotter as I listen to her.

"He would push my back up against the wall... and tell me to put my arms out, palms against the wall...or I'd get hit in the face." Her whispered voice is shaky, but she's speaking. She needs to get this shit out of her. She needs to tell me all the reasons this motherfucker is going to die... "I don't think you'd ever hit me, Dean."

I have to clear my throat before I can attempt to respond to her. "*Never*, Vanna. I will *never* lay a finger on you in anger." It's an easy vow to make. "And I'll fuckin' kill anyone that even tries to threaten you with harm." That one's easy, too.

"I know." She sighs. I truly hope she does. "I'm not afraid of you. Before we... when I hesitated... I wasn't exactly thinking of Jack..." He's the last thing I want her thinking about when she's in my goddamned bed... But I fucking get it. I keep my trap shut as I continue to listen. "Lucinda said you liked it *rough*..." she hesitates.

I try not to crack my own teeth, forcing myself to relax my jaw so I can speak. "Baby, Lucinda said that to get in your head... she read the file... she was trying to trigger you."

Vanna moves in my arms to lean slightly back and look up at me. "I know. I see that now. But, was she...?"

"Lying about that too?" I ask. She lifts her shoulder in a little shrug. "I like whatever you like. I'll do whatever you want to do." I say, before it suddenly occurs to me that maybe there *was* something that I did, that she didn't like. It would be just like Vanna not to fucking say anything about it, God damn it! I reach up to hold onto her arms gently. "Vanna... did I do something wrong? Something you didn't like?"

"Oh, no." She says, seemingly surprised that I even asked.

I let out a sigh of relief. "Fuck... You need to tell me if that happens. Better yet, let me know ahead of time if there's anything you don't ever want-"

"Don't ever tell me to beg."

My heart sinks at her words. The broken wine glasses... The night she ran out on me. "Jesus fuck, Vanna... *I'm sorry.*"

She shakes her head, reaching up to touch my lips. "Stop... I know. You've been nothing but good to me, Dean. And I haven't helped you navigate any of this at all."

Well, that's certainly true, but... "You've got a lot of tells, doll. I should have known better." I sigh.

Her eyes suddenly look sad as fuck. "*People can tell?*" She whispers, as if she's horrified.

"*No.* Fuck... *No.* Not *people.*" I shake my head. "*Me. I* could tell, only that there was something in your past. Something bad. Just, little tells here and there, that clued me in over time. And I *never* said a fuckin' word to anyone about any of it." I swear. "You are safe with me, Vanna. In every fucking way."

She does that other thing she does, now. That thing with her left hand at the base of her throat. Sometimes she does it absentmindedly. Simply touching. Other times, it's as if she wants to dig through her own skin.

"What is this about?" I ask, cocking my chin at her. She seems confused for a split second, which tells me she doesn't even realize she's doing it this time.

"Oh." She says, that forced flittering laugh she does when she's about to avoid something.

God, please don't let her back track on me. She's been so fucking real with me... Vanna, don't go backwards, baby... please...

Her eyes soften when they meet mine again, finding mine searching. Caring. Full of love. Because I *am,* and so they *have* to be.

"It's stupid, really. A forced habit." She tries to make light of this. I keep quiet and hope. "He had this thing... this, *requirement,*" she says the fucking word with a hint of dark laughter about it. A fucking *requirement! What the fuck?* ... "We were engaged... and... people had to *know* that. It was so *embarrassing* to have to *announce it* every time... Thank God he thought it tacky as well. Anyway, I had to make sure his ring was noticed." She hesitates, swallowing hard. "I had to make *very sure.*" When her voice nearly cracks, so does my fucking heart. She takes a moment and clears her throat before she continues. "Anyway, I tried to be subtle about it, at least." She says, bringing her left hand back up to the base of her throat and taps her bare ring finger against her skin... *Making sure I notice.*

I don't think there's anyone I've ever wanted to hurt more, than Jack fuckin' Nero.

"This why you don't want to wear my patch?" I ask, though that answer is obvious now. Jack made her feel like property. His property. To use and abuse however and whenever he wanted.

"I never knew bikers before you. All of this MC stuff was completely out of my realm." She says. "I just didn't see the positive aspects of the whole patch thing at first."

"Because of the *Property Of* shit." I sigh. "I get it. I'll never ask you to wear it again."

Her brows furrow suddenly. "*No.*" She protests.

"*No?* Are you saying you'd consider it?" I ask, surprised. Fuck, she doesn't even know I'm patching back into the MC yet... As fucking president at that. I need to tell her. I don't want to keep any secrets from her, anymore.

"Well, you said you're not a Savior anymore, so I suppose it's a moot point." She kind of chuckles.

"Yeah... about that..." I say, reaching up to smooth back my hair. "We should talk."

"Do we have to?" She asks, her hand drifting down to touch one of my bandaged wrists, picking at it gently. She glances up at me, and maybe I'm fuckin' crazy, but I think that was a *look*. Like, a *look*, look. She slides her fingers from my wrist down to my hand to hold it in hers. I watch as she lifts it to her face, pressing the pad of my thumb to her lips before she touches the tip of her tongue to it, then gently nips me.

Fuck yeah. That was a look, *look.*

"You don't want to talk anymore... what do you want to do?" I ask.

She smirks at me. "Well, you said we had a lot of time to make up for... and look forward to."

"Almost six fuckin' months is a hell of a dry spell."

"Try three *years*." She playfully scowls at me.

"I'm down for rectifying this indefinitely." I grin at her. I'd have gone with *forever*, but I don't want to scare her away with my crazy just yet. She can suspect it, but she can't *know* it. Not yet.

She giggles. "Yeah you say that now." She lets go of my hand and starts to back away from me.

"What would you have me say?" I ask, moving in her direction.

"I thought we were done talking?" She inches her way towards the hall that will lead us back to my bedroom.

"We can be." I say, noticing her pebbled nipples pressing against the fabric of my t-shirt. "You look real fuckin' good in my shirt, doll."

"This shirt?" She teases me, gripping them hem of it and lifting the front of it slightly, only for a moment. Flashing me with what I want to see up close and personal again.

A growl rises up my throat as my fist finds my rock-hard cock again. "Oh, Kitten... you shouldn't tease a wolf."

She lifts her finger to her lips and shushes me. "No more talking." She whispers.

I can't help but grin at her as I stalk her back to the bedroom, watching her turn her back on me and strip off my t-shirt, dropping it on the floor. There are better things I can do with my mouth right now. And the sight of her laying back on my bed, her dark hair fanned out against the comforter. Her body sprawled out waiting for me...inviting me back into her. Those dark hooded almond eyes, giving me that fucking *look*... I'm goddamned speechless anyhow.

Chapter
twenty-six
DEAN

T HERE ISN'T A RECENT STRETCH OF TIME IN MY LIFE WHERE I'VE FELT contentment and happiness, to the degree I've experienced these last few weeks. Since our heart-to-heart, Vanna and I have been spending a lot of time together, falling into a regular routine that seems to have us both feeling lighter. Hopeful of our futures together. Returning to her every night, waking up with her every morning, whether that be at my house or hers, has brought me a sense of peace I previously believed to be unattainable in my wretched life. The restlessness in my soul is calmed when she's in my arms, and I'm home when I'm inside her. Making love to her is like a temporary exorcism of my demons, every time. Losing myself in her, is more freeing than any fight I've ever fought. Any bike I've ever ridden. Any substance I've ever abused, in the pursuit of inner peace.

The little bits of her dark past she's revealed to me, seem to have unburdened her own soul a bit, as well. There's a little ember of light in her eyes now, that wasn't there before, since she let me in on the circumstances surrounding her situation. Since we burned that cursed box together. There are moments when I look in her eyes and can see that she believes I truly love her, with every fiber of my being. Over time, I'll have her believing it whole heartedly. I'm aware we have work to do, and that damage takes time to heal. But I'm all in. And now that I have her, I'm never letting go.

I talked her into a romantic weekend getaway, with no cage fighting. No Viking. No club business. Just the two of us, holed up in my little rustic mountain cabin, six hours away in the smokies. While there, I presented her with the steel pentacle that I welded out of motorcycle frame bars within a tire rim. A representation of our two seemingly separate worlds, melding together, into something both beautiful and strong. She loved it, as well as the cabin. Making me promise to bring her back again to see the snow in the winter. She had me mount the pentacle above the stone fireplace, so that we would have to come back and get it. No excuses, she said. As if I'd deny her anything within my power to give her. Although, I partially suspect her leaving it behind for a while may have had something to do with *exorcising* Lucinda's lingering presence from the cabin. Vanna, leaving behind a little representation of herself. Laying her claim. It's cute, really. Though we did a lot of laying our claims that weekend, having barely left the little one-bedroom cabin at all. Only prying ourselves apart long enough to occasionally satisfy our other ravenous appetites we worked up together.

There are still a few specifics I have to come clean to her about, and I will. I have every intention of being completely open with Vanna about every aspect of my life, both past and present, as time and circumstances permit. As situations are dealt with. Like I'm doing this evening. Right now, as I pull Serene into the lot behind Stogies.

Shutting her down and removing my helmet to place on her handle bar, I dismount her and head for the back door of the establishment. Finding it unlocked, as Viper said it would be, I let myself in.

When I threw Preacher out of the original Saviors MC clubhouse a few years ago, he set up Church in a back room of the cigar shop he owns in town. I'm standing outside the closed double doors to that little conference room in Stogies, now. My back against the wall. Listening to his astounded outrage at the unanimous vote, to not only remove him as president, but to strip him of his voting rights within the MC.

I wasn't expecting unanimous. It seems that Maverick and Kruger have seen the light. Though, I'll have to make that determination officially, myself. For now, Preacher's powerless outrage brings a slight smile to my face, as I light up the CAO Maduro I snagged from the walk-in Humidor. I would have liked to have been able to see his face.

The MC makes quick work of voting Viper into the President's seat to re-place Preacher. Viper then proceeds to call the votes to replace Maverick and Kruger as Secretary and Treasurer with Chopper and Diesel. That goes smoothly as well with no objections, besides Preacher's incessant bitching from somewhere within the room. I smile to myself, knowing Viper let him keep his cut. Preacher's still a member of the MC.

I listen to the hum drum of the official take-over of accounts underway. Maverick, the former Treasurer, doesn't put up a fight and signs everything over to Diesel without a word of protest. From what I can hear, Diesel is none too pleased with the state of the coffers. I expected that, though. Preacher's mismanaged this MC for years. I don't care what he did with the money. But he had to go through Maverick to get it, which is why I'm not too keen on allowing him to remain a voting member either, if I let him remain at all.

As Viper announces that there is another order of business tonight, the double doors swing open and Axel is standing before me with a big smile on his face. He steps aside as I enter the room, and I glance around the packed table of cut wearing bikers. My eyes land on Preacher, to my left, sitting at the end of the long table, among the patch wearing members who haven't earned the right to vote yet.

I can't help but grin at him, as his initially shocked expression upon seeing me, slides into one of immense displeasure. He has to know what's coming. I take a final puff off the Maduro I jacked from his shop, as I step towards him through the cloud of blue cigar smoke. Leaning over Preacher, I extinguish the cigar in the ashtray on the table in front of him.

"Oh, how the mighty have fallen." I smile in his glaring face. For once, Preacher's got nothing to preach about. I shift my focus to Viper and Viking at the head of the table, as I straighten and stand waiting for the rest of the take-over to commence.

"All in favor of the Saviors MC reinstating the full membership of one, Dean Keegan, say aye." Viper calls out to the table of Brothers.

As the ayes raise around the room, I watch Axel make his way over to Viking, who then hands him that familiar scrap of leather I haven't worn in over three years. With a beaming smile on his young face, Axel walks back towards me, my old cut held in his hands. I'm glad it will be Axel that passes it back to me. Probably means more to him, than anyone else in the room.

"The ayes have it, unanimously. Dean Keegan is hereby reinstated, with full voting rights." Viper announces, slamming the gavel once. "Welcome back, Brother." He gives me a slight chin lift, with an even slighter smile, but it's there. Viper's all business. I honestly wouldn't be upset if he wanted to keep the gavel for himself.

Axel opens the leather cut, holding it up for me to slip on over my leather jacket, as the rest of our Brothers pound their fists on the carved wood table and shout their congratulatory remarks. Preacher won't even look at me. Even with his head down, I can see him fuming.

Adjusting the cut on my shoulders, I turn to Axel and give him a quick brotherly hug, before he resumes his seat at the table. I remain standing beside Preacher, my hands folded in front of me as I wait for Viper to initiate the next phase.

"Would you like to do the honors?" Viper asks me with a slight grin.

"Your call, Prez." I say with a shrug. He seems surprised.

Before Vanna, I would have insisted upon carrying out my revenge on Preacher, myself. I find that with the contentment she's brought to my life, my resentment of the man, doesn't run as deeply as it once did. The axe drops regardless, tonight. The hand that drops it doesn't really matter to me all that much, any more. As long as it gets done.

Viking leans over to say something in Viper's ear, but I'm not close enough to hear what it is. As Viper nods in agreement with whatever he said, Viking sits back in his chair, his expression seemingly unamused with my lack of eagerness to exact my revenge on Preacher.

I just give him a subtle, passive shrug.

"Dean Keegan as President of the MC. Yay or Nay." Viper says. "Yay." He adds, the first to announce his vote. I find my eyes sliding back to Preacher, who's shaking his head as my MC Brothers cast their votes one by one.

Unanimously, once again, in my favor. Viper stands up from the seat at the head of the table, slamming the gavel one last time before he places it on the table.

Stepping behind Preacher, I place my hands on his shoulders, and lean closer to his ear. "Gonna need this fuckin' cut you got on, *to come off.* One way or another." I say to him, slapping the sides of his upper shoulders, before I step away from him and walk over to Viper.

We clasp hands and pull each other in for a quick shoulder hug, before I turn to face the men gathered around the long table. One by one, I meet each of their eyes, receiving a mixture of head nods and chin lifts in acknowledgement. I look at Preacher last. He's glaring at the center of the table, at the carved skull and wings.

"Preacher. You have the option to quit the MC and walk away, or be voted out." I say to him. "Either way, works for me. Either way, you leave the cut behind. And you black out your ink."

He pushes himself back from the table and slowly stands up, then turns his head to look at me. "I've worn this cut for thirty-five years." He gravely states.

I nod. "One of the reasons why I don't understand you throwing in the with the Chrome Demons MC." I say. "But you turned the clubs back on the original mission long before they rode into town. Why is that?"

His only reply is a sinister smile. A *go fuck yourself*, grin.

Back in the day, I would have gotten the information out of him, one way or another. But in the grand scheme of things, it doesn't matter anymore. What's done is done. The past is in the past. We can rebuild what once was, again. Perhaps even bigger and better than before.

"Take off the cut." I say, after a moment more of his silence.

"You have no idea what you're walking into." Preacher says, as he slowly removes his cut and places it down on the table in front of him. He turns his head back towards me, glaring darkly. "I tried to run several of you off, for your own damn sakes. Some of you aren't cut out for this... *I'm* not cut out for this..." He stares back down at his cut, shaking his head, the angry look on his face is gone now. "It's not worth it."

"What am I walking into, Preacher? What are some of us not cut out for?"

Preacher shakes his head at me again, as if he's disgusted. But I can't tell if it's with me, or himself, for whatever reason that may be. "I'm out." He says, gesturing to his cut on the table. "You're on your own. All of you. This is still my building. So, see yourselves out, immediately."

I hadn't planned on conducting any further business inside his establishment anyway. I cock my chin at Chopper and gesture for him to grab Preacher's cut. Lifting the gavel, I slam it down once and inform the remaining members of the MC that the meeting is adjourned until tomorrow night, where we will pick up where we left off at The Saviors MC's original clubhouse.

As I leave out the back with Viking, I tell them to hit up Axel, Viper, Chopper, Diesel and Snowy and have them, *and only them*, meet us back at the clubhouse.

"That shit was weird as fuck." Viking says to me, as we mount our bikes.

I strap on my helmet and look back at him. "Sure was. Got a bad feeling about all this now." I admit.

As Viking sends out a group text to our known loyal Brothers, I shoot one to Vanna.

'Gonna be late, baby. Don't wait up. I'm sorry.'

I let out another sigh as I hit send. "All I wanted to do tonight, was get through this one meeting and go home to Vanna." I bitch.

"I'm sure she'll still be there when you get back." Viking grumbles.

Yeah, she will be. I smile to myself.

An hour later, I'm glancing around the table at my MC Brothers.

"Dearly beloved, we are gathered here today..." I sarcastically begin, as my Brothers chuckle around the table in what is no longer our secret meeting room. It's our newly re-established Church at The Saviors' club-house. Though currently, bare bones at the moment. Nothing more than a spare empty room across from the gym. "We need to discuss the *sus-as-fuck* behavior, that went down with Preacher, at Stogies tonight." I continue, to a group of nodding heads and grumbles of agreement. "Maverick, Kruger, any and all prospects... Are *not* to be trusted. Not yet." I say, hard eyeing everyone at the table. "I don't want them involved to any meaningful degree, in any of our business dealings, including the fundraiser next week." I shift my focus to Axel and Chopper. "When you two make the rounds and collect the cash from the vendors, that money needs to be put into the safe I'll have in here, in a few days."

"You think the event is going to get hit?" Viking asks.

"Better safe than sorry. I don't know what else the Demons are planning... But it's something significant for Preacher to have acted so out of character. They're not our friends. I never thought they were. There's no way we're going to be able to intermingle with that type of MC. They're outlaws. We're not. Not anymore, anyway. Not for a while."

The Saviors MC... We've always been a group of rough necks, from different walks of life, with three things in common that united us. One, a love of freedom and motorcycles. Two, we've all got sins to repent for. Some worse than others. And three, we all believe in the original mission my uncle started. Whether it be due to a deep-rooted need to protect the innocent, or a way to earn our own redemptions for what we regret doing in our pasts... Perhaps, a little bit of both. But we're the good guys, now. And no one is going to infiltrate our town and muscle us out. It's not happening. For thirty-five years, The Saviors MC has been a staple in this little town, in this county. It's a safer place because of us. And it's going to stay that way.

"After what happened with the Demons at my Patch party, do you think they're going to try to show up to the fundraiser rally?" Axel asks, sitting a few seats down on the right of the table between Chopper and Diesel. He looks small compared to the two large burly bikers. But he's got his chin up, his eyes focused and his head in the game, all the same. "Maybe not even to start trouble. Just to rep their presence the way they did at the bonfire. Intimidate the citizens, maybe even our vendors."

I nod. "After ousting Preacher tonight... I wouldn't rule it out. Legion isn't going to be happy about his puppet's strings being cut tonight."

"How do you want to play it?" Viking asks.

"I think we need to be real clear, that they aren't welcome in this county, let alone our little town." I say matter-of-factly. "I don't trust our prospects. Not right now. They came in under Preacher, who's clearly been compromised for a while. So as Sergeant at arms, if you need to hire outside security to keep this event safe and running smoothly, do it."

"Preacher wiped the coffers out." Diesel says, turning the laptop he took from Maverick to show me the empty account. Viper and Axel made sure to clear out that room at Stogies before they left, reclaiming all the Saviors property Preacher had in his conference room. "Ain't gonna be able to pay for additional security with seventeen dollars and seventy-six cents." Diesel scoffs.

"Get me quotes. I'll see what I can come up with." I say, glancing at Viking. "Guess it's a good thing I made it to the thirteenth round in Myrtle Beach." I grin at him. "This is probably going to lighten my wallet by at least six grand."

"You can reimburse yourself with the money we raise from the event." Diesel says. "That's perfectly legal. Just get the receipts so I can keep a record of it and make the proper deductions." He turns the laptop back to face himself, and grimaces for a moment, reaching a hand up to grip the wiry beard on his chin. "I know we've got full access to the account now, and I changed the login passwords. But I'd feel better closing this account out and starting a new one. I just don't trust Preacher not to go down to the bank in person at some point. Maybe even Maverick. Something is up with them. Just to throw a wrench into things outta spite."

"I'll go with you tomorrow. Far as I know I'm still down as Vice President on the account. They can't remove me without my signature. At the very least I can freeze it, and we can open a new one." Viper says.

"So, what do we do about the members and prospects in question?" Chopper asks.

"As far as I'm concerned, they're hang arounds at this point. No access to this building beyond the Twisted Throttle. And I think we're going to have to invest in a little recon time on them. See what they're up to when they're not kissing Saviors' ass. Gonna have to test them too, see what they're willing to do on the spot. I'll leave that up to you guys. The hazing process was never my thing." I joke, glancing at Viking, who is a fucking expert on making others' lives miserable for his own entertainment. "I can get Jason to run background checks for us, too. Weed out a few of them quickly that way, also." I look to Chopper, "Get me a list of names and information so I can make that happen asap." He nods in agreement.

"What time should I contact the others for the meeting tomorrow?" Viper asks.

I look back at Chopper. "How long you think it's gonna take you to get the info on the prospects?"

"I'm on it now." He says, pulling out his cellphone and texting. "Gonna let them know if I don't hear back from them within the hour, they can consider themselves out on their asses." He chuckles. "That ought to light a fire under the ones who are serious about joining."

"Let's set the meeting for eight pm tomorrow night. That'll give Jason time to get back to me with anything he might find." I say to Viper. "Tomorrow's meeting will just be a laying down of laws and policies. There will be no talk of the CDMC, nor will there be any talk of getting our original mission back up off the ground. I don't even want to consider approaching the organizations Preacher may have burned bridges with, until we get everything sorted out. The money we raise will stay in the safe, until it's time for us to reach out and reestablish relationships. Until we know who we can trust, I don't want anyone saying much to any of them about anything." The Brothers all agree. "For now, it looks like the Saviors MC, is just us."

"Seven Brothers against the world." Axel smiles, looking around the table at everyone with excitement and pride.

I can't help chuckling at his remark. "Seven against Legion's *legion*... plus possible false Saviors." I shake my head, unable to stop grinning at Axel's optimistic nature.

"Look at us." Axel smiles, gesturing with his arms out to our Brothers. "We've got quality over their quantity, Dean. We've got this."

"Where do we stand on dues?" Diesel speaks up. "The Saviors are tapped the fuck out thanks to Preacher and Maverick. We're gonna need money to open an account tomorrow to start filling the coffers."

I reach into my jacket to remove my wallet and finger through some cash. "I've got six hundred on me now. You can take it to the bank, get things rolling with that." I say, removing the bills and folding them over to toss towards Diesel down the table. Axel picks the money up to hand it to him.

"I got a hundred fifty, myself." Axel says, reaching into his pocket, then handing the cash to Diesel as well.

"Put me down for five hundred." Viking says, doing the same.

Viper kicks in another six hundred. Snowy, three hundred and fifty. Chopper, four twenty-five. And Diesel, a whopping grand, himself.

"That puts us at three thousand, six hundred and twenty-five, bucks." Diesel says, organizing all the cash together as he folds it up and tucks it into the inner pocket of his cut. "We need to see who's willing to cough up what as a show of good faith at tomorrow's meeting, and then what we want the monthly dues to be moving forward."

"Agreed." I say. "Is there anything else any of you want to bring up tonight, that won't be discussed tomorrow?" I ask, eager to slam the gavel and wrap up this meeting. It's getting late and I'm eager to be with Vanna.

"Can I make this room look more like Church?" Axel asks, glancing around the room. I can tell he's been thinking about this for a long time and has some kind of a vision already in mind. I can't help chuckling.

"Knock yourself out, kid." I smile at him. "We're going to need to bring in a few extra seats along the wall in here for the members in question. We'll figure out a more permanent arrangement soon." I look down at the long wooden table with our logo carved into the center of it. The skull with the angel wings. "I think this table will look nice mounted to the wall."

"The fuck we gonna sit at?" Viking asks.

"Eventually, a round table." I reply. "I told you all, when we get things settled with this MC, I don't want to be the King."

CROUCHING DOWN IN MY CLOAK BEFORE THE FIRE I MADE IN MY LITTLE stone pit at the edge of my back patio, I lay a small mirror flat beside it. On top of the mirror, I place the black tourmaline bracelet I made for Dean tonight, setting the dressed candle in the center of it. Lighting the stick of frankincense incense in the fire, I use it's end to light the dressed candle, and stick the incense into the dirt beside it. With the large thorn of a black hawthorn tree, I prick my finger and let a drop of blood bead at my fingertip before I smear my blood on a few of the little polished stones of the bracelet. Closing my eyes, I let my finger linger against it as I chant the spell for protection...

"*With a shield of pure white light, grant him protection day and night. With my blood this shield will hold, no tragic fate, shall unfold. I craft this spell of moon and fire, enchanting this item with my will and desire. Let no harm come to him and from trouble be free. As I will it, so mote it be. Harm to none, nor return on me.*"

A twig snaps somewhere in the darkness beyond my fire, startling me, but it's bright blaze makes seeing through the dark impossible. I jump to my feet and take a few steps backwards in the direction of my back door.

A dark figure moves out of the shadows as my heart begins to race.

"It's just me, Vanna." Dean's voice says, approaching nearer to the fire. "I didn't mean to scare you." In the glow of the flames, I can see his eyes are wide. "What are you doing?"

"A protection spell." I say, pulling my cloak around me tighter. He hasn't realized I'm not wearing anything else yet.

"Your front door was locked. And you didn't respond to my text. I figured you'd fallen asleep, but then I realized I could smell the fire, and walked back here to check." He explains. "It's late."

"The Witching hour." I reply. "I was up making a protection amulet. I was in the middle of charging it for you."

"For me?" He asks, glancing down at the black and white candle covered in herbs and oils, sitting on top of the little mirror on a stone. He squints to see the bracelet around the base of the candle before he looks back at me.

"Yes. I made you a bracelet. For protection. It's black tourmaline... The most protective stone, but it also goes with your aesthetic."

He cracks a smile at me, clearly amused by that last part. "My *aesthetic*?"

I nod, gesturing to his dark biker attire. "Yeah, it'll go with everything you wear. It looks manly, don't worry. It's a masculine stone." I add for good measure.

"So, you made me a magic bracelet?" I detect humor in his tone.

"Are you mocking me?" I demand, automatically placing my hands on my hips and glaring at him.

His eyes widen instantly again. "Holy shit, are you naked under that?"

Oops.

I watch as his expression changes from shocked surprise, to lustful desire as I swoop a finger down the edge of the opening of my cloak, pulling it open slightly to give him another peek at one of my breasts.

"Fuck me..." His whisper escapes on his breath as he looks at me now with a burning hunger in his eyes.

I smile slyly to myself at his choice of words. *Sex magick* would only add to the power of my spell. It is arguably one of the strongest types of magick, and combined with my blood and his physical presence, it could only help, right? I quickly snatch the bracelet and slip it onto my right wrist before I saunter towards him, pushing the hood of the cloak back and allowing it to billow open as I approach him.

His jaw clenches as his eyes take in my bare curves in the flickering light of the fire. I throw my arms around his neck, his eyes staring into mine as I press my body against his. I feel his warm strong hands slip beneath the cloak across my naked back as he touches me, gently at first. Arousal mixed with slight confusion in his eyes.

"Kiss me." I whisper. His lust over powers whatever apprehension lingers from his confusion, as he takes my mouth feverishly, without hesitation. My hand travels up his neck to the back of his head as I kiss him back with an encouraging moan, before I twist my face from his lips to whisper, "I need you."

"I'm right here, baby." He whispers back, kissing my jaw, making his way to my throat.

"I want you." I say, breathily. "I need you, Dean. Here. *Now*." My hand slides down his chest, moving deliberately and quickly south and I lift my leg to wrap it around his waist. My hand strokes his already stiffening cock beneath his jeans as I make my intentions clear.

He grips my thigh as we sink to the ground together beside the fire. I lay back on my cloak, pulling him on top of me as he frees himself. I attempt to pull his face back to mine and kiss him once more, but it's as if he's fighting against me, one arm holding himself up over me, his hand planted next to my head. His other hand patting down his pants and jacket pockets.

"What are you doing? Take me..." I say, wantonly, throwing my legs up around his waist in an attempt to anchor him to me.

"Fuck, Vanna... let me get a damn wrap on." He says, finally finding his wallet and pulling one out. He tosses his wallet to the side of us and brings the square foil to his mouth, tearing it open impatiently with his teeth. I can't help giggling beneath him, telling him to hurry up as he rushes to roll it down his shaft. "Greedy, demanding little thing tonight." He grins down at me.

Reaching back up to him, my hand cupping his face, I pull him down for a kiss. But as Dean invades my body, he invades my mind as well, thrusting inside me hard against the ground. It's difficult to keep my focus on the intention behind the sex magick ritual. I'm losing focus, thoughts of only Dean fucking me are clouding my intentions. I wrap my arm around his neck and pull him to the side, coaxing him to roll onto his back. He gives me what I want and I mount him, hoping that I can focus better if I'm the one riding him, taking charge.

Reining in my thoughts, I reach for his left hand with my right and clasp it tightly, our fingers intertwined and squeezing as I fuck him hard and fast. His free hand gripping my hip, my free hand pressed against his chest.

"Fuck, Vanna..." He groans, "Slow down a little, you're gonna make me come too soon!"

"Shh!" I shush him, squeezing my eyes shut, trying to focus on the spell as I continue to fuck him without mercy. I move back and forth on him, grinding my clit against him as he's deep inside me, and I can feel the pressure building, spiraling quickly in my core.

"Damn it, baby... ain't gonna be able to las..." He begins to speak again, but I put my hand over his mouth to shut him up, keeping it there as I grind down on him harder, making us both moan. He moves his free hand to rub my clit with the pad of his thumb, making me whimper, pushing me further to the edge.

I start to chant the spell over and over to keep it in the forefront of my mind as best I can as I feel the beginning shocks of my impending orgasm. I can feel him thrusting up beneath me, his mouth now closed tightly, his lips pressed together though my hand is still covering his mouth. He rubs my clit harder and faster, desperate to make me come before his own release.

As my orgasm finally rips through me, I throw my head back and cry out, my body convulsing around him. Barely keeping my wits about me, I pull my hand from his mouth and slide the bracelet from my wrist, over our intertwined fingers, onto his wrist. Dean thrusts his hips up once more as his body tenses beneath me, his hand now digging into my thigh almost painfully, as he expels himself inside me with a grunt and a loud groan.

Panting, spent, he lays flat back against the ground, looking up at me dazed and confused. "What the fuck just happened?" He asks, trying to catch his breath.

I release his hand and lean down to kiss his mouth briefly, before I slowly dismount him, watching him wince slightly as his half hard cock slides out of me. I lay down on my back on top of the cloak beside him and look up at the star filled sky. I have no idea if any of that worked, but it was fun trying. I feel him move beside me, probably removing the condom and putting his dick back in his pants. The sound of his zipper confirms that theory.

"Vanna?" His tone inquisitive, as he props himself up on his elbow to look down at me.

"Supposed to let the candle burn out on its own." I say.

I watch his eyes shift to the candle sitting on the mirror beside the fire, then he looks back down at me. "Did we just do some devil shit?"

I burst out laughing, tears in my eyes, and the breath I had just managed to catch is now lost again as I laugh at his endearing innocence. He cracks a grin as he watches me laugh at him, and I can't resist reaching up to stroke his stubbled jaw line. He takes my hand and kisses it, before he notices blood on my finger.

"Shit, baby. You're bleeding."

"It's fine." I say, coming down from my laughing fit. "I pricked my finger for the spell." I explain. "There's blood on your bracelet, too."

"What the fuck, Vanna?" He asks again, looking at me incredulously once more.

"It's not *devil shit*." I laugh again at those words. "I tried to do a protection spell, and make it stronger with blood and sex magick."

"Oh, is *that* what just happened." He grins.

I bite my lip and nod. "Now we just wait for that candle to either burn down or blow out."

"What do we do while we wait for that?"

"Cuddle and look up at the stars?"

"Works for me." He says, pulling the side of my cloak out and laying on top of it. He grabs the other side and pulls it around my body to cover me a bit more, before he lays back, his body against mine, looking up at the night sky. He tucks his right arm behind his head and lifts his left wrist to inspect the bracelet.

"Do you like it?" I ask.

"You made it?"

"Yeah."

"Then I love it. For *oh* so many reasons." He says, his tone playful.

"What reasons?"

"You made it, for starters." He smiles. "And gave it to me in the fucking *weirdest*, hottest way imaginable."

This time, we both laugh.

DEAN

AFTER THE DEVIL SHIT, VANNA RUNS UPSTAIRS TO PUT ON SOME NORMAL clothing, without even looking back at me. I debate with myself whether or not to take off my cut and avoid the inevitable conversation about rejoining The Saviors MC. Must have been too dark outside, or she was too caught up in her witchy shit to notice I was wearing it.

Shaking my head as I think about the weird chain of events tonight, I open her fridge to grab a beer and crack the top off, taking a long, much needed swig. Nico jumps up onto the kitchen island, purring and stretching his head towards me. I hold my fist out to him, which he headbutts in greeting, before I run my hand over his back a few times. It's kind of become our thing. We're cool. He's accepted the fact that I'm going to be around on a permanent basis.

I walk over to her little kitchen table and sit down, exhausted. What a fuckin' day. Lifting my wrist, I examine the spherical black stones of the bracelet she made for me. *For protection*. I can't help smiling, even as I take another swig of beer. It's sweet of her. And her quirky weirdness with this witchy shit only makes her more endearing to me. Even if it was some devil shit we did. It's not like I'm going to get into Heaven when I die. Heaven for me, is being with Vanna. So, if she wants to fuck the Hell out of me, I'm down for it. And I'll worship her until my last breath.

"See, it suits you." She smiles from the kitchen doorway, leaning her head against the door jamb. She's wearing a long t-shirt with kittens on it, that comes down on her body mid-thigh. Her curvy legs are bare, so are her feet. She looks cute as fuck, as always. But I know damn well she can flip that switch to sexy in a fuckin' millisecond. She's got her long dark hair draped over one shoulder as she runs an oval brush through the ends of it. It only takes her another moment to realize what's different. She straightens, her eyes shift to my cut as she places the brush down on the kitchen counter beside her. "What are you wearing?" She asks, her brows pulling slightly together for a moment, before her eyes meet mine again.

I take another sip of beer before I joke, "Don't worry, I'm not naked underneath."

She takes a few steps further into the kitchen towards me. "That's a Saviors MC vest." She states.

"*Cut*, doll. Not vest." I correct her. Not that I care, but if she's going to be my Ol' Lady...

She stares at it, contemplatively. And I can only wonder what she's thinking. "This is what you couldn't talk about." She says, her eyes tipping back up to meet mine. "You said you haven't been a Savior in years... But that day in the cab ride, in Myrtle Beach, there was something you wanted to talk to me about, but couldn't."

I nod. "MC business. And that was before we worked everything out, you and me. I've been waiting to talk to you about everything. I couldn't until things became official."

"With us? Or them?" She asks.

"Both." I watch her as she pulls out a chair and sits down in front of me, her knees parted, the hem of her long t-shirt riding up her thighs a bit. If it were not for her hands fidgeting with her fingers in her lap, weighing down that bit of fabric, I'd know what color her panties are, or if she's even wearing any at all.

I remind myself that I was just inside her, not even thirty minutes ago, and to get a goddamned handle on my urge to fuck her again. I can never get enough of her. But we need to talk about a few things, *first*, at least. Grabbing my beer, I force myself to stop ogling her and take a few gulps, before I start again. "I was voted in as President, tonight." I say, studying her expressions closely.

"That was fast." I watch her mind work for a few moments, before she goes on to ask me, "Why so fast, though? And why you?"

"I asked them that myself." I heave a weary sigh. There's so much I have to get into with her about this. She smiles at me, a sweet smile as if she wants to reassure me about something. "What?" I ask, fighting her contagious beam.

"It's because you're a natural leader. They look up to you. You have an aura about you that's powerful and trustworthy." She says, as if she's stating facts. "I felt it the night we met. I should have been afraid of you, when you beat up Shane, and had your arms around me seconds later. But I trusted you, without hesitation. I think you're the type of man that inspires other men to want to be better. You lead by example and you're honest."

"You think highly of me." I'm not sure if I agree entirely with her assessment.

She gives me a little shrug. "So, what does this ves... I mean, *cut*, mean for *us*? How come you couldn't tell me this was going to happen?"

I finish off my beer, placing the empty bottle down on the kitchen table, before I lean forward to rest my elbows on my knees, hands hanging down between them, as I look at her. "I wasn't certain you and I were going to get to where we are now." I confess.

She gives me a little smirk and a playful scowl. "You were bluffing me with all that *macho bravado man talk,* about killing any guy who touches me because I belong to you?" She teasingly asks, her words full of skepticism.

I can't help cracking a slight grin. "No, I meant *every* fuckin' word of it. And that shit stands forever, doll." I let her know. She giggles at me. "*I ain't playin',* Vanna." I warn her for good measure. She reins herself in, pressing her lips together, gesturing with a wave of her hand for me to go on. "Anyway, the other reason I couldn't tell you, is because it was sensitive information. Couldn't risk word getting back to Preacher..." I stop talking when she scrunches her brows together again.

"But I don't even know Preacher. Who would I say anything to?"

"You work with patch whores who fuck with too many guys. All it takes is one slip to one girl, who mentions it to the wrong guy. I couldn't risk it. There are rules that apply to my life now, that will affect our relationship to a certain extent." Her eyes look more concerned now, and she shifts in her seat, as if she feels the need to brace for some unpleasant news. She doesn't speak, so I continue. "There are only two ways this can go with us, and it's your choice. But there is no middle ground. I can keep you in the dark about everything MC related. You'd still be my girl, go on rides with me, and to *some* events, but I'd never tell you anything that has to do with the Saviors. Technically, you'd be my unofficial Ol' Lady. But you'd stay an outsider."

She stares at me for a few moments as I let that sink in. "Is that what you want?" She warily asks, almost as if she's afraid I'll say yes.

I reach out to touch her knee gently. "The other option, is I make you my Ol' Lady in an official capacity. There are no secrets between us about anything. I tell you everything. And I, as well as the MC, trust you not to speak of anything with anyone outside of the club. That includes Lady Lays, patch whores, sweetbutts, whatever you want to call the girls that hang around the MC. They're protected to an extent by association with us, but they're not family. You would be considered family, as my Ol' Lady."

"I like that better." She says, though her voice is quiet. "What do you want, though?" She asks, as if she really doesn't know.

"I want whichever option keeps you in my life. It's your choice." I say, letting my hand drift down her leg, sliding it back to rub her calf.

"Why do I feel like you guys aren't just a riding club..." I can hear the apprehension in her voice.

I run my hand through my hair with my other hand before I let it fall back down between my knees. I'm not sure if she's going to like hearing this, but... "Technically, we are. But we're all pretty much reformed one percenters... former outlaws. We all come from much rougher MC's. Old habits die hard, doll. This is how we do things. Tight knit loyalty. Full trust, or none at all." I confess.

"Okay." I barely hear her say. "I don't like the idea of keeping any more secrets from each other. That could snowball into other areas of our relationship."

"I wouldn't let it." I try to assure her. But I can see in her eyes that it still doesn't sit well with her. "For what it's worth, and it's still up to you, I prefer option two. But it means my Brothers would have to vote you in. They have to trust you, too. It's not just about me. Telling you everything, is a risk to their lives also." Something flickers behind her eyes, as if she came to some realization.

"That's why Viking gives me so much shit. He knew you were going to be back in the MC, and he doesn't trust me." She sighs.

"He'll come around. He thought you were a distraction. But I don't want to vote you in just yet, anyhow. Not until a few things are settled first." That only makes her look at me suspiciously.

"What things?" She asks, almost as if she's offended.

"So, we're going with option two?" I ask.

She leans back in her chair and crosses her arms at me. "Well, it's not option one."

I can't help grinning at the little bit of sass she throws my way as I rub her leg again. "The Chrome Demons MC are making a push for our territory. Legion and Preacher have been up to something together for a few months now. We don't know exactly what the Demons are up to, but they're bad news. Bad for this town. And we don't want them in it."

"Legion was nice." Vanna says. Her innocence tugs at my heart.

"He's not nice, baby. And if he ever comes to your shop again, you need to call me immediately." I try to warn her without scaring her. "You just need to stay away from anyone wearing the Demons' cut."

"I don't understand." She sighs.

I'm not sure which part she doesn't understand, but both points deserve further reiteration, so I just go into it. "The Chrome Demons MC were originally nomads from out West. Nevada. Arizona. I crossed paths with them years ago. They were known for pushing drugs, getting girls hooked on drugs and prostituting them out." I give her a moment to absorb that ugly bit of information. I can tell she's trying to keep her expression neutral. "They're dangerous, baby. Legion is a wolf in sheep's clothing. I've never met him prior to showing up here. But the fact that he was already in your shop, is of concern to me." He either wants to fuck her, or fuck me through her.

"How do you know they do those terrible things?" She asks.

Fuck. Full disclosure. That's the deal. "I... I was paid to get a girl away from another MC that had been somewhat associated with them. It was a few years ago. That's how I know. I took her out of that environment." I say, trying to be honest, while giving her as little information as possible. This isn't my story to tell.

"Oh my God..." She whispers. "But wait a minute... you were *paid*?"

I nod. "I used to get hired by different people, for a lot of different things. Mostly through the fighting circuits. Headhunters looking for men with a certain level of skill..." I stop myself before I say too much. "But that's not important right now, baby. What's important, is the present situation. I need you to understand that the Demons, that Legion, *cannot* be trusted... Stay away from them."

"Okay," She agrees.

"It's going to get back to Legion pretty quick that I'm in charge now. Which is one of the reasons I'm not too keen on officially making you my Ol' Lady just yet. It puts an unnecessary target on your back. He might suspect you're more to me than a Lady Lay, but he doesn't know for sure."

"A Lady Lay? Why do you have so many different terms for your groupies?" She asks.

"My uncle started that within our MC. He thought it was more polite than sweetbutt or patch whore." I say. "And we treat them with a little more respect than a lot of other MC's. With the Saviors MC coming together again, you're probably going to notice a few more groupies hanging around the Twisted Throttle as well."

She rolls her eyes. "Great. I'm sure Cherry will be thrilled, too."

"Cherry knows the life, doll. You're the one I have to break in." I smile at her, giving the back of her calf a little pat. That earns me another eye roll, even more dramatic than the first.

"Now you sound like Viking." She sighs. "So how do I get your MC Brothers to trust me?"

"Just support the club. Don't back talk me in front of them. Don't ask questions in front of them. Anything you need to know, I'll tell you in private. Anything you have a problem with, you tell me in private." I explain. "They'll come around by the time I'm ready to claim you at the table."

Her eyes widen at that last part. "*Claim me at the table?* What the hell does *that* mean?"

"I make it clear that you're my Ol' Lady, that I want you to wear my cut. That you're trust worthy and loyal to not only me, but the MC. And they vote on it, making you my woman, officially. It's like a biker version of marriage."

She looks relieved. "I thought this was another public sex thing."

I press my lips tightly together, in a serious effort not to laugh at her. To be fair, I can see why she'd worry about that. The *free love* type of partying she's heard about, that wild biker bashes are almost notorious for. What we did on the picnic table at the bonfire. Yeah, I can see how she might be afraid that I'd *do her* on the conference table in front of everyone. I shake my head, losing the battle against my grin.

"Don't laugh at me." She scowls playfully.

"You laughed at me... *Devil shit.*" I remind her, which only makes her laugh again. When she's through with her giggle fit, she takes a breath and looks back at me, trying to be serious.

"So, one day, I'll have a vest like Cherry does, for Axel."

"A *cut*, babe. But yes. Unless you're dead set against it. I'm not going to force you to do anything you don't want to do, doll. I understand your ... apprehension, now." I say, my eyes shifting to glance through the kitchen doorway, towards the foyer, where she keeps Jack's letters in a box in the closet out there.

She reaches down to touch my wrist, her fingers toying with the tourmaline bracelet she gave me. "Okay."

"Do you have any other questions for me?" I ask.

Her eyes lift back to mine again, a wonderment in them. Her expression is thoughtful. "Why are you called The Saviors?" She asks. "Latisha told me that your club does a lot of Charity work, but she wasn't that specific. I know you have the fund raiser rally next week for domestic violence shelters... but the name of the MC sort of implies there's more to you guys

576

than just raising money... And not to be mean, but, you all kind of have a dangerous vibe about you."

I release her leg and sit back in my seat, not exactly sure how she's going to react to this. "We used to do more than just raise funds for organizations centered around domestic abuse. Up until Preacher took over a few years ago, The Saviors MC took part in rescue missions to get women, and their children at times, out of their abusive environments. We also provided free security at safe houses, and escorted victims to their court appearances, so they'd feel safer testifying against their abusers."

Her eyes drop from mine to stare at the patch on my cut. "You did this, too?"

"I did this, and then some."

Vanna's eyes look back up into mine once more. "What do you mean?"

"I was thrown out of the MC three years ago for taking things further. Some think I took things too far. But I don't." She's staring at me, waiting for me to elaborate. There's something behind her eyes, but I'm not sure what it is yet. "What I'm telling you, Vanna, is privileged information. The rescue missions, the security details. We don't advertise that to the public, for the victims' privacy and safety. We don't talk about it with anyone. *And neither can you.*"

She nods her head, though her voice is still quiet when she says, "I understand." She swallows, before she asks, "What did you do?"

"What I'll continue to do." I sigh, hoping she can accept this dark proclivity within me. "I make them pay, Vanna. I make them pay for their crimes against the innocent. In blood and broken bones. I make them pay, in pain and humiliation. I make them feel afraid. So they can experience a fraction of what these women have gone through at the hands of these pricks who were supposed to care for and protect them." I notice she's gone perfectly still at my words, staring at me, but her normal autopilot mode of fidgeting with her fingers has ceased. "Are you afraid of me now? To know I'm capable of this?" I ask. She doesn't respond. "I've broken a man's arms and legs with a baseball bat and left him on his kitchen floor." I say, staring into her eyes, searching intently for some kind of reaction. Nothing. "I've done shit like that more times than I can even count. Hell, I've done worse." I watch her throat swallow again, but she still remains silent. Only blinks. "But nothing is worse than not doing anything." I mutter. "Sometimes, it takes a monster to take down a monster."

Something softens in her eyes at my words. "You're not a monster."

"I'm fucked in the head, Vanna. I know it, but... They deserve everything I dish out to them. It doesn't keep me up at night to know there's someone I put in agony lying in their own blood somewhere. Most of the time, it's in their own damn homes. Just so I can take that feeling of safety from them as well. Like they did to their women. I feel better about the world when I do it. It brings me a temporary feeling of peace."

"That doesn't make you a monster." She shakes her head.

"What does it make me?" I ask, grabbing my beer and realizing it's empty. I put it back down and run both hands through my hair. "You don't have to answer that... I'm afraid to hear the answer anyway." I confess, leaning back in the chair, hanging my head over the back as I move my hands to press my palms into my eye sockets. I may have said way too much, way too soon to her. What the fuck is wrong with me?

"To these women... a *hero*." She says, after a moment. And the word makes me want to throw up...

Psychopath... Deranged Lunatic... I'd even settle for *Vigilante...* But the last thing I am, is a fuckin' *hero*...

"No, I'm not, Vanna." I sigh, dragging my hands down my face and forcing myself to lean forward and look her in the eyes again. "I'm not a hero. And these women have no idea I've done what I've done. I'm a fucked up, violent, self-righteous asshole, with more issues than I care to delve into with you tonight." I say, getting up from the table and walking back to her fridge to grab another beer. I crack the top off, chucking it onto the counter, before I take another long swig. Glancing over my shoulder, I notice she's staring at the rockers on the back of my cut... The skull with angel wings logo.

"You're wrong." She says. "I used to wish for Jack to love me... But then, when things only got worse, there were nights when I wished for someone to take me away from Jack..." I turn to look at her, and find her staring at the floor now. Left hand lightly against the base of her throat. Fuckin' Jack Nero... He's at the top of my *to do list*. She continues, "Other nights, I wished something would just happen to him so that I could get away. I had to make it happen for myself though. I didn't have a hero... I finally had a witness. Only after he and his buddies couldn't cover for him anymore, was something finally done. And even after everything... after trying to kill me... he got seven years. Parole in five... And I'm doing the time right along with him... Hiding. *Waiting*."

"They never get what they actually deserve." I say, trying to keep my voice steady. Thinking of what she endured with Jack makes my blood boil. "Some of them never do any time. And you're right... the women... the kids... they suffer more than what their abusers ever get through the justice system. The victims suffer more... and for far longer."

She looks up at me again. "Why do you do it?"

"Somebody needs to." I mutter.

"No, Dean. I mean, *why* do *you* do it?" She asks.

I turn away from her again, lifting the beer to my mouth and taking another swig. "You don't know?" I ask. "We've got more in common than you think, doll."

She's silent for a few moments, before a single word escapes her lips....
"Madeline."

"Right... *Madeline*." I say my mother's name on a weary sigh.

"Your father beat your mother in front of you... when you were little?" Her voice sounds distant, tight, as if it might crack.

I just nod, at first. Taking another sip of beer before I add, "That's how it started... when I was old enough to attempt to protect her, he'd beat the shit out of me, too. I couldn't ever do a damn thing to help her. Myself. My younger brother... I was *useless*. Ineffective. Weak."

"I'm sorry, Dean. That's a terrible situation to grow up in." She says softly. "*But you were just a little boy... You can't put all that on yourself.*"

Should I even tell her my story only gets worse? That I'm so deeply fucked up for even darker reasons?

"I understand why you do what you do. And for whatever it's worth, Dean, I love you. I might even love you more."

I shake my head. "No, you understand why I have a violent flame that rages inside me. I carry that curse in my DNA. Fuck, even in my goddamned *name*, which I also share with my father. You know I have to quench that rage with fighting... You don't know *why* I actually *do* what I do, though. And probably won't be able to stop."

"I'm listening, if you want to tell me."

I steel myself as I begin to speak about something I haven't spoken of in its entirety before. But I promised her honesty. That I would show her what she needed to see of me. "My uncle was my mother's older brother. He started the mission in honor of her, after her death. He couldn't save her, either. She wouldn't leave my father. Some women... They just *don't* leave. Even when it seems like they can. They just fuckin' *don't*."

"How old were you when she died?" Vanna asks.

"Old enough to know better." I sigh.

"What do you mean?"

Fuck. Here it goes... I close my eyes and just let the words come out. "The day before my parents were killed, I saw my uncle doing something with my dad's motorcycle. I didn't think anything of it, at the time. But I always wondered... Until years later, when my uncle confirmed it." She gives me a curious look, so I go ahead and clear things up for her. "He sabotaged my father's bike, and caused the accident that was only meant to kill him. My mother wasn't supposed to be on the bike with him. He never intended for her to die that day..."

"*Oh*, my God... Dean..."

"I'm just as guilty. I had plenty of time to say something... But I didn't. I was a stupid kid... Too weak to protect my mother from my abusive father... Too fuckin' stupid to open my goddamned mouth... If I would have *just* opened my goddamned mouth! ... I could have... *I could have...*" I stammer... *I could have fucking saved her! "Fuck!* I could have introduced you to her... To my uncle, who never gave up on me and pulled me into the Saviors for a better life." I manage to get the words out. "But he killed himself after years of living with the guilt. Drank himself to death. He blamed himself for my life choices, too. Growing up in a fucked-up environment, turning into a fuckin'..." I stop myself, choking back the words and taking a breath before I say too much. "Anyway, I suppose that's why he left me everything. Hoping I'd keep the mission going... That it would keep me on the straight and narrow... to a point." I open my eyes and look down at my cut. "Better late than never, I suppose." I mutter darkly.

When I turn around to face her, her hand has moved up from her throat to her mouth, her other fist is clenching the bottom of her t-shirt, and her eyes are welling up with tears.

"Don't, Vanna. Don't cry for me." I sigh. "I don't deserve your sympathy." She only shakes her head, unable to speak, I suppose. When she blinks, the tears roll down her cheeks. "Doll, I lost my parents almost thirty years ago. My uncle, nearly ten. I haven't shed a tear about any of it in a long, long time. No reason for you to cry for me." I try to reassure her, but it isn't working. The tears are still flowing and she's silent, aside from her faint, quivering breath and random sniffles. "Maybe I said too much."

She closes her eyes for a moment and shakes her head to object. Her hand moves back to the base of her throat. "N-no." Her voice trembles as she speaks. "I'm glad you told me." She opens her eyes to look at me again. "I'm so sorry for your losses. That sounds so inadequate... But I am. You've lost so much, Dean... and I am so, so sorry."

I try to give her a reassuring smile. "And that's just the first half of my life." I mean for it to sound humorous, though I suppose it isn't all that funny. I grab what's left of my beer and finish it off. She looks at me as if she's honestly afraid to even ask. I don't give her the chance to, though. I don't think either one of us can take any more of my fucked-up life story. Not tonight. I walk over to her and sit back down in front of her, placing a hand on her knee, the other brushing her tears from her cheeks. "You are a light in my dark life, Vanna. Your love is my peace. Your kiss silences my demons. All I need is you, baby, and everything is fuckin' Aces in my world."

Chapter twenty-seven
DEAN

"NOW BEFORE YOU GIVE ME ANY SHIT, DEAN... THE furniture is a gift from me and Cherry." Axel says, as I walk with him towards our newly established conference room on the far side of the building. It's where our gym and large kitchen are located. It's also the side of the building where the twelve, mostly vacant, private bedroom, bathroom combo rooms are. "Just consider it a thank you from us, for letting us live here for nothing all these years."

I don't comment, but I don't feel as though they've lived here for nothing. They help out a lot. Axel's got a day job with a local painter in town and works weekends in the roadhouse for me now. And Cherry runs the bar, does my books and keeps this place neat and clean. She's got a few sweetbutts that help her out, but for the most part, Cherry keeps shit running smoothly for me.

Axel pushes through the set of double doors across from the gym and we step inside. I'm honestly surprised at what he and Cherry were able to accomplish in a day. Not that this room is all that big. But it's big enough to fit the long carved wooden table we reclaimed from

Preacher, which sits ten, as well as the extra seating for an additional twelve more, by way of black leather couches and chairs along the walls on either side of the large table. The style actually matches the bar stools and leather couches in the roadhouse up front. There are a few end tables between a couple of the couches, dark red mahogany wood, like the bar as well. He even managed to paint the walls a neutral shade of muted green.

"Do you like it?" He asks excitedly, hands on his hips as he glances around then pins his focus back on me. "Cherry said the color paint she picked out is *Card Room Green*. Sounded cool, like poker or something." He smiles. "She called it a masculine grey green without being too dark, and it goes good with the wood and leather."

"It looks fuckin' great, kid." I tell him. "How did you two swing this though?" I had told him last night to knock himself out, or go nuts... One of the two. But it was just a figure of speech. I never expected a damn near finished room.

A set of arms wrap around my waist from behind. "I snagged the leather chairs a month ago at an estate sale. I've had them in our storage unit. I figured we might need them in the bar at some point as replacements. I couldn't pass them up because they matched so well." Cherry says, as she gives me a squeeze before she comes to stand in front of me beside Axel. "The side tables we got at the Salvation Army for a steal, too." She adds. "I picked those up today."

"I wish you would have said something a month ago, it's not on you to replace bar seating, Cherry." I say to her, reaching for my wallet. She grabs my arm to stop me.

"Don't you dare try to give me any money, Dean." She frowns at me, a dainty little finger pointed right in my face. "This is a *thank you*, for all you've done for us. Just accept it." She insists, backing up to Axel and hugging her arms around his waist now. He drapes his arm across her shoulders. "Besides, it's for the club, too. The Saviors need a Church."

An hour later, I'm sitting at the head of the table, leaning forward with my hands folded beside the gavel, when my MC Brothers enter the room, gathering around. The prospects, having been made aware that they don't, and won't, have a place at the table, stand back further near the leather seating along the walls. Viper, already wearing the patch declaring him as Vice President of the Saviors MC on his cut, walks up to me and places a wooden box down before me, then takes his seat at my left. Viking, having always been a Sergeant at Arms as well, thus already wearing his patch, takes the seat to my right.

Standing up, I open the top of the wooden box, which contains the new rank patches. As I call my Brothers one by one, I hand them their patches, and they take their appropriate places at the table. Only once they're all seated, do I glance briefly at the prospects and give them permission to sit down on the leather couches along the walls. They keep their mouths shut, already having been informed by Viking, that they are only to speak when spoken to, and that it is a *privilege* for them to even be in here with us.

As I take my seat once again, I allow Diesel to speak on membership dues, and collect another contribution for the coffers from the Brothers who were not at our meeting last night. No one seems to take issue with that at all, and each man hands him over a couple hundred bucks, bringing in another fifteen hundred. We come to an agreement on a monthly due's amount, and I'm about to declare that business settled, when a prospect clears his throat and stands. Viking is immediately ready to give the guy shit, but I put my hand up to stop him and look back at the prospect.

"What is it?" I ask.

"I'd like to make a donation to the MC, sir." The guy with a short sandy colored beard, wearing jeans and a blank cut, says. He looks to be a few years older than Axel.

"Prospects aren't required to pay in until they earn a patch." I remind him. "You're not going to buy your way in, either."

"No, sir. But a prospect should always act in support of the MC in any way he can to prove himself." The guy says.

"So long as we're all clear on that." I eye him, and the other prospects. "Diesel is the one to talk to about monetary donations to the MC. Our coffers are for our MC expenses. It's separate from the fundraising. Just so you're aware of that fact."

"Yes, sir. I'm fully aware. I want to help the club get back on its feet." He nods.

I eye him suspiciously. "What's your name?"

"Rusty. But guys call me Road Rash." Rusty Gunderson. I remember his report file from Jason. He's clean on paper.

Viking scoffs. "Gonna call you *Diaper Rash* till you earn a road name, *prospect*." He taunts him. A couple of the guys at the table chuckle, but I keep a straight face. I never took part in any hazing, but it's par for the course and weeds out the weak. "You're gonna polish my bike this weekend for interrupting this meeting, too." Viking adds.

The prospect only nods, but he doesn't seem fazed.

"See Diesel about your contribution, later." I say to him.

"Yes, sir." He nods, taking his seat on the couch again.

"While you prospects have my attention for the moment," I say, looking them over again, they all seem to perc up a bit now. "Next weekend is the fundraiser. If you're not gonna be there volunteering your time for whatever we tell you to do, leave your cut at the door when you go tonight. If you do show up, we're collecting for Toys for Tots as well, and you better bring some shit kids are gonna like. There will be a box van at the entrance of the rally for you to put everything. Gonna need some of you to step up and man that post and collect the toys from the crowd as they enter." None of them seem to take issue with that demand. "You're also going to stick around after the event, and make sure the lot is cleaned up."

"Including my huge pig smoker." Viking chimes in. "I want that fuckin' grill to sparkle before I tow it home."

"We at least get some pulled pork outta the deal?" One of them asks, a hint of sarcasm in his tone, obviously trying to impress with his ballsy, failed comedic attempt.

Viking stands up, about to give him Hell, but I put my hand up again to stop him and hard eye the snarky prospect with the shaved head and thin, dark goatee.

"You want anything at the event, you fuckin' pay for it. All proceeds from anything Saviors' related goes towards the organizations we're fundraising for. If you don't support the causes we do, the organizations we work with, then you don't belong in this MC. Simple. You don't like it, take that cut off and get out." I glare at him.

He puts his hand up, his expression apologetic. "It was a stupid comment... I'm sorry." He says, "I'll actually volunteer to clean the grill."

"Great. Pick a fuckin' buddy to help you. I don't give a shit who, so long as everything gets done." I snap at him. My tone is harsh, I sound as though I'm more annoyed with him than I actually am. I glance around at the other prospects. "Most of you came in under that prick Preacher... You should know that already puts you at a disadvantage with me." I warn them. "There will be no second chances. You fuck up, you're out. You disrespect a patch wearing member, you're out. You disrespect one of our club girls, you're out. You take whatever shit any of these guys throw your way." I tell them, gesturing to my MC Brothers at the table, who are all sneering at the prospects, playing it up. "No task is too good for you, understand? But you don't take any shit from anyone else outside of the club while you're wearing a Saviors Prospect cut." They all nod in agreement. "Great. Now, we're going to be in here a while going over club business. The Twisted Throttle could use a thorough cleaning. You'll find cleaning shit in the closet near the bathrooms. Those could use some of your attention, too." I say with a mock pleasant smile. "Run along now, Prospects. *Make me proud.*"

They immediately jump to their feet and file out of the room.

"Shut the fuckin' doors behind you!" Viking's loud voice booms after them. The last one to leave nervously grabs the double doors and slams them shut behind him.

I can't help glancing at Viking, who looks back at me, and we all get a laugh out of it.

LATISHA AND I WALK THROUGH THE NEW TEN-FOOT-HIGH CHAIN LINK GATES to enter the Bike Rally, and I'm shocked to see the huge turnout. The lot is packed with people and booths catering to all kinds of needs and entertainment. There's even a Bikini Bike Wash... In mid-October. Not that it's actually chilly out during the day in Eastern North Carolina this time of the year. But it's not summer weather either. I can't help but laugh. It's like these biker babes actually want to be as naked as possible whenever they get the chance. I really do admire their confidence. There are more women walking around in lingerie, leather bikinis and fishnets than I ever guessed there would be in this seemingly proper little town. There are also lots of guys with leather vests and patches to clubs I never heard of before, too. So, there must be a lot of people from out of town.

I look over at Latisha, who is asking a guy where he got his giant neon green plastic party cup from. It reminds me of a huge bong. He points and tells her about ten vendors down, there's a booth with draft beer.

"I can't believe how many people are actually here. This is insane." I say to her.

"They're going to make a killing this weekend." She says. "It's always been pretty busy, but this year The Saviors seem to have gone all out."

As we walk through the crowd, I check out the booths. Clothing and biker gear, specialty leather items, bike parts, booths that advertise custom work for your motorcycle with jars to enter your contact information to win free services. There are food and drink vendors. Even a kissing booth run by a local strip club, where, for a cash donation, you can kiss a stripper. I can't help but laugh. And the line is actually pretty long.

"Oh my God..." Latisha says, grabbing my arm and pulling my attention back to her, she's looking down at a table with about twenty, eight by ten photos, of men's head shots. Some even from the waist up and topless, grinning and flexing for the photos. Some are posing with their motorcycles, others simply have a picture of a motorcycle next to their head shots.

"What is this?" I ask, before I notice a little upright framed sign that says *Bid on a Biker*.

"Apparently you can buy raffle tickets and they're going to auction themselves off later tonight to give the lucky winners a ride on their bikes." Latisha laughs, pulling her purse around to her front to dig for her wallet. "That's so cool! We should totally do this!"

I giggle, looking over the photos. I recognize quite a few of the men I see from working Dean's bar. "Who are you going to bid on?" I ask.

"Viking!" She says, and I don't think she's ever given me a more definitive answer about anything before. I can't help but laugh. "Can I get three raffle books please." She says eagerly to the scantily clad girl working this table.

"Damn girl, it's forty bucks a book." I say. "If you want Viking just tell him, he won't say no to you." I can't help giggling at that last part. Viking is a man whore. And Latisha is not only fun to be around, but she's also pretty. He would not turn her down.

Latisha gives me a wry look. "Dean already told him he can't mess around with me because of my brother. If I win the auction, they can't say shit." She grins at me with a naughty little glint in her eye, which only makes me laugh again.

Looking down at the table of bikers to bid on, I spot a black and white photo of a sexy, scowling Dean, straddling Serene, arms crossed with the slightest smirk on his face like he knows he's hot shit. I buy a book of raffle tickets since it's for a good cause, and put them all towards Dean. When the girl lifts the large, barrel shaped container holding Dean's raffles, it's already half full and the day is just beginning. I glance over at Viking's container, and he's doing just as well.

"You're right, they're going to make a freaking killing here today." I say to Latisha, who just spent one hundred and twenty dollars on a chance to ride

585

on the back of Viking's bike for thirty minutes. She must really have a thing for that asshole. I just smile and shake my head.

"Your boyfriend looks a little jealous of you biding on another guy to ride." The girl says to me, as she grabs the containers and places them back underneath the table.

I look over my shoulder and smile, expecting to see Dean, but he isn't anywhere in sight. When I look back at her, she cocks her chin at a guy across the lot, who happens to be staring at me. I've never seen him before, but he is wearing an MC cut.

"That's not my boyfriend." I say with an awkward chuckle as I turn back to the auction girl. "I bid on my boyfriend, actually." She gives me a surprised look, that I don't really appreciate, but I keep my mouth shut about it.

We spend a little more time perusing the booths and different vendors before we find the place with the bong style party cups. Latisha orders a beer from a woman wearing Daisy Dukes, leather boots and skull pasties on her boobs. That's it. No wonder there are so many guys walking around with these ridiculous cups.

"I've got to bring Derek his wallet, I completely forgot!" Latisha says, pulling out her vibrating phone from her pocket. "Yeah, this is him, wondering where the hell I am. Do you want to meet me by the bike show? That's where Dean and Viking are at. It's all the way in the back."

"Yeah sure, I'm just going to get a drink and I'll start heading that way." I say to her. I watch as she rushes off into the crowd to head back towards the main gate where I suppose Derek is waiting for her. I ask for a bottled water, but before I can pay for it, the guy who had been staring at me, walks up and pays.

"Hey." He says, handing me the bottle of water. His patch says he's with the JoCo Jokers. Their logo is a skull wearing a Jester's hat. He's a few inches taller than me, athletic build with hazel eyes, dirty blonde slicked back hair with a little facial scruff.

"Hi." I say, not wanting to be rude.

"You here with anybody? I haven't noticed a man with you." His eyes roam over me, unabashedly. "Unless you and the black girl are a *thing*." He adds, bringing his hand up to his chin to stroke his scruff. "In which case, I'm down for a little chocolate and vanilla swirl action."

His boldness catches me off guard, and I wonder if I will ever get used to the unfiltered ways of these biker types. "She's my friend." I say, struggling with the cap on the bottle. "But I am meeting my boyfriend here."

"Thought you smiled at me." He takes the bottle from me, twisting the cap to crack the stubborn seal and hands it back to me. "If you got a man, why are you biding on a ride? I'll take you for free, baby. Anywhere you wanna go."

I giggle nervously, feeling really awkward. "Sorry, when the girl said my boyfriend was watching me, I thought it was actually my boyfriend." I try to explain. "And I bid because it's a good cause."

He steps a little closer to me, and I instinctively back up. "You're not wearing a cut or anything saying you're off limits. Is he affiliated with anybody?"

"The Saviors."

"Is he a prospect?"

"No. I should go find him, though."

"I'll walk with you. Make sure nobody bothers you." He winks at me.

I laugh uncomfortably. "Are you friendly with The Saviors?" I ask.

He shrugs. "Never had any issues."

At least that's a positive. I can't see Dean being too pleased with this guy hanging around me though. "Do you know Dean? Keegan?" I ask.

The guy smiles. "Yeah. I know of him." He says, but his smile is off.

"Well, that's him. Thanks for the water." I turn and walk away, but he keeps pace at my side.

"What's your name?" The guy asks.

"Vanna."

"I'm Blade." He says. "I'm good with knives. You got any more clothes you want designer cuts in, you let me know, baby." He reaches over in an attempt to touch my leg through the blue denim of one of the frayed slits across my thigh.

I quickly step further away from him and force an uneasy laugh. "I wouldn't do shit like that in front of Dean." I warn him.

"*Dean* should know better... A girl like you shouldn't be left unattended."

I glance at him as I walk, a bit more hurriedly than before, but *Blade* easily keeps up with me. "Maybe *you* should know better."

Blade is grinning, but looking straight ahead. "That's him, ain't it?"

I look forward and spot Dean talking with a few girls. He's wearing a pair of black aviator sunglasses and a Saviors MC t-shirt beneath his cut. The girls are all wearing Saviors gear, so I'm not too jealous. They might belong to other guys, and at least the Saviors don't seem to poach each other's chicks. Although, when one reaches over to touch Dean's arm flirtatiously, I feel myself getting annoyed. To his credit, he subtly twists out of range of her touch. That makes me smile to myself. He spots me walking towards him, a grin on his face, until he notices the JoCo Joker walking a little too close to me. Dean yanks off his sunglasses and walks through the girls towards us, already scowling at Blade.

"You better mind your manners now." I warn Blade, as Dean fast approaches.

There's no *hello* as he reaches me. I'm greeted with an arm wrapped possessively around my waist, and an intimate kiss on the mouth. If this doesn't shout *claimed*, I don't know what would. Only after his testosterone driven display of Alpha male posturing, does Dean say a word to me.

"Vanna, baby. Where the fuck have you been?" He asks, hard eyeing Blade.

"With Latisha. She had to bring Derek his wallet, so I came looking for you."

"There was a pit stop." Blade speaks up.

Dean's eyes narrow as he sizes Blade up. "And you are?"

"Just an escort. Making sure your lady got to you *unmolested*." He glances at me and winks again, his eyes lowering to my fashionably torn jeans.

"His name is Blade." I say, deciding to leave out the part where this guy touched me, for the sake of keeping the peace at this fundraiser rally. "I literally just met him. I was buying a drink and he jumped in and paid for it."

Dean reaches into his back pocket and pulls out some cash. He peels off a five and shoves it in Blade's vest pocket. "That ought to cover it." He growls.

"What oughta cover it, is a patch on your lady. Not fair giving us guys false hope with a dime piece like this walking around alone, swaying that fine ass and throwing smiles." Blade says. *Is this guy crazy?*

A grin creeps across Dean's face. And it's not the friendly kind.

"No patch means she's available." Blade pushes.

"She's not available to anyone but me." Dean says. "Her *word* should be enough to back you off." Dean releases me and steps closer to the guy. "I know she told you she was with me. There's no game to play here. I'm the lucky fuck pumping my DNA into her every night. This dime piece belongs to *me... Joker.*" I can't help pursing my lips at that DNA line. I was not expecting that. But he definitely went there.

Blade smiles and raises his hands in mock defeat. He glances at me once more. "Lovely to meet you, Vanna." He says, before he turns and walks away.

Dean makes sure he doesn't stop walking before he turns around to look at me.

"Don't bother saying it!" I put my finger up to shush him. "I'll wear a damn *property of* top next time." I expect him to be annoyed, but he only grins at me, putting his arm around my shoulders to walk me back to where The Saviors are set up.

"That *DNA* comment was *a lot.*" I look at him as we walk back through the crowd. "You guys are so territorial. I'm surprised you don't whip it out and pee on us."

Dean chuckles and pulls me in closer to him, leaning into my ear. "*I didn't think you'd be into that.*" He teases me.

When we get to the area they're set up in, Viking is working over a huge smoker that he brought in on a trailer behind his truck. He's got two entire pigs in there. There's a large table that he and Cherry and a few girls from the roadhouse, are shredding meat on and serving up pulled pork sandwiches to the crowd for cash. They've got their own bikini bike wash going on as well, and are collecting donations for entry to the bike show. There's a tent set up with places to sit as well, where Snowy, Chopper and Axel are hanging out with a cooler and beers.

"How are you guys doing so far?" I ask.

"It's a bigger turn out than last year. Every booth here has to pay in. I expect we should have a substantial amount to donate when all is said and done." Dean says. "Speaking of which." He knocks the cooler with his boot to get Snowy and Axel's attention. "Why don't you two make the rounds and start collecting. Everybody has had enough time to make money to cover the cost of entry." They put down their beers and get up to get to work.

"What do you want me to do, boss?" I playfully ask.

"I'm going to send the girls on an ice and beer run, and check in with security. So, if you want, give Viking and Cherry a hand at the table."

"*Yes, sir.*" I smile. He swats my ass as I walk over to Viking.

The day passes quickly. Latisha and her brother Derek stop by to say hello to everyone and hang out under the tent for a bit, before Derek has to go. Latisha opts to hang around a little longer, and I notice her making eyes at Viking quite a few times. I can't help but giggle to myself. Viking makes numerous jokes about me handling his meat the whole time I'm helping him shred and serve up the pulled pork sandwiches and coleslaw plates. By the end of the day, Viking's pulled pork is sold out, and there are seven impressive plastic jugs under the table, full of money from bike show donations, the bikini bike wash and Viking's famous smoked pulled pork sandwiches. I help Viking load them into the back seat of his truck before he locks them up to bring back to the Clubhouse, later. Right now, they're all eager to get off their feet and relax around the fire Axel is starting in a drum, from a busted-up pallet he found discarded behind the lot. The prospects dismantle the tent and pack it into the back of Viking's truck as well, before it gets dark. The sun is starting to set behind the tree line beyond the lot.

There are still a few groups scattered about the lot, packing up their booths to leave. Our group finally settles down with beers and the remaining pulled pork sandwiches that Viking saved for everyone around the fire. Dean asks me to grab him a beer, and when I hand it to him, he yanks me down into his lap. I grab his jaw and kiss him before I cuddle against him and gaze into the fire.

They're all laughing and joking around with each other. Snowy, Chopper, Viking and Latisha are munching on a pile of sandwiches, while Cherry and Axel are off to the side, making out. I think it's cute how into each other they are. Axel doesn't even pay attention to the other girls. He only has eyes for Cherry. I've really come to like her, too. And though I still feel a little like an outsider, at least they seem to have warmed up to me since things became official with Dean. Maybe we'll all be friends someday, too.

Dean squeezes my knee. "You good?" He asks. "You're very quiet."

"Yeah. Just tired, I guess. Was a busy day." I say. "Seems like everybody did well today, though. All the booths and vendors. I had no idea there would be such a huge turnout."

"Yeah, this might have been the best year, yet." Dean says.

The girl from the *Bid on a Biker* auction walks over to us with a big smile on her face as she looks at the guys. "We've pulled the raffles for the twenty lucky ladies that bid on you boys." She says, eyeing each of the guys. When her eyes land on Dean, then me in his lap, the smile suddenly slips momentarily from her face. She clears her throat. "I've got the names and numbers for everyone you guys need to call to set up your *dates* with." She says, un-clipping a page from the clip board she's holding. "These are all the Saviors." She takes a few steps towards Dean and holds the paper out to him. "I've already sent the Jokers their list."

"Thanks, Kimmie." He smiles at her. "I'll make sure everyone gets in contact with the winners and sets it up. You did great today."

She smiles at him again, before she glances at me once more, a kind of sadness in her eyes behind her slipping smile. She shifts her gaze back to Dean. "Well, I'm gonna go, then. Have a great night." She sighs.

"Yeah... you too, doll." Dean says pleasantly. When she walks away, he glances down to study the list. "Alrighty, let's see what we've got going on here... Axel... looks like you're taking Kerry Anne McCormick for a spin."

"Hmm?" He barely twists his face from Cherry's, and I giggle, realizing they're *still* kissing each other.

I look back at Dean, who's smiling at them also, before he looks back at me. "Fuckin' kids." He chuckles, his other hand gripping my leg a little tighter. He clears his throat, shakes the paper and glances back at the list. "Chopper, you've got a woman named Sheila Clancy. Snowy, Barbra Hewlett... Ain't that the lady at the bank?" He asks.

"Yeah, she's a teller." Axel says, before Cherry pulls his face back to hers again.

"And Viking, you've got... *Latisha*..." Dean's voice trails off as he glowers at Viking, silently warning him I'm sure, that he had better behave. I look over at an excited Latisha.

"*Oh my god.*" I can't help laughing, happy for my friend. Viking looks over at her as well, a perplexed, but amused expression on his face.

"*Moving right along...*" Dean sighs, looking back at the list. "The other guys aren't here right now... And I've got..." He hesitates for a moment, and I notice the slightest furrowing of his brow. He clears his throat before he says the name, "Janie Lynn Dawson."

"Oh shit." Viking mutters. Even Axel stops kissing Cherry to turn to look at Dean.

I glance around at everyone for a moment, before I look at Dean, too. "What? Who is Janie Lynn Dawson? An ex?" I ask, wondering what the big deal is.

"No." Dean says. "No, of course not. She's um... a girl. I never met her. I know her grandfather. I thought she moved outta state a few months back." He says, placing the paper down to pull out his cell phone and enter her number into his phone. "Chopper, run down this list and text the guys the names and numbers of the women they have to get in touch with." Dean says, holding the paper out. Chopper gets up and reaches for it, before he sits back down in one of the folding canvas chairs. He pulls out his cell and gets right on it.

Cherry grabs Axel's face and pulls him back to her again, and I guess we're just not talking about this mystery Janie woman anymore. I'll definitely be asking Dean about this later, when we're in private. Like the good *Ol' Lady in training* that I'm trying to be for him. Forcing myself to let it go for now, I glance around the group again and notice they're all a little low on their beers. I get up from Dean's lap and walk to the cooler to grab a few more and hand them out to everyone.

As I do so, the sound of high heels clacking across the pavement, heading hastily in our direction, echoes across the lot. When I turn to see who's walking towards us at such a determined pace, I realize that it's Lucinda, flanked by three of her girlfriends. One of which I recognize from the *kiss a stripper* booth. I roll my eyes and cross my arms before I glance back at Dean. He doesn't look amused by her approach either, but he remains seated, his head leaned back against the chair, hands folded in his lap as he awaits her incoming bullshit. The other guys, besides Viking, avoid looking at her. I wonder if it's because she's such a bitch that they don't even want to invite words with her.

She stops to stand behind Viking, who remains seated as well, and doesn't react to her presence at all. He's sucking the sauce off his fingers from the pulled pork as if it's the only thing that matters in the world right now.

Dean lets out a long, exasperated sigh. "Lucinda. What the hell can I do for you?" His expression clearly indicating he doesn't actually want to know.

She shoots a glare at me as she adjusts the strap of her large, white leather bag on her shoulder. Was I supposed to notice that it's a Prada bag? *Whatever.*

She turns her attention back to Dean. "Did you know you're dating a gold-digging whore?" Lucinda demands. "A bitch who stole all her man's money, sold all his possessions out from under him, while he was locked up and couldn't do shit about it?"

My heart sinks. How does she know about what I did? Those charges were dropped. It should not be on my record at all...

"The fuck are you talking about?" Dean snaps back at her angrily.

"For somebody who fought me so hard in our divorce settlement, I'm shocked you would ever consider dating a woman who *actually did* take her man to the cleaners!" Lucinda reaches into her Prada and pulls out a manila envelope. She tosses it and it lands square in Dean's lap.

All the men look from her to stare at me. It's difficult to read their expressions in the darkness. The firelight dancing across their faces, obscuring their true features.

I can't even speak. My insides are trembling. What has she done?

Dean grabs the envelope and stands, holding it up. "What the fuck is this?"

"She's a gold digger." Lucinda pushes. "The proof is in that envelope!"

He glances at me, scanning me the way he does when he wants to get a read on me. I don't know what he can tell. But he shifts his gaze back to Lucinda after only a moment. "Where did you get this?"

"Read it!" She demands.

"I asked you a fucking question!" He shouts at her, his voice a sonic boom making both Lucinda and I jump at the same time. Even Cherry isn't sucking Axel's face anymore. Everyone is staring at us.

"I hired a private investigator to look into her. Everything in that file is legit!" She shouts back at him.

He looks astounded by her reply. "You fucking did *what*?"

"Just look at it!" She shouts back at him. "Your fucking cock warmer is a gold-digging snitch!"

Dean looks back at me again. He doesn't say anything.

"It's not true." I manage to choke out.

Dean stares at me a moment longer, before he drops the envelope into the fire and turns back to Lucinda as she's screaming at him to take it out. She makes a move to snatch it out of the fire herself, but Viking grabs her around her waist and stops her.

"What are you doing?" She screams at Dean. "The proof is right there!"

He stares at her. Contempt and disdain etched across his face. "This is a new low, Lucinda." He growls at her.

She watches the envelope burn, struggling uselessly to get out of Viking's powerful arms. "Fuck it!" She finally shouts. "There are more copies where that came from!" She punches Viking's arm, but he's unbothered by it. She glances angrily around at the men looking at her. "I'll show you all."

"*No*. You won't." Dean steps closer to her. "This shit is over, Lucinda. This crossed a fucking line." He looks at each of his guys, and they nod in some unspoken agreement. Dean's eyes then shift to meet Viking's. "She can go."

Viking releases Lucinda and she shoves away from him, staggering back to her silent hench bitches. "You're making a huge mistake!" She shouts at him.

Dean runs his hand through his hair and turns around to look at me again. He looks pissed, but I don't think his anger is at me. All I can do is shake my head. None of what Lucinda said is true. It was a complete manipulation of the actual facts.

Dean looks back at Lucinda. "I've made a lot of mistakes, Lucinda. You're at the top of the fucking list, *in bold*." He says to her. She has the audacity to look hurt by his words. "I don't ever want to see your face around here again." His tone is harsh. Lucinda looks like he may as well have slapped her across the face.

"Dean, wait..." She starts.

"For what?" He sounds completely fed up with her bullshit. "For fucking *what*, Lucinda?" Her mouth opens but nothing comes out. "We're over. We've been over. And you need to get out of here. Now." He mutters, as if he's completely disgusted by her.

"Dean!" She sobs.

"Viking." Dean glances at his friend.

Viking nods and turns towards Lucinda and her little posse. "Let's go ladies." He says, moving towards them, his arms out to encourage them to move along. Lucinda shoots me a death glare through her watery eyes as they are escorted by Viking out of the lot.

"Excuse us." Dean says, walking towards me now. He takes my arm gently and leads me away from the group. Once we're behind the brick building and out of ear shot from everyone, Dean pulls me into his arms and holds me tightly against him, stroking my hair. "I'm sorry that happened."

"None of it's true." I say. "She manipulated everything to paint a very different picture of what happened."

Dean pulls back to stroke my face. "I trust you, baby. I don't need to see the paper work."

I stare back at him, impressed, to say the least, that he dropped it in the fire. He could have looked. She was very convincing adding that touch with the manila envelope. But he chose me. It means a lot. "I did sell all of his things when he got locked up." I confess. "Everything. The ring. His furniture. TV's. Stereo system. I took all the money and left the state."

Dean's staring at me, grinning, looking rather amused. "That's fucking badass, Vanna."

I sigh with relief and squeeze him. "So that doesn't make me a gold digger to you?"

He laughs again and kisses me. "No, it makes you an even bigger badass than I already think you are."

"What about your MC Brothers? I couldn't tell what they were thinking."

"I'll handle it." He says. "Right now, if you want me to."

I hesitate. "What if they have questions?"

He puts his forehead to mine. "I said I'll handle it, baby." He reiterates. "You gotta learn to trust me."

I do trust him. Especially after burning that envelope without looking into it, knowing how badly he wants to know the details of my past. He still chose me.

"I do trust you, Dean." I grab the collar of his leather cut and pull him closer to me. "When you burned that file..." I bite my lip and look up at him. "When you chose me over..."

"*Everything*. Always." He cuts me off. "I know you're afraid of word getting back to him. But even if it does, Vanna. Nobody is going to hurt you so long as you're with me." He runs his finger across my lip, before he bends to kiss me. I kiss him back, still gripping his leather cut. He lets me push my tongue into his mouth and I can feel him smile against my lips.

"Do we need to get the fuck outta here, baby?" His growly tone suggestive.

"Yes." I whisper against his mouth. "I want you. Really badly. Right now."

"*Fuck*." He grabs my hand and pulls me back with him to the group without hesitation. Dean clears his throat as we approach them, turning their attention to him.

"Is everything okay?" Viking asks, looking at me first, then shifting his focus back to Dean.

"Yeah. Listen up," Dean says, obviously in a hurry. "Lucinda is a lying bitch. Nothing she said about Vanna is the truth. *I know the truth.* That's all that fucking matters... And if I'm happy with Vanna and she's happy with me, then just be happy for us."

I can't help wondering why they're all grinning at us... Until Viking chimes in, naturally. "You're tenting, bro." He states with nonchalance.

I bite my lip and bring my hand to my face, blocking my eyes from them, embarrassed beyond measure.

"Well, when your woman demands a shot of your DNA, you *oblige* her." Dean grabs his cock and adjusts himself without an ounce of shame. "I'm a fuckin' *gentleman* like that."

The guys laugh at his crude remarks and I can't even bring myself to look anywhere in Cherry's direction.

"All right," Viking says, slamming his hands together and rubbing them up and down a few times. "Dean's *dick brained* right now, that means *I'm in charge*. Let's pack it in and get this money back to HQ."

With that, Dean hauls me towards Serene by my hand. She's parked a couple of yards away behind Viking's truck. He jumps on her and fires her up, I grab his shoulders and climb on behind him. He revs the bike before we take off, and the vibration of the power between my legs kicks up my arousal a little more. I wrap my arms around him and rest my face against his leather cut, as we fly out the back exit of the lot. I suspect we're not going far, since he didn't bother with helmets, which is fine by me because the rumbling and vibration of Serene's powerful motor and exhaust system, is definitely stoking my desire for him. Squeezing my thighs tighter against him, my hand drifts from his abs to his crotch as he turns the bike down a side road. It's all woods. He slows down and hits his high beams on, searching for a spot where we won't get caught, taking a turn onto a dirt path, driving down cautiously but quickly. There's a structure further up. As we get closer, I realize it's a boarded up old church. Dean pulls Serene into the old gravel parking lot, facing the headlights on the structure. He revs the bike loudly a few times before he kicks the stand down, I assume to make sure no one comes out.

"*Keep her running.*" I say in his ear, before jumping off the back of the bike quickly and climbing on in front of him, face to face. I wrap my arms around his neck, lifting my legs up so the back of my thighs are on the top of his and my feet are hooked together behind his back. I pull him to me so that I can kiss him on the mouth. "I want you to fuck me on your bike." I whisper against his lips. A deep growl rumbles up his throat, as he immediately begins fumbling with his belt and fly.

I lean back on Serene's tank to unzip my jeans and pull them down over my ass with my underwear, bringing my legs back around in front of him to get them down around my ankles. Dean grabs my legs and ducks under my bunched up jeans, between my legs, so my feet are behind his back again, ankles bound together by my clothing. He grabs my ass and pulls me a little further down so I'm positioned more under him as he hovers over me. He reaches for the handle bars of the bike and revs her, making me bite my lip as the combination of the cool night air and the powerful vibration of Serene makes me shudder.

"You're so fucking hot." He growls, reaching behind him for his wallet. "Let me slip on a wrap and we'll make this threesome happen!"

"Forget it. I trust you. Just fuck me, now." I demand.

He freezes for a moment, staring down at me. "You want me to fuck you, on Serene... no rubber?"

"In an abandoned church parking lot, no less!" I can't help laughing.

His body, his hard cock, his dark gaze, tells me he wants nothing more than to take me on top of his precious motorcycle, but he hesitates. "Are you... *on* something?" He asks, but it's almost as if the question bothers him, and I can't imagine why that would be.

I nod, peering up at him. "I had an appointment last week, on my lunch break. I was going to wait until your Birthday to tell you, we don't need the condoms anymore." I say, biting my lip and giving him a little naughty smirk. "I'm on the pill."

He gives me a crooked smile, his hand reaching up to run his fingers through his hair for a moment, before he drops it back down to grip my thigh. "Are you sure about this?" He asks, "I mean, I'm clean... I swear. I haven't been with anyone but you, and I had to get tested before the fight in Myrtle Beach..."

I reach up to grab the collar of his leather cut and yank him down to me, kissing him thoroughly again. "Fuck me, Dean... I want you so bad." I whisper against his lips.

"*Fuck*, this is gonna be quick, Vanna." He groans, "I apologize in advance!"

"Just fuck me, Dean!"

"Yes ma'am!" He revs Serene with one hand and angles his cock to slide into me with the other. "*Jesus fucking Christ!*" He groans, penetrating me for the first time without a barrier between us. I whimper beneath him as he fills me, sheathing himself inside me. The momentary discomfort of being taken so quickly is worth it though.

Always the intuitive, observant and considerate lover, Dean revs the bike and holds off on thrusting until he feels me adjust more comfortably around his cock.

My back is arched over Serene's gas tank, there's no other position to be in. No cushion beneath me at all to absorb any shock. Whatever he gives me, I have to take it. Every inch. And I want it all. The pleasure, the pain. I want to feel him actually come inside of me without anything separating us. The thought makes my muscles clench around him.

"Fuck..." he grunts, rocking his hips forward, pushing deeper into me. "So... fucking... *good*... baby..."

I grip his arms as he begins to fuck me faster, revving Serene now and again. There isn't much I can leverage against with my feet bound by my jeans and underwear behind him. I swivel my hips as best I can to grind against him with each of his thrusts. I can feel the pressure climbing, the hot flush over taking my body. I arch my back a little more, pulling up my shirt to expose my chest and abdomen to the cool air, giving him a view of my bouncing tits as he pumps me. He fucks me harder, one hand snaking roughly up my body to feel me and squeeze my tits. Yanking one of my bra cups down, his mouth latches onto my nipple, sucking, as I lean my head back and gasp at the sensation. I notice shadows dancing across the front of the boarded-up church, and realize it's my hair draped in front of Serene's headlights, swaying with each of Dean's powerful thrusts.

He's breathing heavier now, revving her and fucking me faster. "If you don't want me to come inside of you, tell me now, baby." He pants through gritted teeth. I look up at him and bite my bottom lip, moaning as I clench around his cock again. He lets out another groan. "I'm serious, Vanna..."

"Come inside me, Dean. I want to feel you come inside me." I whimper.

"*Jesus fucking Christ...*" He almost whimpers himself, my words driving him to pump me even faster.

"Pretty sure he heard you the first time." I giggle.

"Are you close baby?" He sounds almost pleading.

I smile and slide my hands up his arms to hold onto his shoulders. I'm still climbing, but I'm not as close to the edge as he is. He knows it.

"Fuck." He grunts, dragging his fingers across his tongue and plunging his hand down between us. He finds my clit with his wet fingers and begins to rub me in a circular motion, instantly driving me higher. Pulling me quickly towards the edge with him.

"*Oh God.*" I gasp, digging my nails into his leather clad shoulders as he works me over with his cock and his hand. He gets rougher, making me whimper and squirm beneath him. "*Oh God... yes!*"

"Give it up to me baby," He begs, revving Serene once more before he releases her to grip the side of my thigh roughly. "*Come on baby... come for me...*" He desperately pleads.

His desperation is my undoing. My muscles spasm and clench around him uncontrollably, rippling around his throbbing hard cock. I cry out, raking my nails down his arms and gripping him as my orgasm rips through me. He's only a few seconds behind me, thrusting deeply a few more times, his body tenses as his cock jerks deep inside of me, spurting his hot seed. Dean grips my hips with both of his hands, slamming a final hard thrust into me before he shudders, fully spent.

He slumps forward to rest his face against my chest for a moment while we both catch our breath. I teasingly clench his cock once more while he's still inside me, pulling another groan from him.

"You fucking wreck me, baby. Every time." His voice is low and sated, as he wraps his arms under me. I feel his fingers curling around the back of my shoulders. "I fucking love you." He says on a sigh.

I run my fingers through the top of his hair. "I love you, too."

He twists his head so his chin is between my breasts, his eyes drowsy from a hard come. "Was it good for you?" He asks. "I almost left you behind, I'm sorry."

"Nothing to be sorry for." I say. My body shivers from the slight breeze and sheen of perspiration coating my skin. It's always damper in the woods after dark, adding to the slight chill of this October night.

Dean sits up immediately and tugs my shirt down. He slips out of me and shoves himself back inside his pants, then leans back to help me lift my legs up and over him so he can get off the bike. I grab my jeans and underwear from around my ankles and pull them back up my legs, leveraging my feet against the seat to lift my ass and pull them all the way up. I watch him remove his leather cut as I zip and button my jeans.

"Put this on." He says, holding up the leather Saviors cut for me to get into. "I know it's just a leather vest, but it's all I got that I can give you right now." I bring my leg over the bike and slide off the seat to stand, turning around so he can put the cut on me. The leather is still warm from his body heat. I bring the collar up to my nose and inhale deeply. Smells like Dean and leather, of course. I turn around to face him.

"Aren't you going to be cold?" I ask.

Dean smiles at me, reaching his hand up to touch my face gently. "That doesn't matter."

DEAN

ROLLING OFF OF HER, SPRAWLING OUT ON MY BACK AGAINST THE COMFORTER beside her, my heart thunders in my chest with a life force I haven't felt... maybe ever. I glance over at the raven-haired Goddess in my bed, who's managed to breathe life back into me. Thawed the ice inside my soul. *My* woman. *Vanna*... Fuck, even the sound of her name in my mind, holds the power to quell my demons for a time. The slight, sated smile at the corner of her perfect lips makes me smile as well. I basically ravaged her the moment we stepped inside the house, not all that long ago. I couldn't help myself. That bareback threesome with Serene playing at the forefront of my mind the whole ride home. I was ready for round two before we even hit the driveway. I had to have her again. Nothing between us. Just Vanna and I. God, I'll never get enough of her. She glances at me from the corner of her eyes, her teeth lightly sinking into that bottom lip, the corners of her mouth still in an upward curve.

"What's funny?" I ask.

Her head turns slightly more towards me against the pillow, her hands move down to her inner thighs as she clenches them together. "Nothing is *funny*. I just need to shower." She says, almost bashfully. My little Peony.

I can't help the wicked grin that creeps across my face. "You're welcome to it." I say. "Just tell me *why*, first."

Her eyes widen, so does her smile as she reaches over to smack me lightly. "You pervert." She playfully scolds me.

I roll over on my side to face her, propping my head up on one arm, my other hand reaching over to slide down her thigh, inching further between them. "Tell me... Or *show* me." I growl at her. Her eyes scowl at me, but she's still smiling as she unclenches her legs just enough to allow my hand between her thick thighs. I push my hand further up and feel myself coating her warm, smooth skin. Unable to stop there, I gently slide my fingers slowly up and down the slippery slit of her sex. She lets out a faint, stifled gasp at my touch. And I can't help the groan that escapes my throat in response to that erotic little sound. "Fuck, baby..." I mutter. That's twice in one night I've come inside her. The evidence is all over her... I fucking love it... And I want to do it again.

She clenches her thighs tightly, trapping my hand and hindering my movements, as she giggles. "Are you serious? Aren't your balls empty by now? That's twice in less than an hour. Can a man come dust?" She teases me.

I choose to let that comment pass without remark. "Let me join you, then?" I ask.

She sits up on the bed, looking down at me. Her hair so thick and long, untamed from our wild romp, that it completely obscures her naked back from my eyes as she smirks over her shoulder. "It's *your* awesome spa-like bathroom, Dean." She flirts, letting her legs relax so that I can move my hand freely once more over her body. And I do. I can't help myself. I love every fuckin' inch of her, but right now, I'm all about these sexy, sticky thighs. "I don't want to go home... but, you kind of... ruined my panties too." She says, almost shyly. That makes me grin again.

"You wanted my DNA, doll. You got it." I tease her, making her cheeks flush pink again, evident even in the soft glow of the table side lamp. She closes her eyes and shakes her head slightly. "I've got sweats you can put on, if you really insist on wearing something to bed." I say, semi feigning reluctance in my offer.

She glances back at me. "Maybe we should talk about me leaving some things here, for when I stay the night?" She raises the issue as if part of her fears I'd object. If she only knew what I really wanted. The future I imagine for us. Her insecurities would evaporate. But I don't want to spook her, either. She hasn't mentioned anything about her lease, which is up soon. She either has to agree to buy, or he'll raise her rent until he finds a buyer, and she'll have to move anyway. She should be here with me...

"Bring anything you want." I say, making a study of her reaction. The fact that there is relief in her eyes at my words, bothers me.

"Really?" She smiles.

I let out a sigh. Fuck it. Life's too short. *Carpe Diem* and all that jazz. "Don't buy that shitty house, Vanna."

Her brows furrow for a moment, caught off guard by my apparently unforeseen outburst. But her playful smile returns quickly enough. "I knew you thought my house was shitty." She squints at me.

"It's not *your* house." I say. "And yeah, it's shitty. You deserve better."

"What one can afford kinda dictates a lot." She says with a little shrug.

"I ain't asking you for rent, doll." I say. Her brows lift for a moment, before she glances away from me. Her eyes dart around the room, looking at nothing in particular before she grabs a strand of her own hair to fiddle with between her fingers. She's got so many tells. "What is it?" I already know what she's going to ask, but the motions are necessary. I push myself up to lean back against the head board, folding my hands behind my head as I watch her and wait.

"Did... did you just... I mean, are you... asking me," She stammers, twisting slightly to look back at me.

"To move in with me?" I finish for her. "*Yes.* I am. Will you?"

Her mouth opens as if she's about to say something, but then she closes it, a slightly perplexed expression crosses her features. "Who is Janie?" She suddenly asks. In true Vanna fashion, a hard left turn from the topic at hand. I suppress a sigh. "When you read her name, that she bid on you... you seemed... *affected* by it, somehow. For some reason. What is it? Who is she to you?"

"I've never met her before. Not her, in person. I saw two photos of her once." I say. Vanna is searching my eyes now, and I can see the demons Jack cast inside her, peering back at me through her shimmering dark eyes. Waiting for ammunition from my words to twist her up with. "Actually, it was the night you started working in my bar. Janie's the reason I was late in meeting you that night."

"Why?" Vanna asks, those ravenous devils flickering back at me. I can imagine their sneering little faces, whispering falsities in her mind.

"Her grandfather came to me earlier that night. With an address and two photos. One of Janie and her fiancé." I explain, "The other, of Janie after her fiancé put her in the hospital." Vanna's eyes widen as she seems to realize what I'm about to disclose to her. "I was late in meeting you that night, because I was in the next county, breaking his arms and legs with his own Louisville Slugger. Making sure he wouldn't be there to stop her from leaving him. I was told by her grandfather, that she was leaving the fiancé for good, going to move to another state with some cousins somewhere, or something. To heal. To start over... So, no, I've never actually *met* Janie."

We're both silent for a few moments, before Vanna averts her eyes from me, bringing her arms to wrap around herself. "She wants to thank her hero." She quietly states, but before I can object to that *word* again, she looks back up at me. "How often do they seek you out?"

I shake my head, lowering my arms to my sides. "Never." I shrug. "None of them ever know I'm the one doing it. It's gotta be that way. Or I won't be able to keep doing it. If she should bring it up, I'll deny any involvement. I just hope she didn't go back to him."

Vanna drops her eyes again, barely nodding her head. "I understand. If I were her, I'd want to thank my hero, too." Her voice is quiet.

"For all I know, she could be setting me up for her fiancé." I joke, attempting to end this *hero* talk. Pushing myself off the bed, I walk around to her side. Her eyes shoot up to mine again, full of worry as they follow my movement around the foot of the bed. "A little over six months... He should be fully healed by now and ready for revenge." I tease her, grinning to let her know I'm not serious. She doesn't look amused though. "I'm joking, Vanna. *Relax.*"

I reach down for her to take my hand, which she does, and I pull her to her feet. Wrapping my arms around her, I press her naked body against mine.

"Have the men ever come after you in retaliation?" she asks.

"No. And don't think I forgot about my question, doll. You left me hanging." I remind her.

She's about to answer me, when my cellphone starts ringing somewhere on the floor among the scattered clothes that I tore off the both of us earlier.

"Ignore it." I say. "Do you want to live with me?" I grip her chin gently between my thumb and forefinger, tilting her face up to look at me.

"You don't think it's too soon?" She answers with her own question. "We're just going to skip the overnight bag step?"

Whomever just called, is calling me again. I glance at the clock on my night table. It's a little after ten pm. I'm the fucking President of the MC now. I have to at least check to see what they need. "Hold that thought, babe." I say, releasing her to fish my phone up off the floor from the pocket of my jeans. I toss them on the foot of the bed and glance at the screen. It's Viper. He never calls to bullshit. I hit the green icon and put the cell to my ear. "Yeah, bro. What's up?" I ask. I don't bother trying to sound like I'm not in the middle of something I'd much rather be doing than answering the phone.

"Preacher's dead." Viper says, cutting right to the point. Not at all what I was expecting to hear tonight.

"Well, shit... Hold on." I drop the phone to my chest and look back at Vanna. "Baby, why don't you jump in the shower. I'll be right in there. I gotta talk to Viper first."

"Okay." She says. I can tell she's curious about the call, but she doesn't try to ask about it. I watch her make her way across the bedroom to the bathroom as I sit down on the edge of the bed, slouching forward with my elbows on my knees, I bring the phone back to my ear.

"The fuck happened?" I ask.

"No idea. Gotta be foul play. Cops are over at his place now. Too many for a heart attack or a slip and fall situation." Viper says. "Good thing most of us have alibies for today. It's common knowledge now, that he was thrown out of the club. We're all probably going to be questioned."

The shower in the bathroom just turned on. I want to join Vanna in there, but it's looking like that's not going to happen. "Yeah. That's a real good look for us." I mutter. "They got an approximate time of death?"

"Apparently sometime between seven and nine tonight." He says.

"Shit. He ain't even cold yet. Do all our guys know?"

"Working on it."

My call waiting beeps in my ear, I pull the phone away to glance at the screen. It's Jason Caldwell. "Let me hit you back... Jason's calling in on my other line."

"Ten four." He replies. I switch over to Jason.

"Hey, bro." I answer.

"Preacher's dead." Jason says.

"What happened? Are you on the scene?" I ask.

"Drug induced heart attack. Looks like he over dosed. Found him in his office at home, needle on the desk in front of him. Right on his open Bible." Jason replies. Preacher was a lot of things. But I've never known him to be a drug user. His vice was cigars and whiskey. Not hardcore anything. "His Old Lady found him when she came home tonight, about an hour ago. We'll know more after the autopsy."

"Preacher wasn't a user." I say.

"His Old Lady said the same. Never shot up anything a day in his life." Jason agrees.

"Do I need to come down to the station? I know, being that we just ousted him from the MC and I took over, at least *I'm* going to be questioned, if not the whole MC."

"Nah. Not tonight." Jason says. "I'll give you a heads up if it's looking like it's gonna go that way. You were at the fundraiser, right?"

"I was until I took off with Vanna right around eight thirty. Been with her all night." I say. It's an alibi. Not exactly a strong one though. Multiple witnesses at the rally would have been better. "She's currently showering off the evidence of that fact."

Jason chuckles. "I wouldn't worry."

"I'm not. I was sticking it to my woman, not Preacher." I joke.

"Coroners here. I'll be in touch."

I hang up the phone, then bring up Viper's number to hit him back with the little bit of info I got from Jason, so he can pass it on to our MC brothers. Whether it was suicide, or homicide, I'm not sure. What I am sure about, is that it wasn't accidental.

Chucking my phone onto the night table, I head for the bathroom shower, unable to shake the feeling that this wasn't suicide, either.

Chapter
twentyeight
Vanna

"YOU REALLY DON'T HAVE TO GO WITH ME TO THIS THING." DEAN SAYS, grabbing his Saviors MC cut off the coat hanger by the front door of his house. He's wearing black jeans, black motorcycle boots, a black long-sleeved button-down shirt beneath the leather cut he just slipped on. He's not exactly formally dressed, as I would have expected when one attends a funeral, but he is definitely decked out in black. I guess biker funerals are more casual?

"Well, I own plenty of black clothing. I know I never met Preacher, but if you want me there, I don't mind going to support the club." I offer one last time. He gives me a quick smile.

"I appreciate it, doll. But there's some business I have to attend to, after the funeral. It's best if we just meet up later on." He seems to gently insist. I simply nod. He takes a few steps closer to me, gripping my chin gently in that way he does when he's trying to reassure me of something. "You could hang here and wait for me, if you want. Or better yet, go and start packing your shit. We don't have to wait until the end of the month for you to move in here." He smiles, before he bends to place a kiss against my lips.

"Is there another reason you don't want me there?" I ask. I just can't help feeling like there's something Dean isn't telling me. He's been a little bit off since he got the news of Preacher's passing almost two weeks ago.

"Of course not, doll." He says, moving his hand from my chin to run his fingers through the side of my hair, cupping my ear gently. "Just a lot of MC business. We can talk tonight, if you want to." He drops his hand from me and walks around to the other side of the kitchen island, opening a drawer to dig something out, then returns to me. "Here, this is yours now." He says, holding out a house key. "Will you be staying with me tonight?"

I tuck the key into my pocket and look back up at him. "Do you want me to?"

He gives me a wry look. "Is that a serious fuckin' question, babe?"

I cross my arms and shrug. "You've been a little distant all week."

"*Distant?*" He raises one brow at me, giving me a half smile as he grabs me around the waist and pulls me to him again. His hands slide down to my ass as he grips me tightly, pressing his hips forward against me. "I was inside you this very morning. Been in you every night." He growls. "*Distant?*" The word escapes him with a scoff. "Never."

"Okay." I sigh. "Go handle your biker business." I pat his leather clad chest. "I'll pack some stuff and come back here in a couple hours to get dinner going. Do you have any idea what time you expect to return so I can plan around that?"

"I'll shoot for six. Fair?" He says, after a moment's thought. I nod. "Aces." He smiles. "I'll see you later, baby." He bends to kiss me on the mouth again, before he releases me and grabs his keys off the hook by the front door. As he opens the door, he pauses to look back at me. "Vanna... I'm really happy you're moving in with me." He says, pulling his pair of dark aviator sunglasses out of the inner pocket of his cut.

I give him a little smile back. "Me too."

With one last grin, he slips the shades on his eyes and turns to step out into the bright sunlight of a brisk fall afternoon. I walk to the front door and watch him mount Serene, then take off down the drive way, past the corn fields, past my rental and beyond the pecan orchard, until the road bends and he's no longer in my sight.

DEAN

As I suspected he would be, Legion and his *Legion* of bikers, are in full attendance today. As are a few members of the JoCo Jokers, and the Asphalt Knights. Preacher's funeral looks like it's eighty percent MC's. I'm standing beside his weeping widow, my arm around her shoulders, as she grieves the legally determined suicide of her husband. My crew is in full attendance as well, including prospects. Regardless of how things ended between us and him, Preacher had still been a Savior for thirty-five years. I had been conflicted about the MC showing up to his funeral, until his wife reached out to me and asked that we be here. I simply couldn't deny her tearful request. She'd been a Savior's Old Lady for thirty-five years, too. I'm here, for *her*.

Unseen behind my dark shades, I'm watching Legion, who just so happens to be standing opposite me, on the other side of Preacher's flower covered casket. Though I can't tell for certain, because he's wearing shades too, I'm sure he's hawking me as well. The slightest movement of his head tells me he's searching for someone in the crowd around me. Someone who he expects to be here with me. The fact that my entire crew *is here*, only confirms my suspicion, that he's looking for *Vanna*...

I knew Legion would be here today. And though I hopefully played it off as it being mostly *her* choice in not attending this funeral with me, leaving Vanna home, was the right move. I would have insisted that she not attend today, if she would have decided for herself to accompany me. My gut tells me there's more to this entire situation with the CDMC than we currently know. I have not forgotten that Legion sought Vanna out once before at her job, and made those slick comments to her. That was to get to me, for some reason. As far as I know, he hasn't been around her since. I trust that Vanna would have told me if he had been. I can only hope he lost interest in whatever that ploy was about, when he didn't receive a reaction out of me. And perhaps, with her absence here today, his interest will dwindle further.

That faint curl at the corner of his mouth tells me he's watching me, too.

The minister drones on for another twenty minutes, until it's ashes to ashes, dust to dust time. I walk Preacher's widow up to his casket so she can place her flower on top of it and say her final goodbye to him. I say nothing, only hold her in my arms when she curls back into me for support, weeping against my chest while they proceed to lower him into the ground. When the whole ordeal is said and done, I escort her back to her black limo, and assure her that I will be at her house later, as promised, once the reception concludes. As the limo pulls away, the sound of motorcycles revving up and departing as well, echo throughout the cemetery.

Steeling myself for what's next on today's agenda, I continue to walk across the southern section of the large cemetery, between headstones and over fallen leaves scattered about the manicured lawn. She's waiting for me, near a specific headstone. I spot a woman across the way, crouched before a stone beneath the large oak tree. That could be her, but it's been a while, and I only saw her photo once before. If it is her, she's grown out her hair a bit. The woman I saw in the photo, had a short blonde, pixie style cut. This woman's hair is shoulder length, and now that I'm closer, a more natural shade of blonde.

She stands as I approach her, an awkward smile on her face. "Dean Keegan?" She asks, her blue eyes searching mine.

"Yes, ma'am." I reply. Her smile slips into a more genuine expression now. "Janie, I presume?" I smile back at her.

"Yes, Janie." She tucks one side of her hair behind her ear and gestures to the headstone we agreed to meet at. "Did you have a hard time finding us?" She asks.

"No ma'am. I knew exactly the spot you were describing when we spoke on the phone." I assure her.

"Do you meet women in cemeteries often?" She chuckles as she asks. It's kind of a funny question, I'll give her that. I give her another smile, too.

"No. My mother is buried on the other side of this big old tree." I tell her.

"Oh my." She looks horrified suddenly. "It was thoughtless of me to make a joke like that. I'm so sorry."

"It was funny, Janie. Really, I'm not offended by any means." I try to reassure her. We both glance down at the headstone we agreed to meet at. "I'm sorry for your loss. I didn't know your grandfather passed away... I only met him once, but he left an impression. A good man, who loved you very much."

"You would know, even if your meeting was brief." She says. I don't comment, and quickly steer this conversation in another safer, *less incriminating* direction.

"He mentioned you moving in with some family in another state." I say.

"Yes, I've got cousins and a job in Tulsa, Oklahoma. It's been really great." She sounds happy. I'm glad it worked out for her. "I'm just in town to settle his estate, and then I'm off again."

"Well, you have my number... if you encounter any... *problems*... while you're here." I let her know. I don't need to elaborate on that statement, when Janie looks up at me. Tears almost instantly welling up in her eyes as her lips press together, her chin wobbling slightly. She nods in understanding. I'm not sure what to even do as she takes a few steps closer to me. I've never been in this situation before. She reaches out to me and wraps her arms around my neck, holding me to her tightly. I think, instinctively, I hug her back. Autopilot type reaction. I hold her for a few moments, letting her get whatever this is, out of her system.

"Thank you..." Her voice is tight and shaky as she says those two simple words, but I don't say anything back. I don't know what to say. *You're welcome* just sounds wrong, somehow. She presses a light kiss to the side of my face, and I release her the moment I feel her hold on me loosen. She steps back from me, wiping her eyes.

"Do you want to go for a ride on my bike?" I ask. I don't know what else to fuckin' say, and she won the bid anyway, so, why not that?

"Oh, you don't have to." She says, with a wave of her hand. "I just took a silly chance because I was unsure about just walking up on you in your bar. I just figured if it was meant to be..."

"A silly chance? That's an expensive silly chance." I say, giving her a slightly suspicious, but I hope still nonthreatening, look. "I got a shit ton of bids, doll. How many did you throw in for this to work out?" I ask.

When she giggles at me, I'm relieved. "Okay... quite a few." She admits.

"Then you're getting what you paid for. I insist." I smile. "Come on, she's waiting for us." I say, extending my arm for her to take.

"She?" Janie asks, slipping her hand around my arm without the slightest bit of hesitation. I escort her back across the cemetery in the direction of my bike.

"Serene." I reply, when the distinct sound of a zippo lighter pinging open catches my attention. I already know who it is. When the zippo clangs shut again, I glance to my right in the direction of the sound, as I continue to walk with Janie on my arm. Legion is seated on a concrete memorial bench among a grouping of headstones a few yards away. Watching me. A sneer across his face as he pulls a long drag from his cigarette. Blowing a cloud of smoke, he cocks his chin at me as we pass. I don't bother reciprocating the gesture. No sense in false pretense. I never believed for a moment that the CDMC wanted an alliance with the Saviors.

"Someone you know?" Janie asks, glancing towards Legion as well.

"Not really." I say, allowing him to notice me placing my hand gently over the hand she has looped through my arm. "How long are you in town for?" I ask, hoping it isn't long.

"I leave the day after tomorrow. Cheaper to fly on Tuesdays and Wednesdays."

Aces...

When we get to Serene, I hand Janie the spare helmet and take my time helping her strap it on, checking it to make sure it's secure and comfortable for her. Legion is leaning against a tree in the distance, watching us. Analyzing my interactions with Janie. Probably wondering if Vanna and I split. Or If Vanna and I aren't that serious. Maybe we never were. Which would only be a good thing, for Vanna, to be of less importance to Legion. Of less interest. I'd feel worse about using Janie like this, if she wasn't leaving town in the immediate future. But she is. And so, I am. Even through this slight pang of guilt I feel nagging me in my chest, I know I'd be more than willing and able, to do a whole lot worse in the name of Vanna's safety.

Strapping my helmet on, I sling a leg over Serene, firing her up. "Grab onto my shoulders and climb on, doll." I say to Janie. "Then just wrap your arms around me and hold on tight. There are pedals for your feet right there." I say, dropping an arm to point for her. She places her feet where they need to be and wraps her arms around me. I give Serene a few revs before I kick up her stand. "You ready, doll?" I ask Janie over my shoulder.

"I'm already a little nervous." She laughs, and I feel her adjust her grip on me to hold on a little tighter.

"Don't be." I smile at her. "Feels like Freedom."

BALANCING TWO BOXES ON MY KNEE, BRACED AGAINST THE FRAME OF Dean's front door and one of my arms, I struggle to get the key Dean gave me in the lock and twist the door knob open. Shoving it hard, it swings open a few feet and I'm able to shuffle inside without dropping either box. Not that it would matter too much, it's just clothing. But still. I kick the door shut with my foot and carry the two boxes over to the kitchen island, lifting them up to place them on top of the marble. I could only fit several boxes in the back seat of my little Honda Civic, so I make another two trips to my car to bring the rest of them inside. Dean had told me to clear out whatever drawers I needed, so I spend some time condensing a few of his together, to make room for some of my clothes. The rest I put on hangers, and hang them up in a small section of his walk-in closet.

The last two boxes are full of oils, incense and smudge supplies. I'm not sure how he feels about smoking up his house, so I decide to leave those two boxes packed. I really don't have anywhere to put them. But his house is so neat and tidy, I don't want to just leave them out. He said some of these closed doors were spare rooms. A guest bathroom. An office. Besides the two that happen to be a bathroom, and the other, a laundry room, they're all locked. That's odd. He never told me not to try to open them, though. And if I'm going to be living here...

I walk back down the hallway towards the key rack by the front door and grab the ring of keys there that must be extra's he has for the house and the garages outside. Probably everything for the farm too. Walking back to the hallway, I sort through the keys, looking for ones that seem more *house-ish* than *tractor-ish*. I try a few, until finally, one works. Pushing the door open, I flick on the light to an empty room. Not even storage. Just empty. A room with two windows and a closet. The floor matches the rest of the house, and the walls are a neutral linen color. Total blank canvas.

Wondering if they're all empty, I check the others. One of the remaining two is an office, with a nice desk made from some kind of dark stained wood. The built-in shelves along the walls match the desk and are filled with books. The wood slated blinds that cover the tall windows behind the desk match as well. There's a book on the desk, folded open as if someone had been reading it. *Meditations*, by Marcus Aurelius. I glance around the office for a moment longer, it's pretty classy looking, and I'm curious what other books Dean has in here, but I close the door and move on to the last room nearest the master bedroom.

Twisting the key in the door knob, I push the door open and flick on the light. The room is a pastel yellow, with light pink curtains on the double windows. The floor is a matching pale pink carpet, and along the ceiling, a wall papered border of pink baby elephants, monkeys and giraffes. In the corner of the room, there's something that looks as though it had once been a crib... Only it's completely and utterly destroyed. Like a truck ran it over... Splintered wood, in pieces, just smashed and piled in the far corner of the room...

What the hell is a room like this doing in Dean's house? He told me he didn't have kids with Lucinda... That he didn't have kids, *at all*. Yet, this is clearly a *baby's* room. A baby girl, specifically... Not even the carpet was taken out to match the rest of the flooring in the house, which is the same in every single room, including the other locked ones. This room was intentionally left untouched in his remodeling.

Flicking off the light, I quickly pull the door shut as I back out into the hallway, relocking it. I was going to put my boxes in that first empty room, but I'm not going to, now. I don't even want him to know I looked in that empty room, or he'll assume I did exactly what I just did, and checked out all of them. There has to be a reason for this baby room... Why would he lie to me about kids? Is that why Lucinda wanted to get to know me? Why she wants him back? Is Lucinda's daughter actually Dean's? And why is that crib so horribly smashed up like that, discarded in the corner? That was disturbing...

I hurry back towards the key rack and hang his keys back up, as if I never touched them. And I kind of wish I hadn't now. Glancing at the clock in the kitchen, it's a quarter after five. He told me he'd be back around six. Grabbing my two boxes, I place them against the wall near the entrance to the hallway so they're not in the way. For the next forty-five minutes, I busy myself, and my mind, with preparing something for dinner tonight. I don't even want to think about that baby room right now... that demolished crib...

GLANCING AT MY WATCH AS I KNOCK ON PREACHER'S WIDOW'S FRONT door, I realize it's already a quarter after five. I told Vanna I'd shoot for walking in the door at six tonight. So, I need to make this quick if I'm going to be on time for dinner. She already thinks I'm being distant. I don't want her to start feeling like she isn't a priority. She is.

As much as I despised Preacher in the end, there isn't a part of me that honestly believes Preacher killed himself. Especially not by banging

609

heroin into his arm. They found no evidence of a struggle. No evidence of a break in, and as far as anyone can tell, he was alone. No prints. Nothing pointing to anyone besides himself. But it hasn't sat well with me all week. And the way Legion was sneering at me... Fuck, I hope he read too far into my interactions with Janie today, and drops whatever he's thinking about Vanna.

The sound of footsteps on the other side of the door creak on the floor boards before it opens. "Come in," Preacher's widow says, still wearing her black dress from the funeral, her hair in a now somewhat messy brown bun. She holds open the screen door for me to enter her home. I follow her inside, and she invites me to sit down in one of the floral-patterned chairs in the cluttered parlor room with her.

"What is it you wanted to discuss with me?" I ask. I don't want to make small talk about a man I despised for the last five years. And I'm too short on time to beat around the bush.

"I wanted to make you an offer, before I put the place up for sale." She says, grabbing a tissue from the box on the coffee table between us. "I have no idea how to run the cigar shop."

"You want to sell Stogies to me?" I ask. I'm a little surprised she wants to discuss business the day of her husband's funeral.

"I was actually thinking more like a partnership." She says. "You hire people to run it, we split the profits after monthly expenses."

"What percentage split did you have in mind?" I ask. Legal income is never a bad thing. And Stogies has been an established business for years. There is potential here.

"I can survive with fifty-fifty. I think that's more than fair. I just need it to be someone I can trust not to screw an old lady over." She says. "Pardon the pun."

I nod. "I'll have to bring it to the table for a vote. I've got a lot on my personal plate to be able to take on a fourth business just myself. But the Saviors MC is another story."

"When will you be able to tell me something?" She asks.

"This week. Will have to have Diesel take a peek at the financial records first, though. Do you have access to those? He's going to want to see how well the shops been doing the last couple of years before we can give you an answer."

"All the records are in Preacher's office... but..." She stops talking, closing her eyes as she presses the tissue to her face and takes a quivering breath. "I can't bring myself to go in there yet..."

I do feel for her. "I'm sorry, Ginny. Do you have anyone staying with you? Or perhaps someplace else to stay, if that's easier than being here?"

"My sister, she just ran to the store for a few things. She's staying with me for a couple of weeks."

"Good. Is there anything else I can do for you, while I'm here, before I go?"

"The records are on the shelf behind his desk. Green folders. You can take them all with you. This year's records are still in the office at the shop." She explains.

"All right... I'll go get them and bring them to the clubhouse. Have Diesel look them over the next few days, and I'll get them back to you."

"Alright, thank you." She lifts her arm and points in the direction of the office. "Just back there, first room on the left." She instructs me. "And if you wouldn't mind, would you bring me out his bible? I'd like to read it, please... It's right on his desk... where it's been since this happened. I haven't been able to bring myself to go in there."

I stand up and squeeze her shoulder gently. "Sure, Ginny. I'll be right back."

Walking across the house towards his office, I push the door open and flick on the light. The bible is on the desk, as both Ginny and Jason said it had been. As I make my way slowly into the room, I glance down at the pages in the open Bible, curious as to what Preacher might have been reading before he, according to the Medical Examiner's autopsy report, committed suicide...

It's an Old King James Bible... And as I read the words of the bible verse the book had been open to, my blood suddenly runs cold in my veins...

Mark 5:9 "And he asked him, What is thy name? And he answered, saying, "My name is** Legion, **for we are many..."

Chapter
twenty-nine
DEAN

"ALL IN FAVOR OF THE SAVIORS MC TAKING HALF OWNERSHIP OF STOGIES Tobacco and Cigars Shop, raise your hands." I glance around the table at my fully patched brothers, and it's a unanimous vote. "Looks like we're going into the tobacco business, fellas." I say, slamming the gavel down once. "Diesel, you get everything drawn up, and we'll take it to Ginny and make it official."

"You got it, Prez." Diesel says, gathering the financial records together and shoving them back into the box I brought them in. "I'm just gonna have a prospect make copies for our records and I'll have them brought back to Preacher's widow."

I nod. "Is there any other business we need to discuss before this meeting is adjourned?" I glance around a table full of head shakes and verbal declinations. "All right, meeting adjourned... You're all free to go." I hit the gavel once more. As Brothers get up from the table and exit the room, I reach to either side of me and grab both Viper and Viking by their arms to halt them. "I need a minute with you two. Hang back." I say, just loud enough for them to hear me. Axel notices though, and gives me a confused look. "Shut the door and sit down." I say to him. He immediately closes the double doors and twists the lock, then rejoins us at the table.

"What's wrong?" Axel asks. "How come it's just us?"

"I'm just gonna say what we all suspect. But I don't want this getting out of control. It should stay between the four of us until we know exactly what we're dealing with." I say. They're all looking at me with piqued curiosity. "I'm pretty sure Legion killed Preacher."

"Well, yeah. That's the only thing that makes any sense. And he got away with it." Viper says. "No forced entry. No prints of any kind other than Preacher's and his Ol' Lady's. Even the needle he used only had Preacher's prints on it... But why are you saying that now?"

"When I went to meet with Ginny about this business deal with Stogies, I was in Preacher's office to get the financial records. She asked me to bring her Preacher's Bible." I say.

"Yeah, so?" Viking asks. "What does that have to do with Legion?"

"Because of the page it was open to. Where he *supposedly* placed the needle after banging a lethal dose in his vein. I think it was a warning." I say. "The page was open to Mark 5:9."

"What's the significance of Mark 5:9?" Viking asks.

"Holy shit..." Axel says, having already brought the bible verse up on his cell phone. He looks up at us from his phone with wide eyes. "Are you kidding?"

"The fuck does it say?" Viking demands.

"*Then Jesus asked him, 'What is your name?'*" Axel begins to read the quote off his cell phone screen.

"*My name is* Legion... *For we are many.*" Viper finishes the quote upon realization. He's wearing a similar blood drained expression, to the one I probably wore myself when I first read it. "Fuck..."

"Fuck is right." Viking says with a scoff.

"Call me a conspiracy nut, but that's too much of a coincidence for me." I say.

"Creeper kept grinning at the funeral too." Axel says. "Probably knows even if we found out about it, there ain't shit we can do."

"I don't want him to know we ever noticed this." I say, "That's why I'm only telling you three. He's mind fucking us, at least trying to. He's attempted to involve Vanna in the mental warfare against us as well. Fucking with me through her."

"The fuck you mean he's going through Vanna?" Viking demands. "And why the fuck am I, your goddamn *Sergeant at Arms!* Just hearing about this security threat now?" He throws his huge tattooed arms up at me.

"Maybe because you're always a dick to her?" Axel shrugs. Viking doesn't bother trying to argue against Axel's point, but he looks slightly taken aback by his comment.

"I appreciate the solidarity, Axel." I say to him, before I look back at Viking. "I wasn't sure if he just wanted to fuck her, or if there was something deeper than that." I say to him. "But after the funeral... I'm leaning towards the latter."

"We're going to need the details, Dean." Viper insists.

I let out a sigh, running a hand through my hair as I sit back in my seat. I don't want to go into explicit details and violate her privacy, *our* privacy, as an intimate couple now. "Alright, what I can say, is that the night of Axel's patch party... Vanna and I... we were messing around a little after the fight... Which I believe Legion orchestrated as well." I say. "But there were things Legion said to Vanna weeks later, that had to do with... *specifics* Vanna and I did together that night of the bonfire."

"Could you be less fucking vague for securities sake?" Viking gripes at me. "And when did he talk to Vanna?"

"He went to her job. Bought a bunch of witch shit and was making innuendos." I say.

"Do I need to ask her myself?" Viking demands impatiently.

Fuck no. She'd have my balls for that!

"Under handed comments about getting his hands in her drawers." I sigh. "Shit like that. Gave her his number and address to the Demons' Den too. But for him to have made that specific comment to her... He had to have seen us. He had to have known she would tell me what he said. He had to have known it would piss me the fuck off, and I can only assume it was to get in my head, maybe to provoke me into making a sloppy move on him." I explain. "The funeral actually confirmed my suspicion. He was looking for Vanna there. I could tell he was confused by her absence, since we were all there, Old Ladies included."

"The Bible is another attempt at provoking some sort of a move." Viper says. "He has to know we'd suspect him, even before you found his message. The bible was just to solidify it in our heads. Legion killed Preacher, and got away with it."

"Why would he want to kill Preacher to begin with?" Axel asks. "He wasn't even a Savior anymore."

"Maybe because Preacher failed some task Legion put him to." I shrug. "If you read the rest of that verse in the bible, it goes on to mention demons being cast into pigs, which then run into the sea to drown... Maybe we were the pigs he wanted his Demons cast into... We, as in, the MC. And Preacher couldn't get it done. You guys wouldn't vote the Demons in to patch over to the Saviors. That had to have been Legion's original plan. That fake Savior Prospect I fought that night, I know for a fact I saw him at the Demons' Den. Legion wanted to take over our territory by infiltrating the MC. When we took back the MC, got rid of the members we suspected to be Demons, Preacher not only lost his usefulness to Legion, maybe he also knew too much." I watch as my brothers contemplate my theory.

"It makes sense." Viper nods. "Though, why would Legion choose this MC? This town of all the places he could have gone with? Why the Saviors?"

"That's what we need to figure out." I say. "And if he did in fact, kill Preacher, we all need to watch our backs. Something about him tells me he's not going to throw in the towel just because plan A didn't work out. Legion chose us for a reason. And I don't think it's simply because we're based in a small town with a small police force. There's got to be something more significant in this for him."

"When you spent time out West, Nevada, Arizona. You encountered the CDMC out there." Viking says. "Did you cross paths with Legion?"

I shake my head. "I'd remember him if I had. Even if he was going by a different road name back then." Would be hard to forget his demonic physique and creepy hands. "My dealings with the Demons, was minuscule. The job I did out West that you're referring to, involved another MC entirely. I'd remember Legion if we had ever met before."

My cellphone buzzes in my pocket, and I pull it out to check in case it's Vanna. It isn't. It's Lucinda with a text marked *Urgent*. I'd ignore it, if not for Maddie's existence. Because of Maddie, Lucinda knows I can never ignore her completely. As my brothers deliberate their theories on Legion and the CDMC, I open Lucinda's text.

Maddie needs you. Meet us at your house. Be there in twenty.

Fuck me. "I gotta go." I say, shoving the phone back inside the inner pocket of my cut as I get up from the table. "Let everyone know to watch their backs, but keep the details to yourselves. I don't want anyone going rogue and starting a fuckin' war with the Demons we're not ready for." Even though the psychological warfare between our MC's kicked off the night Legion showed up at the roadhouse, and has continued since.

"Where are you rushing off to?" Viking asks.

"Lucinda just sent me an urgent text that Maddie needs me... She knows I can't blow her off..." I shake my head at my seemingly impossible situation with her.

"Because it's Maddie." Viking sighs.

I nod. "It's Maddie."

When Maddie throws her little arms around my neck, squealing with innocent elation, it's always a bitter sweet moment. Happiness and guilt surge through me simultaneously. I'm not a consistent presence in her life, the way I should be. Though the reasons aren't entirely my fault. Perhaps she realizes this, on some level. And so, she never seems to hold even the slightest grudge against me for my long absences in her life.

Her little body in my arms, I cherish the feeling of holding her for a few brief moments, before I place her back on her feet in my driveway. The moment Maddie ran down my steps and into my arms as I dismounted Serene, I knew she was fine.

Maddie needs you... Just another ploy to get me right where she wants me. The only chain Lucinda has left on me. A little blonde headed girl that isn't even mine. I glance up at Lucinda, standing on my front porch, her arms crossed, looking none too pleased.

"To what do I owe this special visit?" I smile down into Maddie's brown eyes. In the afternoon sun, they look almost golden brown as they peer back up at me. Like the color of a jar of raw buckwheat honey, when sunlight passes through it. Only slightly lighter than the way the sun makes Vanna's dark eyes look.

"I missed you." She smiles, though I know that's not the reason Lucinda brought her to me.

"I miss you too, darlin'." I smile back at her. She takes my hand and tugs me to walk with her back towards her waiting mother.

"We need to talk." Lucinda says, her tone sounding grave. She gives me a look as if to tell me she'd prefer to have this talk alone. Which further confirms to me that once again, Maddie is just a pawn in this situation. Lucinda's trump card. Her guarantee that I'd not only show up, but that I won't flip out on her in Maddie's presence. I try not to glare at her as I unlock my front door.

"Go grab yourself a snack, sweetheart. Momma and I will be right there." I say, pushing the door open for Maddie, then closing it behind her when she steps inside. I give her a few moments to make her way further inside towards the kitchen, before I look back at Lucinda. "What the fuck now?"

Lucinda gestures through the glass of my front door. "Are those moving boxes?"

"I asked Vanna to move in with me. Clearly, she said yes." I reply. "Now, you obviously lied and used Maddie to get me here. So, what is this about?"

"Maddie *does* need you." Lucinda says. "And you're choosing that *witch*, literally, over her." All I can do is stare at her in astonishment for a moment, as I gather my thoughts. Her hypocrisy and manipulation, truly know no bounds.

"Fuckin', *what?*" I shake my head. "Do you even hear yourself? You've kept Maddie from me long before Vanna walked into my life. Try again."

She scowls at me. "The way you treated me when I brought you that file, for your own damn good, by the way! Had me thrown out!"

"Yeah, and I meant it. I want nothing to do with you, Lucinda. Whatever we may have had in the past, it's broken beyond repair. You shattered it when you pulled your shit years ago. When you went after Vanna, you only stomped on the already broken pieces and pulverized them to dust. I'll always be there for Maddie. *Just, Maddie.* So, work your shit out with Daniel... My heart and my wallet, are forever closed to you."

Lucinda glares at me, taking a step closer to get in my face. "You owe Daniel more than what you gave him." She sneers at me.

And just like that, she proves once again, she never really fuckin' loved me.

Vanna

THE PLAN WAS TO USE DEAN'S SILVERADO TRUCK TO MOVE A FEW MORE boxes, since my backseat isn't cutting it fast enough for him. Lucinda's silver Lexus SUV is parked in Dean's driveway when I arrive after work, and I am so not in the mood to deal with her. I pull around it and park near the detached garage where he keeps his bikes. As I get out of my car, Lucinda storms out of Dean's house, pulling a little girl behind her. A little blonde girl, maybe five or six years old. Dean storms out after her but stops short of the steps. Lucinda spots me and starts walking purposefully in my direction.

"Will you take her for a few minutes?" She asks, completely throwing me off. The kid looks scared. I have no idea what's going on, but whatever it is, this child doesn't need to see any more of it.

"Yeah, sure." What else am I going to say? "What's going on?"

"This is my daughter. I made a mistake in bringing her here." Lucinda says, speaking quickly. "Her name is Maddie." Lucinda looks down at her daughter. "Maddie, this is Vanna. She's very nice. Stay with her and be a good girl. Mommy will be back in a few minutes."

The little girl takes my hand reluctantly, as Lucinda goes storming back towards Dean. I look at him for some kind of answer. He just nods and cocks his head slightly to the side, gesturing for me to lead the little girl away.

"Okay, kiddo. Let's go far a little walk." I say, trying to sound upbeat and friendly. "Want to go look at some chickens? Dean has some beside the house over there." I don't know what else to do with her. That's all I've got.

"M'kay." She says, shyly, still not really looking at me. I don't blame her. I'm not exactly comfortable myself. I lead her to the coop towards the side of Dean's house, glancing back to make sure she can't see the front porch from where we are.

"So, Maddie, how old are you?" I ask, trying to make child appropriate small talk.

"Five." She says sweetly, looking at the chickens.

"Oh, so are you in kindergarten?"

"Yeah."

"Do you like school?"

"Yes, it's fun. We paint and count and do our names." She explains.

"Awesome." I say, awkwardly.

She looks up at me and giggles. Her eyes look exactly like Dean's. Her nose is a more feminine version of his... But he told me he never had kids with Lucinda...

"Is Maddie short for Madeline?" I ask.

She nods. Why would Lucinda name her daughter after Dean's mother if she isn't Dean's?

"Maddie!" I hear Lucinda shout from the front yard.

"We're by the chickens!" I call back. I look down at the little girl. "I guess we'd better go." She takes my hand again and we walk back to Lucinda, where her mother basically snatches her from me and is back to ignoring my existence.

"Nice to meet you, Maddie." I wave.

"Nice to meet you too." She says politely. Lucinda beeps her SUV and tells her daughter to get in and wait for her. "But I want to say bye to Dee!" She insists, and goes running to the porch. Dean kneels and scoops her up into his arms, kissing her cheek.

"I love you, monkey!" He tells her. "You remember that always, okay?" He looks like he loves her. How did he not mention anything about this little girl in all the months we've known each other, when he obviously adores her?

"I love you too." She says, hugging him tightly around his throat. He puts her down and she bounds back down the steps to her mother's car and gets inside.

"Is anybody going to tell me what's going on?" I ask.

Lucinda looks at me for a moment. "You're still young, Vanna. Do yourself a favor and find a man worthwhile."

"And why on earth would I take relationship advice from a woman who cheats on her husbands?" I ask. She wants to slap me. I can see it on her face, but she won't do it in front of her daughter.

Instead, she turns back to Dean. "He is going to be here any minute!"

"Don't care." Dean says, pulling out his bowie knife and picking at his finger nail with the tip. He twists it slowly, making the setting sun bounce off the blade.

"Knock it off! Daniel is your brother!" Lucinda shouts at him. "He's your only family!"

Wait a minute... Daniel? As in Daniel... *Dean's* biological *brother? The one that's dead to him... No way.*

I'm about to ask one of them to clear this up for me, when I notice Dean's expression changes instantly from impassive to complete rage. "My only family is that little girl sitting in that car that I paid for!" He snarls at her. "And you fucking *stole* her!"

Stole her?

I stand there with my mouth gaping open, and before I can even raise the question, a motorcycle comes barreling up the driveway and skids to a halt beside Lucinda's Lexus. Dean's expression darkens upon its arrival. The man riding the bike is dressed in black with a full blacked out shielded helmet. I've seen him before. When Dean and I got caught in the rain that day... a few months ago. The night we had our first kiss.

Daniel dismounts the bike, pulling off his helmet and slams it onto the seat. He's a tall man, like Dean. He's got similar features, only he's got a bulkier build. Dean is the more attractive of the two, but Daniel isn't unattractive by any means. A lot of women would find him appealing, too.

Lucinda steps into his path as he makes his way angrily towards Dean.

"Our daughter is in the car, don't do anything to upset her!" Lucinda warns him.

"Daddy!" I hear the little girl shriek with glee as she bolts from the car towards him, throwing her little arms around his thigh. He leans slightly to stroke the top of her little blonde head.

I glance at Dean in time to see a glimmer of pain behind his eyes.

"Go wait in the car, Munchkin. Adults have to talk." Maddie obediently returns to her mother's SUV. "What is going on here?" Daniel demands.

Dean points at them in a seemingly nonchalant manner with the knife, jerking it from one to the other. "You two are trespassing. That's what." He says. "You both know you're not welcome back here."

"This is family land!" Daniel says angrily.

"Not anymore. I bought you out of everything. This is *my* land. *My* money. *My* bike shop. Now, *my* fucking MC. You'd do well to get that through your thick skull." Dean snaps.

Daniel takes a few steps towards him as Lucinda tries to block him.

Dean shoves the blade back in its sheath and jumps down the porch steps. I hurry over to him and grab his arm as they both look like they are ready to start swinging on each other.

"You're just pissed Lucinda jumped ship to me." Daniel sneers at him.

"Oh, I'm over *that*, believe me." Dean growls. "Don't blame me though if she's come to regret that decision."

"Jesus Christ!" Lucinda yells at him. "Can we please just handle this all in court?"

"I sold everything I had at the time to buy you out!" Dean shouts, glaring at his brother. "I struggled for years to make it all work out. You think it's my fault you didn't use the money wisely? You let Lucinda burn through it, huh? Not my fucking problem. Now that I've succeeded, despite you two and the *Hell* you dragged me through. You want what I've built now? It's not going to happen. You've taken enough from me, *brother*." He almost spits the word out of his mouth. "You'll never get another fucking thing from me, ever again. I've had to bounce back twice because of the two of you." He lifts his arm to shove two fingers towards his brother's face. Then I notice Dean glance at Maddie in the SUV, dropping his arm. "Make that *three times*."

Daniel glares at him. "She was never yours."

Dean looks like he could murder someone. That calm seething hate boiling inside him is honestly more bone chilling than when he's actually raging. "But you both let me believe she was mine for a year, didn't you?" He says with complete and utter disdain. "Before you tore my life apart."

"*Oh my God!*" I can't hold back my shocked horror... The mangled crib immediately jumping back to the forefront of my mind... If they did that to him... no wonder... I look at Lucinda, horrified. She sees that I've put it together and shrinks from my gaze, turning back to her husband, trying to convince him to leave. I glance back at Dean, he's still seething, his eyes burning into his brother.

"I didn't know the truth at first either, Dean." Daniel says. At least there's a hint of remorse in his words this time.

"Five months. *Five whole months*, I held her believing she was mine." Dean mutters. "When did you know for sure? The whole time? A few weeks after she was born? Meeting in secret behind my fucking back about her, too? Both of you plotting how to rip her from my life! How to *take everything from me!*"

"She isn't yours!" Daniel shouts back at him.

I can see Dean making a very conscious effort to control himself, taking a long, deep breath before he speaks. "Yeah. I fucking get it. That was made painfully clear to me five years ago." Dean sighs. "You and Lucinda deserve each other."

The car horn beeps as Maddie is running out of patience in Lucinda's vehicle.

"You two should go, this isn't fair to Maddie." I say.

"Stay out of this, bitch. You've got nothing to do with any of this!" Daniel shouts at me, his finger raised and pointing.

Dean goes to lunge at him, but Lucinda and I work together to keep them apart.

"You ever talk to Vanna like that again, so help me God I will lay you the fuck out! I don't care if your daughter is watching." Dean threatens.

"You're a fucking savage!" Lucinda yells at him. "And you wonder why I left you! Why I had to do it the way I did! Don't think I won't get another restraining order!"

Dean looks at her incredulously. "I never laid a hand on you, Lucinda!" Dean says to her, as she tries again to convince Daniel to leave. But then Dean's expression changes, and he grins darkly. "Except for our little *arrangement*, right?" He sneers at her.

She whirls around to glare at him. *"Don't!"* She hisses.

"Oh, come on, fair's fair!" He taunts her.

"What is he talking about?" Daniel looks at Lucinda. She says nothing in response to the question, only continues to plead to leave, now more desperately than ever.

"I fucked your wife, Daniel. Figured I owed you one... Well, more than one." He sneers at Lucinda. "You used to make me *count* the times. What did we make it to?" He says the words with so much hate, I can almost feel that dark emotion radiating off of him, but I have no idea what he's talking about. I just hope it wasn't recent...

Lucinda looks like she could spit fire.

Daniel glares at Lucinda for a moment, then back at Dean. "I'll be in touch with my lawyer."

"Tell him his bike will be ready Tuesday." Dean scoffs.

Daniel shoves Lucinda away from him and storms back to his bike, ignoring her pleas to wait and let her explain. He skids out of the driveway and takes off down the street.

Lucinda's eyes are blazing with rage as she whirls back around on Dean. "You will fucking *pay* for that!" She nearly screams the threat at him.

Dean smiles, but it's a fierce expression rather than friendly. "There you go again, Lucinda. After my wallet. Some things never change." He says sarcastically, then turns and walks back up his porch steps.

Lucinda shifts her focus to me. "Do you want to know the real reason he's so pissed off?"

"I'll let him explain, thanks." I make no attempt to hide my snarky tone. As if I'd trust a word out of this woman's mouth about *anything*. Especially not after what I just learned today.

She smiles at me, but it isn't friendly, either. "I can respect that about you, Vanna, you actually do seem like a standup woman." I definitely was not expecting a compliment, but I brace myself internally for the actual blow. No way in Hell a bitch like Lucinda is leaving on a high note. Not after Dean threw her under the bus in front of her husband.

Lucinda steps closer to me, a nasty little grin on her face. "That big dick he's got, that *shot gun*, ain't nothing but a *cap gun*." She sneers.

I glance at Dean in time to see his body tense, and I notice something subtle changes about his expression. There was a flash of vulnerability in his eyes. It crossed his features so quickly, I would have missed it if I wasn't paying close attention. Most don't get to see this side of Dean. He never lets them. He exudes a screw you, rugged, in your face alpha virility. But in that momentary lapse of self-control, I saw a man who was once broken. Maybe still is. I turn back to Lucinda.

"What the fuck are you even saying?" I snap at her.

"He shoots *blanks*, sweetie." She says in a patronizingly obnoxious tone. "He's so bitter because Maddie isn't his. She was never his *miracle baby*." She mutters, deliberately mocking the term, and I know it's just to hurt him more. "You're still a young woman, Vanna. Don't waste your youth on him. He can't give you what every woman really wants. We tried for years and he couldn't do it."

Ouch. I don't even want to turn around and look in Dean's face. I know that had to hit him hard. "You don't speak for every woman, least of all me." I snap back at her. "He's mine. Now get the fuck out of here before I hurt you, I don't want to scare your kid. And we both know you love that pretty face of yours too much to risk me ripping it off."

She glances back at Dean with a satisfied smirk. The dagger wasn't meant for me at all. It was all him. And she nailed him. She knows it. I don't have to look at him to know he's behind me bleeding from a deep festering wound, she just tore wide open again.

"Don't say I never did you any favors." She smiles wickedly at me.

I say nothing. I watch her get in her car where her daughter has been waiting. I watch them leave Dean's driveway and drive off down the hill. I watch them until they are out of sight, and then some. I do not want to turn around and face him, yet. His complete silence tells me he's not ready to face me either.

I close my eyes to think on all that has just come to light. Everything makes sense now. This was the last piece of the puzzle. Dean couldn't give Lucinda a baby. She had wanted it all from him. The house. The money. The cars. The kid. He gave her all he could, but wasn't able to give her the baby.

My heart breaks when I imagine how happy Dean must have been to learn she was finally pregnant with his child. How devoted and protective he must have been over her. How in love he must have been when that baby was placed in his arms. And then how destroyed he must have been to learn it was all a lie. To have that baby taken away from him. He had to have been utterly devastated. Shattered. Broken, like that locked away crib... And for it to have been his *own brother*... No wonder he lost it and nearly killed him in cold blood. The way Dean looked at little Maddie, the way he scooped her up in his arms and kissed her little cheeks. Maddie is the reason Dean didn't pull the trigger and murder his brother that night. Dean loves that little girl.

I take a deep breath before I turn around to face him. He's leaning against a column on his front porch. His head held low, eyes closed, fist clenched on the railing, white knuckled. His other fist against his forehead.

I don't know what to say to him. Though he must be waiting for me to say something. Dean is never at a loss for words. I have to be the one to break this silence.

"Are you okay?" I ask. "That was... a *lot*."

He exhales a burst of air as if he was holding his breath until I spoke, then releases the banister and turns, slamming his fist into the column. A moment later I watch the calm façade wash over him again as he drops his arms at his sides.

"Vanna, I apologize... I had every intention of telling you about all of this, at some point. When the time was right." He says. "This shit show was not how I wanted to tell you any of it."

"I understand. I'm so sorry they put you through so much. It's so awful. I don't know how they sleep at night."

"Together." He mutters.

"Maybe not tonight, after you told your brother you fucked his wife." I kind of laugh, trying to lighten the mood a bit. "That better have stopped before we met, by the way."

"It did." He sighs. "That sure blew up in my face." He finally turns to look at me and makes his way down the steps towards me slowly, studying my expression as if he's trying to read my thoughts on all I just learned about him and his past. "I don't know how I let myself underestimate her again."

"She's a coldhearted bitch, Dean. Manipulative. You told me so yourself." I shrug. "And you loved her once."

"Never again." He swears.

"I believe you." I sigh. "I'll never doubt you again."

He stops a few feet from me. We look at each other in silence for a moment before he speaks again. "Is it a deal breaker, Vanna?" He asks. I know what he's referring to, but I don't know the right thing to say. I never gave having kids serious thought before, for multiple reasons. I hesitate to answer, searching for the right words. "Vanna, please." He says, and I can see his brave façade slipping before my eyes. "Point *blank*, baby. Just let me have it... Is it a deal breaker for you?"

"No." I say. He looks physically relieved for a moment. "I've never thought about having kids before, so no. It's not a deal breaker for me."

"But that could change... in the future. When you're ready to have children." He says, "I realize the reasons you'd not want to up until now, but when..."

"*If.*" I correct him. "And I still wouldn't call it a deal breaker. I'd call it something to work out."

"Together?" He asks, the desperate hopeful tone in his voice saddens me.

"Of course." I can see the tension physically leaving his body before my very eyes. "I think we're getting ahead of ourselves though. We don't even live together, yet." I try to joke. "Let alone aren't married."

"Is that something you would ever consider?" He asks.

"Dean. Please. I don't want to get into this because of Lucinda." I try not to frown.

He nods. "You're right. I'm sorry. I'm just...*relieved*. I thought maybe you'd see me in a different light." He sighs. "That I'd be somehow... *less* to you."

I reach up to touch his handsome face. "Never. You will always be my charming macho asshole." I tease him.

He takes my hand and turns his head to press his lips to my palm. "I suppose there is a silver lining in all this... We'll save a ton of money on birth control." He grins.

I can't help laughing. "You really are an asshole." I say, before he tugs me to pull me closer to him, wrapping his arms around me until I'm firmly against his body. His expression is serious again, as he leans to press his forehead to mine, closing his eyes.

"*Thank you.*" His tone is low, but I can hear the sincerity in his voice. I have a pretty good idea of what he's thanking me for, but I try to lighten the situation for him.

"I'll call you an asshole more often if you like it so much." I tease him. He smiles slightly, bringing his hands up to gently cup my face between them.

"You know what I'm thanking you for." He says.

I nod, reaching up to hold his wrists. I can feel the tourmaline bracelet I made for him under the cuff of his long-sleeved shirt. That makes me smile. "I know."

"Every time I think I couldn't possibly love you more than I do... I fucking *do.*" He tells me, before he drops his mouth lower to press his lips against mine. We kiss for a few moments before he whispers against my lips, "Let's go get your shit and get you moved in here. There's nothing I want more than that, doll."

DEAN

EXCRUCIATING... HUMILIATING... THAT PRETTY MUCH SUMS UP WHAT IT felt like to have Lucinda rip my guts out and throw them at Vanna's feet. Along with my fuckin' balls. A total massacre of my dignity. Just, guts and balls all over the place.

Yet, Vanna never faltered... Not once. She had my back the whole time. Stood her ground against Lucinda and told her off.

He's mine... She had said... And in that moment, *she* saved *me*...

I've got a bunch of the boxes she's been packing here and there the last week, loaded up in the back of my truck. There's not much left she still has to pack, she claims, though I don't know what's hers and what was in the house when she moved in.

"What about furniture?" I ask, walking back in the front door, eager and willing to grab all I can.

"Just my bed. I don't own any other furniture." She calls from upstairs. I bound up after her to see if I can convince her to either leave it behind, or just let me throw it on the back of the truck. Not that she needs it. I want her in my bed. *Our bed.* When I walk into her room, she's sitting on it, against the pillows propped up on the old headboard. Her knees pulled up under her chin, her arms loosely wrapped around her shins over her long skirt.

"What's the matter?" I suddenly feel a little uneasy about her demeanor. I can tell she's chewing the inside of her cheek as she looks up at me.

"Nothing... just thinking." She says quietly. I move to sit down on the bed beside her, bending a knee up on the mattress to face her.

"I hope not about having second thoughts... I know today was a lot, but baby, I'm still the man you fell in love with. Nothing's changed..." I begin to tell her, before my own demons start fucking with my head... "Has it?"

She looks at me knowingly. "No, of course not." She tries to reassure me. "But you're right, today was a lot. And I can't help thinking back on a few things I just don't understand."

It was stupid of me to think that what happened earlier would be the end of it. That she accepts me, and we never have to revisit any of it again. Nothings ever that easy, but she has every right to ask me whatever questions she wants.

I clear my throat. "Ask me."

She stares at me for a moment, as if she's afraid it's too painful for me talk about. "I don't even know where to begin... I'm curious about everything, to be honest... But, it's up to you, what you want to tell me."

"I don't think any of it should have any bearing on our life." I say. "But I also don't want you to think I'm keeping anything from you... I would have filled you in on a few key things, eventually though. It's just... not an easy subject for me."

"I'm not going to judge you." She says, dropping one of her hands from her legs to hold my hand gently. "I love you, Dean. And I'll still love you, no matter what you tell me."

I decide right then, to tell her everything.

"When my parents died, my brother and I inherited everything, but it went into a trust controlled by my uncle until I turned twenty-five. Then it was on us to keep everything afloat. At first, Daniel was on board with me about keeping the bike shop going and the farm. But he eventually lost interest and wanted to sell everything. I didn't want to. Especially not the house and farm my mother loved. So, my only choice was to buy him out. Which I did. But that put me in a hole financially. I knew it would take time to bounce back, but I worked my ass off to make it happen. Lucinda wanted me to sell everything. She resented me for it. On top of everything else... which, you know now. Anyway, I was struggling. And I guess seeing my brother living comfortably with the money I paid him... What she saw as *our money*. The grass was greener on his side of the fence. She never had faith in me that I'd bounce back. She already saw me as... useless to her..."

"You're not useless at all." Vanna says, a slight frown on her face. "She actually said that to you?"

I swallow hard and try not to look away from her. "She met me when I was more of an outlaw... We got married right before the trust was handed over to us. I settled down after we finally got the inheritance. Joined my uncle's MC, at his encouragement. He wanted to give me something more positive to focus on. To keep me out of the outlaw life. Some of the shit I was doing was probably eventually going to land me in jail. Lucinda wasn't impressed though, and our marital issues started shortly after. We tried to stick it out. Even though she said I broke promises to her... That I lied to her... She looked at me like I was a disappointment... And then when she wasn't getting pregnant... She looked at me like I was less to her." I search Vanna's eyes, and I'm relieved not to see judgment in them, or pity. "It got a lot worse when I bought out my brother. I was home less and less... taking lots of jobs... underground shit... Literally anything I could do to earn fast and large..."

Vanna nods that she understands my meaning, or at least has a vague idea, so I continue, "In my absence... I guess they found each other... But I didn't know it at the time." I take another breath to steel myself. Vanna is patiently listening to me, continuing to look all supportive and nonjudgmental. "Anyway, I'm managing to keep our heads above water... running on fucking empty, but it's working. I'm even managing to earn enough to put in time with the MC. And Lucinda isn't quite as cold as she had been... I start feeling a little bit hopeful again. Like maybe I'm busting my ass every day and most nights, and it's all going to work out Aces for us... Then one night... I come home and she's all smiles... She's fucking *happy*..." I turn away from Vanna and lean forward, elbows on my knees as I run my hands through my hair closing my eyes, fighting to get the words out... "She tells me she's two months pregnant. Not only are things looking up, fucking *finally*... but we got our miracle baby, too."

I have to take a moment before I can go on. I don't know how much time passes before I'm able to get my throat working again to speak, but I continue, "I didn't learn the truth until Maddie was five months old... I didn't think it was weird that my brother was at the hospital when she was born... even though it was at three am... I thought that was what family did... When the doctor put Maddie in my arms, I fell in love with her instantly... She looked up at me and that was fuckin' it. She got Lucinda's blonde hair, but my eyes... So I thought at the time, anyway. You saw my brother..." I scoff and shake my head. God, what a blind fool I was.

"The next five months I'm with her every moment I can be, when I'm not trying to provide for my family. Lucinda all of a sudden doesn't have a problem with me working late hours again... My stupid ass is thinking she's finally come around and believes in me again... Little did I know, it was to get me out of the picture as often as possible, so she could give that time with the baby to my brother. And I'm just happy to be the one making ends meet... Happy to get up and change a diaper or feed her at two am, on four hours of sleep most nights... After all, *that's my little girl*..." My fuckin' voice cracks and I hang my head lower, letting my arms fall between my knees.

Vanna's arms are instantly around me, her head on my shoulder, but she doesn't say a word. I take another deep breath and push on. "Out of the fuckin' blue, her lawyer hits me with divorce papers. I'm served at the bike shop where I'm working that day. I'm not allowed to return to my own house because I have the means to live elsewhere and she's got an infant. She also fears for her safety for some reason, so I'm not allowed within two hundred yards of her or the baby."

I can feel myself getting heated just rehashing this shit in my mind, and I clench my fists against my thighs. "I flipped the fuck out over that bullshit. I go straight home, where she and the baby are supposed to be... I find a note on the table, written on her signature stationary that she used to write me love letters on. Purple paper, with a faded picture of a *jar of hearts*. Along with her letter, there was a DNA test. I'm not Maddie's father. Daniel is. They've been together almost two years. She and the baby are moving in with him, and I'm to sell the house and the businesses and she gets half. Maddie's not my kid... I don't have a legal leg to stand on where she's concerned. They got a restraining order to keep me away from them. I spend a few nights in jail a couple of times for violating it. I don't know how to cope with any of this, so I spiral out of control... Luckily, my lawyer was able to keep Lucinda from completely ruining me financially. She got to take half the money in the account, but because she was an adulterer, she wasn't entitled to any of the businesses, the land, or the house. But none of that shit mattered as much to me as losing Maddie did. I've recovered from the financial hardships... I've yet to recover from losing Maddie."

"You're stronger than anyone I've ever met in my life." Vanna quietly states. "The things you've survived..." Her voice trails off as she squeezes me a little tighter. It's a few moments before she asks, "Are they trying to get money out of you again?"

"Lucinda sees me doing well now... But that buyout I had my lawyer draw up is iron clad. Daniel can't get a penny more out of me. And Lucinda has lost her grip on me. If you're concerned about my ability to keep a roof over your head, don't be. Lucinda never went hungry or unsheltered. I busted my ass to make damn sure of that. I may not be able to give you *everything*... But please believe me, I *want* to. And I'll break my back to do it."

"That's not why I asked." Vanna says.

"I just want you to know it. I *need* you to know it." I glance back at her. "I'm not less than..."

"*I know that.*" She reaches up to stroke my jawline, a pained look in her eyes. "Dean, you have *nothing* to be ashamed of. It's a nonissue to me, really. Nothing has changed the way I feel about you. The way I see you... except that you're even stronger than I thought before." I close my eyes for a moment and relish the wave of relief that washes over me. Vanna lets out a little sigh. "We didn't talk about what I'm going to be contributing financially, before we decided on this moving in thing."

"Ain't looking for a roommate to split bills with, babe." I tell her.

"At the very least you should stop paying me for working at the roadhouse."

"I don't want to talk about money, Vanna. I just want you to move in with me. You're not going to be a financial burden on my life."

"Extra water. Electric. Food." She rests her chin on my shoulder, looking up at me.

"I like showering *with* you. And even if we don't, it's not going to be much of a difference." I say, "And we both work days. Home at night together. It ain't gonna change much. And even if it does, I can easily afford it... You're worth it regardless. You're worth so much more." I think back to when I first met her. How I was willing to pay her to date me. I wonder if she'd still slap me if I told her that, or if she'd understand where I was coming from.

She lets out a slight groan and tucks her chin down to press her head against my shoulder. "I hate talking about money too, but I don't want you to feel used, either."

"I don't. I want you with me. You bring so much good to my life. Even confessing all this twisted shit to you, I feel better about it... I thought it would have been a lot worse." I admit, turning to face her again. Her arms drop from me, falling into her lap as she sits back slightly to look at me as well. "Vanna, you think you summoned me. That I'm in your life to save you... But baby, it's the other way around."

She gives me a wry little smile. "Tell me that if I'm still alive in two to four years."

I try not to glare at her. It's my hatred for Jack that pulls this reaction out of me, not Vanna. The thought of anyone wanting to harm her, to rip her away from me, sets my blood to a boil. "I will. That's a promise." I growl. "Nobody is ever taking you from me, Vanna. Especially not Jack fuckin' Nero."

Chapter *thirty*

Vanna

"SORRY I'M LATE!" I SHOUT AS I BURST through the back door of the shop and shove my purse and car keys into my cubby in the break room. I speed walk into the front main room where Laura is at her desk on the phone. She covers the mouth piece of the cordless and looks at me.

"It's okay. You have a walk in for Reiki upstairs waiting for you. He's only been here about three minutes." Laura says. "Yes, hello I'm here..." she turns her attention back to her phone call. Probably an inventory order.

I hurry upstairs to my Reiki room and open the door, surprised not to see anyone waiting for me in the room or on my table. Was Laura too preoccupied with her phone call not to notice the guy coming back down stairs and leaving? How did she miss that?

I'm about to turn around to go back downstairs, when I feel something cold and sharp at my throat.

"*Don't scream.*" His voice is low and threatening. "Don't do anything unless I tell you to."

My heart sinks to my stomach and I feel like I could faint, or jump out the window, all at the exact same time. What is this? He knows Laura is down stairs. That she's seen his face.

He creeps out from behind the door to shut it behind us, the knife never leaving my throat. "Who are you? What do you want?" I ask, my voice barely above a whisper. "We aren't alone." He steps a little more to my side, though being careful not to let me see his face. I can tell from the corner of my eye that he's looking me over. The knife never more than an inch from me at all times.

"You are just as beautiful as he described." He says, his appraising tone feels degrading. He grabs me by the hair at the back of my head and shoves me forward into the room, roughly slamming me down over the side of my Reiki table.

"Please don't hurt me!" I say, my heart racing as I feel his body press against mine to keep me pinned down against the black vinyl.

"Shut up!" He warns me, his voice is harsh but low. "I have a message for you from your fiancé."

Oh God... Is this really happening?

I have to fight the urge to scream. Jack found me...

The man leans over against my back, so that his mouth is so close to my ear I can feel his hot breath on me. "He says, *'I'm coming for you. You are mine'*." He whispers, then laughs lowly. He places the blade to the side of my face, and I feel his hand run roughly down my body, down to my ass, grabbing me. I gasp and try to move but he presses the knife to my skin, not hard enough to cut me, but enough to let me know he will if I struggle.

"Stay still, bitch!" He threatens me. "Only seen bodies like yours in those thick cunt porn mags." His hand slides up and then down the cleft of my ass over my maxi dress, sliding down further until his hand is pushing between my thighs.

"Stop! Please!" I beg. He doesn't. "I will tell Jack! He'll kill you!" He stops, removing his hand from my body, but not the knife. "You know he's crazy and I'm his property. He'll hunt you down and kill you if you touch me!" I say again. My attacker hesitates for a moment, before taking a step back from me.

"If you make a sound, or this leave this room, I'll cut your friends throat downstairs!" He threatens me. "Give me your cell!"

"I don't have it. I left it downstairs." I say quickly.

"Don't be stupid." He threatens me. I feel the knife lift from my face. The door to my Reiki room opens. Fast, thudding footsteps rush down the stair case and I hear the jingle of the front door. He's gone. My legs give out from under me as I sink to the floor, falling back against the wall.

"Laura! Call the police!" I manage to scream. I hear her scrambling around down stairs, her panicked voice on the phone with 911, telling them to come quickly. She's rushing up the stairs now.

"Oh my God what happened?" She's asking before she even makes it into the room with me.

"That man, he attacked me." I manage to say.

Laura relays that to the operator on the phone, and proceeds to describe him to the best of her memory. I didn't get a good look at him, he stayed behind me mostly. She says he's a white male. Clean shaven. Jeans and a pastel yellow polo shirt. Normal looking guy. Looked to be in his early forties.

"They're on their way." She tells me. "Do you need me to call Dean?"

"Yes, please. Call Dean. I don't have my phone up here." I say, trying to stand up on my shaky legs, Laura grabs my arm to help me up. "I just need a minute."

"Are you hurt?" She asks frantically.

"No... Just shaken up." I say, touching the side of my face and looking at my hand to see if he actually cut me or not. I don't think he did. "I just need a minute. Please, go call Dean." I say once more. Laura hurries back down stairs, and I shut myself in the bathroom until the cops get here.

As I'm describing my attack to the young police officer down stairs in the foyer, I hear a motorcycle roar into the parking lot. Dean is here. I feel a little better already. Within moments he's barging through the front door, storming up to me. His expression a mixture of concern, rage and relief. He blows right by the cop as if he isn't there and wraps his arms around me tightly.

"I dropped everything and got here as fast as I could." Dean says, his voice sounds strangled. The cop excuses himself for a moment to take a call from his department. "Are you hurt?" Dean asks, holding me at arms length now, looking me over. He grabs my chin gently, turning my face to each side, in-specting me for injury.

"I'm not hurt." I say, as he pulls me back into his arms.

The cop returns. "Ma'am, my department has confirmed that at this present time, Jack Nero is still currently incarcerated." I let out an audible sigh of relief. Jack's still locked up... He's found me, but he can't hurt me... yet.

"Jack Nero?" Dean's voice is a growl. "Fucking *Jack Nero* did this?" I squeeze Dean's arm, hoping he doesn't flip out in front of the cop.

"Yes. But unless the guy that attacked me is caught, proving it will be impossible." I say. "He's careful. And the guy that attacked me never said his name directly."

The cop clears his throat. "The more details you can give me, the more we can try to do. I've got a BOLO out on your boss's description of the guy. But if you could finish describing what happened, it will help your case if we get him." The cop explains. He's going over his notes so far. We haven't even gotten to the worst part yet. Dean is not going to take this well. I brace myself for what I have yet to describe.

"You had told me that the perp shoved you over the table upstairs and had a knife to your face. What happened then?" The cop asks. I can feel Dean's body tense up as the officer's words hit him.

"He said he had a message from my fiancé." I explain. "He said *I'm coming for you. You are mine.*"

The cop nods as he writes. "Then?"

I take a deep breath. "Then he put his hands on me."

The cop raises his eyes from his report sheet to look at Dean. Then back at me. "Ma'am, if you wish to tell me in private, it may be easier for you." He looks back at Dean again. "Maybe for both of you."

"*Fuck that.*" The tone in Dean's voice would rattle the Devil himself.

I notice the cop swallow, but he shifts his focus back to me. "It's your call, ma'am."

I hesitate. I know Dean is going to want to know every detail of everything anyway. But it's still hard to talk about.

"Vanna, just tell him." Dean urges me.

"He ran his hand down my body until it was on my backside. He said that he's only seen bodies like mine in... certain porn mags." I sigh. "And then he shoved his hand further between my thighs, trying to touch me... there... you know."

The young cop looks down at his report and writes. I glance up at Dean. I can see the muscles in his stubbled jaw rippling. "Alright, next?" The cop asks.

"I told him to stop. He didn't. I told him I would tell Jack Nero that he assaulted me and that Jack would hunt him down and kill him because I was his property. He let go of me after that. Said if I screamed, he would slit my friends throat downstairs. And then he ran out. I screamed for Laura to call the cops once I heard him run out the door."

The cop keeps writing. "Did anyone see a vehicle? Which way he ran?"

"No." I shake my head. "What happens now?"

"I file this report and we hope we catch him." The cop says.

"Shouldn't somebody be questioning Jack?" I ask.

"He will be questioned. But unless he confesses to putting someone up to this, it's not going to do anything. Not unless we actually catch the guy." The cop says.

"Jack will never admit anything, but at least he's still locked up. What are the chances of actually getting this guy?"

The young cop glances between me and Dean. I know what he's going to say before he says it. Chances are slim. "Unfortunately, ma'am. Without a vehicle description, without any surveillance footage, and just a general description without anything distinct to go on... I'm afraid it's a long shot." He says. "You might want to consider some kind of extra security here. It's a good thing to have cameras in a shop, regardless. Chances are, he probably won't be back. Better safe than sorry, though." The cop reaches into his front pocket and pulls out a card, jotting down the report number for me, and hands it to me. "If you think of anything else, this is your case number." The cop glances back at Dean. "I'm sorry there's not anything else we can do at this point."

When the cop leaves, Dean leans to my ear and finally speaks. "You're done for the day. I'll follow you back to your house on my bike. You'll grab Nico and his things. And that's it. You live with me now." His expression tells me he is not to be argued with right now. "You're not to set foot in that house again."

"Let me talk to Laura before we go."

He nods. "I'll be waiting."

"Come out through the back with me. She's on the back porch."

"I'll be on my bike. I've got nothing to say to her." He still sounds pissed.

"Dean, this isn't Laura's fault." I insist. He doesn't say anything. He kisses my forehead then walks out the front door.

Laura is sitting in her wicker chair, smoking a cigarette on the back porch. And it probably isn't the first one she's had. "Are you okay?" I ask her.

She looks up at me, a sadness in her eyes. "Are you?"

"Yes, but... Dean wants me to go home with him. He's really upset."

She nods. "You should go home. I think I will too. I'm closing up now. I'll leave a note on the door."

"Do you want us to wait until you're in your car? Just to be safe?"

She shakes her head. "No, I'm sure it's fine. The police are still in the area searching. Go home with Dean. It will only take me a few minutes." She extinguishes her cigarette in the ashtray beside her on the small wicker table, then stands up to hug me. "I'm so sorry this happened."

"It's not your fault." I reassure her.

"I should have been paying closer attention." She shakes her head, sullenly. After a few more minutes of reassuring her that I'm okay, Laura goes back inside to lock up, and I walk down the back steps towards my car. As soon as I step into the lot, Dean fires up his bike, ready to escort me home. He watches me walk to my car. A stoic expression on his face.

He's in my rear view the whole ride back to town. I watch him scan the roads as we drive. Looking around for any indication that I'm being followed by anyone.

When we get back to my house, he takes my keys from me and enters the house first. Making me stay in my car with the doors locked until he tells me I can come inside and grab what I need. I put Nico in his carrier, and pack up his food and supplies, and his favorite toy mouse. I'll have to locate his other toys another time. He could have stuffed them anywhere, and Dean is already in a rush to get me out of here. He carries everything out to my car and we go back to his house.

As soon as we are inside, he places everything down in the entryway and walks up to me. "Vanna, we need to talk. You need to take a few days off. At least. For starters."

"I can't do that to Laura, Dean. I'm sorry."

"She should have done a better job protecting you." He growls. "That cop was right. There should be some basic level of security there." I know his seemingly resentful tone is just because he's concerned for me and upset about what happened.

I nod, agreeing with him to calm him down. "You're right. There should be cameras. But she can't afford that. Please don't be mad at her. Neither of us had any idea what was happening until it happened."

"I'll pay for the installation. If you're going to insist on going back there. I insist on this."

"Dean, you should ask her first. I'm sure she would appreciate it, but..."

"It's for your safety. And that's not all. You're also not going back until it's done."

"Let me talk to her about it, okay?" I plead.

He stares at me. "You could have been hurt, badly... *or worse.*" His tone sounds strangled again. "And I have *nothing* to go on. Not a goddamned motherfucking *thing* to find this motherfucker."

"Dean... this isn't your fault either. No one could have predicted this was going to happen today." He's silent now. God only knows what's going on inside his mind. "Dean, he didn't hurt me. I was able to back him off. Jack is crazy and clearly that guy knows it. Just reminding him how Jack thinks of me was enough to stop him. He could have..." Dean grimaces as if he's bracing himself for a word I can't even bring myself to say. "The thought of Jack going after him for it stopped him. He won't be coming back. Jack doesn't want me to be hurt by anyone but him. He's not going to let anyone deprive him of the pleasure."

Dean's fists are clenched, white knuckled at his sides. "If they know where you work, they know where you live." He says. "And we don't know how many are out there."

"He's a disgraced cop in prison, Dean. How many friends could he really have? Cops are only looked at as slightly above pedophiles in prison. It's probably just the one guy."

"We don't *know* that." He mutters. "Give me your keys."

"What? Why?"

"Because on the very, *very* off fucking chance they don't know about me yet, I don't want them seeing your car here. I'm leaving it at your house. I'll walk back. Stay here." I hand him over my keys. "Use this time to call your friend Laura about the cameras. It's nonnegotiable." He says coldly, before he storms back out the door.

DEAN

THIS ISN'T TECHNICALLY AN ABUSE OF POWER... AND EVEN IF IT WAS, I'D DO it anyway. When it comes to Vanna, all bets are off. Between Legion's interest in her, that Bible open to Mark 5:9 mentioning Legion by fucking name, which is just too damn coincidental as far as I'm concerned. And now Jack fuckin' Nero's goon threatening her, I'm not taking any chances with her safety.

She insists on going back to work. Falsely believing she's safe, because that prick Jack Nero is still locked up. I can't keep her a prisoner in my home, even if it's for her own damn good. But that doesn't mean I can't do everything else within my power to keep her safe. Her Boss lady accepted my strong-armed offer to have closed circuit security cameras and an alarm installed in her shop. Part of the deal for footing the bill for this, I have twenty-four-seven access to view the feed on these camera's, for as long as Vanna is employed there. Being able to look in on her any time I feel the need, helps, but only slightly. The shop is still a forty-minute commute from where I spend a majority of my working days, so if anything were to happen, cameras aren't going to rescue her.

But a Savior could...

As I take my seat at the head of the table, in what we've now been affectionately calling *The War Room*, since shit's been stirring with the CDMC, I look at each of the six prospects seated at the far end. Viking, my Sergeant at Arms, at my right. The rest of the brothers aren't here. They don't need to be for doling out grunt work to prospects. I invited them into the War Room to instill the impression that what I'm asking of them, is important. It's not on the same level as the Brothers grabbing a prospect at random and telling them to polish their bike or clean a bathroom. They're in the War Room, that they haven't seen since that first meeting, because their President has a special task for them.

"You've got an opportunity to prove your worth and dedication to the original mission of this MC." I say to them. "Consider it a trial run. I'm not saying you have to do it. But I am saying you're fucking *out*, if you don't."

Viking chuckles beside me. "It's good to be the King." He taunts me. I just scowl at him.

"I'm not asking you to make this an unpaid day job." I turn back to the prospects. "I'm just asking that you make time throughout the week to stop by the shop. Hang out for a bit where your presence will be noticed. I realize we've all got bills to pay. But being a fully patched and vetted member of this MC, means time volunteered guard dogging safe houses on occasion, as needed."

"What happened?" The sandy bearded prospect asks.

"Doesn't matter what the fuck happened, *Diaper Rash!*" Viking shouts at him, slamming a fist on the table loudly. I notice the prospect doesn't flinch. "When the President of this MC has a direct task for you, *you just fucking do it!*"

I clear my throat and look back at the prospect. "My woman was attacked at her job last week, by a man who was sent to do it." I explain. "Cops can't do shit. We can't find him either. It's unlikely there will be a reoccurrence, but..."

"I'm available all day, Thursdays." The prospect, actually named Rusty, speaks right up again. "And I could swing by on lunch breaks and after work the other days she's there. I'd be happy to keep an eye on the First Lady."

I fight the inclination to smile. Vanna isn't officially my Old Lady yet. So, she isn't exactly the *First Lady* either... But I let it slide, since she will be one day, anyway. Giving the prospect a nod of approval, I glance at the other five.

"I can take Fridays." One of them raises their hand. "But can I use my car?"

Viking's large, open palm slams down on the table loudly. "Did you just fucking ask about sitting in a fucking cage?" Viking sneers at him. "Is this a fucking car club? What's intimidating about your fucking Ford Focus? That's a fuckin' chick car, for starters. Are you a goddamned motherfucking *Biker* or not? Because this is an MC!"

"Sorry... I just thought that..."

"Shut the fuck up!" Viking shouts at him again. "Bad asses ride *bikes*, fucker. You need to be noticed in order to intimidate and act as a deterrent! Get it? Your Ford fucking Focus ain't gonna get it done!" He bangs his fist on the table again, then points at each of them. "We could have you all doing a lot fucking worse than sitting in a parking lot a few times a fuckin' week, looking like the tough guys you fuckin' *wish* you were. Pansy ass fuckin' Ford Focus cage lovin' dickwads."

"Are you quite finished?" I ask him.

"That depends on what the next dumb fucker decides to say." Viking grumbles, glaring at all six of them. "Fucking prospects get the grunt work. This is a cake walk and you pricks should be grateful this task, asked of you directly by the fuckin' *President* of this MC, is fuckin' simple. I wanted all these bedrooms repainted. The kitchen and the gym fuckin' detailed with toothbrushes." He gripes, shaking his head. "Do you know the shit I had to do when I was a fuckin' prospect? Let me tell you, you'd have never made it. You want into an MC, you put in your fuckin' time. You do the grunt work with a thank you and a fuckin' smile." He lets out a long, exasperated sigh. "Bitches got shit easy."

I almost want to laugh, but I remain impassive. He isn't wrong. Then again, the MC's that Viking and I rode with, before the Saviors, were one percenter clubs, and a Hell of a lot rougher. I try not to think back on the hazing and grunt work we went through together. One glance at Viking and I might just lose it, so I keep my focus on the prospects.

"Viking's right. I need you to step up. Monday through Friday, ten am to five pm. I'll be paying attention to who shows up, how often and how long. I'll be making appearances myself, so will the other Brothers. I'm not assigning you anything. This is on you to make an impression." I say, reaching into the inner pocket of my cut to pull out six business cards advertising the shop Vanna works at. My cell phone number is written on the back. Walking around the room, I place a card down in front of each prospect. "You text when you arrive. You text when you leave. You fucking *call* if you see anything suspicious." I instruct them, before I take my seat at the head of the table again. "Questions?"

"And don't make him fuckin' regret asking." Viking sneers at them.

"Is this CDMC related?" Rusty asks.

Viking and I glance at each other simultaneously, and he shrugs. I slide my eyes back to the prospect. "Not this specific incident. But the Demons are an ongoing concern. They're not supposed to be around her shop either, so that should be immediately reported as well." I say.

"Isn't this address in the Demons' territory?" One of them asks.

"The Saviors MC does not recognize the CDMC as having any claim to any territory at all in the state of North Carolina." I reply coolly. "Nor do the JoCo Jokers, or the Asphalt Knights." I've made damn sure of that the last few weeks.

"Nomadic Parasites." Viking chimes in. "Roaches."

"How long do we have to do this for?" The one who volunteered Fridays asks.

Viking bangs his fist on the table again before I can respond. "The fuck kind of question is that, *Ford Focus*? You want to be on bathroom duty again?" He points at him.

"But I just cleaned it." He gripes.

"Then maybe I gotta take a piss again, and miss." Viking glares at him. "Unless you want to hold my dick for me to make sure you don't gotta clean it, *again*?" The prospect just sits there, his eyes a little wider than they were a moment ago.

"Until further notice. Same way it works with the safe houses. Anything else?" I glance around at them. They're all quiet. "Great. Coordinate with each other. This assignment starts Monday. I expect to hear from you all, often. If not, I'm taking cuts."

When nobody moves, Viking slams his hand down on the table again with a loud thud. "Dismissed!" He shouts at them, and they scramble up from the table and out the door, remembering to close it behind them on their way out this time.

I can literally feel Viking's eyes boring a hole into the side of my face. I turn to look at him. "What?" I sigh.

"Over kill, no? You said this Jack prick is still in prison. And we both know that other guy ain't coming back to her shop." Viking says.

"Actually, no. I don't *know* that." I reply. "I also don't know if he's the only guy Nero's got on the outside. He's been fuckin' hunting her from his prison cell for years. We both know for him to do that, he's got people on the outside helping. Hopefully, it's just the one. But I don't fucking *know* that."

Viking is looking at me, suspiciously contemplative now, leaning back in his chair, one massive arm resting on the table as he thumps his thumb against the surface a few times before speaking. "This is why she showed up in your bar to begin with. She was looking for some guy to protect her, wasn't she? That's been her plan all along."

I glower at him. "Are you ever going to let up on Vanna?" He only looks back at me for a moment. His response is simply an evasive shrug. "We protect our women. She's my woman. By extension, that makes her your responsibility to protect as well." I point at him. "Especially as Sergeant at Arms of this MC. I need you to get on board with Vanna. We're in love. She isn't going anywhere. You're my Brother. I need you to make this fucking work... For me."

Viking lets out loud huff of air, his bullheaded stubbornness dwindling slightly. "You're just a sucker for a hot dame, Dean. After Lucinda, I worry about you. Those were bad times."

There's no denying that, but, "Vanna's no Lucinda. She loves me, bro." I sigh. "I'm probably going to catch Hell for this shit, too." Vanna doesn't know about the prospects, yet. I plan on telling her tonight, before her shift at the Twisted Throttle. She's got the weekend to come to terms with it before Monday. "She ain't using me. I want her safe. Without her..." I don't need to finish that thought, or sentence. Viking was around when I was going through it with Lucinda. We both remember those dark times.

"Yeah. I get it." Viking nods once as he looks me over. His eyes land on the black bracelet I haven't taken off since she gave it to me. "For you. I'll ease up."

I spend another good hour in the gym, as I have been almost daily now. Expelling pent-up rage on the sand bag, before I head home to Vanna. By the time I get home tonight, Vanna already has dinner on the table waiting for me and greets me at the door with a little kiss. Over dinner she tells me that the security system and cameras have been installed in Laura's shop, and that she's excited to get back to work again. *Hint, hint.* She sends me the information to access the camera's feed on my cell phone, which I then pass on to Axel, who will be setting up a large screen in my Bike Shop so that I can leave the feed running all day while I work. It'll be easier for me to keep an eye on things and still manage to get shit done this way. I even go so far as to upload the app to my smart TV above the mantle of the fire place here, so I can access the footage on the big screen with a click of my remote.

Vanna brings me a beer and sits down on the couch as she watches me review the angles of the cameras on the screen. "This isn't a little much?" She asks, tucking her legs up on the leather cushion and sipping from her wine glass.

"Nope." This isn't even the half of it. And I might as well just rip the band aid off. "I've got prospects on rotation that'll be hanging out in the parking lot, too." I glance at her to see her reaction. She's staring at me as if my words either didn't register, or she flat out doesn't believe I'm this crazy. I am.

"Dean." She looks at me incredulously now. Reality has hit, and she thinks I'm nuts. "*Dean*, this is Laura's shop... You can't just station bikers in her parking lot..."

"Oh, I can and I will." I say. "Laura agreed to the terms, don't worry."

"*Terms?*" Her eyes widen, as if the word alarms her. "What are you talking about?"

"I paid for the equipment. I paid for the alarm system to be installed. I'm paying for the monthly monitoring of that system." I say. "She gets all that, I get access to the live feed, and I get to put men in her parking lot. They won't go inside, unless they have to. They're just going to keep an eye on the place. Act as a deterrent. It's not a big deal. She benefits too." Vanna's looking at me with her wine glass to her lips, but she isn't drinking. She's frozen, staring at me. "There won't be someone there *all the time*, as much as I'd like it. And it's only for as long as you're working there. If you should find something else, or whatever the case may be, no more bikers in her lot. And she can cancel the security monitoring, or switch it over to pay for it herself." I say, shutting off the TV now that I know everything is installed to my liking. "Easy peasy lemon squeezy."

"No rational part of you thinks this is a little extreme?" She asks. "Not to mention totally unfair to your prospects, they're going to be bored out of their minds."

"I hope they are." I smile at her. "Just means you're as safe as I can make you, short of keeping you here." I lift my hand in a gesture of surrender before there's even an argument. "Which I am fully aware and accepting of the fact, that I can't do."

She shakes her head. "This biker rotation of guards can't go on indefinitely. You realize that, right? You're going to have to settle for just the cameras, at some point." She insists, leaning forward to place her wineglass on the slate topped coffee table, before she sits back against the corner of the couch again, looking at me. She drapes an arm over the top of the cushion, bending her elbow to bring her hand to her face, pinching the bridge of her nose. "Some point, *very soon*, I hope. You're going a little crazy with this."

"Pretty sure I gave you ample warning that I was, and am, crazy about you, doll. And I know this can't go on forever... But I'll slit that throat when I come to it." I wink at her.

641

MAYBE IT'S THE FACT THAT THE POLICE OFFICER HIMSELF TOLD ME THAT Jack is still incarcerated, but I think Dean is more shook up about what happened to me at Laura's shop, than even I am. I haven't been back to work in a week, while waiting for the security system to be installed, as per his insistence. It's been a while since I've taken time off work, and I'm starting to miss the shop.

I've been officially living at Dean's house with him, but it still feels like *Dean's house*. My witchy belongings don't really go with his style, so I asked if I could have the empty room to keep my few belongings in. He let me, of course. And it was sweet of him to tell me I didn't have to confine my things to a single room. That *our* home is a home, not a show room. Despite his house looking like something out of an interior design magazine on how to perfectly blend country ranch and rustic cabin together, in one beautiful large open space.

I actually do love his home, and don't want to mess it up. I'm fine with my room. And it gives me my own little space still, should I need a place to retreat to for a time. Nico, as well. Though he seems to have taken a preference to napping on one of the leather chairs at Dean's chess board table, in front of the picture window in the living room. I'm sure he'll love that spot even more, when we've got the nearby stone fireplace going in the coming winter months.

The thought of snuggling up with Dean under a blanket, on that big leather couch in front of a roaring fire, makes me smile to myself. I really do love him.

"What are you smirking about?" Dean asks, walking behind the bar to kiss me on the cheek as I'm drying shot glasses.

"*You.*" I say, playfully elbowing him as he attempts to hold me.

"Good answer." He growls against my ear, making me giggle at the vibration of his deep voice, and the way his scruff tickles me. He releases me so I can look up at him again. "I'll be back in a few. Axel broke the drive chain on his bike so I'm going to show him how to thread a new one and adjust the slack with a rivet masterlink instead of a shitty clip."

I just smile at him. "I have no idea what any of that means."

Dean grins back at me. "I can do it with my eyes closed. I've got a rivet tool in the shop so it won't take long. Viking will be here, though. He knows to watch you."

"Okay, see you soon then."

"Lickety-split." He smiles, bending to kiss me on the lips briskly, then smacks my ass before he goes. I shake my head and chuckle as I watch him go. He raises an arm to grab Axel's attention from across the bar room that he's heading out, and Axel jogs out after him.

Cherry comes up with a tray and asks for three millers, two buds and five shots of Jack Daniels. I load her up and go back to cleaning and drying shot glasses. A few moments later I notice a woman walking into the bar. She doesn't look like a biker babe though. She's wearing a tight pencil skirt and a button up blouse. Black high heels and black, almost cat eyed, framed glasses. Her shoulder length brown hair is loose and frames her face. She kind of has that naughty librarian look to her as she walks up to the bar and sits down near me on a stool.

"Hey there." She says to me with a pleasant smile.

"Hi." I smile back. "Can I get you something?"

"Yes, a double shot of Jager and a Miller Lite, thanks." She reaches into her purse and pulls out a twenty, sliding it to me across the bar. "Keep it."

"You got it." I say, taking the money and putting it in the register. I pour her double shot and crack open her beer and place them down on the bar. She takes half the shot and a sip of beer as she seems to look me over.

"You're new." She says to me.

"Actually, I started working weekends here almost seven months ago. I've never seen you in here before either."

"Oh, I'm not from around here. I'm just visiting on business. I pass through every couple of months. I always make sure to swing by Dean's place. Is he here?" She asks.

"Yeah, he's fixing something on a bike across the lot. Said he'd be back soon." I answer. She smiles big. Too big. *Something is up*, big. "How do you know Dean?"

"We have a little thing going on whenever I roll through town." She grins and then shimmies her shoulders like she just got a massive case of chills, then lets out a little excited squeal. "He's such a fucking fox, isn't he?" She says with too much enthusiasm. "Sex on a fucking stick!"

"He sure is." I force myself to smile. This bitch is here to sleep with Dean. *My* Dean. "Is he expecting you?" I ask. He'd better not be.

"No. Not this time. We were supposed to hook up last time I was in town, a few months ago, but he said something came up and he couldn't make it." She pouts. "I'm not letting him blow me off this time though." I realize this is booty call girl. From the night Dean and I met. He told me he was supposed to meet a fling and called it off that night.

"I'm Vanna, by the way."

She extends her hand to me. "Crystal." She smiles. I shake her hand.

"How did you and Dean meet?" I ask.

"At the hospital. I'm a pharmaceutical rep. I bumped into him in the parking lot outside the ER. He had just dropped someone off and I happened to be parked next to him. I didn't know a tire had gone flat and he offered to put the spare on for me."

Of course, he did. The Chivalrous asshole. "That was nice."

She smiles as if she's reliving those moments in her mind and takes a sip of her beer. "He was so nice. And gorgeous. *Oh my God*, is he *gorgeous*." She laughs for a moment, then waves her hand back and forth as she reins herself in. "Well, you know. You work for him. Anyway, I offered to buy him a drink somewhere as a thank you, told him I had a few hours to kill. We ended up here." She smiles her kilowatt smile again. "We hit it off. He's so charming and funny. Ugh. I couldn't resist him."

"Oh, so he put the moves on you?"

"It was pretty mutual, actually." She laughs. "Best sex of my life. If I lived closer..." She fans herself with her napkin. "I'd probably be *pregnant*." She laughs again.

Wow. "You know, Dean's actually been seeing someone a while now."

She makes a dismissive snorting sound. "Unless he's married to this *someone*, he's still available as far as I'm concerned." She shoots the rest of her shot and chases it with another sip of beer before she looks around for him again. *Thirsty bitch.*

Cherry walks up with another order for drinks. I excuse myself from this messed up conversation to fill Cherry's order and make change for the table. She doesn't seem to recognize the woman, so I don't say anything. While I'm pouring shots, I notice Dean walk in the front door with Axel.

As soon as *Crystal* spots him, she jumps off the bar stool and damn near runs to him, throwing her arms around his neck and plants a kiss directly on his mouth. He immediately grabs her arms and pulls them from around him, stepping back from her and holding her away from him at arms length. As I see him begin to twist his head towards me, I look away and put the bottle of Jack Daniels back on the shelf, acting as though I didn't see anything.

When I turn back to look at them, he no longer has her by her arms and they are standing apart, his hand running through the top of his hair. She has her arms out as if she's asking him about something she doesn't understand. He gestures toward the bar and she turns around to walk back to her beer, Dean following behind her.

"That was not the greeting I was expecting." She says to him. Dean doesn't comment on that statement.

"Was this paid for?" He asks me instead, referring to her drinks.

"Twenty even." I cross my arms.

"Alright. It's on the house." He pulls out a twenty from the inner pocket of his cut and puts it down in front of her.

"Thanks, but I'd rather have another go at you, handsome." She says, attempting to touch him but he leans back and steps away.

"That's not going to happen, Crystal." He says. "We had our fun, but that's over now. Been over."

She glances at me and must notice my annoyance. "What?" She asks, then looks at Dean. "Is she going to rat you out? Pay her off. I've got one hundred on me. Is that enough?" she looks at me.

I laugh at her audacity. "Only a hundred bucks for the best lay of your life?" I sneer.

"Is he dating your friend or something?" She asks. *My friend*? Right... Because compared to her, miss naughty librarian looking booty call lady, there's no way he'd be into me. I look at Dean and gesture with my hand for him to proceed with answering her.

"Vanna is my girlfriend." He says.

Instead of looking shocked or embarrassed, like a normal person would, she looks at me like I'm some kind of gross insect. "*Her*?" She says to him, jerking her thumb at me almost with disdain. I look at Dean and watch his expression change from slightly uncomfortable to outright pissed off.

"Best lay of my fucking life. Ain't giving that up for anything or anybody." He growls.

She has the nerve to look at me with surprise. "Told you he was seeing someone." I shrug. Crystal continues to stare at me as if she's trying to figure out what Dean could possibly see in me.

"Sorry you wasted a trip, Crystal. But I did tell you on the phone last time this thing was done." Dean says.

"I just thought you meant you couldn't make it." She looks back at him with an almost hurt expression now. "Not that you were blowing me off completely."

"I said I can't do it... As in, any more. I apologize if I wa   sn't clear." He shifts his focus back to me. "Baby?" His eyes are searching mine. I know he's worried I'm mad at him. I give him a tightlipped smile. I don't like her. But I can't be mad at him. She threw herself at him unexpectedly. He did what he could do under the circumstances. When it comes to women, Dean does have a bit of a soft spot.

Cherry returns with her tray and another order for a round of shots and beers. I excuse myself from Dean and Crystal to load Cherry up and make change. I can't hear what they're saying over the music and talking in the bar, but I'm not that concerned. Dean made it clear we're together. Hopefully she will leave soon. I grab Cherry's empties off her tray and toss them into the glass bin, then duck under the bar to grab more bottles from the fridge to put on her tray.

"Who's that with Dean?" She asks.

"Someone he used to screw." I scoff. Cherry looks at me, as if she's worried that I'm pissed. "It's fine." I say. "He made it clear we're together. I'm not mad."

"Good. *Incoming*." She says, grabbing her tray and heading off to serve her table. I turn to see Dean walking up to me. I glance past him at Crystal, who is crying into her napkin now.

"What happened?" I ask.

"Apparently she didn't realize she had actual feelings for me until now, knowing I'm off the market." I can tell he feels very uncomfortable, the way his hand is gripping the back of his neck. And the way his brows are pulled together and pitched upward. He doesn't like seeing a woman cry, and it's an awkward situation to begin with. "And now she's *rejected and embarrassed,* she says."

"I guess that's possible." I say, still suspicious of her. I look back at Dean. "So, what now?"

"She asked me to wait with her outside for her ride."

"I'm inclined to believe she's just trying to pry you out of here and away from me, so that you're *less inclined* to be faithful to your girlfriend."

Dean grins at me. "No chance of that, baby." He reaches across the bar to stroke my cheek. "But if you object, then I do too."

"I know you feel bad about her crying. Maybe its genuine. If so, I'd probably want to go outside too, if I were her." I glance at her again, standing near the door waiting, looking teary eyed and depressed. "It's your call. I trust you."

"I can have Viking wait with her, Vanna."

I laugh. "Good idea. Maybe he'll scratch her *biker itch* for her."

"Oh, he'd kill her." Dean says, then appears to instantly regrets his words as he grimaces. "*Fuck.*"

I cross my arms again and glower at him. "Oh, a snug fit, was she? Must have been pretty good sex for you too." I try my damnedest to keep a straight face.

Dean is staring at me, attempting to read me. He can't tell if I'm pissed or breaking his balls and I can see his mind racing to come up with a response. "Uh... I've had better... You... You're the best. I wasn't lying about that earlier, baby." He gives me his best *don't kill me smile.* I narrow my eyes at him, barely holding on to my control as I watch him squirm. It's kinda cute. He swallows. "I'm serious, Vanna. I mean it. You fucking rock my world. The way you fuckin' kiss me... the fuckin' things you do with your hips when I'm inside you... *Fuck...* I'm getting hard just thinking about it."

God damn it. He turns me on too when he says things like that to me. I can't help letting a slight grin slip. "You better." I say to him as I drop my eyes to his crotch for a moment before I look back up at him. "That cock belongs to me. And don't you ever forget it."

He grins back at me, "Never. All yours, baby."

"You're going to make that comment up to me later, too." I push him. I watch as his grin widens and lust darkens his eyes. "With pleasure, Kitten."

I playfully scowl back at him. "That's exactly right." Glancing over in Crystal's direction, I notice she's about to leave on her own. "You can walk her out. On the off chance she actually is genuinely upset. I know a chick crying over you probably bothers you, even if you're not interested." Dean has a heart like that. He gives me a quick peck on the cheek and I watch him walk over to her and escort her out the front door.

Cherry walks up and puts her tray down, coming behind the bar with me to sit on one of the two stools back here. "Everything still cool?" She asks.

"Yeah, it's fine. He's making sure she gets in her ride safe. Apparently, it was more than just sex, on her end anyway."

Cherry rolls her eyes. "You realize that's bullshit, right?"

I laugh. "Yeah, I'm fairly certain."

"If she was anything to him, I'd have heard about her." Cherry says. "But Dean isn't going to slip up. You don't have to worry."

"I'm not." I smile to myself. It feels good to be able to trust a man. I'm not sure I'd be able to, if that man wasn't Dean.

"We're all clear." Dean says, shutting the steel door of the roadhouse and walking back over to me. He bends to kiss me, but I lean back on the pool table, out of range of his lips, and peer up at him. "Oh, come on, baby. You know I fucking worship you. Forget Crystal."

"Worship is more convincing on your knees." I say to him, as I lift my leg and brush it against the side of his suggestively.

He grins at me, that dark, concupiscent grin that always gives me butterflies. He steps closer to me, nudging my legs apart with his knees to stand between them. "Will this earn my forgiveness as well?"

"That depends entirely on you." I tease him.

Dean makes quick, rough work of divesting me of my boots and jeans, folding them over a chair at a table behind him. He slides his strong hands up my thighs and grabs the elastic waist band of my panties, pulling them down. Once off, he shoves them in his pocket.

"Alright, Kitten." His voice is low, growly, as he sinks to his knees in front of me. He grabs my leg, putting it over his leather clad shoulder and kisses my inner thigh, licking and nipping me teasingly, as he inches closer and closer. His strong hand kneads the flesh of my thigh that he has over his shoulder as his other hand wraps around my other thigh, holding me in place. Feeling his hot breath on my sex, I bite into my bottom lip in anticipation.

His tongue slides between my lips and a little gasp escapes me as he sinks into me deeper, then strokes up to flick my clit. He laps at me for a few moments, his tongue swirling before he begins to suck gently in a rhythm that almost immediately brings me to the brink. I moan and reach down to run my hands through his hair, glancing down to watch him. His head buried between my thighs, I can feel the muscles in his shoulder working beneath my knee, the slight bob and turn of his head as he pleasures me with that talented mouth. I throw my head back and close my eyes, as I make a small attempt to pull back from him, testing him, but he grips me tighter holding me in place.

"*Mmm mm mmm.*" He hums in protest, against my body, the vibration makes me quiver. He won't permit me to move, his way of retaining dominance even while pleasing me, and it just turns me on further. I'm getting what I asked for, and he's going to make sure he delivers. I whimper, the pressure building inside me rapidly.

Laying back flat on the pool table, my back arches as my body slowly loses control. Reaching down again, my fingers grip at his wrists as his tongue attacks my clit. My hips swerve in unison with his swirling tongue motions until he gives me that gentle, but consistent, sucking rhythm. This time, he doesn't stop. He doesn't let up at all, and I know he's going to drive me over the edge.

"Oh, yes, yes, yes!" I can't help but gasp.

He grips me tighter, pulling me harder against his face, sucking just a bit more roughly, and that's it. He's worked me over the edge. I cry out and writhe against him as I ride out my orgasm. My body shaking and jerking beyond my control. I'm still trembling and trying to catch my breath when Dean kisses my pussy once more and stands. I hear the purr of his zipper, and the familiar rustling sound of him releasing his cock from the confine of his jeans.

"My turn, Kitten." He growls. I'm still dazed when he grabs my hand and pulls me up so I'm standing on my shaky legs before him, then turns me around and pushes me back up against the pool table like a ragdoll. His boot gently kicks my feet apart, coaxing my legs open for him once more. He pushes me down so that I'm face down on the green felt. "Hold on, Kitten." He taunts me, as I feel the head of his cock bump against my entrance. He slides it up and down against my wet slit, coaxing my lips apart for him again, slicking himself before he pushes into me slowly from behind. I let out a slight whimper as he takes me. At six feet three inches tall, Dean is a proportionate man.

"You feel so fuckin' good, baby." He breathes, moving inside me slowly. His strong hands stroke my hips, digging into my body, sliding up to my lower back, up my rib cage and back down to grip my hips again as he begins to pump a little faster.

I breathe through the temporary discomfort, knowing full well he will bring me back to the pleasure zone with him momentarily. When he takes me from behind, it always feels like he's even bigger and gets deeper. In this position he's in total control, and we both love it.

He grips my ass and gives me an unexpected spank, which causes my body to clench around him as I let out a little surprised gasp. He groans at the sensation it gives his cock. "I love the feeling of you wrapped around me, baby." He growls. I give him a little moan of encouragement, pushing back on him slightly as the pleasure begins to take hold once again. My subtle queue to him that he doesn't have to be as gentle anymore. Dean grips my hips tighter and thrusts into me a little rougher. The pressure inside me begins to climb once again. "Tell me you're mine." He demands, his tone deep with lust.

"I'm yours."

He twists his fist in my hair and pulls my head back as he leans over me. "Do you love me, baby?"

"Yes." I pant.

"Tell me you do." He demands, fucking me harder still.

"I love you, Dean. I'm all yours. I belong to you."

He releases my hair and presses me down between my shoulder blades against the pool table again. His strong hands grip my hips once more as he continues to fuck me harder and harder. "Oh God..." I moan, holding on to the edge of the table as he pounds me mercilessly. As the minutes pass, I can feel the tremors in my body starting, my walls begin to pulsate around his cock. "Oh fuck, *Dean!*" I gasp.

"Give it up to me, baby." The words escape him on a ragged hiss. I imagine he's close to coming too. Holding on until he makes me come again. He hovers lower over me, changing the angle of his thrust slightly, but it's enough to bring me over the edge again. I pull my arms under myself, bringing my upper arm to my face to muffle my own cries as my body shutters and writhes beneath him, my rippling walls clenching around his cock uncontrollably, driving him to the edge of ecstasy as well. He pumps into me hard, then his body tenses deep inside me. He groans loudly and thrusts once more as he shoots his load. His body relaxes after a moment, spent, as he leans forward over me, his hands on the green felt on either side of me supporting his weight. He brushes the hair away from the side of my face. "I fucking love you," he pants, almost a whisper.

I peek up at him and smile weakly. "Ditto."

After another moment he straightens back up, withdrawing from me to tuck himself back in his pants. I turn over and remain leaning against the pool table when I hear the front door of the bar shut.

"*Was someone watching us?*" I nearly shriek, my hands jutting down to shield myself.

Dean is out the front door in seconds as I grab my jeans off the chair and hold them in front of me. Looking around for my underwear, I realize they're still in Dean's pocket. "Damn it." I mumble to myself, pulling my pants on anyway, shoving my feet back in my boots. I walk towards the front door of the bar to see what's going on.

Dean returns before I get to the door. "Nobody out there. Must have been the wind or something." He says. "Are you okay?"

"Yes, it just scared me. I thought the door was locked."

"There's really nobody out there." He reassures me. That would have been really uncomfortable if we had an audience we didn't know about. "There is something I need to do, though, and then we'll go home." Before Dean walks to his office, I get my panties back from him and use the ladies' room while I wait for him to wrap up whatever it is he has to do.

When we meet up again in the empty bar, I can't help wondering. "What did you have to do?"

"Delete the security footage." He winks at me. *Holy shit.* I can't believe I forgot about the cameras. I feel my whole body flush with embarrassment. Dean must be able to read it in my expression, because he smiles again. "No worries, babe. Our impromptu sex tape is no longer." He removes his keys from his pocket and takes my hand, leading me to the front door as he hits the last of the lights off, casting the bar in total darkness. As we step outside, he locks the door behind us, before we walk to his truck. The weatherman had predicted rain, so we opted for the Silverado tonight. He opens the passenger side door for me and closes it once I'm seated inside. I glance around the parking lot as he walks around to get into the driver's seat. I can't shake the uneasy feeling that there might have actually been someone out there.

"It's really not that windy out." I say, as he climbs in and shuts his door. Dean twists the key in the ignition and the truck starts right up. He flicks on the head lights and we both take another gander around the parking lot.

"There was nobody outside, doll. I would have knocked them the fuck out." I don't see anyone out there, either. Maybe it was a random gust of wind.

After a hot shower in *our* awesome master bathroom, I slip on an over-sized t-shirt and find Dean outside on his front porch, instead of in bed. He's kicked back in an Adirondack chair, feet up on the railing, wearing that faded Sturgis t-shirt and a pair of shorts.

"Why aren't you in bed?" I ask. He had gotten out of the shower before me, and I assumed he would have dried off, thrown on some shorts and went right to bed.

"A little wired I guess." He sighs. "Are you okay?"

"Yeah. Just tired. I didn't know where you were." I yawn. Turning to look out into the darkness, beyond his property, I try to make out my old house on the other side of the corn field that separates the two properties. I can barely make out the shape of my former rental home in the distance. "My old house looks even smaller from here." I say.

He reaches down beside him and pulls up a set of binoculars. "Here you go." He smiles at me, holding them up.

"Are you kidding me? You creeper!" I tease him.

He grins. "Oh, come on, it's not like I can actually see in your windows. Look for yourself." He holds the binoculars out to me again. I take them from him, still giving him a suspicious look. He lets out a long sigh. "I used to sit out here and wonder what you were doing when I saw a light on. I used to do that a lot. When I couldn't sleep, it made me feel better to kind of check on you." He tries to explain himself. And just when I start to feel like he's being sweet, he adds, "I've also often wondered if you were ever in there rubbing one out to yours truly."

"Asshole." I smack his shoulder playfully, before I turn around again to take a peek through the binoculars. He's right though, you can't really see inside any windows through all the old lacy curtains at this distance. I imagine just silhouettes, at best.

My heart skips a beat when I think I see a figure on my front porch. I step closer as if that will help me see better, but I can't tell. Lowering the binoculars for a moment to wipe my eyes with the back of my hand, I raise them again and take another look. Nothing now. Maybe my tired eyes are playing tricks? It's dark out. And the clouds blowing across the moon could have cast some kind of creepy shadows. I hand him back his binoculars, watching him place them back down beside his chair.

"You ever rub any out over me, anymore?" I ask him, jokingly.

He looks at me with slightly furrowed brows, as if I should know the answer to this. "*Constantly.*" He says, now wearing a crooked grin. His mock conviction makes me giggle.

"That's actually hot." I say, leaning closer to him so my bare leg brushes against his arm. "The thought of you, your strong fist squeezed around that magnificent cock... Stroking it while you think about me." I say, twisting slightly to rub my leg back and forth against his skin, messing with him. "That really turns me on."

His eye brow arches as he cocks his head and looks up at me. "Oh yeah?"

"Mmm hmm." I bite my bottom lip. As he stands up, I see that his magnificent cock is ready for another round.

"You did this, this is your fault." He teases me, as I back up to the front door at his approach. I turn quickly and swing the door open, laughing as he chases me to the bedroom, where I am tackled and conquered again.

Chapter
thirty-one

DEAN

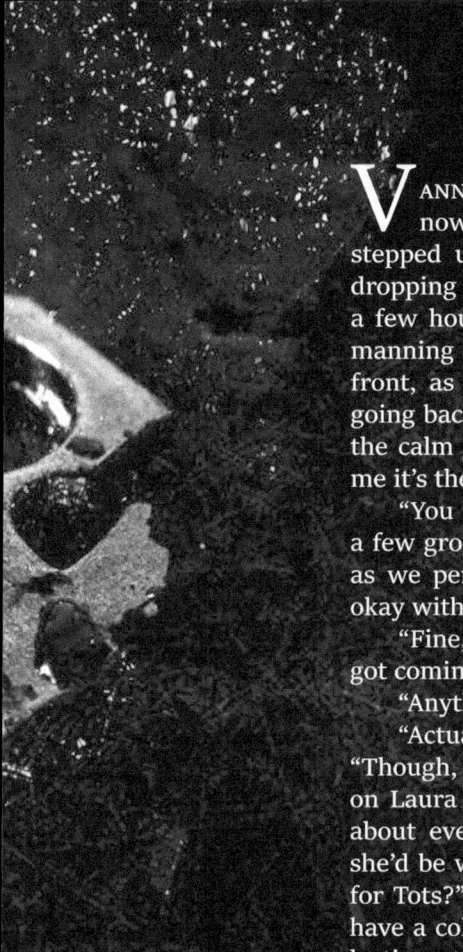

V ANNA'S BEEN BACK AT WORK A WEEK AND A HALF
now, with no incidents. The Prospects have really
stepped up. Between them, Axel, Viking and myself,
dropping by now and then as well, there are only
a few hours, accumulatively, that there isn't someone
manning the shop. All has been quiet on the CDMC's
front, as well, and I'm hoping they're contemplating
going back to wherever they came from. That this isn't
the calm before the storm. My instincts, however, tell
me it's the latter.

"You seem distracted." Vanna comments, placing
a few grocery items in the basket I'm carrying for her,
as we peruse the isles together. "Is everything going
okay with the club?"

"Fine, doll. Just thinking of some things we've
got coming up." It's not technically a lie.

"Anything I can help with?" She asks.

"Actually, yes." I say, an idea springing to mind.
"Though, I wonder if it would be pushing something
on Laura again... I realize I came on strong with her,
about everything that happened... But, do you think
she'd be willing to do a collection in her shop for Toys
for Tots?" I ask. "We do it every year. All the Brothers
have a collection box at their businesses. We start collecting at our fall bike rally, through the second week
of December."

"I'm sure she would love to." Vanna smiles, looking
at me lovingly for another few moments.

"What?" I ask.

She shrugs, before turning her focus back on grocery
shopping. "Nothing, I just never would have guessed
a bunch of *scary bikers* could be so sweet and caring."
She says, glancing back at me. "I'm really glad I got
to know all of you, despite the reasons that brought
us together." She sighs. "You're all really good guys."

I can't help grinning. "We're just a bunch of ruffians
trying to buy our way into Heaven, don't let us fool you."
She rolls her eyes at me, but she's still smiling. "We
make Snowy dress up like Santa and give toys out to
kids, too." Her eyes light up and she smiles excitedly.

"Are you serious?" She asks.

"Yeah, he comes ridding in on his big fuckin' Indian
Chief motorcycle, all decked out as Santa in a leather
cut." I say. "Cherry and the girls decorate the whole bar,

even wrap the stripper poles to look like candy canes. We get a whole bunch of kids every year. It's pretty great."

"That is freaking amazing. I cannot wait to see this!" Vanna says excitedly. "I hope you're not just teasing me."

"I'm not. We actually all really enjoy it." I confess. "Cherry and a few of the girls start wrapping gifts right after Thanksgiving. We get a whole lot of families that show up every year. It's free, though there's a donation box at the door. Parents can take a few pics with their cellphones or whatever, and their kids get to grab a gift from the mountain of wrapped boxes set up behind Snowy." I explain. "Viking's usually a grump because we only let him dress up as Rudolph now... After the *Krampus incident*." Just thinking of that, makes me want to laugh about it again. That did not go over well with the kids...

Vanna actually grabs my arm, and I don't think I've ever seen her look more excited. "*Oh. My. God.* If you're lying to me, I'm going to be devastated. I *have to* see this."

I can't help chuckling. "You will. You can be an elf with Cherry and Axel."

"Do you all dress up?" She asks, enthusiastically.

I shrug. "Not full blown, we all wear green elf hats. Cherry and the girls go all out with decorations and their elf outfits, though. And Viking was a real convincing Krampus that one year... Way too convincing, as a matter of fact." I laugh, remembering the screams of horror upon his theatrical entrance. I had to duck behind the bar because I was laughing so damn hard. Thank God the parents had a sense of humor and thought it was funny as Hell, too. But, never again, after that. Now, he's Rudolph.

"Just thinking of all this makes me want to bake Christmas cookies." Vanna giggles. "What do you all do for Thanksgiving? That's in a few weeks."

"We had it at my house, last year. Cherry helped me cook, and everyone's Old Lady brought something, too. But this year, it's Viper's turn to host at his house."

Vanna's expression is suddenly contemplative, serious. "You'll have to ask him to ask his Old Lady what I should make."

"That's still weeks away, doll."

"I know. But I want whatever it is that I get assigned to, to be *absolutely perfect*. I have to make a good impression." She says, with a determination I can't help but find endearing. Grinning at her as she walks off towards the refrigerated section of the store, I allow myself to feel a little excitement at the approaching Holiday Season. For the first time in a long time, I've got someone special in my life to spend it with.

Vanna

A S WE WALK BACK TOWARDS THE TRUCK, THERE'S A GUY WHISTLING THE tune of Rick Springfield's *Jessie's Girl*, standing right near Dean's Silverado. Dean has the two bags of groceries in his arms, and I've got the truck keys in my hand as we approach. I hit the key fobs lock button twice, making the truck beep, thinking it might get the guy to move out of the way. He doesn't, not until we're right there.

"Can I help you?" Dean asks him, but the guy doesn't say anything, he just keeps on whistling as he finally walks away from the truck, in the direction of the grocery store we just exited, a short distance away.

I hit the key fob again to unlock the doors and pull the passenger side door open for Dean. While he situates the bags on the seat so they won't topple over, I glance over at the whistling man. He's leaning up against the brick wall of the store, staring at us.

"*Jackie's* girl..." He sings.

Dean and I both hear it at the exact same time, as we turn to look at each other. Dean's expression goes stone cold.

"Get in the truck." He says to me, before he turns to the guy. He doesn't stop whistling it, singing those wrong, but significant words now and then, as Dean approaches him. He gets right in the guy's face.

"*Jackie's* girl." The guy says, dead eyeing Dean right back.

"Make a fucking move, asshole." Dean growls at him. The guy only smiles, seemingly unbothered.

"That's Jackie's girl." He says, his eyes shifting past Dean to look at me. Dean's hand drops to the large bowie knife sheathed on his belt.

"Don't fucking look at her. You look at me, or I'll cut your fucking eyes out of your head and feed them to you." Dean threatens him. The guy's eyes slide back to look at Dean. He's grinning at him now, then begins to whistle the song once more.

There's nothing we can do. This guy is technically not doing anything wrong. He could always say he didn't realize he was singing the wrong words. It's not illegal to sing a song in a parking lot, not appearing to bother anyone. We'd look like the crazy people in this situation. I can't even tell if it's the same guy that attacked me in Laura's shop. Dean doesn't move though, he's all up in the guy's face, and I know he's hoping the guy will swing on him and give him a reason to beat him to a pulp on the sidewalk, in broad day light, and probably on camera... I realize, with that thought, that's exactly what this guy wants Dean to do... To get locked up for assaulting him... That would leave me alone, without Dean, even if it's just a temporary window of time...

I rush over to Dean, grabbing his arm. "Come on! He wants you to hit him! He wants to get you locked up."

Dean leans even closer to the guy's face. "Tell your little prison bitch boyfriend, *Jackie*, that I'm really looking forward to getting to know him... very intimately." Dean growls. He reaches into the inner pocket of his leather cut, and pulls out his cellphone. Holding it up in the guy's face, Dean takes his photo. I can see in the guy's expression, he did not like that at all. The surprise in his eyes, tells me that he did not anticipate Dean having a cool enough head to make this move.

"*Checkmate.* Asshole." Dean grins, obviously noticing the shift in the guy's demeanor as well. "I'm gonna say this once... Get the fuck out of my town. There's a whole lot I can do to hurt you with this." He says, showing the guy his own photo, before he tucks the phone back in his pocket. "I guarantee you, that I have more friends in low places than you do... And as soon as we're done here, I'm blasting your fucking face out to every one of them." Dean pats the guy on the shoulder in a friendly fashion. Though, we all know there's nothing friendly about it. He gets close to the guy's ear. "And if I find out, that you were the one that touched Vanna... I'm going to hurt you in ways that you will never recover from. In ways that will make you useless to the fairer sex. And that's only if you even survive what I do to you." Dean's smile is fierce and sharp as a razor, as he lingers a moment longer in the guy's face, making him squirm. When Dean takes a step back from him, removing his hand from his shoulder, the guy immediately turns and walks hurriedly away. He even starts to jog.

"Was that him?" Dean asks me, his voice low and grave.

"I don't know." I sigh. "I never got a look at the guy in the shop. And I couldn't tell if it was the same voice. All this guy did was sing and whistle."

"Yeah. Slick. But not slick enough." Dean says, reaching down to grab my hand. "Come on, I'm taking you home." We walk back to the truck together and get in.

"What are you going to do with the picture?" I ask, as Dean drives us back to his house.

"I'm going to find out who he is. If he's got anybody he cares about. And if I'm lucky enough to see him again, I'll give *him* something to worry about." Dean mutters.

"I don't think you're going to see him again. I think you scared the shit out of him."

"Good. The tables are turning. I've got something I can use now." Dean says, making a turn off the main road to take us towards home.

Dean is on the phone with his cop friend, Jason, out on the front porch, while I put the groceries away. When he comes back inside, I can see that his tension hasn't subsided at all. A mixture of rage and eagerness lingers in his eyes.

"What is it?" I ask, sitting down in the living room in the corner of the big brown leather couch. Nico is curled up on the throw blanket next to me, peacefully oblivious, sleeping soundly.

"I sent the photo to Laura. She said she thinks it's him." Dean says, coming over to sit in the leather arm chair. "She's calling the detective working your case to tell him. He'll probably be in touch with you soon after. Jason's working on pulling the surveillance footage from the parking lot of the grocery store, and I put him in touch with the detective working your case, too. There's a BOLO out now with the photo I sent."

"Isn't that all good?" I ask.

Dean leans forward in the chair, his elbows on his knees as his hands hang down between them. His expression looks like he's afraid to disappoint me. "Laura only *thinks* it's him. Which won't hold up. You never got a look at the guy. So even *if* the cops manage to catch him and question him, he's gonna walk, unless he's dumb enough to confess. Which we both know, won't happen." Dean lets out a frustrated sigh. "This is just another situation where the only justice, is street justice. Which is why I sent his photo out to all my MC friends, too. With any luck, they'll grab him for me first."

I stare at him, remembering his confession about beating a guy with a baseball bat... And he did things like that for women he didn't even know, let alone one he loves. I swallow before I speak, "Dean... you can't get locked up."

"I wouldn't do anything on camera, Vanna. I wasn't going to hit him in the parking lot unless he attacked me first." Dean says, as if that bit of information is rule 101 of the *Ass Kicker's Code of Conduct*. "I don't want to leave you unprotected either. I'm not going to get myself locked up. I haven't even gone to any underground fights."

"I don't know why it didn't occur to me until now, that you could be arrested if caught doing that, too." I shake my head, mostly at my own ignorance.

"Not only that, I don't want to risk an injury that might hinder my ability to protect you." Dean explains. "I've just been blowing off steam at the gym every day before heading home."

When my cellphone rings in my purse, which is sitting on the counter of Dean's marble kitchen island, he jumps up from his seat before I do. "That's probably the detective."

I hurry over to my purse and pull out my cell phone. It is the detective. I relay what happened at the grocery store to him, and he informs me that they ran the guy's photo through their system, but it didn't come back with any matches. Which means he doesn't have a record in our county. That doesn't surprise me, though. If this guy is connected to Jack, I'd imagine they met in prison, which would mean he's most likely from New York, not North Carolina, and definitely not this county. The detective informs me he has contacted the NCDMV and they are in the process of doing a search as well, but if he isn't from North Carolina, it isn't going to turn up anything either. He could have a record in another state, but because of privacy laws and some other red tape, they're unable to run a search. He also informs me that Jack was questioned two days after the attack in Laura's shop, and as expected, denied everything and expressed concern for my wellbeing. When I hang up the phone, I reluctantly repeat all of this information to Dean.

"I guess we should have called the cops. Maybe they could have asked him for his I.D. or something." I sigh.

Dean scoffs. "He probably didn't have any on him. You don't carry I.D. when you do shady shit." He says, dragging a hand across the back of his neck in frustration. "If we did call the cops, they might have brought him in for questioning, sure. Only because of the police report you filed a few weeks ago. But all he'd have to do is deny everything. There's no evidence against him. None. No one who can positively identify him. He'd walk within twenty-four hours, no matter how this played out."

"Well, you scared him off by taking that photo. Even if he knows all of what you just said, he also knows that your *friends in low places*, don't abide by the same rules law enforcement has to follow. He's probably more afraid of your biker buddies, than he is of the cops." I take a few steps closer to Dean and place my hand against his chest. "I'm safe with you, remember?" His eyes look down at my hand on his cut as he brings one of his hands to curl his fingers around mine. He nods. "This guy, he's just a pawn. And you probably knocked him off the chessboard with that photo. That was quick thinking, I would have been too frazzled to think to do that." I reach up to stroke his jawline, attempting to soothe his frustration. "I know I'm safe with you, Dean. I've known it since you grabbed me in that bathroom stall."

"Maybe I should have just cracked his skull against the fuckin' bricks." He sighs. I slide my hands up his chest to wrap my arms around his neck, looking up at him as he wraps his arms around my waist.

"You can't do that, Dean. I need you to keep a level head, like you did today. You can't go to jail. I need you with me." I can tell by his rippling jaw muscles, that he's still thinking about the violent things he'd like to do to this guy. "Are you with me, Dean?" He closes his eyes and lowers his forehead to press against mine.

"Always." He promises.

DEAN

THE LAST THING I FEEL LIKE DOING, IS CELEBRATING MY BIRTHDAY. BETWEEN Vanna's attack a few weeks ago, and whatever is quietly brewing between the Saviors and the Demons, I wish we could just skip over November thirteenth all together. There hasn't been another incident in a few weeks now, with either thorn in my side. That doesn't mean that there won't be. Complacency is not an option. I've been in the game too long, and I've known too many dirtbags, to think that either of these situations have managed to quietly resolve themselves. They haven't. Jack Nero is still a ticking time bomb. And although Legion and his Demons have been quiet, that doesn't mean they aren't making moves in darkness.

I can't even say, that if not for these two looming enemy situations, I'd be able to enjoy the nights festivities in my honor. I've never liked celebrating my birthday. I hate being the center of attention. The only reason I participate, is because the last few years, since Cherry joined our merry little band of misfits, she's taken it upon herself to make a big deal out of our birthdays. Tonight, it's my turn again. She's been excited about it all damn week. Her and Vanna, both. Planning this together. I'm glad Vanna's had something to distract herself with, though. Something besides work. If it's gotta be at my expense, so be it.

The Twisted Throttle is closed to the public for the private gathering of my MC brothers, their girlfriends and Old Ladies, a handful of buddies from the JoCo Jokers MC and their posse of *party favors*. Even our prospects are here... As I quietly slip inside the steel door, attempting not to be noticed right away, the first thing I see is a big golden balloon in the shape of *thirty fuckin' eight* floating above the jukebox in the back. There are tables draped in black and red table cloths with food on either side of the jukebox too, along with about two hundred red and black balloons covering the ceiling of the bar.

Thirty fuckin' eight years. You'd think by now I'd adjust to the whole birthday thing. My mother made a big deal about our birthdays. That ended though, when her life did. It was never really the same after that. When I was on my own, I sure as hell didn't give a fuck. Lucinda barely cared much more than I did, which was fine by me. The only person, other than my mother, to make a damn fuss about November thirteenth, is Cherry, along with Vanna, now that she's in my life.

No one hears the steel door close behind me, over the rock music playing and the boisterous conversations taking place within the space. My plan is just to slip in covertly and avoid being noticed by everyone all at once, but then I spot Vanna walking into the room with another tray of appetizers. I freeze. Staring at her. She's all decked out in black, wearing a long, black leather, high waisted skirt, with a silver zipper that runs the length of it, dead center. The top she's got on is one of those lowcut blouses that show off her amazing curves, yet somehow retain a flowy-ness about them. It's tucked into her skirt, really emphasizing her hourglass figure. And she's wearing those sexy boots that I know hurt her feet, but damn she looks fuckin' good. She places the tray down and turns around, almost bumping into the prospect near her, who's a little too eager to be at her beckoned call. She smiles at him, and it's a radiant smile. She's wearing that deep red lipstick that makes her already perfect white teeth look even brighter. I haven't seen her wear it since our first date, seven months ago. Her eyes are done up in a smokey look like that night, too. She's hot as fuck. And as she gently touches the prospects arm to briefly apologize and walk past him, I swear to God, the little prick just attempted to subtly adjust his fuckin' pants.

I glance around the room and notice he's not her only admirer, either. Forcing down the wave of jealousy that's rising inside of me, I remind myself that she dolled herself up tonight, for me. Only me. They can look and appreciate, but they know she's mine. I know she's mine. And she does, too. As she walks back towards the corridor, I try to peek around the bar to get a look at that fine leather encompassed ass of hers, as it sways back and forth with every step she takes. Note to self, Vanna needs leather pants.

Before I get the chance to really fantasize about that glorious image, Axel spots me and announces my arrival to the room. A roar of Happy Birthday and applause rises up among my friends and MC Brothers. I'm slapped on the back and hugged by a few as I make my way into the bar to the thunderously sung song of Happy Birthday. Viking shoves a beer in my hand, as everyone raises their own beers and shots before they're thrown back in honor of my special fuckin' day. I take a few extra chugs of beer, myself. Wiping my mouth with the back of my hand, I glance around for Vanna. She hasn't come back yet, and Cherry isn't here either. They must be in the kitchen in the back together. I continue to greet my friends and thank them for coming, when I spot Slice, the President of the JoCo Jokers MC, with three of his *party favors* under his arms... *Mary Jane*, *Trippy* and *Lucky*...

Fuck me... I've banged two out of three of these women... almost three out of three if Viking didn't snatch Trippy that night.

The girls are all smiling at me as I approach Slice to say hello. He removes his right arm from Lucky's shoulders, to shake my hand.

"Nice of you to bring the girls." I attempt to sound humorous about it.

"Didn't realize you had yourself an Old Lady." Slice shrugs. "You making it official any time soon?"

As soon as I know what's going on with the CDMC. "That's the plan." I reply.

"She's gorgeous, Dean." Trippy smiles at me. "And so nice. You're lucky." Her words put me at ease. Trippy is still a sweet girl. I find myself hoping that a decent man slaps a cut on her soon.

"Thank you, Trippy. And I know it." I smile back at her. Glancing at Mary Jane and Lucky, I hope they share similar sentiments. "Do you girls think we can keep what we did under wraps?" I ask them. Lucky laughs and agrees right away. Mary Jane makes me fuckin' sweat for a moment. I wonder if she's still mad that I broke her cuffs...

"I guess so. Consider it a birthday present." She finally says to me, and I can fuckin' breathe again.

"Thanks, doll." I force myself to smile.

The birthday cake is wheeled out on a cart draped with a black cloth. It's a triple layered white cake, with what looks like shaved chocolate pieces coating the sides. *Happy Birthday Dean* is written in script in chocolate piping against the smooth white frosting. There's a little red heart next to my name, too. Cherry starts adding thirty-eight fuckin' black candles around the top tier, and I know this thing is going to go from a classy looking cake, to a damn fire ball in a few minutes.

"Do you like it?" Vanna asks excitedly, hugging my arm.

"It's the classiest looking birthday cake I've ever gotten." I smile back at her. I'm not lying. I've had a cake shaped like tits before, an ass, tires... every now and then something normal.

"You have to do the Happy Birthday song for him." A sweetbutt called Candy says to Vanna. "We as a group sang it to him when he walked into the party, but it's on you to sing it to him when you present the cake."

"Oh... okay." Vanna says shyly, rubbing her palms against the swell of her hips. I can tell she's nervous, so I give her an encouraging smile.

"It's okay, doll. Lay it on me." I say.

She clears her throat and starts to awkwardly sing Happy Birthday to me. Her fingers fidgeting in front of her, her voice tight. Candy grabs her arm to stop her as someone in the crowd calls out "Come on honey, you can do better than that!" They all chuckle and I give everyone the death glare. They shut the fuck up immediately.

"If you're his Ol' Lady, you have to *perform* it for him. Not just sing it." One of the other sweetbutts taunts Vanna. I watch as Vanna's face goes white as a sheet, then flushes crimson with embarrassment.

"It's okay, I'll do it again." Candy grins, before she looks at me, flipping her long blonde hair over her shoulder as she licks her lips. "How about a repeat of last year's performance? Everyone seemed to like it, especially you."

Oh, Hell no...

Last time she sang Happy Birthday to me, it was with my *microphone* in her mouth. As a *single*, not to mention, *drunk* guy, yeah, it was amusing for all... Especially me. But I'm hooked up with Vanna now, and that shit isn't going to fly. I don't even want Vanna to know about that.

"That's not going to work for reason's I'd think are obvious. If you're here to start trouble, I'm gonna have to ask you leave. Permanently." I tell her. Glancing at Vanna, she looks surprised by my words. The sweetbutt backs off, though.

"This cake is going to explode if one of you bitches doesn't sing him Happy Birthday, STAT!" Viking bellows impatiently from the side lines.

Vanna turns to glare at him. "Shut up, Viking. The cake isn't going anywhere, you'll get to eat again soon. Relax!" She sassily snaps at him, earning a few chuckles of her own from the party. She turns back to me. "Okay... a performance of Happy Birthday." She says, though it seems to be more to herself than anyone else in the room.

"Don't you have any other talents besides looking like a hot pain in the ass, Vanna?" Viking taunts her again.

I point at him this time. "Shut the fuck up. Or you get no cake." He glowers at me, but he shuts up. I turn back to Vanna, "It's okay, doll. Just sing it to me. I know you have a pretty voice."

"I have talent." She mutters, glaring at Viking. Her eyes dart around the room until she spots something on one of the buffet tables. She storms off towards it, fidgeting with something on a tray quickly, then storms back over to me. I notice she's got two small clam shells pinched between her fingers in both hands, when she squeezes them, they clamp together, making a rapid clicking sound, like a pair of tiny cymbals. Coming to stand before me, she glances over her shoulder one more time at Viking.

"If you want to eat again, maybe you should eat your heart out?" She sneers at him, though there is a tone of playfulness in her voice. He just folds his arms and cocks his chin at her to proceed. She turns to look back at me. "God, I hope I don't bomb at this. I wish someone would have warned me about this little biker birthday tradition." She takes a deep breath, closing her eyes and raising her arms above her head, making the clam shells clatter rapidly as she does so. I realize, somehow, seemingly without moving, her entire body is shimmying for a moment, before she leans forward in one swift motion, whipping her long dark hair and tossing it back. "*Happy birthday, to you...*" She says seductively, in a deeper, more sensual way than before. A few guys in the crowd whoop and whistle, and I realize I'm about to get my first ever Happy Birthday *Belly Dance* performance. *Fuckin' Aces...*

She extends her arms outwards, making those clam shells between her fingers clatter rapidly some more, as her shoulders slowly lift and roll, moving her arms in a fluid motion, like serpents, before she shimmies her chest at me. "*Happy birthday, to you...*" She smirks. Raising her arms above her head again, wrists crossed and fingers still clattering those clam shells, her hips rotate in a vertical figure eight motion, slowly, but exaggeratedly, making her whole body move like a writhing snake now... "Happy Birthday... *Mr. President...*" She winks at me, biting her sexy red bottom lip as she moves that fuckin' body built for sin before me. Dropping her arms, she tosses those clam shells away and spins around quickly, her hair whipping through the air again, smacking me in the face before she dips her fine, leather clad ass low, then brings it back up again, grinding it up against my crotch. I automatically grab her hips and slam her back harder into my groin. She looks up at me over her shoulder, her hands sliding over mine as she swivels her hips some more. "*Happy Birthday, to you.*" When she straightens back up to a round of applause and whistles from everyone in the joint, I don't let her go. I keep her ass pressed to my crotch.

"Gonna need you to stand here for a moment, yet, doll." I whisper in her ear, as I slide one of my hands as discretely as possible between us, adjusting my half hard-on to a less noticeable angle.

Cherry wheels the cake over to me and informs me it's time to make my wish and blow out the candles, or Viking is going to have a stroke. Vanna scoots herself to my side and gestures with her hand for me to go ahead. Aside from when I was a kid, I never bothered to think up a birthday wish before. Staring at Vanna, it's hard to think of a wish even now, when I've got her in my life. She's a dream come true to me. What more could I really want so long as I have her? Taking a breath, I shift my focus to the candles and wish for her happiness and safety as I blow them out.

"Fucking *finally*." Viking chuffs, stepping forward to start yanking candles off the cake with Cherry.

"What did you wish for?" Vanna asks, smiling up at me as she hands me the knife to make the first cut in the cake.

"World peace." I grin back at her, slicing into the cake. She rolls her eyes and grabs a little red party plate and a plastic fork, then takes the knife back from me. Making another cut and placing it onto the plate, she holds it up to me. The inside of the cake is an off-white color, with some kind of cream filling between the layers, containing tiny chocolate chips.

"Let me know what you think. It's not exactly birthday cake." She tells me, handing the knife off to Cherry so she can cut everyone a slice and pass them out. "I made it today from scratch. It's cannoli cake." She smiles. "It's better than birthday cake. And you deserve the best." I smile back at her, and apparently take too long to try her cake, because she grabs the plastic utensil off the plate and forks off a chunk, bringing it to my mouth for me. With a grin at her adorable impatience, I oblige her. And damn, that's fuckin' good. I take the fork from her to stuff more in my mouth.

"You better only make this for special occasions or I'm really going to end up a fuckin' gym rat." I say over another mouthful. She smiles excitedly. Within thirty minutes, that entire three tier cake is fuckin' *gone*. Everyone loved it.

We spend the next hour or so socializing. Vanna definitely earned herself some points with that erotic Happy Birthday performance, too. The sweet-butts aren't giving her any shit, and the guys seem to be looking at her a little differently. Like she belongs among us. Even Viking gives her a little nod of approval. He's probably impressed with her baking skills as well. For a minute earlier, I thought he was going to lick through his paper plate.

When I finally officially introduce her to Viper's Old Lady, Rosita, Vanna's smile brightens the room again as she happily shakes Rosita's hand. The two of them walk off together to discuss Thanksgiving in two weeks, and I can't help but smile to myself. This really is going to work. Vanna is going to be one of us. Rosita was an outsider once, too. With a similar past to Vanna's. One of our rescues, years ago. As I watch our two dark haired beauties smiling and chatting together, I thank Viper for convincing Rosita to join us tonight. She's not really one for crowds. Viper usually ends up flying solo at our MC events, but perhaps our two ladies will become close friends, and we'll see her out and about more often.

"I hope it's not an over step, but I told Rosita that she and the first lady have a few things in common, besides the obvious." Viper says, taking a sip from his beer. "I thought they might both benefit from knowing."

"It's nice to see Rosita out, having a good time." I say. "She's come a long way. And I'm sure it has a lot to do with you, Brother." Viper is usually a rather stoic individual, kind of an asshole at times, but he's doting with his wife. As a man should be. "How's the other mission coming along?" I ask. He glances at me for a moment, hesitating before answering. "It's alright." I assure him.

"Not to steal your thunder tonight, but I completed that mission two and a half months ago, bro." He says with a prideful grin on his face.

"Congratulations." I pat him on the back, ignoring the slight twinge of envy I feel. "Announce it if you want to, I don't mind sharing the spot light. In fact, take it. *Please.* You'll be doing me a favor." I halfheartedly joke. I've been glancing at the time all night, waiting for the chance to snatch Vanna and get her somewhere private. Viper and Rosita might provide the perfect distraction for my disappearing act. Three hours is enough of an appearance at my own birthday party, right?

Viper catches Rosita's attention and waves her back over to him. Vanna rejoins me at my side as well. After a brief discussion between Viper and Rosita, she agrees to allow him to let the cat out of the bag. Sticking my fingers in my mouth, I let out a sharp whistle, grabbing the attention of the room.

"Our VP has something to tell you all." I say, as everyone quiets down and stares in our direction. I throw an arm around Vanna and prepare to make a run for it as soon as he drops the good news.

"Well, I'm not one for speeches, so I'll just out and say it." Viper says, looking down at his wife and sliding an arm around her waist. "Rosita and I are havin' a kid."

As the room roars to life again with an eruption of congratulations and applause, I seize the moment and grab Vanna, herding her down the corridor away from the party.

"What are you doing?" She asks with a playful giggle as I practically shove her down the hall.

"The only cake I'm interested in sinking my teeth into now is this cake right here." I growl in her ear as I squeeze one of her firm ass cheeks over her leather skirt.

"What's gotten into you?" she squeals.

"I'm another year closer to death and just want to feel alive." I tease her.

"I hate it when you talk about your death." The giggle is gone from her voice now.

"It was a joke, I'm sorry." I say, pulling her down another corridor that will lead us to the War Room, gym, and bedrooms. "You want to do this on the conference table or in the gym?" I ask. "I promise to put it in this time if you pick gym."

"No! There are like forty people in this building and anyone can walk in on us!" she protests, starting to resist me and hinder our progress towards a destination.

"The doors lock, babe."

"I'm not doing it in the gym or in the conference room, Dean. And it's rude to ditch your guests." She huffs at me.

"Foods almost gone, cakes definitely gone, I'm fuckin' gone. Party's over." I say, fishing keys out of my pocket. "Our *private party* is about to begin." I pull her to the door of my old club bedroom. I'm not thrilled about her being in here, but I'm out of options since she's vetoed the gym and War Room.

"Is this your old room?" She asks, her tone transitioning from apprehensive to piqued curiosity. "I've never seen inside before."

I jam the key in the lock and twist. "I haven't been in here in a long time." I say, yanking the key back out to stick back in my pocket and shove the door open. Stepping into the small dark room first, I flick on the dim lamp on the dresser by the door and glance around.

It hasn't changed much, but it isn't trashed. The black broken blinds are still on the windows on either side of the bed, which is neatly made, so Cherry must still dust and wash the black pillows and comforter set on occasion in here. The half-naked biker chick posters, along with an American Flag, and some old bike photos, are still tacked to the gray walls. Though, the one corner of the flag has fallen. I hear the door shut behind me as Vanna enters, looking around. Of course, her eyes dart to the smashed picture frames on the dresser first...

"Maybe this wasn't such a great idea." There are a lot of demons in this room... "You deserve better than this. I shouldn't have brought you in here." I turn around to take her by the hand and lead her back out, but she quickly steps away from me, between the side of the bed and the long dresser with the broken picture frames on top.

"Are these photos of Maddie as a baby?" she asks.

"Yes."

"Why are they all broken?" She looks up at me curiously.

"I flipped the dresser over. Collateral damage."

She looks back at the photos, and lifts the one frame that's facing down on the dresser. The one I put my fist through. The photo of Lucinda and I, my arms around her from behind, my hands on her stomach, smiling like the fuckin' fool I was played for. Vanna doesn't ask about that photo. It's mangled frame and shattered glass explain all there is to know. After a moment, she places the picture back on the dresser, face down, then turns around, leaning back against the dresser as she surveys the small, dorm sized room.

"So, this is where you lived for two years?" She sounds contemplative.

"Well, there's a full bathroom over there," I point to the dark room a few feet away in front of me, "and we passed the kitchen on the way here. Turns out a guy with zero will to live doesn't need a whole lot to get by." I shrug. "This was just a place to sleep off the alcohol."

"And sleep with a hundred women?" She asks.

"Not a hundred... and that didn't always happen here... We should seriously get the fuck out of this tomb. I shouldn't have brought you in here. I was thinking with my dick."

She stifles a little laugh, then pushes herself way from the dresser and walks around the end of the bed, brushing past me to the other side. I watch her bend over between the opposite side of the bed and the wall, picking up the tack off the floor. She reaches up to pin the corner of the American Flag back up in its place, then sits down on the bed to look up at it.

I watch her head turn to look at the posters of the scantily clad women strad-dling motorcycles on the wall. After a few moments she looks over at me.

"You know, it's shit like this that used to make me wonder if you were really into me."

"Well, until you, I didn't know about Peonies, doll." I give her a crooked smile.

"So, these are roses..." She sighs, looking back at the women. "You gave me a rose when you first asked me out."

"Would have been a Peony had I known better." I tell her.

"Red roses are lovely." She smiles. "All roses are lovely."

"You're my favorite, doll."

"I know." She says, standing up from the bed and walking in my direc-tion. "So, the color theme of your party is black and red." She smiles up at me. "This is the black." She gestures to her outfit. "The red is underneath."

"Fuckin' Aces... Does this mean I get to unwrap you?" I eagerly ask.

"You *are* the birthday boy." She says in that low seductive tone, reach-ing up to slide her hands beneath my cut at my shoulders to push it down my arms. I shrug out of it and place it down on the chair behind me as her hands move down to undo my belt and jeans. Then I watch her as she takes a few steps backwards towards the foot of the bed, slowly unzipping that long black leather skirt. I unbutton my shirt as I watch her slide the leather down over her hips, bending forward to push it down over her thick thighs, simultaneously giving me a generous glance down her blouse, to the lacey red bra her full, gorgeous tits are encased in. When the skirt hits the floor, pooled around her ankles, she straightens up, stepping out of it, still wearing her boots, and kicks the leather skirt at me with a giggle. I catch it and toss it down on the chair with my cut. The red lace panties that match her lacey red bra barely peek out from beneath the bottom of her blouse.

"Are you going to make me unwrap myself?" she asks, playing with the hem of her blouse, giving me teasing little peeks of those hot fuckin' drawers she's got on. I move towards her, grabbing the hem of her top to pull it over her head, but she grabs my hands. "Nope... boots first." She taunts me, biting her lip as she looks up at me through her dark lashes.

I drop to my knees at her feet, sitting back on my heels as my hands fumble with the laces on her boots. My eyes are pinned on that see through red lace inches from my face. She grabs onto my shoulders to steady herself as she bends one knee, then the other, allowing me to slip her boots off. She runs her fingers through the top of my hair in that soothing way she knows lulls me into calm. I run my hands up the back of her legs, up to her ass, gripping her as I pull her firmly to my face. Pressing my mouth and nose against that red fuckin' lace, I breathe her in deeply. My cock nearly punches a hole in my damn jeans.

"Fuck, baby..." I groan, opening my eyes to look up at her. She pulls the blouse off and lets it fall down on the floor next to me, shaking her dark hair out as it cascades down her arms and back, around the sides of her breasts. Her dark hair. Her perfect complexion. Red is a color for brunettes.

"Are you going to come up here?" she asks.

I shake my head, my nose and mouth rubbing against her as I do so, tickling her, making her giggle and attempt to squirm away from me, but I only tighten my grip on her and breathe her in deeply again. "I'm not ready yet." My answer muffled against her, the vibration of my voice and movement of my lips against the barely-there lace covering her lips, makes her let out a slight whimper.

"I thought you wanted more cake?" she teases me, her hands touching mine, which are still gripping her ass.

"I love your *cherry pie*, too." I say, nuzzling against her again, listening to her little giggly gasps as I do so.

I spend the next forty minutes at least, with my face between heavens gates, until Vanna can't take any more, her delectable body trembling, her fists clenching the black bedding as I stand looking down at her. Undoing the rest of the buttons of my shirt, I slip it off and wipe my mouth with it before tossing it to the chair, or near it. Vanna glances up at me and smiles a sated smile. She watches me shove my pants to the floor, toeing off my boots until I'm more naked than she is. She's still wearing the red bra, though with all her writhing and thrashing about, it's barely containing her breasts anymore, as they rise and fall with her breath. My fist finds my rigid cock. She's so fuckin' beautiful.

"Would you like a birthday blowie?" she asks, sitting up on the bed, running her hand through her dark, luscious locks.

"No... not in here." She looks at me, puzzled, but I don't want to elaborate. "I want to fuck you, now, doll." I growl, before she can ask. Though, I can see it in her eyes, she wants to ask. She wants to know what my aversion to blow jobs is about. This isn't the first time I've declined an offer from her. It's not that I don't want one. Or that I think she'd be lousy at it. Quite the opposite, actually. That fuckin' mouth of hers... I know she'd get me off. It isn't like I haven't jerked off about it either... it's just that... "She used to have to blow me to get me hard enough to fuck her in here..."

Vanna tries not to react, but I can see a flicker of something behind her eyes. Anger towards Lucinda? Pity? God, I hope not pity... I squeeze my dick harder, willing my erection to keep. Vanna's eyes drop from mine, as she looks me over, settling on my cock for a moment. She licks her lips slowly, before her eyes meet mine again, keeping them locked on me as she twists around on the bed, getting on her hands and knees before me. She whips that luscious mane back, her dark hair draping around her back and shoulders as she wiggles her sexy fuckin' ass at me, a playful little smirk pulling at her lips.

"Come fuck me then, birthday boy." She tempts me, lowering her face down against the bed, ass up, all submissive and asking for it in every way. Just seeing her like this makes my balls tight and my cock jerk back to full attention.

Before I know it, I've got my fist in her hair, pulling her back up on all fours, my other hand rubbing the head of my cock up and down her juicy pussy, parting her little slit to sheath myself inside her. I try to take my time, not wanting to ram it in selfishly before she's ready to take me. I can feel her slight tension, so I release her hair and stroke her body instead. The last thing I want is to make her nervous. I know Vanna well enough to know, she probably wouldn't tell me if I was scaring her. Sweeping her hair to the side, I hover lower over her to trail kisses across her shoulder blades, to tell her I love her. I reach around to fondle her lacey breasts, feeling her hand over mine as I gently knead her body. She grips my hand and pulls, and I allow her to guide my hand down her body, down between her legs as she pushes my fingers into her wet folds. I gently stroke her clit as I push the head of my cock against her opening, rocking my hips forward with small thrusts until I'm home, enveloped in the hot, tight center of her femininity. I fuck her slow and steady, savoring the feel of her wrapped around me. When she moans and pushes back on me to give her more, I do. Holding onto her hips, I thrust into her a little harder, a little faster. Until my body is slamming against hers, making the flesh of her sexy fuckin' ass ripple at the impact of every thrust. As her walls begin to clench and spasm round me, I have to slow down, giving her just enough to keep her coming, but barely holding on to the edge myself. I don't want to come yet. I want to make this last. I want to wring every bit of ecstasy out of her that I possibly can, before she pulls me over the edge with her. The way she cries out my name though, is almost my undoing. Panting beneath me, I can feel the pulsing around my cock slow and become more sporadic, as she comes down from her orgasm. I pull out of her and flip her onto her back, before I mount her again, driving my cock home once more. This time, I want to look in her eyes when she comes for me.

Her arms are wrapped around my neck, her legs hooked around my waist as I pump inside her. She's kissing me in that way that always makes the world vanish. Where there's nothing but she and I and there's nowhere I'd rather be than right here, losing myself in her tight, slick heat. I close my eyes only to savor the feel of her for a few moments. All I hear are her sexy little noises. Her gasps and whimpers driving me on, swirling around my brain. The sound of our bodies together, my cock pounding inside her like a piston in a well-oiled machine... *Fuck!* She gets so wet for me. That drives me even madder.

"Dean..." she whispers against my lips.

"Fuck yeah, baby... say my name..." I grunt.

"Dean." She says again.

"Yeah... you're mine, doll... all fuckin' mine... say it..."

"Dean!" This time she's louder, and suddenly her legs and arms aren't around me anymore. I'm the only one holding on.

I stop fucking her for a moment and look down at her. "What, baby? Tell me what you need." I aim to please.

She looks concerned though. "You don't hear that?"

I hear my heart pounding, our ragged breathing. "What, love?" I ask.

A distant crashing sound. Metal on metal, screeching as if something is being dragged across the front lot.

"*That!*" she says with alarm.

I pull out of her and we both scramble to get our clothes on. When I open the door, Viking is already storming down the hall to head for the front lot.

Another loud crash... metal scraping on the pavement...

I rush out of the room, not bothering to button my shirt or fasten my belt, running down the corridor to head towards the front door of the bar. When I get there, it's empty, everyone's gone. I must have been banging Vanna longer than I thought. Swinging the door open, I hit the parking lot in time to see a big black Ford truck peel out and barrel towards the exit of my lot. It hits something one more time, the sound of scraping metal crunching and screeching again, before it exits the lot and takes off down the road, disappearing around the corner down the street.

"*Oh Fuck!*" Viking shouts from behind me.

Glancing around the lot, I realize Serene isn't under the flood light by my shop where I had left her earlier to come to my party...

The steel door behind me swings open again. "*No!*" I hear Vanna cry out as well.

My heart sinks and it feels as if a block of ice is quickly forming in the pit of my stomach. I make my way slowly towards the mangled heap of metal in my lot...

My mind is in denial. I can physically feel it reeling against the reality of the situation... But my heart knows what's happened... and the cracks begin to shatter with every step closer I take.

Chapter
thirty-two

PIECES OF HER BEAUTIFUL BODY ARE SCATTERED ACROSS THE PARKING LOT... The bulk of what's left of her in a twisted metal wreck not far from where I had left her. I sink to my knees beside her... Her life fluids leaking out around her onto the pavement from her utterly broken body... like a pool of blood...

"Oh, baby... no... no... no...no... no..." My throat is tight, my vision is blurry, my voice breaks on her name... "Serene... my sweet, sweet *Serene*..." I place my shaking hand on her scratched up and dented tank. "I'm so sorry, baby..." I whisper to her, hanging my head and slumping forward. It hurts to even swallow as I close my eyes against the burning tears that threaten to spill. No way can I let any of them see me cry, though my heart is as broken as my beautiful Serene.

I can hear Vanna and Viking behind me somewhere, Cherry and Axel too. They're talking frantically between themselves. I think I hear Viking say the address. He must have called the cops. Taking a deep breath, I steel myself. Nearly two fucking years of my time, blood and sweat. Forty-five fucking grand... *Demolished*... all over my lot... right under my fucking nose. I glance up at the security camera beneath the shop sign. The one I installed specifically to watch over Serene when I have her parked in my lot. I'm not surprised to find it broken. Though, I don't need security footage to tell me who could be behind this. This was personal. This went beyond vandalism. This was fucking cold blooded murder. This could only have been the Demons, or Jack fuckin' Nero! I force myself to my feet, gathering my resolve as I do so. I turn around to face my family, my eyes finding Vanna's first. She's already convinced herself as to who is responsible for this travesty. I can see it in her terrified face.

And that's all I need. All I fucking need to chase the sorrow away. Vanna's tear-soaked face. The fear in her eyes, her complexion pale with the horror that must be coursing through her right now. Now, I'm fucking pissed. It's bad enough he murdered my Dame, but he put that fucking look on Vanna's face, too.

I extend my hand to her and she comes to me immediately, burying her face in her hands against my chest as she sobs. I wrap my arms around her and hold her tightly.

"I'm so sorry." She cries, her sobs racking her body. "This is all my fault."

"No, baby." I kiss her head then press my cheek against it as I rock her slowly. "It isn't. We don't know for sure who's behind this. It could be the Demons just as easily." After all, Legion did murder Preacher. I'm sure of it. I stroke her hair along her back to try to soothe her as I look over at Viking.

"Cops are coming." He says simply. I nod.

"What is *that*?" Cherry asks.

I shift my focus to her. She's standing with Axel. He has his arm around her and she's pointing to the light post where I had parked Serene. I turn to see what she's talking about.

There's a knife stabbed into the post... but it's stabbed through something else as well.

Fuck!

"I'll look." I insist. "Viking, take Vanna." I don't want her to see whatever this might be. Whatever it is, it isn't going to be good and she's already scared shitless. I turn Vanna towards him as he approaches and puts an arm around her to keep her with him.

"What is it?" She asks, a tremble in her voice.

"Wait right here." I tell her, before I turn to walk over to the post.

As I get closer, I can see it's a photo of some kind, printed out on a sheet of paper with words scrawled across it, pinned to the post with a switch blade...

My fucking switch blade... That motherfucker was inside the club house... inside my old room... *Fucking Christ...* As I step closer, the photo is even worse than the fact he used my own damn knife.

It's a picture of Vanna and I ... the night I had her on the pool table... the night she thought she heard the door shut once we had finished... As if someone had been watching us. She was right. Someone had been watching us. Taking photos of us... Jesus fucking Christ.

I study the photo. I'm fucking pissed beyond measure, yet somewhat relieved at the same time at the minor fact that, although this is a photo of us fucking, she's not exposed. In the photo her back is arched, her head is back. Unless you know Vanna, it's not an identifiable shot. Her legs are open with one over my shoulder, but thank God my head buried between her legs is shielding her from view. I also never got around to taking her top off.

My eyes shift to read the scrawled message in red ink under the picture. I've read enough of his prison letters to recognize the hand writing.

"You defiled mine. I defiled yours."

I feel the muscle in my jaw pop as I realize how hard I'm clenching my teeth. This wasn't Legion and his Demons... This was Jack fuckin' Nero.

"What is it?" Vanna asks.

I swallow hard, turning around to face her, keeping my body between her and the message so she doesn't see. "Nobody needs to see this." I say. "It's going to be a long night. Cherry, would you be a doll and take Vanna inside and put on some coffee? Axel, I'm going to need you to review the security footage. The cops are going to want to see it, might as well get that ball rolling."

"Sure thing." Axel nods, he runs back to the roadhouse as Cherry walks quickly over to Vanna, attempting to coax her into going with her inside.

"No, Dean, what is it?" Vanna asks, refusing to go with Cherry. She shoves away from Viking, but with one glance at him and an upward tilt of my chin, he grabs her to hold her back. "What is it?" she persists.

Fuck... I don't know what to say to her yet. How many ways is this motherfucker going to violate her? I'm glad I didn't have her more exposed on that pool table. God knows how many fucking cops are going to be looking at this photo for "evidence." Fucking ogling her. She's going to feel humiliated again. And that's my fucking fault. She deserves better than the depraved shit I fucking do with her. I make a vow to myself here and now, I will never put her at risk like this again. Vanna deserves better than what I've given her. I didn't protect her that night. God only knows how many photos he's got. I was thinking with my fucking dick and now she's going to feel violated all over again. She's going to be embarrassed and ashamed, and it's my fuckin' fault! *Fuck! Fuck! Fuck!*

"Baby, go with Cherry. The cops are going to want to talk to you too when they get here. We'll come get you, okay?" I try to sound reassuring.

"Please!" she cries.

Damn it. Is not knowing making it worse for her?

"It's a message, doll. To me. I don't want you to see it just yet." I sigh. "Please, go with Cherry. We'll come get you soon."

Cherry takes Vanna by the hand and leads her back to the roadhouse. Viking knows better than to make a move towards me before the girls are inside behind the closed door.

"Jesus Fuck!" I let out a long exhale that I didn't even realize I was holding, now that the girls are inside.

"The fuck is it, Bro?" Viking asks.

I shake my head. "A picture of me doing Vanna. Anchored to the post with my goddamned switchblade."

"Oh shit." Viking says.

"Motherfucker had somebody inside. Who fucking knows how many times, or what else he's got. What other fucking photos he's got of her. What he's going to do with them. Vanna is going to be fucking mortified!" If I could kick my own fucking ass for being so careless I would.

I can see the red and blue flashing lights on the buildings across the street as the police are arriving. Two squad cars pull into my lot and head over to where we're standing. I pull out my cellphone and take a photo of the "evidence" for myself.

Vanna is going to want to know, as much as I hate it. She has a right, and I know they're going to take it with them. Hopefully she won't have to see it in person.

"Looks like you're having a shit night, Keegan." The cop in the first car says as he climbs out of his squad car. He reaches back inside to turn on his spot light and shines it down on Serene's mangled body... *Fuck*... She's even worse than I thought... A total fucking loss. My heart sinks all over again.

"You could say that, Foster." I mutter depressingly.

The cop, one of Jason's buddies, comes to stand beside me. "The fuck happened here?" He asks. "This doesn't look like a typical hit and run."

I pass both hands through the top of my hair and down the back of my skull, gripping the back of my neck as I stare at the wreckage of what had once been my only steadfast woman. My escape... my only *Serenity*...

"It ain't." I sigh. "It's a lot worse."

By the time we actually walk in the front door of our home, the sun is already rising. We're both beat. Vanna has barely said a word to me since even before the police left. She walks straight into the bedroom without looking back at me, without stopping to grab a water from the fridge, or to pet Nico, asleep on the couch, as she usually does. I can't help but wonder if she blames me as much as I blame myself. I follow her like a lost puppy and stand in the doorway, watching her quietly.

She pulls a t-shirt out of one of her drawers and tosses it on the bed, then removes her boots and strips out of her clothes to change into the shirt. She walks to her side of the bed and pulls the covers back, climbing in and laying on her side, facing the windows. Facing away from me.

"Vanna... I'm..."

"*I can't.*" She cuts me off. "Just go to sleep."

"I'm sorry." I finish anyway.

"I'm sorry, too." She says softly.

"You have nothing to be sorry for."

She scoffs, but she still doesn't turn to look at me. I stare at her beautiful black hair against the pillow under her head. I want to climb into bed beside her and hold her, breathe in those dark waves, but I don't know if I'm welcome to. I don't know if she wants me anywhere near her, after the humiliation she suffered tonight with that fucking photo of us.

"Serene would be tucked in her spot in your garage right now, if It weren't for me." She whispers. I can hear the tremor in her voice. "But instead, she's scrap metal... She's gone. Forever." Vanna sniffles.

"Vanna... what happened to Serene is not your fault." I insist. "She isn't gone forever... I'm going to salvage what I can of her, and I'm going to re-build her."

"You were *crushed*." She cries. "I saw it break your heart."

I swallow hard and nod, even though she isn't looking at me. It did break my heart, but there are worse things I could lose... "I've rebuilt that before, too, baby. I have you to thank for that." I can see her shoulders jerking slightly as she tries to cry silently. That fucking breaks my heart too. "Vanna... please don't cry." I say softly to her.

"You have me to thank for ruining your life." She whimpers. "I dragged you into this mess and he had someone destroy the most important thing to you because of me."

"Baby, I loved Serene... but you're the most important thing to me." I sigh. "You didn't ruin my life. You gave me back life." She doesn't respond this time. She pulls the covers up further, curling herself into them tighter. I worry that this is a wall going up, and not just the blanket. "Vanna... Am I allowed to be near you?" I ask.

"It's your house. Your bed." I can barely hear her faint words.

Shit. "Been thinking of it as *ours*. You live here with me."

She's silent now. I'm not going to let this happen. No fucking way. I walk into the bedroom and around the foot of the bed to her side and kneel down beside her.

"Don't do this." I plead, pulling the cover down to look her in the face, so she can see mine. "Don't let him get between us, Vanna. Not after all we've overcome to be together." She closes her eyes. She doesn't say anything. "Vanna, baby... We're gonna get through this. Please." I press.

Nothing.

I can't help myself. I was going to try to give her a little space, but I can't. I touch her face. I stroke her hair. I try to coax her to look at me. When she still ignores me, my anxiety begins to rise. *Please, please, don't shut me out...* "I fucked up, I'm sorry... The fucking photo. I know you're upset about it. I left you open to this humiliation. I didn't protect you. I know you're upset with me about that..."

"I'm upset about everything, Dean." She says, finally looking at me again. I stroke her cheek gently, moving her hair from the side of her face to tuck behind her ear. "And that embarrassing photo is just as much my fault as it is yours!" Her eyes suddenly go from sorrowful to angry, as she sits up in the bed and shoves my hand away from her. Throwing back the covers she tells me to move out of her way. I rise and take a reluctant step backwards to give her room enough to stand up from the bed.

"What are you doing?" I ask, afraid she's going to start throwing on clothes...

"I instigated our little session on the pool table. We both know it. The photo is my own damn fault. I embarrassed myself." She's looking at me in a way that makes my insides feel like they're twisting up. I'm honestly afraid of what she might say next. "I guess you really do become what you hang with. Spend enough time around *patch whores* in a biker bar, you start behaving like one." She mutters disdainfully.

I don't even know how to respond to that...

"Excuse me." She says, pushing past me, but I grab her by the arm. A reflex. I still don't know what to even say to her. She glares at me for a moment, but her eyes soften slightly as she seems to sense my fear. A sigh escapes her before she speaks again. "I'm just going to take a shower. I need to wash this crap off my face and try to get a few hours of sleep before I have to be at work." She tugs her arm and I let her slip from my grasp. "I really am sorry about Serene." She says, backing away from me. Her bottom lip quivers before she turns from me and hurries into the bathroom, locking the door behind her.

I walk to the foot of the bed, staring at the locked door as I lower myself to sit down on the mattress. Closing my eyes, I slump forward, elbows on my knees, palms pressed to my eye sockets as I listen to the sound of the shower running on the other side of the locked door. She probably thinks I can't hear her crying... But I can... And it kills me.

J UST A MOTORCYCLE...

They don't get it. Serene wasn't *just a motorcycle*. Not to Dean. Not even to me, after seeing the way he was with her... the way he was about her... the way he *still* is about her. Determined to bring her back. Convinced he can somehow salvage what's left and resurrect her. For his sake, I hope it's possible... But I heard the cops. I heard the insurance agent. *A total loss*, they said. Someone offered to call a wrecker to take her to the junk yard, and the look on Dean's face would have stopped my heart had he turned that expression on me. I watched, after the cops left with their collected evidence, as Dean and Viking dragged Serene into his shop. I half expected Viking to crack a joke about a funeral for the bike, but even he seemed to sense that similar words would have been hazardous to his health.

"Vanna... just be glad you weren't attacked again. This is serious." Ethan says, helping me unpack a large box of books and tarot cards in the side room of Laura's shop. "At least it was just the bike."

Just the bike. "You don't get it. She was *real* to him. She became real to me because of him. It feels like a friend died." I try to explain.

Ethan grabs a few books from the box and carries them over to the shelf next to me. "I knew he was too perfect. What is that mental disorder called, where people fall in love with objects? *Paraphilia? Objectophilia*, or something?"

I glare at him. "You're not funny. And it isn't like that. Their connection was spiritual. You know everything has energy. He created her. She was his escape." I snap at him. She was his serenity. His only joy when everything else in his life was falling apart. Dean told me all about it. Explained it to me. When Lucinda was tearing him down, making him miserable, he had Serene to turn to. Rebuilding and modifying and improving her. Turning her into something special and unique. When she was finished, she never stopped being his escape from the pain of everything going on around him. She was his one constant, through all the turmoil, through all the years, through everything, until now.

"From what?" Ethan asks, though his tone is still obnoxiously dismissive.

"A lot. That's all you need to know. He's been through a lot. I'm not going to betray his confidence by giving you the terrible details. But Dean's had a rough life." I shove the remaining books on the shelf, not really caring right now if they're in the correct place or not. Grabbing the empty cardboard box, I carry it to the back room and throw it out the back door onto the porch. I'll throw it in the recycling bin later before I leave.

The sound of a motorcycle roaring down the street makes me pause at the back door, waiting to see if it's one of Dean's prospects, or possibly Axel or Viking. Or maybe it's just someone who happens to ride a motorcycle cruising by that has no affiliation to any MC at all. Ethan slips in front of me and peeks his head out the door.

"Is it the cute one?" He asks.

"Which one is the cute one?"

"The dirty blonde with the blue eyes and short beard." He says. "The young happy one."

"Axel." I sigh. "He's straight, by the way. And *happily* involved."

The prospect Dean calls Rusty, pulls into the back lot, and backs his bike up into a parking space before he shuts his bike down and gives me a quick wave. I wave back and turn to go back inside the shop.

"Drat." Ethan huffs with disappointment.

"Since when are you into bikers?" I take a seat in the chair near Laura's desk and glance at the time bouncing around the screen saver on her laptop. She should be back soon from her lunch break.

"I'm not. But hot is hot. And *Axel* is *hot*." Ethan says, sitting opposite me behind Laura's desk. "You seem a little pissy, Vanna. Are you sure you're just upset about the bike?" He asks, leaning forward to rest his elbows on the desk, propping his chin on his folded hands as he looks at me.

"As long as Jack is still in prison, I'm fine." I've been repeating that to myself for weeks now. Ever since the first attack upstairs. I don't want to get into details about the photo either. It was embarrassing enough to have to explain that to the police. It's embarrassing enough to know that Jack's creep probably has multiple other photos, and who knows how explicit they are. Stupid bitch. What the hell was I thinking that night? What the hell was I thinking with all of this? This whole situation. It's all my fault. The photos. Serene. Dean's impending death, curtesy of Jack Nero...

I was stupid to think everything was going to be okay. That all I had to do was come clean to Dean about the spell, and that once I did, and he forgave me, we would be okay. In reality, it changed nothing, and the wave of guilt that threatens to overwhelm me, crashes over me once again.

DEAN

IVE DAYS. IT'S BEEN FIVE WHOLE DAYS AND VANNA HAS BARELY SPOKEN TO me since the night of Serene's destruction. She checks in with me dutifully when she goes to and from work, but that's it. When I get home from the shop at night, later than usual, granted. I've been working on salvaging Serene between client's bikes and after hours. Vanna is already in bed. Her back to me. Dinner left in the oven. I'm trying to give her space, after the humiliation she suffered with that photo, but I can't let this go on any longer.

I'm staring at the half of my shop I've now dedicated to Serene's parts, spread out across the long work bench and part of the floor, when my cellphone rings. It's Vanna. Calling like clockwork to inform me that she's leaving Laura's shop. I pick up on the second ring.

"Hey, baby."

"Getting in my car now to head to your house." She says.

Your house. Not home. I don't like it.

"How was work?" I try.

"Same as usual."

"I'll be home earlier, tonight." I say, hopeful that maybe she'll wait up for me.

"No rush."

Fuck. I don't like that either.

"I love you, baby." I try again.

"You too. Bye." She hangs up.

You too? Shit... I definitely do not like that.

I'm not losing both of my women to this fucking asshole. If I leave now, I'll beat Vanna home by thirty minutes. Shoving my phone back in my pocket, I walk over to Serene and touch her shredded leather seat. Vanna's name was carved into it. Most likely done with my own switchblade before the bastard plowed into her repeatedly, with a truck we now know was reported stolen and ditched later that night. There was no security footage either, fucker knew the party would be the perfect distraction, nobody checking monitors. Busted all the cameras in the lot strategically before he went in on Serene...

"I ain't giving up on you, baby. We'll be together again." I promise her. "But we can't lose Vanna. I know you understand. You always do." I grip her broken clutch on her bent handle bars for a moment, before I walk away from her. I close up the shop much earlier than I've been since it happened.

As I mount one of my side chicks and hit the starter, I glance at the stain in the lot where Serene bled out on the pavement.

No way this motherfucker is going to win. No fucking way. I kick up the stand and tear out of the lot towards home.

Our home.

I'm in the kitchen, chopping up lettuce, cherry tomatoes, cucumbers and other ingredients for a salad to go with the herb baked chicken breasts I've got going in the oven. Vanna should be home any minute. My plan is to get her to eat with me. Get her to fucking talk to me. I keep glancing at the clock on the wall. She's running a little late. Could be traffic, though. I'm not going to panic just yet. The prospects have all checked in and reported no issues at Vanna's shop.

Once I've got the salad together, I pop open a bottle of Sauvignon Blanc, placing it on the dining room table with two glasses, to let it breathe. Then I sit on a bar stool at my kitchen island, staring at the driveway through the front windows, while I wait for Vanna to show up.

Another ten minutes pass. My fingers are going numb. I've been tapping them hard and consistently on the marble top as I wait impatiently. The idea of installing a fuckin' tracker on her phone is become more appealing by the minute.

I'm about to pull out my cell phone to call her and ask where the fuck she detoured to, when she finally pulls up the driveway. I get up to quickly shut off the oven and pull the chicken out to rest on the stove top for a few minutes, before I greet her at the door.

She gives me a half smile as I open the door for her. "Welcome home, babe." I smile back. "I made us dinner. It's ready. Come sit. I'll get it."

"Oh." She's surprised, but not overly so. "You didn't have to do that."

"I wanted to."

She places her purse on the edge of the kitchen island and walks over to sit down at the dining room table. I have a feeling it's only to humor me, though. Her energy still seems very low. She still feels distant to me.

I pour her some wine before she can object. My hope is that it eventually gets her talking. As she takes a sip, she looks over the rim at me knowingly. I just grin and hurry up to get the food on the table before she pulls some female *'I'm actually not hungry'* bullshit.

It's a few minutes into our meal before she says anything to me. "So why aren't you at the shop?" she asks.

"I miss you." I say, watching for her reaction. I don't get much of one. She seems more into her wine than anything else. "Did I fuck the chicken up?"

She cracks a smile. "No. It's good. I appreciate the effort."

"I just tried to have something done before you got home. I really want to spend the evening together."

"Well, here we are." She says, tilting her glass towards me before she takes another sip. Make that a gulp, of wine. I pour her some more.

"Are you okay?" There was just something off about that last comment she made.

"Fucking peachy." She sighs.

I let that obvious drip of sarcasm slide. "This is the most you've said to me in five days."

She shrugs. "You've been working late."

"Not that late." I counter her. "Since when are you tired by nine at night?" She doesn't answer me. She drinks her wine. "Vanna... you've been avoiding me." I'm just going to be straight with her. "I know I've been staying a few extra hours at the shop this week, but we've never gone to sleep before midnight the earliest. And that's after a round or two of boot knockin', baby. You've barely let me touch you since... since that night."

She scoffs at me. "Is *that* what you miss?"

"I miss *you*. Everything that comes and goes with you. So yeah, I miss being intimate with you too."

"Well, I've got a headache." She says, before another sip of wine. A not-so-subtle way of letting me know I won't be getting any tonight, either.

"Maybe the wine is a bad idea then. Not great for headaches, you know."

She doesn't say anything. She just stares out the window towards the garage. She's being very distant. Bordering on cold, and I can't help but wonder if she's come around to blaming me as much as I blame myself for that photo of us on the pool table together. That would definitely explain her distance from me in bed. I can't really see it being the extra time I've been spending at the shop after hours with Serene.

"Vanna, baby. Talk to me." I press. "If you don't tell me what's wrong, I can't fix it."

"Isn't that what you've been doing all week?"

"Are you upset I've been spending a few hours after the shop closes to work on Serene?" I ask. That would genuinely surprise me. Vanna was devastated over what happened to Serene that night. Why would she be angry with me about this now?

"Serene would be tucked in her spot in your garage right there, right now, if it weren't for me." She says softly, continuing to stare out the window. I can hear the tremor in her voice. "But instead of being in that garage, *right there*..." She takes another gulp of wine.

"Vanna... what happened to Serene is not your fault." I try to reassure her again. "She isn't gone forever. I'm salvaging what I can and I will rebuild her."

"With another bike when the insurance money comes through."

"Right." It's the best I can do. Serene was destroyed beyond repair. The extreme bend in her frame rendered her a total loss.

"Then it won't be Serene." Her voice cracks, she finishes her wine, then grabs her plate and glass to bring to the sink. I grab mine and follow her over.

"Baby... It's alright. And it's not your fault." I say, placing the dishes down beside hers. I try to touch her arm, but she walks away from me, turning to head towards the bedroom. I follow her and stand in the doorway as I watch her.

As she did the night everything happened, I watch as she pulls a t-shirt out of one of the dresser drawers and tosses it onto the bed, then kicks off her shoes and strips out of her clothes to change into the shirt. After she gathers her discarded clothes into the hamper, she walks to her side of the bed, pulling the covers back and climbs in, laying on her side, facing away from me, as she has done these last five nights.

"Vanna... it isn't even seven thirty yet." I say the words on a weary sigh. I can take a hint about the headache comment earlier too. She doesn't want me touching her. That makes me hurt on another level. "Baby, please, talk to me." I try again.

"You can go back to the shop if you want. I understand. I'd want to keep every piece of her too." She murmurs.

"Serene isn't going anywhere. I'm afraid you are."

She sniffles. Shit. Is she crying? "I won't go anywhere. I'm staying in bed until I have to get up for work tomorrow."

"That ain't what I mean, baby. Not gonna lie, you've got me a little concerned, doll."

"I want you to work on Serene. Really. You should. Maybe it helps."

"Are you trying to get me out? Away from you?"

"No. It's your house. Your bed. Do what you want."

Shit. More of that *your* house nonsense.

"Vanna, this is *our* house." I try to gently press. "And I miss you... I feel like you're a million miles away from me."

She scoffs. "You should be so lucky."

"I'd be lost and miserable without you."

"You've survived thirty-eight years without me. You'd be fine."

I don't like the direction this is going. "What is this talk, Vanna?" I ask. She doesn't answer me this time. I watch as she pulls the covers up higher, an attempt to stifle a little whimper. I storm into the room and around to her side of the bed, kneeling before her. She is crying. Her hands tucked under her pillow. Her face turned inward against it as well. I swallow hard. Seeing her cry, knowing she's been blaming herself for days since this happened, breaks my heart, too.

"Vanna, baby... please." She's fucking killing me. I slip my hand between her cheek and the pillow and gently turn her face back to me, rubbing her tears away with my thumbs.

"It's only going to get worse." She whimpers.

"I'm not afraid." I say.

"You should be. Serene was only the beginning. Jack isn't going to stop until he destroys you." She sobs. "And when he does, I'm going to have to live with that, for as long as he lets me live!" She sits up and pushes herself away from me, scooting herself back to get off the other side of the bed. I get up to follow her, but she only sits on the side of the bed and buries her face in her hands to cry harder.

I walk around the bed to be near her again. "Vanna, I'm not going to let Jack hurt you, let alone kill you. He's not killing me either. I know you've seen the scary side of him. And yes, the fucking prick is a goddamned monster. I agree. But you've never seen my dark side. He's not going to beat me. Not when *you* are what's on the line. I will not fail you when it comes to this. I swear it."

She shakes her head. "You can't promise that. And I can't risk losing you."

"What do you mean?" I ask, my anxiety kicking up a few notches. I feel like I'm veering off *I'm Fucked Avenue,* straight over the side of a jagged cliff.

"I mean I love you, Dean. And I can't stand knowing you're going to get hurt because of me. I can't let it happen."

"So, what are you saying, Vanna? You gonna fuckin' leave me? Is that it? Fuckin' run forever?" I pace in front of her, I'm losing my cool. Fast. "Are you? Are you fuckin' leaving me?" I demand. I can't believe we are back here again. After everything. She ain't leaving me. I'll fuckin' chain her to the goddamned bed. "You ain't leaving me, baby. It ain't happening. Better come up with plan fucking B."

"I don't want you to get hurt. Or killed." She cries.

"If you leave me, you will hurt me Vanna. If you leave me, it will kill me." I say, crouching down to face her. "Do you hear me? *You*, you alone, are the only thing that can destroy me. Not Jack fuckin' Nero. *You*, Vanna."

She closes her eyes and shakes her head. "You don't understand."

"I understand that you're scared. I get it. You think Jack is some larger-than-life undefeatable monster." I say, grabbing her hands to hold onto them. "You're stuck on that because of the horrific shit you lived through at his hands. But he isn't larger than life, baby. He's just a man. Not even that. Real men don't hit women, Vanna. He isn't a larger-than-life monster to me. He's a piece of shit who's going to get what's coming to him. I don't beat up women. I beat up women beaters. The Jacks of this world don't scare me." She shakes her head, lowering her eyes from mine. She's not getting it. She's not understanding. "What is it? Tell me, please, so I can reassure you." I plead. "You can't leave me, Vanna. You just can't." I suddenly understand Jack's crazy. As far as being unable to let her go. I can see how a man could lose his mind over a woman, but he took it to a bad place. I'd never hurt Vanna. Jack's already dead for doing that. He just hasn't realized it yet.

"I don't want to leave you." She says, but she still won't meet my eyes.

"Then don't. You can't run forever, baby. We were brought together for a reason. I'm going to end Jack. I promise you. Then you'll be free. We can live happily ever after. You won't have that threat looming over you ever again. I can do that for you. I want to do it. Don't you want that too?"

She nods. Great. I'm far from out of the woods though. She needs to promise me she isn't going to leave me. However, I know myself, even if she does. Now that she's put that fear in me, I'm not going to let myself believe her. I'm going to worry constantly every time she's out of my sight, every time she goes to work, if this is the time she doesn't come back to me.

"Vanna. *You are it for me.* Do you understand me?" I release one of her hands to tilt her face up with my forefinger and stare into her dark watery eyes. "You are my end game. Whether that end is taking Jack down with me, or dying in my sleep in our bed beside you, fifty years from now. You are it for me. My reason for living. My reason for dying. How ever that comes, I accept it." I release her chin to reach for my knife and place the handle in her hand. I force her to wrap her fingers around it as I press the sharp tip to my chest. "If you leave me, Vanna. You may as well cut my heart out and take it with you. It belongs to you anyway. It's useless to me if I don't have you. I don't want to live without you, baby. I don't even think I could. Without you, I give up."

She tries to pull the knife away from my body, but I lean into it to show her I'm serious. The tip pierces my skin just enough to draw blood. The look on her face tells me it did. "You crazy fool!" she snaps at me, attempting to just drop the blade now. I don't let her though. Turning her wrist gently, I force her hand to twist the blade, making the point of the knife in my flesh widen the cut. "You're making yourself bleed!"

"I am crazy. About you, Vanna. Madly in love." I swear to her. "I've got about a gallon and half more that I'm ready, willing and able, to spill for you. I'll spill his, too. I'll make a goddamned bloody mess of it."

"Dean! Please!" She wiggles her other hand out of mine and places it on my chest, her fingers on either side of the blade now. I remove it carefully, only because I don't want to risk cutting her, and place it on the night table beside me.

"What the Hell is wrong with you?" She pulls down my shirt to inspect the small hole in my chest. I already know it's not bad. I barely felt anything. I've been cut worse. Got the scars to prove it. What's one more small one? "Since when did you become such a psycho?" she demands, an almost sympathetic look in her eyes now as she stares back into mine.

"You bring it out of me." I shrug. "I am mad about you, Vanna. Out of my fucking mind. I'll love you like crazy, forever. I've told you, if you leave me, you're just going to have two crazy motherfuckers tailing you. Might as well save yourself the hassle and just stay with me. I'll never leave you. You're stuck. I warned you."

"Warned me?"

"Yes. That night I told you I loved you. That first night you threatened to leave. I told you once I'm all in with you, that's it. Wholeheartedly and permanently. Forever type of deal. You took it. You're stuck with me. I resisted you at first because I knew you would have this power over me. That's what I meant when I told you it wasn't about rejecting you. It was self-preservation. But that went out the window when we finally came together. You're mine, Vanna. And I'm yours. Forever." She isn't crying anymore. She's staring back at me. "You get me, baby?" I ask. She nods. I think I see a hint of a smile. "Good." I let out a sigh. "You have no idea how close you came to living the rest of your life chained to this fucking bed, Vanna. Don't fucking test me like this again."

She shakes her head, but she is smiling, slightly. She thinks I'm joking. I'll let her think that. Because I honestly don't know, myself. I don't think there's a line I wouldn't cross to keep her. Or to keep her safe.

"What are we going to do?" She asks, her voice is quiet.

Thank God we're back to *we*. "We're going to get through this, together. You're going to let me handle Jack. But first, you're going to get me a beer, and a shot of whiskey, so I can try to relax and recover from the stroke you nearly gave me." I sigh, reaching my hand to slide behind her head and pull her towards me. I kiss her lips, tasting the salt of her tears, grateful they've stopped falling and that she isn't leaving me. She kisses me back, her arms sliding over my shoulders as she pulls closer to me and deepens our kiss.

I could not live without this. The heights her kisses take me to... simply her kisses... The rest of her... Fuck. I'm a goner. I knew I would be the moment I had her.

She scoots herself back further onto the mattress, pulling me by the shirt to follow her. I cage her beneath me for a moment, looking down at her. Even with her tear-streaked cheeks and little sniffles from crying, she's the most beautiful thing I've ever seen. I touch her face, sweeping a strand of her dark hair away from her eye, before I run a finger gently across her sexy as sin lower lip. She licks where my finger trailed and bites lightly into it, her dark almond eyes staring into mine, enticing me with the slightest little grin. She reaches up to wrap an arm around my neck, her other hand stroking my jawline, coaxing me to lower myself down against her for another kiss.

I grin back at her. "On second thought, we've been missing out on quite a lot of boot knockin'. And boot knockin' beats beer and whiskey any day." I feel her bare legs slide up the sides of my body and wrap around me as she smirks, her eyes letting me know it's fuckin' on. "I guess that headache went away?" I tease her. She simply nods. I lower myself down to meet her lips once again. "Aces, baby."

Chapter thirty-three

Vanna

"MOTHERFUCKERS." DEAN MUTTERS, AS HE WALKS BACK IN the front door, his thumb angrily jamming the screen of his cell phone. He walks into the dining room and pulls out a chair at the head of the table, sitting down as he starts typing something on the phone again. I know that he's been arguing with the insurance company the last week over the claim with Serene. Glancing at the clock on the wall above the pantry door in the kitchen, it's almost around the time when I usually start cooking dinner. However, that can wait a few minutes. I walk over to the dining room table and pull out a chair for myself to sit with him.

"Are you okay?" I ask.

"Fine, doll."

"You don't seem fine."

His eyes shift up from scrolling on his phone to look at me. I watch his strong shoulders beneath his cut rise slowly with a deep breath, and then fall as he exhales. "Just an issue with the insurance claim on Serene."

"I'm sorry."

"Don't be. You didn't bust her up."

"Not even by proxy?" It's my turn to let out a rueful sigh.

Dean's eyes soften as he leans forward and takes my hand, holding it in his as he strokes the back of my hand with his thumb. "*No*, doll. We've been over this. I thought we put this to bed days ago? You're not at fault for any of this. At all."

"What's the problem with the insurance?" I ask. "They said she was a total loss."

He nods, then shrugs half-heartedly. "Serene was a few years old. They don't take the custom work I did on her over the years, into account. They'll replace her with a stock model one year newer than what she was. No bells and whistles. Nothing for the custom body work, exhaust or engine work I did. So, I'm still out about fifteen grand or so, all things considered." Dean releases my hand to sit back in his chair, going back to scrolling through whatever it is he's looking at. Maybe new motorcycles, but I don't even want to ask.

"I have a little under eight grand left, I can give you." I offer. His eyes dart up from his phone to look at me again, though, this time, they aren't soft at all. It's a borderline glare. "I have it in a shoe box in my room. It's not technically even mine... I stole it from Jack, when I sold all of his things."

"No, Vanna." He almost growls at me.

"I don't *need* it." I say. "It was my escape money. And since I'm not going to run, why don't you just take it for Serene?"

"I'm not taking your money, Vanna." Dean insists. "I appreciate the thought, but no. I can make up what I need in a couple of nights in the ring." He says. "Or one trip to Myrtle Beach."

"No. You're not doing that crazy shit ever again." I frown at him, folding my arms. That whole nightmare death cage match was way too much. If I never have to sit through watching him fight for his life in a ring again, it will be too soon.

Dean cracks a slight crooked grin at my protest. "No promises."

"If you take my escape money, I can't escape." I push, trying to sound playful about it.

He leans back in his chair to look me over. "Baby, if you give me a chance, you're not ever going to want to escape." His words sound like a promise. "Shit's far from ideal right now, under these circumstances, I know. But when everything blows over, doll. And it *will*. When it's just you and me... I'm gonna make you real happy, baby. Gonna do my best to give you everything you want."

His words feel like strong, warm arms around me, and I can't help smiling back at his handsome face. "I believe you." I tell him. "Do we have to wait until things blow over, though? Can't you start right now?" I tease him, giving him an impish little smirk.

He arches a brow at me, intrigued, though his grin is bordering on the salacious side. "What do you have in mind?" he asks, playing up that naughty, gravelly voice of his.

"Pizza?" I giggle.

I watch as his stubbled jaw slides forward, his eyes slightly narrowing as he shakes his head slowly. "Not what I was expecting to hear." He grumbles, though he's still smiling.

"We've been cooped up so much lately." I say, uncrossing my arms to lean forward and place my hands on one of his knees. "Both of us, just to and from work and home. You've been at the shop late almost every night. Can we have a little date? Nobody is going to bother me if you're with me. *Please*, take me out for pizza?" I pout.

Dean lets out a long sigh with mock exasperation. "As if I stand a chance against your powers of persuasion."

"So, yes?" I smile back at him, gripping his leg slightly tighter.

He cocks his chin at me. "Grab a jacket. It's getting chilly out. You want pizza, we'll get you pizza." I give him a playful squeal of excitement, getting up to grab my jacket from the coat rack. As I hurry past him, Dean playfully swats me on the bottom.

THE ONLY DECENT ITALIAN RESTAURANT IN TOWN, WHERE I TOOK VANNA for our first date, has a dress code. I offered to slap on a suit and take her, but she declined and opted for something more casual, which meant crossing county lines in my quest to procure her, her pizza. How could I deny her when I've obviously made her feel neglected? *Please take me out for a quick pizza...* Such a simple request. Shouldn't be complicated at all.

I've managed to keep her in the dark about my intentions since Preacher's funeral. She's most often content to dine at home, even before my security details since her attack. Vanna's usual aversion to nights out on the town, have worked in my favor. It's not that I don't want to be seen with her. I just don't want *her* to be seen with *me*. The straight to work, straight home policy

I've implemented on her over the last weeks since her attack, not only keeps her as safe as I can keep her, without locking her away, it also keeps her off Legion's radar, as well.

The restaurant we're dining in now, is located within the CDMC's stomping grounds. Which is why I opted to take the Silverado instead of a side chick tonight, and swapped out my Saviors MC cut for my old Milwaukee style leather jacket. I'm not a Savior tonight. I'm just a guy taking his girl out for a slice of pizza. Nothing to see here.

"I'm going to use the ladies' room before we go." Vanna says, as we get up from our table, finished with our meal. I drop some cash for a tip and walk her towards the restroom, letting her know I'll be waiting for her by the door after I settle the bill.

"How was everything?" The young girl at the register smiles pleasantly.

"Great. Thank you." I return her smile as I hand her the bill and some cash. I can't help noticing the white Peony flower wrapped in red cellophane resting beside the register. "My girl loves these flowers." I comment, thinking I really should surprise her with a bouquet one of these days. Lousy of me to not have done so already.

The cashier lets out a little chuckle. "I imagine that's why you had it brought over."

Wait...what? Her words catch me completely off guard. "I'm sorry, what?"

She looks up at me, handing me my change with a perplexed expression on her face. "The woman you're with tonight... A man just delivered this for her, from the florist across the street. He said *you* ordered it and wanted it left up front to give it to her before you left. They closed at nine, about ten minutes ago." She explains.

"What did he look like?" I try to sound nonchalant about asking.

She shrugs. "I don't know, he had a scarf wrapped around his neck and mouth. He was wearing a ball cap, too. He just said he was delivering it for you, for her, and walked right back out." She explains. I don't say anything. What is there to say? It wasn't me. She picks up the single flower and holds it out to me, just as Vanna is exiting the bathroom, zipping up her jacket as she starts walking towards me.

I grab the flower from the cashier's hand and place it back down on the counter beside the register. "Keep it... Have a great night." I say, moving quickly to swoop my arm around Vanna and block her from seeing the fuckin' flower. I hurry her towards the door, eager to get her locked in my truck. Even more eager to get her locked in my house. *Our* house.

"What are you doing?" She laughs, as I hustle her towards the exit.

"It's cold out, just getting you to the truck." I say, dragging her out the door and hauling her to my Silverado.

"You're being weird." She says. I pull open the passenger side door and help her in, then slam it shut once she's safe inside. Hopping in the driver's side, I crank the ignition, glancing around for anyone who might be watching. But like that night I had her on the pool table, when that picture was taken of us, I don't spot anybody. Even though this time, I know they're out there.

"I need you to double check something for me." I say, keeping the tonality of my voice low, even though I know Vanna can't hear me. She's in the master bathroom getting ready for bed. I'm all the way on the other side of the house, on the front porch no less, damn near whispering into my cellphone to Jason. "I need you to make sure Jack Nero is still in prison. I just have a bad feeling that something isn't right. Serene was too... personal." So was the white Peony tonight. Had it been any other kind of flower, I wouldn't be able to rule out Legion completely. But I can, because it wasn't just any flower.

There's no way the lackey, Legion, or Jack could have known we were going to that specific Italian restaurant tonight, across the street from a florist. This move with the Peony was made on the spot. By someone with the knowledge of Vanna's favoritism towards that specific flower. The lackey could have seen an opportunity and taken it. But would he be privy to that intimate knowledge prior to the opportunity? It isn't like he can just up and call Jack in prison to run his idea by him on the spot. No... My gut tells me something is rotten in the state of Denmark.

"I thought you said the cop who took Vanna's initial report said he was still incarcerated?" Jason asks. "I've got a BOLO on the accomplice, though nothing so far has come of it. He's still at large."

"The cop called the prison directly. I did an inmate search of his name, he's still listed as incarcerated, there, too."

"Is his earliest release date still posted as two years out?" Jason asks.

"It's not listed at all. Just says he's still inside. No further info. The only date is the date he went in, a little over three years ago."

"Hmmm. That sounds like a system error, or perhaps a data entry mistake. It happens on occasion. Human error, they could have just forgotten to enter it into the system. I'll see what I can find out, though." Jason says. He pauses a moment, before he continues, "Serene happened over a week ago, why are you asking now? Did something else happen?"

I glance through the window I'm standing in front of to make sure Vanna's not through with her shower yet. That she isn't moving about anywhere in the front part of the house where she might hear or see me. She isn't.

"Are you there?" He asks.

"Yeah, I'm here." I proceed to relay the condensed version of the night's events to him. "I don't know, Jay. I'm thinking Jack's out somehow. The flower... Serene... it's too intimate. And I don't want to scare the shit out of her with my theory, unless I have to. Unless he *is* out, somehow."

"I'm looking at his status online now, it does still show him as incarcerated. When inmates are processed, either going in or coming out, there's usually only a two-hour delay before their status is available to view in the system. In some cases, maybe a day. It looks like he's still behind bars, but give me a little while. I'll see if anybody can give me some answers tonight. If not, I'll make a call to the prison first thing." Jason says. "I'd venture to say he's still locked up. Somebody just didn't enter his projected release date. Shit happens."

"I hope you're right... I've got a bad feeling." I say, glancing around the perimeter of the property. The black forest that surrounds the side and back of my house, opposite the farm land. I used to love it for its privacy factor. Now, it's a double-edged sword.

"Maybe the flower was for someone else in the restaurant and the cashier was wrong." Jason says. I shake my head regardless of the fact that he can't see me through the phone.

"It was a Peony, Jay."

"The fuck is a *Peony*?"

I sigh. "A flower of far too much significance."

TOWELING MY HAIR OFF AS I WALK BAREFOOT, WRAPPED IN A ROBE, DOWN the hall towards the front of the house, I spot Dean walking in the front door. He locks it behind him and gives the door knob a pull, double checking the lock before he turns. For a split second, he looks troubled, before a smile crosses his face as he notices me.

"Hey, baby."

"Hey." I smile back at him. I walk over to the fridge for a bottle of water to bring back to the bedroom. I notice he seems to glance around the perimeter of the living room, then the dining room, as he takes a few steps further into the house. "Are you okay?" I ask.

"*Aces.*" He says, though with less enthusiasm than he usually reserves for the use of that phrase. I grab my water and shut the fridge, cracking the cap off and taking a sip as I watch him. He slips off his leather jacket and turns to hang it up on the rack near the front door. He lingers a moment longer to look through the window of the door. Then he turns to walk into the kitchen with me.

"Are you sure everything is okay?" I ask again. He's been acting strange since the restaurant. He nods, wearing a slight smile as he wraps an arm around me, his hand at the small of my back, touching me over the robe.

"I like it when you wear my shit." Dean says. "You got on anything underneath?"

"No."

"Mind if I check?" His grin is slight, though he proceeds to slip his hand inside the robe. His fingers gently skim across my skin until they reach my breast. His thumb strokes back and forth over my nipple, already hardening at his touch, as he cups my breast in his warm, large hand. His grin widens slightly more, at the way my body responds to him. "You know, I could go for a little dessert." He winks at me.

"We didn't bring any home. Could have had Tiramisu or a Cannoli, but you dragged me out of there so fast." I remind him, watching his expression for any sign of acknowledgment regarding his odd behavior tonight.

Dean seems to ignore my statement altogether though, as his hand releases my breast and he moves it slowly down my abdomen beneath the robe, twisting his wrist in the process so his fingers point downward, traveling ever south. With his hand at the small of my back, he pulls me against him and brings his mouth to my ear, growling the words, "I've got your cannoli right here, doll. And I don't need any Tiramisu, when you're my favorite little Italian dessert."

M Y CELLPHONE RINGS A LITTLE AFTER EIGHT FORTY-FIVE AM. I TAKE THE call outside while Vanna is busy sorting clothing from the dryer in the laundry room to put away. I brace myself for what I know I'm about to hear, though I hope I'm wrong. She thinks she's getting ready to head to her Reiki appointments at the witch shop today. I've got a stage four kit to install on a Harley in my shop. My gut tells me our plans are about to drastically change, immediately. And for the foreseeable future.

Closing the door quietly behind me, I step out onto the front porch and hit the answer call icon on my screen, placing the phone to my ear. "Jason."

"I've already got a BOLO on him, Dean. And a squad car at the bottom of your driveway, just in case you went to the shop this morning before I was able to find out and call you." I glance towards the end of the driveway to see the police car just pulling up, parking a few feet from the mailbox.

I knew it, but it still knocks the breath out of me. *How the fuck, Jason?*

"He paroled three weeks ago." Jason tells me. "You can have Vanna file for an emergency order of-"

"How the fuck is Jack Nero out?" My voice is a harsh whisper as I glance back at the door, making sure she isn't looking for me. I walk down my porch steps to pace the gravel of my driveway. "How Jason? I don't want to hear about a useless form that does *jack shit* to protect anyone. I want to know how, as of five weeks ago, he was still in a prison cell several states away! How, as of not even twenty minutes ago when I last checked, the online database *still* has him listed as *currently incarcerated!* The detective working Vanna's case called the prison days after and had him questioned. He was there."

Jason lets out a sigh through the phone. "Yeah. But that's *all* they did. Just asked if he was there. Asked if he had anything to do with the attack.

No further questions. It didn't occur to anyone to ask about his release date. Why would they ask? As long as he was behind bars at the time of the attack..."

"How did he get out two years early?" I demand.

"Good behavior. New York prisons have an overcrowding problem. His case was reevaluated, and with no letters or calls of objection from Vanna or her family..."

"*Fuck!*" I want to slug someone in the face as I clench my fist and continue to pace, occasionally glancing up at the door and front windows to make sure she isn't looking. "Isn't she supposed to get some kind of warning? Aren't victims notified in advance before there's even a parole hearing? Aren't there apparently *useless laws* that give the victims a chance to convince a parole board to let their perpetrators serve the full sentence? How could this have happened?"

"Apparently, Vanna hid herself a little too well... They weren't able to reach her to notify her about the hearing, or his release. The responsibility falls on the victim to stay informed and in touch. They only make so much effort to contact the victims." He explains. "If she was expecting to have two years, minimum, she must have figured she had more time before she had to think about reaching out..."

"She's going to freak the fuck out." I swallow hard, imagining the terror in her eyes when I tell her. And I *have to* tell her, for her own good. I can't shield her from this, for her own safety. She needs to know he's out there. That the danger is real and it's on our doorstep, lurking behind every corner.

"It was most likely Jack Nero, personally, that destroyed your bike." Jason says.

Without a doubt. It was too personal. Too brutal. The handwriting on the photo of me and Vanna looked too similar to Jack's letters from prison. I knew in my gut it was Jack. I should have asked Jason to look into this sooner. I shouldn't have assumed Jack had his fuckin' lackey mail him that printed photo so he could scrawl his warning across it and send it back... The weeks that past between attacks... The fact that the officer told Vanna Jack was still incarcerated... It made sense at the time. But this explains a lot. The brutality exacted on Serene... The way Vanna's attacker backed off her when she threatened to tell Jack... He was afraid because he knew Jack was being released within days. Jack had to have anticipated that the police would only inquire as to whether or not he was still locked up. That they wouldn't bother asking about a release date if all they cared about was whether or not he was in a prison cell in New York that day. Fucker has a set of balls on him, I'll give him that much.

"Dean, we need to talk about a few other things. I have to come by tonight, or you can meet me somewhere." He insists.

"Jay, a man that wants to kill the love of my life is out there, somewhere, waiting... I'm not leaving her side."

"Then I'll come to you, after my shift tonight." Jason says. "When are you going to tell her?"

"I don't know... today... now... I don't fuckin' know." I run my hand through my hair, gripping the back of my neck as I turn to face the woods that surround most of the side and back of my home. "Call your squad car off. I'm not leaving her. She's safe with me."

"I know she's safe with you, but I can spare the car for a few hours if you want it. I can put your house on a watch route for six weeks also. A squad car will drive by just to do a quick sweep of the area at night, randomly. I can do it myself some nights as well."

"Yeah... fine." I say. "Call it away for now... I'm not sure if I'm telling her just yet. A cop car at the end of the driveway is just going to force me to have to when she asks about it... I can't lie to her."

"Alright. Calling them off now." Jason says. "Be smart, Dean. I'll be by right after my shift."

"Yeah." I hang up the phone, shoving it into my pocket as I turn to watch the squad car drive off. When I start to walk back towards the house, Vanna is in the dining room window to the right of the front door, peering out at me, a confused expression on her face.

Fuck me. I was hoping to put this off, at least a little while, to gather my thoughts. Think up the least jarring way to tell her...

"Why was there a police car at the end of the driveway?" Vanna immediately asks, as I walk through the front door and lock it behind me. She's wearing one of her long dresses she typically reserves for the witch shop. Her arms are casually folded, but her eyes are searching mine intently. "Did something happen? Was Jack's accomplice spotted in the area or something?" She continues to ask questions. How the fuck do I even break this to her? She takes a few steps closer to me, her fingers now fidgeting together in front of her. "I know something is wrong. You were acting strange last night. And you only do that thing with your fingers in your hair when you're stressed out." She says. I drop my arm back to my side. "Dean... tell me."

"You're safe with me." I remind her. Her brows furrow slightly as she continues to stare at me. "Do you believe me?"

"Yes." Her quiet response. "What's going on?" A few more moments tick by. A million ways to say it flash through my mind... "Dean? You're scaring me..."

Fuck, baby... it's about to get so much worse... And there's no real way to make this easier on her. I take a breath. "He's out, doll."

"Who is?"

"*Jack*, baby... Jack is out."

She blinks, her head slightly tilts as she looks at me with slight confusion. "That's not possible." Her arms uncross and her hands move to the curve of her hips, her expression sliding into one of defiance. "He has two years. Maybe even up to four." She says with conviction. One of her hands extends towards me, low, palm up in an almost pleading, yet at the same time, insisting, gesture. "You were right there when that cop told us... He said Jack was still incarcerated... You heard him say it, Dean."

"He was released two weeks after. He's been free three weeks now." I say, taking her hand and holding it in both of mine.

"*No...* there's been some mistake... Who told you this?" She shakes her head at me, attempting to pull her hand away from me, but I hold onto her tighter, pressing her palm to my chest with one hand, stroking her arm gently with my other. "He has two years at least, Dean... Four if I'm lucky..." I watch as her expression slowly morphs from denial into desperation. "The Judge... he said so... I was there for the sentencing... he copped a plea with the DA... that was the deal... Seven years, possibility of parole in five... *I have two years still...* and that cop... you heard him, Dean... he said Jack was still in prison..."

"He was, doll. At that time, he was still locked up. He isn't now... It's not a mistake... Jason told me."

"He's wrong... he has to be. There's been a mistake." She shakes her head at me again, pulling her arm from me. I let her hand go, but I follow her as she storms past me, into the living room to grab her cellphone, which is sitting on the slate coffee table. "There's been a mistake." She keeps insisting, grabbing the cell, her finger swiping the screen. "Someone would have notified me about this. If not the parole board, certainly my own mother..." Her voice trails off suddenly, as her face pales upon realization of something I'm not privy to. She sinks slowly to sit down on the leather three-seater. "*Oh God...*" she whispers.

"What is it?" I ask, coming to sit beside her as she slowly places the cellphone back down on the slate coffee table, her hand visibly shaking. "Vanna, what is it?"

"*Oh God...*" She whispers again, her voice full of horror. She brings her trembling hands up to her face, her fingers sliding up her temples, disappearing in her dark hair.

"Baby... talk to me." I persist, gently placing a hand on her lower back.

"My mother... the funeral..." She's still staring at the phone.

"What funeral, doll?"

"She ordered flowers in my name... white roses... and lilies... She signed my name on the sympathy card... I would have *never*..." Her eyes are shifting back and forth rapidly, as if she's speed reading something, but she isn't looking at anything in particular now. She's deep in thought about something that's obviously causing her much distress.

"Vanna, what are you talking about? What funeral?" She's never mentioned any of this to me before.

"Oh God!" She rips her fingers from her hair and slams both hands down on the leather cushion on either side of her. "He's too smart... He knew exactly what I would do!" She jumps up from the couch and starts to pace the room, looking out the windows, then rushing over to them, checking that they're all secured and locked.

I get up to grab her by the arms to stop her. "Vanna, calm down. You're safe."

She shakes her head frantically, looking up at me, her eyes are wide and wild. "I'm not safe... I'm not safe... you're not safe either... not if you're anywhere near me." She says in a panic, gripping my leather cut in her fists. "He planned it. He planned it, Dean. He knew exactly what I would do! I played right into his hands!"

"Vanna... tell me what happened..." I try to keep my tone steady and smooth, for her sake. She needs an anchor right now. A rock. I need to be that for her. "Tell me about the funeral. What happened?"

"Jack's father... he died, a few months ago." She says. "My mother had flowers at the funeral in my name... I was so angry when she sent me the picture... that she wrote a note to Jack and his mother... *with all my love and sympathy*... to that fucking *monster! My* love and sympathy!*"

"You never told me any of this." For her to keep something from me during our relationship, that has clearly caused her distress to this level... It's bothersome to me, to state the least.

"We were in a fight..." she says. "It was after you and Viking came to get me from that bar..."

"Go back to the funeral."

She nods slightly. "I was about to text her back. I was typing out *how dare you*, when she called me. I was so mad at her, I picked up the phone and I yelled at her... but it wasn't her on the other end of the line... It was Jack."

"Jack fucking *called you* and you didn't fucking tell me?" My control is slipping now.

She shakes her head again. "This was before you knew anything... I couldn't tell you... I told you that I changed my phone number... which I stupidly did."

She lied to me then. She told me she was getting incessant calls from telemarketers. I rein in my frustration and take a breath before I speak. This faux pas will be addressed with her later. "What did Jack say to you?"

"He was pretending to be sweet... in front of my mother. She let him call me on her phone... He said I cost him three years with his father... He asked me where I was, and if I could *feel* him getting closer to me... And that he had a surprise for me... *This* is his surprise... He's orchestrated everything... everything!" She grips my cut tighter in her fists. "I need to leave, Dean... You *have to* let me go... He knows who you are. Where you are. Who you care about. He killed Serene... he's going to kill me... he's going to kill you, too."

"You're not going anywhere." I say to her, gripping her arms now and forcing her backwards into the leather arm chair behind her, against the far wall of the living room. I make her sit down as I crouch before her. "You're not leaving my sight until I've dealt with him. You're not going anywhere without me." She shakes her head at me again and I grab her face between my hands, forcing her to look me in the eyes. "I'm dead serious, Vanna. Don't fucking test me." I push down the thought of chains again...

She grips my wrists with her ice-cold fingers. "He knew I'd change my number... that I'd fall out of touch with my family again... That the parole board would be unable to call me either... Dean, he played me... he orchestrated everything... He's a master at isolating me without me even realizing it... until it's too late... He tried to kill me, and my parents still think it was because he loves me so much.... That it was *my fault*... I pushed him to it... That *I* hurt *him!*" Her voice breaks and her eyes start to well up with tears.

"Your parents are fucking assholes. It's not your fault." I try not to glare at her, it's not meant for her. She is right about something, though. Jack is a cunning motherfucker.

She closes her eyes and the tears roll down her cheeks. I wipe them away with my thumbs. "I'm a bad person, Dean... I set all of this in motion..." she weeps.

"You're a fucking angel, Vanna, surrounded by demons." I sigh. "No wonder you were so alone, baby. But you're not now, you have me. And I'll slay all these demons for you." I promise her.

"I made Jack crazy." She whispers, as if it's a confession. "It was my fault... I just wanted him to love me like he used to... But he changed so much after... after..." she leans forward to bring her hands to her face between mine. I remove my hands to hold onto her arms again as she sobs. "After I put a love spell on him... he turned into a monster. Maybe I caused everything..."

"Vanna, I've crossed paths with a hundred Jacks, doll. Trust me, *Magic* has nothing to do with what they are... Jack had the devil in him long before he ever laid eyes on you."

"I know you don't believe in it, but I had to tell you." She whimpers. "I should have told you when I told you about the Knight summoning spell."

I don't want to rehash that. It's water under the bridge, and I still don't believe in any of it, anyway. I'm more concerned with her secrets steeped in actual threats to her well-being. "I have to tell *you*, I'm less than thrilled you've kept this funeral phone call from me for months, Vanna." Had she mentioned his words to me months ago, I would have looked into him then and there, and possibly averted this entire situation. But I'm not going to go so far as to tell her that... She already blames herself enough. "Is there anything else you've neglected to tell me? Any more fuckin' secrets?"

Vanna lowers her hands to look at me with her watery, red rimmed eyes, and sniffles. "Garrett Johnson grabbed my leg when I drove him home that morning, before our fight."

I suck a deep breath in through my nostrils, really reining in my self-control. I release it on a growl of her name. I wasn't expecting to hear that. Garrett Johnson is lucky I've got bigger fish to fry at the moment. "That fuckin' it, *doll*?"

She nods slowly. "What are we going to do?" She whispers.

"I'm gonna throat punch the neighbor next time I fuckin' see him, for one thing." I say. "You're calling Laura and taking an extended vacation, starting now."

Vanna shakes her head with dismay. "I'm going to lose my job."

She has to know she doesn't have a choice. Jack could snatch her at any moment if she's away from me. Her presence puts her friends in danger, too. There's no telling what lengths Jack will go to, now that he's free to carry out his revenge.

"No, you won't. But if you do, so be it. You don't need it. You have me." I can see it on her face, that she wants to protest, so I turn the conversation back towards another matter of importance. "Don't ever lie to me again, Vanna. Don't keep shit from me, either. I will never turn my back on you, no matter what you think you can't tell me. You can tell me anything. I'm not ever going to leave you." I promise her. "I'm prepared to kill a man for you, doll. I think that at least warrants your honesty with me."

She looks down at her hands in her lap. "I'm sorry. I wasn't protecting him. I was protecting you... I didn't want you getting in trouble."

"I understand. *You* need to understand, it's my job as your man to do the protecting. I can't do my job to the best of my ability if you keep shit from me."

"I'll never lie to you again." She sniffles.

"I love you, Vanna." I stroke the side of her face and slide my hand to the nape of her neck, pulling her forward. "Everything is going to work out Aces for us. I promise." I press my lips to hers, sealing that promise with a kiss. "I'll do whatever it takes."

"I'm afraid of what that means." She whispers, sliding herself to the edge of the chair to wrap her arms around my neck, tucking her face against my throat. I wrap my arms around her as well.

"It means after all the shit you've been through, Vanna... All the shit I've been through... We're going to get our happily ever fuckin' after, doll. Even if I have to kill for it."

A majority of the day, I spend on multiple phone calls with my junior bike mechanic, Derek, as he does his best to make repairs on his own in the shop without me. It's frustrating to not be there, to ensure the work is being done correctly. He's good at his job, but I'm going to have to figure something out. I'd hate to have to close shop until this situation is dealt with. I could probably convince Vanna to stay with me at the shop during the day, but I can't see her wanting to spend all day watching me work on bikes. Leaving the house empty would be something Jack would take advantage of, as well. He can't get the drop on me. That's the only shot he's got. Head on, Jack's fucked, but I can tell, he's a patient, cunning motherfucker, just waiting for me to slip up. The only reason he hasn't snatched her away from me, in the three weeks he's been out, is because he *hasn't been here* to do so...

Serene's destruction must have been the announcement of his arrival... His grand fuckin' entrance.

Between business calls, I attempt to comfort Vanna. She seems lost and distant one moment. The next, it's as if she can't get close enough to me, needing to be near me. Wanting me to hold her and assure her everything will be okay, which I do. I think she's checked the locks on all the windows five times in the last few hours, and she's lowered all the wooden blinds where I have them, as well. Though that only makes her getup throughout the day to peek through them.

Towards the evening, I asked her to make us something for dinner. I could have prepared us a meal myself, but I wanted to give her a task to busy her mind with. A temporary distraction, minor as it probably was, but it gave her something else to focus on for a short time.

She spends a good hour curled up in my lap on the couch after dinner, clinging to me for comfort once again. I'm happy to provide it for her, but I know Jason's shift is ending soon. I called Viking to join us as well. Not wanting to subject Vanna to any more stress, I talk her into running a nice bath in the over-sized tub to relax for a little bit.

As I walk into the bathroom, carrying a bottle of wine to refill her glass, I see she's got her long hair twisted up and clipped to the top of her head, and has settled into her bubble bath.

"Will you come in with me?" She asks, peering up at me from billowy white clouds of bubbles as I reach for her hand holding the wine glass. I gently place my hand over hers as I pour her some more.

"Jason and Viking are on their way over now." I tell her, reaching across the tub to the settings, making sure she has the heater on. I set it so her water won't cool down until she hits the drain to get out. "You just try to relax, doll. Let me handle everything." I say, bending to place a brisk kiss on her forehead, before I straighten. "We'll be in the living room. I'll come check on you once we're done."

I partially close the door behind me as I step out, leaving it open a few inches so I can hear her, should she call for me. Walking into the bedroom closet, I grab the Glock I tucked up on the top shelf, and slip it into the waist band of my belted jeans at my back, before I head down the hall to wait for Jason and Viking. Maybe even Jack.

"We both know the likely outcome of this situation." Jason says seriously, adjusting his utility belt as he takes a seat on the leather three-seater couch nearest me. I'm seated in the leather arm chair, opposite Viking, who's in the matching one at the other end of the slate coffee table, a coke in his hand as he listens to our conversation. "You're going to do what you have to do. So will Jack Nero. He doesn't care about the law, though. You need to care, Dean. You need to be smart."

"As long as she's safe. I'll do what I have to do." I mutter, disgusted even more by the justice system that always seems to favor the bad guys. All I want to do is drag my knife across his fuckin' throat. End his life and her nightmare in one swift motion. It would all be over... But then, would Vanna and I... We'd never be together again because I'd go to prison. God forbid I should kill a rapist ex-cop. Serve a life sentence for ridding the world of a truly sick monster. Ain't justice grand...

"Do it in your home." Jason says. "Be fucking smart, Dean. As long as he's the aggressor, *in your home*, you're covered from civil or criminal liability in the use of deadly force."

I nod. "Bait him, then kill him. That's the plan."

"Unless we catch him first." Jason presses his lips together in a firm line for a moment, before he speaks again. "Then he just goes back to prison for a few more years. Free to come back and try again."

"Fuck that shit." Viking grunts, taking a gulp of his coke. "Bust a cap in his fuckin' skull, Dean." He says with a belch.

I look back at Jason. "We want a life together. I want her free of him. I'll be smart about it."

Jason reaches behind his back and pulls out a handgun. A 9mm Ruger. "I don't know what kind of unregistered weapons you might still have... But this one is untraceable. Something a piece of shit like Jack Nero might be able to get his hands on in the street. He probably has a gun, though, Dean." Jason sighs. "But on the off chance he doesn't, you tell the cops he had this on him. That he threatened you with it. Wipe it down, put it in his hand. You were lucky he didn't get a shot off before you took him out. End of story." Jason places the gun down on the slate coffee table.

"We both know the fucker probably has a gun." I say.

"Then you need to shoot first, with one of your legally registered weapons. And not in his back. If he's fleeing, your self-defense claim will be compromised if you shoot him in the back."

"Drag him back in the fuckin' house and blast his chest out with a fuckin' shot gun. Problem solved." Viking says, sounding as disgusted as I am.

"Never shot a guy in the back. Not gonna start with Jack Nero. I want him to see what's coming." I mutter. "But if he punks out, Viking's idea is plan B."

"There's one other thing I want to mention." Jason adds, shifting in his seat to look at me head on. "I know how you can get. You like to abuse the abusers. As much as you want to pull this guy apart, Dean... to make him suffer for what he did... It *can't* look like that. It's gotta look like self-defense."

I just nod. I'll figure that out as this unravels. Jack deserves to suffer for what he's done. For what he's doing. For what he plans to do... But in the grand scheme of things, as long as he is gone forever, that's what's important. Vanna's safety. Her freedom. Her happiness. My gratification at seeing him in pain comes last. I could always pump a few rounds of led into his stomach. That's a bad way to go. Slow. Painful. More than painful... *Agonizing*. Wouldn't have to call the cops right away either. No way really to tell how long I let him suffer before I bust a cap in his twisted heart, and plant a wiped down gun in his cold dead hand...

"I've got to head back to the station." Jason says, standing up from the couch. I get up to shake his hand and thank him. "I'll see what I can do about those orders of protection. I know you see them as useless papers, but at least it paints a picture in your favor for self-defense, prior to this shit storm when it goes down."

"You're right. I appreciate you looking out." I say, walking him to the door. After Jason leaves, I sit back down on the leather three-seater and look over at Viking. "Pull the prospects off the witch shop and have them guard the house instead. I'm gonna need at least two of them, for a solid block of five hours, daily. Gonna get my shut eye during the day, so I can be up at night and wait for him."

"Roger that." Viking says.

"There might be days, I'll have to go to my shop to handle shit Derek can't. Those hours, I'm gonna need you here, inside the house with Vanna." I tell him. "She can't ever be alone."

"Alright. If I were you, I'd do all my traveling in a cage, Bro. Retire the bikes until this is over. Running you off the road and killing you on a motorcycle would be too easy for him. He ain't gonna be able to run you down in your truck." Viking says.

I nod. "Fair point." Reaching into my back pocket to grab my wallet, I pull out a couple of bills and hand them to Viking. "I need you to give this to Snowy and Chopper, for their girls. I'm closing the farm stand, probably until spring. I don't want Veronica and Jessica anywhere near here with Jack lurking around out there. God forbid either of those girls gets hurt." I explain. "I'll throw the chain up tomorrow to block off the lot. As far as the MC goes, I need you and Viper to take the reins until this shit is done."

"You got it." Viking says, folding up the money and tucking it into the inner pocket of his leather cut. "You sure you don't want anyone here at night?"

"I gotta make the prick think he's got a shot at taking me down. It's gotta happen inside for self-defense to hold up. He isn't gonna break in with guards outside. He's crazy. Not stupid. In fact, he's a cunning bastard. I might have to come up with another idea. For now, we gotta play it like this. Fuckin' waiting games. No telling where he's been hiding these last few weeks. I can't be hunting for him and leaving Vanna vulnerable. Fucker has to come to me."

"Alright. Axel and I will handle shit at the Twisted Throttle, don't worry about that." Viking says.

I nod. "What day this week are you free to wait here with Vanna for a few hours?" I ask. "There's something I have to do at my lawyers office that can't wait long."

Viking looks at me. "Fuckin' Lucinda and Daniel again?"

"Yeah... I just need to make sure I have everything in order, and I'd rather get it out of the way sooner rather than later." Especially now, but I say it like it's no big deal.

"No problem. Just let me know when your appointment is, and I'll be here to babysit the first lady." Viking says.

Getting up to shake his hand, I give him a shoulder hug and a mutual slap on the back in gratitude, then walk him to the door. I watch him take off on his motorcycle, before my eyes slide towards the dark perimeter of trees around my house. I can't help but wonder if Jack's out there. Watching and waiting. I'd never admit this to Vanna, simply for the fact that she's so terrified about him being free. But in a way, I'm glad the fucker is out.

He's more accessible to me now. Part of me wants to unlock every window and door in this house, just to make it easier on him to walk into his death.

You want our lives, Jack? I've got one thing to say to you... *Molon Labe, motherfucker.*

Chapter
thirty-four
Vanna

ACK'S FINGERS DIG PAINFULLY INTO THE FLESH just above my ankles as he yanks me down the mattress. "No! Please!" I cry, trying to pull away from him. He leans over and back hands me across the face, snapping my head to the side. The pain exploding in my cheek makes my eyes water. I try to turn over and crawl away from him, but he grabs me by the back of my hair and yanks me back so that I'm kneeling on the edge of the bed, my back to him.

"Don't bother trying to get away you little bitch!" Jack snarls at me. "I'm going to give you what you deserve!" I can hear him undoing his belt with his other hand while the one in my hair twists painfully. I try to reach back and grab his hands to stop him before he rips my scalp.

"Jack, please! You're hurting me!" I cry out. He shoves me forward, hard. I land sprawled out, face down against the mattress. At least it isn't the hard wood floor this time. The sound of his belt sliding quickly through the belt loops of his pants makes a zipping sound behind me. I look over my shoulder at him as he folds it and grabs it with both hands, pulling it so that it makes a loud snapping sound.

"You think you can tell me no? You ungrateful little whore!" He shouts at me. "I'm going to beat you until you beg me to fuck you!"

"No! You don't have to!" I plead, scrambling to get up before he can swing the belt at me. I hear the belt whip through the air before the leather bites into my upper thigh. I scream out in pain as I turn over onto my back and push myself back up the mattress to get away from him. He raises his arm with the belt again. "Jack please! Please stop!" I whimper. He swings his arm down with the belt again, whipping me across the front of my shin. He strikes me with such force, I can feel it in my bone. Reflexively, I bend my knee to cradle my leg in pain. All I can do is sob, it hurts so much.

He snatches my ankle roughly again, dragging me back down to him once more. I curl up as he rains down strikes on me, hitting my shoulders, my stomach, my back as I continue to cry in fear and pain, pleading with him to let up.

"Stop, please, Jack..." I can barely hear my own voice through the tightness of my throat.

"You want to get fucked yet, you slut?" Jack shouts at me.

"Just do it..." I whimper. I hear the sound of the belt hit the floor and suddenly he's on top of me, pinning me down on the bed, his knees ramming my legs apart, his hands squeezing my wrists so hard I wonder if they will snap. "You're hurting me! Stop hurting me! I'll give you what you want!" I plead with him. He releases my wrists only to wrap his hands around my throat. "No Jack! *No! No!*" I hate this the most, when I can't breathe. There's nothing more terrifying... I thrash beneath him, but he keeps squeezing tighter, I claw at his hands as he squeezes harder still, jerking me up and down as if he wants to snap my neck as well.

"I'll kill you, Vanna! I'll kill you, Vanna!" He keeps repeating... I can't breathe... I can't get him off me... Jack is really going to kill me this time...

"Vanna! Vanna! Wake up!"

That's not Jack's voice...

"Vanna! Wake up! It's a nightmare, baby!"

My eyes snap open and I gasp for air, nearly panting. I can see in the dim light that Dean is above me, his hands on my shoulders. He must have been shaking me awake. I sit up and cling to him, immediately sobbing into his chest. He wraps his arms around me tightly, holding me close to him as my sobs rack my body.

"*Shh...shhh...shhh...* You're with me, I've got you." He whispers gently. "You're safe, Vanna. No one is going to hurt you. It was a dream, doll... just a nightmare... you're safe." Dean strokes my back and kisses my head, rocking me gently as I cry it out in his arms. He keeps reminding me that no one can hurt me now, that he's here and that he will protect me.

After a while my body stops trembling and my tears stop flowing. I twist my face so that my cheek can rest against the damp fabric plastered to Dean's chest, as I stare at the little clock next to dim lamp on the night table. It's a little after midnight, again. I've had a nightmare every night, since I found out that Jack was released from prison. After five days with barely any sleep, I'm exhausted and drained. I sniffle and take a quivering breath.

"I'm so tired..." I barely hear myself speak.

Dean holds me tighter, pressing another kiss to my head. "I know, baby. I'm sorry." His voice is almost a whisper, too.

"Will you please stay with me?" I ask. "At least until I fall asleep again." Dean has been staying up nights, only catching a few hours of sleep during the day when there are prospects keeping watch outside. My sleep has been so sporadic, sometimes I'm still so tired, I lay with him then, too.

Dean stands up to make his way to his side of the bed, nearest the door. I watch as he slips out of his cut, chucking it to the foot of the bed, then removes the gun tucked behind his back and places it on the night table beside him. He sits down on the edge of the bed and removes his boots, then leans back against the headboard, bringing his feet up on the bed.

"Come here, doll." He says, lifting his arm. I scoot across the bed so that I can curl into his side under his arm, and rest my head against his chest. I wrap my arm around his abdomen and close my eyes. Dean strokes my hair and back soothingly, and I listen to the strong beating of his heart until sleep finds me, for a time, once more.

DEAN

SEVEN DAYS INTO THIS STAND-OFF WITH JACK, THE LANDLINE IN MY HOUSE rings. I jump out of the leather arm chair in the living room, to grab it before it rings again and wakes Vanna. She's actually sleeping soundly tonight. I've got music playing in the bedroom softly for her. A song she's come to love after all the times I've referenced it to her throughout the more turbulent stints of our relationship, as a reminder of my unyielding love for her. *Scorpions, Still Loving You,* on repeat.

I already know who it is that's calling. It's two am. And anyone who would be calling me, would be doing so on my cellphone. Not my barely used landline. Not at two am. Placing the receiver to my chest, I listen for a few moments to determine whether or not the single ring had woken Vanna... But I hear nothing from the back of the house, only the faint music of the rock love ballad. I bring the phone to my ear, settling back down in the leather arm chair, staring into the darkness of the living room, my eyes shifting from each window, to rest on the unlocked front door. I can hear him breathing on the other end of the line.

"Were you hoping she'd pick up the line, Jack?" I growl into the phone. I've been getting his photo texts of Vanna these last few nights on my cell. Some from that night on the pool table. Some of her through the windows of our home... Jack trying to bait me into a fatal mistake... I haven't told her about any of them. I haven't responded, either. This is his first call to the house, and I already know it's because he's getting desperate.

"Dean Keegan." I can hear the dark grin in his voice. "Dirtbag biker ex-traordinaire. Giovanna has really been slumming it since I've been away."

"Oh, come on, Jack." I taunt him back. "She seems rather impressed with my humble abode... Why don't you come inside and have a better look around? Perhaps my interior decorator will impress, since my landscaping seems to have left you wanting." He chuckles, but doesn't respond. "You want me to roll out a red carpet for you? The doors open, Jack. Let's *Netflix and kill.*" No response. "And here she had me thinking you were some kind of a badass. Gotta say, Jack. I'm unimpressed... Hell, I'm down right disappointed."

"Were you disappointed when you found your motorcycle? Your pride and joy destroyed that night in the parking lot?" Jack prods at me, an incontestable sneer in his voice. "All banged up. Shattered and bent, torn apart and slashed up. That was just a preview, Dean... Of what's to come."

A preview of what's to come... He's talking about Vanna...

That shit gets to me, and I need a brief moment to rein in my seething rage. In my silence at his words, I hear him chuckle darkly through the phone again. Vanna was right when she called him a monster. The man is a subhuman, twisted creature.

"Next time, Dean, you'll get to *watch*." He nearly whispers, forcing me to really listen to his words. "*Demolished*. Like your precious Serene... Imagine what that *looks* like... Imagine what that's going to *take*."

I can feel my mind slipping dangerously into blackout rage territory. I force myself to breathe as calmly as I possibly can. But he can probably feel my rage through the line. I'm sure of it. He knows he's fucking my brain up. Fucking me real hard. Without a wrap either.

"I'm taking her back, Dean." He tells me, as if it's a cold, hard fact. "I was her first. And I'll be her last." Another sinister laugh, before he adds, "And *you* get to *watch*."

Had Jack's words been a physical slug to my core, he would have taken the wind right out of me with that one. Jack Nero knows what he's doing. He knows what to say to slither right under my skin. To twist my guts up with his words and make my blood boil. I believe him. His intentions, that is. I will never let it happen, but he would hurt Vanna just to break me. Make a disgusting spectacle of it to punish me for touching his play thing... Destroy me via the destruction of her... I couldn't take that. He knows it.

As I stare into the darkness beyond the front door, it's evident this man has no fear. At all. I'm just an obstacle to him. He's smart, too. Trying to taunt me into storming outside to attack him, leaving myself wide open to him. He knows where I am. I don't know where he is. I could step outside and he could cut my throat. Blow my head off. Take me out in whatever way he sees fit, clearing his way to Vanna.

No... I need to be smarter than Jack Nero. Vanna deserves to live a happy life. And I want to be around to make sure she gets it. To be the man that gives it to her. I promised her that. I have words to live up to...

"You're a sick fuck, Jack." I speak slowly, fighting with everything in me to stay calm. "That shit ain't gonna happen... You see, Jack. There's nothing I wouldn't do to protect her. *Nothing*. Not a line I won't cross. Not a life I won't take. Especially yours, Jack. And I look forward to it. I'm going to take you apart. And I'm going to enjoy it." I say, letting him know he doesn't scare me, either. Not one iota.

"Step outside. Take your best shot. I'm coming for her." He taunts me, but I can hear in his voice, he knows his plan to set me up again has failed. It's my turn to taunt him. To bait him into my house where I'm legally covered to take this motherfucker out.

"Well, until you do, Jack, I'll be coming *in* her. Every night. Like I've been for months now. In my bed, where she sleeps beside me. Because Vanna is *mine*, Jack. *All mine.*"

The only thing I hear is a slight shuffling sound, leaves beneath boots maybe, before the call ends. I hang up the phone and place it down on the rustic wooden side table, leaning forward to run my hands through my hair. The motherfucker could be anywhere. An icy feeling in my gut tells me, he isn't far. I have to make a move to turn the tables... This can't go on for much longer. Vanna's nerves are shot... We've both got a life together we want to live...

A loud crash of shattering glass and Vanna's terrified scream has me leaping over the leather three-seater couch. Darting down the hall towards the bedroom, gun drawn, I'm ready to blow a smoking hole through Jack's twisted heart.

Flipping on the bedroom light, Vanna is backed against the headboard, still under the covers which she has clutched to her body. The bedroom window is shattered, the cobalt blue curtains billowing into the room, glass all over the floor near the foot of the bed on her side. Among the broken glass on the hardwood, there's a brick with a flower strapped to it...

A vibrant red *Peony.*

Fuckin' prick can't even let her have her favorite flower...

F OR THE FIRST TIME IN ALMOST TWO WEEKS, DEAN LEFT THE HOUSE TODAY. He's been gone for a few hours now, since mid-afternoon. The sun has already set. Though I already have a baked pan of ziti in the freezer, I opt to make a whole new tray from scratch, just for killing time's sake. And it will be enough to feed the three prospects standing watch outside, as well as Viking, who is inside waiting with me for Dean to return. Or as he not quite so affectionately calls it, *babysitting* me.

Since I'm not allowed to step foot out of the house for any reason, I ask Viking to bring the prospects their plates of food and sodas, while I set the tray on the dining room table with plates and utensils for Viking and I. Knowing how he is with food though, I scoop a portion out onto another plate and wrap it up, setting it aside for Dean. Viking, while in extremely impressive physical condition, built like a tank and just as big, is a bottom-less pit. He's also a serial dater. Which I intend to distract myself with, from the tension of our current situation, and question him about over dinner.

By the time I get back to the dining room table from putting Dean's plate in the warm oven, Viking has half the baked ziti on his plate and is already going to town on it. I shake my head in amazement and sit down at the end of the table, lifting my wine glass to take a sip. These last few weeks, I've really taken a liking to wine.

"You date a lot." I say, breaking the silence between us. He shoves a fork full of ziti into his mouth and shrugs. "What's that about?"

"Bitches like me." He replies simply.

"Yeah, but you're always with a new one. Every time I see you with a girl it's a different girl." Viking grins and looks at me suspiciously. "What?" I ask.

"Is Lancelot coming up *short*? I can give him some pointers for you if you want me to." He jokes obnoxiously.

"You're so funny. *No.*" I roll my eyes at him. "*Lancelot* doesn't need any pointers, *FYI*. He happens to be *quite* the skilled lover."

Viking winks at me and digs into his food again. "Defending his honor, that's good." He says around a mouth full of food, before he audibly swallows. "The way Dean goes to bat for you, you should be loyal to him." He has the nerve to point at me with his fork as he speaks.

I glare at him. "I *am* loyal. I'm not interested in your giant dick."

My words catch him off guard as he almost spits out his ziti to laugh at me. "Relax, Vanna. Dean is a brother to me. I'd never make a pass at you." He says. "Besides, you're the one who kissed *me*. Remember?"

"Just to make him jealous." I mumble, taking another sip of wine.

"Why are you asking me about the women I date?"

"I'm just curious if they're still alive after sex with you." I shrug.

Viking simply stares at me for a moment, as if he's genuinely contemplating my words. "I suppose that is a valid question." He says, before he turns his focus back to his food, devouring another mouth full. We sit in relative silence for the next few minutes as he eats, before he looks back up at me. "So, you love him." Viking says. I can't tell if it's a statement or a question, though. Just to make myself clear, I decide to respond.

"Of course, I love Dean." I say. "I'd do anything for him." Viking nods. "Why are you asking me that? You think I'm using him?" I wonder if Viking will ever accept me into their little biker family.

"I don't want to see him hurt again." Viking says. "Lucinda was bad for him. I saw it from the very beginning. It was a bad situation for a long time even after her... I'll never forgive her for a lot of shit... Even if he does, some day. Lucinda is poison, and on my eternal shit list."

"I'm nothing like Lucinda." I don't bother trying to hide my annoyance.

"That's my point. The way Dean is about you. I've never seen him like this before. He'd literally cut his heart out for you. I just hope you know that." Viking says. Actually, I do know that... Forcing my hand to stick him in the chest with a knife is still fresh in my memory. "You can really hurt him." Viking adds. "*Don't.*"

I remind myself again, that Viking is Dean's best friend, and is only looking out for him. There's no reason for me to be offended or insulted by his words. "I have no intention of ever hurting Dean. I really do love him."

Viking stares at me as he chews. Looking at me as if he's trying to detect any type of waver in my resolve about how I feel about his best friend. His brother by choice. He won't though. I do love Dean. Viking nods, then goes back to his plate. I suppose I've passed his cross-examination.

We're both quiet as he finishes his plate and goes for another large helping of the baked ziti. I shake my head in bewilderment at his ability to seriously pack food away, before I glance out the window in time to see a set of headlights coming up the long driveway. It looks like Dean's Silverado. "I think he's back."

Viking drops his fork with a clatter against the plate, as he stands and looks, his hand lingering by the large hand gun at his hip. When he is satisfied that it is Dean, he sits back down and grabs his fork. I get up and go to the front door to welcome Dean home. I haven't seen him in hours and have missed him. We've been nearly inseparable these last two weeks. He parks the truck under the spotlight in the drive way and walks to the house, scanning the property as he makes his way to the front door. I unlock it and let him inside. His lips are on mine before he even crosses the threshold, wrapping an arm around my waist he continues walking forward, backing me up as he closes and locks the door behind him.

"I'm eating." Viking says, interrupting us. Dean and I both smile against each other's lips before we part.

"When aren't you?" Dean teases him, releasing me.

"Touché." Viking casually replies.

"Smells great. Anything left for me?" Dean asks, as we walk together back to the table.

"Of course, I saved you a plate just to be safe." I smile. "Sit down. I'll get it for you."

Dean slides into the chair at the head of the table and leans back. He looks tired. I wonder what he's been doing the past several hours since I saw him last.

"You take care of everything you needed to with the lawyer?" Viking asks him.

Dean lets out a long, exasperated sigh. "Yeah. Couldn't wait." He says. I grab the plate out of the warm oven and remove the foil from it, then grab a glass as well and bring it to the table, setting them both down in front of Dean. "Thank you, baby." He looks up at me with a tired smile. I run my fingers through the top of his dark, slicked back hair, before moving to get the bottle of wine to pour him some. "Did you eat?" He asks.

"No. She had wine." Viking rats me out.

"I'll have a little now, thank you." I scowl at him. When I move to pour Dean some wine, he quickly places his hand over the top of the glass and asks for a bottle of water instead. Of course, he doesn't want to impair himself, not even in the slightest. After I grab him a bottle from the fridge, I take a scoop of what little remains of the baked ziti and sit back down with my plate. I let Dean get a mouth full or two of dinner down before I ask him, "What did you have to do today? I've missed you."

"*Biker business.*" Dean grins at me, giving me a little wink before he glances at Viking, who rolls his eyes at the term he deems corny and annoying. "How are you two getting along?" Dean asks.

"She cooks good." Viking says with a slight shrug, spearing more ziti with his fork. A compliment. It must not have been too bad for him to babysit me. "Shame you guys missed Thanksgiving at Viper's. I was looking forward to Vanna's dessert... Speaking of which, *is there* any dessert?" He stares at me expectantly. I look back at him, astounded, then at Dean, who simply shrugs as if Viking's appetite is normal.

"Seriously?" I can't help shaking my head at the both of them.

DEAN

WHILE VANNA BUSIES HERSELF IN THE KITCHEN WITH CLEANING UP AFTER dinner, I take the opportunity to talk with Viking quietly at the table.

"Vanna is going to hate this." Viking says, keeping his voice low.

"I don't have a choice. This has gone on long enough." I quietly sigh. "She'll eventually forgive me."

"And if he kills you?" Viking presses.

I look at him for a moment, making sure he meets my eyes. "Then I need you to promise me, that you will protect her. That you'll kill this son of a bitch for me. To avenge me and to save her. That's my dying wish, Bro. Can you promise me that?"

Viking looks away from me as he leans back in his chair, bringing his hands up to run them across the shaved sides of his head, folding his hands over his blonde, braided mohawk style ponytail. He lets out a long sigh, and I can't recall a time I've seen him look more distraught. Placing my arms folded in front of me on the table as I lean forward, I try to get him to look at me.

"Viking, I need to know you're going to be there for me. You're the only man I trust her to, if I can't be here. I *need* you, bro." I say quietly, but gravely. He shifts his eyes back to me, and though his expression tries to hide it, his eyes can't. He's worried about me. He's angry with me, too. "I'm not planning to die, brother... It's a *just in case* request." He lowers his arms back down to rest his forearms on the table as well.

"You should just let me go to the fucking cabin and wait for him. I'll end his life." Viking grumbles, I touch his shoulder briskly to remind him to keep his voice down. If Vanna knows I'm planning on leading Jack to the cabin, there's no way I'll be able to just drop her off and leave her at the clubhouse. I'd have to lock her in a room like a prisoner, and I don't want to have to do that to her.

"I need to know you're with Vanna. That you'll keep her inside and safe. If I know that, I can focus on what I have to do about Jack. No distractions if she's safe with you." I tell him. "It's got to be me."

"How do you even know he's going to follow you?" Viking asks.

I glance over at the sink to make sure Vanna is still occupied. She's still scrubbing pots and rinsing dishes and placing them in the dishwasher. "Had my truck looked over while I was out. There's a tracker on it. There's probably a tracker on Vanna's car, too."

"Why didn't you just yank it out and toss it? Stick it on some random car?" He demands. "We can go sweep Vanna's car right now and yank hers off, too."

"So he can just run over to Walmart, get another one and do it again? Fuck it. I'll use it against him." I say.

Viking let's out a long sigh as he shakes his head. "How are you so sure he's going to follow you?"

"I'm not." I admit. "But I have to take a shot. I'm going to have Vanna pack two bags, put Nico in his cat crate. Gonna make a mad rush show of getting the fuck outta Dodge. Toss everything in the back of my truck and peel the fuck out of here. I'll make a fast pit stop at the clubhouse, while he's probably scrambling to get to whatever vehicle he's got stashed somewhere, drop Vanna and the cat off with you, and book it to the mountains. Hopefully, he believes she's with me and I'm taking her away. He's an ex-cop. I'm sure he's looked into me. He knows I own a cabin in the Smokies. As soon as I hit I-40 West, he's going to know that's where we're headed. Only it'll just be me."

Viking is staring at me now. "This is about more than just luring him out, Dean... You want time with him. Jason told you it has to look like self-defense if you're going to keep your ass out of prison." Viking obviously feels the need to remind me.

"I'm going to put a bullet through his heart. I'm going to look him in the fuckin' eyes when I do it." I say. "There won't be behind the back bullshit. But that doesn't mean I'm going to do it right away."

"I know you want to torture him, Dean, but..."

"When the fuckin' cabin burns down..." It pains me a little bit to say this. To have plotted this scenario out. The cabin has been in my family for so long, but it's a means to a much-needed end. "And he's just a charred body, they're not going to be able to tell what the fuck happened to him, before I put him out of his misery. I won't break any of his bones... But there's plenty I can do with a fuckin' knife... As far as the authorities need to know, we fought... Knocked over an oil lamp. Cabin went up, he shot at me, I shot at him. He went down, I got out of the fuckin' cabin before it burned to the ground. Whatever I do to him, the fire will cover up." Viking continues to stare at me. I just shrug. "When my bullet takes him in the chest, maybe he falls backwards into the lamp, gets the oil all over him. It's my word against his charred up remains. He's the one who came looking for trouble. The orders of protection against him, his prior record of violence against Vanna, his letters from prison, her police report of the attack and harassment.

711

That all works in my favor. So, there might be an investigation, in the end, they won't be able to disprove my story. He's the disgraced ex-cop who tried to kill Vanna at least once. I'm the Savior who raises money for charities and has worked with organizations to protect victims of domestic abuse. One of my best friends is a high-ranking officer of the local police department." I take a deep breath and let it out. "The only people who know I'm fuckin' crazy are my closest friends... And I'm leaving you all out of this. I just need you to look after Vanna. I don't intend to die. But if I do, I need your word... Don't let me die thinking she's next, Gunther, please. Let me go knowing my best friend, my Brother, is going to keep her safe and finish what I started."

"*Fuck...* don't *Gunther* me, Bro." Viking groans, but I can see the conflict in his eyes as he stares back at me for another few moments. He finally shakes his head slightly as he says, "I fucking hate every part of this damn scheme, Dean."

"But you'll do it?" I press him.

He lets out another long, exasperated sigh. "You have my fuckin' word." He grumbles. "But you better not fuckin' die."

"I really don't plan on it, Bro."

"If you do, I'm gonna fuck your chick, Dean." Viking scowls at me. "You can die knowing *that*, too."

M Y HANDS ARE SHAKING AS I LISTEN TO THE BITS AND PIECES OF conversation taking place behind me, between Dean and Viking. I know I haven't heard every detail... But I've heard more than enough to know that I can't let him do this.

Shutting the dishwasher and turning it on, I grab a hand towel from beside the kitchen sink and wipe my hands, before hanging it on the handle of the oven door to dry. Whatever else Dean and Viking had to say to each other, has been said. I watch as they both get up from the table, Dean walks Viking to the front door, where they exchange a mutual brotherly shoulder hug and a fist bump, before Viking leaves on his motorcycle. As Dean watches him go, I walk to the bedroom to change into my nightgown. It's nothing fancy, but it's prettier than an over-sized t-shirt. A sleeveless midnight blue satin that comes down mid-thigh. Stripping off my panties, I chuck them into the hamper, before making my way into the master bathroom to brush my teeth and hair before bed, as I normally do.

When Dean comes to stand in the bathroom door way, I notice the way he looks me over, but he doesn't comment on my choice of sleepwear.

"Are you okay?" He asks. "I didn't think you'd be turning in so early. It's only seven." He gestures to the clock on the night table in the bedroom behind him, by chucking a thumb over his shoulder, before he drops his arm back to his side and hooks his thumb in the front pocket of his jeans.

I run the brush through my hair once more before I place it down on the stone countertop and look up at him. "Why did you go to the lawyers today?" I ask. "I thought maybe it had something to do with Lucinda and Daniel... but I feel like I was wrong in that assumption."

"Not exactly." He says. "I wanted to make sure there wasn't any kind of clause that would grant them entitlement to anything, should something... happen."

"Should what happen?" I ask, as Dean leans against the door jamb, his eyes lowering to look me over again. He doesn't seem to be checking me out though. His gaze isn't appraising, or lustful. He's just *looking* at me, as the moments tick by. "Dean? Why did you really go to the lawyer today? What couldn't wait?" I ask again. "Look at me, damnit."

"I am lookin' at you, baby. You look beautiful." He says. I take a few steps closer to him so that I can look up into his face.

"*What did you do?*" I try once more. He pulls his thumbs out of his denim pockets and reaches out to skim his hands down the sides of my body, until they come to rest gently on my hips. I reach up to place my hands against his chest and give him a pleading look. "Tell me."

"We aren't married, Vanna." He sighs, and I watch as the expression in his eyes shifts from reluctance, to what looks like regret. "We might never be."

"What's that supposed to mean?" I demand, though I know damn well what he means. He removes his hands from my hips to place them over my hands on his chest, wrapping his fingers around mine to hold my hands tighter against him.

"Nothing in life is a guarantee, doll. I just want to be able to give you the best life I can. I promised you that. I intend to keep that promise, no matter what. Aside from a trust for Maddie, and the Saviors MC clubhouse... It's all yours, doll... Keep it all. Sell it off. Whatever is best for you... But it's yours to decide... If we were married, you'd automatically get it. But since we're not, I had to take care of it... In case Jack does manage to k- "

"Shut up!" I cut him off before he can fully say those dreadful words. "Just shut up, don't even say it." I close my eyes tightly, wishing I could will this entire situation away, as I've wished for months now.

"Vanna... I'm not planning on dying. This is just a precaution." Dean sighs. "I want to live out the rest of my life with you, doll. That's the plan. The fuckin' dream, baby... But-"

"Stop talking." I shake my head, pulling my hands from his to hold onto the sides of his hard body over his cut.

"But I just..."

"Dean, I love you." I say, opening my eyes to look up at him again, his handsome face etched with an expression of slight confusion now. "I love you, just stop talking." When he's about to open his mouth again, I grab his face and pull him down to me, pressing my mouth to his, effectively stopping him from whatever he was about to say. I don't want to think about Jack right now. I don't want to think about what may or may not happen. I don't want to acknowledge that Dean is right... Nothing in life is guaranteed. But we're both here, in this moment together. Alive and in love.

"Vanna, baby..." He mumbles against my lips. I wrap my arms around his neck, one of my hands at the back of his skull as I kiss him deeper, my tongue seeking his, my body pressing against him. His arms wrap around me, his hands running over the satin on my body, moving down to towards my lower back as I bend one of my knees to lift my leg and wrap around him. His big, hot hands continue their journey down, until they're gripping my naked ass. "No fuckin' panties?" Dean growls against my mouth. Before I know it, my bare feet are no longer touching the stone tiled floor. He has me in his strong arms, my legs wrapped around his waist, our kiss never breaking, even as he moves us to the bed, sitting down on the mattress. I reposition myself so that my knees are against the comforter as I'm straddling his lap. Shoving at his cut to get it off his body, he releases me to shrug his arms out of it, then tosses it to the foot of the other side of the bed. As I continue to kiss him, I undo the buttons of his shirt until it's loose enough for him to yank over his head, along with the wife beater beneath it in one move. Our mouths come together hungrily again, and I fumble with his belt to get it undone as well.

"What's gotten into you?" He asks.

"You." I say, yanking at his jeans to get them open. "In a few moments, anyway." I tease him.

"Shoulda left you all my shit sooner." He jokes.

"Shut up, I don't want your shit... I just want *you*... I'll always, only want *you*."

He grabs me and twists me down onto the mattress so that I'm on my back and he's on top of me. "Hold that thought," he teases, getting up to quickly strip off the rest of his clothes and boots at the foot of the bed. I push myself back up the mattress, watching him strip, admiring the way the muscles in his chest and arms ripple with every movement his powerful body makes as he sheds his clothes. When he crawls back over me, I cup his whiskered jawline and pull him back down to me for another kiss. His strong, rough hands slide along my body, gripping my hips and thighs before he shoves his hands up under the hem of the nightgown, forcing the satin up over my body, until my breasts are exposed to him, and there is nothing between our bodies where we are touching. I bend my knees to bring my legs up against the sides of his body, wrapping them around him, opening myself to invite him inside as my hands slide from his sexy jawline, to his strong shoulders. His skin is smooth and hot under my touch as I grip and feel his body as well, the hard muscles moving beneath. I tug gently at his neck, and he knows I want him on his back. Sliding his hands under to wrap his arms around me, he rolls to his side, pulling me with him until he's on his back and I'm on top of him again, straddling his lap, my sex pressed against the base of his rigid cock. I sit back against his rock-hard thighs, taking his cock in one of my hands. I slide my hand up and down his shaft, watching him watch me, as I run my other hand through my hair, pushing it back out of my face.

"You're so fuckin' beautiful, baby... lose that nightie... I wanna see every bit of you." He growls beneath me, his hands sliding up my thighs under the satin that fell back down my body in my upright position. Releasing his cock to pull the night gown off and toss it to the side of the bed with his cut, I watch his intense expression as I bring my hand back to his shaft, gently working him again as he leans back against the pillows, folding his hands behind his head. Rubbing my thumb against his slit, I smear the precum beading at the swollen head of his cock, before I bring my thumb to my mouth and taste him. His eyes seem to darken lustfully. "Jesus fuck, doll..."

I scoot myself back a little bit, lowering myself down to kiss along his chest, licking his black scorpion tattoo. He flexes his muscles as I kiss and tease down his body, letting my hair fall to the side to sweep against him. His hands move to my hair, gathering it up together in one fist as I move further down, nipping gently at his hip. I drag my tongue over his sculpted abs, then along his impressively cut Adonis belt, before I bring my lips back to the center of his lower stomach, slowly placing kisses further and further down. Running my hands up his hard thighs, I grip his cock once again, stroking him as I look back up to his face.

"Do you want me to stop?" I softly ask, watching him carefully. Any will to object he may have had, dissolves when I let my breath hit his manhood. My Gently twisting my wrist, I slide my fist up and down the length of him.

His expression is tense, but he slowly shakes his head, moving his hand from behind his head to gather more of my hair into his other fist, before he rests his arm at his side against the comforter beneath us.

Holding eye contact with him, I bring my lips to his head, and place a little kiss against the velvety soft skin of his frenulum, then stick out my tongue to trace a vein along the hard length of his cock. His eyes are fixated on me, the desperation behind his gaze growing, his lips slightly parted. My tongue slides back up towards the tip of his cock, and I take his head inside my mouth, giving it a little suck before I pull it out with an audible pop.

His teeth bite into his lower lip for a moment as he sucks in air through his nostrils. "*Fuck.*" The word escapes him on a hiss of breath. I slide my tongue against his shaft, getting him wetter to work him a little harder, then I rub his frenulum against my moist lips. Slipping the head of his cock back inside my mouth, I swirl my tongue around him, giving him another moan. The vibration causes him to push his hips up, his hand fisted in my hair gently pushing down, wanting to get his cock deeper inside, but he doesn't force it. Even though I know he could. I reward him by taking his cock into my mouth a little further, continuing to stroke him.

"Fuck, Vanna..." His words burst forth as his hips thrust upward again, seemingly reflexive and beyond his control. I hum a little teasing laugh, my tongue stroking against him. When I pull up again, my lips tight around him as I increase my suction, he lets out a groan as I pull him out with another lip pop. His fingers grip my hair tighter. His other hand against the mattress, digs into the comforter, eyes desperate now, a dark need in them.

"Do you want more?" I whisper, letting him see me swirl my tongue around his head with an open mouth.

"Yes." He pants.

I slide my free hand, palm up, between his legs, pushing against the mattress beneath him to cup his balls gently, massaging him carefully as I take him deeper into my mouth. He groans at the sensations as I move up and down on him now, my lips sealed tightly around him, each time taking him deeper. His fist slams on the bed once, before he grips the comforter again, losing himself in the pleasure. His grunts and groans as I work him turn me on. I remove my hand from stroking him, taking him all the way down as I fight the urge to gag.

"Fuck! Shit!" He gasps, his hips slightly bucking off the mattress as I come up for air. I stroke and twist my fist around his cock, looking back up at him, both of us breathing a little heavier now. "Jesus fuck, Vanna... you're gonna make me come in your throat." His voice is a harsh whisper. "Is that what you want?"

"Is that what *you* want?"

"I want everything."

I giggle. "Well, we've got one shot at a time." He seems to consider my words for a moment, warring with himself, whether he wants me to suck him off or fuck him. I place another teasing kiss against the velvety head of his cock. "I love you, Dean. Whatever you want..."

"Ride me, doll." He says definitively, after his moment of consideration. "That way you get something out of it too... I want some of that tight little pussy." He releases my hair and it drapes down the side of my body as I move back up to straddle his cock. He rolls his bottom lip into his mouth, teeth sinking into it as I sink slowly down, impaling myself on his rigid manhood. His hands slide up my thighs to my waist, gently holding onto me as I settle down on him, taking his whole length in one slow motion. With a groan I can feel him flex his cock inside, before I start to gently rock back and forth on him, adjusting to the stretch of him filling me completely. We haven't had sex since he told me Jack was out, a little over two weeks ago. We've both been so stressed... But I couldn't not make love to him tonight, knowing what's about to happen. What has to happen, in order to bring this nightmare I've been living, that I've pulled him into, to an end... I push those thoughts out of my mind for now... For now, right now, I'm in the moment with Dean. My love. Who loves me to death...

Leaning slightly forward, I place my hands against his powerful chest as I fuck him, rocking and swiveling my hips as I thrust and move up and down on him, staring into his dark, hooded eyes. His hands move up my body to cup my breasts, the rough pads of his thumbs toying with my pebbled nipples. As I ride him a little harder, a little faster, I can feel the pressure building up inside of me as I clench my muscles around him, making him groan in response. His hands slide from my breasts, around to my back as he sits up, forcing me more upright. Burying his fingers in my hair, he pulls my mouth to his and kisses me deeply, almost aggressively, his tongue sweeping through my mouth. When his hands drop to my hips, he grabs me and pulls me harder down onto his cock, one of his arms wrapping around my lower back to keep himself deep inside me, mashing my body up against him. All I can do now in this position is grind on him, the head of his cock slightly bumping my cervix, my clit rubbing against his body. I place my hands on his taught shoulders, feeling his arms flex as he pulls me against him with every rock forward of my hips, as if he can't get deep enough. But I've taken him to the hilt. I move on him as fast as I can, clenching around him, pulling groans out of us both. That pleasure spiral coils inside of me as his arms encircle me even tighter. One of his strong hands curling up over the back of my shoulder. His rough jawline scrapes across my skin as he brings his mouth to my neck, my throat, kissing and licking me, until I feel his teeth sink into the base of my neck. I let out a little whimper as the sensation of him leaving his mark on me shoots a quivering pang of pleasure throughout my entire body.

"Come for me, baby. I want to feel you coming on me." He growls against my throat, flexing his cock inside me again, thrusting upwards. The pulsing of my walls rippling around his hardness is beyond my control now. I cling to him tightly, my body convulses as my climax shatters my existence, making me writhe against him as I cry out my orgasm into the crook of his neck.

In an instant, I'm somehow whirling through the air, landing on my back again against the mattress, most of my hair hanging off the side of the bed. Dean is on top of me, his arms curled under me, his hands holding onto the back of my shoulders, anchoring me beneath him as his body presses down on me. His mouth takes mine again in another passionate, dominating kiss. His body curls into me, driving his cock deep inside me again, thrusting at a steady pace. I feel his arms slide further up my shoulders and neck, his fingers seeking the back of my hair as they curl into it, tugging my head back until my scalp tingles. His mouth moves from my lips to my fully exposed neck and throat, licking and kissing, sucking as he fucks me harder and harder. I hook my heels behind his powerful thighs, my hands reaching up behind his arms to hold onto the back of his shoulder blades. The pressure builds inside me rapidly again. The sandpapery roughness of his stubbled jaw scraping against my skin as he moves to kiss and suck the other side of my neck, shoves me closer to the edge.

"I fucking love you, Vanna..." his breathy words in my ear, before I feel his tongue swirl around it, his teeth sinking into my lobe. That spiral inside me curling tighter and tighter, making me gasp and moan as he pumps me harder still. I cling to his back, trying not to dig my nails into him too deeply as I feel his muscles working beneath his hot, damp skin, fucking me with everything he's got. His mouth takes my open mouth again, his tongue thrusting inside to dominate mine once more, before he breaks our kiss to look me deeply in the eyes. His are impossibly darker, his expression intense. "Do you love me, baby?" he asks with a need I'll never deny him.

"Yes... yes, I love you, Dean... More than anything in this world..." The expression in his eyes seems to soften slightly at my words.

"There's nothing I wouldn't do for you." He tells me, as if I'm unaware.

"I know." I whisper... There isn't anything I wouldn't do for him, either...

Chapter
thirty-five

DEAN

Sitting up out of a dead sleep, my heart pounds frantically in my chest. I stupidly fell asleep in bed beside Vanna after our love making. Between the few hours a day I actually do get sleep, and our rigorous romp in the sack, I must have just conked the fuck out. I'm fairly certain Jack isn't going to attempt breaking in here, but I'd rather not leave that shit to chance.

Glancing to my side, I realize she isn't in bed with me. Panic begins to seize me once more, until I notice the light on under the closed bathroom door. *Fuck!* Relief washes over me as I will my heartrate to slow down. Getting up out of bed to throw on a pair of boxers, I grab my jeans off the floor and pull them back on as well, buckling the belt and adjusting the sheathed knife at my side as I walk down the hallway towards the kitchen for a much-needed drink. The glowing digital clock on the stove reads a little after nine pm. I haven't been asleep long at all. Must have just been a thirty-minute nap.

As I switch on the kitchen light, I notice there are four bowls of cat food on the floor, along with three larger bowls of water up against the base of the kitchen island. On top of the kitchen island, Nico's bag of cat food and a box of his favorite canned food is sitting side by side, with a note in Vanna's handwriting...

One can for breakfast, one for dinner, fill dry food only once a day, litter box is in the laundry room...

Fuck my life!

I sprint back down the hall to our bedroom, bursting through the bathroom door, only to find it vacant... *"Fuck! Vanna!"* My blood thunders in my ears, a block of ice feels like it's forming in the pit of my stomach. I try to calculate how long she's been gone as I race around the room to throw my clothes back on. Grabbing my cellphone, I try to call her. It seems to ring forever as I continue to pull my clothing and boots on in a mad rush. "Pick up! Pick up! Vanna, please!"

"Hello?"

"Baby!" I freeze in my tracks, listening intently. *Does he have her?* "Where are you?"

"I have to do this... I can't put this on you... I'm sorry." I can hear the highway through the phone, the air coming through a cracked window in her vehicle. I force myself to take a deep breath, trying to remain as calm as I can in this completely fucked situation.

"Baby... I *need* you to turn the car around and get back here, *now*." I say as calmly as I can possibly manage.

"The only way to get him to the cabin, is if *I* lead him there. I'm going." She says with a determination in her voice that tells me I have indeed entered the ninth circle of Hell.

"Vanna, for the love of fuck! Get your ass back here, now!" I shout at her.

"I love you."

"Baby, please... I'm begging you." Literally, as I drop to my knees beside the bed, elbows on the mattress. Closing my eyes, I clutch the phone with both hands holding it to my head, as if I can will her back here by some magical force. "Come back, Vanna... Don't do this."

"I took your gun... I *can* do this. I have to... it's *my* mess."

I swear to Christ I'm going to have a coronary... "Doll... You need to come back and let me handle this... Baby, please, just turn the car around..." I beg her again.

"I can't, Dean. I love you too much to-"

"If you love me you'll turn the fucking car around!" I damn near scream at her.

A moment of silence before she speaks again. "You know where I'm going. And I do love you, jerk. You can't talk me out of this. I'm doing this *because* I love you. Jack won't believe I'm tough enough to pull the trigger... I am, now. I'll beat him there... and I'll do it."

"It ain't in you to kill a man, Vanna. It just ain't. Not even Jack." I try to tell her. No response. Plan fuckin' B. "Alright... then just, pull over somewhere. I'll meet you... we'll do this together, okay?" I'm willing to say anything at this point. She doesn't need to know that I'll drag her back, kicking and screaming and chain her to the bed in the clubhouse if I have to. To keep her prisoner until this is over. I'll fuckin' do it. I should have already done it!

"I have to conserve my battery. My cell phone charger isn't working." This situation just keeps getting better.

"Vanna, please, *please*..." I don't know what else to say to her. "I love you, don't do this..."

"I love you, too. Everything will be okay. I've got this." With that, she ends the call.

Glancing at the night table, she indeed took my Glock. I shove off the mattress and get to my feet, storming into the closet to grab the unregistered 9mm Ruger Jason gave me, as well as my Desert Eagle semi-automatic. Tucking the Deagle into my waist band, I throw on my leather jacket and tuck the Ruger into the inner pocket, before I sprint back down the hall to grab my truck keys and hurry out the door.

Pausing by my truck, I attempt a final hail Mary. On my cellphone, I bring up the last photo text of Vanna I received a few nights ago. A picture of her petting Nico on the living room couch through the front porch window. Tapping the cellphone number that sent the photo, I hit the green call icon and hope to God the motherfucker answers...

After a few rings, the line picks up. "Where are you, you son of a bitch?" I demand. "I'm outside waiting for you. Come and get me."

A sinister laugh before he replies. "Did you really not anticipate this?" Jack taunts me. "Running is what she does. I've just been smoking the fox's den... waiting for the little vixen to bolt... To play right into my hands, as she *always* does. She's been mine since she was a teenager... You still think you know her better than I do?"

I swallow the painful lump in my throat as a cold chill takes over my body. "Are you already there?" I manage to ask through the strangling feeling. The only response I get is a low chuckle, and a click as Jack disconnects the call.

Vanna's got at least a thirty-minute head start on me... Which means she'll be at the cabin by a little after three am. Jumping in my truck, I crank the ignition, throw it into drive and slam on the gas, spitting gravel and barreling out of my driveway.

I pray she takes the route I took her last time. The scenic route, that takes about thirty minutes longer than her GPS app will. That's my only shot at beating her there... My only shot at taking on Jack without her in the line of fire.

If there truly is a God in Heaven, please... let me beat her there...

Vanna

L AST TIME DEAN TOOK ME TO THE CABIN, THE SIX-HOUR DRIVE, FELT LIKE A six-hour drive. Somehow, this time, the hours and the miles seem to fly by as if I were in some kind of a time warp. There are no street lights on this winding, Smokey Mountain road, as my car climbs up towards Dean's little rustic cabin nestled in the woods. The digital clock on my car reads two thirty am. I should be close. Glancing down at my cellphone, I see that it has seventeen texts from Dean, one bar left and no signal. Part of me wishes I would have called him back before I lost service. Just in case this doesn't go as planned. If Jack was keeping an eye on my car, and there is a tracker, he shouldn't be far behind. Even with the several wrong turns I made on these dark roads, mostly thanks to the faulty signal up here, I should still beat him. Dean won't be far behind, either. If I can't pull the trigger... I can at least hold a gun on him until Dean arrives. I've felt strangely calm about this entire situation. Like I've been in an odd, almost tunnel vision like trance. Smooth sailing the whole way here. Has Jack finally pushed me over the edge? Or is it because I truly love Dean... And this needs to happen?

Switching on my bright lights, I keep an eye out for the little metal sign to the right of the entryway. It isn't paved, none of these little trails to cabins are. They're just winding, dirt and stone paths up into the woods. And far apart at that. Dean's cabin property is fifty acres on its own. The moonless night sky and thick, black forest make these winding roads unidentifiable. Especially when I've only been up here once. After a few more miles, I spot the little crooked sign that reads 1789, leaning against a tree at the foot of the opening. Taking a breath to steady my now slightly increasing nerves upon seeing the address, I turn the wheel to the right and pull into the path, heading slowly up towards the cabin.

After about a minute, I drive through an open split rail fence with a *For Rent* sign nailed to one of the posts... I don't remember there being a split rail fence anywhere on Dean's property. And he never said anything to me about ever renting it out to anyone. Especially not with the furniture his grandfather built by hand. And certainly not with his grandfather's Civil War rifle and the Pentacle he made for me, still over the fireplace inside... If he planned on renting it out, why would he have let me leave it up here? Why wouldn't he have brought that gun home with us, at the very least? He wouldn't risk tenants stealing that rifle. It has to be worth something.

As the cabin comes into view within my headlights, I realize immediately, that this isn't Dean's cabin at all. It's twice the size of the log cabin Dean brought me to last time.

Shit... Did I remember the address wrong? I can't even call him. There are no cars in the driveway. The place looks empty as I turn my car slowly, lighting up the front of the cabin. There aren't even curtains on the windows. It's totally vacant. I look for a number on the cabin, but there isn't one. Turning my car around, I head back down the driveway and look back down at the metal sign leaning up against a big pine tree. 1789. That's the number I remember seeing last time I was up here. At least, I think it is...

Grabbing my cellphone, I bring up my map and double check where the pin is dropped. It seems as though his property is another mile up the road. I must have remembered the wrong number. Pressing my foot down on the gas pedal gently, I make a right and continue another mile up the curving dark road until I come to another driveway. Cutting my wheel to the right once more, I head up the dirt path through the dense woods.

The gravel clearing in front of the small one bedroom, one bathroom, log cabin is vacant. All the lights inside are off. Dean's cabin appears to be empty as well, but I'm not taking any chances. Cutting the wheel sharply to the left, I circle to pull the back of my car up to the tree line, leaving the headlights on to illuminate most of the driveway, and the front steps of the cabin. Realizing I forgot to bring a hair tie, I reach into my glove box to grab two bobby pins, pinning the sides of my long hair back on either side of my temples, so my hair won't fall in front of my face. Then I reach into my purse and carefully remove Dean's gun, knowing full well he always keeps it loaded, and that there's no safety.

Stepping out of the car, I listen intently to every little noise. There's a slight, chilly breeze that barely rustles the fallen leaves littered all over the ground. The forest is too dense, but I can hear it slicing through the bare branches above. Wisping through the evergreens and pines. I walk slowly around my car, keeping close to it, clutching the gun in my hands. My sneakers crunch on the gravel with each slow, deliberate step I take towards the cabin.

If Jack was nearby Dean's home when I made my break for the cabin, the odds are in my favor that I beat him here. Even with my wrong turns. I was the only one who knew I was making a break for the cabin when I did.

In the distance, through the clear crisp cold night, I can hear the sound of an engine approaching. A truck of some kind. It could be Jack... If he was watching me, he'd know where I was heading before Dean was awake to realize... Dean won't beat Jack here. I rush to the other side of the cabin, away from the headlights of my car. Maybe my car will draw Jack's attention in that direction, opposite of where I'm now standing in the shadows, and I'll be able to get the drop on him...

My heart slams against my ribcage rapidly. As I listen intently, the unnerving sound of heavy footsteps rushing somewhere across the gravel driveway startles me. *I'm not alone...*

I whirl the gun around towards the source of the sound, in time to see a black figure dart towards my car, jumping into the driver's side door. The headlights cut off as I squeeze the trigger. The gun explodes. So does a hole through my windshield. The shot was loud, but not deafening and I hear a man's voice hollering in pain, cursing.

Keeping the gun aimed in his direction, I take a few steps forward, about to tell Jack to get out of my car, when something slams into my right side so hard, it knocks every bit of air out of my lungs, and I'm suddenly on the cold hard ground. Gravel digs into the side of my body through my thin denim jacket, as someone crushes me under their weight. I'm slightly dazed as I attempt to bring the gun back around towards them, but they grab my arm tightly, slamming it back down against the gravel several times. My knuckles smash against the jagged edges of the hard rocks I'm pinned down against, until I can no longer hold onto the weapon and it topples from my grasp.

"I didn't think you had that in you, Giovanna!" Jack's voice humorously sneers above me, before he back hands me across the face. I must still be stunned, because I barely felt his slap and continue to struggle to fight him off me. I try to kick him away from me and scream, but as I let out a shriek, the hard barrel of Dean's gun slamming into my forehead catches my scream in my throat. "Get up, baby." The black figure hovering over me with Jack's voice demands. "We don't have time for this shit right now." I don't move. The sound of heavy footsteps crunching towards me makes me slide my eyes in their direction.

"This fuckin' bitch shot me! Grazed my fuckin' arm!" The man says angrily.

Jack ignores him. "I'm not going to ask you nicely again, sweetheart... Get up and get in the cabin. Our other guest is about to arrive." In the darkness, I can still see that he extends his hand to me. My heart begins to race again as I reach up and take it, letting him think he's helping me up. I know he's going to kill me. He's going to kill Dean. As I stand up, I yank his arm with all my might and bring my knee up towards his groin. I miss my target, but he still lets out a grunt upon impact. Angered, he jams the barrel of the gun into my stomach, making me hunch over momentarily in shocked pain. He snares my hair in his fist, yanking my head back so hard I nearly lose my balance backwards. "I see the company you've been keeping has rubbed off on you." He snarls in my ear, before he starts to drag me to the cabin steps by my hair. I grab at his wrist and try to fight, pulling away from him as he drags me, even though it feels like he's going to rip my scalp off. The barrel of Dean's gun is jammed under my chin now, and I instinctively freeze.

"I'm trying to be a gentleman about this, Giovanna..." Jack warns. A gentleman... I spit in the darkness of his face. He chuckles, removing the gun from my chin to wipe his face off on his arm. "I see I've got some work cut out for me. Those white trash bikers have corrupted the proper lady I used to know. But she's still in you, darling. We'll bring her back out." I can hear the threatening smile in his voice. "Grab her. Get her inside!"

I fight and I flail, but between the two of them, I'm over powered and dragged, kicking and screaming, into the cabin. Once inside, Jack tosses me down on the love seat in the living room, to the left of front door, holding the gun on me as he speaks to his accomplice. "Pull her car around the back, then get in here, fast." He demands. His lackey, as Dean calls him, rushes back out the door of the cabin. I watch as Jack's shadowed figure in the dark cabin moves to sit beside me on the love seat. The cushion beside me sinks under his weight, and I flinch as his hand slides over my thigh, gripping me over my denim jeans firmly, but not violently. "I've missed you, my love." He says softly. I say nothing as he strokes my leg. A few moments later, the lackey is back. "Alright, let's get ready for Giovanna's *Savior* to arrive." Jack announces, mocking the word as he jumps back to his feet.

A bright, high lumens flashlight is suddenly shinning directly in my eyes, blinding me, as I raise my hands to block out the painful light. My wrists are grabbed and cuffed within a second, and as I open my mouth, a cloth is jammed roughly inside. I continue my attempt to scream as the sound of ripping duct tape behind me sends another surge of panic through my body. I'm unable to spit out the cloth before it's wrapped around my mouth. Jack squeezes my face to smooth the tape against my skin, shushing me as he does so. He grabs the chain between the cuffs and yanks me painfully by my wrists to my feet, before he swings me around, shoving me back down into a wooden chair against the back wall of the living room area, facing the front door.

"You make a sound... A move... I'll make this experience so much worse for the both of you, Giovanna..." Jack growls sinisterly, wrapping a rope tightly around me a few times as he binds me to the chair. "You have no idea how bad this could get." He hands something to the lackey before he heads back out the front cabin door. The cold, sharp feeling of a blade at my throat keeps me still. In the dark, he could easily cut my throat if I struggle.

"Just like old times, eh baby?" The man growls, pressing the knife against me a little harder. "I'm gonna make you pay for knickin' my arm with that bullet... We're gonna finish what I started in that room with you." The lackey says, and I swallow down the bile that wants to rise up my throat. I try not to give him the satisfaction of a single sound as he turns off the flashlight and positions himself behind me, using me as a human shield. He crouches down low, his face right behind my ear. His breath pants on me. Even through my hair, I can feel it against the side of my neck. He's excited. One of his finger's curls into my hair, pulling it back, exposing my ear to his panting breath. He jams his disgusting tongue into my ear canal and I attempt to jerk away from him as he snarls, "Ain't just gonna be *Jackie's* girl tonight..."

725

DEAN

"I T'S ABOUT GODDAMNED TIME YOU CALL ME BACK!" I SHOUT INTO THE phone as I glance at my gauges on the dash of my truck. I'm honestly shocked I've still got enough fuel to get up the mountain, with the way I've beaten the absolute fuck out of my truck to race here. I'm only twenty minutes out from her now.

"Local police checked the cabin. Vanna's not there. Neither is Jack Nero. They said the place is empty. No fresh tire tracks. Nothing. Place is still buttoned up tight." Jason informs me.

"The fuck do you mean, nobody's at the cabin? She should already be there!" I slam my foot on the gas harder as I weave around the few cars on the road at three am. That's about the only thing I've got working in my favor tonight.

"They were there thirty minutes ago. Walked around the whole place. Cabin number 1789, right?" Jason says.

"Yeah, but... Something ain't right..." Did she have to stop for fuel? Did he grab her at a gas station along the way? Did she get lost? Could he have run her off the road? Taken her to a different location? A million scenarios race through my mind, and none of them good. Vanna would have called me, texted me, if she had come to her senses and decided to turn back for home.

"I've got more bad news..." Jason adds. I just brace myself. I don't even want to ask. "We're still two hours behind you."

Fuck...

I hang a sharp right off the main drag, onto the long winding road that will take me up to the cabin, and gun it. "What happened?" I ask, but all I hear in response is garbled incoherent semblances of words, then a beep as the signal is dropped. I place the phone down on my passenger seat. It's useless now. So is my cavalry. The reasons don't matter. All that matters is that I get to Vanna.

Twenty minutes winding up pitch black mountain roads at a suicidal speed... It's a damn good thing I know this mountain like the back of my hand. As I take the final bend that will lead me to my cabin, I spot something that makes my blood run cold and my foot slam on the breaks, bringing my truck to a skidding halt. 1789... Only the sign is a mile away from where it should be at the end of my driveway.

The cops didn't find anyone at my fucking cabin, because they went to the wrong one!

Jesus Christ... Jack has her... He's been at the fucking cabin and has had her for at least a half hour... A lot can happen in thirty minutes... My mind drags me back to his sick letters... His revenge fantasies... I could fucking puke... I force my mind to focus on what I have to do to save her, even though I'm trembling with a mixture of rage and terror coursing through my body.

I could stash the truck and hoof it to the cabin in an attempt to get the drop on him, but that would take a lot longer. That would be more time she'll be forced to endure his vengeance... My mind keeps pulling me back to all of the sick possibilities that could be happening right now in that cabin... He hasn't killed her yet, though... Vanna is alive. He wants me there to see it. Which means if I drive right up, he's not going to kill me right away either...

Unless he was bullshitting me. Just saying that shit to get in my head...

Fuck! Fuck! Fuck!

I slam my hand against the steering wheel... Every fucking moment I waste, something horrible could be happening to her. I don't have the luxury of time to strategize now. Slamming my foot back on the gas, my truck lunges forward and I speed the last mile up the mountain, banging a right into the driveway and barreling towards the cabin.

Jack wrote those sick letters for three years straight... He meant every word. Whatever he plans to do with Vanna, it isn't going to be quick. I have to believe that what he said to me on the phone that night, is true. He meant it when he told me I would watch... And we'd both have to be alive in order for that to play out.

My truck takes every bump and dip in the driveway as if they aren't even there. I'm going too fast to even feel them, and within seconds I'm at the gravel clearing in front of the cabin, sliding to a halt. Killing the engine, I jump out of the truck, yanking the Desert Eagle from my waist band as I raise the weapon, ready to kill anyone and anything that isn't Vanna.

I can hear her muffled screams from inside the cabin. She sounds desperate. Terrified. They've got her gagged, I can tell she's screaming through something. The motion sensor lights don't turn on as I approach. Jack must have taken them out when he switched the cabin number to fool the cops. I scan the dark shadows in front of the cabin, my weapon follows my gaze as I press forward, up the steps. There's a good chance Jack is outside, waiting to get the drop on me. I try to listen as intently to my surroundings as I can, though Vanna's screams from inside are tormenting me, twisting me up inside. One of them must be inside with her. I storm forward, bringing my boot up to slam against the wooden door. It busts open with a crack and a bang as I step through the threshold, gun still aimed and at the ready. She's still screaming. An almost painfully high lumens tactical flashlight strobes in my eyes from across the small room, obstructing my vision, and far too close to her to risk taking a shot. I remove my finger from the trigger, though I keep my gun pointed in that direction. Vanna's screams are suddenly cut off, and a man's voice warns her that he'll cut her if she doesn't shut up. It isn't Jack.

"Step away from her, and I promise I'll make your death quick and relatively painless." I growl at the dark form behind the strobing light.

I drop one hand from the gun to slip my knife from its sheath. Jack thinks I can't hear him sneaking up behind me, but the gravel outside gives away his approach.

"Ain't gonna be anything quick and painless about tonight." The lackey jeers back at me. "And we both know you ain't gonna take that shot with her right here. You can't see accurate worth a shit right now. And even if you did shoot me, I've got a knife to her fuckin' throat. I'll cut her dead before I drop."

The floor board behind me creaks, and I whirl around with the knife gripped like an icepick horizontally in my fist, slashing throat level into the darkness behind me. The blade embeds into the door frame, within the same second, there's a bang, and two sharp prongs are embedded in my chest. Fifty thousand volts of electric current courses through me with sharp zaps and incessant clicking, as I attempt to bring the gun back around in front of me. But the motherfucker's police grade taser is doing what it was designed to do... incapacitate me. Five seconds of sharp pain and muscle spasms beyond my control. Five seconds feels like thirty, and I know I've only got a fraction of a second to rip these fucking prongs out of my body, before he hits me again with another dose of electric current. Before I can come out of it, he hits me again, twice more, and in the process, I lose my guns, my knife...

In the split second of consciousness I have left, I watch through the strobing light, as Jack's dark figure slams something into my head, just before it all goes black.

"Fuck... he's coming out of it already... hurry up!" Sounds like Jack's voice...

My eyes snap open in a now lit cabin, and I attempt to lunge at whatever body is nearest... Something is restraining me. I realize that I'm on the floor, hand cuffed with my hands behind my back, to the old steel steam pipe radiator beneath the window in the front of the cabin. The pipe coming out vertically at the side of the radiator, is long enough between pipes affixed to the wall, that I'm able to sit up on my knees and jerk forward. Testing if the old pipe has any give. If I can rip it out of the wall. The cuffs bite into my wrists. The pipe doesn't budge. *Fuck.*

I search for Vanna. She's behind them on the other side of the room. Still tied to a chair and cuffed. Still gagged by a rag and duct tape. Eyes wide with terror. I glare up at the two figures standing before me. Both wearing black t-shirts and black cargo pants. Tactical boots. One I'm already familiar with. The lackey from the parking lot at the grocery store a few weeks ago. The prick who attacked Vanna in her shop. The one who threatened to cut her throat when I barged in. I shift my focus to Jack. He's grinning down at me, like a hunter might gaze upon a wild animal ensnared in a trap. And that animal is pissed the fuck off. I can tell he's appraising me. Sizing me up. He looks different than his mug shot. Meaner. I've probably got an inch or two on him, but he's ripped. Fuckin' shredded. Prison bodied. I can tell even through the clothes he's wearing, Jack's all lean muscle with a crazy glint in his icy blue eyes. Up until he murdered Serene, I'd been hitting

728

the gym pretty hard. Harder than I usually do. Now that I'm looking at this bastard, I'm glad I keep myself in fighting shape.

"So, what now?" I ask. Jack's expression remains the same. That creepy ass slight grin doesn't waver. He doesn't speak either.

"The *party's here!*" Jack's lackey announces... His words make my stomach churn... I've heard that expression before... In another disturbing situation... Nineteen men... Three women... "What now, is we get this fuckin' *party started.*" His lackey sneers at me, taking an aggressive step forward and slugging me in the face. Vanna let's out a muffled shriek as the lackey leans a little closer to me. "*Checkmate.* Asshole." He taunts me with my own words. I spit the little bit of blood pooling in the corner of my mouth at his boot.

"Bet you've been jerking off about that." I chuckle. "Couldn't wait to say it, huh?"

"Been holed up in this shit cabin for weeks. Bored out of my fuckin' mind. But I ain't gonna be bored, or jerking off now... Got your bitch here to take care of that for me." He grins down at me with satisfaction. I try not to show any reaction to his disturbing words, but my eyes slide back to Jack, who looks a little less pleased than he did a moment ago. A slight glimmer of hope remains, that he's not onboard with the lackey's intentions for Vanna.

"That the plan, Jack?" I scowl at him. "You gonna let this filthy piece of shit touch our girl?" It sickens me to even say those words... To refer to Vanna as *our* girl. She's *mine* and mine alone. But I'll say whatever I have to in my desperate attempt to stop this. Though, Jack still doesn't respond to me.

The lackey moves to slam his boot into my gut, and I brace my core for the blow, letting out a short grunt of air on impact. He storms over to Vanna with that fuckin' knife, cutting off her ropes. Grabbing her by the back of her hair, he yanks her up out of the chair, dragging her closer to me, but he stops short, in front of the love seat.

"*Our* girl is right." He chuckles darkly. "Though this won't do... I like it when they try to tell me to stop... when they scream... pretend they don't want it." He places the knife on the side table behind Jack and reaches a hand in front of her face. Tearing off the tape roughly from her mouth, she lets out a little whimper from its harsh removal, and he pulls the cloth from her mouth. She breathes heavily, and I'm sure it's from a mixture of fear and finally having access to unrestricted air. The lackey twists her hair in his fist, forcing her face to turn to his as he attempts to kiss her. She fights him, shoving her cuffed hands up in his face, attempting to push him away from her. I glance briefly at Jack, trying to fight my instincts to react. He's watching me intently, though I can't read him as we listen to Vanna struggle with the lackey behind him. I swallow hard and hope whatever love he might have left for her, outweighs his desire to watch me suffer through having to witness this scum have his way with her, too...

"Get off of me!" She shouts at the prick, as he manhandles her down onto the love seat behind Jack, shoving her torso over the arm of the couch.

He rips her head back by her hair and slams his crotch against her ass, grinding on her and laughing while he looks at me.

"She like it from the back, Keegan? You get to fuck her in the ass yet?" He taunts me. Vanna reaches for the knife with her cuffed hands as he dry pounds her, but it's still too far. I try to ignore the sick, taunting descriptions of what he's planning on doing to her, as I look back up at Jack. He's grinning at me now.

"And you claim to love her." I mutter with disgust. "Three years... all this careful planning... You had me fooled, Jack." The sick smile slides off his face, his expression gone vacant now, as we both listen to this prick molest and manhandle Vanna. I force myself to remain glaring at Jack. To not react to what I'm hearing going on behind him on that couch. Vanna's whimpers and demands for this fuckin' rapist to stop, to get off of her. Jack's eyes bore into mine and mine into his. We both hear the guy undoing his belt. His fly. Fabric ripping. Vanna's shouts shifting from anger to pleading fear...

"*You're pathetic.*" I tell him, before I lower my eyes to look back at Vanna. I fight the urge to throw up as I see that this rapist piece of shit has her on her back now, positioned between her legs as he rips her jeans open wider, attempting to pull them down over her hips. She's trying to kick him away from her, shoving and clawing at him, but he grabs her by the throat and squeezes. Her hands immediately go to her throat to try to pry his fingers from it, while his other hand wrestles to get his dick out of his pants. I fight against the cuffs with all my might, even though I know it's useless. They're not going to snap like this... and this fuckin' pipe ain't giving me an inch. He's got the cuffs on me too tight. Even if I bloody up my wrists for lubrication, which I'm sure I'm doing right I'll never be able to slip my hands through them... I'm five feet away from her... And I can't stop it... I can't save her... I'm fucking useless!

"*No! No! No! Please!*" Vanna cries out... And I can feel myself dying a little inside... "*Jack! Please!*" Jack's sick smile slices across his features once again, as he finally springs into action, a crazy look in his eyes. He raises my Desert Eagle in his hand and turns, taking a few quick steps to stand beside the couch. Extending his arm, holding the gun to the would-be rapist's head, Jack pulls the trigger, blowing the bastards brains out with a loud bang. Vanna lets out a blood curdling scream as his body falls forward onto her. Jack yanks his corpse back and lets the body hit the floor in a crumpled, bloody heap. She's crying and trembling, her hands shaking so hard the cuffs rattle as she covers her face and sobs.

"It's okay, sweetheart... I saved you." Jack says to her, in a tone that sounds as though he's trying to be loving. "Look, I'll make the ugliness go away..." He moves to the end of the area rug, bending to grab it by the edge. Lifting it up, he walks forward to toss the rug over the dead pricks body, covering his corpse from view. Jack moves back over to Vanna, sitting near her as she scrambles to tuck herself into the corner of the couch in a terrified ball. Her head tucked behind her knees, her arms curled over her head. He reaches out to stroke her hair, shushing her calmly. "I would never let him hurt you, Giovanna." He says the words like he actually means them. I watch as he

730

reaches into his pocket and pulls out a set of small keys. "Give me your hands, sweetheart." He says to her, but she's too afraid to move. I don't even know if she can hear him. If she's in shock. He moves closer to her and unlocks the cuffs, pulling them off her wrists gently. "Is that better, my love?" he asks her softly, as if he fucking cares. "Look at me, baby." He coaxes her, caressing the denim over her leg. *"Don't make me ask you again..."* That loving tone now has an edge to it, and Vanna peeks her head up from behind her knees to meet his gaze. "Your jacket is covered in that scums blood, honey. Let's get that off of you." She timidly complies with his request, moving slowly and cautiously as she turns to place her feet down on the hardwood floor, leaning forward slightly as he helps her remove the blood-stained garment. She glances at me, checking to see if I'm alright, but she does so briefly, as if she's afraid of Jack noticing her concern for me.

"M...may I please... use the bathroom, Jack?" her voice trembles as she asks, "H-his blood is all over m-my neck... I want to wash it off." Jack immediately jumps to his feet, holding out his hand to help her stand up. The chivalric gesture seems absurd to me when offered by the likes of him. She places her hand in his and gets up to stand on shaky legs. He wraps his arm around the small of her back to steady her.

"No funny business, Giovanna. I'm trusting you to be a good girl in there. You freshen up and come right back out here." He says to her, like he's talking to a teenaged girl. "You try anything... There will be consequences." He warns her, reaching with his other hand to grip her face roughly, twisting her head towards me. "If you try *anything*, sweetheart..." he lets his words hang between them. Letting her fill in the blanks with her own imagination of what he's going to do to me. I don't care what he does to me. I stare into her terrified eyes, wishing she could read my mind, telling her to *run*. There's a sliding window in the bathroom... If she lifts the sliding portion out of the tracks, she could remove the glass quietly. It would give her that extra inch and a half to squeeze out of it. She could escape if I can keep him distracted long enough. I left the keys in my truck... But she suddenly looks like she doesn't want to leave me...

"*Go,* baby." I tell her. "It's okay, Vanna... Just... Go, baby." *Please hear me, Vanna... Go...Run...*

Jack and I both watch her walk into the bathroom, closing the door quietly behind her. The sink turns on, and I anxiously try to work the cuffs behind my back, attempting to kink up the chain, though it's probably useless. Especially when I'm cuffed around a pipe. I'll never be able to snap the swivel in this position. It's physically impossible. I grab the pipe with my hands and attempt to pull it from the wall again. It ain't budging. I'm not getting out of this... All I can do is hope she gets out.

The water turns off after a few minutes of her absence. A sinking feeling in my gut tells me she won't leave me... *Damn it, Vanna...*

Chapter thirty six

Vanna

My entire body is still shaking when I close the bathroom door behind me and stand before the sink in the small bathroom. Holding onto the cold edge of the porcelain, I stare at myself in the mirror. I look like a terrified mess. There's blood splattered all over my neck and in some of my hair. The sticky blood is all over the top of my blouse as well. I turn on the sink and wet a hand towel, wiping off my skin as best as I can.

Jack murdered the lackey. I watched his brains spray out the side of his head... His dead body fell over on me, dumping more blood and brain matter onto my chest... Before Jack tossed him on the floor like nothing... He blew part of a man's head off, and he didn't even flinch.

As I wipe at my skin vigorously, I turn my head towards the shower. There's a raised sliding window in the stall. I'm not sure my hips would fit through it, though... And if I made a run for it, Jack would certainly kill Dean within minutes.

"Go, baby...go..." Dean had said. He wants me to run.

I turn back to look at myself in the mirror. *No.* I'm not running. Dean and I get out of this together... or we don't. I'm not leaving him. He would never leave me.

Dropping the blood-stained towel, I open the bathroom cabinets, searching for anything I can use as a weapon against Jack. Anything I can use to get Dean out of those cuffs if I can't get the keys from Jack. I rummage through the cabinet beneath the sink as quietly as I can. I know I don't have much time... Jack will come in here any moment. I feel something with a curved handle in the darkness and grab it, pulling it out into the light.

An old straight razor...

Opening it up, I touch the blade. It isn't that sharp, but with enough force, I might be able to do some damage. Standing up, I quickly shove it into the front pocket of my ripped jeans and check to see if it's noticeable. That rapist piece of shit ripped the fly beyond use, but the button on my jeans is still intact. As I shift in front of the mirror, I'm afraid that Jack might notice there's something in my pocket. My jeans are somewhat tight. Even if he doesn't, he might catch me reaching for something... Pulling the straight razor back out of my pocket, I tuck it into the cuff of my blouse, curling my hand so that it doesn't drop. Jack knows when I'm afraid, I wrap my arms around my abdomen... he might not suspect anything if I walk out there like this... Looking back in the mirror, I practice my posture with the weapon, making sure he can't see it. That I look somewhat *normal*, all things considered. Running my hand through my hair, my finger snags on one of the bobby-pins I slipped in earlier. My heart rate increases for a moment as I place the razor on the sink and reach up with both hands to tug the hair pin halfway out, loosening its grip on my hair.

If I can get close enough to Dean... there's a chance...

"Giovanna, darling! Do I need to come in there?" Jack calls to me from the other side of the door, startling me.

"No, I'm almost done... I'm coming out!" I quickly respond. I grab the old straight razor, folding it open, before I tuck it back up my sleeve. Taking a deep, quivering breath, I attempt to settle my nerves and step out of the bathroom. Jack is standing a few feet from the front door. The knife Dean tried to stab him with, is still stuck in the frame. I glance around the room for other weapons I could possibly grab, but Jack seems to have made them all disappear. My eyes settle on Dean for a moment. He's still on his knees, cuffed with his hands behind his back to the old radiator. There's a profound sadness in his eyes as I look into them. He had been hoping I'd have gone out the window when I had the chance. As if I could ever leave him behind. I shift my focus back to Jack. To what I have to do to get us out of this.

"Come here, sweetheart." He smiles. I walk slowly towards his outstretched, beckoning hand. The straight razor is cradled in mine, tucked up my sleeve. I pretend to fidget with the cuffs of my blouse as I approach him, hoping he doesn't suspect a weapon. Lowering my eyes timidly from him, I bring my arms across my stomach, the way Jack has always been used to seeing me when he knows I'm frightened. I notice the blood and brain matter on the floor and hold myself a little tighter as I step around it. Perhaps Jack will think I'm merely sickened by the sight of it... Which isn't far off from the truth, anyway. "It's alright, my love... just blood." Jack says. When I'm within range, I drop my arm and let the straight razor slide from my cuff, through my hand. I grip the handle before it drops to the floor and quickly swing it up at Jack's throat. He manages, within a second, to reflexively lean back just in time for me to barely graze him.

The room is dead silent for a moment. The seconds feel like minutes as Jack's expression turns dark again... Dark like that night he tried to kill me. He grabs my arm with the straight razor, squeezing my wrist painfully, as he brings his other hand to his throat, then examines his fingers. A little bit of blood coats his fingertips, but it's a superficial wound. I didn't cut him deep enough. Not by a long shot.

Dean is shouting before the back of Jack's hand collides with the side of my face, snapping my head sideways. He rips the straight razor from my grasp and throws it across the room with an angry shout.

"Oh, you disappoint me, baby!" Jack snarls, before he slugs me in the stomach. I keel over, trying to breathe, as he grabs me again, yanking me upright by my hair. Slapping me across the face, he then shoves towards the back of the couch. I topple over it, landing on my back on the floor in front of the stone fireplace, the back of my head smacking against the stone hearth. Dazed, and still trying to breathe normally, I try to push myself up. I can hear the cuffs around Dean's wrists clattering madly against the steel radiator as he shouts desperately for Jack to stop, to fight him instead. I look up in time to see Jack yank Dean's knife from the door frame, and storm around the side of the couch. As he rounds it, Dean kicks his leg out, tripping up Jack and sending him crashing to the floor. Going for Jack's knees, Dean slams one of his boots down on him. Jack shouts out in pain, rolling away from him, towards me. I try to take advantage of Jack's momentary distraction and go for the knife in his hand, jumping on top of him, even though I can barely see straight. We struggle for a moment, but it's no use. Jack is too strong, too fast. A former cop, with years of experience subduing criminals resisting arrest, Jack gets me face down on the hard wood floor quickly. Wrenching my arms behind my back, making me scream as it feels like he's going to dislocate both of my arms, I feel the bite of the handcuffs around my wrists again before he finally gets off my back.

"Yeah, that's right, you fuckin' pussy, come at me!" Dean shouts. I twist my head in time to see Jack storm back over to Dean, slamming his boot into Dean's stomach, forcing grunts out of him with every brutal stomp.

"Stop it!" I desperately scream, struggling to get up with my hands cuffed behind my back. "Jack! Please! Stop it! I'll do whatever you want! I give up! Stop!" I manage to scramble to my feet and throw myself in front of Dean, blocking Jack's assault on him. He grabs me, spinning me around to face Dean, then kicks me behind the leg, shoving me down on my knees before him. Dean is breathing heavily, but his eyes are still full of fight and rage as I look into them. Jack pulls my head back and I feel the cold blade of a knife at my throat again. Staring into Dean's eyes, I watch as terror seeps into his expression.

"I should spray him with your fucking blood! Let that be the last thing you ever see of each other! You bitch!" Jack shouts vehemently. The blade of the knife drags across my throat, slowly cutting me. A drip of warm blood trickles down my neck. The cut burns, but it's just a scratch. He didn't press down. Jack suddenly releases my hair, pulling the knife away from my throat, before he shoves me forward into Dean's chest. I fall against him, and I can hear his heart thudding rapidly. "Kiss him goodbye, Giovanna..." Jack mutters, his tone full of disgust. "These are your last moments together." I hear him take a few steps back from us, moving towards the love seat. Glancing over my shoulder as I attempt to straighten myself up, I see Jack sit down on the love seat, staring at the steel pentacle above the fireplace. When I turn back to face Dean, he looks tormented... defeated... slowly shaking his head with despair. His eyes are bloodshot, glassy, and there's blood in the corner of his mouth.

"I love you, Dean." I tell him, leaning forward to kiss his cheek. I slide my face against his rough whiskers, moving closer to his ear as I whisper, *"Pull the bobby-pin from my hair... and please, please forgive me."* I move slightly back, turning my head so that he sees it hanging loosely by a few strands of hair at my temple.

"Why didn't you run?" He whispers back, his voice tight, straining to say the words. Leaning forward, I feel him press a kiss to my temple, before he grips the pin between his teeth and pulls it out. I watch him tuck the pin inside of his cheek with his tongue, before I lean forward to press my lips to his, kissing him hard and desperately. *"I love you more than anything in this world, Vanna... You stay alive..."* he whispers against my lips. *"Do you hear me? You stay alive... no matter what."*

"Times up." Jack mutters behind me. My lips are still pressed to Dean's when Jack rips me away from him, yanking me back up to my feet by the biting cuffs. Dean lunges forward, but Jack slams him back against the radiator with a boot to Dean's chest.

"Please stop hurting him, I'll do anything you want, Jack. I give up. I'm not going to fight you anymore." I try not to cry.

"Yeah. You will do everything I want." He slips Dean's knife up under the front of my blouse, jerking his arm violently forward, tearing my shirt wide open. The now tattered fabric hangs off my body, exposing my bra and bare torso to Dean. "I promised your boyfriend he'd get to watch." Jack growls against my ear. He grabs what's left of the fabric of my blouse and tears at it, jerking me nearly off balance, leaving it hanging from my cuffed wrists behind my back. The rage is back in Dean's eyes. The muscles in his jaw rippling as he fights against the cuffs some more. "If you disobey me one more time, Giovanna... I give you my word, I'll spill his guts on the floor and let him bleed out. Do I have your word? Are you going to be a good girl and accept your punishment for all the bad you've done?"

I nod frantically. *"Yes. I promise."*

Jack tucks the knife in his belt, then grabs my wrists and undoes the cuffs again. They clatter to the ground, and he pulls off what's left of my shredded blouse, tossing it at Dean. I feel him slip a finger under my bra strap, stretching it away from my skin, he lets it slip off his finger and snap back against my body. "Lose the bra." He demands. "Now." I reach up behind my back to unhook the clasp, letting the bra fall forward down my arms, slipping off, landing at my feet. At Dean's knees. Jack stands closer, his arms wrap around me to cup and fondle me in his hands. Agony mixes with the rage in Dean's eyes. I almost can't bear to look at him. "Did you enjoy these?" Jack taunts him. "Well-endowed as she is." He squeezes me almost unbearably hard, the pain forcing a whimper from me.

Dean rails against the cuffs again, swearing at him. Jack seems to ignore his words as his hands skim down my body towards my ripped jeans. He rests his chin on my shoulder, stopping his hands descent to gently stroke my lower abdomen. His fingers lightly teasing delicate circles around my naval. I squirm slightly. "She has amazingly soft skin, doesn't she?" Jack says, nuzzling his face in my hair. "She's also quite ticklish around her bellybutton. Did you know that?"

"I know every fucking inch of her." Dean growls, his tone dripping with hate.

Jack doesn't respond to him. He presses a kiss to my shoulder that makes me shudder, but not in a good way. His hands begin to travel south again, and I feel his fingers undoing the button of my jeans, pulling the denim apart. As he slides his hand inside, Dean's pained expression twists further into excruciating agony. I squeeze my eyes shut, unable to look at him anymore. All I can hear is his ragged breathing, the cuffs clanging against the steel radiator, Jack's groan in my ear as he moves his hand inside my jeans. I clench my fists at my side and try to think of anything else, but it's impossible with Jack whispering in my ear about how much he's missed me... How often he jerked off in the prison cell I sent him to, thinking about this moment... All the things he's going to do to me...

"Open your eyes, *Vanna*..." Jack demands, saying my name like it's a curse word. "I want you to watch him, watch you, come for *me*."

"I'm going to fucking kill you, Jack!" Dean snarls at him. "You're going to die tonight!"

Jack only chuckles again, grabbing my hand and forcing it against his crotch. I can feel his hardness over his pants. He's enjoying everything about this twisted situation. And it's only going to get worse. Especially for Dean. I can't let this happen in front of him. "Who do you belong to, *Vanna*?" Jack demands, grabbing me roughly between my legs. "Tell him!"

"*You*." I gasp. He snares my hair in his fist and yanks my head back again.

"Louder." He snarls, pushing his hardness against my hand.

"*You, Jack*." I say again, curling my fingers to stroke him a little more. "I've missed you... nobody's ever fucked me like you have, Jack." I'm desperate to turn this situation around. This can't happen in front of Dean. And I need to buy him some time if there's even a chance he can get out of those cuffs. Twisting to face Jack, I find his expression somewhat surprised by my words. "I'm sorry... I've thought about everything for three years. I'm sorry I didn't understand that you loved me." I tell him, moving my hands to undo his pants. He grabs my wrists with both of his hands to stop me. "You should punish me for my stupidity. I deserve it, Jack." I move closer to press my body against him. "Don't you think I deserve it?" I whisper, pleadingly. "You should bend me over the bed, like old times... use your belt... remember? You liked that." His grip loosens on my wrists, and I slide my hands up his body, to his neck, pulling him down as I bring my mouth to his, kissing him.

In an instant, his arms are wrapped around me roughly, his fingers digging into me, his returning kiss is aggressive, dominating. His teeth scraping and biting at my lips every now and again. I can literally feel his emotions skating between love and hate as he kisses me in this savage, violent way. When I pull back from the kiss slightly to look him in his cold blue eyes, they're heated. "Come on, Jack... what we have is too intimate to involve him." I tilt my head in Dean's direction. "He's not going anywhere, anyway. He couldn't even save me from that rapist... *You* did, Jack. *You* saved me." He reaches up to gently stroke the side of my face. "You kept me safe... I see now, that you always have."

"You've always been mine..." Jack says. I drop my hands from his shoulders to take one of his in mine, gently tugging him in the direction of the bedroom.

Forcing myself to smile sweetly up at him, I coax, *"Make me yours again, Jack. I want to be yours."*

I TRY NOT TO DWELL ON THE THINGS I JUST WITNESSED BETWEEN VANNA AND Jack... I know she didn't mean a word of it... She did what she did... She's doing what she's doing... to save our lives. But Jesus fuck, did her words, her actions, tear me up inside. I don't have time to think about any of it right now. Not if I want to stop what's about to happen in the bedroom. She's counting on me to stop it.

Sweeping the hairpin out of my cheek with my tongue, I twist my head around as far as I can, bringing my hands around to the best of my ability. I've got one fucking shot to spit this pin into my cuffed hand, or it's all over for us. Jack's going to fuck her, snap back to psychotic, and kill her. Then walk right in here and blow my brains out like he did the lackey. At which point, he'll be doing me a favor...

Holding my breath, I let the bobby-pin drop from my teeth, sending up a silent prayer that it lands in my hand. The fact that I didn't beat Vanna to this cabin, that I didn't get the drop on Jack, and that this fucking hairpin just ricocheted off the side of the cuff and dropped to the floor, is all the evidence I need to know, beyond any shadow of a doubt, I'm destined to burn in Hell for all of my wrong doings when I leave this miserable fucking planet. And that might very well be today.

The sharp crack of what sounds like a whip rings out from the bedroom, followed by a muffled, clipped little shriek...

Motherfucker!

Ramming my hand as hard as I can through the cuff, my fingers reach for the pin. I manage to touch it, pinching it between my two finger tips, and curling it up into my hand. As the whipping sound carries on in the bedroom, I shove my thumb inside the bobby-pin, bending it open, and get to work on picking these cuffs. It takes a solid fucking minute to get the cuffs off. Knowing Jack's beating her in the next room is thoroughly fucking with my ability to concentrate. When I get to my feet, I nearly stumble. I've been on my knees for so fucking long, my legs are painfully stiff. I glance around the room for a weapon. Jack's got my gun, my knife. He tossed the Glock and the Ruger outside in the dark, citing "Too many weapons to keep track of." I don't have time to go searching for those. Besides... a fuckin' bullet would be too quick for him. There are more ways than one to make self-defense work for me. Jack deserves to die by knife, or my bare fucking hands.

Another cry from Vanna as she's struck again... I hurry over to the lackey's body, crouching down to search him for a weapon. He's got another folding blade in his pocket. I snatch it from him, shoving it in my own pocket as I move quickly and quietly towards the bedroom. Leaning up against the wall in the partial shadows, I glance into the room.

The fucker is standing over Vanna. She's still wearing her jeans, but he's got her on her knees on the floor, bent over the foot of the bed, shaking... Her arms tucked up under her chest, her face down in the mattress to muffle her cries... Pink and red welts, crisscrossed and marred all over her naked back and shoulders from the leather belt he's been beating her with. He's breathing heavy, as if this sick shit really pulls his balls tight. His hand gripping his junk over his pants as he admires his handy work on her... My fuckin' blood is at a boil.

"Pull those jeans down, baby... I want to put some marks on that perfect, lily-white ass." Jack pants, gripping his dick harder in anticipation. As Vanna moves to do what she's told, I notice Jack still has my gun tucked in the back of his waistband. I ain't gonna let this sick fuck hit her again. She's taken enough abuse to buy me time to get out of those cuffs. I wait until she's slowly sliding the denim down over her ass to him. I know the sight of those black lacey panties between those pale, perfect globes of hers as the denim slowly slides down, is one Hell of a fuckin' distraction. He ain't gonna look away. Jack takes a quivering breath, his hand excitedly wiggling the belt at his side, getting ready to raise it to whip her again...

Fuck that shit.

As he swings his arm back with the belt, I charge him, slamming him up against the wall a few feet away from where he was standing behind Vanna. Momentarily stunned, it's a piece of cake to pin him against the wall and grab the gun from his waist band. I ram the barrel painfully into that tender little spot between a man's jawbone and his ear. Jack winces, though he's still grinning that creepy ass psychotic smile in my face. I shove him so his back is flat against the wall, then I drive my knee up into his fuckin' balls. Hard. He lets out a groan and wants to crumple over. I ram my gun harder into that painful nook behind his jaw, slamming his head back, forcing his icy blue eyes to mine.

"That's for *Serene*." I growl in his face, as he tries to catch his breath through the pain. "Everything else I'm gonna do to you... Is for Vanna, you sick, *sick* fuck." I can hear Vanna behind me, moving slowly. I imagine she's in a bit of pain as well. "Are you alright, doll?" I ask, briefly glancing over my shoulder at her. She's standing, pulling up her ripped jeans, buttoning them to keep them up the best she can, before she crosses her arms in front of her chest. "There are some old t-shirts in the dresser, baby. Go put something on... then go wait for me in the truck."

"I'm not leaving you." She says stubbornly. And though there's a tremor in her voice, I don't doubt her. She's not going to leave me. In fact, she probably saved us both, getting Jack to lower his guard.

"What's about to go down, baby... I can't have any distractions." I press the gun harder into Jack, and he lets out a hiss through gritted teeth. I smile at his pain as I remove my forearm from his throat, in order to pull the late lackey's knife from my pocket. Flipping it open with one hand, I bring the blade up to his throat, pressing it against him. Removing the gun from him, I hold it out behind me, speaking to her as I continue to scowl in his face. "Take this, Vanna. And stay in this room. Don't come out until I tell you." I feel her hands gently take the gun from mine. "It's loaded, doll. Be careful."

"I know." I can hear her sit back down on the foot of the bed. "I shot the lackey earlier." She sighs. Good for her.

"This one's got a bit more of a kick. So, hold on tight if you have to use it. Just in case it isn't me that comes through that bedroom door."

Vanna is suddenly by my side, the barrel of the gun against Jack's forehead. She's got tears welling up in her eyes as she stares at him. Her bottom lip trembling.

"Vanna... don't."

"I'm not willing to risk it not being you, Dean." She whispers, her voice tight as she speaks. "I'm sorry, Jack. For whatever I did to you to make you this way." Tears roll down her face. "I really did love you, *once*..."

Fuck... She's gonna smoke his ass. Blow his damn brains out... I can't let her kill him. It ain't in her to do this, and still be the same Vanna I love on the other side of it...

"Vanna... baby...." I sigh, distracting her with my words, as if I'm not about to simultaneously disarm her, and temporarily incapacitate him, in one swift move.

I twist to bring my hand up quickly, shoving the gun up and out of her grasp as I grab it, then bring my elbow back down, with all of my might into Jack's solar plexus, knocking the wind out of him again. He grunts loudly upon impact and keels over. I shove him hard to the floor between Vanna and I. She's stunned, looking at her empty hand, then at Jack on the floor, gasping for air. She finally settles her eyes on mine.

"He's done things that deserve worse than a bullet in the head. He's done things, baby... that if I don't do this... this way... *my way*... I'm never going to be able to move past." I try to explain to her as he wheezes on the floor between us. "If you kill him Vanna... he takes something of both of us with him. And I don't want that... I don't want that for you... And honestly, baby... I've lost so many pieces of myself throughout the years, I can't let this piece of shit take another one with him. He's done things to us tonight, that if I don't get to take him apart... These things are going to haunt me for a long, long time."

Her dark, glassy eyes stare at me for a steady moment, as if she's trying to understand my words. I'm not sure if she fully does, but she nods, at the very least, in agreement. "Okay." She whispers.

I spot my other knife on the dresser beside the bed. Stepping around her I grab it, then come back to stand before her.

"Stay in here." I say, handing her back the gun. "*I will* let you know when it's safe to come out." Kissing her briefly on the lips, I then turn to Jack. Bending to grab him by the back of his shirt, I haul him towards the door as he attempts to scramble to his feet. Shoving him outside into the short hallway, Jack hits the wall and stumbles to the floor again, landing on his ass. I grab the bedroom door, slamming it shut on Vanna, as Jack glares up at me. With a sweep of my arm, I chuck the dead lackey's knife at Jack. The tip of the blade sticks into the hardwood floor with a thunk, mere inches from his inner thigh. "Pick it up, *bitch*." I growl at him.

That crazy smile returns to his face, as his fist wraps around the handle of the knife, ripping it out of the floor board as he gets to his feet. He changes his grip on the knife, holding it like an icepick as he gets into a fighting stance. Jack either has no idea what he's doing... or this motherfucker actually has some knife fighting skills. Either way, I'm taking Jack Nero apart.

Raising my hands to fight, I hold my own blade with the tip facing my enemy in a hammer grip, my other hovering within range of my throat. I move towards Jack, swiping the blade through the air between us, as he backs up towards the open space in the front of the cabin, giving us a little more room to dance.

He seems to be watching me, beginning to mimic the way I keep my blade in constant motion in front of me, random patterns he cannot predict as we circle each other. I don't attack him yet, though. I want to wear on his psyche. Force him into a mistake, so I can cut him and cut him good. As the moments pass, he grows more impatient, and it isn't long before he lunges at me. Coming in hot, his right arm raised, gripping the knife as if he thinks he's going to plunge it down into the left side of my neck, I jump back out of range of his blade, slashing out with my own quickly, across his forearm. As his arm comes down, missing me, I rebound and back hand slash across his bicep, then shove his body away from me, rocking him off balance before he even realizes he's cut. He regains his footing. The slight tightening around his eyes, the way his lips part to reveal clenched teeth as he sucks in air, tells me he can feel the burn of those cuts I just gave him. Crisscrossing the blade in front of me once more, I gesture with my free hand and a smile, beckoning him to try again.

"What's the matter Jack, nobody taught you how to shank a guy in prison? Did you spend all your time in solitary, you pussy?" I grin at him, flicking my blade towards him tauntingly. He jumps backwards, scowling as he swipes back at me. Our blades meet briefly between us with a clang. "Are you afraid, Jack? I barely grazed you... Don't get all knife shy on me now. We're just getting started." His eyes shift past me, glancing towards the kitchen. I can't let him get past me in there. Too many potential weapons, including a block of kitchen knives.

He grabs the deer antler bowl from the side table behind him, and hurls it at me. I knock it away and it shatters against the front door as he charges me again, slamming his foot into my abdomen, rocking me backwards as I swipe my blade at him, cutting him across his chest deeply. He continues to follow through with his charge like a mad man... and well, he is exactly that. His knife stabs through my leather jacket, into my left bicep. Gripping his wrist to prevent him from driving it all the way through, I can't help the painful groan that escapes me as I grit my teeth and bear it. Jack twists the blade in my arm to open the already deep wound wider, his other hand gripping my wrist that's holding my blade. He pulls the knife out of my arm and moves to stab me in the chest and I grab his wrist again, though my arm is significantly weakened now.

We struggle against each other, each of us attempting to drive our blades into the other. His eyes are wild. Fuckin' crazy. His panting breath hisses through his clenched teeth inches from my face. I'm not even sure if he realizes how deep the cut is across his chest. Blood seeping into this torn clothing, dripping on the floor between us. I allow him to force me back towards the kitchen another step or two, his boots now standing in his own blood. I shove my knife harder towards him, in quick stabbing bursts, making him brace expectantly for another and another, as he fights to keep my blade from reaching him. Instead of another forceful attempt at stabbing him, I jerk my knife backwards, simultaneously pivoting my body to the side as I throw him off balance and he slips in his own blood.

Staggering to keep himself upright, I swipe my knife deeply across his forearm, cutting across his wrist, through the tendons that control grip. His blade falls from his now limp fingers, and Jack immediately drops to snatch the knife back up with his other hand, as if he's totally unfazed by the serious wound. While crouched down he swipes the blade at my legs, making me jump back again towards the front door of the cabin as he lunges at me, wildly swiping the knife. I'm backed against the door now, using my own blade to block his stabs and slashes, a flourish of sharp metal and clanging as our blades collide. I manage to jab him a few times in the process with the tip of my blade, before I'm able to kick him back and shift my position away from the door, towards the living room.

I can feel the sharp burning on my own person as well, where he managed to swipe me a few times in that brief bladed skirmish... My hands, my chest as well. Though, nothing too deep. He makes another leap at me, swiping his blade with a murderous glint in his eye. Jack doesn't care if he dies in this knife fight, as long as he takes me down with him. I however, have something to live for. I counter block him with my blade again as I jump back. My right foot lands on something that makes my leg slide out, throwing me off balance... The fucking handcuffs I discarded haphazardly on the floor in front of the radiator. Taking advantage of my momentary unbalance, Jack slams his blade down against mine, the force knocking it clean out of my grasp. *Fuck!*

He wastes no time in swiping at me again, forcing me to jump out of his strike zone, and now I'm backed against the stone fireplace. His next strike narrowly misses slashing across the inside of my wrist. The little black bracelet Vanna made me, isn't so lucky. The black rounded stones scatter across the hard wood floor at our feet. Jack charges through my guard, bringing the knife up horizontally towards my throat for the kill. I block that kill strike with my good arm, grabbing his wrist and pushing back on him as he presses his whole body into his arm, forcing the blade closer and closer to my throat. Blood from the puncture wound in my bicep has been running down my arm, coating my hand, but now I use it to my advantage. Bringing my bloody hand to his face, I smear my own blood in his fucking eyes. He lets out a shout as it stings, blurring his vision. He jumps back, trying to rub the blood out of his eyes, and I lift my boot to nail him in the gut, shoving him back from me as I fall back aainst the stone fire place, the top of my shoulders slamming up against the mantle. I know that if I go for my knife on the floor, he'll stab me in the back. I reach backwards over my head for anything I can use as a weapon on the mantle... A candle stick... the Bronze End of the Trail statue... *Anything!*

As Jack manages to get a bloody eye open, my hands feel the cold steel rim of the pentacle I welded for Vanna. I grab it as Jack comes at me again with the knife, but he's un-steady in his attack, sliding on the black, spherical stones on the floor beneath his boots. His footing slips from beneath him and he trips, falling to his knees before me. I bring the steel pentacle up over my head, slamming it down over the top of his skull, dead center of the star. In that same moment, he plunges his knife into my inner left thigh, releasing the blade to bring his hands to the rim of the pentacle. I stagger aside and rip the protruding weapon from my leg, dropping it on the ground to grip my hands as best I can around my now profusely bleeding thigh.

Jack struggles to shove the jammed pentacle off of his head, but he can't... It's stuck... Wedged on his skull tightly, the top of his nose is crushed by one of the steel bars of the star across his face. Blood gushes down his face as he continues to struggle. He knows he's wide open to attack. Completely vulnerable. He's panicking... flailing about and shoving at the steel circular frame as he lets out shouts of frustration... He knows he's in trouble... But so am I. Blood flows far too steadily from the gash in my leg. Jack got me good...

I quickly move to the chair against the wall, grabbing at the remnants of the ropes they used to restrain Vanna. Sitting down in the wooden chair, I tie a rope tightly around my leg above the wound as I watch Jack have a meltdown about his own predicament. The sweat beading up on his forehead is running down his face, mixing with the blood I smeared around his eyes, making it drip right into them again. Not only can he not get himself free, he can't even see anymore.

"Any last words?" My voice sounds oddly casual even to myself. Though it's mostly due to exhaustion. I've shed considerable blood in this fight. Pushing myself up from the wooden chair, I limp towards him. As I move, the blood is still trickling from my wound... I don't have time to fuck around. I need to end this, once and for all. For Vanna. *Forever.*

As he hears me approaching him again, he abandons his attempt to un-wedge himself, dropping his hands to the floor as he feels around the planks, searching blindly and frantically for his knife. He finds it, but it isn't going to do him much good now. Swiping at the air, threating to kill me still, I make my way around him. He's breathing so raggedly, shouting in such a frenzy, he doesn't even know where I am. I grab the rim of the pentacle around his skull, like a big ol' steering wheel...

"*Checkmate,* asshole... *She's mine.*" I mutter to him one last time, before I twist the pentacle with all of my might, listening to the cracking of bones in Jack's neck as he goes eternally silent.

I let his body fall forward onto the floor. The rim of the pentacle preventing his face from touching the ground, his neck bent at a most unnatural angle...

Grabbing the throw blanket off the chair in the corner, I toss it over the top portion of his corpse... Vanna doesn't need to see this.

In the dead silence of the cabin now, I can hear my own blood dripping steadily from my fingertips onto the wooden plank floor with a steady tap... tap... tap...

Clearing my throat, I call out to her. "It's all over, doll... You're safe... You can come out here, now... And bring that belt with you..." I'm gonna need it...

Chapter thirty-seven

Vanna

K NIVES CLASHING, MEN SHOUTING AND
grunting, hisses of pain and things
breaking... That's all I hear as I pace in the
bedroom behind the closed door, clutching Dean's
gun to my chest, against the old t-shirt I dug
out of a drawer. Until I hear Dean call out... *It's
all over, doll... You're safe...*

Bring that belt with you...

I drop the gun I've been clinging to onto
the bed and grab Jack's belt off the floor. Flinging
the door open, I hurry towards Dean. He's
leaning against the back of the couch, his back
to me as he attempts to shrug out of his leather
jacket. The lights are off in the living room now,
and as I make my way around him to look him in
the face, my eyes don't get that far... *Oh, God...*

"*Dean...*" I barely hear my own voice. The belt slips from my fingers, the buckle clattering against the hard wood floor. He's covered in blood. I can't tell what is his and what is Jack's, except from the obvious wounds across his torso, his arms. The sickeningly sweet, yet strong metallic smell invades my nostrils. I don't even know what to do to help him, but I can tell there is a pretty serious gash in his left thigh. His pant leg is soaked, dark blood seeping into the fabric of his already dark gray jeans. Even the rope he's already tied around his thigh is red with blood. There is a small pool of blood on the floor beneath his left boot as well... His wrists are torn up and already bruised from the handcuffs... I force myself to lift my eyes to his. He looks tired, but content.

"Gotta get a belt around my leg, baby." He sounds exhausted, as he brings his hands to fumble with his belt, unbuckling it and pulling it through his pant loops. "Gonna need you to help me get it tight, okay, baby?" I help him wrap it around his upper thigh and slip the belt through the buckle as he pulls, hard. So hard, I can tell it's really digging into his flesh as he groans in pain. "Put the prong through the lowest hole you can, Vanna." He sounds as though he is struggling. I quickly do as he says. "Now, grab that belt." Dean says, cocking his chin towards the belt I dropped beside me. "I need another tourniquet on my arm. Gotta slow all this bleeding down more, as much as I can."

I freeze, staring at him. *Oh my God.* Is he bleeding out right before my eyes?

Dean gives me a weak smile. "I'll be okay, baby." He says, leaning a little more against the couch now. "I need you to get me Jack's belt, though. It's important."

It's important. He says it like it's a bill that needs to go out to the mailbox on time. I can see it in his eyes though, he's trying to hide it. It's beyond important. It's vital.

I grab the belt off the floor and sling it around his arm above the wound on his bicep, pulling it as tight as I can. Dean grimaces but manages to focus through the pain enough to slip the prong through, and I finish securing it for him. The belt strap hangs from his arm awkwardly, and I wonder if this is enough.

"There's rope, on the chair." I say quickly, moving to rush into the living room, but Dean grabs my arm with his other bloody hand.

"Don't go in there, Vanna... Jack's dead... you don't need to see it." I catch a glimpse of a throw blanket over something on the floor. We don't have time to argue. I can see it in his eyes. There's a growing urgency behind them.

"What now?" I ask nervously, fighting my own anxiety.

"My keys are still in my truck. Pull it up to the front porch." He says, leaning slightly forward to inspect the bleeding on his leg. His eyes meet mine again. He gives me another faint grin as he sits down now on the back of the couch. "I love you, baby... Go get the truck."

I can't tell by his expression whether the belts are working or not. A horrible feeling in my gut tells me it's the latter. I turn and hurry out the front door and down the porch steps, dashing towards the Silverado. Entering through the passenger side door, I slide to the driver's seat, grabbing and twisting the key in the ignition before I'm even fully behind the wheel. I throw it into reverse and hit the gas as the tires spin, kicking up dirt and gravel. Throwing it back into drive, I cut the wheel as I near the cabin, positioning the passenger side door right at the steps of the porch and throw it into park. Hurriedly, I slide back out the way I got in, rushing back up the steps and bounding back inside the cabin where I had left Dean.

He's still sitting on the back of the couch, crookedly, his shoulders hunched forward, staring down at the floor. He looks up at me as I enter, a weak grin across his face. "Probably gonna have to do some witchy shit on that pentacle thing I made you... to get the bad juju off it after all this. I definitely did some devil shit with it." I have no idea what he's joking about, and right now, it can wait. I need to get him to a hospital.

Rushing over to him, I grab his leather jacket and duck under one of his arms so that he can lean on me. I take most of his weight as we make our way slowly down the steps towards the truck. With what seems like his last bit of strength, he grabs onto the handle inside the door and we manage to get him into the passenger seat. I drape the leather jacket over him and shut the door, rushing to the other side and jumping in behind the wheel.

"Which way is the hospital?" I frantically ask.

"A right at the end of the road, take it thirty miles down. There will be signs. Just follow them." He says tiredly. "You got this, doll." I throw the truck into drive and hit the gas, tires spitting gravel at the cabin behind us now as I barrel down the hill and out to the road. "Doin' good, baby." He says in that reassuring tone of his. I glance over at him as I speed down the road. He's leaning back against the head rest, but his face is turned towards me, his heavy-lidded eyes staring at me. Dean's posture is somewhat slouched and crooked, one hand resting in his lap on top of the leather jacket. His other hand laying across the seat of the truck between us, palm up. I reach down to grab it and hold his hand. As his fingers curl through mine, I can't help noticing how cool and clammy his hand feels. Only a few hours ago, when we were making love, they had felt so strong and warm.

"*Dean?*" I try not to let my voice crack. I can't get the words out. I'm afraid to even think them fully, let alone say them out loud.

"Everything's gonna work out Aces for you, baby." He says quietly, giving my hand a gentle squeeze. I'm aware he's not being gentle intentionally, though. He just lacks the strength to squeeze my hand any harder.

"Dean... *please...*" My voice is tight, and my eyes are starting to sting with tears as my heart begins to race faster. I want to look at him, but I have to focus on the road too. I'm taking the curvy mountain roads as fast as I can without killing us both for sure, glancing at him every second I can spare.

"Vanna... need you to call Jason, when we get to the hospital. Officer... Jason Caldwell." Dean says. "Tell him... tell him what happened." He sounds weaker by the moment.

"Stay with me, Dean." I plead, pushing the gas pedal down a little more.

"Always, baby." I glance at him in time to catch his slight smile.

"I love you, Dean." I whimper. "I love you so much it hurts."

"I know you do, baby." He says. "I love you, too. Despite all this, you're still the best thing that's ever happened to me."

I glance at him again. He's still staring at me. "I'm sorry I wasted so much time... We could have had so much more time together." I cry. I can't believe I ever doubted his love for me. I'm such a damned fool for not taking a chance on him sooner. For not trusting him that his feelings were genuine.

"Baby, I'll never leave you." His thumb lightly strokes my hand.

"Promise me." I demand, as if simple words will keep him alive if he does so. "Promise me you will stay with me. I can't lose you, Dean." I can hear his breathing becoming a bit shallower. I make it to the main road and turn right at the sign directing us towards the hospital, then I glance back at Dean. He's sitting a little lower now, but his face is still turned towards me. "Don't just look at me, promise me!" I'm trying not to sound harsh, but if he dies on me, I don't think I'll ever be able to handle it. I will never get over losing him. Especially not like this. The weaker he gets, the higher my fear rises.

"Gave you my heart and soul, doll. Long before tonight..." Dean says, almost a whisper now. "Love never dies."

Love never dies... but people do... He does believe he's dying. Dean might be dying right here beside me... *Oh, God... Oh, God...* I hold his hand tighter. I've got the petal to the floor, maxed out at 99 miles an hour on the straight run towards the hospital. There are very few cars on the road at this early morning hour. We should be there in a few minutes.

Please God, don't let him die!

"Dean, I will never forgive myself if you die. Do you hear me? I won't ever move on from this. I *need* you. *I need you with me.*" I beg him, squeezing his hand tighter still. "Please hold on. I'm doing the best I can."

"You're safe now, doll. Kept all my promises." He smiles weakly. "But I'm sorry... too... Jack... got the drop on me... all this... is on me. Not you, baby... You were right... I probably just should have taken the gun from you... and shot him."

Blue and Red lights flash inside the interior of the truck reflecting in the mirrors. There's a cop behind us now. I'm speeding. Breaking the law. But I'm not pulling over. Dean doesn't have that kind of time. I slap on the emergency flashers, hoping the cop behind us will understand that something is wrong and realize I'm speeding towards the hospital.

"Baby?" Dean's voice is weaker still.

"Yes?"

"You're gonna be okay, Vanna... I promise you that."

I refuse to let this be goodbye... "I will never forgive you if you leave me!" I cry. "Never!"

He gives my hand another light squeeze. "I knew there was a chance... something like this could happen."

"Dean! *Please!* Don't..." I'm going to crash if I can't see with the tears flowing from my eyes.

"But as long as you made it out alive... and whole... I can live with it... or not." He chuckles weakly.

"It's not funny, God damn it!" I cry. "You can't leave me, please..." The entrance to the hospital is fast approaching on the right, I let off the gas, flick the blinker so the cop sees it, and hit the breaks to slow down. As I cut the wheel, the back of the truck nearly fishtails as I jump on the gas again to speed us towards the ER. *"We're almost there! Hang on!"*

"You know I love you, baby, right?" He asks, as if he needs to hear it...

"If you love me, stay with me!" I shout at him, slamming my hand on the horn as I skid the truck to a halt under the over-hang of the ER entrance. I slam it into park, leaving it running as I drop his hand, about to jump out of the truck.

"Vanna, wait." Dean says, reaching to stop me. There's an urgency in his voice. I turn back to him, worried we're almost out of time. "Kiss me and tell me you love me." He's smiling, but I can see the sorrow mixed with love in his eyes... He knows this might be his final request.

My heart shatters into a million pieces as I grab his face and press my lips to his. *"I love you."* I whisper against them between kisses. And I've never meant anything more in my entire life. "Dean Keegan, *I love you*, I love you, I love you..."

I feel his breath escape him on a sigh against my lips. *"Aces*, baby." Dean whispers back. "I love you, Vanna... And I'll love you, for..."

He stops talking...

His lips slip away from our kiss... his face falls through my hands as his body slumps over onto the seat...

I'm screaming for help before I even get out of the truck. As I scramble out and run around the front of the truck to the other side, yanking Dean's door open, the cop that was following us is right by my side. He's saying something but I can't understand him. I barely hear him. I'm reaching inside, pulling at Dean, but he isn't moving now. Full panic is hitting me like a tidal wave as I'm begging for anyone to help us. Someone grabs me around the waist and hauls me away from Dean as two guys in scrubs with a stretcher pull him out of the truck and hurriedly wheel him inside. His leather jacket falls to the ground.

The cop is telling me to calm down, but I can't. I have to go with him. *"Please! Please!* Let me go! That's my husband!" I lie, but I'm desperate. The cop releases me and I grab Dean's jacket, clinging to it as I sprint after them through the double sliding doors. They must have already taken him in the back to assess his injuries because he's not in the waiting area.

"Where is he?" I ask, rushing up to the front desk. The receptionist looks past me to the cop standing just behind me. She doesn't say anything, but she buzzes me through the door. The cop follows me. I don't know if he gave her some signal to let me through. I don't care right now. I spot Dean and run over to the side of his stretcher. They're already hooking him up to IV's and checking his vitals. "I'm here, Dean! I'm right here!" I grab his hand for a brief moment before the cop pulls me away from him again.

"Give them some room miss, so they can help him." He says.

"What happened?" One of the ER personnel asks. "How did he sustain these injuries?"

749

"He was stabbed, beaten. His leg is really bad." I say quickly, looking past her at Dean again. His eyes are still closed. He looks really pale... And as they cut open his shirt, under the bright lights of the ER, he looks so much worse than he did in the dim cabin or the dark truck. His torso is full of bruises and knife wounds. "Is he going to be okay?" I manage to ask through my trembling voice.

"How long have the ropes and belt been on his leg?" One of them asks as they place an actual tourniquet on his leg before removing the ropes.

"About thirty minutes. Maybe a little longer. I don't know. I got him here as fast as I could."

"Okay Ma'am. We're going to have to move him to Trauma. You will have to wait. Someone will update you as soon as possible."

"What's going to happen?" I ask, fearfully staring at Dean. They're putting an oxygen mask over his face now.

"We're going to have to get some blood into him, once he's stabilized, he'll be transported to the OR for surgery."

"Is he going to be okay?" I desperately ask again.

"Wait outside, please." She doesn't answer me, but glances at the cop, who gently takes me by the arm to lead me into a separate waiting room from the outside lobby. I stare at Dean as they move him once more, this time out of my line of sight.

"She didn't answer me." I whisper, mostly to myself as I sink down in a chair in the small waiting room, holding on tightly to Dean's leather jacket. I realize my hands and arms are covered in Dean's dried blood.

"I don't think they can legally answer that question, miss." The cop tries to sound reassuring. I look at him for the first time. He's young, maybe a few years older than me. He kind of reminds me of a cleanshaven older version of Axel.

"I'm sorry I sped. I didn't have a choice."

He shakes his head. "Let's not worry about that, right now. Why don't you tell me, exactly what happened to you two."

"I'm supposed to get in touch with Officer Jason Caldwell. I don't know if I'm supposed to say anything else beyond that. I'm sorry. I don't know what I'm supposed to do now... Please, call Jason Caldwell..." Another wave of panic hits me as I begin to sob, curling into myself as I burry my face in Dean's jacket.

Dean might die. He might be dead already. He was talking like he knew he was dying. He wouldn't take his eyes off me in the truck, as if he wanted to make sure I was the last thing he saw... He told me that love never dies and that he would never leave me. That his heart and soul belonged to me... He meant his spirit would stay with me. Dean knew he was dying... And I'm the one that did this to him. The reason he sacrificed himself. He put his life on the line for mine. This is all my fault. If Dean dies, I'm the one that killed him.

A loud rapid beeping alarm begins to go off somewhere in the ER where I can't see, and a robotic sounding female voice comes over the loudspeakers,

"*Code 1000, MTP... Code 1000, MTP...*" I pick my head up in time to see two ER doctors rush past the little room I'm in, hurrying in the direction Dean was taken. One of them saying something about a *massive transfusion protocol... A white male going into Cardiac Arrest...*

No... No...No...

"Please, please don't let him die!" I cry out loud, praying to a God I hope can hear me. I feel arms wrap around me tightly, someone trying to comfort me. I wish it was Dean, but it isn't... It might never be Dean again... The arms around me now, belong to the cop that followed us to the hospital. He's sitting beside me, pulling me towards him. Telling me that it's going to be okay...

Chapter thirtyeight

Vanna

M*ADELINE KEEGAN... IN MEMORY OF OUR BELOVED MOTHER...* It's a gloomy, damp December day, as I kneel down in front of the white marble headstone beneath the big old oak tree in the center of the cemetery. The coldness of the hard ground seeps through the denim of my jeans right into my knees, but I lean forward to wipe a few dead leaves away from the lower ledge of the marble footer. I place the bouquet of red and white roses inside the cemetery vase attached to her headstone. Arranging the flowers, my eyes drift to the grave on her left...

Dean Keegan is buried beside Madeline... And as I stare at that name, carved in the black granite, my eyes well up with tears, and my heart breaks all over again. I know now that it's completely, humanly possible, for a person to die of a broken heart. I can feel it. As sobs rack my body, and I squeeze my eyes shut against his name on that grave stone... I understand how the one's left behind can be swallowed up whole by the darkness left in their lover's absence. How their grief could be so all consuming, life without them is simply unimaginable... Unbearable... Unlivable...

As I reach over to touch Dean Keegan's name carved in black granite, strong arms wrap around me, a warm hand takes mine and gently pulls it back from the headstone. A whiskered jaw presses against the side of my face. And a deep, baritone, growly voice whispers, "That ain't me, doll... I'm right here beside you, where I'll always be, still loving you."

Twisting around in his embrace, I bury my face against his leather clad chest, holding onto him tightly. "You came so close to dying..." I can barely speak through my tears. Dean presses his lips to my temple as he holds me closer, tightly in his arms.

The brief investigation into Jack Nero's death cleared our names of any wrong doing. The gun powder residue on Jack's body, proved he murdered the lackey himself at point blank range. The blood on the taser as well as the handcuffs and knives, along with the medical reports of both of our injuries, further proved that Dean and I acted in self-defense. No charges were brought against us, and that young cop never wrote me up for speeding.

We learned later that day, Viking and Jason were t-boned in Viking's truck on their way up to follow Dean to the cabin. Axel borrowed Cherry's mustang to pick them up and rushed to the cabin while Viking's truck got towed back to town. They missed us by an hour and a half. Made the same mistake I did with the cabin number also, and apparently, so did the cops doing the welfare check early on. Another bit that showed Jack's premeditated plans to torture and kill us. So did the stolen car that was found in the woods behind Dean's cabin, with a trunk containing more rope, duct tape and a baggie full of tranquilizers.

It also had the lackey's wallet in the glove box. Turns out, his name was Aaron Hopper, from Gila Bend, Arizona. How Jack and Aaron came to know each other, is still a mystery. I suppose it doesn't matter now. They're both dead.

While Officer Jason Caldwell spent a majority of the time with the local police, Viking and Axel barely left my side in the hospital while waiting for word on Dean. After his cardiac arrest scare and a massive blood transfusion, Dean was put on a propofol drip to remain sedated while the doctors stitched him up. Once he was out of recovery from surgery, they removed the drip and put him in a room. We were finally allowed to see him. It took a few hours for Dean to come out of it and wake up, but I was by his side when he did, holding his hand the entire time. We spent four days in the hospital before he was allowed to be discharged. I've barely been able to step away from him since. Like he might disappear on me somehow if I'm not right here beside him. Like this is all a dream and I'm going to wake up and realize he didn't make it...

"Come on, doll, let's get you up off the cold ground... Had I known my father's headstone was going to set you off like this..." Dean says with a penitent sigh, carefully getting back to his feet as he takes my hands and pulls me up with him. He shifts his weight off his injured leg as his hands move to grip the collar of my coat, pulling it more closed around me from the cold. He gives me a crooked, rueful smile. "Maybe I should have brought her Christmas Bouquet on my own... Introduced you two on our Easter visit."

I wipe my eyes and shake my head, not sure what to say, really. Seeing his name carved on a headstone in the cemetery just drove it all home all over again, how close I came to losing him. "I'm sorry, I'm fine." I force myself to say, "I'll give you a few minutes alone with your mother." Kissing him briskly on his stubbled cheek, I turn to walk a few yards away to sit and wait on a stone bench beneath a large fir tree. When I look back at him, Dean is still watching me. After a moment, he shifts his gaze back to his mother's grave, saying words I can't hear. I watch him press his fingers to his lips, then bend to place his hand on the top of her headstone. He lingers for a few moments, before he takes a single white rose from the Bouquet that we brought her, and straightens. I watch as he seems to stare at it, before tossing the rose at his father's grave. Without a backward glance, he turns and begins his slow return to me.

"Are you sure you feel up to going to dinner tonight?" I ask him, "The doctor said you need to take it easy on that leg for another three weeks... Another five would be better."

"I'm fine, doll." He says, coming to stand before me. "You've been my dutiful little nurse for weeks now."

"Well, it's also *Christmas Eve*... The restaurant is probably going to be packed."

"That's why I made a *reservation* over a week ago, doll." He winks at me, reaching for my hand. "From now on, there will only be happy memories about Christmas Eve." I smile at him as I place my hand in his, and we walk together across the cemetery towards his truck parked a few yards away. "Unless you don't want to be seen in public with a *gimp*." He teases me, exaggerating his slight limp for a moment.

I give him a playful frown, squeezing his hand tighter. "You better watch your mouth, mister... that's my hero you're talking about."

Dean grimaces slightly at being referred to as my *hero*, and doesn't comment. Though after a moment, as he opens the truck door for me to climb inside, the corner of his mouth curves up ever so slightly.

LIFE'S TOO SHORT NOT TO SHOOT FOR HAPPINESS. HAPPINESS IS FAR TOO rare not to grab a hold of it with both hands when you find it. And Love... love's worth risking it all for...

Thought for sure I was a goner on our way to the hospital that night. Bleeding out on the passenger seat of my truck, making damn sure that Vanna was the last thing my wretched eyes would ever gaze upon... I was content to die that night. Not that I wanted to, but she was safe. I completed the mission. Fulfilled my promise to her that I would end him, his reign of terror on her life. I'm not sure what happens after we die, but I think my soul would have been at peace knowing she was free. That I did all I could to make sure she had the best shot at happiness I could give her, even without me by her side. I'd like to think I'd have been able to look in on her from time to time, though. Taken up the role of her *guardian angel* or some shit...

But I'm alive today, here on this earth, *with her*, holding her hand, kissing her lips... And life's too damn short not to shoot for happiness...

Vanna's inside the house now, getting ready for dinner at that ritzy Italian joint I brought her to on our first date. Old habits die hard, as I'm once again hiding out on the front porch, this time calling Cherry's number on my cell.

Waiting for her to pick up, I test my left leg to see what it can do. The doctors removed the stitches and staples earlier this week, said everything was healing up just fine. The skin around the healing wound is tight, the muscle deeper inside aches slightly at being stretched a bit, but I'll manage. I can pull this off. I'm no stranger to a little bit of pain or discomfort. She's worth it anyway.

"Is everything set?" I ask Cherry when she answers the phone.

"Yes, I'm here now, they finished it just this morning, everything looks great, Dean. Really beautiful."

Aces... I paid extra to make sure this would all happen by Christmas Eve. A week and a half was really cutting it close...

"How about the arrangement?" I ask. "Is it perfect, too? Is it going to work?"

"Gorgeous, and yes." I can hear her amusement at my eagerness in her voice. "I'll be waiting with Axel outside until you two are seated. I met with Kimberly earlier so she knows what's going on. You shoot me a text when you're ready."

Taking a deep breath, I let it out slowly, hoping to settle my increasing nerves. "I can't believe I'm doing this again..."

"You're not." Cherry's smile is evident in her voice as she reassures me. "*It's Vanna.*"

EAN RESERVED US THE SAME TABLE IN THE UPSCALE RESTAURANT WE originally sat in on our first date. He's a handsome devil in that same black sports jacket and deep reddish burgundy button-down collared shirt. He's got his hair buzzed low on the sides and slicked back tighter on top, like he did that night as well. His sexy facial scruff is trimmed a little shorter, slightly more than a five o'clock shadow. As per his request, I'm wearing the black mesh nude illusion dress he claims unhinged his jaw that night. And although I didn't have time to do my hair into long, old Hollywood style waves this time, I'm wearing my makeup the way I wore it that night for him, as well.

The pretty restaurant is all done up for Christmas time. Hundreds of crystal snowflakes and icicles dangle from the ceiling, catching the light from candlelit dinners. There are tall, slender Christmas trees decorated in the corners of the rooms and to either side of every entry way. The window we're seated in front of, is trimmed with garland all around it, adorned with more icicles, snowflakes and opulent golden ornaments. And the tables all have a small vase with a few red roses, and pure white peonies.

Dean notices me touching the soft white petals as I admire the flowers, and cocks his chin towards them. "You know, there are a few myths about the Peony flower." He grins at me as our plates are cleared away from the table.

"You don't say." I smirk back at him.

"Well, there's the one where Aphrodite turns a bashful nymph into a Peony for banging Apollo." He says, matter-of-factly.

I stifle a laugh at his summary of what he got from the story. "Uh huh."

"Then there's the one about the Greek physician of the Gods, who almost gets his ass whacked, but Pluto has compassion for him and turns him into one, too." he adds.

"That's right." I almost giggle.

Dean clears his throat, grabbing his wine glass and takes a sip, before placing it down on the table again. He leans back slightly in his chair, leaving his hand on the table cloth, his fingers touching the base of his wine glass. "Not sure if you know this either, doll... But Peonies also symbolize romance, true love and a happy marriage."

I look at him with playful suspicion. "I'm pretty sure *I* told you that."

He smiles and asks, "Have you heard the story about the *Knight* and the Peony?"

"No... Is there one?" I'm admittedly curious...

"You don't know it?" His grin widens as he looks at me satirically. "And here I thought you knew *everything* there was to know about Peonies."

I give him a skeptical look of my own. "Why don't you share this Knight's tale with me then?" Leaning back in my chair, I cross my arms to sit back and listen to this myth I've never heard of before.

"Alright, well the story goes as this... Way back in medieval times, there was a Knight that fell in love with a maiden, but she kept herself way up in this tower, all alone, looking out across a terrible view. Nothing but a gnarly, dark forest of thick, thorny vines, no matter where she looked." Dean says, all the while wearing the slightest of grins. "Just a godawful view."

"That sounds terrible." I play along with him, battling my own urge to smile at what I suspect is a made-up story of his own.

"Oh, it was. For the Knight too, he was down there all up in that miserable shit. And for the fuckin' life of him, he just couldn't reach her." Dean continues, shifting slightly in his seat, still fidgeting with the stem of his wine glass.

"Was the tower too high?" I ask, uncrossing my arms and leaning forward to place my elbows on the table, resting my chin across my folded fingers as I look at him intently.

"That, and she couldn't see him, not among all the darkness that was around them." He says, but then clears his throat again before he goes on. "You see, his armor didn't shine. It was all tarnished from battles he'd previously fought."

"So, the Knight was hidden from her by all of the darkness? That's sad." I pout at him.

"Tragic, doll. Really." Dean's brows knit together as he nods, feigning concern and sympathy for the Knight.

I giggle. "So, what happened to the Knight and maiden?"

"Well, the Knight knew about the Gods turning people into Peonies, but he said fuck that shit, don't turn me into a flower. The fuck am I gonna be able to do for her as a flower?" He jerks his head back slightly at the absurdity of it all, shaking his head in disagreement with the Gods' seemingly go-to approach.

"Right." I press my lips together, rolling them inward to prevent myself from laughing. After a moment, I ask him, "So, what *did* the Knight do to win her love? Did the Gods help him at all?"

"Fuck, no."

"This story gets more tragic by the minute, Dean." I stifle a laugh. He bites his own lip and lifts a finger up for me to wait a moment, before he proceeds with the rest of his story.

"Well, the Knight knew he might not be able to give her *everything*, but he had more to offer the fair maiden than a flower could... He also knew that the maiden would definitely notice a Peony... If a Peony is a stand-alone flower, even among roses," He gestures to the little vase on our table, "then a Peony among the ugly, gnarly, thorny vines, would *surely* be noticed by the maiden."

"That makes sense." I humor him. "But where, *oh where*, did the Knight get a Peony from in such a dark, horrid forest?"

"How do fairy tales explain the unexplainable?" He grins at me in that cocky way of his, lifting his shoulder in a slight shrug. "Fuckin' *Magic*, doll."

I have to hold my breath to keep from laughing. Closing my eyes for a moment, I press my hand to my mouth and sit back in my seat. When I have a handle on my composure, I open my eyes again. Dean looks like he's struggling not to laugh either. "Please, do go on." I encourage him, placing my hands in my lap.

He takes another sip of his wine, nodding as he places it back down on the table cloth. "The Knight slashed his way to a clearing where he hoped the maiden might be able to spot him."

"And did she?"

"Not at first."

"Well then, if the Gods didn't help the Knight, what Magic did the Knight possess himself, to win the maidens heart?" I curiously ask.

"He was the *Knight of Wands*, doll." Dean winks at me, and I have to suppress another giggle. "Upon raising his Morning Star Weapon, it transformed into a big Peony... A pinkish white one, so she'd see it better, you know, contrast the darkness."

"Of course. And did she *finally* see him?"

"She saw the flower and came down from her tower to get a closer look at its beauty." He explains. "When she stepped outside, the Knight gave her the peony. And she was so touched by the gesture, she asked him to remove his helmet so that she could see him and place a kiss upon his cheek. Of course, he obliged." Dean says, with a sly smile now, leaning towards me. "As it turned out, the Knight was a rather good-looking motherfucker, and she fell in love with him right on the spot... *Love at first sight* type shit."

"Well, that's sweet." I smile back at him.

"Yup. He gave her a flower, and she gave him *her* flower." He grins devilishly at me before he adds with a growl, "*All night long.*"

I can't help shaking my head as I look back at him. "You are such a rogue sometimes, Dean, I swear it."

He casually shrugs, sitting back in his chair again. "So, that's how the Peony came to symbolize romance, true love and a happy marriage." He grins, proud of his bogus myth as he grabs his wine glass and finishes it off.

"Beautiful. And did they live happily ever after in the tower?"

"Fuck, no." He shakes his head. "That place was a dump. She deserved better. The Knight threw her on the back of his mighty black steed and they rode off into the sunset, back to his place." Dean smiles, lifting a hand to run his fingers through his hair. "*There*, they lived happily ever after."

I can't help but notice that he takes another deep breath, which quivers slightly as he exhales, dropping his hand from his hair to grab his napkin. He wipes the hand off with it that he just ran through his slicked hair. I try not to look at him suspiciously, but something is off about him. And now that I think about it, he's seemed a little off since we got here. Not quite jittery, but... tense? Even through his joking. I pick up my wine glass to take another sip, watching him pull his cellphone out of his inner pocket. Whatever he does with it is quick, because it's right back in his pocket again.

Our waiter returns to the table, about to pour some more wine into his glass, but Dean juts his hand out to cover the rim. "Hold that thought a minute, bro... Might not be having any more wine tonight." Dean says, giving the guy a *look,* which has him walking away rather quickly with his bottle of wine.

"Are you okay?" I ask, wondering if he suddenly feels sick or something.

"*Aces*, doll... Fuckin' *Aces*." But he doesn't sound like he's *Aces*. He stares at me intently for a moment, tension radiating off of him. His dark eyes are fixed on mine, and I can see the flame of the candle on our table flickering in them.

Placing my glass down, I glance around the room for a moment, wondering what's going on with him. He reaches across the table, laying his hand against the white cloth, open, seemingly in wait for me to place my hand in his. I do, and he gently curls his warm fingers around mine, stroking my skin with his thumb in that loving way of his. I peer back up into his handsome face, now wearing a slight, crooked smile.

"You saved my life." He quietly states, but when I start to protest, his hand holds mine tighter. "I'm not talking about the cabin..." He closes his eyes for a moment, as if fighting off the awful memories of what happened there that night. I try not to think of them, either. Dean opens his eyes to look at me intently again. "I'm talking about since the moment I laid eyes on you... I know we've had our ups and downs... that you didn't always believe me when I've told you that I love you... And now that we're where we are, together... On the other side of all of it... Do you believe me when I tell you now, that I love you?"

"Yes." I give his hand a gentle squeeze in return. My answer broadens his smile a little more. "I love you, too."

"I know I said things about my life, and my intentions for you in my life..." He hesitates, clearing his throat again as he glances over his shoulder briefly, before turning his attention back to me. "But I love you more than anything, Vanna. More than I ever thought a human heart capable of... I'm crazy about you. I adore you... And the *moment* is the moment, and it's the moment, doll."

759

"It is?" I glance over his shoulder in the direction he looked a moment ago. The hostess is walking over to our table, carrying a large Boquete of white and pale pink peonies. Dean gives my hand a squeeze before he releases it and quickly stands up from the table as she approaches us.

"Sir, these were was just delivered for you." The pretty brunette smiles as she hands them over to him. His hands seem slightly tremble for a moment as he takes them. She gives him a quick wink before she walks away, and Dean, staring into the Boquete, taking another deep, quivering breath, turns back to me again.

"*Fuck...* here goes..." he whispers under his breath, looking back up to meet my eyes again. My breath hitches in my throat as he steps forward, slowly lowering himself until he's on bended knee before me...

"*Oh my God...*"

Is this happening? Is this *really freaking happening* right now? Is this *the moment?* I don't know what to do with myself as I try not to fidget anxiously in my seat, or look at the other people in the restaurant who are surely staring at us... Yep, they are... Now *I'm the one* having to take a deep breath to gather myself...

"Vanna, baby," Dean says, his voice pulling my focus back to him.

My eyes meet his for a moment, before they shift to something that sparkles in the middle of the Boquete he's holding between us. In the center of the only deep burgundy peony surrounded by pale pink and white ones... The flower matches Dean's shirt. I don't know if that was on purpose or just a coincidence but... "*Oh my god.*" The words just tumble out of me again. That's a sparkling diamond ring... I lift my eyes once more to meet his, and he suddenly doesn't seem so nervous, wearing a smile on his handsome face that reaches those deep, penetrating, dark eyes of his.

"I want to marry you, Vanna..." Dean professes. "I want a life with you. I want to be your provider and protector, forever. I want to make you happy for the rest of your life. Nothing could ever make me happier than having you as my wife... So, what do you say, doll? Will you do me that honor? Will you marry me, Vanna?"

"Yes." I barely manage to squeak out at first. I know he heard me, by the expression of love and happiness on his face, but, "Yes." I say again, holding my left hand out to him. "I'll marry you, Dean... I want to marry you, too."

"*Aces*, baby." He grins, plucking the ring eagerly from the center of the burgundy peony. Wincing slightly as he rises, though his smile never falters, he places the flowers on the table and takes my hand, gently pulling me to stand with him. Gripping my left hand gently, he slides the ring onto my finger, then brings my hand up to his lips to press a kiss against it. Wrapping his arms around me, as I wrap my arms around his neck, he bends to press his lips to mine. I barely hear the people in the restaurant applauding. I'm too wrapped up in my future husband's searing kiss, and his warm, strong embrace, to notice anything or anyone, but Dean Keegan in this moment. *Our* moment.

DEAN

V ANNA ROLLS OVER IN OUR BED, TANGLED NAKED IN THE SHEET AS SHE snuggles up against me. Placing her cheek against my bare chest, she bends her knee to drape her sexy thigh across my lower abdomen. My arm curls around her shoulder to hold her tighter against me. I watch as she lifts her left hand again, to admire the ring I gave her earlier tonight, when she agreed to be mine, officially and forever, as my wife. And though we just made love, my heart still feels like it's racing, in a state of euphoric bliss, over the fact that she said *yes*.

"*Vanna Keegan...*" she whispers in the darkness, moving her hand in the lambent glow of the moonlight emanating through the windows beside our bed. My mother's radiant cut diamond, now Vanna's, catches the light and sparkles on her finger. "I like the way that sounds."

"Me too." I press my lips against her head, breathing her scent deeply into my lungs. Smiling at the fact that this woman is like oxygen to me, and that I'm no longer fearful of her having such power over me.

"I suppose this means you'll have to meet my family." I can hear the trepidation in her voice.

"Do you not want me to?" I ask.

"It's not that." She lets out a little sigh laced with uncertainty. Twisting her body against me now so that her chin is on my chest, she looks at me as I look down at her. "My relationship with them is so screwed up."

Untucking my arm from behind my head against the pillows, I reach down and wrap my fingers around her hand on my chest. "I don't have to meet them if you don't want them in our life. I'm not marrying your family, doll. It's whatever you want. Can't say I'm all too impressed with the way they've treated you." I'm less than impressed. In fact, I've got a few choice words I'd like to say to them about it, but I'll bite my tongue if she wants me to. I have every intention of striving to be everything Vanna will ever need. Vanna doesn't respond, though. She shifts her body to rest her cheek against my chest once more. "Are you upset?" I ask.

"No. How could I be upset tonight?"

I shrug, grinning to myself as I tell her, "Women are complicated."

She giggles and gently bites my peck, making me squirm slightly at the sharp, unexpected sensation and we both chuckle. After a few minutes of quietness in the dark, she speaks again. "It's after midnight... *Merry Christmas.*"

"*Happy Yule.*" I reply.

"I have a present for you."

"You are the gift in my life, baby."

"And you're mine, but I made you something anyway." Her tone is almost gleeful.

Before I can say anything else, she pushes herself up over me, her smooth thigh sliding further across my lower torso until she's straddling me between her legs, looking down at me as I gaze up at her. In the moonlight I can tell she's giving me a little smirk, then leans forward and over to the night table, pulling the drawer open to retrieve something. Whatever it is though, can't be better than her voluptuous breasts in my face. And I can't help myself, capturing one in my mouth, skimming my hands up her soft, curvaceous body, built for loving me. I cup both of her breasts, pressing them against my face, and suck gently on one of her pebbled nipples. She lets out a little prurient moan that stirs my primal need to have her again, hardening my cock beneath her. The night table drawer shuts with a faint clap as she sits back on me once more, her sex against my shaft, pinning it down between us. I rock my hips slowly, feeling my hardness slide between her hot, slick heat as I groan and take her other breast into my mouth. Teasing it with my teeth as I flick her pebbled peak with the tip of my tongue, I pull another little gasp of pleasure from her. A low growl rumbles up my throat as the urge surges through me to take her back down to the mattress and drive myself deep inside her once again.

"Give me your left hand." She insists, her fingers encircling my wrist and pulling my hand away from her breast, herself. She slips something familiar over my fingers, onto my wrist, and I smile against her soft flesh, releasing her nipple from my mouth.

"Is this what I think it is?" I ask, sliding my other hand back around her to bury my fingers in her long, silky hair. Pulling her mouth to mine, I feel her little smile against my own, before I kiss her deeply, having my way with her mouth for a moment. *"Devil shit... on Christmas morning?"* I tease her. She gently captures my bottom lip between her teeth, then gives it a little suck of her own. She giggles and releases me, trailing tantalizing kisses along my jawline until she whispers in my ear...

"For the last time, Dean, it *isn't* devil shit."

"I wouldn't care if it was, doll..." I confess, relishing the sensation of her lips against my throat now. "You're my little piece of Heaven I'd sell my soul to keep."

A FEW WEEKS LATER

"YOU NEED TO GET OVER TO VANNA'S OLD HOUSE. ALONE. AND *RIGHT now.*" Jason said to me earlier, the urgency of the matter coming through loud and clear. He'd called me while I was at my shop working on Serene. After establishing that Vanna was fine and at work, oblivious to whatever the Hell was going down at her old run-down farm house rental, I left the shop in Derek's capable hands and rushed straight over.

Now, as I pull up to the old house, Jason's squad car is in the driveway, the front door left slightly ajar. I dismount my side chick and walk up the porch steps, hand on the gun tucked behind my back, just in case. Pushing the bottom of the door with my boot to swing it open, Jason's standing in the foyer wearing his police uniform and latex gloves. From what I can tell just from the entryway, it looks like the house was ransacked.

"Don't touch anything." He tells me, "Just, brace yourself, and follow me."

"You know, I prefer the whole ripping off of the band-aid to be done quickly as opposed to slow and painful." I say, following Jason upstairs to what once was Vanna's bedroom.

"You'll know in a few seconds. Vanna's landlord, Richard Blackthorn, was reported missing about a month ago. A detective in his home town up in Maryland called to request that the local department here swing by his rental property and peek around. See if anything was amiss before he made the trip down here to investigate."

Now I know why she never got her security deposit back... "I'm guessing some shit's amiss then... and it's got something to do with Vanna." I say, stopping behind him when he rounds the corner of the railing and pauses in front of Vanna's old bedroom door.

"Both of you..." Jason sighs. "I'm glad I'm the first one on the scene... I haven't called this shit in yet. I'm going to let you take the worst ones, but you can't touch anything else. The fact that you've been dating Vanna will explain your prints all over the house, but not your prints all over any of the evidence we'll have to leave behind for the sake of this guy's case."

"Yeah... This doesn't sound good." I mutter, more to myself than to Jason. He pushes the door open with his boot and steps into the room. I follow him in.

I don't know what I was expecting to see... But it wasn't this sick shit... I'm glad the motherfucker is six feet under... burning in the Hell I sent him to.

"Jesus fuck..." I run a hand over my mouth and the stubble of my jaw as I take in the twisted fucking shrine of a room that only Jack fuckin' Nero could have been behind. This motherfucker was right under my nose for god-damn weeks... Living in her old house.

There are photos of Vanna all over the walls, all over the floor. What looks like a pair of her panties she must have left behind accidently, wadded up on her old bed. I don't want to think about what the fuck he was doing with those. As I take a closer look, some of the pictures are from that day I had her on the pool table at the Twisted Throttle. Those are definitely coming with me. No way I'm letting her go through that humiliation again... These are *worse,* far more explicit than the one he left with his note the night he murdered Serene.

"I think it's safe to add Mr. Blackthorn to Jack's body count." I glance at Jason.

"I gotta call that detective and let him know about this." Jason says. "How long do you think you'll need? Forensics is the next call."

"I'm taking everything she isn't fully clothed in. Not thrilled about the fuckin' panties... but I'll leave 'em for the DNA evidence." I sneer at the sight again. "Give me thirty just to play it safe, I don't want to rush and miss anything that's going to humiliate her later. He's done enough to her." Even in death, the sick fuck manages to strike again.

Jason hands me a pair of gloves. "Thirty minutes. I'm gonna check the rest of the house." He says, before he leaves me alone. I take every bit of time I've got to go through every photo, carefully collecting the ones no one should ever see. Most of which, are taped to the ceiling above the bed. For good measure, I check the drawers in the old dresser, and come across the camera with the zoom lens and chip containing all of the photos. I tuck that into my pocket as well, when I spot something that damn near takes the breath right out of my fucking lungs like a slug to the gut.

A piece of paper among Jack's maps and photos of Vanna on the floor, partially tucked under the dresser. A piece of paper that's so much more than what first meets the eye.

Reaching down, I snatch the paper up and stare at it with horror coursing through my body...

I'm sure it was the sender's intention that this piece of paper, was never meant for anyone's eyes but Jack's. I'm more than confident, the sender never anticipated that I would ever find out about this, let alone lay my eyes upon it...

No other but I, would see the heart stopping, gut churning, significance of it...

Vanna's home address, written in an all too *familiar* feminine scrawl, upon a purple sheet of Stationary paper... A *purple* sheet, depicting a faint picture of a *jar of hearts*...

As if that wasn't unnerving enough, now knowing *she* did this to Vanna and I... That *she* sent a psychopath after the woman I love, in hopes of tearing us apart forever... Nearly getting us both killed in the process... As if that treachery wasn't bad enough...

The words written above Vanna's address, in a more masculine hand, paint an even darker picture, still...

I've read enough of Jack's letters to know this isn't his handwriting.

Reaching for my wallet, I remove the Demons' Den Club House card Vanna handed me months ago, when *he* visited her shop. Placing the card with the hand written phone number on top of the paper, I compare the writing to the disturbingly significant words, scrawled above Vanna's address on the jar of hearts stationary.

A cold chill runs down my spine as I read those ominous words one more time...

"The Party's Here..."

"Turn your Demons into art,
your shadow into a friend,
your fear into fuel,
your failures into teachers,
your weakness into reasons to keep fighting.
Don't waste your pain.
Recycle your heart."

—Andrea Balt—

If you enjoyed Savior Book 1, please consider
taking the time to leave a review on Amazon.
Reviews go a long way to help us
Indie Authors connect with other readers
who may enjoy our work.

To keep up with my future projects and events,
check out my website at

www.JenniferSaviano.net

Where you will find detailed Content & Trigger Warnings
Autographed Books and Merch
Links to my Social Media Accounts
The Saviors MC Spotify Playlist
& Sign up for my Newsletter